Berkley Street Box Set Books 1 - 9

Written by Ron Ripley
Edited by Emma Salam

ISBN-13: 978-1724549648
ISBN-10: 1724549642
Copyright © 2016 by ScareStreet.com
All rights reserved.

Thank You and Bonus Novel!

I'd like to take a moment to thank you for your ongoing support. You make this all possible! To really show you my appreciation for purchasing this book, I've included a bonus scene at the end of this book. **I'd also love to send you a full length horror novel in 3 formats (MOBI, EPUB and PDF) absolutely free!**

Download your full length horror novel, get free short stories, and receive future discounts by visiting **www.ScareStreet.com/RonRipley**

See you in the shadows,
Ron Ripley

Berkley Street
Book 1

Chapter 1: Shane, September 1st, 1982

Shane Ryan had never seen a bigger house.

Their new home looked like a castle, with two towers and tall, narrow windows. Shane counted six chimneys. A pair of giant, thick trees stood on either side of the wide front door. A thick stone wall, nearly as tall as Shane's father, protected the whole property.

"What do you think, kid?" his father asked as he parked the car in the long driveway.

"Is it a castle?" Shane asked.

His mother let out a pleased laugh, and his father shook his head.

"No, kid. The Andersons, well, they were really wealthy. They wanted it to look like a castle on the outside, but on the inside, well, it's a regular house."

"Oh," Shane said, trying not to sound disappointed. "So no secret passages or anything?"

"Who knows?" his mother said, gently slapping his father on the arm. "Who knows?"

"Yeah," Shane's father said, winking at him in the rearview mirror, "Who knows?"

"Come on," Shane's mother said. "Let's go inside."

His father turned the engine off, and Shane dutifully waited for his mother to open the back door of the Cadillac before he got out. The September air was warm and still smelled like summer. Shane saw the grass in the yard was freshly mowed and all of the windows shined. Each gray stone seemed to glow in the sun.

"How big is the yard?" Shane asked, looking around.

"Well," his father said, following his son's gaze, "you could fit eight of our old yards into the front yard."

"Wow," Shane said, turning and looking at the expanse of grass.

"In the side yard there's a garden," his mother said, "there's also a pond in the backyard."

Shane felt his eyes widen. "A pond?"

"Yup," his father said happily. "And you know what else, kid?"

"What?" Shane asked.

"It's full of fish. We can go fishing whenever we want."

"Wow," Shane whispered. "Wow."

Shane's parents laughed happily, and he followed them up the front walk. His father took out the house key, unlocked the large door and opened it. Shane stepped into the biggest room he had ever seen.

A huge set of stairs stretched up into darkness, and dim pieces of furniture filled what he realized was a hallway. Close to where Shane stood, a tall grandfather clock ticked away the time.

And behind the tick of the second hand, Shane heard whispers.

Someone whispered in the walls.

Chapter 2: Shane, March 20th, 2016

The fan hummed steadily.

Shane sat up in his narrow bed as the cool air dried the sweat on his body. He took long, deep breaths and looked at the clock.

Six in the morning.

He closed his eyes and forced away the last remnants of his nightmares. He reached over to his bed table, took the bottle of whiskey and glass off of it and poured himself a small shot.

Shane drank it quickly and returned them both to their place.

My security blanket, he thought bitterly. He got out of the bed, took the three steps to his bathroom and climbed into the shower. Shane turned on the water and forced himself to stand under it until it warmed up. Finally, with the water tolerable, he scrubbed himself rigorously and then rinsed off.

The bare minimum to get clean and rid himself of the stench of fear and sweat.

Once out of the shower, he dried off and looked at himself in the mirror.

Thin face. Haggard eyes. No hair.

Alopecia areata, he thought, running a hand over his smooth scalp. His pale skin looked sickly in the light of the fluorescent lamp above the mirror. *Unexplained hair loss.*

Pretty sure I can explain it, Shane thought angrily.

With a shake of his head, he forced himself to focus on his morning routine. He brushed his teeth, went back into his bedroom and got dressed. A pair of jeans and a black tee shirt. Running shoes and a pullover sweatshirt of dark gray. Absently he rolled the wedding band on his ring finger as he walked to his kitchenette.

Oatmeal for breakfast. Strong coffee. Vitamins. A banana and two pieces of rye bread toasted.

No matter how much he ate, though, he wouldn't get up over one hundred and forty-five pounds.

Tall and thin, he thought. *Just like dad.*

Shane put his wallet in his pocket, took his phone and his keys, and left his apartment. The noises of the world fell in around him, and he did his best to ignore them. He took his walk alone in the early morning light. The streets were clear of snow, although salt and sand crunched beneath his feet.

Winter had slipped by New Hampshire and snow had been a rare sight. Ice, however, had visited more than once, and the streets were always treated for it.

Shane fought the urge to stop at the Paki's corner store for a pack of cigarettes, but he walked by. He reached the top of Library Hill, walked around the Soldiers and Sailors Monument, and made his way back to his apartment on Locust Street.

Once inside, he poured himself a fresh cup of coffee and went to his laptop. He powered it up, logged into his work account, and looked to see what needed to be translated.

Among the work emails, he found one from O'Connor Law Associates.

Oh, Jesus, what now? He thought, opening the email.

His heart leaped at what it said.

Dear Mr. Ryan, the email began.

> *We are pleased to inform you the proceedings regarding your family's home at 125 Berkley Street have finally finished.*
>
> *The house is yours, per your parents' wishes, and your uncle and aunt have exhausted their financial and legal options.*
>
> *Please call my office at your earliest convenience so we might sign the appropriate paperwork and give you the keys to your home.*
>
> *Sincerely,*
> *Jeremy O'Connor*

Shane sat back and stared at the email.

The keys to my home.

My home.

Shane leaned forward and jotted the number for the firm down on his notepad.

Book 1: Berkley Street

Now I'll find them, he told himself, joy and rage twining together in his heart. *Now I will find them.*

Chapter 3: Shane, September 15th, 1982

"Are you awake?"

Shane sat up and turned on his light. His heart beat quickly, and he looked around his large room. The curtains were drawn on the tall windows. His books were lined neatly on his shelves. Legos were scattered across the floor by the old fireplace.

"Are you awake?" the voice asked again.

Shane twisted around in his bed. Neither his mother nor his father was in his room.

He was alone.

He couldn't tell where the voice came from. His mouth was dry, so he swallowed, wet his lips with his tongue, and said in a low voice, "I'm awake."

"Good," the voice said.

It came from behind his dresser.

"Why? Why is it good?" Shane asked.

"Because they don't want you here," the voice said. "They don't want you. Here."

His heart thumped heavily, and he managed to ask, "Who?"

"Don't ask," the voice said. "I want you here. I'm lonely."

Shane tried to speak but couldn't. The sound of his blood as it rushed through him nearly drowned out his own thoughts. "Why are you lonely?" Shane whispered.

"I've been here a long time. Such a very long time."

The bureau started to move, inch by inch, into the room. It swung out slowly from the wall, and a dark shadow appeared.

It took Shane a moment to realize there was a passage in the wall.

A soft scrape slipped out of the darkness, and it was quickly followed by a sigh.

The speaker stepped into the room.

A girl. Perhaps eight or nine.

And dead.

Dead, dead, dead.

She smelled like death, and her skin was shrunken, pulled tight across her bones. Her lips were stretched in a gruesome smile, and long teeth protruded from her yellow jawbone.

"I'm lonely," she said, stepping into the room. Bits of fabric fell from her ragged, gray dress. Her brown hair was tied back with a faded red bow, and the bones of her feet cracked as she walked. "I'm lonely. I want to play."

Shane closed his eyes, opened his mouth, and screamed.

Suddenly his bedroom door was thrown open and bounced against the wall, and Shane opened his eyes. His father and mother charged into the room, their faces puffy with sleep and their hair disheveled.

"Oh my God, Hank," his mother said, pointing to the bureau.

"What the hell?" his father asked. His father walked to the bureau as his mother hurried to Shane.

Shane sank into his mother's arms and shook as she held him tightly. From the protection of his mother's embrace, Shane watched his father.

"There's a passage," his father said, looking back at Shane and his mother. "Fiona, there's a passage here."

"What?" she asked. "Are you sure?"

4

"Positive. Looks like we put his bureau against a door of some sort. Couldn't even tell. You'd think it was part of the wainscoting. Hell, I did."

Shane's father leaned into the dark hole the dead girl had come from.

His father backed out and looked at his mother. "It's a real passage, Fiona. I can't see much in there right now, but I thought I saw lights. It's just wide enough for someone to walk through."

"Servants' passage?" she asked.

"Must be," he answered.

Shane watched as his father pushed the bureau back into place.

"It wasn't in any of the forms, Hank," Shane's mother said. "There wasn't anything about servants' passages. Just their quarters."

"Yeah," his father said. "I know."

Shane's shakes slowly went away, and his father came and sat down on the bed beside him.

"Did you get scared, kid?" his father asked.

Shane nodded.

"Would have scared me too," his father said.

"There was a girl," Shane whispered.

"What?" his mother asked.

"A girl. A dead girl," Shane said.

"Shane," his father started, and Shane heard the 'now you're seven, so you need to be a big boy' voice, but his mother interrupted him.

"Hank," she said, her voice harsh. "Not now."

"Okay, Fiona. Okay," his father said with a sigh.

"Is there a way you can block the bureau so it won't pop open again?" his mother asked.

"I'll figure it out," Shane's father said, nodding.

"Good. Shane," his mother said. "Do you want me to lie down with you for a bit?"

Shane clung to his mother and nodded.

Chapter 4: Standing in Front of Hell

Shane smoked steadily as he leaned against an old oak tree and looked at his house.

His monstrous familial home.

His hand shook as he tugged the cigarette out of his mouth and exhaled.

The keys he had picked up from the attorney sat heavily in his pocket. Shane wanted to go through the gate. He wanted to walk up the driveway and unlock the front door. It was his right, and his responsibility to enter the home. He sighed and took another drag from the cigarette.

An older man walked towards him from the dead portion of Berkley Street. He had an older German shepherd on a short leash; the dog's brown and black fur glistened in the mid-morning light.

The older man frowned as he looked at Shane, and Shane knew what the old man saw; a middle-aged man who leaned against a tree and smoked a cigarette. A man who stared at a house empty for decades.

Shane looked, he knew, like a criminal.

The older man, whose skin was pale, and his hair gone, adjusted his grip on the dog's leash and paused half a dozen feet away from Shane.

"Hello," the old man said, and Shane heard the authority and command in his voice.

He's used to being obeyed, Shane thought. He fought the desire to make the conversation difficult for the old man.

"Hello," Shane said simply. He finished his cigarette, stubbed it out and held onto the butt. Once he was sure the embers were out he slipped the remains of the tobacco into his pocket.

The stranger looked at him curiously.

"Do you always police up your cigarettes?" he asked.

"Yes," Shane nodded. "Ever since I saw a drill instructor crawl up one side and down the other of a kid who tossed his butt onto the ground."

The old man chuckled.

"I quit a long time ago," the stranger said. "But I experienced something similar."

"Nice weather for a walk," Shane said, conversationally. He wondered when the man would get to the point.

"Do you live around here?" the old man asked, politely but pointedly.

Shane nodded.

"Do you mind if I ask where?" the stranger said.

Shane looked at the man. He could see the stamp of the Marine Corps on him. The man's back was ramrod straight, his eyes steady. He was probably in his seventies, but Shane suspected the man could still hold his own in a fight.

"I don't mind at all. I live there," Shane said, nodding towards his house.

The stranger frowned, confused. "No one lives there, son."

"I do. Now. I lived there before too. A long time ago, though," Shane said.

The man's eyes widened slightly. "Are you the Ryans' boy?"

"I am," Shane said. Impulsively he offered his hand and introduced himself. "Shane Ryan."

The stranger shook it. "Gerald Beck."

"A pleasure," Ryan said.

"This is Turk," Gerald said, patting the top of his dog's head. "He and I are both retired."

"Police dog?" Shane asked.

"No," Gerald said, shaking his head. "Just an old dog. He came from a shelter up in Enfield. He's a little jumpy sometimes. I try not to walk him by your house too much. Tends to upset him."

"But you saw me loitering?" Shane asked, grinning.

Gerald chuckled and nodded. "Yes. I did. I'm a nosy old maid sometimes."

"No problem with it," Shane said. He looked back at the house. The windows seemed to look back at him. A shiver danced along his spine and Shane returned his attention to Gerald. "So, you're a Marine?"

"Yes," Gerald said proudly. "Infantry. Korea and Vietnam. First Marine Division. You?"

"Forward observer, America's Battalion," Shane said. "Did a couple of tours in Afghanistan. One in Iraq."

Gerald looked at him for a minute. "Fallujah?"

Shane nodded.

"We had heard you joined the military. I wasn't close to your parents, so I didn't know what branch," Gerald said apologetically.

Shane smiled at the man.

"I heard there was some difficulty with the house in regards to ownership," Gerald said.

"It's cleared up now," Shane said.

"You thinking about whether or not to go in?" Gerald asked.

"Yeah," Shane said softly. Then with more determination, he said, "Yes."

"Well," Gerald said, "when you're done, you're welcome to come down and say hello. I live up the road at one sixty-six. Just ring the bell. I've always got coffee on. It's just me and Turk in the house."

"I will," Shane said. "Thank you."

"You're welcome, son," Gerald said. He started to walk away, and Turk followed him. Gerald glanced over his shoulder and called back, "Anytime."

Shane raised a hand and nodded with a smile. He waited a few minutes after the older man, and the dog had left before he straightened up. Shane focused on the front door and started to walk towards it.

Chapter 5: Graduation, Parris Island, South Carolina, 1994

Shane sat with Corey's family. He smiled at Corey's mom, who was fawning over her son, and looked out over the parade ground for his parents. They had promised they would make his graduation from boot camp. They had even reserved rooms on Parris Island.

Shane felt proud; he had earned the title of United States Marine, and it was Family Day. He wanted his family there.

Where are they? He asked himself, peering through the crowd of people.

He couldn't see them.

Drill Instructor Allen came from around a group surrounding Davidson and made his way to Drill Instructor Carter, who stood off to one side and chatted with Ramirez. Allen leaned in close, said something to Carter, and the two Drill Instructors turned and looked at Shane.

Shane stiffened.

It didn't matter if he had just graduated, those men were still NCOs, and they could make life hell until he shipped out.

A wave of nervous fear ripped through him as they walked closer.

"Private Ryan," Carter said.

"Aye, sir," Shane said, standing up quickly. Out of the corner of his eye, he saw Corey tense.

"Come with us, Private," Carter said.

"Aye, sir," Shane said. He quickly followed the two Drill Instructors to a distance away from the rest of the class, to where the chaplain stood alone, a look of concern on his face.

"Private Ryan," the chaplain said. "We've received some news about your parents."

"Sir?" Shane asked.

"Your parents are missing, Private Ryan," the chaplain said.

Shane blinked and shook his head. "What are you saying, sir? Missing? On the road somewhere?"

"From your house," the chaplain said in a gentle voice. "They've vanished."

Shane closed his eyes and shook his head.

The house, Shane thought numbly. *It took them.*

He suddenly felt hands under his arms. They gripped his biceps firmly and applied just enough pressure to support him. Although he wanted to drop to his knees, Shane found he couldn't.

"Easy, Ryan," Drill Instructor Allen said in a soothing tone. "Easy. It's alright."

"How long?" Shane managed to ask.

"At least a week," the chaplain said. "Your parents were just gone, though. From what I was told, everything is there. Their wallets, money. The car. The police aren't sure what happened."

Shane tried to stand on his own but his legs wouldn't obey.

Drill Instructor Carter leaned in to help.

"You're okay, Marine," Carter said. "You're going to be okay."

Shane knew he would be, but it didn't make the vanishing of his parents any easier.

7

Book 1: Berkley Street

Chapter 6: Finding Courage

It took Shane another ten minutes to build up the courage to even cross the sidewalk and step onto his property.

His uncle and aunt had fought him since his parents had initially disappeared. They had even hinted at Shane's possible involvement in their vanishing.

The courts, of course, had found it to be a baseless accusation. The United States Marine Corps could confirm he had been present at the Recruit Training Depot at Parris Island, South Carolina, the entire time.

Shane had never liked his Uncle Rick or his Aunt Rita. At one point he had even hated them after the court cases had begun. He didn't any longer, though. They weren't worth his time or effort. He had allowed his lawyers to handle the case, and they had.

The house was his.

The house was *his*.

If a house like this can belong to anyone, Shane thought.

With a grimace, he squared his shoulders and stepped across the sidewalk to the asphalt of the driveway and started the long walk to the front door. Shapes flicked in and out of the various windows. He told himself to ignore the shadows of birds and clouds.

But he knew neither of those had reflected in the old glass.

Nothing ever reflected in the old glass.

Even the sun was defeated by the house.

Shane felt the urge to spit but found his mouth to be dry. He kept his breath steady and approached the house carefully.

The keys shook in his hands as he took them out of his pocket and stepped up to the front door.

He slid the key in, heard the lock tumble, and he twisted the doorknob.

It opened easily, as though it had been only yesterday when he had last been inside, instead of the day he had left for boot camp.

A soft breeze rolled over him and carried with it the scent of lilacs. His mother had hated lilacs and despised how the house was never quite free of the smell. The house was cold as he stepped in.

And the door closed quickly behind him of its own accord.

Shane managed not to jump.

I need to get the power turned back on, he thought, looking around. Sunlight filtered in through the tall, narrow windows, but Shane knew he needed electricity. And water and sewerage, and all of those other things. Someone had suggested he contact a plumber, in case the pipes had burst over all the cold New England winters, but Shane knew he didn't need to worry about it.

Nothing would happen to the house.

He looked around and saw the furniture still placed exactly as he remembered it. Everything was absent of dust, as though someone had cleaned the home just for him.

And they probably have, Shane thought with a sigh.

He walked slowly through the first floor. He passed into and out of the parlor, the dining room, the living room, the game room, and the butler's pantry. He ignored the second floor and the basement. He needed more sunlight, and more courage than he had at the moment.

He stood in the kitchen and looked out the back door. A wide porch swept out towards the backyard and the pond. Behind him, he heard whispers, low voices.

He couldn't understand any of what they said, but he knew it wasn't pleasant.

He had heard it all before.

Long before his parents had vanished.

He focused his attention on the pond. What little light was left in the day seemed to be swallowed by the water.

Shane stiffened, focused on the center of the pond and stared.

Just beneath the water, he saw it. A strange white shape which twisted and undulated. Shane caught sight of hair and the glitter of eyes.

She watched him.

She remained.

Shane turned to the counter, went to the sink and threw up the coffee and protein bar which had served as lunch. He spat several times into the sink to rid his mouth of the taste.

Suddenly the pipes clanked under the cabinet, and he took a nervous step back.

"The water's on, Shane," a voice whispered from behind him.

He snapped around but saw nothing.

The faucet groaned, and water splashed loudly into the sink.

With a shudder, he turned around and saw the water. It came out of the tap quickly. After a moment of shock Shane took a step forward, pulled up the sleeves on his sweatshirt, and started to rinse the vomit down the drain.

Something cold brushed his ear and an old voice hissed, "Welcome home, Shane."

Shane did his best to ignore it and focused instead upon the wretched, acidic smell of his own bile.

It was better by far.

Chapter 7: Shane, May 3rd, 1983

Shane was ready.

In three more days he would be eight years old. He wasn't going to be scared anymore.

He wasn't going to have to sleep with the light on anymore, or with the bedroom door taken off the hinges

Shane wasn't going to be afraid anymore.

The grandfather clock downstairs in the main hallway struck midnight and Shane waited. After the last chime, he heard someone scratch behind his bureau. He listened closely.

The type of scratching would reveal who had come through the passage.

Light scratching meant it was Eloise.

Heavy scratching meant it was Thaddeus.

Shane closed his eyes and tilted his head as he listened.

Thaddeus, Shane thought.

The scratching got louder and in another room he heard a bang.

The bureau hissed as Thaddeus pushed it out into the room.

The entry into the passageway was black.

Thaddeus breathed heavily in the dark.

"Go away," Shane said firmly.

The breathing grew heavier.

"Go away," Shane said again.

The toe of a worn boot protruded from the darkness.

"Go away!" Shane shrieked.

A second boot appeared, and the breathing became faster.

"I said, *go away!*" Shane screamed, and he launched himself from his bed. Yet he did not run for the safety of the hall and his parents' bed. Instead, he ran into the darkness, and he heard the surprise catch in Thaddeus' throat, and then Shane ran into the ghost.

Or rather, he ran through him.

Shane slammed headlong into the wall of the passage, and as he fell dizzily to the floor, Thaddeus rushed past him.

Enraged, Shane got to his feet and chased after the ghost.

Behind him, the passage slammed shut, and Shane was plunged into darkness.

His sudden inability to see caused him to stop. His rage quickly gave way to fear, and Shane realized he was trapped in the walls of the house with the dead.

He took a cautious step back, stumbled, fell and hit his head. Stars exploded in his eyes, and he struggled back to his feet. He couldn't tell which way would lead him back to his room.

He had no idea.

Cautiously Shane started to walk. He reached out both hands, so the fingers touched the rough wood of the narrow passage's walls. He took a few steps and pushed against the walls. He sought out a handle, one to open the door into his room.

He couldn't find anything, though.

He took a few more steps and tried again.

Nothing, he thought, and he realized he was going to be too afraid to do anything soon.

His breath started to race and he turned around again. He retraced his steps, sought out the handle, and when he didn't find it, he took a few more steps.

Still nothing.

Shane started to panic.

Something moved in the darkness behind him, and then a moment later another sound came from in front of him.

Shane sat down heavily, closed his eyes, put his hands over his ears, and he screamed.

He continued to scream until his voice hurt and his brain felt like it was going to explode.

His scream filled the small passage and soon he could feel rather than hear someone pound on the wall.

Shane stopped, put his hands down, and he heard, "Shane!"

It was his mother.

"Mom!" he screamed, crawling towards the part of the wall she had hit.

"Shane, stay where you are," she said firmly. "Your father's found an entrance in here, and he's getting the door open."

When the last syllable had slipped out of her mouth, a crack of bright light appeared a few feet from Shane on the left. He crawled to it. He panted as he reached the door. His mother leaned in, grabbed hold of him tightly and pulled him out into bright light.

Bright daylight.

She held onto him tightly, and Shane's father sat down heavily in a chair.

They were in the library on the second floor, across the house from Shane's room.

"How did you get here?" his mother asked, pushing him away slightly to look at him.

"I don't know," Shane said, sniffling back tears. "I don't know. I chased the ghost back into the passage, but then the door closed. I've been screaming. They were coming for me."

"Hank," she said, looking at his father.

"We've been looking for you," his father said. The man looked exhausted. "Your screams have been coming through every room in the house. We kept trying to find you."

"I want them all sealed up today, Hank," his mother said.

"I haven't even been able to check them all, Fiona," his father argued.

"I don't care," she snapped. "Close them up, Hank. Close them all up."

Shane's father opened his mouth to add something but closed it when he saw his wife's stare.

"Sure," his father grumbled. "Sure. I'll close them up today."

Book 1: Berkley Street

Chapter 8: In the House

The temperature in the house dropped steadily.

Soon Shane could watch each breath he exhaled. He stuffed his hands in his pockets and wandered absently through the front hallway. Pictures of himself and his parents hung on the walls. The photographs taken prior to their arrival at the house showed Shane as a little boy with a big smile.

After they had taken up residence on Berkley Street, however, his eyes had taken on a haunted look. His smile was not nearly as wide. His face was pale.

Life at the house had been difficult.

Shane paused at the bottom of the stairs and looked up.

His bedroom was at the top of the stairs and to the left. The closest room to his parents'. He could see how his door remained off the hinges, and he wondered if it was still propped up in the hallway of the servants' quarters or if someone had moved it.

Part of Shane wanted to go up the stairs and examine the rooms. In theory, no one had been in the house for nearly twenty years. Shane could smell a hint of death beneath the scent of lilacs, and he knew it wasn't new death. Not some animal trapped within the walls or a chimney. Nor was it an animal that had lived out its time and died.

The smell of death was the house's smell, no matter how much the ghosts had sought to mask it with lilacs.

Shane turned away from the stairs and walked to the front door. It was time for coffee with Gerald.

The knob turned easily in his hand, and he left his home. He didn't bother to lock the door.

The house would take care of itself.

Something flickered in the corner of his eye as he followed the driveway to where it met the road. As he walked along the stone wall which wrapped around his property on his right, Shane heard a noise.

Shane heard the whisper of someone's feet in the grass on the other side of the wall.

Whoever it was kept up with him and Shane didn't bother with questions. They would speak if they wanted to.

And they did.

"Where are you going?" a young man asked in German.

"To a neighbor's for coffee, Carl," Shane said, answering in kind.

"Come home soon, Shane," Carl said with a chuckle. *"We've missed you."*

Shane ignored the way his stomach twisted at the dead man's words. With a tired sigh he continued on his walk. It felt strange, Shane realized, to be in his old neighborhood. Some of the houses had changed, of course. Different colors and new roofs. None of it was so drastically altered, however, enough for him to not know exactly where he was. Soon, he found himself at Gerald's and he paused. The house in front of him was a well-built Victorian, a Painted Lady. The trim and clapboard, the spindles on the porch and the shutters on the windows, were all variations on the color purple.

The house's brilliant façade was stunning in the sunlight.

Shane felt oddly excited as he walked up to the front door and rang the bell.

From behind the door, he heard the electronic chime and the sudden, sharp bark of Turk.

A few moments later Gerald's voice came through the wood.

"Who is it?" the older man asked.

"Shane Ryan," Shane answered.

The deadbolt clicked, a small chain rattled, and the door opened.

Gerald smiled and stepped back. Turk sat a few feet away, and his tail thumped loudly on the old wooden floor. The house smelled strongly of coffee.

"Come in, Shane, come in. Here to take me up on my offer?" Gerald asked.

"I suppose I am," Shane said, stepping into the house. "I hadn't planned on it, but I suppose I am."

Gerald closed the door behind him and said, "Just go through the first door on your left. I've already got some coffee in there."

Shane nodded, turned left into the first room and took a seat in a high-backed leather arm chair. Gerald and Turk followed him in. Turk lay down in front of the fireplace, even though the hearth was unlit. Gerald walked to a small marble table, where a silver coffee urn stood.

A moment later, the older man carried the drink over to Shane, who nodded his thanks.

"My apologies, Shane," Gerald said as he sat down in a second leather armchair. "I don't take cream or sugar myself, so I tend not to have either one in the house, unless I know my kids are on their way to visit."

"No worries," Shane said. "I drink my coffee black."

Gerald nodded his approval and for a minute, the two men drank the warm, dark brew in silence.

"Well," Gerald said, "I have to ask. Why have you come back to the house now?"

"Like you said earlier," Shane said, "there was a bit of a dispute in regards to ownership. My aunt and uncle didn't feel it was right for an eighteen-year-old to own a house like mine."

Gerald frowned. "Why not?"

Shane shrugged, took a drink and said, "All I can think of is they wanted the house because of the trust fund. You see, my parents established a fund for the upkeep and care of the house, should anything happen to my dad. He wanted to make sure my mother would have a place to live. I don't think either of them expected it to go to me so quickly."

"So if your relatives had won ownership, they would have been able to live free in the house?" Gerald asked.

"Essentially," Shane said, nodding.

"And where were you going to live?"

Shane smiled. "My father and my Uncle Rick weren't close. In fact, they really didn't care for each other much at all. Uncle Rick and Aunt Rita really couldn't have cared less what happened to me after they got the house."

Gerald snorted derisively. "Mighty Christian of them."

"Funny you should mention Christian," Shane said. "Uncle Rick's a pastor at a place called the Holy Child Baptist Church down in Massachusetts."

Gerald laughed and shook his head. "Well, there's a fine joke for you."

Shane took a drink and then he grinned. "I don't much care for either of them. They tried to declare my parents dead, long before the legal time. They also pulled a lot of underhanded tricks. They hired a private investigator to see if I had something to do with the disappearance of my parents."

"Weren't you in boot camp at the time?"

Shane nodded.

Gerald snorted in disbelief, and Turk glanced up at him.

"Nothing to worry about, Turk," Gerald said, smiling at his dog. "Here's to you, Ryan, and welcome back to the neighborhood."

"Thank you."

"Will you be moving back in tonight?" Gerald asked.

Shane shook his head. "Tomorrow. I've got a few things to wrap up for work and then I'll take a few days off to get situated at home again."

"What do you do for work?" Gerald asked.

"I'm a freelance translator," Shane said. "Mostly non-fiction books. Military history stuff."

"You don't say?" Gerald said, nodding his head. "Impressive. What language?"

"Languages," Shane said, smiling. "German, French, Spanish, Italian. Just the basics."

"And you make good money, I assume?" Gerald asked, leaning back in his chair.

"Good enough," Shane answered. "And what about you, what did you do?"

"Worked in the defense industry. Perfected ways to kill people at a distance," Gerald said, shrugging. "There's no nice way to say it."

"No," Shane agreed, "there usually isn't."

Chapter 9: Shane, June 3rd, 1983

Shane sat in the back seat of the Cadillac, his arms crossed over his chest as he glared out the window.

His mother glanced back at him. "How was it?"

Shane looked at her, thought about something mean to say, but then turned and looked out the window again. He watched the trees of Greeley Park go by as his father guided the car towards home.

"Shane?" his mother said.

"I don't want to talk about it," Shane said.

"We're just curious is all, kid," his father said.

"I'm not crazy," Shane said, still looking out the window.

His father signaled to turn onto Swart Terrace.

"We didn't say you're crazy," his mother said quickly. "Dr. Wolfe doesn't think you're crazy either."

"Yes he does," Shane said. He looked at his mother. "He told me there aren't any such things as ghosts."

"Well come on, kid," his father said in a joking tone, "you know there aren't."

"I know what's in the house," Shane said angrily. "I know Eloise is dead. I know Thaddeus is dead. And there are others. They're in the walls. And there's the girl in the pond."

His parents looked at one another nervously and remained silent as his father turned into the driveway.

After the engine was shut off and they all got out and started to walk to the front door, Shane's mother asked, "Do you want to switch your bedrooms tonight?"

"It won't matter," Shane said.

"Why not?" his father asked.

"They don't care what room I'm in," Shane said, stepping over the threshold. "When they want to talk to me, they talk to me."

His mother tousled his hair as his father closed and locked the door.

"How do you know?" she said. "Don't you think they'll leave you alone if you're, say, in our room?"

Shane shook his head.

"No?" his father asked, chuckling. "Tell you what, kid, after dinner you can go to sleep in our room, and your mother and I will stay in there with you."

Eloise laughed from behind the grandfather clock, but Shane's parents didn't hear her.

"Sure," Shane said.

"Okay," the relief in his mother's voice was clear.

Shane went and played with his Star Wars figures in the kitchen while his mother got dinner ready. It was unusually hot for June according to Shane's father, so his mother heated hot dogs and baked beans while his father conducted some business over the telephone in the library.

Soon Shane had to put his toys away, and he ate dinner with his parents at the small table in the kitchen instead of the larger one in the dining room. His mother gave him a quick bath, got him into a pair of Superman pajamas, and soon he found himself in the middle of his parents' giant bed.

"What do you want to read tonight?" his father asked, leaning in the doorway as his mother sat down in the bed beside him.

"There's a Wocket in My Pocket!" Shane said, snuggling against his mother.

"Okay," his father said with a grin. He left the room and returned a minute later with the Dr. Seuss book. He carried it to a chair under the windows and then he brought the chair close to the bed. The evening sun poured in through the tall windows and filled the room with light.

Shane yawned, rolled a little in the cool sheets and pressed himself closer to his mother. He closed his eyes and listened to his father read.

Shane heard a soft hiss, and he opened his eyes.

The lights were off in his parents' room, the shades were drawn, and the sun had set a long time ago. He had fallen asleep while his father had read the book.

His parents liked to sleep with the door closed, so the room was dark.

The hiss sounded again, and it was quickly followed by a loud squeak.

'Shane," Eloise said.

He started to pant.

'Shane," she said again.

Another squeak sounded and something clattered on the floor.

"Do you hear me, Shane?" she asked, but it wasn't in English.

A different language. He didn't know what it was, but he *understood* it.

"Yes," Shane said, answering in the same tongue. It came easily to him, as easily as English.

"I want to play, Shane," she said, and something scratched across the floor.

"Hank," Shane's mother said tiredly.

A loud groan sounded.

"Oh, Jesus, Hank," his mother said, and Shane felt her sit up in the bed. Her hand stole out and found him.

"What?" he asked sleepily. "You okay, Fiona?"

The bed shifted slightly as his father sat up as well.

"What's going on?" he asked with a yawn.

The groan was followed by a scratch and a squeal.

Then something rushed across the hardwood floor and slammed into the doorframe.

"Damn it! Shane!" his father said angrily.

"He's in bed with us," his mother snapped.

"What?" he asked. "Watch your eyes."

Shane closed his eyes, and the light was turned on.

"Holy Mary Mother of God," he whispered.

Shane opened his eyes and saw his mother's long, dark brown chest of drawers pushed up against the door. Near the left corner of the room, one of the servants' doors had been opened. The thick coffin-head nails his father had used to close all of the doors lay on the floor. They were laid out in a neat row.

In the dark doorway stood three of Shane's small Star Wars action figures. Stormtroopers. Each of them had a blaster, and each blaster pointed at the bed.

"Shane," his father began.

"Hank," his mother said. "I've been holding onto him since I first heard a noise. He hasn't been out of this bed."

His father shook his head. "It doesn't make sense."

"Yes it does," Shane said, sinking back into the middle of the bed and looking up at the tin paneled ceiling.

"What do you mean?" his mother asked.

"Eloise is angry," Shane said, closing his eyes. "She wants to play with me, but you won't let her."

"Who's Eloise?" his mother said.

Shane opened his eyes and looked at her. "She's a little girl."

"And, and she's dead?" his mother asked.

"What killed her?" his father asked, and Shane could hear the doubt in his voice.

"The house did," Shane said.

"What?" his father asked, surprised. "What do you mean the house killed her?"

"The girl in the pond," Shane said. "She told the house to take Eloise, so it did."

"How do you know?" his mother asked.

"Eloise told me," Shane said.

"When?" his father asked.

"This morning," Shane said, closing his eyes and pulling the sheet up around him. "This morning. Where?" his father asked.

"In the butler's pantry," Shane answered. "There's another door in there."

His mother said something, but Shane couldn't quite make it out. Sleep stole over him, and he wondered what the dead would do next.

Chapter 10: Trespassing

Rick and Rita Ryan sat in their rented car a few houses down from the house which rightfully should have been theirs. Rick's obnoxious younger brother, Hank, had left everything to that spoiled brat Shane.

The same Shane, who had turned away a full scholarship to the Harvard Divinity School so he could join the Marines.

Shane, Rick and Rita agreed, was as stupid as Hank and Fiona had been.

And while Rick didn't particularly care for any of *those* people, he didn't particularly care as to where Hank and Fiona had disappeared to. At first, he had thought perhaps Hank had gotten himself into some financial trouble, and he and Fiona had taken off. It didn't explain the house, though, or why it was left to Shane.

After some thought, Rick and Rita had agreed Shane must have done something to his parents. In fact, they were positive and that somehow the boy had managed to convince the Marines and the government he was actually in South Carolina at basic training the whole time.

Rick knew better.

The boy had made his parents disappear.

It made perfect sense. The boy had been troubled ever since they had moved into the house. Rick and Hank's mother had told him so. Shane probably snuck back, murdered his parents and then he hid the bodies on his way back to South Carolina.

He was trained to be a killer, after all.

"There he is," Rita said.

Rick shook away his thoughts and looked to where Rita pointed.

Shane walked out of the yard, turned to the right and made his way up the street. Rick followed his nephew's progress until he crested a small rise and disappeared from view.

"Do you think he'll be gone long?" she asked, looking over at Rick.

"Has to be," Rick said confidently. "Kid doesn't even have a car. Must be walking to that hole of an apartment of his."

Rita nodded her agreement, pulled her peroxide blonde hair into a ponytail and asked, "Ready?"

"Yes, let's get it done," Rick said. He patted his coat pocket to make sure he had the car keys before getting out. Rita did the same, and a moment later they hurried across the street. They reached the sidewalk, crossed it and entered the property.

The first thing Rick noticed was the lack of noise.

No birds sang in the trees. No squirrels ran across the yard.

The house and everything around it were oddly silent.

Rita didn't seem to notice. She made a straight line for the front door.

Rick shook off his worries, hurried after her and caught up just as she turned the knob. Together, they entered the house.

"Good God," she said, "he left the place unlocked."

"What does he care?" Rick asked, closing the door behind him. "He didn't have to work for any of this. My brother did."

Rick swelled up self-righteously, and Rita gave him a pat on the arm.

"That's why we're here," she said proudly. "He doesn't deserve this stuff. Not the way you do."

Rick nodded in agreement.

The floor above them creaked as someone walked across it.

Rick saw Rita's eyes widen, and he felt his own do the same.

Behind them, the deadbolt clicked into place.

The room darkened, as though the sun was on a dimmer.

"Rick," Rita said uncomfortably. "No one's here, right?"

Rick shook his head. "Can't be. We watched this place all day, and the only one in or out was Shane."

All of the doors on the first floor slammed closed simultaneously, and the hallway was plunged into darkness.

Rita reached out and took hold of his arm. She pulled herself closer as she asked, "What the *hell* is going on, Rick?"

"I don't know," he answered.

And then someone took hold of his other arm. The grip was cold as it burned his flesh through his clothes.

"Yes, Rick," a soft, feminine voice said, "what is going on?"

"Oh, Jesus Christ protect us!" Rick yelled, ripping his arm out of the thing's grasp and stumbling into Rita.

"Who's here?" Rita demanded, tugging Rick closer to her.

The voice remained a short distance from them and chuckled. "A better question is, why are you here, in my house?"

The temperature sank quickly, and Rick shook with both chills and fear. Rita screamed and let go of his arm.

"Rita?!" Rick yelled, swinging his arms wide, trying to find his wife. His heart beat erratically and his breath came in great gasps. The panic attacks he had gotten a hold of decades earlier in his life came back, a great, terrible force. Waves of fear slammed into him, and he stumbled over his own feet. "Rita!"

"Not as lively as when she left you," the voice said. "No, not by far."

Rick turned away from the voice, stumbled into something heavy on the floor and fell headlong over it. He threw his hands out in front of him, his fingers broke and his knee crumpled as he landed. An involuntary scream was ripped out of his throat, and he groaned as he rolled onto his back.

A few feet away, a door opened, and a single, long rectangle of light spilled into the hallway.

It framed Rita perfectly.

Or what was left of Rita.

Her face was gone. Neatly removed, as though a surgeon had freed her of the burden of flesh. Her eyes were now lidless and stared straight up. An old porcelain doll sat beside his wife's mangled face. Its legs were spread, the dress it wore was a faded yellow and with expansive ruffles. The doll's blonde hair was neatly brushed and braided.

The doll looked at him, blinked, and grinned with bright white teeth.

Rick tried to look away, but brutally cold hands gripped his ears and forced his horrified gaze back to his wife's corpse.

"This house is not yours," the same feminine voice said from behind him. "It is mine. You were not invited in. You shall not be allowed out. But I think, dear Richard, you will live a little longer than your wife. Although you shall regret it."

And Rick screamed as the owner of the voice slowly peeled his ears from his head.

Chapter 11: Shane, November 6th, 1985

Shane lay in bed and listened to his parents argue.

He was sure they believed he was asleep, but they had woken him up.

He listened to the clock by his bed tick away the seconds, his father's voice clearly audible above it.

"I'm only saying it's a possibility, Fiona," he said.

"Really, Hank?" she said angrily. "Really? You're ready to think our son has some sort of supernatural, psychic abilities, but you won't admit to ghosts?"

"There's no evidence concerning ghosts," his father said defensively.

"Oh," his mother sneered, "and what 'evidence' is there about psychic phenomenon?"

"Lots," he snapped. "Places like Harvard and Yale, they're all doing tests in the field. It's documented. They can even repeat it in laboratory settings."

"So," she said. "You would rather believe our son has been doing all of this crap himself instead of thinking maybe, just maybe he might be right about the dead being here?"

"Come on, Fiona," his father said. Shane recognized the tone. It was the 'you know I'm right, let's not argue' tone Dad used to try to get his mother to calm down.

It never worked, and it didn't work this time either.

His mother got angrier.

"Shut up, *Henry*," his mother said.

Oh no, Shane thought. She had used his father's given name. The name he hated.

"Jesus Christ," he said. "We've never seen any of the stuff done. It's always when he's asleep or was about to sleep. It's definitely more in line with psychic abilities than it is with ghosts."

"What the hell is it going to take to get you to believe it?" she demanded.

"I need to know Eloise and Thaddeus were real," his father said defensively. "Prove to me they were real, and we can start to discuss the possibility of there being ghosts here."

Shane's mother said something Shane didn't quite catch, but he knew it wasn't pleasant. His dad didn't respond. He never responded when she said something really mean.

Evidence, Shane said to himself, closing his eyes. *I need to go to the library. I'll be able to get evidence there, I bet. The librarians know everything.*

Chapter 12: Shane, November 7th, 1985

It took Shane twenty-five minutes to walk from St. Christopher's School to the library, which was on Court Street, tucked behind the newspaper office and the canal. The air was cold, and he thought he might use the payphone to call his mom for a ride home when he was done.

It all depended on whether she was in a good mood or not.

She hadn't been angry with him before he left for school in the morning. She had even given him permission to go to the library. But she was definitely still mad about the argument with his dad, even though she didn't realize Shane had overheard most of it.

Maybe she still won't be mad at dad, he thought. He hurried to the library doors, pushed them open and walked in. Inside, it was wonderfully quiet.

He had been to the library several times with his mother and once with his father, but this was his first visit alone.

A pretty, older woman with black and white hair stood behind the long circulation desk. She punched date cards in a machine. The clunk of each stamp seemed entirely appropriate for the library.

After a moment, the librarian looked up, saw Shane and smiled.

"Good afternoon," she said. "May I help you?"

"I'm trying to look up the history of a house," Shane said. "Could you help me?"

"Well," the librarian said, putting the date cards down. "I can't, but we have a special librarian who knows how to find everything there is in the library. I'll bring you to her, okay?"

"Okay." Shane said, nodding.

"Good," the librarian said, "Follow me."

She walked down the length of the desk, and Shane kept pace with her as she headed towards a desk in the center of a larger room. An overhead sign said "Reference Desk" written on it in large red letters.

A woman much younger than the librarian, and possibly even younger than his mom, sat at the desk. A large, black bound book was open in front of her. She looked up over her glasses as Shane and the librarian approached.

"Tina," the woman smiled, inserting a slip of paper between the pages before closing it.

"Hello, Helen. This young man needs help finding out information on a particular house," Tina turned to Shane and said, "Good luck!"

"Thank you," Shane said, smiling.

"So you need help?" Helen asked.

"Yes, ma'am. I do," Shane answered.

"Excellent. You are in the right place, young man," she said with a grin. "Now, what house do you want to know about?"

"My house," Shane said. "I live at one twenty-five Berkley Street."

The smile on Helen's face dropped away. She cleared her throat uncomfortably and asked, "Did you say one twenty-five Berkley Street?"

"Yes, ma'am," Shane said.

Helen's skin grew pale. She licked her lips nervously. "How long have you lived there?"

"A couple of years," Shane said.

"Oh," she said. "I grew up on Chester Street."

"Hey," Shane said with a smile, "Chester Street is right next to Berkley."

Helen nodded. She managed a small smile and then asked him, "So, what would you like to know about your house?"

Shane grew serious. "I'd like to know if anyone ever died at my house."

For a long moment, Helen didn't answer and Shane was worried he had asked an inappropriate question.

Finally, she took a deep breath and asked, "Why do you want to know if someone died in the house? What's happened?"

Shane looked at her and whispered, "You know, don't you."

Helen opened her mouth to reply, closed it, and then she nodded. "Yes. Yes, I do know."

"How?" he asked her.

She glanced around before she leaned forward and said, "I went in, once, when I was a little girl."

"What did you see?" Shane asked.

"When my parents were talking with Mrs. Anderson I was allowed to play in her parlor. The room was dark, and out of the shadows, I heard another little girl."

"Eloise," Shane whispered.

Helen nodded her head. "Yes. Eloise. We talked for a while. She wouldn't come out of the shadows. She didn't want to scare me. I thought she had something wrong with her. After a little while, she went away, and I went into the kitchen. I told my parents and asked how long Mrs. Anderson's granddaughter was visiting."

"Eloise lives there," Shane said. "She never leaves."

"No," Helen said. "She never leaves."

"Did she die there?" Shane asked.

"Yes," Helen said, nodding. "Yes, she did. I'm not sure how. No one is. There is a small book, in the Stearns Room, about your house. Are you old enough to read it?"

Shane nodded.

Helen looked at him closely for a minute and then she stood up. "Yes. I think you are, too. Come with me. I'm sorry, I didn't even ask you your name."

"I'm Shane Ryan," Shane said, extending his hand the way his father had taught him.

Helen smiled and shook it. "Helen McGill. Follow me, Shane."

She led him to the back of the library, along the rear wall to a room guarded by a pair of large, wooden doors. She took a key ring out of her pocket, unlocked the door and pushed it open. A tall room was revealed. Bookshelves were protected by glass fronts and narrow windows looked out over the canal's small waterfall. A long table, occupied by half a dozen leather chairs, stood in the room's center.

Helen turned on the light, walked over to a bookcase and slid the glass protector out of the way. She bent down, reached in and withdrew a slim book. Helen looked at it briefly before she stood up and walked to the table.

"Sit down, Shane," she said, pulling out a chair for herself. Shane sat down at the table beside her.

She put the book down and opened it.

Shane leaned forward and saw a black and white picture of his house beside a faded picture of a different, smaller house.

"This house," Helen said, tapping the picture of the strange home, "was at one twenty-five Berkley Street before yours. The Andersons purchased the property in nineteen thirty, and then they added on and changed it into the one you live in now."

"When was the first one built?" Shane asked.

Helen turned the page to 'Chapter I.'

"According to whoever wrote this," she said, "the original house was built in eighteen-fourteen. It was sold several times and each time the house was changed just a little bit. Things were added on."

She turned the page to a curious illustration.

"Do you see this?" she asked, tracing a thick line with her finger.

"Yes," Shane said.

"Each wide line is a secret corridor," Helen said. "As the house was built, and wealthier people bought it, they made sure their servants couldn't be seen. The servants were able to walk to any room in the house without bothering the owners. And that was the way they wanted it. By the time the Andersons bought and finished the house to the way it is now, they made sure the doors the servants used couldn't even be noticed when they were closed."

Shane nodded. "I know. It's terrible. My father thinks he sealed all of the doors, but we keep finding them."

Helen looked at him, swallowed nervously and said, "I'm going to tell you a secret, Shane, okay?"

"Yes," he answered.

"The house makes more doors," she said in a low voice. "Eloise told me all those years ago."

"Helen," Shane said nervously, "do you know who Thaddeus is?"

Helen's hands shook, and she turned several pages to another picture.

Shane looked at an old photograph of a boy about his own age. The boy wore an old-fashioned suit, worn boots and he smiled at the camera. He held a small rifle in his hands and behind him was the pond at Shane's house.

Shane knew it was the pond because he could see the dead girl in it. The girl with no name who stayed right below the surface and watched him in the yard.

"Do you see her?" Helen whispered.

Shane nodded.

"Not everyone does," Helen said, closing the book on the disturbing photograph. "Thaddeus swallowed some water while swimming in the pond and later, when he fell asleep, he died. They call it dry drowning. A little water in the lungs is enough to kill."

"She killed him," Shane said. It wasn't a question, and Helen didn't take it as one.

"She did," Helen agreed. "I can remember looking at the pond as a little girl. Mrs. Anderson made sure I never was allowed near it. Sometimes, from my window, I could see the fish swimming in the water, or the watermen near the edges. Once in a great while ducks would land on the water, but they'd fly away soon after, and there'd always be a dead duck floating."

"She doesn't like ducks," Shane said, nodding. "I've seen a couple of dead ducks before my dad fishes them out. He says they died naturally, but I know she killed them. I don't know why, though."

Shane looked at her. "Could you do me a favor, Helen?"

"What is it?" she asked.

"Could you write down the names of Eloise and Thaddeus for me, and when they died?" he said.

"Sure," she said, slightly confused. "Why?"

"My dad doesn't believe there are ghosts in the house," Shane answered. "He thinks I'm the one who keeps moving things around."

Helen frowned. "Does your mom believe you?"

Shane nodded. "He said he might believe in ghosts if my mother could prove people had died in the house."

"A lot of people have died at one twenty-five Berkley Street, Shane," Helen said in a grim voice. "Eloise and Thaddeus are only two of them."

Shane sighed and said, "I was afraid so."

Chapter 13: Whispers in the Walls

Something was wrong.

Shane could feel it.

With the morning sun on his back and his few possessions in the truck he had rented, Shane stood in the open doorway.

The house felt *wrong*. It smelled wrong.

Blood, Shane thought. *I can smell blood.*

His hands itched to hold a glass of whiskey as he stepped into the house and walked forward. The sun shined down into the rooms off the hallway, and some of the light spilled out onto the beautiful hardwood floor.

And Shane saw the stain. Not a large stain, just a few drops a dozen steps in. He walked slowly to the spot and crouched down.

Blood, Shane thought. He reached out and touched it. It was dry. He straightened up and looked around.

Whispers came from behind the massive grandfather clock and as Shane took a step towards it, the pendulum started to swing. The hands moved backward, playfully.

"Eloise," Shane said.

A giggle sounded, and the whispers stopped.

The clock's hands changed directions.

"Eloise," Shane said again.

"Hello Shane," Eloise said, her voice slightly muffled. "You've been gone a very long time."

"I know," Shane said. Fear crawled up his legs and settled in his stomach.

"Why?" Eloise asked, tapping on the wall on either side of the clock.

The noise brought back memories of his childhood and Shane shivered.

"I wasn't allowed." Shane said. He cleared his throat. "Did anyone come in here yesterday?"

"Yes," Eloise answered.

"Did they leave?" Shane asked.

"No," she said.

"Well," Shane said, anger slowly replacing his fear, "where are they, Eloise?"

"Here," she said. "In the walls, and in the basement. In the attic and in the pond."

"How many people came in?" he asked.

"Two," Eloise said.

Shane closed his eyes and took a deep breath. A moment later he opened them and asked, "What happened to them?"

"Carl happened to them," Eloise said cheerfully.

Shane's breath caught in his throat. "Carl."

"Carl," she repeated. "We've all missed you so much, Shane. Where will you be sleeping tonight? In your room?"

"Yes," Shane said softly, turning to look back at the stain on the floor. "Yes. Where else would I sleep?"

For the briefest of moments, he wondered who had died at the hands of Carl, and then he pushed the thought away.

I'll find out soon enough, he sighed. He turned around and headed for the door. He needed to bring his things in.

Book 1: Berkley Street

Chapter 14: Shane, December 12th, 1985

Shane's father finally believed in ghosts.

It wasn't because Shane had gotten the information from Helen, the librarian. It wasn't because his mother had double checked the information with Helen, the librarian. It wasn't even his father going down himself to the library.

No. It wasn't any of those.

It was what had happened in the morning. Down at the pond.

The weather had been a little warmer, and the sun and wind had cleared the snow from the surface of the pond. The ice, revealed, shined brightly, and his father had wondered if he could see the fish under the ice.

Shane had stood a safe distance away from the pond. He didn't trust it. Especially after Helen had told him about Thaddeus.

So Shane stood in snow that covered up to the tops of his moon boots. He moved his toes around and listened as the Wonderbread bags on his feet crinkled. The bags were an extra layer of warmth and protection, insisted upon by his mom.

Shane pretended to smoke and exhaled great clouds of his breath into the air as he watched his dad, who crept carefully out onto the ice.

Shane's mother had left the house earlier, shortly after he got home from school, to get the groceries. His father had been home since a furnace technician had come out and double checked the furnace and the oil line. If his mother hadn't gone to get food, then Shane's father never would have gone out on the ice.

She wouldn't have let him.

Shane's father knew it as well, and he had sworn Shane to secrecy.

Shane had agreed, but he also knew if his father did something foolish he'd have to tell his mom.

Shane didn't want to disappoint his mother, and a lie would upset her.

"Oh damn!" his father yelled, and Shane watched as his father suddenly sank to his knees in the pond, the ice cracking loudly beneath him.

"Dad!" Shane cried out.

"I'm okay," his father said, twisting around to face Shane. He forced a smile. "I'm just freezing and wet. I'll be fine."

The smile vanished though, and he stumbled back. A look of pure terror filled his face as he struggled towards the shore. He jerked back again, and he looked down, let out a terrified scream and practically ran out of the pond.

Shane stepped towards him, and he pointed back to the house.

"Inside!" his father yelled. "Inside now!"

Something sickly and white reached up out of the water from behind him.

Shane turned and sprinted for the basement door. Behind him, he heard heavy footsteps crash through the snow. Just as Shane made it inside, his father rushed in behind him and slammed the door shut.

The man breathed raggedly and shook from head to toe. Water dripped from his jeans and leaked out of his boots. Shane watched him take cautious steps to the washer and dryer, strip down and then dig a pair of sweats and fresh socks out of a wicker laundry basket. Within a minute, he was dressed, and he left his wet clothes where they lay.

"Come on, Shane," his father said hoarsely. "Let's go upstairs."

Shane kicked off his snow gear, pulled the bread bags off of his feet, and dutifully went up into the kitchen. His dad opened a cabinet, took out some alcohol and poured himself a large drink. Shane rarely saw him with alcohol, and he had never seen him upend a glass and empty it in one gulp.

His father's hands shook as he put the glass on the counter.

For a long, silent minute he gripped the edge of the counter and looked down at the sink.

"I'm sorry," he said after a minute. "I'm sorry, Shane."

"Why?" Shane asked.

His father turned and faced him, his lips pressed tightly together and nearly white. "For not believing you about ghosts. About the ghosts here."

"What did you see?" Shane asked in a low voice.

"A girl," he answered quickly. "I saw a girl in the pond. She grabbed my leg. She tried to pull me in."

The man turned back to the glass and the bottle and poured himself another drink.

"I'm sorry," his father whispered, and Shane nodded as the glass was emptied again.

Chapter 15: Why He Returned

Shane was afraid.

He sat in his old bed, a book beside him. His cigarettes and lighter stood beside his bottle of whiskey and a tumbler. Shane had made sure to move the bureau away from the servants' door. He had removed the nails from every door he could find.

Soon Shane would have to speak with them. Almost all of them.

And he didn't want them in a bad mood.

They're grumpy enough as it is, he thought with a sigh.

He looked down at his book, *The Moon is Down*, by John Steinbeck, and he wondered idly if he could concentrate enough to read. He doubted it, and he doubted they would give him the opportunity.

Eloise was pleased he had returned. Carl was happy he had come back. And the old man, well, who knew with the old man.

The real question, however, was whether or not Shane would be allowed to find his parents. Or at least, learn what had happened to them.

Shane leaned back against his pillows and looked at the lights in his room. He had three of them plugged in, as well as his fan which droned on slowly as it oscillated from left to right and back again. For decades, the lights and fan had helped him sleep. In the Marines, he had been too exhausted to not sleep well. On the rare occasions where sleep attempted to avoid him, well, the raucous noise of his Marine brethren had lulled him into rest.

Shane closed his eyes, listened to the white noise of the fan and waited.

He didn't know if he had fallen asleep or if they had waited only for him to seem at rest. Regardless as to what occurred, his thoughts were brought back into focus by the strained squeak of the servants' door.

Memories of childhood, of his screams as they ricocheted off walls, it all came back to him with brutal force. The fear evoked by the hidden portal was visceral and primal. Shane was no longer a man of forty returned to his parents' home, but a child of eight, trapped in the Star Wars sheets of his bed.

Shane forced himself to keep his eyes closed. Silently he counted the seconds as they dragged by, carried along with the scratching of his old bureau on the wood floor.

Seven seconds exactly and the noise ceased.

"Shane," Eloise said.

"Hello, Eloise," Shane replied, keeping his eyes closed.

"Why won't you look at me?" she asked playfully. "Are you afraid, Shane?"

"Always," he answered truthfully.

The dead girl laughed and a boy asked, "Why have you come back to us, Shane?"

Thaddeus, Shane thought. "I need answers," he said aloud. "I need to know where my parents are, Thaddeus."

"Hmph," Thaddeus said, and Shane could picture the dead boy's frown. "Your parents are exactly where she wants them to be."

"Who is 'she'?" Shane asked, his heart beating excitedly.

"The girl in the pond," Eloise whispered. "She is she."

"Yes," Thaddeus said. "She likes your parents where they are. They're nearly quite mad, you know."

Shane stiffened and opened his eyes.

As he did so, the lights flicked out, and the fan stopped. Shane's breathing was terribly loud.

The room was black, too dark for him to see anything.

But he could smell them. The stale air odor which lingered about the two children. He knew it well.

"May I see my parents?" he managed to ask after peered into the darkness for a moment.

"You may," Thaddeus said, chuckling, "or you may not. It is her decision, Shane. Not ours."

"How do I ask her permission?" Shane asked.

Neither of the ghosts answered him.

"How do I ask for permission?" Shane snapped, trying to keep the rage and excitement out of his voice.

"You don't want to ask, Shane," Eloise whispered. "You don't ever want to talk to her."

"No," Thaddeus agreed. "Best to forget about your parents, for now, Shane. They will keep, and you must as well. Not everyone is pleased to see you've returned."

Chapter 16: Investigation

Detective Marie Lafontaine stood on the corner of East Stark Street and Berkley Street. She adjusted her scarf and looked out at Berkley Street, first to the left, and then to the right.

In Brighton, Massachusetts, a middle-aged woman had reported her parents missing. Richard and Rita Ryan. Ages sixty-seven and sixty-eight respectively. Both were recently retired. Richard had sold his share of his wife's family's car dealership, at a loss, to pay for a decades-long legal battle which he had lost.

A legal battle over the property of his missing, and legally declared dead brother.

A black Toyota Nissan Sentra, rented to Mr. Ryan, had been found abandoned on East Stark Street. The car had faced the house which Mr. Ryan and his wife had so recently lost the battle for.

The car had been ticketed twice for being parked overnight. Finally, an alderman who lived on Berkley Street had called to complain. The car was towed to the impound lot, its information put through the system, and Mr. Ryan's information had popped up. Another cross-check showed the man and Rita were listed as missing persons.

The discovery of the car, parked so close to the house, brought with it a concern of foul play. Especially since ownership of the house had been so heavily contested and for such a lengthy period of time.

The house was now owned and occupied by Shane Ryan, son of Hank and Fiona Ryan, who had mysteriously vanished while Shane was in South Carolina at Marine Corps basic training.

Marie looked at the house and felt uncomfortable, sickened.

Something was wrong with it. Something was off. She wasn't quite sure what it was, but she could feel it. A knife blade of doubt and fear in her stomach.

Marie opened the door of the unmarked Impala, leaned in and took the microphone out of its cradle. She keyed it.

"Base this is Four Three," she said.

"Four Three this is Base, go."

"Base, approaching number one two five Berkley Street for interview."

"Good copy, Four Three, check back in five."

"Copy, out," she said.

Marie hung the microphone back up and closed the door. She pushed aside her jacket, adjusted the volume on her handheld radio, and crossed Berkley Street. She walked directly to the front door of the house, rapped on it sharply, and waited.

Several moments passed and she raised her hand to knock again when the sound of a lock's tumbler interrupted her. She lowered her arm and took a cautious step-down.

The door opened, and an exhausted-looking man answered the door. She estimated him to be in his late thirties, perhaps a hundred and fifty pounds and almost five ten. Her critical eye roved over him and identified his worn and faded blue jeans, a patched black sweater, and new running shoes. He lacked any sort of hair from what she could see. Not by choice, but by a physical ailment.

"May I help you?" the man asked politely.

Marie nodded. "Mr. Ryan? I'm Detective Lafontaine with the Nashua Police Department, I was wondering if I could ask you a few questions?"

"Sure," he said, stepping aside. "Come on in. Too cold out to chat on the front step."

"Thank you," Marie said as she walked into the massive foyer. She kept her reactions under control, but she was impressed at the size of the house. It looked even bigger on the inside than it did from the street, and the house was huge when viewed from the curb.

"So," Mr. Ryan said. "What can I help you with, Detective?"

"I'm here because a car your aunt and uncle rented was found nearby," Marie said.

Shane frowned. "You mean Rick and Rita Ryan?"

"Yes," she said.

"I don't know why it would be," he said. "I haven't spoken to either of them since my grandmother's funeral in nineteen eighty-seven."

"So you haven't seen either one of them?"

He shook his head. "No. We're not exactly on good terms. They know they wouldn't be welcome here."

"Why exactly?" Marie asked, although she already knew the answer.

"They wanted my parents' house," Mr. Ryan said, gesturing at the home. "They've been trying to get it since my parents disappeared over twenty years ago."

"They've been trying to get you out of the house?" she asked.

Mr. Ryan chuckled and shook his head. "No. I haven't been living here. Not in the house. Because of the legal issues the house has been empty."

"Where have you been living?" Marie said.

"On Locust Street. Little studio apartment," he answered.

"And do you live here alone?" she asked.

Mr. Ryan nodded.

"Do you work outside of the house?"

"No," he said. "I do freelance translating. All of my work is done online. I walk a bit each day, but otherwise, I spend most of my time indoors."

"Is your car in the shop?" Marie asked. "I didn't see it outside."

"I don't own a car," he replied. "I don't like to drive."

Marie glanced around the hallway and then she asked, "When did you move in?"

"Three days ago," he said.

"The house is spotless," Marie said, registering a curious looking splatter on the wood floor. "Did it take you a long time to clean it?"

"What do you mean?" he asked.

"You said the house was empty this whole time," Marie said, smiling. "There must have been a lot of dust."

"No," Mr. Ryan said with a shake of his head. "There wasn't. The house takes care of itself. I didn't have to clean anything."

"Oh," she said. *This place has been scoured. He's full of it. Someone's been cleaning.*

Her nose wrinkled slightly at a metallic smell. *Old blood?* She thought. Marie smiled and offered her hand and he shook it. "Well, thank you for your time, Mr. Ryan."

Marie took a business card out of her wallet and handed it to him. "This is my number at the station, Mr. Ryan. Please call me immediately if you hear from either your aunt or your uncle."

The man nodded his head as he took it. He held it loosely in one hand and walked her to the door. He opened it for her and nodded good-bye.

When Marie reached the sidewalk, she keyed her radio and said, "Four Three to Base."

"Go ahead Four Three, this is Base."

"Finished at one two five Berkley Street. En route to station."

"Good copy, Four Three."

"Four Three out."

Marie returned the radio to her belt and glanced back at the house.

In the far, upper right window a young man watched her carefully.

She waved, and he waved in return.

Marie turned away and thought, *He said he lived alone.*

She would have to check out some of what Mr. Ryan had said, and learn why the house stank of blood.

Chapter 17: The Little Place of Forgetting, August 1st, 1986

Shane sat in the library on the second floor of his house. He usually didn't go into the library. Neither did his parents. The room had come fully stocked with books, but they weren't anything his parents had ever been interested in reading. The library was usually off limits, since his mother had a 'weird feeling' about it.

When Shane had woken up a few hours earlier, the rain had poured down from dark clouds. His father had left for work, and his mother had gone to visit a friend, and Shane had been given permission to stay at home.

Which was better than a visit to Mrs. Murray, where his mother would spend the better part of the day.

Shane had wanted to finish the tank model he had started the night before. Unfortunately, he had left the cap off of the glue, so he couldn't complete it. He couldn't paint it either since he had forgotten to buy new paints.

For about an hour he had wandered around the house and tried to stay out of most of the rooms. Eloise had loosened a few of the doors, and he could hear her in the walls. The old man who lived in his parents' bathroom had filled the second floor with groans for most of the morning.

The only room Shane hadn't been into was the library.

And so he had gone there to escape Eloise and the old man, Thaddeus and some of the others whose names he didn't know. He wasn't afraid of them, at least not during the day. At nighttime, he was terrified, but it wasn't his fault. They opened doors constantly.

The only one he was afraid of during the daytime was the girl in the pond. The unnamed girl. The one who had tried to drown his father, and who always got closer to the surface when Shane was in the backyard.

So, in an effort to avoid the wanderers in the walls and the murderer in the water, Shane had decided to visit the library.

And he was *thrilled*.

The previous owner had been Mr. Anderson. Shane's father said the man had filled the library with books. They were great books. Books all about wars and military and history.

All of the things Shane loved to read about. Most of the books were old. Some of them printed in foreign languages, and there were dictionaries for all the languages too. Shane could figure out what they were about if he wanted to.

When the clock on the library's mantle struck ten, Shane stretched. On the floor in front of him was a German to English dictionary. Beside it was a slim book. Shane had figured out the title.

Letters of German Students in the World War.

It had taken him a long time.

A cool breeze suddenly ran along Shane's back.

He twisted around to see what it was.

All he could see were bookshelves.

And it didn't feel the same as when Eloise or Thaddeus moved past him.

He held his hand out and felt the cold air against his skin. He moved his hand a little to the left, and the breeze disappeared. Back to the right and he found it again.

Shane twisted around and started to follow the air. Soon he felt it on his face, and it seemed to issue forth from a bookshelf. When he reached it, Shane touched the books on the shelves and found only the ones on the bottom shelf were cold.

A secret door, Shane thought. He was excited. This wasn't a secret door the dead had told him about. Or one his father had found. No one knew about it but himself.

Shane stood up, and he looked at the bookshelf carefully. Then he found what he sought, a small, smooth bump at the back of the center shelf. He reached in and pushed on it.

A loud click sounded, and the whole bookcase swung out half an inch.

Excited, Shane took hold of the edge and pulled it back. The whole thing moved easily and silently.

Behind it, a tall, dark wood door was revealed. A slim metal handle protruded, and Shane grabbed it. He twisted up and down, but the door didn't budge. Then he pulled it to the left, and the door slid on tracks into the wall. A hole was revealed, set within the floor. The walls were smooth, a push-button light switch the only thing marring the surface.

Shane turned the light on and down the length of the hole, lights flickered into life. Electric bulbs in wire cages.

Shane leaned forward slightly and looked down.

Perhaps twenty or so feet down, he saw a skeleton, clad in a suit, and curled up on the floor of the hole.

Shane shivered, turned off the light and closed the door. He looked at the bookcase as he was about to close it and saw something written on the backside of it.

My Oubliette, the first sentence said. *My little place of forgetting. I shall forget he existed, and so shall the world.*

Shane's hands shook as he closed the secret door and he wondered who the person was.

Book 1: Berkley Street

Chapter 18: Carl and the Remembering

Once more Shane sat in his room.

He had found the picture, which his parents had hidden from him in his father's sock drawer when he was fourteen.

The photograph was in a tramp art frame, a cunning piece of woodwork made from scraps. Some man had crafted it in the Great Depression and made it as a gift for Mrs. Anderson. The picture within was older than the frame, and the photo was of a handsome young man in a German uniform. The photograph had been taken at some point during the First World War, and the man's name had been Carl Hesselschwerdt.

A Stormtrooper, a skilled soldier who had survived four years of combat before he suffered a wound and had been captured by American Marines. Eventually, Carl had immigrated to the United States shortly after the economic collapse in America. He had been a scholar, had come to New Hampshire, and then he had disappeared.

Vanished until Shane had found his remains in nineteen eighty-seven, at the bottom of the oubliette. It had taken Shane a long time to find Carl's picture, to find out who the dead man had been.

Shane made sure to remember, and Carl loved him for it.

And now Shane sat in his room and waited for Carl to visit.

A flicker of light announced the dead man's arrival.

A moment later Shane caught a glimpse of Carl in the slim shadow along the wall by the closet.

"*How nice it is to have you home, Shane,*" Carl said in German.

"*It is, in a way, nice to be home again, my friend,*" Shane said, replying in German. It was a curious sensation to know he was now older than Carl had ever been.

Carl stepped out of the shadows. He was slim and rather short, but the suit he wore was well-cut, the shoes glowed with a curious light, and Shane had to remind himself the man was dead. Had been for eighty years.

And Carl, for some unknown reason, was vicious when he wanted to be.

Carl looked to the bed table, saw his own photograph and smiled. Shane remembered the night his parents had taken the photo away. Carl had been displeased, and his parents had not slept well.

Not for a long time.

In spite of their belief in ghosts, neither his mother nor his father believed Shane when he had told them Carl wanted his image placed in the open again.

"*Thank you, my friend,*" Carl said. "*Thank you for remembering.*"

"*Always,*" Shane said, smiling. "*I was wondering if perhaps you could assist me, Carl.*"

"*Of course. How?*"

"*I am seeking a way to find my parents,*" Shane said.

Carl looked at him for a long moment before he answered.

"*I can show you the entrance,*" Carl said hesitantly, "*but it will be dangerous for you. Not nearly as dangerous as it was for them, yet it will be dangerous nonetheless.*"

Shane nodded.

"*We had a bit of trouble, several days ago, Shane,*" Carl said.

Shane frowned. "*What sort of trouble?*"

"*Your aunt and uncle,*" Carl replied. "*They came in uninvited.*"

The image of the blood on the floor and the stink of it in the air flashed before Shane's eyes. "*Carl, did you do something to them?*"

"*I did.*"

Shane took a deep breath and asked, "*What, my friend, did you do to them?*"

"*I killed them.*"

"*And their bodies?*" Shane managed to ask.

"*Within the oubliette.*"

"*The police were here,*" Shane said. "*They will return.*"

"*They will not find the bodies.*"

"*I saw the evidence,*" Shane started to say.

Carl held up a hand. "*The old man has scrubbed the floor, and the dark ones have hidden the scent.*"

Shane shivered at the mention of the dark ones. He had blessedly forgotten them. The little, half-seen things, the unknown dead who scurried from shadow to shadow even in the brightest part of the day.

"*It is through them you must pass,*" Carl said, and not without compassion.

"*What do you mean?*" Shane asked, a cold sweat erupting across his brow.

"*The domain of the dark ones. The root cellar. Beneath the butler's pantry. Your parents heard them, and down they went,*" Carl said.

Shane felt sick to his stomach.

"*The root cellar,*" Shane whispered. "*They went into the root cellar.*"

Carl nodded.

In English Shane said, "I told them not to."

"*I know.*"

"I told them never to go into the root cellar. I told them to board it up. To buy cement, to fill it."

"*I know, my friend,*" Carl said sadly.

"*Are they here? Are they dead?*" Shane asked, switching back to German.

"*She will not tell us.*"

"*Will she tell me?*" Shane said.

Carl took a nervous step back. "*You cannot, Shane. No one speaks with her.*"

"*I have to know.*"

"*Then go to the root cellar,*" Carl said grimly. "*You will have a better chance there than with her.*"

Shane's heart beat so loudly, the sound of it nearly drowned out his own breath as it raced in and out of his lungs. "*I'll have to, won't I?*"

"*I cannot go with you,*" Carl said, fear thick in his voice. "*I went down once for you.*"

"*I know,*" Shane said, smiling tightly. "*I know. And I thank you for it. I do not ask you to come, Carl.*"

Shane let out a shaky laugh.

"*You will wait until the morning?*" Carl asked.

"*I will.*"

"*Will you speak with me?*" Carl said. "*It has been a long time since I have had the pleasure of your company.*"

"*Yes,*" Shane said, nodding. "*Yes. It has been far too long.*"

"*When last we spoke you were joining the United States Marine Corps,*" Carl said. "*Tell me, how was it? Did you taste the bitter draught of war, my young friend?*"

"*I did,*" Shane answered. "*And I would rather be in combat than preparing to descend the ladder into the root cellar.*"

He looked at Carl, pleased to have the ghost with him once more. After a moment he said in a low voice, "*I'm afraid, Carl.*"

The dead man nodded. "*You should be, Shane. You should be.*"

Book 1: Berkley Street

Chapter 19: Shane, October 1st, 1986

Shane was alone in the house.

Specifically, he was alone in the butler's pantry. He glanced at the boxes of dry goods, the different cans of soup and vegetables, some bags of chips, some of his father's beer and his mother's wine.

Shane focused his attention on the far left corner, though. The dark shadow where the servants' door remained hidden. He stood perfectly still and waited.

Soon, the door opened.

It swung out into the room, and an ancient hinge screamed. Shane winced and turned his head slightly. Someone spoke, and Shane strained to understand the words.

"What do you want, child?" a man asked in German. Shane had been studying the language from the books found in the library. But for some reason, he found he understood a great deal of it, especially when he heard people speak it.

"I wanted to talk to you," Shane said hesitantly. He shifted the picture he had hidden behind his back from one hand to the next, the wooden pyramids on the frame smooth beneath his skin.

The ghost snorted. *"About what would you have me speak, child?"*

"I found something," Shane said, pausing between words to make sure he was speaking correctly. He remembered the skeleton at the bottom of the oubliette. He recalled what had been written on the door, how the dead man would be forgotten.

From behind his back, Shane pulled the photograph in the curious wooden frame. A photograph of a young man in a soldier's uniform. He had seen the ghost before. He recognized his lean face in the younger man's.

The dead man said nothing for a long time.

Shane's hands shook as he held the picture out and waited to see what would happen.

Finally, the ghost asked in a whisper, *"Where did you find it, child?"*

"In the parlor," Shane answered. *"It was on a low shelf, by the fireplace. I almost didn't see it."*

He stepped out of the darkness and once more Shane recognized the suit he had seen at the bottom of the oubliette. The ghost looked up from the photograph to Shane and asked, *"Would you like to know my name?"*

"Yes," Shane said.

"I am Carl Wilhelm Hesselschwerdt, and I was murdered by Mr. Anderson," he said.

"I'm sorry," Shane responded.

Carl smiled. *"You've no need to be sorry, Shane. You will remember me?"*

Shane thought of the lonely skeleton and the horrible thing Mr. Anderson had written, and Shane nodded. *"I'm going to put the picture by my bed."*

"Thank you," Carl said with a sigh. *"Thank you."*

Chapter 20: The Morning Arrives

While the nightmares had not gotten worse with his return to the house, they had not gotten any better either.

Shane put his toothbrush back, ran his hand over his bald head, and left the bathroom. He went to his bedroom, poured himself a second shot of whiskey and downed it quickly. For a moment, he contemplated a third, but then he put the tumbler back on his bed table. Shane made his way to the kitchen to make some breakfast.

Dishes rattled in the cabinets and Shane sighed.

"Why are you here?" the old man asked, his voice seeming to come from all corners of the room at once.

"To eat breakfast," Shane said.

"I'll not accept sass, young man," the old man said, and the empty chairs at the table shivered.

"Don't ask stupid questions," Shane replied. He wasn't in any mood for the old man's harassment.

"What are you doing back at the house?" the old man said. "I am curious. Tell me why."

"I want to find my parents," Shane said, taking a drink of coffee.

"Ask her," the old man said, chuckling. "Ask her what she's done with them."

"You ask her," Shane said, cutting the ghost's laughter short.

The doorbell rang.

Shane frowned and looked at the clock on the stove.

Six thirty.

He took a bite of his toast, washed it down with a bit more of his coffee and stood up. He made his way to the front door and had just about reached it when the bell rang again.

Shane rolled his eyes at the sound, waited for it to finish and then he said through the door, "Who is it?"

"Mr. Ryan," a woman said. "This is Detective Lafontaine, and I'm here with a warrant to search your premises."

Shane groaned inwardly, undid the locks and opened the door.

Detective Lafontaine stood on the doorstep with a dozen other police officers and forensic personnel behind her. They all looked terribly serious.

For a moment, Shane had an urge to crack a joke, but he resisted.

Detective Lafontaine had an extremely severe look on her attractive face, and Shane wondered what she might look like when she wasn't being a police officer. In her hand, she held a warrant, which she offered to him. Shane nodded, accepted it, and stepped out of their way. She came in and stood beside him as he opened the warrant and read it.

Any and all evidence relating to the disappearance of Richard Michael Ryan and Rita Joan (Sanderson) Ryan, Shane saw.

Of course, he thought, managing to keep his sigh bottled up. *Of course.*

"Mr. Ryan," the detective said. "Is there anything you'd like to tell us before we begin searching the house?"

"No," Shane said honestly. "But I am going to go back to the kitchen and finish my breakfast. You're welcome to join me for a cup of coffee. Any of you are."

He folded the warrant and tucked it into his back pocket. Detective Lafontaine followed him into the kitchen.

"Do you want coffee, Detective?" he asked.

"Yes please," she said, shrugging off her coat and hanging it on the back of one of the chairs.

Shane brought down a mug, filled it and handed it to her.

"Sorry," he said, setting it down on the table, "I don't have cream or sugar."

"Thank you," she said with a polite smile. "I drink it black."

Shane returned the smile, politely, and sat down.

"So, Mr. Ryan," she said after taking a sip, "you haven't heard from your aunt or uncle?"

Shane shook his head. "If I had, I would have let you known, Detective."

"And they're not here?"

Again he shook his head.

"Is anyone else living here with you?" she asked.

"No," Shane said. "Just me and the ghosts."

She frowned. "What do you mean?"

"This place is haunted," Shane said, leaning back in his chair. "Has been since before I moved in."

She raised an eyebrow.

"Don't believe in ghosts?" Shane asked her.

"No," she answered. "No, I don't. You do?"

"Of course, I do," Shane answered. "And if you lived here, Detective, you'd believe in ghosts too."

"I'll have to take your word on it, Mr. Ryan," she said, giving him a tight smile.

A moment later, a young woman hurried into the kitchen. "Detective Lafontaine?"

"Jen?" the detective asked.

"Um, there are secret passages in the house."

The two women looked at Shane.

He put his coffee mug down and smiled at them. "Servants' passages. They run through the walls of the house. Just be careful, though. Some of them don't go where they're supposed to."

"What do you mean?" the detective asked.

"Just what I said," Shane said. "They don't go where they're supposed to. You think the passage from the pantry leads up to the floor above. You go up a few steps and suddenly there's a wall. Tomorrow, though, it might go all the way up, or it might go down into the cellar."

Detective Lafontaine looked at him with a suspicious frown, then she turned her attention back to the technician. "Check them out, and make sure you guys work in teams. It's an old house and who knows what's in the walls, or how safe they are."

"Okay, Detective," Jen said, and she left the kitchen.

Detective Lafontaine looked at him. "How long were you in the military?"

Shane knew the question was meant to catch him off guard, but it didn't.

"*Twenty years,*" he said in French. "*When did you move to the States?*"

Her eyes widened in surprise. "When I was six. How did you know? I don't have an accent."

"You do," Shane said, hiding his satisfaction. "Only a hint of one, though. I'm a linguist, Detective. I listen to people and how they talk. It's how I knew you were born in Canada, Quebec City, if I hear it properly."

She nodded, chuckled and took a sip of her coffee. "Well done, Mr. Ryan. Well done."

He gave her a short bow.

"So," she said, settling back in her chair and crossing her legs. "Twenty years in the Marines. Did you do language work there, too?"

Shane nodded. "Later on, though. My first enlistment I was all gung ho. I went straight zero three eleven, infantry. When my captain learned about my language skills though, he browbeat me until I got a slot in the language program. Saw some combat here and there, working as an interpreter. Running and gunning when I had to."

"How many languages do you speak?" she asked.

"Speak?" Shane said. "Seventeen."

"Seventeen?" Marie asked, incredulity in her voice.

Shane nodded and smiled. "Not as difficult as you think. Languages can be grouped into families. As for myself, I read and write fluently in the romance languages, but I focus my translating work on German, French and Spanish too. Just the languages I like. With my pension from the Marines and translation jobs, I do okay."

A yell from the pantry startled them both.

Detective Lafontaine was up and out of her chair before Shane, and she opened the pantry door. An older police officer stumbled out, his eyes wide and his face pale. Once in the kitchen, he paused and blinked his eyes.

"The kitchen?" he asked.

"What's wrong, Dan?" Detective Lafontaine asked.

"The kitchen?" he repeated in a lower voice. Then he looked at the detective and said, "Marie, I was in the library."

"Okay," she said.

"Marie, the library's on the second floor. Other side away from the kitchen. I walked three steps to the right and saw another door. I went through it, and I found myself in there," he said, jerking his thumb back at the dark interior of the pantry.

Marie frowned. "You're kidding."

Dan shook his head.

The technician, Jen, hurried into the room. "Detective, Bob's missing!"

"What?" Marie asked, twisting around to face her. "What do you mean?"

"He went into a passage in a bedroom upstairs, and the door closed behind him. When we opened it, he wasn't in the passage," Jen said, her face pale.

"Why the hell did he close the door?" the detective snapped, frustrated.

"He didn't," Jen said softly. "It closed by itself."

"What room?" Shane asked, taking a step towards the technician. "What room did he go into?"

"It had a fan in it," Jen started.

"Damn it," Shane spat. "Parlor."

Without waiting for anyone he hurried out of the kitchen and heard the others follow him. He made straight for the parlor, and when he opened the door, he saw a young man. The man's hair was white, and he sat on the floor by the hearth.

"Oh my God," Jen said as she came in behind Shane. "Look at his hair."

Bob seemed to notice them for the first time, his eyes wide and unfocused. The room stank of fear.

Jen, Dan and the Detective all raced to Bob, who continued to sit numbly on the floor.

"Bob," Dan said, squatting down. "Bob."

Bob looked at Dan.

"Bob," Dan repeated. "What happened?"

"She wanted to know who I was," Bob said hoarsely. "And what I was doing in the house. In the walls. She plays in the walls."

"Who plays in the walls?" Detective Lafontaine asked gently.

"Eloise," Bob said. He looked at Shane. "She took my hand and dragged me through the floor. Straight down. The girl wants us to leave you alone."

"How old is this girl?" the detective asked.

Bob blinked. "She's eight, I think. I couldn't really tell. But, she'll never get older, Marie."

"What?" Detective Lafontaine said. "Why not?"

"Because she's dead. She said they're all dead here," Bob whispered. He pointed a trembling finger at Shane. "He's the only living one here.

Chapter 21: Forced to Wait

It was nearly eight o'clock in the evening when the police finally left, empty handed.

And Shane couldn't go into the root cellar. As much as he wanted to find information on his parents, he wanted to be alive when he did it.

If he descended into the root cellar at night, he would risk his life needlessly.

Shane would have to wait again.

The police had found nothing, however, just as the dead had promised him. He felt bad for the man named Bob, and for Dan as well. A few others had been frightened, but not to the extent of those two.

Detective Lafontaine would be back. The house had both intrigued and enraged her. She wanted to know more.

So did Shane.

He grabbed a bottle of whiskey and a tall glass out of the cabinets and carried them upstairs to the library. He turned on the light, adjusted the thermostat in the room and smiled at the loud clank the steam radiator made, as the furnace rumbled into life far below him in the basement.

Shane sat down in the large chair behind the desk, set his glass on the leather blotter and poured himself a drink. He sipped the whiskey slowly, and the liquor went down as easily as water. Soon, he would make his way to bed, make sure all the lights worked properly, and turn on the fan before he faced the nightmares again.

First, though, he told himself. *First, we'll have a little more whiskey.*

The day had been long. Terribly long. He had been able to get some work done, but only a bit. The police and their technicians had more questions than Shane had answers for when it came to the house. The police had not, of course, found the remains of his aunt and uncle. Nor had they found any traces. Not even with black lights or anything else in their bag of tricks were they able to find anything.

The dead had made sure of it.

The police had remarked on it.

Something, the police had said, should have been found. Not just evidence of his aunt and uncle, but evidence of people having lived in the house for decades. Even old blood would have shown up.

Yet not a single drop had been visible.

Detective Lafontaine told him she would be back soon, and Shane didn't doubt her.

He sighed and then he took a long drink of whiskey. Within a few minutes, he finished the glass, put it down beside the bottle and closed his eyes.

The floor creaked, and the stench of mildew and rot filled the library.

Shane opened his eyes.

It was ten past nine. He had fallen asleep.

His nostrils flared, and he realized the smell hadn't been part of a dream. The library actually stank. Shane sat up straight and looked around the room and then he froze.

On the floor by the desk were small, wet footprints. They circled the desk and then led out the library door and into the hallway.

Cautiously, Shane got to his feet and followed the trail. The tracks seemed to have started at the desk itself, as though the owner had suddenly appeared. In the hallway, the prints turned to the right, towards Shane's room. He found a large puddle just outside of his doorway, but the trail continued on to the left and did not enter.

Part of him breathed a sigh of relief as he followed the footprints farther down the hall, towards an empty front bedroom. Just before the closed door, however, the footsteps disappeared.

Shane stopped beside them and looked at the wall. A large, gilt-framed painting of a forest hung upon the wall. The piece of art was huge, perhaps four feet in width and another seven in height; the woodland scene was dark and grim; terrible things hinted within the shadows.

The canvas rippled in front of him, and a cool breeze slipped around the edges.

Shane licked his lips nervously and reached out. He had never liked the painting. In fact, he had avoided it as much as possible as a child.

Perhaps there's more to it, he told himself.

He reached out with his right hand and as he slowly traced the frame with his suspicious fingers, he immediately discovered a small protrusion. The tiniest hint of a lock he had suspected would be there.

Shane pressed it gently, and the painting swung out effortlessly into the hall.

A cold, foul wind slapped him and stung his eyes. They swelled up with tears as he took a cautious step back. He blinked them away to see what he had exposed.

Narrow stairs which led up. Straight up.

"Don't," a voice said, and Shane recognized it as the old man's. "Don't."

The voice was behind him, and Shane fought the urge to turn around, to see if he would finally catch sight of the ghost who owned the voice.

Instead, Shane managed to whisper, "Why?"

"Simply, don't," the old man said sadly. "At least not without the benefit of the sun, Shane."

Shane opened his mouth to ask why again, but closed it instead.

"Go to bed, Shane," the old man whispered. "Worry about this problem tomorrow."

Shane nodded and closed the painting over. With a nervous swallow, he went to his room and got ready for bed.

Chapter 22: Shane, October 27th, 1986

"Where did you get the picture?" his father asked.

"It was in the parlor," Shane answered. He sat on his bed and looked at his mother and father. He was confused. "Why? What's wrong with it?"

"Nothing's wrong with it, Shane," his mother said. "We just don't think your fascination with war is healthy."

Shane frowned. "I'm not fascinated with war. I like to read about history. Military history."

His father sighed. "Shane, we don't mind you reading about history. It's having a soldier's picture on your bed table. It's kind of strange. You don't even know who the man is."

"Yes, I do," Shane said.

"Really?" his mother asked skeptically. "Who is he?"

"Carl Wilhelm Hesselschwerdt," Shane answered.

His father laughed, and his mother gave him an amused smile.

"Well," she said, "you've certainly created an interesting name for him."

"I didn't," Shane said defensively.

"How do you know his name then?" his father asked between chuckles.

"He told me."

The humor vanished from his parents' faces.

"Don't be funny, Shane," his father said angrily.

"I'm not," Shane said, trying not to snap. "He told me his name. He died here."

"Did you find out about him at the library?" his mother asked, concern in her voice.

"No," Shane answered.

"Where then?" his father demanded.

"Here. He told me his name here," Shane said.

"Yes," his mother said quickly, "but, how did you know he died here?"

"Oh," Shane said. He scratched the back of his head, hesitated a moment and then he said, "Well, I found his body."

"Jesus Christ!" his father snapped, turning away and starting to pace the room.

"Where?" his mother asked and Shane could hear her trying to keep her voice calm. "Where did you find the body?"

"In the library," Shane said.

"No," his father said, turning to look at him. "You're wrong about the body. I've been in there plenty of times, Shane. There's no body."

"Yes, there is," he said angrily.

"Then show us, Shane," his mother said.

Shane got up from his bed and stomped his way out into the hallway, and into the library. He flicked on the light and went directly to the bookcase which served as a secret door. He reached in, found the switch and unlocked the case. As it popped out slightly, he took hold of the edge and pulled it the rest of the way out.

Behind him, his parents gasped in surprise, but he ignored them both. Instead, he grasped the handle of the pocket door and slid it open. Shane turned on the light and glanced down into the oubliette.

Carl's body still lay on the bottom.

Shane stepped back and gestured to the oubliette.

His mother and father moved forward and looked down. His mother turned quickly away, but his father remained and stared down. After a long moment, he too, turned away.

When both of his parents looked at him, Shane said, "It's called an oubliette; a little place of forgetting. Mr. Anderson killed him. Pushed him in and let him starve. This is the only way in or out. Carl won't tell me why he was killed."

His parents remained silent as Shane went and turned off the oubliette's light, closed the door and then the bookcase.

"We should remove the body," Shane's father said.

"No!" Shane shouted. "He doesn't want his body moved."

Both of his parents looked at him in surprise.

"We're moving the body, Shane," his father said firmly.

"And we're taking the photograph out of your room," his mother added.

The chair behind the desk was suddenly thrown into the back wall, and his parents cried out in unison.

Shane looked at them both, angry.

"Carl doesn't like what you're saying," Shane said in a low voice. "He doesn't like it at all."

Shane turned on his heel and left the library. Anger boiled in him, and he made his way to his bedroom.

Behind him, something broke in the library and his parents shrieked again in surprise.

Shane smiled angrily.

Carl wasn't happy. Not one bit.

Chapter 23: Getting a Cup of Coffee

Shane could feel something wrong in the house.

He stood in the main hallway and listened. Just below the white noise of the appliances and the neighborhood, he could hear angry murmurs.

This is not a good time to go into the root cellar. Or up the stairs behind the picture.

Anger at waiting longer to discover the fate of his parents boiled up within Shane, but he pushed it down.

Need to take a walk, he told himself. *Maybe it'll be better when I get back.*

He left the house and felt better as he made his way down the driveway. He actually smiled upon reaching the sidewalk. Shane shoved his hands in his pockets, looked up and down the street and decided to turn left towards Main Street.

He set a steady pace for himself and enjoyed the cold air on his face and in his nose. Within a few minutes, he reached Laton Street and headed to Raymond Street, where he turned again at Temple Beth Abraham and nearly bumped into Gerald and Turk.

"Shane," Gerald said happily, Turk's tail wagging as Shane patted the dog's head.

"Gerald," Shane said, shaking the man's hand. "Beautiful weather for a walk."

"It is indeed," Gerald said. "How goes it with the house?"

"Okay," Shane answered. "A little too busy yesterday; the police stopped by."

"I saw them," Gerald said.

"Evidently, my aunt and uncle got themselves lost," Shane said without much sympathy. "They left their rented car parked nearby and the police thought maybe they were in the house."

"Well," Gerald said, shaking his head. "What an unpleasant welcome to the neighborhood."

"An extremely unpleasant welcome," Shane agreed.

"What are you up to now?" Gerald asked.

"Just out for a bit of fresh air. Sometimes the house is a little too much to handle."

Gerald nodded sympathetically. "Would you like to walk back to my house? My niece should be stopping by soon."

"Trying to set me up?" Shane asked with a grin.

"No," Gerald said, laughing. "She is about your age, but, to be completely honest, I'm not sure if she even likes men."

"Fine, then," Shane said, "so long as I'm safe."

"I think you are," Gerald said, smiling.

"Lead on then, Marine," Shane said. He fell into step with Gerald, and they walked back to the older man's house. Turk trotted along easily and paused occasionally to mark a tree or bush.

Within a short time, they turned back onto Berkley Street, well past Shane's house, and made their way to Gerald's home. Parked at the curb was a large, black Dodge pickup with someone in the driver's seat.

"There she is," Gerald said with a chuckle. "She's always early. Too early, sometimes."

As they neared the truck, the driver's side door opened and Gerald's niece got out.

"Detective Lafontaine," Shane said, surprised.

She looked surprised as well, and decidedly different. She wore a pair of jeans tucked into calf-high black leather boots, and a snug gray sweater. Her hair was done nicely, and she wore a little bit of makeup.

The detective was extremely attractive.

"Marie," Gerald said, stepping forward and giving his niece a hug. "Thank you for coming over today."

"You're welcome, Uncle Gerry," she said. She squatted down and scratched Turk easily behind his ears. She looked up at Shane. "So, you know my uncle."

"I do," Shane said, nodding.

She stood up and shook her head. "I should have known. He's a busy body, and you're both Marines."

"Busy body," Gerald snorted. "Only a little bit of one."

"Come on, Uncle Gerry," she said. "Make me some of the sludge you pass off as coffee."

"Are you okay with Shane having coffee with us?" Gerald asked. "I invited him along."

"It's alright," Shane started to say.

Marie held up a hand and stopped him.

"Mr. Ryan, well, Shane, I do want to speak to you tomorrow about your aunt and uncle," she said, "but, we couldn't find a thing in your house. Do I think you did something? No. Do I think something happened to them in your house? Yes. For right now, though, let's have some coffee with my uncle before he gets too senile."

"A little too much sass from you, young lady," Gerald said, leading Turk up to the front door.

"You love it," she said, chuckling as she followed him, and Shane, in turn, followed her.

All of them went into Gerald's kitchen, and Turk laid down upon a floor mat at the back door. The dog occasionally opened an eye to make sure all was as it should be, and then he went back to sleep. Shane and Marie sat at the kitchen table, and Gerald hummed to himself as he made the coffee.

Soon the coffee maker hissed and gurgled, and Gerald took a seat.

"So, you two know each other," Gerald said.

"We do," Marie replied.

"Officially," Gerald said.

She and Shane both nodded.

"Alright then, let's introduce you two unofficially. Shane, this is my niece Marie Lafontaine, a detective with the Nashua Police Department," Gerald said. "Marie, this is Shane Ryan. He's my neighbor, and he works as a translator."

"There," Gerald said with a grin, "you two are introduced."

"A pleasure," Shane said honestly, and he extended his hand over the table. Marie gave a curt nod, shook his hand warmly and offered a small smile.

"Now this isn't about work," Marie said, "but I have to ask, were you serious about your house being haunted?"

"Of course," Shane said.

Marie looked doubtfully at him.

"Don't discount it, Marie," Gerald said gently. He stood up and went to the cabinet above the coffee maker. He took down a trio of blue ceramic mugs. As he filled each one, he continued. "The house is haunted. Has been haunted for as long as I've lived here."

"Uncle Gerry," Marie said, laughing. "There's no such thing as ghosts. Even the stuff we saw yesterday can be chalked up to fear and confusion."

Gerald brought the coffee to the table, set a mug down in front of each of them and then sat once more. After a moment of silence, Gerald asked, "Marie, did you listen to the house when you got there yesterday?"

"No," Marie said, smiling. "I didn't *listen* to the house."

"What about the yard?" Gerald asked.

She shook her head. "Why?"

"I ask because if you had, you wouldn't have heard anything," Gerald said.

"Am I supposed to?" she asked, frowning.

"Listen now," Gerald said.

Shane listened as quiet settled over them. Beyond the windows and door, he heard birds. They called out loudly for spring, and their songs filled the air. He could even hear a squirrel yell.

"What?" Marie asked. "What am I supposed to be listening to?"

"You hear the animals?" Gerald asked. "The birds and the squirrels?"

"Yes," she said, a tinge of anger creeping into her tone. "Of course, I do."

"You won't at Shane's house," Gerald said. He took a drink of his coffee. "You won't hear any birds there. Nor any squirrels."

Marie laughed and shook her head. "You're crazy, Uncle Gerry."

Her voice trailed off though as she realized he was serious.

"Come off it," she said, frowning. "You can't be serious."

She looked from her uncle to Shane, and Shane nodded. She picked up her mug, took a sip, and then she said, "Why?"

Gerald looked at Shane and waited.

"The house is haunted," Shane said. "It has been since I moved in, and, from what I've read, it was haunted long before me, too."

"Who haunts it?" Marie asked. Her tone of disbelief had been replaced by a more professional curiosity.

"Not one, but many," Shane said.

"You told me you lived alone," Marie said. "Tell me, who's the young man I saw the day before yesterday?"

"Upstairs window?" Shane asked.

She nodded.

"Probably Carl," Shane said.

"And how long has he lived with you?" Marie asked.

Shane smiled. "Carl's dead, Marie. He's a ghost. He's been there for a very long time."

"Did you see him in the upper right window?" Gerald asked.

"Yes," Marie answered.

"I saw him for the first time in nineteen sixty-eight, when your aunt and I were looking at this house," Gerald said softly. "Mr. Hall, who lived across from me, said he had been seeing Carl since the early forties."

Marie looked from her uncle to Shane and shook her head. "I really can't believe this."

Shane shrugged. "If you like, come home with me after coffee."

She raised an eyebrow.

"Sorry," Shane said, chuckling, "definitely came out wrong. If you'd like to visit after coffee, we'll see if Carl, or any of them, are up for company."

"Fair enough," Marie said. She drank some of her coffee and grimaced. "Jesus, Uncle Gerry, did you drain your oil tank and run it through the coffee maker?"

"Just for you," Gerald said with a chuckle. "Just for you."

Chapter 24: Shane, September 19th, 1987

"Are you sure you're going to be okay?" Shane's mother asked him for the fourth time.

He managed to not roll his eyes as he nodded. "Yes, mom."

His father adjusted his tie as he looked over at him.

"We're just worried about you in this house alone," his father said. "Well, at night at least."

Shane glanced out the front sitting room's window at the treetops lit by the sun as it slowly set. He looked back to his parents and smiled. "I'll be okay."

His mother gave him a worried smile, and his father said, "Alright, kid. No girls, though, okay?"

Shane shook his head, and his mother slapped his father's arm, and not playfully.

"Enough, Hank," she said. She looked at Shane. "Listen, you have the number for the Hunt Building. Call it if you have any trouble. Or go over to Mrs. Kensington's house."

Shane nodded.

He wouldn't have any trouble. At least not until he slept. The dark ones, the ghosts in the root cellar, were the only ones who bothered him now. They slipped in when his parents were asleep. When the other ghosts were lost in their own memories.

But I'm supposed to talk with Carl, tonight, Shane reminded himself. They would work on practicing Shane's German.

"I'll be okay," Shane said. He smiled. He knew he would be okay, but he couldn't explain it to his parents. If they knew he was going to spend most of the night in a conversation with Carl, whose picture his mother constantly hid, they wouldn't be happy.

"Alright," his mother said with a sigh. She gave him a quick kiss, wiped off the faint trace of lipstick it left behind from his forehead, and then she hugged him tightly. "Alright."

His father gave him a pat on the head and then Shane watched them leave. The limousine was at the front door and in a moment, the large black car pulled away with his parents inside.

With his parents gone, Shane left the parlor and went upstairs to the library. He found a copy of *Sturm* by Ernst Junger, and he sat down in the chair with it. Patiently, he looked at the words and carefully translated each sentence in his mind. Line by line, paragraph by paragraph. He worked his way through the first page, and then the second.

His eyes grew tired, and he stifled a yawn as he tried to stay awake.

He was always tired.

He never felt as though he had rested.

The dead were too noisy.

The light went out, and the door clicked shut.

Shane heard the lock turn.

His hands started to sweat, and he put the book down on the desk. His heart threatened to beat its way out of his chest, but Shane forced himself to breathe. He needed to be in control.

Something or someone would be in the room soon, and it wouldn't be Carl.

He could *feel* the difference in the air.

"Shane," a female voice said. "Shane Ryan."

It wasn't Eloise. A hint of darkness stained the voice and filled him with fear.

"Shane," the female said again, dragging his name out in the darkness.

He realized the room was completely black. He couldn't see anything. He felt as though he had been thrust into a box and the lid slammed shut.

The oubliette, Shane thought. *This is what it would feel like to be in the oubliette, with no way out.*

"Who are you?" Shane whispered.

"Vivienne, or Nimue," the female said, laughing easily, frighteningly. "You should read *Le Morte D'Arthur*, Shane. I draw my name as easily as he drew the sword."

Shane had read *The Death of Arthur*. "You're not the lady in the lake."

Vivienne snorted in disgust. "What do you know? You're still clinging to your meat. Come to the pond, Shane. Come down and swim with the ducks."

"You don't like ducks," he answered.

"I hate them!" she spat, and Shane reeled back in surprise and horror. A stench had suddenly enveloped him. The odor choked him, and he nearly threw up as he pushed himself back away from the desk.

He wanted to jump out of the chair, but he knew he couldn't.

The room was too dark.

She was in the room, and who knew how much bigger the room could get. The house followed no rules.

Shane could literally become lost in the library.

"You'll visit me soon," Vivienne whispered, her voice suddenly close to his ear. "Yes, you will, Shane. You'll have no choice. You will visit me soon."

The light in the room flared into life, and he turned away. He rubbed at his eyes and a moment later he was able to see again.

Shane was still in the chair, but it was by the door instead of behind the desk.

Wet footprints dried slowly on the hardwood floor.

Shane took a deep breath and wondered if he could make it to the relative safety of his bedroom.

Chapter 25: Introductions are Made

Shane had barely finished his morning medicinal shot of whiskey when the doorbell rang.

Jesus Christ, he thought. He put the glass on the bed table and hurried down the stairs. *Who the hell is here this early?*

Shane needed to get into the root cellar.

He needed to look for his parents.

It can't be Detective Lafontaine, he thought as he reached the door. *Six thirty is way too early.*

Detective Marie Lafontaine stood at the doorstep dressed in her 'civilian' clothes. Once more Shane was impressed with just how attractive the woman was.

"Shane," she said, nodding her head. "Is this too early?"

"No," Shane said, stepping aside to let her in. "I'm just surprised."

"Well," she said as he closed the door, "I drink coffee pretty early in the morning."

Shane looked over at her and saw her smile.

He chuckled, shook his head and said, "Yeah. I didn't think about the time."

"So," she said, looking around. "Since I'm not here on official business, are you going to introduce me?"

"Yes," Shane said.

Marie looked at him. "Did you have a drink?"

"I have a drink every morning," Shane said. "And every night."

"You might have a problem, Shane," she said. There was no condemnation in her voice, no tone of judgment.

"I do have a problem," he said tiredly. "I grew up here. This house is a nightmare, with brief moments of respite."

"Then why did you come back?" she asked.

"I need to know what happened to my parents," he answered.

Marie frowned. "What do you mean?"

"Your uncle didn't tell you?" Shane asked.

She shook her head. "He plays things close to the vest."

"Fair enough. Follow me into the kitchen," he said. "I'll tell you in there. Have you had breakfast?"

"Yes," she said.

He led her in, pulled out a chair and fixed his toast, coffee, oatmeal, and his water. "Coffee?"

"Please," Marie said. "Yours is a lot better than Uncle Gerry's."

"Thanks," Shane said, chuckling.

"When did your parents disappear?" she asked after he had gotten everything ready and sat down across from her.

"When I graduated from boot camp, basic training down on Parris Island," Shane said. "They were supposed to see me graduate. They never showed up. My father didn't go to work for a few days, and his boss got nervous. My dad never missed work. Not if he could help it. The police came, checked out the house, found it unlocked. But, no sign of my parents, though. It's been almost twenty-five years."

"Did you ever find out what happened?" Marie asked.

Shane shook his head. "It's the only reason why I'm back here. Some of the dead are alright, like Carl."

"Carl?" she asked.

"He's probably the young man you saw in the window," Shane said. "He shifts his form from young to old and back again. I don't think it's intentional. Anyway, I was going to start looking for my parents this morning. I didn't expect you to be here quite so early."

"Shane," Marie said, looking at him with concern. "We went through the house the other day. We didn't find anything or anyone. And we're experts at finding stuff."

"They're still here," Shane said softly. He drank some of his coffee, and he gave her a small, tired smile. "I doubt they're still alive, but they're still here."

Marie looked at him for a moment and then she asked, "Where do you think they are?"

"I don't know. I know where they went in, and so I can only follow," he answered.

"What do you mean?" Marie asked. "Went into where?"

"Into the house," Shane said.

"They were already in the house when they disappeared, right?" she asked.

"Yes, but you can disappear into the walls. Places and rooms which shouldn't exist, but they do anyway." Shane finished his coffee.

"You're not making any sense, Shane," she said.

"She doesn't seem to know anything," Carl said from behind Shane.

Marie stiffened, her cup shook in her hand and splashed coffee onto the table.

"Not about this, no," Shane answered.

Carl's voice moved from behind Shane, his next words spoken from near the sink. *"Do you wish for her to see me? She shall, perhaps, understand you a little better?"*

"Are you throwing your voice?" Marie asked, looking at him with a confused expression.

"No," Shane answered. "I'm not."

Carl suddenly appeared, the edges of his body hazy, as though viewed through a camera with a scratched lens.

Marie's eyes widened with fear, and the coffee mug fell from her hands and struck the table loudly.

Chapter 26: Shane, December 31st, 1988

Shane was home alone, his parents now comfortable with the idea. It didn't bother Shane too much. It was better to be awake in the house than to be asleep. Occasionally the dead startled him, but being awake when it happened was much easier to handle. When Thaddeus or Eloise slipped into his room and whispered in his ears, the initial fear was terrible.

With his parents at Mrs. Kensington's New Year's Eve party, Shane was free to do what he wanted. Within reason of course.

Shane knew his limits. An entire pack of Oreo cookies and a gallon of milk was unacceptable for a snack. Perhaps he could get away with half of each. He was hungry.

He whistled as he took a handful of cookies out of the package and then went to the fridge. Shane took out the gallon, stood there with the refrigerator door open and drank long and deep. When he finished, he wiped his mouth with the sleeve of his sweatshirt, returned the milk to its proper place in the fridge, and closed the door.

With a satisfied belch, Shane left the kitchen and popped an entire Oreo into his mouth. He made his way to the second floor and headed towards the library.

From the third floor, he heard the groan of old hinges.

Shane stopped and listened.

The noise sounded again and slowly shifted into a long, drawn out squeal.

He had been to the third floor only a few times but he had never stayed long. The temperature up there was always colder, the walls barren of decoration. None of the lights worked, even though an electrician hired by Shane's father said they should. The doors in the hall were always locked, too.

They were *always* locked.

Shane walked to the small, hidden door at the end of the hall. He opened it and took a step back. The lights were on in the stairwell.

He stood in the doorway long enough to finish his cookies. Shane brushed his hands off on his jeans and then he climbed the stairs. Another door stood at the top, he opened it and stepped into the third-floor hallway.

Light spilled out of every wall sconce. Out of the four doors in the hallway, the last one on the left was open. Not a little, or only slightly. Not half, but fully open and against the wall.

Shane heard music.

A violin.

The music drifted out of the open doorway and slipped down the hall. Each note followed the other gliding off the bare plaster and along the worn wooden floor.

Shane approached the open door carefully. The music gradually grew louder and soon he was only a step away. For a moment, he paused, took a deep breath, and moved forward to look in.

Shane blinked and shook his head.

A set of stairs stretched up in front of him. They led to a fourth floor, but there wasn't a fourth floor. At least not when you looked at the house from the outside.

The strange stairwell was dim, and Shane could barely see a door at the top. The sound of the violin came through it and rolled out and around him.

Shane took a moment to build up his courage, and then walked up the stairs.

The music increased in both tempo and volume.

The unseen musician seemed to sense his approach.

Shane paused for a moment, and so too did the music. The last note hung in the air and lingered.

Shane, in spite of the trepidation he felt, smiled and continued up the stairs.

The music started up again.

The door at the top of the stairs was tall and narrow, barely wide enough for Shane to pass through if it was unlocked. He reached out and took hold of the cut crystal doorknob, found it warm and the edges smooth, as he carefully turned it.

The latch clicked loudly, and the door swung into the unknown room.

The music washed over Shane as he stepped into a dimly lit space. Thick rugs covered the floor, and stacks of written music were piled around the room haphazardly. The room, like the door, was tall and narrow. It was also long and barren of windows. On the wood-paneled walls, dozens of violins and their bows rested on individual shelves.

The end of the room was hidden in a shadow behind a solitary floor lamp. The music came from the darkness; a pure, beautiful sound. Shane's heart ached with each note.

He cautiously walked forward, and the music stopped.

"I'm sorry," Shane said softly. "I don't mean to interrupt."

"*You're not interrupting, Child,*" a man said. The language wasn't German, or French, but something else. Similar to French, but not the same.

"*Will you continue to play?*" Shane asked, and he couldn't keep the surprise out of his voice as he heard himself speak the man's language.

"*Of course, I will,*" the man chuckled. "*I had heard of your ability to speak, but I did not know it would include my own.*"

"*What am I speaking?*" Shane asked.

"*Italian, Child,*" he said.

"*Are you dead?*" Shane asked as politely as he could.

The man laughed. "*Yes. I am dead. Long dead, I am afraid.*"

"*May I ask your name?*"

"*You may, and I will even tell you. Roberto Guidoboni.*"

"Why are you here?" Shane asked.

"My music," Roberto said. A beautiful note escaped the shadow. "I feared I would not be able to make my music after my death, and so I built myself this room. I put my violins in it, and when I was sure death was near, I locked myself in."

"But," Shane hesitated, then he continued on. "But, this room doesn't exist. It shouldn't even be part of the house."

Roberto laughed. "Well, it did exist. It was a secret room in my house, yet it burned. Later, when Anderson purchased my home, my room remained, and the new house kept me here. She lets me play. When it suits her."

"The one in the pond?" Shane whispered.

"Yes," he answered. "The one in the pond."

"Will you... will you still play?" Shane asked, hopeful.

"I will. You are not afraid of the dead?"

"Not all of the dead," he said.

Roberto chuckled. "Well said, Child. Well said. Would you look upon me as I play?"

"Yes," Shane answered.

"Excellent."

The light shifted slightly, and suddenly Shane could see Roberto Guidoboni.

A skeleton clad in rags.

He sat on a high stool, the tattered remains of house slippers on the bones of his feet. He tucked a violin under his chin, somehow worked his fingers around the neck of the instrument to place them on the strings, and carefully drew the bow back in one long, graceful motion.

Shane sighed and sat down on the floor. He closed his eyes and listened to the music the dead man created.

Chapter 27: The Root Cellar

"Marie," Shane said gently. "Marie, are you alright?"

She turned her attention away from Carl and stared at Shane. She blinked several times and then she asked, "Is this real?"

Shane nodded.

"How?" she said, looking over at Carl and then back to Shane. "How can this possibly be real? There are no such things as ghosts."

"Will she be well?" Carl asked.

"Yes," Shane said. "I think so."

"What are you speaking?" Marie asked. "Is it German?"

"Yes," Shane said.

Marie looked at him, shook her head and said, "This is real."

It wasn't a question.

"Yes," Shane said.

"Okay," she said. The muscles of her jaw tightened and relaxed several times before she nodded. "Okay. Does he speak English?"

"He does," Shane answered.

"Will he?" She asked.

"No," Shane said, trying not to smile.

Marie frowned. "Why not?"

"He doesn't like to," Shane said.

"Well," she said, "does he know where your parents went?"

"No," Shane said. "Just where they went in."

"And where did they go in?" she asked.

"The root cellar."

Marie stood up. "It's in the pantry, right?"

"Yes," Shane answered, standing up as well. He walked to the pantry and opened the door. He turned on the light and pointed to the trapdoor which led down. "I need to go down there."

"Let's go," she said.

"What?" he asked.

"Let's go," she repeated. "I need to see what's down there."

"Tell her it isn't safe," Carl said, stepping towards them.

"It's not safe," Shane said. "Not at all."

"I know," Marie said, smiling tightly. "I figured it wouldn't be. Will your friend be coming with us?"

"No," Shane answered. "It's not safe for him down there."

"He's afraid?" Marie asked, surprised.

"Yes," Shane said. "Just because he's dead doesn't mean he wants to vanish from the world. Are you sure you want to go down there with me?"

"Absolutely sure," she said.

"Okay," Shane said. He walked into the pantry, bent down and pulled up the trap door.

A terrible wave of cold air rushed out of the darkness, and Shane staggered back. He and Marie coughed and wheezed at the stench of old death heavy in the air.

"Jesus Christ," Marie hissed. "It didn't smell like this yesterday when we opened it."

"I don't remember it ever smelling like this," Shane said. "Or it being this cold either."

He took a small LED flashlight off a shelf, turned it on and pointed it down the ladder. The darkness tried to eat away at the cone of light, which revealed a hard-packed dirt floor. Shane looked over at Marie.

"Ready?" he asked her.

"Yes," Marie said, nodding. She slipped a hand into her pocket and took out her own flashlight. Marie grinned at him. "Better than a boy scout."

Shane smiled. "Yes, you are."

He looked back down the ladder, ignored the nervous rumble of his stomach, and descended into the root cellar. When he reached the bottom, he pointed the flashlight at each of the walls. They were made of large, rough cut stones with small niches carved in them. In the far left corner, a stone had been removed, and blackness awaited.

Marie reached the floor and a moment later, her flashlight's beam joined his.

"There?" she asked him.

"Yes," Shane said with a nod. He walked forward, and Marie was barely a step behind him. Finally, just a few steps away from the darkness, the light cut through it. A small, oval doorway was revealed, absent of any door, though. The floor beyond was made of smooth stone, and it gently sloped down.

The walls and ceiling were of the same type of stone and the passage turned slightly to the right. Within a few feet, the remainder of it was hidden. The foul smell and cold air of the room emanated from the tunnel.

"This wasn't here," Marie said.

"No," Shane said in agreement. "It wasn't. I've never seen it before, and I thought I had seen just about everything this house had hidden."

Something splashed in the distance, and Shane stiffened.

"What is it?" Marie asked. "What's wrong?"

"Did you hear the splash?"

"Yes," she said. "Is it bad?"

"More than likely," Shane said softly.

"Well," Marie said, taking a deep breath, "only one way to find out."

Shane nodded and stepped into the tunnel.

Instantly it felt as though the walls would close in on him and he had to crouch slightly or else he would hit his head on the ceiling. He reached a hand out to steady himself and pulled it back quickly.

"What's wrong?" Marie asked.

"The wall," Shane answered. "It felt wrong."

"Oh Jesus," she said after a moment. "Feels like mucus."

"Yeah," he said. He continued forward. He followed the path of his own flashlight as the passage curved. And it continued to curve and descend in a tight circle.

"I hope we don't have to come back up this way," Marie said after a minute.

"Why not?" Shane asked.

"I'm having a hard time not slipping right now," she answered. "Can you imagine what it'll be like going up this path?"

"No," Shane said. "I can't."

After a long time, the floor leveled out and the passage straightened. Slowly, it widened as well. The walls disappeared, and only the floor remained. No matter where they pointed the flashlights, they only found darkness and the stones upon which they walked.

"Shane," Marie said after a few minutes of walking.

"Yes?" he asked.

"Is there something up ahead?" she asked.

Shane moved the beam of his flashlight towards hers, and he saw a small shape on the floor. He hurried forward and came to a sharp stop.

"It's a belt," Marie said. She stepped past Shane and squatted down.

A long, dark brown, leather belt lay curled on the stones. The silver buckle was face down. She reached out to turn it over with her flashlight.

But Shane already knew what the buckle had engraved on it.

"'H R,'" Marie said, looking up at him.

"Henry Ryan," Shane said. "Well, he preferred Hank."

"Your dad's?" Marie asked.

Shane nodded. "Yes. I gave him the belt on his birthday when I was fourteen."

"Why is it here?" she asked, looking at him.

"He loved to wear it," Shane said sadly. "He wore it all the time. He said a man always needed to wear a belt or suspenders. And he hated suspenders. He always had it on."

Reverently, Marie picked up the belt and handed it to Shane.

"Thank you," Shane said softly. He took the belt, wrapped it into a tight loop and slipped it into his back pocket.

Marie stood up and looked around the darkness. "Well, which way from here?"

Her flashlight flickered and went out.

"Take my hand," Shane said quickly, extending his free hand to her.

Marie clasped it just as his own flashlight was extinguished.

Over the sound of his own heartbeat, Shane heard the slap of something wet against stone. It was repeated, rhythmically.

"Something's walking," Marie said.

He tightened his grip on her and fought down a wave of fear.

"Do not let go," he whispered. "No matter what you do. Do not let go."

The walker drew closer.

"What is it?" Marie asked in a low voice.

"I think it's the girl in the pond," he said softly, unable to keep a quiver of terror out of his voice. "We need to leave."

The darkness pressed down upon them, and Marie asked, "How?"

Before Shane could answer he caught a bit of music.

A violin playing part of Schubert's *Death and the Maiden*.

Shane turned towards the sound. It grew louder, if only slightly. "Do you hear it?"

"Hear... wait, is someone playing a violin?" Marie asked.

"Yes," Shane said excitedly. "We need to get to it."

"Let's go, then," Marie said, as she led the way towards the instrument.

They moved at a steady pace. The music became louder, and so did the sound of the walker. The force's pace quickened as they drew closer to the musician.

Suddenly, a thin, horizontal line of light appeared in the darkness ahead of them.

"Run!" Shane hissed.

The two of them ran for the light, which grew faintly larger and revealed the bottom of a wooden door.

The walker ran.

Shane slammed into the door, found the cut crystal knob and twisted it violently. The lock clicked, as they stumbled in. Light blinded him, and he rolled across a carpeted floor. The music stopped, and Shane shouted, "The door!"

The door slammed shut, and he panted as he lay on the floor.

Chapter 28: With the Musician

Marie rested her head against the cool wood of the door and her hands on plush carpets. She slowly got herself under control, opened her eyes and looked down.

Water seeped beneath the door and into the fabric of the carpets.

Marie stared at it for a moment, confused, until something heavy hit the door. She pushed herself backward and bumped into Shane. They both stared at the door.

She could worry about the room they were in later.

The real threat was on the other side of the wooden door.

The walker, for who else could it be, knocked.

A voice from behind Marie, and it wasn't Shane's, said something in what sounded like Italian.

Another knock was the only response.

The tone of the speaker changed from courteous to angry. The Italian was spoken quickly.

The door shuddered in its frame. Once. Twice. Three times.

And then Marie could hear the presence leave. The slap of the feet grew fainter.

Shane stood up and said, "Marie, I'd like to introduce you to our host. Roberto Guidoboni."

She turned and froze, horrified.

Roberto Guidoboni was dead. A skeleton clad in rags as he held a violin. He bestowed upon her a death's head grin and spoke to her in soft, delicate Italian.

Marie stood shocked, not quite sure what to say.

Stunned, she let Shane guide her to an ancient armchair. He murmured for her to sit down, and she did, unable to take her eyes off of the skeleton, though. Shane sat down on the floor beside her and spoke in Italian to Roberto.

The skeleton bowed his head and placed his violin between his shoulder and his chin. His fleshless fingers danced across the neck and the bow flew along the strings.

A deep, beautiful rhythm filled the room, and Marie shook as her adrenaline high crashed.

Book 1: Berkley Street

Chapter 29: Shane, January 20th, 1989

Shane hurried through the snow, but he wasn't going to make it.

Keith and Matthew were too close. He could hear Christopher, larger and slower, laugh as Shane tried to get home.

Shane passed his wall and made it to his driveway.

He needed his front door, though. The steps at least.

Halfway to safety, Keith's hand landed on Shane's shoulder. The older boy grabbed Shane's parka and jerked him backward. Shane grunted as he landed hard on his backside. He scrambled to his feet and found the other three boys in front of him. Keith stood in the middle, the tallest of the three and the leanest. Matthew was slightly thicker and a little shorter. Christopher, red-faced from the race through the snow, was the shortest and the widest.

And Shane stood alone in the driveway against them.

His mother was gone, at least until four.

She had a dentist appointment.

His father was still at work.

Shane was alone.

"Why'd you run, freak?" Keith asked, sneering.

"Leave me alone, Keith," Shane said. He hated the sound of fear in his own voice, but he knew the three boys wanted to beat him up. There was no one to stop them.

Shane would fight, and he would lose.

"Leave me alone, Keith," Matthew said, pitching his voice high and mimicking Shane. Keith and Christopher laughed.

Keith took off his gloves and dropped them into the snow.

"I like the way it feels on my knuckles," Keith explained. "You know, when the blood hits them."

Shane shrugged off his backpack and held a strap tightly in his right hand. His heart beat quickly. All three of the other boys were bigger and older than Shane. They had picked on him ever since he started middle school.

They always seemed to know when neither of his parents were home.

Keith cracked his knuckles and grinned.

"Hit him!" Christopher said excitedly. "Hit him, Keith!"

"I will," Keith said happily, raising his fist as he stepped forward.

A loud groan spilled out from the house and washed over them.

They all froze.

"What the hell just happened?" Matthew asked, looking around.

Shane looked around nervously. The house seemed to have darkened. A shadow had slipped over it. Some of the trees bent in different directions.

"You need to leave," Shane whispered. "Something bad is going to happen."

Christopher laughed. "Yeah, Keith's going to beat you up."

"Knock it off," Keith said sharply, lowering his hand. "Something's wrong."

"You need to go," Shane said, desperately. All of the trees were moving now. "*Please,* you need to leave."

A whisper, indistinct, raced across the snow. A shadow slipped into the driveway and stopped in the center. It blocked the way to the street. The way to safety.

"We need to get inside," Shane said in a low voice.

"What?" Matthew asked, surprised.

"All of us need to get inside now," Shane said. "We have to go in."

"Why would we go in with you?" Christopher said, grinning. "You want a beating inside your own house?"

Keith saw the shadow in the driveway. The shadow over the house. The way the trees moved. The bully looked at Shane.

"Can we?" Keith asked in a low voice.

Shane nodded. "Just run. The door's open."

Keith turned and ran for the door, and Shane followed him. Matthew followed and with a snort of disgust, Christopher did too.

Keith reached the door, opened it and led the way into the house. A moment later, Shane and the others piled in.

Shane closed the door, and something outside screamed.

"Holy Jesus!" Christopher said, stumbling backward and crossing himself.

"Lock the door," Matthew said nervously.

"It won't matter," Shane said, feeling better as he took off his backpack. "Not if it really wants to come in. It usually doesn't though, and if it does, it doesn't like what happens."

"What happens?" Keith asked.

"Carl happens," Shane answered. He removed his jacket, opened the hall closet and hung it up. He took off his boots and put them on the boot tray by the door. When he was done, he looked at the three boys. They had wanted to hurt him a few minutes earlier, but *it* had come. The thing in the yard. The thing he hated.

These were just boys. Stupid boys.

And Shane wasn't mad at them.

"Do you guys want something to eat?" He asked.

The three of them looked at him in surprise. After a moment, Keith nodded.

"Okay," Shane said. "Just take your boots and jackets off. You can call your moms in the kitchen."

He waited as they shed their backpacks and winter gear. Soon all of them stood in their school uniforms and stockings.

"Come on," Shane said. He passed through them and led the way to the kitchen. Upstairs, a door slammed, opened, and then it slammed again.

"Is your mom home?" Matthew asked.

"No," Shane said. "No one's home but me."

"What?" Christopher asked. "Who made that noise then? Who banged the door?"

"Probably the old man," Shane said, gesturing to the kitchen table. "Sit down."

"What old man? Your dad?" Keith asked.

Shane shook his head. "No. The old man. The old ghost. He spends a lot of time upstairs. He's a real pain. All he does is complain."

Keith and Matthew looked nervously up at the ceiling towards the second floor, but Christopher laughed.

"You're full of it, Shane," the boy sneered.

"Shut up, Chris," Keith snapped.

Christopher looked at him in surprise.

"So," Keith said, looking at Shane, "this place is really haunted?"

Shane nodded.

"Bad?" Matthew asked.

"Yeah," Shane said, taking down four short glasses. "Bad. I have to sleep with the lights on and the door off of the hinges."

"You're a liar," Christopher said angrily. "There's no such thing as ghosts."

The back door rattled.

Shane looked at him and for the first time realized he didn't have to be afraid of the older boy. Of any of them.

"Do you want milk or water?" He asked.

"Milk," Keith and Matthew said.

"You need to tell me how you're doing this," Christopher said, his face going red. "You need to tell me."

"Knock it off!" Keith yelled.

"No," Christopher said, his voice getting higher. "No! There's no such thing as ghosts!"

All of the windows darkened, as though someone had painted each pane black.

"There are," Shane said softly. "And there are a lot here."

"How many?" Matthew whispered.

"At least six, maybe more," Shane answered. "And yes, they can hurt you."

Christopher opened his mouth to speak and then he stopped. His eyes widened in surprise, and his blonde hair stood straight up. He got up from his chair, and Shane realized someone had the boy by the hair.

Christopher started to cry, and he wet his pants.

"Carl," Shane said, and he hoped it was the dead German. *"Please let him go."*

"Fine," Carl said, and Christopher sat down hard in his chair, the wood creaking beneath his weight.

Keith and Matthew looked in horror at their friend.

"Carl doesn't like bullies," Shane explained. "And he doesn't like people who make too much noise."

When none of the three boys responded to the statement, Shane walked to the pantry, opened it and asked, "Do you guys want Oreos?"

Chapter 30: A Glass of Wine

Shane poured the red wine into a glass and handed it to Marie, who accepted it gratefully. Her hands shook slightly and for a minute, he was worried he might have to help her hold the glass steady enough to drink from.

But, she managed.

"She will be fine," Roberto said, playing a small piece on his violin. *"I can tell."*

"Yes, I think so," Shane agreed.

Marie looked from Shane to the skeleton and back to Shane.

Well, Shane thought. *I hope she'll be alright.*

"How are you holding up, Marie?" he asked her.

"Okay," she said. She took a long drink from the wine glass and looked at him. "This is all real."

"Yes," Shane said.

"And your parents disappeared down here twenty odd years ago?" she asked.

"Yes."

She frowned and after a moment she said, "Can I see the belt?"

"The belt?" he asked, and then he remembered. "Oh, yes."

He reached into his back pocket and pulled it out.

She took it from him and examined it. "Shane, this hasn't been down here for twenty years. Hell, I don't think it's been down here for more than a few weeks."

"What?" he asked, squatting down beside her.

"Look," she said, "the leather should be rotted, and the belt buckle should be covered in muck."

"That is your father's belt, is it not?" Roberto asked.

Shane looked over at him and nodded. *"How do you know?"*

"He was wearing it when I saw him," the dead man answered.

Shane straightened up. *"What? When did you see him?"*

"I am not sure," Roberto said apologetically. *"Time is...it is not as I remember it. Nothing is."*

"When do you think you saw him last?" Shane asked, trying to fight down his hope, knowing it to be futile.

"A week ago. Perhaps two," he answered.

"What did he say?" Marie asked. "Does he know something?"

Shane nodded. "He says he thinks he saw my father a week or two ago. *Roberto, was my mother with him?"*

"No, Shane, I am sorry to say. I have not seen her in quite some time. He is searching for her. But the girl, she keeps them apart."

Shane passed the information on to Marie. She finished her wine and stood up.

"Ask him where your father was headed," she said.

Shane did so, and he translated Roberto's response. "Into the attic."

"Can we get there?" She asked.

"It depends on which one," Shane said. "There are several, from what Carl has told me."

Outside of the door came the sudden sound of wet feet on stone.

"Quickly," Roberto said. *"You must leave, Shane."*

Shane turned to the door he had entered when he was only a boy. *"Thank you, my friend."*

Roberto nodded.

"Come on, Marie," Shane said. "We need to leave."

He led the way out. Narrow stairs led down to the next floor. With Marie close behind him, he hurried down to the hallway at the bottom. Behind them, someone banged on the door to the stone room.

Roberto yelled in Italian at the stranger.

Shane reached the hall and waited for Marie.

"Where the hell are we?" She asked, looking around. "I don't recognize this place."

"The servants' quarters," Shane said.

"These weren't here yesterday," Marie said as they headed to the exit which would lead them to the second floor.

"I know," Shane said. "A lot of things weren't. They might not be here tomorrow."

Shane opened the far door and led Marie down the next flight of stairs.

"Are we on the second floor now?" Marie asked.

"Yes," Shane said.

"How?" she said, turning around to look at him. "How is it even possible?"

"What do you mean?" he asked.

"We never went up, Shane," Marie said. "Never. We went down. And down. And *down*. We even came down out of the damn musical skeleton room. We never went *up*."

"No. We didn't."

"Then it's not possible," Marie said angrily.

"Everything's impossible until it isn't," Shane said, shrugging his shoulders. Downstairs, the grandfather clock struck the hour.

Noon, he thought. His stomach rumbled in agreement.

"So, Detective Lafontaine," Shane said. "Do you feel like having lunch?"

Book 1: Berkley Street

Chapter 31: Shane, February 10th, 1988

Shane put the phone back in its cradle and for the first time in a long time, he looked at himself and realized he was afraid.

His parents weren't going to be home. The car had broken down in Connecticut, and they couldn't even find a car to rent.

Shane was going to be alone in the house, overnight.

They had called around to the neighbors, but no one had answered.

He felt panic well within him but he tried to ignore it.

Then again there wasn't any place safe. Not at night.

He started to sweat, and he left the parlor. Shane quickly went upstairs and went into the library. He turned the light on and went to sit in the leather armchair behind the desk.

The house was silent.

Shane couldn't hear anything. Not the old man, not the violinist. Not Thaddeus and not Eloise. Even Carl was absent.

The house didn't settle, and the air was cold. He couldn't hear the furnace or the wind which bent the tops of the trees in the pale light cast by the February moon.

The silence terrified him.

Shane swallowed nervously, got up from the chair and walked to a window. He looked down on the back yard. In the center of the pond, beneath the ice, he knew the dead girl waited. She wanted him, and he didn't know why.

It doesn't matter why, he told himself. *You just can't let her get you. You can't.*

As he stood in the window, something moved and caught his eye.

Someone walked into the yard from Chester Street. It was a man, from what Shane could see. He carried a backpack and was dressed in warm clothes. His winter coat was blue, and so was the knit cap he wore. It looked like he had on black pants and work boots.

And suddenly the man changed direction. He walked towards the house instead of away from it.

Is he going to try and break in? Shane wondered. *Can't he feel how wrong the house is?*

The man stepped closer to the house, out of Shane's sight.

With a sigh, Shane returned to the desk and the chair.

Something scratched in the walls.

The noise became louder, and soon it sounded as if dozens of people ran through the servants' passages. Within a moment, silence returned.

A scream raced through the house and exploded out of the iron heating vents set in the library's floor. The scream ended abruptly, and laughter followed.

Shane sat stiffly in the chair while he listened.

The sound of footsteps returned, this time in the hallway.

Shane looked out the open door and waited. Soon the feet drew closer, laughter echoed off the walls, and something heavy was dragged along the floor.

The first shape that Shane saw, was nothing more than a shadow. Dark, far too dark for the hall. It crept into the doorway and was only two or three feet high. The vague semblance of a head turned towards him. Eyes the color of an electric blue spark looked at him, and then the head turned away. The shadowy creature moved forward and passed beyond the doorway.

Others followed, though, and they carried the man who Shane had seen in the back yard.

He was stripped naked and his limbs were bound together in rusted wire. When his head appeared Shane stifled a scream as he saw the man's wild, terrified eyes. A black shadow had wrapped around the man's mouth and kept it tightly closed.

"Are you dreaming, Shane?" a voice asked him. Cold, a terribly cold breath stung Shane's ear and he couldn't bring himself to turn and see who spoke to him.

He shivered uncontrollably and gagged at the smell of rot which filled the room.

"Where do you think he will end up?" the stranger asked. "Will you guess?"

Shane managed to shake his head.

A cruel laugh, filled with malice rang out, and Shane nearly wet himself with fear.

"He will go up and up and up," the voice said. "Far and away. Alive and not dead. Dead and not alive. You'll understand one day, Shane. Yes. I promise one day you will understand."

Shane closed his eyes and fought the urge to run.

Warmth returned to the room, and the smell of rot faded. Shane could no longer hear footsteps, or the man being dragged down the floor.

Muffled laughter drifted down from the unused servants' quarters, and Shane desperately wished for his parents to return home.

Chapter 32: Alone

Marie Lafontaine had left and promised to return after her shift the following day.

Shane sat on his bed, a glass of whiskey in one hand and his father's belt in the other. He took a small sip and examined the silver buckle.

It was his father's. Shane was certain of it.

The leather was the same as well.

And neither of them was old.

Shane drank a little more.

How is this even possible? He wondered. *My father can't be alive. No matter what anyone says. Maybe trapped, spiritually. But they can't be alive.*

He put the belt down on the bed, finished his whiskey and poured himself another.

The phone in the library rang sharply.

Shane nearly spilled his liquor.

The phone rang again.

He looked out his doorway at the hall.

For a third time, the harsh sound of the telephone cut through the air.

Shane emptied his glass, put it on the table and got up from his bed. Silently, he walked out of his room and to the library.

The black phone on the desktop rang again, which was incredibly interesting.

The phone was an interior line only. No connection to the outside world, only to a phone in the kitchen, and one in the servants' quarters.

And there was no power to the phone. There hadn't been any since Shane had moved into the house as a boy.

Shane walked to the desk, sat down, and picked up the receiver.

"Hello," he said.

"Hello?" a woman asked frantically. "Oh my God, can you hear me?!"

Shane's hands shook. "Yes. Yes, I can hear you."

"Oh thank God," she said, weeping. "Please, I don't know where you are, but I need you to call the police. My husband and I are trapped in our house. We've been down here for days, and we can't get out."

"Mom?" Shane whispered.

The woman choked back a cry and said, "What? What did you say?"

"Mom," Shane said a little louder. "It's me, Shane."

There was silence on the other end, but Shane could hear his mother breathe.

"Is… is this some kind of trick?" she asked, her tone unsure. "You can't be my son."

"You're Fiona Ryan," Shane said softly. "My father is Hank Ryan. His real name is Henry. He hates it. You only call him Henry when you're mad at him, like when he didn't believe us about the house."

His mother let out a moan. "You can't be Shane. You're too old. You can't be. I can hear how old you are."

"I am old," Shane said. "I'm over forty now, mom."

"No!" She screamed. He jerked his head away from the phone. She spoke again, and he listened once more. "No. No, my Shane is in boot camp. He's graduating in a week. We're going down to South Carolina to see him."

"Mom," he said, his voice growing hoarse, "you've been gone for years. So many years."

The line went dead. Shane sat in the chair and held the silent phone for a moment before he hung it up.

Yet as soon as his hand left the cold handle the phone rang again.

He looked at it cautiously, but by the third ring he picked it up.

"Hello," he said, trying to keep the hope out of his voice.

The harsh laughter which greeted him told him he had failed.

"Shane," a girl said, her voice sounding as if she were speaking from beneath water. "Shane, your parents miss you. Do you miss them?"

Shane hung up the phone and left the library. He closed the door, but even through the thick wood he could hear the telephone ring.

Chapter 33: A Visitor

Someone knocked at the door, and Shane forced his eyes to open.

He was drunk.

Good and drunk. He wasn't sure if it was early afternoon or early morning. Or maybe neither if the clock in the parlor was broken.

He chuckled at the idea of it and managed to get to his feet. He staggered out of the room and into the main hall. Someone knocked again, and the knock was followed by the doorbell.

Shane winced at both sounds, but he still found the image of a broken clock funny. He laughed as he opened the door and then he choked on the laughter.

Christopher Mercurio stood on his doorstep.

He wore the school uniform of Nashua Catholic Junior High School. He even had the trendy, bowl haircut the cooler kids had worn. Christopher Mercurio, the boy who had bullied him in school, even after having hidden in his house, was soaked through as he looked at Shane.

Thoroughly wet, just as he had been when the police had pulled his body out of the pond when Shane was fifteen.

Christopher looked terrified. Confused.

"Am I dead?" he asked Shane.

Shane quickly sobered up.

"Yes, Christopher," Shane said. "You're dead. You have been for a long time."

"She told me I was," Christopher said, and he began to cry. "She told me I can't go home to my parents as they won't want me because I'm dead."

Shane couldn't think of anything to say, so he didn't.

"She killed me, Shane," he said.

"I know."

"You told me not to go near the water," Christopher said, moaning. "You told me not to."

"I know," Shane said sadly.

"I didn't listen to you," the dead boy said, starting to weep. "I wish I'd listened."

"I'm sorry," Shane whispered.

Christopher nodded, wiped his tears away with a wet hand and then he sniffled loudly. "Shane."

"Yes?"

"She's angry," Christopher whispered. "She didn't like it when you hung up on her."

"Did she make you come and tell me?" He asked.

The dead boy nodded.

"Will she let you go now?" Shane asked.

"No," Christopher whimpered. "She never lets any of us go. She says she won't ever let your parents go."

"Are my parents alive, Christopher?" He asked.

"I don't know," the dead boy answered. "I can't tell. I wasn't sure I was dead until I saw you. You're old, Shane. You're bald, too."

Shane nodded.

"I didn't know I was dead. Not for certain. None of us do," Christopher said.

"Are there a lot of you down there, with her?" He asked.

"Yes," the dead boy said. "I'm not sure how many, but there are a lot of us."

"Oh," Shane said.

"She's angry, Shane," Christopher said. "She's so angry. You need to leave, Shane. She's going to hurt you."

"I can't leave. I need my parents," Shane answered.

"She won't let them go," the dead boy sighed. "None of us can go."

Christopher turned and walked away from the door. Shane watched as the dead bully turned to the right and continued on around the house. Back to the pond.

Shane closed the door and returned to his whiskey.

He needed to get drunk again.

Chapter 34: Shane and the Furnace, February 29th, 1988

Shane liked to be in the basement. The basement was safe.

Nothing, as far as he could tell, was in the basement.

Yes, it was dark. Yes, there were lots of spiders.

But there weren't any ghosts, and Shane appreciated it tremendously.

The furnace was his favorite part of the basement. The old, oil-run machine was gigantic, a monstrosity which would have looked at home on an old battleship. Shane could picture it running the propeller of some ancient warship.

It was warm by the furnace too. Waves of heat rolled off the hot cast iron casing, and he could catch sight of the flickering red and orange flames as the oil burned.

Shane lay on his back on top of an old woolen army blanket. His book, something by a Chinese general named Sun Tzu, was beside him. He had a bookmark at a page where the general had declared, 'All warfare is deception.' And Shane had a feeling the man knew what he was writing about.

Shane yawned and looked up at rafters and noticed a small box tucked above one of the cross beams. He got to his feet and squinted to try to get a better look at it. He could just make out a single word.

Map.

"Shane!" his mother yelled down the stairs. "Time for lunch!"

"Okay, Mom!" he called back up. He turned towards the stairs.

"And don't leave your book and blanket down there this time," she said.

Shane groaned inwardly, turned around and picked up both of his things. He grumbled to himself and went upstairs.

I'll have to look in the box later, he promised himself, and he turned off the light as he left.

Chapter 35: Remembering

Shane fell out of the chair and landed on the parlor floor with a thud.

Pain blossomed in his head, but he got to his feet.

"The box," he said to the silent room. "The *box!*"

He hurried out of the room, legs unsteady as he approached the main stairs. He cut around to the left, found the hidden pocket door and slid it back. He flipped on the lights and walked quickly down the stairs into the basement.

The air was warm and dry, the furnace rumbled, and there were fewer spider webs than Shane remembered.

He went to stand in front of the furnace where he used to lay down his blanket and looked up.

There was the box. The one with the word *map* written on it.

The one he had never come back to look at.

Shane reached up and grabbed the box. It was an old cigar box. *Hoeffler's Havana's.* A buxom Cuban woman smiled at him and held out a glowing cigar. Shane ignored the advertisement's offer and hoped there was more than old cigars in the box.

There was.

Folded into a neat square was a thick piece of paper.

Shane took it out, set the box on the floor at his feet and unfolded the map. Six-floor plans were sketched out in minute detail. The top left plan had the legend, *Main Floor*, written beneath it. The second, *Second Floor.* Then *Servants' Quarters,* followed by *The Music Room, Where We Fear to Tread,* and *Her Room.* In the far right corner was a small square labeled, *The Root Cellar.* A question mark was beside it.

Shane carried the map upstairs and into the kitchen. He laid it on the table, started a fresh pot of coffee and returned to the map. He held onto both edges of the table and looked down at the paper. He needed to see how to get to the fifth floor, and from there to the sixth.

Nowhere in the Servants' quarters did he see a door marked stairs.

He looked at the second floor and stopped.

The painting, he thought. Set in the wall was a door he had only seen once. The door behind the painting. The stairs which led to the fifth floor.

A quick examination of the fifth floor showed another set of stairs which led up to her rooms.

"*Where did you find it?*" Carl asked, and Shane nearly jumped.

He turned and saw his dead friend in the chair across from him.

"*The basement,*" Shane answered. He walked over to the coffee, resisted the natural urge to offer the man coffee, and poured himself a cup. He sat down at the table, had a drink and looked at Carl. "*Did you know of it?*"

"*Of it? Yes. Where it was? No. I did not know where you might be able to find it if it even existed anymore.*"

"*Who made it?*" Shane asked.

"*A boy named Herman. A very smart boy. When he realized what was happening in the house, he mapped what he could and then he fled. Not before his mother killed his father, though.*"

"*When was this?*"

"*Nineteen fifty-two,*" Carl answered. "*His father was the chauffeur. His mother was a scullery maid. All of them lived together on the third floor.*"

"*How did he find about all of these?*" Shane asked.

"*He traveled them,*" Carl said.

"*Is he still alive?*" He asked excitedly.

The dead German shrugged. "*I do not know, my young friend.*"

"*What was his last name?*" Shane asked.

"*Mishal,*" Carl answered. "*Herman Mishal.*"

Chapter 36: With the Benefit of Years

Herman Mishal took off his glasses, pinched his nose and sighed to no one in particular.

His wife, Bernadette, looked up from her book.

"*Are you alright?*" she asked in Hebrew.

"*Yes,*" he said with a smile. "*I'm tired. And I do not feel especially well.*"

The cordless phone rang, and both he and Bernadette looked at it, surprised.

It was well after ten and the phone never rang after eight. Not unless it was an emergency with one of their children.

Herman put his glasses back on and looked at the caller id.

It read 'unavailable.'

He frowned and answered the phone. "Hello?"

"Hello," a man said. "I hate to bother you this late, but I'm looking for a man named Herman Mishal. Do I have the right house?"

"You do," Herman said. "But, it is terribly late. Perhaps you can call back tomorrow?"

"Sir," the stranger said, a note of anxiety in his voice. "Could you spare me just a minute? Please? It's about my parents?"

"Who is it?" Bernadette asked.

Herman shrugged his shoulders. "Well, you have an advantage. You know my name, but I don't know yours."

"I'm sorry. My name is Shane Ryan."

Nothing about the name was familiar to Herman. "I don't think we know each other, Mr. Ryan."

"We don't," Mr. Ryan said. "But you can help me. I know you can."

"How do you know that?" Herman asked. The mantle of therapist dropped over him.

"I found your map," the man said.

Herman shook his head, confused. "Map? What map are you talking about?"

"The map of the Anderson House."

A chill ripped through Herman and his mouth went dry.

"Herman?" Bernadette said fearfully. "Are you alright?"

He held up a shaky hand to her and nodded slightly. He cleared his throat and asked, "How did you come upon that map, Mr. Ryan?"

"I first saw it when I was a boy," he said. "But I remembered it a little while ago, and I found it in the basement, by the furnace."

Herman's heart pounded against his chest. He whispered, "Where are you, Mr. Ryan?"

"I'm in my house," the man said. "One twenty-five Berkley Street. I need to know how you made it through to her."

"Mr. Ryan," Herman said. "Do you know Nashua at all?"

"Yes," he replied.

"My wife and I live at twenty-six Sherman Street. Would you like to bring the map to me so we can discuss it?"

"Yes," he said, sighing. "Yes. When?"

"Right now," Herman said.

"Yes. I'll be there soon," Mr. Ryan said. "Thank you."

The man disconnected the call, and Herman hung up the phone.

"Herman," Bernadette said sharply. "Why did you invite a stranger here, especially now?"

Herman looked at his wife and smiled weakly. "He lives in the Anderson House."

Her eyes widened, and she closed her mouth tightly. She marked her place in her book, set it aside and stood up. "I'll go put on some coffee."

"Thank you," Herman said. He looked down at his hands, at the fingers which still ached from when they had been broken by *her*.

By the girl in the pond.

Chapter 37: Looking for a Ride

Gerald didn't sleep well.

Age, memories, being a widower.

It all contributed to his insomnia.

Turk, of course, had no such concerns or worries. The dog put his head down on his crossed paws, and fell asleep.

Gerald looked over at the German Shepherd and smiled. Turk lay on his side in front of the hearth, and occasionally his back leg kicked out. Gerald closed his book, set it on the coffee table and picked up his bottle of beer. It was warm, and barely palatable, but he drank it anyway.

The doorbell rang, and Turk was up and on his feet in a heartbeat. The dog's hackles were raised, and his lips pulled back as he growled. His old, yellow teeth still looked fearsome in the room's soft light.

Gerald put the bottle down, opened the drawer to the side-table and pulled the Colt .45 out. He chambered a round and stood up. The doorbell rang again as he left the room and went to the front door.

He stayed out of the sidelights, kept the weapon down by his leg and called out, "Who is it?"

"Gerald, it's me, Shane."

The younger man's voice was urgent and desperate.

Gerald slipped the safety on and stepped up to the door. Within a moment, Shane stepped in, and Turk greeted the man with a lopsided smile while his tail thumped steadily on the floor.

"What's going on?" Gerald asked, gesturing towards the study with the pistol.

"I need a favor," Shane said, dropping into a chair.

The man looked pale, as though he hadn't slept in days and something had run him ragged.

"What?" He asked, returning the Colt to the side-table before sitting down again.

"Could you give me a ride?" Shane asked desperately. "I can give you money for gas, I just, I just can't wait for a taxi."

"Shane," Gerald said, trying to keep his voice relaxed. "Is everything okay?"

The younger man shook his head. "I found a map, in the house. It might lead to my parents. Or, at least, where their bodies are."

Gerald rubbed the back of his head. "A map. What kind of map?"

Shane reached into the front pocket of his sweatshirt and withdrew a folded piece of paper. His hands shook has he handed it over.

Gerald looked at it and tried to make sense of the drawing.

"Shane," he said, "your house doesn't have six floors."

Shane nodded. "I know. It's not supposed to, but it has a lot of things it shouldn't. And this map was made by someone named Herman."

"Herman Mishal," Gerald whispered. He looked down at the paper in his hands. "I remember him. He was a younger, Jewish fellow. But he was a hell of a baseball player. What happened to his parents was terrible."

"I'm sorry," he said, shaking his head and forcing himself to return to the issue. "Shane, where do you need a ride to?"

"To Herman Mishal's house," Shane answered.

Gerald blinked several times and then he asked, "Are you serious?"

He nodded. "I spoke with him maybe ten or fifteen minutes ago. I told him what I had found. He said to come right over. He lives here in Nashua. Twenty-six Sherman Street."

"You need a ride to Herman Mishal's house?" Gerald asked.

"Yes," Shane said. "Please, Gerald."

"Of course," Gerald said, standing up. "Let's go see Herman."

Chapter 38: Meeting the Mishals

Shane was out of Gerald's old Buick before the car was even put into 'park.'

Herman Mishal's house was a small New England cape with a breezeway connecting the main structure to the two car garage. The light of the half-moon glowed in the pale blue siding, and smoke curled up from the chimney.

From either side of the front door, the exterior lamps cast their yellowish light onto the snow, and Shane approached the door excitedly.

He paused though, as he heard Gerald turn off the car's engine. He waited until the older man caught up with him before the two of them walked up the steps.

Nervously, Shane knocked on the door.

A moment later it opened, and a woman who looked to be slightly younger than Gerald smiled at them.

"Come in, please," she said, stepping aside.

Both Shane and Gerald murmured their thanks and entered the house. Warm air wrapped around them, as did the smell of coffee. Every wall, Shane noticed, was lined with bookcases, and each bookcase was neatly organized.

The woman smiled at Shane and said, "We like to read."

Gerald chuckled and nodded his head. "Yes, ma'am, it certainly seems like you do."

"I'm Bernadette Mishal," she said, offering her hand.

Shane and Gerald each shook it in turn while introducing themselves. Bernadette looked at Shane and said, "You live in the house?"

"Yes," he answered.

She nodded, and then she smiled. "Come with me, please. Herman is waiting for you."

They followed her down a narrow hallway, and into a small room. Like the hall, the room was lined with bookcases. Some of the shelves, however, were occupied with family photographs and antiques. The shades were drawn over the room's two windows, and a pair of well-worn reading chairs flanked a small table.

A small, delicate man sat wrapped in a blanket. He marked his page and set his book down on a side-table before he smiled at them.

"Forgive me, please," he said. "I cannot easily get up and out of the chair. I am Herman Mishal."

"Shane Ryan," Shane said, stepping forward and offering his hand.

Herman slipped a hand free of his blanket and carefully shook it.

The older man's fingers, Shane saw, had been severely broken at some point and not set properly.

"Don't be afraid of hurting them," Herman chuckled. He shook out Gerald's hand and nodded to Bernadette. The woman left the room and returned a moment later with a pair of folding chairs.

Shane went to help her, and she looked over her glasses at him sternly.

"Thank you," she said, smiling impishly, "but I am quite adept at doing things my husband should."

"... *wicked girl,*" Herman said, and Shane managed to catch only the last of what the man said. It was a language he hadn't heard much of before.

"*... only for you, Herman,*" Bernadette said. "*Should I bring the coffee now or would you rather wait?*"

"*If you don't mind,*" Shane said, trying out the language, getting used to the harsh sounds and the tricks of the tongue, "*I would prefer a cup of coffee now.*"

All three of them looked at him in surprise.

"You speak Hebrew?" Herman asked.

"I do now," Shane said.

"*What do you mean you do now?*" Herman asked, pronouncing his words carefully. "*Did you not speak it before?*"

"No," Shane said, shaking his head. "*But if I hear something, especially the older I get, the easier languages become.*"

"Impressive," Herman said softly. He smiled. "My apologies, though. My wife and I tend to speak Hebrew primarily in the house, so it is only natural for us to lapse into it. I hope I didn't offend either of you."

"No offense taken," Gerald said, smiling.

Bernadette finished setting up the pair of chairs and he and Gerald each sat down. She slipped out of the room to fetch the coffee.

"So," Herman said, sadness in his voice. "You found my map."

Shane nodded.

"And you want to know if it's real," Herman continued, "and whether or not you can use it to retrieve your parents."

"Yes," Shane whispered.

"I can assure you it is real," Herman said. "But as to whether or not you can use it to find your parents, well, I don't know. First, though, may I see the map?"

Shane took the map out, fought down the urge to keep it to himself, and reluctantly handed it over.

Herman freed his other hand from the blanket, and Shane saw those fingers were just as twisted as the others.

The man opened the map, which shook ever so slightly in his grasp, and he sighed sadly. He looked upon the paper for a long time, and then he nodded, folded the map, and returned it to Shane.

Shane tucked it away.

"Did you really make it?" Gerald asked.

"Yes," Herman said, smiling gently. Bernadette entered the room with a small serving tray and four cups of coffee, a sugar bowl and a small pitcher of cream. She handed a cup to each man, added cream and sugar to Herman's and then she turned to Shane and Gerald.

"Would either of you care for cream or sugar?" she asked.

"No thank you," Shane said, taking a cautious sip. The coffee was hot and rich. He sighed happily.

"No thank you, ma'am," Gerald said.

She nodded, put her own cup down on a small table and added sugar. She left the room with the tray and returned a moment later. After she had taken her seat, Herman smiled at her and started to speak.

"I made the map when I was thirteen years old," he said, his voice strong. "I lived in the servants' quarters at one twenty-five Berkley Street. My father, Barney, was the Andersons' butler. My mother, Anna, was a maid. My father was not Jewish, but my mother was. She was insistent about my being raised in the faith, and my father adored her. He was not terribly fond of the Lutheran church."

Herman smiled. "We moved into the estate when I was ten, and we lived there together for five years. The Andersons were kind enough to ensure I received a proper education. Mr. Anderson, who was truly a frightening man, discovered my love of books, and he was kind enough to grant me unrestricted access to his library.

"A little too bellicose for my taste," Herman said with a sigh, "but the books were of the best sort. The way they were bound and written. The array of languages. Anyway, I'm rambling."

"When I was thirteen," he paused and took a sip of his coffee and smiled his thanks to his wife, "I discovered secret ways within the house. They branched off from the servants' passages running through the walls. There were rooms I knew you couldn't find from the halls. Whole floors magically appearing.

"I tried to tell my parents, but neither of them was terribly imaginative, and they merely patted me on the head and told me to concentrate on my studies and not on fairy tales. As time passed, though, I decided to map out my travels. I felt like Shackleton, exploring the great unknown. Sherlock, investigating mysteries. Watson, keeping a journal of all I experienced."

Herman sighed and looked down at his twisted hands. "There was so much more, though. A danger lurking in the walls. One I never expected or even dreamed of. You found it, though, didn't you?"

Shane nodded. "You kept a journal?"

"I did," Herman said. "I have it put away in a safety deposit box. When I pass away, it can be read."

"I remember you," Gerald said, nodding to Herman. "I remember you were one hell of a baseball player."

Herman grinned a youthful, boyish grin. "I loved baseball. I still do. My poor Bernadette has suffered through years of it. When the Red Sox finally won the World Series, she told me I shouldn't ever watch the sport again."

"He didn't listen," Bernadette said. "He was yelling again at the television on opening day the following season."

Herman chuckled, adjusted his glasses and said, "Yes. I yell at the television."

"He doesn't understand they can't hear him," she said.

"It's why I don't watch football anymore," Gerald said. "They don't listen to me."

Herman nodded. "Very true. And yes, I was a fair baseball player. You ask, I suppose, because of my hands?"

"Yes," Gerald said.

The gleam in Herman's eyes died and all the humor was gone from his voice. "She did this."

"Which she?" Shane asked, leaning forward.

"The girl in the pond. Vivienne," he answered.

"How?" Shane asked in a whisper. "How did she do it?"

Herman closed his eyes, took a deep breath and then he said, "She possessed my mother."

Shane's hands shook so badly he had to put his coffee cup on the floor. He clasped his hands together and looked down at his feet.

"It happened to you?" Herman asked.

Shane nodded. "Not with my mother. One of the neighbors who came over to find her lost cat.

Chapter 39: Shane, August 15th, 1988

Shane had known Mrs. Kensington since he had moved into the old Anderson house. She had been the first neighbor to welcome them, and the first to become friends with his mother. Occasionally, he would even go to her house after school if his mom felt particularly uncomfortable about the house.

Mrs. Kensington, in turn, rarely visited their home.

She was never at ease, or so Shane had heard her say. Something bothered her. She couldn't, she had told his mother, quite put her finger on it.

Shane could, of course, and his mother could as well.

On Monday morning, Shane sat at the small kitchen table. In the hall, the grandfather clock struck seven, and he yawned.

Too early, he thought. But the three of them were supposed to be going to Wells, Maine to enjoy the beach.

Shane didn't like the beach, though. Not since he had read *Jaws* and seen the movie. He had even told his mom, but she had said he couldn't stay home alone for the week. His parents had rented a house right on Moody Beach, and Shane was going to be there. He could read all day from the safety of the rented home's porch and not have to worry about sharks.

With a sigh, Shane pushed the last of his egg onto his toast, ate both in one large bite that his mother would have reprimanded him for, and stood up. He chewed as he walked, which certainly would have earned him a second scolding, if not an outright punishment, and carried his plate to the sink. He rinsed off the yolk, put the dish amongst the others, and walked to the back door.

He opened it and looked at the backyard.

As always, it was quiet outside, but he couldn't see the girl in the pond. Some mornings, she lurked near the surface; a hideous white form beneath the water. While others, she disappeared completely.

Nothing, though, and Shane smiled.

"Captain!" A voice called out, nearly startling Shane.

He looked to the right, and he saw Mrs. Kensington. The woman wore a pair of khaki gardening shorts, a button down blue shirt, and a wide-brimmed sun hat over her pinned up gray hair. She was short and stout and at times she looked almost like a bulldog the way her jowls would hang down. But her smile was always genuine, and she made the best chocolate chip cookies Shane had ever eaten. He didn't mind the pair of Birkenstock sandals she wore, which she had probably purchased just after the end of the nineteen sixties. For some reason, they drove his father crazy though.

As did the name of her orange cat.

Captain.

"Captain!" She called again.

Shane watched as she approached the pond, but since he couldn't see the girl in the water, he didn't worry too much about it.

He didn't think the cat was in the yard, either. Most animals stayed away from one twenty-five Berkley Street. And those few who wandered in usually ran away after a minute or two on the property.

Mrs. Kensington's head turned towards the pond and Shane heard her say, "Captain?"

He could hear the rustle of the tall grass around the water's edge, and evidently Mrs. Kensington heard it as well. She took a step closer.

"Captain," she said. "What are you doing by the water?"

A white, swollen hand, streaked with mud and filth, suddenly shot out of the grass, latched onto Mrs. Kensington's thick ankle and pulled.

Shane threw open the screen door as Mrs. Kensington was jerked into the water. The splash was loud and frightening. He heard her cough and splutter. She slapped at the water, and a scream was ripped from her.

He hurried down the back steps and sprinted to the pond. Mrs. Kensington clung to the bank and dug her fingers into the grass. She pulled up great clumps of it as she dragged herself forward. She was wet and filthy, and when Shane finally reached her, he quickly helped her to her feet. He hauled her back to the house and got her into the kitchen.

The screen door slammed behind them as he led her to the table. Shane sat her down in the seat he had so recently vacated and ran to the sink. He poured a glass of cold water and carried it to her before grabbing a hand towel off a hanger by the fridge.

Mrs. Kensington was covered in mud, her clothes stained with it. She looked dully at the glass in front of her. Shane wrinkled his nose as he got closer. The mud stank of rot and filth.

"Here, Mrs. Kensington," he said, holding the towel out to her.

She blinked several times before she turned and looked at him. Her face was slack, her eyes vacant. Her hat, he noticed, was gone and strands and clumps of her gray hair had escaped the bun she had tied it in.

"Mrs. Kensington?" Shane asked.

She smiled.

A cold, hard smile.

Her eyes focused and locked onto him.

"Hello Shane," she said, and yet it wasn't Mrs. Kensington who spoke.

It was Vivienne.

"This body is old. It is fat," the dead girl said as she pushed away from the table and stood on uncertain legs. "However, it will suffice."

She licked her lips.

"Oh," Vivienne whispered. "She likes you, Shane. She does. Dirty little thoughts about a dirty little boy."

Vivienne laughed, and it was a harsh, painful sound.

Shane winced and took a cautious step towards the hallway.

"Where will you go?" She asked. "To a bedroom? It's what she wants. Shall we give it to her, Shane?"

The door between the hall and the kitchen slammed closed.

Vivienne blocked his path to the back door.

"No," she said softly. "I don't think we'll give her anything except your death, Shane. A brilliant memory of her murdering you. A gift to your mother as well. Do you think dear mother will make it from the bathroom to the kitchen without falling? I'm certain she'll race naked as the day she was born when she hears Mrs. Kensington scream.

"And Mrs. Kensington will scream, Shane," Vivienne hissed. "When she sees your body, and realizes it was she who killed you."

Vivienne lunged at him.

Shane didn't try to slip to the right or to the left.

Instead, he charged at her.

Vivienne's eyes widened in surprise, and a small grunt escaped her lips as he struck her solidly in the chest.

Shane was small, but he had faced more bullies than he cared to remember.

And none of his tormentors ever expected him to charge at them.

Vivienne was dead, but she was still nothing more than a bully.

She staggered back, and Shane raced for the back door.

Which slammed shut.

Vivienne screamed with rage, and he spun around to face her.

"You'll pay," she spat.

"Shut up," Shane said, grinning.

Her eyes widened and her face reddened. "What?"

"Shut up," Shane repeated. "Shut up. You're nothing. A dead brat. Nothing else. And you smell like dead fish."

Vivienne shrieked and blood exploded out of Mrs. Kensington's nose. The older woman's body lurched towards him, and Shane waited until the last moment to move. He ducked easily under the flabby arms and let out a frightened laugh as Vivienne slipped and slammed into the wall.

The door to the kitchen burst open, and Shane's mother ran in.

She had on her bathrobe, but water dripped from her body and from her hair. She looked at Mrs. Kensington in surprise and said, "Beatrice?!"

The woman came to a stop, shuddered, blinked, and stumbled back into the wall.

The entire house shook, and Shane heard the front door slam open, and his father yell.

The world went black in front of Shane, and he felt himself fall.

Chapter 40: What to do about the Map?

Shane cracked his knuckles nervously. He caught sight of Herman's fingers and stopped.

Herman chuckled. "Don't worry about my feelings, Shane. Your nervous habit won't bother me."

Shane smiled his thanks.

Herman pulled his blanket around him and settled back into his chair. "When I was fifteen years old, my mother made the mistake of going too close to the pond. Well, at least that is what I assumed happened. No one saw her prior to the murder, you see."

"I was home, after school, and I was practicing with my violin. My mother came into the apartment, and she was… well, she was different." He sighed and closed his eyes. "She smelled. That curious, foul smell peculiar to the pond behind the house. I should have known then something was wrong. But, I was fifteen. I was focused solely upon my violin. And when I wasn't seeing Schubert's music, I was picturing the upcoming game against Dracut High School.

"I first realized something was amiss when my mother ripped the violin out of my hands. She had a grin, a smile full of teeth which didn't look quite right on my mother's face. Before I could ask her what was wrong, she struck me on the head."

"Herman," Bernadette said.

He opened his eyes and smiled at his wife. "I am alright, my love. Thank you."

"Now," he continued, "she struck me on the head. A terrific blow which knocked me off the stool and onto the floor. Before I could get to my hands and knees, she struck me several more times. She shattered the instrument, I am afraid, and I must have been knocked unconscious. I later awoke to excruciating pain. My mother was stomping upon my fingers with her heels.

"It was then my father entered the apartment. I must have been screaming. He was followed by one of the gardeners. It was he who pulled me away from my mother while my father attempted to gain control over her. Or, rather, the evil inside of her."

Herman paused and smiled sadly at them. "Unfortunately, the girl in the pond had quite the grip upon my mother. When he grabbed her, my mother tore his throat out with her teeth.

"The gardener was a smart man and instantly realized something was wrong. He slammed the door shut and locked it. Since my mother was Jewish, they called for a Rabbi. Unfortunately, the closest Rabbi was at Temple Adath Yeshurun in Manchester. I was brought to St. Joseph's Hospital, for my hands to be looked at. By the time the Rabbi reached the Andersons' house, my mother had died.

"She choked to death on my father's heart."

"Good God," Gerald said, crossing himself.

"I did not appreciate God for quite some time," Herman said. He looked at Shane. "Did she speak to you, when she tried to kill you?"

Shane nodded. "She told me some of the things Mrs. Kensington was thinking."

"Yes," Herman said. "She did the same with my mother. Who knows what was truth and what was fiction. I can only assume she used a fine mixture of both. The most hurtful lies are those with a bit of honesty in them."

Silence fell over all of them for a few minutes.

"Well," Herman said. "Since we have now established our credentials regarding one twenty-five Berkley Street, how may I help you, Mr. Ryan?"

"I need you to explain your map to me," Shane said. "I need to get to her."

"Why?" Herman asked.

"Because," Shane said with a sigh. "She still has my parents."

And he explained to Herman and Bernadette and Gerald what had happened to his mother and father.

Chapter 41: Marie Finds She Must Believe

It had taken Marie ten years to beat alcohol. She had moments, of course, where she wanted a drink. Hell, moments when she *needed* a drink.

But every alcoholic wrestled with the need.

Marie had never, however, been so close to breaking her sobriety.

Something was wrong with the Anderson House. Something inside of it was bad. She had enough problems when she went through withdrawal to understand hallucinations and delirium.

What she had experienced in the Anderson House was real. Terrifyingly real.

She got up out of her chair, walked over to her bonsai trees and inspected them. She had already taken care of her miniature grove in the morning. When she stood in front of the trees, though, she felt peaceful.

It helped take her mind off the rum and coke.

She glanced at the clock on the wall.

One, she read. Her stomach growled, as she gave it a pat. It was time to eat, and she was hungry.

Nevertheless, her experiences with Shane Ryan dominated her thoughts.

None of it could be real, and yet it was. She couldn't deny it.

I want to, she thought, turning away from the trees. *Oh, Christ do I want to.*

Because if she couldn't deny it, she had to accept it. And if she accepted it, it meant she had experienced an event the likes of which she had scoffed at for years.

How many calls did I get when I first joined the Nashua Police Department where nothing had been found? People adamant they'd heard something, seen something? She thought.

The jokes with the other cops about people who drank too much, as they sat in their favorite bar and consumed massive amounts of alcohol to deal with the other, more horrific events. Painful crimes which had been all too real.

And now this, she thought.

Marie walked back to her chair and sat down. She looked at the television and realized she didn't want to watch anything. She glanced over at her computer. Her screensaver, a photo of her trees, cast a soft light over her desk.

She had played solitaire for hours, and contemplated playing a few more. She had to be at court for the Jubert case at nine. Otherwise she was free.

Free to sit and obsess over the Anderson House.

After court, she told herself. *After court, I'll go back and see Shane. We'll figure out what's going on. I'll talk to Uncle Gerry, too. He's been on Berkley Street for as long as I can remember.*

I bet he knows something.

Marie stood and went to the kitchen. She needed something to eat before she played another hour's worth of solitaire.

Chapter 42: Shane, April 9th, 1989

Shane no longer let his parents put his bureau in front of the door that Eloise and Thaddeus used. For some reason, the noisy piece of furniture being pushed across the floor was worse than when either of the ghosts whispered in his ear.

He stayed out of the pantry, if he could help it, and away from the root cellar's trap door at all costs. Occasionally he could hear the dark ones whisper.

And it was never pleasant.

Ever.

The library was safe. So was the parlor. He didn't trust the kitchen, not since Mrs. Kensington had been possessed by Vivienne.

He felt badly for Mrs. Kensington, too. She couldn't look at him and, not surprisingly, his mother didn't have the woman watch him anymore.

I don't need watching, Shane thought. He tied his sneakers and stood up. A glance out the window showed dark clouds. The sun was hidden, and by the looks of the clouds, there might be a thunderstorm.

Downstairs a door slammed.

Shane turned away from the window and looked out into the hallway.

Both of his parents were out, and the ghosts hadn't slammed any doors in a couple of years.

With the exception of Vivienne.

"Carl?" Shane said softly.

Carl didn't answer.

"Eloise?"

Silence.

"Thaddeus?"

He knew better than to call for Roberto. The musician barely heard anything. He played too often and was too far away. Occasionally, Shane would catch a bit of music, but only once in a great while.

Shane walked out of his room to the top of the stairs.

Heavy scrapes dragged through the air, and someone slammed a piece of furniture down.

Shane walked a few steps down.

"My friend?" he whispered in German.

Still Carl didn't answer.

The old man in his parents' bathroom moaned and caused Shane's heart to leap.

His head started to pound, and he walked down to the main hall.

More noise came out of the parlor.

The door, he saw, was closed. The light flickered in a mad rhythm from under it and shadows shifted crazily across the wood floor.

Shane nervously licked his lips and reached for the door.

Something cold and hard grasped his wrist and stopped him.

Surprised, he looked to the right, and a moment later a man appeared. An old man stood tall and gaunt. He wore a black suit and his white hair hung past his shoulders. His blue eyes shined, and his lips parted to reveal a mouthful of broken, yellowed teeth.

"Away, boy!" the man hissed, and Shane recognized the voice.

The old man.

The old man. The one from his parents' room.

"Away!" the old man said again. "You don't know what's in there. You don't want to know. Get out!"

A deep, hideous voice screamed through the parlor door. The thing said a name Shane didn't catch, but evidently the old man did.

A second later his wrist was free, and the man from the bathroom was gone.

Before Shane could move the door to the parlor was ripped open, and death stood in front of him.

A skeleton, bones yellowed, lurched towards him and Shane stumbled backward. It was barren of clothing, yet wisps of black hair clung to its skull. The dead man howled while reaching for Shane as he scrambled out of the way. The skeleton's bones scraped across the floor, and Shane got to his feet and ran.

He sprinted down the hall, tripped over his own feet and slammed into the wall by the kitchen door. A look back showed the skeleton only a few paces away.

Shane lunged for the kitchen, but a bony hand locked onto his shirt collar and jerked him back. A terrible chill swept through him and Shane shivered violently. His stomach churned, and the Fruit Loops he'd eaten for breakfast rushed up his throat and burned his mouth as he vomited over the floor.

The skeleton shrieked with glee and Shane felt himself being lifted off the floor and thrown back down the hall. He struck the wood, and his head spun. He gasped for breath as he was elevated again and darkness finally rushed over him.

***

Pain woke Shane up and made him realize he was alive.

With a groan, he pushed himself up from the floor. He rubbed his eyes with the palms of his hands until stars exploded behind his eyelids. The iron tang of blood filled his mouth, and his nose hurt. Shane got to his feet and walked haphazardly to the sitting room's main bathroom. The grandfather clock struck one, and he dimly realized he'd been knocked out for hours.

Shane turned on the light and leaned over the old porcelain sink. He ran the cold tap, splashed water against his face and rinsed out his mouth. Blood circled the drain and a piece of his tooth clattered against the metal.

Shane probed his teeth with his tongue but couldn't feel anything exceptionally painful. Everything was sore, and he felt as though someone had beaten him.

Someone did, Shane thought with a sigh. *They were just dead.*

He rinsed his mouth out once more, cleaned the blood and turned the water off as he straightened up. He looked at his reflection and blinked several times.

I'm different, Shane thought.

It was almost horror flick different.

His face was swollen. Both eyes were black and blue. One whole cheek was swollen and red. The other was scratched.

And all of his hair was gone.

Every single strand on his head.

All of it was gone.

His eyebrows were gone. The eyelashes. The hint of a mustache and the few scrawny hairs which had populated his cheeks. All of them were gone.

Shane looked down at his arms and saw they were smooth and bare as well. He leaned over and pulled up the leg of his pants. Horrified, he watched as his leg hair fell and clung to his sock and his sneaker.

He let his pants' leg fall and sat down on the toilet. The skin of his scalp was warm and smooth under his hand, as though he had never had hair.

For the first time, in a long time, Shane cried.

Chapter 43: A Decision is Made

"Are you sure about this?" Bernadette asked, fixing his tie for him.

"Of course not," Herman said. His stomach twisted nervously. Fortunately, he had not been able to eat anything. If he had, he would have been in the bathroom, on his knees, with a sincere worry as to whether or not he would be sick.

"Then why?" She asked, looking at him.

"I must," he said. *"Not only for him but myself, my love. His parents are dead, of course, but he should know for certain."*

Bernadette nodded, finished his tie, and stepped back. She smiled at him proudly. *"So handsome, my beautiful husband."*

Herman blushed, as he always did. As he always would.

"Are you ready?" she asked.

He nodded.

Bernadette put on her coat, took her purse and the car keys off the shelf by the back door, and led the way out.

A few minutes later, they were in their old Chevy sedan and Bernadette took her time. Berkley Street was only a few minutes away, and Herman knew she had no desire to see him return to the house.

His stomach twisted around and seemed to push against his ribs.

The fear grew with every rotation of the tires. With every foot, every inch they drew closer to the house. To where his mother, possessed, killed his father and eventually herself.

Gluttony, Herman thought.

He remembered the Rabbi and of being forced to go and live with his mother's sister. A kind woman, but not his mother.

No, not his mother.

Tears welled up in Herman's eyes, and he quickly blinked them away.

Bernadette didn't bring him to the Anderson House, but instead she drove to Gerald's house. When she pulled into the older man's driveway, the door to the house opened, and Shane Ryan hurried out.

The man looked tired, battered.

Herman, who had spent a lifetime as a therapist, could only imagine the prolonged horror the man had suffered through.

Bernadette turned the engine off and looked at Herman.

"Is Gerald going in with you?" she asked.

"I don't believe so," Herman said. "Let me ask, though."

He opened the door and got out of the car.

"Good morning," Shane said.

"Good morning," Herman said, smiling in an effort to hide his growing fear. "My wife would like to know if Gerald will be accompanying us?"

"No," Shane answered, shaking his head.

Bernadette got out of the car. She had the keys and her purse. "I will ask if I can stay here with Gerald then."

"Are you certain?" he asked her.

She smiled. *"What do you think?"*

Chapter 44: Going into the House

Shane stood with Herman in Gerald's kitchen.

Gerald, Turk and Bernadette were in the study.

Shane looked at the old man with the crippled fingers and asked again, "Are you sure about this, Herman? I just wanted to know the best way into the house."

"I'm sure, Shane," Herman answered. "And, quite honestly, I am the best path into the other rooms of the house. I knew them all when I was a boy. I may have forgotten one or two, but I doubt it.

"They were terrifying."

Shane nodded in agreement.

The doorbell rang and Turk barked from the study.

A moment later, Gerald exited the room with a frown on his face. He hurried to the front door, peered through the sidelight and let out a surprised, but pleased laugh. Quickly he threw back the deadbolt and let Marie Lafontaine in.

"You weren't supposed to be over until later this afternoon," Gerald said, giving his niece a hug.

She grinned as she nodded. "I know. The Jubert boy pled out. I didn't have to testify."

"Shane and Mr. Mishal were just about to leave, but Mr. Mishal's lovely wife is going to keep me company," Gerald said.

Marie looked at her uncle shrewdly. "You know all about what's going on at Ryan's house, don't you?"

For a moment, it looked as though Gerald would deny it, but then he said, "Yes. I know exactly what has occurred."

"I don't mean to sound rude," Marie said, turning her attention to Herman, "but how do you fit into this?"

Shane looked at the man and saw a mischievous grin steal across his face.

"I'm looking to purchase the home so I might turn it into a school for wayward girls," Herman said evenly.

Marie's eyes widened for a heartbeat before they narrowed.

"No, my dear lady," Herman said, chuckling. "Nothing of the sort. I make jokes when I am afraid, and right now, I am petrified. As to how I fit into the grand scheme of the Anderson House, well, I lived there as a boy before young Shane did. The house claimed my parents, but in a far different fashion than the way in which it took Shane's. I, at least, have the cold comfort of knowing they died. Shane does not."

The simple truth of Herman's statement struck Shane viciously, and he dropped his chin to his chest.

Herman had summed it up succinctly.

Shane had no idea what happened to his parents. He could only hope they were dead. Part of him, the childish part, wished to find them alive. To find them thus, however, would mean they had spent decades in hell. They would be insane. No one could survive it.

No one.

Shane lifted his chin up. "Thank you, Herman."

"Mr. Mishal," Marie said, offering her hand, "I'm Marie Lafontaine. I'm going to help today."

Herman shook the hand carefully. "I am Herman, Ms. Lafontaine. We are going to need all of the help we can get. Let us walk to the Anderson House, and I will tell you what I know of the fourth floor."

Chapter 45: Herman, August 27th, 1947

"You play beautifully," Herman said to the skeleton in the small music room.

The dead man held a violin loosely and stared at Herman with empty eye sockets.

Doesn't he speak English? Herman wondered. He only spoke English and Hebrew, and he doubted the dead man spoke Hebrew.

Herman wracked his brain and tried to think of a way he could communicate with the musician.

A grin stole across Herman's face. Even though he knew the skeleton couldn't understand him, Herman asked, "May I?"

He pointed to a beautiful, dark stained violin. A bow lay beside it on its shelf, and there was a small jar of resin with it as well.

The skeleton held up its violin in what Herman thought was an inquisitive way.

"Yes," Herman said, nodding. "I can play."

The musician gestured to the wall and nodded.

Happily, Herman picked up the bow. Carefully he added some resin and then he picked up the violin. He tucked it under his chin, adjusted his fingers, and picked out the first part of Schubert's Death and the Maiden, which he was sure he had heard from the room.

After the first few bars, the skeleton joined in, and soon the room was filled with the music of Schubert.

They played together for a long time until sweat gathered at the base of Herman's neck and ran down his spine to pool in the waistband of his underwear. Eventually, the two of them worked their way through the entire piece, and when it was finished the skeleton said, "Bravo!"

The word startled Herman, and he laughed at his own fear.

The musician chuckled as well.

"Can I, can I go through the door?" Herman asked, gesturing with the bow to the door beside the skeleton.

The musician's laughter stopped, and he looked from the door to Herman and cocked his head questioningly.

Herman nodded.

The skeleton pointed to the door with his bow, then brought it back to the violin quickly and dragged it across the strings in a harsh, discordant note. He pointed to the door again.

"Yes," Herman said after a moment. "Something bad is beyond the door."

"Si," the musician said, speaking for the first time. "Il Male. Il Male."

Herman nodded.

From his seat on a high stool, the skeleton pointed at the door, to a whistle which hung beside it.

A dog whistle? Herman thought. He put the violin and the bow back and stepped to the door.

The musician said something he didn't catch, but Herman felt he understood the gist of it.

The whistle was important.

Herman took it down and looped the long string over his neck.

"Il Male," the musician said, and then he teased out a long, high-pitched note from his violin.

"Blow the whistle," Herman said, bringing it up to his lips, "if I see something bad. Il Male."

The musician nodded and repeated the note. When he finished he said, "Il Male."

"Thank you," Herman said. He opened the door and stepped out into a forest.

Chapter 46: Searching for the Entrance

"A forest?" Marie asked as Shane opened the door and led the way into the house.

"Yes," Herman said, stepping inside. "A forest."

"How can a forest be inside of a house?" she asked, confused. She closed the heavy front door and looked at Herman. "How?"

"There are rules, of course," Herman said slowly, as if he picked each word carefully from a giant mental dictionary before he answered. "We know of how things go up, and therefore, they must come down. We know there is a finite amount of space within an area, such as this hall. These are absolutes, correct?"

Marie nodded.

"Excellent," he said. "No, the issue is not a lack of rules within the confines of the house, but *new* rules. Different rules. A room is as large as she wishes it to be. The dead may or may not leave. The dead may or may not be dead. The rules are hers, so we must learn them."

"Now," Herman said, "we must proceed to the second floor."

Shane looked at the older man and instead of going up the stairs, he said, "Herman, are you alright?"

Herman turned to face him, and Shane saw how pale the man's face was. Beads of sweat gathered around the man's temple and a nervous hand adjusted his small, black yarmulke on his head.

"No, Shane," Herman said with a tight smile. "I am not alright. I am terrified at what I'm going to find. This house, not surprisingly, features rather prominently in my nightmares."

"I understand," Shane said.

The older man nodded his head. "I'm sure you do. Now, Ms. Lafontaine, would you be able to lend me your arm? I am always rather cautious with stairs."

"Yes," Marie said, stepping up to his side.

Shane looked at both of them for a minute, the detective and the retired therapist. *They're both here to help me.*

An odd mixture of humility and strength washed over him. Shane smiled a moment later after he recognized it.

He had felt the same thing every time he and his Marines went into combat.

Nothing can beat us, Shane thought, as he led the way up the stairs.

In a short time, they stood before the door to the servants' quarters, and Shane tried the doorknob. It was locked.

"Locked?" Herman asked.

"Yes," Shane said.

"Do you have the key?" the old man asked.

"There isn't one," Shane answered.

"Ms. Lafontaine, could you please go to the window for me?" Herman asked.

"Sure," Marie answered. She walked to the large window at the end of the hall. It, like all of the others in the house, was huge. The sill was nearly a foot deep, and white panels lined the sides.

When she reached the window, Herman said, "Could you please press on the lower left corner of the bottom right panel?"

She leaned forward, pushed on the panel and let out a surprised laugh as the panel swung in. Cautiously, she reached in and pulled out a key and an old baseball.

Shane looked over to Herman and saw the man was smiling.

"Could you bring them both over?" the old man asked.

She nodded and the panel clicked closed as she returned to the servants' door. Herman accepted both the key and the baseball from her.

He looked longingly at the ball and smiled gently. After a moment, he said, "This was my favorite baseball. My absolute favorite. It is signed by Roy Campanella. Do you know him?"

Both Shane and Marie shook their heads.

"A pity," Herman said. He slipped the ball into a pocket of his coat. "I will tell you all about him when we are done here."

The man turned to the door and, with surprising dexterity, considering the state of his fingers, fit the key into the lock.

The door opened effortlessly for him. The faintest strands of music drifted down to them, and a huge smile appeared on Herman's face.

"The musician," he whispered. Then, in a louder voice, Herman said, "Come, we must see the musician for only through his room can we get to the fifth floor. Lead on, young man, lead on."

Shane nodded and went up the stairs.

The hallway on the third floor was dimly lit. A single bulb flickered randomly in the sconce by Roberto's door. The air was cold and stale, and Marie coughed uncomfortably.

"It will be better when he realizes we are here," Herman said.

Shane was about to ask him what he meant, but Roberto answered the unasked question.

All of the lights in the hall burst into life, warmth flooded the air, and the musician's door sprang open. It nearly hit the wall, but it stopped a hair's breadth from the plain plaster.

Music exploded into the room, and Herman laughed happily. He put the key in his pocket and turned to face Shane.

"He is pleased," Herman said, his eyes shining with excitement. "Oh, Shane, Marie, I have not seen the musician in decades. The music we would play together. I learned how to play Vivaldi here, and waltzes. Ah, Marie, the waltzes I could play. And I could dance as well."

The old man went silent, and he looked down at his hands.

"What she took from me," he whispered. "What she took from me."

Shane reached out and put his hand on Herman's shoulder.

The older man looked at him, blinked and said softly, "What she took from us both, eh, Shane?"

Shane nodded. "Do you want to lead the way?"

"Yes," Herman said. "Yes, I do."

Chapter 47: A Meeting of Old Friends

Herman could hardly contain his excitement as he navigated the last few steps to the musician's closed door. Marie was directly behind him, a firm hand on his lower back to make sure he wouldn't fall should his twisted hands refuse to retain their grip on the banisters.

At the last step, he let go of the right railing and knocked gently on the door.

The lock clicked, the doorknob turned, and the portal opened.

Herman looked into the room of the musician and fought back tears.

The walls were still lined with shelves. Each shelf had its violin and its bow. The light was on at the end, and the musician sat upon his stool. The skeleton played beautifully, as always, and the music pulled at Herman's heart.

Shane and Marie entered the room and closed the door behind them.

The musician lowered his violin and looked at them with his hollow eyes. He said something in a language Herman didn't understand.

"He says 'hello, my friend'," Shane said.

Herman wiped a few errant tears away and looked at the younger man. "You understand him?"

Shane nodded. "He's speaking Italian. His name is Roberto Guidoboni."

"Roberto," Herman whispered.

Roberto chuckled and spoke again.

Once more Shane translated.

"He's happy to see us, and hopes Marie doesn't find his appearance too distressing," Shane said.

"I don't," Marie said, although her face was pale.

Roberto spoke again, for a longer time, and when he finished, Shane nodded. He said, "He has often thought of you, Herman. He remembers the music the two of you played together. And he wonders what has brought the three of us to him."

"Could you tell him we need to enter the forest?" Herman asked.

Shane did so.

Roberto looked at the door which led to the forest, and then he looked back to them and spoke.

"He wants to know if we're certain of traveling through the forest," Shane said.

"Yes," Herman answered. "We have no choice, not if we wish to find what happened to your parents."

Shane relayed the answer.

Roberto brought the violin up to his chin and played a few notes. The door to the forest glowed. The lock clicked, and the door swung open.

Marie gasped in surprise and Shane said, "Damn."

"We came through the door," Marie said. "But it was only stone and darkness."

"Because you were in a passage," Herman said. "You can only get to the forest from this room, or from hers. No other way. Shane, will you be kind enough to take the whistle? The one hanging by the door?"

Shane walked to the door and took the whistle down. It was a seaman's whistle, long and thin and attached to a twine cord. Herman shook his head as Shane held it out to him.

"You wear it," he said.

"What is it for?" Shane asked, slipping the long cord over his neck, allowing the whistle to rest against the center of his chest.

"An emergency," Herman answered.

"Buona fortuna, amico mio," Roberto said, and Herman didn't need it to be translated.

He smiled at the musician and stepped through the door, into the forest.

Chapter 48: A Difficult Journey

When the door closed behind them, Shane realized they were locked in the forest.

It was a strange thought, the idea of being locked into something like a forest, but, then again, the Anderson House was far from normal.

He had never quite comprehended just how abnormal it was, though.

The forest, unlike the property around the house, was not silent.

It was filled with the sound of crows, their harsh and dangerous calls in the perpetual twilight.

The air was cold, and the leaves of the trees had changed colors. Yet without the benefit of the sun, the colors were muted and blunt. Shane could faintly smell rot, as though somewhere among all the foliage, some dead animals slowly went the way of all flesh.

"This place is bad," Marie said.

"Very much so," Herman said. He looked at Shane and Marie. "There is nothing delicate about this place, nothing beautiful. In my youth, I came upon the bones of others who had gone before us."

"What do you mean, others?" Marie asked. She looked around. "There are bodies here?"

Herman nodded.

Shane shook his head and let out a sharp laugh.

"What?" Marie asked.

"I wonder if my parents are here, among the trees," he said. "If they died here."

"Is there any way you'll be able to find out?" Marie asked.

"I don't know," Shane said. He felt miserable, as though someone had hung the proverbial millstone around his neck.

"Shane," Herman said.

He looked at the older man. "Yes?"

"I don't believe your parents will be here, in this forest," Herman said. "She would have taken them to her room. It is what she did. I found others there, in her room. Those with whom she had been especially displeased. If she snatched both of your parents, as the dead have told you she did, then they will be in her room. Not here. Not on the forest floor."

Shane looked at Herman for a long time, and then he nodded. "Thank you."

Herman smiled. "Now, let us move quickly. As I said, the rules in the house are different. She has done something, I am not quite sure what. Time, all of it, is different."

"I'll take point," Shane said, "unless you remember the way."

"The way is simple and straightforward," Herman said. "There is but one path and it leads to her room."

Marie looked around, and then she pointed and said, "Is it there?"

Shane followed the line of her finger and saw a slim trail which started between a pair of tall, thick elm trees.

"Yes," Herman said, his voice low. "Yes, Ms. Lafontaine. There it is."

Shane looked at it and felt fear creep into his belly. It was the same fear he'd felt in Afghanistan and Iraq. The same fear which had gnawed on his stomach in Bosnia.

This won't be a stroll through the park, he told himself. *She's waiting. They're all waiting.*

He wished for Carl. Or Eloise and Thaddeus.

Hell, Shane thought. *Even the old man.*

Someone who had dealt with Vivienne more than either he or Herman had.

But such a person wasn't available.

Shane took a deep breath and then his first step.

The second was easier. And within a few feet, he passed through the trees and stepped onto the trail.

The trees closed in around them. Dead brush and wicked briar climbed up between the trunks. They limited what he could see, magnified what he heard.

An angry grumble joined the voices of the crows. Shane could hear Herman and Marie behind him as he scanned the trail from left to right and back again. Occasionally the growth on either side fell away and revealed things he didn't wish to see.

The bones of a child, clad in the remnants of clothing so old he couldn't tell when the child might have been from.

A dog's skull looked at him from a pile of ash.

A woman's skeleton, her tattered dress gathered around her. Her skull was off to one side of a tall tree, and a rough noose still hung from a low branch.

The remains of cats and other animals. Squirrels dead beneath trees. Even the skeleton of a horse, still in its harness and hooked to a two-wheeled carriage.

"Don't look too much," Herman said gently. "You will be drawn in. It is part of the trap. The desire to see what is beyond the path. To learn who they were."

"What happens if you leave the path?" Marie asked.

"I suspect the path vanishes," Herman answered. "No matter what we see we must remain upon the trail. We risk a prolonged death if we deviate. Or at least that is what I believe will happen."

"Well, let's not find out," Marie said. After a moment, she asked, "Herman, what led you in here to begin with?"

Herman paused and then answered, "The ragman."

Chapter 49: Herman, July 14th, 1947

At the edge of the Andersons' property, where it ran into the conservation land of Greeley Park, Herman had found the perfect spot.

The dead end of Chester Street was marked by a large oak tree. The tree was about a foot from the stone pillar which marked the property line of the Andersons. Rose, the kitchen maid, had given him an old flour sack and Herman had tied it up between the stone and the tree.

When it hung down, it made the perfect target to practice his pitches.

Herman paced off the distance from the sack and used a piece of wood to mark the spot where the pitcher's mound would be. He'd even been able to gather up a dozen beat-up baseballs from behind Holman Stadium. They were piled in an old milk bucket and waited for him.

The old flour sack hung limply from its cords, and Herman gave it a nod.

He wasn't throwing to the sack, he was throwing to Harry "the Horse" Danning, the greatest Jewish catcher ever to play in the big leagues.

Herman took a ball out of the bucket and sighed happily at the feel of the old leather in his hands. The stitching soon found its way underneath his fingers and Herman grinned at the Danning.

He went into his windup, let the ball go at just the right moment, and watched with satisfaction as it slapped into the center of the sack. The burlap snapped up and around the ball and dropped it in the tall grass.

"Well, you've got a hell of a good arm there, kid," a voice said from behind Herman.

He turned around and saw the ragman. The old Greek stood with his arms crossed over his broad chest, and he nodded approvingly. At the intersection of the street the ragman's old chestnut mare stood with her head down as she nosed around the grass. His wagon stood still behind her. Buckets of old rags, ready for use, stood open to the warm summer air. Other rags, which needed to be cleaned, were in closed buckets.

"You want to play for the big leagues, maybe the Boston Braves, yes?" the ragman asked.

"Sure I do," Herman said with a smile.

"Who do you throw to there, hm?" the man said.

"Danning," Herman answered.

"Ah, the Jew," the Greek said, nodding. "Yes. He is a very good catcher. Very good. Even though I am Greek, I would throw to him too."

The man laughed, and the sound echoed off the trees and the back of the Anderson house. Herman grinned.

"Got a lot of rags today?" Herman asked.

"Just enough," the ragman said. "Just enough. Tell me, who is in the kitchen today?"

"Rose."

"Ah," the ragman said. "The pretty one?"

Herman blushed slightly as he shrugged. "Maybe."

"Yes," the Greek chuckled. "The pretty one. I will not tell her, do not fear. We men, must not let them know, or they get too strong, yes?"

"Sure," Herman said, grinning.

"I will go up and leave Niki here, yes?" the Greek asked.

"Sure, she can stay," Herman answered.

"She will cheer you on," the ragman said, nodding his head with mock seriousness. "Yes. She will make certain Danning gives you the right signals. No curves, young pitcher. Only fastballs. I know they cannot hit your fastball."

Herman smiled and waved as the Greek whistled and turned towards the house. The man started to cut through the backyard, as Herman bent down to take another baseball out of the bucket. He tossed it easily from one hand to the next as he pictured Danning and the signal for a fastball.

With his foot against the board, Herman went into his windup and put everything he had into the pitch. The ball hit the burlap with so much force the fabric cracked loudly in the July air.

"Hey, hey boy!" the Greek yelled frantically.

Herman turned quickly to look.

The ragman splashed into the pond and pointed towards the center. "There's a girl in here, quick, fast as you can, to Rose! Get help!"

A girl? Herman thought.

Confused, he could only watch as the Greek plunged deeper into the pond.

And then a pair of hands, pale white and swollen with rot, came out of the water, and Herman gasped.

Someone is in the water!

He ran towards the pond and saw the ragman bend down to grasp the hands, and when he did, the Greek shrieked.

The sound pierced Herman's skull and caused him to stumble. He tripped on a small stone and fell into the grass. The ragman continued to scream as Herman struggled to his feet and caught sight of the man as he was dragged beneath the water.

The back door to the house opened up, and Rose raced out, followed by Herman's father. Movement in an upper window caught Herman's eye and he looked up.

Mr. Anderson stood in his library window, lit a cigar, and then he turned away.

Silence filled the air.

Rose and his father stood on the back steps, looks of horror on their faces as they looked at the pond. Other members of the staff joined them and the minutes ticked away.

Herman took a cautious step towards the pond.

"Herman, no!" his father yelled, and Herman stopped. As he looked to his father, the man shook his head. "No."

A moment later a curious 'pop' sounded, and the body of the ragman sprang to the surface of the pond. It floated face down, and Herman knew, without any doubt, the man was dead.

One of the gardeners came around the side of the house and called out to Herman's father, who nodded and descended the stairs. Together, the two men approached the pond. The body of the Greek drifted towards them as if guided by some unseen hand.

The two men stood patiently at the bank and waited. Herman gave the pond a wide berth and walked to them. When he reached his father's side, he stole in close to the comfort of the large man's side. A heavy arm wrapped protectively around his shoulders, and together the three of them waited.

A few moments later, the body finally came to rest in the reeds.

"Hold tight, John," his father said as he let go of Herman.

"Alright, Barney," John said. When Herman's dad stepped towards the body, John moved forward. Herman watched as the gardener hooked his hands through the back of his father's braces and got a good grip. "Go ahead, Barney."

The man stepped down, one foot at a time, into the water. With each movement, he was poised to flee, and Herman had never seen his father act in such a way.

Finally, with a deep breath, he reached out, grabbed hold of the Greek's shirt and pulled.

John and Herman's father fell back onto the bank, the body of the Greek coming out of the water easily. It lay limply on the shore beside them.

"Damn him," John muttered. "Why doesn't he drain this God forsaken pond?"

"He likes to watch them die," Herman's father said, pushing himself into a sitting position. He looked down at the body and sighed. "He likes to watch them die."

Chapter 50: Walking towards her Room

"Who is she?" Marie asked.

"Hmm?" Herman said.

"The girl in the pond," Marie said. "Who is she?"

Shane looked back at Herman. "Did you ever find out?"

The older man was silent for a few minutes, and Shane thought he wasn't going to answer. But then the man spoke.

"Yes," Herman said. "I did find out."

Both Shane and Marie kept silent and waited for him to elaborate.

Finally, Herman took a deep breath and said, "Her name is Vivienne Starr. I would like to tell you her wickedness came about from abuse. From some horrific incident in her life. Or, conversely, I would enjoy telling you she was a spoiled child who died terribly, and thus became the way she is.

"Neither, however, would be true," Herman said with a sigh. "She was always a wicked child, from what I have been able to learn. A foul wretch. One who pulled the wings off butterflies, not out of curiosity, but from a distinct desire to inflict pain."

"How long has she been here?" Marie asked.

"She and her family purchased the home which was built here in the early eighteen hundreds," Herman said. "They moved in during the summer of eighteen fifty-six."

The treetops shook, and Herman said, "Stop."

Shane did so.

The trees shook again.

"Telling stories, Herman?" a voice whispered from above. A woman's voice. "We taught you better."

The older man's face paled, and he swallowed nervously.

"What is it?" Marie asked in a low voice.

"My… my…" Herman's hand shook has he wiped the sweat off of his brow. "It is my mother's voice."

"Not only her voice," the woman said. "But all of her."

Shane caught a glimpse of something pale dart from one tree to another. He watched it and tried to get a closer look.

"It cannot be," Herman said, his voice growing stronger. "My mother was buried."

"This is not my flesh," the woman laughed, and Shane watched her drop down behind a tree. She peered around it, a pretty face framed by dark brown hair. With a wink at Shane, she disappeared back behind the tree. "I have no flesh. No body. Nothing."

"And why would my mother be here?" Herman asked.

"Who says I was ever allowed to leave?" his mother said, laughing. "And, what's more, why do you think you shall ever leave, my darling boy?"

"I will not be trapped here," he said defiantly. "She will not keep me here."

"Did you ever pitch to Danning, little man?" a man asked, and Shane watched as Herman stiffened. "I think not. The girl in the pond, yes, she saw to it. I think your fingers remember, yes?"

"The Greek," Herman whispered.

"Ah, Vasiliki Tripodis," the dead ragman chuckled. "Vasiliki Tripodis, and dead I am. Drowned by the girl. Should you be drowned, Herman, for bringing them here?"

"Yes," a deeper male voice said. "You've been ever so willful, my son."

"Is this real?" Marie asked in a low voice.

"I'm afraid it is," Herman said, his voice low and despondent.

Shane knew it as well. The old man's dead had come for him, and Shane wasn't sure if they would be able to stop the ghosts.

"Where are my parents?" Shane asked. He looked around and caught sight of bare flesh as the naked dead dashed from tree to tree. "Are they here too?"

The dead simply ignored them.

Instead, they continued to speak to Herman.

"Did you think you could come back and not suffer?" the man's mother asked. "Did you, Herman? You escaped once. She shall not let you away a second time. Oh no."

"And don't you wish to be with us, Herman?" his father asked. "We could be a family again. Who did they send you off to when the girl killed me? It was your mother's sister, was it not? It could only have been her. Unless they sent you to the Protestant orphanage, although I very much doubt they would have taken in a Jew."

"Come, Herman," Shane said, taking his eyes away from the forest. "We'll continue on."

"Damn it!" Marie yelled, and Shane turned in time to see a stocky, hairy man land on the path behind them. The man was naked, and he gave them all a lurid grin.

The Greek, Shane thought. He brought the bosun's whistle up to his lips, and as he blew a shrill note on it, Marie reached into her coat and pulled out a small automatic pistol.

She fired twice, the report of each shot loud and painful. Shane turned his head as he winced. His ears rang, and the stench of gunpowder filled his nose.

"Shane," Herman said.

Shane straightened up and looked around.

The forest was gone.

The three of them were in a narrow, dimly lit corridor. The roof was several feet up, and the walls were mere inches away on either side. Thick dust covered everything, and Shane had no idea where they were.

"Shane," Herman said again. "Look."

The older man pointed a crooked finger behind him, and Shane twisted around.

Half a dozen feet away a small door, painted white, marked the end of the hall. A brass doorknob, set into a plate made of the same metal, waited for one of them to turn it.

"Where does the door lead to?" Marie asked.

"It leads to her room," Herman said. "We will find Vivienne behind there if she is not busy in her pond."

Chapter 51: Shane, October 31st, 1990

The Halloween party was in full swing, and Shane had slipped away.

He knew what real ghosts were. What real monsters were. It still surprised him how his parents could be so nonchalant about it all at times, but then again, the dead didn't bother them.

Only him.

He didn't mind Eloise or Thaddeus. Carl was his friend. Even the old man, as frightful as he was, still had tried to help him. Roberto was always pleasant, on the rare occasion when Shane saw him.

But then there was the skeleton who had torn apart the parlor. The one who had caused his hair to fall off and never grow back.

The dark ones in the root cellar.

And the girl in the pond. The one who had possessed Mrs. Kensington.

The one who wanted him dead.

The one who had tried to drown his father.

Shane hated her.

He stood out in the backyard, by the pond. The lights of the house spilled out of the windows and cast long rectangles out over the grass.

Shane looked into the water and saw her. In the center of the pond, directly beneath the surface.

She waited.

She wanted him to get closer. To step up to the reed-lined bank where she could steal forward and snatch him into the water.

Part of him wanted to. Part of him wanted to fight her, to beat her. He felt he could, and part of him knew she feared him.

She must, Shane thought.

The water rippled, parted, and Vivienne rose up from the center. His stomach churned as her head appeared and nothing else.

Pale, wet blonde hair clung to her head, and Shane saw she wasn't more than thirteen or fourteen.

She glared at him.

"Come into the water, Shane," she said, her words skipping across the water like stones. "Come to me."

"Come out and see me," Shane said, clenching his hands into fists. "Would you like to go to the party?"

"An engagement?" she asked with a snicker. "Are you formally asking me to go with you, Shane?"

"Careful, my young friend," Carl said suddenly.

Shane didn't turn to look for the German, but he nodded.

"She seeks your death, of this I am certain."

"You're probably right," Shane said. *"I don't know if she can, though."*

"What are you saying?" she demanded. "I know you're talking to the German about me. Stop it!"

Carl said nothing more.

"Would you prefer I speak of you in English?" Shane asked.

"I would prefer you never spoke again," she snapped. She moved closer and her head cut the water like a bloated shark fin.

"You need to leave my house," she hissed. "Leave it or die."

"No," Shane said.

Vivienne grinned, and someone in the house screamed.

Not a playful scream, but one full of terror.

"You'll leave soon enough, Shane," she whispered and slipped back beneath her water.

He turned and sprinted for the house. In a moment, he was inside of the kitchen, and there was a man on the floor. Blood exploded out of his mouth as he vomited repeatedly and others were gathered around the man. They tried to help him as Shane's mother spoke frantically on the phone with someone.

"What happened?" Shane asked the person nearest to him, a woman he vaguely remembered having been introduced to.

"We don't know," she said in a shaky voice. "He was fine one minute, getting a beer out of the fridge, and then he just screamed and clutched his stomach. He's been throwing up blood."

The man collapsed onto his side, and someone caught him. The man looked at Shane, and his eyes went wide with fear.

"You!" the man gasped, and threw up again.

Shane staggered back as the man's bloody bile struck him in the face. The woman steadied him, and the man screamed again.

Shane watched the light flee from the man's eyes, and the Anderson House claimed another life.

Chapter 52: Going In

"Do we knock?" Marie asked, and Shane laughed in spite of the fear in the air.

Herman chuckled, the sound rife with anxiety, and said, "Yes. Shane, will you?"

Shane stepped forward, raised up his fist and knocked loudly several times.

No one answered.

He reached out, grabbed the doorknob and twisted. With a grunt, he pushed the door open.

A bright light burst out of the room, and Shane turned away. He blinked and rubbed at his eyes and finally was able to look in.

Dolls were piled haphazardly all over the furniture in the room. The bed and a rocker, a dresser and a side chair. Each of them was buried beneath dolls. Some of the dolls were ancient, nothing more than old cornhusk toys in rag clothing. Others were new as if taken fresh from a toy store shelf.

The room smelled sweetly of lilacs, and Shane remembered how much his mother hated the smell.

He took a few more steps into the room and Herman and Marie followed him. The detective walked to the left, the pistol still in her hand as she examined the dolls and the furniture.

"It has been a very long time," Herman said.

Shane looked at the man.

Herman smiled nervously. "A very long time since I was in this room. She has added to her collection."

"Why all the dolls?" Marie asked, finishing her circuit of the room.

"Trophies," Herman replied. "Mementos of those she has killed."

"*Shane!*"

Shane, Herman and Marie turned to the door.

Carl, flanked by Eloise and Thaddeus, stood in the doorway, just inside the hall.

"*You must leave,*" Carl said, a note of desperation in his voice. "*She's coming. She's coming! She heard you in the forest. She knows you are here. You must flee, my friend!*"

Shane looked at Herman and Marie. "She's coming."

"What can we do?" Marie asked.

"Try to find my parents," Shane said, his voice suddenly raw. "Help me find my parents."

"We will," Herman said, nodding.

Shane turned to the dead. "*Thank you, my friend, but I must know where my parents are.*"

Carl looked at Shane for a moment and then he said, "*We will hold her off for as long as we can.*"

The door slammed closed.

Shane looked around the room.

"Herman," he said, "is there anywhere she might hide someone here?"

"The wardrobe," Herman said, gesturing towards a corner with his bent and crooked fingers.

"Wardrobe," Shane started to say, and then he stopped himself.

What he had assumed was molding for a window was in actuality the frame of a wardrobe built into the wall. Dolls were piled in front of it, and Marie stepped towards it. She put her weapon away and pulled down the dolls. Without a word she threw them onto the bed and Shane and Herman stayed out of her way.

Screams ripped through the room's closed door, and Shane jerked around.

The harsh sounds of a fight, vicious howls, and voices raised in anger, pushed their way through the wood.

A look back showed Marie as she cleared the last of the dolls.

The wardrobe's wide door opened of its own accord, and the noxious smell of old death bled into the room.

"Oh Jesus," Marie said, taking a stumbling step back.

"Shane," Herman said, reaching out a hand to steady him.

Shane shook his head as he stepped forward. The noise of the fight in the hall vanished, replaced by the thunderous beat of his own heart.

For all intents and purposes, the wardrobe's interior looked much as it should though it was barren of clothes. Shane's mother and father, however, hung from meat hooks set in the back of the piece of furniture.

They were dressed in their pajamas, their bodies thin husks, mummified. Between them stood a small marble plant stand. Upon the pale stone was a black house phone, similar to the one in the library.

The one through which he had spoken to his mother. If it had been her and not Vivienne.

"Shane," Marie said, "Shane we have to leave."

The words slowly pierced his sorrow. His rage grew, however, as he looked up at the bodies. Silence filled the hallway, and suddenly the door blew off the hinges.

Book 1: Berkley Street

Chapter 53: Vivienne Returns to Her Room

Shane turned slowly and faced the door.

Once more, he heard nothing except his heart. Vaguely he saw Marie rush past him and drop to the floor. Herman lay on his back, part of the door upon his small chest. Blood spilled from several cuts on his face.

He's hurt, Shane realized dully. Yet he could only remain focused on the doorway.

Focused on Vivienne.

She stood and grinned at him. Her long blonde hair was in a pair of ponytails, each tied with a bright blue ribbon. The blue matched her eyes.

She wore a white dress, the hem of which reached the floor while the sleeves ended at her wrists. On her hands, she wore a pair of brilliantly white gloves.

"Hello Shane," she said, stepping into the room.

"Vivienne," he said, his voice harsh.

She smiled. "You're upset?"

"Quite."

"Your parents?" she asked, feigning innocence.

"Yes."

She looked past him and into the wardrobe. "You know, they look remarkably well for being so dead."

From the corner of his eye, Shane saw Marie pull Herman farther from the doorway.

"They do," Shane agreed. "I was curious, though."

"Oh," Vivienne said, smiling sweetly, "about what?"

"Does your body look as well preserved?" he asked.

The smile vanished from her face. "Mine will look better than yours when I am finished with you, Shane Ryan."

"I doubt it," Shane replied.

Her nostrils flared as she took a step closer.

"I'm going to flay you alive," she whispered. "I've hated you for so long, Shane. Ever since you came here. Ever since you first slept in your room. I pushed them all to you, and yet you won them over. How?"

"I was never a spoiled brat," Shane answered. Her face went red, and he smiled. "Oh, you don't like names, do you?"

"I'll teach you," she spat. "I *will* teach you!"

Shane stood his ground as she lunged forward. She thrust her hands into his stomach and squeezed.

Nothing happened.

She looked up at him in surprise, a surprise which he was sure his own face mimicked.

"No!" She shrieked angrily. "No!"

She withdrew her hands, shoved them in again, and still nothing happened.

"The house is yours," a voice said in Italian. *"The dead have fought for you, and thus have made it yours."*

Roberto's violin began to play in the distance. A victorious march.

Shane reached out and put his hand on Vivienne's shoulder.

It was solid beneath his hand.

And everything about Vivienne flashed before him.

The wretched, vile girl; he saw her torture the hens and gut the cow. He watched her poison the serving girl and smother her infant brother. A burning image of her preparing to set the house on fire, the gleeful grin upon her face as she held up a flaming brand.

Her father, a great, tall, somber man. Miserable at what he had wrought with his own loins.

82

Shane saw her father come into the room and rip the torch from her small hand. Vivienne screamed at him in rage as her mother cowered in a corner, with a giant leather bound bible held up before her.

Vivienne laughed even as her father grabbed her by her shoulders, looked at her with a terrible inner pain, and picked her up.

The laughter and joy in her face vanished as he walked with fierce, stiff steps towards the pond.

Suddenly, she realized what he intended to do, and fought him. Great tufts of hair were ripped from his head. Blood sprang forth from a dozen cuts made by her nails. She sank her teeth into his back, yet he remained resolute.

He walked steadily down the bank, through the reeds and into the water. He tore her from his shoulders and thrust her into the pond.

The man wept as he drowned his daughter. Her white dress grew heavy and pulled her down as she thrashed. Fish scattered through the water, her eyes full of fear and rage as Vivienne tried to free herself. Her blonde hair slipped free of the ribbons to float like a halo about her pale face.

Shane shuddered and shook his head. He looked down at the beastly child in his hands.

Vivienne's mouth went slack with shock.

He tightened his grip, and she screamed.

Foul, dirty pond water burst from her lips and drenched his clothes.

"Marie," Shane said, looking over at the detective. "Get Herman to your uncle's."

Without a word she picked the small, old man up easily and hurried out of the room with him.

Vivienne tried to wrench herself free of Shane's grip, but she failed. She looked up into his face, and the wickedness which had filled her blue eyes vanished, replaced by terror.

"Where do you think you're going, young lady?" he whispered.

"Let me go," she hissed, trying to pull away again. "Let me go!"

Shane grabbed her other shoulder and squeezed. A sense of grim satisfaction slipped over him as she screamed. Her knees went weak, and only his tight grip kept her upright.

"Your parents are still here," she gasped. "Still here. Did you know?"

Shane kept the same amount of pressure on her, but he said, "I did not know, Vivienne. Why do you mention it?"

"Because I can free them, yes, yes I can. I can free them. They cannot leave the house, but they won't be trapped here. Not with me. I will let them go, if you will do the same," she said desperately, a whining tone in her voice.

"Will you?" Shane asked softly.

"Yes," she said, "just let me go, and I will free them."

Shane let go of one shoulder. "Free them first, Vivienne, and you shall follow."

"No," she said, grinning viciously. She screamed in pain as he tightened his grip with the other hand.

"Yes!" She shrieked. "Yes, fine!"

"Where are they?" Shane asked.

"In the bed tables drawer," she said. "Bring me there."

With his grip firmly on her shoulder, he half pushed, half dragged the dead girl over to the bed-table.

"Open it," he snapped.

Vivienne flinched, but she opened it as ordered.

A long, low moan escaped the drawer and something cold brushed past him.

He heard his parents weep as they fled the room.

"Freed," Vivienne said triumphantly. "Freed. And now for me, Shane Ryan."

"And what will you do? Where will you go?" he asked lightly.

She frowned, confused. "Why back to my pond, of course. I will keep my pond as I always have."

"So I thought," Shane whispered.

He looked at her for a long moment, until she finally demanded, "Let me go!"

Shane smiled. "I don't think so."

"You promised!" she screamed.

"No," Shane said, clenching his free hand into a fist and raising it above his head, "I never did."

He suddenly felt the power of the house, of all the bound dead flow through him. A deep, powerful energy surging inside of him. Beneath his hands, Vivienne was solid; a real form. An entity which could suffer and die; one which could be forced out of a world and into the next.

The power of the house, the energy of the dead who were loyal to him. All of it gave him a strength which no one, living or dead, could stand against.

As the spirits and the house surged inside of him, Shane discovered he could beat a ghost into oblivion.

Chapter 54: Two Weeks Later

"I spoke to Bernadette this morning," Marie said, taking a drink of her coffee.

"Herman is alright?" Shane asked, washing the last of the lunch dishes.

"Yes," she said. "The hospital will be releasing him in a few days. Uncle Gerry is still upset."

"About the whole 'adventure'?" Shane said, glancing over his shoulder at her.

"Of course," she said with a sigh.

"It's the Marine in him," he said, putting the last plate into the drying rack. He wiped his hands on the hand towel, hung it up to dry and went to the table.

"How are you feeling?" she asked.

He shrugged. "Partly in shock, I suppose."

"Have you had any luck getting back to her room, to recover your parents' bodies?"

"No," Shane said, rubbing the back of his head. "I haven't even been able to get to Roberto's room. No word from Carl, or Thaddeus or Eloise. Even the dark ones have been silent. I'm more afraid of the house now than I was when they were all raising a ruckus."

"Still drinking?" Marie asked.

"Yes," Shane answered. "The house may be quiet, Marie, but it doesn't mean my nightmares have gone away."

"Well, I'll say it again," she said as she stood up. "I'd be happy to sponsor you if you want to start the program, Shane."

"Thanks," Shane said. "I appreciate it."

"Listen, give me a call tomorrow. Maybe we can get coffee at some place other than your house or my uncle's," she said, grinning.

"Sounds good, Detective."

She chuckled. "I'll see myself out, Shane. Have a good day."

"You too, Marie," he said. He watched her leave the kitchen, waited for the front door to open and close, and then he walked to the pantry. Quickly he opened the door, lifted up the trap and descended into the root cellar.

He stood on the dirt floor and waited. Within a moment, the room darkened, and a voice said, "What do you want?"

"Answers," Shane snapped. His anger flared, and he fought back the urge to swear at the dark one.

"What answers do you think we have?" the dark one asked sulkily.

"Whatever ones I want," Shane answered angrily. "Have you found Carl and the others?"

"No."

"What of the old man?" Shane demanded.

"One of my brothers saw him in your parents' bathroom. And," the dark one hesitated.

"And what?" Shane asked.

"We saw your parents," it answered.

"Where?" Shane said excitedly.

"The library."

Shane turned around quickly and nearly slammed his head into the ladder. Hand over hand he quickly climbed up, flipped the trapdoor back into place and ran out the pantry. He took the stairs two at a time, grabbed hold of the banister and turned sharply towards the library.

The door, which he had closed earlier, was open.

The lights were on.

A fire burned in the hearth.

He stumbled over his own feet and nearly fell as he went into the room, and when he caught himself, he saw them.

Both his mother and his father.

Hank and Fiona Ryan.

Dead, but still they were there.

Each sat in a chair. Each held a book and a glass of wine.

They looked worn and battered, far older than he remembered, yet he knew it was from their time in hell with Vivienne.

His parents smiled at him.

Shane dropped to his knees and began to weep.

* * *

The Lighthouse
Book 2

Book 2: The Lighthouse

Chapter 1: Squirrel Island

The dawn was breathtakingly beautiful, and for that Mike Puller was extremely thankful. The strong, powerful scent of the Atlantic was heavy in his nose as the waves pounded against the boulders of Squirrel Island. Behind him, the Lighthouse stood tall and majestic. The keeper's house, which was painted the same stark white as the lighthouse, was empty.

Waiting. Mike thought, shuddering. *Waiting for me.*

He reached his hand into the breast pocket of his work shirt and removed the letter he had written. The short note was tucked into an envelope, which in turn was sealed in a pair of Ziploc sandwich bags.

For a moment, Mike held the letter, the plastic cool and thin beneath his fingers. Finally, he sighed, put the letter on the pier beside him, and put a large stone on the bag. The light gray of the rock contrasted sharply with the dark wood of the pier. The construction was new, not yet weathered by Atlantic storms or the Nor'easters which come down from Canada. A light wind came in from the east, but not enough to do more than flutter the loose edge of the sandwich bag.

Mike got to his feet and quickly undressed. The early June air was surprisingly warm. He folded each item of clothing as he took it off and soon he had a neat, tidy pile beside the gray stone.

He climbed down from the pier, stepped onto a large boulder, and then strode into the piercing cold of the ocean. Instantly he shivered, his body attempting to rebel against the sudden change of temperature. His flesh seemed to crawl and pucker simultaneously. At first, his legs refused to move, his hands gripping at the stones. Each and every muscle urged him to step back towards the lighthouse. Self-preservation screamed at him to get out of the Atlantic.

Mike ignored it, and overrode the need to live.

He couldn't stay on Squirrel Island.

No, Mike thought, stepping further out. *She made that perfectly clear.*

His foot slipped, and he plunged down into a crevice. For a moment, he struggled to free himself, the surface of the water only inches from his head. A wave rolled in, pushed him back, and Mike relaxed.

It's easy, he told himself.

Michael Patrick Puller opened his mouth and inhaled.

Chapter 2: Going for a Ride

Marie Lafontaine held on tightly to the side of the boat.

Jesus, am I going to be sick? she wondered.

Amy glanced over at her and asked, "You doing alright, Marie?"

Marie hesitated, then nodded. "You didn't say the waves were going to be this rough."

Amy shook her head, grinning. "This is called a 'calm sea,' my friend. You should see it when it's rough."

"There's a reason why I live in a city, Amy," Marie said, trying to keep focused on the lighthouse which drew rapidly nearer. "So, what made you decide to purchase a lighthouse?"

"I bought the island," Amy said. "I wanted a little peace and quiet plus the price couldn't be beat."

"How much did you pay?" Marie asked.

"A dollar," Amy answered smugly.

"What?"

"One United States dollar," Amy said.

"Wow," Marie said.

"Not really," Amy replied. "The Squirrel Island lighthouse is on the national registry of historic buildings."

"What does that mean?"

"It means," Amy said, "there are certain things I can do and certain things I cannot. Also, part of the purchase contract requires me to bring the lighthouse up to code, maintain it, and ensure its survival."

"Oh," Marie responded.

Amy nodded, guiding the boat toward the pier which extended from the island. "I hired a contractor to live out here for the first couple of weeks. He and I both agreed it would be easier for him to do the repairs that way. I haven't heard from him in a few days, and I want to make sure he hasn't taken off with all of the supplies and equipment. Plus, I wanted to show my cousin the lighthouse.

"You know," Amy said, glancing at her and winking, "do a little bit of the whole, look at what I've got and you don't."

"Real nice," Marie said, shaking her head. "I thought we were done with one-upping each other in high school."

"No, not at all," Amy said with a laugh. "You might have been, but I wasn't."

"So this is your way of saying you've won because you've got the most stuff?" Marie asked.

"Exactly," Amy said sweetly.

"Thanks," Marie said, grinning. "You're such a good cousin. I'm happy you've got your own little island, literally, but I wish it wasn't so far from the shore. Or have to ride in a boat to get there."

"Stay put," Amy said, laughing. "Let me get the boat secured."

Marie watched, impressed as Amy brought the small vessel in, side-bumping against the pier gently.

"Amy," Marie said, straightening up. "Are those clothes?"

Her cousin looked away from the pier's edge. "Yeah. That's strange."

The clothing was folded neatly, stacked beside a bowling ball sized stone. A plastic bag of some sort was under the rock.

Suicide, Marie thought instantly. She had seen how suicide victims often left their clothes. Orderly piles. One last effort from a confused mind to organize something and make sense of some small part of the world.

"Amy," Marie said.

The tone of Marie's voice caused Amy's eyes to widen in surprise. "What?"

"Once you get this boat tied up, I want you to stay in it, okay?" Marie asked.

"Why?"

"Please," Marie said, "this is the cop talking now. Something bad has happened here, and I don't want you to be the first one to see it."

Amy nodded. She threw a loop of thick rope around a piling, pulled the slipknot tight and turned the engine off completely. With the absence of the diesel's rumbling, the sound of the Atlantic filled Marie's ears. Her queasy stomach was forgotten as she grabbed hold of the pier and climbed out of the boat.

Her legs quivered for a moment, her head spun, and she slowly looked up and down the length of the pier. On the island, the lighthouse stood tall. A small house, which was attached to it, had closed shutters over the windows and a faded blue door.

Marie walked to the pile of clothing and squatted down.

Work boots, Marie thought. *Blue jeans. Socks. Boxer briefs. T-shirt. Sweatshirt. Note.*

She reached out, carefully tilted the stone back and slipped the Ziploc bag out from under it. There were two bags, and then an envelope.

'*Ms. Amy Kahlil.*'

"Marie," Amy called. "What's going on?"

"Hold on," Marie said. She opened the bags, slipped out the envelope and broke the seal on it. Inside was a single piece of white notebook paper.

> *Dear Ms. Amy,*
> *I'm sorry. She doesn't want me here. She won't let me stay. I have to leave. She won't let me call. She won't let me stay.*
> *She won't let me stay.*
> *Mike Puller*

Marie put the letter back in the envelope and stood up. She looked around the pier and then stopped. A flash of white caught her eye, and she turned to the left. A wave rolled in, slapped the stones loudly, white foam breaking apart. She stepped closer to the edge and peered down.

Only a few inches beneath the surface of the water was a body. His arms were outspread, and he was naked and covered in thousands of minute crabs. The creatures crawled over him, pulled off tiny pieces of flesh and devoured them, fighting one another as they did so.

Marie's stomach churned, and she closed her eyes. She had regained her composure before she called out, "Amy."

"Yeah?"

"Call 911, please," Marie said, opening her eyes and turning away from the body.

"Why?" Amy asked, a hint of panic in her voice. "What's wrong?"

"Your handyman killed himself," Marie said bluntly, walking over to her cousin.

Amy's eyes widened, and her face paled. "I can't call," Amy whispered. "Mike and I communicated through emails; for some reason, there's no cell reception out here."

Marie frowned. "Alright. Head back to shore, get a hold of the police. Tell them there's been a suicide and that I'm here. Make sure you tell them I'm a detective with the Nashua police department. Got it?"

Amy nodded. "Should we do anything?"

"Nothing to do," Marie said.

"Shouldn't you come back with me?" Amy asked. "I mean, if he's dead, why do you have to stay here?"

"Because I don't want anyone else to show up," Marie replied. "We don't need someone to decide they want a look at the lighthouse and find a body. Okay?"

"Yeah," Amy said. "Okay."

Marie watched her cousin get the boat ready to go, and then she waved goodbye as Amy backed the boat out and headed back towards the shore.

Once Amy was gone, Marie walked up the pier to a small patch of overgrown grass in front of the closed-up house. There was a fresh lock on the door, and the shutters as well. She walked around the house and found a pile of boards of various sizes beneath a tarp. The windows on the back of the house were shuttered and locked. A tall brick chimney rose up, and a large amount of seasoned firewood was neatly stacked.

A dull-gray metal bulkhead was beside the chimney, and this, too, was secured shut.

It's like he was trying to keep something or someone from escaping, Marie thought.

She moved on to the lighthouse and found that its door, painted the same as the house's, was also locked tight. On the far side of the lighthouse, she found a single-person tent. In front of it was a fire pit, a cooler off to the right. A rustling sound came from the interior of the tent and for a moment Marie's breath caught in her throat. Cautiously she bent down, took hold of the loose flap and pulled it back.

A middle-aged woman sat in the semi-darkness. She wore a plain, soft blue dress. Her hands were neatly folded in her lap, and her salt and pepper hair was pulled back into a loose bun. Her features were fine, gently rounded with age. Crow's feet spread out from the corners of her light gray eyes as her full lips parted in a smile. Her teeth were slightly yellowed, and a little crooked.

The edges of the woman were fuzzy, and even in the dimness of the tent Marie could almost make out the back fabric of the interior straight through her.

She's a ghost, Marie thought with cold certainty. The hair on her neck stood on end, and her back was rigid with fear.

"He left," the woman said.

"He did," Marie managed to say.

"You should too."

The woman vanished, and Marie let the tent flap fall noiselessly back into place.

Trust me, Marie thought, hurrying back to the pier. *I'll be leaving here just as soon as I can.*

She sat down by Mike Puller's clothes, avoided the crabs and their feast, and waited impatiently for Amy to return.

Chapter 3: A Surprise Guest

Shane Ryan sat on his back steps and lit his first cigarette of the day. It wasn't enjoyable, and it wasn't refreshing, but it definitely took the edge off the morning.

Which is the whole point of the thing, Shane told himself. He tapped the ashes off into an ashtray, took a drink of coffee and enjoyed the warmth of the sun on his face.

"Shane," Carl said.

He turned his face to the left and saw his dead friend. In German, he said, "Good morning, Carl."

"Good morning to you, my young friend," Carl replied in the same language. "You have a guest."

Shane took a pull off of the cigarette, looked at Carl warily and asked, "Alive or dead?"

"Alive," Carl answered. "It is your friend, the policewoman."

"Marie?" Shane asked. He picked up his coffee and stood up. "At six in the morning?"

"Yes," Carl said. "She should be ringing the bell in a moment."

The grand old doorbell of the house chimed as Shane stepped into the kitchen. He put the cigarette out in an old coffee can by the sink and hurried out to the main hall and the front door.

When he opened it, Marie was standing on the doorstep.

"Come on in," he said, stepping aside. "You pick the most ungodly hour to come calling, you know."

"I know," Marie said, smiling at him as she entered the house. "I also know you get up early."

"Very true," Shane said. He closed the front door, saying, "Come on into the study."

They entered the room and once Marie had sat down in one of the club chairs, he did the same.

"Everything okay?" he asked.

She opened her mouth, hesitated, then said, "I have a favor to ask."

"Sure," Shane said. "What do you need?"

In quick, short sentences, with the words seeming to tumble out one on top of the other, she told him about the Squirrel Island Lighthouse, a suicide, and a ghost.

"My cousin's really upset," Marie said. "I mean, I'm not too happy about seeing the crabs feasting on a corpse, but she's invested in this place. She can't have a malicious spirit haunting it."

She can, Shane wanted to say, but he kept the thought to himself. "Agreed. Now tell me, Marie, what would you like me to do about it?"

"I was thinking about how you got rid of your ghost here," Marie said. "I was hoping you'd be able to do the same at the lighthouse."

Shane sat back in his chair, frowning. He reached up, rubbed the back of his head and said, "It's not as easy as that."

"I didn't think it would be," she replied, "but I thought if anyone could do it, it would be you."

He smiled. "I appreciate the confidence, I do. I think the only way I could help is if I actually went to the island and stayed in the lighthouse for a while."

"What would that do?" Marie asked.

"Let me get to know the woman there," Shane said, his smile fading. "Once I get to know her, maybe get a grip on who she is, I might be able to make her leave. I can't guarantee it, though."

"I know," Marie said. "But I'd be happy as hell if you'd try."

"For you," he said gently, "I'd be more than willing to try."

She blushed slightly, reminding him again of how she was more than a detective. Once more his heart ached at the memory of what they almost had.

Marie's blush faded, and she smiled. "When do you think you could go?"

"If you want to hang around for about half an hour, forty-five minutes tops," Shane said, "I can get everything I need. I mean, there is internet service, right?"

"Yeah," Marie said, nodding. "It's strange. There's a booster on a new solar array in the lighthouse, and it helps with getting a direct satellite connection, but there's no cell reception."

"We can keep in touch through email," Shane said, getting to his feet. "I'll bring my laptop and the essentials."

Marie stood up and smiled at him. "Thank you, Shane."

She gave him a strong, fierce hug, and he returned it happily.

"You want to wait down here?" he asked. "Or up in the library?"

Marie shook her head, stepping out of his embrace. "No. Not me. Your ghosts still scare the hell out of me."

"Me too, sometimes," Shane said seriously. "Alright, I'll see you in the car then."

"I'll grab some food from Jeannotte's Corner Store, do you want anything?" Marie asked.

"A carton of Lucky Strikes," Shane said, "and a box of matches. Everything else I need is here."

"You need to quit smoking," she said as she left the room.

"Yeah," Shane agreed, following her out. "Later."

She shook her head and made her way to the front door. Shane turned and went up the stairs. He had to pack.

Book 2: The Lighthouse

Chapter 4: A Meeting with Amy

Shane had never been a fan of the ocean. Or water, in particular. Not since the house and the girl in the duck pond.

He had smoked half a pack of cigarettes as he and Marie sat at a picnic table in a rest area. Amy was on her way, according to Marie.

The sooner, the better, Shane thought. He looked out over the Atlantic, and in the clear, bright sunlight of the morning, he could see the lighthouse. It was small from where they sat, and the idea of being on an island in the middle of the ocean turned his stomach.

He took out a cigarette, lit it off the one he was finishing, and sighed.

Marie glanced at him. "You okay?"

He shrugged. "Don't particularly care for water."

"Why?" she asked.

"Aside from the dead girl in the pond," Shane said, "I don't like the idea of being a lower member of the food chain."

"What?" Marie asked, confused.

"Sharks," Shane said. "I don't want to be eaten by a shark."

She laughed, saying, "Shane, there aren't any sharks here."

"Yes, there are," Shane said, exhaling a long stream of smoke. "Listen, there are constant sightings of great whites off the coast of Massachusetts, and the damned things come up here, too."

Marie shook her head. "Shane, you're not going to get eaten by sharks."

"Not if I stay out of the water," he agreed.

She rolled her eyes, then turned her attention to the entrance of the rest stop as a large, black Cadillac SUV pulled in. The driver, hidden by the vehicle's tinted windows, shut off the engine and then opened the door.

A woman who looked to be roughly Marie's age got out and waved.

Marie returned the wave and stood up. Shane did the same, examining the driver.

She was tall and lithe, dressed in a flower print summer dress. Her skin was a delicate tan as if she spent the perfect amount of time in the sun and not a second more. She walked delicately, yet with a commanding presence. She was a confident person, and Shane heard it as soon as she spoke.

"Amy," Marie said happily, embracing her.

"Hey Marie," Amy said, grinning. "And you're Shane?"

"I am," Shane said, offering his hand.

She shook it, her grip strong. "You're going to help me with this problem of mine?"

"I'll do what I can," Shane responded.

"I do appreciate it," Amy said. "Do you want to talk here, or somewhere else?"

"Here, if we could," Shane said. "If you don't mind. Not too many places allow you to smoke inside anymore."

"So long as I'm upwind, I don't mind at all," Amy said, smiling.

They all sat down at the table, and Shane looked expectantly to Amy.

"Okay," she said, brushing a lock of light brown hair behind her ear. "I'm sure my cousin has given you the basics of what happened the other day?"

Shane nodded.

"Right," Amy said. "Good. I did a little digging in the town library, and over in the historical society. Turns out the lighthouse has a bad reputation. Suicides. Murders. People vanishing."

"For how long?" Shane asked.

"Ever since the first stones were laid for the foundation," Amy said, frowning. "And let me tell you, all of the rumors have come back in full force since Mike's unfortunate death."

"What do you mean?" Marie said.

"I went to hire another couple of contractors," Amy explained. "Told them what I wanted, and they were all gung-ho and ready to work until someone who was nearby asked if it was for the Squirrel Island lighthouse. When I told them that it was, one of the contractors asked if the rumors about Mike Puller's incident were true. Again, I said it was. And that was that. Word has spread like wildfire, and I can't find anyone from Pepperell, Massachusetts to Kennebunk Port, Maine who'll do the work for me."

"That bad?" Shane asked.

Amy nodded. "A few of them said that as soon as the place was cleared of its bad luck, they'd be happy to come do the work for me."

Marie snorted derisively. "They won't even work in teams?"

"No," Amy said, shaking her head. "I offered that too. Even wanted to bring an exorcist, but the guys said it wouldn't do."

"It won't," Shane said.

The two women looked at him.

He lit a fresh cigarette and sighed. "Exorcisms do pretty much one of two things. They either send some poor lost soul out into the big bad world, which is just as bad for them as it is for us, or they make a mad ghost even madder."

"Oh," Amy said, surprised.

Shane nodded.

"What's your suggestion?" Amy asked.

"Let me stay on the island for a while," Shane said. "I'll figure out what's going on. Then, well, we'll see what happens. I might be able to convince the spirit there to leave."

"Really?" Amy said. "Are you serious?"

"Yes," Shane said. "But remember, I said 'might.' I'm not guaranteeing anything."

"Do you want money for this?" Amy asked.

"No," Shane said. "Just make sure I have food and come out if I ask you to. I do my work remotely, so I should be good there. I've got a carton of cigarettes. Two-fifths of whiskey, and the complete works of Raymond Chandler. I'll be good for a little while."

"If you're sure," Amy said, "I can bring you out there right now. You coming for the ride, Marie?"

"Hell no," Marie said decisively. "I don't like boats, and the last trip hasn't changed my mind."

Shane grinned and said, "Alright, then. Let's get my gear out of your car and into Amy's."

They stood up from the picnic table, and Shane looked out once more at the lighthouse.

How bad could it actually be? he wondered. He shook his head, took a final drag off the cigarette and stubbed it out.

Chapter 5: Squirrel Island Lighthouse

Shane was alone.

Amy had given him a quick tour, helped him put his belongings in the keeper's house, and then was on her way back to the mainland.

Shane had an itch at the base of his skull, as though someone was staring at the back of his head.

Someone probably is, he thought. He walked down to the edge of the island and strolled along the perimeter. In the distance, he could make out sails and people out in their small boats and yachts. A ferry made its way from some island to the next and Shane shook his head. He enjoyed the beauty of the ocean. The power which lay beneath the waves.

But he was respectful of it as well. He'd been aboard ships on training missions, and had seen deep-sea storms throw destroyers and battleships around like bath toys. While a rogue wave wasn't likely, he knew full well how one could rip everything on Squirrel Island out into the depths.

Let's not get too morose, he chided himself.

When he reached the pier, he followed the old path from the water's edge up to the keeper's house. He had already taken the locks off of the doors and windows, thrown open the shutters and set up his belongings.

There hadn't been much to it.

He had a sleeping bag, his pack of cigarettes, whiskey, books, and laptop. A change of clothes were kept in his pack. Canned food and bottled water had been stocked up for the unfortunate Mike Puller, and they were still there for Shane.

Whose future fortunes have yet to be decided, Shane thought, grinning. He went in, sat down on his sleeping bag and looked at the afternoon light as it played across the interior of the room.

Where he was making his camp had once been the living room for the keeper and his family. Off of it was a kitchen, a small stairwell leading to a loft bedroom, and a small office. The house was barren of furniture. The cabinet doors had long been removed from the kitchen's cabinets, and the dull white walls were a maze of cracks. The stairs leading up looked iffy at best, and Shane wasn't certain he wanted to go into the cellar without a shotgun.

The whole place felt *off.*

He reached over, grabbed his pack and pulled it to him. He rifled around in it, pushed aside a sweatshirt and smiled. He brought out his iron knuckles, the deadly weapon which had served him so well in Rye and Mont Vernon.

He slipped them on and nodded to himself. *Play it safe. Play it smart.*

Sighing, Shane settled back against the wall, closed his eyes, and relaxed as best he could. Sooner rather than later, it would be night, and he suspected the island would be far more active then.

The soft creak of an unoiled hinge woke Shane up from a fitful sleep.

Beyond the windows, he could see the night sky and the wide-reaching arc of the lighthouse's beam. He heard a soft whir followed by a click as the lantern above completed its rotation.

Yeah, Shane thought, sitting up. *That sound could get old real quick.*

He reached over, found his pack, and pulled out the camp light he had purchased on the way up to the shore. With a flick of a switch, light burst out and filled the room.

Damn! he thought, setting the lantern down clumsily and rubbing at his eyes. White spots exploded behind his eyelids. *Stupid. Way to blow your night vision.*

After a minute, Shane dropped his hands, blinked, and looked around the room. It was eerie, frightening in a new way. The walls seemed to breathe; the house felt like a living entity around him.

Shane shook his head, picked up his water bottle, and had a long drink of the warm liquid. When he finished, he wiped his mouth with the back of his hand, sighed and thought, *Suppose it's time to get another look at the place.*

Shane got to his feet and stopped.

The floor above him creaked. Footsteps crossed the loft and paused at the top of the stairs. Shane took a deep breath and turned to face them. As he did so, the unknown intruder descended the stairs. Each step creaked, squealed beneath some weight. Soon, the visitor reached the bottom and stood, unseen, in what was the former living room.

Shane waited.

"Who are you?" a woman asked. Her voice was cold, brutal and unforgiving.

"My name's Shane," he replied. "May I ask yours?"

She didn't answer. She didn't walk away either.

"I've been asked to speak with you," Shane said.

Still, she remained silent for a few more moments.

"I am Dorothy," she said finally. "And you are not welcome. None of you are. Leave, or I will make you go."

Her footsteps went up the stairs, across the floor, and silence fell over the house again.

Great, Shane thought. *I'm not welcome. This should make it a hell of a lot more difficult.*

Chapter 6: Drunk at Sea

Dane, Scott, Courtney, and Eileen all relaxed comfortably in Scott's father's yacht. All of them were more than a little drunk, and it took Scott quite a while to realize they that had lost their anchor and were drifting along with the current. The understanding of their situation helped to take the edge off his inebriated state.

At twenty-two, Scott was not a sailor nor had he ever been. He had always been far more interested in the young ladies that a yacht attracted rather than the yacht itself. Scott didn't have any of the necessary licenses to operate a yacht or even a boating license.

Oh my God, Scott thought, getting shakily to his feet. *I am absolutely screwed.*

He looked out at the expanse of the Atlantic and tried to see something, anything which looked like the shore. Running aground would be terrible, especially since his father had quite expressively forbidden Scott from even *thinking* about the yacht, let alone taking it out.

Better to beach the damned thing than sink it, Scott thought. Gripping the handrail he made his way to where Dane lay with his thick arm wrapped around Eileen's equally thick waist.

"Dane," Scott said, nudging his friend with the toe of his boat shoe. "Dane!"

Dane opened one eye, which rolled drunkenly until it focused on Scott. Dane grinned and slurred, "What's up?"

"We're screwed!" Scott snapped. "That's what's up."

"Not yet," Dane argued, closing his eye. "Too much whiskey."

Scott pushed Dane roughly. "Don't pass out!"

Dane opened both eyes and sat up a little. "What're you being such a pain about?"

"The anchor's gone!" Scott hissed.

"Bull," Dane said, struggling to look around. "We're fine."

Dane got up, glanced around, stopped, turned his attention to the sails, and said softly, "Jesus, Scott."

Scott helped his friend to his feet, steadied him as best he could, and together they stood at the rail. A wide beam of light passed over them, moved in a wide arc to the left, vanished, and then reappeared.

"Holy Christ," Dane said.

"What?" Scott asked. "What's wrong?"

"That's the Squirrel Island lighthouse," Dane said. "We're miles from where we should be, Scott. And if we don't get in on the lee side of the island, the breeze'll run us straight out and up along the Maine coast."

"What do we do, now?" Scott asked, feeling panic creep into his voice.

Dane tried to turn towards the wheel, stumbled, caught himself, and sank to his knees. He stuck his head between the upper and lower bars of the rail and vomited straight into the Atlantic. Again and again, Dane threw up, until Scott, feeling sick from the sight and smell of the bile, turned away. Finally, when Dane had finished dry-heaving, Scott helped him up.

"There's a pier, on the island," Dane managed to say as they reached the wheel. "You need to drop the sails while I steer, can you do that?"

"I think so," Scott said. "But why?"

"We'll run aground if we don't take the sails in and get the engine started," Dane replied. "Wake Eileen up, she knows a little about sailing. Tell her we need an emergency anchor. Then wake Courtney up, have her fire up the engine."

"We can't just beach the yacht?" Scott asked.

Dane's expression was one of horror. "There's no place to beach her, Scott. Squirrel Island is nothing but rock, and I don't know this area. I don't know where the shoals are, or where anything is along this stretch of beach. She won't beach. She'll break up, and if we don't pull our act together, we're going down with her."

Fear, it seemed, had burned all traces of the alcohol out of Dane's system.

Scott managed to wake both of the girls up. Soon, they were all frantically – if somewhat drunkenly – getting the yacht ready. The sails came down, Eileen managed to fashion an anchor from a length of the line and a small, spare anchor found below deck, and Courtney got the engine running.

With the motor powering the yacht, Dane guided it in close to Squirrel Island, and when they were a short distance away, he yelled out to Eileen. Eileen gave a thumbs up, and heaved the anchor overboard. Seconds later, the anchor struck bottom and the yacht, *A Father's Dream*, came to a gentle stop as Courtney cut the engine.

The anchor line went taut, then slackened as the yacht floated easily at anchor.

Scott sank down to the deck and let out a long sigh. *Thank God he's away for the weekend*, Scott thought, imagining what his father's reaction might be if he ever learned of the debacle. He shuddered at the idea of how angry his father would be. The man had never struck Scott, but Scott believed that could quickly change.

Dane and the girls came over to him.

"Unbelievable," Courtney said, her face flush with excitement. "That was great!"

Scott raised an eyebrow. "I would definitely not describe it as 'great.' Or anything other than terrible. It's not your father's yacht, sweetheart."

She stuck out her tongue and sat down across from him.

"Hey, isn't the lighthouse supposed to be automated?" Eileen asked.

"I don't know," Scott replied sulkily. His head was starting to hurt.

"It is," Dane answered. "There aren't any more manned lighthouses. At least not on the East Coast."

"Then, why is there a light on in the house over there?" she said, pointing out at the island.

"I don't know," Dane answered softly.

Scott twisted around, saw light streaming out of a window. His stomach rumbled. "Wonder if they have any food."

Courtney said, "Right! I'm starving."

Dane shook his head. "No. I'm not going ashore. I'd rather stay right here. I don't trust anyone squatting on an island. Something's not right."

"God, Dane," Eileen said, looking at him. "You are such an old lady sometimes."

"Do you guys not watch the news?" Dane asked.

"About what?" Scott said, laughing. "Crazies living on islands where they can't even get cable? Get over it, Dane."

Scott pulled himself up and stood, holding onto the rail. A wave of sickness flooded him, but he waited a moment, and it passed as quickly as it had arrived. "Come on. Let's get the jolly boat down and over to the pier."

"You know," Courtney said, "I heard somebody actually bought the place. I bet they're working on it out here."

"Where's their boat, then?" Dane asked grumpily. "How the hell are they getting back and forth to the island? And why would they stay the night?"

"They probably just left a light on, you big baby," Eileen said, laughing. She walked over to the jolly boat and said, "Come on, let's get this in the water."

Scott and Courtney went to help her and after a short, sullen silence, Dane did as well.

Soon, the four of them were crowded into the small jolly boat with Scott on the oars. It took less than five minutes to row to the pier, but it was enough to drench Scott in sweat and put an ache in his arms. He was more than happy to ship the oars, and he watched as Dane secured the boat to the pier and then helped each of them up and onto it.

When the four of them stood together, they looked up to the lighthouse and the keeper's house. Both of them were a soft, gentle white in the darkness of the night. The barest hint of a path led from the end of the pier to the front door of the keeper's house. The light in the window was bright, yet not nearly as powerful as the beam sent out by the lighthouse's lantern.

"Ready?" Eileen asked.

Scott and the others assented as she started up the path, the rest following her confident lead. A cool wind set a chill into Scott's flesh, and he realized the June night was unseasonably cold. He shivered, suddenly conscious of the light clothing he was wearing.

Christ, I hope it's warm in there, Scott thought.

The walk was blessedly short, if slightly uphill, and they came to a stop before the door. Eileen boldly knocked on it.

"Who is it?" a man demanded from the house, his voice coming through the door and out of the window.

"My name's Eileen," she said loudly. "My friends and I are in a jam. Our yacht is at anchor a little off the island, and we're hungry. We only planned for a day trip, and something happened. We can't get into the harbor until morning. We don't know the coast around here and, well, we didn't plan for anything really."

The lock slid back, and the door opened. An older man, perhaps in his forties, stood in the doorway. He was bald and lean, his skin pale. He wore only a pair of shorts, and was in good shape. On his right breast, he had a large tattoo: the eagle, globe and anchor of the United States Marine Corps. On his left breast, in spiderlike script, he had the words *Until Valhalla.*

The man studied them in an awkward silence, then stepped to one side, saying, "Come on in."

They all said thank you, and walked into the room.

It was of a decent size, with a door on the back wall, and another on the right. A set of narrow stairs led to a second floor. The room was in rough shape, the plaster on the walls looking as if it would come tumbling down at any moment. The only light was a Coleman camping lantern. On the floor was a sleeping bag, a backpack, and a laptop, along with some other odds and ends. The man, evidently, was not expecting company.

Their host closed the door, but he didn't lock it.

"My name's Shane," he said. "Take a seat. I've got some food in the kitchen. Not much, but it should be enough to quiet your stomachs until you leave in the morning."

"Anything would be great," Courtney said.

Shane nodded and left the room. He returned a minute later with an armful of bottled waters and a box of packaged peanut-butter crackers. Quietly, he handed them out, kept a package of crackers for himself along with a bottle of water and sat down on his sleeping bag.

Scott ate the food quickly and drank the water the same way. The fear of losing his father's yacht had made him ravenous.

Shortly, when the food was gone, Dane said, "Shane, why are you here?"

Shane took a drink of water, capped the bottle and put it down beside him before he answered. "I'm here because of some ghosts."

"Really?" Courtney asked excitedly. "Like, real ghosts? Is the place haunted?"

Shane nodded. "Yeah. It's haunted. You may all want to get back to your yacht before the dead take notice of you."

Scott snorted. "What are they going to do, scare us and keep us awake all night?"

Shane smiled at him politely. "No. They may, however, convince you to commit suicide, or outright kill you. Keeping you awake really isn't on their bucket list."

Everyone chuckled, then the humor faded as they realized Shane was serious.

"You're joking?" Dane asked.

Shane shook his head. "Not about this. Some ghosts aren't exactly pleasant or generous. Some aren't misunderstood or unable to move on because of some horrible personal tragedy." Shane's voice was cold and hard.

"Some simply like to hurt people," he continued. "Some of them refuse to accept death and instead, begin to punish those around them. Whatever the reasons for this place's dead, they don't matter right now. What does matter is all of you getting out of here and being safe. I can't give you much more; I don't expect to be resupplied for another couple of days, and I really don't like to be hungry."

Dane scoffed. Eileen closed her eyes and snuggled up against him.

Scott looked at the bald man. *I don't know if I believe him or not.*

Courtney looked at Shane and said, "The ghost here. Is he bad?"

"She," Shane corrected gently. "It's a 'she.' And I do believe she is. I'm here because she convinced the contractor hired to fix the place to drown himself. No one's going to be able to live here if she keeps doing that."

"I heard about that," Scott said. "What I heard, though, is that he went for a swim and got caught in the rocks and drowned."

"Well, what actually happened," Shane said coldly, "is she harassed him to the point where he killed himself."

"How?" Courtney asked. "How can someone talk someone else into suicide?"

"Lots of ways," Shane said softly. "Sleep deprivation. Fear. Isolation. All of those factors are here. Suicide, he believed, was the only way he could escape her."

"How do you know that?" Dane asked.

"He left a note," Shane replied.

"There was no mention of a note in the news," Courtney said. "Why wouldn't they say there was a note?"

Shane shrugged. "I'm sure it sounded crazy. And who wants to have their loved one's madness splashed all over the evening news?"

"So," Dane said, "who's the ghost?"

"Her name's Dorothy," Shane answered. "I don't think she likes me."

"Could she hurt you?" Eileen asked.

"She'll definitely try," Shane said. "She might succeed, too. Ghosts can cause a hell of a lot of damage when they want to. Even kill you if they've got enough power."

Scott shook his head, Dane laughed, and Eileen grumbled as she adjusted herself in the young man's embrace. Courtney glared at Dane.

"This isn't funny, Dane," Courtney said angrily.

"Oh come on!" Dane said, chuckling. "You don't believe this crap, do you? I mean, seriously? Ghosts? And they can hurt you, too? That's absolute bull, Cort, and you know it."

Shane gave Dane a hard, angry look. Then, in a low voice, thick with disdain he said, "I don't care what you do or don't believe. But you're in here as a courtesy. Keep running your mouth and you can leave. Be respectful. You don't have to agree. Just be polite."

The cold, harsh tone of the man forced a nod out of Dane.

"We should get back to the yacht anyway," Scott said. He stood up, stretched and added, "Thanks for the food and water, though."

Shane nodded.

Scott looked out the window as the others stood up and he whispered, "What the hell?"

Chapter 7: A Painful Realization

"What?" Dane asked. "What's wrong?"

"The jolly boat's gone," Scott said.

Dane got to his feet. "Where the hell did it go?"

Eileen looked up at Dane and asked, "Didn't you secure it?"

"Of course, I did!" Dane snapped, anger dancing in his eyes. He turned to face Shane and said, "Alright, who else is on the island, and why in God's name would they steal the boat?"

"Oh no," Scott said softly, cutting off any reply Shane might have been readying. On the pier stood a naked man, and Scott could see the yacht through the man.

Dane choked back something, took half a step backwards and fell onto the floor. Both of the girls scrambled to their feet, crowding around Scott at the window.

"Why is he naked?" Eileen asked.

"Yeah, oh Jesus," Courtney gasped. To Shane, she said, "Why can we see through him?"

Shane picked up his water bottle, drank some and then said, "Because he's dead."

Courtney sat down, her back against the wall so she could face the bald man. Scott joined her, and Eileen did the same as Dane got into a sitting position. Courtney asked, "Who is he?"

"If he's naked and at the pier," Shane said, "then, more than likely, he's the contractor who committed suicide last week. Mike Puller, I think that was his name."

"Why is he here?" Courtney asked.

Shane shrugged. "Depends on the person. Depends on the place, too. If this woman is as strong as she seems, then she has bound him here. Possibly others as well. I'll find out soon enough, I guess."

"How are we supposed to get to the yacht?" Dane asked, his voice small.

"Is there a second boat?" Shane asked.

"No," Scott answered. "Just the one."

"We can call for help, right?" Eileen said, looking around as she dug her phone out of a pocket.

"It won't work," Shane said. "No reception here."

"I always have reception," Eileen said. She frowned. "This can't be right. I don't have any reception. None!"

"She doesn't want us to use phones," Shane said. He picked up his laptop, tried to power it up and shook his head. "Great. Nothing on mine now."

Scott checked his phone, as Courtney and Dane did the same.

Absolute zero, Scott sighed. His phone wasn't even turning on.

"Damn it!" Eileen said, dropping her phone to her lap. "It just died!"

"If they're all dead," Shane said, "it means she's draining them."

"What?" Dane asked, confused.

"There's a theory that ghosts are energy," Shane explained, "and they can drain the charge out of a battery to give themselves extra strength."

"Great," Eileen muttered.

"Could we swim to the yacht?" Scott asked Dane.

Dane shook his head. "No. Not this close to an island. We wouldn't be able to get through the surf, and if we did, there's no accounting for the currents around us. I'm a decent swimmer, Scott, and even I wouldn't risk it."

"Is someone coming here for you?" Eileen asked Shane.

"Couple of days," Shane replied. "Sooner, I hope, when I don't contact them tomorrow morning."

"This is insane," Scott said. "We can't be trapped on an island."

"We can," Shane disagreed. "And it seems like we are."

"What are we going to do about food?" Courtney asked.

"I brought enough for myself for a week," Shane said. "If we ration it we can stretch it between the five of us for a couple of days. We may need to make it last for three, but I hope not. I hate being hungry."

Silence filled the small room, broken only by the steady click of the lighthouse's lantern.

"Why is it so cold?" Courtney asked.

"You don't want to know," Shane said. He stood up. "There's wood out back, I'll bring some in and get a fire going. It'll fight off the chill, and give us a little peace of mind."

Scott watched the older man go through the doorway in the back wall, then an unseen door was opened. The others looked at Scott, and Scott shrugged.

The place felt vile, and the situation seemed even worse.

Chapter 8: The Dawn Arrives

Shane sat on the front step of the keeper's house. He was dressed, smoking a cigarette and finishing the last of his morning whiskey.

"Good morning," a young woman said.

Shane twisted around and saw Courtney, who had her black hair cut in a pixie style. She was exceptionally pale, her eyes large and green. She was short, perhaps no more than five feet tall and lithe, Shane realized, was the best way to describe her.

"Good morning," Shane said. He moved over to the right and patted the stone beside him. "Take a seat. Need a cigarette?"

"No, thanks," she answered, sitting down beside him. She smelled of the ocean and sweat, alcohol and fear.

"Whiskey?"

Courtney's eyes widened a hair, and she laughed. It was a good, rich sound which made Shane smile. "No. Thank you, though. You always drink whiskey first thing in the morning?"

"Breakfast of champions," Shane said, getting out another cigarette and lighting it. He exhaled and added, "I have terrible nightmares. Absolutely foul. Whiskey is the only thing that takes the edge off."

"I'm sorry to hear that," Courtney said.

Shane grinned. "No worries. I'm essentially a functioning alcoholic."

"Do you have alopecia?" Courtney asked suddenly.

"I do," Shane said, surprised. "Don't meet too many people who know about it. They either figure I'm a diseased freak or a freak who Nairs all of his body hair."

Courtney chuckled. "No. My younger sister has it. Not as serious as you, though; patches here and there on her head."

"I'm sure it's rougher on women," Shane said. "Men can usually get away with being bald. Society still can't turn away from a woman who has a bald head, either by choice or by nature's design."

"She's lucky," Courtney said. "Our mom has figured out how to comb and pin her hair so Andrea isn't made fun of."

"How old is your sister?" Shane asked.

"Twelve."

"How are you even old enough to drink, if you have a twelve-year-old sister?" Shane asked.

Courtney blushed slightly. "I'm twenty-six, but I look younger than I am."

"You look good," Shane said, taking a long drag off of his cigarette.

Her blush deepened.

"Scott doesn't tell you that nearly enough, I'm sure," Shane said.

She raised an eyebrow.

Shane grinned. "Common fault among men. Especially when they're between the ages of thirteen and forty-two."

Courtney laughed. "And how old are you?"

"Forty-three," Shane replied. "Old enough to know better, dumb enough to forget every so often."

"Well," Courtney said, "I'm willing to listen whenever you want to say it."

Shane let out a pleased laugh, nodded, and said, "Sounds like a deal to me."

A pleasant silence wrapped around them and the Atlantic went about its ageless motions. A short distance away, the yacht bobbed at her anchor, a reminder of how the four travelers were trapped with him.

"Shane," Courtney said.

"Yeah?"

"How did you get involved in this? I mean, why are you here?" she asked.

"It's a long story," Shane said. "But, if you want to hear it, let me get some coffee going on the stove, and we can sit in the kitchen, and I can tell you my long, sad story."

Chapter 9: Miserable

When Scott woke up on the hard floor of the keeper's house on Squirrel Island, he instantly knew the previous night had not been a bad dream.

Oh, Christ Almighty, he thought miserably, *Dad is going to kill me. Straight up murder me, bring me out to the middle of the Atlantic, and dump my body. Just as soon as he gets another boat.*

He got up slowly, his body aching from the poor and painful sleep of the night before, and stretched. The smell of fresh coffee widened his eyes a little, and he stepped over Dane and Eileen. Both of whom snored loudly as they spooned. Scott went into the kitchen, and he saw Shane had a fire going on the small wood stove. Shane sat with Courtney, the two of them sharing a cup of coffee.

A spike of jealousy drove through the morning haze of Scott's brain and the emotion burned violently as Shane gestured to him.

"Come on in, Scott," the older man said. "Take a seat. Sorry about the lack of hygiene here, but I have only the one cup."

Courtney took a last drink, passed the tin mug to Shane, and Shane got up and went to the stove. He used a t-shirt to take the bluestone percolator off the iron heating plate and poured the dark, rich liquid.

The smell was phenomenal and went a long way towards easing Scott's jealousy.

"Take a seat," Shane said, passing the cup to Scott. "And I'm sorry, but I don't have any sugar or cream. Don't use the stuff myself."

"I think it'll be alright this morning," Scott replied, sitting down between Courtney and Shane.

The older man, who was wearing a pair of blue jeans and a black tee shirt, rummaged in a box on the countertop. He pulled out a bulky, brown plastic bag of some sort and handed it to Scott.

Scott accepted it with his free hand, read the label on the package and said, "What's an 'MRE?'"

Shane grinned and leaned against the counter. "In theory, it is a 'Meal Ready to Enjoy.' The newer generations, they aren't half bad. The ones I first ate when I joined the service, well, those were of dubious culinary delight."

"This says vegetarian lasagna," Scott said. "So, it's a dinner?"

"It is a fifteen hundred calorie meal," Shane corrected. "I hope you're not going to be burning through so many calories today that you'll need more than one of those a day. I found a case of them out back, tucked behind the wood. Looks like Mike Puller either shopped at the local Army surplus store, or he had a buddy who could get him the stuff for free. Either way, this stretches out our food supply."

"What's in it?" Scott asked. "Just the lasagna?"

Shane shook his head. "No. There'll be a powder mix for a beverage, some sort of snack, a bread product, and a desert. Also some matches, gum, wet-wipes, and a heater for the food. Lots of stuff we can use. If we have to."

"Did you eat yet?" Scott asked Courtney.

She nodded. "A little bit. Something called a Ranger bar. Basically a chocolate protein bar."

Scott was going to ask a little more, but his stomach growled. He took a sip of his coffee, winced at how hot it was, and blew on it to cool it down a little.

"I'm going to take a walk," Shane said. "I'll see you both in a bit."

When he had left by the back door, Scott turned to Courtney and asked, "What the hell were you doing in here with him?"

Courtney frowned at him. "Really, Scott?"

"Yeah, I mean, you got up and left me in there?"

"You were asleep," she said, her eyes going cold with anger. "What did you want me to do, sit there and hold your hand while you slept?"

Scott felt his face redden.

"And all I was *doing*, Scott," she said in a low voice, "was getting some coffee and a little to eat. What did you think I was going to be doing? Making out with him? You know, you act like you're in high school sometimes."

Scott forced himself to take a drink, in spite of how hot it was.

"I don't come down on you when you talk to a woman," Courtney continued, "so you sure as hell better not give me a hard time for talking to a man."

"Fine," Scott mumbled. "I'm sorry."

"Fine," Courtney snapped. She got to her feet.

"Where are you going?" Scott asked.

"Back to sit with Eileen and Dane. They're better company asleep than you are awake," Courtney said, and Scott groaned as she left the room.

Smooth, Scott, he chided himself. *Real smooth.*

Book 2: The Lighthouse

Chapter 10: Wandering Where He Shouldn't

Dane had disengaged himself from Eileen's arm and slipped out of the house as he heard Courtney's voice raise up.

Dude will never learn, Dane thought, easing the front door closed. *Always harassing her. Told him before how Courtney won't put up with that.*

He looked around the front of the island, frowned at the sight of the yacht not a quarter mile off the pier, and turned his attention to the rest of Squirrel Island. Especially its lighthouse. The last time he had been in a lighthouse had been on the Marginal Way in Ogunquit, Maine. And he had still been in grammar school.

Dane walked over to the front of the lighthouse and saw the padlock on it was undone. The whole place was open for exploration. He grinned, slipped the padlock out of the latch, set it on the ground beside the door, and let himself in. The circular room he found himself in was dimly lit and wider than it seemed from the outside. A metal staircase wound its way up, protruding from the wall. From several windows scattered along the lighthouse's length, morning light drifted in.

Around the base of the building were boxes of supplies. Mostly electrical wiring, paint, all of the necessities needed to bring the buildings up to code and make them livable. There was even a stack of one-gallon water jugs, maybe thirty or forty altogether.

Dane walked over, grabbed one of the gallons and opened it. He drank long and deep from the tepid water.

Even though it's warm, Dane thought, *it still tastes damn good.*

He continued to drink for a minute, and when he had his fill, he capped it and returned it to the floor. He looked at the staircase, grinned, and started up it. The old metal groaned slightly beneath his weight, and a bit of panic flashed through him as he feared the whole assembly might pull out of the wall.

But it held.

With a sigh of relief, Dane continued up the stairs. Several times he hesitated, contemplated a retreat to the ground level again, but with each moment of hesitation, he shook off his fear.

When he reached the top of the lighthouse, he found himself beside the giant lantern. The old brass fittings were dull, and some were green with age. A radio with a handheld microphone was on a shelf, and the view from the top was nothing less than spectacular. Dane could see the coastline clearly, other boats and small ships sailing in the morning breeze. Down below, appearing deceptively close, lay the yacht. As he watched, the yacht swung out wide to the extent of her anchor, the line going taut.

"It's beautiful up here, is it not?"

Dane screamed with fear and surprise. He twisted around, his heart pounding.

A middle-aged man stood by the exit. He wore a thick knit sweater, corduroy pants, and heavy boots. He had a reddish brown beard, trimmed neatly, and a black cap usually seen in old pictures of early merchant captains.

However, the similarity ended there, for the man's eyelids were stitched open, the eyes black and the skin of his face cracked above the beard. His lips looked hard, as if formed from twisted plastic, the line of his mouth grim.

And Dane could see through him. The world behind the man was opaque, as though swaddled in fabric, but the man *felt* terribly real.

Dane cleared his throat and whispered, "Yes. It is beautiful."

"My name is Clark, and I am the keeper," he said. "I must ask, why are you here?"

"Um," Dane said, then he found his voice and said louder, "We went adrift last night. Put another anchor out and came in on the jolly boat. Trying to figure out what we're going to do now because someone stole the jolly boat last night."

"No one stole the jolly boat," Clark replied. "The others slipped your line last night and sent her out. She came back, of course."

"The boat's back?" Dane asked, surprised. "We can leave then!"

"Are you a shipwright?" Clark asked, a note of bitter humor in his voice.

"No," Dane said, slightly taken aback. "Why?"

"Alas, the scraps you'll find will not help you any," Clark chuckled. He turned his blank gaze out onto the water. "She came in hard, as they always do, and broke apart on the rocks."

Dane took a deep breath, prepared himself to ask another question and then thought, *Wait a minute. This is bull. I bet this is all a set-up. Some hidden camera. I bet it's just some sort of projector. There's no such thing as ghosts.*

"Sure they did," Dane said, relaxing slightly, glancing around and trying to spot the projector. *Just a joke. A bad one, but still a joke.*

An expression of surprise flickered across Clark's ruined face.

"Listen," Dane said, grinning, "you have yourself a good day. I'm heading back down to the keeper's house to see what other crap Shane has cooked up."

He stepped towards the stairs and Clark whispered, "Stop."

The word was spoken with authority, harshness, and a coldness which instantly brought Dane to a standstill.

"Where do you think you're going?" Clark asked.

"Out," Dane replied.

"No. We are bound here, for her to harness our strength. To build up her own." Clark said. The hands which had been kept clasped behind his back came out. They were thick, their backs and palms spider-webbed with fine, almost lace-like scars. And in the right hand was a knife of terrible, frightening design. It was curved like the moon in its last quarter. A deep gray handle, with a mirror image curved to the blade, was gripped tightly by Clark.

If, if this real, Dane thought, trying not to allow fear to dominate him, *then he's a ghost and he can't hurt me. Ghosts can't hurt me. They can't hurt anyone. Even the guy who offed himself, he did it himself. That's all. Be strong. No fear.*

No fear.

Dane straightened up and took a step closer to the stairs.

Clark advanced as well, saying, "I am the Keeper of the Lighthouse, and you will not leave until you have my permission to do so."

Dane let out a laugh, and then a moan of surprise and pain.

Clark's empty hand had swung out and smacked Dane solidly on the right cheek, the ghost's cold hand knocking Dane back and into the glass. He caught himself on the slight edge, horror growing in his heart.

"No, you shall go nowhere without my permission," Clark growled. "I am the Keeper, as surely as I was once captain. And let me tell you, my boy, there is nothing quite as fearful as a captain on his ship, or a Keeper in his lighthouse."

How can he hit me? Dane wondered, ignoring Clark. *How is it even possible? If he's a ghost. They can't hurt you.*

They can't hurt me.

But they did, Dane thought, reaching up and touching his sore, throbbing cheek. *He hit me hard.*

"I need to leave," Dane whispered. "I need to go back to my friends."

"No," Clark stated. "There's work here that needs doing. You look like a strong lad. Welcome to the Squirrel Island Lighthouse, boy."

"No," Dane whispered, then screamed, "No!"

He rushed for the stairs, but Clark met him there easily. The knife was a blur in Clark's hand, and he stepped deftly to one side. A sharp, terrible pain erupted in Dane's belly.

Dane fell sideways, landed first on his knees, then his hip, and finally his side. His head thunked loudly against the wooden floor, and he panted as he lay there. Fearfully, he reached down, touched his stomach, felt a warm, sticky liquid, and let out a sob.

When he brought his hand back up to examine it, he saw there was dark, rich blood upon it.

"Careful, lad," Clark said sympathetically. "It's a wicked blow I've dealt you. Reach much farther down and you'll feel your innards, which the Lord, in His magnificence, never meant for us to embrace."

Dane sobbed and felt something slip out of his stomach. He heard it slap wetly on the floor.

I'm going to die here, Dane realized morosely. *Oh God, I'm so sorry for everything I've done. I'm so, so sorry.*

"If you're praying, son," Clark said, putting his knife away and folding his arms over his chest as he stood there, "I'd say don't waste your breath. You will not leave this place. No, you're here forever, just like the rest of us. Since I've brought you over, though, well, you'll be with me."

Clark grinned. "Which is good. We have a great deal of work to be done in this lighthouse if we're to be getting it shipshape and Bristol fashion. Yes, a good deal of work."

Dane wanted to scream again, needed to scream again, but the pain was too intense. To even speak would have caused intense agony. Instead, all he could do was bleed out on the aged floor, and wait to die while his murderer kept a careful watch.

Chapter 11: And So It Begins

Shane stood on the pier and looked out at the yacht.

I need to get them off of this island, he thought. *This place is bad, and it's going to be too much for them. Might be too much for me.*

He reached back, patted the iron knuckles in his pocket, and sighed.

Yeah, Shane told himself, *it's going to get bad. I can feel it.*

A scream ripped out from behind him and Shane twisted around. Something stood at the top of the lighthouse. The shape was the barest hint of a person from where Shane was.

Why in the hell would one of them scream like that?

Courtney and Scott came out of the house, followed by the young woman, Eileen.

But not Dane.

Dane, Shane thought. He pulled the iron knuckles out, slipped them onto his right hand, and rushed up the slight incline to the lighthouse and found the door still locked. He kicked the door with all his strength, putting his foot close to the padlock. The force of his blow snapped the screws of the latch, and the wood ripped as the deadbolt tore through the aged and weathered wood.

The door sprang inward, bounced off of the inner wall, and shivered to pieces. Only a long, ragged edge was left, hanging madly from the old rusted hinges. Shane ran straight for the stairs and raced up, ignoring the way the metal quivered beneath his feet, or how the old bolts in the brick walls groaned.

Shane threw himself through the opening at the top of stairs and came to a sharp stop.

Dane lay on the floor, eyes wide in death while blood leaked out onto the floor. The young man's guts were in a slipshod pile, spilling out of the gaping hole in the boy's belly.

Shane's attention snapped from the dead youth to the ghost who stood off to one side, close to the mammoth lantern which served as the lighthouse's beacon.

The man smiled at Shane. "You're a fighter."

Shane nodded.

"They boy's dead."

"So he is," Shane said. "You killed him."

"It was required," the man said soberly. "Name's Clark. Clark Noyes. I'm the Keeper."

"Shane Ryan," Shane replied. "I'm here to find out why that was required."

"You'll need to speak to Dorothy," Clark answered. "If Dorothy will speak to you. You've been to sea, and not like this lad. No pleasure trip, aye?"

Below them, someone called his name and Shane yelled down, "Stay outside!"

"What ship?" Clark asked pleasantly.

"Depended on where I was and when," Shane replied warily, trying to keep his attention from Dane's pale, bloodless face. "Did a tour with the Sixth Fleet, though, Mediterranean."

"Sailor?"

Shane shook his head. "Marine."

Clark grinned. "Excellent. Well, if you'll excuse me, Shane, I've work to do, and so does this lad. As you can see, the lighthouse is in sorry shape. We'll have her righted soon enough, though. That we will."

The man vanished.

Work to do, Shane thought. He returned his gaze to Dane. The boy was dead. Undeniably so. But it seemed as though his spirit wouldn't be allowed to leave.

Dane had been enslaved.

Chapter 12: Horror

Scott stood outside the broken door of the lighthouse with both Courtney and Eileen. None of them spoke. They had all heard the scream. A terrible sound Scott was sure would haunt him for the rest of his life.

When they had raced outside, they had seen Shane down on the pier.

But no sign of Dane.

None.

Then Shane had run up to the lighthouse, kicked his way in, and gone after Dane. Scott and Eileen had hesitated at the entrance.

Courtney had not.

She had stepped into the old building and called up to Shane, who, in turn, had told them all to stay outside.

And so Courtney had gone back out, stood beside Eileen, and together the three of them waited, not so patiently, for answers. Scott could vaguely hear a conversation going on between Shane and someone else, but he couldn't make out any of the words.

It only lasted for a few minutes, and then Shane had called to them.

"I'm coming down now," Shane said from the top. "You need to stay back from the door. This isn't going to be pretty, and it sure as hell isn't going to be nice. Courtney?"

"Yes?" she said loudly, and Scott felt anger and jealousy rear their heads again as the older man said his girlfriend's name.

"Behind the house, by the wood, is a blue tarp. Grab it, will you?" Shane asked.

"Sure," Courtney said, and she hurried away.

"What's going on?" Eileen called out, desperation in her voice. "Is Dane up there with you?"

"Yes," Shane replied.

"Oh, thank God," Eileen said, her shoulders dropping in relief. Then she said, "Is he hurt?"

"He's dead," Shane answered.

"Oh Jesus Christ," Scott whispered. Eileen sank down to the ground, put her back against the old bricks of the lighthouse, and stared dully out at the Atlantic. And then Courtney was back, carrying the blue tarp with her. It was balled up in her arms. She glanced at Eileen and frowned.

"What's wrong?" she asked her friend.

Eileen shook her head.

"Dane's dead," Scott replied.

"What?" Courtney asked. "What do you mean he's dead? How can he be dead? We heard them talking up there."

Scott shook his head, unable to give her an answer.

"Courtney?" Shane called.

"Got it," she answered. "Now what?"

"Spread it out right in front of the door, please," he said. "And don't look, okay?"

"Okay," Courtney said. She brought the tarp to the door, stretched it out, and then turned to Eileen. "Come on, hon, let's go inside."

Her expression was one of dazed confusion, Eileen allowed Courtney to help her stand up. Together they went to the keeper's house.

Scott was alone.

"All set?" Shane asked.

"Yeah," Scott said. "And the girls went inside."

"Good," Shane said. "You may want to go inside too, Scott."

"No," Scott responded, his voice sounding oddly mechanical to his ears. "He's my best friend."

"Alright," Shane said. "Be ready."

A moment later, Scott heard Shane's footsteps on the stairs. They were heavier than before, and the man came down steadily. Soon, Scott could see him. Shane walked carefully, stepping on each riser. Once again, he was bare-chested, and blood stained his hairless flesh.

Dane Wesser, Scott's best friend, was limply draped over Shane's shoulder. Dane's body flopped and jiggled curiously, lifelessly with every step Shane took.

When the older man reached the ground floor, he grimly exited the lighthouse and gently placed Dane's body on the tarp. Scott could see why Shane was shirtless. The black tee shirt he had been wearing earlier was on Dane's stomach. Dane's braided tan belt had been removed from his khaki shorts, looped around the shirt and cinched tightly.

"Why?" Scott asked softly.

"Why what?" Shane asked, getting down on his knees.

"Your shirt?"

"To keep his intestines in," Shane said bitterly. "He was gutted like a fish."

Scott felt the urge to vomit, but he kept it under control. Silently, he watched Shane wrap the tarp around Dane, and then roll him carefully and gently in it. When he had finished, Shane looked up at Scott and said, "Will you help me move him?"

Scott nodded. "Where?"

"We'll bring him around the back. There's an old shed, it's seen better days, but it's empty. We can put him there until someone comes and gets us later, alright?"

"Yeah," Scott whispered. "Yeah, alright."

"Good."

Not really aware of what he was doing, Scott helped to pick up Dane, whose body was incredibly unwieldy, and together he and Shane went around the lighthouse. In the back was the shed, its door wide open and hanging cockeyed off of its hinges.

Shane backed in and said, "Here, on the right."

They maneuvered in the tight confines of the small structure and put Dane's body on a shelf that kept him off the ground and was barely long enough to fit him.

"Thanks," Shane said as they left the shed and he closed the door, sliding the latch in place. "Will you do me another favor?"

"Sure," Scott said numbly. "What is it?"

"Go in, grab a t-shirt out of my bag and bring it down to the pier?" Shane said. "I need to wash myself up. Salt water isn't great for it, but I won't waste what little fresh water we have."

"Yeah," Scott said. "I can do that."

"Thanks," Shane said. He hesitated, then he added, "Listen, I'm sorry this happened to your friend. I truly am, Scott."

Scott nodded, and Shane left for the pier.

Scott stood outside the shed a little longer. Then, with a shudder, he went into the keeper's house. He needed to get the shirt for Shane.

And he needed to tell Eileen about where Dane's body was.

His body, Scott thought, and tears filled his eyes. *Oh Christ, his body...*

Chapter 13: Down at the Pier

Shane was thankful the weather was warm, and that the breeze coming off of the ocean was equally warm. He had managed to scrub Dane's blood off of his body, and he sat on the pier, air-drying. The salt water had left an unpleasant residue on his flesh, but it was far more preferable than the remnants of Dane.

He took his cigarettes out, lit one, and exhaled as he looked at the water. The waves smacked the large stones at the base of the island. The water was rough, angry. A glance at the yacht showed it at the end of its tether.

It'll break free soon, Shane thought glumly, and he wondered when Marie might get out to them. He needed the kids, and the body, off of the island.

He heard footsteps on the path behind him and he turned quickly.

Courtney was approaching, holding his gray t-shirt in her hand.

"Fantastic," Shane said around his cigarette. "Thank you so much."

He got to his feet and walked towards her. She gave him a small smile as she handed it to him. He could see the fear and concern in her eyes.

After he had put the shirt on, he sat back down on the pier and she joined him. Several minutes of silence passed by before she asked, "What happened?"

"Dane was killed by a ghost," Shane said.

Courtney shook her head. "How? I mean, come on, how can a ghost hurt someone?"

"I don't know how," Shane said, then to himself, *No, she doesn't need to know.* "I just know they can. It's like bumble bees. They look like they shouldn't be able to fly, but they do. I don't know how a ghost can hurt someone, but they do."

Courtney hesitated, then she said, "How was he killed?"

"Badly," Shane answered. "We're going to leave it at that."

She nodded, accepting the reply. "Scott's not taking it well."

"They were good friends?" Shane asked.

"The best. They'd been friends since first grade," Courtney said.

Shane shook his head, finished his cigarette, and pinched out the butt. He stripped the paper off of the filter, tore up the filter, and then put the debris in his pockets.

"Most people would have thrown it in the water," Courtney said.

"Hm?" Shane asked.

"Your cigarette butt," she said. "They would have tossed it into the ocean."

"Old habits," Shane said, smiling. "They die hard."

The waves moved in, struck the rocks, broke apart, and then repeated the pattern.

"It's beautiful out here," Courtney said softly. "Too bad it's terrible, this place."

Shane nodded his agreement. "I have to find Dorothy."

Courtney frowned. "Who?"

"The ghost I spoke to last night before you all showed up," Shane clarified. "Clark, the one who killed Dane, he said she's in charge. I need to speak with her. But I need to find her first."

"Where do ghosts hide?" Courtney asked. "I mean, this is a small island. Where can they be?"

"Lots of places," Shane replied. "We've got the lighthouse and the keeper's house. The shed, and the pier. There has to be a cistern or something like it."

"For the water," Courtney said, nodding. "Yeah. There wouldn't be a well. They would have had to bring it in and store it here."

"And there's the cellar," Shane said, glancing back at the house. He saw Scott in the window, watching them.

"Scott's keeping an eye on you," Shane said.

"I know," Courtney said, sighing. She didn't bother to look. "He gets a little jealous. It's what I get for dating a guy four years younger than me."

"Strange that he gets jealous," Shane said.

"Why?" she asked.

"You don't strike me as the type of person who'd cheat," Shane said. "I think you'd be more likely to tell him you were done and move on if you were interested in someone else."

"Yup," Courtney agreed. "That's me. He knows it too. I've told him. Doesn't mean he's listening to me, though."

Shane nodded.

"So," she said, "what do we do now, wait for your friends to notice you haven't written or replied?"

"Yes," he said. "Not much else to do about it. Just going to try and keep the rest of you safe. If I can."

"Thank you," Courtney said softly. "For all of us. I don't think either Eileen or Scott will see it that way, but I do. Thank you."

Shane nodded, trying not to look in her green eyes. After a pause, he said, "I need some coffee. How about you?"

"Sure," she said.

They both got to their feet and began the short walk back to the keeper's house. Scott was no longer at the window.

"Will you start looking for Dorothy right after coffee?" Courtney asked.

"Yup," Shane answered.

"What do you need?"

"Iron knuckledusters, light, and a whole lot of luck," Shane said.

"Where are you going to start?" she said.

"The cellar," Shane said.

They lapsed into silence, turning up the path towards the keeper's house. The sounds of their footsteps were swallowed up by the waves. Soon they reached the front door, and Courtney opened it for him. Shane smiled and nodded his thanks.

When he entered the house Shane saw Scott and Eileen sitting in the living room. Both of them were exhausted, deep shadows beneath their eyes, stubble on Scott's face.

"I'm going to make coffee," Shane said to them. "And I'll heat up some food. You'll both need to eat. Letting your bodies get too hungry or thirsty isn't the way to last this one out. Understood?"

Scott nodded.

"Eileen," Shane said sharply. The young woman looked up, surprised. "Did you hear me?"

"No," she said softly. "I wasn't paying attention."

"You need to," Shane said grimly. "This place isn't nice. It isn't friendly. Whatever is here, hurts people. I need you to pay attention. I need you to eat. All of you. Not eating and not drinking is going to get you hurt, and probably me."

"Do you need help getting the food ready?" Courtney asked.

Shane nodded. "Any help would be great, Cort."

She blushed slightly at the nickname and passed by him to go into the kitchen. Scott's face reddened too, but it was from anger and not attraction.

Good, Shane thought. *Maybe it'll help him to pay more attention to her.*

Chapter 14: Angrier and Angrier

Scott didn't care about Shane having gone racing into the lighthouse after Dane. He didn't care the man was making them food.

All Scott cared about was the inappropriate amount of time Courtney, his girlfriend, was spending with a forty-something-year-old guy. Dane being dead didn't help Scott's attitude.

But it's all about 'Cort' now, he thought angrily. The pet name caused his anger to flare and his hands to itch. He had never wanted to hit anyone as badly as he wanted to hit Shane Ryan.

It would have been worse if Shane was actually hitting on Courtney in front of him. Shane wasn't though.

No, Scott fumed, *she's attracted to him. To a God-Damned forty-year-old!* he snarled inwardly. *Christ, she's in there helping him cook! She won't even let me near the stove at her place.*

Briefly, he contemplated sucker-punching Shane, but with the idea came the realization that if he didn't knock the man out, Shane would probably beat the hell out of him.

I just want to leave this place, Scott complained to himself. *Get good and far away, then we can figure out what the hell happened to Dane.*

The thought of his friend twisted his gut and Scott dropped his chin to his chest.

"Scott," Eileen whispered. "Did you hear that?"

He was about to say 'no' when he did hear something. A creak followed by a soft groan.

From the second floor.

Another creak filtered down, then a third.

Someone's walking up there, Scott realized.

Eileen turned toward the kitchen door, and he stopped her.

"Wait," he whispered.

She looked at him, surprised, and she asked in a low voice, "Why?"

"What if the person up there is a friend of Shane's?" Scott asked. "I'm having a hard time believing all of this ghost stuff. Especially after Dane was killed."

Eileen hesitated, then she shook his hand off of her. "I don't believe it."

Scott watched her leave the room, and then he turned his attention to the stairs. The steps drew nearer. He got to his feet and walked softly over to the railing. The wood was cold and smooth beneath his hand. He held onto it as he peered up into the dim light of the second floor.

A man appeared, and Scott took a nervous step backward. It was the naked man he had seen on the pier the night before.

"Scott," Shane said, suddenly at his side.

Scott stared at Shane, unable to speak briefly. Then, finally, he managed to stutter out, "He's see-through."

"I know," Shane said. "Go on back, please. Let me speak with Mike here."

Scott could only nod as he backed up and found himself between Eileen and Courtney. In horrified, but fascinated silence, they watched the scene before them unfold.

Chapter 15: A Conversation

Shane slipped the iron knuckledusters onto his right hand, and he waited for the man at the top of the stairs to speak.

"You should leave," Mike Puller said.

"I'd like to," Shane replied. "Can't though. No reception for the phone. And someone decided to mess around with my ability to connect with the internet."

"She wants you gone," Mike said, moving a step closer.

"She can want me gone until Hell freezes over," Shane said pleasantly. "I'll leave as soon as I can."

"You'll leave now," Mike said, advancing another step.

"No," Shane said. "I won't kill myself like you did, Mike."

The statement caused the man to hesitate. "How do you know my name?"

"I'm a friend of Amy's cousin," Shane said. "I was asked here."

At the mention of Amy's name, Mike Puller lowered his head. "I'm sorry she has to carry this weight. I didn't want her to."

Puller fixed his eyes on Shane. "Doesn't mean you get to stay."

"I stay because I want to. And I'll leave when I want to. Do you understand me?" Shane asked. He drove all semblance of politeness from his voice. "I'm going to find out what the hell is going on, and then you're all going to leave. Am I understood?"

Puller chuckled. "You have no idea who you're dealing with."

"Cliché much?" Shane asked him.

Puller glared and raced down the stairs at him. Shane slipped to one side, and Mike Puller spun around and snapped, "Think you're clever? Think she won't find out about you?"

"Dorothy had best forget about me," Shane said softly, "and worry about learning to live with the living."

"The island is hers," Puller stated matter-of-factly. "The lighthouse is hers. The keeper's house is hers. You had best remember all of that."

"Go," Shane said. "You're boring the hell out of me. Go put some clothes on."

Mike Puller snarled with rage and hurled himself at Shane.

Shane didn't bother stepping aside. He adjusted his position, raised his right fist up and brought it smashing into Puller's face. The ghost's eyes went wide as the iron struck him.

A short scream pierced the air, and Mike Puller vanished.

Shane lowered his arm and wondered, tiredly, *When is Amy going to check her damned email and see I haven't written in?*

He sighed as he walked away from the stairs. Courtney, Eileen, and Scott all stared at him as he approached.

"What's wrong?" he asked them.

"You punched a ghost," Courtney said.

"Only worked because of the iron I had on. These knuckledusters," he said, slipping them off and putting them back into his pocket, "their iron, and a friend of mine gave them to me. Back when we had a little run-in with some other, equally unpleasant ghosts.

"Come on in the kitchen," he said as he passed by them. "I'll tell you what little I know about what can slow a ghost down."

They followed him, and as he and Courtney finished the preparation of the MREs, he told them about iron, and how to use it.

Chapter 16: Going Down

Scott was sulking in a corner, they had survived the night and the morning had slipped by uneventfully. Eileen lay on the sleeping bag, and Shane wasn't sure if the girl was awake or asleep. She was quiet, and she had cried again after they had eaten. Courtney had spoken with Scott, and whatever it was had resulted in his new bad mood. Courtney sat beside Eileen, her hand on her friend's shoulder. When Courtney saw Shane looking at her, she smiled.

Shane smiled back.

"When are you going to go into the cellar?" Courtney asked.

"In a little while," Shane replied.

"What do you think you'll find there?" she said.

"I'm hoping I'll find Dorothy," Shane said.

"Are you nervous?"

"Of course, I am," Shane said gently. "I'd be a fool not to be. I don't know what I'll run into down there. I know I've got a minimum of three ghosts to deal with, possibly more. It all depends on how many others Dorothy and Clark have bound to them. No, I'm not looking forward to this at all, Cort."

"Do you need me to go downstairs with you?" she asked. The fear was thick in her voice.

Shane smiled at her. "No. No, but thank you. I want you, Eileen, and Scott up here, where it's safe."

He stood up and stretched.

"Shane," Scott said bitterly, "what do we do if you get taken?"

"Set the house on fire," Shane replied. "And hope someone sees you and comes out to investigate."

He left them, passed through the kitchen, and went out the back door.

It was nearly mid-day, and the sun was strong and true. The island was warm, smelling sweetly of saltwater, and Shane wondered what he would find in the cellar of the house.

He walked around to the bulkhead, pulled it open, and set the locks. The stairs which led down were steep and narrow, the ledge of each barely more than ten inches deep. Webs clung to the corners, as did shreds of grass and the carcasses of long-dead insects. At the bottom was a tall, narrow door made up of long, thin boards bound together with old iron. Like the doors of both the lighthouse and the keeper's house, the door before him had once been blue as well.

Shane took a deep breath, calmed his heart rate, and armed himself.

Carefully, he descended the steps, reached the bottom, and thumbed the latch, swinging the door open.

Nearly pure darkness waited for him inside. The smell was rank and musty, a foul odor which threatened to burn the insides of his nose and caused his eyes to water. The daylight illuminated a small patch of earth which served as the cellar's floor. He stepped in cautiously, allowing his eyes to adjust to the limited light.

After several minutes of trying to adjust to the dark, he could make out rough shelves of canned and jarred food. In the ceiling above, he could see joists and the faint outline of a trap door. His skin crawled as he stepped in further. To the right, he saw four small boxes, one stacked on top of the other. At the bottom of the pile, though, was a fifth, larger box.

Shane stared at them. Blackness pulsed around them and sought to pull him closer. To drag him in.

"What are you?" he asked softly.

"We're death," a little girl answered.

"So our father called us," a boy added.

"Our mother too, Frederick," a different girl corrected.

"Yes, Jane," Frederick said.

Another child, an infant, let out a wail.

"You've awakened the baby," the little girl chided.

"Jillian," Jane said, "the baby never sleeps."

"It's why we're here," a man said.

"Yes, grandfather," Jane agreed. "It is why we're here."

"Why are you down here?" Shane asked.

"Punishment," their grandfather answered. "The children for being children. And myself for having the audacity to try and come between them and the discipline their parents sought to administer."

"They killed you," Shane said softly.

"Poison," the grandfather said sadly.

"Drowning," Frederick said cheerfully.

"Strangulation for the girls," Jane said.

"Who did it?" Shane asked.

"Father and mother," Jillian said, sounding as if she believed Shane to be a little too stupid.

Shane held back his exasperation and asked, "Could you tell me their names?"

"Mother and father," Jane said. "We knew them as nothing else."

"My son-in-law was Clark Noyes," the grandfather said. "My daughter was Dorothy."

"Where is she?" Shane asked. "I've come down here for her."

"Down here?" the grandfather asked, surprised. "Why would she be here?"

"She doesn't like the cellar," Jane said confidentially.

"She *hates* the dark," Frederick said. "Grandmother used to punish her by locking her in the cellar. For days on end, she would weep in the darkness. The door would be locked, and Mother would starve. Her disobedience kept her stomach empty, kept her in the cold depths. Grandmother sought to teach our Mother, although she would not learn.

"But, in the end, Mother took her anger out on Father. But only after Mother and Father had punished us," Frederick finished, laughing.

"How?" Shane asked.

"In the lighthouse," Frederick said, seeming happy to have Shane to speak with. "Oh, in the lighthouse, all the way up at the lantern. She brought him his coffee one dark night and knocked him unconscious. A terrible blow."

"Oh yes. She strapped him to the light, face first. She stitched his eyelids open, and over hours and hours she burned out his eyes. We could hear the screams from the top of the tower down here in our wooden tombs."

"It took days for him to die," their grandfather added. "I'm not even sure how many, only that he suffered tremendously. He would grow silent, and then my daughter would think of some new punishment for him. Some horrific bit of torment to inflict as much pain as she could on him."

Shane swallowed uncomfortably at the idea of torture. "Do you know where I could find her? Would it be in the lighthouse?"

"No, not the lighthouse," the grandfather replied. "Not if she can help it. She despised the lighthouse."

"Where then?" Shane asked.

"The second floor," Frederick answered.

Shane stiffened. "The second floor of the keeper's house?"

"Yes," she replied.

"It's only a large room up there," Shane said softly. "There's nothing."

"Perhaps not now," the grandfather said. "When we first moved into the keeper's house, there were two bedrooms in the loft."

"Mother's room looked out over the sea," Frederick said.

"She loved to see the shore," Jillian added.

Of course, it's the second floor, Shane thought numbly. *It's where she came down from. Just because the cellar felt bad didn't mean she was down here.*

The bodies are here.

Her own father and children, whom she murdered.

It's the death and the torture I felt. Their memories are sifting up through the stairs and into the back of the house.

And she's upstairs.

Upstairs!

"Thank you, for your time," Shane said as politely as he could. "I must go upstairs. I must see if Dorothy is in her room."

A scream from above cut him off and he was plunged into darkness as the cellar door slammed closed and locked itself.

Shane knew exactly where it was, and he threw himself at it, battering the wood as he sought to claw his way to freedom. A second scream rang out, and he managed to rip the old and rotten door off its hinges.

Biting back his anger, Shane went barreling up the stairs and into the sunlight.

Chapter 17: Dorothy Comes In

Courtney did her best to ignore Scott. He had tried to pull the whole 'I'm your boyfriend, you can't talk to him' speech earlier, but Courtney wasn't having any of it.

She sighed, shook her head, and focused her attention on Eileen. Her friend was still laying on Shane's sleeping bag, in and out of sleep, from what Courtney could tell.

Courtney removed her hand from Eileen's shoulder, brushed back a bit of hair from her friend's forehead, and felt an unnatural heat emanating from her flesh.

Oh no, does she have a fever? Courtney thought.

Muffled voices came from the cellar.

Children's voices.

Courtney looked over to see if Scott had heard them as well. His wide-eyed, surprised expression was enough of an answer.

Footsteps came down the stairs, and Courtney turned in time to see a woman finish her descent from the second floor. The woman's face was cold, merciless. There wasn't hate in her eyes, only disdain and disgust.

"This is my home," the woman said, facing them.

Courtney gasped, shivering as she found herself looking *through* the woman.

"We don't want to be here," Courtney said, her voice not nearly as confident as she would have liked. "We want to leave."

"But I don't want you to leave now," the woman said, smiling bitterly. "I like your company. In fact, I'm not sure I want any of you to leave. Ever. There's so much work to do to get the lighthouse ready. I need to be stronger. And for that, I need you. All of you."

She walked into the room, towards Courtney.

Courtney scrambled to her feet. Her heart beat ferociously in her chest and the impulse to run and fling herself into the Atlantic threatened to destroy her self-control.

"Get out of here," Courtney said, mustering all of the force she could. "Leave us alone."

"Soon enough," the woman said softly, "I will leave you all alone. But not yet."

Courtney was suddenly in the air, thrown back against the wall. Her breath was knocked from her, and she collapsed to her hands and knees. With her head spinning and gasping for air, Courtney heard Scott scream in terror. Beneath them, a door slammed shut.

Managing to take a deep breath, Courtney looked up and saw the stranger kneel down beside Eileen. Eileen, in turn, was sitting up, a groggy, confused expression on her face. Then she screamed as she saw the woman, who let out a pleasant, almost beautiful laugh.

Courtney tried to get to her feet, but only managed to collapse onto the floor. Her head spun too much from the force of the throw and she couldn't regain her balance. In horror, she watched as the stranger reached out, grasped Eileen by the head and smiled.

Eileen screamed again, tried to twist away, but the ghost kept a firm grip on her.

Something shattered outside, and the sound of running feet could be heard.

The woman slipped her thumbs onto Eileen's eyelids, and Courtney couldn't turn away as the stranger began to pry Eileen's eyes out of their sockets.

Eileen's screams turned to shrieks while Scott vomited and wept. Shane thrust open the back door. Courtney crawled forward, determined to stop the woman.

Then Shane raced out of the kitchen and past her.

"Dorothy!" he yelled.

The woman snarled at him. "You're all going to die," she hissed. "And sooner rather than later."

Even as Shane reached Dorothy, she grinned and twisted Eileen's head sharply to the left. The result was instantaneous and sickening. A dry, brittle snap.

Eileen's shriek ended abruptly, and she went limp.

Shane dove at Dorothy, his right hand smashing through her. With a howl of pure hatred, she vanished. Shane landed hard, rolled, and thudded against the wall, small pieces of plaster dropping onto him.

Courtney finished her crawl to Eileen. Her hand shook as she reached out, touched Eileen's neck, and sought a pulse.

There was none to be found. Dorothy had killed her.

Blood dried slowly on her friend's cheeks, her eyelids misshapen after the destruction of the orbs beneath.

Courtney began to shake uncontrollably. She pushed herself back and sat down. Shane moved closer, wrapped an arm around her, and pulled her in close. He said nothing.

She suddenly remembered Scott and looked over to him. He was passed out on the floor.

She relaxed into Shane's arms, smelled the sharp tang of blood on him. Courtney closed her eyes, felt sorrow and rage well up within her, and let out a long, angry sob.

Shane continued to hold her, and he let her cry. He didn't offer up soothing words, and he didn't pull away. He quietly stroked the back of her head, held her, and began to sing softly in a language she didn't know.

The steady thump of his heart accompanied the song, and Courtney wept for her murdered friend.

Chapter 18: Disbelief

Half an hour had passed since Eileen's death, and Scott's world continued to crumble

He stood in silence and looked out of the window at his father's yacht. He watched as it drifted away, the anchor line snapped and the sails furled. It rode the current, out towards deeper waters.

Maybe it'll be found, Scott thought numbly.

Everything was happening all at once. The yacht. Dane's murder. Eileen's murder.

And now this? he thought, turning to look at Courtney.

"How can you do this?" he asked her in disbelief.

Her face was stern, eyes red from crying, skin around them puffy. She had streaks of Eileen's blood on her, her arms folded across her chest.

"What do you mean?" she said coldly.

"How can you break up with me?" Scott asked, shaking his head. "I mean, how can you do it here? You couldn't wait until we got back to the mainland?"

"What?" she asked in surprise.

"Yeah," Scott said. "You don't think this is hard on me, too? Couldn't you think of me? You know, maybe that I shouldn't have to deal with the end of a relationship in the middle of all this crap?"

"What are you, fourteen?" Courtney snapped. "Jesus Christ, Scott, act your age."

"Why are you breaking up with me?" Scott demanded. "I thought everything was fine."

"Everything was fine," Courtney said. "Because we were dating. We're not engaged. We were dating. And now we're not."

"Is it because of Shane?" Scott asked in a low voice, not wanting the older man to hear him.

"Part of it, yes," she said. "Mostly, though, it's you acting like a teenager. And, you know, passing out instead of trying to help Eileen really doesn't qualify you as 'continued boyfriend' material."

His face burned with embarrassment. "It was a little too much to deal with."

"I managed to make an effort," Courtney said, biting off each word.

"This is garbage," Scott said angrily. "Our relationship isn't done until I say it's done. You'll see once we get back to the mainland. You're just stressed out."

He stopped as her expression changed.

Hatred filled her eyes.

"You listen to me, Scott," she whispered. "I've had one bad relationship where the guy wasn't going to let me go. He broke my wrist and my arm, then he cracked two of my ribs. He ate through a straw for months because I shattered his jaw with his laptop. He'll never, ever have children because of what I did to him. And let me tell you, *Scott,* you come near me, and I *will* hurt you. Do you understand me?"

Scott licked his lips nervously as he stepped back, bumping into the wall. He nodded. "I'm sorry."

"Shut up," she spat. "Just shut up." She turned around and went into the kitchen.

Scott stood alone in the living room. From outside, he heard the wind pick up, and the waves become louder. Slowly he sank into a sitting position. He dipped his head, closed his eyes, and asked himself, *How the hell did all of this happen?*

Book 2: The Lighthouse

Chapter 19: A Good Idea Gone Bad

George Fallon steered his boat with one hand and kept his beer steady with the other. Vic Nato and Eric Powell sat in their seats, drinking their own beers. The fine, cooling spray of the Atlantic misted over them as George's new Boston Whaler, *Terminal Fleet*, cut through the water.

It was nearly six in the evening, and the sun had already begun its descent. But they were only five minutes from Squirrel Island.

"Pity about Mike," Eric said, raising his voice slightly to be heard over the thrum of the Whaler's powerful engine.

Vic, who didn't know Mike, stayed silent.

George, who had known Mike Puller since the first grade, spoke up. "Hated the guy."

"He was alright," Eric said defensively.

"Sure he was," George said, "if you were a broad. Otherwise, nah, he'd just as soon steal from you as work with you on a project."

"I heard," Vic chimed in, "he had screwed Nate Verranault on a job up in Bangor."

George nodded. "One of many. He found out what Nate bid on the carpentry, went in and told the owner he could do it in half the time, and for half the money."

"Didn't he go to prison for that one?" Vic asked.

"No," Eric said grumpily, "he went to Valley Street jail in Manchester. He didn't even do two years."

"Only because it was under five grand that he got away with," George said, chuckling. "Anyway, we'll be there in a minute or two. Got your phones all charged?"

Both Vic and Eric raised their beers in assent.

"Think this'll boost the website?" Eric asked.

George grinned. "Damned right, it will."

The three of them, with help from Vic's girlfriend, had started up a website. It specialized in photographs of death scenes. Accidents, murders, suicides. As long as death was involved, the pictures went up on the site. They had come onto the idea early one morning, talking about a construction accident Vic had seen.

All the wackos and weirdos who had come out of the woodwork, George thought. *Everyone trying to get a look, trying to take pictures.*

And the site is a damned goldmine, George grinned. With the money they made from subscriptions and advertisements, they were all enjoying life. George's new, 2017-model Boston Whaler was a prime example of it.

"There's the pier," Eric said, bringing George out of his pleasant reminiscing.

The new structure extended out into the ocean. George, who had been operating boats since his father stood him up behind the controls of an old speedboat when he was four, guided the Whaler in easily. Vic put his beer down, got to his feet, and was over the side in a moment, securing the boat to the pier as George turned the engine off. Eric, slightly unsteady on his feet, managed to get onto the pier and George followed.

"This the place?" Vic asked.

"Got to be," George said. "Only pier on the island."

"What the hell?" Eric said softly.

George turned towards Eric and saw the man was staring at the island. When he followed Eric's line of sight, he gasped in surprise.

At the end of the pier, sitting on a rock, was a boy of perhaps ten or twelve. He wore a pair of dark blue pants, battered shoes, and a collarless, button-down shirt. His skin was tanned, his hair bleached blonde by the sun. Sharp, bright blue eyes stared at George. The boy's face was thin and drawn. Between his narrow lips and clenched in his teeth was the stem of an unlit pipe.

The boy reached up, took hold of the briarwood bowl and took it out. He pointed at the three men, one at a time, with the pipe's stem.

I can see through him, George realized in surprise.

"Jesus Christ, George," Vic said softly. "Is the kid a ghost?"

"I think so," George whispered.

"This is awesome!" Eric said, barely able to keep his excitement contained.

George took his phone out, turned on the camera, brought it up, and snapped several pictures.

"Someone recording this?" Eric asked, fumbling with his own phone.

"I got it," Vic replied, holding his cellphone up.

The boy gave them a confused look, put the pipe back in his mouth, and said around it, "You're all going to die."

Eric chuckled, and Vic let out a laugh.

George felt his stomach tighten. He lowered his phone and asked, "What?"

"Die," the boy repeated. "Do you understand? We're going to kill you. All of you."

"Hey," George said to Eric and Vic, "maybe we should leave?"

"Are you kidding?" Eric asked.

"Come on, George," Vic said, grinning and glancing over at him. "Can you imagine the hits on the site when these go up? The video will probably go viral."

George looked back to the boy, who had gotten to his feet.

"No," George whispered, "this isn't going to go viral. This isn't going to go anywhere. He's going to kill us."

"Ghosts can't kill people," Eric said, grinning.

For the first time, George could hear the slur in Eric's words. The man had drunk more than George had known. A glance at Vic showed he was too giddy with the idea of being an internet sensation to recognize death was at the end of the pier. Death in the form of a little boy with an unlit pipe in his mouth.

The boy smiled. A quiet, disturbing smile which reminded George of his worst nightmares. The smile was a promise of pain, of misery, of pure terror right before the moment of death.

"We need to leave," George whispered. He left his friends on the pier and got back into the Whaler.

"Get in!" George shouted at Vic and Eric as he tried to start the boat's engine.

Vic and Eric looked at him, and the engine sputtered.

"Come on!" George said frantically, trying to start the boat again.

"George," Vic called, "relax, man, ghosts can't do anything."

George looked up at him and was about to argue the point when he saw the boy. The ghost was walking down the pier, humming softly to himself.

George recognized the tune. It was an old sea shanty, one his grandfather had used to sing. The boy was at the refrain.

I'll go no more a-roving with you, fair maid, George thought, hearing his long dead grandfather's voice.

"This is great," Eric said. "Absolutely fantastic!"

George tried again to start the engine, and again it refused to do more than sputter.

Vic continued to record, turning to follow the boy as he came to a stop in front of Eric. The boy looked up at Eric, who, in turn, bowed his head slightly to look into the boy's upturned face.

"You, on the boat there," the boy said, not turning away from Eric.

"Yes?" George asked, unsure of what else to do.

"You were smart," the boy said pleasantly. "You're the one who wanted to go. For that, you shall."

George hesitated, then he tried the engine again, and it started.

"Get in!" he shouted. He climbed up, untied the boat before he jumped back down.

"No," the boy said, his voice carrying with it a note of deadly seriousness. "They don't get to leave. Just you."

George went to protest, but he stopped.

The boy, with his right hand straight as a knife's blade, plunged it straight into Vic's stomach.

Vic stiffened, dropped the phone, and gasped in shock and pain. He convulsed slightly, tried to breathe but couldn't. The ghost grinned and turned his arm gently to the right.

Vic's scream echoed off of the stones, and the door to the keeper's house was flung open.

Enough! George screamed to himself. He turned the wheel hard to starboard, slammed the throttle down, and the Whaler fairly leaped away from the pier and back to the open sea.

More of them in the house, he thought frantically, aiming for the mainland. *Oh, Jesus, there's more than one.*

Fear drove him away, and he abandoned his friends to their fates.

Chapter 20: Things Get Worse

Shane had heard far too many screams. The newest one was completely unexpected.

He had finished moving the unfortunate Eileen into the shed to lay alongside Dane, who had already begun to decompose in the June heat.

He had rinsed the taste of death out of his mouth, spat it out on the ground, and thought he had heard the sound of an engine.

Shane straightened up and thought, *Did they send someone a day early?*

He grinned, thrilled with the idea, and he hurried to the front of the keeper's house. He quickly ran around the corner as Courtney was coming out the front door. Down on the pier, Shane saw three people. Two of them were men, and one of them a child. The men were alive, and the child was not. A large, deep-sea fishing boat turned away from the pier and raced out into the sea.

Shane's excitement at a possible rescue vanished.

"Stay up here, Cort," Shane said, motioning for the young woman to stay back.

She gave him a nod and Shane ran down the slight rise to the pier. He held his horror in check as the child, a boy with a pipe, pulled his hand out of one man's stomach. As the stranger collapsed to the pier, the boy advanced on the second man, who backed up, holding his hands out in front of him.

"Stop!" Shane yelled, his boots hitting the wood of the pier.

The boy turned, grinning around the stem of the pipe. Behind him, the man turned and ran, diving into the ocean.

Shane watched as the boy's shoulders slumped and he turned fully to face him. The boy took his pipe out of his mouth, pointed at Shane, and said, "You've ruined my fun, you have!"

"Have I?" Shane asked, catching a glimpse of the man swimming away. "Let me call him back."

"The other? I think not. He's too afraid, he is."

The swimmer dipped beneath a wave and didn't appear again.

"And," the boy grinned, "he didn't swim out far enough. Not nearly. There are a few of us in the rocks beneath the waves. He's joined them now."

119

Shane forced his thoughts away from the drowned man, glanced at the man lying on the pier and saw he wasn't dead. Severely injured, but not dead.

"What's your name?" Shane asked.

"Ewan," the ghost said, and he spoke a sentence in a different language.

Gaelic, Shane realized, translating it quickly.

Shane replied in the same. "I would have to argue, Ewan. I *do* know who my father is."

Ewan's eyes widened, and then the boy grinned. Still, in Gaelic he said, "So you speak the mother tongue, do you?"

Shane nodded.

"It is a pleasure to hear it," Ewan said, smiling pleasantly. "Never did I expect to hear it again. I have been here a long time, Shane Ryan."

"You know my name?" Shane asked, keeping an eye on Ewan as he took a small, careful step towards the downed man.

"We know your name here," Ewan said. "We were told to expect you."

Shane stopped and looked at the boy. "Told by whom?"

"By Dorothy, of course," Ewan said. "She knew you were coming. I wouldn't worry about the man behind me, Shane. He's not long for this world, although he shall be in mine soon enough, don't you know it?"

"What did you do?" Shane asked softly, hoping the boy was lying.

"I pushed and pulled, prodded and poked," Ewan said in a sing-song voice. "I rearranged a few things. To be honest with you, Shane, I'm surprised he's still breathing air."

"Is there no way to save him?" Shane said.

Ewan shook his head. "And it is not his fate to be saved. Fear not, each of us has our destiny. His is to be here, with us."

"And what is mine?" Shane asked.

"None of us have heard about your fate, Shane. Not even Dorothy. But she would like to pretend she has," Ewan said with a wink. "Now, if you will excuse me, I have a bit of a schedule to keep."

Before Shane could react, Ewan turned around, took hold of the man on the pier, and dragged him into the ocean.

Shocked, Shane could do nothing more than watch as the man vanished into the depths.

What the hell is going on here? Shane wondered. He remained there for another minute until he heard Courtney calling his name.

Shaking his shock off, Shane turned and made his way back up to the keeper's house.

Chapter 21: A Phone Call is Made

"So," Uncle Gerry said, sitting down and smiling at her. "What's new with you?"

Marie Lafontaine shrugged, relaxed, and said, "Not much."

"Have you seen Shane lately?" her uncle asked, a falsely innocent note in his voice.

"I did, as a matter of fact," she replied, frowning. "Why do you ask?"

"No reason," he said, dropping a hand to his dog's head and scratching the German Shepherd between the ears. "None at all."

"You wouldn't be pushing to have us start dating again, would you?" she asked.

"Would I ever do such a thing?"

"You would," she answered, "and you have."

"I thought you two would get along well together," Uncle Gerry said.

"We do, and we did," Marie said. "We're not compatible."

"You make it sound like a chemistry problem," he said.

"If you want to boil it down, Uncle Gerry," she said, sighing, "that's exactly what it is. We like each other. We have a good time when we go out. I don't want to date him. He doesn't want to date me. Even if we did, and if we got married, there is no way in hell I would live in his house. Pretty certain he won't leave it either."

Uncle Gerry harrumphed, took a drink of coffee, and shook his head. "Too bad. I'd like to see you married, someday."

"How about I just shack up with someone for a while?" she asked teasingly.

He rolled his eyes. "Don't get me started, Marie."

She chuckled and said, "Back to the first question, yes, I saw him earlier this week. You know Amy bought the lighthouse, right?"

"Your cousin on your father's side?" Uncle Gerry asked.

Marie nodded. "Yeah. She had a little bit of trouble with her contractor and Shane said he'd help her out."

"Has he said how it's going?" her uncle asked.

"No," Marie said. "I have to call Amy in a little bit. They're supposed to keep in touch with one another. No cell phone reception on the island, so they're using e-mails."

Turk, her uncle's dog, stood up and looked patiently at Gerald.

"Really?" Uncle Gerry said. "I just poured my coffee."

"Why do you talk to your dog?" Marie asked. "You know you sound crazy, don't you?"

"What do you want me to do?" he replied, putting his mug down on the coffee table. "He asked to go out, you want me to ignore him?"

Marie shook her head as her uncle stood up, wincing slightly.

"Come on, Turk," Uncle Gerry said, motioning to the dog. "Let's go."

Turk walked slowly behind her uncle, and soon she heard the back door open. She took her cell out, pulled up Amy's number, and dialed it.

After two rings, her cousin answered.

"Hey, Marie!" Amy said cheerfully.

"Hey Amy," Marie said, grinning. "Any word from Shane?"

"Hold on," Amy replied. "I'm just getting to this morning's emails. Had a late start to the day."

Marie listened to the clack of fingers on a keyboard, then Amy said, "Okay, here we go. Hm, looks like there's nothing going on. He says he's checked the house, and the shed. No ghosts yet. Shane also said he'll be checking the lighthouse itself. He'll shoot me an email as soon as he finishes up with it.

"And," Amy said happily, "I'll send you a text as soon as the email comes in. You worried about him?"

"Of course," Marie replied, surprised.

"You two a couple or something?" Amy asked slyly.

Marie found herself blushing. "No, Amy. Christ, you and my uncle Gerry are absolutely terrible about Shane."

"Even without his hair, he's a pretty good-looking guy," Amy said, snickering.

"Lay off," Marie said. "Anyway, you'll shoot me a text?"

"Guaranteed," Amy replied.

"Great," Marie said. "Thanks, Amy."

"No," Amy said, "thanks for sharing him. I really appreciate what you're both doing to help me out."

"You're welcome. I'll talk to you soon," Marie said. She ended the call and put the phone away. From the back of the house, the rear door opened and the click of the dog's claws on linoleum could be heard.

Uncle Gerry and Turk came into the room, resumed sitting at their previous seats, and her uncle said, "Were you talking to someone, or was I hearing things?"

She grinned. "No, you weren't hearing things. I gave Amy a quick call. Shane's fine."

"Good," Uncle Gerry said. He leaned back into his chair, saying, "Tell me, what's new and exciting in this fair city of ours?"

"Nothing," she said. With a sigh, she began to tell him about the rise in gang violence and drug-related crimes.

Chapter 22: Feeling Isolated

Scott had never felt so alone before. Not even when he had been forced to sleep in the musty old sub-basement of the Upsilon-Upsilon House when he was a pledge.

Courtney was asleep on the kitchen floor. Scott sat on the countertop, and Shane stood in the doorway of the living room. The older man lit a cigarette, inhaled deeply, and then let out a long, steady stream of smoke.

Didn't even ask to see if I minded, Scott thought angrily.

Shane looked at him, and Scott turned his head quickly.

"Come on," Shane said. "Let's go out front."

The tone of the man's voice told Scott it wasn't a request, but an order. A command from a man who seemed to have been used to commanding.

Angrily, Scott got up and followed Shane outside. Once in the cool, night air, Shane gestured for Scott to sit down. Scott sat on the front step and glared at Shane.

Shane's face was a perfect mask of calm. His eyes shined in the starlight. The anger in the man's gaze forced Scott to swallow nervously, his own emotion subsiding. He lowered his eyes, cleared his throat, and asked, "Why'd you want me out here?"

"Because we need to talk," Shane answered.

"About what? 'Cort?'" Scott said, spitting out the last word.

"It would be best if you calmed down," Shane said softly. The deadly seriousness in the man's voice made Scott swallow uncomfortably. "Do you understand me?"

Scott nodded.

"Good. This is not about Courtney. Whatever is going on between you two, is just that; something going on between the two of you," Shane paused a moment as if allowing Scott to comprehend what he had said. "This is about the three of us, this island, and the ghosts who are here. I want to move us out of the house and into the lighthouse soon. I don't trust the house anymore, not with Dorothy living upstairs. I'm not certain as to who's in the lighthouse, but we'll move in and find out."

"Dane was killed in the lighthouse," Scott said in a low voice.

"Yes," Shane agreed. "And Eileen was killed in the house. Got five other ghosts in the basement, one on the second floor, and possibly one in the lighthouse. Let's not forget there are at least three dead from the pier. There are ghosts and bodies all over this damned island. I would feel better about going into the lighthouse. If you want to stay in the keeper's house, then I'll give you some supplies, and you can wait it out there."

"I will. I'm not leaving the house for anything. I don't want to be in the lighthouse. It's where my best friend died. What about Courtney?" Scott asked, finally looking up at Shane again.

Shane shrugged. "I think she's a smart woman. She'll make up her mind and go where she thinks is best."

A spark of hope ignited within Scott. He straightened up. "When are you moving into the lighthouse?"

"In a bit," Shane said. "I'm going to try and get a hold of the owner again, see if the internet connection is back up."

"I don't even know why it would be out," Scott said angrily. "Even without any phone service we should be able to go online."

"Regardless," Shane said, finishing his cigarette and rubbing the butt out on the ground. "I'm moving in. First, I'll divvy up the supplies."

Without another word, Shane slipped past Scott and returned to the house. Scott sat on the front step, looked out at the haze in the sky, and smiled.

She'll stay with me in the house, Scott told himself, nodding. *I know she will.*

Chapter 23: Getting Worried

Shane still couldn't access the internet. The laptop wouldn't power up. And neither would his phone. He stood in the kitchen, both of the devices on the counter, and he tapped his fingers lightly. The urge to light up another cigarette was strong, but he resisted.

God forbid I run out of the damned things, he thought.

Courtney snored suddenly and opened her eyes tiredly. She blinked several times, then rolled over and went back to sleep.

Shane smiled at her.

Her presence alone made him happy, which was strange.

And she's way too young, Shane thought, shaking his head. It felt odd to be attracted to someone her age. He let the thought slide away and focused on the task before him. He needed to get his supplies into the lighthouse. Above him, he heard noises, and he wondered if Dorothy or the naked Mike Puller might wander down the stairs again.

Why will the lighthouse be safer? he asked himself.

Because Dorothy's not here, and she's the worst one around.

He looked at the stack of MREs on the counter. Adding them to the food he had brought, between the three of them, they had enough to last four days.

If we stretch it, he added silently.

Bottled water had been found in the basement of the lighthouse. All they needed to do was either wait for Amy, or whoever she sent, to rescue them from the island.

"Shane?" Courtney asked tiredly.

He turned and smiled at her. There were sleep lines on her right cheek, from where she had rested her head against his rolled up sweatshirt.

"Hey," he said. "How are you feeling?"

"Like I've been thrown down a flight of stairs," she answered, yawning. Then, in a darker tone, she asked, "Where's Scott?"

"Living room," Shane answered. He took a bottle of water out of his bag and handed it to her. She nodded her thanks, opened it, and took a long drink.

When she had finished, she asked, "What's going on?"

"I'm getting ready to move my stuff into the lighthouse," he replied.

"Why?"

He explained his reasons quickly and at the end she nodded. "I'll go with you."

"You don't feel safe here?" Shane asked.

She shook her head. "Not to sound corny or anything, but I feel safer with you."

He felt his face go red, and she smiled at him.

Scott walked into the kitchen. He looked coldly at Shane, then he turned his big, lovestruck eyes to Courtney.

The affection was not returned.

Whatever feelings she had for him before this are gone, Shane realized.

"Shane's moving into the lighthouse," Scott said. "You and I are staying here."

"I think you're a little confused," Courtney said. "You're staying here, and Shane and I are going to the lighthouse."

"I figure we can set up a—" Scott paused, furrowed his brow and said, "I'm sorry, what did you say?"

Courtney repeated herself.

Scott's face went nearly purple with anger. His eyes, rage-filled, moved rapidly from Courtney to Shane and back to the woman.

"You can't go with him," Scott sputtered, nearly choking on his words.

"I can," Courtney replied, getting to her feet. "And I will. If Shane says it's not safe here, then it isn't safe here, Scott. Not only does he know a lot more about this stuff than we do, but he's also the only one who's been able to do something about it."

"So that makes him more of a man than me?" Scott snarled.

Shane kept a careful eye on the young man.

"No," Courtney answered. "It means we should stick with him because he knows what he's doing."

"I'm not going in there with some twisted, bald psycho," Scott spat, "and definitely not with any whore!"

Shane stepped forward. Scott raised a fist, swung clumsily at him, and Shane blocked it easily. A casual movement of his left arm and Scott's punch bounced haphazardly away.

Shane's punch was not clumsy, and Scott didn't block it.

The blow was delivered precisely, and with the barest amount of power to let Scott know he had been hit. The younger man's head snapped back, his teeth clicking together loudly. Scott stumbled into the living room, but Shane didn't follow.

He stood in the doorway, his hands held loosely at his side.

"Are you done?" he asked as Scott straightened up. A small trickle of blood leaked out of Scott's right nostril.

"You hit me," Scott said with surprise.

"You tried to hit him!" Courtney yelled.

"Shut up!" Scott said, stepping forward and pointing at her.

Shane reached up and took hold of Scott's index finger.

"Stop it," he said softly to the young man.

"You and your whore—"

Scott didn't finish.

Shane bent the finger back sharply, causing the young man to screech and collapse to his knees, arm above his head. Shane was close to breaking the digit, but he held back.

"Scott," Shane said, relaxing the tension.

Scott looked up, tears of rage and pain mingling freely in his eyes.

"Are you listening to me, Scott?" Shane said.

Grimacing, Scott nodded.

"Good," Shane said. "Now I want you to understand something, in case you haven't figured it out on your own. I do not appreciate you calling Courtney names. Is that understood?"

"Yes," Scott replied through clenched teeth.

"Excellent," Shane said. "Here's a little information for you. I served in the Marines for twenty years. I did some exceptionally bad things. And I liked them. I liked them a lot. I can hurt you in ways which will never show, and I can cause you pain you can't even imagine."

Shane bent the finger back a hair's breadth and Scott whimpered.

"Do you believe me, Scott?"

"Yes," the young man whispered.

"I'm glad." Shane let go of Scott and the young man instantly cradled his injured finger. "I'm going to leave you enough food and water for several days. If I hear anything about someone coming to take us off of this island, then I will tell you. If you're in trouble, come on over to the lighthouse, or yell for me. If you get afraid, come on over to the lighthouse. I won't hold a grudge."

Scott got to his feet, glared at both Shane and Courtney, then he turned and left the house by way of the front door.

Shane went back into the kitchen, where Courtney was already dividing the food.

"I'm sorry," Shane said.

"Don't be," Courtney said, giving him a grim smile. "He's a jerk."

"Fair enough," Shane said.

In silence, they prepared to go over to the lighthouse.

Chapter 24: In the Waterman

George Fallon sat alone at the bar of the Waterman. He had finished three bottles of Budweiser, and three double shots of whiskey. Behind him, the lights of the wharf glowed brightly against the night sky. A few regulars were in the bar, but there was a new bartender, some young guy that George had never seen before.

George didn't look at him too much.

He'll cut me off soon, George thought dully. *And then what'll I do?*

He couldn't drive the image of the kid on the pier out of his head.

George couldn't forget about how he had abandoned his friends.

Are they even alive? he wondered. *What did I do?*

The bell over the entrance rang, and George glanced into the mirror behind the bar. Around the bottles of top-shelf liquor, he saw an attractive blonde woman walk in.

George couldn't be bothered with her, though. He needed another drink.

He looked up to the bartender, but the caution in the kid's eyes told George he'd be lucky to get a seltzer water.

"You look like a drinking man," the blonde said as she sat down next to George.

He nodded and straightened up a little. She smelled of sweetness and roses.

"What are you drinking?" she asked him.

"Whiskey with a beer chaser," George answered.

She smiled and let out a light, beautiful laugh. "I like the sound of that."

She raised a perfectly toned and tanned arm, gesturing for the bartender. The young guy hurried over.

"Hello," the bartender said, smiling. "What are you drinking tonight?"

"Give me a pair of whiskeys and two beers. Whatever you have on tap," she answered, putting a small purse on the bar.

The young guy frowned and said, as politely as he could, "Miss, I was about to shut him off. He's too drunk to drive anywhere."

"Don't worry about that," she said, almost purring. With a delicate hand, she opened her purse, took out several twenties and handed them over. "I'll be taking him home tonight. And I don't need the change."

The bartender, George saw, was no fool. He nodded, got the drinks, gave George and the woman a pleasant smile, and went down to the other end of the bar.

She raised her whiskey and George did the same.

"To new friends," she said, and they clinked their glasses together.

He knocked the drink back and was impressed to see she did the same.

"So," George said, taking a drink of beer, "what's your name?"

"Let's have a little mystery, right now," she said with a wink. "My only question for you is, do you have a boat, and is it big?"

George let out a laugh, finished half of his beer and said proudly, "Sweetheart, ain't nothing small about George Fallon."

"I was hoping you'd say something along those lines," she said, grinning. "Drink up, George, then maybe you can take me out on your big boat."

George finished his beer, and she signaled to the bartender for another round.

Things are looking up, George thought drunkenly.

The bartender set another whiskey in front of him, and George smiled as he picked it up. All thoughts of Vic, Eric, and even the little ghost were gone from his mind as he looked at the woman beside him.

Yes, George thought, knocking it back. *Things are looking up.*

Chapter 25: In the Lighthouse

Shane didn't like the lighthouse. Granted, he disliked the keeper's house more, but the lighthouse was a close second.

Courtney felt the same way.

"You okay?" he asked her.

She nodded, her gaze traveling up the stairs. "Do we need to go up there?"

"Maybe tomorrow night," Shane answered. He sat down beside her, draped his arms over his raised knees, and looked up to where the young man, Dane, had been killed.

"Why tomorrow?" Courtney asked. "Why not today?"

"I'm hoping someone will come and check on me in the morning," Shane said. "I haven't checked in since I arrived."

"And if they don't come?" Courtney said.

"Then I break the lantern," Shane said. He fished out his cigarettes, lit one, and blew the smoke away from her.

"Why not now?" Courtney asked.

"It's too risky," Shane said.

She was silent for a short time before she said, "Because if you shatter the light and there's already a rescue crew on its way, they might not be able to get to us."

He nodded. "Exactly. If we break it tomorrow during the day though, whoever monitors the light on the mainland will send a boat out immediately. It has to be standard procedure because the lights are always on, they have to be for safety. Which means there has to be a boat on standby at all times. More than likely, a Coast Guard patrol boat. Maybe even a cutter. But there'll be one ready."

"And they'll take us off the island," she said softly.

"I hope so," Shane said.

"What about the bodies?" Courtney said, looking at him. "Eileen's neck was broken. Dane was ripped apart."

"I'll deal with the fallout of their deaths," Shane said, the cigarette trembling in his hand briefly. "I don't want to go to prison for a couple of murders I didn't commit, but I'd rather be alive than dead and trapped here forever."

"You think that's what happens?" she asked softly.

"I do," Shane said. "When I was up there, the ghost who killed Dane said he needed help to clean the lighthouse. I'm assuming that was why he killed Dane."

"What? Like some undead indentured servant?" she asked, her voice quivering with a hint of revulsion and fear.

"Exactly."

"What if he needs more?" she asked, trembling. "What if one isn't enough?"

Shane reached out a hand, and Courtney took it.

"We're in here together," he said softly. "We'll be okay. We know what to look out for."

She hesitated and then asked, "What about Scott?"

"Scott has a choice to make," Shane said gently, without any malice. "He can come and be safe with us, or he can sulk in the keeper's house. It's really his decision."

"Yeah," she whispered. "You're right."

Courtney leaned against him, pulling his arm up and around her shoulders.

"What do we do now?" she asked.

"Now," he answered, "we wait to see what happens, if anything."

"Do you think it'll be a quiet night?" she asked hopefully.

"No," he said with a shake of his head. "I think someone will come in, and they'll be coming for us. Maybe more than one of them. But we'll be okay."

"How do you know?"

He kissed her forehead lightly. "I know."

She nodded her acceptance of his statement, closed her eyes, and rested her head against his chest. Shane enjoyed it. He felt strong, but he knew the dead were coming and he needed to be prepared.

Of that I have no doubt, he thought, sighing.

Shane tugged the knuckledusters out of his back pocket, slipped them on, and flexed his fingers.

The girl fell into a light and fitful sleep, waking occasionally to look around and adjust her position.

Shane remained awake.

He chain smoked, careful not to drop ashes on Courtney. The base of the lighthouse was cool, the bricks and stones stained with age. Gallons of water were stacked along one portion of the wall, various tools and equipment a little further along.

Who'll pay us a visit tonight? he wondered. *And how many?*

What's Scott doing? Shane thought. *Will he survive the night?*

Chapter 26: In the Keeper's House

Scott had literally backed himself into a corner. He sat on the floor in the kitchen, knees pressed against his chest. He was able to see into the living room and out the back door from where he was.

Shane and Courtney had taken the only light with them. Every few seconds, the house lit up with the glow of the rotating lantern in the lighthouse.

Scott shivered, not from the weather, but from the steady creak of the floorboards above him. He wasn't alone in the house.

Stop, he thought, staring at the ceiling. *Oh God, won't you please stop walking?*

He pictured the woman, Dorothy, and how easily she had killed Eileen.

She's going to come down here and kill me, Scott thought, panic building up within him. *I know she is. She's going to do the same to me. She's going to pop my eyes and snap my neck. Or worse. Oh, Jesus! It's going to be worse.*

Go to the lighthouse, he thought. *Go. Just go. No shame. Shane told me I could. Even Courtney wasn't being a jerk. Just go. Go. Go!*

Scott hyperventilated as he sat in the kitchen, staring at the ceiling. He let his legs go slack, and he tried to stand up. As soon as he did, the noises above him changed.

The footsteps paused, then they moved away.

Towards the stairs, Scott realized, scrambling to his feet. *She's coming down.*

Trying to get a handle on his fear, Scott turned to the back door. He had left it open to make certain he could run if he needed to.

Yet as he looked at the exit, a small boy blocked the doorway. The child was thin, see-through, a wicked apparition. As the dead youth stepped into the kitchen, the door slammed closed behind him.

"No," the boy said gently, "you'll not be leaving this way. Not tonight, no."

The stairs groaned with an unseen weight.

I can make it to the front door, Scott told himself, each breath shallow and nearly futile. He took two small steps towards the living room, and when the boy didn't follow, Scott's courage was bolstered. He turned his back to the ghostly intruder and hurried into the living room.

As he entered it, the naked ghost of the man who committed suicide grinned at him.

"It's not so bad here, Scott," the man said, taking a step forward. "You'll like it here. I know I do. Oh, the promises she's made. You'll do your time like I'm doing mine, but when it's done. When it's done, Scott, yes, *then* we'll have our glory."

Scott stifled a scream and raced for the front door, he shoved it wide open, stumbled over the threshold and fell face first into the grass. He got back up and let out a shriek.

Dane stood before him.

His friend wore the clothes he had died in. The shirt was slashed open diagonally, and his belly was sliced open the same way. Scott could see into his friend's stomach. He could see the intestines, gray and bloated like a hideous, coiled worm.

Dane winked at him and asked, "Why are you running, Scotty?"

Scott tried to answer, to form words, yet his lips only trembled.

"You know what they say about running, don't you, Scotty?" Dane asked pleasantly.

Scott could only shake his head in reply.

"They say not to," Dane said. "And do you know why?"

"No," Scott whispered.

"Ask why?" Dane said, grinning.

"Why?"

"Because you'll die tired," Dane said. He laughed, shook with pleasure at himself. Scott turned and threw up as his friend's intestines spilled out onto the ground. Hot bile splashed onto Scott's hands and forearms. The thick beef stew he had eaten cold from the MRE was hot and stinking in front of him. When he looked up, he saw Dane's ghostly innards on the ground.

Scott scrambled backward, got to his feet and looked around desperately. The naked man was in the doorway to the keeper's house. Behind Dane was the lighthouse.

The lighthouse, Scott thought frantically.

I need to get to the lighthouse.

Dane wasn't going to let him by. Scott could see it in his dead friend's eyes.

Scott looked over his shoulder and gasped.

Eileen was only a few feet away. Blood trickled down from beneath her misshapen eyelids. Her neck was wrong, something off about the way she held her head. Her dead lips spread into a wide smile before she said, "How do I look, Scott? Still pretty enough for your best friend?"

Scott tried to run, but his feet became tangled up together. He fell, hit the ground hard, and rolled down the small hill towards the pier. As he rolled, he caught sight of others on the pier. Twenty of them, maybe more.

He flung his arms out, managed to stop himself and got up, his stomach aching and his head pounding. His eyes locked onto the door of the lighthouse, and he launched himself towards it.

A terrible cold slammed into him, knocked him to his knees and swarmed, over him. Hands pulled at his limbs, his clothes. Yanked his hair out of his head and smothered his screams as the breath was stolen from his lungs. Hardened fists slammed into his flesh, sought out the soft parts of his body and punished him, relentlessly, without mercy.

Scott could hardly think, and part of his mind screamed for the solace of unconsciousness. No such peace was granted.

When he felt as though he could bear no more, it ended.

The cool grass caressed his face, and dimly Scott realized he was naked. Completely stripped of his clothing.

He shivered uncontrollably, a piercing cold pulling at his nerves, threatening to pull each delicate, sensitive tendril from him.

"Look at me."

Scott lifted his head and saw Dorothy. She stood before him, her face hard and impassive. There was no hint of sympathy. No whisper of mercy.

Through her, he could see the lighthouse, the tall structure was a place of sanctuary.

And I said no, he thought, tears welling up in his eyes.

Dorothy bent down and reached for him.

Scott closed his eyes and managed a hoarse scream as she pried open his mouth, and tore the lips off.

Chapter 27: Listening to Things Best Left Unheard

Courtney slept through most of it, thankfully.

She lay on the stone floor of the lighthouse, her head on Shane's lap as he drank his whiskey straight from the bottle. He moved it out of the way as she sat up swiftly, her eyes wide and full of horror.

"What was that?" she asked, all vestiges of sleep gone from her.

"Scott," Shane said. He capped the whiskey and put the bottle down.

"What are they doing to him?"

"Torturing him," Shane said bitterly.

She looked at him, her face pale. "We need to do something."

"All I could do now," Shane said, "is kill him, if I could even get close enough. There are too many of them."

"What?" she said. "I thought there were only a few."

Shane shook his head. "I looked out when I heard his first scream. There's at least thirty, maybe more by now. I can't be sure."

"Oh my God," she whispered. "Is there any way we can stop them from getting in? From getting to us?"

"I don't think so," Shane answered. "Our best bet maybe my knuckledusters, but I wanted to poke around the tools and see if there's anything which could help."

"Okay," Courtney said, standing up. "Let's look."

Shane got to his feet and walked with her to the pile of equipment left behind by the unfortunate Mike Puller.

Most of what they found was fairly common. Nail gun, compressor, and nails by the thousands. For nearly twenty minutes they moved aside the different tools and supplies.

"Look at this, Shane," Courtney said.

"What's that, Cort?" Shane said, glancing over.

Beneath a pile of boards was an old, short bookcase. On it was a few stacks of books and the old photo albums the Victorians had favored. Shane walked over, squatted down, and looked at the volumes. Most of the titles dealt with ships, maritime law, and coastal soundings. Three of the books were ledgers, taller and thinner than the others and with the marbled boards so common for the time. Two of the leather bound books were photograph albums, each equipped with a pair of brass hinges and matched clasps to keep the covers closed.

Courtney took one of the albums and sat back, opening it while Shane slipped one of the ledgers off of the shelf. He stood up and opened the book carefully. It smelled of the sea, and old, dry paper. The ruled green, horizontal lines, bisected by double red lines on either margin, were filled with neat, orderly sentences.

It's a journal, Shane realized. The first entry was September 9th, 1881.

"Oh Jesus Christ, Shane," Courtney whispered. She held the album up for him to see.

A glance at the sepia toned image showed a pair of children. Twin boys, each dressed in short pants and ruffled shirts. Between them was a woman, dressed in a long, dark dress, eyes closed and propped up in a casket between them.

Mother, was written beneath the photograph.

Shane turned over several of the heavy pages. Each page had a single photo. The others in the images were all alive. He opened the album to the center and stiffened.

"Cort," he said softly, handing it back to her.

She took it, looked at the photo it had been left open to, and quickly closed the album. Courtney's lips were pressed tightly together, and she swallowed several times before she managed to say, "Dorothy."

Shane nodded.

Courtney put the album back on the shelf. She took a deep breath, let it out slowly, and then asked, "What have you got there?"

"Someone's journal," he replied.

"Whose?"

"I don't know," Shane said. He looked at the front-end paper and found only a stamp for a bookstore in Concord, New Hampshire. At the end of the book, on the last page, he saw a name and an address. He read them both out loud,

"'*Dorothy Miller, Squirrel Island Lighthouse, Maine.*'"

"Shane," Courtney said, concern heavy in her voice.

"Yes?" he asked, closing and tucking the book beneath his arm.

"Why are you smiling?"

Shane hadn't realized he had been. As soon as she pointed it out, his smile spread into a grin. "This is what I need."

"Why?" Courtney asked.

"It'll tell me what I need to know—" he began, but a pounding on the door cut him off.

His heart thudded in his chest, and he handed the book to Courtney.

"Stay behind me," he said.

She slipped behind him, resting a small hand on his back.

The hammering on the door continued.

"Who is it?" Shane called out.

The knocking stopped.

"It's Scott."

"What's going on, Scott?" Shane asked calmly.

"I'd like to come in," the young man replied.

"I don't know about that," Shane said.

He doesn't believe he's dead, Shane thought. *He doesn't believe he can just come in.*

"Why not?" Scott asked, a confused tone in his voice.

"I'm pretty sure you're dead, kid," Shane answered.

Scott hesitated before he said, "No, I'm not."

"Think about it for a while," Shane said, kindly, "and then get back to me in the morning."

"What if they come for me?" Scott said.

"They already did."

"I'm not dead," Scott said softly, his voice barely audible through the door.

Sadness crept up into Shane's heart, and he said, "You are, Scott. I'm sorry, kid."

A plaintive wail ripped through the lighthouse. Silence followed, and after several minutes, Courtney put her head against Shane's back and cried.

Shane turned around, took her into his arms, and guided her to the wall. They sat down, and Shane comforted her as best he could.

Chapter 28: Whiskey and Bad Decisions

George was drunker than he had been in a long time. It helped him forget about Vic and Eric. And the blonde cougar on his arm aided as well.

She kept him steady and on his feet as they wandered down Main Street towards the marina. The touch of her hand on his arm, the power of her scent, the alcohol he had consumed, all of it made him giddy. Continuing on down the road, she guided him, gently but firmly.

"What's your name again?" George asked, impressed at how little his words slurred as he spoke.

She gave him a wink. "Mystery."

"'Mystery?'" George repeated, chuckling. "That's a hell of a handle. Why'd your parents name you that?"

Mystery laughed, shook her head and told him, "You are a funny man when you drink, George."

He straightened up with the compliment. *Nobody's told me I was funny before. I must be, though. Mystery's the best.*

Ahead of them, George caught sight of the gate to the marina. Powerful street lights illuminated the newly painted white boards and the salty smell of the Atlantic, always strong, hammered through his drunken nose. The rich, intoxicating scent of the salt water made him grin.

"What's the smile for?" Mystery asked.

"The ocean," George said. "I love it. Always have."

"Do you work it?" she asked.

George shook his head and nearly knocked himself over, but Mystery's surprisingly strong grip kept him from falling.

"Nah," he said, "I'm in construction. You know. Hammer. Nails."

"Hammer? Nails?" She leaned in and whispered into his ear, her breath hot against him. "Sounds suggestive, George. Where's this boat of yours?"

"Right this way, sweetheart," he answered, wobbling as they reached the gate and opened it.

The small gatehouse, tucked off to the right and in a deep shadow, suddenly glowed with light.

Both George and Mystery stopped, the woman turning her head away and putting a hand up to block the harsh glare which threatened to blind them both.

George was too drunk look away. He merely squeezed his eyes shut.

The door hinges of the gatehouse screamed as it was opened.

"George?" Dell Fort called out. "Is that you?"

"It is," George snapped. "Turn the damned light out, Dell."

A moment later, the partial darkness returned, and George opened his eyes.

"Christ, George," Dell said angrily, "it's after two! Why the hell aren't you at home?"

Dell's sentence ended when he stepped closer and saw Mystery on George's arm, her head still turned away.

"Ah, hell," Dell muttered. "Go on in. Keep it quiet, though, alright? The McCormicks are in their boat. Those old farts complain if someone answers a phone call after nightfall."

"You got it, Dell," George said, grinning.

Dell waved them on and turned away.

Mystery pulled George close and murmured, "I almost thought our night was ruined."

A thrill raced through George, and he breathed heavy as he answered, "No one's ruining it. I'll take her out, away from shore. McCormicks won't complain then."

"I was thinking the same," she said softly.

George staggered down the pier towards *Terminal Fleet*, his steps misguided by equal parts of alcohol and lust. Mystery's hold on his arm quickened his pace.

Chapter 29: Close to Dawn

Courtney awoke, hungry and miserable. She lifted her head off of Shane's lap and sat up. He closed the ledger he was reading and smiled softly at her.

"How are you feeling?" he asked her.

"Terrible," she replied. She could smell whiskey and cigarettes, sweat and concern, which she found strangely comforting.

"Understood," Shane said. He picked up a bottle of water and passed it over to her. "Rinse and spit out the first mouthful. The rest will taste better."

"Spit where?" she asked, opening the bottle.

He grinned. "Anywhere you like, Cort. We won't be here much longer, one way or the other."

A chill raced through her at his words. She did as he said with the water, and found he was right. She drank all of the water quickly.

"You've figured a way out?" she said softly. "Or are we out of luck?"

"A way to stop Dorothy, and the others," he said. "And I'll be smashing the absolute hell out of the lantern if I can't do what I'm planning."

"How are you going to stop her?" Courtney asked.

Shane lifted up the ledger. "With this. All three of them, actually. Everything she was, she wrote in here. And when she was afraid someone might read her words, she wrote Latin. She was a smart woman. Angry, but smart."

"You read Latin?" Courtney asked, surprised.

"Yup," Shane said, smiling. "Lots of other languages too. But what she wrote in Latin, is the key to the power over her."

"What do you mean?" Courtney asked.

"Here," Shane said, opening the ledger up. He flipped through several pages, stopped and said, "Let me read this to you,

"We have been here too long. Far too long. Ione has left us. The willful girl, and I doubt I shall see my eldest daughter again soon. This leaves me with the task of caring for

my beastly husband and the remainder of our wretched children. My father will not survive long. He will move on to the next world, either by God's will or by my hands."

A painful terror gripped Courtney's empty stomach, and she whispered, "She planned her father's death?"

"His, and the death of her children. Her husband as well," Shane said. "She hid the bodies. Both to avoid punishment and out of shame. There's more. Revelations about past sins, and those she wished to commit. By hiding them from all others, even in her private thoughts, she's shown there is a power over her through them."

"What are you going to do?" Courtney said.

"Find her and bind her to the physical world," Shane said.

"What then?" Courtney asked.

"I'll break her," Shane said. "Break her and cast her to Hell, because I'm pretty sure she's headed there when all is said and done."

He set the ledger down, grabbed an MRE, and opened it, passing it over to her. She dumped it out onto the floor in front of her, spotted a package of crackers and another of peanut butter.

"Breakfast of champions?" she asked tiredly.

"You've no idea, Cort," Shane said, smiling. "I ate those damned things for years, out in the field. And when you're hungry, and you can't stand the sight of them, you still choke it down."

She tore open the peanut butter, ate some of it from the small container, and then said, "You're a strange man."

"Me?" he asked, surprised.

"Yes, you," she said. "Here you are, retired military and ghost hunter, and you read Latin."

"More than just Latin," he said in a voice suddenly tired and worn.

"Really?" she said, opening the crackers. "What else?"

"French, Spanish, Portuguese, Russian, Greek, German," Shane said. "And a whole lot more than that."

"How can you read all of those?" she asked, surprised.

"Read, write, and speak," Shane said. "I don't know how, exactly. Languages are easy. I hear it, and I can speak it. And if I can read it, then I can write it."

"That's amazing," Courtney said. "What do you for work? I mean, you can't be a full-time ghost hunter, right?"

"Right," Shane said, smiling. "I'm a freelance translator. Plus, I have my pension from the Marine Corps, in the end, so everything's working out pretty well. Even this."

"What do you mean?" Courtney said, her heart fluttering.

"I got to meet you," Shane said softly. "I wish there wasn't so much death around us, but I'm pleased we met. Exceptionally pleased."

"Me too," Courtney said, and she took out a cracker to eat, her smile too big to hide.

Chapter 30: Seeing the Sunrise over the Atlantic

George felt as though a thousand little fists were hammering against his head. His mouth was painfully dry, and when he tried to move, he found he couldn't. He cracked open an eye, but the sun was breaking the horizon, filling the Atlantic with its powerful light.

I'm on the boat, he realized dully.

He tried to move again and was able to roll over onto his back. Blinking he tried to focus, and he saw he was on the deck. In the chair so recently occupied by Vic, sat Mystery.

Even after sleeping in her clothes, and on board a Boston Whaler, she was stunning. She sat with her legs crossed delicately and sipping from a bottle of water. When she saw he was awake, she adjusted her mirrored sunglasses and smiled at him with full, red lips.

"Good morning, George," she said pleasantly.

"Morning," he replied grumpily. In spite of his efforts to sit up, he couldn't. Something held him back. *I'm so hung over.*

"You, my fine, fat friend," she said, grinning, "can drink a lot of whiskey. I was impressed. I thought for certain I'd have to roll you out to your boat, but you made it."

George closed his eyes. Licked his lips, swallowed once to try and moisten his throat, and then said, "Where are we?"

"We are windward of Squirrel Island, looking at the back of the lighthouse and the keeper's house," she replied.

George stiffened and kept his eyes shut. "You're kidding, right?"

"Not at all," Mystery said happily.

"Why the hell did I bring us out here?" he asked with a groan.

"You didn't," she said. "I did."

George opened his eyes and looked at the woman. "Why, in God's name, would you do that?"

"Afraid, are you?" she asked, her voice taking on a dangerous calm.

"No," George lied.

"Of course, you are," she said softly. "You left your friends out here to die. You know it."

Did I talk when I was drunk? he thought frantically. *Good God, what did I say?*

His panic must have shown because Mystery laughed, a pleased and joyous sound.

"No, you fat, cowardly drunk," she said, smiling. "You said nothing. Well, at least not about the lighthouse. No, not a word. But I know."

Terror took over him. "I know all about your abandonment of your two friends," she said. "I agree, they were stupid not to have gotten back into your boat. Your own effort, perhaps, should have been greater, to get them to go away with you. And, failing to do so, you should have remained."

Her face went hard as she leaned forward. "You should have remained. You have caused me a great deal of inconvenience, *George*, and you shall suffer for it."

"I didn't do anything," he said, his voice was hoarse with fear.

"Liar," Mystery said, lounging back in the chair. "Liar, liar, liar. You'll get yours, though, George. You will indeed. I expect her to be here soon. Very soon."

"Who?" George whispered.

"My great-grandmother," the woman said sweetly. She adjusted her sunglasses, tilted her head back slightly and said, "Watching the sun rise over the Atlantic is always an occasion to treasure. Always."

George writhed on the deck, trying to get up.

"Give it up," she said, yawning. "I've trussed you up like a Thanksgiving turkey. You won't be going anywhere. Not until she arrives and decides what to do with you."

"What will she do with me?" George whispered.

"If you're lucky," Mystery said, smiling softly, "you'll drown and be on your way."

"And if I'm not?"

"If you're not," she said, the smile fading away, "you'll drown and be here until the end of time."

Book 2: The Lighthouse

Chapter 31: Risking a Look

Shane stank.

His body smelled of old sweat and fear. Although he had managed to clean up a little with some wet-wipes he had brought along, it hadn't made much of a difference.

She doesn't smell, he thought, looking at Courtney.

He pulled out a flameless heater from an MRE and prepped a bag for coffee.

"You look like you know what you're doing," Courtney said, coming over and sitting down next to him.

"Looks are deceiving," he said with a grin. She had been crying again earlier, but it was to be expected.

I'll worry if she doesn't cry, he thought.

"Not in your case," she said confidently. "Everything you are is right out front, isn't it?"

Shane could tell the question was rhetorical, but he nodded in agreement anyway. "I don't see a need to hide anything. Not anymore. I played things pretty close to the vest for a long time. Can't really tell your friends the house you lived in killed your parents."

Her eyes widened, and she said softly, "Oh my God, I'm so sorry."

"Don't be," Shane said, sighing, "it was a long time ago."

He shook the bag with the coffee in it and added water to the flameless heater's bag. Once the chemicals in the heater reacted, he slipped both the containers into a cardboard sleeve, propped them up against the wall at an angle, and relaxed a little more.

"Did you sleep at all?" Courtney asked.

"A little, here and there," he said.

"How much is a little?"

"Maybe an hour altogether," Shane said. He tried not to think about how tired he felt.

"Do you want to sleep now?" she asked.

"No," he said, shaking his head. "It would only make it worse. Better to stay up until everything is done."

"What do you want to do after the coffee?" Courtney said, glancing over at the door.

"Take a walk," Shane replied. "I want to see if we can find some more iron somewhere."

"Where would we find iron?"

"We'll take a quick look around the house," Shane said. "Then we'll go down by the pier. We'll do it together, though. They may be a little cautious around me, and we'll have to work with what we have."

"Yeah," Courtney said, "I'm not leaving your side, Shane."

"Glad to hear it," he said, smiling. "Coffee's about ready. Want some?"

"God yes," she said, sighing.

Shane poured the brew out into their sole cup and handed it to her.

"Thanks." She blew on it to cool it down, took a sip, and winced. "Damn, that's strong."

"We need it to be," Shane said. "Sometimes, when we were out in the field, and we were all jonesing for a caffeine fix, we'd take the instant coffee from the MREs and use the crystals like they were chew."

"I have no idea what that means," she said, grinning.

"You know, chewing tobacco?" Shane asked. When she nodded, he said, "Well, we would stick a pinch of the instant between our gum and cheek. Sort of suck the caffeine out of it."

"Sounds absolutely disgusting," Courtney said.

"It was," Shane said, smiling as he remembered. "But you do what you need to do."

"And what we need to do today is find iron?" she said.

"If we can," Shane said, nodding.

"What if we can't?"

"Hope like hell that we can," Shane said with a shrug of his shoulders.

Together they drank the coffee, ate some less-than-appealing breakfast, and got ready for the day. Shane gave Courtney one of his clean t-shirts to wear and politely turned his back while she changed. She extended him the same courtesy while he switched out all of his clothes.

"Ready?" Shane asked her, his hand on the latch.

She nodded.

"Remember, we go everywhere together."

"Got it," Courtney said grimly.

"Okay."

Shane took a deep breath and opened the door. The sun had come up only a short time before, and the wind was stronger than it had been. The waves were in a frenzy, the whitecaps mad as they danced along the breadth of water between the mainland and the island. The pier and the stones suffered beneath each wave.

Shane stood still and looked out at the island.

He saw nothing out of place. No one walking around, no ghosts waiting for them.

"Alright," he said, glancing back at Courtney.

His eyes widened.

What remained of Scott stood behind her, and smiled at Shane.

Chapter 32: In for Rough Weather

The Boston Whaler pitched and rolled with the ocean. The waves were getting larger, and George could see them from his position on the deck.

She'll be swamped soon, George thought, depressed.

The mystery woman was either unaware of the danger or didn't care. She continued to lounge in her seat. He could see the knuckles on her hands whiten as the boat rose up, and then followed the curve of a wave down.

"How are you feeling, George?" she asked pleasantly, no hint of concern in her voice.

He didn't respond.

"Oh, you don't want to talk now?" she said, laughing. "I couldn't get you to shut up last night. The promises you made."

George kept his comments to himself. He was afraid. Not of her, but of whatever was coming from the island for him. He had no doubt about it. Somewhere, something was on its way.

And I'm going to die, he thought.

Mystery stood up suddenly, a triumphant smile on her face. She retained her balance and poise as the boat rolled with the waves.

"Great Mother," she said respectfully, taking off her sunglasses.

Without knowing why George twisted to see who the woman spoke to.

A middle-aged woman, her face harsh and severe, had arrived, somehow. Her hands were clasped loosely together in front of her, and she looked disdainfully at George.

George's heart lost all sense of rhythm, beating erratically as he looked through the new arrival. The edges of her body had no clear sense of definition, and the world beyond was disturbed, as though by a gossamer curtain.

George struggled as panic flooded him, and his frantic efforts brought a cold smile to the Great Mother's face.

"His fear is palpable," the new arrival said. "You've done well, girl. Exceptionally so. Soon we'll have enough to put the lighthouse to right."

"Thank you, Great Mother," Mystery replied, a sense of awe in her voice. "Do you require more?"

"A few. Just a few."

George continued to struggle, his hands and feet numb from hours of being bound. All of his attempts were useless. Finally, he let out a cry and closed his eyes as he gave up.

"Bring him to the island," the Great Mother said. "I must put the newest of the help through their paces."

The Whaler's engine started up, and George felt the boat begin to move. He risked a look and opened an eye. He saw Mystery at the helm, her back was to him.

"I'm sorry, George," she said over her shoulder, and there was no true note of sympathy or apology in her voice. "You will not be drowned today. Something worse, I'm sure, but at least you won't be drowned."

George shuddered.

I'd rather drown, he thought miserably. *Dear God, please kill me now.*

God didn't answer, and George began to weep.

Chapter 33: Uninvited and Unwanted

Shane closed the door carefully, never taking his eyes off of Scott. Or rather the horror which had been Scott. The dead had mangled the young man. His clothes were gone, but he wasn't naked. It was worse.

Scott was nothing more than a bloody sketch of what he had been prior to his death. His eyes were gone. Destroyed sockets seemed to stare at Shane. He had been flayed, all of the muscles laid bare for the world to see. Teeth were broken, shattered remnants of what they had been. Each finger was a twisted horror, a nightmare idea of what the digits should be.

What did they do with the body? Shane wondered. *Did they drag it down into the ocean after? Did they stuff it down amongst the rocks for the crabs and fish to eat?*

"Why'd you close the door?" Courtney asked, confused. "I thought we were going out."

"We will be," Shane said, keeping his eyes on Scott as he answered her. "Cort, do you trust me?"

"Yes," she said, frowning.

"I'm going to tell you to do something, and I need you to do it exactly as I say. Do you understand?" Shane asked.

She nodded, fear replacing the confusion.

"Good. Without looking around, I want you to sidestep to your right and never take your eyes off of me. When you reach the wall, sit down, close your eyes, and keep them that way until I tell you to open them."

He saw her swallow nervously, but she did as she was told. Shane kept his attention fixed on Scott. Finally, he said, "How are you, Scott?"

The destroyed visage focused on him, and the mouth moved as Scott said, "I won't lie, Shane. I have been a *whole* lot better."

"Kind of figured that out," Shane said. "Are you in pain?"

"No," Scott answered. "Got to tell you, it wasn't pleasant."

"I don't imagine it was."

"Thanks for opening the door, by the way," Scott said cheerfully. "For some reason, I couldn't get through it last night."

"Why are you here?" Shane asked.

"I've come for the little whore," Scott said, laughing. "Dorothy wants you. Wants you all to herself. And, from what I hear, she's going to make an *example* out of you. I'm really looking forward to watching that."

There was no more joy in Scott's voice, only hatred.

"Oh yes," the young man said softly, "I will enjoy watching you suffer. Watching you die. There's been some talk of keeping you on, but I hope she won't. I hope she sends your rotten soul straight to Hell."

"She might," Shane said. "You really can't rule anything out."

"No, you can't," Scott said, nodding in agreement. "Anyway, I've come to get Courtney."

When Scott turned his head to look at her with eyes no longer there, Shane attacked. He threw himself across the short distance which separated him from Scott. He brought the knuckledusters smashing down on Scott.

The young man screamed a sound of pure rage which instantly gave Shane a headache. Scott disappeared, and Shane lost his balance, tripped, and slammed into the thick wall of the Lighthouse. He knocked over some of the equipment but caught himself before he fell.

"Courtney," Shane said, standing up and looking at her. "He's gone now."

She opened her eyes, anger and fear combined within them. She got to her feet and went to Shane. Her body shook, her face was pale, but she exuded strength.

"Where did he go?" she asked.

"To wherever they hid his body, I'm assuming," Shane said, flexing his hands and letting out a deep, shuddering breath.

"I need something to protect myself with," Courtney said. "I need it now."

Shane nodded his agreement. He turned his attention to the lighthouse door. The latch was iron. The hinges were iron.

He went to a tool bag set on the floor by the bookcase.

"Are we going to go into the house to look?" Courtney asked.

"No," Shane said, pulling the bag open and rummaging through it. "Look at the door."

"What about it?"

"The hinges, the handle. Hell, even the straps on the boards, they're all made of iron," Shane said, shaking his head at his own ignorance. He took a pry-bar and a two-pound sledge out of the bag. He carried both over to the door and looked at the hinges.

"Pinions," he said, pointing at them.

Courtney's smile was cold and knowing. "They'll pop right out."

"Yup," he said. He fit the edge of the pry bar beneath the lip of the pin on the first hinge and banged it out. He did the same with the other two hinges, handing all three of the pins to Courtney. Then with the door held in place only by the latch and luck, he put the tools down and took the door out of the frame. He set it against the inner wall and examined it.

The wood was old but still strong.

This'll take some work, he sighed.

"What's wrong?" Courtney asked.

"Nothing," Shane said, smiling at her. "Hold onto those pins, alright?"

"Sure," she said. "Are we putting the door back up?"

"No," Shane said, shaking his head. "I'm going to get one of these hinges off, try to make you a club of some sort."

Courtney nodded. She examined the pins and then asked, "So, think these would work too?"

"In a pinch," he replied. "I'd rather you have something with a little more reach. I don't think they're going to come at us individually. They'll probably swarm. Dorothy's not stupid, she'll have seen we have at least a little iron. That'll keep her about as honest as possible. Which isn't much."

"No," Courtney said bitterly, "it's not."
"Alright," Shane said, picking up the sledge. "It's going to get loud."
Courtney smirked. "That's how I like it."
Shane laughed, caught off guard. "Okay, then. Sounds good to me."
He lifted the sledge and brought it down hard on the door.

Chapter 34: The Forecast

With her morning run finished, Marie was in her den. She was stretching and cooling down as the news played out on the small television. The forecast was calling for high winds, possible rain, and thunderstorms, with a high-wave warning for the coastal communities.

She frowned as she straightened up. *It's been too long without any word from him. Or from Amy about him,* Marie thought.

Calm down, she told herself. *Amy said she'd let you know as soon as she heard from him.*

You could always call her. There is rough weather coming in.

Marie nodded to herself, went to her coffee table, and picked up her phone. She dialed Amy's number, but after three rings, it went to voicemail. Marie left a message asking her cousin to call back.

Still holding her phone, Marie went and sat down on the edge of her couch. She turned up the volume on the television.

A yacht had been found drifting off the coast of Maine. The anchor line had snapped, and the Coast Guard was out looking for the crew. No one had been reported missing, but the yacht had left its berth three days earlier. According to the news report, the boat had been spotted anchored close to Squirrel Island, but that had been the last reported sighting.

Marie frowned.

An abandoned yacht, last seen near Squirrel Island. Where Shane Ryan is investigating the ghostly connection to a suicide.

Jesus Christ, she thought, *Amy better get back to me soon, or I'll be going up there myself.*

The idea of being on the ocean again churned her stomach.

I can't leave him out there. And what if the crew is there, too?

Marie turned off the television, got up, and went towards the bedroom. She needed to shower and get to work. In her head, she calculated how long it might take to charter a boat out to the Squirrel Island Lighthouse.

Chapter 35: An Unexpected Guest

The weapon was ugly. A length of board cut down to roughly two feet. One end was wrapped tightly with strips of one of Shane's t-shirts. The head of the bludgeon was a pair of hinges, beaten and battered into shape.

"Swing it," Shane said, stepping back after he had handed it to Courtney.

The muscles in her forearms stood out as she lifted it up into the batter's position. She set her feet, her mouth set grimly. She took a deep breath and gave a swing that made Shane's eyes widen with appreciation.

"Damn," Shane said, chuckling. "You would have hit it out of the park."

She winked at him, lowering the weapon. "Played softball in high school, and at Rivier University in New Hampshire."

"It shows," Shane said. "How does it feel, though?"

"Rough," she said. "Wouldn't want to try and hit a ball with it, but I think I can crush anything that steps up to me."

"Good. You've got the pins still, too?"

She nodded. "Back pocket."

"Okay, keep them there. If you lose the cudgel, use those. One in each hand," he said.

"Got it."

He picked up the last item he had made. It was the third hinge, bent into a crescent shape. He had threaded strips of cloth through the nail holes and made a rough pair of knuckledusters for his left hand.

"So," Courtney started to say, and then she stopped. She pointed out the open doorway and Shane turned to look.

A boat was at the pier.

Is it the same boat from yesterday? Shane wondered dazedly. *Did he come back for his friends?*

"Should we go down there?" Courtney said cautiously. "It's the same boat as yesterday."

"Is it?" Shane asked.

Courtney nodded. "*Terminal Fleet.* I saw the name."

He caught sight of a woman wearing sunglasses and a large hat, her blonde hair pulled into a ponytail. She was also wearing what looked like an oversized man's sweatshirt. For a moment, she ducked down, and when she came back up, she was dragging a man. A man whose hands and legs were bound behind his back. She pushed him over the side of the boat, and Shane heard his body thump on the wood of the pier.

"Oh Goddamn," Courtney hissed. "They'll kill him."

Shane nodded and led the way out of the lighthouse. With Courtney at his side, he jogged down, keeping an eye out for the dead. Inwardly he groaned as the boat's engine shifted gears and it peeled away from the pier.

"Shane," Courtney said.

He turned partially and saw Mike Puller. The man closed in on them, and when he was close enough, Courtney swung.

Mike shrieked as the head of the cudgel connected, the man vanished.

Courtney grinned. "It works."

They picked up their pace, and soon their feet were pounding on the pier. When they reached the bound man, Shane dropped to a knee, took out his work knife, and flicked it open with one hand. The stranger's arms and legs were zip-tied, and Shane cut them away quickly.

The man whimpered, rolled onto his side, and looked up at Shane.

"We're going to die," the stranger whispered.

"That's a given," Shane replied. "But let's make sure it's not today."

He helped the man to his feet, the stranger grimacing. Shane let the man lean on him, and he said, "Ready, Cort?"

She nodded and led the way back to the lighthouse.

Thankfully, they were left alone.

Chapter 36: At the Marina

Dell Fort was tired and in a decidedly bad mood.

Frankie McCrory had called in sick for the first shift, which meant Dell had to cover for him.

I'm so tired, Dell thought, dumping three packets of sugar into his fresh coffee. He added cream, put the container back into the mini-fridge in the gatehouse, and glared out the front window. He had the gates unlocked and open. A few of the natives had been in to check on their boats and there were too many of the summer folk for his liking.

They pay the bills, Dell, he reminded himself. With a sigh, he took a drink, winced at how hot it was, and put his mug down. Movement caught his attention, and he looked down at the end of the marina. George Fallon's new Boston Whaler, *Terminal Fleet,* was coasting into its berth.

Dell smirked. George had been out all night with his lady friend. Dell waited, hoping to catch sight of her.

"Dell!"

The sharp, waspish voice of Mr. Webb forced Dell to turn away from Fallon's boat and look out the front window. Mr. Webb, gangly and unkempt, per usual, held up his monthly bill.

"What is it, Mr. Webb?" Dell asked. Long ago, he had given up trying to be polite to the man. Webb was a colossal pain, no matter how nice Dell was.

"You raised the berthing fees again," Mr. Webb snapped.

"Mr. Webb," Dell said patiently, "I didn't do anything of the sort. The Marina Association did, though. They raised the berthing fees for everyone. Not just you."

"I didn't think it was just me," Mr. Webb said. "And I know it's you."

Oh, Jesus, Dell thought, *why the hell did Frankie have to call in sick today?*

"Mr. Webb," Dell said, "if you'd like to lodge a complaint you'd be better off writing a letter or sending an email."

"Don't you tell me what to do, Dell Fort!" Mr. Webb yelled, his voice rising to nearly a shriek. He shook the bill at Dell, turned around, and stomped off to the beat-up Ford station wagon he drove. Dell watched as black smoke billowed out of the car's exhaust and Mr. Webb puttered out of the parking lot.

The man has more money than God, and he complains because the Association raised his berthing fee by ten dollars a month, Dell thought.

His inner monologue was interrupted by another person, but this one came from the pier. It was a woman, her blonde hair pulled back in a messy ponytail and a large, tan fisherman's cap on her head. She wore mirrored sunglasses and a dark blue sweatshirt that was way too big for her. The hem of the shirt hung down to the mid-thigh of her khaki capris. Her hands were tucked into the front pocket of the sweatshirt.

When she passed by the gatehouse, Dell saw "Fallon Construction" in white letters on the back of the pullover.

Dell shook his head as she passed through the parking lot and up Marion Street. He glanced up the marina, but he didn't see any movement on board the Boston Whaler.

Must have been one hell of a night, Dell thought. He took up his coffee, took a sip, and winced. *Still too damned hot.*

Chapter 37: At Squirrel Island

The man's name was George Fallon, and he was scared to death.

With good reason, too, Shane thought.

Courtney sat beside Shane, and George was across from them. He had deep marks on his wrists from the zip-ties. He had drunk nearly a gallon of water, and he constantly looked out of the open doorway.

"You said there's wood around here?" George said finally.

Shane nodded. "Round the back of the house, there's a pile of lumber for the construction work."

"Yeah," George said. "Would make sense. Mike wouldn't have rented a boat to go back and forth each day. Would have cut into his profits."

"Why are you asking about wood?" Courtney asked.

"I'm in construction," George answered. "All of Mike's tools are in here. Lumber's out back. I can build a door."

"It won't do much good," Courtney said. "Doors and walls don't stop them."

George's shoulders slumped, and he sighed unhappily.

"Who was the woman?" Shane asked. "The one who dumped you here and stole your boat?"

"Don't know," George said. "Met her in a bar last night; thought my luck was changing, especially after what happened here. We got drunk, she asked me for a ride on the boat, and I said yes."

"But why did she bring you here?" Shane asked.

"She said her great-grandmother was upset that I had gotten away," George said, his voice dropping to a whisper. "They're supposed to kill me."

Shane stiffened. "Her great-grandmother?"

George nodded.

"What did the woman look like?" Shane asked.

"You saw her," George said.

Shane shook his head. "Not really. Tell me."

George described her. "Attractive, blonde, tanned. Good walk, great laugh."

"How old?" Shane asked, his voice tightening.

"Forties, maybe?" George said. "Can't really remember too well, right now."

Shane stood up, anger pulsing through him. He walked over to the tools, picked up the two-pound sledge, and went to the stairs.

"Shane," Courtney said, "what are you doing?"

"I'm going to go smash the lantern," he said, starting up the steps.

"Why?" she said. "I thought we were going to wait and see if they were coming for you today."

"They're not," Shane said.

"How do you know?" Courtney asked.

Shane paused and looked at her.

"I know," he said angrily, "because the woman that dumped George on the island is the same one who hired me in the first place. No help is coming, Courtney. Not from her."

Gripping the handle of the sledgehammer tightly, Shane made his way up the top of the lighthouse.

Chapter 38: Reassurances

Marie Lafontaine looked at the ID on her phone when it rang and saw it was Amy.

"Hello?"

"Hey, cousin!" Amy said cheerfully. "I'm sorry I didn't answer the phone when you called. The damned thing never even rang."

"Everything alright with it?" Marie asked, leaning back in her chair and closing the file she had been working on.

"Yes," Amy answered. "It's Squirrel Island. The reception is terrible."

"What's going on out there? How's Shane?"

"He's looking devilishly handsome," Amy said, laughing. "I didn't think a man could be completely bald and still be attractive, but he is."

Marie shook her head and rolled her eyes at her cousin's antics. "You've always been too much, Amy."

"Says you," Amy said cheerfully. "Anyway, your fine-looking friend, Mr. Ryan, is not only rooting out the problem of the ghost but doing some fine construction work as well."

"That's a relief to hear," Marie said, and she meant it. She felt a weight slip off of her shoulders. "I was afraid I'd sent him into something he couldn't handle."

"Nonsense," Amy said. "He's a strapping young man."

Marie laughed. "Amy, he's as old as we are."

"You wouldn't know it by looking at him."

Marie sighed. "Cousin, you're too much. Anyway, so he's doing okay, then?"

"More than okay," Amy replied. In a serious tone she said, "Marie, I'll let you know if anything goes wrong. But he's doing well. He's a little upset about not having an internet connection, but other than that, everything is going exactly as planned."

"I'm glad to hear it," Marie said. "When are you picking him up again?"

"Two more days," Amy said. "He said everything should be wrapped up by then. Do you want to meet me here and we'll pick him up together?"

"Yes, I'd like that," Marie said.

"Then it's set," Amy said. "I'll talk to you tomorrow, and we'll make all the plans."

"Great."

They ended the call, and Marie returned to her work. She whistled to herself and felt far better than she had before.

Chapter 39: Calling for Help

Shane was angry.

A deep, chilling anger which he nursed and cared for. He ground his teeth and made his way to the top of the lighthouse. He switched the two-pound sledgehammer from his left hand to his right, the grip awkward with the protection he wore on his hands.

Can't risk taking it off, he thought, squeezing the wooden shaft of the tool tightly. *Too dangerous.*

When he had reached the lantern, he examined it closely.

So many people saved by such a simple idea, Shane thought. He raised the sledge and swung it with all of his strength. The lens shattered easily, reflective material exploding outward from the force of the blow. Shane breathed deeply, then struck it twice more.

He brushed fragments of glass off of himself, frowning at tiny nicks and scratches on his arms from the flying debris. Still holding tightly onto the sledgehammer, Shane went down and joined Courtney and George. Shane dropped the tool onto the floor, kicked a few shards away, and sat down next to Courtney.

"What the hell did you do that for?" George asked, confused.

"Coast Guard must monitor the lighthouses, right?" Shane said.

George nodded. "Yeah. They monitor all of them. It's a federal offense to mess around with them."

"Good," Shane said. "It's the only chance we have for getting off this island alive."

Comprehension brightened George's eyes. "They'll send a boat out to see what happened."

Shane nodded.

"Still, you're probably going to end up doing some time for the vandalism," George said, grinning.

Shane smiled. "More than happy to. That means I'll be alive."

"Don't worry," Courtney said, reaching out and taking his hand. "I'll come and visit."

"Fair enough," Shane said. "That alone, makes it all worthwhile."

"Ahoy the lighthouse!" a voice called from outside.

Shane let go of Courtney's hand and quickly stood up. Two long strides carried him to the open doorway, and he looked for the speaker.

Clark, the lighthouse keeper, stood a short distance down the path. Dane was beside him, a terrified expression on his face. Both men were difficult to see in the bright morning light.

"Mr. Noyes," Shane called back. "What can I do for you?"

"You can first let me compliment you on your manners, my Marine," Clark said cheerfully. "Ever polite you are. Well done, sir."

Shane inclined his head slightly. "Many thanks. Now, back to my question, if you will."

"Ah, yes," Clark said, nodding. "Business. My wife, Dorothy, well she has laid a claim on the man who has come to you this morning. A relative of ours brought him here specifically for my wife. You've no right to keep him from her."

"I have every right," Shane said coldly.

"You'll not send him out, then?" Clark asked, frowning.

"No," Shane said, shaking his head.

Behind him, Shane heard George let out a shuddering breath.

"Anything else, Mr. Noyes?" Shane asked.

"Yes," Clark said, his voice going cold, anger creeping into it. "I see you went ahead and broke my light."

"I did."

"Will you be repairing it?" Clark demanded.

"Of course, I will see it is repaired when I reach the mainland," Shane answered.

"Damn your eyes!" Clark snarled, taking a step forward even as Dane shrank back. "Do you have any idea of the danger you're putting those ships and crews in?"

"I do," Shane said.

"You're a monster," Clark hissed.

Shane laughed, surprised at the comment. "Ah, Mr. Noyes, at least I didn't condemn a boy to an eternity of servitude to care for a flashlight."

"It's a lighthouse, you twit," Clark said, his voice low and thick with anger. "And it needs to be cared for."

"It will be," Shane said, all humor gone. "You'd best run along to your mistress now, Mr. Clark. Go be about her business since she won't let you be about yours."

"My mistress has plans for you, Shane Ryan. She will teach you to have a civil tongue, or she will take it out." Clark turned and walked to the keeper's house, Dane following quickly behind him. Once they had disappeared into the small home, Shane left the doorway and returned to his seat.

"They were dead," George said after a minute.

Shane nodded.

"The lighthouse keeper," Courtney hissed, her voice filled with both anger and bitterness, "and the others, they've murdered everyone."

"Shane," George said, his voice thin and fearful. "What's going to happen?"

"We're going to fight," Shane answered. "First, I need some more coffee. Then I need to read the rest of Dorothy's journals. I need to know more; I need to know her better."

"Who is she?" George asked. "And why the hell do you need to know her better?"

"She's the one in charge," Shane said. Courtney started to help him prepare the coffee. "I need to understand her better so I can figure out how to destroy her. Hey, we've got powdered cream and sugar from an MRE, if you want a cup of coffee."

Dazed, George nodded.

Shane whistled the Marine Corps hymn as he worked beside Courtney, her hand occasionally brushing his.

Book 2: The Lighthouse

Chapter 40: Bad News

Amy pulled on an old t-shirt and a battered pair of shorts after she had taken a quick shower. She had washed off the stink of the bar, the sweat of George, and the dirty smell of the Marina. In the bathroom, she ran the hair-dryer and then unplugged it before she wandered tiredly out to her bed.

With an exaggerated sigh, she flopped down, adjusted the pillows and wondered if she would be able to get any sleep. She was excited.

Everything is nearly done, she thought, closing her eyes and smiling.

The locket on her chest suddenly felt like an ice-cube against her skin.

"Oh Christ!" she shouted, jumping up off of the bed pulling the chain up over her head. Pain screamed through her hand as she cast the locket onto the bed, the latch springing open and the bit of broken mirror, within the metal, started gleaming.

Dorothy appeared in the room, her dead face shrouded in a mask of silent rage.

"Great Mother," Amy whispered, backing up nervously and sitting down in the chair at her vanity.

"Child," Dorothy said, no affection or care in her voice. "I am displeased."

Panic wormed its way into Amy's heart. "What is it? What's wrong? What did I do?"

A small smile appeared on Dorothy's face. "You accept blame. And for that, you are forgiven. So few can do so."

A minor tremor of relief passed through Amy, and she whispered, "What have I done wrong?"

"You left too quickly," Dorothy said, the smile vanishing. "Shane and his young woman rescued the man you left for me. They are within the lighthouse. The keeper is in a rage for they have broken the light.

"And you know what shall happen without the light?" Dorothy asked, her voice growing cold.

"Nothing," Amy whispered. "Nothing will happen."

Dorothy nodded. "I will continue to be bound to the island, restricted to these brief excursions. I will not have enough souls to thrust me forward, to release me. I *need* the dead. I do not believe I can stress this enough, Child."

"I know," Amy whispered. Then she frowned and said, "The light. Why would they break the light?"

Dorothy looked at her coldly. "What do you think will occur when the lighthouse does not shine this evening?"

"Oh God," Amy said in a small voice as she straightened up. She felt panic rise up within her throat.

I'm going to fail her! she thought frantically. *I can't fail her! I can't!*

"Someone will come," Amy moaned. "They'll be rescued!"

"Stop it, then!" Dorothy commanded. "This may be only a way for me to reach out and speak to you, but I promise, there are many other ways in which I can hurt you. And I will, in my own time."

Amy swallowed dryly, nodded and said softly, "I will, Great Mother."

Without a word or a gesture, Dorothy vanished. Amy's body trembled, and it took her a few minutes to gather up the courage to stand up and walk to her bed. Her hand shook as she picked up the locket and held it tightly in her palm.

The small piece of jewelry had passed through generations to her.

I will not fail you, Great Mother, Amy thought, closing the locket. It was no longer bitterly cold, only cool and comforting as she slipped it back over her neck. *The lighthouse will be restored, and we will be great keepers again.*

She climbed onto the bed, pulled a sheet over her, and sighed.

I've got a couple of hours, she thought. *Get some rest, then find the Coast Guard and have a little chat.* She smiled, closed her eyes, and let herself search for sleep.

Chapter 41: Seeking the Way

I have played at this game for far too long. Five children with that witless oaf. The only child worth a damn gone to the mainland. And who can blame her? Certainly not I. And my hated father, the proverbial albatross about my neck. Would that he had gone down with his ship off the Grand Banks. A watery grave would have been best, and might still be if I can break my oafish husband of his sentimentality.

Fool.

Perhaps one day he will read these journals. Will he be intelligent enough to understand half of what I've written? A third? A quarter?

Yes, perhaps a quarter. But I distract myself with my complaints. I must remain focused on my task. I must not be distracted; it will lead to my ruination.

The oaf must be convinced of the danger the children present. And my father as well. He may balk, and if he does, he shall join them. I've no qualms about manning the lighthouse on my own; I have done so with a new babe in my arms and the oaf drunk with his damnable rum.

Can you imagine it, dear journal? A silent house? A well-kept house without the noise of children or old men? No husband to dirty the sheets. No children to scream for more food. No father to ask for help to the outhouse.

See the lighthouse, her brass gleaming, her bricks white and red so the world will see and know of the danger.

No child suckling at the breast. No husband's rough pawing. No father demanding fealty.

None of it.

None of it.

None of it!

Shane closed the journal. It was nearly noon.

Courtney was stretched out by the tools, her mouth partially open as she slept. Her long lashes kissed the skin beneath her eyes. Her short hair was disheveled.

Beautiful, Shane thought. He put the journal down, took out his cigarettes, and lit one. He tilted his head back a little, exhaled towards the ceiling, and then looked to George.

The younger man sat a little back from the doorway, staring out at the ocean. He had a small cudgel in his hands, the top of it studded with iron nails pounded out of the remains of the lighthouse door. Shane noticed how the man had lost his dazed look, a hard expression on his face.

"George," Shane said softly.

The man looked at him, his eyes dark and haunted.

"How are you holding up?" Shane asked.

George shrugged. "Got nothing to compare it to. Part of me doesn't even believe any of this garbage is real. I mean, come on, ghosts? But then there's the part of me that saw everything, and it's saying, 'Don't be stupid, Stupid.'"

Shane chuckled, nodding. "Yeah. It's a little rough."

"You seem to be doing pretty well with it," George said, looking back out the front door.

"Well, I also grew up in a haunted house," Shane replied.

"Things went bump in the night?" George asked.

"Yeah," Shane said bitterly, "and they eventually killed my parents."

George blushed, and he said, "Sorry, man."

"It's alright," Shane said, upset with himself for mentioning it. *More tired than I thought.*

"So this isn't your first time?" George said.

"No," Shane said. "Not by a long shot. I helped out on a couple of other hauntings, thought I could help with this one, too."

"These ones tougher than you thought?" George asked.

Shane nodded.

"I didn't really think the place was haunted," George said after a short time. "We, me and my friends, we had a website. Murder scenes. Suicides. Stuff like that. People ate it up. Hell, it was how I bought my boat. When we heard about Mike's suicide, we decided we'd come out, get a little video footage. Maybe some pictures of the whole place. We figured we'd do well with this one. The island being isolated and all."

"That's why you showed up yesterday?" Shane asked.

"Yeah," George said, sighing. "Vic and Eric got out of the boat, saw the kid, and started to click away. I told them to get back in the boat. I told them."

George stopped, and Shane waited patiently. Long minutes had passed before George spoke again. When he did, his voice was raw.

"I feel terrible about leaving them," George said, staring out the door. "But they didn't listen to me. And I ran. I had to."

No, Shane thought. *You didn't have to.*

But he kept his opinion to himself.

"I'm worried," George said softly. "Worried I'm going to see them here."

"You might," Shane said.

George's head snapped around, his eyes wide with fear.

"What?" he hissed.

"You might," Shane repeated. "We've already seen the new dead. But I need to see the old dead, and I may be gone for a while."

"What are you talking about?" George asked.

"In the cellar of the keeper's house are five ghosts. The children and father of the ghost, Dorothy."

"Why the hell are they down there?" George said.

"She put their bodies in the cellar after she had murdered them," Shane answered. "They'll be able to tell me more about her. If they have a mind to speak to me."

"You're going down there?" George asked.

"Yes."

"While knowing there are ghosts in it?" George said.

"Yes," Shane said. "I need everything they can give me."

"Information?" George said.

"Yeah," Shane said softly. "And an edge."

"Why do you need an edge?" George said, confused. "I thought we just had to wait until the Coast Guard shows up about the busted light?"

"We will," Shane said. "But I'm going to kill her, too."

George opened his mouth to reply, but he was too surprised for any words to come out.

Chapter 42: Light's Out

Lieutenant Sid Cristo was sitting at the desk outside of the captain's office, playing a losing hand of solitaire. He always played house rules, on the off chance he might actually travel down to one of the casinos in Connecticut, and he rarely won. The captain had been on conference calls all day with command down in Boston, and then with someone else from the Coast Guard Academy in New London.

Sid frowned as he turned over his last hand. He flipped all of the cards over, gathered them into a pile, shuffled, and laid out another game.

As he finished, the door to the office opened.

Sid looked up and was surprised to see an attractive older woman walk in. The dress she wore was short and snug, leaving little to the imagination. She gave him a near-perfect smile, closed the door, and said, "Hello, I've come to tell you there's a technical issue at the Squirrel Island Lighthouse. The contractor I have out there says the wiring may say the light is out."

The solitaire hand was forgotten. "The light's out?"

"No," she said, shaking her head but still smiling. "The wiring may say it is."

"Ma'am," Sid said, "there's no 'maybe.' The light is either on or it's out. The wiring won't send a false signal."

She stepped up closer to the desk, revealing a lot of her ample chest, and winked at him. "Well, even if it is, we don't have to worry about it, do we?"

Sid felt uncomfortably warm, his attention drawn to a locket hanging from around her neck.

"Ma'am," he said, forcing himself to look her in the eyes, "it is something we need to worry about. When the automated system does its check, it'll kick back an alarm here. We need to take care of it as soon as possible."

"Maybe," she said, her voice still seductive, "I should speak with your commanding officer?"

Sid grinned. "Ma'am, I think that would be a wonderful idea."

He pushed himself away from the desk, stood up, and walked to the commander's door. He knocked, opened it, and said, "Captain, we have a person here who wants to speak with you."

Captain Ellen Root glanced up from her desk. "Show them in, please, Lieutenant."

Sid looked back at the civilian, saw the shocked expression on the woman's face, and smiled as politely as possible. "Ma'am, Captain Root will see you now."

He managed not to snicker as she walked dejectedly past him.

Sid sat back down at his desk, looked at the hand he had dealt himself, and started to play.

Chapter 43: A Decision Must Be Made

Amy lay on her bed and stared at the ceiling. She fought the urge to chew on her fingernails, a nervous habit she'd broken herself of twenty years earlier.

Damn it, she thought, sitting up. *What am I going to do? She needs them.*

The desire to see the lighthouse controlled by her family once more burned with the intensity of a fever in Amy's breast. The power of life and death on such a grand scale. There was no greater power in the world, and she and Dorothy would ensure the family had it again. She got up and paced about her bedroom.

When the Coast Guard gets out there, George may still be alive, she told herself. *I don't have to worry about Shane or that girl who's attached herself to him. Just George. George can say I kidnapped him. Threw him there. No one will believe ghosts did any of it. But George can mess it up. He can mess all of it up.*

Amy walked to her closet, flipped on the light, and found an old pair of jeans and sneakers. The sweatshirt she had taken from George's boat lay on the floor. She picked it up, pulled it on, and then dressed quickly. She pulled her hair back in a ponytail, wrapped it around and tucked it up as a bun. A battered Boston Red Sox baseball cap kept her hair up and out of sight.

On her dresser, she found an old pair of black sunglasses and tucked them into the pocket of the sweatshirt. She went over to the bed, knelt down, and pulled her gun safe out. It was a newer model, one equipped with a thumbprint scanner. Amy pressed her right thumb down, heard the satisfying click of the lock letting go, and opened the safe.

She took the small, Glock 9mm out, removed the two fully loaded magazines and a holster, and then locked the safe again. She slid it back under the bed before she stood up. Quietly she loaded the weapon, chambered a round, and made sure the safety was on. The spare magazine went into her back pocket, the pistol into the holster, and the holster into the small of her back clipped to her jeans.

She left the bedroom and grabbed her wallet out of her purse. A quick check showed her license to carry a concealed weapon was in there and up to date. She put the wallet in the front pocket, took the sunglasses out, and put them on.

Amy looked at herself in the mirror by the front door. She didn't have any makeup on. She had washed it all off after her failed attempt at seduction in the Coast Guard's office. Without the makeup, and with her hair put up and away, she was barely recognizable.

They still might recognize you, she cautioned herself, and she nodded in agreement.

True, she replied, *but this task needs to be done.*

She took her keys and left her house. Amy had to get to Squirrel Island as soon as possible. There was a lot of killing she had to do if she was going to correct the situation.

And I have to do it before the Coast Guard gets there, she reminded herself. *Also need to get rid of the bodies. I can't forget that. The souls may remain, but the flesh must go. Yes, it must go, or else no others will be harvested.*

I need to make sure the crops come in, Amy thought, chuckling.

She grinned to herself, broke into a whistle, and made her way to her car.

Chapter 44: Going into the Cellar

"Do you have to go?" Courtney asked softly.

Shane nodded in reply.

"Will you be safe?" she said.

Shane smiled. "I don't know. I hope so. There's no real choice here, though."

"I know." Courtney was standing beside him, her arms folded across her chest as they looked out the doorway at the Atlantic. "You don't need any help?"

"I don't know," Shane said honestly. "I hope I won't, but if you hear screaming, well, I wouldn't mind an assist."

"I'll listen for you. What about him?" she asked, nodding towards George. The man was asleep, propped up between the wall and some of the construction equipment.

"Be careful," Shane said. "They want him more than they want us. I don't know why, but they do. It might just be because they're upset we brought him in here. Don't trust him, though. He'd sell us out in a heartbeat if he thought he could get home safely."

"Will you be careful?" she asked.

"I'll do my best," Shane said. "I've no desire to die here, Cort. Plus we've been having a good time getting to know each other. And I'd like to keep getting to know more about you."

She smirked at him, the tiredness and fear falling away easily, if only briefly. "I like the sound of that, Shane. Make sure you come back here alive and well."

"That's the goal," Shane said. "Alright, wish me luck."

"Luck," Courtney said. Then she reached up, took hold of his face, and pulled him in for a kiss. It was quick but full. No sisterly gesture.

Christ, am I blushing? Shane thought as she let go, his face burning.

"Come back soon," she said.

Shane could only nod, and he stepped out of the relative safety of the lighthouse.

The midmorning air was cool, a strong wind coming in from the east. The waves were still choppy, though not nearly as rough as they had been earlier in the morning.

He glanced around.

Nothing yet, he thought, and he made his way to the keeper's house. He worked around to the back of the building, saw the bulkhead was still open and walked quickly to it. At the top of the narrow stairs, he looked down at the remains of the door. Wood littered the steps and darkness waited for him.

Shane walked down into the cellar and stood in the pale rectangle of light cast by the sun. His own shadow stretched out before him.

"You're back," the grandfather said.

"I am," Shane replied.

"The children aren't here," the unseen ghost said, sadness in his voice. "Their mother came down earlier, in spite of her fear of this place, and frightened them all. They're hiding."

"I'm sorry," Shane said.

"Why have you returned?" the old man asked.

"To ask your name," Shane said, "and to hear what you would tell me about Dorothy."

"My name is Wyatt," the grandfather said. "And what would you like to know about her?"

"Whatever you can tell me," Shane responded, easing himself down into a sitting position on the floor.

"Tell me your name first," Wyatt said, the voice coming closer.

"Shane."

"Well, Shane," Wyatt said, "it is a pleasure. I've had no one but my grandchildren to speak to for a long, long time. I love them, but the conversation of children grows tiresome."

A shape glimmered and Wyatt appeared. He wore a thick, cable-knit sweater, his hair trimmed close to the sides of his head and a little long on the top. On his face, he had impressive muttonchops, the gray hair long and well-cared for. His pants were of some dark material, his shoes worn and black. The hands which extended from the ends of his sweater were large and thick.

"You look as though you are a man of action," Wyatt said as he sat down across from Shane.

"At times," Shane said.

"I appreciate that," Wyatt said, smiling. The expression faded from his face as he looked at Shane.

"I've been dead a long time," Wyatt continued, "though I'm not sure quite for how long exactly."

Shane opened his mouth to tell him the year, but the other man held up a hand and stopped him.

"I don't want to know," Wyatt said. "I'm afraid it would drive me mad, and I'm nearly there already, you see."

Shane hesitated, waited to see if the man would say any more, and when Wyatt didn't, Shane asked, "Will you tell me about your daughter?"

"Let us call her Dorothy, aye, lad?" Wyatt asked softly. "It pains me to think someone I brought into this world would murder her children and family."

"Dorothy it is," Shane said.

"Many thanks," Wyatt said. "What would you know of her?"

"Is she afraid of the cellar because of her husband, or for some other reason?" Shane asked.

"From Clark, not at all," Wyatt said, "her fear is from her mother, I'm afraid."

Shane waited.

"I was a sailor," the man continued. "Away more than I was home, it seemed, and I cannot tell if Dorothy had the devil in her, or if my wife couldn't bother to be a mother. I learned later, much later, of the punishments my wife doled out. She would lock Dorothy in the cellar for days on end. No food. No water. Starved nearly to madness. It was the only way to discipline her, so my wife said. No amount of beatings seemed to silence the girl's tongue. But the cellar, the darkness and hunger. When Dorothy was released, she was cowed. At least for a short time.

"Either way," he continued, "it seems as though Dorothy was marked. She could feign love. Affection. She could act any role you like. There was nothing in her, though. No spark. She was cold. I've known dogs with more affection than Dorothy Noyes showed the world."

Wyatt cleared his throat, looked past Shane briefly, and smiled tiredly. "It was she who convinced Clark to kill the children. How she did it, I know not. The hard truth is she did, and thus their small bodies are here with me."

Shane looked at the boxes and said in surprise, "Your bodies are still here?"

"Aye," Wyatt said bitterly. "She boxed us up and shipped us out to the mainland. We were kept in darkness, bound in a place where the children screamed and wept. Only recently were we returned to the island, although I cannot say by whom or why."

"My sister Ione," Jillian said, startling Shane as she stepped out of a shadow.

"What?" Wyatt asked, looking at his granddaughter.

The girl, no more than twelve, walked forward and took a seat beside the man. She wore a long nightshirt, the large, heavy curls of her light blonde hair falling to her shoulders. Her face was angular, the cheeks high. Jillian smiled nervously at Shane.

"My sister Ione," she said again. "It was she who had kept our bodies for Mother. Then Ione's grand-daughter returned them."

"How do you know?" Wyatt asked.

"I saw her," Jillian said. "Just once. Ione and her husband were arguing about the boxes, and about how long they would have to keep them in their own cellar."

"What did she say?" Shane asked.

"Until mother called us home," Jillian answered.

Shane looked at Wyatt and said, "When did Dorothy die?"

"I'm not certain," Wyatt replied. "Shortly after she killed Clark, she sent our bodies away."

"You should ask father," Jillian answered. "Mother bound his body with chains and cast him into the ocean, right off the pier."

"Your father's a little upset with me," Shane said. "I broke the lantern."

"He'll speak with you," Jillian said confidentially in a low tone. "He despised mother. I can remember the names he called her when he was dying. They were terrible. Even dead I blushed to hear them."

"Shane," Wyatt said, "why do you want to know?"

Shane got to his feet and smiled at them. "I want her to leave the island."

"She'll never leave," Wyatt said, shaking his head. "It is a fool's errand to try and make her. And how would you? She is much too strong."

"I'll make her," Shane said. "I may need help, but I'll make her go."

"I'll help," Jillian said softly.

"Thank you," Shane said.

"As will I," Wyatt said. "I'm sure the other children will as well. Perhaps even those who have died at Dorothy's hands."

"I would appreciate all of it," Shane said. He glanced at the door and then looked back to Jillian and Wyatt. "She threw him off the pier?"

They both nodded.

"Okay," Shane said, sighing. "I guess I'll go and talk with Clark."

"Come back soon," Jillian said shyly, "I like talking with you."

Shane nodded, smiled, and left the cellar.

Chapter 45: A Time for Action

Amy left her car in the parking garage, cut through an alley between a lobster shop and an antique store, and came out half a block away from the marina. Her disguise was simple and complete. Few people, if any, would recognize her in such plain attire.

I always dress well, she thought, smirking. *They'll never think it was me. And besides, I am on a mission. The family will be returned to the lighthouse. We will be the keepers again, even if we have to wash the island in blood to do it. Who lives. Who dies. What ships make port. All of it will be ours to decide.*

Her smirk faded as she thought of her great-grandmother, the woman hard and brutal, but driven.

She pushes me to greatness, Amy reminded herself. *She won't let me fail.*

A quick peek at the gatehouse showed it was empty, the guard probably on his rounds.

Amy relaxed slightly, set her eyes on George Fallon's Boston Whaler, and moved quickly to it. Her sneakers were almost silent on the worn boards of the dock, the pistol a warm, comforting presence against the small of her back.

When she reached the end of the dock, where the Whaler was tied up, she bent down and went about untying the line.

"Miss?" a voice said from the boat.

Amy stiffened, looked up, and saw the guard who had been on duty early in the morning. He stood on the deck of the boat.

"Yes?" she asked, smiling as she stood up. Out of the corner of her eye, she saw the line snake down and into the water. Her smile broadened.

"Have you seen George around?" he asked. "I came aboard, thinking maybe he was sleeping one off, but he's not here, and he never passed by the gate house. I'm coming up to the close of a twenty-four-hour shift. I haven't seen him at all."

"No," Amy said, "I don't imagine you have. Did you check under the seats?"

"What?" the man said, confused. He twisted to look back and when he did, Amy quickly drew her pistol.

Chapter 46: A Bad Decision

Dell hadn't made too many bad decisions in his life. Joining the Navy had been one of them. Three years of misery and chipping paint. Marrying Mollie Grace, which had been another. Turning his back on the woman who had left George Fallon's Whaler alone in the morning wasn't working out so well either.

Christ on a crutch, Dell thought, staring at the flat, black semi-automatic pistol in her hand. The weapon didn't move, the end of it fixed firmly on his belly.

Dell had seen a man get shot in the gut while on liberty in Hong Kong.

"Miss," Dell said, licking his lips nervously, "I ain't got nothing to steal."

"Step back," she said softly. She didn't wave the gun about. Instead, she made sure it stayed on him.

She'll kill me if I don't do as she says, Dell realized.

Keeping his expression neutral, Dell took a careful step backward and down. He kept his hands at his side, where she could see them.

"Take a seat," she said.

Dell did so.

She climbed aboard easily, her movements graceful. She sat down across from him, the pistol resting on her leg, but still pointing at him.

"What's your name?" she asked, smiling.

"Dell, miss."

"Dell," she said, nodding. "Tell me, can you pilot this boat?"

"Yes, miss," Dell answered.

"Fantastic," she said. She grinned pleasantly at him. "So can I. What you're going to do, Dell, is pilot this little rig out to Squirrel Island."

"Did you kill George there?" he asked suddenly.

"No," she said, laughing. "No. George is alive and well. I promise you that. I also promise you that if you pilot this boat to the island for me, everything will work out for you too."

"And if I don't?" Dell asked nervously.

"Well, Dell," she said politely, "Like I said, I can pilot this boat, too. And, in case you can't figure out what that means, Dell, it means I won't hesitate to put a couple of bullets into your chest and dump you over the side when we're windward to Squirrel Island."

"I'll bring us to the lighthouse," Dell said quickly. "No mistake about that."

"Good," she said, a smile still on her face. "Get up to the helm then and take us out. The sooner we're done, the better we'll all be."

"Yes, miss," Dell said. He stood up on stiff and awkward legs. With a painfully dry throat and his heart thundering against his ribs, Dell went to the helm.

Bring her out there, Dell, he told himself, *bring her out there and be done with her.*

Aye, he thought, *best plan there is.*

Dell started the engine and backed the boat slowly out of her berth.

Chapter 47: A Discussion

Shane walked around the front of the keeper's house, wary for any of the dead who might be wandering. All he saw was Courtney in the doorway of the lighthouse. She lifted a hand in greeting, and he waved and smiled at her.

Her smile was tight and forced.

She worries, Shane thought, turning his attention to the pier. The young woman's concern made him feel cared for, a curious sensation. Even when he had briefly dated Marie Lafontaine it had been more physical than anything else.

Focus, Shane scolded himself. He followed the path down to the pier, walked to the end of it and sat down. His legs hung over the side, and a fine mist was picked up by the wind and cast on him with each wave as it broke. Clumsily he took out his cigarettes, lit one, and enjoyed the potent chemicals in the smoke.

"Clark Noyes," Shane said, speaking towards the ocean, "can you hear me?"

"Aye, you git," came Clark's voice from behind him, "I can hear you."

Shane twisted slightly, saw Clark standing a few feet back and asked politely, "Will you sit with me, Clark?"

"Tell me why you have a mind to speak with me now," Clark said warily. "You ruined my light."

"I ruined your light," Shane replied, "because Dorothy wants the rest of us dead. And, no offense now, but I have no desire to be dead yet."

Clark nodded. "Aye, understandable."

"As for why I want to speak with you," Shane continued, "I want to know how you died."

Clark raised an eyebrow over one charred eye, then he grinned, the cracked lips twisting obscenely. "I like you, Shane, I do. And if my foul bride wants you dead, well, perhaps we can upset her a bit in that regard."

Clark walked forward and took a seat beside Shane.

The cold emanating from the ghost was highly unpleasant but bearable.

"I have to tell you," Clark said after a minute of silence, "I loved being a keeper. I enjoyed the solitude. I am not a good man, Shane. Nor am I a pleasant one. Are you looking to see remorse in me?"

"No," Shane answered truthfully. "I've known a lot of bad men, Clark. Not many as bad as you, mind you, but bad enough. And one or two worse. God judges. Not me."

"Just and true, and true and just," Clark said, nodding. "Now, you want to know how I died?"

"I do."

"My wife," Clark said, looking out over the Atlantic. "My blushing bride. My own Eve, the lover of the serpent. She killed me. Tortured me first, though I deserved it."

"How did she torture you?" Shane asked, already knowing the answer.

"The light," Clark said bitterly. "My own light. Burned the sight out of my eyes. Starved me. Bled me. Gelded me. Thus my body is now the horror you behold."

"Why are you still here?" Shane asked.

"She bound me," Clark said, his voice thick with anger. "A soul to keep the lighthouse working true. Nothing more than a slave."

"And what of her?" Shane asked. "Did she work the light after your death?"

"Not for long," Clark spat. "The coastal watch, they found her out. And she killed herself, damn her! She bound herself to the island, made sure she would be here."

"And you never were able to care for the lighthouse again?" Shane asked.

Clark shook his head. "Even with the binding of the man, Dane, she hasn't let me back in! And then you went and broke the thrice-damned light."

"I did," Shane agreed, keeping an eye on the ghost. "I did. But I've already told you, in order to be rescued. They'll be coming today, tonight the latest, to repair the lantern. And if you help me, Clark, I'll be able to shatter Dorothy the way I did the light."

Clark looked at him warily. "How?"

"You feel that anger inside of you? That hate?" Shane asked.

Clark nodded.

"I'll need some of it, the part you hold against her," Shane said softly. "The part all of you hold against her."

"And what will happen?" Clark said. "When you have this?"

"I'll break her," Shane replied grimly. "I will pull her apart and drive each piece like a nail into Hell."

Clark stared at Shane for several long minutes. Shane tightened his grip on the knuckledusters, readied his make-shift weapon, and waited.

"Can you do it?" Clark asked finally.

"I can," Shane answered.

"Have you done it before?" The skepticism in Clark's voice was thick.

"Once," Shane said, "and that little girl was a hell of a lot worse than Dorothy could ever think to be."

Clark raised an eyebrow, then a cold, hard smile crept onto his face. "The lighthouse will be mine?"

"The lighthouse and the whole damned island for all I care," Shane said truthfully. "I'll not chase you from it. I only want Dorothy, she's the one pulling the strings here."

"Aye," Clark said softly, "that she is. A mad witch playing at Fate."

In a louder voice, Clark said, "You'll have my help, Shane. For my lighthouse, and more than a bit of revenge."

"Fair enough," Shane said. He stood up. "If you'll excuse me, I have others to speak to about Dorothy."

"There are those you don't know," Clark said, standing. "They won't heed your call, nor believe you."

"Will you help?"

"To put my bride in Hell?" Clark asked, then with a wicked grin he said, "Of course I will."

The ghost vanished, and Shane was alone on the pier. He looked out at the Atlantic, saw the sun moving steadily towards the western horizon and thought, *Will they come tonight for the light? Will it even matter in the end?*

He shrugged, unable to answer his own questions, and turned to walk back to the lighthouse.

Chapter 48: An Uneasy Alliance

Courtney stood in the doorway of the lighthouse, watching Shane. The man was walking slowly along the pier, his head bent down. She had seen him speak to the ghost, and while she knew Shane would tell her what was said, she still burned with curiosity.

A grumble behind her caused her to take her attention away from Shane and to George Fallon.

The man was sitting up, yawning and rubbing at his eyes. When he lowered his hands, he nodded to her and looked dejectedly at the doorway.

"What's going on out there?" George asked tiredly.

"Shane's on his way back," she answered.

George nodded. He sighed and said, "I wish I'd never come out here."

Courtney didn't reply.

"How'd you get on the island?" he asked.

"Bad decisions," she answered. "Ones that seemed like they were good ideas at the time."

"Same here," George said.

"Hello," Shane said, stepping into the doorway and resting a hand on the small of Courtney's back.

The touch was gentle, but firm, and sent a thrill of excitement through her.

"What's going on?" she asked, her voice steady.

Shane quickly explained how Clark had agreed to help.

"I'll need to try and find some of the others," he continued. "Dane and Eileen, even Scott, if he'll listen to me."

"Will it work?" George asked, his tone one of disbelief.

Shane nodded. "What are the names of your friends?"

"Vic and Eric," George said. "But how is it going to work?"

"You're in construction, right?" Shane asked.

George nodded.

"So you know what a power converter is, AC to DC when you need the electricity in a pinch?" Shane said.

"Sure," George said. "What's that got to do with this place?"

"I think that I'm some kind of a power converter," Shane said. "Before, when I had enough information, when I had the backing of other ghosts, I was able to channel it. And that power, well it forces the dead, like Dorothy, into a somewhat physical form I can handle."

George shook his head. "That doesn't make any sense at all."

"Do ghosts?" Courtney asked. "I mean, seriously, do ghosts make any sense to you whatsoever? They shouldn't even be here, let alone be capable of hurting someone. But they are, and they do."

George didn't respond.

"Whether it makes sense or not," Shane said. "It's what happened."

"And you've done it before?" George said doubtfully.

"Once," Shane replied.

"You managed to get rid of the ghost?" George said.

"If I hadn't," Shane said coldly, "I wouldn't be here."

"How can you do something like that?" Courtney asked. She looked at the man before her as he hesitated before answering her.

"I think it has something to do with my house," Shane said slowly, seeming to pick each word with care. "I never had a great knack for languages before we moved to Berkley Street. I could speak English, of course, but nothing else. Then, the more time I spent at the house, and the older I got, the more I understood. The more I could speak the different languages. It felt like something was unlocked in my head."

"I've done research on what I did at my house," Shane continued. "There are skills, like mine, which have been recorded. Others who can channel energy. There are a few accounts online. Usually they pass along a family line. My parents didn't say anything about it, and my grandparents on both sides were dead."

"So maybe this is genetic?" Courtney asked.

"That's what it looks like," Shane said, nodding. "The stories I read talked about how most benevolent ghosts don't have a problem with people who possess my ability. It's the bad ones, like Dorothy, who really don't care for us. I don't think she's realized what I can do. I don't think she would leave me be."

"So what are you going to do?" George asked, skepticism still in his voice.

"I'm going to learn more about Dorothy," Shane said, looking at Courtney, "if I can really know her, then I'm almost positive I can do it again. Make her, well, touchable."

Courtney moved closer to Shane, tilting her head slightly to look at him. "You're going to go speak with more?"

Shane nodded.

"Do you need help?" she asked.

Shane smiled at her, teeth stained by coffee, but the smile was genuine.

"No, thank you," he said gently. "I'd rather you were here. They seem to avoid the lighthouse, although I'm not quite sure why."

"Okay," Courtney said. She looked over at George. The man was looking listlessly at the floor. To Shane, she said, "You'll be careful?"

"As careful as I can be," Shane said. He leaned in and gave her a soft kiss. "I'll be back."

Courtney nodded, her back cold after he took his hand away and left the lighthouse. She glanced at George, saw the man was still concerned with the floor, and sat down inside the doorway. The ocean stretched out beyond the island, but in the distance, she saw a boat.

It was heading toward the island.

Chapter 49: Terminal Fleet

"There's a boat," Courtney said.

George looked up past the girl, out the doorway and onto the Atlantic.

She's right, George realized. A boat was steadily making its way to the island. The closer the boat came, the more familiar it looked.

"Oh my God," George whispered.

"What?" Courtney asked.

"That's my boat," George said, recognizing the antennae array and the Gadsden flag snapping proudly off the aft of *Terminal Fleet*. "That's *my* boat!"

He got to his feet, his heart beating excitedly.

"George," Courtney said, standing up. "Didn't she steal the boat? The woman who dumped you here?"

A chill raced through him as he realized the girl was right. He was nodding when the boat got close enough for him to see the one piloting it.

"But that's not her," George said excitedly. "That's Dell! That's Dell! He's the gatekeeper at the marina!"

George raced out of the lighthouse, pushing past Courtney. He stumbled, nearly fell, but caught himself. He hurried down the path to the pier, his feet hitting the wood at the same time as Dell pulled the Boston Whaler in alongside.

"Dell!" George shouted.

Dell raised his hand in greeting, a smile of relief on his face.

Then a shot was fired, and George watched as the top half of Dell's face exploded outwards. Blood, bone, and brain sprayed outward.

Someone was screaming, and George realized he was the one making the noise.

The smile never left the ruins of Dell's face, even as he collapsed to the deck. From one of the seats, the woman who had marooned George on Squirrel Island stood up. In her hand was a small, black, semi-automatic pistol. She shook ever so slightly as the boat ran aground slightly and came to a sharp stop.

A broad, happy smile was plastered on her face, and she waved cheerfully to him.

"Hello, George!" she said, stepping onto the pier and keeping the pistol on him. She quickly made the boat fast, stretched, and said, "You have an appointment to keep with my great-grandmother. She's not one you want to anger, I might add. No, she's worse than Bruce Banner when she's angry."

She raised the pistol a little, so George was staring at it rather than her.

"No," the woman said, "let's find her, shall we? We don't want you being any later than you already are. She wants one of her newly dead to kill you, George. The dear woman enjoys watching their initiations. Tremendously."

George went to speak, but only a moan came out. A warm liquid rushed down his pants and he realized he had wet himself.

Chapter 50: Interrupted

Shane had only left Courtney a few minutes earlier when he heard the gunshot, followed by a brief, horrified scream.

All plans to meet with the dead were cast aside as he turned and ran back towards the pier. When he reached the edge of the lighthouse he paused, crept around the building, and looked down at the pier.

A boat, whose engine he had never heard, was tied up to the pier. George was there, his shoulders slumped as Amy pointed a handgun at him. A quick glance at the boat showed a body near the helm.

Shane pulled his knuckledusters off, stuffed them into his back pocket, looked around, and saw a fist-sized rock on the ground. He picked it up, found the weight to be good, and took a long look at Amy.

She and George were talking, but the wind carried their words away.

When she brought the pistol up a little higher, Shane stepped out and threw the stone. It raced through the air, a perfect, elongated arc.

With a flat crack, it smashed into the side of Amy's head. Her legs collapsed beneath her, and she fell with a thud to the pier. Her hand let go of the pistol, and the weapon slid off the wood and into the ocean.

George sat down, his shoulders shaking.

Christ, Shane thought as he walked back to the path, *he's absolutely worthless.*

Courtney came out of the lighthouse and joined Shane.

"Did you just hit her with a rock?" she asked.

"Yup," Shane said.

"That was an awesome throw!"

Shane grinned. "Thanks. I was trying to hit her in the chest, though."

"Whatever works," Courtney said. "We've got a boat now."

"Oh damn," Shane said, surprised. "We do!"

The two of them walked quickly down onto the pier. George was staring at the boat.

"What's wrong?" Shane asked, dropping to a knee and checking Amy's pulse. She had a welt on the side of her head, and blood trickled from her nose.

"She killed Dell," George said, his voice low and hoarse.

"She didn't kill you," Shane said harshly, "and she didn't kill us. That your boat?"

George nodded.

"Well let's get the hell out of here," Shane said. He picked up Amy and draped her over his shoulder.

"Okay," George agreed. Courtney helped him to his feet.

"You won't be using this little boat," a voice said from the Boston Whaler.

Shane looked for the owner, and he saw the young boy with the pipe who had killed George's friends. The boy stood on the deck, pipe in his mouth as he grinned.

"And why won't we?" Shane asked.

"She's sinking, she is," the boy said. "When your bonnie lass there shot the pilot, well, the boat ran aground. She sprang a good and healthy leak, and not one to be fixed without a dry dock."

Shane looked at the boat and saw the boy was right.

It is sinking, Shane thought. As he watched, it had sank perhaps half an inch, and then half an inch more. In silence, they all stood where they were and after several minutes the boat had settled down as far as she would go.

"That's a little bit of a disappointment, is it not?" the boy asked gleefully.

Shane wanted to strangle him.

"It is," Shane agreed, his voice tight. "But that's alright. It's better to finish the job myself than leave it to another."

The boy took the pipe out of his mouth, laughed pleasantly, and pointed the stem at Shane. "That, my fine bucko, is an excellent way to look at this particular situation. You've no love for Dorothy?"

Shane shook his head.

"Aye," the boy said, and then he winked. "Neither do I. She's a right foul beast, she is. I heard your little talk with Clark Noyes. You mean to do her in."

"I do," Shane said.

"Good," the boy said, returning his pipe to his mouth. "Good. I'll see you at the end, then."

The boy vanished.

"I am more than a little upset," Courtney said.

Shane nodded. "Same here."

George began to cry.

Chapter 51: George Makes a Move

George spat on the ground outside of the lighthouse, his back against the brick wall. Behind him, inside the building, Shane and Courtney sat with the woman, Amy. The one who had tried to kill him.

Not once, George thought miserably, *but twice. How would Shane like it?* George thought. *If someone was trying to kill him?*

He felt ashamed at having cried in front of them, but at least Amy hadn't seen it.

The sun was sinking rapidly on the horizon, the waves of the Atlantic reflecting the day's last light. The chrome and steel of his boat shining as well.

George straightened up as he looked at *Terminal Fleet*.

The antennae which still stood tall in the evening light.

The radios! he thought excitedly. George glanced back into the lighthouse. Shane and Courtney sat close together. Against the back wall, her hands bound behind her back, Amy was still unconscious.

I'll check the radios, George decided. *Maybe then Baldy won't sneer at me.*

George nodded to himself and quickly walked away from the building. He hurried down the path, moved as quietly as he could across the pier, and reached his Boston Whaler. He paused and looked at it, wincing at the sight of it.

Christ, he thought, sighing, *I'll have to have a salvage crew come out, lift her, and tow her back in.*

He scrambled aboard and came to a sharp stop.

Dell's body was on the deck. Mercifully, the man was face down, but the remnants of his skull and brain were splattered over the helm. Hundreds of flies crawled about the exposed flesh while what looked like thousands had already begun to feast and lay eggs on Dell. The entire boat stank of death. George turned and vomited onto the pier, clutching the side of the Whaler.

With bile dripping down his chin and clinging to the corners of his mouth, George turned back to the wreckage of Dell and the radios.

"Oh Christ, Dell," George whispered, "I'm so sorry this happened to you."

Gingerly, he stepped over the body and threw up on the deck as he tried to wipe dried brains off of the two-way radio.

"It won't work," a woman said from behind him.

George twisted around, his sneakers slipping in the blood and bile, and he sat down on Dell's head. Bone cracked loudly, and the flies took to the air, buzzing around him angrily.

Fresh tears sprang into George's eyes, and he scrambled away, his pants wet with blood and urine.

A young woman stood near the port side. She was pretty, but her eyes were closed, and it looked as though she had been crying as well.

Something's wrong, George thought, squinting.

Oh, he realized, *I can see through her.*

Right through her.

She took a step forward and he crab-walked backward until he bumped into the starboard side.

Her eyes looked deflated, and her neck was bent oddly to one side.

"There's no service here," the young woman said. "None. It's why we couldn't get any help. There's no way to get in touch with anyone."

"What happened to you?" George whispered.

"Me?" she asked, smiling. "Oh, Dorothy happened to me. She put out my eyes and broke my neck."

"Why?" George asked, his voice barely audible.

"Why not?" the young woman asked, shrugging. She stopped a foot away from him and said confidently, "I will tell you this, though."

"What?"

"This is how it felt," she whispered, and before George could move she grabbed hold of his head.

Frozen thumbs worked their way up to his eyes and pushed.

George screamed.

Chapter 52: Then There Were Two

A loud, horrified scream jerked Shane's attention away from the unconscious Amy. As he and Courtney looked to the door, he said angrily, "Damn it!"

Courtney didn't ask why.

Both of them could see George was gone.

Shane kept a tight grip on his temper, and he stood up and went to the door. He glanced around and saw movement on the defunct boat.

Eileen stood over George, her hands on his head.

"What's she doing?" Courtney asked, fear thick in her voice.

"Killing him," Shane said. He put his hands gently on Courtney and turned her away. George's screams ended abruptly. Shane shook his head.

"It's too late," Shane said softly. He and Courtney sat down slowly.

For several long minutes, they were silent.

Book 2: The Lighthouse

And then Amy let out a grunt, rolled from her side onto her back, and opened her eyes. She blinked several times, the camping light close to her and shining brightly.

"Hello, Sunshine," Shane said softly.

Amy's eyes focused on him, and her face paled. She went to move her arms and couldn't. Shane watched the color drain from her lips as she pressed them tightly together. The dark, dried blood on the side of her face stood out boldly.

Amy looked at him, wet her lips and said, "Hi Shane."

"Courtney," Shane said, "this is Amy. Amy, this is Courtney."

"A pleasure," Amy said, forcing a smile. "I don't suppose you'd do a girl a favor and untie me?"

"No," Shane said. "You're all trussed up, and I'd like to keep it that way."

"Why?" she asked, feigning ignorance. "Why would you keep me tied up?"

"Who do you think hit you with a rock?" Courtney snapped.

"You did?" Amy asked, glaring at Courtney.

"I did," Shane said, correcting her. "I have more than half a mind to drown you, Amy, but I don't want to add another body to this damned place."

"That would be murder," Amy said. She focused her attention on him.

"And so it would," Shane agreed. "I'd sleep alright. You, Courtney?"

Courtney nodded.

"So, you know where we stand on the whole murder issue, Amy," Shane said. "I know where you stand on it, too."

"Shane," she said, her voice low and seductive. "You don't think I could have had anything to do with murder, do you?"

"Amy," Shane said, leaning closer. "I have something I want to tell you."

"What?" she asked, smiling at him.

"I guarantee you I will beat the brains right out of your head," Shane said coldly, "if I think, even for an instant, that Courtney is going to die here."

Amy sat back sharply. "She's going to kill all of us."

"Dorothy?" Shane asked.

Amy nodded.

"I think you're mistaken," Shane said sincerely.

Amy looked at him, confusion on her face.

"I already told you," Shane said, "I'll kill you. Not Dorothy."

"You don't understand!" Amy shouted.

The sudden violence in her voice caused Shane to recoil briefly.

"What don't we understand?" Courtney asked, her knuckles whitening as she tightened her grip on her cudgel.

"My family," Amy said, a mad gleam creeping into her eyes. "This island is ours. This lighthouse, it is ours. All of it. Even the dead. It is our purpose, our divine mission, to ensure the light forever shines. By controlling the light, we decide who lives, who dies upon the seas, and who will drown within the depths."

"Each death grants Dorothy strength. With each soul trapped on the island, her power grows. And the more dead upon the island," Amy continued, grinning, "the stronger my great-grandmother becomes. Soon, she shall be able to leave the island, to travel freely to the land, where her power will grow ten-fold. Thus, we ensure the safety of the light."

"And what about me breaking it?" Shane asked, taking out a cigarette.

Amy sneered. "A mere speed bump in our goal. The Coast Guard will come out. They will fix it. We will guard it. Dorothy will see to it."

Shane blew streams of smoke out of his nose, grinned at her, and said, "Are you planning on being alive for this whole deal, or are you expendable, too?"

"She won't sacrifice me," Amy spat. "I brought the lighthouse back into our family. I returned her children to her."

"Her children?" Courtney asked, looking at Shane. "Dorothy had children?"

Shane nodded.

Courtney switched her attention to Amy. "Why does she need her children?"

Amy smiled and remained quiet.

"Now, you decide to shut up?" Shane asked. "No. I don't like that."

"And what will you do about it, Shane?" Amy asked softly, laughing. "Will you torture it out of me?"

"Yup," Shane said, nodding. "I hate how sweaty I get, but I'll deal with it."

Amy's eyes widened. "You're joking."

He shook his head. "Not in the least little bit. Courtney?"

"Yes?" Courtney asked.

"I'm going to ask you to turn around and watch the doorway for me. I'll gag the murderer here, but you're still going to hear some things," Shane said apologetically.

Courtney looked hard at him, hesitated, and then nodded. "Alright."

She turned around and faced the doorway.

Shane took his cigarette out of his mouth, slipped his shirt off, and smiled at Amy. He returned his cigarette to its proper place, twisted the shirt into a tight length and got to his feet.

Amy pushed herself backward as far as she could go.

"Stay away from me!" she snarled, jerking her head from side to side as he got closer. She kicked at him, but the blows were weak, bouncing impotently off of his shins and knees.

He extended his arms, and as the shirt neared her mouth Amy screamed, "Wait!"

Shane stopped. The shirt was only a few inches from her head.

Panting, Amy glared at him.

"Is there something you want to tell me?" Shane asked softly.

She nodded.

"Well?" he said.

Amy closed her eyes and whispered, "She needs to have the children placed at the cardinal points."

"Of the compass?" Shane asked.

"Yes."

"Why?" Shane said.

"It locks the power in," Amy replied. "All of the strength Dorothy's gathered over the years. All of the deaths. The fear and horror. It feeds her. With it, she'll be able to power the lighthouse's lantern even if there's no power in the solar batteries. Even if the backup generator has been run dry. She'll be able to keep the light shining.

"She'll be able to save the ships," Amy whispered, finally opening her eyes again.

"Well," Shane said, unraveling his shirt. "She's more civic-minded than I thought."

"God told her what to do," Amy said, the fervent gleam returning to her eyes. "It is our mission, Shane. You can't stop it. You mustn't."

He shrugged, finished his cigarette, and stubbed it out on the stairwell. Sighing, he slipped the shirt back on and said, "Courtney."

"What's up?" the young woman asked, stepping away from the doorway.

"We need to go down to George's boat, together," Shane said. "There should be some emergency supplies, a flare gun, and all that good stuff."

"Okay," Courtney said. She switched the cudgel from one hand to the other.

"Why do you need the flare gun?" Amy asked.

"So we can signal the Coast Guard," Shane said. "If they're not on their way already, the flare gun will definitely light a fire under them."

"You can't," Amy said, horrified. "She's not ready yet."
"Perfect timing then," Shane said with a grin.
"You can't!" Amy shrieked.
Shane winked at her, turned away, and said to Courtney, "Ready?"
Courtney nodded, and together they left the lighthouse. Behind them, Amy screamed furiously.

Chapter 53: Waiting for Dorothy

Amy dropped her chin to her chest and sobbed. She was enraged.
They'll try and ruin it all, she thought. *They'll destroy every last bit of it. Everything!*
The temperature in the lighthouse dropped and the locket around her neck grew cold, her breastbone aching painfully from the touch of the metal.
Amy whimpered and forced herself to look up.
Dorothy stood in front of her. Beside her was the shattered remains of a man. Amy kept her eyes focused on her great-grandmother.
"Amy," Dorothy said.
"Yes?" Amy's voice was barely above a whisper.
"You came back to finish off George?" Dorothy asked.
"Yes."
"But you did not," Dorothy said.
Amy couldn't respond. She shivered with fear.
"One of the new children did," Dorothy said after a moment. "The one named Eileen. She took care of George for us."
Amy looked up at her great-grandmother, unable to contain her surprise. "She did?"
Dorothy nodded.
"What about Shane?" Amy asked fearfully. "What about the girl, Courtney?"
"What of them?" Dorothy asked. "We've only to slay them both. He will look like a murderer, and then another suicide. It is a task which is easy enough to manage."
"And what about me?" Amy asked. "Will you untie me?"
Dorothy shook her head. "You must stay bound. Perhaps for a day, perhaps less. You need to be found as you are. Only then will you be able to play the role of victim. The deaths of the man named George, his colleagues, and those from the yacht. All of them can then be laid at the feet of Shane. It is he who will be the suicide victim this time."
Amy nodded. "So I wait."
"So you wait," Dorothy agreed. "Now this one and I must carry out the rest of the task. Be at ease, child; you have done our family proud."
Amy blushed with pride. Dorothy and the mutilated man vanished. The locket on around her neck grew warm. Soon the chill of the room was replaced by the warm June air.
Smiling, Amy closed her eyes and did her best to ignore the discomfort of her arms and wrists.

Chapter 54: A Missing Light

Chief Petty Officer Al Arsenault looked out at Squirrel Island.
The lighthouse was dark. The signal from the island's service program was correct. Something was wrong with the lantern.

He turned away from the window, picked up the phone and called Captain Root at home. Al quickly informed her of the situation, and the Captain responded in the same fashion. In less than two minutes, the phone call was over, and Al turned to Seaman Mauser.

"Mauser," Al said.

The young man looked up from a battered paperback. "Chief?"

"Call down to Zucci, let him know we need the patrol boat readied," Al said, sitting down at his desk.

"Aye, Chief," Mauser said.

Al took a drink of his coffee. Mauser made the call, then he looked over at Al and said, "Zucci wants to know who we need?"

Al put his mug down and said, "We'll need at least a two-person tech crew. Light's out on Squirrel Island. May be just a couple of wires, or it may be the lantern itself."

Mauser nodded and relayed the information, then hung up the phone. "Anything else, Chief?"

"Yeah," Al said, finishing his drink. "Put another pot on, will you, Mauser? Looks like it's going to be a long night."

"You got it, Chief." The young man got up and left the office. Al went to the window again and looked out at Squirrel Island. He'd been there a few times, and each occasion was something he'd rather forget.

The place was cold.

Bad luck, Al thought. *A Jonah's place if ever there was one. Nothing but death there. The quicker this is done, the better.*

Mauser returned a short time later. "Coffee should be ready in about five, Chief."

Al nodded his thanks, but he didn't move away from the window. The lighthouse was a dark silhouette against the stars. The sea had calmed down, the waves no longer rough.

Al yawned, and the phone rang. Mauser answered it and said, "Zucci says the boat's ready whenever you are. The crew is already aboard."

"Good," Al said, turning away from the window. "Tell Zucci I'll be down there in five minutes."

Mauser nodded and relayed the message.

Al took his travel mug off of his desk and brought it into the staff room.

Well, he thought, *let's get this done with.*

Chapter 55: Strange News

Marie Lafontaine sat in her chair, a glass of wine in her hand as she watched the ten o'clock news. She was only half listening, more focused on whether or not she could finish her drink before she had to go to bed. The day had been long and frustrating. A witness had recanted their statement, and another person had overdosed on heroin.

In the tot-lot playground on Ash Street, Marie thought, shaking her head.

The words 'mysterious disappearance' were spoken by the newscaster and caught Marie's attention. She listened as the reporter talked about how a gatekeeper at a marina in Maine had disappeared from work.

The news station used a stock photo of the marina. Beyond the docked boats and wooden pier, Marie caught sight of something which sent a bitter fear through her. The Squirrel Island lighthouse formed part of the backdrop.

Marie picked up her cellphone and called Amy. It went right to voicemail. She ended the call, got up, and walked over to her laptop. Marie did a quick search for more information on the disappearance, but she received nothing more than the man's name and basic history.

She frowned and then searched for information on the empty yacht which was found. The articles she found all agreed on one particular point.

No bodies had been found. No lifeboat. No distress signal sent out.

The crew was still missing.

Did Amy get this guy to bring her out to the island to check on Shane? Marie wondered. *But wouldn't he have told someone?*

Something's wrong, Marie realized. *Terribly wrong.*

She knocked back the last of her wine, put the empty glass on the desk beside the laptop, and made her way to the bedroom.

It was time to drive to Maine.

Chapter 56: Slipping Away

Although Courtney felt better to be with Shane, she wasn't naïve enough to believe all of her troubles would be solved by being with him.

Mom always told you to rely on yourself, Courtney thought. *Don't expect a prince to come and rescue you.*

Courtney looked at Shane and grinned.

No, she thought, *he's no prince. More like a hired gunman than anything else.*

And Courtney liked that about him.

As they made their way towards the pier, she forced herself to pay attention. George's boat was still visible, still partially submerged.

And still completely useless, she thought, sighing.

They reached the pier and Shane led them swiftly to the boat. At its side, he paused, turned, and said, "Stop here, Courtney."

"Why?" she asked, halting a few feet from him.

"Because it's bad," he said. "Terribly so."

"I can help," Courtney said, the words coming out quickly.

"You do help, and you will," Shane said, not looking away from her. "I just don't think you need to see any more bodies."

"More bodies?" Courtney asked. "I thought it was only George."

"And the man who brought Amy here this morning," Shane said.

"What about him?" Courtney said.

"She blew his brains out," Shane said. "Bullet to the back of the skull. Exit through the front. His brains and skull are everywhere."

"Oh," Courtney said. She glanced at the boat, but she didn't try to look in it. "You'll be able to find what you need without me going on board?"

"Yes," Shane said. "Stay here, and stay safe."

She nodded. Shane stepped forward, embraced her, and then stepped away. She watched as he climbed up onto the deck. Soon he was gone, and she could hear him rummaging through the interior of the boat. Long minutes passed, and she shifted her attention constantly from the boat to the pier, from the pier to the lighthouse, from the lighthouse to the cabin, and then back again.

"Got it!" Shane called up.

Courtney heard his feet on the ladder and in a second, he was back on the deck. He had an emergency kit in his hands. She took it from him, and he climbed down to stand on the dock. They sat down, opened the kit, and looked at the materials inside. Among the emergency supplies, they found a small strobe light, emergency rations, a flare gun, and a compressed emergency raft with instructions on how to inflate it. It even had a collapsible paddle.

"Perfect," Shane said softly.

"How so?" Courtney asked.

"The raft," Shane said, looking at her. "We're going to inflate it, get you a life vest from the boat, and send you out a little off shore."

"What?" Courtney said in disbelief. "You can't be serious?"

"I am," Shane said. "If you're in the raft, you can't be grabbed by the dead. They won't even care. You'll be able to use the flare gun, and someone will come and pick you up."

"What about you?" Courtney asked. "You can't stay here by yourself."

"I have to," Shane said. "I have to take care of Dorothy, and you need to tell whoever picks you up that it's Amy's fault. All of it."

"Do I try to tell them about the ghosts?" Courtney asked, and winced at how ridiculous it sounded even to her.

"No," Shane said, shaking his head. "Don't tell them about the ghosts. Tell them how you became trapped here, and how she kept you a prisoner."

"Not much of a stretch there," Courtney said bitterly.

"No," Shane agreed, "not much at all."

"And if they ask me if she killed my friends," Courtney said, "I'll tell them yes."

Shane nodded.

"Are you going to be safe?" Courtney asked him, worry spiking through her as she looked at him.

His face was harsh, the light of the stars and the moon etching shadows on his pale skin. "Probably not," Shane said. "But we'll make it work."

She wanted to say more, but she didn't.

"Alright," Shane said softly, "let's get this started."

He picked up the raft, pulled the cord, and a sharp hiss sounded as the rubber inflated rapidly. With an easy motion, he dropped it onto the opposite side of the pier, holding onto a long, nylon tether.

Silently Courtney picked up the emergency rations and the flare gun.

"Here," Shane said, passing the tether to her. "Hold this for a second."

When she took it, Shane scrambled back onto George's boat and came back quickly with a life vest. He helped her put it on, tightened the straps across her chest, and smiled at her.

"As soon as you're in the raft, I'll pass the paddle to you. I want you to make your way about a hundred yards out. More if you can. Once you're there, fire off the flare gun, and move out a little more, okay?" he asked.

Courtney nodded.

"Good," Shane said, smiling. He took her face in his hands, looked into her eyes, and said, "Be safe. Don't worry about me."

She went to nod, but he held her still, bent forward, and kissed her full and long on the lips.

"No fear, Courtney," he whispered. "Fear kills."

Shane let go, and Courtney went to get into the raft, heart beating fiercely.

Chapter 57: Amongst the Enemy

Only when Shane turned to walk back up the pier did he realize Courtney had left her cudgel.

Too late, he thought grimly, picking the weapon up. He looked back at her in the bright orange circular raft. The strobe light, attached to the top by a cord, pulsed brightly in the night sky. *Too dangerous to call her back.*

He shook his head at his own forgetfulness and pushed aside thoughts of her being dead because of it. With the cudgel on his shoulder, he reached the end of the pier and paused.

I need to go back into the cellar again, Shane thought. *I need to tell the children what their mother's plan is.*

He turned to walk up and around the side of the house and saw them.

Four men.

One was George Fallon, whose eyes were gone. The others were the man's friends. Both of them looked as well as could be expected, but Shane knew they had been drowned. The fourth was the man who brought Amy back to the island, and the majority of his forehead and orbital sockets were missing.

"And where are you going?" George asked, blindly staring at him.

"Wherever I want," Shane replied pleasantly. "And yourselves?"

"She wants you dead," George answered. "It's not fair that you're alive, and we're dead."

"You know," Shane said, moving the cudgel off of his shoulder, "I have to say, life, in general, isn't fair. So, I'm not particularly surprised that death isn't fair either."

"You're going to kill yourself," one of the other men said, "whether you want to or not."

"Interesting statement," Shane said. "Do you have any intention of backing that up?"

The man who had spoken grinned maliciously and walked forward.

Are they stupid enough to attack one at a time? Shane wondered. When the other three remained where they were, Shane grinned and said, "Thank you."

The approaching man paused, confused. "Why?"

Shane swung the cudgel, full force at him, and the ghost screamed as it tore through.

As their friend vanished, the other three men attacked.

It came fast and hard, and though they lacked the brutality and effectiveness of the Mujahedeen he had faced in Afghanistan, the men were no less determined.

A searing pain ripped through his left arm, and it felt as though someone was trying to tear the muscle off of his bone. Another blow struck his leg and dropped him to a knee while a third blow struck his shoulder, his fingers springing open, the cudgel falling to the ground.

Grimacing, Shane swung his numb right hand, the iron knuckledusters causing the faceless man to vanish. An explosion of pain erupted behind his eyes, and Shane screamed angrily, lashing out with his left hand. The gauntlet made from the hinge shattered George, leaving Shane with the last ghost.

Shane spat on the ground and looked at the man, who glared at Shane.

"How did you do that?" the man hissed.

"Do what?" Shane asked. "Send your little buddies away?"

The man nodded, looking around as if he was expecting help.

"Iron," Shane said, grinning, the pain in his head receding. "It does a body good."

Before the man could respond, Shane threw himself forward, the knuckleduster passing through the man.

Shane was left alone on the path, his body aching.

Cellar, he told himself. *Get to the cellar, and then deal with Dorothy.*

Chapter 58: Shock and Horror

Amy was half in and out of sleep when a cold, hard slap woke her up.

Her eyes snapped open, and she found Dorothy above her. The woman's face was a mask of rage.

"Who is he?" her great-grandmother roared.

Amy scrambled backward. "Who?"

"Shane, Shane Ryan!" Dorothy hissed, slapping Amy again.

Amy winced, tears springing to her eyes. "I don't know! My cousin said he had grown up in a haunted house, I had to bring him in because she offered. I couldn't say no! Why what's wrong?"

"He did more than grow up in a haunted house," Dorothy said angrily, turning away. "He knows about iron. He knows how to use it."

"What about iron?" Amy asked. "I don't understand."

"Iron stops us," Dorothy said. She looked back at Amy. "For the weak ones, they are wounded. Too weak to move forward and attack. The stronger we are, the quicker we recuperate."

"And if you were hit with iron?" Amy asked fearfully.

Dorothy smiled grimly. "A few minutes, perhaps more. Still, it is not a pleasant experience."

"What are you going to do?" Amy asked.

"About the intrepid Mr. Ryan?" Dorothy said.

Amy nodded.

"I'm going to kill him," Dorothy replied. "And not quickly, either. I will drag him down to the water's edge and drown him by inches."

Amy smiled and whispered, "I would like that."

Dorothy looked at her approvingly and left the lighthouse.

Amy watched her great-grandmother go and wished she could watch Shane die.

Chapter 59: A Change in Plans

Since there was no bad weather on deck and no heavy fog for the dawn, Al didn't feel any particular pressure in getting the patrol boat out to Squirrel Island faster than he needed to.

Zucci was at the helm, and the rest of the boat's crew went about their work. Harper and Kaplan sat below deck, more than likely arguing about who the Patriots were going to have start the season for defense Al scratched his right forearm compulsively, irritated he had forgotten his nicotine patches at home.

I need to keep some in my locker, he thought.

A sharp flare, bright red, launched up into the sky. It reached its peak and slowly arched.

"Chief, did you see that?" Zucci called back to him.

"Aye, Zucci," Al said, getting to his feet. "Adjust your course, get the men on their lights."

The call went out over the communication system, and men and women scrambled to their lights. Sharp, powerful lights exploded from the helm, the beams crisscrossing the waves and the dark water.

"Strobe to starboard!" someone yelled.

All of the lights swiveled on their mounts, picked through the water and across the whitecaps. A yellow life-raft could be spotted, with what looked to be a single person in it. The lights settled on the raft, and the occupant waved their arms.

After several minutes, the boat was as close as it dared to get to the raft. The rescue team was over the side in a matter of moments, and shortly after that, they were back aboard, along with the raft's sole occupant. A young woman, barren of makeup and looking exhausted.

She smiled wearily, tears in her eyes. "Thank you."

Gwen Ouellette, the boat's paramedic, came forward and did a quick, cursory exam as a rescue blanket was wrapped around the young woman.

"She's good, Chief," Gwen said. "We'll have to bring her to the hospital for a full checkup when we get in, though."

Al nodded and stepped forward, dropping down into a squat next to the seated woman. "Hello, miss, I'm Chief Petty Officer Al Arsenault. Can you tell me how you got out here?"

In straightforward, clear sentences the young woman, Courtney DeSantis, told him about what happened to the people who had been aboard the yacht, *A Father's Dream*. She told him about a man trapped on Squirrel Island and the woman named Amy who was there to kill him.

Al stood up, a cold feeling in his stomach. Those who had been around Courtney looked at him.

"Zucci," Al said.

"Chief?" the man asked.

"All ahead, full speed to Squirrel Island," Al said. "Get someone on the horn to base, have them call this in to the city's police. We'll do what we can when we get there."

"Aye aye, Chief," Zucci said.

Al walked over to the stairs and called down, "Kaplan!"

"Aye, Chief!"

"Open the weapons locker."

Al could feel the eyes of the crew on him, but he ignored them and turned his attention back to Squirrel Island.

Chapter 60: On the Road

Marie drove a little over the speed limit, not wanting to have to stop and explain to a State Trooper why she was in a rush.

Or why I think I'm in a rush, she corrected herself. She didn't know for a fact if either Amy or Shane were in trouble. The coincidence was a little too much for her, though.

A missing yacht. A missing gatekeeper at a marina. No word from Amy. Silence from Shane, Marie thought. She checked her mirrors, signaled left, and went around a minivan.

Are you overreacting? she asked herself. *Are you worried something has happened to them? Are you worried they've made a love connection?*

Marie shook her head, chuckling. *No, that's definitely not it. More power to them. I doubt either of them is looking for more than a good time.*

With the travel lane free of the troublesome minivan, Marie got back into it.

It's likely nothing more than Amy having a night on the town, she thought. *How many times has she forgotten her phone at home? Or even forgot to charge it? Or just plain turned it off when she's been having a little too much fun?*

Amy was wilder than Marie would ever be, and she still couldn't understand how the woman did it.

Like all good cops, Marie had a scanner in her car. It was a necessity to her as much as an iPod was to the younger generation. She had the scanner turned down, but loud enough for her to hear. Occasional calls went out. Mostly the mundane, everyday chores of any police force. Moving violations. A rare report of a fight. A domestic assault call and the fear that goes with it.

The scanner squawked as she neared the coast. Some unknown dispatcher at a Maine State Police barracks called out, "We have the Coast Guard reporting a possible 207 at Squirrel Island. I say again, the Coast Guard is reporting a possible 207 at Squirrel Island."

Marie stiffened as she drove. Her foot suddenly grew heavier, and the accelerator went down accordingly.

207A, she thought numbly. *Possible kidnapping.*

Marie no longer worried about the speed limit.

Book 2: The Lighthouse

Chapter 61: Changing Tides

Amy, from her position in the lighthouse looking out the doorway, had seen the flare go up. And she had seen the lights from, what was more than likely, a Coast Guard patrol boat searching the ocean.

She hadn't worried about the rest. All of her great-grandmother's plans were unraveling.

He has to be stopped, she told herself, her thoughts ricocheting madly about her head. *She won't be able to do it alone. Not with the Coast Guard coming. Something has to be done. I have to help.*

After a great deal of struggling and wrenching of her muscles, Amy managed to get her knees up to her chest and her hands under her feet. With her hands in front of her, she was able to find a shard of the broken lantern and cut her bonds.

Amy looked around the scattered tools left by the deceased Mike Puller, and she found a heavy pry bar. The dull blue metal was scratched and pitted, the hooked end of it sharpened to a fair edge.

Good enough, she thought, *to remove Shane's head!*

Clutching the tool tightly in her sore and throbbing hands, Amy made her way out of the lighthouse. She looked around and listened.

From the keeper's house came the sound of something breaking. As though boxes were being broken into.

The children! she thought frantically. *He's in the cellar! He's trying to find the children. If he gets the bodies, she won't be able to bind them here. If she can't bind them, then all of it will have been for nothing!*

Everything will be done.

Shaking with rage, Amy crept along to the keeper's house and made her way to the cellar. In spite of her trembling arms, the pry bar was steady in her hands.

Chapter 62: With the Children

Shane wanted to weep.

The remains of Dorothy's children were pitifully small. He had found a folded tarp near the stairs, and he had spread it out. The last bones, those of the baby, were put with its siblings.

"Why are you sad?" Jillian asked softly.

"I am sad you're dead," Shane answered, keeping a tight rein on his tears. He brought the ends of the tarp together, picked it up, and found the load to be terribly light.

"You don't have to be," Jillian said.

Shane didn't reply as he carried the children up the narrow stairs and into the starlight. He brought them out several feet into the yard and set them down. The wind shifted and carried with it the stink of the bodies in the shed.

Christ, he thought, *I'd forgotten about that smell.*

"I've had enough of you, Shane Ryan!" a woman said.

Shane turned and saw Dorothy. She stood off to the right, far more solid than she had been before.

"Fair enough," Shane replied. "I'm sick of you as well."

"Alas," she said, smiling wickedly, "there is nothing you can do about it."

"Says you," Shane said. He cleared his throat, spat to one side. "You look strong tonight."

"Stronger than I have ever been," Dorothy sneered. "See who I have around me."

She gestured, and the dead appeared around her in all of their horrific glory.

Scott and Dane, Eileen and George. Clark and the boy, Ewan. Jillian, holding a baby, and her grandfather standing beside her. And more. Perhaps another twenty or twenty-five.

Shane didn't bother to count them all.

They'll either side with me, or they won't, he thought.

Shane was armed only with the knuckledusters, having left the makeshift gauntlet and cudgel in the cellar. He took a single step forward and looked to Clark.

"Why are you looking to my husband, Shane Ryan?" Dorothy asked, laughing. "He is my creature. They are all my creatures, bound to me for eternity."

Jillian looked at her mother and walked over to stand behind Shane.

And her grandfather.

And Clark.

Ewan and others followed. The more who left her side, the fainter she became.

Dorothy's face grew cold and harsh.

"This means nothing," she snarled, left only with the newest of the dead, the naked Mike Puller and others beside her. Those too weak to break her hold on them. "I'm still here. And so are they. They'll regret this night, mind you, and I will kill you slowly, Shane Ryan. As slow as I can."

"In the darkness, Dorothy?" Shane whispered.

Her eyes widened, and her face paled.

"No," he said, his voice growing louder. "You'll do nothing in the darkness. But those you murdered will."

"And what will they do?" she asked, a tremor in her voice. One she tried to hide beneath bravado.

"They will give me the strength they deny you," Shane answered.

He crossed the short distance between them quickly.

Mike Puller stepped back nervously, as did the others.

"Do your worst," Dorothy hissed. "I've felt the sting of iron before, and it is no worse than that of a bee."

"Not yet," Shane said softly as if speaking to a lover. "Oh, not yet, Dorothy."

Behind him, he heard Jillian speak.

"We give this to you," the girl whispered.

Terror and pain, violent fear, all of it ripped through him. All of the horror Dorothy had visited upon her victims. The decades of living a nightmare denied salvation or damnation, pummeled Shane.

He grunted, remained on his feet, and absorbed all of it. Every shred of their experiences. It felt as though his blood burned in his veins, as if his lungs would explode, as though the bones would shatter. Shane tilted his head back and screamed, a long, drawn out sound which threatened to drown out the ocean's great voice.

And then it changed.

The scream became a gasp, the gasp a laugh, the laugh a shout of triumph.

Dorothy stood in front of him, as real as the island beneath his feet.

"No," she hissed, looking at her hands. "This cannot be. What have you done?!"

She remained silent as he lunged forward, grabbed hold of her, and dug his fingers into her flesh. She let out a shriek as the fingers pushed through the dress, through the skin, pierced the muscles and gripped them.

With a howl of savage glee, he ripped his hand back, tattering the muscles.

Dorothy tried to jerk away, but Shane didn't let her. He wrapped his hands around her neck and squeezed.

She batted at his arms, grabbed a hold of one of his pinkies and pulled it back, the bone snapping loudly.

Shane bit back a scream, the pain immediate and intense. Stars exploded around the corners of his vision and she wrenched herself away from him. She looked for a way out, but the dead who had sided with Shane made a circle around them. The ghosts kept the two of them contained.

When Dorothy saw she had no escape, she let out a shriek of pure rage and threw herself at him, parts of her arm flapping grotesquely. Shane caught her, grunted at the effort to keep his balance and punched her solidly with his good hand. Something crumpled beneath the blow.

Dorothy's fingers clawed at his face, a thumb catching his lip and slipping into his mouth. The vile taste of her curious flesh made him gag even as she tried to rip his cheek away from his skull.

Shane jerked his head back, threw his fist against her head again and watched as her entire jaw slid to the right. She stumbled and he caught her by the hair, jerking her head back.

Her throat was exposed and as she struck at him, each blow feebler than the last, Shane leaned forward, brought his hand up and began to dig his fingers into her neck.

Chapter 63: Disbelief and Rage

Amy had observed everything which took place between her great-grandmother and Shane. The permanently bald man had looked as though he would collapse, and then the unthinkable had happened.

Dorothy had taken on some sort of physical form.

Shane's obvious scream of pain, and the way he had collapsed, had thrilled her. It had looked like he would succumb to whatever power Dorothy exerted. And then he hadn't.

His screams of pain had become triumphant exultations.

And he had forced, somehow *forced* Dorothy to become real.

There, but not quite.

Exhilaration had filled Amy, and she had tightened her grip on the pry bar. Excitement raced through her as she prepared to watch her great-grandmother destroy Shane.

Yet the opposite had occurred.

Shane had attacked Dorothy. Had literally begun to rip her to shreds. Great chunks of the woman had been cast aside. Those few ghosts who had remained by her great-grandmother's side had fled while those who had betrayed the woman remained behind Shane. All of them pulsed with some strange glow. Their hollow voices rose up in cheers and taunts. They called for Shane, encouraged him, and made certain Dorothy could not escape. Some pushed and kicked at her, and the air vibrated with their excitement.

When Shane bent Dorothy back and tore at the flesh of her neck, Amy froze with horror.

Numb, she watched as Shane let out a howl and he wrenched up with both hands.

Amy's great-grandmother vanished completely.

With a silent rage Amy was spurred to action.

Raising the pry-bar above her, Amy ran forward and brought the sharpened end down, stumbling at the last moment. She slammed the tool into Shane's right shoulder, knocking him forward.

Chapter 64: Gunshots in the Night

When Dorothy vanished, a collective sigh reached Shane's ears. A second later, a terrible pain blossomed in his shoulder.

Shane staggered forward, stumbled and fell. He twisted as he landed and looked up. Through the windows of the keeper's house, and around the sides, a light flashed. A curiously bright illumination. *What the hell was that?* he wondered numbly.

Then he saw her.

Amy had gotten free, and she held some sort of tool in her hand, the top of which was wet.

That's my blood, Shane realized.

She charged at him, and he rolled to one side, lashing out with a foot. He missed her leg as she missed his head.

He managed to get to a knee, and then tried to push off the ground with his right hand. His wounded shoulder wouldn't bear the weight. With a grimace, he slipped down, and he saw her raise the tool up for another attack.

I'll have to meet it head on, he thought dully.

A semi-automatic pistol barked three times, muzzle flashes coming from the left.

Amy stiffened, took a step towards him as someone emptied the rest of the magazine into her.

She collapsed lifelessly to the ground beside him.

Shane looked at her body and thought, *Thank Christ.*

And then passed out.

Chapter 65: At the Dock

Marie made it to the Coast Guard's dock only a few minutes after their patrol boat had docked. Chatter on the scanner had talked about a shooting on Squirrel Island, about a wounded male victim and a dead female assailant. The State Police were sending a boat out to process the crime scene. The Coast Guard was bringing the victim in to be transported to the hospital.

Marie pulled her car in beside an ambulance. All of the vehicle's lights were on, the paramedics in the back.

She had put the car into park, left the keys in the ignition, and hurried to look in the ambulance. Both paramedics were in the back, as was a young woman. The young woman was holding Shane Ryan's hand. He was sitting up on the gurney, shirtless, dirty, and bloodied. When he saw Marie, he nodded.

The paramedics glanced over, and one of them said, "We can't fit any more in here, ma'am."

Marie showed the man her badge and the paramedic shrugged.

"Are you okay?" Marie asked.

"Yeah," Shane said. "They just started a morphine drip for the pain. I'll be useless in about two minutes."

"What happened?" Marie said, glancing at the girl.

Shane shook his head. "Later."

Marie nodded. "Meet you at the hospital?"

"Sure," Shane said, closing his eyes.

Marie turned to leave but stopped as Shane called out, "Hey, Marie."

"Yeah?" she said, looking back at him.

"I will tell you one thing," he said.

"What's that?" she asked.

"No more favors for your family."

Before Marie could ask him what he meant, the paramedics closed the door and the ambulance's engine roared to life.

Chapter 66: Back on the Island

Shane stepped onto the pier and winced. The injuries from his fight with Dorothy were still fresh, only days old. He glanced back at the boat they had chartered and saw Courtney. She stood off to one side with her arms crossed over her chest. Shane knew she had a small piece of iron hidden in her hand. The pilot of the small boat leaned back in his seat, yawned, and checked his phone.

Shane waved to Courtney and she smiled nervously as she returned the wave.

Sighing, Shane turned back to face the island, and started walking along the pier. By the time he reached the path up to the buildings, he could feel the dead gather around him. The air was cold, his exhalations a soft white cloud. He ignored both the lighthouse and the keeper's house, walking around to the back. The door to the shed where he had stored the bodies of Courtney's friends leaned haphazardly, the entire structure leering at him.

A shiver rippled through him, the air growing painfully cold around him as he came to a stop in the spot where he had destroyed Dorothy. The earth beneath his feet felt wrong, the grass a corrupted yellow stain amongst the vibrant green of the rest of the yard.

"Hello," Shane said.

The air around him twisted, folded in on itself and opened and closed, and Ewan had stepped forward. Jillian was with him, the strangulation marks on her neck a vivid red in spite of her translucent nature. The boy had his pipe in his mouth, a wry smile on his lips.

"So," Ewan said, "you've gone and done in Dorothy."

"With your help," Shane said. "I couldn't have done anything without it. Without all of you."

"Right and true," the boy said, "but you were the one who faced her down in the end."

"Thank you," Jillian said softly, looking at him shyly.

"You're welcome," Shane said. He looked from Jillian to Ewan then said, "Will you all be well now?"

"As well as the dead can be," Ewan said seriously.

"I can help you move on, if you wish it," Shane said.

Jillian's eyes widened hopefully, but Ewan's didn't.

"I, myself," Ewan said, "am quite pleased to be here. To look out at the Atlantic, to drift through whatever life this is. There will be others though who might wish it."

Jillian nodded. "I know I do, as well as my siblings."

Shane looked at the tarp where the remains of the Noyes children were tucked away near the house.

He looked from Ewan to Jillian and said, "Thank you, Jillian, for your help."

The girl blushed and for a moment her form lost some of its opaqueness. "I, thank you, Shane Ryan, my siblings and I would like to see what is beyond this island."

"I hope you shall," Shane said. "Good-bye."

The two children said farewell and vanished.

Shane walked over to the tarp, picked it up and carefully carried it away from the house. He set the package down, pulled back the canvas and looked at the remains and swallowed dryly. From the pockets of his cargo pants he took a small bag of salt, a bottle of lighter fluid, and a book of matches. He scattered the salt over all of the bones, then doused them with the flammable liquid. When he finished, Shane stood up, lit a match, and dropped it onto the remains.

The result was instantaneous. A curious, light blue flame arced up to the sky. The fire was smokeless and burned quickly. Soon, nothing remained except ashes.

For a few minutes, Shane stood still, then he pinched the bridge of his nose, wiped his eyes and left the backyard. Long strides returned him to the pier, and then to the boat.

The pilot looked up disinterestedly from his phone and raised an eyebrow. At Shane's nod, the young man put the phone away and started up the boat.

Courtney reached out and took Shane's hand, gently pulling him down to sit beside her. She asked softly, "How did it go?"

"Well enough," Shane replied. "They make me sad."

She nodded, then said, "What now?"

"Now, we go home," Shane said. "Which reminds me, where do you live?"

Courtney grinned. "I live in Manchester, over on the west side. A few minutes from St. Anselm College."

Her grin slipped away and a nervous smile replaced it. "Do you think you might want to get together, maybe have dinner with me?"

"I'd love to," Shane said, squeezing her hand.

The pilot backed the boat away from the pier and headed to port, the lighthouse a silent sentinel. Shane looked at it for a moment, until he saw Clark Noyes standing and watching.

Shane turned his head away from Squirrel Island and looked to the mainland.

Chapter 67: Coffee with Uncle Gerry

"How are you holding up?" Uncle Gerry asked, looking over the top of his coffee mug at her.

"Alright," Marie said. She picked at a thread on the old sweater she wore.

Her uncle looked at her doubtfully.

Marie sighed. "I'm upset."

"About your cousin?" he asked.

She nodded. "The fact that she was responsible for so many deaths, and she nearly killed Shane."

"And how is the young Marine?" Uncle Gerry asked, dropping a hand down to pet the top of Turk's head.

"One," Marie said, grinning tiredly, "he's not young. He's in his forties."

"Still young to me."

Marie shook her head and chuckled. "Two, he's okay. Healing."

"Will you be seeing him later on?" Uncle Gerry said. "Perhaps for dinner?"

"No," Marie replied. "I won't."

Her uncle frowned.

"There's nothing between us, my dear uncle," Marie said. "And, to be perfectly honest, I'm more than happy on my own. I've got a good routine. A good life."

"He's a good man," Uncle Gerry said.

"Without a doubt," Marie responded. "But I don't want a relationship with him, and he doesn't want one with me. Sure, we're friends and I value his friendship, but it won't move beyond that. He's, well, he's got too much baggage, Uncle Gerry. He's too damaged for me. If I'm going to have a relationship, the person has to be okay with who they are. They need to have made peace with their past. Shane is almost happy with who he is, but he certainly hasn't been able to put the past behind him."

"I'm not saying he has to, or that he even should," she continued. "I'm just saying he isn't what I'm looking for in a partner."

Uncle Gerry put his coffee mug down and looked at her silently for a moment. Finally, he said, "What you're saying makes sense. And it's a mature view. I do have one question."

"What's that?" she asked.

"Can I still be friends with him?"

Marie let out a surprised laugh, Turk's ears perking up at the sound.

"Yes," she said, smiling at her uncle, "of course you can!"

"Excellent," Uncle Gerry said, grinning. "Now, tell me about the case you're working on, the one about the body found behind the Holocaust Memorial downtown."

Marie picked up her own coffee, took a sip, and started to give him the gruesome details.

* * *

The Town of Griswold
Book 3

Book 3: The Town of Griswold

Chapter 1: Looking for a Place to 'Shine

John and Jimmy Quill drove along Route 111. They had 'Irish-ed' up their coffee with a good dose of bad whiskey, and they were feeling fine as the sun rose. John steered with one hand, held his travel mug with the other, and kept watch on his side of the road. Jimmy, younger by two years, examined everything which passed by on the passenger side.

"John," Jimmy said, breaking the silence.

"What's up?"

"On the right, about two hundred feet, slow down," Jimmy said, rolling down his window to get a better look.

John pulled off onto the shoulder, came to a stop. A narrow road, the pavement cracked and in desperate need of repair, turned off and into the shadows. "What's this?"

"Don't know," Jimmy answered.

John watched as his brother pulled out his phone, punched in their position, and waited to see what results showed up. With a flick of his wrist, John put on the hazard lights and kept an eye on the mirrors, making sure no cops showed up to ask what he and Jimmy were up to.

After several minutes, when John was finally feeling a buzz from the whiskey, Jimmy said, "Here it is, bro. Place called Griswold. Used to be a lumber town. Shut down sometime in the thirties."

"What's there?" John asked, peering down the tree-lined road which led into darkness.

"Couple of buildings, maybe. Cellar holes. An old church," Jimmy replied. Holding the phone out, he said, "Here, take a look."

John took it and looked at the crisp, black-and-white image on the screen. A clapboard church, a good-sized building, was the dominant feature in a town.

"That church," John said, grinning at his brother, "that church looks perfect."

Jimmy nodded, smiling. "Yeah, it sure as hell does."

John took his foot off the brake, made sure no one was coming up on them and pulled wide into the street before he cut hard to the right.

The street leading into Griswold was a mess. Every few feet John's old, restored Dodge pickup bounced along. John winced with every bump and thud.

Damn, he thought, *I sure as hell better not break a damned spring.*

Tree limbs slapped at the sides and the windows, but John continued to push on. The world consisted of nothing more than broken asphalt and the crowded road.

Then the forest opened up around them, and the town of Griswold appeared. Two buildings stood tall: the church, and a long but low structure with a faded sign that proclaimed it to be the Griswold Country Store. The remains of a few other buildings stood on either side of the narrow street, and empty plots stood close by. Hints of other roads branched off through the forest, which had encroached on the town. Young trees, no more than twenty or thirty years old by their size, were along both sides near the back.

"We could do it here," Jimmy said, looking around.

John nodded his agreement. "For a while at least. Eventually, they'll figure it out."

"Yeah," Jimmy said, sighing. "They always do. But it might take a little longer here."

"Will you be able to get the Chinaski brothers to help?" John asked. "They've got access to the college's trucks, right?"

"Yeah," Jimmy said. "Both of them still owe me for the bet they lost on the last Red Sox game. I'll tell them I'll get rid of the bet and the interest."

"Sounds good," John said. "We'll have to come back and check it out before we set up, though. Make sure nobody's squatting here."

Jimmy nodded his agreement as John started to turn the truck around. It took a few tries in the tight confines of the overgrown street, but he managed. As he pointed the truck back the way they had come, he looked in the rearview and almost hit the brakes.

For a second John thought he had seen a young woman by the church.

Probably a deer, he told himself, shaking his head. John pushed the thought out of his mind and guided the truck back towards Route 111.

Just a deer.

Chapter 2: At Berkley Street

The doorbell rang, and Shane stepped out into the hallway. He looked around and said, "I'm serious. Best behavior." When no response was forthcoming, he walked to the main door and opened it.

Courtney DeSantis stood on the front step. She was stunning in a pair of jeans and a light gray sweatshirt, well-traveled hiking boots on her feet and a pack slung over her right shoulder. She brushed a strand of dark purple, almost black hair out of her eyes and smiled at Shane.

Shane grinned back at her, stepping aside and saying, "Come on in."

She did so, eyes darting from left to right. "Wow. This is a big place."

Shane nodded as he closed the door. "You like it?"

"I do," Courtney said, turning around and kissing him swiftly on the cheek. "I like you, too."

Shane felt his face heat up and thought, *What the hell, it's like I'm fourteen all over again.*

She saw his expression and laughed. "You're too damned cute, Shane."

Shane chuckled. "I've been called a lot of things, doll, but never cute."

"Good," she said happily. Courtney shivered slightly and said, "Are there a lot of ghosts here?"

"A few," Shane said.

"Want to give me the tour later on, once we get back?" she asked.

"I'd love to," Shane said. "You sure you're okay with that?"

She raised an eyebrow. "After Squirrel Island? Yeah, I'm okay with your house."

"Good," Shane said.

"You need to pack or anything?" Courtney asked.

"No," Shane said, shaking his head. He gestured to the corner by the main door. His old backpack was on the floor, filled with the few items necessary for a day trip up into the North Country. "Already took care of the packing this morning."

"Nice," she said, smiling. "So, want to know where we're headed?"

"Yes," Shane said, grinning. "I thought it might be nice to know."

She punched him playfully in the arm. "Place called Griswold. Ever heard of it?"

"No," Shane said, grabbing his backpack. "Small town?"

"Small and unoccupied," Courtney said. "It's a New England ghost town."

"Sounds good," he said. "I don't think I've ever been to a ghost town before."

"Then it's an adventure," she said, winking. "So, ready to go?"

"Yup," Shane said, nodding.

"Great!" she yelled, stepping forward and kissing him again. "Let's go!"

Shane grinned foolishly, shook his head, and opened the door.

Book 3: The Town of Griswold

Chapter 3: Waiting on Jimmy

Three days after John and Jimmy had decided the ghost town was the place to set up their distillery, John was in front of the abandoned general store. He sat on the lowered tailgate of the pickup, some of his camping gear scattered about the bed and his rifle across his legs. The weapon was broken down, and he had taken a short break from cleaning it. He glanced at his watch, saw Jimmy was twenty minutes late, and shook his head angrily.

John picked up his phone and called his brother.

Jimmy answered on the fourth ring. "What's up?" he asked.

"What the hell do you mean, 'what's up?'" John snapped. "Seriously, Jimmy? What the hell? You're supposed to be here with me."

Jimmy yawned loudly and asked, "Where?"

"Griswold," John said, biting off the word.

"Oh," Jimmy said. Then repeated, "Oh! I didn't think it was today. I thought we were doing it Thursday."

"It is Thursday, moron," John said, his anger rushing out of him. "Jimmy, what did you do?"

"Me and Erica scored a couple of nail-heads yesterday, well, Tuesday," his brother replied.

"You told me you weren't going to do any more heroin," John said.

"It was right there, Johnny, bro," Jimmy said, chuckling. "Listen, Clint came over with them, he gave us friend prices and we were off and chasing the dragon. We got a little lost. I'm good now, though."

"Why, you mainline it all?" John asked, disgusted.

"No, no needles this time," Jimmy said. "Told you I wasn't doing that anymore."

"You also said you were going to stay away from heroin completely, *James*," John said, the anger returning.

"Christ, John," Jimmy said, his voice low and apologetic. "It was just once."

"I'm not watching you get another shot of Narcan because you OD'd, Jimmy," John said. "Anyway, when can you get your nasty self over here?"

"Um," Jimmy grunted, "give me half an hour. So, yeah, nine?"

"Okay," John said. "See you then."

He ended the call and put the phone back on the truck bed.

Why is he so stupid? John wondered, sighing. He reassembled the weapon, checking the action on the bolt. When it was whole again, he set it down beside the phone and looked around the small town.

Not even a bar, he thought. *Where the hell did they drink? How could you even live in a place like this without alcohol?*

John shook the questions away, got off the tailgate, and stretched. He walked over to the old church and looked through the broken windows. A few pews remained inside, cockeyed and covered with the filth of years. Scurrying sounds told him there were rodents within, and that they could see him.

Have to get a cat or two, John told himself, wandering away from the building. He stuffed his hands into his pockets and followed the barest hint of a path which led around the back. The young trees were widely placed, and John moved through them easily. There was deer scat, and the bark was stripped from some of the lower branches.

Damn, he grinned, *might be able to get some fresh venison out of season.*

The path moved around cellar holes, the remnants of chimneys on the ground around them. Grass grew up among the red bricks and crumbled mortar. Soon, he found himself at the general store. He walked closer for a better look.

John stopped. He jerked his head to the right, towards his truck.

Someone's here, John thought. He examined everything closely. His eyes sought out tell-tale shadows, the straight lines that gave away humanity.

Nothing, John thought. The hair on his neck was standing up, his heart beating quickly. *No, there's something here. I can feel it.*

Jimmy would have said John's 'spider-sense' was tingling, and in a way, Jimmy was right. John's ability to read a situation from the subtle clues around them had saved the brothers from arrests, repeatedly.

A shadow fluctuated near the pickup. Near the back of the truck, where the rifle was. And where his phone was, too.

And the damned bullets! John thought angrily. He kept a tight rein on the fear trying to boil over in him. With slow movements, he pulled his hands out of his pockets, taking his SOG folding knife with him. He put his thumb on the quick-flip for the blade and focused on the shadow he had seen.

Even though he was only a short distance away, John couldn't tell if there was a big animal or a small person by the back of the truck.

One way to find out, he thought.

"Hey!" he yelled. "Get away from my ride!"

The shadow flinched but didn't leave.

Anger flared up in him, and John took a step closer to the pickup.

"I know you can hear me!" John shouted. "Now get away!"

Again, the barest hint of movement, but the shadow remained where it was.

With the barest pressure from his thumb, the blade of the knife sprang out, clicking loudly. He reversed his grip on the weapon, so the back of the edge ran parallel to his forearm.

John took a deep, calming breath, exhaled through his nose, and advanced towards the truck. He went at it wide, making sure he could see the person before they could rush at him.

When he came abreast of the pickup, he stuttered to a stop.

A young woman crouched at the back of the truck. Her clothes were tattered, a vivid red mark around her neck, and the sun shining through her to the ground behind her. John's grip on the knife loosened and he dropped it.

The young woman's brown eyes were wide, she opened her mouth and in a voice full of fear she whispered, "Run."

John wanted to ask why, but something struck him in the back of the head, and he fell forward. The ground rushed up to greet him as he passed through the cold air the young woman occupied.

Chapter 4: Jimmy's Late Again

When Jimmy pulled into the defunct main street of Griswold, he saw John's pickup. But he didn't see his brother. Frowning, Jimmy parked alongside John's truck, turned the engine off, and got out.

"John!" Jimmy called out. His voice echoed off the two buildings before it was swallowed by the forest around him. He cupped his hands around his mouth and yelled out, "Johnny!"

Silence answered him.

Jimmy went to John's truck, opened the door, and saw the keys in the ignition. He walked to the back and looked in the bed. Some of John's camping gear, his bolt-action Enfield rifle, and his cellphone.

"What the hell?" Jimmy murmured. He looked around the town, glanced down, and froze.

There was blood on the asphalt and the grass that grew between the cracked pavement.

Oh, no, Jimmy thought. He turned back to John's truck, grabbed the rifle out of the bed, and went back to the vehicle's interior. In the glove box, he found a box of cartridges and several loaded clips. He stuffed everything but one clip into the front pocket of his sweatshirt. With a quick motion, he put the clip into the rifle, chambered a round, and went to the blood on the pavement.

Jimmy dropped down into a squat and let his eyes roam slowly outward, searching the street until he spotted another splash of blood. He got up and walked carefully, eyes flicking from the pavement to the town around him. Each step was cautious, and he followed the blood trail as quickly as he could.

It led steadily on toward the store.

Was the door always open? Jimmy wondered. *Or is there a squatter? Did someone get the jump on John?*

Jimmy increased his speed, more blood leading him to the store's small porch. A long streak across the old, worn wood showed where his brother was probably dragged.

Through the doorway, Jimmy could see little. The darkness seemed to undulate, and fear dripped out of the building, making Jimmy's mouth dry and his throat tight.

What the hell's in there? he asked himself. *It doesn't matter. John's in there. Someone's got your brother. Get him back.*

Jimmy brought the rifle up to his shoulder and tucked his cheek against the cool wood of the stock, smelling the gun oil.

Go, he commanded, and he went.

He moved in quickly, crouching slightly to present a smaller target. A quick step to the right and he stopped, listening. The sound of something tearing reached his ears. Jimmy let his eyes adjust to the darkness, trying to focus on the sound.

To the right a little more, Jimmy thought. He adjusted his position and was able to make out a counter, and damaged shelves.

Someone whistled.

A happy tune interrupted by more tearing noises.

Behind the counter. John is behind the counter.

Jimmy moved carefully, but the floor beneath his feet was old and traitorous. After his third step, a board let out a shriek.

The whistling stopped.

"You, behind the counter," Jimmy said forcefully, "stand up where I can see you."

"Would you see me, boy?" a deep voice asked. The hatred in the words reminded Jimmy of his father and weakened his knees.

"You heard me," Jimmy said, managing to keep the fear out of his voice. "Get up or I come over and put a hole in you."

The stranger chuckled. "How can I refuse such a demand?"

Jimmy kept the rifle aimed at the counter and waited.

A heartbeat later, the individual stood. And stood, and stood.

He was tall, well over six feet. Thinner than anyone living Jimmy had ever seen. The man's eyes glistened with the light from the doorway. He was pale and shirtless, his chest concave. His head was thin, sparse brown hair clipped short, which highlighted his long face and nose. His hands were below the counter.

Jimmy took careful aim at the man's chest. "Mister, you're going to raise your hands up where I can see them, or I'm going to blow your back all over the wall behind you. I'm not asking, I'm telling."

"I believe you would," the man said, nodding approvingly. He raised his hands up as commanded.

In his left, he held a leg. In his right, he held an arm. John's arm.

Jimmy recognized the tribal tattoo around the bicep. It was the same one he had on his own.

Blood dripped from the limbs, and it looked as though they had been ripped from John's sockets.

John, Jimmy thought numbly. Then he squeezed the trigger on the Enfield. The sound of the shot deafened him briefly, the flash of the muzzle ruining his vision in the dimness.

But Jimmy fired all five rounds, and even without looking he knew he put all of them in the man's chest. Or he thought he had.

The stranger laughed, and something heavy hit Jimmy in the head, knocking him back. Jimmy tripped over his own feet, fell, and hit the floor. The air rushed out of his lungs, and his back screamed out in pain. Gasping for breath Jimmy got onto his side, dug another clip out of his pocket, and spilled the rest onto the floor.

He slammed the clip home, got to his knees, and was knocked over again as something crashed into his chest.

Before he could regain his breath, the Enfield was ripped out of his hands, and he was picked up. Cold hands grasped either arm and lifted him off the floor. Blinking, Jimmy tried to see, kicking out with his feet but encountering nothing.

"You are a wiry fellow," the deep voice said. "I think I should like a hunt. You look like you enjoy a good hunt. Have you ever been the prey, hm?"

Jimmy continued to struggle, but the man squeezed him tighter. A scream of pain tore its way out of Jimmy's throat. He went still.

The man loosened his grip and said, "Now, you haven't answered my question."

"Why?" Jimmy said furiously. "Why did you kill him?"

"Because I can," the man replied in a bored voice. "And, well, it has been a long time since I have. He woke me up, you know. I heard him cleaning his rifle. Such a clear and delicate sound. Nearly as sweet as a songbird. I'd been asleep for quite some time. Dreaming you know. Now, answer my question."

"What question?" Jimmy snapped.

"Have you ever been prey?"

"What?" Jimmy asked. "No. Why would I be?"

"So, a new experience for you," the stranger said happily. "I do so love virgins. Ah, perhaps I should introduce myself then. I am Abel, Abel Latham. And you are?"

Jimmy remained silent, but Abel squeezed, and Jimmy gasped out, "James! James Quill!"

Abel relaxed his grip and said, "I knew a Quill once. I didn't like him. How appropriate then, wouldn't you agree, James?"

"I don't know," Jimmy said, taking in great, deep breaths.

"I suppose not," Abel said, sighing. "Now, are you ready?"

"For what?" Jimmy asked, his mind racing. *How do I get away? I have to get away. I have to get the cops here.*

"For the hunt," Abel said. He chuckled. "You will run, I will follow. Not right away, mind you, for where is the fun in that? No, you will run, and you will hide. I will hunt you. I will find you. And then, I shall see how pretty your insides are."

Abel let go, dropping Jimmy to the floor. Jimmy's entire body howled in agony.

"Run," Abel said. "Run as fast and as far as you can, James. I'll be coming after you soon."

Jimmy scrambled to his feet, launched himself out the door, and sprinted to his truck. He jumped in, started the engine, and slammed the pickup into drive. The sharp, iron tang of blood was in his nose, and a glance down showed he was splashed in it.

Worry about it later. Later, he told himself. He crushed the gas pedal beneath his foot and raced along the road, branches slapping at the truck. For more than a minute, he drove recklessly back toward Route 111. A mirror broke off, the road curved sharply again, opened up, and Jimmy slammed on the brakes.

He was back in Griswold.

Abel stood on the porch of the country store, wearing only jeans and boots. His thin arms were folded across his chest, and Jimmy realized there was something wrong. It was almost as though he could see the darkness *through* Abel.

The tall man waved and called out, "Run, James! Run!"

Jimmy panicked. He got out of the truck and sprinted for the tree line. Behind him, his pickup rolled forward slowly. As he reached the trees, Jimmy heard a dull crash. Without looking back, he knew what had happened. His truck had hit John's, but it didn't matter. None of it did.

He's going to kill me if he catches me, Jimmy thought frantically, and he plunged deeper into the forest.

Chapter 5: In the Diner

The diner was small, with a good morning crowd, and Shane and Courtney had drawn more than a few disapproving looks. They were obviously not father and daughter, and Courtney looked younger than her age.

The waitress was cold and gave Shane a withering stare. He recognized it for what it was, and why, but it took Courtney a few minutes to realize they were the focus of several people's attention.

"Why are they looking at us?" Courtney asked in a low voice.

"Two reasons. First, my lovely locks," he said, running his hand over his bald head, "and second, because you look like you're at least twenty years younger than me."

"Seriously?" Courtney said. She looked around, shook her head and turned her attention to the menu.

The waitress came back with a cup of coffee for Shane and orange juice for Courtney. She put his mug down hard, splashing coffee onto the Formica of the table, and she gave Courtney a pitying look. Then the waitress left without waiting to see if they were ready to order.

"Wow," Courtney said, a note of discomfort in her voice. "That was pretty bad."

"I'm a dirty old man," Shane said, shrugging. "At least that's what she's thinking, and most of the others. I've been stared at for years because of my hair. And, when there was all the angst in the news about Iraq some people would frown at me when I was in uniform. Not too many, though."

"It's not right," Courtney said, closing her menu and putting it down. "Who cares about the age difference? They're not dating us."

"People like to judge, doll," Shane said. He put his menu next to hers. The coffee was strong and hot, and it made him smile. "I'm not bothered by them."

The waitress returned, ignored Shane and said to Courtney, "What'll you have, sweetheart?"

"Two eggs over easy, with a side of bacon and wheat toast, please," Courtney said, glancing at Shane.

The waitress wrote it down quickly on her order pad, then, without looking at Shane, she said, "And you?"

"The same, please," he answered.

The waitress left.

"Damn," Courtney said. "She gets no tip."

"Tip or no tip, it's not going to change the way she thinks," Shane said. "But I'd like to tip anyway. Being a waitress is tough. Couple of my friends in the Marines, their wives picked up waitressing jobs to help make ends meet. Long hours, bad pay, and a whole lot of idiots."

Courtney shook her head. "Still not happy about it."

Shane winked at her. "You don't have to be."

He glanced out the window of their booth and saw dark storm clouds. The trees on either side of the road bent back with a sudden, surging wind.

When he looked back to Courtney, he asked, "So why a ghost town?"

"Why not?" she said.

"Squirrel Island."

Her face paled, and her lips tightened. "I don't think there are really ghosts in this town."

"No?"

She shook her head.

"Fair enough," Shane said. "I hope there aren't."

"Me too," Courtney said softly. "I wouldn't mind meeting a spirit on my own terms, but I don't want to be surprised by one again."

"Yeah," Shane said, picking up his mug and taking a drink. "Not a whole lot of fun."

They lapsed into silence for several minutes. The waitress arrived, smiled at Courtney, served them both, and left.

"She does not like you," Courtney said, taking a bite of her toast.

"Nope. I'm robbing the cradle," Shane said.

"You're a brat," Courtney said, grinning. "Maybe I should tell her I stole you out of a nursing home."

"That'll work," Shane said with a chuckle. "Ask her if my senior discount applies to your meal, too."

Courtney laughed, wiped her mouth with her napkin, and said, "Maybe we could see if one of them could help you back to the car."

"We're not at a bar," Shane said with mock seriousness, "and I have never been too drunk to walk."

"No?"

He shook his head. "I either walk or pass out. No half-measures for this Marine."

Courtney's happy laughter filled the air, and Shane forgot about the looks of the wait staff and other patrons.

Chapter 6: Trying to Hide

I'm lost, Jimmy thought. He couldn't tell if it was good to be lost, or bad. It all depended on whether or not Abel was in the woods.

Jimmy had found a small brook, slipped down a washed-away bank, and had hidden himself among the exposed roots of a pine tree. He had taken a drink of water and examined the front of his shirt. There was plenty of blood, but it wasn't his. Whatever Abel had hit him with had left its mark.

What the hell did he use? Jimmy wondered. *Oh, damn.*

Jimmy bent over and retched, all of the water he had drunk burned its way back up and out of his throat.

He hit me with John's parts, Jimmy thought, and he threw up again. He dry-heaved several times, spat out the foul taste of bile, and rinsed his mouth. Wincing, Jimmy forced himself to drink more water. The day was too warm, and his body was already in agony over what he had done the night before.

The air around him darkened, and for a heartbeat, he feared Abel had found him. A glance up to a hole in the canopy showed him storm clouds.

He frowned. *No forecast of rain today.*

Nothing about your brother being murdered by some unholy creature, either, Jimmy thought bitterly. *You need to get your act together, and you need to get out of here. Figure out a way to come back and kill whatever Abel is.*

Anger spiked in Jimmy's heart, and a fierce rage burned within him.

He forced himself to settle back into the cool depths of the root system. The various insects he ignored, closing his eyes and focusing on clearing his mind. It was still muddied with the aftereffects of the heroin and the drinking.

Jimmy kept his eyes closed, and he listened. The sounds of the forest were normal over the soft noises the brook made. The different birds called out to prospective mates or argued with rivals. Squirrels yelled at everything. A twig cracked the careless step of a deer close by. The air was warm, almost heavy. There was a charge in it as well, the tiny hairs on his arms standing up as an electrical current seemed to ripple through.

A thunderstorm, Jimmy thought. *If it's strong enough, it'll break the back of the heat. Cool it all down.*

The squirrels were the first warning Jimmy had. They stopped their angry chatter. When he noticed it, the birds ceased their passionate calls. Even the brook muted itself.

Jimmy didn't have to wonder why.

Within several minutes, Abel walked silently about thirty yards away. The trees were shadows through the man. His head scanned to the left and to the right, searching for sign of Jimmy's passage.

He knows what he's doing, Jimmy realized as he watched Abel. The killer paused and looked, inspected branches and leaves.

Same as I would do, Jimmy thought. Which was why, after his initial blind run into the forest, he had slowed down and forced himself to think. Jimmy was lost, but he hadn't left much of a trail to follow. He'd spent too many years hunting with John to make such an amateur mistake.

Abel paused, turned his back to Jimmy's hiding spot, and waited.

He knows I'm near, Jimmy thought, fighting to keep his heart rate under control. *He's trying to make me break for it. You can't, Jimmy, you can't. Be cool.*

Fear and panic fought for control within his mind and eventually Jimmy managed to calm himself. Abel still stood with his back to Jimmy's pine tree. The ghost's back was crisscrossed with raised, white scars. There wasn't a place on his back which wasn't old and knotted tissue. Abel was clad only in old jeans and boots, a grim figure. A few vivid scars danced along the back of Abel's biceps and down his forearms.

After several long minutes, Abel turned and moved off to the right.

Run! A fearful part of Jimmy demanded. But he resisted it, kept his mind focused on the way Abel had gone. If the man was trying to draw Jimmy out, Jimmy had to wait. There was no other choice to be made.

Slow, Jimmy told himself. *Go slow. Wait.*

Jimmy nodded, listened to the squirrels take up their arguments once again, and waited to see what else the morning would bring.

"I know you're out here, James," Abel said, his voice echoing off the trees and gripping Jimmy's spine with a fist of fear. "What do you think I will do, when I find you, hm?"

He's trying to spook you. Flush you out, Jimmy told himself, his heart a thunderous roar in his ears.

"You are ever so entertaining," Abel continued. "Far more than your brother. He screamed a little, to be honest, but who wouldn't, eh?"

Jimmy bit the inside of his cheek to keep his mouth shut.

"Can you imagine the pain of having an arm torn from its socket? Or a leg?" Abel asked, chuckling, his voice rolling out through the forest. "It is far more difficult than it seems. Perhaps if I had roasted him first, it would have loosened the limb up. Is it not so with a chicken?"

Jimmy closed his eyes, tears spilling out onto his cheeks. *Christ, I hope he died quickly.*

Silence stretched out, and briefly Jimmy held out hope Abel would be gone.

"I did not die in such a fashion," Abel said, shattering Jimmy's hopes. Abel's voice was slightly farther away, but still too near.

"No," Abel said, "I died peacefully, in my sleep. Granted, I was chained to the chimney of my own house. Imprisoned by my own sister. But I have forgiven her. Is that not what we do for the ones we love? Is it not what God commands us to do, even for our enemies?"

Jimmy didn't answer.

"Will you?" Abel asked, laughing cheerfully. "Will you, young James, forgive me for your brother's death, and for your own as well?"

Abel didn't ask any more questions. Or proclaim or expound upon anything else.

"He's gone," someone whispered, and Jimmy nearly screamed.

A young woman had appeared in the brook, her clothing shredded. Around her slim, pale neck was a vivid red mark, as though someone had tried to garrote her.

No, they succeeded, Jimmy thought numbly.

He could see a minnow swimming in the brook. Through the young woman.

I can see through her. Right through, Jimmy thought. Then his eyes rolled up to show their whites, and he passed out beneath the exposed roots of the pine tree.

Chapter 7: The Ghost Town

"You look like you've done that more than once," Courtney said appreciatively.

Shane finished the adjustments on his straps, made sure the pack was comfortable on his back, and grinned at her. "Yeah, more than once."

He stopped and his grin turned into a smile. "Here, put these on."

Shane reached into his shirt, pulled out his dog tags and handed them to her.

Courtney smiled, blushing. "So, guess this makes the whole dating thing official?"

"Guess so," Shane said, heat spreading over his cheeks. He watched, happy as she slipped the tags on over her head and tucked them into her shirt.

"How many years were you in the Marines?" she asked as he stepped forward and double checked her pack.

"Twenty years," Shane said.

"Hell, you enlisted when I was what, two?" she asked, winking.

Shane gave a mock grimace. "Basically."

"Why?" Courtney said, her face serious. "Why did you join?"

"I joined because I felt I had a duty to," Shane answered. "I feel everyone should do something for their country, either serve in the military or contribute to society. I reenlisted because my parents were missing and the Marines are my family."

"Once a Marine, always a Marine?"

Shane nodded. "To this day. Until I die. They'll be at my funeral."

"Pretty intense," Courtney said. "I don't get it, but it's kind of cool."

"Kind of like me?" he asked, smiling.

"You're more than cool," she said, standing on her tiptoes to kiss him. "Now, let's go see what a New England ghost town looks like."

Book 3: The Town of Griswold

"Okay," Shane said. They left the car parked on the side of Route 111 and above them the late morning sun was hidden by a bank of newly arrived dark clouds. The road leading into the town of Griswold was a maze of broken pavement, with grass growing in the breaks and trees pressing in close on either side.

Shane felt uncomfortable the further they traveled. Eventually, the birdsong petered out, the normal sounds of the forest vanishing. The air was heavy to breathe and colder than it should have been.

You're paranoid, he told himself. *This place is fine, even if it is haunted. If there were deaths, they would have been reported, would have been in every book and on every site about haunted places.*

Courtney reached out, took his hand, and squeezed it. Shane's anxiety lessened, and they followed the road deeper into the forest. Freshly broken branches lay on the asphalt, and hung in splinters from the trees.

"Someone's been through here," Shane said, glancing around. "Maybe even today."

"How can you tell?" Courtney asked.

"The trees," he replied.

"What? Oh, wow, I didn't even notice the branches," she said. "That's crazy. Probably someone checking it out like we are."

Shane nodded, but a curious sound caught his attention. He titled his head to the right and listened.

An engine.

He looked at the sides of the road. Shane making sure they had a way to get off of the narrow asphalt passage should a vehicle come barreling up towards them.

"Do you hear something?" Courtney asked.

"Yeah," Shane said. "It sounds like an engine. Car, probably a truck, given the marks on the trees."

Courtney nodded.

The road curved slightly, and when it opened up, they found themselves in the town of Griswold. The remains of chimneys reached into the sky. Cellar holes could be seen, and two buildings remained. A church and a general store. A pair of trucks were in the center of town, one of them still running. Its front end was pressed up against the driver's side door and part of the truck bed.

"Oh Jesus," Courtney said softly. She let go of Shane's hand and cautiously moved forward toward the pickups. Shane walked beside her, eyes flickering from place to place, searching for whoever owned the vehicles. Shane turned the engine off of the still rumbling truck.

"Stay close," Shane said. Courtney nodded and followed him as he went around to the other side of the pickup. He reached in, opened the glove box, and pulled out the registration.

James Michael Quill, Shane read. He returned the paper to the truck and made his way to the other pickup. He repeated the process and read the name printed on the other registration. *Jonathan Patrick Quill.*

"Shane," Courtney said in a low voice.

He looked at her. She had taken a step away and was looking into the bed of Jonathan's truck.

Shane joined her and saw a few pieces of camping gear and a cellphone.

"Damn," he muttered. "Alright, do you have your phone?"

She raised an eyebrow at him. "Want me to call 911?"

"Please," Shane said. He glanced around. "Soon as you get through, tell them we're going back to the road. Something's wrong here, and I don't want us mixed up in it."

Courtney nodded in agreement, pulled her phone out of her back pocket, and dialed the number. Frowning, she tried to dial again.

"What's wrong?" Shane asked.

"Hold on," she answered. She pressed the power button. Then held it down. A concerned expression crept onto her face. "My phone's dead. I charged it this morning, right before we left. I wanted to make sure I could get a lot of photos."

"I didn't bring mine," Shane said.

She looked at him in surprise.

"I'm with you," he explained. "Nobody else I want to talk to."

Courtney blushed in spite of the situation they found themselves in.

"Okay," Shane said, reaching into the truck's bed, "let's see if this cell works."

He picked it up, tried to turn it on, but nothing happened. Still holding the phone, Shane walked up to the truck, leaned in, and found a charger plugged into the lighter. He connected the phone to the charger. Nothing happened.

Shane leaned in, turned the key which was still in the ignition, and nothing happened. Not even a click from the starter. His heartbeat quickened. Silently he pulled the whole charger out of the lighter and carried it to James' truck. He plugged the power cord in, and the phone remained dark. Shane tried to start the pickup, and like Jonathan's, it was dead.

"We need to leave," Shane said, backing out of the cab.

"Bad?" Courtney asked.

He nodded. "Yup. All the batteries are dead."

"What does that mean?" she said, glancing around uncomfortably.

"Ghosts are energy," Shane explained, reaching out and taking her hand. He started back towards the road which would take them to her car. "They can boost their own strength by draining batteries."

"You think this place is actually haunted?" she asked. Her voice had a hint of fear.

"Yup," Shane said, resisting the urge to look over his shoulder as they passed into the tunnel of trees. "I don't know if it's only one ghost, or a hundred. All I know is there are two pickups and at least two missing men. We get out of here, charge your phone, and head to a police station. I think there's a state police barrack around here somewhere."

They moved quickly along the cracked asphalt, the trees sinister as they loomed on either side. The interlocking branches above them were the bars of a cage. None of the familiar sounds of the forest greeted them. Only silence, and a cold in the air which ripped the breath from Shane's lungs.

The road curved, ever so slightly back towards the way they had come, and when it opened up, Shane and Courtney came to a sharp stop.

"Oh my God," Courtney said, despair creeping into her voice. "You've got to be kidding me."

Shane stared at the trucks of the Quill brothers, the general store and the church, the cellar holes, and the solitary chimneys spitting both gravity and time.

Suddenly, painfully he remembered the passages in the walls of his home, the unorthodox and insane ways in which they moved. Old, childhood fears threatened to swarm over him. To devour his adulthood and his sanity.

"Shane," Courtney said, "you're holding my hand too hard, handsome."

Her voice smothered the memories, and he relaxed his grip. "Sorry, doll."

"You okay?" she asked.

"Yeah," he said, sighing, his voice quivering briefly. "For a second there, I felt like I was back in my house."

"How?" she said.

"This," he said, gesturing to the town. "Following a path which should have brought you one place, but ends up bringing you back to where you started."

"Damn," she said, shivering. "Did it get colder?"

"A lot," Shane said. Before he could say anything else, the door to the church opened. Only an inch or two, but enough to be noticeable. "Courtney, look at the church."

She did so, frowned, and asked in a whisper, "Wasn't the door closed before?"

"Up until about a minute ago," Shane agreed. As they looked at the building, a small dog peeked its head out and looked at them. It was followed by a little boy's head. The child's hand sneaked out and beckoned to them. The boy's cherubic face was worried, and his hand moved quicker.

"We should go," Courtney said.

Shane looked at her. "Why?"

"I think the kid wants to tell us something."

"He's dead," Shane said as the boy ducked back into the church, the dog following a second later.

Courtney nodded. "He's really little, though. Maybe six or seven. And I don't think he wants to hurt us."

Shane looked around. "Alright, maybe he can tell us something. If he doesn't try to kill us."

"Kids aren't evil," Courtney said, reprimanding him gently.

"Remind me to tell you a little more about my childhood, later," Shane said bitterly.

She squeezed his hand, and he followed her lead towards the little boy. The door opened more to admit them, and then closed with a soft click once they stood inside. In a shadow off to the right, Shane could make out the shapes of the child and the dog.

"Hello," Shane said in a soft voice.

"Hello," the little boy replied.

"This is my friend Courtney, and I'm Shane."

"My name's Andrew," the little boy said, "and this is my dog, Rex."

"It's very nice to meet you, Andrew," Courtney said, squatting down and smiling. "Why did you want us to come in here?"

"Abel is outside," Andrew said fearfully. "He's hunting."

"Hunting what?" Shane asked.

"A man," Andrew said, slipping further into the shadow. "Abel only hunts people."

Chapter 8: Jimmy and the Girl

Jimmy opened his eyes, stared at a network of roots over his head, and realized he hadn't been dreaming. The girl he had seen in the brook was beside him, looking down at him with concern. He could still see through her. Part of him wanted to pass out again, but he resisted.

Sitting up, Jimmy looked at her and whispered, "Can you hear me?"

She nodded. In an equally low voice, she said, "You need to leave. Abel will be back soon. He knows you are near."

"I tried to leave," Jimmy said. "I couldn't."

"It's glam," the girl said. "Nothing more. But if you cannot see through it, you cannot leave."

Jimmy shook his head. He wanted to ask what the hell 'glam' was, but he didn't. "Where do I go then?"

"What is your name?" she asked, ignoring his question.

"Jimmy. James," he answered. Then, for the sake of being polite, he said, "What's yours?"

"Eugenia," the girl replied. "Come, James. Follow me."

She moved down to the brook and Jimmy went after her. He stepped carefully into the water, his sneakers soaking up the cold liquid quickly. Eugenia followed the brook, the banks gradually rising on either side until they were in a gully. Young trees grew up tall, hiding them further. The path of the water was thick with double backs and gentle turns, centuries of movement having carved out the passage. Occasional deadfalls blocked the way, and while Eugenia passed through them easily, Jimmy had to climb over, under, and occasionally go around them.

Every splash caused his heart to race and fear tried to choke the breath from him. He caught himself focusing on Eugenia. The girl's brown hair was long and tangled. Her body slim in the tattered remains of her dress. Jimmy noticed her feet were bare, vivid cuts upon the soles when he occasionally caught a glimpse of them.

I'm with a ghost. A dead girl who looks like she was murdered, Jimmy thought, trying to understand the situation. It was farfetched, unrealistic. A slice of fantasy which made him wonder if he had snorted a bad bit of heroin from Clint.

No trip has ever been this real, and I've never even heard of somebody having a ride like this, Jimmy thought glumly. *It has to be real.*

The banks lowered again, sank down until the stream was nearly level with the forest floor. To the left, Jimmy saw the remains of a house. Stone walls lacking a roof. A fieldstone chimney standing tall. Windows hidden by shutters and a door closed against the world.

Eugenia started towards the front of the building, paused, glanced at Jimmy, and then went around to the left. Jimmy continued to follow her, and he saw a portion of the stone wall had fallen. Eugenia went through the hole, and Jimmy scrambled over the pile of stones which marked the impromptu entrance.

He found himself in the house's single room. The fireplace was on the far wall, opposite the front door. Leaves littered the ground. Fir and pine saplings grew up in clusters. The remains of a chair and table lay by the wall Jimmy had climbed through. The stone walls of the house were barren of decoration if they had ever had any.

Eugenia stood in the center of the room and smiled nervously at him. Jimmy felt uncomfortable looking through her as if it violated her in some way. He glanced around, saw the front left corner would keep him hidden from anyone looking in through the hole in the wall, or any of the windows.

Tiredly, Jimmy walked over to the corner, scooped out some of the leaves, saw the floor was only earth and sat down. Eugenia hesitated, then came over and sat down across from him.

"How are you feeling, James?" she asked, shy concern in her voice.

"Cold. Tired," he answered. A wave of grief washed over him. "And my brother's dead."

"I am sorry," Eugenia said. "I told him to run, but it was too late. Abel was too fast. Your brother woke him up."

"How?" Jimmy asked, confused. "I mean, how do you wake a ghost up?"

"Some of us never sleep," she said sadly. "Abel rests. Fitfully at best. But when your brother cleaned his rifle, the sounds woke Abel. The man loved his weapons. He was a creature bred for war."

Jimmy closed his eyes. He could picture John with the old Enfield. His brother had a habit of cleaning his guns when he was bored, and it had cost John his life.

"Why?" Jimmy whispered, opening his eyes to look at her. "Why did he have to kill him though?"

"He likes to kill," Eugenia said. Her fingers reached up and traced the mark on her neck. "Kill and torture. To inflict as much pain as he can. He reveled in it during life. And in death as well. Your brother is not the first Abel has killed since his own death decades ago."

Jimmy shivered, glanced up at the sky, and realized it would rain soon. He leaned forward, stretched out and grabbed the remains of the table. It moved easily, two of the legs still attached as he dragged it to him.

Eugenia watched as he turned it over to look at the top.

It was made from two wide planks of pine joined together. The joint still held, with no visible crack.

"This'll work," Jimmy said, smiling at the girl. He crouched down a little more, slid the table over himself, and propped it between a pair of stones in the wall. Carefully he let go and smiled as it remained upright.

A moment later the rain began, and Eugenia smiled at him. "You're clever," she said appreciatively.

"I try," Jimmy said, "but it usually gets me in trouble."

"So too for my brother," Eugenia said sadly.

"Your brother's dead, too?" Jimmy asked.

She nodded. "Andrew. He and his dog Rex, they are in Griswold. They may yet come home, but he is probably hiding from Abel."

"Why?" Jimmy said. "Can a ghost hurt another ghost?"

"Oh yes," Eugenia whispered. "Terribly. I always thought, though, that if I was married, then I would have a husband to protect me from Abel."

"I'm sure a husband would," Jimmy said, smiling politely.

The rain became heavier, the drops slapping the wood above Jimmy's head and rolling down the sides. A chill wind picked up, spinning leaves around the interior of the house.

The forest grew darker, and in the distance, Jimmy thought he heard Abel singing.

Chapter 9: With the Boy and the Dog

The shadows in the church had deepened and the heavy rain hammered on the roof. Leaks sprang up everywhere, tiny rivulets coming down from the ceiling. Shane and Courtney sat close together and near Andrew. The ghost dog, which Shane had truly believed to be an impossibility, roamed around the church while Andrew looked at them seriously.

The boy's brown hair was thick with curls, his brown eyes large and observant. The child's nose was upturned, like a pug's, and his face rounded. He wore a flannel shirt and corduroy pants, but his feet were bare. They had vicious, open wounds on the soles and above the collar of his shirt was a horrifically vivid red mark, a sign of strangulation.

Shane kept his eyes from it as much as possible. He tried not to think about the pain that had been inflicted on the child.

"Why are you here?" Andrew asked.

"We came for a hike," Shane explained. "To go exploring."

A smile flashed across the boy's face. "I like exploring."

"So do I," Courtney said. "Do you still do a lot of exploring?"

Andrew hesitated before he nodded.

"How far do you go?" Shane asked. "Just the town?"

"No," Andrew said, shaking his head. "I can go all sorts of places. All the way out to the falls and back."

"Do you ever go up the road?" Shane said. "To Route 111?"

"You mean the big road?" Andrew asked.

Shane nodded.

"No, not anymore," Andrew said. "It's too far. And when we get there we can only look at the cars on the road. We can't walk there."

"Your dog goes with you?" Courtney asked, smiling at Rex.

"Of course," Andrew said, grinning. "So does Genie."

"Who's that?" Courtney said.

"My sister, she's older than me," Andrew said happily. Then he frowned. "She was here earlier, but then Abel woke up. She tried to get the other man to run, but he didn't. Abel caught him. Then Abel caught the other man, too."

"Is he hunting them both?" Shane asked.

"No," Andrew said sadly. "The first one, he killed. I saw it. He ripped off the man's arms and legs. His head, too. He's hunting the second one."

"Can we get out of here?" Shane asked.

"Of course," Andrew said, smiling.

Shane tried to remain patient as he said, "How?"

"The road," Andrew replied.

"The one we came in on?" Courtney asked.

Andrew nodded.

"But we tried," she said. "It brought us back here."

The boy frowned. "He turned you around, then. He doesn't want you to leave."

"How can he turn us around?" Shane said, his frustration growing.

Andrew shrugged. "I don't know. He did it when he was alive, too. He tricked people. Lots of people."

"How?" Shane asked.

"Some said magic and sorcery," the boy whispered, leaning in close. "But he would slip a powder into their drinks, and talk and talk and talk. We saw it many times."

"You and your sister?" Shane said.

Andrew nodded. "They would come out to our house, to eat and drink."

"Your house?" Courtney said. "Why your house?"

"Why?" Andrew asked, confused. "Because Abel is our father."

Chapter 10: College Kids

Trooper Glenn Jackson was a three-year veteran of the New Hampshire State Police. He enjoyed the work, liked the people he met, and didn't mind when he had to deal with an idiot trying to set speed records. The accidents were tough, though, and out of the few deaths he had seen, only that of a four-year-old girl still gave him the occasional nightmare.

He had the air-conditioner on in his interceptor when he spotted the Nissan Maxima parked at the entrance to the abandoned town of Griswold. Glenn rolled his eyes, threw on his sirens, and pulled in behind the car. The back windshield was plastered with decals. Stickers proclaimed the sanctity of the earth, asked for diversity, tolerance, and said the driver was a proud student of Keene State College. There were also a couple of Minions from the movie of the same name, an Army of One sticker, and one that asked if he had hugged a tree lately.

I have not, Glenn thought, responding to the last decal's question. He called in the stop to dispatch, informed them he was going to Manchester for his twenty and would report shortly.

Dispatch gave him the go ahead, and Glenn checked his mirrors before he pulled out. Too many officers were injured and killed because people didn't pay attention to them. The heavy rain didn't make it any easier.

As he prepared to pass by the road which led down into Griswold, he slowed down. He wanted to go on into Manchester and have his break, but something stopped him.

Part of him wanted to forget he had even seen the Nissan, but Glenn remembered how two years earlier, Donnie Matterhorn had ignored a car parked in the same place. They had never found the driver. Not even a trace beside a pair of old hiking boots in front of the abandoned Griswold General Store. The boots had been identified as those of the driver, Thomas Jeremy Speidel, Jr. by his girlfriend.

Donnie was still upset about not checking Griswold out. There was always the chance he could have stopped something. No one brought it up. They didn't have to; Donnie talked about it whenever he had a couple of drinks in him, which was why he was at AA twice a week and only six months sober.

When it was clear, he swung the interceptor wide and eased onto the road that led into Griswold. He moved along slowly, left his lights on with his windshield wipers squealing, and he winced as each branch slapped his car.

God help me, he thought, *they're going to need to detail the car when I leave here.*

Glenn shook his head, focused on the road in front of him, and followed it until he arrived in the center of the old town. What he saw through the rain wasn't encouraging. Not in the least.

A pair of trucks were in the middle of the town, the front end of one up against the other. They weren't mud-runners, tricked-out country boy rides made for the backwoods and old logging roads. The two pickups were relatively new and well cared for. They even had plates and looked to be registered.

Glenn pulled up, put the interceptor into park and tried to call the information in. There was too much feedback and distortion in the call, which meant an electrical storm was building up in the clouds. Frustrated, he turned off the engine before he got out of the car.

I'll try again in a minute, he thought. Glenn pulled on his slicker, winced at the cold water as it struck his face, and walked to the pickups. He made his way around them and came to a stop.

Blood, he thought. He had seen enough blood on asphalt to recognize it, even with the heavy rain washing it away.

Call it in, a small voice said, but he ignored it.

The blood trailed off towards the country store, and he took several steps toward it when he heard the squeal of ancient hinges.

He dropped his hand to his pistol, as he turned and caught sight of a bald man. Glenn kept his hand in place as the stranger stepped out of the front door of the church.

"Sir," the man said, holding his hands up so Glenn could see he was unarmed. "We need to leave here right now."

"What's your name?" Glenn asked, keeping an eye on the man.

"Shane Ryan, sir."

"Shane," Glenn said, "I want you to come over to me, keep your hands where I can see them. I'd like to know what's going on here."

"You won't believe me if I tell you," Shane said earnestly. But he walked towards Glenn, arms raised. The rain struck the man sharply, but he gave no sign that it bothered him at all.

"Is that your car up on Route 111?" Glenn asked.

Shane shook his head. "My girl's. She's in the church."

"Call her out here," Glenn started to say, but a loud crack in the forest cut him off. He drew his weapon easily as he twisted toward the sound, dropping to a crouch.

"Get in the church now," Shane hissed.

A wave of fear slammed into Glenn, and he didn't know where it came from. Some primal, instinctual part of him screamed for him to run. To get back into the interceptor and leave.

Instead, Glenn got to his feet and used his free hand to press the call button on his radio.

Nothing happened.

He tried again. And again.

The radio was dead.

"Church. Now, trooper!" Shane snapped, and there was such authority in his voice that Glenn was moving towards the church before he realized it. Shane had already fallen back to the building's door, holding it open for Glenn as another crack ripped through the air. Glenn holstered his weapon, slipped into the church, and stepped away from the door as Shane closed and locked it.

"What the hell is going on?" Glenn demanded, staring hard at Shane.

"Sit down, son," Shane said. "Keep out of sight."

Glenn opened his mouth to argue but closed it when he saw a young woman. She sat on the floor against the wall, her pretty face pale and drawn. Beside her, half-hidden by shadow was a little boy and a dog.

He could see through them both.

Chapter 11: Trooper Glenn

Shane saw the panic explode across the young trooper's face, and he threw himself at the man. As the officer turned to run, Shane slammed into him, wrapping his arms around the man and locking his hands behind the trooper's back.

The man struggled, but Shane held on. He got his feet under him, lifted, twisted, and threw the cop down. Shane went up on his toes, pressing his entire body weight down upon the younger man's chest and pinning him to the floor. With his mouth next to the trooper's ear, Shane hissed, "You need to stop. Right now."

The man's struggles increased. He slammed a knee up into Shane's ribs, causing Shane to gasp but not lose his grip.

"He'll kill us!" Shane whispered fiercely, and the statement seemed to burrow into the other man's fear. Instantly the man calmed down.

With a raw voice, the trooper said, "You can let go."

Shane heard the rationality in the tone and released his grip. He got up and looked at the officer warily.

The man took a deep breath, adjusted his body armor under his shirt, picked up his 'Smokey the Bear' ranger hat. The young man put it back on his head and kept his eyes away from Andrew and Rex as he shrugged off his wet raincoat.

"If it's easier," Shane said softly, "look at me until you're used to it."

He saw the man swallow nervously, nod, and then fix his attention on Shane.

A third large crack ripped through the town.

"What the hell is that?" the officer asked.

"Andrew's father, near as we can tell," Shane said. "What's your name?"

"Glenn. Glenn Jackson."

"Glenn," Shane said. "This is Courtney. The little one is Andrew. His dog is Rex. What unit were you with?"

Glenn looked at him with surprise and said, "Second of the 80th, Field Artillery. How the hell did you know I was in?"

"Pretty good bet," Shane said, smiling. "Most cops have been. And you can spot it when you know what to look for."

"You?" Glenn said.

"Marines. Lifer," Shane responded.

Glenn nodded. He glanced nervously at the door and said, "So, want to tell me what in the hell is going on here?"

Shane did, as quickly and concisely as possible, and with as much information as possible.

Which isn't all that much, Shane thought, sighing as he finished.

Glenn looked at Courtney, who nodded, and then back to Shane. He didn't look at the boy or the dog. Silently, Glenn took his radio off his belt, tried to broadcast and wasn't able to. He waggled the piece of equipment at Shane and said, "Can you explain how this is dead?"

"Ghosts are energy," Shane said. "They pull the juice out of whatever is nearby. Cellphone batteries, radio batteries, car batteries."

Glenn stiffened at the last and said, "Car batteries."

Shane winced. "Did you turn your cruiser off?"

"Yeah," Glenn muttered. In a louder voice, he said, "You're telling me the car won't start if I go out there?"

"Yes," Courtney said. "Both of the trucks are dead outside."

"All because a ghost named Abel is stealing the juice?" Glenn asked, looking hard at Shane.

"Yeah," Shane answered.

"I don't believe it," Glenn said, shaking his head. "It's too much. I feel like you guys are trying to pull a fast one on me."

"We're not," Shane answered.

"I know you're not," Glenn said sharply. With a sigh, he added, "I'm saying it feels like it."

"Sorry," Shane said.

Glenn nodded.

"When do you call back in?" Shane asked.

Glenn looked at his watch. "Not for another hour."

"What'll happen if they can't reach you?" Shane said.

"They'll dispatch another patrol car to me," Glenn replied. "Maybe even someone from Goffstown, which is the closest town with a police force near here. There's a catch, though."

"What?" Shane asked, not liking the tone in the man's voice.

"The storm," Glenn said, looking up at the leaking ceiling. "If it turns out to be an electrical storm, then they might overlook the lack of a call-in. We've got a new radio system, and thunderstorms play hell with it and the GPS that's installed in it. Between the storm and lunch, they might wait a bit longer before starting to worry."

"Alright," Shane said. He shook his head. "I was hoping we might get the cavalry, get us out of here before Abel figures out we're inside the church."

"He'll be looking for you," Andrew said softly, stroking the head of his dog. "He knew of the first and is hunting the second. With the new car, he will be searching for a third."

Shane watched as Glenn shook and kept his eyes averted.

"Andrew," Courtney said. "Is this the safest place to be?"

Andrew shook his head. "The best place is home. He is afraid of home. And of my aunt's house."

"Why?" Glenn asked, his eyes wide with fear.

"Home is where they caught him," Andrew said knowingly. "My aunt's house is where they put him to await his own death. Bound and chained."

"What did he do?" Glenn said.

"Killed us. And mother," Andrew said sadly. "They found him stoking the fire, preparing, he told them, to return our flesh to the ash from which we were created."

"Jesus," Courtney whispered.

"Doesn't matter," Shane said. "How long would it take us to walk there, Andrew?"

"An hour," Andrew said. "But you can't go."

"Why not?" Courtney asked.

"Because he's on the street outside. Can't you feel him?"

And suddenly, Shane realized he could.

Book 3: The Town of Griswold

Chapter 12: In the House of Latham

Jimmy was cold. He continued to sit under the broken table, and Eugenia was across from him. The rain fell through her, splattered on the leaves beneath her, and reminded him of the strange, almost dreamlike quality of his new reality. Jimmy shivered and gathered the leaves close around him, piling them up on his legs and lower body. He put the hood of his sweatshirt up, and then pulled his arms in from the sleeves. Jimmy put his hands under his arms and tried not to think about the chill.

The occasional peal of thunder caused the ground to shake, and bolts of lightning stitched the sky. It was dark, exceptionally so, and a ripple of fear ran through him.

You're going to die here, Jimmy, a little voice told him. *Abel is going to kill you.*

Jimmy tried to shove the voice away, but it only snickered and hovered on the edge of his thoughts.

"Are you alright, James?" Eugenia asked, concerned.

"Yeah, I mean, yes, I'm okay," Jimmy said, forcing a smile. "I'm doing alright. Thank you."

"You're welcome," she replied. She looked around the walls, touched the mark on her neck, and then smiled as she turned her attention back to Jimmy. "Have you ever thought about marriage, James?"

"Me?" he asked, laughing. He shook his head. "No. Not me. I'm too young to think about marriage."

"I thought about it," she said, sadly. "All of the time."

Jimmy thought about something, anything to talk to her about, and finally decided on the only subject which seemed to have any importance.

"Eugenia," he said.

She smiled. "Yes?"

"Can I ask you how you died?"

Eugenia nodded cheerfully. "Yes. My father killed me. He strangled me."

"Did he cut your feet after you were dead?" Jimmy asked hopefully.

She shook her head 'no,' and caused him to sigh dejectedly.

"Great," he muttered. Jimmy looked around before he asked, "Is there a way for me to get out of here?"

"Yes," she said. "There are many. But Abel knows them all. It is best to wait. He may fall asleep, or even forget you are here."

"Has he done it before?"

"Once," Eugenia said. "A long time ago. A young man slipped away."

Jimmy leaned forward. "Will you tell me how?"

She paused, and then said, "The brook continues on down to Charles' Lake. Once there, the young man followed the shore to the edge of Griswold."

"Why the edge?" Jimmy asked. "What's important about the edge?"

"Abel cannot go past it. None of us can," Eugenia said. "We are bound within Griswold, unable to move past its boundaries."

"Why?" Jimmy asked.

Eugenia shrugged. "I don't know. Abel may, but if he does, he has not told me. Or the rest of us."

Jimmy frowned. "There are more of you?"

"Yes," she said.

"How many?"

Eugenia bit her lip as she concentrated. "Seven. Perhaps eight now who wander the forests."

"Wait, what do you mean by 'perhaps'?" Jimmy asked.

"I'm not sure if your brother has passed on, or if he is here," she said sadly. "Sometimes, they remain. Like myself and my brother, Andrew. In addition to our father, there are four others. I do not speak with them. They hide. For years on end. They fear him."

"Do you?" Jimmy said in a low voice.

She nodded. "He is a terrible man. He is evil. He thrills at the thought of pain, of death. He is foul. When he was alive, he smelled of death, a terribly sweet scent of slow rot."

"Sounds great," Jimmy said sarcastically. He remembered his own father, the way the man had stunk prior to his passing. A foul stench the doctor's attributed to the cirrhosis of his liver.

"Why?" she asked, confused.

Jimmy chuckled. "I'm sorry. It doesn't. I was being sarcastic."

"Oh," Eugenia said. She smiled and said, "Will you make for Charles' Lake?"

"I'll have to," Jimmy said. "But not yet, later on. At dusk, I'll go to the brook. I can follow it in the dark and not get lost."

"Yes," she said, nodding. "It is a wise course of action. It makes me sad, though, to think of you leaving. I enjoy your company."

Jimmy grinned. "I like your company, too, Eugenia."

The young woman smiled happily, and the rain became heavier. Jimmy hugged himself tighter, yawned, and waited for dusk.

Chapter 13: Waiting for the Rain's End

Glenn sat with his back against the wall. His right side was colder than his left, the boy and the dog sitting in the shadows near him. He shivered at the thought of them and bit back the panic in his mind.

I need to leave, he thought, looking at Shane. The older man sat beside Courtney. *I need to get out of here.*

Shane's eyes were closed, as were Courtney's.

Glenn couldn't tell if they were awake and resting, or if they were actually asleep. The last time he had risked a look at Andrew he had seen the boy closely watching *him*. A fact which had caused Glenn to throw up in his mouth. He had swallowed the foul bile rather than spit it out.

Water continued to leak through the roof, striking the old leaves and the abandoned pews. The wind occasionally blew rain in through the broken windows while it howled through gaps in the walls.

I'm in a nightmare, Glenn realized. *This isn't real. None of it. Why else would I be with a ghost kid and his ghostly puppy? What the hell, Glenn, get a grip. Wake yourself up!*

He squeezed his eyes shut and thought, *I'm going to count to ten, and then I'll open my eyes and I'll be in my car, up there, safe and sound away from Griswold.*

One. Two. Three. Four. Five. Six…

A cold breeze caressed his face and interrupted his count. His eyes snapped open and locked on a woman in front of him. And although she looked to be in her thirties, she was exactly like Andrew.

Dead.

Glenn let out a high, piercing shriek, scrambled to his feet, and raced to the door.

Chapter 14: Awoken in Church

Shane's eyes snapped open, and if he'd had a rifle it would have been up and ready, safety off and finger on the trigger. But he didn't.

All he had was himself, and he was on his feet even as Glenn reached the door, ripped it open, and fled the safety of the church. As the man ran outside, Shane saw why.

A woman stood where Glenn had been sitting. She, like Andrew, was dead. She looked at Shane, shrugged, and vanished. Courtney got clumsily to her feet, rubbing her eyes and asking, "What the hell is going on?"

"Glenn," Shane said, walking to the door. He closed it over and paused to look out onto the deserted main street. Courtney joined him, slipping in front so she could see. Together they watched as Glenn reached the cruiser. In a moment, Glenn was in the vehicle, the rain pounding on it as he slammed the door closed.

Lightning flashed, and a terrific roll of thunder shook both the earth and the air.

A second lightning bolt lit up the entire town, and Shane saw someone standing by the woods.

"Shane," Courtney whispered fearfully.

"I see him," Shane replied.

The man was terrifying. He was tall. Taller than anyone Shane had seen before. He was bare-chested and wearing boots with his jeans. With a concave chest, the man gave the illusion of weakness, but Shane could tell, how strong he was just by the way, he walked.

"Close the door, Shane," Courtney said softly. "Please."

Shane nodded, leaving it unlocked before stepping over to a window to the right of the door. He crouched down, sat a little back, and watched the scene unfold.

Glenn remained in the car, seemingly oblivious to the giant of a ghost approaching him. Shane could picture him, trying to start the car, attempting to reach someone on the radio. Shane knew none of it was going to work.

Suddenly the hairs on Shane's neck stood up, and a glance showed Andrew and the dog had come to stand beside him.

"There is Abel Latham," Andrew whispered. "My father."

Shane looked at the tall man and nodded.

"The officer should have stayed here," Andrew added sadly. "Abel does not care for people. But he despises the police."

"Why?" Shane asked, never taking his eyes off of the advancing.

"The sheriff of Griswold," Andrew answered. "It was the sheriff's decision to poison Abel. And he did it, happily. He loved my mother and hated Abel. When I first died, and before they killed Abel, I heard the sheriff and Abel speaking. Abel had been terrible, foul-mouthed and mocked the sheriff."

"The sheriff took out his pen knife. It was not nearly as sharp as my father's knives. But he took my father's boots off and cut his feet the way he had cut mine and my sister's. He put the boots back on when he was finished. There was no need to treat the wounds, as far as the sheriff was concerned. He wanted Abel dead. As did we all."

Andrew sighed. "My father knew it was the sheriff who wanted to poison him. He knew it was the sheriff who did it. It's why he hates the police so very much."

"I wish he'd stayed dead," Shane murmured. He looked around for Courtney and saw she had returned to her previous seat.

"Watch," Andrew said softly, excitement thick in his voice.

Shane watched.

Abel reached the interceptor, walked around to the passenger side, and peered in. The man waved, went to open the door, and found it locked.

"Now that is not very nice," Abel said, his loud voice carrying. "You should let me in."

Shane couldn't hear Glenn's response, but he assumed it was a 'no.'

Abel straightened up, shrugged, and said, "Alas, I must take you out."

The man took hold of the cruiser's passenger side door and ripped it out of its frame.

Glenn's reaction was instant and violent. The sound of fourteen or fifteen shots from the man's sidearm filled the air. Leaves and branches fell from the trees and Abel let out a laugh which shook the forest. A lightning bolt, followed by thunder, punctuated his mirth.

Shane could hear Glenn scream as Abel bent down and reached in. Abel's words were lost, muffled by the interior of the car, smothered by Glenn's terror.

He reappeared shortly, dragging Glenn out by a shoulder. The young state trooper writhed in the dead man's grip, desperately trying to free himself as he screamed. Abel's smile was gigantic, broadening as he slammed Glenn onto the hood of the car, which crumpled beneath the force of the blow and the weight of Glenn's body. The young man's screams ended abruptly. Shane watched as Abel went to the man's feet, carefully undid the knots on each boot, and then tossed them onto the ground. He stripped off the socks and examined each foot.

"Very nice," Abel said happily. "Your arches are magnificent. I am sure they are sensitive to a tremendous degree, are they not?"

When Glenn didn't reply, Abel shrugged and dragged the young man off of the car's hood. Shane winced as the officer's head bounced off the pavement, and winced again as Abel dragged him towards the country store.

"Can we do anything?" Courtney asked in a horrified whisper.

Andrew answered for him.

"No," Andrew said sadly. "He is lost to us. My father will have his way with him."

A scream, sharp and brutal, pierced the air.

"Oh God, I hope it's quick," Shane said softly.

It wasn't.

Chapter 15: Jimmy Leaves

Jimmy drifted in and out of sleep for hours. The rain continued its steady assault upon the land while lightning tore the sky apart. Thunder shook the earth and the trees, the rumblings sending tremors through his heart.

When he awoke again at dusk, the rain still beat heavily, and Eugenia smiled sweetly at him. He returned the smile, moved the table off of his head, and shuddered at the initial rain drops that struck his face.

Oh man, Jimmy thought, standing up. He winced, pain shooting through his legs. Reaching out he put a hand on the stone wall, steadying himself. Both feet were asleep, the uncomfortable sensation of pins and needles churning his stomach. The realization that he had not eaten since *before* he'd gotten high the night before made his belly complain, and Jimmy tried to ignore his sudden, ravenous hunger.

"Are you unwell, James?" Eugenia asked with concern.

He managed a weak smile, nodded, and said, "Long day sitting around and doing nothing."

"'Idle hands do the Devil's work,'" Eugenia said, "but, in this case, I believe they saved you."

"Me too," Jimmy said. He took a cautious step, bit back a curse, and forced himself to move forward. For several minutes, he paced back and forth, making certain of his footing before he had to go down to the brook and travel through it to Charles' Lake. He closed his eyes, pictured the lake in his mind, and then focused on a map he had seen years ago. The nearest town was Webb, right on the border of Griswold, but even Webb would be a hike along the shore. The Charles wasn't a popular spot. Too cold and the locals were too unpleasant.

Jimmy grinned, turned to Eugenia, and said, "Feel like showing me down to the brook, Eugenia?"

She smiled and said, "Yes, I do."

The young girl passed noiselessly in front of him and through the wall. Jimmy hurried after her, climbing out the way he had come in. He found her waiting for him. When she saw him, Eugenia gestured and led on.

Jimmy followed.

It took only a few minutes to reach the brook again. Jimmy stumbled over a root, almost fell, but caught himself. He hissed at the cold water and the way the rain continued to beat on his face. Vainly he tried to pull the hood of his sweatshirt further down, but it was pointless, and he let go.

"May I go with you to the end?" Eugenia asked.

"Sure," Jimmy said. "I like your company, and I appreciate your help."

She lowered her eyes and murmured, "Thank you, James."

"You're welcome." He started cautiously, making sure of his footing on the smooth rocks and loose sand. Soon he was slipping, his feet numb in the water as the darkness descended. The moon and starlight were smothered, suffocated by the storm clouds. The thunder and lightning continued, and Jimmy found himself praying he wouldn't be electrocuted.

Desperately he wanted to climb up one of the banks and make his way on dry land, but he knew he couldn't. Abel would find him.

Eugenia walked near him, her voice soft and constant. She spoke sadly of being seventeen and of never having been married, of never being a mother. She had hoped to have been married in Griswold's church, a great wedding with a tremendous, store-bought cake from Concord.

Jimmy listened with half an ear, more intent on not falling and splitting his head open and drowning in the darkness. When he heard a question, he gave an answer, agreed with observations, and continued to offer up silent prayers. He lost track of time, knew only pain and hunger, and caught himself counting his steps. The numbers drifted in and out of focus, and suddenly the forest opened up.

Jimmy stumbled to a stop in the center of the brook and looked out at Lake Charles. Lightning flickered and showed him the darkened shore. A few boats were out in the center of the water, their lights bobbing as they rode out the storm.

"Oh thank Jesus," Jimmy said, fighting back tears. "Oh thank you, God."

Eugenia stood beside him. She looked at him earnestly. "James."

"Yes?" he asked.

"Will you, will you come and visit me?" she said, her eyes pleading.

But Jimmy was too tired and hungry to lie. "Probably not."

She dropped her head down, her chin resting on her chest.

"I'm sorry," he said sincerely. "Really, Eugenia, it's too dangerous for me. Abel, he'll kill me."

She nodded, brought her head up, and said softly, "I know."

Eugenia threw herself at him, a cold weight slamming into his chest and knocking him down into the water. His mouth was open in surprise, and instantly he was choking on it, drowning. He tried to get up, but Eugenia was on him and held him under. Jimmy thrashed his arms, kicked his legs, and bucked under her. To no avail.

Stars exploded around his vision, blackness crept in as his lungs demanded air. Eugenia remained on top of him, her face a mask of sadness.

Then he heard her voice above the frantic beating of his own heart.

"I will have my wedding, James."

Chapter 16: In the Darkness of the Church

Courtney had fallen into a fitful sleep and lay against Shane. She had wept for nearly two hours. The entire time Glenn was tortured. It had been long and drawn out. Abel had started with the man's feet, of that Shane was certain. Then, after he had grown bored with them, he had moved on to strangulation.

Even through the rain, and interrupted only by the thunder, Shane had heard Abel choke Glenn into unconsciousness repeatedly. The man had screamed and begged until his voice had broken.

"He's moving him," Andrew whispered.

The boy stood by the window, watching the store.

How strong are they? Shane wondered suddenly. *With this storm raging? Can they feed directly off of the lightning?*

He thought they could. Both the boy and the dog were looking far more solid than they had before.

"Where will he take him?" Shane asked, keeping his voice a whisper.

"I don't know," Andrew said, coming over to sit across from him. "I never knew. None of us did. It does not pay to follow Abel too closely. Even the others do not know where he has hidden them. I have heard my sister say it is because of the shock of death, how horrible it is."

"Could be," Shane agreed. "How are you feeling?"

Andrew looked surprised at the question. "I feel quite well, Shane, thank you very much for asking."

Shane smiled. "You're a polite young man."

Andrew straightened up with pride. "Our mother made certain to raise us well. Father, too, before he went mad."

"Is that what happened?" Shane asked gently.

Andrew nodded knowingly. "When he first started to behave strangely, our mother said it was because of the war."

"He was a soldier?" Shane asked.

"Yes," Andrew said proudly. "He killed many and more, so he would say when he drank."

"Where?"

"Everywhere," Andrew replied. "When he was in France, he killed Germans. When he was in Turkey, he killed Greeks. When he was in Greece, he killed Turks. He killed whomever they asked him to."

"And he liked it," Shane said softly.

"More than anything," Andrew said. "He needed more, so he said. He needed more death. To smell the blood, he said. To feast on the pain."

"Was this when he went mad?" Shane asked.

Andrew nodded. He put his hand on the dog's head, scratched it and said, "Yes. I'm not sure if he killed others before mother left to visit grandmother. She never thought he would hurt us. Nor did we. But one night, as we sat in the house, he looked at us, apologized, and said he could wait no longer."

"Do you remember your death?"

"If I think about it, I do," Andrew said with a brave smile. "But I don't. I think instead about my mother and Rex. Rex died the same night. I think he tried to stop Abel, but Rex was only a puppy."

"A very brave puppy," Shane said. "Much like you are a very brave boy. You were a true friend to bring us into the safety of the church."

Andrew grinned. "Thank you."

"Thank you, Andrew," Shane said. Silence passed between them for a few minutes, and then Shane asked the boy, "How long will it take?"

"For Abel to hide the bodies?" Andrew said.

"Bodies?"

Andrew nodded. "There was the police officer and the one before him. The one with the rifle."

One of the brothers, Shane reminded himself. "Yes. How long for the bodies?"

"He is stronger tonight," Andrew said. "It will be quick. An hour, perhaps two. Why do you ask?"

"I was wondering if we could slip away," Shane said.

A look of fear flickered across Andrew's face, and he shook his head. "You have to wait. At least until morning. Perhaps longer."

"Why?" Shane asked.

"There's still one more for him to find," Andrew said. "He'll still be looking for the other man. The one he let out into the woods."

"Come on," Shane said, groaning. "I'd forgotten about him. How will we know if he got away?"

"If Abel goes to sleep," the boy said, "then we'll know."

"And if he doesn't?" Shane asked.

"Then you might die here," Andrew said sadly.

Chapter 17: The Storm

Gordon Bay sat on a log which had washed up onto his small section of beach on Lake Charles. The rain pounded down around him and on him, smacking against his poncho. In his hand, he had an all-weather flashlight and a shotgun across his lap. The wind whipped the normally placid lake into a frenzy, raising whitecaps on the small waves slapping at the shore.

The flicker of light from the electrical storm gave the land and water a graphically nightmarish quality. All of it reminded him of why he had moved to the lake, to begin with.

From where he sat, Gordon could see the brook, the one he had followed and fled the town of Griswold from. A terrible storm had raged on the night of his escape when the man Abel had hunted him through the woods and screamed in a terrifying mixture of rage and frustration.

Gordon longed for his pipe, to sit in his front room and smoke a relaxing bowl of the new Cavendish blend he'd received in the mail. The sudden storm and its ferocity had made such an act impossible.

My place is here, he reminded himself. *Waiting and hoping.*

The last time such a storm had occurred, surprising everyone, a man had gone missing in Griswold. Vanished, leaving only his shoes behind.

And you know why, Gordon thought. *You know he has a thing for feet.*

He yawned, the storm slowing down around him. Gordon glanced once more at the brook, stood up and followed the white stone path from the beach up to his small house. Once inside the mud room, he set his shotgun down, undressed, and hung his wet clothes up to dry.

He pulled on his robe, put on his slippers, and picked up his weapon again. Absently, Gordon carried it with him into the kitchen, poured himself a beer, and brought both the drink and the shotgun into the front room.

He turned on the television, sat down in his chair, and settled in to watch the news. A newscaster he didn't know out of Portsmouth was talking about a missing state trooper. The man had vanished earlier in the day, and, according to unnamed sources within the state police department, there wasn't even a signal coming from the trooper's car or cellphone.

Gordon took a drink of his beer.

A second newscaster came on to report on a pair of notoriously troublesome brothers. The Quill brothers, out of Goffstown, had a history of run-ins with the police, and there was some speculation as to their having had a hand in the disappearance of the as-of-yet unnamed state trooper.

Terrible, Gordon thought. He put his beer down on the coffee table, picked up his pipe and tobacco pouch and filled the bowl. Soon he had it packed, lit, and was smoking steadily. He washed the sweet taste of the Cavendish down with the cold beer and wondered if the weather forecast would actually be right.

Their batting average is pretty terrible, he thought and nodded in agreement with himself. *And you're getting a little strange in your old age, Gordon.*

He snorted at the idea and took another long pull off of the bottle, quickly followed by a drag off the pipe.

Gordon had the bottle on its way up to his mouth when the sensor light in the back yard burst into life. He quickly put the drink down and stood up with his shotgun. Long strides carried him to the plate glass window which looked out over the lake.

Down on his beach, he caught sight of a coyote, bedraggled and thin, sneaking out towards something large that had washed up. Gordon clamped down hard on the pipe.

That's a body, he thought coldly. *A goddamned body.*

By the time he reached the mud room and pulled on his boots, the rain had stopped completely. He was smoking furiously, great, pale clouds drifting up to the storm clouds passing overhead. Still holding onto the shotgun, Gordon hurried to the beach, his approach scaring away the coyote.

When Gordon reached the body and turned the young man over, he could see it was already too late. The man had drowned. Quickly he searched the man's pockets, found a wallet and the license.

James Michael Quill, Gordon read. *One of the brothers on the news.*

Gordon stood up and looked down sadly at the young man. Then a cold, mind-numbing thought stole over him.

Was he in Griswold? he wondered, looking up towards the brook. *Was he there? Was his brother?*

Shapes moved in the distant shadow, and the clouds broke open for a second. The pale moonlight shined down and illuminated a man and a woman. Then both were gone.

Fear shook Gordon to the core.

Chapter 18: Gordon Bay, Griswold, August 1st, 1975

Gordon had a hard time with people. They made him nervous. He tasted steel in his mouth whenever he had to speak with them. He would sweat uncontrollably when with them for too long, and longed for solitude at all times.

Wasn't like that before 'Nam, he thought morosely.

Book 3: The Town of Griswold

Gordon found the only people he could associate with were other veterans, and even then only when he was drinking. He sat in his Plymouth Valiant, his pipe in his mouth and the lingering aftertaste of Budweiser on his tongue. The sun had set hours before, and the exterior, fluorescent light on the side of the VFW Club filled the small parking lot. A few other cars and trucks were around him, the owners drinking cheap beer and bad whiskey.

Don't judge, he told himself. *You were doing the same half an hour ago.*

Gordon had been planning to spend the better part of the night at the bar, but he hadn't been able to shake his blues.

Two years since Angelo was killed, Gordon thought sadly. *Will you do it today? Maybe,* he told himself. *Maybe.*

Clenching the pipe between his teeth, Gordon started the engine, backed out of the lot, and headed along Route 111 toward his apartment in Manchester. He drove slowly, high-beams on to cut through the darkness. The clouds obscured the night sky, and the air was heavy with humidity. There was an electrical feeling in the atmosphere, as though the seemingly innocent clouds contained a fierce storm.

Suddenly his lights illuminated a young boy and a puppy, the pair standing on the side of the road. Gordon blinked and they were gone into the darkness.

What the hell? he thought, jerking the car over to the shoulder. *I know I'm not seeing things. There was a boy there. And a dog.*

Gordon put the Plymouth in park, leaving the lights on and the engine running as he got out. He stood on the road, the heat of the day being slowly released by the asphalt. On the right, where he had seen the boy, there was a driveway.

No, Gordon thought, correcting himself. *It's a road. It leads into Griswold.*

He took the pipe out of his mouth, exhaled a long stream of smoke, and looked at the road. Something heavy crashed in the woods to the left of the road. Too heavy for a boy and a dog.

Where the hell are his parents? Gordon wondered. *Are they squatting down in Griswold? Hell, is he living alone?*

The last thought chilled him, and Gordon stood still, thinking. Finally, he put his pipe back in his mouth, went to the car, and turned off the lights and the engine. He went to the trunk and unlocked it. Stuffing the keys into his back pocket, Gordon opened the trunk and flipped up the old wool blanket he had folded in the back. He had a small .32 caliber revolver there, and a box of shells.

Silently, he broke the weapon open, loaded it, spun the cylinder to make sure it still moved properly, and then put the box of shells in his breast pocket. With the pistol in his left hand, Gordon closed the trunk and headed for the road. The light which slipped through the clouds was thin, the half-moon and the stars weak.

Gordon felt the weight of the pistol in his hand and smiled grimly. A pleasant feeling washed over him, a familiar one he had enjoyed in Vietnam. He had an undeniable thrill, a sense of power. A memory of Mike Kenefick flashed through Gordon's mind.

The strongest man in the world, Mike had said, *is the one who's pointing a gun at you, kid. Don't ever forget that. Ever.*

Gordon knew it was true. He felt it every time he wrapped his hand around the grip of the pistol.

The darkness increased ten-fold when he started down the road leading into Griswold. He slowed down, making certain he didn't trip on deadfall, and he paused constantly to listen. The hair on his arms stood on end and he felt an uncomfortable surge of fear the deeper he went.

A small yip, the noise of a rambunctious puppy, came from ahead of him, and Gordon pressed on. Sooner than he had expected, Gordon walked into the center of Griswold. The clouds had thinned out, and he was able to see what remained of the town. A pair of buildings, scattered chimneys.

Watch your step, he told himself. *Where there are chimneys, you'll find cellars. Stick to the road.*

He glanced around, saw the door to the first building on the left was closed, but the one on the right was open. The second structure, Gordon realized, was a church, the cross on the top briefly highlighted by the moon.

A cloud, thick and pregnant with rain, swarmed over the sky and a thick rain fell. The drops were cold, brutally so, and in the space of a heartbeat, Gordon found himself shivering.

Where the hell did this come from? he thought angrily. He made for the church, thinking, *I'll wait it out.*

Gordon jogged the rest of the way, his clothes clinging to him uncomfortably. He reached the building, pushed the door open a little more, and went in. Water dripped down from the decrepit roof, and it took him a minute to find a relatively dry spot. Then he remembered why he had walked down into Griswold.

The boy and his dog, Gordon thought. He walked around the church, stepping over fallen pews and through piles of leaves that were older than he was.

Nothing, Gordon thought. *Not a damned thing.*

He listened to the rain and shivered, wondering where the boy and dog were, and if they were safe.

You can't look for him in the rain and the dark, Gordon, he told himself as he sat down. *But as soon as the rain stops you can.*

Gordon put the pistol in his lap, rested his hands on top of it, and settled in to wait.

Chapter 19: Waiting for Andrew

Shane woke up quickly and realized Courtney was in front of him. She smiled tiredly, her face a pale shadow in the dimness of the church. Thin moon and starlight fell through the broken windows and cracks in the roof.

"Do you want some water?" she asked, holding up a bottle.

"Yes, please," Shane said. She took the cap off and handed it to him. "Thanks."

He drank the tepid water slowly, looked around, and said, "Did Andrew leave?"

Courtney nodded. "A little while ago, with Rex. He said he was going to see what Abel was up to."

"How are you holding up?" Shane asked, examining her carefully.

"I'm a mess," Courtney said honestly. "I won't lie. I'll have nightmares the rest of my life, however long that is. I didn't, I … Damn, I didn't think someone could scream like that."

"I know," Shane said in a low voice. "The first time you hear it, it breaks you. Kills a little something in you."

Courtney hesitated and then asked, "You've heard people scream from being tortured before?"

Shane nodded, thought about telling her, then he didn't. *Some things need to stay buried. Forever.*

"What'll we do if Abel is gone?" Courtney asked. "Will we leave?"

"Yes," Shane said. He drank a little more. "If he's gone, or asleep, we can take the road back to Route 111."

"What about Glenn?" she whispered.

"We tell the police what happened," Shane replied.

She looked at him, eyes wide with surprise. "What?"

"We don't tell them Abel was a ghost," Shane clarified. "We tell them the truth. We came down into Griswold for a little hiking. The trucks were here when we arrived. A mad man chased us into the church. Glenn arrived, was attacked by the man, and we stayed hidden in the church."

"What if they ask me about Abel, what he looked like?" she asked.

"Tell them the truth," Shane said. "You didn't see him. I did, and we ran because I said to run. I saw him. I can give a description. They're going to hold us. They're going to interrogate us. As long as you don't tell them about any of the supernatural elements, and you stick to the basics, everything will work out, doll."

"Okay," Courtney said, and then she repeated the basic story.

"Good," Shane said, nodding. "We stick to that. I'll offer up details about Abel."

"This is terrible," Courtney said, anger flaring in her voice. "He killed him!"

"I know he did," Shane said gently, holding out a hand. She took and squeezed it. Pain flared up in his fingers, but he ignored it.

"All I wanted was a nice day," she said, her voice shaking with rage. "That was it. I wanted a nice, normal day. Instead, there's another psycho ghost."

Shane waited.

She looked hard at him. "Why?"

"I don't have an answer, Courtney," he said. "Any answer would sound trite and contrived. He's dead. We're not. We need to get out of here as soon as Andrew says we can. Nothing more. Nothing less."

Courtney nodded, crossed the short distance between them, and huddled up next to him. She had a sweet, powerful scent which reminded him of safety and he pulled her in closer, holding her tightly.

"How are you doing?" she asked shortly.

"Better with you in my arms," Shane answered.

She chuckled tiredly. "What a perfect answer."

"Really?" he asked, surprised.

"Really, Shane Ryan," she said, resting her head against his chest. "Really."

Chapter 20: Gordon and the Church, August 1st, 1975

Gordon awoke with a shudder.

Damn it, he thought, *I fell asleep!*

The rain still thundered against the roof, still made its way in to splash against the floor, the leaves, and the tumbled pews.

He made sure the pistol was still in his lap and then checked his watch. The luminescent hands showed it to be 11:14 p.m.

Quietly, he pulled out the knob on the watch's side and wound the timepiece.

Forty, maybe fifty minutes, he thought. He yawned, looked around and the yawn froze on his face. The boy and the dog stood by the open front door, looking at him in surprise.

Lightning split the sky and the boy, and the puppy glowed for a moment. It was then Gordon realized he could see through the child, and the dog as well.

Gordon pressed himself against the wall. *Holy Mary, Mother of God*, he thought frantically, *he's a ghost.*

"Who are you?" the boy asked in a whisper.

Gordon swallowed nervously, then answered, "I'm Gordon."

"Whisper, Gordon, and be gentle in your speech," the boy said softly, "he feels you near but doesn't know where you are."

"Who?" Gordon asked.

"Abel, my father," the boy replied.

"Oh," Gordon whispered. "Is that bad?"

The child nodded his head seriously, eyes wide.

"Okay," Gordon said. "Um, what's your name?"

"Andrew. Andrew Latham."

"Andrew, were you at the roadside earlier?" Gordon asked even though he was certain the boy had been.

Andrew nodded. "We like to watch the cars go by. Usually, we aren't seen. And we are never followed. Until tonight."

"I was worried," Gordon said. He wanted to add, *I shouldn't have been since you're already dead.* But he didn't.

The boy smiled shyly. "Thank you."

Gordon nodded. "You're welcome. Tell me, Andrew, do you think you could help me get back to the road? It's a little too dark for me to see."

"You can't," Andrew said sadly. "Abel is there, on the road, waiting. The only way out is the brook, and we will have to ask my sister for her help. She knows the path best to it. I have … Well, I have forgotten."

"A brook?" Gordon asked, confused. "How do I get back to the road by a brook?"

"The road?" Andrew said. "No, not the road. The lake."

"Lake Charles?"

Andrew nodded.

"In the dark?" Gordon said.

"Yes."

"Great," Gordon said angrily. "Well, your sister can bring me there?"

"Yes," Andrew said. "I'll find her."

Gordon wanted to ask another question, but the boy ran out of the church with the dog close on his heels.

With a sigh, Gordon leaned his head back against the wall, shifted the pistol from his left hand to his right, and scratched the back of his head.

What in the hell is going on here?

Chapter 21: Trooper Martini

State Trooper Sergeant Henry Martini kept his head about him. The New Hampshire police community was in a frenzy. Glenn Jackson had been missing for over twelve hours. Worse, they didn't even know where Glenn's interceptor was. No one could get a read off of its GPS.

Every off-duty cop in New Hampshire, Maine, Vermont, Massachusetts, New York, and Connecticut was looking for him. They were scouring back roads, garages, warehouses, rivers, ponds, lakes, quarries. People known to have anti-police sympathies were getting some rough treatment by out-of-state members of the thin blue line. Correctional officers were leaning on prisoners.

Henry had been on vacation when the text messages and calls had come in. He had left the house he and his wife had rented at Ogunquit, made his way back to the barracks and gotten the low-down on the situation.

The last call Trooper Jackson had made had been about a car near the abandoned town of Griswold. No one had gone into Griswold, though, because the road was too narrow to fit a Prius, let alone an interceptor.

Henry didn't believe it, though. He knew Donnie Matterhorn, and how the man still felt guilty about the hiker who had gone missing. Glenn had gotten Donnie's sector because Donnie couldn't handle driving by Griswold anymore. Once, when Henry had gone to bring Donnie home from the drunk tank in Milford, Donnie had said something Henry had chalked up to being hammered.

Donnie had told him how he occasionally saw Thomas Speidel, the missing hiker, standing at the entrance to Griswold late at night.

And what if Glenn remembered Donnie and Thomas Speidel? Henry wondered, pulling up behind the Nissan Maxima Glenn had called in.

Henry put on his lights and called in his location. He grabbed his light and stepped out into the cool air. Long strides carried him to the road which led down into Griswold. He turned on the Maglite and flashed its powerful beam down into the darkness. On either side of the road he saw broken branches at car height, scattered leaves twigs littered the old and cracked asphalt.

Anger built up in him as he looked at the trees on either side of the road. *They didn't look,* he fumed. *God damn them! They didn't look down the road!*

Enraged, Henry ran back to his interceptor to call it in.

Chapter 22: Meeting Andrew's Sister, August 1st, 1975

"Are you ready?" Andrew asked in a whisper when he returned.

Gordon nodded, got to his feet, and went to where the boy stood by the door. Andrew smiled at him, and Gordon smiled back. His breath came out in great white clouds. The air at the door was brutally cold.

The clouds had vanished and left behind the light of the moon and stars. Gordon could see easily. He glanced at the road which led back to Route 111, and he wondered if he might be able to make it.

"He's still waiting," Andrew said.

Gordon swallowed nervously, nodded, and said, "Lead on then, Andrew."

Andrew and the dog, who he called Rex, went into the street. With the passing of the storm, the boy had become fainter. He wasn't as solid as when Gordon had first seen him. Andrew's steps were tentative, cautious. The puppy mimicked the boy's attitude, remaining near the child. Finally, once he had reached the center of the street, Andrew motioned for Gordon to follow.

With a deep breath, Gordon left the safety of the church, the pistol in his hand. Long strides carried him to Andrew's side.

"Follow me, quickly and quietly," the boy whispered.

Gordon nodded.

The boy smiled, turned, and ran towards the far tree line. Gordon kept up with him, worried he might step on a branch and give himself away to the unseen Abel. A small part of him didn't believe the boy, but a deeper, more primal portion of his heart told him Andrew spoke the truth.

Gordon never hesitated but slipped into the edge of the forest. Andrew moved silently through the trees, disturbing nothing with his passage. Gordon, however, wasn't so lucky. His feet made far too much noise as he ran.

Soon Gordon found himself stumbling along, barely able to see. Too little of the moon's light breached the canopy overhead, and Andrew was little more than a shape flitting in front of him. Trees loomed up out of the darkness, and more than once he slammed into them.

This is ridiculous, he thought angrily, tasting blood in his mouth after bouncing off a birch.

Someone screamed from behind him, a sound full of rage and fury. And madness.

Gordon's heart threatened to shatter his ribs as fear spurred him forward.

Then he was falling, arms swinging wildly as he plummeted into the cold water of an unseen stream. Gordon pushed himself up, gasping for breath.

"Here," Andrew whispered, "sit still and be quiet."

Gordon sat down in the cold water and forced himself to breathe through his nose. A young woman appeared out of the darkness, following the water towards them. The sight was disturbing, her legs moving but not disturbing the surface of the stream. When she drew nearer, Gordon saw a horrific red line around her neck, and it was only then he realized Andrew had one on his neck as well.

"You are Gordon?" Andrew's sister asked.

Gordon nodded.

"I'm Eugenia," she said. The young woman looked at him closely. "You're a killer."

Gordon hesitated before he said, "Yes."

Eugenia nodded. "We've enough killers here, Gordon. I will lead you away if you will."

"Please," he replied.

She smiled at him tightly. "Stand then, and we will leave. You must be stealthy. Abel has realized you have slipped away and into the woods. He has yet to realize we are helping you."

"Well," Gordon said, standing up, "let's keep it that way."

Chapter 23: Meeting Again

Some officers carried a .410 shotgun in their trunks. Henry Martini had an AR15 Bushmaster. After calling in his position he took out the rifle, loaded it, and made his way to the road leading down into Griswold. Protocol required he await backup.

Within three minutes, an unmarked car squealed to a stop behind his interceptor. A pair of cops hurried out, leaving the doors open. One was a young male, the other was an older female, both African-Americans. The male jogged over to Henry as the female went around to the trunk of the car.

The man offered his hand, and Henry shook it.

"Dwayne Reynolds."

"Henry Martini," Henry said. "Nashua?"

Dwayne nodded. The woman came towards them with a riot shotgun. She had a City of Manchester patch on her uniform.

"Janet DeMilo," she said. "You called in."

It wasn't a question. "Yeah. Glanced down the road. Definite signs of a vehicle."

"Alright," Dwayne said. "I'll take point if you two want to flank."

"Sounds good," Janet said, and Henry agreed as well.

They went down the road quickly, Dwayne moving several feet in front while Henry took the left and Janet the right. The three of them kept a steady pace, the cracked and broken asphalt wet beneath their boots. Minutes passed before they reached the curve in the road, and they slowed down.

Tension filled the air between them and for the first time, Dwayne glanced back at Henry and Janet. Henry gave the younger man a nod, and Dwayne moved forward at a crouch.

When the road straightened out, the sight which they stumbled upon caused Henry's stomach to flip. Glenn Jackson's interceptor was parked close to a pair of pickups. The trooper's vehicle was a mess. It looked as though an extremely large child had taken an equally large hammer and smashed the car. A pair of uniform boots lay on the asphalt near the interceptor in a sea of broken glass.

Book 3: The Town of Griswold

All three of their radios squawked at the same time, the State Police dispatcher requesting an update.

Janet reached up to her shoulder microphone, pressed the talk button, and said, "Send a team down into Griswold." She looked at Henry and glanced at the boots.

Henry nodded. "Tell them it's Jackson," he said grimly.

Dispatch asked for confirmation, and Janet gave it.

Henry looked from the defunct general store to the church and then brought his weapon to bear on the church's door.

Someone was opening it.

"Church!" Henry snapped.

Janet dropped to a crouch, the shotgun tucked firmly into her shoulder while Dwayne took up a position at Jackson's car, covering them both.

"Hands!" Janet yelled, her voice booming out. "I want to see hands, and I want them now!"

A pair of hands were thrust out into the open, and a man called out, "There are two of us in here. Male and female."

"Both of you come out," Janet snapped. "Hands where I can see them. When I tell you to, you will turn around and get on your knees. Understood?"

"Yes, ma'am," the man replied. The door opened completely, and the man came out first. His arms were fully extended, fingers spread wide. He took one step out, and one step to the side. A young woman followed, mimicking him perfectly. Yet while he looked calm, she was nervous.

Together the pair walked forward, and when they had crossed roughly half the distance to Henry and the other officers, Janet called out to them again.

"Stop and turn around," Janet said.

The man and the young woman did so.

"Knees," Janet ordered.

The young woman had a little trouble, but the man didn't. In a moment, the two of them were on their knees, arms and hands still straight up in the air.

"Hands on your heads," Janet snapped.

Both did as they were told.

"Dwayne," Janet said.

Dwayne holstered his sidearm, took his handcuffs out, and waited for Henry to take his out as well.

Henry watched as Dwayne approached the male first, going in from the left, keeping out of the line of fire. The man made no effort to resist as Dwayne cuffed him. With quick movements, Dwayne slipped over to the young woman and cuffed her.

From Route 111 came the sound of sirens, quickly followed by the sound of branches being smashed. Seconds later, cruisers and SUVs filled the narrow confines of Griswold's main street. Police spilled out, quickly moving towards the two buildings. Henry slung his weapon and went to take charge of the handcuffed male while Janet did the same with the female. Dwayne was already with another team surging into the church.

When Henry helped the male to stand he looked at the man for the first time, and nearly stumbled back.

It was Shane. Shane Ryan from the shooting at Old Nashua Road and the Roy house.

Shane looked Henry in the eye and said, "Trooper Martini. This is a bad place to be."

Chapter 24: The Interrogation

Shane's head hurt. It hurt a lot.

No, Shane corrected himself. *It hurts like hell.*

He was in a small interview room with a bottle of water. A small camera in the upper left-hand corner of the room stared down at him, the red light blinking occasionally to remind him people were watching.

Probably lots of people, he thought tiredly. He had been in the room for seven hours. For six of them, he had been questioned relentlessly about the disappearance of Trooper Glenn Jackson. Shane stuck to the story he had come up with, and he didn't try to get fancy and add details.

Keep it simple, stupid. One of the finest things he had ever learned in the Marine Corps.

Shane closed his eyes, pinched the bridge of his nose, and tried to focus on something, *anything* other than the headache nestled uncomfortably behind his sinuses. The door to the room opened, but Shane didn't look. He heard two sets of boots, the pair of chairs opposite him were pulled out, and a new set of police sat down.

Someone closed the door, and still, Shane kept his eyes shut.

A young woman spoke in Spanish. "Do you think he's good for this?"

Another woman answered, speaking Spanish as well. "Doesn't matter. He knows something one way or another. More than what he's saying."

"Wonder what he's thinking of," the first woman said.

"Who knows, Angela," the second said. "And really, who cares?"

"We should," Angela said angrily. "Have you seen the preliminary report on the scene?"

"No," the other woman said, "I came in half an hour ago. Just finished getting the low down."

"Lisbeth," Angela said, lowering her voice, "they said there are gallons of blood there. From two distinct individuals."

"Damn."

Shane opened his eyes and looked at the officers. They were both middle-aged women, dressed in button-down shirts with empty shoulder holsters. Both women had their dark brown hair pulled back in ponytails, their eyes deadly serious.

"You want to start?" Angela asked, still speaking in Spanish.

Lisbeth nodded. In English, she said, "What's your name?"

"Shane Ryan."

"Shane," Lisbeth said, "what can you tell me about what happened to trooper Glenn Jackson?"

Shane repeated the same story, without variation. Both officers frowned at him when he finished.

"Your friend tells almost the same story," Lisbeth said.

Shane didn't reply.

"You don't think that's a little odd?" Lisbeth asked.

Shane shook his head.

"You don't want to add anything?" Lisbeth said.

He looked at her but didn't reply.

"Now's your time, Shane," Angela said. "We just want to know what happened to the trooper. Any help you can give us will go a long way."

"We understand things happen," Lisbeth said, picking up the line. "Accidents always happen. It's why they're called accidents."

"We just want to know where he is, what's going on with him," Angela said, smiling warmly. "You can understand, right?"

Shane kept his mouth closed.

The smile vanished from Angela's face, replaced by an expression of sadness. "Really, Shane?"

"You know," Lisbeth said, "I've seen your record. All of your information came up when we punched your name and social in. Did you know that?"

Shane waited.

"We know you were a Marine," Lisbeth continued. "A career man, too. Looks like you did some regular grunt work, then some Arabic and Pashto language work, even some intelligence gathering."

"Glenn was a soldier," Angela said. "Saw some time in Afghanistan."

"So," Lisbeth added, "we're kind of wondering why you don't want to help us. You being a Marine and all. You gave decades of your life for this country, and it's looking like Glenn gave his for it. Why don't you tell us what happened? I mean, was it the Quill brothers?"

"We know they had some trouble with the law," Angela said. "Especially the younger one, James."

They want me talking, Shane thought. *They think I did something. They want to tease it out of me. Whatever it is.* He wanted to tell them. He burned to speak of it. *But it won't do any good.*

Shane yawned, and Lisbeth's face went cold.

"Are we boring you, Mr. Ryan?" she snapped.

Shane looked at her with disinterest, then he looked at Angela. In perfect Spanish, he said, "I'm tired. I had a hell of a night, and I listened to some terrible stuff. I told you what I know."

He looked at Lisbeth, satisfied to see a glimmer of surprise in her eyes. Continuing on in Spanish he said, "I feel horrible about the young officer's disappearance. If I could help you, I certainly would. But I can't. Pretty soon you're either going to have to let me go home, or you're going to have to hold me as a material witness. Either way, I don't care. Let's make a decision and be done with it."

Lisbeth glared at him, but Angela looked at him with interest. In Spanish, she asked, "Where did you learn to speak Spanish, Mr. Ryan? The Marines?"

Shane nodded. "The men I served with."

"You sound like you're from Puerto Rico," Angela said appreciatively. "Your accent is perfect."

He tilted his head in thanks.

"You said there was a man who grabbed trooper Jackson," Angela said, continuing in Spanish. "Can you give me a description?"

Shane did, the women's eyes widening slightly.

"Why didn't you do anything to help?" Lisbeth asked, her voice hard.

Shane looked at her, waited until she blinked, and said, "I had my girlfriend with me. When I first saw the attacker, he smashed through a window without any hesitation. That tells me he's either unbelievably strong, insane, or cooking on something. I'm not a young man anymore, officers. I know my limits, and if I had to sacrifice myself, it was going to be for Courtney."

Lisbeth switched to English, the disdain in her voice plain. "Pretty cold, Mr. Ryan."

"I made a decision, officer," Shane replied. "I'd make the same one again."

"This isn't really getting us anywhere, is it?" Lisbeth asked coldly.

Shane shook his head.

"Why don't you tell us a little more about what happened?" Angela asked.

"There's nothing more to say," Shane answered.

"Come on, Marine," Lisbeth sneered. "Nothing else you want to add? No little tidbit you'd like to share with us? You're telling me you didn't notice anything special, with your keen eyes?"

Shane laughed, shook his head, and said, "Ma'am, if I didn't think I'd lose a couple of teeth, I'd tell you what I've been able to notice about you."

Lisbeth's face became a hard mask and Angela's hand stole out, gripping the other woman's arm tightly. A knock sounded, and the door opened. An older man Shane hadn't met gestured to the two officers. The women stood up, ignored Shane and left the room.

Shane settled back into his chair, closed his eyes and tried to ignore the pain in his head.

Chapter 25: Running, August 2nd, 1975

Somewhere in the darkness of the forest, the man called Abel searched for Gordon. Moonlight passed through Eugenia, flickered on the water, and allowed Gordon to follow the young woman. He had a stitch in his side and every breath hurt.

Behind him, and off to the left, he heard a tree crash. It was a terrible, foreboding sound. One that spurred him on.

Andrew and the dog had vanished, leaving Gordon alone with Eugenia. Occasionally she would look back at him, a concerned expression on her face.

She's asking if I'm worth it, Gordon told himself. A small voice denied the truth of the statement, but Gordon knew better. *Abel can hurt her, I'm sure. And she's wondering if I'm worth the possibility of pain.*

Seriously, am I? he wondered, trying to get control of his breath.

Evidently she decided he was because she continued to lead him along the stream.

Gordon tripped over either a submerged stick or protruding stone and fell with a crash into the water. Something cold gripped him, dragged him up and pressed him against the bank.

"Silence," Eugenia hissed.

Gordon closed his mouth, shivering with a chill which was more from fright than the water's temperature. Memories of Vietnam swarmed over him, patrols in the dark. Ambushes. Blackness lit by muzzle flashes and followed by screams from wounded men.

He closed his eyes, bit on his tongue to keep himself quiet, and was able to get control of his fear. The shivers subsided, Eugenia removed her hands, and Abel passed by them, unseen. Each footstep sounded like a tree being felled, a terrible cold sweeping through the air. For a split second ice formed on the top of the water, and it became painful to breathe the air.

Then the ice melted, warmth returned to Gordon's lungs, and Eugenia sat down on the bank beside him. She looked at Gordon closely before she whispered, "He hunts for you still."

Gordon nodded.

"Why did you come into Griswold?" she asked shortly.

"I saw your brother," Gordon replied in a low voice. "Up on the edge of the road. I thought he was lost. Abandoned. I was worried about him."

She looked at him intensely. "You came because you were worried about my brother?"

Gordon nodded.

Several minutes of silence passed between them before Eugenia finally broke it. "I will make sure my father doesn't take you, Gordon. You will reach Charles' Lake alive and well."

"Thank you," Gordon whispered.

"You're welcome. Now come," she said, standing up. "Abel will soon realize he passed you by, and he will double back."

"Okay," Gordon said, sighing. *We sure as hell don't want him to come back. Not at all.*

Chapter 26: Courtney and Trooper Martini

Courtney was exhausted and barely able to keep her eyes open. An empty chip bag lay on the table in front of her, as did half a cup of water. She was in a small, narrow room, and she hadn't seen Shane in almost seven hours. The police hadn't allowed her to call anyone, and they hadn't asked her if she wanted a lawyer.

They had found new and interesting ways to ask the same question. She had stayed true to the bare-bones story Shane had told her to recite. The police didn't seem to believe she had anything to do with Jackson's disappearance.

But they think Shane did. Courtney wanted to tell them the truth, about the ghost boy and dog, about being trapped in the church by the dead.

I can't, she thought morosely. *Who's going to believe me?*

The room's solitary door opened and a middle-aged state trooper entered alone. He closed the door behind him, nodded to her, and sat down across from Courtney at the table.

His name tag read, *H. Martini.*

"Hello, Courtney," he said. "My name is Trooper Martini. We met briefly in Griswold when we were taking you into custody."

"I remember," she said.

He settled back into the hard plastic chair, looked at her, and said, "I've met Shane before."

"You have?" Courtney asked, surprised.

"Yes," Martini said. "There was an incident at a home earlier this year. One which resulted in a shooting, unfortunately."

"The Roy house," Courtney said softly.

Martini raised an eyebrow. "He told you about it?"

She nodded. "Did he tell you what happened?"

"He wasn't in much of a state to talk when I first met him," Martini said. "And, from what I've been reading, the two of you were in a rather difficult situation a few weeks ago? The Squirrel Island Lighthouse?"

"Yes," Courtney said.

"It seems like a whole lot of death and destruction follows Shane around," Martini said offhandedly.

Courtney stiffened and said angrily, "We didn't have anything to do with the deaths on Squirrel Island!"

"I know," Martini said soothingly. "I know. I was making an observation. How much do you know about Shane Ryan?"

"Enough," she answered, sounding far younger than she had meant to.

The trooper smiled kindly at her. "I'm just concerned, Courtney. That's all. You seem like an extremely intelligent young woman, and I'm worried you're getting mixed up with a man who, well, seems to have trouble follow him around."

Courtney bristled. Goosebumps raced along her arms and rage chased away the exhaustion. She leaned over the small table and said, "There are things you don't know about, Trooper Martini. Parts of this world that aren't what they seem."

He nodded, a patronizing look of concern on his face. "I've seen and heard all sorts of strange events in my life, Miss DeSantis, I doubt you've anything to tell me which would cause my hair to go white."

"What do you know about Squirrel Island?" she demanded.

He shrugged. "Only what I read in the report. Some rumors of it being haunted. Same sort of situation with Griswold. Urban legends and scary stories to tell around the campfire or during Halloween."

"It's true," Courtney spat, unable to stop herself. She wanted to see the man's face change, a look of surprise replace the expression of fatherly concern.

Martini merely raised an eyebrow. "Is it now? Are you telling me a ghost caused Glenn Jackson to disappear?"

Courtney nodded, her face feeling flush. She crossed her arms over her chest and looked down at the table.

"And Shane didn't have anything to do with it?"

She shook her head.

"What about the Quill brothers?" Martini asked. "Did they have anything to do with it?"

Courtney looked up. "The guys who owned the trucks?"

"Yes."

"No," she said. "They were gone long before Trooper Jackson showed up. We never even saw them."

"So, you're saying we shouldn't be looking for this guy Shane described to us?" Martini asked. "We should be searching for a ghost, maybe?"

"You should," Courtney said coldly. "Because the man Shane saw is a ghost."

Chapter 27: A Chance Meeting, August 2nd, 1975

"There's someone ahead of us," Eugenia whispered, stopping him with an icy touch.

"Abel?" Gordon asked softly.

She shook her head. "This one is alive. We must be careful."

Gordon nodded. Most people didn't camp in the woods around Griswold. It never felt right.

Moving as quietly as he could, Gordon advanced up the stream. He caught sight of a tent in the moonlight, and then Eugenia stopped him again.

"Get in the water!" she hissed, pulling him down. "He's coming!"

Gordon allowed her to move him, and in a moment he was as low as he could be. The cold liquid passed over him, slapping occasionally at his face and his mouth. He breathed slowly through his nose, Eugenia gone. Gordon's eyes fixated on the tent, and he wondered why she had told him to hide.

The answer came seconds later. A tall man, taller than any Gordon had seen before, eased out of the shadows near the tent. The man was terribly pale, as though he had spent decades in a cell, locked away from the world. He was shirtless, clad only in pants and boots. Gordon watched as he passed around the front of the tent, and it was then he realized he could see through the man.

Oh, Christ, Gordon thought, understanding why Eugenia had made him hide. *It's Abel.*

The ghost continued around the tent, and when he turned, Gordon saw the man's back was a single mass of scar tissue. Abel made a complete circuit around the tent, finally coming to a stop in front of it. The man squatted down, leaned close to the closed flap, and whispered, "Hello."

After a moment of silence, he repeated the word, his voice a little louder. Again there was no reply, and Gordon heard Abel chuckle.

"My," Abel said, his voice cheerful, "whoever you are, you sleep exceedingly well."

To one side, out of her father's view, Gordon saw Eugenia. She watched Abel carefully.

Gordon returned his attention to Abel and saw the man reach out and unzip the tent. Still, the person inside made no sound. Even when Abel laughed, crawled in, and came back out, dragging a sleeping bag behind him.

Whoever it is has to be drunk, Gordon thought, hopefully. *What's going to happen? What can I do? Jesus, how do you stop a ghost?*

All coherent thought was driven out of his head a moment later as the sleeper awoke. The scream torn out of the man's mouth ricocheted off of the trees, punctured the peace of the night, and shattered the moonlight. Dark clouds swarmed the sky and plunged Gordon into a darkness his eyes couldn't pierce.

But his ears continued to work. Even as a hard rain began to fall, Gordon could hear perfectly well. Every scream, every cut, every laugh from the dead man's mouth.

Gordon would remember them forever.

Chapter 28: Martini Leaves the Room

Henry wasn't sure what to make of the young woman. She had seemed truthful, adamant, and enraged. All at the same time.

He left the interview room and shrugged when Detective Larson caught his eye. Larson walked over, looked at him, and said, "So, what did the little princess have to say?"

"Not much," Henry said. "The only thing she added was that we should be looking for the guy Shane described. Except the guy is a ghost."

"What?" Larson asked, incredulous.

"Yup," Henry said, sighing. "I kid you not."

Larson shook his head. "Insane. Listen, head over to the break room. Grab a cup of coffee. We've got a briefing in ten. We're sending out more teams into the woods before it gets dark. We need to see if we can find any trace of Glenn."

Henry nodded and turned to leave when he saw Donnie Matterhorn. Donnie was looking at him with wide eyes and a face which was far too pale.

"Donnie?" Henry said, stepping towards the older man. Donnie was turning an AA coin over repeatedly in his hand.

"Henry," Donnie said, his voice raw. "Got a minute?"

"Sure," Henry said. "Couple, actually. What's going on?"

Donnie leaned in and asked, "What did the girl say?"

Henry frowned, but he gave Donnie a quick rundown of what Courtney had said. When he finished, Donnie said, "Do you have a description of the man?"

"Who?" Henry asked, confused. "This ghost man that she said exists?"

Donnie nodded quickly.

"Sure, I guess. The male, Shane, he described the person as tall. Extremely tall," Henry started.

Donnie cut him off. "Were there scars all over the man's back? Was he wearing only pants and boots?"

"Yeah," Henry said softly. "Yeah, that's exactly what he was said to be wearing."

Donnie reached out, grabbed hold of Henry's bicep, and said, "Follow me."

Henry was half dragged down the hallway, to a side door, and a thin set of stairs which led them down into the basement and the old storage cabinets. Hundreds of files waited to be sent up to Concord, and Donnie went right to the back. Henry watched as the man moved aside boxes and reams of unused paper.

Finally, Donnie sighed with what sounded like relief and revealed a tall, narrow filing cabinet. The man pulled a key out of his pocket, fit it into the lock, and opened the top drawer.

"It's here," Donnie said, pulling a file out. "Right here, Henry. Look at this."

He handed the old manila folder to Henry, who took it cautiously. The file was thin, but when he opened it Henry found several pages of onion paper. They were stapled together, and the date on the top page read *August 2, 1975*.

Henry looked at Donnie, and the older man nodded, gesturing towards the file.

Conscious of the oil on his fingers, Henry moved the first page carefully, making sure he could read it in the pale light of the old bulbs hanging from the ceiling.

Witness Statement (08/02/1975)
Bay, Gordon M. (11/14/1953)
Laton Hotel
Railroad Square
Nashua, NH

Statement taken by Trooper Daniel Waters.

    My name is Gordon, Gordon Bay. I was in the town of Griswold on the night of August 1st to August 2nd. I came in to report a murder. I was walking through Griswold, following the stream, well, the brook, that leads into Lake Charles. There were two men. One had crucified the other between a pair of trees and he was, oh Jesus, he was torturing him.

    The killer, he was huge. I don't think I've seen a taller guy. I mean, easily over six and a half feet. And he was shirtless. His back was just all scars, terrible like someone had worked on him for years. All he had on was a pair of work boots and old jeans.

    And, I didn't do anything. I couldn't do anything. It was too much. I just couldn't do anything. The screams were terrible. I mean, I heard and saw some stuff in 'Nam, but nothing like this.

    Nothing.

    When I saw him, he was working on the guy's feet. He had a knife, real small. Maybe a pen knife. But he was cutting away, whistling to himself. It was terrible.

    Absolutely terrible.

Findings of Trooper Daniel Waters. (08/02/1975)

    Shortly after the conversation with Gordon Bay, Trooper Eli Collins and myself went to the town of Griswold. We located the brook which runs to Lake Charles and followed it. Eventually, we did come to a single person tent, belonging to one Leonard Waye of Manchester, NH.

    A hiking pack, along with several days' worth of canned goods were discovered. A pair of Chippewa boots were found a few feet away from the tent. They were placed next to a birch tree (see photograph attached).

    There was a large amount of blood evidence. The ground between the birch tree and an elm was saturated with blood (see photograph attached). In addition to the blood and boots, we found what looked to be holes large enough for railroad spikes in the trees. At the time of the initial investigation, we were unable to reach the holes as they were at least seven feet off of the ground (see photograph attached).

> *Neither Trooper Collins nor myself saw any sign of a ladder or any other tool which may have been used to reach the height mentioned.*
>
> *We have since established that Mr. Waye is twenty-two years of age, a nature enthusiast, and employed by the Manchester High School as a janitor. He owns a 1968 Dodge Dart and lives in a boarding house operated by Lynn Raleigh. He has no debt, outstanding warrants, or known associates of questionable morals. Conversations with his supervisor and landlady have given a picture of a man who is punctual and respectful.*
>
> *At this time, we have not recovered a body, although the blood evidence would suggest Mr. Waye is dead. There is an APB out for both Mr. Waye and the man the witness described. The witness is not a suspect at this time.*
>
> *Conversations with the witness, his employer, and members of the V.F.W. have established him as a quiet man who avoids confrontation. He is a returned veteran from Vietnam where his role was as an infantryman.*
>
> *We are awaiting the arrival of his military records to ensure Mr. Bay was not discharged dishonorably, or investigated for any crimes while in the Army.*
>
> *At this point in time, Mr. Waye is considered a missing person, and will be until he either reappears or his body is discovered.*

Henry shook his head, read through the witness' description of the assailant again, and then he looked at Donnie.

"Donnie," Henry said, "what the hell is this?"

"The man," Donnie said, licking his lips nervously. "The man your witness claims she saw. The man Gordon Bay saw. The man *I* saw."

"What?"

Donnie nodded. "Back when Speidel went missing, when the boots were found, I went there, and I saw *him*, Henry. Tall. Too tall. Pants and boots, a scarred back. I thought I was going crazy. I could see right through him. Like he was a double image on an old photo. He was there, but he wasn't. It was, it was terrible."

"How did you find this?" Henry asked.

"I thought I was going crazy," Donnie said. "And before I got sober, I was in the V.F.W., having a couple of drinks. This old guy walks in and the bartender asks him how he is, you know, the usual small talk."

Henry nodded.

"So, they get to talking, and the bartender tells this old guy about what happened with Speidel. The old guy shakes his head, starts talking about how Griswold is haunted. I figured it's just a regular bull session, you know?"

"I know," Henry said.

"Well, another guy rolls up, drops down onto a stool, picks up on what they're saying and chimes in. I hear him telling them about how he'd actually seen the killer ghost back in the seventies. Tells me how a guy went missing, and aside from his camping gear, the only thing left were his boots."

"Damn," Henry said softly, looking down at the file in his hands.

"Yeah. Damn. So, the bartender asks the other guy if he ever reported it to the police. The new guy, he says it was the first thing he did when he got out of Griswold. Went right to the barracks in Manchester and told them all about it," Donnie said. "When I heard that, I went home, got cleaned up, and managed to sober up pretty quick. By the time my seven a.m. shift rolled around, I was good to go. It was that day I found the file, and I decided to get sober."

"Is he still alive?" Henry asked, tapping the file. "Gordon Bay?"

Donnie nodded. "Heard from him last night. He's the one who found James Quill's body."

"What?" Henry said in surprise. "I didn't even know about Jimmy Quill being found."

"Yeah," Donnie said. "Last night. Looks like he drowned in Lake Charles. Body washed up on Gordon's property."

Henry thought for a moment, looked down at the paper, and said, "Do you think we could stop in and see him?"

"I know we can," Donnie said. He pulled his cellphone out of a back pocket and started to dial.

Chapter 29: Free to Go

When Shane was let out of the interrogation room, he was sore and tired, and his head still hurt. The ache had become a steady, unending throb which stretched from his sinuses down to the back of his head.

All I want is a cigarette, he thought, *and a fifth of whiskey.*

Courtney was already out, and she hurried into his arms when she saw him. She looked as worn out as he did. He kissed the top of her head and tried to ignore the looks of disapproval from the gathered police. When Courtney let go of him, Shane took her hand, and they went and gathered their belongings from the clerk.

Outside, the air was warm, light clouds partially hiding the sun. They walked down the stairs, reached the sidewalk, and came to a stop.

"Hungry?" he asked.

Courtney nodded.

"Want to walk up the road a bit? There's a restaurant where we can grab something to eat, then figure out how to get to your car."

"Sounds good to me," she said, sighing. She looked up at him and asked, "What's going to happen?"

"I don't know," Shane replied. "They may eventually charge us with obstruction if they think there's evidence of it. Mostly I think they'll bring us back a few times to question us."

"Great," she said sarcastically.

"I know," Shane said. He gave her hand a squeeze, and they began to walk. After several minutes of silence, he spoke again, hesitantly. "I'm going to go back."

"Where?" she asked. "The police station?"

He shook his head. "Griswold."

"What? Why?" she said, stopping.

Shane looked at her. "He has to be stopped."

"Abel?"

Shane nodded.

"It's done, Shane," she said, anger creeping into her voice. "We're both alive."

"I know," he said. "But he killed the trooper. And I think he killed the two brothers, too. He has to be stopped. I can do something about it."

She pulled her hand out of his and looked hard at him. "Give me a break, Shane. Find someone else to do it. You can't."

Anger pulsed in him, but he kept his voice calm. "I have to."

"Why?" her voice was cold.

"I'm a Marine," Shane said. "And I can. I have to."

"You'll die." Her words came out flat and hard.

"I might," Shane agreed.

"I can't go back in there," Courtney said.

"I wouldn't ask you to. And I can't have someone else die. Not when it can be avoided."

Tears welled up in her eyes. "I like you a lot, Shane. A real lot. I don't know how much is because of Squirrel Island, or because of you, I just know I like you. But I'm not going to hang around while you risk your life. Not for this."

Shane nodded. He was surprised to feel his gut wrench and twist beneath his skin.

"Will you be able to find a ride home?" she asked him after a moment of silence.

"Yeah," Shane said softly, smiling sadly at her.

She nodded, not looking at him. "Okay."

Courtney turned and walked away from him, her head down and her arms across her chest.

Shane didn't watch her leave. Instead, he faced the other way and made his way towards the heart of the city.

I'll call a cab, he thought, his head hurting worse than before. *But I need a drink first. A good, hard drink.*

He walked quickly and kept his eyes open for a bar.

Chapter 30: Gordon Entertains

Gordon opened the door and saw Donnie with a state trooper he didn't know.

"Come on in, gentlemen," Gordon said, stepping away. Both of the men did so, Donnie leading the other to the kitchen table. Gordon joined them after he shut the door. He went to his seat, sat down, and looked at Donnie.

"Gordon, this is Henry Martini," Donnie explained. "He was down in Griswold earlier. We've got a couple of missing men."

"One's a statie?" Gordon asked.

The two men nodded.

"Henry wants to know what you can tell him about your experience in Griswold," Donnie said.

Gordon swallowed uncomfortably. "It's a little hard to discuss."

"I'm patient, Mr. Bay," Henry said pleasantly.

"Call me Gordon, please."

"Alright, Gordon, take your time," Henry said. "I'd like to know what you saw."

Gordon cleared his throat, looked down at his feet, then back up at the two men. After a moment's hesitation, he began to speak. He told them everything. About seeing the dead boy, Andrew, and the dog. He talked about how he had hidden in the church, and then how he had followed Andrew into the woods. Gordon told them of Eugenia, and of hiding in the brook, before following it. Finally, he told the two troopers of Abel Latham and the unknown camper. He told them of how the ghost had carried the stranger out of the tent.

"It started to rain then," Gordon said. He stood up, got a drink of water, and returned to his seat. "A hard rain. The type you want to hide from. Even when you're home, you know it's a bad rain. Lightning followed close on its heels, and thunder, of course. With every strike of lightning, Abel grew stronger. Firmer. He glowed as he worked. The stranger was crucified, between a couple of trees. It was brutal. Horrible."

"I'd seen men hurt," Gordon said, looking from Donnie to Henry. "I've seen them tortured and killed. This was more than anything I'd seen before. A terrible job. When Abel went to work on the man's feet, I couldn't take any more. I ran. Ran."

Gordon shook his head. "Eugenia led me along the brook. And it took a while. A long while, until I reached Lake Charles. Even then I thought Abel was right behind me."

"Do you know what happened to the body?" Henry asked.

"No," Gordon said softly. "I wish to God I did. I used to pray that someone would find the bones, at least give some peace to him."

Silence fell over the men, and Gordon broke it a short time later, saying, "Can I ask why you're interested?"

He saw a glance pass between the two troopers, and finally, Donnie spoke.

"There are two men missing," Donnie said. "One of them is the brother of the man you found. The other is a state trooper. We had a couple in custody earlier."

Henry nodded, adding, "Evidently, Donnie here, thought you might be able to help. You see, the man we had in custody, well, the one we had brought in for questioning, he gave a description which matches yours perfectly."

"Abel?" Gordon asked, his voice suddenly hoarse and weak.

Henry looked at him, and then said, "Seems like it."

Gordon's mouth went dry, and his hand shook as he lifted his glass up for another drink. "You didn't believe him?"

Henry shook his head. "I didn't. I'm not sure I still do. Have there been others who reported seeing this man, Abel, to the police?"

"I don't know," Gordon said, looking to Donnie.

"No," Donnie said. "When I first overheard Gordon here, I went through the old files in the barracks. Then in Concord. Nothing. Not a damned thing. Seems like only Gordon, Shane Ryan, and the girl, Courtney, have seen Abel before."

"No," Gordon said softly. "We're just the only ones to live and report it."

Both of the officers looked at him, confusion on their faces. Gordon stood up, went over to his desk, opened the bottom drawer and pulled out a thick envelope. "You may want to look at this."

He handed it Henry and said, "I'm going to put a pot of coffee on. I think we'll be here a while."

Chapter 31: Home on Berkley Street

Shane's wallet was significantly lighter after his taxi ride from Manchester to Nashua.

When he closed the door behind him and walked tiredly towards the kitchen, Carl appeared in the hall.

"My friend," Carl said pleasantly in German. "How was your adventure?"

"Terrible," Shane said.

Carl frowned and followed him into the kitchen. Shane made his way to the liquor cabinet, pulled down a fresh bottle of whiskey, and opened it. He took a tumbler out of the dishwasher, filled the glass, and then carried it and the bottle to the kitchen table. With a drawn out sigh, he settled down in his chair and emptied the tumbler as quickly as he could.

As he poured himself a fresh drink, Shane looked at Carl, who was eyeing him with concern.

"May I ask," Carl said, "what happened?"

Shane gave the man an abridged version of what had occurred.

Carl scratched the back of his head, confusion plain on his face.

"Tell me," Carl said after a short time, "what is it she would have you do?"

"Let someone else worry about Abel Latham," Shane said, trying to keep the bitterness out of his voice.

"But you are a man," Carl said, shaking his head. "You must do what a man would. You can do no less."

"I know," Shane said. He hesitated before he poured a third shot. *Who cares? No one alive is going to see me falling down drunk.*

"I am sorry for you," Carl said.

"She is a nice young woman," Shane said. He hesitated and then added softly, "I was happy with her, Carl. I was very happy. I never thought I could be. It sounds melodramatic, I know. But we got along. She didn't mind the way I am. Nothing I did bothered her. Except for this."

"My young friend," Carl said gently. "I am truly, truly sorry for you. She seemed like such a nice, young woman."

"She is," Shane replied. "An extremely attractive and nice young woman. She deserves better than a broken man haunted by his childhood."

"That is the whiskey talking," Carl said, scolding him. "You should not drink as much as you do."

"I know," Shane agreed. He knocked back the third drink and set up a fourth. "The problem, Carl, is I just don't care. I may later on. But not right now. Right now, my dear friend, all I want to do is drink and forget about her."

"When will you be going after this ghost? This Abel?" Carl asked.

"The sooner, the better," Shane said bitterly. "I need to know more about him. If I'm going to hurt him, that is."

Carl nodded. "I'm afraid you are correct. With whom shall you speak, my young friend?"

Shane shrugged. "Someone who knows more, I figure."

The whiskey kicked in, a hard blast to his stomach that caused him to wince.

"Perhaps you should not drink so much?" Carl said, his voice laced with concern.

"You're right," Shane said bitterly, pouring himself another drink.

Carl gave a short bow and left the kitchen. Shane was alone at the table, with only the whiskey for company.

Fine with me, Shane thought.

He drank a little more. The screams of Trooper Glenn Jackson echoed through his head. Shane pictured Andrew's feet, and a vivid image of Jackson being tortured burned into his thoughts. Shane shuddered. He dug his cigarettes out, lit one, and exhaled a large cloud of smoke. The tobacco felt good, adding a pleasant, familiar aftertaste to the liquor.

The door to the pantry opened, startling him, as it always did.

Eloise looked out. The little girl eyed him carefully before she asked, "Do you want to play, Shane?"

Startled, Shane laughed and smiled at her. "Why?"

"You're upset," Eloise answered, taking a cautious step into the kitchen. The temperature in the room dropped significantly. "Carl has told us what happened. I thought you might like to play. Playing always made me feel better."

Shane considered it for a moment, tapped the head off his cigarette into the glass ashtray and nodded. "Yeah, Eloise. Yes. I'd like to play. What are you thinking of?"

"A tea party," the little dead girl said excitedly. She clapped her hands, pigtails bouncing. "You can have real tea, and I will have to pretend. We can sit here, at the table, just like grown-ups!"

"I think," Shane said, grinning, "a tea party is exactly what I need."

He stood up, a little unsteadily, and walked over to the stove. Shane got the tea kettle, filled it, and set it on a burner. Eloise skipped over to him, smiling.

"Shall it be a grand tea party, Shane?" she asked in a happy voice.

"The grander, the better," Shane replied, talking around his cigarette. "Hell, we'll even get some cookies out."

Eloise laughed and clapped her hands, watching him intently as he got everything ready for their tea party.

Chapter 32: Investigating the Unexplained

Tom Coach had been a reporter for fifteen years. He'd started off in print and been smart enough to shift into online work when the times changed.

Print's dead, he thought. It was a phrase he had repeated to himself many times when he had to get out and do some legwork for an article. Not only did he write columns for the Nashua Telegraph, the Manchester Union Leader, and the Concord Monitor, but he had his blog as well. He covered politics because New Hampshire was all about the presidential race, but Tom had started his career in crime. And crime was still his passion.

He had managed to get his hands on an illegal scanner, one which allowed him to monitor everything going on where he lived. Tom had heard about the Quill brothers, and he had heard the calls about Trooper Glenn Jackson.

Then there was nothing.

No more chatter on the scanners. None of his former sources would tell him what had happened to Jackson or to John Quill. James Quill's body had washed up on a private beach on Lake Charles. The State Police, the Manchester Police, and the Goffstown Police were all keeping a tight lid on the story.

Too tight, Tom thought. He adjusted his backpack and brought his binoculars up. From where he was parked, he could see the State Police interceptor parked across the road which led down into Griswold. Tom frowned. *I'm going to have to go in through the woods.*

He sighed, put his binoculars in the side pocket of his pack and shook his head. Tom was prepared for the hike, of course. He even had extra supplies in case he got lost.

Not likely, he chuckled. *But stranger things have happened, and best be prepared. What's that phrase Franklin used to say? "An ounce of prevention is worth a pound of cure?"* Tom shrugged, *Always prepared.*

With his car parked at the Mobil Station up the road, where he had given the clerk twenty dollars to make sure the vehicle wouldn't be towed, Tom had hiked the half-mile up Route 111. He walked down the gentle grade, through the tall grass in desperate need of mowing, and entered the woods. The air felt heavy, too humid to be comfortable.

Tom ignored it as best he could. The police were hiding information. No reporters were allowed into Griswold. The pretense was that the entire town was an active crime scene. He scoffed at the idea.

They've had plenty of time to process it, Tom thought. *They're just holding onto it for some reason. All the anti-cop violence going on, I bet that's the angle they're trying to hide.*

It had been a long time since he had been out actively seeking information on a story, and excitement filled him as he moved further into the woods. He followed a thin game trail, which led steadily to the northeast. Every few minutes, he checked the compass he had brought along, making sure he was keeping to the right course.

Griswold, or what was left of it, would be coming up shortly. He remembered when he had moved to Goffstown and how the retirees had talked about the ghost town. Stories of it being haunted. Unexplained disappearances. The strange, abnormal thunderstorms which erupted over it.

Tom snorted derisively. *Man the things people invent.*

The trail opened a little, and he heard the sound of water. He paused, pictured the map of the area in his head. There was a brook to the left of Griswold's main street. The water ran all the way to Lake Charles.

And there's no other water here, Tom thought with a grin. He continued on, and soon he saw the remains of a house. It had been built of stone. There were still closed shutters on the windows and the door hung crazily in its frame. One wall was partially tumbled, the roof was gone, but the chimney still stood tall.

Tom stopped and looked at the home. *I wonder who used to live here,* he thought. He walked closer and peered in. Leaves littered the floor, hiding it from view. A broken chair lay on its side, as did a table.

"Why are you here?" a voice demanded from behind him.

Tom let out an involuntary shriek and jumped. He turned around too fast, tripped and stumbled into the wall. He caught himself even as a stone fell inside.

He saw a young man standing by a birch tree a short distance away. The man looked strange, his clothes soaking wet. Wet hair clung to his forehead and his eyes bore into Tom's.

Tom took a cautious step back, hands out until they found the chill stone of the house.

Cold radiated from the young man, washing over Tom and causing him to shiver. The stranger didn't look right. Something was off about him, but Tom couldn't place it. But he knew he was afraid.

"Are you going to answer me?" the young man asked harshly.

Tom managed a weak smile and said, "I'm just out for a hike. That's all. On my way to Lake Charles, figured I get a little exercise in, you know?"

"This is private property," the stranger said.

"No," Tom said defensively and tried to put a little authority in his voice. "This is public property. What's your name?"

"James. Tell me yours."

"Tom," he replied. He stared at James for a minute. "You look familiar. What's your last name?"

James sneered. "Quill. But I don't know you, Tom."

"James Quill," Tom said, shaking his head. "You're not James Quill. He's dead."

"I am," James agreed, taking a step forward.

It was then Tom realized what was wrong with the man. He wasn't whole. Wasn't completely solid. He looked like a hologram from a science fiction movie. There but not.

"Ghosts aren't real," Tom said defensively.

James raised an eyebrow and in a bitter tone asked, "Would you like to meet my wife, Tom?"

A cold hand touched Tom's arm, and he screamed, wetting himself. He jerked away and turned. A young woman stood close to him. Around her neck was a terrible mark, as though someone had hung her. She smiled at him and stepped forward on bare, silent feet. Her dress was old, faded. And she was as thin and unreal as James.

Her smile faded. "My husband is right. This is private property. Why are you here?"

Tom's heart thundered in his chest. He stuttered as he answered her, "I'm a reporter. I'm just a reporter."

His right arm went numb, and his pulse became erratic. Pain flared in his face, and he thought frantically, *Oh dear God, I'm having a heart attack!*

He groaned, dropped to the ground, and sat there. His breath came in gasps, a tight fist closing around his chest. Tom's heartbeat was a thunderous roar in his ears.

James came closer and stood beside his wife, the dead couple looking down at him with disinterest. Their voices were faint but clear.

"Is he dying?" James asked.

"Yes," the young woman answered. "He's having a heart attack."

Then she added, "I don't want him to stay here. He can't haunt our home."

James sighed. "What do you want me to do?"

"Help me drag him," she answered. "There is a little hill not far from here. At the bottom, he will no longer be in Griswold."

"Fine," James said.

Tom felt both of them grab hold of his arms, pulling him away from the house. Stars exploded around his eyes, and each breath was a struggle, a battle.

I'm dying, Tom thought, tears springing to his eyes. *Christ almighty, forgive me of my sins. I'm so sorry. Please forgive me.*

James and the young woman dragged him unmercifully across the ground. Vaguely Tom felt stones and branches beneath him. Then they were moving him up a small hill. When they reached the crest, they pushed him unceremoniously down the other side.

Tom rolled, gained momentum, and eventually crashed into the rotten trunk of a fallen tree. He glanced up at the top of the hill, expecting to see them looking down at him, but they were gone.

His heart still beat, but it felt more like a five-year-old hammering on a drum set than his great organ pushing blood through his body. Then it began to fail.

Tom gasped as he lay on his back, staring up into the branches and leaves. Birds sang, squirrels called out, and Tom knew he was dying.

Fear and panic battered away at his thoughts, refusing to let him calm down. His heart missed a beat. Then two.

Blackness crept in around the edges of his vision, then stole towards the center, and finally he was blind.

His heart stopped, and his last thought was one of terror.

What if I'm stuck here? What if there's no place to go?

Silence answered him.

Chapter 33: Talking about Griswold

Henry finished his third cup of coffee and sat back in his chair.

Gordon had been right. Henry and Donnie were still in the old man's house, the three of them sitting at the kitchen table. The information which had been in the envelope was spread out over the table. And it was disturbing.

Abel Latham, born circa 1890 along the Maine-Canadian border, had served in the First World War. Not as an American soldier, but as a member of the French Foreign Legion. He had been, by all accounts, a huge man. Well over six feet tall, thinly framed, but extremely strong.

Henry pulled a page closer to him and reread the description of Abel.

> *Abel Latham was nearly a head taller than most of the men in the town of Griswold. He worked as a supervisor of a lumber team. Abel was exceptionally strong, often moving logs by himself when two or three other men might be required to. He had an obsession with his feet, and it was not uncommon for him to be seen with his boots off and a penknife in hand, trimming away calluses and dead skin. Reports given later stated he was a fair man, though given to bouts of both depression and madness.*
>
> *When depressed, it was difficult to rouse him for work.*

> *When the madness took him, he would sneak away and be gone for days, often returning in an extremely pleasant mood. He would refer to these times as his 'regeneration,' when all would be made new.*
>
> *No one was quite sure what he meant by it until after he murdered his family.*

Henry put the page down and looked at Gordon and then Donnie. "Abel Latham murdered his family," he said.

Donnie nodded.

"Yes," Gordon said. "There is a belief that he may well have been responsible for other deaths, in the mill cities and lumber towns. Places where people could disappear and never be thought twice of again."

"This is miserable," Henry muttered. "How many?"

Gordon shook his head, and Donnie said, "They have no idea. I've tried to do a little research, but there were too many transients. No way to keep track of everyone. It wasn't strange for somebody to pick up and go."

"Is there a way to get rid of him?" Henry asked.

Donnie looked over to Gordon, and Gordon answered the question.

"There are ways to stop him," the older man said hesitantly. "Slow him down, if he's coming at you. But from what I've read, he would have to be bound, and I don't even know if that's a real thing or not."

"How do we slow him down?" Henry asked. "If he's to be stopped, we need to know that."

"Salt," Gordon said. "There was a blog, active up until a month or so ago. Local folks. They said the best thing to stop a ghost is salt and iron."

Donnie looked at him. "What, you throw salt at him? Or iron?"

Gordon gestured to the corner by the door, and Henry saw a double-barrel shotgun.

"I pack my own shells," Gordon said. "They're loaded with rock salt. It's enough to send the spirit packing for a while."

"You're sure of that?" Donnie asked.

Gordon shook his head. "It's what the blog said."

"What's the name of it?" Henry asked, taking his phone out.

"It was the Leonidas Group or something like it," Gordon said. "But it's been taken down."

Henry frowned. "Don't suppose they said who they were or anything?"

"They did," Gordon said. "They even had their address posted if people wanted to stop by. Last name was Roy. Lived out in Mont Vernon."

Henry put his phone down on the table, shook his head and said, "Roy?"

Gordon nodded.

Donnie looked at Henry and said, "What is it?"

"Remember the shooting a little ways back in Mont Vernon?" Henry asked.

Donnie's eyes widened. "Holy Mary Mother of God. The Roys. Brian and Jennifer."

"You know who else was there?" Henry said.

Donnie shook his head.

"Shane Ryan," Henry said. "The guy we had in for questioning today."

Book 3: The Town of Griswold

Chapter 34: Uninvited Guests

Shane was good and buzzed by the time he finished his tea party with Eloise. He sat alone in his study, the last cigarette of his pack in his mouth, unlit. There was a fresh carton in the kitchen, but it was too far to travel when he couldn't feel his legs.

I could ask Carl, Shane thought, grinning. *He might do it. He might not. Too tired to call for him.*

Shane looked at the lighter on the table beside him, reached out, and missed it. He swore, and the cigarette fell out of his mouth and onto his chest. Shane frowned and thought, *I am not that drunk.*

He patted around his chest for a moment, picked the cigarette up, and returned it to his mouth. For a moment, he eyed the lighter, and then figured he would wait.

Don't want to light myself on fire.

The doorbell rang.

Tiredly, Shane looked to the study door. Carl appeared a moment later, passing easily through the thick wood. "You've guests, my friend."

"How many?" Shane asked in German.

"Three," Carl replied. "Men. Police, from what I can see."

The doorbell rang again.

Shane rolled his eyes.

"Will you answer it?" Carl asked.

"Sure," Shane said, pushing himself upright. He hesitated and then got to his feet. For a second, he swayed unsteadily, but he shifted his weight and maintained his balance precariously.

"And if they arrest you?" Carl said.

Shane chuckled. "Then I'll sober up in jail tonight. Not worried about it, Carl. So don't."

Carl shook his head and slipped away.

For a third time, the doorbell rang, and Shane yelled out, "I'm coming!"

Carefully he made his way out of the study, down the hall, and to the front door. He opened it, saying, "Come in, gentlemen."

The three men looked at him warily as they entered.

Shane put a hand out to the wall to keep himself upright. "Follow me."

He led them back to the study, dropped into his chair, and watched them as they entered the room. They sat without waiting for permission.

Shane sighed and examined the men. One he knew. Henry Martini, the State Trooper. The other man, a little older than Martini, had the bearing of a police officer, and Shane thought he had seen the man at the barracks in Manchester. The oldest of them Shane had never seen before. But on the man's jacket was an American flag pin, the Vietnam War campaign pin, and a small, blue-enamel combat infantryman's badge.

He's a hard case, Shane thought. He glanced at what remained in the whiskey bottle, considered it for a moment, and then decided against it.

"You're drunk," the old man said.

"Almost," Shane said. "But I plan on getting drunk, and remaining so for several days."

"We'd rather you didn't," Martini said.

Shane waited to hear why.

Martini cleared his throat and then introduced the men. After he did so, the veteran, Gordon, said, "You've seen Abel Latham."

"Yup," Shane responded. *Guess I'll need the drink.*

He reached out to pour it and Donnie said, "Don't."

A bolt of anger raced through Shane. "Donnie, this is my house. I'm going to drink as much as I want."

Carl came into the room and stood behind the visitors.

"You're too drunk already," Henry said.

"I will take the bottle away from you until we're done," Donnie added angrily.

Shane smiled. "Best if you don't try, Donnie. I'd hate for us to get off on the wrong foot."

Picking up the bottle, Shane started to pour the drink, and Donnie stood up.

In German, Shane said, "My friend, if you would."

Carl stepped forward, put his hands on Donnie's shoulders and pushed him back down onto the couch. Donnie's exclamation of surprise filled the room as Gordon and Henry looked at him in shock.

"What the hell just happened?" Henry asked uncomfortably.

Donnie was rubbing his shoulders, glancing around nervously. Carl still stood behind him.

"That was my friend, Carl," Shane answered, lifting his glass and taking a drink. "Carl is dead. Has been for an extremely long time. But he is my friend. This is my house. And if I want to get so drunk that I wake up in my own puke on the floor, that's what I'm going to do."

"Unfortunately," he continued, "your arrival has sobered me up somewhat, and I don't particularly want to be sober right now. I have extremely bad coping skills, as you can see by the nearly empty bottle of whiskey at my elbow. Now, if you gentlemen will kindly explain to me what it is you want, we can all be about our business, whatever it may be."

He drank a little and waited for someone to speak.

Henry finally broke the silence. "Can you tell me what happened at the Roy house?" he asked.

The question surprised Shane. "There was an intruder."

"There's more to it than that," Henry said. He leaned forward. "I know it. They ran a paranormal website. Something happened."

"Sure," Shane said, "something did happen. Why are you asking me?"

"Because," Gordon interrupted, "their website said something about being able to get *rid* of a ghost."

Shane set the half-finished drink on the table. "Are you telling me you think Abel Latham is a ghost?"

"I know he is," Gordon said tightly. "I saw him in 1975 when he wanted to hunt me down. What I want to know, what we want to know, is if the things the Roys said on their website are true?"

"Iron, salt, bindings?" Shane asked.

The three men nodded.

"Yeah," Shane said. "They work. Iron and salt beat back a ghost. Disrupts their energy. Bindings are a little trickier. You need to have someone who knows what they're doing, or it'll go south real quick."

"Do you?" Donnie asked.

Shane shook his head. "I don't know anything about it. Don't even want to try."

"Is there someone who could?" Henry asked.

"Yes," Shane said. "But they're kind of leery going in after someone. It's hard to bind a soul. You don't have a lot of time to do it, and when you are, the spirit in question is usually struggling. They prefer to work with haunted items. Makes life a little easier. And a whole lot safer."

"Oh man," Donnie muttered. "Is there any way to deal with Abel?"

"Sure," Shane said. He cracked his knuckles nervously. "Try to figure out who he was. Talk to the ghosts of those he's killed."

"What good will that do?" Henry asked.

"You get someone who can channel them, sort of juice up," Shane said softly. "If there's enough, then the person can try and stop him."

"Do you know anyone?" Gordon asked.

Shane nodded.

"Who is it?" Henry asked.

"Me," Shane said, chuckling. "I can do it. But we need to find the bodies. It'll be the easiest way for me to try and talk to the dead."

"No one's ever found the bodies," Donnie said dejectedly.

"I know," Shane said. "Doesn't mean we don't try."

"When do you want to start?" Henry asked.

Shane picked up his whiskey and drank the rest of it.

"In the morning," Shane said, putting the tumbler back. "I'm going to need to sleep this one off."

Chapter 35: Looking for Help

The next morning Shane sat on the hood of his car, smoking and nursing a cup of coffee. He was parked in the center of Griswold. The state police interceptor was gone, as were the Quill brothers' trucks. The place was quiet, but not unnaturally so. He could hear birds and squirrels, the normal noises of the forest.

He had arrived first, shortly after sunrise. As he looked at the remnants of the town, he heard an engine and turned his attention to the road. A large, black Dodge Ram drove into the town, pulled up alongside his car, and the driver shut the engine off. Henry, Donnie, and Gordon climbed out of the truck, the older man wincing.

Shane stood up, stubbed out his cigarette, and field stripped the butt, tucking the papers into his pockets. The three men carried shotguns. Shane had his iron knuckledusters.

"So," Henry said, "we need to find a place no one has found in eighty years, right?"

Shane nodded. "About the size of it."

"Any ideas?" Gordon asked.

"Yeah," Shane said. "When I was here before, the dead told me when Abel was caught he was preparing a fire, to 'offer up their ashes to God.'"

"What?" Henry said.

"Hold on," Donnie said. "You said ashes?"

Shane nodded.

"You know," Donnie said. "I think I know where they might be."

Everyone looked at him.

"Southeast, near a hill," Donnie said, nodding. "There's an old smithy. Big old furnace so they could heat the metal up."

"Okay," Shane said. "Do you know the way?"

Donnie reddened. "No. I've only ever seen it on a map."

"Let's find it then," Shane said. He slipped on his knuckledusters, got his bearings, and started towards the back of the church.

The other men fell in behind him.

There was no talk. No idle chatter. They moved along quietly, each deep in their own thoughts. Shane let his eyes rove over the woods as they walked. For a short time, they followed a game trail, before it peeled off towards the west. Half an hour passed, then another, and finally they came upon the remains of the smithy.

The stone walls had either fallen down or been pulled down. A hearth the size of Shane's kitchen stood at what would have been the back. The chimney reached up from the slope of a small hill. The air around them was significantly colder than the rest of the woods.

Shane shivered and saw the others were chilled as well.

"This is it," Shane said softly. "You can feel it."

They nodded.

"Where are the bones?" Donnie asked.

"Can't you smell it?" Gordon said. And Shane realized he could.

The scent of death was in the air. A faint hint of rot.

"I can smell it," Henry said. He stepped off to the right, looking around.

Shane closed his eyes and inhaled deeply. His stomach turned painfully, rejecting the smell. But Shane tried to focus on it, turning to the left.

He opened his eyes, saying, "Come, this way."

A sparse path led around the hillside, all the way to the back. Granite stones protruded haphazardly from the earth, and the path ended at a large boulder. Donnie walked up, pushed the rock, but nothing happened.

"Further up," Gordon said, nodding. Shane looked and caught sight of the path about twenty feet beyond.

They picked their way through the granite, coming out near the trail's continuation. Once again, they followed it until it hooked sharply to the left around a large, black walnut tree.

Shane rubbed the back of his head and then smiled at the men around him. The smell was terrible by the tree.

"Don't suppose anyone here has a flashlight?" Shane asked.

Henry reached into a back pocket and pulled out a small, LED Maglite. He handed it to Shane.

"Sure you want to go in first?" Donnie asked.

"Of course not," Shane said, laughing and turning on the light. "Might as well get it done, though, right?"

No one answered.

"So," Shane said, clearing his throat. "If I come back, and I'm dead, shoot me and run like hell."

The men nodded.

"Good," Shane said softly. He turned his back on them, walked around the tree, and found what he had suspected.

A hole, large enough for a man to walk through, was in the side of the hill. The rank smell of decay was heavy around it. Shane's hand shook as he got out a cigarette, tore the filter off and broke the remainder in half. He tucked one piece up each nostril, the smell of tobacco smothering most of the stench. He shined the light into the hole and saw the floor slanted down a short distance before it turned into stairs.

Shane entered the hillside, moving carefully. The roof of the tunnel was tall, large enough to allow Abel Latham to walk easily when he had been alive. The passage continued its descent, turning sharply to the right. Hugging the left wall, Shane went around cautiously. All he saw was the continuation of the tunnel.

Shane traveled further in. He navigated three more turns, each of them to the right until he came to a large door. The wood was rough, the hinges made out of ancient leather. A piece of rope served as a handle. In the confines of the tunnel, trapped by the dirt walls, the smell of death was nearly suffocating.

Shane shined his light on the rope, grasped it, and gave the door a tug. The bottom left edge dragged in the dirt, but it opened.

In silence, Shane stood in the doorway, letting the light play across the room.

At the far end was the back of the blacksmith's hearth. There was a small, iron door. It was large enough to thrust body parts through. On the stone floor in front of the makeshift cremator were body parts. Shane counted four arms, an equal number of legs, two torsos, and a pair of heads.

He moved the flashlight's beam from the dismembered bodies to the walls and felt a sickening feeling in his stomach, fear and disgust ripping through him. Rough shelves lined the walls. Ten shelves on each. And on the shelves were shoes.

Shoes and boots. Footwear for ladies and for men. Children as well. Not a few pairs, but perhaps hundreds. Maybe more. So many it caused Shane's heart to ache as he looked at them.

He stepped into the room and began to count. He couldn't stop himself.

I have to know, Shane thought. Tears filled his eyes, and soon they spilled down his cheeks. Some reached the corners of his mouth and left a bitter taste on his lips. The smell of death was forgotten, the cigarette pieces more annoyance than comfort, yet he left them in. He had to count.

For several long minutes, he gathered the numbers to him. When he finished, he stepped out of the room and closed the door. He followed the tunnel back out and soon stood with the other men.

"Shane," Gordon said, turning Shane towards him. "Are you alright?"

Shane shook his head. He pulled the cigarette pieces out and stuffed them into his pocket. Henry took his light back, and Shane got out a fresh cigarette, he lit it, and exhaled shakily into the morning air.

"What did you see?" Donnie asked gently.

"The remains of Jackson and Quill," Shane said, his voice surprisingly calm.

"Anything else?" Henry asked.

Shane looked at him, nodded, and said, "Three hundred and forty-two pairs of shoes."

Chapter 36: In Bad Company

Courtney had cried herself to sleep.

When she awoke, her face felt puffy, and she tasted tears on her lips. She lay on her back in bed. Her stomach felt empty, but she didn't want to get up. Instead, she kept her eyes closed and tried to move as little as possible.

A knock sounded on her door, and Courtney said tiredly, "Come in."

Her roommate, who had also been Elaine's cousin came in. Sherry, like Courtney, had not had an easy time with Elaine's death. Sherry's boyfriend had helped her, much like Shane had helped Courtney.

Courtney sighed and looked at her roommate.

"You okay?" Sherry asked, coming in and sitting down on the edge of the bed.

Courtney shook her head.

"What's up?" Sherry said, concerned.

With a shuddering breath, Courtney told Sherry the abbreviated story about the hiking trip. She told her all about being questioned by the police. And then Courtney told Sherry how Shane had decided he needed to go back and try to help the police find the body of Trooper Jackson.

"Why are you crying then?" Sherry asked, confused.

Courtney blinked, shook her head, and said, "Because the murderer's still out there. And because I told him I couldn't be around him if he was going to risk his life."

Sherry's eyes widened, and she said, "Courtney, you didn't tell me everything about the lighthouse, and, well, I don't want to know anything else about it, but you told me Shane did some pretty awesome stuff."

Courtney nodded.

"I think," Sherry said hesitantly, "he's programmed to do heroic things, you know? I don't think he can stop himself. He was a marine, right?"

"Yeah," Courtney said softly. "Twenty years."

Sherry shook her head. Tears crept into her eyes and she said hoarsely, "He helped to stop the woman who killed Elaine?"

"Yes," Courtney whispered.

"He has to do this, hon," Sherry said, her voice raw. "I understand if you're nervous about being in a relationship with someone who's taking risks, but he's taking them for the right reasons. He wants to help. Damn, girl, he's a hero. A real hero."

Courtney sat up and looked at Sherry. "You think so?"

"Yes," Sherry answered. "I do. I'm not saying to start the relationship up again or anything like that, but you've got to understand who he is."

Courtney sniffled, smiled tiredly, and said, "You're putting your psych degree to good use."

"I try," Sherry said, leaning forward and pulling Courtney in for a hug. "I'm making tea. You want some?"

"Yeah," Courtney said, wiping her eyes as Sherry let go and stood up. "Be right out."

Sherry nodded and left the room. Courtney picked her phone up off of the bed and sent Shane a quick text.

I'm sorry. Still friends?

His reply came a few minutes later.

Always.

Chapter 37: At the Crematorium

Shane was sober and tired. He wanted to sleep, but stood outside the entrance into the hill and smoked a cigarette instead. Soon, he would have to go back into Abel Latham's trophy room, and he hated the thought of it. The chamber reminded him of the pictures of Nazi warehouses, filled with the belongings of the murdered.

Shane took a deep, shuddering breath, and forced himself to calm down. His hands trembled when he took out a fresh cigarette and lit it. He exhaled slowly into the warm air.

Shane thought about Courtney, about the text message she had sent, and he smiled. A wave of happiness swept over him and Shane felt like a teenager with a crush.

This is stupid, he thought, still grinning. Shane let a long stream of smoke out through his nose. *Maybe, just maybe we can get back together. Maybe we can try again. I won't do anything like this again.*

Shane sighed. His hands relaxed slightly and he thought about the situation.

The others would return soon. Armed with more iron and salt. Donnie had brought up the idea of an exorcism, but Gordon had rejected the idea.

You'll only free him of the binding to Griswold, Gordon had explained. *Imagine taking a serial killer out of prison, handing him a road map, keys to a car, and saying, 'Have fun!' That's what happens when you exorcise a ghost.*

Shane had nodded his agreement, impressed with how much the man knew.

The darkness of the entrance kept drawing Shane's attention back to it. *I need to go in. I need to speak with them.*

Henry wanted Shane to wait, had asked him to not go in until they had returned.

I don't think it's a good idea to wait, Shane thought. *Not with Abel. I can feel it.*

There was an uncomfortable weight in the air, an oppression making it difficult for Shane to breathe. He walked to the entrance and passed into the darkness. His right hand trailed along the wall, and he took his time as he went, careful not to trip. Once more he descended, and soon he couldn't see at all.

He soon found the door, his fingers discovering the rope pull. Shane let himself in, ignoring the rotting stench of Jackson and Quill as best he could. He took a single step into the room, sat down, and looked at the dull, orange glow of his cigarette's tip.

Spikes of cold wedged themselves into his flesh, burrowed into his joints and caused him to cringe. He took out another cigarette, lit it off of the one in his mouth, and switched them out. His body was one mass of goose bumps, and he shivered continuously.

In silence, he waited.

"I wish I could smell that," a man's voice said.

"I wish I could give you a smoke," Shane answered. He looked to the left, where the words had come from. "My name's Shane."

"Theodore," the man said. "Why are you here, in this place?"

"I've come for help," Shane replied.

"With what?" Theodore's voice came from in front of Shane, as if the dead man was sitting across from him.

"With Abel Latham," Shane said.

Whispers and curses raced around the room.

Theodore, it seemed, was their spokesman.

"You'll not get much help here," Theodore said grimly. "He is too strong. Even for all of us combined. Have you seen the storms?"

"The thunderstorms?" Shane asked.

"Yes," Theodore answered.

"Sure," Shane said. "I was here the other night."

"They are his."

"What?" Shane asked, confused. "How are they *his*?"

"He calls them to him," Theodore answered, lowering his voice. "He creates them, from us."

A fresh stab of fear punctured Shane's chest, and he asked, "He uses you?"

"Yes," Theodore said bitterly. "When he is hunting, he is a great leech. Sucking us dry, pouring it into the sky, and pulling the clouds in. Every lightning strike increases his strength. He is too adept at his craft, Shane. Far too many of us fear him, and are too afraid to resist him. And for those of us who would fight him, he is too strong."

Then Theodore repeated, "Too strong."

Whispers of agreement filled the air.

"Do you know how to stop him?" Shane asked in a low voice.

"No," Theodore said. "Not even how to slow him down, else we would have done it."

"Yeah," Shane muttered. "Do you know where he's buried?"

"No," Theodore replied. "I doubt it is in hallowed ground."

"Yeah," Shane agreed. "Me too."

The cold vanished from the room, and Shane knew he was alone with the trophies and the corpses. Faintly he heard someone calling his name.

"Coming out!" Shane yelled, and stood up. He needed to tell the others what he had learned and decide what to do next.

Chapter 38: Brainstorming

None of the men had been particularly pleased with Shane's message.

Not that you expected them to be, Shane thought. He sat on Gordon's porch. The older man was beside him, and they both had a beer. From their seats, they could see the brook which

Gordon had followed years earlier to escape Abel, a story Gordon had told Shane after the troopers had gone to work. They would report finding Jackson and Quill's bodies.

"So," Gordon said, interrupting the silence. "What are you thinking?"

"Wondering if salting and burning Abel's body is an option," Shane said.

"You didn't mention it to Henry or Donnie."

"I did not," Shane said. "They have enough to worry about right now. I figured I could talk to you about it. Especially since you know about salt and iron."

Gordon nodded.

"Do you know where he's buried?" Shane asked.

"No," Gordon said, shaking his head. "No idea. We'll have to dig around a bit. I'm hoping someone claimed his body."

Shane looked at him. "Why?"

"How hard do you think it'll be to get onto the prison's grounds, find the right grave, dig it up, and get rid of it without someone with a rifle noticing?" Gordon said.

"Christ," Shane grumbled. "Didn't think about that."

"It's alright," Gordon said, taking a drink, "I did."

"We'll need to do it as quickly as we can," Shane said after a short time.

"Why's that?" Gordon asked.

"Did you see the news about the dead reporter?" Shane said.

Gordon shook his head.

"Yeah, online writer," Shane said, finishing his beer. "Dead of a heart attack on the Griswold line."

"Damn," Gordon said softly.

"Yup. Guessing someone scared him to death," Shane said. "Trouble is he won't be the last. Plenty of people are going to want to inspect Griswold. Had an issue like that with some men on Squirrel Island. They ran a website for death-junkies."

Frowning, Gordon stood up, went over to the door, and lifted the lid on a cooler. He took out a fresh pair of beers. He popped them both open, carried them to the table, and passed one over to Shane.

Shane nodded his thanks, took a swallow, and said, "So, guess we need to figure out where old Abel Latham's body is."

"There is a graveyard in Griswold," Gordon said after a minute of silence.

Shane looked at the older man and waited.

Gordon cleared his throat uncomfortably, stared out over the water for a moment and then continued. "Not a nice place. Dark. Even for a place in the woods. There's a bad feeling when you go there."

"How bad?"

"Bad," Gordon said grimly. "Real bad. Kind that makes you wish you had more than a pistol on your hip. Maybe a priest, if you believe in God."

"Don't know if a priest would be any help," Shane said. "Not unless he was okay with desecrating a grave."

Gordon snorted his agreement, took another drink from his bottle, and said shortly, "You look like a hard man, Shane."

"When I have to be," Shane admitted. "You don't look like a shrinking violet yourself."

"I'm not," Gordon agreed. "Vietnam kind of rubbed most of the soft spots away."

"It happens," Shane said, nodding.

"And you?"

Shane smiled. "Let's just say I've had an interesting life, Gordon, and we'll leave it there."

"Sounds fair to me," Gordon said.

They finished their beers in silence.

"Want to wait for Henry and Donnie?" Gordon asked.

"Not at all," Shane said. "You?"

"Nope. I've got a spare shotgun if you want it."

"I'd appreciate it," Shane said, standing. "How will we get in?"

"Same way I got out," Gordon said, getting to his feet. "The brook. Let's hope we can follow it back when we need to."

Shane nodded his agreement and went inside to get armed.

Chapter 39: Looking for a Thrill

"Come on," Bonnie whispered. "It'll be fun!"

Erick looked at his girlfriend and shook his head. In a low voice, he replied, "There are cops crawling all over the place."

"That's what makes it exciting," she said, pulling on his arm. "Come on. Your parents are home. My mom's home. The janitor's locked the church up."

Erick shifted his weight, keeping an eye on the cruisers and police in the center of Griswold. He and Bonnie had snuck down from 111 to have a look at the murder scene when the police had raced down the road and piled out of their cars. The sun was getting close to setting, and the two of them had been behind a chimney for almost an hour. Twenty feet away was a cellar hole, something he and Bonnie could slip into. They'd be able to make-out. If the cops didn't catch them.

It's like she wants them to, Erick thought, glancing at her. Her pink-streaked blonde hair was piled up in a ponytail, and she wore a shirt too small for her chubby frame.

He smiled and felt a fresh line of sweat break out on the back of his neck.

Well, maybe we could make out for a little while, he thought.

Bonnie saw his smile, pulled on his arm again, and winked at him. Erick nodded, and the two of them got to their feet. He kept an eye on the police, barely noticing the white medical examiner's van which pulled in.

They sneaked across the short distance, clambered down into the cellar hole and lay on the ground, panting.

"That was so hot," Bonnie whispered, rolling over onto him. "So damn hot."

Erick forgot all about the police, the stories of how Griswold was haunted, even why they had gone down to look in the town, to begin with. All he could think about was Bonnie.

Before he knew it, the sun had set, and the lights of the cruisers had vanished. Crickets sang out loudly, barn owls ripped the night with their cries, and bats winged their way through the air. Erick and Bonnie lay on their backs, staring up at the night's sky. The stars had come out in force and the moon shined down brightly.

Life is good, Erick thought happily, Bonnie nestling into the crook of his arm.

For the first time in hours, Bonnie pulled her phone out. She held it up above them for a selfie and then said, "What the hell?"

"What's wrong?" Erick asked, yawning.

"My phone's dead," she said angrily.

"How?" he asked, looking at her. "I thought you had charged it before we left."

"I did," Bonnie said. She shook the phone, tried to turn it on, and nothing happened.

"Let me see what time it is," Erick said. He took his phone from his pocket and found it was as dead as hers. "Damn."

"What?" she said, glancing at him.

"Mine's dead too."

"Hey," Bonnie said, sitting up. "I think the cops left."

Erick joined her and looked at the trees. There were no flashing lights illuminating the leaves, or work lights set up. He had watched cop shows like *Law and Order* for years, and he didn't see any of the lights he expected.

"Did we make out through all of it?" he asked Bonnie.

"I guess so," she said, standing. "Yeah. No one's here."

Erick got up as well and saw they were alone. "Wow."

"Do you have your flashlight?" she asked.

Erick almost responded with, *What, the one you always make fun of me for carrying?*

But he knew that wouldn't be the best way to answer her. Bonnie got angry easily. Instead, he reached into his back pocket and pulled out the small SOG flashlight he carried. Erick grinned at her. "Want to check out the church first?"

She shook her head. "I heard they were killed in the store. I want to see the blood."

A thrill of excitement raced through him, and Erick laughed. "Yeah. Let's do that."

The flashlight's beam danced in front of them as they crossed the distance between the cellar hole and the old country store. Night sounds filled the air, and Erick thought he could smell the heavy, iron tang of blood. It reminded him of his first hunt with his father, a large doe shot cleanly through the heart.

The scent of its blood had been thick in the fall air, the body steaming. Erick vividly remembered the sight of the offal tossed aside, the quick, efficient way his father had field dressed the deer. A smile crossed Erick's lips, and the light soon illuminated the front of the store.

Bonnie stopped, and Erick did as well.

"Did you see it?" she asked in a low voice.

"What?" Erick said, glancing around. "Did I see what?"

She shook her head. "I thought I saw a woman, looking out of the left window."

Erick pointed the flashlight at it, but he didn't see anything. "Might have been shadows."

Bonnie didn't say anything. Finally, she spoke. "Yeah. Probably."

She led him toward the store, but she moved cautiously. Erick didn't push it. She had been in a good mood, which was a lot better than when she wasn't.

A whole lot better, Erick thought.

They stepped into the building and stopped several paces in. The smell of the blood was heavier, and the dark stains on the floor told a grim story that churned Erick's stomach. Bonnie squeezed his hand tighter as she looked around.

"What the hell happened in here?" she whispered.

"Something bad," Erick answered. "Something really bad."

She nodded, tugged on his hand, and together they advanced a little further into the room.

"Who are you?"

The words were spoken harshly, and Bonnie screamed while Erick choked with surprise. They slowly turned around, Bonnie letting go of his hand.

A middle-aged woman stood in the doorway. She was barefoot, dressed simply in a sweater and a dress which came down to just above her bare ankles. Her dark hair was pulled back into a tight bun, her face hard. Around her neck was a vivid, red scar.

And Erick could see the world through her.

Bonnie didn't scream again. She shrieked.

A sound so loud that Erick clapped his hands over his ears as he winced with pain. Still screaming, Bonnie ran out of the store through the dead woman. The ghost didn't seem to care. Her eyes were fixed on Erick.

"Answer my question, young man," the woman repeated.

He dropped his hands down to his sides, the flashlight falling to the floor and shining brightly through her. His fingers trembled, and his palms began to sweat. Erick rubbed at the side of his nose nervously, stuttered and managed to whisper, "We were looking for ghosts."

"There aren't any ghosts here," the woman said. "What absolute nonsense."

Erick blinked, confused. "But you're a ghost."

Her eyes widened. "I am not. I am Emily Ross, forty-seven years old and the school teacher for the town of Griswold!"

He nodded. "Yeah. You're dead. Nobody's lived in Griswold for, I don't know, eighty years or something."

"You're a liar," the woman hissed, clenching her fists.

"No," Erick said, shaking his head. "Really. You're dead."

Her face became a mask of rage, and she let out a furious howl. An invisible force threw Erick backward, smashing him into an old counter. Pain exploded in his lower back, and an agonized gasp pushed past his lips as he dropped to his knees. The joints cracked loudly against the ancient floor, and the woman was upon him. Bitterly cold hands wrapped around his throat and squeezed.

Erick fought for every breath, managed to get a hand on the counter and pulled himself up.

She tightened her grip and twisted to the right.

Erick tried to free himself, but there was nothing he could do.

His head was pushed up and to the right, his neck extending farther and farther. He saw the plain, open framework ceiling.

My neck is going to … and he never finished the thought.

His vertebrae cracked, the noise loud in the curious stillness of the night.

Chapter 40: Desperately Seeking Safety

Bonnie ran.

She had never moved so quickly, or so blindly in her life. Erick was forgotten, and only fear remained. It propelled her forward, across the cracked asphalt of Griswold and into the woods. Some primal part of her mind was focused on escape, adrenaline thrusting her into the darkness of the forest.

Bonnie ran until her foot caught on some unseen branch, and went tumbling across the forest floor. She cried out as she struck a tree, coming to a hard stop. For a long time, she lay on her back, panting. Slowly, she realized she could hardly see. The trees hid the night sky, and the forest was quiet. Terribly, horribly quiet.

Where's Erick? she asked herself, sitting up. *Didn't he follow me?*

"Erick?" she whispered.

He didn't answer her.

"Erick?" she repeated, a little louder.

Silence was the only reply she received.

I'm lost, she realized, standing up slowly. *I'm lost!*

She began to hyperventilate, and she reached out, finding the tree she had struck. Bonnie grabbed hold of the cool bark and pulled herself closer to it. Once her back was firmly pressed against it, Bonnie closed her eyes. Her entire body shook, fear running rampant through her.

Bonnie opened her eyes, hoping she would be able to see something, but all that greeted her were dark shapes.

Chills burst through her as a cold hand touched her hand, traced the line of her neck and lingered on her shoulder. She screamed, and someone slapped her in the mouth. Instantly, she tasted blood, and she went silent.

"Keep quiet," a voice said. It was a man's voice, and he was directly in front of her. She couldn't see him.

"I'm lost," she whined.

She was slapped again, the blow leaving her head ringing.

"I said be quiet!" the man spat.

The cold hand played with her hair.

"You're not a very pretty girl," he said shortly.

Bonnie whimpered and whispered, "Erick."

"Erick?" the stranger said, chuckling. "Your young man, I suppose?"

She nodded.

"Don't worry about him," the man said, and she could hear the pleasure in his voice. "He's run into someone, and I do believe she's killed him."

A sob exploded out of Bonnie's mouth, and again the man slapped her.

"Shut up," he said, exasperated. "You mewl more than a newborn kitten."

The hand took a handful of hair and pulled back slowly, taking Bonnie away from the tree. She fell, and he jerked her back to her feet. A scream started and he slapped it away.

Bonnie began crying, stumbling along, the stranger dragging her through the darkness.

"Good God," the man said angrily, "you never shut up."

He stopped her and struck her violently, smashing her down to her knees. Sharp sticks dug into her, and she screamed.

The blows continued.

The stranger paused, sighed, and said sadly, "You know, you're not worth the effort."

Before Bonnie could wonder what he meant, the man hit her again. And again. He struck her hard and fast, driving her to the forest floor. Bonnie felt bones breaking, blood leaking from her ears. What felt like booted feet hammered into her ribs and back and skull. She couldn't move and could hardly breathe. Bonnie gagged on blood, vomited, and heard the man's laughter over the sound of her own heartbeat.

His laughter stopped abruptly, replaced by a song.

"'Give me that old-time religion, give me that old-time religion, it's good enough for me,'" the man sang.

Faintly, beneath the terror and pain, Bonnie had an absurd thought.

He has a beautiful singing voice.

The thought echoed in her mind as he slowly beat her to death.

Chapter 41: Moving through Darkness

Shane and Gordon were armed with shotguns and flashlights duct-taped to them, the beams aimed down the length of the barrels. Each man carried twenty rounds for the shotguns and backup batteries for the flashlights. They walked along the slim beach, side by side, toward the brook which Gordon had used to escape from Griswold decades earlier.

Gordon's steps slowed the closer they got to the unmarked border of Griswold.

Shane looked at the older man and asked, "You okay?"

Gordon nodded. "Just afraid."

"No shame in that," Shane said. "I'm scared, too. I don't want to go back, but Abel needs to be gotten rid of. He's done too much damage."

"Yes," Gordon said softly. "I hope our boots don't end up in his collection."

Shane snorted. "Same here."

They reached the point where the brook met with the lake and the two men paused to look into the forest. A narrow path ran along the left-hand side of the brook.

"This leads back into Griswold," Shane said. He glanced at Gordon. "When will we know to turn toward the town?"

"There's a house we'll pass," Gordon said, shining his own light along the brook. The water twisted and turned the light into various shapes and sizes. "Once we see the house, we turn to the left. There should be an old trail. Might be hard to see with only the flashlights, but it should still be there."

"Will that take us into town?" Shane asked.

Gordon shook his head. "No. Right to the burial ground."

"Good," Shane said. "I really don't want to see Abel anytime soon."

"Same here," Gordon said. They looked at the brook. "Well, I'm ready. You?"

Shane nodded and led the way into the woods.

They kept the brook on their right, the water a soft chuckle of sound as it moved along its bed. Every thirty or forty feet, they paused, making certain they were still traveling the right way, and to let their arms rest; the heavy shotguns were kept at shoulder height so the flashlights could illuminate the way.

"We should be close now," Gordon said.

"Okay." Shane felt uncomfortable, as though someone was watching them.

Someone probably is, he reminded himself. The thought was not comforting.

They moved further along the trail and soon the remains of a house could be seen at the edge of the flashlight's circle. Wordlessly, Gordon turned towards it, and they left the safety of the brook behind them. The building was little more than two crumbled walls and the remnants of a fieldstone chimney. A path followed the footprint of the house and led them deeper into the forest. Around them the darkness was complete, the silence disturbing and heavy.

"Hello?" a voice asked from the darkness.

Shane and Gordon stopped.

"Hello?"

To the left, Shane thought, swinging the barrel of the shotgun towards the speaker. The flashlight's powerful beam fell upon a teenage boy. The teen wore a t-shirt which said he was the world's best Patriots fan, and a pair of jeans that were far too tight. His neck was also bent crookedly.

"Oh no," Gordon said, sighing.

"Hello," Shane said, keeping the shotgun leveled at the teenager's chest.

The teen looked at him, confusion in his dead eyes, his chubby face desperate.

"Where am I?" the boy asked.

"Griswold," Shane answered.

"Why?" the teenager said, shaking his head. "I'm not supposed to be down here. They said there are ghosts down here. I need to go home."

"Then go," Shane said gently. "Go home."

"I can't!" the boy sobbed, choking. "I tried and I can't! I get close to the road, and there's a wall, I can't go by it. Oh, Jesus, I can't go through it. I can't even see it! I thought I'd walk to Lake Charles, but she told me I can't."

"Who?" Gordon asked gently.

"The woman," the boy said, sniffling. "Even Bonnie doesn't know what's going on."

"Who's Bonnie?" Shane asked, shifting his weight but keeping the shotgun level.

"She's my girlfriend," the teen replied. "She sits by a tree crying. Someone beat her up. I just want to go home, okay? Can you help me? Can you help us?"

"We'll do what we can," Shane said.

The teenager nodded and passed by them, a cold wake following him.

In silence, Shane and Gordon continued on. Soon Shane heard someone crying, soft, hiccupping sounds.

Bonnie, he thought grimly.

The sound was oddly frightening, it slipped around the trees and assaulted his ears from all sides.

"Look," Gordon said, gesturing with his shotgun.

Shane looked, and he saw a cemetery. It was small, perhaps not even a full acre. A short, wrought-iron fence ran across the front of the burial ground. Shane could see thirty or forty stones standing upright.

They stopped a short distance from the gate, which hung only by a single hinge, the other broken and ruined.

"We're thinking in there?" Shane said, nodding towards the headstones.

"Yes," Gordon replied.

"Well," Shane said, "no time like the present."

Gordon nodded, opened his mouth to reply, then closed it suddenly, his eyes widening with surprise.

Shane was about to ask him what had happened when he saw for himself. Another ghost had appeared. A young woman, wearing a simple dress and shirt, the open collar revealing a hideous garroting scar. She stood barefoot before them, an angry expression on her face.

"Eugenia?" Gordon whispered.

The anger on her face fled, replaced by a look of confusion. Warily she asked, "How do you know my name?"

"It's me, Gordon," he said. "You helped me."

For a heartbeat longer, the confusion remained on her face, and then she smiled. "Gordon. I did not expect you ever to return to Griswold. Never. Have you returned to die?"

Maybe, Shane thought, shaking his head. *Maybe we both have.*

Chapter 42: The Decision Made

Courtney remembered how to get to Shane's house. And if she hadn't, she still had it programmed into her GPS. She had tried calling him several times, but it kept going to voicemail.

He's probably working, she thought, putting the car in park and getting out. She had a nice bottle of wine and hoped he would take a break long enough to entertain her.

And let me apologize, Courtney sighed. She felt terrible about having broken up with him.

Holding onto the wine tightly, she walked up to the front door and knocked once. As she raised her hand to knock a second time, there was a click and someone let her in. She stepped inside but didn't see anyone.

An uncomfortable feeling crept over her. "Hello?" she said nervously. She walked in a little further, and the door shut behind her.

Boy, she thought, jumping at the sound, *that was pretty stupid, Courtney.*

"Is anyone here?" she asked, trying to keep the fear out of her voice.

It didn't work. Her voice sounded like it had gone up two octaves.

"There are lots of us here," a voice said. It sounded like it belonged to a little girl.

Courtney looked around and caught a glimpse of a child. The girl stood half in and half out of a shadow at the end of the long hall.

"Hello," Courtney said, forcing herself to smile, her heart beating madly. "I'm looking for Shane."

"He's not here," the girl said. She took a step closer. "Who are you?"

"I'm Courtney. Who are you?"

"Eloise," the little girl said. "You shouldn't be in our house, Courtney. You made Shane sad. We don't like it when he's sad."

There was a barely contained anger in Eloise's words. A door to Courtney's right opened up, revealing a study. The lights were on, but the leather club chairs were empty. She glanced at Eloise and then hurried into the room. Courtney closed the door before she sat down in one of the chairs.

"I'm quite surprised to see you, *fraulein*," a man said, and Courtney screamed in surprise.

A man stood off to the left of the hearth, looking intently at her. He was neatly dressed, his hands behind his back as he watched her. Courtney could see through him as he walked towards her and sat down in a chair across from her.

"My name is Carl," he said politely, his English heavy with a German accent. "I must say, we are all quite surprised at you being here. Our young Miss Eloise is right. None of us are especially pleased with your injuring of Shane's emotions. In addition to that, he has gone off to Griswold. To face off against this particular sadist. I do not know if he is with the men who visited him, or if he is facing the beast alone. Alone would be more in keeping with his personality however. Don't you agree?"

Courtney tried to answer, but her mouth wouldn't form the words.

Carl politely waited for a moment before he continued. "Well, I can only assume you have either spoken with him since he left or else you came here to make amends." He smiled at her. "You see, I am not nearly as young as Eloise, so I can see what the answer might be, yes?"

Courtney nodded.

"It doesn't mean that, Carl!" Eloise yelled from the other side of the door.

Courtney jumped and looked nervously towards the hall.

Carl waved his hand dismissively. "She cannot come in, not unless I give my approval, and I do not. Shane has established certain areas for us."

"Oh," Courtney whispered.

"Ah, you can speak," Carl said, chuckling. "Excellent. I'm certain my dear Shane would have mentioned if you were a mute."

The door rattled in the frame, and Eloise screamed, "Let me in!"

"Das ist genug, Eloise!" Carl snapped.

Eloise muttered something unintelligible, and the door went still.

Carl cleared his throat. "Now, you cannot stay here, Ms. Courtney. Do you understand?"

"Sure," Courtney said. "I mean, I guess. I need to leave the house since Shane isn't here."

"Exactly," Carl said, nodding cheerfully.

"Alright," Courtney said, standing up. "Well, I'll come back when Shane's here."

She looked over at the door. "Um, is it safe to go out there?"

"Into the hall?"

"Yeah," Courtney said.

"No," Carl said, the smile vanishing from his face. He looked at her coldly. "It is not safe at all. You have two choices before you, young miss. Either the hall and Eloise, or the window and the yard."

"What?" Courtney asked. "You can't make her leave me alone?"

"Of course, I could," Carl said. *"Aber warum sollte ich?"*

She shook her head confused.

"'But why would I?'" Carl asked softly. "You have hurt my friend, a man who did much for me, even as a child. I am not inclined to help you, even if you have made an apology to him. You will risk the ire of Eloise, and of the things in the yard if they are awake. I will neither hinder nor help you. Make your own way."

The dead German vanished, leaving Courtney alone in the room. She glanced at the tall window which looked out towards the road. From where she stood, Courtney could see her car parked in the driveway.

The doorknob rattled, and the high, sweet laughter of a child came through the keyhole.

"You're all alone, Courtney," Eloise said in a sing-song. "All alone. Come into the hallway, Courtney. I want to play. I'm *lonely*."

The little girl shook the door in its frame and Courtney ran for the window.

Chapter 43: An Unexpected Situation

Donnie had an AA meeting, leaving Henry to drive to Gordon's house alone. The lights on his pickup cut through the dark country road the old man lived on. Henry cruised along slowly, tired and sore from the long day in Griswold. They had to process the scene at the makeshift crematorium, and he and Donnie had lied. The two of them had reported the discovery as being done solely by themselves.

No one would have wanted to hear that Shane Ryan had been involved. The man had left a bad taste in the mouths of more than a few cops. And there were others who believed Gordon had been involved with the disappearance he had reported back in 1975.

What a mess, Henry thought with a sigh.

Reflector-laden posts, the markers for Gordon's driveway, appeared suddenly on the left and Henry signaled before he turned. Gravel spit out from under the pickup's tires, striking nearby trees loudly. When his headlights hit the end of the driveway, the motion-sensor lights around Gordon's home flickered into life.

Henry came to a stop and saw Shane's vehicle parked next to Gordon's.

Where the hell are they? Henry asked, looking at the dark house. None of the interior lights were on. *Christ, are you kidding me? Are they fishing or something?*

Angrily, he put the truck into 'park,' shut off the engine and got out.

Henry heard the slap of waves against the beach and the cry of night birds. A hot spike of rage punched through him.

They left, Henry realized. *I bet they went back into Griswold. But why? And where?*

He dug his phone out of his pocket and sent Donnie a text message.

Both of the idiots are gone, it read. *I'm at Gordon's. Meet me as soon as you can.*

Henry put the phone away and got back into his truck. He wanted to go into Griswold, to try and find the men, but he knew better than to wander around in the woods at night, alone.

Especially since the damned place is haunted.

Death waited in the woods, of that, Henry was certain. He'd seen what had happened to Jackson, and John Quill. Somehow James Quill had drowned, and Henry suspected Abel Latham had something to do with it. He glanced at his watch.

Another hour until Donnie's done, Henry thought with a sigh. He closed his eyes, made himself comfortable in his seat, and waited for something to happen.

Chapter 44: A Little White Lie

Donnie didn't particularly enjoy lying. And he didn't like to admit to people he was good at it. It was one of the issues his first wife had brought up at marriage counseling. She could never tell when he wasn't telling the truth.

Never, Donnie thought. *Never told the truth to her. Surprised she didn't figure it out.*

Book 3: The Town of Griswold

He popped the truck into neutral and let it glide the last thirty feet into Griswold. The headlights lit up the front of the general store. Glenn Jackson had died in the store. John Quill too. Their boots had been found inside, on the counter, reminding Donnie of his own, terrible mistake.

It had been more important for me to get to a glass of scotch than to do my job, Donnie thought angrily. *Not now. Not tonight.*

The truck slowed down, and Donnie brought it to a stop. He turned off the lights and the engine. For a moment, he sat there, staring at the building. Then Donnie turned and took his shotgun down from the rack in the back window. He had spent an hour getting the shells ready, and his pockets were weighed down with them.

Donnie had lied to Henry about the AA meeting, and he had lied to Karen, his third wife, about why he was loading shells.

Lies, lies, lies, he thought dejectedly. Donnie loaded both barrels of the shotgun, locked it down, and got out of the truck.

Time to finish him, Donnie thought. He had done a little research on ghosts. Iron and salt were supposed to take care of them, he had confirmed that much. Most of what he had read said the ghost couldn't come back once they had a blast of salt.

Shane's full of it, Donnie told himself. *He's too drunk to even realize it.*

Donnie had considered a priest, but he was a lapsed Catholic, and he doubted a priest would have gone with him to exorcise an old, abandoned town.

Taking a deep breath, Donnie walked to the country store.

You're ready, Donnie thought. *You're ready. You're going to do what needs to be done.*

He crossed the threshold, looked around the interior, and wondered how he would talk to Abel Latham.

Like any other perp.

"Abel Latham!" Donnie shouted. "Abel Latham, come out with your hands up!"

The building rumbled, as though a hand grabbed it and shook it.

Donnie planted his feet and waited.

The darkness at the far wall pulsed, throbbed, and a soft groan filled the air. A chill swept over him and Donnie shivered.

Keep it together, Donnie thought. *This isn't anything. Not a damned thing.*

He adjusted his grip on the shotgun, and Abel Latham stepped forward.

The ghost was tall. Taller than most men. He was bare-chested, wearing only an old pair of jeans and an even older pair of boots. Abel grinned at Donnie, his flesh disturbingly bright in the darkness of the building.

Above them, thunder ripped through the night sky, and lightning burst in the air.

"And what is your name, little one?" Abel asked, sitting down on the counter.

"Don't worry about it," Donnie said briskly. "Listen to me. You're all done here. You're going to leave and never come back."

"I must confess," Abel said, his voice thick with sincerity, "it is something I long to do. Alas, I cannot. I am bound to Griswold, by what means and for what reason I do not know. But here I am, and here I'll stay. Not to be moved by the likes of you."

Donnie brought the shotgun up to his shoulder and took careful aim at Abel.

"I will make you hurt," Donnie said coldly. A second roar of thunder nearly drowned out his words, and another lightning strike caused him to blink. Rain began to hammer the roof and Abel laughed.

"You can do nothing, little one," Abel said pleasantly, "but I am amused. And pleased, too. It is so nice of you to present yourself to me. The last man here was far less entertaining than I thought. I would like you to run. Would you like that?"

Donnie pulled the trigger, yet as he did so Abel suddenly twisted away to the right. And Donnie's shot missed.

Before he could bring the weapon to bear, it was ripped out of his hands and Donnie screamed as the index finger on his right hand was bent back and broken by the trigger guard. An excruciating pain sent him to the floor. He heard the weapon tossed aside and felt a cold, freezing arm wrap around his neck. Donnie tried to fight back, but there was nothing he could grab, no one he could strike. Desperately he tried to breathe, and he felt himself being dragged backward.

Suddenly the rain was striking him in the face, and he was thrown to the ground. Abel Latham stood over him, grinning.

Abel's happy laughter was muffled by the rain and he said, "You're an extremely interesting man. I do want to know your name."

"That's too bad," Donnie replied through clenched teeth.

"Apparently," Abel said, chuckling. "But let us play, shall we? I am a hunter. You, my little friend, are my prey. Do you know what that means?" Donnie shook his head.

"It means it is time for you to run, my little friend," Abel said happily. "Time to run."

Donnie scrambled to his feet, and he ran as Abel Latham prepared to hunt him.

Chapter 45: The Rain Arrives

The rain slammed into them. There was no warning, each drop hammering down through the trees and striking the men roughly.

"Jesus help me," Gordon grumbled.

Shane hunched his shoulders against the drops, looked at the graveyard, and said, "Let's get this done. I don't like the way this storm feels."

Thunder ripped through the air, followed quickly by a flash of lightning.

"Agreed," Gordon said. The older man led the way into the small cemetery. Shane went to the left and Gordon to the right. The beams of the flashlights shined upon headstones slick with the rain. Shane read name after name, dates for both births and deaths. He saw mothers and fathers. Husbands and wives. And children. Too many children.

Shane made his way through row after row, as did Gordon.

"Shane!" the older man called out.

Shane hurried over to where Gordon stood.

"What's up?" Shane asked.

Gordon pointed with his shotgun into the woods behind the cemetery, the flashlight showing a tall, narrow stone. "Might be it."

Shane nodded. "Outside of sanctified ground, but still close enough to the dead."

Together they passed through the last portion of the graveyard, walking cautiously to the marker in the woods. When they reached it, Shane saw three words carved into the rough, pale gray stone.

Abel Latham, Murderer.

"Here he is," Shane said softly.

Gordon nodded. He opened his mouth to speak, but the thunder interrupted him. The rain increased and for split second, as the lightning lit up the storm, Shane thought he heard the sound of a scream. He glanced at Gordon and saw concern on the man's face.

"Did you hear a scream?" Shane asked.

"Yeah," Gordon said, turning away from Abel's grave. He reached out and turned off his flashlight. Shane turned off his as well. Quietly, the two men stepped into the woods, got down, and kept watch.

Shane's eyesight slowly adjusted to the darkness. Thunder roared, and he closed one eye to preserve his night vision. The temperature in the air dropped. Not slowly, but violently. Shane shivered; his and Gordon's breath coming out in clouds. Neither of them spoke. They only waited.

Faintly, beneath the thunder and the lightning, muffled by the heavy rain, the sound of someone running could be heard. It was a frantic, frightened sound, the sound of the hunted.

A heartbeat later, the prey came into view.

Donnie, Shane realized.

"Donnie!" Gordon hissed.

The man stopped with a terrified expression on his face. Water streamed down his skin, dripping from his chin as he looked around frantically.

"Here," Gordon said, standing up and waving.

Donnie saw him and sprinted towards them.

Behind him, in the black woods, the hunter called out happily, "Where are you, little one? Why will you not play with me?"

Abel Latham's laughter echoed off of the trees and the headstones.

Donnie fell into them and dropped to his knees, panting.

Gordon remained upright, weapon facing out. Shane slapped a hand over Donnie's mouth, keeping the man's ragged breathing silent. The moisture of the trooper's breath was hot and wet against the palm of Shane's hand.

After a moment, Donnie reached up and patted Shane's hand. Shane took it away, wiped it on his wet shirt, and brought his shotgun to the ready position.

"Little nameless one," Abel sang out, "where are you? I've so many wonderful things for us to do together. Oh, I do indeed!"

And then the killer was there. He was crouched over, unaffected by the rain. A slim wraith moving through the night, through the storm on which he fed.

"I know you came this way," Abel said, walking slowly. "I will find you. We will play. Are you ticklish, little one? I've a sharp toy to find out. Will you enjoy it?"

Abel chuckled. "I think not. But I shall, little one. I shall enjoy it, *tremendously.*"

Chapter 46: Trying to Escape

Courtney knew the door out of the study wasn't an option. Carl had made it known that remaining in the room was not a possibility either. Standing at the window, she tried to get her heart in control. It thumped madly in her chest, frantically trying to beat its way out.

Fearfully, she looked out at the yard. Night had come, and she didn't know how. Time had passed strangely in the house. She looked at her phone, but not surprisingly it was dead.

Let's go, she told herself, putting the cellphone back in her pocket. Her hands shook as she reached up, took the cold metal of the latches in her hands and unlocked them. Courtney took hold of the sash and pushed the window up.

A terrible, painful wind struck her, forcing her to close her eyes. Unintelligible whispers assaulted her ears. Fear settled in her stomach and made her shake from head to toe.

You need to leave, Courtney thought. *You need to go before they come in here. Before they do something bad. You shouldn't have come. You should have waited for Shane to get in touch. Why did you come?*

She pushed the terrified, frightened voice away, opened her eyes, and climbed out the window. Courtney dropped several feet to an unkempt flower bed and looked at her car. She dug her keys out of her pocket, hit the 'unlock' button, and nothing happened. Again she tried to unlock the car.

Courtney took a deep breath as she put her keys away.

Alright, she told herself. *All you have to do is cross the yard, get to the driveway, and make it to the street. You can do this.*

She stepped away from the house and jumped as the window slammed shut, locking loudly. Courtney looked over her shoulder and screamed.

A little girl stood against the house. Beside her was a boy, who looked to be only a few years older. Both of them smiled at her, and neither expression was pleasant.

Courtney twisted around to face them, walking backward nervously.

"I'm leaving," Courtney whispered.

"I don't want you to leave," the little girl said, and Courtney recognized the voice.

"Eloise," Courtney said, clearing her throat nervously. "Eloise, I have to go. I'll be back later when Shane is home."

"Maybe you'll be here when he gets home," Eloise responded.

"Perhaps you could stay for a longer time altogether?" the boy asked.

"Thaddeus has a wonderful idea, don't you agree, Courtney?" Eloise asked.

Courtney shook her head. "No, I don't think it's a good idea at all."

Eloise and Thaddeus separated, Eloise on the left and Thaddeus on the right. With each step, the distance between them grew. Courtney had a difficult time keeping an eye on them both. She continued to walk backward, reaching out with a hand to make sure she didn't bump into her car.

"Shane and I had a tea party," Eloise said.

"Did you?" Courtney asked politely, her mouth uncomfortably dry.

"We did," Eloise said, nodding. "Except he didn't drink tea. Oh no. He drank *whiskey.*"

The dead child's pronunciation of the word was harsh and cruel. In that one word Courtney heard a promise of pain and misery.

Fear, which she had managed to control on Squirrel Island, overwhelmed her. Courtney turned her back on the children, sprinting for the driveway. But she was already there.

Her knee slammed into the wheel well of her car, and she shrieked in agony. Blood instantly soaked her capris and it felt as though her kneecap had been sheared off.

Damn it! She thought. Instead of trying to get around to the driver's side Courtney grabbed hold of the passenger side handle and ripped the door open.

A cold weight slammed into the small of her back and slammed her into the car. She hit her injured knee and let out a howl as the pain exploded in her leg again. Courtney climbed across the interior, trailing a smear of blood behind her. Grunting with the exertion, Courtney got into the driver's seat as the passenger side door was slammed closed with enough force to shake the car.

She jammed the key into the ignition and started the ignition. In a heartbeat she had the car in gear, and the tires squealed as she raced out of the driveway.

Chapter 47: Escaping Griswold

Gordon literally sat on Donnie to keep the man still.

Abel had lingered nearby for some time. Shane could tell the murderer suspected Donnie was near, but the storm which fueled the ghost also hid his prey from him.

Finally, after a disturbingly long time, Abel had moved on, still calling out to Donnie.

"Next time," Gordon hissed, getting off of Donnie, "I swear I will cut your throat."

Horrified, Donnie looked from Gordon to Shane.

Shane shook his head. "First rule of hiding, don't make any noise."

"You don't understand," Donnie began.

The matching expressions on Shane and Gordon's faces silenced Donnie. The trooper looked around nervously before asking, "Can we get out of here?"

"Yes," Gordon answered. "It'll be a little harder now with him looking for you."

"We won't be able to use our lights," Shane added. "Best bet will be for all of us to move, hand on shoulder, front to back. Gordon?"

The older man nodded. "I'll take point. Do you have the back?"

"Yes," Shane said. "You're the monkey in the middle, officer. You keep your right hand on Gordon's right shoulder. I'll keep my left hand on your left shoulder. Fair enough?"

Donnie nodded.

"Well," Gordon said, "no time like the present."

They quickly got in line, and Gordon led off. He kept a steady pace, and their footsteps made Shane wince.

We're too loud, Shane thought. He felt Donnie tremble beneath his hand. *And he's too afraid.*

It took longer than Shane remembered to get to the brook. When they reached it, there was a collective sigh of relief.

"This is the easy part," Gordon said softly. "We follow the water to Lake Charles. Once we're on the beach, Donnie, my house is off to the left."

"Okay," Donnie whispered. "Follow the water."

Whatever steel was in the man before, Shane thought, *it's been broken. He's done in.*

Gordon went into the water first. Donnie and Shane followed. The rain and noise of the brook hid the sound of their passage, and Shane relaxed. He listened to the forest as best he could. Someone yelled in the distance, and the sound sent a bolt of fear through him.

Abel, Shane thought. The man had realized his prey had slipped away.

The memory of the shelves of shoes flashed through his mind, and Shane pushed the image away. He knew what would happen if they were caught.

Shane focused on his steps. *Left, right, left,* he thought. He ignored the water as it sloshed in his shoes. *Keep your ears open. Eyes wide, boy. Don't relax. You're not safe. Not until you're out of Griswold.*

Donnie slowed down, and Shane prodded him with the shotgun. The shriek Donnie let out caused Shane's eyes to widen.

In the distance, Abel Latham let out a howl of pure joy.

Shane heard Gordon break into a run, and Shane unceremoniously slapped Donnie in the head.

"Run, moron!" Shane screamed.

Donnie ran.

Abel's laughter echoed off the trees, ringing out proudly in the night air. The rain increased while thunder and lightning bracketed the ghost's ecstatic cries.

Shane's feet slammed into stones and branches, yet somehow he kept his balance. Donnie stumbled repeatedly in front of him, and each time he slowed down Shane hit him.

"Have you found friends, little one?" Abel called out, his voice far too close.

Angrily, Shane adjusted his grip on the shotgun, found the switch for the flashlight and turned it on. He skidded to a stop, swung the weapon up and to the right in time to catch sight of Abel Latham cresting a bank.

"And who are you?" Abel asked happily.

"Shane," Shane answered, and he fired both barrels. And Abel Latham vanished as the salt struck him.

Chapter 48: On the Beach

The roar of a shotgun woke Henry up. Instantly, he flung the door to his pickup open, and he tumbled out. He had his pistol drawn, the safety off. The lights had flicked on, and his shadow followed him as he ran around the side of Gordon's house.

Beach, Henry thought. He sprinted down a narrow path, reached the sand and looked around. Far to the left, he saw a trio emerge from the woods. They staggered out onto the beach and moved towards him.

Henry jogged forward and recognized Donnie, Shane, and Gordon. He flicked the safety back on and came to a stop.

"What the hell happened?" Henry asked, looking at Donnie and unable to keep the shock out of his voice.

Donnie looked old. Far older than he had been only a few hours earlier. There were lines around the man's mouth, and his eyes darted about fearfully.

Gordon spat on the ground and walked by him. Shane broke open the shotgun, pulled a pair of spent casings out, and dropped them in his pocket.

"This *idiot*," Shane snarled, his voice filled with hatred, "almost got us all killed."

Donnie winced and whispered, "I was afraid."

"No shame in being afraid," Gordon said angrily. "None at all. Been afraid a whole lot. But you don't *scream* like a little girl. I'm going inside for a drink. Maybe two. Hell, maybe a whole damned six pack."

"What happened?" Henry said.

Shane's voice quivered with rage as he told Henry everything that had happened since he left, including how Donnie's scream had led Abel Latham back to the three of them.

"The shotgun stopped him?" Henry asked, surprised.

"Yeah," Shane said. "He's probably madder than hell right now. And when we go back in, he'll recognize me for sure. If I die, I can guarantee I'll be coming back to find Donnie here, and the rest of his short life will be absolutely miserable. Now, if you'll excuse me, I'm going to get drunk with Gordon. Hopefully drunker."

Shane walked past them, leaving Henry with Donnie.

They stood in silence for a short time. Finally, Henry said, "You lied to me, Donnie."

Donnie didn't reply.

"You could have been killed."

Donnie looked at him, his expression one of sheer exhaustion. In a hoarse voice, Donnie said, "I thought I could take him. I mean all this crap about ghosts. I thought I could handle it. I'm a cop. I should have been able to handle him."

Henry shook his head. "There's a reason why I wanted to bring Shane in. He knows a little more than us."

"He's a punk," Donnie muttered.

"Doesn't matter what we think of him," Henry said sharply. "The thing is he knew what he was talking about. He had a plan. I don't like that he went off with Gordon. But they went in together. You went in alone."

Donnie looked down at the beach.

"And he's right," Henry continued. "Abel's going to recognize him. What's worse, Donnie, is that Abel's going to be expecting something now."

"What?" Donnie asked, surprised.

Henry nodded. "Think about it. You went in there and you challenged him. Then, when he finds you again, you're with a guy who's got a shotgun loaded with rock-salt. He knows someone is after him. He knows to be looking for us."

"Do you really think so?" Donnie asked.

"Yeah," Henry said. He shook his head. "Come on. Rain's letting up, and we're both soaked now. Let's get in and warm up a bit. Figure out what's next."

Henry turned away and behind him, Donnie said, "I know what's next."

"Oh yeah?" Henry asked, walking towards the house.

"Bye, Henry," Donnie said.

Henry turned around in time to see Donnie put the barrel of a snub-nosed .38 into his own mouth.

"Donnie!" Henry yelled, but the sound of the pistol drowned him out.

Chapter 49: Out for a Walk

Gerald maneuvered along the sidewalk with the help of a cane and Turk's patience. Occasionally, the German Shepherd looked back at him as if to say, *Hey Gerry, technically, I'm older than you are. If you do the math.*

"I'm moving as fast as I can," Gerald said to the dog. Turk's ears twitched, as if in disbelief, but he made sure his pace matched that of Gerald's.

"What was that?" Marie asked.

Gerald smiled at his niece. "Sorry, Marie. I was replying to Turk's disdainful glance."

Marie chuckled and shook her head. "If I didn't know better I'd think you were losing your mind, my dear uncle."

Gerald chuckled and the three of them continued on their walk. He looked around as they moved along the sidewalk.

The sun had set, and the lights on Berkley Street were lit. Porches were absent of people, although the curious glow of television sets flickered behind the windows. Gerald sighed and shook his head.

Such beautiful weather and no one is outside enjoying it, he thought.

They neared Shane's house and looked at it sadly. Gerald had hoped Shane and Marie would have been more than friends. Shane's home was still an oddity, a structure avoided by most people in the neighborhood.

"Do you think they know why?" Gerald said suddenly.

Marie glanced over at him. "Do I think who knows what?"

"The people around here," Gerald said, pausing. He gestured at the other houses with his cane. "Do you think they know why they avoid the house? Even those who don't know anything about the building, or its history, they don't walk by it. I've seen people cross the street to avoid it. I'm curious if they know why."

"Probably not," Marie said. "In fact, most people don't notice anything outside their immediate circle."

Someone shrieked and both Gerald and Marie looked to the opening of Shane's driveway. Turk's ears perked up and a low growl emanated from his throat. Within a few seconds a car door slammed shut, an engine started, and a small, black car tore out of Shane's driveway.

It raced by them, and Gerald was able to catch sight of a young woman, her face a portrait of panic and fear.

"Who was that?" Gerald asked, more to himself than looking for an answer.

"Her name's Courtney DeSantis," Marie said.

"Do you think something's wrong with Shane?" Gerald said, glancing at his niece.

"No," Marie answered. "I think she may have gotten an introduction to Shane's ghosts."

"Yes," Gerald said, nodding. "I think you're right."

He began to walk again, Turk's tail wagging cheerfully. Marie kept her pace slow. They looked at Shane's home and saw lights on in the first floor.

"So," Gerald said, smiling at Marie, "how have you been getting along with Shane?"

Marie shook her head, laughing. "Oh leave it be, Uncle Gerry."

"I can't," he said, grinning. "I like you both. Therefore I think you would be good for each other."

"We're about as good as oil and water," Marie said with a sigh.

"I am sorry to hear it," Gerald said.

Marie glanced back at Shane's house and said softly, "So am I, Uncle Gerry."

Chapter 50: In the Early Hours

"I've seen too many cops in the past few days," Shane said, holding his glass out to Gordon. The older man uncapped the bottle of bourbon and poured a healthy dose of the amber liquid.

"At least they're not looking at you for Donnie's suicide," Gordon replied, adding liquor to his own glass. He left the cap off as he put the bottle down on the table.

"True." Shane took a drink, his eyes widening. "Damn, that's good."

Gordon nodded. "I don't buy the cheap stuff."

"I appreciate that."

The back door opened, and Henry walked in. With a sigh, he dropped down heavily into an empty seat at the table. Henry looked at both of them before he said, "They're gone now."

"All of them?" Gordon asked.

"Yeah," Henry replied tiredly. He frowned at the glasses in their hands. "It's four in the morning."

"So?" Shane asked politely.

"Shouldn't you stop drinking?" Henry said, anger creeping over his face.

"I don't see any reason to," Gordon said. "We've got a few hours yet before we can slip back to Griswold and try to do what we should have done last night."

"Will we be getting more help?" Henry asked, looking at Shane.

"Not that I know of," Shane answered.

"Why not?" Henry demanded.

"Listen," Shane said, pausing to take a drink, "this isn't a movie, right? So there's no cavalry. No one's going to come and help us. There are no secret organizations to call. Sure, there are some folks out there who deal with this sort of thing, but not on this scale. It's dangerous, and, as we've all seen, it can cost you your life. Whoever we called would want all of the information up front, and once they had it, they'd say 'thanks, but no thanks.'"

"We're doing this alone," Gordon said. Then he looked at Shane, "Unless you actually know someone who will help?"

Shane shook his head. "No one I'm willing to ask."

"What about the girl who was with you?" Henry asked. "Courtney DeSantis?"

Shane gave the trooper a cold look. "I'm not bringing her back into Griswold. She and I barely made it out last time, if you remember, trooper. I won't be responsible for her death."

Henry shook his head angrily. "Fine. Whatever. So it's the three of us?"

"Against the world," Gordon said.

"Well, what do we need to have so we can finish this?" Henry asked.

"Shovels," Gordon said. "Salt. An accelerant, and some matches."

"Plus the shotguns, the loaded shells," Shane added, "and steel wool, if you've got it."

"I do," Gordon said, a quizzical look on his face. "Why?"

"Let's say for luck, alright?" Shane replied.

"This is insane," Henry muttered. In a louder voice, he said, "Do you have another shotgun, Gordon?"

The older man shook his head.

"You can use mine," Shane said. "I'll carry most of the gear. We'll bring one shovel and rotate out using it. I'd rather have two on guard than two digging."

The other men nodded in agreement.

"What happens when we get the grave dug, and the coffin opened?" Henry asked.

"Pray like hell Abel's bones are actually in there," Shane said. He took his cigarettes out and looked at Gordon. The older man nodded and Shane tapped out a pair. He held one out to Gordon, but the man shook his head.

"No, I don't smoke," Gordon said. "But I don't have a problem if you want to smoke in here."

"Appreciate it," Shane said. He left one cigarette on the table, put the other in his mouth, and lit it.

"You didn't ask me," Henry said coldly.

"It's not your house," Shane replied, blowing smoke towards the ceiling, "and I don't care."

His face tight with anger, Henry asked, "What do we do if he's not in the grave?"

"We get the hell out of there," Shane said around the cigarette.

"And if he is?" Gordon asked, playing devil's advocate.

"We dump an entire box of salt on his bones, douse them with lighter fluid, and burn him," Shane answered.

"How is that going to do anything?" Henry said, confused.

"It's going to shut him down, completely," Shane said. "From the lore I've read, Abel will be cast from the earth, so long as everything is burned."

"If it's not, he'll still be here?" Henry asked, looking from Gordon to Shane.

"Yes," Gordon answered. "We won't have to worry about it, though."

"No?" Henry said. "Why not?"

"Because he'll kill us," Gordon said. "He'll kill each of us, and if we're lucky, it'll be quick."

Shane finished his drink, looked at the empty glass, and then smiled sadly at Henry as he said, "It won't be, Trooper Martini. So don't get your hopes up."

Chapter 51: Back into Griswold

Shane was carrying an old backpack, and it was heavy. Over one shoulder he carried a long-handled shovel. He followed Gordon while Henry was behind him. The ground was wet from the storm of the previous night and the sun pierced through the leaves in some places. Around him, the air was heavy and uncomfortable.

Shane still had a slight buzz from drinking with Gordon.

Hell, I'm sweating like a pig, Shane thought. He pulled a bottle of water out of a pocket on the backpack and drank deeply. *Can't dehydrate. Not now.*

Shane put the water away, shifted the shovel on his shoulder, and listened to the forest. The animals ignored the men and called out in their own way. Above him, Shane could catch glimpses of the sky, and it was free of clouds.

Here's hoping Abel's asleep, Shane thought, *and not waiting for us to come back.*

Gordon turned away from the brook, leading them in towards the center of Griswold. The forest was thick around them, young trees growing in tight groups between the older ones. Elms and oaks, young birches between thick pines. Ferns sprouted up in various places, and occasionally a chipmunk darted by. Squirrels yelled at them from the trees, and the random bird added their cries to the mix.

It's almost peaceful, Shane thought. *The fact that there's a homicidal ghost is the only drawback.*

The forest opened slightly, revealing the cemetery. It was smaller, more pitiful in the light of day.

Gordon stopped a few feet beyond the tree line, and Shane went to stand beside him, Henry in the back.

"Here we are," Gordon said softly.

"Where's the grave?" Henry asked.

Gordon pointed to where the small marker could be glimpsed.

"Will it take long to get to the coffin?" Henry said.

"Don't know," Gordon answered.

"Yes," Shane said, heading towards Abel's marker. "Digging a grave takes longer than you might think."

Chapter 52: Courtney Returns

Courtney had a difficult time breathing as she sat in her car. She had made the decision to return to Griswold. Courtney was back in a place she had sworn never to return to it. But the ghost, Carl, had told her how Shane was going to confront Abel Latham, possibly alone.

I can't let him do it alone, she thought, shivering. *I can't. No matter how afraid I am, I have to help him. He helped me. Saved me. I love him I have to make sure he's okay.*

Still, fear gripped her. She took Shane's dog tags out from her under her shirt, brought them up to her lips and kissed them quickly, as she might a cross.

Alright, Courtney, she thought. *You can do this. You've done it before with Shane. If you get to him, everything will be alright. You know that. Remember the lighthouse. Remember getting out before.*

You can do this.

Courtney took a long, deep breath, kissed the dog tags once more, and slipped them back into her shirt.

She looked out at Griswold and the scene was hauntingly familiar. An abandoned pickup sat in the center of the ghost town. A small sedan was parked beside it. She stared at the vehicles, the engine of her car idling. Her hands clung to the steering wheel and she tried to get control of her heart which beat rapidly. Rain pounded down upon the car, blurring the world beyond the windows.

Shane's here, he needs my help, I know he does, Courtney thought. *This is how I can show him how much I care. This will show his ghosts that I care.*

She nodded to herself, forced her hands to let go of the steering wheel, and she turned the engine off. On the seat beside her was a small piece of iron. Courtney picked the cold metal up, clutched it and got out of her car. She winced at the force of the rain, stumbled, and dropped to her bad knee, the one injured in her flight from the dead children.

"Damn it!" she muttered. Courtney held onto the door and pulled herself up. Her knee ached with a dull throb. A glance down showed fresh blood on her pants, the cloth torn and stained.

Come on, Courtney, she scolded herself, *you can do this.*

She pulled her phone out of her back pocket, tried to shield it with her body, and typed in Shane's number. As she got ready to hit 'send' the phone blinked.

Low battery, it read.

Courtney frowned, and before she could make the call the phone died. The screen became black. *What the hell?*

A cold, terrible realization stole over her.

Oh no. Oh no, no, no, she thought, her inner voice filled with panic. All of her resolve left her and she dropped her phone as she turned back to the car.

But the sound of gunfire ripped through the storm and Courtney turned towards it.

Shane, she thought, and began to search for the man.

Chapter 53: Looking for Shane

After seeing Courtney DeSantis leave Shane's house, Marie had become concerned about the man. When she left Uncle Gerry's place Marie returned to Shane's and knocked on the door. No one had answered. The house was silent.

It was then that she did a search for him, to see if his name popped up anywhere in the State's law enforcement system.

Marie wasn't terribly surprised when it had. He was with the State Police. Marie had called the State Police barrack in Manchester and told them she wanted to speak with Shane. A trooper named Henry Martini had requested a delay. Marie was told Martini was investigating several murders, and evidently, Shane was assisting them.

They didn't tell her how. The staties had been pretty tight-lipped on the phone about it.

But, she thought, sighing, *They usually are. Always need to do it in person with them.*

Marie had thought the polite refusal to send Shane along was odd. Usually, they would send the individual along.

After their flat out refusal to assist, Marie had tried to think of a reason why. It was then she had remembered the murdered State Trooper, Glenn Jackson. He had been killed and found in an abandoned town.

One of New Hampshire's ghost towns.

Marie Lafontaine thought of all of this as she pulled into the driveway of Gordon Bay. After she had made the decision to find Shane and check on him, Marie had gone to the State Police Barracks in Manchester. The troopers on duty had told her what had happened the night before and how Gordon Bay had been friendly with the trooper who had committed suicide on the beach.

Marie parked her car next to Shane's and got out. She went up to the front door, knocked on it, and waited for a reply. When no one answered, she knocked harder.

Frowning, Marie went around the side of the house to the building's rear. She climbed the porch and banged on the back door. After a minute, she leaned closer, peered through the glass, and tried to see inside. On the kitchen table, she saw an empty bottle of bourbon and a pair of tumblers. A box of shotgun shells stood open on the counter.

What are they hunting? Marie wondered, stepping back. She turned and looked out over the lake and saw multiple sets of shoe prints in the sand.

Marie looked at them for a moment, then returned to her car. She sat down, pulled out her phone, and did a quick search for Griswold. In a minute, she was on a website which talked about various ghost towns of New Hampshire. Griswold was one of them.

It spoke about a ghost named Abel Latham, and how he had killed his own children before he was lynched. The last reported sighting had been by a man named Gordon Bay.

Griswold, Marie thought. *But how do you fight a ghost with a shotgun?*

She turned her attention back to her phone and typed her question in.

Book 3: The Town of Griswold

Chapter 54: Things Best Left Covered

Shane had dug graves before. More than a few. Some he had been afraid would eventually be his own. But he had never dug *up* a corpse before.

First time for everything, he thought.

Shane stood a few feet from Abel Latham's marker, holding the shotgun. Gordon was on the other side, keeping watch. Henry was in the grave, shoveling away. They were only a few feet down.

Shane straightened up. The forest had gone quiet.

"Gordon," Shane said softly.

"I know," Gordon whispered. Henry didn't seem to notice their exchange, as he kept moving earth.

"What are you doing?" a voice asked.

Shane jerked his head around and saw Andrew. The boy stood in the cemetery with his dog, Rex.

"Oh Jesus," Henry said in surprise.

"We're digging up your father's bones," Shane answered.

Andrew walked closer, bringing the dog and a chill with him. He peered down into the grave and said, "You shouldn't."

"Why not?" Shane asked.

"He's not alone," Andrew replied, looking at Shane. "They buried them with him."

"What?" Henry asked. "Buried who with him?"

"His best friends," Andrew said. He reached down and stroked the top of his dog's head.

Suddenly, Andrew looked around, "This isn't right. Something is wrong here."

Before Shane could ask Andrew what he meant, the boy and Rex vanished.

Shane felt uncomfortable, and he turned back to look at Gordon and Henry. The older man shook his head. Henry shrugged and began to dig again.

Shane adjusted his grip on the shotgun, scanned the tree line and thought, *Who the hell could Latham have had as best friends?*

Chapter 55: Going into Griswold

Marie sat in her car, the engine idling. She looked down the road which led into Griswold, the trees on either side of the broken asphalt battered from the passage of vehicles over the past few days.

What are you going to do down there, Marie? the voice of reason asked. *You don't have salt. You don't have iron. You didn't bring a priest. How in the hell are you going to help Shane if he's hunting a ghost?*

Marie sighed. *I'll figure it out.*

She took her foot off of the brake and drove down into Griswold. Soon, she was parked beside an abandoned car and a truck. The car looked familiar, but Marie couldn't recall where she had seen it. The pickup had a small 'Troopers are your best Protection' sticker in the rear window. The rifle rack in the pick-up was also empty.

Ignoring the car, Marie went to the truck and looked in the driver's side-window, saw the door was unlocked, and there were shotgun shells on the passenger seat.

I bet they're loaded with salt, she thought. Marie opened the door, reached in and picked up the five shells. She tucked them into a pocket and glanced at the two buildings which still stood. A church and a country store.

Word was the blood evidence showed that both Jackson and Quill had been killed in the store, Marie told herself. *Whoever had the shotgun would have gone inside, if they were hunting a ghost.*

Marie crossed the short distance to the store and went in. On the floor, she found the shotgun, a double-barreled weapon. Marie broke it open, found the right shell had been fired and extracted it, dropping the empty casing on the floor. She reloaded it with a fresh shell from the truck, secured the weapon, and examined the place quickly. Across the room from the front door, there were fresh marks on the wall.

Walking over, Marie squinted and saw several large pieces of rock salt embedded in the old wood. *Now, where are you, Shane?* Marie wondered, leaving the store. Marie stood out in the sunshine, adjusted her grip on the shotgun, and listened.

Chapter 56: Pay Dirt

Shane was back in the grave, his turn with the shovel when he struck the old coffin.

A dull thud sounded.

Oh thank God they didn't bury him too deep, Shane thought. His shoulders hurt, and his back ached. Sweat dripped steadily and unpleasantly down his spine. He reached up, grabbed his water off the edge of the grave, and had a drink before he said, "I've found it."

Henry came over and looked in while Gordon remained where he was.

"What do you need?" Henry asked.

"For this to be over," Shane said. "Get me the hatchet in the pack, please."

Henry nodded, set the shotgun down, and opened up the pack. A moment later, he handed the hatchet down to Shane.

"Thanks," Shane said, passing the shovel up to Henry. With the hatchet in hand, Shane slipped the leather hood off it, spread his feet wide, and began to hack at the old wood of the coffin's top. Several hard blows and Shane was through to the interior. Patiently, and carefully he widened it, making certain the light of day would shine upon the casket's dubious treasure.

Soon, Shane pulled pieces of wood away, throwing them out of the hole. Finally, he could see clearly.

The remains of Abel Latham lay in the confines of the casket. Little remained of his flesh, the clothes rotted on his large frame. Tucked between the corpse and the coffin's sides were other shapes.

Unable to see it clearly, Shane squatted down, pried up another length of wood, and the sun fell fully upon the unknown item.

"What the hell is that?" Henry asked.

"It's his best friends," Shane said softly. "There are dogs buried in here with him."

Nearby, a dog let out a long and angry howl.

Chapter 57: A Storm Arrives

Marie walked along the broken asphalt of Griswold's main street. She looked from left to right and back again in an effort to find Shane. Her footsteps were loud, but the forest was quiet around the town, broken only by the sound of a howl from off to the left.

The shadows vanished as thick clouds rolled in suddenly from the east, and she looked at them. They were dark, speeding across the sky.

That looks like rain, she thought, frowning. *There wasn't anything in the forecast about rain.*

Another howl rang out, quickly joined by a second and a third.

Coyotes? Marie wondered. She knew it couldn't be wolves. New Hampshire hadn't seen any wolves in decades.

A man yelled, the cry coming from the same direction of the howls, and Marie turned sharply to the sound.

The howls rang out again, and the unknown man shouted in an angry voice.

I bet that's Shane, she thought. *What the hell has he gotten himself into this time?*

Tightening her grip on the shotgun, Marie ran towards Shane's position. Above her, the sky continued to grow darker, and a few drops of rain fell. Quickly more arrived, and soon the storm struck the land. The roar of thunder caused the ground to shake, and lightning lit up the underbellies of the clouds.

Marie's hair was plastered to her head, her clothes clung to her, and several times she slipped, nearly losing her balance.

Again the howling commenced, and someone screamed.

Marie caught sight of a slim path leading into the woods, and without hesitating, she ran towards it.

Chapter 58: Abel Latham's Friend

"Get me out!" Shane snapped at Henry.

The dogs were howling, each cry nearer than the last.

Henry reached down, grabbed Shane's hand, and helped him to climb out of the grave.

The rain was cold, the drops painful and hard as they struck bare skin. Gordon had stepped closer to them. Henry looked around, and Shane said, "Henry, keep an eye on Gordon. He knows what he's doing."

The trooper hesitated and looked as if he might argue, but then Henry shook his head and dropped to a knee. Shane grabbed his backpack and pulled out his knuckledusters. He slipped them on before he found the bag of steel wool from Gordon's house.

"What the hell?" Henry asked.

Shane looked and wished he hadn't.

Abel Latham's best friend was only a few feet away. It was the ghost of a large, black Irish wolfhound, and it wasn't alone. Shane counted four of them, and they were spread out.

Four, Shane thought. *And two shotguns. Four rounds altogether. Plus my knuckledusters.*

The dogs charged.

Shane dropped the bag as a great hound charged at him. He brought his right hand up and waited.

It only took one of the animals mere seconds to reach him. Amid the thunder and the lightning, Shane heard and saw the shotguns. Two of the dogs vanished, and then Shane felt a tremendous pain as the dog who had charged him latched onto his leg. Teeth, excruciatingly cold, punctured the flesh of his thigh.

The dog growled and tried to rip the muscle from Shane's bone, and Shane screamed with fury. He brought the knuckledusters down onto the hound's head, and the beast vanished. Shane stumbled to the side, nearly tumbling down into the grave. Henry shouted, and one of the dogs was on him, knocking the man down.

The trooper clung to his weapon and tried to beat the dog back, but the barrel passed through them.

More howls raced through the night, and the dogs were once more rushing out of the forest.

Oh no! Shane thought angrily. *The bones! I've got to burn their damned bones. We're too close to the grave!*

"I remember you!"

Shane turned and saw Abel Latham, the ghost striding out of the forest. The dead man grinned wickedly, but not at Shane.

Abel's attention was focused solely on Gordon Bay.

Chapter 59: In a Nightmare Once More

Gordon's hands refused to listen to his brain. His feet and legs mutinied as well. Immobile, Gordon stood and watched as Abel came towards him, the man's long legs devouring the distance between them.

Gordon could hear Henry Martini screaming. Below the high pitched shrieks of pain issued from the trooper, Gordon could hear the deeper voice of Shane Ryan. The curiously bald man was yelling one word over and over again.

Reload, Gordon thought. *He's telling me to reload.*

Then Abel was next to him. A massive hand, shimmering with a curious light, reached out and wrapped itself around Gordon's throat.

The shotgun fell from his hands, and only after Abel began to squeeze did Gordon regain some control over his limbs. He reached for the deathly cold hands squeezing at his flesh, but they found nothing to grab. Only cold air as Abel slowly choked him.

Abel smiled up at him. "You have run for a long time," Abel chided. "Quite a long time. I had to punish my children for their betrayal. It is a father's duty, as distasteful as it is."

The ghost's grip tightened, and Gordon felt excruciating pain with the crushing of his larynx. His body shivered, his legs kicking out at nothing. Blackness swarmed over him as his eyes rolled up into his head.

Will he add my boots to his collection? Gordon wondered.

But there was no answer.

Chapter 60: Desperation

When Gordon's legs began a mad, frantic tap dance in empty air, Shane knew the man was as good as dead. Shane turned his attention to Henry, the dead dog still mauling the trooper.

Henry was no longer fighting back. He wasn't doing anything at all.

The man was curled in a fetal position, but his body was limp as the dog jerked at it.

Stay strong, Shane thought, keeping his own fear at bay. He dropped to his knees, picked up the bag of steel wool with one hand, and grabbed the pack with the other.

"What are you doing, little one?" Abel asked.

Shane looked up and saw Gordon's lifeless body dropped to the ground. The old man flopped limply with all of the grace of a gutted fish.

"I saw you last night, did I not?" Abel said, grinning. The grin faded. "You shot me. It was not a pleasant thing for you to do."

The dogs growled from behind Shane, and he stiffened.

"Hold, my little friends," Abel said, chuckling.

Shane spat nervously on the ground. "Thanks."

"Don't thank me yet," Abel said, "We would like to play with you. It is a game, rather like hide and seek. Would you like to play?"

"No," Shane said, glancing at the open grave. "Not particularly. Pretty sure I wouldn't come out on top."

Abel smiled, nodding. "I am afraid that your chances would not be good. What is your name?"

Oh, what the hell, Shane thought. "Shane. Shane Ryan."

"And why are you here, Shane?" Abel asked politely.

"I was really hoping I'd be able to send you straight to Hell," Shane said honestly.

Abel laughed approvingly. "Oh, Shane, I do like you. I will make a deal with you. I will kill you quickly when I catch you. No torture. I believe we could have quite the hunt together. You seem to me an admirable prey."

Shane laughed in spite of his fear. "Damn, seems okay to me, Abel."

The ghost's reply was lost in the roar of a shotgun.

Something tore into the back of Shane's shoulder and he grunted. He held onto the backpack and the steel wool as he rolled to the right, and down into the grave. A jagged piece of rotted wood thrust up into his left bicep, and Shane bit back a scream as he sat back.

He hunched over Abel Latham's bones and bit back the pain as he shook out the bag of steel wool onto the corpse's belly. Shane hurriedly dug out a box of salt from his backpack. He ripped the tab open and dumped the contents onto Abel's remains. Throwing the box aside, Shane found the matches. With the heavy rain falling on him, Shane hunched over and put the flame to the steel wool. The shredded fibers caught fire instantly, the flames leaping to his hands and burning his fingers where the steel wool dust coated them.

Burn, Shane thought, grinding his teeth. *Go on and burn.*

Chapter 61: A Bad Shot

Marie had hit one of the dogs with a load of salt. Unfortunately, she had been aiming at the ghost of Abel Latham. She had also caught Shane with part of the shot. The second round had also been for Abel. The ghost had moved at the last second, and she had missed.

Abel had not been happy. Not in the least.

"She's mine!" Abel screamed, and the dead dogs remained where they were.

The rage in his voice had literally caused the hair on the back of her neck to stand up, and she dropped a pair of shells as the ghost came towards her.

Then she had smelled smoke.

How can there be fire in the rain? she thought numbly, trying to reload the weapon again.

"You're mine!" Abel shouted. "Oh, the pain you'll feel, woman."

Marie got one shell in, snapped the weapon closed, and brought it up. She took careful aim at the ghost and didn't have time to pull the trigger.

The ghost was there. His face twisted with rage and he backhanded her, the force of the blow terrifying in its strength. Marie stumbled backward, lost her grip on the shotgun, and dropped it as she fell.

In an instant, he was beside her, kicking her with heavy boots. Each strike sent a bolt of pain through her as he worked on her thighs. She tried to twist away, but the kicks landed on her arms and her stomach.

A look of calm replaced the rage and each blow was precise, designed to inflict as much pain as possible. Marie gasped for breath, and everywhere she turned he was there. Beating her ruthlessly.

Then the blows stopped and Marie looked to see why.

Abel Latham was grinning. His attention no longer focused on her, but on a young woman limping towards him.

It was Courtney DeSantis and she held something in her right hand, a piece of metal. Rain poured down her face, her hair clinging to her scalp. Her expression alternated between fear and rage.

"Where is he?!" Courtney demanded.

"Who, little one?" Abel asked, chuckling and advancing towards her. "Hm? Of whom do you speak?"

"Shane," Courtney snapped.

"Oh, my new friend," Abel said, nodding in understanding. He gestured behind him. "Yes, he is in my grave."

One of Abel's great dogs launched out of a shadow, teeth barred and a snarl deep in its throat. Courtney swung at the animal, striking it with the iron and dispatching it.

As the dog vanished, Abel lunged at the young woman, caught her arm and bent it back snapping it easily. Courtney's eyes widened in terror, a bit of iron falling from her hand.

Then the fear fled from her face, and with a grimace, she tore her broken arm free from the murderous ghost's hold.

Abel laughed in genuine surprise.

"Never," he said, shaking his head as he reached out and grabbed her by the other arm, "Never in all of my years has someone slipped from my grasp. Well done, little girl. Well done."

Courtney let out a shriek as he took her broken arm in his other hand.

"However," Abel said as he scooped her up, "I've no time for wounded prey. No pleasure in hunting the injured. This, little one, is a mercy."

With a twist of his wrist, Abel broke Courtney's neck, the pop of its snapping was loud and disturbing.

Dear God, Marie thought, *she's dead. Oh Shane, she's dead.*

He dropped Courtney's limp body to the floor, turned back to Marie and said, "Now, my dear, where were we?"

Abel lifted a foot to prepare a kick, smiling broadly.

I'm going to die, she thought, but before she could gather her wits about her, Abel came to a sudden stop.

He stood still, a look of shock on his face and Marie could see why.

Abel Latham was burning.

Small holes appeared on his chest and neck, the edges lined with bright green embers as ghostly blue flames ate at his flesh. The holes became gaping wounds, blackness revealed.

Abel opened his mouth, and Marie could see blue tongues of fire. The curious flames licked at his teeth and burned his lips.

The ghost screamed a deep, powerful cry which shook Marie to her bones.

Abel stepped forward, collapsed onto one knee and threw his hands up to his face as his eyes exploded. Marie watched as the flames ate his fingers, inch by inch. A hole in his stomach expanded from the size of a baseball to a basketball, and finally, it burned through his entire mid-section.

Marie got her wits about her and shuddered with revulsion as Abel's screams were cut off as his lower jaw vanished. Flames roared and erupted from the top of his head with the power of a geyser. A crackling sound filled the air and sparks flew from the ghost's flesh.

With Abel silenced, Marie heard someone coughing.

Shane, she thought. Then, shaking her head, she called out, "Shane!"

Marie climbed to her feet, muscles throbbing with pain. For the first time, she saw the dark, oily smoke as it rose up from the open grave. Shane had been able to light a fire in spite of the heavy rain.

Marie pushed her fear and revulsion away and forced herself to run past Abel Latham as he vanished.

Book 3: The Town of Griswold

Chapter 62: Returned from the Grave

Shane kept his face close to the side of the grave, his breath coming in great, painful gasps. The smoke which came off of Abel's burning remains scorched Shane's lungs.

He had tried to climb out, but the fresh wound in his shoulder had stopped him. As did the crumbling sides of the hole. With each cough, a scream attempted to fight past his lips. His pants were on fire, his flesh heating up beneath the fabric. Shane reached down, slapped out the flames and was rewarded with more burns on his hand and fresh fire on the pants.

I'm going to die, Shane thought, coughing and squeezing his eyes shut. *I am going to die in this grave.*

Fantastic.

A hand grabbed him by the back of the shirt and a woman screamed, "Climb!"

With the unknown woman's help, Shane scrambled up and out of the grave. He half crawled as she dragged him away from the smoke and flames. Tears ran from his eyes, mucous from his nose, and saliva from his mouth. His stomach churned and expelled the water he had drunk earlier.

Through the smoke and tears, he saw the remains of Abel Latham. The ghost's boots, nothing more.

Finally, the woman stopped, and Shane collapsed onto his side.

"Oh, no," he muttered, his voice raw and barely audible. Wincing, Shane rolled onto his back and looked up at the sky.

Already the rain had stopped, the clouds splitting open for the sunlight to pierce Griswold's darkness.

"Shane."

Shane recognized the voice, turned his head and saw Marie Lafontaine. She knelt beside him, a look of concern on her face. Her hair was soaked and clung to her head.

He smiled at her and asked, "How does my hair look?"

She blinked, laughed in surprise and said, "You don't have any."

"Christ," he said, sighing, "I must look like a mess then."

Marie opened her mouth as if to speak, and closed it instead.

"What is it?" Shane asked.

She shook her head, gave him a tight smile and said, "Nothing that can't wait. Too much excitement and I'm afraid you'll send yourself into shock."

He wanted to ask her what she meant, but the cold, calculating part of him knew Marie was right. *Whatever news she has,* Shane thought, *can wait.*

"Shane," she said, bringing his attention back to her, "you've got some severe burns here, not to mention smoke inhalation. Nothing you can't survive, but I'm going to need to get help. My phone's back in the car."

"Sure," Shane said, opening his eyes. He smiled at her. Shane didn't feel any pain, which was a bad sign. His body wanted to go into shock regardless of the control he was trying to exert. He reached out, and she took his hand. "I've never had a better friend, Marie."

She gave him a small, tight smile as she nodded.

"Marie," Shane said, grimacing, "there's something that needs to be done, if you can."

"Sure," Marie said, "what is it?"

"Nearby, there's an old blacksmith shop. The hearth is built into the side of a hill. If you go around it," Shane said, "you'll find a small path. At the end of the path, there'll be a cave. It should be easy to spot. The bodies of Jackson and Quill were found there."

"What do I have to do in there?" Marie asked.

"There should be bones in there," Shane answered. "A box. Probably a small box. Burn it. Whatever bones, whatever looks human, burn it. There's more salt and lighter fluid in my bag. Light it all up, Marie."

"Okay," she said softly. She shifted her weight and Shane suddenly saw a body behind her. It was crumpled, the neck twisted and somehow wrong.

Dead, Shane thought. *Someone new is dead.*

"Oh, Shane," Marie whispered.

"Who is that?" he asked, his voice sounding like metal dragged across gravel.

"It's … Courtney," Marie answered.

He closed his eyes.

"Courtney."

"Yes," Marie said.

"And she's dead," Shane said.

"Yes."

Shane fought against the shock welling up within him. He pictured Courtney, her delicate body and the steel within her.

And she's dead, he thought. His chest ached as he clamped down on his sorrow, as he refused to give voice to it.

"Shane," Marie said.

He opened his eyes.

"Shane," Marie repeated.

"Yes?" he asked, and his mind threatened to turn each word into a shriek of rage and grief.

"Do you need anything before I leave?" Marie asked

"Yeah," Shane said, nodding.

"What?"

"I really *need* a cigarette," he whispered.

Chapter 63: Burning Down the Dead

Marie made the call to 911 and looked around for the hill Shane had spoken of. She could see little through the forest, but she caught sight of a trail. Branches were broken back, widened by the passage of dozens of people. She had worked enough crime scenes to recognize the signs of a police investigation.

Marie, with Shane's backpack in hand, jogged to the opening. She moved quickly along it and within a few minutes arrived at the hill and the remains of a blacksmith's shop. Shreds of yellow caution tape clung to a few trees alongside a trampled game trail. It curved around the base of the hill and went up to what was probably once a hidden entrance.

Marie entered it, darkness surrounding her. She pulled her keys out of her pocket and clicked on the small LED flashlight attached to the ring. The illumination was sickly, as was the smell which filled the moist air of the corridor. Soon she reached an open door and what she saw sickened her.

A teenage boy and girl, each stripped bare, lay on the floor, one atop the other. The smell in the room informed Marie that they were undeniably dead. Beside them stood a small boy and a dog. She could see through both of them.

"They were killed by the others," the boy said sadly, glancing at the bodies. "My father brought them here, to save some bones, and to add to his flock, if you will."

"Why?" Marie asked in a low voice.

The boy shrugged. "Who knows why Abel Latham did anything? Are you here to burn them?"

"Yes," Marie answered.

"To burn the bones?"

"Yes," she said.

The little boy turned and pointed at the back wall, saying, "There."

His small finger directed her to the fireplace. She realized it was the back of the one in the blacksmith's shop. To the right of it was a brick with the letters 'AL' carved into it.

"The brick hides his trophies, those that weren't destroyed by another hunter," the boy said sagely.

Marie walked forward, put the bag down between her feet, and worked her fingers in around the edges of the bit of masonry. Within a minute, she had pried it out. The brick was hollow, and in it were five small finger bones and the jawbone of a small dog. She reached in, took them out, and dropped the empty container to the floor. When she picked up the backpack, Marie saw the boy and the dog stood by the bodies.

In silence, she carried the bones over to the bodies and placed them on the girl's breast. Quickly, before she changed her mind, Marie retrieved the bottle of lighter fluid. She opened it, emptied the entire contents onto the bones and the bodies, and found the matches.

Marie hesitated, then struck the match and set fire to the dead.

The boy and the dog vanished, and Marie was alone with the makeshift funeral pyre. As the bodies burned she thought of the Quill brothers who had been killed when it all began.

The medical examiner owes me a favor, Marie thought tiredly. *He can say the brothers were infected. Cremation is necessary, unfortunately.*

Yes, she sighed. *Cremation is necessary.*

Chapter 64: Going Home Again

"Are you alright?" Marie asked.

"Yeah," Shane said, nodding. She had stopped the car in his driveway, and the two of them looked at the house.

"Shane," Marie said.

He looked at her and smiled. "Really, Marie, I'm good. Thank you."

She nodded and went to put the car in 'park.' Shane reached out and gently touched her hand, stopping her.

He shook his head. "You don't need to come in."

A look of relief flashed across her face as she asked, "Are you sure?"

"Yeah," he said, nodding, "I'm sure. You've done enough."

"Want me to call and check on you?" she said.

"That'd be great, my friend." He opened the door, grabbed his bag, and said, "Thank you, again, Marie. I appreciate it more than I can say."

"Shane," she said.

"Yeah?" he asked, pausing.

"I almost forgot to give you these." Marie reached into her breast pocket and removed a set of dog tags.

He took them from her and looked at them. They were his. The ones he had given to Courtney.

"Thank you," he whispered.

Marie smiled and nodded. "I'll talk to you soon."

"That you will," he said. He got out of the car, closed the door, and went up to his house. He stood and watched her leave, waving once. After she had left, Shane let himself in and stepped into the hall.

Carl drifted out of the study and looked at him. His eyes widened at the sight of Shane's arm in a sling. In German, he asked, "Shane, are you alright?"

Shane held up a finger, and Carl closed his mouth.

"I want to know, Carl," Shane said softly in German, "who chased her from the house?"

"They were angry with her for hurting you," Carl said.

Shane closed his eyes, sadness welling up within him. He swallowed roughly, blinked back tears, and whispered, "She is dead."

"Oh my God, Shane," Carl said, horrified. "They were worried about you, that is all!"

Shane nodded. "Tell me who, please, my friend."

Carl hesitated and then said, "Eloise and Thaddeus."

Shane forced himself to open his eyes. In a loud, firm voice he called out, "Eloise! Thaddeus!"

At the far end of the hall, they appeared from a shadow. They had been listening. Their heads were lowered. Neither of them said a word.

"You chased her," Shane said.

They nodded.

"Made her run," he added.

"Yes," Eloise whispered.

"She hurt you," Thaddeus said. "We wanted to hurt her."

Tears fell from Shane's eyes. It pained him to speak. "She did. Please go, and hide from me. Carl will let you know when you can come out."

The two children fled the hall.

"I'll be upstairs, Carl," Shane said in German. "I need to get drunk."

Carl bowed, and returned to the study.

Shane carried his bag up to his room. He dropped it on his bed, dug out his fresh bottle of whiskey, and opened it. The liquor was familiar and comforting as he drank it straight from the bottle. When he finished, Shane set it down on the bed table and got out a fresh pack of Lucky Strikes. He lit a cigarette, exhaled through his nose, and walked to the windows.

Silently, he drew the curtains, the room becoming dim, lit solely by the sunlight drifting in around the old fabric.

The room was cold, comfortingly so.

He went and sat on his bed. He finished the cigarette, stubbed it out in the ashtray by the whiskey, and took another drink. Cautiously, he stretched out on the bed. Most of the burns didn't hurt, but a few did.

He took his dog tags out of his pocket and looked at them for a moment. They felt charged, almost as if they had a small current of electricity running through them. Shane sighed, and then he set them on the pillow by his head. They smelled faintly of Courtney's shampoo.

As he adjusted himself on his bed, he heard a noise and caught a hint of movement in the corner by his armoire.

Shane nearly sobbed as he closed his eyes. In a voice raw and thick with emotion, he said, "Come to bed, Courtney."

"I miss you," she whispered.

"I miss you, too," he replied softly.

A heartbeat later, a cold but familiar form pressed up against him. Courtney sighed, and Shane waited for sleep to come.

* * *

Sanford Hospital
Book 4

Book 4: Sanford Hospital

Chapter 1: Waiting for Death

Ray Antonio laid in bed listening to the world around him. He could do little else. In 1945, near the end of the war, a German shell had taken his legs off at the thigh. At ninety years old, Ray didn't have the strength to use his prosthetics, or even hold himself up in a wheelchair.

Ray was waiting for Death to finish what it had started 70 years earlier.

His room smelled of antiseptic, the mustiness of old age, and despair.

Sully O'Hare had passed away the day before, and they had cleaned out the man's belongings. Nothing more than a few pictures. A couple of mementos from Sully's life before ending up in Sanford Veteran's Hospital.

I'll have another roommate soon, Ray thought. *If I even make it that long. Let's see how well I handle Stage 4 breast cancer.*

Breast cancer.

Ray sighed and stared up at the drop-tile ceiling. He had long ago memorized the pattern of dots in the panels. The television didn't interest him. Too many scantily clad women. Too much violence. The America he saw from his bed wasn't the America he had fought for.

That America was dead and buried, along with his wife and three children.

He drifted in and out of sleep for a while, finally opening his eyes when the sky beyond his window was dark. The parking lot was sparsely populated with the cars of the late night shift, the sickly yellow lights of street lamps illuminating the exterior of his small world. The Hospital had grown quiet, the ambient sounds of machinery filling the crisp air.

Ray looked from the window to the closed door of his room and stiffened.

A young woman stood silently by his bureau. She wore a nurse's uniform from when he had been a boy. The starched white clothes, the cap with its bright red cross, highlighted and helped to define the woman's sharp features. Her lips were full, her eyes wide set and almond-shaped. Small curls of light brown hair slipped out from under her cap, and Ray knew she had a hard time keeping it in check. She had her hands in front of her, delicately small and clasped politely.

When she saw him looking at her, the young woman smiled.

It was then Ray realized he could see straight through her to the back of the door where his blue bathrobe hung.

Ray pushed himself upright and looked with surprise at the young woman.

She took a silent step further into the room.

"Who are you?" Ray asked, his voice harsh from lack of use.

"A friend," she replied. "Just a friend, Raymond Antonio."

The use of his name sent a chill racing through him, and Ray noticed how cold the air in the room was.

"A friend?" Ray said. "Well, what's your name, miss?"

"Ruth," she replied, walking closer to the foot of his bed. "Ray, I've come to help you."

"I don't need any help," Ray snapped. "I thank you for the offer, though."

"Oh, but you do," Ruth said, nodding her head "You do. You just don't realize it. You're too close to it. So was your friend, Sullivan. He didn't want to leave either, but you have to trust that we have your best interests at heart."

"What are you talking about?" Ray asked, fear creeping into him. "What happened to Sully?"

"I want you to know, Ray, how I want to help you," she said. "I helped Sullivan, even though he didn't want it. He couldn't *see* how he needed my help."

"Sully's dead!" Ray said angrily. "Did you kill him?"

"No," Ruth replied. "Well, I helped to set his spirit free. His soul is at peace, now."

"What did you do?" Ray demanded. "Tell me!"

"I merely eased his passing," Ruth whispered said. "And do not worry, Raymond. I will help ease yours as well."

"The hell you will!" Ray barked. "I'm not dying today, and you won't be the one to decide."

"But you will," Ruth said. "And, more importantly, *I will*. I know my task, and whether you think it's your time or not, Ray, I have decided it is."

As she finished her short speech, Ruth headed towards the side of his bed. Ray grabbed the red call button for the nurse and tried to twist away from her. He moved too quickly and fell onto the floor. Ribs cracked loudly, and his head bounced off the old tile. Ray continued to press the button, twisting around to see where Ruth was.

She passed through his bed, anger flashing across her face.

"This wouldn't have happened," she said, her voice cold and flat, "if you had laid still."

The dead nurse leaned over him, reached down and thrust her hand into his chest.

Ray howled with fear and pain as she grasped his old heart and squeezed.

Chapter 2: Brett Goes Running

The call button for room 9 went off and jerked Brett Pelletier upright, causing him to knock over his coffee cup. The tan-colored liquid splashed out onto the floor but Brett didn't pause to clean it up. Instead, he launched himself from his chair at the nurse's station and sprinted towards room 9 as the patient howled.

"Hey Doctor Pelletier, he probably just has to go to the bathroom," Karen said without moving from her seat in front of the television.

Brett ignored her.

In a moment, he was at the door to the room and pushed it open. Faintly, he registered the fact that the wood was cold beneath his hand. The sight in front of him caused him to stop sharply and forget about the curiously cold door.

Sergeant Raymond Antonio, US Army, World War Two veteran, lay on the floor. The call button was in his hand, his faded pajamas loose on his thin frame. The man's mouth was open, toothless without his dentures. His eyes were wide, back arched. Ray's dark skin a shade too pale. And a woman was kneeling beside him.

Except she wasn't whole.

She was more of an image than a reality. Like someone was using the room for a movie screen.

Her hands were in Raymond Antonio's chest, a frown on her face. She looked up to Brett and nodded.

"He's fine now, Doctor," she said. "Better, really, than he has been in a long time. But he should have taken his medicine without complaint."

Then she vanished, leaving Brett in the room with a corpse and an image that he couldn't accept as real.

Chapter 3: At the Manchester Veteran's Hospital

Shane Ryan sat in the main waiting room of the VA Hospital in Manchester. He had his arms folded across his chest and his head bent down. Around him, people talked, a television played, and he did his best to stay calm.

In his back pocket was a folded and creased letter from the Department of Veterans Affairs. The message inside had informed him that as of the first of September, he could receive treatment for his burns at the newly reopened Sanford Veteran's Hospital. Since the VA was able to offer him treatment, the letter had continued, the government would no longer pay for any services obtained through private doctors or institutions.

"Son, are you alright?"

Shane lifted his head and was caught off guard. A man in a monk's robe stood in front of him. The man was short, his head was shaved, and he looked like he had endured a hard life. His face was etched with wrinkles. One eye was cloudy, the other was clear, the iris a bright blue. Several small scars worked their way up the side of his face and into the scalp.

"Yes, Brother," Shane said, gathering himself. "I am. Thanks."

"May I?" the monk asked, nodding to the chair beside Shane.

"Sure."

The man sat down and offered his hand to Shane. "Dom Francis Benedict."

"Shane Ryan," he said, shaking the hand. He looked at the monk and said, "Never thought to see a monk in here."

"Well," Dom Francis said, smiling, "part of the rules of my order require that we reach out to those in need. And since I'm a veteran too, I figured this was a good place to be. Plus, my Abbot gave me permission."

"You're a vet?" Shane asked, unable to keep the surprise out of his voice.

Dom Francis nodded. "Army. What about you?"

"Marines," Shane replied. "Career man. Legged it for a while. Too long, actually."

The monk chuckled. "Yeah. It's definitely not easy on the knees or the back. What'd you do after you were infantry?"

"Linguistics," Shane said, "mostly Pashto and Arabic."

In Pashto, Dom Francis said, "I'm impressed. Not too many can speak it."

Shane laughed, shaking his head and saying in English, "Okay, I need to know, how did *you* learn Pashto?"

"I was an 18 Delta," Dom Francis said, smiling softly.

"Special Forces?" Shane asked.

Dom Francis nodded. "Fifth. Spent a little bit of time in Afghanistan."

"Damn," Shane said appreciatively. "Yeah. I did a few tours there as well. What made you shift from the Army to religion?"

"Combat," Dom Francis said. "I was weapons. I got hit pretty badly on my last rotation through. I decided if I made it out, I was going to join the Benedictine monks. I went to school at St. Anselm's in Manchester before I enlisted. What about you, how'd you learn Pashto?"

"Honestly," Shane said, "I just picked it up listening to some of the interpreters speak it."

Dom Francis raised an eyebrow. "Can you do that with any language?"

Shane nodded.

"Are you sure?" the monk asked in Chinese.

"Of course, I'm sure," Shane said, answering in kind.

Dom Francis smiled. "Did the Marines know about your special ability?"

"No," Shane said, shaking his head. "And I was perfectly happy with them not knowing either. They would never have let me out."

"I'm surprised they let you out anyway," the monk said. "There aren't too many who can speak Pashto. Even when I was medically discharged, they gave me a hard time. They wanted me to stay in at a desk."

"Not for you?" Shane asked.

"No," Dom Francis said. "Definitely not for me. I joined Special Forces to get out and see the world. Free the oppressed. All the good stuff. Not to sit there and teach."

"What do you do now?" Shane said. "When you're not here?"

"Teach," he answered, with a wry smile.

Shane laughed until his sides hurt, and he was still laughing when his name was called. He wiped a tear from his eye as he stood and held out a hand to the monk. "A pleasure, Dom Francis."

The man shook it as he stood up. "I'll be around. If you ever need to talk, you can leave your name here, or call up to the college. Ask for Dom Francis. Don't ask for Benedict. There's got to be ten of us who took the name."

"Will do," Shane said. He turned away from the monk and walked across the small waiting room to an office. A middle-aged woman smiled wanly at him and then closed the door after he had entered the room.

Shane waited until she sat down before he took his own seat, and he looked at her as she organized some papers on her desk.

"So, Mr. Ryan," the woman said. "My name is Meg Kane. What can I help you with today?"

He reached into his back pocket, took out the letter and passed it across to her. "Could you explain this to me, please?"

She picked up a pair of reading glasses from the top of her desk, put them on and quickly scanned over the page. After a moment, she nodded, put her glasses down and returned the letter to him.

"It's fairly self-explanatory, Mr. Ryan," she said. "The Department of Veteran Affairs is now able to offer you the care you were previously receiving from private practitioners. We have several newly established medical sections in Sanford."

"Sanford Hospital," Shane said angrily.

"Yes," Ms. Kane said, her voice tight.

"I doubt Sanford Hospital's ability to deal with something as specialized as burn aftercare," Shane snapped.

"Well, Mr. Ryan," Ms. Kane said, looking down at her desk and rearranging some papers. "The point is, we will not be paying for any burn care outside of the Sanford facility."

"I saw that," Shane said, trying to keep his temper. "And what I'm concerned with, Ms. Kane, what I'm saying to you is, this is New Hampshire and not Maryland. I highly doubt the VA is going to have the skilled personnel at Sanford that it does down in Bethesda in regards to burn treatment and skin grafts. Wouldn't it make more sense to leave me in the care of the physicians who have been treating me?"

"If you don't want the VA to treat you," she said stiffly, looking back up at him, "it is obviously your choice. The VA will not, however, pay for you to go elsewhere when it is able to provide for you at its own facility."

"If I could afford private insurance," Shane said angrily, "do you really think I would be at the VA for anything?"

"I'm sorry you feel that way, Mr. Ryan," Ms. Kane said coldly.

Shane leaned back into his chair, took out a cigarette and lit it. Ms. Kane looked completely dumbfounded.

After a moment, she said sharply, "Mr. Ryan, you cannot smoke in here!"

He smiled at her, took a long drag off of the cigarette and said sweetly, "I'm sorry you feel that way, Ms. Kane."

In less than two minutes, he was escorted out of her office by security, the cigarette still in his mouth as he waved goodbye to Dom Francis Benedict, who was laughing by the front desk.

Chapter 4: Brett Keeps Quiet

The night after Ray Antonio died, Brett was back at work for his shift. A sense of anxiety hovered around him.

Was she real? he asked himself. *Did I imagine it?*

He had heard rumors of a ghost. *But what old building doesn't have a ghost story or two?*

Officially, Ray had died of a massive heart attack. Not unusual for someone who had been born in the early part of the 20th century.

Hell, Brett thought, *it wouldn't be unusual for someone like me, born in the eighties.*

But Brett knew it wasn't a heart attack that had killed Ray. A ghost had killed him, and Brett wasn't able to tell anyone about it.

Be a good way to lose the job, he thought angrily. It had taken him three years of applications to make it into the system. *Telling people you saw a ghost kill Ray, well, that's how you end up in the nuthouse.*

Brett walked into the nurse's station and nodded to Karen. The older woman waved, asking, "Doctor Pelletier, are you feeling okay?"

"Fine," Brett said, forcing himself to smile. "Little tired tonight."

"Antonio?" she said.

"No," Brett said. *Not the old man. The ghost with her hand in his chest, yeah. But not Ray.* "Couldn't sleep, is all."

"Sorry to hear that," she said, turning her attention back to the television and the news program. "Kind of tough trying to get used to this shift. You'll be okay, though."

"Thanks, Karen," Brett said. He walked to the back desk, put his lunch bag under it and flipped open the file to look at the patients on the ward. The staff referred to 'E' Ward as 'God's Waiting Room'. Most of the patients moved into E were on death's doorstep. It seemed like the slightest breeze could send them on their way.

Out of all of the other wards, E had the highest mortality rate. Even for a place with critically ill patients. On Brett's first day at work, a Vietnam vet had died from liver failure. The county coroner, laughingly, had told them he should have his own office in the building with the rate the vets were dying off.

Brett hadn't found the joke to be funny then, and it was even less so as he remembered it.

He shook the memory away and focused on the men who would be under his care for the night.

She said Ray was better, Brett thought. He stared hard at the list. *She was acting out of mercy. Twisted, but still a mercy. So who would benefit from her 'gentle' touch?*

Brett picked up the list and walked over to the desk. He sat down beside Karen, who glanced at him.

"What are you reading that for?" she asked.

"Just looking at specifics," Brett answered. "One case of mesothelioma, and two of stage four cancer. Myeloma and leukemia"

"Why do you even care?" Karen said, looking back to the television.

Brett held his tongue, not wishing to fight with someone he was going to have to spend the unforeseeable future with.

"Just want to be thorough, Karen," Brett said, keeping his tone light and pleasant.

"Okay, Doctor," she said, taking a drink from her travel mug. "Knock yourself out."

Brett didn't answer. Instead, he read the list.

And who was Ray Antonio? Brett thought. *What would make him worthy of the ghost's attention?* He tried to remember Ray's file. Raymond Antonio had suffered from Stage 4 breast cancer. Double amputee for over seventy years. He had never had any visitors. No phone calls. No letters.

Raymond Antonio had been alone in the world.

Alone and dying, Brett realized.

He took a pen from the holder on the desk and went through the list. Three other men matched the same criteria. A trio of men to watch and keep safe. Safer than the rest, at least. Pedro Martinez, Logan Tran, and Howard Case. Three men from different wars, each with a separate malady.

And not a friend in the world, Brett thought. He closed the file, put it aside and stood up.

"Where you headed?" Karen asked without looking at him.

"Checking on the patients," Brett said.

She snorted. "Have fun with that, Doctor."

Brett resisted the urge to yell at her, looped his stethoscope around his neck and left the nurse's station. He walked towards Pedro's room to check on the man and to let him know he wasn't alone.

Chapter 5: Going to Sanford

Shane was not encouraged by what he saw.

Sanford Hospital was old, with the distinctive architecture of the late Victorian period. Tall, wide windows with ornate ledges and brickwork. The roof was still slate, and in spite of the fact that it had recently been renovated, Shane couldn't help but wonder if there was even heat on all five floors. Ivy grew up along the front doors, the roots of the vine had dug themselves in deep, the individual leaves a deep, rich green. A few men and one woman sat on the long granite steps leading up to the entrance. They were smoking, and Shane smiled when he saw them.

He had gotten a good chewing out for smoking in the Manchester VA.

Worth it, Shane thought, chuckling. *Definitely worth it.*

He followed the narrow, one-way road around the right of the building to a large, surprisingly well-kept parking lot at the back. A newer looking docking bay at the hospital's rear was occupied with a red ambulance, the lettering on the side stating the vehicle was from Milford.

Shane turned his attention away from the emergency vehicle to the parking lot. He read the signs posted on the various lamp posts and saw one which read "D" Ward Parking.

That's me, he thought. He guided his car to an open space, backed in and shut the engine off. Pocketing his keys he got out, locked the door and started towards the front of the hospital. He caught sight of a few others walking around, some were pushed in wheelchairs, others moved along with the help of canes or relatives. Shane saw men older than himself, and younger.

He sighed and focused on the hospital.

Why? he wondered. *Why the hell did they put a hospital way out here, to begin with?*

The question remained unanswered as he reached the front of the building. He waved hello to the smokers, paused and pulled out his own cigarettes. As he put one in his mouth and lit it, Shane asked, "How is it here?"

An older African-American man shook his head.

"What branch?" a woman asked.

"Marines," Shane answered.

"East Coast or West?" another man asked.

"East," Shane said.

"Blake Cassidy," the man said, offering his hand.

Shane shook it.

"This is Alan Moore," Blake said, nodding to the African-American. "And Judy Witherspoon."

"Pleased to meet you all. Shane Ryan."

"So, you're a Parris Island Marine," Blake said.

"Yup," Shane said.

"You there before they put the barracks up?" Blake asked.

Shane nodded.

"Fine, fine," Blake said, stubbing out his cigarette and slowly field stripping it, peeling away the filter's paper cover and putting the remains in his pockets. "Sanford is worse."

"Damn" Shane said, exhaling smoke through his nose. "Are you serious?"

All three of them nodded.

"Best to hope they don't admit you," Judy said.

"That good, huh?" Shane asked.

The three nodded in unison.

"Great," Shane said, sighing. "Great."

He finished his cigarette, field stripped it as always and walked up the stairs. The old doors were heavy; a solid, almost comforting weight.

When he entered the building, Shane paused. He could smell sickness and death beneath the strong odor of cleaning products. The lobby was narrow and occupied by a single desk. Behind it was a young woman who looked worn and tired, as though she had been chained to the piece of furniture for years.

Maybe she has, Shane thought.

He walked to the desk and stopped in front of it. In silence, he waited for her.

She was texting on her phone, glanced up at him and smiled. Her name tag read, 'Jane S.'

"May I help you?" Jane asked.

"Yes, miss," Shane said. "I'm Shane Ryan. I have an appointment with Doctor Georges."

"Dr. Georges called in sick today," Jane said apologetically. "We have Nurse Platte covering for him."

"Okay," Shane said. "Where do I find Nurse Platte?"

"She's on B Ward," Jane said. "Second floor. The elevator is out today, so you'll have to use the main stairs."

"Tough day?" Shane asked.

"No," Jane said, sighing. "It's pretty normal."

"Great," Shane muttered. He turned, saw the tiled stairs which led up to the second floor, and he headed towards them.

When he reached the first landing, he found himself at a pair of doors. Above them was a sign, B Ward. He pushed them open and walked in. The floor was polished to a high sheen, the lights were bright, and the area looked well-cared for. A male nurse sat at the main station and looked up at Shane.

"Hello," Shane said, "I'm here to see Nurse Platte."

The man nodded and called out over his shoulder, "Nancy, you've got a patient."

From a back office, a woman appeared. She looked to be in her sixties, her gray hair pulled back in a loose ponytail and glasses on her face. The woman was short, round, and Shane could see she wouldn't take any grief from anyone.

"You're Mr. Ryan?" she asked, her voice like broken glass on gravel.

"Yes, Ma'am," Shane answered.

"Right this way," she turned around and went back to the office. Shane hurried after her. She sat down and nodded to him. Shane took the seat and waited.

Nurse Platte picked up a file, scanned through it, closed it, and said, "You're here for burn treatment?"

"Yes, Ma'am," Shane said.

She put the file down, took her glasses off and looked at him. In a low voice, she asked, "Is there any way you can afford to go back to where you were?"

He shook his head.

"Dr. Georges is a nice enough man," she continued, "but he shouldn't be doing most procedures. Hell, I don't even trust him to take someone's temperature properly."

"Great," Shane muttered. "I don't have a choice."

"Alright," Nurse Platte said. "I will do my best for you. I promise you that, Mr. Ryan. However, even in the best of facilities, there is a high chance for infection when caring for burn injuries."

"Yeah," Shane said. "I know. Okay, what now?"

"I'm going to send you to the lab, make sure you have all of the blood work up to date," she replied. "Then I'm going to admit you and schedule you for tomorrow morning. Eight o'clock."

"Why so soon and so early?" Shane asked, surprised.

"Best to get it done sooner rather than later," Nurse Platte said. "Dr. Georges usually doesn't start drinking until lunch time."

"Usually?" Shane said.

She nodded. "Usually."

Chapter 6: Brett Keeps an Eye Open

After having checked on Pedro, Brett went into Howard Case's room. He found Howard asleep, but the man's roommate, Bill "Doc" Kiernan, was awake. The younger man's pale skin and short cropped red hair, like his name, spoke of his Irish heritage. His green eyes sunk in their sockets above high cheekbones, confirmed the diagnosis that Bill was not long for the world.

"Hey, Doc," Brett said, walking in and sitting down. "How are you, tonight?"

"Well," the young man said. "I just turned thirty last week and I'm dying, how about yourself?"

"Can't complain too much when you put it like that," Brett said.

"Sure, you can," Bill said, grinning. "One of my drill sergeants told us that we had very few rights in the Army. One of them was the right to complain, and that we should do it as often and as much as we could possibly get away with."

Brett laughed. "Sounds like good advice. How are you feeling tonight?"

"I'm dying, Brett," Bill said, the grin faltering for a moment. "Other than that, I'm feeling okay."

"I wish there was more I could do," Brett said sincerely.

"Don't worry about it. You do what you can, and I appreciate it. I know Howard does, too."

Brett nodded.

"Anyway," Bill said, sighing, "anything new on E Ward?"

"No," Brett replied, shaking his head. "No new arrivals. No new staff. What about you, what's the rumor mill got going during the day?"

"Well," Bill said, adjusting himself on his bed. "Let's see. Heard we got a new patient downstairs on B Ward. Poor guy's going under Dr. George's knife in the morning."

"How did you hear about him?" Brett asked. "Kind of far for word to travel, isn't it?"

"Guess he's completely bald," Bill said. "No hair anywhere. The nurses were joking about how they weren't going to have to shave him."

"No hair at all?"

"Zero," Bill said.

"Guy probably has alopecia," Brett said, more to himself than to Bill.

"What's that?" Bill asked.

"Unexplained hair loss," Brett said. "An autoimmune disorder."

"Might make it tough to chat up some of the ladies," Bill said with a grin.

Brett nodded, chuckling as he stood up.

"That's true. Very true. You need anything, Doc?"

"A cure for whatever cancer I got from those Iraqi burn-pits would be nice," Bill said. "But, if you don't have that lying around, make Karen get up and bring me a cup of coffee to wash my pain meds down."

"You got it," Brett said. "Tell Howard I said 'hello' when he wakes up."

"Will do."

Brett left the room, and checked in on Logan Tran. The man and his roommate were asleep. He did the rest of his rounds, ended up back at the nurse's station and found Karen upright in her chair with her eyes closed, fast asleep.

He shook his head in disgust and sat down in his own seat. Quietly, he picked up the newest Jack Reacher novel and opened up to his bookmark.

Chapter 7: Feeling Good

Shane walked up the main stairwell. He had managed to get out to his car, have a couple nips of whiskey, and then slipped back inside. The security guard was an old Marine, and he and Shane had talked about Okinawa, less than reputable drinking establishments, and the best ways they had eluded the arrest by the Shore Patrol.

It was a quarter to midnight, and Shane knew he wouldn't be able to eat or drink anything else prior to his surgery in the morning. The fact that they were putting him under the knife didn't bother him as much as the risk of infection did. He had no idea about the whole skin grafting procedure, but he knew there were dangers to any surgery.

That'll be my luck, Shane told himself, passing the landing for the third floor and heading towards the fourth. *I'm going to die on the operating table of a backwater VA hospital because I don't have private insurance.*

His body burned through the alcohol quickly, and he considered, briefly, a second trip to the car. He shook the idea away and focused on the stairs. The plan was to tire himself out enough so he would sleep.

Preferably without nightmares, he thought, sighing. He paused on the steps, adjusted the pull-strings of the pajamas they had issued him, and then continued on. Soon he passed the fourth floor, and he reached the end of the stairs at the landing for E Ward. He hesitated in front of the doors, then he pushed them open and stepped onto the fifth floor.

Shane noticed the temperature immediately.

It was easily ten degrees colder than the rest of the building. The ward was filled with the ambient noise of different medical equipment. A curious, unidentifiable stench hung in the air, but the two people at the nurse's station didn't seem to notice.

The nurse, in fact, looked as if she were asleep. Beside her was a man in a doctor's coat, and his head was down, intent upon the book he was reading. Only when the doors whispered closed did the man look up.

His eyes widened in surprise, and he hastily put the book down. The man looked to be in his early thirties. His face was round, as if he enjoyed pastries more than he should. The man's brown hair was messy and his ears, which were more pointed than curved, protruded sharply through the locks.

"Can I help you?" the man asked.

"Not really," Shane replied. "I'm just out for a walk."

"You're the man who came in today," the doctor said.

"Yeah," Shane said warily. "How'd you know?"

"Your alopecia," the doctor answered. "It made the rounds of the hospital. Even came up here to some of the patients."

Shane shook his head. "Glad I can help people gossip."

"Beats what the last guy was known for," the doctor said.

"Oh yeah?" Shane asked.

The doctor nodded. "Syphilis."

"Unreal," Shane said, laughing in spite of himself, "yeah, guess it does."

A soft clink echoed through the ward.

Both Shane and the doctor looked down the left wing.

"No!" The shout came from one of the closed rooms.

Shane turned to the doctor, but the man was already out from behind the desk and racing down the hall towards the voice. Without hesitating, Shane ran after him.

The doctor slammed open a door and barreled into the room. Shane was close behind him. Close enough to see a woman in an old nurse's uniform standing beside the bed of another patient, an old man. His skin a sickly yellow, and wisps of white hair clinging to scalp.

She snapped her head up at Shane and the doctor, anger and determination on her face. Shane groaned inwardly as he saw the wall through her. *Not again.* Her hands were over the mouth of the patient, and he struggled weakly beneath her.

"You're too loud," the nurse spat, and she flicked her hand towards the door.

Shane felt himself thrown backward, his feet leaving the floor as he went hurtling into the hallway. He stumbled and caught himself only to have the doctor slam into him. Shane's head struck the cement wall and everything went dark.

Chapter 8: On the Wrong Floor

"Hey," a man said. "Can you hear me?"

Someone pried open one of his eyelids and Shane jerked his head away. He blinked, tried to see, but his eyes wouldn't focus, so he closed them again.

"Yeah," Shane mumbled.

"What's your name?"

"Gunnery Sergeant," Shane responded.

"Come on, your name, not your rank," the stranger said.

"Shane. Shane Ryan," Shane said.

"Stay awake, Shane," the unknown man said. "You've got to do that for me, Marine."

"Damn," Shane said, the word slurred as it exited his mouth. "I'm tired."

"No rest for the wicked, Marine," the man said. "Keep those eyes open. Come on."

Grumbling, Shane did as he was told. The world came into focus, and he saw a young man squatting beside him. The stranger was wearing pajamas and a robe with Looney Tune characters all over it.

"What's going on?" Shane asked, frowning at the slow tempo of his speech.

The young man smiled. "You can call me Doc, Shane. Listen, you hit your head pretty hard when you came out of Pedro's room. Doctor Pelletier said some crazy stuff about ghosts, but I'm more concerned with your head right now. Think you can help me out?"

"Sure," Shane said. "What do you need?"

"How many fingers do you see?" Doc asked, holding up one hand.

Shane counted seven fingers, which didn't seem quite right, but he told Doc the number anyway.

"Yeah," Doc said, chuckling. "I never would have made it into the service if I had seven fingers. No, you've got a concussion, Marine. No surgery for you in the morning."

"The hell," Shane said. He yawned, closed his eyes and tried to rest against the wall.

"No, no, no," Doc said, shaking Shane's shoulder to keep him conscious. "No one's given you the okay for sleep. You've got to stay awake for me. You need to be awake until they get a gurney up here for you, and that's going to be in a little bit. They're trying to get a service elevator up and running to bring you and Brett downstairs. If they can't, well, you're going to be in the Waiting Room until tomorrow sometime."

"You got spare beds up here?" Shane asked, looking at Doc.

"Two as of right now," Doc said. "Pedro died."

"Pedro?" Shane slurred. "Who's Pedro?"

"The man in the room you and Brett ran to," Doc answered.

"She killed him," Shane murmured.

"Who killed him?" Doc asked sharply.

"The nurse," Shane said, trying to force his eyes to focus on Doc. "The dead nurse killed him. She was smothering him when we went in."

"What the hell are you talking about?" Doc asked, his voice low.

Shane closed one eye and was able to see Doc clearly with the other. Taking a deep breath, Shane said, "There was a ghost. In the room. She was killing him. Pedro. When we went in. When we went in, she threw us."

"Bull," Doc hissed. "There's no such thing as ghosts. Brett was seeing things."

Shane shook his head and instantly regretted it. Pain exploded behind his eyes and churned his stomach. He managed to calm down, looked at Doc and said, "A ghost in Pedro's room. She killed him. Mad we were interrupting her."

Doc licked his lips nervously, glanced around as if to make certain no one else was close by and he whispered, "Did Brett see this ghost too?"

"Yup," Shane answered. "Hey. Hey, Doc."

"Yes?" Doc said, the tone of his voice leveling off. "What do you need?"

"You said no surgery for me tomorrow?"

"Not with a concussion," Doc said. "Plus you're talking like your brains are really scrambled up there. Traumatic Brain Injury is what you're sounding like, Marine."

Shane waved the comment away. "Already been checked for TBI. Hit an IED in Helmand Province. You know. I don't know. Anyway. No surgery?"

"No. No surgery."

"Good," Shane said, sighing. "Do me a favor."

"What?" Doc asked.

"My keys are in my robe pocket," Shane said. "I got a fifth of whiskey in the trunk. Bring it up will you?"

Before the younger man could reply, darkness swept over Shane, and the world went still. He felt hands lift him up. Someone adjusted his head, and he could feel them carrying him.

Shane smiled in spite of the pain in his head and his back. *No surgery*, he thought, chuckling. *No surgery. Dr. Georges will have to cut into some other poor sap tomorrow.* From a distance, he heard Doc or someone else speak his name.

Shane laughed and said one word in reply.

"Whiskey."

Chapter 9: Brett talks with Shane

Shane sat in a chair and stared at the television. He had the volume muted, barely registering the show; something about finding and rebuilding vintage muscle cars.

Shane had suffered a few concussions before, and he hated them. His head ached, his mouth was dry, and he was exhausted but couldn't go to sleep.

There was a knock at the door, and Shane managed to say, "Come in."

Brett entered, a swath of painfully bright light blinding Shane.

"Sorry about the light," Brett said, hastily closing the door.

"It's alright,"

Shane picked up the remote and turned the television off. "Came to check on your newest patient?"

Brett nodded, pulled the room's other chair over and sat down. "How are you feeling?"

"Miserable," Shane said, sighing. "How about you?"

"Not as bad," Brett said. "At least I don't have a concussion."

"Yup," Shane agreed. "What's on your mind?"

The man cleared his throat uncomfortably, scratched the back of his head and said, "Did you see anything when we went into Pedro's room?"

"Yeah," Shane said.

Brett waited for Shane to continue, but when he didn't, he stammered, "I mean. Well, did you … did you see a woman?"

"A nurse?" Shane asked.

A look of relief filled Brett's face. "Yes. Oh my God, yes, a nurse."

"Yes," Shane said. "I saw her. I saw her smothering Pedro. She threw us out of the room."

"Oh, thank you," Brett said. "I was worried you hadn't. I hoped you had."

"I did," Shane said. "Have you seen her before?"

"Yes," Brett whispered, nodding. "The other night when Ray, another patient, died. Or was killed, I guess. Can ghosts kill?"

"Ghosts can do a lot." Shane stared at the wall for a moment, then he looked back to Brett.

"I was thinking," Brett said, "could she be the reason there are so many deaths on E Ward?"

"Definitely," Shane said. "Who's the guy called Doc?"

"Bill Kiernan," Brett said. "Combat medic. Did a few tours in Iraq and Afghanistan. He helped out when you and I were down."

"Yeah," Shane said. "You may want to talk to him about this ghost, too. I vaguely remember mentioning it to him when he was treating me."

"Is it that bad?" Brett asked.

Shane shrugged. "Depends on whether or not he believes me. Feel him out. If he thinks I'm crazy, don't say you saw her too. You don't need the grief. If he sounds like he thought I was telling the truth and I'm not insane, you might want to see if he's seen or heard anything strange."

"Are we safe?" Brett asked softly.

"I don't know," Shane said truthfully. "I think that's something we need to figure out."

"Is there a way to get rid of her?" Brett said. "I mean, can we even do that?"

"Sure," Shane said. He winced. "There are a few ways. I can't really wrap my head around everything right now, Doctor."

Brett nodded and stood up, straightened his coat and pants and turned towards the door. "You'll be able to fill me in later?"

"Yeah," Shane said. "Hey, you going to speak to him now?"

Brett paused and nodded.

"Think you could ask someone to send me some coffee since I'm stuck here for a while?"

"Will the caffeine help you stay awake?" Brett asked with a small smile.

"No," Shane answered, "but a full bladder will."

Shane picked up the remote, turned the television back on, and tried to find an interesting show to watch.

Chapter 10: Matias Hears the News

Matias Geisel was an old man.

In August, he had turned ninety-four. He had been moved into the Sanford Hospital on October 7, 1998. When the facility had closed in 2001, shortly after the terrorist attack in New York City, he had been moved down to Roxbury, Massachusetts. Then, with the reopening of the hospital, he had been shifted back. Matias was Sanford's oldest resident, and he knew all about the Nurse.

One day, Matias told himself, *she'll come and claim me. Return me to the dust from which we all come. One day.*

He dealt himself a fresh hand of solitaire, breaking in the new pack of playing cards his great-grandson had brought him earlier that day.

Matias's room was on A Ward, tucked in a corner by the back stairs. The staff had done him that courtesy, allowing for visitors to slip in and out at will. Having served in three wars – the Second World War, Korea, and Vietnam – the folks at Sanford cut him a lot of slack.

Someone knocked on his door frame, and Matias looked up from his chair. Nancy Platte stood in the hall, smiling in at him.

"Nurse," Matias said, a great grin breaking across his wrinkled face, "Come in, come in."

"Oh Lord, Matias," Nancy said in her harsh voice as she carried a pair of coffees from Dunkin Donuts into the room, "I've told you before not to call me 'Nurse'."

"And you'll tell me again," Matias said, smiling. He cleaned the cards off his tray, stacked them neatly on one side and gestured for Nancy to sit. He straightened up as best as he could. "How are you?"

"Fine," Nancy said, opening the lid on his coffee to let the steam out and placing it in front of him.

"Thank you," Matias said. "How was your ride in this morning?"

"Good," Nancy replied. "Nothing too drastic. A Little bit of traffic on Route 3, not much more. Did you hear the news?"

Matias shook his head.

"Another death on E Ward last night," she said, sighing.

Matias frowned. "She's busier than usual."

Nancy raised an eyebrow.

"Oh allow an old man his beliefs, however foolish, Nurse," Matias said, smiling. "I've been here a great deal longer than you."

"I know," Nancy said. "I find it hard to believe the ghost of a nurse is acting as Sanford's grim reaper."

Matias shrugged. "Believe it or don't. It happens nonetheless. Anyway, tell me what happened, please."

Nancy did so, taking the occasional pause to sip her drink. Finally, she said, "There was no mention of a ghostly medical practitioner, Matias."

"Perhaps not."

"The elevators are out again," Nancy added. "In fact, one of the patients I admitted yesterday is stuck on that floor. They've decided to monitor him up there for now. Maintenance is waiting on a representative from the elevator company to show up."

"What was the patient admitted for, if you don't mind my asking?"

Nancy grinned. "Violating all sorts of laws with this, but he's supposed to be having a skin graft done."

Matias frowned. "Isn't that the domain of Dr. Georges?"

She nodded.

"Evidently, someone has given the patient a reprieve," Matias said.

"Evidently."

"It would be best if Dr. Georges died," Matias grumbled. "People suffer enough without his assistance."

"That's not nice to say," Nancy said, scolding him gently.

"The truth rarely is," Matias said, smiling sadly. "Now, tell me what else has gone on in this fine facility since you came in yesterday."

As Nancy filled him in on all of the rumors and gossip, Matias drank his coffee and listened happily.

Chapter 11: Dr. Georges Goes for a Drink

Angelo Georges only had a problem with alcohol when he couldn't get enough of it.

Whistling to himself, Angelo closed and locked the door to his office. From the bottom drawer of his filing cabinet, he took out a new bottle of Bailey's Irish Cream. He smiled, nodded, and opened it. Angelo added a healthy dose of the liquor to his coffee, took a sip from the bottle, and then put it back into the drawer.

He drew the shades, turned the light down low and settled down in his chair. With his mug in hand, Angelo relaxed, enjoyed the pleasant, familiar burn of the alcohol and felt relieved. The day was nearly done, and soon he would be on his way home.

No more surgeries and Helen is away for the weekend, he thought with a grin. *I'll be able to drink without being subjected to her constant nagging.*

He lifted the mug in salute and enjoyed a long sip.

The shade rustled, and the room chilled noticeably.

Angelo frowned, stood up, and went to the window. He moved the plastic aside, checked to make sure the latch was secure, and then shrugged.

Curious, he thought. *Wonder if the window needs to be redone. Didn't they just put these in?*

Angelo returned to his chair, sat down again and finished his coffee. Instead of retrieving the Bailey's from the cabinet, Angelo opened the center drawer of his desk, reached into the back and grabbed one of the nips. It was a small bottle of vodka, and when he opened it, his mouth watered.

Pavlov's Dog, he thought, chuckling. *Ah well.*

The light flickered, sputtered, and then burst. He could hardly see. *What the hell,* he thought. He put the nip down on the desk, stood up and felt himself thrust back into the chair.

Hands pressed down on his shoulders, a terrible cold penetrating the fabric and settling into his flesh. Fear and panic rose in his throat, the muscles tightening, his heart pounding. Again he tried to rise from the chair, and once more he found himself incapable of moving.

Sweat burst out on his brow and under his arms, his breath raced in and out, and desperately he tried to rein it in.

"You are an unrepentant drunk," a woman whispered in his ear.

He shivered, for although the words were close to him, Angelo could feel no breath upon his flesh.

"You know you are a drunk," she hissed. "I hate your drinking, Doctor. Your habit. Your predilection. I will have no more of it, do you understand, *Doctor?*"

The last word was pronounced with venomous hatred, so much so that Angelo found himself unable to reply.

"What?" she hissed. "Has the cat got your tongue?"

He shook his head.

"I am fed up, quite frankly," she continued, "of your interference. Your drunken ineptitude has caused my patients to die sooner than they should. You, *Doctor*, do not get to choose. Only I do. Out of all of the physicians here, you are the only nuisance. I have had enough of you getting in my way."

Angelo found his voice. "I'll leave. I promise, I'll leave."

"You will," the Nurse said. "Only not in the way you plan."

Her hands passed through his clothes, sunk into his flesh and found the nerves. The pain was immediate and excruciating.

Angelo opened his mouth to scream, but the stranger jerked a hand free and clamped his lips together. What should have been a piercing shriek was nothing more than a squeal, a sound eking out into the office.

Someone passed by in the hall and Angelo kicked at his desk.

They continued on their way.

No! he thought desperately. He tried to free himself, but the pressure she exerted was too much. She pushed her hand deeper inside him, the agony unbelievable. Stars exploded around his eyes, vomit rushed up his throat and smashed against his lips. Inadvertently he inhaled, taking in a deep breath of bile and alcohol.

Angelo couldn't breathe, he was suffocating in his own vomit.

Panic caused him to throw up again.

He fought against her, but it was no use. Her strength was incomprehensible. She was of a single-minded purpose.

"You'll die, Doctor," she said, her voice low and hard. "You will drown in your own bile."

The cold hand within his chest sought out and found a lung. Angelo felt each individual finger creep around the organ, settle in, and squeeze. The grip on his mouth tightened, his teeth grinding and then breaking in his mouth. He shook violently, yet she kept him in the chair, pressing him down.

The Nurse never relented, and Angelo took a long time to die.

Chapter 12: Misery Loves Company

Shane held an icepack to his head and smoked a cigarette. Doc had found an electric fan for him, and it blew the wispy evidence out of the open window. Shane took a final drag, ground the butt out in the window sill and sat back.

"Are you alive in here?" a raspy voice asked.

Shane twisted in his seat and saw Nurse Platte walk into the room.

He smiled at her. "Almost alive. Really looking forward to the all-clear so I can lie down and get some sleep."

She nodded, paused and raised her head slightly, her nostrils flaring. "Were you smoking in here?"

"Yeah," Shane said, turning his chair around to face her. He switched off the fan.

Nurse Platte frowned. "You're not supposed to."

"Getting a concussion wasn't on the agenda either," he grumbled, "but here we are."

She shook her head.

"Did they get the elevators fixed yet?" Shane asked.

"No," Nurse Platte answered.

"Can I go back to my room?"

"Not yet," she said.

"Why not?" Shane said. "Am I not allowed to walk down the stairs?"

"If it was one flight of stairs," Nurse Platte said, "we'd let you go. But not four."

"I can't even go home."

"I know," she said. "The doctor will be able to see you tomorrow morning so long as the elevators are good."

"And he'll be sober?" Shane asked.

"I'll make sure of it," Nurse Platte said, and the tone of her voice left no doubt that she would.

"So," Shane said, "you'll let me walk down the stairs tomorrow, even if the elevators are still broken?"

She nodded.

"Good."

Nurse Platte was silent for a short time, and Shane could see that she wanted to ask him a question. Finally, after several minutes of hesitation, she said, "I spoke with Doc Kiernan."

Shane waited.

"He told me you thought you saw a ghost."

"Yeah," Shane responded. "I didn't think it. I know it."

"Mr. Ryan," she said cautiously, "you suffered a concussion. And, given your history of them, and your combat experiences, maybe it was a hallucination."

"I know what I saw," Shane said with a sigh. "Please don't doubt it, Nurse Platte. I'm not here to convince you otherwise. I don't really care. All I want is to have the skin graft done, go home, and get back to murdering my liver with whiskey. My lungs need a couple of packs of unfiltered Luckys, too."

"You won't say anything to the other patients?" she asked.

"Not a word," Shane said. "These men are dying. I'm not about to mess up the rest of their days with some ghost stories. They've all got enough to think about."

"Thank you," she said, smiling with relief. "I do appreciate it."

"You're welcome." He shifted the ice pack from one side of his head to the other, wincing as he did so.

"I've got to go back to my floor," Nurse Platte said, smiling. "One of the other girls called in sick. I'm picking up part of her shift."

"I'll see you later." he said.

Nurse Platte nodded, waved goodbye, and left the room.

A few more hours and I'll be able to go to sleep, Shane thought. *Even walk down the stairs.*

"Good afternoon," a woman said, and Shane almost fell out of his chair in surprise. He looked up and went completely still.

The Nurse stood by his bed. She was opaque, a small, polite, and business like smile on her face.

Shane cleared his throat, gave a short bow and said, "Good afternoon."

"What are you doing on E Ward?" she asked.

Her tone was firm. Completely professional.

"I suffered a blow to the head," Shane said. "They won't allow me to go down to my room until the elevators are fixed, or until twenty-four hours have passed."

She nodded.

"I'm sorry you were injured so," the Nurse said. "But you were interrupting, which was rather rude, I might add."

"Please accept my apologies," Shane said. *Can I get away from her, if she attacks?*

"Apology accepted," she said. She narrowed her eyes at him and added, "Make certain it does not happen again."

"I'll do my best," Shane replied.

She looked at him, shook her head, and then turned to leave.

"Excuse me," Shane said.

"Yes?" she said, pausing.

"May I ask your name?"

She frowned. "I don't see why this is of any importance, but, if you must know, my name is Ruth. Ruth Williamson."

Shane watched as she turned and left the room through the right wall.

Ruth Williamson, Shane repeated to himself. *Let's see what we can find out about you, Nurse.*

Chapter 13: Matias, Sanford Hospital, June 2nd, 1967

"I didn't think it would come back," Matias huffed, his feet bare and up on the examining table.

"It did," Doctor Jack Neal said. He took the cigarette out of his mouth, tapped the head off into the ashtray on the counter, and shook his head. "It's a fungus, Matias. You contracted it in the Pacific first, right?"

Matias nodded.

"Well," Jack said, putting the cigarette back between his lips, "looks like the heat of South East Asia has brought it back out. Most of the time, I tell people to take better care of their feet, but this doesn't have anything to do with it. You came by it honestly."

"That's a relief," Matias said sarcastically.

"Don't be smart," Jack said. "We'll do what we can, as always. I'm more worried about the way the hip wound is healing."

"Why?" Matias demanded. "What's wrong with the hip?"

"I think the pins we put in may not have been as sterile as they were supposed to be," Jack said, sighing. "To put it bluntly, Matias, we may have to go in, lance the wound, drain the infection, and maybe even open you back up to scrape the pins free of any debris."

Matias held his tongue, keeping the anger within.

"Matias," Jack said, sighing and stepping back. He folded his arms across his chest and shook his head. "You know I wouldn't tell you if it wasn't necessary."

"I know, Jack, I know," Matias said. He carefully moved his legs off the table, wincing as he adjusted his position. "I've been under the knife enough. I'm not looking forward to another operation."

"Well, make sure you send a thank you letter to Vietnam," Jack said, sitting down on a stool. "I'm certain they'll appreciate it."

"No need," Matias said. "I've got the sniper's skull in my study."

Jack looked at him in surprise. "You don't!"

"I do," Matias said. "My fire-team mailed it to me when I was in Germany for the first leg of the trip home."

Jack shook his head. "There is something fundamentally wrong with the Marines."

Matias shrugged. "Perhaps."

"Listen, I'm going to admit you," Jack said. "I'd like to lance the wound today. I'll be able to tell by the discharge whether or not we should go in and scrape it clean."

Matias rolled his eyes. "You picked a good time. Debra's got the kids with her down in Boston."

"Really?" Jack said innocently. "How fortuitous."

Matias looked at him, and then said, "Jack, have you been speaking with Debra?"

Jack's face reddened.

"The pair of you, thick as thieves, eh?" Matias asked.

"Did you think I wouldn't consult with my sister?" Jack replied.

Matias shooed the doctor away. "Go get me my room. Better to have it done now."

Jack grinned, stubbed out his cigarette in the marble ashtray by the door and left the room. A few minutes later, he returned with a large, male orderly. The man pushed a wheelchair in front of him, and Matias frowned.

"My orders," Jack said. "I don't care how stubborn you are. The only bed we have open is on E Ward, and I won't have you limping your way there."

"What do you mean?" Matias asked. "There's the elevator."

"Only if you're in the wheelchair," Jack said. "I'll make you walk the whole way up if you won't take a seat."

"When I'm better, Doctor," Matias said, "we're going to put on the gloves and go a couple of rounds."

"Excellent," Jack said, smiling. He turned to the orderly and said, "Don."

Don brought the wheelchair to the table and waited as Matias put himself in it. The pain was terrible, and it must have shown on his face.

"We'll have you better in no time," Jack assured him. "Go on upstairs. Rest. I'll be along shortly."

Matias could only nod in reply.

In a short time, Don had wheeled him from A Ward to E Ward and brought him into Room 8. A terribly old man lay asleep on one of the two beds, and the room was lit with the afternoon light. Don pushed the wheelchair directly to the unoccupied bed. Matias got onto the bed and took a deep breath.

"Are you alright, sir?" Don asked.

Matias nodded. "Well, enough. Thank you."

"Do you need a nurse to help you get into your bedclothes?" the orderly asked.

"No," Matias said, shaking his head. "Thank you, but no."

"Alright, sir," Don said, and he put the wheelchair in a corner before he left the room, closing the door behind him.

Matias carefully bent over, untied his shoes and left them under the bed. With equal caution, he brought his legs up onto the mattress, made himself as comfortable as possible, and looked over at his companion.

Each breath was a wheeze for the old man, the tell-tale rattle in his chest a sound Matias had heard all too often.

He's dying, Matias thought. *Maybe not tonight. But definitely tomorrow. How old is he? Damn, he looks old enough to have ridden with Roosevelt and the Rough Riders.*

Turning his attention away from the old man, Matias looked around for something to occupy his attention. There was a deck of cards on the table between the pair of beds. Beside the table was a folded lap desk. Matias reached over, grabbed the cards and the desk. He dealt out a hand of solitaire and began looking for a home for the three of clubs.

The door swung open.

Matias looked up, saw a nurse, and frowned. *I told him I didn't need help.*

The thought died as Matias realized he could see through the woman. She seemed to be more of an afterthought. An idea of a woman, or a memory of one. Her uniform was old; antiquated.

Book 4: Sanford Hospital

She smiled pleasantly at him as she passed by, a wave of cold air preceding her.

Matias shuddered, the hackles on his neck standing up and the pain in his hip increasing exponentially.

She made her way directly to the old man in the other bed. As she neared him, Matias's roommate gasped and turned slowly in his bed. When she came to a stop beside the bed, the man's back was to her.

Matias' horror grew as he watched her reach out with both hands, placing them in the center of the old man's back. A heartbeat later, she pushed her fingers further into the man's flesh, and soon she was wrist deep in his elderly form.

The old man gasped, shivered, and the death rattle stopped.

For several minutes longer, she remained where she was, her hands still hidden within him.

Matias stayed where he was, fear gripping him.

Finally, she withdrew herself and turned around. Once again she smiled at Matias, pausing for a moment at the end of his bed.

"Craig is feeling much better now," she said sweetly. "Much better. I'll come by later and check on you as well."

Matias remained perfectly still as he watched her leave the room and thought, *I hope not.*

Chapter 14: A Visitor

The elevators had been fixed, and Shane had been moved from E Ward down to A Ward.

At six o'clock in the morning, he woke up, sweating profusely and panting from the nightmares. Even after all that he had been through, the terrors of his childhood remained with him; plagued him every night.

He sat up in the hospital bed, jonesing for a cigarette and a shot of whiskey. Shane got up quietly, conscious of the man sleeping in the other bed, and went into the bathroom. He washed up quickly, pulled a fresh pair of issue pajamas on, and slipped his feet into his sneakers. When he left the room, he nodded to the nurse on duty and got the 'okay' from the old Marine security guard to go outside for a smoke and a nip.

As soon as the doors closed behind him, Shane took out his cigarettes and lit one up. He smiled at the taste of tobacco and made his way down the stairs to the back lot. In a few minutes, he was enjoying the pleasant burn of whiskey and wondering how much longer he was going to have to stay at Sanford.

"Shane!"

Shane looked and saw Doc Kiernan. The dying medic hobbled toward him, leaning heavily on a cane.

"Hey, Doc," Shane said. "Want a drink?"

"You have whiskey in your car?" Doc asked, laughing.

"You don't?" Shane responded, winking.

"Hell, I don't even have a car," Doc said. He leaned against the side of a pickup parked next to Shane's vehicle. With a nod of thanks, he accepted the bottle from Shane, gave the mouth of the whiskey a cursory wipe, and then took a long drink. He coughed, shook his head and held the bottle back out to Shane.

Chuckling, Shane took it back. "What are you doing out here?"

"My morning walk," Doc said, wiping tears from the corners of his eyes. "Or, rather, my morning shuffle."

"Bad?" Shane asked.

"Bad," Doc confirmed. "You know, I was in some hot places. First battle of Fallujah, went in with the Marines. Hajii threw a lot of lead at us."

"He had a habit of doing that," Shane said.

"Yeah," Doc said. "It's why I didn't think I'd die at thirty from something as stupid as a burn pit."

Shane nodded. "Couple of guys I served with, they're sick. Down in Bethesda, getting tested. How come you're not there?"

"Sanford is fine with me," Doc said, accepting the bottle as Shane handed it to him. The man paused, took a drink and passed it back. "There's no cure for what I have. They can't even figure out what's going on with me, other than I'm dying. So, why let them run tests? My family's up here. They can visit a hell of a lot easier than traveling down to Maryland."

"True enough," Shane said. He sipped at the whiskey. "How long have you been here?"

"About a year now," Doc said. He hesitated, then asked, "Do you remember what you said to me when you hit your head?"

"Yeah," Shane said. "I saw a ghost."

Doc looked at him carefully. "You're sure?"

Shane smiled. "I'm sure."

"I've seen her, too," Doc said shortly. "I didn't tell you earlier because I wasn't sure how well you'd handle it. You had a concussion and were definitely suffering from some trauma."

Doc smiled wanly. "I talked with Brett last night. He thinks she may have had something to do with Dr. Georges death, too."

"What?" Shane asked. "Dr. Georges?"

"Yes," Doc said. "You didn't hear about him?"

Shane shook his head, and Doc quickly filled him in on the doctor's death.

"They think it was an aneurysm from drinking?" Shane asked when Doc had finished.

Doc nodded. "They won't do an autopsy or anything. They found him in his office when he didn't show up for an appointment. The light was broken, vomit in his mouth. Looks like he choked on it."

Shane snorted and shook his head. "Guess I lucked out."

"How do you figure?" Doc asked, surprised.

"He was supposed to work on me today," Shane said. "Word was he had a problem with his alcohol."

Doc looked at the whiskey bottle in Shane's hand.

"I don't have a problem," Shane said. Then he grinned, "Besides, I'm not operating on anyone."

He took a last drink, capped the bottle and put it away. After he locked the car up Shane got out a fresh cigarette and glanced at Doc. "Will this bother you?"

Doc shook his head. "Light up. Those'll kill you eventually."

"If I'm lucky enough to live that long," Shane muttered.

"What?" Doc asked as they began the walk back to the building.

"Nothing. Nothing," Shane said. "I'm running my mouth. Anyway, why do you think the Nurse killed Dr. Georges?"

"No one knows why. Usually, she's seen up on E Ward. Rarely downstairs. People think she's, well, like Death. She comes and snatches people up when it's their time," Doc said.

"But she's only been seen up on E Ward?" Shane asked.

"Yup," Doc said. "She's kind of like an open secret, you know? Some of the staff know about her, but they won't talk about her. They say it brings the morale of the patients down."

"So I've heard," Shane said.

Doc glanced at him, but when Shane didn't offer up anymore, he continued on. "Anyway, some of the patients have seen her. They don't like to talk about her. You know, kind of like, 'Speak of the Devil and the Devil appears.'"

"Yeah," Shane said. "I understand. My question is, has anyone ever tried to stop her?"

"What do you mean?" Doc asked. "Like an exorcism or something? Some of that new-age hippy crap about telling the Nurse she's dead and needs to go towards the light?"

Shane laughed. "No, nothing like that. I mean, bound her to something, or found where she's buried then salt and burn her bones."

"Jesus Christ," Doc said, shock on his face and in his voice. "Sounds a little barbaric, man."

Shane shrugged. "Whatever gets the job done."

They started up the handicapped ramp toward the back door.

"Guess I don't have any doubts now," Doc said as they reached the automatic opener.

"Doubts about what?" Shane asked, opening the door for Doc.

"About you being a Marine," Doc replied, grinning. "Only a Marine would be okay with digging up a body, dumping salt on it and lighting it up like a barbecue."

Shane's laughter echoed through the hall as they entered the hospital.

Chapter 15: What Dreams May Come

Shane woke up in his bed.

Not a hospital bed.

His bed.

He looked around the bedroom, a wave of confusion threatening to overwhelm him.

This isn't right, Shane thought. *It's too big.*

Everything was oversized. The dresser was too tall, the door was too big. Even his bed was gigantic. He threw the blankets off, looked down at his legs and stopped.

His legs were small. Small and covered with fine, light brown hair.

Cautiously he held up his hands and saw they were proportionate to his legs, and there was a fresh scab on the back of his left index finger. He had cut it when reaching into a grate for one of his action figures.

When he was twelve.

I am not twelve, Shane thought, forcing himself to get up. The wood floor was cold beneath his feet. He looked around the room at his Star Wars toys, his GI Joe action figures, and a stack of comic books. *I am not twelve.*

"Hello."

Shane looked up and saw the Nurse.

She stood in his room, in front of his door.

"Hello," Shane answered, and his voice was that of a twelve-year-old. "Why are you in my room?"

"I've come to check on you," Ruth said. She took a step further into the room. "You are my patient."

Shane glanced around, trying to see something he could defend himself with.

There was nothing.

"I appreciate your concern," Shane said, "but I'm really okay."

"I think perhaps I am the better judge of your medical condition," she said in a patronizing tone.

"You need to stay away from me," Shane said, putting as much force into his young voice as possible.

Ruth paused, wagged a finger at him and said, "You will have to take a more respectful tone with me, young man, or else I'll make sure they withhold your dessert."

Fear began to eat at Shane. Desperation filled him as she started to walk towards him again. A hypodermic needle appeared in one of her hands while a glass vial was suddenly visible in the other.

"You need to take your medicine," she said, stopping at the side of his bed. Ruth inserted the needle into the vial, drew a dark, foul substance into the instrument, and smiled at him. "It will only hurt for a moment."

"No!" Shane yelled. He twisted on his bed and launched himself off it towards the windows. Behind him, Ruth commanded him to stop. He leapt without looking back.

***

Shane swore as he hit the tile of the hospital room floor. With his chest aching, he turned and saw the Nurse standing beside his bed. A mixed expression of anger and disappointment was on her face.

The door to the room swung open, and she vanished.

Brett hurried into the room, followed by Doc Kiernan.

Shane managed to get to his feet by the time they reached him.

"Are you alright?" Brett asked.

"Fine, now that she's gone," Shane said.

"Who?" Doc asked. "The Nurse?"

Shane nodded.

"Why was she in here?" Brett said.

"To give me my medicine," Shane said bitterly. He sat down on his bed. "In my dream, no less."

When the two men looked at him in confusion, Shane told them what had happened.

"But why did she target you?" Brett asked. "No offense, but other than Dr. Georges, everyone else who's died was old or dying."

"Evidently, I'm special," Shane said.

"Or else she's killing more than we know of," Doc said in a low voice.

Shane and Brett looked at him.

"Honestly," Doc said. "Think about it. What do we know about her, other than that she's said to wander around E Ward offing those already on death row? What if that's not true? What if she's just kept herself busy for however many years? What if she kills whoever she thinks needs killing?"

Shane sighed. "What a terrible idea."

Brett nodded his agreement.

"I didn't say I liked the idea," Doc said. "I was only throwing it out there."

"You may be onto something," Brett said. "I'll have to look into it. See how many fatalities there were over, say, the past year."

"Go back farther," Shane said.

The men looked at him.

"Farther," Shane repeated. "Her uniform is about a hundred years old. Means she was here, or nearby, around the end of the First World War. Possibly during the Influenza Epidemic right after the war. I don't know if there are records going that far back, but look into it, Brett, if you can. I won't be out of here for at least another day or two. Longer if they don't find someone to do the skin graft."

"You should be out by tomorrow," Brett said.

"Good," Shane said, unable to keep the relief out of his voice.

"Going to leave us to our fate?" Doc asked.

Shane shook his head. "Hell no. I've got some stuff at home I'll bring back. Maybe even find a friend or two who might be able to help. If I'm lucky. If not, well, then I'll bring enough material to make sure the Nurse doesn't come back anymore."

"Like what?" Brett asked.

Shane gave them a hard, small smile. "Gasoline and a good supply of matches."

Chapter 16: The Order of St. Benedict

Dom Francis Benedict felt physically ill when he looked at the Sanford Hospital.

This place is bad, he thought, examining every aspect of the building with a critical eye. *This place is downright terrible.*

A small part of him urged retreat, a return to the car and a quick trip back to the college. But only a small part.

I place my life in your hands, Oh Lord, Francis thought, and he walked to the front of the hospital. When he entered the building there was a terrible chill to the air, a foul scent hiding behind the normal smells of a hospital. He paused in front of the main desk and a young woman looked up from her phone. It took her a moment to realize he was a religious man, and when she did, she hastily put her phone down.

She smiled nervously and said, "Good morning, Father."

"Good morning," Francis said, smiling. "But it's Dom Francis, or Brother if that's easier. And don't worry, this isn't Catholic school. You're not in trouble for looking at your phone."

The young woman blushed. "That obvious?"

Francis grinned and nodded. "I'm here to visit with some of the residents. I usually start with the oldest, if they have a desire to speak with me."

"Hm," she said. "That would definitely be Matias Geisel, but he's not Catholic. I think he's Lutheran."

"I'm not here to convert," Francis said gently.

"Oh, okay," the young woman said. "Well, he usually has visitors, but he may want some more company. He's in Room 20, A Ward. Just go up the stairs, through the double doors and take a right. Matias is in the last room on the left."

"Thank you very much," Francis said. "I didn't get your name."

"Sarah," she said. "Sarah Hall, Brother."

"A pleasure, Sarah," Francis said. He waved goodbye and followed her directions. The hallway leading to Matias Geisel's room was filled with myriad sounds, a veritable cacophony. People talking, televisions playing, announcements over the speaker system. A couple in another room were arguing, and Francis had to focus on the reason he had come to Sanford.

He knocked on the door.

"Come in!" a voice called out.

Francis did so, and he found an extremely old man sitting alone in an easy chair. Framed photographs lined the walls, covered his bureau, and gave a brief glimpse into the vast family Matias Geisel enjoyed.

Matias had a rollaway table in front of him, a half-finished game of solitaire dealt out. He had a fresh cup of coffee and a piece of toast as well, and he looked pleasantly surprised at Francis.

"I have to say," Matias said with a grin, "this isn't something I expected when I awoke this morning."

"I'm glad," Francis said. He walked closer, shook Matias' hand and introduced himself.

"Have a seat, Dom Francis," Matias said, gesturing towards the room's other chair.

Book 4: Sanford Hospital

"Thank you," he said as he sat down. "I'm here to visit and to talk."

"Me in particular?" Matias asked with a raised eyebrow.

"No," Francis said, smiling. "Everyone who would like a little conversation."

"I never say no to a little conversation. Or even a lot," Matias said, winking. "You must be from St. Anselm's College."

Matias nodded. "I am."

"Yes, I've only seen a few Benedictine monks, and they have all been here in New Hampshire," Matias said. He took a sip of his coffee and then said, "I'm being terribly impolite. Would you like me to see if someone could bring you a cup of coffee?"

"No, thank you," Francis said. "I had some this morning when I broke my fast. Too much and I'll never be able to sit still through evening prayers."

Outside the room's single window, clouds settled in front of the sun, casting a dim shadow over the two men. Matias reached out, found the switch for the lamp on his end table and turned the light on.

"I don't appreciate the dark anymore," Matias said. "Too many years of doing things most men should never have to. You have the bearing of a military man, Dom Francis. I've never seen it in a religious way before."

"I was in the Army before I took my vows," Francis said.

"I suppose that explains it then," Matias said, chuckling.

The light flickered, went out, came back on, and flickered again.

Both men looked at it.

A moment later, the bulb shattered, glass embedding itself in the lamp shade and scattering across the floor. The temperature in the room plummeted. In the dim light, Francis's breath came billowing out in great clouds.

The sensation of unease which he had felt when he had first walked into the building magnified a hundred fold and Francis stood up.

"Sit down," Matias said gently. "We can't do anything against her, not if she's set her mind to it."

"Who?" Francis asked, looking over at the old man.

"The Nurse," Matias said. "Now sit. Please."

Francis sat.

The room grew colder, goose bumps erupting on Francis's entire body. Then, from the left wall, a figure emerged. A woman, dressed in a nurse's uniform Francis had only seen in books. She looked at them both, a stern expression on a face which was undeniably pretty.

"Father," she said, looking at Francis.

He didn't bother to try and correct her. Francis was trying to accept the reality of her presence.

"I must ask you to be sparing with your time with Mr. Geisel. He is old and I've not yet decided if he's to have his appointment today or not," the Nurse said. She smiled at Matias and said to him, "It may be today, Mr. Geisel. It may not. Best to be prepared."

With a nod to them both, she turned and left the way she had come. The room slowly warmed up, and Francis looked at Matias.

Matias picked up the call button for the nurse on duty, pressed it and looked at Francis. "Would you like a cup of coffee now, Dom Francis?"

Francis could only nod as the image of the dead nurse etched itself into his memory.

Chapter 17: Visiting Some Friends

Nurse Platte had been upset when Shane left the hospital. It was only after he had promised to return for treatment, that she had discharged him.

Shane enjoyed a large drink of whiskey and two rapidly smoked cigarettes before he left the parking lot. He picked up a coffee from a gas station and sent a request for assistance via text.

The response had been quick.

Come on by.

Thirty-seven minutes later, he pulled into a driveway on Old Nashua Road, parked the car and shut the engine off. He walked up the stairs of the farm house, stepped onto the porch and knocked on the door.

It opened a second later, and Brian Roy stood in front of him, grinning.

"Shane," Brian said, holding out his hand, "how the hell are you?"

"Terrible," Shane replied, shaking Brian's hand and then pulling the man in for a hug. They clapped each other on the back.

"Come on in," Brian said, stepping away from the door. He turned and called down the hallway, "Jenny, Shane's here!"

From the kitchen, Jenny said, "Hi Shane!"

"Hey Jenny," Shane called back. Brian closed and locked the door. Together they walked into the small den. Shane plopped down in a chair while Brian went to the loveseat.

"This," Jenny said, "is as domestic as I'm getting today."

She sat with Brian on the loveseat and Shane looked at Brian. "You doing okay?"

"Fair enough," Shane said.

"Tell us what's going on," she said.

Shane settled back into the chair, and told them about Sanford Hospital. He kept the bit about Nurse Ruth invading his dream for the last.

The color drained from Jenny and Brian's faces.

"Jesus," Brian said after a moment. "I've never even heard of anything like that."

"I have," Jenny said, and both Brian and Shane looked at her. "I've been reading through different books from a friend's library. One of them talked about ghosts and demons conducting psychic attacks through dreams."

"Did they say how to defend yourself against the attacks?" Shane asked, leaning forward. "I've got to go back up there, and more than likely it'll be for a little bit. I'd rather not have her choke me to death in my sleep before I can figure out what to do with her."

"There was," Jenny said, "but I'll have to look it up. I don't remember, and I sure as hell don't want to give you the wrong name."

"Yeah," Brian said. "That would be a pain."

"Be right back, I want to check the books upstairs." She got up and left the room. Shane looked at Brian, at the scars on the man's head and the glitter of steel-capped teeth in his mouth.

"Man," Shane said, "you look like an extra from an apocalyptic movie. What the hell happened?"

"Just some trouble with a ghost," Brian said.

"Looks like you got worked over pretty good," Shane said.

"More than pretty good," Brian said bitterly. "I do research every once in a while, but it's Jenny who does most of it. She works hard. And don't let her kid you about reading a little bit. She's reading about a book a day. Sometimes more if they're smaller."

"Wow," Shane said.

"Wow is right," Brian said.

"What's wow?" Jenny asked, walking back into the room. She had a small book in her hand.

"I was telling Shane how much you read," Brian said.

She grinned. "Yeah. A little bit."

"I guess so," Shane said, chuckling. "So, what's the deal with psychic attacks? I've never dealt with this before."

"It's not common," Jenny said. "There's stuff about it in ghost lore, but usually it takes an incredibly strong ghost."

"Okay," Shane said. "But you know, I've faced off against some miserable spirits. And they were strong. Really strong. No one tried to reach in my head before while I was asleep."

"There are a lot of factors," Brian said. "From the research I've seen, one of the biggest is voluntary energy sharing. I don't know how this ghost of yours operates, but look at Josephus."

Jenny scoffed at the mention of the dead man's name.

Brian nodded. "Yeah, Babe, I feel the same way. But the point I'm trying to make is all of his power must have come from the other spirits he kept there. He was an energy vampire. Stealing the power. So while he was strong, he wasn't as strong as he could have been if they had given him their energy voluntarily."

"What we're thinking," Jenny added, "is that your ghost is getting her boost from the willing, and that really makes all the difference in the world when it comes to being able to attack psychically."

"She might fit the bill," Shane said after a minute. "She's been operating for a long time at Sanford. And I think she's got a lot of support there. And that could do it?"

Jenny nodded. "Yes, as long as she's able to feed off their energy, yeah. Definitely."

"Like we said," Brian added, "voluntary is the key."

"Great," Shane said, sighing. "So, how do I keep her from ripping me apart while I sleep?"

"Couple of different ways to defend yourself," Jenny said. She opened the book, flipped to a page near the end and nodded to herself. "The only one I think has some real merit, and some actual testimony from reputable ghost sites is the herb, betony. I know there's a new herbal shop in Nashua, so you may be able to find it there. If not, you'll have to call around."

"What do I do with it?" Shane asked. "Wear it like a charm?"

Jenny shook her head. "No. Sprinkle it around your pillow. It probably wouldn't hurt to scatter it around your bed either."

Shane took his phone out, brought up the notepad app, and entered 'betony'. "Thanks, Jenny."

"You're welcome," she said. "I wish there was more we could do without putting my man-child here in harm's way."

"No worries there," Shane said, grinning. "I've got a couple of hard-charging veterans up at Sanford. We'll get it done."

"I'm sure you will," Brian said. He looked down at his hands and sighed.

"Something wrong with the drink?" Jenny asked with a wry smile.

Brian nodded.

Shane looked at him and asked, "What?"

"No whiskey in it," Brian said, and Shane laughed as Jenny slapped her husband on the arm.

Book 4: Sanford Hospital

Chapter 18: Matias Waits Alone

Matias knew he would die. Everyone did.

He had seen hundreds of men killed. Thousands wounded. He knew what it was like to choke the life out of a man, and what it meant to try to pick up the pieces of a friend killed by artillery fire.

Matias had been a killer – one of the finest. He didn't suffer from nightmares or regrets. Matias knew plenty of men and women who were afflicted with post-traumatic stress, but he wasn't one of them. He had found peace in war. Without a doubt, Matias had been a war-junkie, one of the few who constantly sought out strife.

The wound in his hip had ended his relationship with war and forced him to build one with his wife.

He reflected upon all of it as he looked at the pictures in his room, photographs of his children, grandchildren, and his great-grandchildren. In the top drawer of his dresser was a photo-album filled with pictures of friends, most of them dead. A few of the younger ones, those with whom he had fought in Vietnam, remained.

Matias sighed, turned his attention away from the memories and looked at the lamp. Raphael, one of the orderlies, had been kind enough to clean up the mess and replace the bulb. The curious Benedictine monk, Dom Francis, had stayed for some time, and Matias had explained what he knew about the Nurse.

Francis had listened intently, absorbing all of the information. When Matias had finished, Francis had thanked him and left, saying he would return soon.

Matias had no other visitors for the day, which wasn't unusual. His grandchildren and great-grandchildren were active in various athletic events, and so his children were busy with them.

Matias smiled and wondered what videos they would bring to him.

He shivered suddenly, and he realized the room had gotten colder. The light flickered, and Matias turned it off. He was left in near total darkness, only a faint bar of illumination slipping in between the door and the floor.

Something passed through the light, a faint shadow.

"Hello, Mr. Geisel," the Nurse said.

"Good evening, Nurse," Matias said. His voice reflected his fatigue. "To what do I owe this pleasure?"

"I've come to tell you that I'll be administering your medicine soon," she said. "I wanted to be certain you knew."

"I don't particularly want any medicine," Matias said. "In fact, I'm fairly positive I don't need any."

"Mr. Geisel," she scolded, "you will take your medicine, as per my orders."

"I thank you for your concern, Nurse," Matias said, mustering as much authority as possible, and applying it to his tone. "But I will decide my own course of treatment."

Before she could reply, the door opened and light filled the room. Matias turned his head away and closed his eyes. He heard the click of the switch and the overhead fluorescents flickered to life.

"Oh Jesus," someone whispered, and Matias opened his eyes.

He looked through the Nurse and saw a young woman, one of the new third shift nurses, standing in the doorway. Her eyes were wide with surprise, her jaw open.

"Who are you?" the new woman asked, fear in her voice. "What are you doing in here?"

The Nurse turned to face her and said in a harsh voice, "Mr. Geisel is my patient. You will do well to leave the room and leave his care to me."

The young woman shook her head, and although Matias could hear a tremor of panic in her voice, she said, "You need to leave."

"It's alright," Matias said hurriedly. "Leave the room, please."

"No," the new nurse said, strength replacing the panic. "No. Nurse, you are not on duty on this floor. You have no authority or control over Mr. Geisel's treatment. You need to leave now."

"I am tired of people questioning my treatments," the Nurse snarled. "Leave. Now!"

"No," the young woman said. "You will not treat Mr. Geisel."

"How dare you!" the Nurse Spat, enraged at the challenge. "How *dare you!* I know what is best for *my patients!*"

"No," the new nurse stuttered. "No."

The temperature in the room plummeted.

"No one," the Nurse hissed, "interferes with me. *No one denies me!*"

The ghost became a blur of motion. In less than a heartbeat, she crossed the distance between her and the young woman, and she smashed into the living nurse as the door slammed shut. The new nurse was hurled into the wood, her head smacking obscenely against it.

She groaned as she sank down to the floor, a small smear of blood trailing down the door.

Matias grabbed the panic button and jammed his finger into it.

The Nurse leaned over her, grabbed the woman by her throat and lifted her up. The young woman's eyes rolled in her head as spit gathered in the corners of her mouth. Someone tried to open the door but it wouldn't budge. They pounded against it.

The Nurse slammed the young woman into the door repeatedly in reply. Soon, she was limp in the Nurse's hands. The door shuddered, both from the blows outside the room and within it.

Fragments of bone became embedded in the wood and long strands of the young woman's black hair were caught there as well. The whites of her eyes were distinctly visible between her half-closed lids. Her pink scrubs became stained with her blood and at some point, she had lost control of her bladder. Her legs twitched, her feet went into spasms, and her fingers danced about madly as if she were frantically typing out a letter.

Slowly Matias heard the people on the other side of the door as they yelled to him and to the newly dead nurse. Matias tried to answer, but his voice refused to obey him.

Finally, the Nurse dropped the young woman's body to the floor and turned to face him once more.

The look on her face was cold and hard. She smoothed out her uniform, looked at him and said, "Mr. Geisel, I am the only nurse in charge of your care. I know what you need, and I shall administer it. All others will be warned, and then punished accordingly."

The Nurse vanished, and the door was thrust open and struck the woman's body. It was pushed across the floor, smearing blood on the linoleum.

Chapter 19: Home Again

Shane had found betony at the shop off of Main Street in Nashua. The herb, which he had bought in bulk, smelled like black tea.

It could smell like manure, Shane thought as he got out of the car with the bag in hand, *as long as it does the trick.*

He went up the stairs and into his house, closing the door behind him. Shane looked around the hallway and came to a stop. "Hello!"

A second later, Eloise appeared from a dark corner. The dead girl smiled and waved at him. Shane returned the wave and approached the ghost.

"Where is everyone?" he asked, sinking into a squat to speak with her.

Eloise shrugged. "I was playing hide and seek with Thaddeus, but I was the one who was hiding."

"Do you know why Thaddeus left?"

"Yes," Eloise said, her voice, dropping to a whisper. "Courtney and Carl are fighting."

Shane frowned. "Where?"

"Your bedroom. She doesn't want him in your room."

"Great," Shane said, sighing. "Just what I need."

He got to his feet and went up the main staircase to the second floor. As he approached the door to his room, the air became painfully cold, hurting his lungs with each breath.

Damn it, he thought. The doorknob was nearly frozen as he grabbed and twisted it, shoving the door open. Shane shivered as he stepped into the room, the muscles in his jaw tightening.

Carl and Courtney stood a few feet into the room, their forms pulsing with energy. Courtney's body reflected her death, her neck with a curious crick in it.

Carl stood thin and tall, and he and Courtney glared at one another.

"Enough!" Shane snapped. "You've made my bedroom a god damned freezer!"

The two ghosts looked at him, shame and surprise on their faces.

"I don't want to know why you're fighting," Shane said, holding up a hand. "I really don't care. Carl, I've asked you not to enter the room when I'm not in it. I'll meet you in the study shortly, please."

Carl hesitated for a moment, and then gave a short bow before he vanished.

The temperature in the room warmed noticeably.

Courtney looked at him and his heart ached at the sight of her.

She smiled. "How are you?"

"Tired," Shane replied. He put the bag of betony on his dresser and went to his bed. Quietly, he sat down and took off his shoes.

"Did they do your skin graft?" Courtney asked, sitting down beside him.

"No," Shane answered.

A cold finger traced the line of his jaw. Softly she said, "I love you, Shane Ryan."

Shane choked back a sob and managed to whisper, "I love you too."

Chapter 20: Back at Sanford

Brett paced Doc's room, nervous and afraid of the Nurse. There hadn't been any more reports, no strange deaths after an unknown aide's 'epileptic fit'. The one which caused her to repeatedly slam the back of her head into the door and keep three adults from opening it.

"Brett," Doc said. "Calm down, you're making me anxious."

Brett looked over at the younger man and frowned. "Sorry."

He sat down in a chair and glanced at the empty bed.

"You need to relax," Doc said. "At least a little bit."

"It's difficult for me," Brett said. "There's a murderous ghost on the loose in the hospital."

"And evidently, she's been here for a while," Doc countered.

Brett nodded and rubbed his temples. "I know we've always had deaths on E Ward. It's expected. But why downstairs? Why Matias?"

"He's old," Doc said. "Maybe she thinks it's time?"

"And the young woman? The aide?"

Doc shook his head. "She got in the way? I don't know, Brett. I really don't. But you pacing back and forth isn't going to solve anything. Anyway, have you gotten any word from Shane?"

"Yeah," Brett said, easing back into the chair. "He said he had something to help keep her at bay. Should be back tomorrow with it."

"Good."

Silence arose between the two men. After several minutes, Doc said, "How the hell does someone get involved with ghosts?"

"I have no idea, but he seems to know what he's talking about."

"Yeah," Doc said, grinning. "I was thinking about that earlier. Guy was a career Marine, usually not your ghostly type."

"No," Brett agreed. "Then again, I haven't had a whole lot of experience with ghosts. You?"

"Not really," Doc said. "Thought there was a ghost in my house as a kid, but who knows, you know?"

"Yes," Brett said, sighing. He stood up. "Alright, I've got to do my rounds, make sure everyone's okay. Karen's almost asleep at the desk."

"Sure thing," Doc said, lying back on his bed. "I'll be here. Writing my movie."

Brett paused and looked over at Doc. "Your movie?"

"Yeah," Doc said, smiling. "A bio pic. My exciting life. Lots of action, car chases, gun fights, beautiful models. You know. The normal American experience."

"Am I in it?" Brett asked.

"Everyone's in it."

"Who's going to play you?" Brett asked.

"Ryan Reynolds."

"And who's going to play me?" Brett said.

"Samuel L. Jackson," Doc said, snickering.

Brett laughed. "But I'm white."

"Doesn't matter," Doc said, putting his hands behind his head and looking up at the ceiling. "It's a requirement. Every movie has to have Samuel L. Jackson in it, and he's playing you."

"You're out of your mind, Doc," Brett said, shaking his head.

"Only all of the time," Doc said. "Talk to you soon."

Brett waved goodbye and left the dying man behind. The hallway was filled with the noise of machines, respirators, and monitors. He walked to the nurse's station and found Karen asleep. Her head lolled to one side, she snorted, and a thin line of drool spilled out one of the corners of her mouth.

How do you keep your job, Karen? he thought. Brett wanted to walk around the back of the desk and push her onto the floor, and then ask her if she was okay, but he didn't.

An uncomfortable sensation tickled the back of his neck. Brett slapped at it, but it happened again, and he turned around.

His heart skipped a beat before it began to hammer against his chest.

A tall man, cadaver-like in appearance, stood by the elevator door. The man was naked, his pale flesh covered in liver spots. Thin wisps of white hair clung to his head. Equally sparse hair hung from his cheeks and chin. His nose was long, almost dagger-like, the eyes close-set on either side of it. They were gray and cold and lifeless.

Brett could see the elevator door through him.

The tall man's long fingers twitched along the sides of his bare thighs, each hand looking like an anxious spider.

Brett gulped.

The man stared at Brett and whispered in a low, raspy voice, "Name."

Brett shook his head.

"Name."

"Brett."

"Jacob."

Jacob's head twitched, his upper lip curled into a sneer. Nearly black teeth were revealed, terrible incisors that reminded Brett of the horror movies he had watched as a teenager.

"Brett," Jacob said.

"Yes?"

"Leave the Nurse alone," Jacob said, and there was a deadly tone in his gritty voice. "She has a task to carry out. As do we all. I will make *you* my task if you do not allow her to do hers. Am I understood, Brett?"

Brett nodded.

"Good." Jacob looked past Brett at Karen. "Wake her up. Before I kill her. I hate sloth."

"Alright," Brett whispered.

Jacob nodded, turned, and stepped through the elevator door.

Brett's body trembled and he stood in place for a moment.

What's going on? he finally asked himself. *How many ghosts are there? What am I going to do?*

Then Brett remembered Jacob's threat. Still trembling, Brett hurried around the desk to wake Karen up.

Chapter 21: A Struggle Within

Francis sat on his narrow bunk in his room at the residence. He held his rosary in his hands, the feel of the wood comforting. His thumb traced the familiar image of Christ on the crucifix.

He had prayed for nearly two days, attempting to come to a conclusion as to what had to be done. When he had first returned from Sanford Hospital, he had gone immediately to the Abbot. They had spoken for hours about what Francis had seen, and what it meant to the patients at the facility.

The Abbot believed it was Francis' decision when it came to the ghost. If he was to defend the sick and wounded from the dead nurse, or to let her do what she willed.

Francis' initial reaction had been to fight. It was what he did best. Yet he had continued to pray on the issue. *Was that a battle God wanted?*

A single memory from his first deployment in Afghanistan leapt forward in his mind. Francis recalled a house with an old man in it, a tired and sick Afghani who the local Mujahedeen had come to kill.

Francis and his team had stayed with the man and fought off the Mujahedeen. The Afghani had died in his sleep during the firefight.

Their lives must run their course, Francis thought. *She does not decide. Only God can, and God has put me in her way.*

Francis stood up and slipped his rosary into his pocket. He needed to eat, and then speak with the Abbot about taking time off to return to Sanford Hospital and battle the Nurse.

It will be good to fight again, he thought.

Chapter 22: On the Stairs

Ian Hays had been an orderly at various Veteran hospitals for over twenty years. He knew the routines, and he liked them. Ian kept his mouth shut, did his job, and went home. He never complained, paid his Union dues, and made sure he made it to at least one Red Sox game in the spring, one Patriots game in the fall, and one Bruins game in the winter.

Ian stifled a yawn, walked up the back stairs towards B Ward and resisted the urge to slip into an empty bed and sleep. He had picked up a shift for another orderly, and while the additional hours were nice, Ian knew he was going to suffer for it in the morning.

He turned the corner of a landing and shivered.

Seriously? he thought. *Who the hell put the air-conditioning on?*

Ian continued up, and the cold increased. Finally, he stopped on the landing in front of B Ward and looked around.

This is terrible, he thought. *Cold like this is going to drift out into the wards and chill the folks.*

The door to the ward opened and Ian glanced over to see who it was.

When he did, his breath caught in his throat.

The Nurse stood in front of him. Her expression was full of malice, her shoulders hunched.

"What are you doing?" she demanded.

Ian's thoughts raced. He had heard of others bumping into her, and he tried to remember how they had gotten away from her.

Honesty, Ian thought. *I'll be honest.*

"It's cold in here," Ian said. "I'm trying to see what's wrong. I don't want the patients to be cold."

"But I do," she remarked.

Ian blinked, shook his head and said, "I'm sorry, what?"

"I want them to be cold." She took a step forward. "Too many haven't been listening."

"Oh," Ian said, stepping back. He put his hand out and grasped the railing.

"I don't like it when people interfere," the Nurse continued. Her eyes narrowed. "I don't like it at all."

Ian became aware of the stillness in the stairwell. A curious silence washed over them.

"No one should ever interfere with me," she whispered. The Nurse stepped forward, placed her hands upon his chest, and pushed.

Her strength was incredible, and Ian found himself falling. His sneakers lost their grip on the old, green tile, and for a moment Ian felt like an Olympic diver as he hung in the air.

Then he smashed into the stairs, tumbling down and yelling out. Ian hit the landing, rolled and smashed into the old electric radiator against the wall. He struggled to regain control over his feet, but the Nurse was there.

Painfully cold hands gripped him, lifted him up until he was above her head, and she hurled him down the next flight. Everything slowed down, as though someone had suddenly hit the half-speed button on a DVD player.

Minutes, it seemed, passed as he hung in the air, and then the floor rushed up to meet him.

Chapter 23: Shane Prepares for the Nurse

"Where are you going?" Carl asked in German.

Shane looked up from the desk in the library. The ghost stood by the door with an inquisitive expression.

"Back to the veteran's hospital in Sanford," Shane explained, also in German.

"What's going on there?"

"There's a ghost who seems to think she decides when it's time for a patient to die," Shane replied. He looked down at the items before him. A pump-action shotgun and twenty shells, loaded with rock-salt, the iron knuckledusters, several boxes of salt, lighter fluid, matches, a lighter, and a bag of steel wool. "Everything but a Bible," Shane murmured.

"What was that, my young friend?" Carl asked, moving further into the room.

"Nothing," Shane said. He collapsed into the desk chair. From a pocket, he took out his cigarettes and lit one. "This one is going to be difficult, I think."

"How so?" Carl said.

"She's decided she knows best," Shane said, exhaling the smoke through his nostrils. "And, from what I can figure, there are those who agree with her. Both the living and the dead, it's the only way she's been able to operate so freely for such a long time. If that's the case, then it means I may be facing more than this nurse."

"Will you have assistance?"

"I hope so," Shane said. "There's Brett on E Ward, the floor she likes to roam around on. Plus there's Doc, a combat vet who's dying of God knows what. He's set. I think there may be one or two more. If we can work together and get it done, yeah, it'll be okay."

"And if not?" Carl asked.

"Then all of this," Shane said, gesturing to the material on the desk, "well, it may be enough to get me out of the building and into the car. Then again, it may not. I'll find out when I try."

Carl nodded. "Have you told the others?"

"What others?" Shane asked, confused. "The people at Sanford?"

"No," Carl said. "The rest of us here. Have you informed them of your intentions? Have you let them know you may not be returning from this excursion?"

Shane shook his head.

"If I may ask, my friend, but why?" Carl asked.

"Why would I?" Shane said. He looked at the shotgun. "I either make it back or I don't, Carl. No need to worry anyone."

"Let us worry, my friend," Carl pleaded. "We are your family, are we not?"

"Yeah," Shane whispered. He picked up the weapon, double checked the loads were in and said again, "Yeah."

Chapter 24: Talking about Ruth

"How are you doing?" Nancy asked.

Matias looked at the younger woman and smiled. "I'm doing well, considering how old I am."

She frowned. "I meant with what happened to the aide."

"I know what you meant," Matias said gently. "It was a sad sight, and I am sorry she died in such a way."

"That's it?" Nancy asked, shock in her voice.

Matias nodded and said, "Is there something more you would like me to express?"

She shook her head. "I don't understand."

"Don't try to," Matias said. "Let it be."

Nancy hesitated, then said, "No. No, I can't let it be. Matias, how can you be so cold?"

"I'm a killer, Nurse Platte," he said softly. "I may be old, but I am still a killer. If I could have stopped the death, I would have."

"Regardless, you couldn't have stopped her seizure," Nancy said. She took a sip of her coffee, the Styrofoam container shaking in her hand.

"It wasn't a seizure," Matias said.

"Of course, it was," Nancy said. "What else could it be?"

"You're asking the wrong question," Matias said. "It is not a question of what, but of who."

"You're saying she was murdered?" Nancy asked, dumbfounded. "By who? You? There was no one else in the room, and you certainly don't have the strength to do the damage she did to herself."

"The Nurse did it."

Nancy scoffed. "I've told you before, Matias, there's no such thing as a killer nurse roaming the hallowed halls of Sanford."

"Is it really so difficult for you to accept?" Matias asked, his own voice rising. "Do you think such an entity could not exist?"

"I don't know," Nancy snapped. "But I highly doubt a ghost could kill someone, Matias. It's absurd."

"Perhaps," Matias said. "But I will tell you this, Nancy. Last night was not the first time I have seen the Nurse. I pray it is the last, mind you, although I doubt it. She will inevitably be the death of me."

Nancy put her coffee down on the table, stood up and walked to the new door. She looked at it for a moment before she turned around and faced him. "Mark in maintenance told me they asked if you wanted a different room. You refused."

"I did," Matias agreed.

"Why?" she demanded.

"This was my room before, and for an exceptionally long time," Matias said. "Why would I move because of death?"

"But it was a terrible death," Nancy said in an imploring tone.

"Do you know so little about me?" he asked.

She frowned, a look of confusion flickering across her face. "What do you mean?"

"Have you ever looked at my file?" Matias said.

Nancy shook her head.

"What war do you think I fought in?"

"World War 2," she said. "You're the right age for it."

"You're correct," Matias said. "I also fought in the Korean War."

"Alright," she said. "You fought in two wars."

"And Vietnam."

Nancy hesitated and then said, "Three?"

He nodded.

"Why?" she asked though she feared she already knew the answer.

"Because I liked it," Matias said. "Because, quite frankly, I was good at it."

"What?" she asked.

"Haven't you ever wondered what I did?" Matias said.

"No," she said, shaking her head. "Why would I?"

"Perhaps you should have."

"Matias," Nancy said. "Lots of men feel guilt over their roles. It doesn't mean they did anything."

"Nancy," Matias cut in. "I did something. Lots of somethings. I killed men with my bare hands. I killed them with knives. I shot them. Garroted them. Blew them up. And I drowned them."

Nancy looked at him, horror growing in her eyes.

"I killed them when I was a teenager, as a man in my twenties, thirties, and forties," Matias continued. "I butchered them in their sleep, then I went home and raised a family. Baseball? Wonderful. Taking out a guard by puncturing his lungs? Fantastic. Are you beginning to understand?"

"Yes," she whispered.

"As you can see," Matias said, "I had an extremely marketable skill set. I happened to remain with the Army for the entire time. Don't believe that I did it for love of country. First, it was the thrill of fighting, then it became an addiction. A need. Had I not been injured so severely in Vietnam, I would have done as much time there as possible."

A long silence filled the room and the horrified look on Nancy's face saddened him.

"You really don't care?" she said softly.

"It's not that I don't care," Matias corrected. "It doesn't bother me. The manner of her death depresses me. But it doesn't bother me."

Slowly Nancy walked back to the chair, sat down and picked up her coffee. She brought the cup up to her mouth, and then, without taking a drink, lowered it. Nancy looked hard into Matias's eyes.

"You're telling me the truth about the Nurse?"

"Yes," Matias replied.

"Do you know who she is?" Nancy asked.

"I know who she was," Matias said. "Or, rather, I know a good deal about who she was."

"Why was she here yesterday?" Nancy said.

"She warned me that it would be my time soon," Matias said.

"What?"

"My time to die," Matias said. "She said she had made the decision."

"What? Why?" Nancy asked.

Matias shrugged. "I wish I knew."

Nancy nodded her agreement. "Tell me."

"Tell you what?" Matias asked.

"Everything about yesterday," Nancy said. "I need to know."

Matias nodded, and he began to talk.

Chapter 25: Sweet Dreams

Karen Conlon loved the beach.

She lay on her back, sunglasses on and the warm sun beating down. In the background, she heard the crash of waves and smelled the strong, pungent scent of the Atlantic Ocean. The towel beneath her was thick, brand new and purchased especially for the trip to Ogunquit. The radio was playing a soft R&B song she didn't quite catch, but it had a beat that made her smile. She adjusted her position slightly and wondered how the day could get any better.

A shadow fell across her face, and Karen opened her eyes. Through the dark lenses of her sunglasses, she saw a woman. A nurse.

What in God's name is she wearing? Karen thought. *Damn thing looks like it came out of a costume shop!* It reminded Karen of the uniforms early nurses had worn. *Really early nurses.*

"Hey," Karen said. "Not to be a jerk here or anything, but you're standing directly in my sun."

"Your sun?" the woman asked. Her voice was sweet, melodic. "I didn't know it was yours alone."

"It's not," Karen snapped. "But, you've got the whole beach to stand on. So, go stand somewhere else. You're blocking me from getting a tan."

"I don't want to stand on the whole beach," the strange nurse said. "I want to stand here. Next to you."

"What are you, some kind of weirdo?" Karen asked, pushing herself up into a sitting position. She took off her glasses and looked at the woman. "Come on. Get out of here or I'll call the lifeguard over, and he'll deal with you."

"What lifeguard?"

Karen turned around to yell to a lifeguard, and she realized there wasn't one. In fact, there wasn't anyone on the beach other than herself and the mystery nurse.

Karen looked around quickly. There were dunes, but no houses behind them. Waves and the expanse of the ocean, yet no ships sailed on it. Even the lighthouse was missing from the Point. Her mouth went dry, and she clambered to her feet. She stood up and saw her towel was gone.

"What's going on?" Karen asked, her heartbeat quickening.

"You're being called to task," the nurse said, all trace of pleasantness gone from her voice. "You have been lax in the care of your patients."

Karen's anger flared. She pointed a finger at the stranger and said, "You listen to me—"

Before she could continue, the nurse looked at Karen's extended digit, and Karen screamed.

Horrified, she watched as her finger bent backward at an unnatural angle. The bones broke crisply, and a pair of jagged ends suddenly protruded from her skin.

Gasping in pain, Karen dropped to her knees. She held the mangled finger in front of her as she began to hyperventilate.

The stranger smiled and asked, "Do you remember what the term hematemesis stands for?"

Karen shook her head. The pain was tremendous, a terrifying weight crushing her.

"Do you remember Sergeant Allen O'Hare?"

"No," Karen said, gasping. "What are you talking about?"

"He was a young man, little more than a boy, really, at Sanford last month," the woman explained. "He bled out. He called for you to help him. In the end, as I sat beside him, he called for his mother. Nothing more than a whisper. He could barely breathe; his throat raw. Do you remember now? The floor covered in blood?"

Karen remembered. The mess. The blood everywhere. The organs falling apart.

"He died," Karen said, holding her injured hand. "Why does it matter?"

"Because," the stranger said. "I didn't wish it. I hadn't decided it was his time."

The woman straightened up. "Hematemesis, Nurse. What is it?"

Karen shook her head.

The stranger leaned in close and whispered, "Bloody vomiting."

Karen felt her stomach cramp, and she doubled over, the strong taste of blood filled her mouth. She opened her mouth to scream and vomited instead.

Chapter 26: A Disturbing Event

Brett sat at the nurse's station, frustrated as he shook Karen again. She opened her eyes, glared at him, and went back to sleep. No matter how many times he woke her, the woman refused to stay awake.

Brett resisted thoughts about the Nurse. He had a recurring fear about the dead woman stepping out of the room, and the old man from the elevator joining her.

Karen groaned beside him, and he glanced over at her. She twitched in the chair and let out a whimper.

Bad dream, Karen? Brett thought angrily. *Maybe you shouldn't sleep on your shift.*

He turned away from her and focused on the crossword puzzle from the day's paper. Brett tapped the pen on the desktop, whistled softly to himself, and was promptly interrupted by Karen. The woman hacked noisily, and Brett twisted to face her.

She needs to wake up, he thought, reaching out for her.

As his hand touched the light blue shirt she wore, Karen jerked upright. Her eyes snapped open, and she screamed, "No!"

No other words followed.

Instead, Karen fell forward, grabbed the edge of the station. She opened her mouth wide and vomited.

A dark red, arterial blood sprayed out of her mouth. It dripped from her lips and down her chin. The fluid stained her scrubs and misted out over the paperwork and the monitors.

Karen stumbled back, short of breath, and Brett watched as she caught hold of the chair. She looked at him, terror in her eyes, and she vomited again. The blood launched from her mouth and caught his neck and chin, soaking him instantly. The smell struck him like a fist.

She's dying, Brett realized. He stepped forward, tried to take hold of her arms and she let out a scream. Her eyes darted about madly and for a third time she threw-up. Karen began to fall, and Brett eased her to the floor. He reached up under the desktop and hit the panic button.

She tried to roll onto her back, but he stopped her, forcing her to remain on her side. He kept her head tilted slightly, and she convulsed in his hands. From the rooms he heard patients calling, asking what was going on.

Doc arrived shortly and knelt down in the blood. He pried open Karen's mouth, swept it with a finger and pulled out the tip of her tongue. Wordlessly Brett plucked a pen from the desktop and slipped it between Karen's teeth.

"Brett," Doc said. "Look at her pants."

Brett did so, and he shuddered at the sight. The groin and rear were both stained with blood, more of the fluid leaking out onto the floor.

"She won't make it," Brett said.

Doc nodded.

"I don't think she's even here now," Brett continued.

Doc nodded.

"It's alright, Brett," Doc said, putting a hand on Brett's shoulder. "She's okay where she is. They always are."

In less than a minute the elevator doors opened, and the crash team raced out. Soon they had taken over, and Brett and Doc were removed to a separate room to be quarantined until it was determined what exactly Karen had died from.

Chapter 27: Going into the Hospital

Shane had gone through half a pack of Luckys by the time he reached Sanford. When he parked in the back lot, the sun had already begun to set.

Shane sat in the car for a minute and wondered, *Maybe I should have come up in the morning.*

Then a cold voice, which reminded him distinctly of Drill Instructor Allen, said, *Are you afraid of the dark now?*

Yup, Shane thought. But he got out of the car anyway. He went around to the trunk, opened it, took out his backpack and slung it over his shoulders. Shane slammed the trunk closed, and the sound echoed through the nearly empty lot. He turned and faced the building. Somewhere, a ghost waited. She didn't hide. She didn't need to. Sanford Hospital was hers, and it was Shane's responsibility to challenge her.

The men in Sanford were his brothers-in-arms. He couldn't leave them to die at the hands of the Nurse.

Shane got out a fresh cigarette, lit it, and realized he wasn't alone.

A young man stood in the shadow beneath a faulty lamp, and Shane knew the chill in the air wasn't from an early autumn breeze.

Shane exhaled into the sky and asked, "Want a smoke?"

The stranger shook his head and stepped forward. He was young, maybe in his mid-twenties. His pajamas, decorated with the logo of the New England Patriots football team, were stained with blood; massive amounts of it. It looked as though someone had mopped up a casualty scene with them. The man's lips and chin glistened with the liquid, his brown eyes fixed on Shane.

Shane watched as the young man drifted in and out of focus, like an old movie's bad special effect.

"I know why you're here," the stranger said, his voice low and hard.

"You do?" Shane asked.

The young man nodded.

"Please," Shane said, taking the cigarette out of his mouth and smiling at him, "let me in on the secret."

The stranger didn't smile. "You're here to stop the Nurse."

Shane chuckled. "Yeah, you're right about that. Well done. How'd you find out?"

"The Nurse told us," the young man said angrily. "You can't stop her. She's the only one who knows what she's doing."

"Hold on there, chief," Shane said. "I'm going to say 'no' to that one. Seems like she's killing whoever she wants, regardless of whether they're sick or not. She shouldn't be the one who decides when someone dies. She needs to stop."

"Try to stop her then," the stranger sneered. "We will protect her right to grant death to whom she sees fit."

Shane slipped the backpack off one shoulder and slid it around to the front of his chest. From an exterior pocket, he removed his knuckledusters. He put them on, flexed his fingers several times, and then said, "Why don't you go back to the Nurse and tell her someone will be along shortly to speak with her."

The young man stepped forward and the temperature dropped several degrees. He clenched his hands into fists, and the lights around them flickered. "You're going to leave her alone."

"Take a hint," Shane said coldly. "Go away. Find someone else to bother. I've got things to do."

The stranger sprang at Shane, hands outstretched.

Shane treated him as he would any other headstrong opponent. With a quick step forward he slammed the knuckledusters into the dead man's face.

The lights leaped back to their former brightness, the air instantly grew warmer, and the young man disappeared.

Shane's hand trembled as he raised the cigarette back to his lips, took a long, desperate drag off it and thought, *Well, now I know she's not the only ghost around.*

Chapter 28: Matias, Sanford Hospital, October 21st, 1980

Matias hung up the phone and rubbed the back of his neck.

"Everything alright?"

He looked up at his roommate, a man named Albert Chevalier.

"Yes," Matias said. "Thank you. I've an old injury in my hip and my wife's afraid one day they'll have to take the leg. So she worries."

"So does my ex-wife," Albert grinned, flashing a smile full of yellow teeth and partial dentures.

"Does she?" Matias asked, swinging his legs up onto his bed.

"Yes, she does," Albert said. "If I die, then the money stops. It's kind of nice to know at least one person's praying for me on Sunday."

Matias chuckled. "What are you here for, Albert?"

"Shrapnel," Albert replied. "I was in supply in Danang. One day the Viet Cong mortared us. That was, oh hell, eleven years ago now? Each year I come back, and they do an x-ray, see if any more of it can be taken out."

"And what about this year?" Matias asked.

"Oh yes, yes they can," Albert said, sighing with satisfaction. "Looking forward to it. I work for the State of New Hampshire as a truck driver hauling materials for all the new constructions they're doing on the highways. They hate it when I have to go in for surgery. Messes everything up."

"Does it?"

Albert nodded. "Especially when I schedule it during everyone's vacations."

Matias smiled and shook his head. "I am getting the impression you are not a popular man."

"My good sir," Albert said with mock indignation, "I have no idea what you mean."

The two men chuckled and after a minute, Albert asked in a serious tone, "What about you, what are you here for?"

"Something's gone wrong with my hip," Matias said. "They think there may be bone fragments mixed in with the old shrapnel. They won't know until they do a secondary x-ray. Even then they may not be able to get it all out."

"Do you mind me asking what happened?" Albert said.

"No," Matias replied. "We were patrolling, and doing some basic counter-sniper work. Evidently, the sniper disagreed with it."

"Korea?" Albert asked.

"No," Matias said, smiling. "Vietnam."

"Damn," Albert said appreciatively. "I had you pegged for the Second World War, maybe Korea. Sure as hell didn't think you'd have done time in Vietnam."

"I did," Matias said. "Ended my career as well."

Someone's scream cut off Albert as he started to speak. Both men looked at one another, and they quickly got out of their beds. Matias felt certain they looked foolish hobbling quickly to the door, but it didn't matter.

Something was wrong.

In spite of his limp, Matias reached the door first. He pulled it open and both he and Albert looked out into the hall.

A man who looked younger than both of them scrambled backward, terror etched on his face while his brow glistened with sweat. Up and down the hallway men looked out of their rooms, but none of the staff could be found.

"No!" the man on the floor shrieked. "It's not my time!"

"What the hell," Albert whispered.

Matias had no answer.

The nurse he had seen years earlier, the dead woman in the old uniform, stood a short distance from the screaming man. She gave the patient an understanding smile, and it was then Matias realized how cold the temperature in the hallway was. Some of those who watched turned away and closed their doors. Soon only a handful of men, including Matias and Albert, remained.

"It is your time, Jonathan," the Nurse said patiently. "We've discussed this. It was no mere dream, our little conversation. I wanted you to prepare. To make your peace with God and your family. I will wait no longer. It is time."

"Help me!" Jonathan screamed, looking around desperately. "Please!"

Matias tried to leave the room, but with a hand gesture from the Nurse, he and Albert were thrust backward. The door slammed shut. A heartbeat later, a terrible, keening wail rose up.

In silent agreement, Matias and Albert grabbed hold of the door and tried to pull. Regardless of how hard they pulled, the two men were trapped in the room. Panting, they finally gave up the effort. They stood, heads hanging down, and listened. They could do nothing more.

In the hallway beyond, the Nurse had murdered Jonathan.

Albert and Matias turned away from the door. They exchanged no words as they returned to their beds.

Matias reached out for the phone, but Albert stopped him.

"It's a ghost." The man's voice was hoarse. "Do you think anyone will do anything?"

Matias put his hand down. "No."

Albert laid down and stared at the ceiling.

Matias remained upright on his own bed. He looked at the door.

Where's the staff? he wondered. *Why weren't they here? Why was it Jonathan's time?*

When will it be my time?

The thought was cold and unpleasant.

Yes, he thought. *When will it be my time?*

There was, of course, no answer.

He winced, brought his legs carefully up onto the mattress and stretched out. Matias left the light by his bed on, and so did Albert.

In the stillness of the room, Matias couldn't help but wonder how Jonathan had been killed.

Chapter 29: Doc and Brett in Isolation

"Have they said how long we'll be in here?" Doc asked, yawning as he sat up.

Brett shook his head. "They'll get through the blood tests pretty quickly I assume. They had to isolate the entire ward, clear people out. Last I heard there was a scrub team going in there."

"Good," Doc said, getting off the bed. "I like you, Brett. But I don't know if I want to end up spending a couple of days stuck in here with you."

"Thanks," Brett said, chuckling. "You're a real pal."

"I know," Doc said, grinning. "So no real word as to what's going on?"

"No," Brett said. "Nothing."

The room was small and hermetically sealed. The lights were exceptionally bright, and the room was a comfortable 72 degrees Fahrenheit. Whatever Brett or Doc wanted, someone would bring to them. The only trick was they couldn't leave until someone cleared them.

The door to the room opened, and someone walked in. They passed through the secondary seal and came to a stop outside the third seal.

"Hello," the stranger said. Brett thought it was a man, but he couldn't be sure. The voice was muffled since the stranger wore a full-body bio suit. And the facemask was tinted.

Brett glanced at Doc and saw the man's attention was fixed on the visitor.

"Hello," Brett said, standing up. "What's the word?"

"The word is you're still going to have to be in here for a while," the stranger said apologetically.

"Damn," Doc muttered.

"We wanted to tell you," the visitor continued, "that you need to stop."

"What?" Brett asked.

"You need to stop," the visitor repeated.

"Stop what?" Brett said.

"Interfering with the Nurse," the stranger said. Brett heard anger, low and hard, within the person's voice. "She's doing what she must. Doing what is right. You do not interfere with her, do you understand?"

"Hey–" Doc started, but Brett cut him off.

"Hold on," Brett said, stepping closer to the thin plastic separating them from the visitor. "Who are you? What ward do you work on?"

"None of those answers are necessary, Brett," the stranger said. "You will do well to remember, however, that there are those of us who support the Nurse and her work. And we will ensure she continues to do so without interruption from the likes of you."

"She's murdering people," Brett hissed. "Killing them!"

"She stops those who would stop her," the stranger said calmly. "And she ushers others to the next world. She is as a nurse should be, do you not agree, Brett?"

"No," Brett snapped. "I don't. She shouldn't be killing anyone."

"Regardless of how you feel about the Nurse," the visitor said, "you will no longer attempt to interfere with her. This is the last warning you shall receive."

Without another word, the stranger turned around and passed out of the room.

Brett shook his head, hardly able to understand what had happened. He went back to his bed and looked at Doc. The young man sat and stared at the door. Finally, Doc looked at Brett. "What the hell was that about?"

"I don't know," Brett said in disgust. "But I know it won't stop me. She can't kill anyone else."

Doc nodded, picked up the remote and turned the television on. Quickly, he flipped through the channels, stopping on New England Cable News. Then, without looking at Brett, Doc sighed and said, "Don't worry, Brett. We'll be out of here soon."

"I hope so," Brett said and glanced back at the door.

Chapter 30: Getting Reacquainted

Dom Francis locked the door to his blue Camry. He heard a noise and turned around.

A bloody young man, with his arms outstretched, charged a bald man. The bald man stepped forward and punched the attacker in the face and he vanished.

Francis stood completely still and stared at the man who remained. He watched as the man exhaled a cloud of smoke into the evening sky.

"Shane!" Francis called, recognizing the bald man.

Shane twisted around and smiled wearily. He raised a hand, waved hello and began to walk to Francis. Francis met him halfway and paused as he was about to speak. Shane wore what looked like brassknuckles on his right hand.

"I'm surprised to see you up here, Dom Francis," Shane said, offering his iron-clad hand.

Francis shook it. "I came up to expand my ministry. Why are you here?"

"Treatment," Shane replied. "Except the doctor who was supposed to work on me is dead."

Francis looked at Shane and hesitated briefly before he said, "Do you know why?"

Shane nodded.

"Does it have something to do with a nurse?" Francis asked softly.

Shane's eyes widened. "Yeah. As a matter of fact it does. How do you know?"

Francis quickly told the other man about his meeting with Matias, and of how the Nurse had come in.

"Yeah," Shane said, nodding. "Doesn't seem like she's particularly fond of people interfering. And the guy you just saw, well, he wasn't too keen on the idea either. There are a few others in here who want to get the Nurse to move on, though. Have you done this before?"

Francis shook his head.

"What did you bring?" Shane said.

"Only my faith. I could think of nothing else," Francis said. He nodded to the pack Shane carried. "What have you brought?"

"Hopefully enough to do the job," Shane said. He put his backpack on the hood of the nearest car and opened it.

Francis peered in and whistled appreciatively at the double-barrel, sawed off shotgun. Shane had also removed the butt of the weapon, so it fit neatly in the pack.

"It's loaded with salt," Shane explained. "I figured it was such close quarters I wouldn't need accuracy as much as radius."

"I agree," Francis said. "These are all for dealing with a ghost?"

"Yeah," Shane said. He zipped up the pack and slung it over one shoulder again. "I had been hoping it would be only one ghost, but the way it's looking right now, I don't think that's going to be the case."

"You're probably right," Francis said. He looked at Shane and asked, "Are you planning on doing anything tonight?"

Shane shook his head. "When I was here last time, the Nurse came to me in my dreams, and she was going to finish me off that way. I'm worried she'll try to do the same with Brett and Doc if she figures out what we're planning on doing to her."

"How are you going to stop her?" Francis asked.

"I had been hoping, originally, to get a hold of her and beat her to death," Shane said without any hint of sarcasm in his voice. "But if there's one ghost who likes her, then there has to be more. If that's the case, I don't think I'd be able to do it. I wouldn't be strong enough."

"So, what are you going to do?"

"The next best thing," Shane said, finishing his cigarette. "I'm going to find where she's buried. I'll dig her up, salt her down, douse her with lighter fluid, and then light her up."

"And that will get rid of her?" Francis asked, incredulity thick in his voice.

"Yup," Shane said. "It always does the trick."

"You've dealt with ghosts before?"

"More times than I would like," Shane said, his voice taking on a hard edge. "It would probably be best for us to go inside now. I don't want to be out here any longer than I have to."

"Why?" Francis asked. "You think they'll be back?"

"Yeah," Shane said. "Depends on how far away their bodies are. Or parts of them. Or if they're attached to some item. Lots of variables."

Francis frowned. "You know what, come in with me, you can meet my friend Matias. If anyone knows about the Nurse, I'm sure he will."

"Fair enough," Shane said.

The two men left the parking lot, heading for the front of the building.

"How are you feeling?" Francis asked after a minute of silence.

"Me? I'm fine."

"And your arm?" Francis said.

"Hurts," Shane said. "But I was told by my previous doctor that a little bit of pain was a good thing. It means that the tissues are healing. All I really need is that damn skin graft."

"Think you'll get it soon?" Francis asked.

Shane shook his head.

"Why not?"

"Because," Shane said, "I get the distinct impression that I'm not winning any popularity contests here."

"Not a shock, Shane," Francis said, shaking his head.

"No," Shane agreed. "Usually isn't."

The two men walked into the building.

Chapter 31: Running into Nurse Platte

Meg Ward was one of the few female patients in Sanford Hospital, which meant she had a room all to herself.

And she hated it.

At sixty-eight, Meg liked company, and she didn't get nearly enough of it as far as she was concerned.

And, she thought, frowning, *they keep closing my door.*

I should probably open it, she thought, contemplating the task. Then she shook her head. *Nope. Too much effort.*

Meg picked up the remote control, turned the television on and flipped through the channels. There was nothing but news on. She had napped through all of her game shows.

Well, she sighed. *This is turning into a wasted night.*

Meg turned off the television and then picked up her crossword puzzle book and pen.

Halfway through number thirteen down, she realized she was cold. Meg paused, pulled her blanket up around her swollen legs.

Stupid diabetes, she thought angrily. *My legs used to be stunning.*

With the blanket tucked in, Meg went back to her crossword.

Soon she was shivering.

The room's cold, she realized. Her breath puffed out. *What the hell is going on here?*

A shape stepped out of the shadow by the door and Meg stiffened.

Oh Mary, Mother of God, she prayed, *Pray for me.*

The Nurse moved closer into the room. Her face was hard, unforgiving. Whatever beauty and compassion had been there in life had been stripped away by death.

The crossword puzzle book fell from Meg's hands as she watched the Nurse approached the bed. Meg closed her eyes and screamed as cold fingers wrapped around her neck.

Don't fight it, she told herself. *Don't. It'll be done soon.*

Yet as the dead woman began to squeeze the life from her, Meg fought. She writhed and twisted on the bed. The Nurse kept her pinned down, in spite of Meg's efforts. Her breath was stolen from her and pain exploded in her head.

"No," the Nurse said in a low voice. "Not yet."

Then the hands were gone and Meg fell out of bed. She crashed to the floor and screamed hoarsely. Meg rolled onto her back, gasping for air. The door to the room was thrown open and Zoe, the second shift nurse, rushed in.

The younger woman knelt down beside her, asking, "Meg? Are you okay?"

Meg nodded. Zoe helped her sit up.

"What happened?" Zoe asked. "Did you fall out of bed?"

"The Nurse," Meg croaked.

Zoe smiled, a strange glimmer flickered in her eyes. "Really?"

Meg looked at Zoe in surprise.

"What was she like?" Zoe asked. Her tone was ecstatic. "You're so lucky, Meg! I wish I could meet her!"

Meg glared at the young woman and snapped, "Good. Maybe next time she'll try and kill you."

Zoe patted her hand. "Oh, it's alright, Meg. You're fine."

The nurse stood up and smiled down at Meg. "You really don't know how blessed you are for her to take an interest in you."

Horrified, Meg watched as Zoe left the room, whistling.

Meg turned away from the door, got onto her knees, and for the first time since she had been a little girl, she said her prayers before getting into bed.

Chapter 32: Matias and Francis have a Chat

"You've returned," Matias said, smiling at the young monk.

"I said I would," Francis said, sitting down with a thump.

Matias nodded. "I didn't doubt you would, Dom Francis. I am merely surprised to see you this soon."

Francis chuckled. He said, "You have a new door, I noticed."

"Yes," Matias said soberly. "There was a rather bad death."

"Here?" Francis asked, surprised. "In your room?"

"Yes," Matias said. "Here, in my room. The Nurse beat a young aide to death."

"I'm sorry," Francis said softly. He looked at the door and bent his head, offered a short prayer for the unknown woman, and then crossed himself before he returned his attention to Matias.

The old man looked far worse than he had previously.

In a careful tone, Francis asked, "Matias, why did the Nurse kill the woman in your room?"

"She was here for me, to tell me to make my peace with God, essentially," Matias answered. "The young aide attempted to stop her."

Francis nodded. "Are you alright?"

"Yes," Matias said, smiling sadly. "Unfortunately, I am. I am not terribly burdened by remorse or anything of the sort, Dom Francis."

"I didn't think you were," Francis replied honestly. "But I wanted to be certain."

"I do appreciate it," Matias said. "I must ask, have you thought of a way to stop the Nurse?"

"No," Francis said, frowning. "All I can think of is my faith, but I believe it would be more for my own protection rather than stopping her."

"I would have to agree," Matias said.

"I did meet someone in the parking lot who I believe does have the knowledge to stop her. His name is Shane and he has experience in this area. He had to stop off at an office so he'll be joining us shortly," Francis said. Suddenly, he felt uncomfortable, as though someone was listening to them. He waited a moment, but heard nothing more.

"You believe this man, Shane, can help us?" Matias asked, leaning forward.

Francis nodded. "I do. I truly do."

"And these men, the ones on E Ward," Matias said, "you believe they can help us, too?"

"I know Shane believes it," Francis said. "And I believe Shane."

"Fair enough," Matias said.

Francis hesitated, then asked, "Do you know much about the Nurse?"

"I know a bit," Matias said. "I don't know if it would be much."

"Anything's better than nothing at this point," Francis said.

The old man nodded. "Yes. I suppose you're right. From what I have heard she was a nurse here at the end of the First World War."

"Sanford is that old?" Francis asked, surprised.

"Yes," Matias replied. "Older, even. I have heard it was built a short time after the end of the Civil War."

"Considering the architecture, it would make sense."

"It would," Matias agreed. "In any case, she was a nurse here. Sanford's primary purpose was to care for those who were damaged by war. Those men who had lost their minds either from wounds or from what they had witnessed."

Matias adjusted himself on the bed before he continued.

"There were stories of men dying, the severely wounded, those who were madder than the rest. Some merely died, others," Matias said, shaking his head, "she helped on their way."

"For how long?" Francis asked.

"Not terribly long," Matias clarified. "Shortly after the end of the war, there was a great flu epidemic. A pandemic ripping through the globe. New Hampshire was not spared. Nor were the men in Sanford."

"Did she die of the flu?" Francis asked, unable to keep the surprise out of his voice.

"Oh no," Matias said softly. "She was killed, so the story goes."

"Accidentally?"

Matias shook his head. "No. The story is that there was some sort of incident involving a patient. The patient was violent and attacked the nurse. Evidently, the orderlies were so distraught they beat the man to death."

A knock on the door interrupted them. Without waiting for Matias to respond, the person on the other side pushed in.

"Nurse Platte," Matias said, surprised. "Whatever are you doing here?"

"An issue arose on E Ward, Matias. I had to stay late. I wanted to check on you before I left," she said, and Francis heard genuine concern in her voice.

"Thank you, Nancy," Matias said. "I am quite well."

"This gentleman here isn't tiring you out, is he?" she asked, looking pointedly at Francis.

Matias shook his head. "Not by any means. I don't sleep much lately, as you well know. And I could do with a little tiring out."

"Alright then," the woman said. "I still have to be in for my regular shift, so I'm heading home."

"Drive safely," Matias said.

"I always do," she responded. She waved at Matias and left the room.

"She doesn't like me," Francis said.

"You're in good company, Dom Francis," Matias said, reclining in his bed. "She dislikes only the finest of men."

Francis chuckled and looked at the playing cards on the tray.

"So," Francis said, "you play anything other than solitaire?"

A devilish gleam entered Matias's eyes, and he said, "I play everything. Is there a game you have in mind?"

"Poker," Francis said, picking up the deck and shuffling the cards. "Is there any other game?"

Chapter 33: Waiting for Them

He stood at the far end of 'A' Ward, tucked away in a shadow and his attention fixed completely on the old man's door.

He had been at his post for nearly an hour and hadn't seen a single person enter or exit Matias' room.

He has a guest, you know this, the watcher told himself. *Do not become lax.*

Even as these words echoed in his thoughts, the main doors to A Ward opened, and three men stepped out into the hallway. The watcher recognized two of them. One was a new hire who worked on E Ward. The other was Doc Kiernan, who had been at Sanford long enough to understand the Nurse; who the third man was, the watcher didn't know, and he didn't care.

He merely made a mental note. His keen eyes saw the backpack on the man's shoulder. The man's bearing, the way he moved, all of it spoke of a man who knew the business end of a weapon.

Weapons, most likely supplies, the watcher thought. *A large caliber weapon with the way the bag hangs. Possibly a cut-down shotgun. He's the one to watch. The scars on his face. Combat veteran. Definitely a threat here.*

The one she needs protection from.

The watcher slipped his phone out of his back pocket, keyed in a number and sent a text.

Three new arrivals. New hire from E, Doc from E. Third unknown. Bald and armed. Looks like he knows his business.

Within a moment, the watcher's phone vibrated, the signal of a new text. He paused, watched the three men enter Matias' room, and then looked at the response.

Excellent. Keep me informed.

The watcher erased the text message, returned the phone to his pocket, and focused his attention to Matias' door.

Chapter 34: Matias, Sanford Hospital, March 10th, 1998

He was angry. Angrier than he had ever been in a long time.

"Dad," Michael said, "I'm sorry, but Patricia doesn't want you in the house. She says she can't parent when you're there."

Matias looked coldly at his son.

"Michael," Matias said bitterly, "your wife lacks any sort of ability in regards to parenting. My presence has no bearing on the issue."

Michael's face reddened and his lips tightened. Oscar turned away, hiding his smile. Michael glared at his younger brother but didn't say anything.

"Do not attempt to make excuses," Matias continued. "I know I am a burden, and especially so to your wife. However, I do wish I had been given a little more advanced warning about what was going to happen. I would have preferred to have been placed in a home a little further from New Hampshire."

Michael nodded, and Oscar looked at Matias.

"Dad," Oscar said. "We made the decision, Michael and me, to put you here in Sanford. When I get discharged, I'll be back in New Hampshire. Plus, whether you like Patricia or not, she is the mother of your grandchildren. I know you'll want to see them. And Michael too once you're done being mad at him for not letting you stay at his house."

Matias knew Oscar was right, but he was still angry. Glancing at Michael, Matias asked, "Will you bring the children to see me?"

"Dad," Michael sighed. "Of course I'm going to bring the kids to see you."

Matias was partially mollified by the new information. He took a deep breath, let it out slowly and said, "I understand why I can't stay with you, Michael. I do. Your wife irritates me. I am afraid I let it get to me."

"Don't worry about it, Dad," Michael said.

"Hey," Oscar said, reaching into a pocket. "I picked something up for you."

Matias watched as his youngest son took out a pack of Bicycle Playing Cards. Oscar deftly tore the plastic wrap off of it, broke the seal with a thumbnail and handed it to him.

"Thank you," Matias said. He slipped the cards out and enjoyed the feel and the smell of the new deck.

"Listen," Oscar said. "Michael and I are going to make a run down to Manchester for a few things. We'll be back soon, okay?"

Matias nodded, forced himself to smile and said, "Yes. Sounds fine."

He watched his sons leave the room and close the door behind them. After a moment, Matias removed the jokers and the introduction card and set them aside. He shuffled slowly, the cards slick against his fingers. Once he had them thoroughly mixed, he dealt out a solitaire hand on the bed tray and began to play.

The temperature in the room dipped slightly, and Matias shook his head.

Can't the VA ever get anything right? he wondered, focusing on the cards and trying to ignore the new chill.

"I know you," a woman said.

Matias straightened up, surprised someone had managed to get into the room unnoticed. He turned around and stifled a gasp. Matias clutched the remnants of the decks of cards as he looked at the dead nurse he had seen years before.

She eyed him carefully, nodding to herself.

"Yes," she said. "I have definitely seen you before. It was here, was it not?"

"It was," Matias said, surprised at how steady his voice was.

"You have come back."

He nodded.

"How interesting," the nurse said softly. "Don't you agree?"

"What is?" he asked.

"How you've come full circle," she said, smiling. "This is where you'll die. Didn't you know that?"

Matias had feared the same ever since Michael had told him about the move to Sanford.

"Yes," Matias said in a whisper. "Yes, I suppose I did know it."

"Oh good," the nurse said happily. "It always makes me sad when people don't believe me."

"Is it today?" Matias managed to ask.

"No," she said, smiling. "Not today. I'm not sure when. But it is not today. Does that ease your conscience?"

"A bit," he said, his mouth dry.

"Very good. I will see you on occasion," she said, and she turned and left the room.

Matias sat in silence, and for the first time in a long while, Matias felt fear.

Chapter 35: The Forces Gather

The small room was crowded. Shane stood with his back against a wall while Dom Francis sat in the room's only chair. Matias reclined on his bed while Brett and Doc used the other as a couch. Shane's backpack was on the floor between them all.

Introductions had been made, and an awkward silence filled the room.

"Let's not all talk at once, eh?" Matias asked.

Shane could hear the trace of a foreign language in the man's words. English was not Matias's first language, nor the only one he spoke.

"I think perhaps Shane should lead off here," Dom Francis said, and he sounded more like a combat veteran than a Benedictine monk.

All of the men looked to Shane, and he inclined his head towards them.

"I've brought with me a few tools that I know work for certain," Shane said, gesturing toward the pack on the floor. "Inside there's salt, flammables, a shotgun with shells loaded with rock salt, and something new."

"I'll bite," Doc said. "What's the 'something new'?"

"I'm very glad you asked," Shane said. "It's a herb called Betony. The lore on the plant says it can stop psychic attacks in your sleep if you sprinkle it around your pillow. I'm figuring if we spread it around your beds as well, you'll be safe."

"Psychic attack?" Matias asked. "I don't know of anyone who has been assaulted in their sleep."

"I have," Shane said. "When I was here and fell asleep on E Ward, the Nurse came into my dream. She was definitely looking to do me some harm, and if I hadn't woken up, I know she would have."

"You'll leave the betony here for Doc and Matias?" Dom Francis asked.

"Yeah," Shane said. "At least I planned on it."

"What else are you thinking?" Dom Francis said.

"I'm not scheduled for my skin graft," Shane continued, "but I'm not exactly thrilled with the idea of going home and leaving you all to the tender mercies of the Nurse."

"Appreciate it," Doc said.

"You'll stay somewhere close by?" Matias asked.

"Yes," Shane said, nodding. "I'm going to stay here in the building. Up on E Ward. She obviously likes to visit there more than anyplace else. I'm going to try and figure out a way to draw her out. I think that if I can get her out, talk to her a bit, I might even be able to find out where she's buried."

"And if she doesn't want to talk?" Doc asked. "If she just wants to kill you?"

"That's what my bag of goodies is for," Shane said. "I'll at least be able to protect myself. Give me enough time to get out if I need to."

Shane looked over at Brett. "So, Doctor, what's the deal? Do you think I could sneak into a room here?"

Brett shook his head. "No."

"What?" Shane asked.

"You can't," Brett frowned. "Listen, security has tightened up over the past couple of days, and I don't know if it's because of the increase in deaths or not."

"Do you think security is in on it?" Doc asked. "I mean, it seems to me like there are more people who know about the Nurse than we thought, right? How else would she get away with this mayhem for so long?"

"Damn it." Shane rubbed the back of his head. "I really thought I could grab a bed here somewhere. Anywhere."

"No," Brett apologized. "We have a few empty beds, but security has actually been checking everyone's pass cards, IDs. You name it, they're checking. A couple of the staff who regularly park in the visitor section at night had their cars ticketed. So I'm going to go out on a limb here and say you'd probably get tossed out on your ear, if not arrested for trespassing."

Shane groaned and shook his head.

"What now?" Dom Francis asked.

"Evidently," Shane said, "I sleep in my car. I was hoping to bunk down in here, and that way set up some sort of watch. Do you guys think you could swing that yourselves?"

"I think so," Brett said, nodding. "I can try and have Doc and Matias here room together, at least for tonight, then we can work on stretching it out if we have to."

"Is there anything else we can do to protect ourselves from her?" Matias asked, looking at Shane.

"Two of the big things are iron and salt," Shane answered. He looked around the room, examining it. "The problem is, the Nurse pretty much comes and goes as she pleases. She moves through the doors, which means we could have the thresholds salted. But when I look at the ceiling, I see the vents. The heating system. The AC. You've got cables and wires running out of the walls. Hell, I bet the drop ceiling just cuts straight across the whole ward. I don't think there's any real way to stop her from entering the room."

"So how's the betony going to help?" Doc asked, a note of concern in his voice. "Seriously, why is she going to bother going into our heads when she can come into the room?"

"I don't know," Shane replied. "I'm trying to close off avenues of attack for her. If one of you stays awake and she shows up, I'm hoping you can scream for help."

He looked at Matias and Doc. "Let's be honest, this entire situation is terrible. Her decision to not kill you tonight is pretty much up to her; and whether or not you two can get away. The last thing I can do is leave either my shotgun or my knuckledusters."

Matias laughed and Doc shook his head.

"No," Doc said. "Pretty sure they'd throw us out, dying or not, if they caught us with either one of those things. We've lasted this long."

Matias nodded. "We shall last a little longer. We'll keep watch and use the betony to sleep as peacefully as we can."

"Which brings us back to the question of where you're going to stay," Doc said.

Shane shook his head. "I don't know. I suppose in my car, in the visitor's lot. I don't want to drive back to Nashua only to drive back in the morning. If something happens I want to be nearby. I've already given my number to Brett here."

"May I have it as well?" Matias asked.

"Yeah," Doc added, "we should all have it."

"Will do," Shane said.

"Hold on," Brett said, looking at Dom Francis. "What about religious items?"

"I'm not sure," the monk answered. "I don't think they would do anything to prohibit the Nurse or any other ghost who chooses to come in. The items might offer you spiritual comfort, but since the Nurse doesn't seem to be a demon, I don't believe your religious faith will have any effect on her."

"Great," Brett muttered.

"Sorry," Shane said. "I do have a question for you guys, though. Does anyone know *where* the Nurse is buried?"

None of them did.

"Alright," Shane said. "Do you think there's any way one of you can find out more information about her?"

"I might be able to," Brett said. "I mean, if she worked here, which she must have at some point, then there should be something in the system about her. Sanford managed to put all of its records in the online database last year. I can do a search, see if anything comes up."

"Good," Shane said. "I couldn't find anything online as to where she might be buried. If you can dig that up, it'll work out a lot easier for us."

"How so?" Matias asked. "How will knowing where her body lies help us?"

"Because then we'll be able to stop her," Shane said.

"I'm sorry," Matias said. "How exactly will we stop her again?"

"We find her," Shane said, "dig her up, salt her bones, douse them with lighter fluid and then light her up."

"And that will stop her?" Matias asked.

Shane nodded. "Yup. And there's a bonus to it too."

"What's the bonus?" Dom Francis asked.

"It'll be a bonfire," Shane said, grinning. "Hell, we could even bring marshmallows if we want."

No one thought the joke was funny.

Chapter 36: Who is the Nurse?

Brett wanted nothing more than to clock out. He was stressed and ready to go home.

With a sigh, Brett signed out and he headed for the back stairs. He stifled a yawn as he pushed open the door and walked the six long flights to the hospital's basement. When he reached the bottom landing, Brett took out his key card, swiped it, and let himself in to the rarely-used portion of Sanford.

A long, narrow corridor, lined with too many doors and populated by few lights, stretched out in front of him. No one else was in the basement with him, and it made him feel worse.

Should have brought some coffee with me, he thought. Brett stepped into the corridor, let the door click shut behind him, and he walked to the far end. He found the records room unlocked, and he let himself in. His hand groped along the inside of the wall until his fingers discovered the light switch. Closing his eyes, Brett turned the overheads on. The bright gleam of the fluorescents penetrated his eyelids, and he turned away in spite of his preparation.

When he dared to look, he found the room smaller and more cluttered than he remembered.

Someone had left half a donut on a paper plate, and the sight of the stale pastry made his stomach rumble, reminding Brett of how hungry he was.

Quiet, he told himself. *You'll eat soon enough.*

He went to the desk, pulled out the chair and sat down. Quickly he powered up the computer, the ancient desktop's tower whirring and clicking. Brett rolled his eyes, threw away the old donut and waited several minutes until the monitor flickered to life. Once it seemed properly warmed up, he logged in and gained access to the hospital's record system.

He would have preferred to have done the research upstairs, but the idea of someone looking over his shoulder didn't please him. The fact that there was a living breathing person helping the Nurse sent a shiver down his spine. Brett could understand how a ghost would help her, but not how someone still upright and taking in air could.

Don't worry about it, Brett told himself. *Let's get the information and be on our way.*

He tapped his fingers on the desk, looked at the computer, and then brought up the search screen. He thought about how to research the Nurse, and then he thought, *Why not try her name?*

Brett typed in 'Ruth Williamson' and hit 'enter'.

The screen went black, flared white, and then showed a screen with a blank entry form. It asked for the password.

Password? Brett thought. *How do I know what the password is?*

He rubbed the back of his head, stared at the computer and thought for several minutes. Brett typed in all of the basics from around the hospital. "Surgical1", "Admin1", and "Sanford2016". Finally, Brett shrugged and typed in 'The_Nurse'.

The screen flickered, and a document appeared.

It was simply titled, The Nurse.

Brett leaned forward and began to read.

> *We welcome you to a Brotherhood of like-minded caregivers. By your dedication to the lives and deaths of our Veterans, you have been selected to join a group which has existed since the end of the Great War. While it is no easy task to care for our wounded Veterans, those whose protection President Lincoln charged the Department with, it is far more difficult to have the strength to help usher our wards into the next life.*
>
> *Here, in Sanford, where the sick and the cast-off are gathered, it is sometimes necessary for us to be the merciful hand of Death. You, at some point, have done this task, on your own, and it has been noticed. You may have believed yourself to be acting in the dark, but it was not so.*
>
> *She noticed.*
>
> *The merciful Angel, the Nurse, our beloved Ruth Williamson.*
>
> *It was she who first took up this burden when the men had returned from the Great War. The men broken by combat, sick to death from gas and wounds which would not heal. Then came Influenza, and death nearly as terrible as that upon the field of battle.*
>
> *Trapped here as they were, weakened as they were, our Veterans were all too easy prey for Influenza, and a thousand other lingering deaths.*

> *The Nurse took the burden of death upon her own frail shoulders. From the first case of Influenza, she realized what needed to be done. She knew she alone had the strength to choose who lived and who died.*
>
> *Several of us rallied to her, and under her careful leadership, we began to winnow out those who she knew would not survive. We helped her and stood watch outside of rooms as she entered and removed the chaff. We found whatever it was she might need; hypodermics, scalpels, poisons. If she requested an item, we would procure it.*
>
> *She, alone, had the strength to serve as God's Angel of Death.*
>
> *A terrible and glorious strength was in her.*
>
> *Never did the doctors suspect her. They believed, in their arrogance, that nothing could have been done to help those who died.*
>
> *Our beloved Nurse was not long for this world, however. In 1920, shortly after the crisis had passed, she was killed by a patient. It is a statement of how much the Veterans loved her that she was buried in the cemetery at the edge of the grounds, beneath the shade of the graceful elms.*
>
> *She lies with many of the men she had cared for and many more of those she had chosen to move on into the next life.*

Brett pushed himself back from the monitor.

She's here, he thought, blinking. *She's buried in the lot.*

He shook his head in amazement, leaned forward to read more of the document, but paused as he heard a door open. Brett twisted in the chair and looked down the length of the hall to the opposite end. The door was closing, and someone was walking down the hallway towards him.

For a brief second fear spiked in him, but when he realized he couldn't see through the new arrival, Brett relaxed. He waved and the person waved back before they stopped at one of the locked doors.

Brett turned back to the computer and tried to find his place.

"Hey, Brett!" a voice called.

Brett turned again, saw the unknown person back in the hallway, something small and black in their hands.

"What?" Brett asked.

Two suppressed shots answered him, the bullets smashing into his chest. He slumped slightly, tried to catch his breath but discovered he couldn't. Warmth spread out across his breast.

Oh, Brett thought numbly, *I'm dying.*

Chapter 37: Preparing for Battle

"Do you think it'll work?" Dom Francis asked.

"What's that?" Shane asked. He passed the whiskey over to the monk.

Dom Francis accepted it, took a long swallow and then said, "The betony."

"I hope to hell it does," Shane said. "Otherwise, the Nurse will pick off both Matias and Doc Kiernan, and we won't be able to do anything about it. At least if they're awake when she comes they might be able to do something. Anything to get away and to give them a fighting chance."

The monk nodded.

They sat in Shane's car, passing the bottle back and forth while Shane indulged in chain smoking. When the meeting with the others had wrapped up, Shane and Dom Francis had walked out to the parking lot together. Neither of the men had wanted to leave, so the decision had been made to hang around in one of their cars.

Since Shane couldn't smoke in the monk's vehicle, the only logical choice was Shane's own ride. For hours, they had talked about the military, their first taste of combat, and how different the world was outside of the armed forces. The conversation had then drifted, wandering from education to families, and finally to ghosts.

And Shane had told Dom Francis everything.

It had been good to tell his whole story. The struggle of growing up in the house on Berkley Street, the nightmares that continued to plague him, and even of the death of Courtney.

Dom Francis returned to the subject after he passed the bottle back to Shane.

"You said she's a ghost now?" Dom Francis asked.

Shane nodded. "Yeah."

"Can you tell me how her ghost is with you?" the monk said. "Not her death, but how she became bound to your tags."

"I don't know how exactly," Shane said. "All I can do is guess. At some point, when she was dying, she must have focused on my dog tags. I'm sure there are books out there on how a person becomes bound to an item, but I haven't read any of them."

Shane cleared his throat, rubbed at his eyes and said in a hoarse whisper, "It's tough, you know?"

Dom Francis waited for Shane to continue.

"I mean," Shane said, stumbling on the words, "it was hard to lose her. Really hard. I buried friends. Saw them wounded. Lost my parents. All sorts of crap. Yeah, it hurt, but not like this. Not like this at all."

Shane closed his eyes and sighed.

"I swear," he whispered, "it feels like someone reached in and tore a chunk out of my heart."

"I'm sorry," Dom Francis said.

Shane nodded, wiped his eyes again and said, "Well, she's with me in one way at least."

He looked at Francis. "You know, I feel like I killed her."

"How so?" Francis asked.

"If I hadn't been there in the first place," Shane said, "she wouldn't have come. If she hadn't come, she'd be alive."

"You know better than that," Francis replied. His voice was firm. "You can't think like that. You'll end up second guessing yourself about everything, and it'll cost you. And considering what you do on the side, it'll more than likely be your life."

Shane cleared his throat and said, "Enough of that talk, huh? Tell me, what do the Catholics have to say about ghosts?"

"You know," Dom Francis said, "the Catholic Church doesn't say anything against ghosts, contrary to what many people believe."

"Really?" Shane asked, surprised. "Honestly, I thought they would have been against the whole ghost idea."

"Why?" the monk asked, grinning. "Spirit is a pretty essential part of our faith. And there are more than a few mentions in the Bible about ghosts. Anyway, I suppose my point is I'm curious about how ghosts come about. I don't mean any disrespect concerning Courtney."

A wave of sadness washed over Shane as he heard her name.

"It's alright," Shane said. "I know you didn't. I wish I had an answer for you."

"Have you asked Courtney if she wants to leave?" Dom Francis asked. "I know it sounds silly, but in some of the haunted house movies I watched as a kid, they always said to ask the ghost if they need help going to the light."

"I haven't asked her, no," Shane said. He took a long drink of whiskey. "She knows she's dead. There's no light she's avoiding. Pretty sure she'll make her way along when she's good and ready."

They were silent for a minute, and then Dom Francis said, "If you were to wear your dog tags, would she come with you?"

Shane nodded. "Yeah. That's how it works. She's bound to them. If I were to mail them to Timbuktu, she'd go along. She doesn't have a choice, not until she either frees herself, or someone does it for her when she's ready."

"Can she free herself?" the monk asked.

"Honestly, I have no idea," Shane said.

Faintly, Shane heard the sound of a siren, and as he twisted in his seat to look out the back window, Dom Francis did the same. An ambulance raced up the road, its lights flashing and the siren screaming louder. When it reached the main lot, the vehicle went silent, but its emergency lights continued to spin. The ambulance cut around into the back lot and sped to the rear bay.

Shane watched as the driver deftly cut the wheel and reversed into the parking space. Both doors opened, and the paramedics inside leaped out. They ran into the building and disappeared.

"Do you think it's for one of our guys?" Shane asked, looking at Dom Francis.

"I hope not," the monk said. He frowned. "They'd call, right?"

"It's why we gave them my number," Shane said. The phone rang and he took it out.

He answered it. "Hello?"

"Shane? It's Doc."

"What's going on?" Shane asked.

"Someone murdered Brett!" Doc said. His voice was tight. "He was shot. Two rounds, center mass."

"Anything we can do?" Shane asked, pinching the bridge of his nose.

"Stay where you are," Doc said. "I think you'd draw too much attention if you came inside."

"Alright," Shane said. He ended the call.

"Who was it?" Francis asked.

"Doc," Shane replied, putting his phone away. "Brett's been killed."

In silence they looked at the ambulance, and Shane wondered who had murdered the man.

Chapter 38: Parking Lot Troubles

The air didn't feel right.

Shane had gotten out of his car to stretch, but the strange scent in the morning breeze, and Brett's murder left him uncomfortable. Dom Francis had gone inside the building to check on Matias and Doc.

It's a musty smell, Shane realized, tilting his head back a bit and inhaling deeply. *Like someone's opened an attic that's been closed off for years.*

He sensed an electrical charge in the air, static electricity building up around him.

Carefully, Shane leaned into his car and took out his backpack. He scanned the parking lot while he grabbed his knuckledusters and then his shotgun. Shane slipped the iron over his fingers and put the shotgun in the crook of his arm. He looked back at the hospital.

If I fire this off, he thought, *I am going to have an incredible amount of explaining to do.*

But, having to explain myself beats being dead, Shane told himself, grinning. From the pack, he pulled out a handful of shells and stuffed them into his back pocket. He looked around and tried to see where he might be able to establish some sort of defense for himself.

Shane knew nothing offered him protection, then he grinned.

There, he thought, *the far end of the parking lot. A clear field of fire.*

Shane checked quickly for any vehicles in motion, and when he saw it was clear, he moved towards the open pavement. As he did so, the air at the edges of his vision flickered, light paled and intensified.

The dead were coming.

He picked up the pace, his heartbeat quickening. A smile slipped onto his face, and he felt a familiar, joyous sensation.

The thrill of a fight; the chance to destroy something. All of it spoke to a deeper, darker part of him.

Remember who you are, Shane thought. *They don't know who it is they're dealing with. Or what you've done.*

By the time Shane reached the far end of the lot, five spirits had appeared. They were all men. One of them was the bloody young man he had beaten the night before, and another was an old, naked man. The rest of them were of various ages and races, yet all five wore the same expression, one of anger and determination.

Shane understood them perfectly.

He came to a stop a short distance from them and nodded.

"Good morning," he said.

"You're Shane," the old, naked man said.

"And you're Jacob," Shane replied, remembering the man's name from the story Brett had told.

A smile flickered across the old man's face. "I am."

"What can I do for you, Jacob?" Shane asked.

"You can die!" the young, bloody man spat.

Jacob held up a hand, and the young man took a cautious step back.

"He is impetuous," Jacob said. "He is, however, correct. If you don't leave the Nurse alone, you will die."

Shane shrugged. "I appreciate the warning, but I can't leave her alone. She's killing people."

"So did you," Jacob said. "I can smell death on you. It taints you."

"I imagine it would," Shane said. "You're never exactly the same again."

"None of us are," Jacob agreed. "Will you leave the Nurse to her business?"

"Nope," Shane said. He brought the shotgun up and put a round into the bloody young man, who vanished.

Jacob's laughter rang out in the morning air, and the rest of the dead swarmed towards Shane. He managed to get the second shot off, eliminating a middle-aged Asian man before the others were on him.

A fist slammed into Shane's head, causing his left eye to instantly darken. Silently Shane struck out with the knuckleduster, his hand passing through a cold form. A blow to his bicep deadened his arm, forcing him to drop the shotgun. Grimacing from the pain, Shane struck another ghost before he staggered several steps back.

Jacob remained and a smile appeared on the old man's face.

"You've fought our kind before," Jacob said.

"Once or twice," Shane said through clenched teeth and bent down, picking up the shotgun.

"You will not relent?" Jacob asked.

"Not a chance," Shane said.

Jacob nodded. "I admire your determination. It will be the death of you. Perhaps not at our hands, but eventually, and more than likely, at the hands of our kind."

"Yeah," Shane agreed. "Pretty much how I've figured it, too."

"We will see you again soon," Jacob said.

"Could you do me a favor?" Shane asked.

"What is that?" Jacob said.

"Is there a way for you to put some clothes on?" Shane said. "This is distracting as hell."

"Keep your humor," Jacob said, smiling coldly. "It will warm you when you bury your friends."

Jacob vanished, and Shane heard someone call out to him. Shane twisted around, brought the shotgun up and pulled the trigger. Dom Francis jerked to the right even as the weapon's hammer fell on a spent casing. There was nothing to shoot and Shane collapsed to the ground, sitting down hard on the asphalt. He let the shotgun drop into his lap and he looked at Dom Francis.

"I'm so sorry," Shane muttered.

The monk approached him with cautious steps. "Are you alright?"

"I need sleep," Shane said. "If there had been a round in the chamber you'd be picking rock salt out of your gut."

Dom Francis nodded as he came to a stop, squatting down beside him.

"What did you find out?" Shane asked. "Was it the Nurse who killed Brett?"

Dom Francis shook his head. "No. He was shot to death."

Shane stopped and looked at the hospital. No one had come out when he had fired the shotgun. No one had even seemed to notice. And now, he knew why.

It was more than the dead and one living person helping the Nurse.

Much, much more, Shane thought, and he opened the shotgun and reloaded it.

Chapter 39: Getting Away

"What now?" Dom Francis asked.

They stood at the back of the parking lot, leaning against Shane's car. Shane stretched, his back aching.

"I need some sleep," Shane said. "Some real sleep. I'll head home, rest and then come back."

"What about Matias and Doc?"

"They won't be any better or worse if I'm not here," Shane said. "At least for a few hours. It seems like no one's too worried about them, since they're both dying."

Dom Francis nodded. "What are you going to do about your surgery?"

Shane's burns had been discussed in depth while they were in the car. "I'm going to have it scheduled for here."

"Are you out of your mind?" Dom Francis asked. "Seriously. Have you lost it?"

"No," Shane said. "I want to see if I can get a shot at the Nurse."

"With the shotgun?" the monk asked.

"Or the knuckledusters, either one," Shane said.

"It's not just the dead we have to worry about," Dom Francis said. "Brett was murdered by a living person."

"I know," Shane said. "I think I might be able to get someone to talk if they attack me."

"That's a big change," Dom Francis said. He frowned and shook his head. "I don't like it. You're the only one who really knows what to do here, Shane. If you die, or become incapacitated, then we'll be out of luck."

"No," Shane said. "You'll do fine. I know it. But hey, this is my decision. I'll get a little rest, then be back and get ready to take care of the Nurse."

"You have the gear here," Dom Francis argued. "Can't you do it today?"

"Not like this," Shane answered. "You have my number?"

The monk nodded.

"Good," Shane said. He straightened up and offered Dom Francis his hand. The man shook it.

"Come back soon," Dom Francis said.

"I will," Shane promised. The monk stepped away from the car, and Shane climbed in.

Chapter 40: No Help in Sight

Shane had left Sanford Hospital with a cold, uncomfortable knot in his stomach. Part of it was fear, the rest was anger. A miserable, energy-consuming rage.

He had expected the dead to raise their hands against him, and against the others. In a way, he enjoyed it. A battle with ghosts lacked the burden of morality while it freed him to use violence.

But, the sudden and deadly intervention of a living person made him grind his teeth. He was also enraged with the way the battle in the parking lot had been pointedly ignored by the staff of the hospital. Shane knew how loud the shotgun was, how the sound of the shots had rung out through the morning air. And no one had gone out to investigate. Not a single person. Even after Brett's murder, the security hadn't even come out. Rage filled Shane's mind, a dangerous undercurrent he knew he had to control. *Security is in on it. Probably most of everyone in there. At least staff.*

He doubted the entire hospital was involved. But there were definitely enough people to ensure that the dead operated with impunity.

Shaking his head, Shane turned onto Berkley Street, drove to his home and pulled into the driveway. He took only his phone and keys with him as he left the car.

When he entered the house, he paused and listened. Above him, somewhere on the third floor, he heard a violin, and he smiled. The Musician had been quiet for far too long. Shane lit a cigarette, closed the main door and walked to the kitchen. He grabbed a protein bar out of an open box on the counter, tore the pack open and ate it in a rush. He washed it down with a drink of water from the faucet, then he took out a fresh bottle of whiskey.

"Shane," Courtney said softly.

"Hey," Shane said, his throat dry and his voice raspy. He turned and faced her. She held back to a shadow, a hint of her body. "How's it been?"

"Quiet," Courtney answered.

"No more fighting between you and Carl?" he asked.

"A little," she replied. Shane watched as she moved to the right, standing beside the pantry door. Her form pulsed, alternating in solidity. "Are you hurt?"

"Not much," he said. He took another drink.

She stepped forward, her neck at its odd, disturbed angle, the brutal reminder of her death at the hands of Abel Latham. Courtney frowned. "You're drinking too much again."

He shrugged and took another swallow.

Sadness replaced the frown. In a whisper, she said, "You're going to kill yourself."

"Always a chance," he replied. Shane capped the bottle and put it beside the protein bars. He finished his cigarette and stubbed it out in the ashtray by the sink.

"You're tired," she observed.

"Exhausted."

"Will you come to bed?" she asked, and the question was like a knife, pushed deep into his guts and turned slowly back and forth.

Words failed him, so he nodded instead. She led the way out of the kitchen, and he followed her back into the hall and up the main stairs. Out of the corner of his eye, he caught sight of some of the others. Eloise and Thaddeus looking nervously at him. Shane waved hello to them, and they slipped away quickly.

Carl met them on the second floor, barely containing an expression of disdain.

"You need to rest," Carl said, ignoring Courtney.

"He is," she snapped.

Carl raised an eyebrow in surprise.

Shane nodded.

"Did you tell him he had a message?" Carl asked.

Shane saw Courtney stiffen, and a small smile crept across Carl's face.

"What message?" Shane asked.

Courtney shot an angry look at Carl and then said, "Someone from the Sanford Hospital called and said they had an opening for you tomorrow for the skin graft."

"Alright," Shane said. "I'll listen to it, later. I need to sleep now. Didn't sleep at all last night."

"Was it bad, my friend?" Carl asked in German.

"Yes," Shane replied, answering in the same. "One of the living helped them. There's a man dead, and I'm sure there'll be more before this is through."

Shane switched to English and said, "I'll see you for lunch. Or dinner. Or whenever I wake up, Carl. Please make sure the others are quiet. I am not in the best of moods."

Carl gave a short bow and vanished.

A cold touch reminded Shane of Courtney's presence, and he looked down at her small form.

"You need to rest," she repeated.

Shane nodded. An ache settled into his heart as he looked at her, her once elfin features blurred by death. She smiled at him, and there was only love in the expression.

For a moment, he wondered if she ever blamed him for her death, if she ever held him responsible for her murder.

With a sigh, Shane followed her into his bedroom and hoped he would be able to sleep.

Chapter 41: Alone in His Room

"You have to keep him home today," Matias said.

His youngest son's confusion came through in the phone. "Why? He loves to see you."

A pang of remorse punched through Matias and he nodded. Then, remembering he was on the phone he said, "And I love to see him. But we've had a murder here. Several, in fact, and I could not live with myself if he was hurt."

"Are you serious?"

"Very," Matias replied. "Now listen. Under no circumstances are any of you to come and see me. Not until I call and tell you everything is alright."

"Dad," his son began.

"Alright?!" Matias demanded.

"Sure, dad, sure." His son's tone was placating. "I'll let everyone know."

"Thank you," Matias said. "Good bye."

He didn't wait for his son to reply before he hung up.

Matias shivered in bed and turned his eyes away from the phone.

The call had been difficult to make, but Matias knew it had been necessary.

As much as he longed for the companionship of his family, Sanford was too dangerous. He had dealt with many tragedies in his life, he would not suffer the death of a grandchild or great-grandchild caused by his own negligence.

He was alone in the room. Doc had been moved out shortly after Brett's murder, returned to E Ward. Matias looked at the betony scattered around his bed. More of the herb was on his pillow, and for a moment he wondered if it would be better to wipe the dried bits of leaves away.

Why not let her come in your sleep? he asked himself. *Would it not be easier? Is that not what she wants? What you want, after all?*

Matias couldn't argue with himself. The idea of death didn't normally bother him. For some reason, however, the thought of dying at the Nurse's hands filled him with fear. It was an unusual sensation for him and one that he didn't find particularly enjoyable.

What bothered him even more was the fact that if she killed him, his death would most certainly not be the last.

She will continue to intervene, he thought. *When nature should be allowed to run its course, however brutal it might be.*

Matias looked at his cards and realized he had no desire to play, nor any interest in the television or the stack of Jack Reacher novels that Nurse Platte had so thoughtfully brought in to him.

I only want this finished, Matias thought. *I want her gone, sent to either Heaven or Hell, I don't care which.*

Matias yawned, turned a little to the left and looked out the window. Beyond the clear glass, he could see the night sky. The stars shined brightly, the crescent moon glowing a curious yellow. Autumn would quickly run its course and winter would settle in brutally upon New England.

The idea of the cold weather sent a shiver through him, and Matias shook his head. He had never been fond of the cold.

Best not to think about it, he thought, chiding himself. *Stay alert and focused on the Nurse, and whoever she has as an assistant.*

Really, he thought. *What chance do I have? If I close the door, she can pass through it. Or a nurse or an aide, even a janitor or someone on security could come in and finish me off.*

Panic ate at the edges of his reason. He fought back the urge to call for a nurse, to ask to be brought to another room. To be given some sort of living companion who wouldn't try to shoot him in the chest.

Matias let out a short, harsh laugh.

Is this what you've come to? An old, frightened man trying to hide from death? he asked himself.

Let them come for me, Matias thought, closing his eyes. *Let them come. I will live, or I will die. But I will fight, and I will finish this task if I can.*

Chapter 42: Never Alone

He passed by Matias' door several times, peering in as he did so.

Always, the Watcher saw the old man awake, eyes looking at some distant point.

It wasn't until well after midnight that the old man was finally asleep.

The Watcher hesitated by the door and stared hard at Matias. When the old man didn't react, he moved into the room.

He walked quietly, each step carefully placed. If Matias was to awaken, the Watcher would smile and ask the old man how he was.

But Matias didn't wake.

Instead, he snored gently, a bit of saliva gathering in the corner of his mouth.

Soon, the Watcher thought, backing out of the room. *The Nurse will usher you along, and you will find the peace you need.*

When he reached the hallway, the Watcher glanced to the nurse's station and saw Nurse Emily there. She nodded and looked down.

The Watcher closed the door to Matias' room and went to the supply closet. From it, he withdrew security tape and carried it back. Silently, the Watcher sealed the entry. Then, from his breast pocket, he removed a small sign and attached it to the door.

The message, written in bold black letters on a red background, declared the patient in the room to be quarantined.

No one will listen to your screams, Matias, the Watcher thought, returning the tape to the supply closet. *Pity you? Yes. Listen? No.*

Chapter 43: A Time for Violence

Dom Francis Benedict had given up violence when he had taken his vows.

He had forsaken it after leaving the Army. Years of fighting had cost him; emotionally and spiritually. He had been able to separate himself from it, as all good soldiers can, but after he had become a civilian, he remembered what he had done.

Dom Francis recalled who had done it, too.

Occasionally his dreams were haunted, filled with bitter memories of the past.

He sat on his small cot in his austere room. His previous life was boxed away, left with his brother in Vermont. The sole decoration on his walls was a crucifix.

Dom Francis looked at the image of his Savior and thought, *Must I resort to violence?*

He did not expect an answer, and he wasn't disappointed when none was given.

Dom Francis got off of his cot, knelt down on the floor and crossed himself. He let his chin drop to his chest, and he sank into prayer.

Time passed, and he continued to seek guidance.

Then, a flash of memory.

He was crouched on a hilltop, making sure he didn't silhouette himself against the night sky. The rest of the team was around him and the enemy approached. They had come upon a caravan coming in from Pakistan. The men below them, burdened with supplies, chattered in Pashto. Some complained and their friends mocked them. They were almost home to their village. From there, the supplies would go out to various Taliban units.

Weapons, ammunition, information.

All of it would be used against Coalition troops and Afghanis who had allied themselves with the United States.

Dom Francis and his team had struck quickly, killing every member of the caravan. Some of the supplies were destroyed. Others were booby-trapped. Dom Francis had helped to sow destruction in order to save others.

He opened his eyes and saw the sun had risen.

A single beam of sunlight pierced the clouds, passed through the clear glass of his window and fell upon the small bedtable beside his cot. The light illuminated his Bible, and the small red book of the Rule of St. Benedict.

The petit volume glowed.

With his joints aching, Dom Francis got to his feet. Carefully he went and picked up the book. It fell open in his hands and his eyes latched onto a paragraph.

"Thanks to the help and guidance of man, they are now trained to fight against the devil. They have built up their strength and went from the battle line in the ranks of their brothers to the single combat of the desert."

She may not be the devil, Dom Francis thought grimly, closing the small book, *but she certainly does his work for him.*

He returned the book to the bed table and looked at the crucifix. Dom Francis crossed himself and thought, *There's work to be done.*

He left the safety of his room to prepare for battle with the Nurse.

Chapter 44: Leaving Berkley Street

"It's dangerous at this hospital?" Courtney asked.

Shane sat on the edge of his bed, his shades drawn against the morning light. He lit a cigarette and replied, "Yes."

"And the operation is dangerous?" she said.

Courtney was close by, the room cold and causing him to shiver occasionally. He couldn't see her in the darkness, and he was thankful.

"Yes," Shane said.

"Then why are you going?"

"So I can use myself as bait," Shane explained. "I need more information. Someone has to know where her body is."

"But they want to kill you," Courtney said, her voice coming closer.

"Some of them do, sure," Shane agreed.

"I want to come with you," Courtney demanded. "I can make sure no one interferes with the surgery."

"I don't know if you're strong enough," Shane said gently.

The door to the bedroom opened with a thud, light from the hall causing him to wince. Then it was slammed shut, shuddering in its frame.

"I'm strong enough," she declared. "I get stronger each day. The children, they help me."

"Eloise and Thaddeus?" Shane asked, surprised.

"Yes," Courtney answered. "They say it is their penance to care for me after they chased me away."

Shane had no reply for the statement. He held himself responsible for her murder.

"Shane," Courtney said softly. "Do not blame yourself for my death."

Shane's throat tightened, and he couldn't reply.

"Will you let me come with you?" she asked.

He nodded.

"Then put them back on," Courtney whispered.

In the darkness, Shane stretched out his hand and found his dog tags on his pillow. The metal was cold and familiar, the chain was a comfort as he slipped it over his head and let it hang around his neck.

Courtney sighed.

"When will we leave?" she asked.

"Soon as I'm showered and dressed," Shane answered. He finished his cigarette, stubbed it out in the ashtray on his nightstand and stood up.

It was time to go to the hospital.

Chapter 45: Waking Up Alone

Sunlight woke Matias up. He was surprised he had slept through to the morning.

He straightened up as his body complained; aged joints and bones upset at being disturbed. Matias looked to his tray and saw there was no breakfast.

Evidently, I haven't slept as late as I thought, he told himself. Matias glanced at the clock on his bureau and paused. *Quarter past 7? Breakfast should have been delivered. Hm, perhaps they're late.*

Matias turned himself partially on the bed and saw the door.

It was closed.

Frowning, Matias picked up the call button for the nurse and pressed it. A moment later, the speaker above his bed squawked.

"Yes, Matias?" a woman asked.

"Marilyn?" Matias asked.

"No. My name is Irene," she said. "Marilyn's been moved up to another Ward."

Matias hesitated, pressed the reply button and said, "Irene, my door's been closed, and there's been no breakfast. Is everything alright?"

"We're all fine out here," Irene replied. "Did you forget that you're under quarantine?"

"What?" he asked, surprised.

"Yes," she said, her tone one of sympathy and patience. "Last night you were quarantined. You were exposed to a toxic chemical. One of the janitors accidently trailed it into your room. We have to keep you isolated for a brief time."

"No," Matias said, "this is unacceptable. I need my door open."

"Now, now," Irene said soothingly. "We'll bring your food in shortly. We have Mark suiting up right now."

"Mark?" Matias asked. "Why aren't you? And what about Nurse Platte? Does she know about this?"

"I'm not trained to work in a hazmat suit," Irene replied. "And Nurse Platte is busy. She said she'll check in on you later."

"I would prefer you or Nurse Platte," Matias said.

"I know," Irene said. "Listen, I don't want to alarm you, but the chemical you were exposed to, has been known to induce hallucinations, both audio and visual. And, because of your age, there really isn't anything we can prescribe to help you with them."

Matias didn't respond. He didn't have to.

He knew there was no chemical, toxic or otherwise.

They've isolated me, Matias thought. *Have they done the same to Doc on E Ward?*

"Matias?" Irene said.

"Yes," Matias said, sighing.

"Mark will be in shortly. Let us know if there's anything we can do to make you comfortable," Irene said, her voice full of sympathy.

"I will," Matias replied. He set the call button down on his bed.

This was deftly done, he thought. *A chemical, one which induces hallucinations. Should the Nurse come and I call for help, who is to believe me? An old man, seeing a dreaded rumor. They might feel terrible about my passing, but they will think I was old and that my body couldn't withstand the shock of the toxin or of the hallucinations it induced. Clever. Quite clever.*

The door to his room opened. A man in yellow, protective gear entered the room. Matias could see it was Mark behind the clear plastic of the face plate and the man carried with him a tray of food. Beyond the door was a small foyer made of heavy plastic sheeting.

For a moment, Matias considered the possibility of a real chemical spill.

Then Mark was at his bedside, putting the tray down on the table.

"Anything else?" Mark asked.

Matias shook his head.

"Don't worry," Mark said with a smile. "This will all be over before you know it."

"I hope so," Matias replied, picking up a piece of toast.

"I know it will," Mark said. "The Nurse will arrive soon."

Matias stopped mid-bite and looked at Mark in surprise.

Mark nodded. "Yes. She'll come for you and you will know peace, Matias."

The man patted Matias's leg affectionately and left the room.

Matias put the toast back onto his plate. He had lost his appetite.

Chapter 46: Preparing for Battle

Dom Francis walked into the Lithuanian Club, and the conversation stopped.

Several old men sat at the bar, and Uri Popovich looked at him in surprise from behind the same.

"Francis," Uri, the large man, said, coming around and offering his hand. "What the hell are you doing here?"

Francis shook it and said, "I need a favor, Uri."

"Sure, anything. You name it."

"I need a shotgun and your loader," Francis said.

Uri blinked, and the men at the bar suddenly had stunned expressions.

"Damn," Uri said when he found his voice again. "No offense, Francis, but what do you need a weapon for? I thought you gave all that up when you left the Army."

"Can you accept that I need it, without explanation?" Francis asked his old comrade in arms.

"Sure," Uri said, grinning, half of his teeth gold. "You know that. You could have walked in and asked for an RPG, and I'd get it for you."

"I know, my friend," Francis said. "And I thank you. But all I need is the shotgun and the loader."

Uri turned to the bar and said, "Gary."

One of the men nodded.

"Mind the shop, will you? I've got to go upstairs for a minute," Uri said.

"Sure," Gary replied.

"Come on, Francis," Uri said, and he led the way to a set of stairs tucked away in a deep shadow. Francis followed him to the second floor, where Uri lived and repaired weapons. Various tools for gunsmithing, as well as more than a few weapons of different makes and models, were set neatly on the workbench. To the right of Uri's equipment was a riotgun- a fast-shooting shotgun with a drum magazine.

"Take it," Uri said, gesturing towards the weapon while he went to a cabinet.

Francis picked the weapon up, the weight familiar and comfortable in his hands.

From the cabinet, Uri withdrew the loader and several boxes of empty shells. He set them on the table and then took out a large black duffel bag. Francis watched as Uri placed the items into the duffel, and then held his hand out for the shotgun. After he had handed it over, Uri asked Francis, "What type of shot do you need?"

"Nothing," Francis said.

Uri shrugged, zipped up the bag and handed it to Francis.

"Francis," Uri said.

"Yes?"

"What are you loading it with?" Uri asked.

"Rock salt."

Uri looked at Francis, confused. "Rock salt?"

Francis nodded.

"What the hell are you shooting with rock salt?" Uri said.

Francis smiled. "I'm hunting the dead, Uri."

Uri narrowed his eyes and stared at Francis for a moment.

"You're serious," Uri said finally.

"Yes," Francis responded.

"Hm," Uri said. He scratched the back of his head and then said, "Anything else you need for it?"

"Do you have any iron?" Francis asked.

"Iron?" Uri repeated. "No. Wait. Yeah, yeah I might."

Uri left the room and returned a short time later. He carried a length of dark wood, one end of it wrapped in iron bands with pointed studs.

Francis laughed and shook his head. "What is that?"

"World War One trench weapon," Uri said, grinning. "It was used to convince German troops to surrender peacefully."

"I can see how it would be effective," Francis said. He unzipped the duffel and Uri put it in with the other items.

"Anyone else," Uri said, "and I'd say they were on a bad acid trip. But you, I know you're telling me the truth, and it scares the hell out of me. Be safe."

"I'll be as safe as I can, my friend," Francis said. Once more they shook hands and Francis followed him out.

When they reached the main floor, and Francis walked to the door, he heard one of the men at the bar ask in a low voice, "What's going on?"

"Francis is going to save the world," Uri said, holding the door open for Francis to exit.

Not the world, Francis thought, stepping out into the morning light, *but hopefully some who are in it.*

Chapter 47: Returning to Sanford

The parking lot was empty when Shane pulled into it. He had an unpleasant taste at the back of his throat, a symptom of the fear he felt.

Shane knew he would be at risk when he was on the table, waiting for the surgery.

Am I really scheduled for a surgery? he wondered. *Or are they taking the bait and are ready to finish me off?*

Hell, Shane thought, *with the VA running their own security, they could make up any reason they want and never have to even involve the local police. They could kill me and no one would be the wiser. And since I don't have any real family left, they could bury me here somewhere.*

As soon as the thought ended, Shane straightened up in his seat.

Bury me here. He looked out the window at the wide expanse of the hospital's grounds.

There has to be some sort of burial ground here, he realized. *Every hospital had one. It might not be taking any new residents, but a Nurse who died decades ago. One who gave her life to this place? Yeah, I bet she's buried here. Somewhere.*

I need to find out where the cemetery is, Shane thought. *Matias probably knows. Or Doc. One of them has to.*

He got out of his vehicle, grabbed the bag he had packed for an overnight, and closed the door. He headed for the front of the hospital, glancing back occasionally. No ghosts appeared, and he couldn't see any sign of the cemetery either.

You'll find it, Shane thought.

When he reached the main entrance, he walked in and found a different receptionist than the first time he had arrived. The man wore a name tag which read, "Mark".

"Hello, Mark," Shane said.

"Good morning," Mark said, smiling. "How may I help you, today?"

"Evidently, I have a surgery scheduled for six o'clock," Shane said. "The message said to be in by nine since I have to fast for eight hours prior."

"Very good," Mark said. "What's your name?"

Shane gave the man his name, date of birth, and social security number. Mark quickly typed all of the information into the system, found Shane's file, and nodded.

"Yes," Mark said, "you need to see Nurse Platte first, and then she'll have someone show you to your room. She's in the office; follow this hall back, turn left at the second door and you'll find her there."

"Thank you," Shane said, and Mark waved as he walked away.

When he reached her door, Shane found it closed, so he knocked on it. A moment later, it opened, and Nurse Platte gave him a weak smile.

"Come in, please," she said, returning to a cluttered desk. "Take a seat."

Shane did so and thought, *I wonder if she knows what's going on. Is she part of it?*

"You look a little frazzled," Shane said.

"Not a little, a lot," she said. "They're still investigating Brett's death, but it doesn't seem like they're going to solve it."

"Was anything stolen?" Shane asked.

Nurse Platte nodded. "Several discs which were loaded with personal information. Social security numbers, military records; everything someone could want in order to establish themselves somewhere else with a new identity."

"Great," Shane said, shaking his head.

"Yeah," Nurse Platte said. "We all viewed it the same way. Right now it's a matter of damage control and fielding all of the questions about financial security. Not only from the men and women here, but their family members and people we've treated who aren't residents. It's a mess."

Then she smiled at him. "Well, we're not here to talk about the hospital's newest problem. We're here to talk about your upcoming skin graft."

"Yup," Shane said.

"It'll be a straightforward procedure," Nurse Platte said. "We'll get you upstairs, get you well-prepped before surgery, and make certain everything is going to work out well. Do you have any questions for me before I send you up to D Ward?"

"No," Shane said, shaking his head. "No questions."

"Good," Nurse Platte said, standing up. "I'll be by your room in a few hours to check on you."

"Thanks," Shane said, standing up. He left the room and went back to the elevators. After he had pressed the 'up' arrow, he waited for several minutes until the doors opened and he stepped in. His finger hesitated over the 'D' button, and then he pressed the one for E Ward instead.

Need to check on Doc, Shane thought to himself. *I've got to make sure he's okay.*

Chapter 48: A Visit from the Abbot

Francis sat on the floor in his room.

He had spent nearly two hours carefully loading shotgun shells with rock salt. With the preparations finished, someone knocked at his door.

"Come in," Francis said without looking up.

The hinges creaked, and the unknown individual gasped in surprise.

Francis looked to the doorway and saw Abbot Gregory. The older man adjusted his glasses, shook his head and said, "Francis, what are you doing?"

Francis tried to think of a way he could explain the situation delicately to his superior and found there was none. Sighing, Francis told Abbot Gregory everything.

The abbot listened intently, eventually moving to sit upon Francis's cot. Abbot Gregory's back straightened, and he took his glasses off, absently wiping them off with the cuff of his sleeve. Finally, when Francis finished, the abbot put his glasses back on.

The older man looked at Francis and asked, "Do you need anything else?"

"What do you mean?" Francis said, confused.

"You have the shotgun and the ammunition," Abbot Gregory said patiently. "You have iron. Have you any iron rings for your fingers?"

Francis looked down at his hands as if to confirm what he already knew about his lack of additional iron, and then looked up and asked, "Do you have some?"

"Yes," Abbot Gregory said, a small smile playing across his face. "The college has existed for over one hundred years, Francis. We have had our share of difficult spirits. It is not something we usually speak of, and there are few in the Order who have sufficient strength and wherewithal to battle the dead. But just because there are few of us, doesn't mean that there aren't any. You have, from what you told me, moved beyond the realm of a simple monk."

Francis looked at his Abbot. "You're saying there are members of our Order who have fought the dead before?"

Abbot Gregory nodded. "Indeed. Not many, mind you, for God does not call us all to this purpose. Evidently, He has called you."

"How come I've never heard of this before?" Francis asked. "I've never even read anything of the sort. Were records kept?"

"They were," the older man said. "There are books, journals which are kept in my quarters, and within the special collections of the library. You may read them, when you are ready. Some will test your skills for they have not been translated from either French or Latin."

"Thank you," Francis said.

Abbot Gregory sighed, looked down at his hands and continued. "Well, you are more, now, Francis. You have passed through to a place many will never reach. There is a strength within you, a gift, which will allow you to battle those who have either intentionally or accidentally aligned themselves with evil."

"You, you're alright with this?" Francis said, gesturing towards the ammunition and the weapons.

"Quite," the older man said. "It is new, and I would not have thought to employ a shotgun, but upon reflection, it is no surprise that you would. You were a soldier, Francis, and in your heart, you still are."

Francis nodded.

Abbot Gregory stood up. "I have a set of rings here, in my quarters. I will bring the box down to you, and you can find a pair which fit."

"A pair of them?" Francis asked.

The abbot nodded. "One for each hand. It is best to be prepared, should you lose your weapons."

Francis watched the man leave the room, and thought, *Everything would help. Every. Last. Bit.*

He loaded the drum magazine and waited for Abbot Gregory to return.

Chapter 49: Visiting Doc

When the elevator doors opened onto E Ward, Shane felt uncomfortable. An unpleasantness hung in the air, and it was cold. Terribly so. Shane stepped out onto the floor, hesitated and waited to see if anything would happen.

The woman at the nurse's station smiled politely at him. "Are you alright?"

"Yes," he answered. "I'm here to see Doc."

"He's in his room," she said. "Do you know the way?"

"I do," Shane said. He turned and headed for Doc's room, nodding 'hello' to the few men he passed. Doc's door was open, and Shane paused long enough to rap on the doorframe and wait for Doc's reply.

"Come in," Doc said, looking up from his bed. He smiled wanly at Shane. "How are you?"

"Alright," Shane answered. "How are you holding up?"

Doc shrugged. "Little bit upset. Wish I knew why the hell Brett was shot."

"You don't think it had anything to do with the Nurse?" Shane asked, surprised.

"Part of me does," Doc said. "But then I wonder why someone would go so far as to shoot him. I don't know. I'm tired. They've got me on a new round of medication they think might help."

"Might?"

Doc nodded. "Might's better than not at all."

"True," Shane said.

"So, you back for your skin graft?" Doc said.

"Yeah. Tonight, as long as I make it through all the tests," Shane told him.

"Have you been drinking?" Doc asked.

"Of course," Shane said.

The younger man sighed. "They probably won't want to do it. Did you fast at least?"

"No," Shane said, shaking his head. "I'm doing it now. Surgery isn't scheduled until six."

"Tomorrow morning?" Doc asked.

"Tonight," Shane answered.

"That doesn't make any sense at all," Doc said softly. He looked at the door, and then back to Shane. "You need to watch yourself."

"I will," Shane said.

"I'm serious," Doc said earnestly. "They never do surgeries after four, not unless it's an emergency, and I figure yours isn't."

"Not life or death, no," Shane said.

"Then why are you here?" Doc asked, confused. "I'm being serious, Shane. Brett was shot. Murdered. Not by a ghost, but by a person. Why risk it at all?"

"I'm hoping to get someone to try something," Shane said. "That way, I can find out where the Nurse is buried."

"Can't you just look it up?" Doc asked.

"I tried," Shane said. "All I found was an obituary, and all it said was she had died at Sanford. Nothing else. It's like someone went in and stripped the information off the web."

"So you're putting yourself out there as bait?" Doc said.

"Yes."

"Still?" Doc asked. "After what happened to Brett?"

"Especially because of what happened to Brett," Shane said grimly. "Listen, Doc, whoever it was who killed Brett is obviously okay with what the Nurse is doing. I'm not. In order to prevent any more deaths like Brett's from occurring, I have to get rid of the Nurse. The only way to do that is to salt and burn her bones. Which is what I'm going to do."

Doc shook his head. "Well, be careful, okay?"

"I will be," Shane said, standing up to leave.

"What ward are you on?" Doc asked suddenly.

"D Ward," Shane replied. "Going to come and visit me after my surgery?"

"Yeah," Doc said. "Figure I'll make sure you're okay."

"Sounds like a plan to me," Shane said. He left the dying man's room and went in search of his own.

Chapter 50: Ready to Leave

Matias had eventually eaten his breakfast, and then his lunch. He would need his strength for whatever was to come.

Mark had returned for the tray, smiled at him with fanaticism, and left the room.

When the man exited, Matias listened carefully. The door clicked shut, but it remained unlocked.

Matias took a deep breath and laid back against his pillows. He stared at the ceiling.

Will you be able to do this? he asked himself. *Can you?*

Better to die trying, than to wait for it, he answered.

Matias took the blankets and sheet and cast them off. He looked down at his legs, wasted sticks existing where pillars of strength had once been.

Useless, he thought bitterly. *But you're not. Forget them. Carry on.*

Grabbing hold of the side rail, Matias carefully eased himself out of the bed. The effort was agonizing, his arms screaming, stomach clenching. Finally, he reached the floor, and when he did so, he lay upon it for a long time. It was cold beneath him, but he didn't care.

He realized he had wet himself with the effort, and Matias didn't care about that either. Pressing his hands flat against the floor, Matias pushed himself up. He managed to sit and rest his back against his bed.

I need to get to the door. Beyond the door was the plastic foyer, and after that barrier, the hallway.

Maybe I'll have a heart attack and die before I ever reach it, Matias thought. *Then I won't have to worry about what to do next.*

Maybe, he thought scornfully. *And maybe the cavalry will come to my rescue.*

Matias pushed all of the thoughts to the back of his mind as he carefully lay back down on the floor. Fixing his gaze upon the door, he began to drag himself forward.

Chapter 51: Getting Prepped for Surgery

Shane wore the uncomfortable hospital smock reluctantly. Soon, he knew, they would come in and begin the blood work and conduct the various other tests which let them know if he really was ready for the surgery.

I'll probably get an earful for all the alcohol in my system, he thought. *Oh well.*

He straightened up in the bed and felt the dog tags slide across his chest. Shane smiled, reached up and held them. It was a comfort to feel them, and to know that somewhere, somehow, Courtney was with him.

He picked up the remote, tried to turn on the television and found it didn't work. Shane rolled his eyes and thought, *Typical.*

He tried several more times, then he pressed the call button for the nurse. A moment later, a young woman entered and smiled at him.

"What can I do for you?" she asked.

"The television's shot," Shane explained. "Do you have a book or magazine I can look at? Even a paper?"

"Sure," she said, smiling. "I'm sure we can find something."

"Thanks," he said and watched as she left the room.

Several minutes passed and the nurse didn't return. Instead, the room grew colder. The light of the bed lamp weakened, flickered, and went out, leaving Shane in semi-darkness.

He twisted in his bed, slipped a hand under his pillow and pulled out the knuckledusters. Quietly Shane slipped them on, felt the strength of the cold iron against his flesh, and waited.

A moment later, Jacob entered the room.

"You've returned to us," Jacob said.

"Had to," Shane responded. "I'd rather not be here."

"The feeling is mutual," Jacob assured him. "Tell me, why are you here?"

"Surgery," Shane explained.

Jacob frowned. "And will you leave our Nurse alone when you are done?"

"Not a chance in Hell," Shane said.

"It will cost you your life," the dead man said after a minute of silence.

"It could," Shane agreed.

"Your determination is foolish," Jacob said, anger creeping into his voice.

"Usually is," Shane said.

"Then leave," Jacob urged. "Go. Find another facility for your operation. We will let you go in peace."

"Can't," Shane said.

"Can't or won't?" the old man asked.

"Either. Maybe both," Shane said, shrugging. "The point of the matter is this, I'm going to destroy the Nurse, then no one else will have to worry about being killed before their time."

"You don't understand anything," Jacob said with a bitter tone. "You don't know what it's like to cling to life, and all the while lacking the courage to kill yourself. The Nurse takes that burden from us. We will not have to suffer with the sin of suicide over our heads. She has accepted the responsibility of our deaths."

"You swallowed the lie hook, line, and sinker, didn't you," Shane said softly.

"It is no lie," Jacob snarled. "You have been given a choice. Will you stay and suffer the wrath of those who support her, or will you leave and live until your time has come?"

"Wrath sounds good to me," Shane said. "Now, if you're not here to cheer me up for the surgery, you should probably go."

The old man didn't move, and Shane tightened his grip on the knuckledusters.

Then Jacob turned and left the room.

The light flickered and came on.

A knock sounded and the door opened.

A young woman walked in. She held a couple of paperback books in her hands, and she smiled at Shane.

"Here you are," she said, bringing the books to the bed table and setting them down beside the lamp's base.

"Thanks," Shane said, and reflexively his right hand lashed out as the young nurse swung her fist at him.

Metal clashed against metal and Shane yelled as something plunged into his left shoulder. She kept her grip on the handle of a knife, the blade of which was buried to the hilt. As she tried to pull the weapon out Shane latched onto her wrist, keeping the knife trapped in his body.

His body shrieked, pain exploding across his nerve endings and setting his brain on fire. Shane ignored the injury, and the grating sensation of metal against bone, and swung his left fist at the nurse's face.

Shane's blow lacked any strength and bounced harmlessly off her forehead.

Then a powerfully cold sensation surged through his body and the woman let go of the weapon. The young nurse stumbled back as Courtney took shape in the room. The light flickered, and the bulb exploded. Cries of surprise could be heard from the hallway.

She's drained the whole floor, Shane thought numbly.

With the room lit only by what little light came in through the window, Shane saw the young nurse catch herself on the wall. She stood and gasped, trying to catch her breath.

"Who are you?" she hissed, staring at Courtney.

Courtney said nothing. Instead, she stepped forward and grabbed hold of the woman's blouse. Shane saw a small, grim smile appear on Courtney's face, and then her arm was a blur. Courtney hurled the woman across the room, where the cinderblock wall stopped the young nurse violently.

Shane heard something break, and the woman slid limply down to the floor. A trail of smeared blood remained on the wall. For a heartbeat, the woman remained upright, and then silently she fell to the left, landing with a thud.

Shane watched as Courtney walked over and knelt down beside the woman, looking at her.

"She's alive," Courtney said, glancing at Shane.

Shane struggled and sat up. He ignored the knife hilt which protruded from him. Wincing, he got out of the bed and forced himself to sit down beside the young nurse.

"Nurse," he said.

She didn't respond.

"Hey!" Shane shouted.

Her breathing was ragged. Reaching out, Shane pulled up an eyelid. Only the white was showing.

Great, he thought. *Pointless now. And I've got a damned knife in me.*

"She's dying," Courtney said in a low voice.

"Let her." Shane grimaced as he shifted his weight. "I hope it hurts like hell."

Courtney vanished and Shane was left alone, wondering what to do next.

Chapter 52: An Exodus

Francis pulled the car over on the side of the road leading up to Sanford. From where he sat, he could see the building, and something curious.

Buses.

Three were parked in front of the facility, and others could be seen idling on the road reaching around to the back lot. Francis could see patients being brought down the stairs. Staff members helped them into the buses, and as Francis watched, the first bus was loaded, the doors closed, and the vehicle pulled away. Soon it passed by him, and then it was followed by the second, and the third. In less than half an hour, fourteen buses traveled down from the hospital to the main road.

The building had been emptied out.

Why? Francis thought. *Why have they left? Is Matias still there? And what about Doc?*

He waited for a minute, then he started the car again and turned on the radio. Francis checked the stations until he found a news report.

"The information being given out is pretty slim right now, folks," a male reporter said. "All we know is that the authorities at Sanford Hospital said there has been some sort of chemical leak. The patients and staff are being evacuated. We'll let you know as we learn more. But, as of right now, you can go to Manchester West High School, which is where the patients are being brought."

Francis turned off the radio and shook his head. *Decent cover story,* he thought, and drove up to the back parking lot.

Shane's car was there, near a light.

Francis frowned, shut the engine off again and looked at the tools he had brought: the shotgun, the extra rounds, the war club from Uri, and the rings on his fingers.

Abbot Gregory had allowed Francis to pick a pair of them, as he had promised. Each ring was made of thin iron and stamped with crosses. The metal was snug against the index finger of each hand, and Francis felt better knowing they were there.

He got out of the car, went around to the passenger side and took out the extra rounds and the shotgun. He felt odd, carrying a weapon while still wearing his simple robes. But a deep, powerful part of him knew it was justified, and he was doing what was right.

Turning around, Francis walked towards the back of the building. A bay door had been left open, and he quickly walked up the concrete steps. Emergency lights were on, and Francis realized there was hardly any ambient sound. He moved quickly along the corridor and found a jacket. A security badge was clipped to it, and Francis pulled it off. He held the thin plastic card in his hand and soon had a use for it.

Francis came to a secured door, but the electronic reader accepted the swipe from the card and buzzed him in.

He found himself on the first floor, A Ward, and he took a moment to familiarize himself with the hallway. Francis tried to remember where Matias' room was, and as he looked down the hall, he saw a door with a quarantine seal around it.

Matias, he thought.

Francis quickened his pace and as he advanced he heard a noise. He twisted around in time to see an old woman. She moved towards him and Francis saw she was dead. Her face was wide, her eyes half-closed and the gray hair on her head pulled back in a loose bun. She wore a gray nightgown, clinging to her large frame.

Francis brought the shotgun up and sighted down the barrel.

Chapter 53: Matias in His Room

It took an exceptionally long time for Matias to crawl the length of his room. By the time he reached the door, he could hardly breathe. With a gasp, he rolled onto his side and pressed his back against the wall, resting his head on the floor. He closed his eyes and tried to gather his breath and his wits back to him.

The way my luck is running, Matias thought grimly, *Mark will return and find me out of bed. Wouldn't that be a kicker?*

Finally, Matias opened his eyes again and looked at the door. The handle was only a few feet off the floor, but it would be a challenge to reach it.

And open it, Matias thought, *and then get out.*
How are you going to get out of the building, Matias? he asked himself.
One problem at a time, he thought.

Matias got into a sitting position, looked at the door handle and reached up for it.

The metal was cold in his hand as he gripped it tightly. His heartbeat increased, his blood thumping in his ears as he pulled it down. Cautiously he pulled the door back, a quarter of an inch at a time, listening intently.

The sound of a shotgun jerked his hand away from the door handle and caused him to fall backward.

Chapter 54: Doc Arrives

A shotgun blast stunned Shane. Within a heartbeat the door opened, and Doc came into the room, wide-eyed.

Doc looked around, saw the body and said, "What the hell happened? And who the hell is shooting in here?"

"She tried to kill me," Shane said, waving towards the body, "and I don't know."

"Jesus, man, do you have a knife in your shoulder?" Doc asked. "Where is everyone on this floor?"

"Yes. No idea," Shane said through clenched teeth. "Listen, Doc, if you could help me with this, I would really appreciate it."

"Yeah. Right," Doc said, shaking his head. "Sorry. Can you follow me?"

Shane nodded. Together they left the room and went out into the empty hallway. No one was at the nurse's station. From what Shane could see, no one was anywhere. Someone fired the shotgun twice more.

"Wait here," Doc said, and he hurried around the nurse's station. Shane held onto the counter top with his right hand, and he could feel the blood seeping around the edges of the knife blade. Doc reappeared thirty seconds later with a large first-aid box. He set it down, opened it, and pulled out a pair of scissors.

"So," Doc said, cutting away at the fabric, "you come here often?"

"Is this your bedside manner?" Shane asked, wincing as Doc reached the knife and worked his way through the cloth.

"Yup," Doc said, removing the shirt. "You like it?"

"No," Shane said, "but please don't let that stop you from fixing me."

"I never allow constructive criticism to interrupt my work," Doc said. He put the scissors down, took a compression bandage out and said. "Can you say, 'ah'?"

"Ah?" Shane asked, and when he did Doc grabbed the knife and pulled it out.

Shane's voice became a scream of rage and pain. Doc slapped the bandage on him, and as Shane's vision pulsed in time to the throbs of the wound, the former medic taped him up.

"How's it feel?" Doc asked.

"Like crap," Shane grumbled.

"Good," Doc said. "At least you feel something there."

The medic rooted around in the first-aid box for a moment, grunted in satisfaction and pulled a small hypodermic needle out.

"Tetanus," Doc said, and without ceremony, he took the cap off and stuck the needle in Shane's deltoid.

"Doc, you have the absolute worst bedside manner," Shane said. He looked down at himself. "And I am now bloody and in a pair of boxers."

"Well," Doc said, dropping the needle onto the desk. "It could be worse."

"How so?" Shane asked.

"You could be wearing tighty-whities," Doc replied.

Before Shane could comment, another shotgun blast echoed through the hospital.

Doc glanced at Shane's hand and asked, "Will those actually work?"

Shane looked down at the knuckledusters and nodded. "You bet, Doc."

"Okay," Doc said, "let's go find out who's gone haywire with a shotgun."

Shane nodded and walked toward the stairs.

"Where are you going?" Doc asked, stopping by the elevator.

"Power's out, Doc," Shane said, glancing over his shoulder. "Think you can get the elevator to work without it?"

Doc frowned and followed Shane. Together they reached the stairwell and Doc slipped in front of Shane. The former medic removed a key card from his pocket and swiped it through. The emergency power allowed the door to open.

"Where'd you get the card?" Shane asked as they entered the stairwell.

"Ask me no more questions, I'll tell you no more lies," Doc said, starting down the stairs. The shotgun was fired again, the sound echoing up from the bottom of the stairwell.

"Doesn't sound good," Doc said, looking over at Shane.

"No," Shane agreed, "it sure as hell doesn't."

Chapter 55: Francis Finds Matias

The world was silent.

Occasionally the dimness of the ward was lit by the muzzle flash of the shotgun, and Francis knew he was smiling. His heart kept a strong, steady beat within his chest, and he felt the blood flowing through him.

A man stepped out of a room, a look of pure hate on his face. He was missing his left arm at the shoulder, but he still looked as though he could inflict serious damage on Francis.

Francis pulled the trigger, rock salt exploding out of the shotgun and ripping through the ghost. As the spirit vanished and the rock salt shattered against the wall, Francis turned and realized he had reached Matias' room.

He let go of the weapon with his left hand and grasped the door handle. With a jerk, he twisted it and pushed into the room.

Matias was lying on the floor.

Suddenly the ability to hear rushed back to Francis and the old man's labored breathing filled his ears.

Francis dropped to his knees, setting the shotgun down beside him.

"Matias," Francis said, and the old man looked at him with wide eyes. His lips were blue, his face pale.

"Dom Francis," Matias whispered, his voice barely audible.

Francis went to speak, but a scream tore out of his mouth instead of the kind words he had meant to say. Something unspeakably cold grabbed him and threw him aside.

Francis watched as the Nurse reached into Matias' chest, her hand plunging in all the way up to her wrist.

Matias opened his mouth in silent shock, his eyes glazing over as his back arched.

Francis tried to move but found he couldn't. Fear immobilized him.

"Peace," a voice he recognized as the Nurse's said. "He is nearly done. And it is not yet your time, Father."

Francis remained silent, unable to respond.

Matias relaxed, then went limp. For a few seconds longer, the Nurse kept her hand in Matias's chest. Finally, she withdrew it and looked to Francis.

"You should return to your home, Father," she said. "There will be others who will need your comfort before I give them mine."

The Nurse vanished, and Francis tried to gather his strength, but he failed.

Chapter 56: A Gathering

When they reached A Ward and exited the stairwell, Shane could see the door to Matias' room was open. Plastic wrap for quarantine control was in disarray. The smell of gunpowder was heavy in the air.

"Oh damn," Shane breathed as they reached the doorway.

Doc pushed past him, hurrying to Matias' side. Shane watched as Doc checked the old man's vitals, but it was no use. Matias was dead.

"Dom Francis," Shane said.

The monk was on his knees, head bent. His hands were clasped together on his lap, and a riot shotgun with a drum canister lay on the floor beside him.

"Dom Francis," Shane repeated.

The monk lifted his head and in his eyes Shane saw a deep sadness.

"What happened?" Shane asked.

"She killed him," Dom Francis replied. "I couldn't stop her."

"Look at me," Doc said, command and authority in his voice.

Dom Francis did so.

Doc checked the monk's pulse, his pupils, and his neck. With a sigh, Doc settled back on his haunches and said, "You're fine, physically."

Dom Francis nodded. "I know. Shaken, is all. I thought I'd be able to save him from her."

"You and me both," Shane muttered.

"Now what?" Doc asked, looking from the monk to Shane. "Seriously, what do we do now? This place has been abandoned, so I don't think we're going to get any help if we call anyone."

"Not looking to call anyone," Shane said. "All I want to do is get to my car, get my gear bag and find her grave."

"You still want to do that?" Doc asked, shocked. "After everything we've gone through?"

"Yes," Dom Francis said, getting to his feet. "Shane is right. We need to finish her off. I doubt the hospital will be closed for very long."

"You guys have some issues," Doc said, using the wall to support himself as he stood up. "But I guess you're right. We should finish it. We can't risk her coming back. And, you know, I really don't want to wake up with her standing over my bed one day."

"Alright," Shane said. "Got a question you might be able to answer."

"Go ahead," Doc said.

"Do you know if there's an old graveyard around here. Maybe something in a back corner, tucked away?" Shane asked.

"Sure," Doc said. "About a quarter mile away, up through an old road. I think they used it for the hospital, back before it filled up and people changed their minds about letting the government bury their family members."

"Alright," Shane said. He looked over at Dom Francis. "You okay to do this?"

The monk nodded, and then he asked, "You've done this before?"

"A couple of times now," Shane said. "Yeah."

"Did anyone die before?" Dom Francis said.

Shane nodded and whispered, "Yes."

With the painful memory of Courtney's broken body in his mind, Shane turned away and headed for the parking lot.

Chapter 57: The Plan

"I don't know what to expect here," Shane said as the three of them stood at his car. He had gotten a pair of pants on, but nothing else. His shoes were in his room, and he had found a zip-up hoodie in the trunk, along with the collapsible shovel he left in there for the winter months.

"What do you mean?" Doc asked.

"Before," Shane explained, "there were always at least a couple of the dead who were willing to help me. This is not the case here, as we've found out. In fact, they would much rather work against us. Stop us from ending the Nurse. Thing is, other than the Nurse, none of them have really tried to kill us. But, I'm concerned about what they might try to do if we get too close to her grave."

"Can't we use the shotguns to stop them?" Doc asked.

"Sure," Shane said. "Shotguns come in handy. But how fast can you pull a trigger?"

"What?" Doc said, looking at him. "What do you mean?"

"You've been in combat, right, Doc?" Dom Francis asked.

Doc nodded.

"You ever know the bad guys to wait patiently for you to draw a bead on them, or come at you one at a time?" the monk said.

"Damn," Doc said, sighing. "No."

"And these aren't ordinary ghosts," Shane said. "Most are former military. Yeah, some may not have seen combat. These were guys who suffered from post-traumatic stress, battlefatigue, whatever you want to call it. These were combat vets. They don't have fire superiority, but they have strength in numbers. Hell, I had to face five of them."

Doc took a deep breath, let it out slowly and said, "So what do we do?"

"We go as carefully as possible. And remember," Shane said grimly, "we've still got to dig her up. Pretty sure she's not going to be laid out all nice and neat for us in some crypt. Life is never that easy."

"How is this going to work then?" Doc asked. "I mean, are we going to lay down covering fire while you dig, or what?"

"How am I going to dig, with my arm like this?" Shane asked.

"How are you going to walk a quarter mile without shoes?" Dom Francis asked.

"Carefully," Shane replied.

"Are you sure you don't want to try and get them out of your room?" Doc said. "Seriously, Shane, we can wait."

"It's not a matter of time," Shane said. "It's about who might try to stop us in the building before we ever get to the cemetery. Anyway, can you handle a shotgun, Doc?"

He nodded, picking the weapon up. "Yeah. No problem there."

"What's the plan, then?" Dom Francis asked.

"Pretty straight forward," Shane said. "Once we get to the cemetery, we find the Nurse's grave. Next, comes the digging, and here's hoping we won't be interrupted. When we have her grave opened up, we salt her bones, dump some lighter fluid on her, and light her up."

"Easy enough," the monk said. "Except for when it all goes to crap."

"Exactly," Shane said, nodding.

"Boy," Doc said. "You guys really know how to inspire confidence."

"We try," Dom Francis said grimly.

"Alright," Shane said. He winced as he put his gear bag over his good shoulder. With his right hand, he picked up the shovel and said, "Let's get this done."

Doc took the lead since he knew the way to the graveyard. Shane tried not to think about how his feet were cold, or about how hard and uncomfortable the ground was beneath them. Occasionally, he winced as sharp rocks bit into the tender flesh of his insteps. Soon, he felt himself bleeding and he knew he would have to get a round of antibiotics to make sure nothing became infected.

At least I don't need a tetanus shot, he thought, shaking his head.

What if they know the nurse didn't stop me? Shane wondered. *Won't they be back tomorrow? Won't they wait until I'm sedated?*

At the memory of the surgery he needed, Shane glanced at his arm. There was hardly any pain, but the injury he had sustained in the fight against Abel Latham in Griswold was a serious one.

"You okay?" Dom Francis asked.

Shane nodded. "Yeah, I'm good."

"You know," Doc said over his shoulder. "I'm surprised they didn't wait until you were knocked out to try and do you in."

"Me too," Shane agreed. "Maybe she was too nervous."

"She seemed like she had her act together," Dom Francis said. "I think she may have been a little too zealous."

"Lucky for me she was," Shane said, and then he gasped and hopped on one foot for a moment.

The other two men stopped, and Doc said, "Sit down."

Wincing, Shane did so.

Doc squatted down, picked up one of Shane's feet and shook his head. "Hey, you're going to need to stop soon. You're cutting your feet to pieces."

"How far are we from the graveyard?" Shane asked as Doc put his foot down.

"It's over the rise there," Doc said, gesturing towards the road. "Seriously, you should wait here, let us go up there and do what needs to be done."

Shane shook his head. "You two haven't done this before. Plus there's no telling what you're going to run into in there."

"Shane," Dom Francis said. "I'm former special forces. Doc here was a combat medic. Add to that the iron we're carrying, plus the shotguns. I think we're looking pretty good."

Shane hesitated, and then he nodded. "Alright. I'll make a deal with you two. You leave me here for a bit, then I'll make my way up to you."

"Shane," Doc started.

"No," Shane said, shaking his head vehemently. "It's either this or I limp along with you. Or, better yet, one of you gets to carry me. And I am a hell of a lot heavier than I look."

"Fine," Doc said, frowning as he took the gear bag from Shane. "Rest. But do not hurry up to us. Got it?"

"Sure," Shane said, stretching his legs out and wincing at the pain. "Sure."

He watched Dom Francis and Doc head off up the narrow road, and he tried to ignore his feet as they throbbed.

Chapter 58: Francis and Doc on the Road

Francis felt himself slip easily into the old, familiar rhythm of a patrol. He scanned from left to right, and back again. His eyes picked out likely spots for ambushes, as well as areas where he might be able to establish a successful defense. Everything came sharply into focus; each leaf, every tree branch. His ears picked out and identified a hundred different sounds.

On the wind, he smelled sickness, and Francis knew it was Doc. The man had been on E Ward, and Francis could only imagine what horrific disease ate at the young man. Francis had friends who had contracted rare, terminal diseases, others who had suddenly sprouted unknown cancers.

Job hazard when slogging through third world cesspools and warzones where dictators and warlords used chemical weapons on friend and foe alike, Francis thought.

He adjusted his grip on the shotgun and looked over at Doc who was focused on the road and the large cemetery that had appeared. The burial ground was hemmed in by trees, but no fence; although it looked as if there had been some sort of barrier before. Chunks of cement with broken pieces of black metal protruding from them, formed the rough outline of where a wall would have been. A light fog hung at knee level, most of the stones cropping up from the mist. Here and there Francis saw small crypts as if some mournful person had sought to immortalize their loved one.

"This is a sacred place," Francis said softly. "How many people are buried here?"

"Over two thousand," Doc said.

"How do you know?" Francis asked, surprised.

"I counted them," Doc answered, his voice filled with sadness. "Each and every one of them."

"I'm impressed," Francis said. Then, he said, "Do you know where the Nurse's grave is?"

"Ruth Williamson," Doc said. "Of course, I do."

And he brought the shotgun up and pulled the trigger.

Chapter 59: Shane's in Pain

Shane lay on his back, and he looked at the stars.

My God, he thought, *I can't believe I'm lying here. I should be up there with them. Bleeding feet or not.*

Slowly he sat up, his body complaining bitterly. The wound in his shoulder seeped blood, and the cuts on his feet did the same.

The blast of a shotgun interrupted his self-critique.

Silence followed.

Enough waiting, he told himself, and he managed to get to his feet. A wave of pain-induced nausea rolled over him, and he spread his arms wide, trying to maintain his balance. For a second, it seemed as if he might fall, but he didn't.

Shane took a deep breath, let it out slowly, and focused on the narrow road. Each step was an effort, and he knew he was leaving bloody footprints behind him.

Ignoring the agony, Shane continued on.

Doc and Dom Francis were going to need his help.

Chapter 60: The First Battle in the Grave Yard

Francis had been shot at many times. He had even been hit on occasion. So when he saw Doc bring the shotgun up, Francis immediately turned away.

There wasn't enough time to get completely out of the blast radius, however, and he felt some of the rock salt strike him in the back and the side. The pain was impressive in its intensity and immediacy.

Francis didn't try shooting back, it merely would have been a waste of ammunition. So instead, he threw his own shotgun at Doc and rushed him. The dying man reacted as most people would. He shied away from the thrown weapon, and he didn't try to put another load of rock salt into Francis.

As Doc avoided the shotgun, Francis reached him, wrenched Doc's gun free and threw it aside. The young man was much stronger and quicker than Francis had been lead to believe.

Doc lashed out with a fist and caught Francis in his newly wounded side. And, if Francis had been a regular guy, the blow would have been enough to put him down.

No, Francis thought, turning himself towards Doc. *I'm not a regular guy.*

He brought the heel of his hand up, smashing it into Doc's chin. The clack of his teeth against each other was grating, and Francis smiled.

I was a bad man, Doc, Francis thought. *Long before I was ever a good one.*

The fight was short and brutal.

When Francis was done, he stood over Doc. The former Army medic lay on his back, both eyes swelled shut and his breath coming in great gasps. Francis's fists had mashed Doc's lips, giving them the shape and appearance of swollen, bloody sausages. As Francis looked down at the man, he realized he had blood on his robes.

You can never come back from this, Francis told himself. *Your time as a monk is done. Your peace is ended.*

Accepted, he thought, and he squatted down beside Doc. He picked up Doc's left hand and said, "Can you hear me?"

Doc nodded.

"Good," Francis said. "Can you speak?"

"Yes," Doc said, the word barely intelligible. "What do you want to know, Dead Man?"

"Why?" Francis demanded.

"I'm dying," Doc said, chuckling and grimacing at the same time. "I wanted to help as many people as I could."

"Where is the Nurse buried?" Francis asked.

Doc spit blood at him.

Francis took hold of Doc's left pinky and broke it.

Doc's shriek echoed off of the headstones.

"Where is the Nurse buried?" Francis asked.

Doc shook his head.

Francis broke the man's left ring finger.

Doc sobbed and vomited.

"Where is she buried?" Francis asked again.

"A crypt," Doc gasped. "And she's going to kill you for this. She's going to *kill* you."

"Maybe," Francis said. He dropped Doc's mangled hand and stood up. He grabbed Shane's gear bag, picked up his shotgun and looked around the cemetery. In the curiously peaceful light of the night sky, Francis could see four separate crypts. He contemplated another round of questions with the recalcitrant Doc, but he shook the thought away.

Too much time, Francis thought. *And torture never feels right.*

Francis left the traitor on the ground and walked towards the nearest crypt to see if he could find the Nurse.

Chapter 61: Reaching the Cemetery

Shane's feet had gone numb by the time he reached the cemetery, and he didn't know if he was stumbling from exhaustion, pain, or a combination of the two.

He caught sight of Francis as the man entered a nearby crypt, but Shane couldn't see Doc anywhere. Moving into the low hanging fog, Shane heard a sound, nothing more than a whimper, but he turned towards it and saw Doc crawling towards the edge of the cemetery.

"Doc?" Shane asked. He wanted to hurry to the man, but an uncomfortable feeling whispered for him to stop.

Doc looked up, a wheezing laugh escaping his mangled mouth.

"Have you come to die, Shane?" Doc asked. "You must have. She's here. Waiting for you. Waiting for the monk. You think she needs the dead to help her? Not the Nurse. She needs no one and nothing. You'll die. But not before she's played with you a bit."

Shane's skin crawled at the man's words, most of which were difficult to understand.

"You sided with her," Shane said softly, finally understanding.

"Long before you were here," Doc said, crawling again. "Oh yes, Shane Ryan. I chose her, and I am pleased I did. So many of us, staff and patients, even a few family members. We all chose her."

Shane stared down at the man and watched him crawl.

Shane tightened his grip on his knuckledusters.

There's the sweet-spot, a calm, cold voice told him. *Right there, where the skull meets the top of the C-Spine. Or the temple. A single blow and he'll be dead. One punch and he won't pass the word to any of the Nurse's twisted little devotees.*

Shane relaxed his grip, turned away from Doc and limped towards the crypt he had seen Dom Francis enter. As he walked, the fog began to dissipate. The air grew colder and the stars and moon shined brighter.

She's coming, Shane realized, trying to quicken his pace. *She knows we're here.*

Dom Francis stepped out of the crypt again, quickly bringing the shotgun up.

"Shane," the monk said. "You look like crap."

"Like looking in a mirror," Shane said, nodding towards the wet spots standing out starkly on the monk's robes.

"True," Dom Francis said. "You run into the traitor?"

"Yeah," Shane said. "Why are you checking the crypt?"

"Little weasel said she was in one of them," Dom Francis paused and looked around. "It's colder."

"She's around," Shane said. He searched the graveyard, surveying the three other crypts.

"Why is she waiting?" the monk asked.

"To kill us," Shane replied. "I think she's expecting us."

"Too bad for us," Dom Francis muttered.

"Yup," Shane agreed. "Ready to try door number two?"

"Of course," the monk said.

"You shouldn't," a feminine voice said from behind them.

As they turned around, the Nurse stepped forward, slapping the shotgun out of Dom Francis's hands. He swung at her, but with a flick of her wrist, he was thrown backward, striking a small headstone and tripping over it.

Shane, unable to run, stood his ground.

The Nurse looked at him sympathetically.

"Why are you struggling against me?" she asked him, genuine curiosity filling her voice. "You are alone in this world. I seek only to give you peace. To grant you rest."

"I don't mind being alone," Shane said. "And peace and rest, they don't particularly interest me."

"You are unloved," she said sadly.

Shane's dog tags grew cold, and he smiled at the Nurse.

"No," he whispered, "I am loved."

A high-pitched wail pierced the night, and Courtney launched herself out of the dog tags.

Chapter 62: Fighting Among the Stones

Shane knew he was running on adrenaline and little else.

He doubted Courtney would give him much time to get to the Nurse's crypt, but he found himself drawn to watch the battle between the ghosts.

The Nurse was strong, incredibly so. She had survived and thrived for decades, and whether she realized it or not, Shane knew she had fed on the energy of the ghosts around her.

Courtney had none of these in her favor. But she was angry.

Shane watched as Courtney slammed into the Nurse. There was no finesse. No deft and able moves, nothing 'Hollywood' about the fight between the two dead women.

A glow wrapped around them, pulsing in time to the punches Courtney was landing. The Nurse staggered back, a look of surprise on her face. And as she tried to regain her balance, Shane limped as quickly as he could to the next crypt.

In the light of the moon, he read the name carved in the granite mantle above the door.

Ruth Williamson.

Shane smiled grimly, and when he reached the door, he found it locked.

Worry ate at him as he dropped his gear bag and dug out his collapsible shovel, glancing over his shoulder at the battle behind him.

The Nurse had managed to straighten up, and she shied away from Courtney's blows. But they weren't having any effect, and the Nurse was realizing it. Even as he watched, Shane saw her look of surprise and shock being replaced quickly by annoyance, and then anger.

He lifted the shovel and smashed the lock. The old metal sheared away, and a wave of dizziness caused Shane to stagger forward, slamming against the door. It swung open, and he fell into the crypt, landing heavily on the tiled floor.

He felt the knife wound keenly, more blood spilling out and soaking his hoodie He pushed himself back up, reached out and grabbed his gear bag. From it, he pulled out a lighter and for a heartbeat he stared at it. A glance outside showed the battle between Courtney and the Nurse had shifted. Courtney was moving backward with the Nurse advancing toward her.

Leave, Courtney, Shane thought. *Leave.*

He shook his head, needing to focus. This was going to hurt.

He opened his hoodie, clenched his teeth and ripped the bandage off. Blood pulsed out of the wound in time with his heartbeat, and he let out a shaky, tired laugh.

"Okay," he whispered. "Do it."

Shane flicked the lighter, and he brought the bright flame to the wound. He let himself yell as he cauterized the wound, the smell of burning flesh hard in his nose. His hand shook as he dropped the lighter to the floor and a cold sweat broke out across his brow.

"Shane!" Courtney screamed.

He looked out the doorway, and he saw Courtney. She backed towards him, Ruth grimly pressing towards her.

"Run, Courtney," he said.

She glanced at him, and he nodded.

A look of sadness flickered across her face, and she vanished.

Ruth paused, looked around, and then continued on toward the crypt. When she reached the doorway, she stopped, and she was clearly irritated.

"Shane Ryan," she said in a firm, maternal tone, "you have been an extremely difficult patient."

Shane chuckled, the absurdity of the statement too much to handle. His chuckle turned into a laugh, and his belly hurt from it. Tears spilled from his eyes, and he had to catch his breath. Finally, he stopped and looked at the Nurse. Her look of irritation had been replaced with one of concern.

"You're going mad, aren't you," she said sadly.

"Probably," Shane said. "But I'm still going to cook you up."

"No," the Nurse said, gently, "you're going to your well-deserved rest, warrior."

A shotgun blast ripped through the night air, and she vanished.

Dom Francis stood a few feet away, leaning against a headstone.

"She'll be back," Shane said, getting up.

The monk nodded. "Light her up. I'll cover you."

"You got it," Shane said, and he turned to find her bones.

Chapter 63: Ruth Williamson Returns

Francis didn't know how many rounds he had left. Getting thrown into a granite headstone hadn't helped his short term memory retention.

He wanted to move closer to the crypt, but he couldn't. Not only because he had a better field of fire from where he stood, but if he tried to move from his position, he would probably fall down.

It had been a tremendous effort to stand, and only his strength of will had allowed him to shuffle a few feet to the front of the crypt. Once there, he had been able to enjoy a clear, sure shot.

The air shimmered to the left of the crypt and the Nurse appeared.

Oh no, he thought, looking at her face. *She is decidedly unhappy with me.*

The Nurse took a step forward, and Francis shot her.

And once more, she vanished.

This is going to get old fast, Francis thought, his head starting to pound. *She's going to figure it out, and I'm going to die.*

"How's it going?" Francis called out.

"Found it!" Shane yelled back.

"Little good it will do you both," the Nurse hissed from behind Francis.

He tried to spin around, but instead he fell to the ground, which saved him. As she stepped closer, glaring at him, Francis managed to bring the shotgun up and fire again.

"Hurry!" Francis shouted, struggling back into a sitting position.

"Really?" Shane yelled. "Because, you know, I thought this might be a good time to start writing my memoirs."

A crash sounded, and Shane let out a harsh laugh.

Francis looked into the crypt and saw Shane. The man stood triumphantly by a sarcophagus, and the Nurse appeared behind him.

Francis shot her, and some of the rock salt caught Shane high in the back.

Book 4: Sanford Hospital

Oh no! Francis thought as Shane leaned against the sarcophagus. Horrified, Francis watched as Shane slid down to the floor.

Ruth Williamson snatched the shotgun out of Francis's hands and snarled, "I've had enough of you meddling with my patient, *Father.*"

She cast the weapon aside and grabbed hold of him by the front of his robes.

"You've left me no choice," she said, a hint of sadness in her anger. "I have to euthanize you."

"Sure," Francis agreed, and he punched her. He fell against a headstone as the iron sent her back to her bones.

Better hurry up, Shane, Francis thought as darkness closed in around the edges of his vision. *I've got nothing left.*

Chapter 64: The Homestretch

Shane pulled himself up, dragging his gear bag along as well. Holding onto it tightly, he looked into the open sarcophagus. The physical remains of Nurse Ruth lay in front of him. She was dressed in what had been a beautiful gown, her hands neatly folded over her stomach. On her head was perched a nurse's cap. Her skin, ancient and parchment-like, clung to her bones, accentuating all of them. Dried flowers were scattered about her.

Too bad you're crazy, Shane thought. He removed the lighter fluid from the bag, popped the cap and sprayed the body down. When it was empty, he dropped the can onto her body and took out the steel wool.

Not taking any chances here, he told himself, and he sprinkled it over the corpse.

"Why are you desecrating my body?"

Shane turned around and saw the Nurse. She stood with her arms folded across her chest, and she looked displeased.

Shane shrugged.

A look of sympathy came onto her face. "You really are a mad man, aren't you?"

"Some people say I have a few mental issues," Shane replied. "I disagree, personally. You know? Everyone's a little crazy. Once in a while."

She nodded her head. "It is why I want to grant you your peace, Shane."

"You know," he said, "I really do appreciate the gesture. But I'm not too thrilled with the idea of dying right now."

"Dying is easy," she said comfortingly.

"I'm not ready," Shane said.

"It's because you're afraid. We're all afraid of the unknown," she said, her voice filling with compassion. "I'm here to help you be unafraid. To know that there is a better place for you."

"Well," Shane said, taking a deep breath and letting it out slowly, "I guess the question I have right now is, do I have a choice?"

She shook her head. "I am afraid not. It is your time, Shane. None of us can argue with that."

Shane nodded.

He took out a cigarette, his hands shaking as he put it in his mouth. Fumbling around he found his lighter, snapped out a flame and lit the cigarette. As he exhaled, the Nurse frowned.

"Perhaps," she said, giving him a cold smile, "I should let you live and suffer with the cancer growing in your chest."

Shane inhaled deeply, the smoke calming.

"But," she added, "I will enjoy killing you."

"Fair enough," Shane said. He took one last drag on it, then flicked the cigarette onto her remains.

The result was instantaneous.

Some of the steel wool burst into flames, which lit the lighter fluid and sent a blue flame ripping through the sarcophagus.

The Nurse screamed and lunged at Shane, slamming him hard against the stone. His breath rushed out, and he gasped for air. She pressed him there, even as she started to burn bright blue. He could feel flames against the back of his head, and he fought against her, trying to move away from the fire.

Only when her own interior flames destroyed her arms, did she fall back, and release him from the threat of immolation.

Shane fell to the floor and rolled away from the ghost as she burned.

She twisted her face towards him, her eyes turning into smoldering orbs.

"Why?!" she howled. "Why?! I was doing God's work!"

"Why?" Shane repeated. "Because you're not God! You're not anyone! I hope you burn in Hell!"

Her response was lost as the flames devoured her, and he was left alone in the crypt as smoke filled the enclosure. Coughing, Shane rolled over and crawled to the door. Tears streamed down his face as he reached the open air.

He lay pressed against the cold grass, struggling for a breath free of the acrid smoke. Shane twisted his head to one side, and fear rippled through him.

Ghosts stared down at him.

Hatred filled their dead eyes, but none of them advanced.

Spitting the foul taste of the Nurse's burning corpse out of his mouth, Shane sat up and saw why the dead remained where they were.

The ghosts of Matias and Brett stood between him and Dom Francis's unconscious body.

No, Shane realized, *they're not standing, they're hovering.*

Matias and Brett were several inches off the ground, and their expressions were cold and hard.

Without looking at Shane, Matias said, "Rest now. They will not touch you. Not when we are here."

"Are you strong enough?" Shane asked, his voice little more than a croak.

Brett nodded, and Matias smiled.

"They ask themselves the same question," Matias said. "I will say yes, and I am eager for them to try to find a definitive answer."

"Okay," Shane said, letting his head drop back to the grass. "Whatever you say, Matias."

Shane tried to crawl, but exhaustion swept him into unconsciousness.

Chapter 65: Awake and Alert

Francis woke up to the night sounds of the woods around the cemetery. He was on his back and looked at the night sky.

An owl cried out, and a dark shape soared by.

Get up, Francis thought. And he did. Muscles screamed and protested, dried blood cracked and wounds which had scabbed broke open. *Find Shane.*

Francis got to his feet, using a headstone to steady himself. He wobbled as he walked, staggering towards the open crypt. A foul, burnt stench filled his nose and he pushed the unpleasant sensory input to the back of his mind.

Shane was stretched out in the grass, in front of the open door. The man was unconscious, and had fresh burns along the back of his neck. Blood and dirt caked the soles of his feet.

Francis bent down and picked Shane up. He put him in a fireman's carry, slinging the man across his shoulders. Shane grunted, but didn't wake up.

Standing up, Francis took a deep breath. He adjusted his own body weight, turned and headed towards the road. The old ability to separate his mind from his body's actions returned, and Francis found himself able to remain above the physical pain. His pace increased and he was soon at his own car. He set Shane down on the trunk, unlocked the backdoor and then put Shane in.

He let the unconscious man lie across the seat, tucking Shane's bare feet up before closing the door. Francis paused, caught his breath and fought back a spike of pain from his various injuries. He took in a long, slow breath through his nose and exhaled the same way. With one hand on the roof of the car Francis thought, *I need to get us to a hospital. Then I need to go back to the Order.*

I have a decision to make.

He focused his mind again, and then Francis got into his car. The engine started when he turned the key, and the car moved when he shifted into 'drive'.

Francis smiled.

Everything's going to be fine, he thought, and he left Sanford Hospital.

Chapter 66: Francis Makes a Move

"Are you quite certain, Francis?" Abbot Gregory asked.

Francis nodded, not quite trusting his own voice to contain the raw emotion flowing through him. His small travel bag was packed and on the cot beside him. The linens had been stripped and sent to the laundry. Abbot Gregory stood in the doorway, his hands clasped together.

"Where will you go?" Abbot Gregory said, concern in his voice.

"I'll be asking a friend if I can stay with him for a bit," Francis replied.

"And if he says no?" the abbot asked.

Francis smiled wryly. "Well, then, Abbot, I'll figure it out."

Abbot Gregory nodded, then he stepped into the room. "Hold out your hand, Francis."

He did so.

The abbot dropped the two iron rings Francis had used at Sanford into his open palm. He looked at the older man, confused.

"I have spoken with the older members of the Order," Abbot Gregory explained. "We feel you are not done with the unquiet dead, and so you will need these."

"What if someone else does?" Francis asked, looking down at the rings.

"Then we will have more forged," the abbot said.

"Thank you," he said as he slipped the rings onto his fingers. "Thank you very much, Abbot."

"You are quite welcome," Abbot Gregory replied. "Will you send us your address as soon as you have it? I have forwarded your request to withdraw from the Order, and while I am certain it is forthcoming, we will need to know where to send the permission."

"As soon as I know," Francis said, "I will let you know."

"Excellent," the old man said. "Now come, I will give you a ride to where you need to go."

Francis nodded, stood up and took his bag off the bed.

"St. Joseph's hospital in Nashua, Abbot," he said. "My friend, Shane, is there. I must speak to him."

Abbot Gregory nodded. "Let us be on our way, then, Francis."

Holding onto his bag tightly, Francis followed Abbot Gregory out of the room, and out of the Order.

Chapter 67: At St. Joseph's Hospital

I am going to be paying these bills forever, Shane thought, staring up at the ceiling.

Well, a cold voice in his head replied, *you could be dead.*

Shut up, Shane told himself.

"Hello," a voice said.

Shane turned to look at the doorway and saw a young nurse. She was pretty, a tall, thin woman who looked to be in her mid-twenties.

"Hello," Shane replied, returning his attention to the ceiling. His body ached in spite of the morphine that dripped through the intravenous line. He knew he could tell them, but part of him was afraid to have the dosage increased. *Alcohol is enough of a problem,* he thought. With a sigh, he scratched at his left shoulder, where they had put the nicotine patch to help with his cigarette cravings.

"How are you feeling?" she asked, coming into the room to stand beside his bed.

"Peachy," Shane answered. "Think I can go home now?"

She smiled and shook her head. "Not yet. The police were here again while you were sleeping."

"That's nice of them," Shane said.

The smile on the woman's face became a frown. "They're concerned about who stabbed you."

"Stabbed me?" Shane said, feigning surprise.

"Yes. Are you going to tell them who stabbed you?" she asked.

"Why would someone stab me?" Shane said, stifling a yawn. The young nurse sighed in exasperation.

"The police would like to see you later on if it's convenient," she said.

Shane looked at her. "It's not. Tell them I said 'No, thank you.'"

"Shane," she started, and he frowned.

She blushed slightly. "Mr. Ryan, they have to investigate the crime."

"There was no crime," Shane said. "Nothing happened."

"You were burned, given a concussion, and stabbed, and nothing happened?" she asked.

"Exactly," Shane said.

The nurse shook her head and left the room without saying another word. A few minutes later, the dog tags shifted on his chest, and Courtney was there. She looked at the room's door and said, "She's pretty."

"She's not you," Shane said.

Courtney smiled down at him. "Shane Ryan, you know exactly what to say."

"Glad you think so," Shane said. He looked at Courtney and blinked away tears.

She smiled at him. "All will be well." Shane shook his head. His heart hurt too much to speak. Courtney reached out, her touch cold against his cheek. Goosebumps raced along his flesh. He cleared his throat.

"Thank you, for everything," he whispered.

"You're welcome," she replied. Her finger traced the line of his jaw.

A knock sounded on the door, and Courtney vanished.

"Come in," Shane said.

Dom Francis entered a moment later, carrying a travel bag and wearing street clothes.

"Dom Francis, what's going on?" Shane asked in surprise.

"I've left the Order," Dom Francis said, smiling apologetically. "And call me Frank, please."

"Sure, Frank. Do you need help or something?" Shane said.

Frank nodded. "I, well, I need a place to stay."

"And you want to stay with me?" Shane asked, surprised.

"Yes," Frank said, then added hurriedly, "if it's not too much trouble."

"No," Shane said. "It's not any trouble at all. It's just, well, I'll need to talk to you about the other residents in the house."

"Are they difficult?" Frank asked.

"No. No, Frank," Shane said, "They're dead."

The expression of surprise on Frank's face made Shane laugh, and Frank soon joined him. Their laughter filled the small room, and Shane wondered what it would be like to have a living person in the house again.

* * *

Kurkow Prison
Book 5

Chapter 1: Kurkow Prison

"It's a steal is what it is," Pete said.

Ollie glanced at him. "How, exactly, is it a steal?"

"Come on!" Pete grinned as he stepped away from the sedan. "Look at it, Ollie!"

"I am," Ollie said. "Damned thing looks like a money pit to me."

"No!" Pete said. He spread his arms wide as if trying to encompass the entire structure. "Look, part of the beauty of the deal is that we *don't* have to fix it all up."

"What?" Ollie said, staring at his brother. "Pete, have you lost your mind? Honestly, what part of it looks like a good deal?"

Ollie left the car then went and stood by Pete. "I'm going to tell you what I see, okay? I see acres of lead paint. I see miles of asbestos-wrapped pipes. I see lakes of foul, nasty water. The place is a superfund site without any funds to clean it up. What the hell are you thinking? Do you want to open a bed and breakfast? A museum? For God's sake, man, what the hell do you want to buy this for?"

"First," Pete said, holding up a thin finger, "I want you to hold onto the bed and breakfast idea. Might be a great way to put a spin on it. And, second, don't be mad, I already bought the place."

Ollie turned his attention away from the prison and looked at his brother. He tried to speak, but the words refused to exit his mouth.

Pete took a step back, holding his hands up in front of him, palms out.

"Oliver," Pete said, "they were practically giving it away."

"What was the price?" Ollie hissed.

"Well," Pete stammered.

"Price!" Ollie screamed.

"Two!" Pete yelled.

"'Two' what, Peter?"

Pete loosened the collar of his shirt. "Million."

For the first time in his life, Ollie felt faint. He took a step back, trying to catch his breath. Pete reached out to help and Ollie snapped, "Don't."

"Okay."

"You already signed the paperwork?" Ollie asked, exhaling slowly.

Pete nodded.

"How much did they want down?" Ollie grumbled.

"Twenty percent," Pete said.

"Twenty percent," Ollie repeated. "Twenty percent!"

Ollie straightened up and focused on the prison. The building was huge, stretching for two entire blocks. Three fences wrapped around the perimeter and each fence was topped with razor wire. Old guard towers were on each corner, and the prison was three stories tall. The windows, protected by heavy metal grating, were unbroken, and for that Ollie felt thankful.

He turned and glared at his brother. "You used my part of the inheritance."

"I had to," Pete said.

"Fine," Ollie said. "Fine. We'll make a go of this, whatever the hell it is you're thinking about. But this is how it's going to work. You, my dear, stupid brother, are going to be in there, with the crews, going through the place. My inspector is going with you."

"What?" Pete said, crestfallen. "Gordy hates everything I do!"

"I don't care," Ollie snapped. "Gordy won't try and hand me a polished turd and tell me it's a diamond. He goes with you. He'll make notes. He'll tell me whether or not your little plan is feasible."

"It's a great plan," Pete said, grinning. The grin vanished and was replaced with a somber expression. "You'll see, Ollie."

"I better," Ollie said, "or you are going to be in for a world of hurt."

Without waiting for his brother to reply, Ollie turned away from both Pete and the prison and walked back to the car. He sat down hard in the passenger's seat and sent Gordy a text.

Ollie closed his eyes and tried not to think about the financial mess his brother had gotten them into.

Chapter 2: An Honest Day's Work

"What have you got going on today?" Frank asked.

Shane looked up at him, the morning light causing the milky portion of his right eye to glow. A fine stubble of light brown hair had started to grow on the former monk's head, and the scars on his face stood out crisp and sharp.

Shane shook his head and shrugged. "I have absolutely no idea. I've taken a break from any translation work. The past couple of months have been a little too much, physically and mentally."

Frank nodded, pulled out a chair and sat down at the table.

"Why?" Shane asked. "What's up with you?"

"When I left the Order I reached out to a few friends of mine," Frank said. "Told them I'm looking for any work. Not too much, my knees can't handle it, but I'll do some day labor."

"Someone gave you a call?" Shane asked.

Frank nodded. "Guy I knew in high school. Ollie, he wants me to work on a crew that's going to look at demoing the old Kurkow Prison."

"Where the hell is that?" Shane leaned back in his chair, knocked the head off his cigarette and said, "I've never heard of the place."

"Old prison, upstate, New Hampshire. It's a little town called Gaiman, right along the Canadian border." Frank said.

"That's a long ride," Shane said.

"Yup," Frank said, grinning. "So, you feel up to a little honest, manual labor?"

"Hell no," Shane replied. "But I'll go anyway. I could use the work. Get out of the house for a bit. How much is your friend paying you?"

"He hasn't told me yet," Frank said. "But I think he wants me to babysit his brother Pete."

"Hard to handle?" Shane asked.

Frank shook his head. "Impulsive."

"Ah." Shane stubbed out his cigarette and nodded. "Yeah. Alright. When do you want to leave?"

"Soon as you're ready," Frank answered.

Shane stood up. "I'm ready now."

As Frank got to his feet and Shane turned to leave, Courtney appeared in the doorway. She shimmered in the pale light thrown by the overhead kitchen lamp, and she had an expression of concern on her dead face.

"Where are you going?" she asked.

Her voice sounded strange, almost too faint.

"I'm going out for a bit," Shane said. He smiled at her. "Frank and I will be home soon enough."

"Take me with you?" she asked.

Shane shook his head.

354

Courtney's form solidified as she demanded, "Why?"

"I won't risk losing you," Shane said, his voice gentle but firm. "You are not a trinket for me to carry around and to lose."

For a moment, Shane thought she might yell, but instead, she vanished.

When she did, Shane shook his head and led the way out of the house, pausing only for himself and Frank to grab their coats out of the hall closet. Once they were outside, Frank glanced over at him.

"What's going on?" the former monk asked.

"Wish I knew," Shane said. "Want to drive since you know the way?"

Frank nodded and caught the keys with one hand when Shane tossed them to him.

Shane felt sadness well up within him as he wiped the snow off his car on the passenger side. Frank did the same on the driver's window. Shane brushed the snow off his hands, the flesh red from the cold, and felt his attention drawn back to the house.

Courtney stood in his bedroom window, her crooked neck glaring in the morning light. A harsh and bitter reminder of her death at the hands of Abel Latham.

"Hey," Frank said, his tone gentle. "You alright?"

"No." Shane sighed and got into the car. Frank climbed in, started the engine and closed the door.

"Want to talk about Courtney at all?" Frank asked.

Shane shook his head, closed his eyes, and tried not to think of the young woman who had given her life for him.

Chapter 3: Gordon Capullo and the Prison

Gordon Capullo sat in his Super-Duty pickup and waited, a cup of tea in one hand and the morning paper in the other. He had spent most of his adult life in vehicles, traveling from one job to another. Constructing homes and buildings, then inspecting the same. The interior of the Super-Duty reflected his nomadic job.

A mint scented air-freshener was clipped to one of the vents over the radio. On the passenger side floor was a trashcan, strapped in with a bungee cord. His metallic green thermos, filled with traditional Chinese tea, protruded from a cooler packed with a variety of healthy snacks.

Beneath the cooler was a copy of the day's Boston Globe, another of the Boston Herald, the Washington Post, the New York Times, and the Manchester Union Leader. A reprint of the classic Batman by Bob Kane was tucked between the cooler and the back of the seat.

The only items missing from the truck were his wife and his dog, and Gordon had buried both of them years earlier.

Gordon took the Telegraph off of his lap, turned the page, glanced over an op-ed piece on one of the Presidential candidates, and wished Libby was still with him. He looked at the cell phone on the seat beside him and felt a wave of sadness wash over him as he remembered how he would never receive another text or call from her.

Sighing, Gordon closed the paper, folded it back into its original form, and put it beneath the cooler with the others. He started up the truck to let the heater run for a few minutes, and he looked out the windshield at the prison.

Gordon was old enough to remember the accident which had closed the facility. And the investigation into the incident. The wave of suicides that had followed.

The crunch of wheels on snow caught his attention, and Gordon turned to see a small, black sedan pull in beside him.

He didn't recognize the man in the passenger seat. A bald man, perhaps in his forties, his face etched with lines of grief and anger. Scars climbed up out of the man's shirt, sprawling across his neck and up the back of his head.

The driver's side door opened and Gordon laughed out loud.

He turned off the truck's engine and got out.

"Frank!" Gordon called out.

"Gordon," Frank said, laughing and walking around the front of the car. "Ollie didn't tell me he had you on this job."

The two men shook hands and hugged. Gordon stepped back and looked at the younger man.

"Who else would he hire?" Gordon asked. "You look good, Kid. Better than I was led to believe."

"Oh?" Frank said, raising an eyebrow. "Who's been talking smack?"

"Who else?" Gordon sighed and shook his head. "Pete of course."

Frank rolled his eyes. "Peter."

The passenger side door opened, and the bald man got out. Frank stepped aside and said, "Shane Ryan, this is Gordon Capullo. The whole reason I joined the Army."

Gordon shook Shane's hand, the other man's grip firm and polite. "A pleasure, Shane. And, Frank, you best keep that information to yourself. Your mom's not so old that she wouldn't hit me upside the head with a frying pan."

"True," Frank said, chuckling. "She's got a good throwing arm too. I could never outrun her. Luckily, she only used the wooden spoons as projectiles."

"Anyway," Gordon said, folding his arms over his chest to keep his hands warm in the cold air. "What are you doing up here? Last I heard you were in a religious order."

"I was," Frank said, the humor leaving his face. "Things didn't work out, so I left."

"You or them?" Gordon asked.

"Me," Frank said. "All me. The Order was great. They took care of me, I just couldn't stay there anymore."

"Did Ollie call you, too?" Gordon asked.

Frank nodded. "I had put the word out that I was looking for work."

"You're going to help with the demo?" Gordon said.

"Yup," Frank answered. "So is Shane."

"Is this your regular line of work?" Gordon asked.

"No," Shane said.

"What do you usually do?" Gordon said, and he saw Frank glance at Shane.

Shane grinned. "Usually?"

"Yeah," Gordon said.

"I kill ghosts," Shane replied.

The response caught Gordon off guard, and he let out a surprised laugh.

Chapter 4: Meeting the Boss

Shane had an instant dislike for Pete when the man showed up.

After their brief conversation, Shane and Frank had retreated to the car, while Gordon had gone back to his truck. As the time passed other vehicles arrived. Pick-ups and vans, contractors ready to look at the property.

The snowfall was light, and it was well after ten in the morning when a black Cadillac Escalade pulled into the small parking lot. The vanity plate on the SUV read, 'P-Dawg,' and the man who got out of the vehicle swaggered as he walked.

"That," Frank said in a low voice, "is Pete Dawson, Ollie's brother."

"Thus, P-Dawg?" Shane asked.

Frank nodded.

Shane and Frank got out of the car as Gordon and the men exited their own vehicles. Pete, Shane noticed, had on all new clothes. Jeans, work boots, and a Carhart jacket that looked as though they were fresh off the shelves. Pete looked like an unattractive male model in the working gear, someone unused to any sort of physical labor.

His dark brown hair was clipped in the latest fashion, and his beard was trim and neat as well. It was cut to highlight the line of his jaw and to hide the weakness of his chin. The man's brown eyes were narrow and close to one another.

"Good morning!" Pete said, grinning, and his voice was grating, reminding Shane of the squawking of a duck.

There were some grumbled replies, but Gordon returned the grin, saying, "Nice of you to show up, Peter."

Pete flinched at the words. "Well, traffic was rough on two ninety-five."

"Ah," Gordon said, nodding. "It wasn't for us. But we all got here at nine when we were asked to be here."

Pete cleared his throat. "Sorry about that, fellas."

"Anyway," Gordon said. "I don't know if I speak for everyone else, but I'd like to see what it looks like in there. Then maybe we can all get down to basics, huh?"

"Good idea," Pete said. With all of the bravado of a small town mayor, Pete led the way through the lot. They came to a narrow corridor formed by old and rusted wire fence. Razor wire was strewn across it, and Shane had an uncomfortable feeling.

"What's up?" Frank asked, glancing at him.

"Feels like we're being watched," Shane replied.

Frank looked up at the walls and the glass behind thick, cage-like steel.

"Yeah," Frank said. "Sure does."

Pete stopped at the doors. They were ancient in appearance, scarred and battered. A thick, iron chain was looped through the handles, a massive lock keeping them closed.

Shane looked at the chain. Rust from the links had stained the front of the doors, giving them the appearance of being blood stained.

He was distracted as Pete stood there and patted down the pockets of the new jacket.

"What's wrong, Peter?" Gordon asked, his voice thick with disdain.

Pete jerked around. "Ah, I think I left the keys in my other jacket."

"Not just the key to the lock here?" Gordon asked as some of the men groaned.

"No," Pete said. "Um, the keys to all of the different rooms and stuff."

Someone muttered about the whole job being a waste of time, and Gordon raised a hand. The men became silent.

"I have a pair of bolt cutters in my truck," Gordon said. "We can at least get inside and get a feel for the work that needs to be done. This way the day won't be a waste for the rest of us. If you're okay with it, Peter."

Pete nodded and the men stepped aside as much as they could, pressing themselves against the fence to let Gordon by. While the older man was gone, Pete took the opportunity to introduce himself to some of the men he didn't know.

"Frank!" Pete cried out. "I haven't seen you since you got out of the Army. What the hell happened to your face?"

"RPG hit a rock near me," Frank said. "You'd be amazed at how much it hurts."

"Can you even see out of your eye?" Pete said, leaning in for a closer look.

"Yes," Frank said, and Shane could hear the tightness in Frank's voice. "Yes, I can. Pete."

"Good, good," Pete said, and then he turned to Shane. He offered his hand, and Shane shook it. "Damn, what happened to your hair?"

Shane fought the urge to light a cigarette and put it out on Pete's tongue.

"You wouldn't believe me if I told you," Shane replied.

"Try me!" Pete grinned.

"I was trapped in the walls of my house with some ghosts as a boy," Shane said. "All of my hair fell out, and it never grew back."

Pete continued to grin as if waiting for a punch line. When one didn't come, he straightened up and looked around. "Okay, alright. Um, hey, here comes Gordon."

Shane turned and saw the older man. Gordon carried a well-used pair of red-handled bolt-cutters. As Gordon passed by, Shane's attention was drawn back to the iron chain.

Why iron? he wondered. *Where the hell would they even get iron, and why?*

Shane stiffened. "Pete."

Pete looked at him, "Yeah?"

"Are there any ghosts in here?" Shane asked.

The man smirked. "Why, you afraid?"

Frank put out a hand, restraining Shane.

Before Shane could speak again, there was a loud, sharp crack as the bolt-cutters severed a link. The chain rattled as one of the men pulled it out from between the handles.

All of Kurkow Prison seemed to sigh.

A wave of cold air rolled over them, the doors bowing out for a heartbeat.

"What the hell was that?" one of the men asked.

"Something bad," Shane said in a low voice.

Pete glanced at him. "What could be bad about cold air?"

As the last word left the man's lips, the windows on the first floor of the prison exploded outwards.

Chapter 5: More than He Bargained For

Pete was not happy.

And he knew, without a doubt, that Ollie wasn't going to be happy about it either. But for a completely different reason than his own.

He stood inside the entryway of Kurkow prison with four others; Gordon, Frank, Shane and a metal scrapper named Quincy.

The rest of the men who had come in to give bids on various parts of the job had left.

All of them, Pete thought, shaking his head. *Ollie's going to be livid.*

Pete looked at Gordon, who leaned against the wall, his arms crossed over his chest. Shane stood beside Frank, smoking and watching Pete. Shane's eyes were hard, and it seemed as if the man saw everything.

Pete didn't like it.

"What are you looking at?" he snapped.

Shane exhaled smoke through his nose and replied, "Apparently, not a whole lot."

Pete bristled. "What?"

"Is he deaf as well as stupid?" Shane asked Frank in a low voice, tapping the head of the cigarette off onto the floor. "That would be unfortunate. One affliction's enough."

Frank chuckled, and Pete jerked his head around to face the man.

"What?" Pete demanded.

"You'd do well to calm down," Gordon said. "I'm here. Quincy's here, and both Shane and Frank have hung around. I suggest we get started so we can all get home, and you can get this project started."

He's right, Pete thought. He nodded. "Fine. Yeah. Ok."

"Great," Gordon said, straightening up. He took a notebook out of his breast pocket and unclipped a pen from it. "Where do you want to start, Peter?"

"Um, here?" Pete said, hating how indecisive he sounded. "Yeah. Here. These offices should be a good place."

They all looked at him.

"What?" he asked. "What's wrong?"

"Peter," Gordon said, "it's your job to lead us through. Show us the rooms, so we can start to compile the information. In this case, since Quincy is the only one here to bid on a job, you let him take a look. As for me, I'm here to look at wiring, pipes, and all that good stuff. And, from what I gathered, Frank and his friend Shane are here to help with any demo or work that needs done so the contractors, or myself, can look at what we need to. Or, really, the one contractor."

Pete's face went red.

"Yeah," Pete said, "I didn't think the guys would run because of a little broken glass."

"A little?" Shane asked, chuckling. "That's quite an understatement. Personally, I'd qualify the breaking of a prison's windows as a lot of broken glass. But hey, I like to exaggerate I guess."

"I'm getting tired of your mouth," Pete said, pointing at Shane. "You'd be smart to shut it."

"Maybe," Shane said.

Shane's grin was terrible, and Pete realized it could only be worse if Shane's teeth were stained with blood.

"And maybe," Shane continued, "I'll snap your finger off at the knuckle if you don't point it somewhere else."

Pete dropped his hand. Without a word, he turned around, spotted the closest door in the foyer and walked to it. He grabbed the doorknob, which squealed as he forced it to the right. Pete strained, put his shoulder into it and popped the door open.

He stumbled into the room and a shiver ripped through him as he came to a stop in the center. Old papers fluttered in the breeze which came through the glassless windows. A desk, painted a sickly green, was on its side, the drawers scattered on the floor. The walls were painted a dull yellow, and fluorescent lights hung askew from the ceiling.

Gordon went around Pete to the nearest window and squatted down. He leaned close, examined the paint for a moment, and then took his glove off, scraping at the sill.

"I can't tell you for sure without a test," Gordon said, straightening up and brushing his hand off on his pants leg. "But I'm positive you're looking at lead paint, Peter. Probably layers of it."

Pete groaned, but he didn't say anything. He forced a smile and said, "That's alright. Gordon, I figured as much."

Gordon nodded and walked away.

Oh man, Pete thought. *Ollie told Gordon everything he was afraid of.*

"Hey Pete," Quincy said, his accent thick. The man was from some small town on the Maine, New Hampshire border, and it sounded as if French Canadian had been his first language.

"Yeah?" Pete asked.

"You got a lot of these in here?" Quincy asked, kicking the desk with a steel-toed boot. The sound was hollow, falling dead on the cinder block walls.

"I don't know," Pete answered. "Why, they worth anything?"

Quincy nodded. "Not too much, but they'll sell. Last year, huh, I salvaged two hundred from a school in Bangor. Shipped 'em all out to some studio in Los Angeles. Good money, yeah."

"Good," Pete said, perking up. "Real good."

He was about to say more, but Shane had turned around and walked to the doorway. The man's shoulders were tense as he tilted his head to the left.

"You look like a dog listening for his master to come home," Pete said, chuckling. The sound died though as Shane glanced over his shoulder at him. There was a brutal mixture of disdain and caution on the man's harsh face.

"We need to leave," Shane said in a low voice. "And we need to do it right now."

"What?" Pete started, but Frank cut him off.

"Why?" Frank asked, stepping over to Shane.

Shane returned his attention to the foyer as he said, "Because something's coming."

Chapter 6: Getting Out

Behind him, Shane could hear Pete speak. He didn't pay attention to the man, or to the words he spoke.

Somewhere beyond the next set of doors, which were chained just as the first had been, came the sound of someone walking.

The steps were loud and harsh, dominating the stillness of the prison.

Shane stepped out into the foyer. He reached to his back pocket, and his hand stopped as his fingertips grazed the worn material of his Levi's.

His knuckle-dusters were at home.

All of the iron is at home, he realized.

"Is there someone in here?" Gordon asked.

"There better not be," Pete snapped.

The footsteps advanced towards the chained doors.

"Gordon, get the chain off that door," Pete ordered.

"Don't," Shane said, his voice low. "We all need to get out of here."

"Like hell," Pete said, walking out into the foyer. He looked at Quincy and said, "Hand me those bolt-cutters."

The young man shrugged, picked the bolt-cutters up from where they rested against the wall and brought them to Pete.

"It's time to leave," Shane said to Frank.

Frank nodded. "Come on, Gordon."

"What's going on?" Gordon asked, an unsure expression on his face.

"We need to go," Frank said. "I'll fill you in outside. I promise. You just got to trust me on this one."

Out of the corner of his eye, Shane saw Gordon nod, and the two men left.

The footsteps came to a stop on the other side of the doors.

Quincy took a nervous step back.

"Do me a favor, kid," Shane said in a low voice.

Quincy looked at him.

"Grab me some of that chain from the first set of doors, will you?" Shane asked. Quincy nodded and hurried out of the room. Shane was alone with Pete. The other man was wrestling with the bolt-cutters, trying to get them to work.

"Leave it," Shane said, putting all of the authority he could muster into the words.

Pete straightened up in surprise, and he looked over at Shane. "Why? That guy's right on the other side. I swear I can hear him breathing."

Not likely, Shane thought. Quincy came back in, a length of the chain rattling in his hands. Shane nodded his thanks, accepted the metal and said, "Go outside with Frank."

"Aha!" Pete shouted, and the bolt-cutters snapped through a link. In a matter of seconds, he had severed a second. "Nothing to it!"

Shane watched as Pete dropped the bolt-cutters and unthreaded the chain from the handles.

Part of Shane wanted to back out of the room and leave Pete to his fate.

But he couldn't.

I don't hate him that much, Shane thought. *At least not yet.*

Pete dropped the chain to the floor, slapped his hands together in satisfaction, and jerked the right-hand door open.

In the dim light of the hall beyond, the walker was revealed.

He was huge. Easily six foot six, if not taller. He wore a dark blue uniform, the pants bloused at the tops of his boots. His skin was a putrid green, his eyes bulging from their sockets. The man's tongue was swollen, the tip of it protruding from between black lips. And he was bald in random patches across his head.

Pete's horrified scream told Shane that he could see through the man as well.

Shane moved forward even as Pete tripped over his own feet and fell hard onto the floor. Without hesitation, Shane stepped over Pete's prostrate form. When he was between Pete and the ghost, Shane began to swing the chain in a slow circle.

The links cut through the air with a soft hiss, and the dead prison guard smiled at him, a gruesome action which revealed gray teeth.

"You need to stay where you are," Shane said. "We're leaving."

The guard shook his head and spoke, his words surprisingly clear.

"No, you're not," he said. His voice was harsh and brutal. "You're going down into the hole. You shouldn't be up here. Only the warden and the screws are allowed up here."

"Pete," Shane said, "get out."

Pete didn't reply, but Shane heard him scramble out of the building.

"All alone, punk," the guard said.

"I'm leaving," Shane said, taking a cautious step back.

The guard stepped towards him. He flexed his hands and shook them out with all of the ease and confidence of a professional boxer.

This one likes to hurt people, Shane thought. *He must have been real popular with the prisoners.*

Shane took another step back, and the guard lunged at him.

Rocking forward, Shane gave the chain some slack, and it lashed out, smashing into what would have been the guard's chin. As the iron penetrated the ghost's form, the guard shuddered, screamed, and vanished.

Shane's heart beat against his ribs with enough force to be painful. The chain was heavy in his hands, and he took a deep breath to calm himself.

Farther down the hallway, he heard the sound of footsteps racing towards the foyer.

Shane turned and sprinted for the exit.

Chapter 7: Giving a Little Lesson

They were in a diner five miles down the road from Kurkow Prison.

Shane finished up his eggs while Frank doodled on a napkin. The other three men watched both of them with dazed expressions.

Putting his fork down, Shane looked at Frank. He shrugged and continued to work on a stick figure. The little man was running out of a building, his hands in the air and a thought bubble which read 'Ghost!'

"Am I really that pretty?" Shane asked.

Pete blinked first. "What?"

"Just wondering why you're all staring at me. Well," Shane said, leaning back. "Not really. I know why. What do you want to know?"

"How did you stop it?" Gordon asked.

"Iron," Shane said. "It's one of the few things I know of that can get the job done. Requires you to be up close and personal though, which I am not a fan of."

"Does it destroy them?" Quincy asked.

Shane shook his head. "No. It sends them back to either their bones or whatever they've attached themselves to. In this case, it was pretty damned close by."

"So that was him you heard running towards you?" Gordon asked.

Shane nodded.

"Why?" Pete asked, his voice raw. "Why are there ghosts there?"

"Maybe because of the accident," Gordon suggested.

"Yeah," Shane agreed. "Care to enlighten me? I don't know any details."

Gordon nodded, and he began the story.

"I can give you the basics, but not a whole lot more. If you want the finer points, well, you'll have to reach out to some of the survivors," Gordon said.

Shane took a cigarette out and placed it unlit between his lips.

"In nineteen seventy-four, there was an accident at the prison," Gordon continued. "No one was ever told exactly what happened. Or how it happened. But it boiled down to this. The day had begun as usual with the night shift guards preparing to leave while the day shift guards were getting ready to trade out the posts. The police who did the investigation believed that's why so many of the prisoners were actually saved. Double the amount of guards."

"What was the accident?" Shane asked.

"Some sort of gas," Gordon said. "Word has it that the gas slipped out from the basement. An accident, a mixture from some of the chemicals stored down there. Prisoners and guards suffocated, poisoned by the gas. When they retrieved the bodies, they were so contaminated that people got sick from being around them. In the end, the authorities decided it would be best to burn the corpses. But all in all, they don't know how the whole thing started."

"How many died?" Frank asked.

"That's the other thing," Gordon said, leaning back in the booth. "They think most of the prisoners were saved."

"Think?" Shane asked. "Didn't they do a head count?"

"They said they did, but a couple of hundred got out. Mostly the hard cases, so they said, the ones down in solitary and the others on death row." Gordon shook his head. "Other than that, they didn't say."

"How did they die?" Shane asked. "Do they even know what the chemical agent was?"

"No," Gordon said. "And they blocked any release of information about the investigation."

"How?" Quincy asked, looking around, confused. "I mean, I thought in America they can't do this sort of thing, yes?"

Shane snorted.

"What?" Pete asked. "What's funny?"

"Nothing's funny," Shane said, taking the cigarette out of his mouth. "The problem is that if you're going to really work on the place, you're going to have to do some digging."

"If I work on the place," Pete murmured. A forlorn expression settled on his face. "I can't get the money back that I deposited. I have to make it work."

"I can't work with ghosts around," Quincy said. There was fear in his eyes, and Shane didn't think any less of the young man for it. "No. No, I can't."

"What?" Pete started, but Shane interrupted him.

"No worries about that, Quincy," Shane said, smiling. "No worries. No shame in it, alright?"

Quincy nodded. He pulled his wallet from a back pocket, took out a ten dollar bill and put it down on the table. When he stood up, Quincy looked at Pete.

"If you get a place without ghosts, Pete," Quincy said. "Then I'll come."

"And I won't call you for the work," Pete snapped.

Quincy shrugged, waved to the others, and left.

Silence fell over the remaining men for almost a minute, before Peter broke it, asking, "How do I get rid of ghosts?"

"There are professionals out there," Shane said.

Frank looked at him.

"What about you?" Pete asked, his face brightening. "You seem to know what you're doing. Hell, you got rid of that one quick enough."

"And it came back," Shane replied. "Listen, getting rid of them isn't easy. It's not like those shows where you can just wave some burning sage around, and the damned things leave."

"You said you killed ghosts," Gordon said.

Shane sighed. "I do."

"And he's good at it," Frank said. "Extremely good at it."

"Will you?" Pete asked. "Please? I don't know how much it would cost, but would you?"

Shane hesitated, and then he said, "Tell you what, let me dig into the history of the prison for a few days, and I'll let you know. If I think it's too much, then no, I won't. If it's something I think can be done, then we'll work out a price."

"Thank you!" Pete said, extending his hand.

Shane shook it and felt as if he had just made the worst decision in his life.

Chapter 8: Mulberry Street, The Adams House

Dorothy Adams had been retired for exactly three days, fourteen hours, and seventeen minutes.

And she was going stir-crazy.

She had never been a knitter or someone who enjoyed crocheting. Reading was enjoyable, but Dorothy had exhausted the local library's supply of new books. And while her pension would allow her to live comfortably, there wasn't a great deal of what she saw as 'financial wiggle-room.'

Dorothy left the kitchen, walked into her small family room and sat down on the couch. Taz, her black and white cat, looked up at her with tired eyes.

"What's wrong, handsome?" she asked.

Taz got up, stretched, and walked over to her. He smelled her blouse, sneezed, and then climbed onto her lap, dropping down. He was heavier than she remembered, and she considered whether it might be better to limit his food.

No, she decided. *He's seventeen years old. He can eat whatever he wants.*

She scratched between his ears and the cat purred. Dorothy smiled and looked out the bay window onto Mulberry Street. She knew she was alone on the street. Over the years, the other families whom she and Jonathan had known so well had either broken up, moved away, or passed on.

The new residents were strangers to her. Men and women who worked full-time jobs far from their small town. Their children were in daycares or at school. The only people Dorothy could expect to see over the next few hours were either delivery drivers or the mailman.

And Dorothy was alone.

Jonathan had died years before, working as a guard at Kurkow Prison.

She closed her eyes against the memory of it. Each fall and winter, and into every spring she was reminded of the horror. Through the trees lining her backyard the prison could be seen. A huge, abandoned structure.

They didn't even let me bury him, she thought. Dorothy sighed and closed her eyes.

All of the bodies had been burned. Contaminated by whatever had killed them. And she had been left alone to raise their son.

A bitter taste rose up in her throat at the thought of Jon Junior. He had been so unlike his father. A calm and peaceful boy, a place of refuge when his father stormed against them both. He had even stood between Jonathan and Dorothy on those nights when his father had had too much to drink.

Those nights when the belt would come out, Dorothy remembered. *When he would beat me.*

But Jon Junior would stop the beatings, the abuse.

Then the world had changed with Jonathan's death. Dorothy had to go to work and her time with Jon Junior had become less and less.

It was because of that, she thought, anger rising to the surface. *If I had been home more, then he never would have joined the Marines. And if he hadn't joined the Marines, he wouldn't have been in Beirut. He wouldn't have died in the bombing.*

My little boy wouldn't be dead.

Dorothy let out a long, shuddering breath, opened her eyes and focused on the world beyond her bay window. The sky had been darkening since a little after dawn, storm clouds moving in with a promise of snow. Dorothy had tried to watch the news, but none of the weathermen on the various channels seemed to have any idea how much snow they might be in for.

A honeymoon snowstorm, she thought with a wry smile, remembering the old joke with a smile. *You know it's coming, but you don't know when, how much, or how long it'll stay.*

She chuckled to herself and watched a car pass by the house, the driver holding a cell phone up to their head.

Foolish, Dorothy told the driver. *That's a good way to cause an accident. Or get a ticket.*

But as soon as she finished the thought, the vehicle was gone, leaving her alone with Taz on Mulberry Street. She smiled at the cat, scratching his back.

Taz went quiet, his body stiffening. He got to his feet, all of his hair standing on end. His eyes narrowed to slits, and his ears laid back against his skull. The purr was replaced by a low, angry growl.

"What's wrong?" Dorothy asked him.

The cat jumped from her lap, landing with a thud on the floor. He sank down low, his tail snapping back and forth.

"Taz," Dorothy said. "What's going on?"

He fixed his eyes on the doorway that linked the kitchen and the family room, the growl growing louder.

Dorothy got to her feet and looked at the cat. "What's gotten into you?"

Taz scooted backward, never taking his eyes off the doorway.

Dorothy shook her head and went into the kitchen. The air was colder than the rest of the house, and she checked the window over the sink. It was closed, and the storm glass was down over the screen. She stepped over to the back door and saw that it was locked. Frowning, Dorothy pulled the curtain aside to make certain the screen door was still closed, and when she did, she gasped.

Jonathan stood on the back porch. He was a few feet away from the door, his shoulders slumped beneath his uniform shirt.

The shirt she had ironed the morning of the accident.

His skin was green, his lips swollen. From between them, his tongue protruded, looking like a dead snail half out of a broken shell. His yellow eyes widened in surprise when he saw her. Then he grinned, revealing crooked teeth, the enamel no longer white, but gray.

Dorothy backed away from the door, terrified, the curtain dropping back into place.

The grin on Jonathan's face was the same he had worn whenever he was drunk.

Whenever he would take his belt off and loop it around his hand, the buckle swinging free. The grin which proceeded the abuse.

He's not real, Dorothy told herself. *Jonathan's dead. His body cremated. His remains somewhere unknown. He isn't a ghost. Ghosts aren't real. You know that. If the dead could come back, my little boy would have returned to me.*

She clasped her hands together to try and force herself to calm down.

And Jonathan came through the door.

He didn't open it. He didn't break it down.

Just passed through it, gliding into the kitchen.

"Hello, Darling," he said, his swollen tongue and discolored lips somehow forming the words.

Dorothy backed into the table, grabbed the edge with her hands and eased herself into a chair. The room had grown cold enough for her to see her own breath.

"You're dead," she whispered.

"Yes," Jonathan said, stopping a few feet away. "Very dead."

"How are you here?" she asked, still whispering.

"I don't know," he replied. "I've been at work for a long time. There was an accident, and we died. So many of us. And so many of us have been there, at Kurkow. Waiting, wondering when our shifts would end. When the sentence would end. And they ended today."

"Oh," she said in a small voice.

"I've come home," Jonathan said, and there was no affection in his voice. His grin widened, a horrific rather than an endearing expression.

"What can I do for you, Jonathan?" she asked, her legs shaking as she got to her feet.

"You're going to help me, Dorothy," he said, an old and terrifying humor filling his voice.

"How?" she whispered.

"Do you remember how *gentle* I was?" he asked, his words coming out in a rush. "Do you remember how I worked off that head of steam I'd build up at Kurkow?"

Dorothy nodded, petrified.

"Do you remember how much it would please me?" he hissed. "Do you recall how you would entertain me?"

"Yes," she whispered.

"Then entertain me," he said, stepping forward. Before she could react, his hand lashed out and wrapped around her throat, the touch cold and brutal. Pain exploded in her flesh, his fingertips like needles as they drove into her muscles. Her windpipe was closed off, and she gasped, desperate for breath.

Jonathan lifted her with one hand and threw her against the wall. Her head put a dent in the drywall, the paint cracking and falling to the floor as she slid down. The phone was jarred from its cradle, slapping the tile with a loud crack.

Jonathan chuckled, took the receiver and ripped the cord out of the base.

Dorothy's head spun, and she had a difficult time focusing. When she could see straight, she found Jonathan standing over her, smiling. He waggled the phone's receiver at her, the yellow plastic seemed dull in the pale light of the kitchen.

"I know it's not my belt, darling," Jonathan said, "but I think it will suffice."

Dorothy screamed as he brought the handset crashing down onto her shoulder, the clavicle snapping.

Over her own shrieks, Dorothy could hear him whistling as he struck her again, and again, and again.

Chapter 9: Getting Help

"Where are you going?" Frank asked.

"Mont Vernon," Shane answered.

"Why?"

Shane sighed. "I've got a couple of friends out there. They've done the whole ghost thing before, too. It's always good to have another set of eyes look at the problem."

Frank didn't say anything. Instead, he stared out the window while Shane drove. Finally, Shane glanced at his friend and asked, "You okay?"

"Hm?" Frank said. "Oh, yeah. Sorry. No, I'm good, man. I was just thinking it might not hurt for me to go and see if I could speak with the Abbot."

"What abbot?" Shane asked.

"The head of the Order," Frank explained. "The one I used to belong to."

"Why?" Shane said. "Can he help us?"

"He might be able to." Frank tapped on the seat for a minute. "See, before I left the Order, he explained to me about how some brothers had fought against the dead before."

"Seriously?" Shane asked.

"That surprises you?" Frank shook his head and laughed. "Hell, with all of the things you've seen and done, and the idea of monks fighting ghosts surprises you?"

Shane chuckled. "Yeah, I guess it does. It shouldn't. But it does. Whatever. So, you think he might be able to give us some advice, too?"

Frank nodded.

"You know, we've got to pass through Manchester on the way back," Shane said. "That's where the Order is, right?"

"It is," Frank said, "but I don't want to drop in unannounced. He may not be around, and it would be considered impolite."

Shane shrugged.

"I'll give him a call when we get back to Nashua," Frank continued. "You sure it's okay?"

"Yup," Shane said, then he grinned. "You'll like them."

"Your friends?"

Shane nodded. "Yeah, they're funny. Good people, you know?"

"I'm familiar with a few," Frank said, grinning.

Shane glanced in the rearview mirror and saw dark clouds had swarmed over the morning sun. "Looks like another storm is coming in."

Frank sighed and said, "Let's hope it isn't too bad."

Here's hoping Kurkow isn't too bad either, Shane thought, and he returned his focus to the highway.

Chapter 10: Mulberry Street Isn't Nice Anymore

On a normal day, George Vlade got home half an hour before his wife Jess. When she was headed home and route eighty-nine was bumper to bumper, that half an hour might stretch into an hour, or even two.

With the storm settling in over Gaiman, George had a feeling he would be eating dinner alone.

Probably sleeping alone, too, he thought, sighing. Jess' work down at Dartmouth Hospital often kept her late. And with the storm dumping an inch of snow per hour, it wouldn't be safe or practical for her to try to make it home.

George dropped his briefcase on the kitchen table, ignored the three new messages on the answering machine, and went directly to the fridge. He took out a bottle of spring water and enjoyed a long drink before he returned it to the shelf. Into the silence of the house, he let out an appreciative belch, and then opened the freezer. He looked into the crowded shelves, realized nothing tasty was going to materialize and closed the door.

George walked over to the pantry, took out a box of Cheerios and poured himself a bowl. He hesitated, wrestling silently with his inner child, and gave in. From the baking shelf he pulled out a box of sugar, and he poured an excessive amount over the cereal, grinning the entire time.

Whistling, George put the sugar and the Cheerios box away, got the milk out of the fridge and drowned the cereal in it.

When the milk was safely in the cool depths of the fridge once more, George got himself a clean spoon, and left the kitchen. Unlike most days, George succeeded in not spilling the contents on himself and sat down in his chair. He put the bowl down for a minute, found the remote, and turned the television on.

Nothing.

He tried the power button again, frowning.

Finally, the television came on, but there were no channels.

George let out a disappointed sigh, dropped the remote to his lap and picked up his food.

You know, he thought, shoveling a spoonful of cereal into his mouth, *all I wanted was to see the highlights. That's all. Just a few highlights from yesterday's game.*

Oh well.

He continued to eat, moving the spoon as fast as he could from the bowl to his lips. In several minutes, he was done, tipping the bowl up to drink the remaining milk. Jess hated it when he did that, which made the act all the more enjoyable.

George put the bowl and the spoon down on the side table, picked up the remote and tried it again. After searching, he found he could get in a single channel.

The local news, which he despised.

Well, he thought, dropping the remote down. *I guess it's better than nothing.*

He watched and listened as a bleach-blonde newscaster, squeezed into a red dress three sizes too small, gave a rundown of local events.

"There have been some very strange situations today," she was saying as he reached down and turned up the volume. "All of the windows on the first floor of the old Kurkow Prison seemed to have been broken, although authorities are not saying what caused the breakage to occur. This has brought out speculation from some longtime residents of Gaiman about whether or not there might be a repeat of the disaster which had closed the facility in the seventies."

What? George thought. *What disaster?*

But the reporter wasn't forthcoming with any other information. Instead, she moved on to the winter festival in Concord, which might or might not be affected by any inclement weather.

George got out of his chair, took his empty bowl and carried it into the kitchen. As he put it in the sink, he shook his head, thinking, *Why weren't we told about a disaster in the town? Shouldn't that have been shared when we purchased the house?*

He opened his briefcase, took out his phone and checked it for messages. There was a single text from Jess stating that she would be staying at Dartmouth, and reminding him to take his blood-pressure medication. George rolled his eyes, sent a response telling her to be safe, and put his phone back on the table.

God, he sighed. *I hate that damned medicine. My libido is getting absolutely murdered by it.*

George went back into the front room and went straight to the fireplace. He put in a couple of lengths of wood, stuffed the gaps with crumpled up newspaper and lit them with a long fireplace match. With the smell of sulfur stinging his nose, George smiled and stood up.

"Do you know what it's like to be cold forever?" a deep, pained voice asked from behind him.

George twisted around, surprise and shock rippling through him.

A pair of men stood in the room, and George shivered in the sudden cold. The men were short and stocky, broad-shouldered and with almost identical faces. Their thick noses were pressed close to their faces, the foreheads longer than what they should have been. They wore matching clothes as well, what looked like denim shirts and pants. Over the left breast pocket of each was a stenciled number.

George's stomach rumbled and threatened to eject his dinner. The sight of the men was hideous as well as surprising.

Their skin lacked any sort of normal pigmentation, stained, instead, a foul green. Each man's tongue was black, peeking out between bulbous lips.

And as George looked at them, he realized at times he could see through each. Their forms ebbed and flowed, moving from solid to faint image and back to solid. The men stood by the front door, and George knew he wouldn't be able to get past them.

Even as the realization settled over him, the two men moved, one to the left and the other to the right. George was trapped in the room with them.

He licked his lips, his hands trembling. Out of the corner of his eyes, he sought some sort of weapon with which to defend himself, and he found it. Leaning to the right, George reached out, his hand finding the cold, comforting brass handle of the fireplace poker.

"What are you?" he asked, his voice higher than normal.

The two men grinned.

"We're brothers," one of them said.

"Best of friends," said the other.

"Murderers," they said together.

"And not by accident," began one.

"But by design and for pleasure," finished the other.

"It has been a long, long time since we've killed," one of them whispered.

And they advanced towards him.

George stepped back, felt the heat of the fire against his legs and stopped. He raised the poker into a batter's position, wrapping his left hand around the brass below the right.

"Stay back," George said. "Stay where you are!"

The men laughed.

"Or what?" one of them asked. "We're dead. You can do nothing."

"But we," the other hissed, "we can do whatever we want."

The dead prisoner on the right rushed towards George, and George shrieked, swinging the poker at the man. The heavy iron head of the poker passed through the prisoner's head, and the ghost vanished.

The second prisoner stood up straight, surprise on his face.

"How?" the prisoner began to ask, but George didn't let him finish. He raced forward and slammed the poker with enough force so that when it passed through the second ghost, the iron slammed into the wall.

George left it hanging there as he went stumbling back, found his chair and sat down. He stared at the poker. As his thoughts slowed down, George was able to focus. Finally, he stood up, walked out to the kitchen and took his laptop out. He carried it back into the television room, pulled the poker out of the wall and sat down. George powered up the laptop. Soon he was online, and he accessed the Google's homepage.

With a shaking hand, he typed in a short sentence.

How to stop a ghost

George hit return, and he waited for the results to appear.

Chapter 11: A Chat Between Brothers

Ollie sat in his chair, swirling the rum and coke around, the ice cubes clattering against the sides of the glass. Pete was at the bar, pouring himself another vodka tonic.

Pete's third.

Ollie took a drink and watched his brother. Pete's hands trembled, as he splashed a bit of the vodka onto the bar's top. Pete muttered, grabbed a paper towel and wiped up the spilled liquor with awkward motions. When he had finished, he went and sat down across from Ollie.

Pete didn't look him in the eye.

On the television screen above the mantle, there was a recap of the Sunday football games. Ollie had it on mute, waiting for Pete to finally tell him how work on the prison had gone.

Pete's silence wasn't encouraging.

Ollie sighed, picked up the remote and turned the television off.

"What happened today?" Ollie asked.

Pete looked up, took a drink, and then looked back down at the thick, burgundy rug which lined Ollie's man-cave. "Nothing. Why?"

"Nothing?" Ollie repeated. "You haven't looked me in the eye for more than a second since you came in here an hour ago. If Beth and the kids weren't downstairs in the playroom, I'd be slapping you. Tell me what the hell happened at Kurkow today. Did you get any quotes? Was Gordon there? How bad is it?"

Pete cleared his throat, drank the vodka tonic down in one long swallow, and rose up from his chair.

"Sit your ass down," Ollie said between clenched teeth, "or I am going to punch you in the mouth."

Pete sat down.

"Did you get any quotes?" Ollie demanded.

Pete shook his head.

"Was Gordon there?" Ollie snapped.

His brother nodded.

Ollie felt his anger rising. "How bad is it?"

Pete didn't reply.

"Answer me!" Ollie shouted.

His brother winced, turned his head away and muttered, "It's haunted."

Ollie laughed in surprise, then in relief. He shook his head, took a long drink and then said, "That's it? That's the big thing you were worried about?"

Pete nodded.

"Good God, Pete," Ollie said, getting out of his chair and heading to the bar. "Grow a pair, will you? So, that is why you didn't get any quotes today?"

"Yeah," Pete answered.

"Did your guys actually see a ghost?" Ollie asked, chuckling.

"The guys didn't," Pete said. "But they were there when all of the windows on the first floor blew out."

Ollie went quiet. He put the empty glass on the bar and turned to face Pete. "Say that again?"

Pete wiped his nose with the back of his hand and said, "I figured you would have seen it on the news."

"It was on the news?!" Ollie shouted. He forced himself to calm down. "I don't watch the local crap. Tell me what happened."

"Not much to tell," Pete said, staring back down at the floor. "We cut the iron chain off the front doors, and as soon as we did, the windows all blew out. Knocked us all down."

"And then the guys left?" Ollie asked.

Pete nodded.

"Gordon too?" Ollie said, turning away and pouring straight rum into the glass. He carried his drink back to his chair.

"Um, no," Pete said. "Gordon, your buddy Frank and a friend of his, and one scrapper stayed on."

"What happened next?" Ollie asked.

"We went inside, looked around a bit, then," Pete paused, cleared his throat and said, "then I cut the chain off of the interior doors."

"After the whole incident with the chain on the front doors?" Ollie asked, surprised.

Pete nodded. "I, ah, I could hear footsteps. I thought maybe someone was on the other side. You know, squatting."

"Squatting?" Ollie asked. "In an abandoned prison."

Pete blushed with embarrassment.

"Anyway," Ollie said. "You cut off the next chain. What happened then?"

"There was a ghost," Pete whispered. He looked up, and Ollie could see the genuine terror in his brother's eyes. "It was terrible."

Ollie waited for Pete to continue.

"I, I was frozen, afraid," Pete said, his voice hard to hear. "That's when Shane, Frank's friend, did something. He hit the ghost with the chain, and it vanished."

"A chain?" Ollie asked, confused. "A steel chain?"

Pete shook his head. "No. Not steel. Iron. Both sets of doors had been locked with iron chains."

Ollie's phone rang, and he picked it up off the coffee table.

"Hey Gordon," Ollie said.

"Hey, you got the news on?" Gordon replied.

"No."

"Put it on. Channel nine."

"Hold on." Ollie bent over, grabbed the remote and turned the television on and turned up the volume.

"Right now the police are investigating a series of break-ins in downtown Gaiman," a young woman said. "No one is quite sure why the sudden spike in crime, although there is some speculation that it may have something to do with the strange occurrence at Kurkow Prison earlier today."

"Break-ins?" Ollie asked.

"It gets worse," Gordon said, his voice grim.

"As of right now," the woman continued, "the police are also investigating the murder of Dorothy Adam. There is no sign of forced entry, and the recent retiree was beaten to death. Anyone with any information is asked to contact the New Hampshire State Police, Barracks F, or to call the tip line of their local police station. I have been told that there is going to be a thorough investigation after the storm has passed. At this time though, the scene is secure, and the police are urging the public to stay indoors and off the roads."

Ollie turned the television off and said, "Is there more?"

"I don't know," Gordon replied. "But whatever we let out of Kurkow is raising hell in Gaiman. Has Pete heard back from either Frank or Shane?"

Ollie repeated the question to his brother.

Pete shook his head.

"He says 'no,'" Ollie said.

"Alright," Gordon said, sighing. "Listen, let me know as soon as you do what those two guys have to say. I think we let a genie out of a bottle here, Ollie, and we're going to have a hell of a time putting it back in."

"Sure," Ollie said, "I'll let you know, Gordon. Thanks."

He ended the call and looked at Pete.

"What did he mean about Frank and Shane?" Ollie asked.

"Evidently," Pete whispered, "Shane knows how to kill ghosts."

Chapter 12: At Mont Vernon

Shane and Frank stood on the porch, and Shane knocked on the door.

"Do they mind when people drop by?" Frank asked.

"Yeah," Shane answered.

"A lot?" Frank said.

"We might catch a twelve-gauge worth of rock salt," Shane said.

Frank looked at him.

"No," Shane said, shaking his head. "I'm not joking. Brian and Jenny aren't the most trusting of folks."

Footsteps approached the door from inside the house, and Shane heard Brian call out, "Who is it?"

"Brian, it's Shane! I've got a friend with me, too."

The door opened a sliver, then all the way. Brian stood in the doorway with a sawed-off, double-barrel shotgun in his hand. The man grinned at him, steel-capped teeth catching the hall light and shining. He had a knit cap on over his otherwise bald head, and a Boston Bruin's hoodie sweatshirt.

"Come on in," Brian said, propping the shotgun in a corner. "How are you?"

Shane shook his friend's hand and then gave him a quick hug. "I'm alright. Brian, this is my friend Frank."

The two men shook hands and then Brian closed the door.

"Is Jenny home?" Shane asked.

Brian shook his head. "No. She's in Nashua, doing some research at the library. What's up?"

"I've got a strange question for you," Shane said.

Brian chuckled. "What other kinds are there? Come on into the kitchen, I was just finishing up the dishes. Tell me what's going on."

As they walked down the hall, Shane told Brian what had happened in the prison, with Frank filling in any details he forgot. By the time Brian was done with the dishes, he was leaning against the counter, arms folded across his chest, he was shaking his head.

"That sounds absolutely terrible," Brian said. "What do you need to know?"

"The answers to two questions, really," Shane said. "Is it possible to get rid of an entire prison's worth of ghosts? And, if not, is there a way to make sure they're all in there and seal it up again?"

"Okay," Brian said, biting on his lower lip. "Let me ask you this, why do you want to empty the prison?"

Frank explained the situation with his friend Ollie and his brother, Pete.

"Damn," Brian muttered. "Well, it may come down to them having to take a loss on this. Seriously, guys. You're talking about sealing the prison again, and then working through it, section by section. You'll need a medium who can spot the ghosts and someone who can bind them. Plus you have to think about the danger factor here. I mean, you've got the ghosts of prisoners. Some of whom, I think we can assume, were not incarcerated for stealing lollipops."

Shane nodded.

"That being said," Brian continued, "you'd have to defend yourselves, which means a big group. You'd need at least two to three shotguns. Plenty of iron, and a whole lot of patience. You can't rush a job like this."

"And what about sealing it off?" Frank asked. "Just closing up the whole damned building?"

"It would be your best bet," Brian said. "Now there's no way the ghosts can get out, right?"

"What?" Shane asked, confused. "What do you mean? I thought they were bound to where ever it is they died? Or at least to their bodies or an object?"

Brian shook his head. "Not necessarily. I mean, yes, most of the time that's true, but there are plenty of recorded incidents where ghosts have traveled. Especially if the property used to belong to them, or to the town."

"The town," Frank whispered.

"What?" Shane asked.

Frank nodded, looking from Shane to Brian. "The town. Gaiman was a prison town. Most of the people there worked in the prison, or for the prison. I think I read somewhere that some towns used to actually rent the prisons to the state."

"If that's the case," Brian said, "then they could easily drift out into the town. You're looking at a huge area to cover in order to get them back into the building."

Frank groaned and shook his head.

Shane sighed, the scar at the base of his skull itching. He scratched at it and said, "That is some bad news, my friend."

"Sorry about that," Brian said.

Shane shrugged and looked over at Frank. "So, what do you want to do? Ollie's your friend."

"Bring the information back to him and Pete," Frank said. "Then, if they still want to push the issue, well, I guess I can go talk to the Abbott."

"Abbott?" Brian asked.

"My boy here used to be a monk," Shane said, grinning.

"Honest to God?" Brian said, looking over at Frank.

"Yes," Frank said, nodding.

"And what'd you do before that?" Brian asked.

"Special Forces, weapons specialist," Frank said.

Brian opened his mouth, closed it, shook his head and then let out a laugh.

"Damn," Brian said, turning around and opening a cabinet door. "If that doesn't call for a drink, then I don't know what does."

The clink of glasses filled the kitchen, and beyond the windows, the snow continued to fall.

Chapter 13: Ollie Looks for an Angle

Ollie wasn't a rich man, but he wasn't struggling either. Over the years, he had made a decent amount of money by flipping houses, renting out apartments, and being able to find a way to make a good return on almost anything.

And I'll be damned if I don't do it now, he thought. Ollie had finished a call with Frank, and Frank had told him what Shane had said. Ollie, in turn, had asked for a couple of days to think about it.

Ollie tapped his fingers on his desktop, organized the papers, tapped his fingers a little more, and then looked at his computer. A smile spread across his face, and he straightened up. His fingers hammered on the keys, and he soon had a page of results that broadened his smile into a grin.

Ollie picked up the phone, glanced at the monitor and dialed the first number he saw.

It rang twice before it was answered by a woman with a youthful voice.

"Thank you for calling the Granite State Paranormal Society," she said.

"Hello," Ollie said, "I was wondering, does your organization contract out?"

She hesitated, then asked, "Are you talking about having us investigate a home?"

"Sort of," Ollie answered. "You see, I've recently purchased a large structure, and I've been led to believe that it may or may not be haunted. I was wondering if I were to fund you for the evening if someone from your organization would be willing to investigate it."

"Oh," she said, pleased surprise in her voice. "I believe that is definitely something we could do. I'm sorry, I didn't get your name."

"Oliver Dawson," Ollie said. "And you are?"

"Emma," she said.

"Fantastic, Emma," Ollie said, leaning back in his chair. "Now, is it possible you could send along your fee schedule, and we can get this ball rolling? I'd like to have you guys in there as soon as possible."

"I can definitely do that," Emma said, excitement thick in her voice. "And we can pretty much go in whenever is good for you."

"That, Emma," Ollie said, smiling, "is exactly what I wanted to hear."

Chapter 14: The Granite State Paranormal Society

The Granite State Paranormal Society had four founding members. Emma Schloss, Cherilyn Falte, Melissa Tork, and Gwen Nolt. Each of them had studied English Literature at the University of New Hampshire, where they had founded their own paranormal society after watching the first five seasons of Ghost Adventures on the Travel Channel.

The transaction with Ollie Dawson had moved along at lightning speed. Gwen had gone to meet him with the proposal, and she had returned an hour later with a signed check for a thousand dollars.

All they had to do was go to Kurkow Prison in Gaiman, New Hampshire.

The four young women were crammed into Emma's beat up Jeep Cherokee. Most of the room was taken up by their investigative equipment. Some of the gear had been purchased, but most of it had been cobbled together by techies who had harbored crushes on the girls.

"There it is!" Gwen said, pointing from the back seat.

Emma jerked her head away from Gwen's hand, the Cherokee jumping in its lane on the highway. Melissa slapped the hand down, and Gwen yelped.

"Yeah, Gwen," Cherilyn said. "We can all see it. Sticks out like a sore thumb."

"The place is huge," Gwen said, her voice filled with awe.

"So's your mom," Cherilyn said, snickering. Then she yelped as Gwen punched her.

"Hey!" Emma said, looking in the rearview at her two friends. "Knock it off. I'm having a hard enough time driving without you two messing around back there."

"Yes, Mom," Cherilyn and Gwen said in chorus.

Emma rolled her eyes and resisted the urge to stomp on the brakes so she could send the two into a tumble.

"This exit here," Melissa said, nodding.

"Thanks," Emma said. She signaled, double checked the lane and eased the Cherokee down the ramp. The State plow drivers had done a less than admirable job with the road.

Several times the vehicle slipped, the back end kicking out a bit to first the left, then the right.

No, you don't, Emma thought, correcting the skids before they could get out of hand. *You're not going to do anything like that at all.*

She stepped on the brakes with light pressure and eased the Cherokee to a stop at the end of the ramp. To the right was the prison. Emma steered towards it, finally coming to a parking lot in front of the facility. When she put the Jeep in park, she looked at Kurkow in silence, and she realized the others were doing the same.

The building seemed to squat on the land. Every aspect of the structure was ugly. Hideous. A monstrous blemish that spoke of foulness and despair.

There was nothing about the prison which spoke of rehabilitation.

Nothing in its aura that said its purpose was anything other than punishment.

"This place," Melissa said in a low voice, "this place is haunted."

Emma and the others nodded their agreement.

For a moment, Emma wondered if the thousand dollars were worth it.

Yes, she thought. *You know it is. If we want to do something other than work regular day jobs for the rest of our lives, this is the first step. You know it's worth it.*

"You guys ready?" Emma asked.

A chorus of 'yes' was the reply, and the four of them got out of the Cherokee. They stretched their legs and Emma noticed that they all kept their attention fixed on the prison. The windows, Emma saw, were all broken on the first floor. And as Oliver Dawson had said, the front doors were open and unlocked.

She considered the foolishness of doors left unlocked in the modern world, and then she grinned. *And who's going to break into a prison? Nobody.*

"How do we want to start this?" Cherilyn asked.

"We've got plenty of daylight," Melissa said. "We should probably go in and see about doing a basic sweep. Find out what rooms are open, what areas are accessible."

They all nodded in agreement.

"I've got a digital recorder ready," Gwen said, pulling a small silver device out of her pocket. "You know, if we get any cold spots or anything."

Emma was about to give a smart-aleck response, but when she took another look at the building, she kept her comment to herself. *We could definitely get a cold spot in there during the daylight.*

There was a lot of snow on the ground, some of it gathered into drifts and some of those drifts as high as Emma's knees. The four of them slogged through the snow and made their way to the open front doors. Each of them entered the foyer and found, as Oliver had said, the next set of doors open.

Snow had slipped into the prison, a gradual slope leading to the hall beyond the next pair of doors. The temperature within, Emma realized, felt colder than outside.

How are we even going to be able to find any cold spots? she wondered.

"Wow," Melissa said, "this is decidedly unpleasant."

"One of us is going to have to go grab a kerosene heater or something," Gwen said. "There's no way we're going to be able to set up a camp in here without one."

"Yeah," Cherilyn said, stamping her feet. "It is *cold* in here."

"Let's not split into teams today," Emma said, turning and facing her friends. "We don't know how bad it is in here, and I really don't want to find out what the reaction time is for emergency services this close to the Canadian border."

"Sounds good to me," Cherilyn said.

"Take the lead, fearless leader," Gwen said, saluting.

Emma rolled her eyes, saying, "Come on."

With the others following close behind her, she led the way into the prison. Their feet were loud on the tile floor. Soon they passed through various steel doors, each one frozen open. Before Emma knew it, they were in the cell blocks themselves.

She stopped, an uncomfortable feeling sweeping over her. The doors to all of the cells were open, the bars painted a dull gray. Even in the cold, Emma felt as if she could smell fear and rage. Old desperation settled on her, the belief that she would never know what it would be like to be free again.

"This is horrible," Gwen whispered. "Absolutely horrible."

Emma could only nod. She didn't trust her voice. There were too many emotions fighting within her.

"I'm going to turn the recorder on," Gwen said.

Emma heard the click of the machine, and Gwen said in a loud voice, "This is Gwen with the Granite State Paranormal Society beginning our investigation of Kurkow Prison."

When she finished, Emma started to walk again. She moved at a slow pace. Part of her wanted to look in each cell as she passed, but a deeper, more primal part of her refused to allow her head to move so much as a quarter of an inch.

Someone whispered.

Emma stopped, half turned and asked in a low voice, "What?"

The others looked at her in surprise.

"What do you mean, 'what'?" Cherilyn asked.

"One of you just said something," Emma said.

They shook their heads.

"I thought you had said something," Melissa said.

"Not me," Emma said. "Did you hear what it was? I mean, what was said?"

"Hello. That's what I said. And I say it again. Hello."

The voice came from the right, and Emma looked into the cell.

A young man stood in the cell. His throat was slit from ear to ear, the flesh separated in a grin which mimicked his own. Blood, which looked fresh, stained his pale skin and the denim shirt and pants he wore. His sleeves were rolled up his forearms, revealing muscles and tattoos, as well as the fact that Emma could see through him.

From the corner of her eye, Emma saw Gwen's hand lift up, shaking as she held the digital recorder closer to the ghost. He looked at it, shrugged, and then turned his attention back to Emma.

He's cute, she realized, her thoughts numb. *Strange. Even with his throat slit, he's cute.*

He smiled at her.

"What's your name, Beautiful?" he asked, his voice almost a purr, sultry as it slipped past his dead lips.

"Emma," she whispered.

"I'm Tommy," he said, taking a small step forward. When she didn't back away, his grin broadened, and he took another slow and cautious step towards her. "It's a pleasure to meet you, Emma."

"A pleasure to meet you, too," she said. One of the girls tugged on her arm, but Emma jerked the limb free. With a blush, she adjusted her coat and asked Tommy, "Why are you here?"

"I'm dead," he replied. "They wouldn't let me leave."

"Who?" Emma asked.

"The others," he said, waving his hand around.

"Um," Gwen said off to one side, "how did you die?"

"I tripped," Tommy said with an exaggerated sigh.

"Really?" Gwen asked in surprise.

"No!" Tommy said, laughing and shaking his head. "Good God no. They cut my throat."

"Who did?" Emma asked.

"The other prisoners," he answered.

"But why?" Emma said. "Why would they do that?"

"For one thing," Tommy said, "we were all dying. And, for another, even in prison they don't like rapists."

As the last word slipped out of his mouth, Tommy lunged at Emma.

Chapter 15: George Gears Up

George hadn't slept well the night before.

He had spent hours researching ghosts on the internet, and he had learned far too much. His sleep hadn't been restful either. George had slept on the bathroom floor, wrapped in the down comforter and a line of salt across the threshold of the door and the window. He had even added salt to a bag and taped the plastic up over the air-vent. When he had finally drifted off to sleep, it had been with the brass handle of the iron poker in his hand.

George wasn't taking any chances.

He walked around the kitchen, going about the process of preparing his morning coffee. All the while holding onto the poker. George had called into the office earlier, letting them know he would be working from home for the day. He had texted Jess the same, and she had said the snow was terrible down in Dover. Twenty-two inches of snow overnight.

In storms, past George would have been upset if she had spent more than one night away.

This is different, he reminded himself, carrying both his drink and his weapon to the table. *This isn't a girls' night out. This is her staying safe. Being safer there than at home with me.*

And he hated it.

George sat down hard, rested the iron poker across his legs and waited. He hadn't bothered to shovel the walkway, or to snow-blow the driveway. None of it mattered.

At least not until I can figure out what to do about those ghosts, he thought. A chill raced through him, and he took a drink. The two ghosts had been prisoners at one time, their matching prison uniforms had shown him as much.

If they were prisoners, George had reasoned, then they had probably come from Kurkow. Some of his morning had been spent searching the news sites, and he had come across several describing the events of the previous day in Gaiman.

The unexplained breakage of hundreds of windows in Kurkow Prison, George remembered. *So how many ghosts left the prison? Was it only those two? Where there more? A lot, a little?*

George stood up, leaving his mug on the table but carrying the poker. He paced around the small kitchen for a minute, then made his way into the television room. Walking to the sidelight to the right of the door, he looked out onto Monument Street.

The road was untouched, all of the snow pristine and unbroken.

Plows haven't been through, he realized. *Why? What's going on?*

The harsh sound of metal on metal caused him to jump, and George unlocked the front door and opened it. His breath and the heat of the house caused the glass on the storm door to fog up, and he wiped it away with his hand. George peered down to the left, towards where Monument intersected with Dell and swallowed back a cry of dismay.

Jammed up against a car was a plow, an old International truck with the cutting edge on the front mounted plow buried in a half hidden car. It wasn't the sight of the accident which had caused George to be upset.

What bothered him was the driver, a young man in his twenties or thirties. He wore a gray Patriots hoodie and a black knit cap, and his mouth was open in a silent, horrified scream.

Two ghosts had the man by the arms, and they were dragging him out of the broken, driver's side window. George watched as the young man kicked and flailed, the ghosts laughing, expressions of sheer joy on their faces. Soon they had the driver out and in the snow, and George saw them thrust the man's face down. They thrust his head in the snow until the young man ceased to move.

Then they held him up, shook him, and when his eyes opened, George could hear them cheer.

Then they shoved his face back into the snow.

George reached out, took hold of the handle to the storm door, and then he stopped.

"Don't," a voice said, from outside.

George looked to the right and saw an older man, a guard. He stood by the house, arms folded over his chest. His face was an abomination, like the others George had seen.

"Stay inside," the guard said, glancing over at George. "Those two they were car thieves. They got carried away in fifty-four and killed a man. Looks like they're repeating themselves. If you go out there, son, you'll end up dead."

"Will they leave?" George whispered.

"No," the guard answered. "There's a man we need to see. Some payback for all of us, prisoners and bulls alike. Best to stay inside, son."

In silence, George nodded, stepped back, closed the door, and locked it.

The guard was right, there was nothing George could do.

Book 5: Kurkow Prison

Chapter 16: Running through the Prison

Emma's lungs screamed for oxygen as she ran. The harsh sound of her own breathing, the pounding of her footsteps on the grating, and the thumping of her blood were all she could hear.

The other girls had run off, each fleeing Tommy.

But the other girls didn't have to worry about him. Tommy, Emma found out, only wanted to touch *her*.

As she ran, Emma heard laughter, and she jerked her head around to see ghosts in their cells. Men of various shapes and sizes, prisoners for the most part, although there were a few guards interspersed.

And all of them were cheering. Their hideous faces green, tongues black. All of them shouted encouragement to Tommy, who was only a few steps behind Emma.

He could catch me, Emma realized. *If he wanted to, he could grab me. But he doesn't want to. Not yet. He wants something more.*

This is a game.

The shock of understanding caused her to stumble, and she slipped to the right, screaming in agony as she bounced off the wall. Emma spun, caught herself on the railing and managed to push herself away.

"Run, Emma!" Tommy howled, his words filled with glee. "Aren't you having fun?"

Emma suddenly wished pepper-spray could work on a ghost.

Her throat burned with the effort to take in enough oxygen, and her legs shook, but Emma forced herself to run. Ahead of her, she saw a stairwell encased in heavy gauge wire, and she made her way to it.

"Will you go down?" Tommy asked. "Will you? Don't you know who was down there, Emma? The truly bad men were downstairs. The ones who made me look like an angel. Those men who ate their victims before they were dead. Men who killed for pleasure."

When Emma reached the stairs, she didn't go down them. She went up, racing through a short, skinny man. Passing through him left her skin crawling as if she had been rolling in a pile of ant hills.

"Ah," Tommy said, "we're going up!"

Emma wracked her brain as she ran, forcing herself to plumb her memories. *What can stop a ghost? What can make them turn away?*

Salt. Iron. Sage. She snorted, reached the next landing and raced onto it. There were fewer ghosts. They were all similar to Tommy, men with their throats cut. Murdered before whatever accident had decimated the prison population.

No sage here. Emma thought. *And no salt. Need iron. Iron. Was there some at the front? Can I get back to the front? Where are the girls?*

The last question had finished, and Tommy grabbed hold of her arm.

She screamed, his dead hand horrifically cold. Her skin crawled at his touch as he dragged her down to the floor.

"Enough running, Emma," he whispered in her ear. "I want to play a different way."

She screamed as his hands wrapped around her throat.

Chapter 17: A Surprise Phone Call

When his phone rang, Shane picked it up and looked at it. It was a New Hampshire number he didn't recognize, and he almost put the phone down without answering it.

Midnight and someone's calling, Shane thought, rolling onto his back. *If it's a wrong number, they deserve to know. Probably some sort of emergency.*

"Hello?" he asked.

"Hello," a male said, his voice thick with nervous energy. "Is this Shane Ryan?"

Shane closed his eyes. "Yeah. This is. Who's this?"

"Pete Dawson."

Shane sat up, sleep chased away by curiosity.

"What's going on?" Shane asked.

"I have a situation, with Kurkow," Pete said.

Shane shook his head. "Yeah. I know."

"No," Pete said, his tone becoming desperate. "You don't know. I told my brother about it."

"Yeah, and your brother told Frank he would think about it whether or not to send us in," Shane said, yawning.

"That's just it," Pete said. The words rushed out one after the other. "Shane, he isn't thinking about it. He hired some amateur group to go in there to see if there's really a ghost or not. I think he's looking for an angle."

"He sent in someone else?" Shane asked. His heart thudded against his chest. "When?"

"This morning, but he told me they wouldn't be out until tomorrow. They had to go in there overnight," Pete said. "They've been in there since the early morning, Shane. All their equipment is still in their car. I, well I went by. But I can't go in! I can't!"

"Alright," Shane said. "Relax. I need you to do something for me."

"What can I do?" Pete asked. "Because I can't go in there!"

"Pete!" Shane snapped. "Get a grip and listen to me. You're going to go to the nearest twenty-four hour Wal-Mart, and you are going to buy me a very large amount of rock salt, kosher salt, whatever. It has to be salt."

"Why?" Pete asked. "What for?"

"Just do it. Also, you need to pick up some flashlights, too," Shane said. "Not the rinky dink little things, I'm talking full-on police issue LEDs that can blind you. You getting all this?"

"Yeah," Pete said, and Shane was pleased to hear a note of calm in the man's voice. "I hear you. Salt and flashlights."

"Good," Shane said. "Now, do you know how many people were in this group your brother hired?"

"Four, I think," was the answer.

"Okay. Then I want four emergency blankets. If they're trapped in the prison, it's going to be brutally cold in there for them. Got all of it?"

"Yeah," Pete said. "I've got it."

"Good. Now go get it. Frank, and I'll be up there as soon as we can," Shane said. "Make sure you stay away from the prison. Meet us at the diner where we had lunch."

"Okay," Pete said, and he hung up the phone.

Shane put his phone down, got out of bed and left his room. He walked down the hallway and knocked on Frank's door.

"Who is it?" Frank asked.

"Shane."

"Come in," Frank said.

"You get a lot of visitors I don't know about?" Shane asked, grinning.

"No, although some of the ghosts knock once in a while," Frank said. He smiled and asked, "What's up?"

Shane opened the door. Frank was sitting up in bed, a bible in his hand and the light on beside him.

"What's up?" Frank asked.

Shane recapped his conversation, and by the time he had finished, Frank was out of bed. The former monk pulled on a pair of jeans and slipped into his boots. "I'll be ready in about three minutes."

"Same," Shane said. He left the room shaking his head. Going into a haunted prison at midnight during a New Hampshire winter was something he had never wanted to do.

Halfway down the hallway, Courtney appeared. Her form fluctuated from solid to a faint outline. A sign of her anger.

"Where are you going now?" she demanded.

"I have to go to a prison," Shane said, passing by her and entering his room.

"A prison?" she asked, following him. "Why a prison?"

"There are ghosts there," Shane answered. He started to get dressed. "And some people who are in trouble. Or if they're not, they will be."

"How many ghosts?" Courtney asked.

Shane shrugged.

"Will you take me with you?" Courtney said.

Shane began to say 'no,' but then he changed his mind.

"Fine," he said, picking up his dog-tags and sliding the cold chain over his head. He tucked them under his shirt. "It would be good if you came with us."

"Us?" she asked, bristling. "Who else is going?"

"Frank is," Shane said. He picked up his boots, carried them to his chair and sat down. Courtney stared at him.

She remained silent for a minute, then spoke again. "Watch yourself, Shane Ryan. Something is coming."

He shook his head, his shoulders sagging. "Go to sleep, Courtney. Rest. I'll let you know when I get to the prison."

She started to speak, stopped herself, and then the dog-tags became terribly cold for a heartbeat. When Shane looked up, he found he was alone in the bedroom. Courtney had slipped away, placing herself in the dog-tags once more.

Shane put on his right boot, tied it, and sat back in the chair. He put his left leg up on his right and picked at the frayed ends of the cuff.

She's going mad, he thought. *She can't deal with being dead anymore. I need to remember to talk to Brian and Jenny about her.*

With a sigh, Shane got to his feet. He looked around the room, turned off the light and walked out towards the library. In that room, he would find his weapons, the tools of the trade. Part of him longed for the feel of the knuckle-dusters in his hand, the weight of the shotgun against his shoulder. He wanted the bag full of shells loaded with salt and the iron rings. Shane wanted all of it, and the freedom to use them all.

He needed to go up to Kurkow Prison, not only to rescue the people trapped inside the building but to fight the dead.

Shane grinned, for he was in love with the violence.

Chapter 18: Return to the Prison

At a little past two in the morning, Shane and Frank pulled into the parking lot in front of Kurkow Prison. It had taken nearly two hours to drive from the bottom of the state to Gaiman, near the Canadian border. Shane stopped his car beside a beat-up old Jeep Cherokee, which looked to be more rust and Bondo than actual metal. The back of the vehicle was loaded with boxes and bags as well as loose pieces of electrical equipment.

Book 5: Kurkow Prison

The license plate, green and white and with the image of a moose on the left, read, *GSPS – 1*.

They both got out of the car, and Shane shivered at the electrical charge in the air. He could feel the energy of the dead, and when he looked over at Frank, Shane saw the other man could sense it as well.

"This is bad," Frank said, opening the back door and taking out a duffel bag.

Shane nodded, walked around to Frank and waited as the man put the black bag down and unzipped it. In silence, Frank doled out the equipment. Each of them slipped on a headlamp, flicking the 'on' switch over to the red so that their night vision was preserved, and they could still see. Pump action shotguns followed, and each of them strapped a small hip pouch with extra rounds onto their belts.

Frank passed the knuckle-dusters over to Shane, and then took a pair of iron rings out of the bag for himself.

Shane tossed the bag back into the car, closed the door and asked, "You ready?"

"Yeah," Frank said, nodding and chambering a round into the shotgun. "Let's get this done. We're looking for four females?"

"Yup," Shane said. He turned around and spotted Pete's vehicle a short distance away. Pete had followed them from the diner after handing off the salt and flashlights. Pete flicked the headlights from low to high and back again. Shane raised his hand up. "Okay. Let's go."

Frank took the lead, the snow on the ground trampled by the women who had entered the prison.

The doors were open when they got to them, and Frank stepped through, moving off to the left. Shane entered close behind him, taking the lead and passing through the next set of doors. He advanced a few steps and paused, listening.

The prison was silent.

"Courtney," Shane whispered.

The dog-tags pulsed with a chill, and then Courtney stood before him. She looked with a nervous expression on her face. "This is not a good place, Shane."

"I know," he whispered. "I need a favor. But if you can't do it, then don't do it."

"What is it?" she asked.

"There are four women in here, living women," Shane said.

Courtney's eyes widened in disbelief, and then they narrowed. "In this place?"

Shane nodded.

"You want me to find them?"

"Yes," Shane said. "We're going to wait here."

Courtney vanished.

"Will she find them?" Frank asked doubt in his voice.

"She will," Shane replied. He sank down to one knee, keeping the shotgun ready, and the knuckle-dusters heavy in his back pocket. Shane watched the right while Frank settled down behind him. As they waited, the silence of the prison was soon broken.

Shane could hear voices. Men talking and laughing. Someone cheered.

Shane tried not to think about what might be so entertaining to the dead.

Courtney reappeared. Her expression was grim.

"There is only one woman alive here," she said. There was anger in her words, hatred as well.

"Where?" Shane asked.

"The next floor up, the cell across from the stairs," Courtney said. She hesitated, then added, "I would go quickly, Shane, I don't think they want her alive much longer."

381

"Thank you, Courtney," Shane said, and he felt a pang of sorrow as she left him again. He could feel the sudden cold of the dog-tags against his skin as he stood up. Shane glanced at Frank, who nodded, and the two of them started towards the stairs.

Chapter 19: Waiting

Pete sat in his Escalade, the engine running and the heat on. Bags from Wal-Mart, holding the emergency blankets Shane had told him to purchase, were on the passenger seat beside him. He had forgotten to give them along with the salt and flashlights, but then again, he hadn't seen much of a need for the blankets anyway. From where he sat, Pete could see the Jeep Cherokee, Shane's nondescript sedan, and the prison.

A few minutes earlier, Frank and Shane had disappeared into Kurkow, and Pete's heart had been racing in his chest ever since.

The town of Gaiman was falling apart, and Pete didn't know how long it would be safe to sit in his Cadillac.

I have to wait, he told himself. *I have to. They're counting on me. All of them. Frank and Shane, and those girls. Oh hell, why did Ollie send them in there? Why didn't he believe me?*

Pete shook his head. *No, he did believe me. That's why he sent them in there. He just didn't believe it would be bad.*

And Pete knew it was bad. He had a scanner in the Escalade, something he used to avoid speed traps and accidents on routes eighty-nine and interstate ninety-five. Pete had been listening to the chatter on the State Police band for most of the night.

Most of it was about accidents from the snow. Cars off the roads, SUVs spinning out. Telephone poles and trees down. Some of the calls were about Gaiman.

Concerned family members had called in. They had tried to reach loved ones, but there was no contact. People wanted to know if the power was out, and if so, could the police check on their relatives. The police couldn't do health and welfare checks yet, too many accidents on the roads. The checks would have to wait.

The power wasn't out. All of the phone lines were up. The cell phone tower was still standing, still processing calls.

A woman had been found beaten to death in her home, and a plow driver had been discovered in the street, half a dozen feet away from his plow. The man had been smothered in the snow.

Pete had finally turned the scanner off.

The dead were out there, in Gaiman. He knew the town was theirs. And they knew it as well.

Pete sighed, turned his attention back to the prison, and screamed.

A pair of men stood in front of the Escalade, and Pete was certain they were dead.

They had the same bloated distortion to their faces as did the man in the prison. Under the discoloration, he could see they were twins, and they wore matching prison uniforms as well. Smiles spread across their faces.

Pete threw the Cadillac into reverse, smashed the gas pedal to the floorboard and raced backward. The men ran towards him as he shifted into drive, cut the wheel hard and sped towards the road that would take him out of Gaiman.

Frank, Shane and the four members of the Granite State Paranormal Society were forgotten, the blankets tumbling onto the floor of the passenger side.

Chapter 20: Disheartening News

Oliver Junior had suffered a nightmare, his screams and cries filling the hallway between their rooms and waking up Ollie and Beth. Beth had gone into the boy's room to comfort their son until the nightmares went away.

Ollie adjusted himself on his bed, pulled the blankets up around his shoulders and closed his eyes when the cell phone rang. It was a dull, grumbling sound, the vibration of the phone against the wood loud and annoying.

Ollie sighed and sat up.

He didn't need to look at the caller ID to know who it was. Only Pete would call him at almost two thirty in the morning. Ollie answered it and rolled back onto his pillow.

"What?" he snapped.

"It's bad, Ollie," Pete said, panting into the phone.

"What's bad?" Ollie asked, then he shook his head. "Hold on. Are you drunk again?"

"No," Pete said, almost moaning. "Oh God no, Ollie. It's the prison. Kurkow. It's really bad."

"What the hell are you talking about?" Ollie said, trying to keep a rein on his anger.

"You sent those ghost hunters in," Pete said.

"So?"

"So," Pete cried, "they never came out!"

"They're not supposed to, you idiot," Ollie said, sighing. "Seriously, Peter. I told you, they need to study the place overnight. I'm going back to sleep now. I suggest you do the same."

"Oliver!" Pete yelled. "They never set up their stuff!"

"What?" Ollie asked, opening his eyes. "What stuff?"

"Their ghost detecting gear," Pete said. "I went by, to check on them, and they went in the prison, but none of their equipment was with them. It's all still in their car."

"Did you go in and look for them?" Ollie asked, sitting up.

"No," Pete whispered.

"No," Ollie mocked. "Of course you didn't. What did you do, Peter, other than call me up?"

"I talked to Frank and Shane," Pete said. "They went in there, too."

"Okay," Ollie said. "Frank and his friend went in there. Great. Where are you now?"

"Pulled over on route eighty-nine, just over the Gaiman town line," Pete said.

"Did you talk with Frank?" Ollie asked.

"No."

"Did you call them to see if they went in there or not?" Ollie asked.

"I watched them go in," Pete said. "I was across the street."

"Did they get the Granite State people out?" Ollie said.

"I don't know," Pete whispered.

"How could you not know?" Ollie asked, and then he answered his own question. "You ran, didn't you?"

Pete was silent.

"Of course you did," Ollie said, disgust rising in his voice. "Of course you ran. What happened?"

"I saw some ghosts," Pete said. "I had to leave before they did something."

Ollie snorted. "Sure."

"You don't understand, Ollie!" Pete said, his voice rising an octave. "I've been listening to the scanner. Bad things are happening in Gaiman. People are dying!"

"You know who might be dead?" Ollie snapped. "Those investigators from the Paranormal Society. Or they might be hurt. Either way, Pete, it means we can get sued. It means we're on the hook for all sorts of financial obligations. Not only that, you sent two other people in there to get the first four out! And then you ran! Now that's six, count 'em, Pete, six people who could sue us!"

"I'm sorry," Pete said.

"You're always sorry," Ollie spat. "Good God in Heaven, get back to the prison!"

"I can't," Pete said.

"You have to!" Ollie ordered.

"No," Pete whispered, and he ended the call.

Ollie looked at his phone in surprise. Pete had never hung up on him before.

Beth appeared in the doorway to their bedroom, yawning. "What's going on?"

"It's Peter," Ollie said, putting the phone down hard on the bed table. "It's just Peter being Peter."

Beth climbed back into bed.

"Oliver okay?" Ollie asked.

"Yes," Beth said, yawning, "just a bad dream about ghosts."

"Ghosts," Ollie said, shaking his head. He wrapped an arm around his wife and said, "Funny, Pete was complaining about the same thing."

Chapter 21: Leaving the Nest

A scream woke George up from a fitful, uncomfortable sleep. He sat up in the bathroom, the night-light spilling over him. George wrapped his hand around the handle of the poker and listened.

Someone screamed again, closer.

George stood up, stepped over his line of salt on the tiled floor and into the hallway. Quick steps brought him to the front door, and he peered out into the night. Mrs. Geisel was running in the street.

Her hair was in disarray, her nightgown in tatters, and her feet bare.

Behind her was a large, fat ghost, and it was the ghost who let out a scream. The look on its face was one of malicious delight. He was, as far as George could tell, pleased with the game he had created.

For the first time since he had arrived home the day before, George opened the front door and left his house.

The brutal cold in the winter air struck him like a fist, knocking the air out of his lungs and causing his eyes to water. His hand cramped up around the handle of the fireplace poker, but George focused on Mrs. Geisel.

Mrs. Geisel twisted away from the prisoner, stutter stepped and then jerked herself to the right as the fat prisoner tried to catch her.

The dead man came to a stop and stared at George.

"Mrs. Geisel," George said, his voice loud and abrasive in the night air. "Please come over here to me."

Mrs. Geisel backed away from the prisoner, glancing at George and then returning her attention to the fat man.

"I'm just trying to have fun," the prisoner said, his voice high for a man so large. "I just want to play with her. I won't hurt her much, I promise."

The prisoner's fingers twitched, and he took a cautious step forward.

George was amazed to see the ghost's feet didn't disturb the snow. The fat man licked his lips and took a larger, bolder step towards her.

"Come on," the ghost whined. "Let me play. It's been so *long*."

"My house, please, Mrs. Geisel," George said. She nodded and passed by him, stinking of urine and fear.

George understood and wondered if his own pants were still dry.

He took a cautious step back, and the ghost lunged at him.

Gripping the poker like a baseball bat, George swung the tool upwards. The iron passed through the ghost on an arc, and in a heartbeat, the fat man was gone. Flickering movements around the edges of his vision told George more of the dead were coming.

Without waiting to see how many there were, George turned around and ran after Mrs. Geisel.

Chapter 22: Finding the Woman

Shane moved up the stairs with gentle steps, the shotgun ready, and the red light of his headlamp illuminating the way. Frank was close behind him, the two of them moving in rhythm.

When they reached the next floor, Shane almost came to a stop, his stomach churning.

He had stepped into a slaughterhouse.

To the left of the stairs was a pile of clothes. Shredded and in tatters, stained with blood and flesh. Hanging from an empty light fixture were a trio of heads. All women. Their long hair had been knotted together, their tongues pulled out, and their eyes were gone. The flesh of each neck was shredded as if someone had torn the heads free of the bodies.

And they did, Shane thought. He moved forward while Frank stepped to the right. The floor around them glistened, blood congealing on the steel. Massive amounts of the liquid which told Shane that the women had taken a long time to die.

There was little left of the women themselves. Bits and pieces scattered along the walkway as far as he could see.

He clenched his teeth and focused on the cell in front of him, the one where Courtney said the last woman was.

The sole survivor of the little trip into the depths of Kurkow.

Shane moved closer and saw a young woman on the floor of the cell. She was naked, covered in blood and a thousand small cuts.

And she was alone.

Shane slipped into the cell, dropped to a knee and checked her pulse. It was there if ever so faint beneath his fingertips. She was slight, her dark hair a massive tangle of knots and blood. Shane set his shotgun on the steel frame of the bunk and stripped off his jacket. He wrapped her in it then picked her up and put her over his shoulder.

Adrenaline pumped through his system as he picked up his shotgun, the woman's weight negligible. He stepped out of the cell and looked at Frank.

Frank nodded and then snapped, "Down!"

Shane crashed to the floor, pain ripping up from his knees while Frank's shotgun roared. Twice more the weapon sounded out and then Frank yelled, "Move!"

Shane got to his feet, wincing at the agonized protesting of his joints. His ears rang, and lights flashed in his vision. He turned toward the stairs, caught himself before he slipped in a small pile of gore he had missed before, and went down to the first level. Behind the pain and the partial deafness from the shotgun blasts, Shane heard Frank reload.

Shane exited the stairwell, focused on the door at the far end and moved towards it. A shape stepped out into the hall, and for a heartbeat, Shane thought it might be Pete. When he realized he could see through it, Shane pulled the trigger. The shot wasn't perfect, but enough of the rock salt from the load hit the ghost.

Behind him, Frank fired again, all five rounds.

"Weapon!" Frank yelled.

Shane paused, handed off his shotgun and took Frank's. Frank fired twice more and then they were at the door and into the foyer.

"Reloading," Frank said, "keep moving."

Shane nodded, shifted the girl from one shoulder to the next, and exited the prison.

"Damn!" Shane spat.

"What?" Frank asked behind him.

"Pete's gone!"

"What?! Oh, come on!" Frank said disgust thick in his voice. The shotgun roared again.

Shane seethed with anger as he broke into a jog. He reached his car, ripped the door open and threw the shotgun onto the car floor. Shane put the young woman in the back seat and climbed in after her. Frank closed the door as he passed, and then got into the driver's seat.

"Keys?" he asked.

"Ignition," Shane answered. He pulled the girl in close to him, wrapping himself around her, trying to keep her warm with his own body heat. The engine started, Frank turned the heat up to its maximum, and backed up.

The young woman shivered, and Shane nodded.

"Can you hear me?" he asked.

Her head moved a fraction of an inch.

"Okay, listen," Shane said, "I'm going to start rubbing you, I'm not getting fresh. I need to keep you warm and get the blood circulating in your hands and feet, or you're going to lose them to frostbite. It's going to hurt."

"It's okay," she murmured.

"Okay," Shane whispered.

Chapter 23: Pete's Surprise

For the first time since Peter Dawson had purchased a cell phone, he had turned it off.

The iPhone lay on the dashboard of the Escalade, and it looked as lonely and forlorn as Pete felt. He had never hung up on Ollie before. Not once in their entire history together. But Pete knew he couldn't go back to the prison. There was no way he could go into Kurkow and see if everyone was okay.

The ghosts wouldn't let him.

He knew that. Pete also knew they would hurt him.

They'd probably kill me, he thought, sighing. He wiped his nose with the back of his hand. *Or they'd do something terrible to me first. Torture me. Who knows what.*

The glint of headlights caught his attention and Pete looked in his rearview mirror. A car was approaching, racing along route eighty-nine in spite of the black ice and the snow drifts forming along the edges. In less than a minute, the car sped by him, and Pete saw it was Shane's car.

And as he registered whose vehicle it was, the car's brake lights flashed red. Then the white reverse lights flared, and the wheels were cut hard, the car racing backward towards him.

Before he could do anything to stop it, Shane's vehicle smashed into the front of the Escalade. Pete howled as his head snapped forward, striking the leather wrapped steering wheel. He could taste blood in his mouth, and one of his back molars throbbed.

Then the driver's side door was ripped open, and Pete was dragged out of the SUV and into the snow. He fell down, tried to get up and a blow knocked him back to the pavement.

Instead of trying to get up, Pete rolled onto his back and looked up.

It wasn't Shane standing over him, but Frank.

His brother's old friend had his fists clenched, his face a mask of fury, the scars dancing in the starlight.

"Why did you leave?" Frank hissed.

Pete didn't answer him. He watched as the tension drained from Frank's shoulders, the rage on his face replaced by an expression of calm. Even his hands relaxed.

"Tell me, Peter," Frank said, his voice low. "Tell me why you left."

"I was afraid," Pete whispered.

Frank closed his eyes and Pete saw the man's Adam's apple bob up and down as he swallowed. "Where are the blankets Shane told you to pick up?"

"Passenger side," Pete said.

Frank turned away from him and went around to the other side of the SUV. Pete could hear Frank get the bags out. Soon he passed by the Escalade and went to the back of Shane's car. He opened the door, and Pete sat up.

Frank tore the blankets out of their packaging, snapping them open and then leaning into the car with them. He was wrapping someone up.

Pete grabbed hold of the Cadillac's door and pulled himself to his feet. He cleared his throat, and when Frank didn't look at him, Pete asked, "Where's Shane?"

Frank remained focused on the person in the backseat. "Here."

"Is he okay?" Pete asked.

Frank shot him a withering look. "He's fine."

"What about the Paranormal Society?" Pete asked, trying to see inside the back of Shane's car without leaving the protection of the Cadillac.

"There's one here," Frank said. He closed the door, bent down and picked the trash up from the road. He stuffed it all into one plastic bag and walked back to Pete.

"One?" Pete asked, confused. "There were four of them. Are they okay?"

"No," Frank said, throwing the bag of trash at him. "They're dead."

Pete blinked. "What?"

"Dead," Frank repeated. "Dead. Their heads are hanging from a light fixture inside the Prison. I'm not exactly sure if all of their body parts are there as well, but they might be. You can tell Oliver if you want. In fact, you should. And tell him that I'll be coming soon to speak with him."

Pete's heart skipped a beat.

Memories flashed before him. Frank had been a terror in middle school and high school. A kid who would fight for any reason, at any time. Someone who didn't mind a little bit of pain to get in close and hurt someone.

"Tell him I'm coming," Frank said, nodding. "And it'll be soon."

Pete watched Frank walk to Shane's car. The man paused, looked down at the fender which hung half off, and then reached down to tear it away. Frank threw the molded fiberglass onto the road's shoulder and got back into the car.

Pete shivered and got back into his vehicle. He found his phone on the floor and picked it up. Pete held it for a moment, then put it down.

Ollie can find out for himself, he thought, and he closed the door.

Chapter 24: By the Fire

George's world had shrunk down to what he could see of Mulberry Street from his windows, and the relative safety of his home. For almost two days, he had existed alone in his new environment, a desolate life where he had witnessed one death and nearly suffered his own.

But now he had a companion in misery.

Mrs. Geisel.

She was wearing some of Jess' sweats and wrapped up in an old comforter. Mrs. Geisel sat in front of the fireplace, her cheeks and nose still red from her time in the cold.

George had tried to speak with her several times, all to no avail. She hadn't responded to any of his questions or offered up any information. Eventually, George had stopped with the inquiries.

He placed a cup of warm milk on the floor beside her, set another log on the fire and retreated to the couch. The shades were pulled, and salt lined the window sills and the thresholds. He had found another container of the blessed spice in the pantry when looking for hot chocolate.

"Charles is dead," Mrs. Geisel murmured.

George looked at her in surprise. He was about to ask her a question when she spoke again.

"The fat man killed him," she continued. She picked up the cup of milk, took a drink and then looked at it for a minute.

George waited for her.

She turned to face him, her eyes swollen and red. "Do you have any idea what's going on?"

"Not really," George said. His voice sounded strange in his ears, like metal being dragged across metal.

"What did you do to stop them?" she asked. "Nothing we tried worked."

George picked up the fireplace poker. "This is made of iron. It can send ghosts away, just like salt can keep them out."

She glanced around the room, nodding. "How did you find out about the iron?"

"I was just lucky. I picked it up and swung at it," he hesitated, then added, "It was a ghost. There were two in the room with me. I think the other one was just as surprised as I was. When they were gone, I looked up ghosts online."

Mrs. Geisel finished her drink and set the cup on the floor. She held her hands out towards the fire, and George saw they trembled.

George had always thought Mrs. Geisel was in her fifties. Perhaps a little older. As he looked at her in the dim light thrown by the fire, he realized she was older than he thought. Wrinkles were gathered under her neck and crow's feet spread out from her eyes. There was a good deal of white hair interspersed in her black locks. Fear and exhaustion added to her aged appearance.

"I don't believe I know your first name," George said.

She gave him a wan smile, revealing capped, bright white teeth. "Merle."

"A pleasure, Merle," George said. "Do you need another blanket, perhaps something more to drink or to eat?"

Merle shook her head. "No. Thank you, though. My feet hurt, as do my hands, but I take it as a good sign. The question now is what shall we do."

"Do?" George asked.

"Oh yes," Merle said. "We're not the only ones alive on Mulberry Street, George. Not by a long shot."

"You want to rescue them?" George said, unable to keep the incredulity out of his voice. She smiled. "I do indeed."

George looked from her to the fire and stared into it for a moment. Blinking his eyes, he shook his head. He opened his mouth, the word 'no' forming on his lips, but instead his voice said, "Yes. Let's do it. Soon as the sun's up."

Merle nodded her approval and George was left alone with his thoughts, wondering why he had agreed to leave the house again.

Chapter 25: Lost in the Storm

"Damn it!" Frank snapped.

Shane turned his head and asked, "What's wrong?"

"I'm lost," Frank barked. "Sorry. It's snowing again. I got turned around somehow."

"Great," Shane muttered. His entire body ached, not only from holding onto the young woman but from the minor accident with Pete's SUV.

The girl was asleep, her breathing slow and normal. She wasn't resting easy in his arms. Now and again she kicked, struggled, and bit down. None of which were pleasant to experience.

Shane consoled himself with the knowledge that she was unaware of her actions. With a grunt, he shifted his body and tried to get comfortable. Beneath the blankets Frank had beaten out of Pete, Shane was sweating.

Frank stopped the car and mumbled to himself. Shane turned his attention back to the girl. In the darkness, he couldn't make out more than a silhouette of her face, which was almost cherubic in form.

"Oh no," Frank whispered.

"What's wrong?" Shane asked.

"We're back in Gaiman," Frank said.

"What?!" Shane said. "How the hell did that happen?"

"I must have turned off the wrong way," his voice faded. "Wait. No, no I didn't. Oh, crap."

"What?" Shane said, his anger rising.

"The route cuts back," Frank said. "Doubles right back on itself to follow whatever river this is to the bridge. It led us right into a small pocket of land belonging to Gaiman."

Shane closed his eyes. "How fast until we can get out of here?"

"I'll let you know," Frank said, and Shane felt the car lunge into motion.

The young woman whimpered, her eyelids flickered and her eyes locked onto Shane. For a moment, they were cloudy, unable to focus.

When they did, she let out a loud, sharp gasp.

She struggled against him, and Shane let go immediately. He thought she was going to sit up, but after she tried, the young woman collapsed back onto the seat.

"Are you okay?" Shane asked.

She nodded, her eyes closed. "Where are my friends? Are they in here with me?"

"You're in the backseat of a small sedan," Shane said. "And I'm the only one back here with you. Can you tell me who you are?"

"Emma," she said.

"Emma, my name's Shane. My friend, Frank, is going to drive us to the closest hospital," Shane said. "You were in the cold for a long while."

"I know what happened," she said, her voice low. "We were caught by the dead. I was dragged into the cell because they were bored."

"Who was bored?" Shane asked.

"The ghosts," Emma answered. "They've been bored for decades. We were 'entertaining' them."

"Shane!" Frank yelled.

Shane shoved himself up, twisting at the same time to look out the windshield.

A line of ghosts stretched across route eighty-nine, all of them prisoners. The car's headlights shined through and illuminated them at the same time. The engine revved and the car raced forward.

"What's happening?" Emma asked, trying to sit up.

"Stay down," Shane ordered. He reached into his back pocket and took out his knuckle-dusters. The shotgun, even loaded with rock salt, would be far too dangerous in the close confines of the car.

And then the decision was out of his hands.

Frank drove the car through the line of the dead, some of the prisoners reaching in. As Frank lashed out with an iron ringed hand, Shane did the same with his knuckle-dusters. Ghosts screamed with fury, and one managed to get into the front passenger seat.

"Give her back!" the dead man screamed. "She's ours!"

"Out," Shane snarled, driving his fist into the ghost's face, the iron causing the ghost to vanish.

Emma managed to sit up as Frank guided the car around a curve. For a second, the headlights shined upon a small, green sign on the side of the road. It read, *Welcome to Cornish, New Hampshire*.

Frank slowed the car down and Shane sagged back into the seat.

"What happened?" Emma asked again, the words mumbled through her swollen lips.

"Roadblock," Shane answered.

Wincing, Emma turned and looked out the back window. "I don't see anything."

"They were dead," Frank said over his shoulder.

"I don't understand," she whispered. "Where are my friends? How were the ghosts out?"

Shane reached out, helped to pull a blanket closer around her and said, "Rest, Emma. You'll know it all soon enough."

Emma blinked, nodded, and leaned against Shane.

He could smell her blood and feel the tiredness of her body. A sudden, painful ache filled him, and Shane closed his eyes against the tears.

He missed Courtney.

Chapter 26: An Old Friend

"Shane."

Shane sat up, his eyes bleary. He looked around and saw they were pulled over on the side of the road. A glance at the radio's clock showed it was 3:33 in the morning.

"Yeah?" Shane asked.

"I have an idea," Frank said.

"What's that?" Shane rubbed at his eyes and yawned.

"I have an old friend up here, right outside of Cornish. Former Special Forces medic. He could treat the girl if he's home," Frank said.

"Why him?" Shane asked, stifling another yawn.

"You want to bring in a female, in obviously bad condition, to a hospital and then try to walk out?" Frank asked.

Shane's shoulders dropped. "Damn. Yeah, you're right."

"You want to ask her what she wants?" Frank said.

"Sure," Shane said. He turned to the girl, tapped her on the shoulder and said, "Hey, Emma."

When she didn't respond, he raised his voice and shook her a little harder.

Still nothing.

She was asleep, or unconscious.

"He's nearby?" Shane asked.

"Half a mile up on the left, we turn onto a dirt road, then a quarter mile further in and we're there," Frank said, nodding.

"Alright, let's do it." Shane lifted Emma up, pulled her close and made sure the blankets were wrapped around her. He held onto her as Frank moved back onto the road and found his way to his friend's house.

It took less than five minutes before they pulled into a driveway. Powerful lights eliminated all shadows, and cameras were mounted on each corner of the house and the barn which stood on the left.

Frank turned off the car's headlights, picked up his cell phone and dialed a number.

"Asa," Frank said. "It's Francis. I've got a male friend and an injured female."

Frank listened, nodded and said, "Thanks."

"We good?" Shane asked.

"Yeah," Frank said, putting the phone away. "He won't shoot us now. Let's move."

In less than a minute, Shane had Emma in his arms, and he was close behind Frank. By the time they reached the front door, the unseen Asa had started to open it. When Shane stepped into the house, the smell of antiseptics and cleansers stung his nose. The walls were painted white and absent of any decorations. The door clicked shut behind them, and Shane turned to see an older man standing beside it.

Asa held a large hunting rifle, a powerful scope attached to it. He held the weapon with easy familiarity, and he wore a long, white bathrobe. His feet were bare, his white hair long and falling well past his shoulders. The man's face was thin, his blue eyes bright. His nose looked like a hawk's bill, his lips thin.

"Hello, Francis," Asa said, and Shane was surprised at the musicality of the man's voice.

"Hello, Asa," Frank responded. "This is my friend, Shane, and the young woman he's carrying is Emma."

Asa nodded. "Follow me."

The man's footsteps were silent, Asa moved with the grace of a dancer.

He's dangerous, Shane realized. *Terribly so. Someone would never hear him sneak up on them.*

Asa paused at a gun rack, cleared the chambered round from the rifle and hung the weapon up. He dropped the unspent bullet into a box of the same and opened the door to a room beside the weapons.

When Asa flicked on the lights, Shane winced, blinked several times and then gasped when he could see again.

He was in an operating room. Everything gleamed beneath the strong lights.

"Wow," Shane whispered.

One corner of Asa's mouth curled up in a small smile. "Thank you. It has taken me quite some time to accumulate the materials. You would be surprised at what the government regulates and tracks. Now, please set the young lady on the table and step out of the room. I will let you know if I need any assistance."

Shane put Emma down and paused. Frank took him by the arm, saying, "Come on. She's in the best hands now."

With a reluctant nod, Shane followed Frank out of the room. Asa closed the door behind them.

"This way," Frank said, gesturing towards a small room nearby. It contained a pair of chairs and a wall of monitors. Each monitor had a different view of the area around the house. There were also some monitors whose cameras were tracking game trails and nearby roads.

"Paranoid much?" Shane asked. He sat down, exhaustion creeping in on him.

Frank chuckled as he took a seat. "Little bit. He wasn't like this before Afghanistan. Traumatic brain injury from a roadside bomb. Made him paranoid. Fortunately, he's still a brilliant medic."

"He's good?" Shane asked.

"The best," Frank said. "He's the one who stitched my face back together. Plastic surgeons worked on the rest, but they said if he hadn't done the initial work, well, it would have been a lot less pretty."

"Fair enough," Shane said. He looked around the room and found a single book on the small table between the chairs. Leaning forward, Shane picked it up and read the title. *Meditations*, by Marcus Aurelius. "And he's a stoic."

"Yeah," Frank said. He rubbed at his eyes and then closed them. "He'll get us when he's done."

"Okay," Shane said. He shut his eyes, let out a sigh and tried to relax. As sleep climbed up to claim him, a sudden, painful thought grabbed him.

If the ghosts were on the road, he told himself, *then the town is overrun.*

The thought kept him awake for a long time.

Chapter 27: Early Morning in Gaiman

Jess' sneakers were a little big on Mrs. Geisel, but she could move around in them. She held onto the fireplace shovel while George remained master of the poker. Both he and Mrs. Geisel were bundled up against the cold and stood by the back door.

"I spoke with Evie Marchinko before everything happened at my house," Merle said, her voice hard. "I'm not sure how she's managed since then, but I know she was still alive as of yesterday morning."

"And she's the house to the right of yours?" George asked, glancing out the window at the building in question.

"Yes," Merle said, "that's right."

George looked at the house. It couldn't have been more than a hundred feet away, but there was a fresh layer of snow covering everything, and he didn't know if there was ice beneath it. He also wasn't sure how many ghosts were watching his house, if any.

It would be foolish to think they're not, he told himself. *I don't know if sending them back to wherever they came from hurts, but they certainly don't like it.*

Gripping the poker, George looked at Merle, gave the woman a tight smile and asked, "Are you ready?"

Her face paled at the question, but she nodded and forced a smile.

George felt his resolve weakening, so he grabbed the doorknob, twisted it and jerked the door open. He entered into the chill air and kept his eyes focused on Evie's house.

One step in front of the other, he told himself. *One step in front of the other.*

George didn't focus on anything more than that. Lifting the right foot and putting it down, lifting the left foot and putting it down, and repeat. Soon they were on the street, then across it, and finally, they were walking up to the side porch.

Merle went first since she knew Evie better than George did.

The older woman knocked on the glass. When no one answered, she knocked a little louder.

"Who is it?!" Evie yelled from inside. George could hear the panic in the woman's voice.

"Evie, it's Merle," Merle said. "I'm with George from across the street. We've come to get you and the children."

"How?" Evie demanded. Her volume had lowered, but the fear was still there.

"George has set up a safe place in the house," Merle said, and George was impressed with the calmness which emanated from her. "We can all be safe there together until someone figures out what's going on."

"The door's opened," Evie said.

Merle went into the house, and George followed. They entered the wrecked remains of a kitchen. The table and chairs were smashed, cups and plates and silverware littered the floor.

Evie was crouched in the corner between the refrigerator and the wall, her children pressed in behind her. George remembered a woman with bright red hair, a round face and dour clothes, someone whose body had gone to pot long ago.

The woman George saw in the kitchen only had the ginger hair he remembered. Her pale skin was splotched with red, a trio of identical scratches down her left cheek. It looked like she had lost ten pounds in the last three days, and also found a strength George doubted she had known about prior to the current situation. In her chubby hands, she held onto a cast iron frying pan, and George smiled.

"You've kept them away with that," he said.

A little girl peered over her mother's shoulder and said, "She's made dozens disappear."

"Not dozens," Evie whispered. "But a lot. They wanted my girls. They wanted to do things to them."

"I'm glad you did. It was good," George said. "Really good. I never thought of a cast iron frying pan as a weapon."

"I saw what you did with the poker," Evie said. "We were watching out the window."

George nodded. "Listen, do you have any food and extra salt?"

Evie frowned at the second part of the question. "Sure. Why?"

"We need it, dear," Merle said, smiling. "Let's gather up what we need quick as we can, alright?"

Evie paused and then straightened up. "Okay. Salt and food are in the pantry. I'll grab the kids' coats and stuff."

"Alright," George said, "but let's hurry. I don't know when the ghosts will be back."

Fear spurred them all to greater efforts.

Chapter 28: Answering Some Questions

The sun was up when Asa stepped into the small observation room and said, "She wants to speak with Shane."

Shane nodded his thanks, stood up, stretched and went to the small operating theater. He found Emma on the bed, the back of it raised slightly, and the safety bars on either sides of her in the upright position. She had several white hospital blankets on her and an IV drip as well. Asa had also hooked her up to a monitor, which beeped at a slow and steady rhythm.

Emma's face was puffy, but all the cuts had been cleaned and bandaged, giving her the appearance of a boxer who had come out on the losing end of a bout. Her eyes followed him as he entered, and since there was no chair for him, Shane stood.

He smiled and said, "Hello, Emma."

She offered a weak, tired smile in return and when she spoke her voice was small and difficult to hear. Shane heard the painkillers working their magic, fighting off shock and keeping her from sinking under its weight.

"Where are my friends?" she asked.

"They were killed," Shane answered.

Tears welled up in her eyes, but she blinked them away.

"Did they suffer?" Emma asked.

"I hope not," he said.

"Me too," she said, sighing. "I suffered. You know, I had heard, once, that people who have a traumatic incident usually don't remember it. Some sort of safety mechanism for the brain."

"That's a lie," Shane said.

"Figures," Emma said. "Thank you."

"For pulling you out of there?" Shane asked.

"And for bringing me to this hospital," she added.

"You're welcome," Shane said. "But you're not in a hospital. This is a friend's house."

Emma shrugged. "Whatever works. He's got some awesome drugs. I don't feel good, but I don't care that I don't feel good."

"I'm glad to hear it," Shane said.

Emma closed her eyes and was quiet. Shane turned to leave and stopped when she asked, "How did you know to use salt?"

Shane faced her again and said, "Those weren't the first ghosts I've had to deal with."

"Ah," she said, a small smile playing on her face, her eyes still closed. "I wish I had known there were a lot of them."

"We did know," Shane said, anger creeping into his voice. "We were supposed to go in there. We were just waiting on the call."

Emma opened her eyes. "You were supposed to?"

Shane nodded, not trusting himself to speak calmly.

"Then why did he send us?" she asked, confused. "If you knew what you were doing, and how many were there?"

"I don't know," Shane answered. "But we're going to talk to him. He's got at least three deaths on his hands, maybe more."

"How could he have more?" she asked. "Did others go into the prison?"

Shane shook his head. "No. The town of Gaiman owned the prison. And the ghosts are loose within its borders."

"Oh my God," she said, and Shane had to strain to hear her. "How many people?"

"I don't know," he answered. The bitterness and rage he felt towards Ollie Dawson tasted like steel in his mouth. "But we're going to find out."

Emma closed her eyes again. "Hit him for me."

"I will," Shane said. He stood by the bed for several minutes, making sure she had fallen asleep before he went back to the monitoring room. Frank and Asa were there, Frank raising an eyebrow.

Shane sighed as he dropped into his seat. He yawned, rubbed at his eyes and said, "I want to knock your friend Ollie's teeth out."

"Is he the one responsible for this girl's condition?" Asa asked, and Shane heard an angry tightness in the man's voice.

"Indirectly," Frank said. "He sent them into a place he had been warned about."

"Them?" Asa asked, and Shane could see the man struggled with his temper.

Frank nodded.

"Can you tell us the extent of her injuries?" Shane asked.

"Yes," Asa answered. "All of her toes have been broken, as well as several of the larger bones in her feet. Both knees were dislocated, and all the ribs on her left side were cracked. She has suffered extensive internal injuries and a fracture of the left orbital socket. Both pinkies were broken, and the thumbs dislocated."

Asa took a deep breath, looked down at the floor and added, "And she was assaulted."

Frank pushed himself up out of the chair and walked around the room for a minute, cracking the knuckles on his hands.

Shane clenched his teeth, breathing rapidly through his nose.

"She cannot be moved," Asa continued, "at least not without an ambulance. When she wakes up, I will, of course, offer her that option. I will also offer her the choice of remaining here until she is well enough to travel home in a vehicle other than an emergency one."

Shane nodded.

"Thank you, Asa," Frank said.

Asa offered them a grim smile. "It is not much of a burden, although I must say that I wish I could go with you when you speak with this Oliver Dawson."

"Yeah?" Shane asked.

Asa nodded. "As a medic, I have the requisite knowledge for inflicting the maximum amount of pain while causing the least amount of physical damage."

"That," Shane said, "is something I would like to see."

"Do you want to see him now?" Frank asked, turning to look at Shane, his hands balled into fists.

"If I may," Asa said, standing up. "Both of you would do well with two to three hours of sleep. Also, a large amount of snow fell again while I was caring for Emma. I would advise you to rest. I will wake you up in three hours, and have a meal ready for you."

Shane didn't want to, but he knew the wisdom of it. He looked to Frank and the former monk nodded his agreement.

"We would appreciate it, my friend," Frank said.

"Then come," Asa said, standing up. "My home is Spartan, but it is comfortable."

Shane got up and followed his friend and the strange medic out of the room, wondering what the day might bring.

Chapter 29: Merle Has Information

George poured the last of the chicken noodle soup into a cup and carried it out into the television room. The fire burned brightly in the hearth, the flames casting out much needed warmth over Evie Marchinko's two little girls who were asleep in a Coleman sleeping bag. Their mother was wrapped in an old blanket, sipping a hot toddy from an old china cup.

Merle was standing by the wood logs that she and George had brought in together and stacked beneath the front window. She inspected the line of salt on the sill, nodded to herself and smiled at him. The expression showed her exhaustion, as did the black circles beneath her eyes.

"Soup's here, Merle," George said, easing himself down onto the floor.

"Thanks," she said. Merle sat beside Evie, accepted the cup from George and bent over it, inhaling. "Funny. I never thought chicken noodle soup could smell so good."

"I didn't think I'd ever be hungry enough to eat half a stack of saltines," George confessed.

Evie took a drink and then asked, "Why?"

"Why what?" Merle asked. George could hear the effort it took for her to keep her voice calm.

"The ghosts," Evie said, looking at Merle. She kept her voice low, but it was tinged with desperation. "Why are they here? Are they in all of Gaiman, and why isn't anyone coming to help us?"

"I don't know," Merle answered.

"I called the police," Evie said. "And they told me they had lots of other problems to deal with, and that they'd send an officer out as soon as they could."

George shook his head. He had never thought to call the police, and by the look on Merle's face, he could see the idea had never presented itself to her either.

"When did you call?" Merle asked.

"This morning," Evie said, her voice rising a little. Then she took a deep breath and continued. "I called this morning because a couple of them had come into the house. They said terrible things. They were going to hurt my girls. That's when I grabbed the frying pan."

"You did a great job," George said. "A fantastic job, Evie."

She nodded, brushed a lock of red hair away from her forehead and said, "But why are they here?"

"I think I know why," Merle said.

Both George and Evie looked to her. Evie's surprise mimicking his own.

"When the town first brought the prison in," Merle said, "the guards and the staff had to drive in from places like Concord and Goffstown. Some as far as Nashua. The town figured it would be in their best interest to put in a few houses, so they built Mulberry Street."

"Wait. What?" George said.

Merle nodded. "This entire street. It's why all the houses are all one type. Easy to build prefabs. The whole place went up in about a month. Then the prison's staff and the guards moved in. They could see their homes when they were at work, and the prisoners could see the freedom that the guards enjoyed. Everyone in Kurkow was fixated on Mulberry Street."

"That's why there were guards here too," George whispered.

Merle nodded.

"But why are there so many of them?" Evie asked. "I mean, come on, did a whole bunch die at once or something?"

"Yes," Merle said, and she told them about the accident at Kurkow Prison. "Lots of rumors really, about what happened at the prison. Small towns are good for that. And no one knows for certain, of course, because no one bothered to tell the residents. What's passed down over the years is that there was an accident in the basement. They kept chemicals down there. Some for the cleaning equipment they used, since they did all of their own laundry, and some for finishing wood."

"What?" George asked, confused.

"Kurkow used to put out some excellent furniture," Merle said, shaking her head. "Gave the prisoners something to do. A way to earn money. And for some, it was a way to learn a trade so they could get a job when they got out."

"And they think it was the chemicals?" Evie asked.

Merle nodded. "Yes. I heard from one man, who survived, that a cloud came up from the basement. Men choked to death on it. It became a mad house. Prisoners being murdered even as the guards tried to get everyone out and to safety. A lot of guards died, too, trying to save those men."

"Did the man who did it get punished?" George asked.

"No," Merle said. "They never learned who it was. Or how it happened. The bodies were so contaminated by the gas that they were cremated instead of being interred."

"Is that why they look the way they do?" Evie whispered.

"Must be," Merle replied. She glanced at the window and George did the same, wondering how many of the dead were roaming Mulberry Street.

Book 5: Kurkow Prison

Chapter 30: A Visit from an Old Friend

Ollie finished up a Skype session with his property managers down in Boston and stood up to stretch. He enjoyed the early morning discussions. His employees tended to be more truthful, less prepared to lie in front of him about rental issues or property damage.

Ollie left his small office, listened for Beth and the kids and then remembered she had said something about an appointment at the dentist. He shrugged, walked down the center stairs and turned off towards the kitchen when the doorbell rang.

Frowning, Ollie went to the front door, looked at the closed circuit monitor and saw two men. One of them was lean and bald, the other was Frank.

Ollie hesitated a moment, then thought, *Oh, what the hell. I've got at least an hour until the next conference call.*

He reached out, flipped back the deadbolt and opened the door.

"Frank!" he said, extending his hand.

Frank smiled at him, shook the offered hand and stepped in when Ollie motioned for him to do so.

"Ollie," Frank said, "this is my friend, Shane."

"Nice to meet you," Ollie said, shaking Shane's hand.

Shane gave him a tight smile and a nod, not saying a word.

Damn, Ollie thought. *Guy doesn't have any hair at all. What the hell type of a freak is he?*

"What brings you by?" Ollie asked, closing and locking the door.

"Pete didn't tell you we were going to stop in and say hello?" Frank asked.

"Well, you know Peter," Ollie said, waving his hand dismissively. "I'm surprised he can remember where he lives some days. Come on, I was just going to the kitchen. Doctor's got me on this damned, gluten free diet, which means Beth's watching what I eat like a hawk."

They went into the kitchen, and Ollie pulled a banana out of a bowl, peeling it as he looked at the two men.

"How is Beth?" Frank asked, sitting down in the breakfast nook. Shane took his jacket off, put it on the seat beside Frank and rolled up the sleeves of his shirt.

"She's good," Ollie said, tossing the peel into the compost pot by the sink. "She's out with the kids right now."

"Oh," Frank said. "That's too bad. I was hoping to see her. Think they'll be back soon?"

"Not likely," Ollie said around a mouthful of banana. "The kids are going to the dentist, which means a trip to the toy store after. It'll probably be lunchtime before I see any of them. Good for work."

Ollie finished the fruit, washed his hands in the sink and wiped them off on a dishtowel, asking, "So, what brings you by? I was going to call you later on about the prison. Pete said you guys swung in there last night. Anything exciting?"

"I guess you could say that," Frank said, nodding to Shane.

Ollie turned to look at the hairless, quiet man and saw Shane step towards him.

***

Ollie woke up with a horrific headache and the coppery taste of blood in his mouth. He was sitting in a chair in the center of the kitchen. Frank was still in the breakfast nook. Shane was by the sink.

"What the hell happened?" Ollie asked, wincing. He probed the back teeth with his tongue and found sharp edges.

"I punched you," Shane said. His voice was hard, the look in his eyes murderous.

Ollie tried to stand up and found he couldn't. His hands, he realized, were tied behind him and his legs were bound to the chair.

"What are you doing, Frank?" Ollie demanded, looking at his friend.

There was no friendship in Frank's eyes.

"Last night," Frank said, "you sent a team of amateurs into Kurkow Prison."

"So?" Ollie snapped. "What business is it of yours?"

Shane punched him, a calculated blow to the side of Ollie's knee that sent needles of pain through him.

"It is our business," Frank continued, "because Pete asked us to check on them. And we're glad he did."

"What, you upset that someone else got your payment?" Ollie sneered.

Shane's next blow was to the groin, and Ollie couldn't scream as he vomited the banana onto his own lap.

"It might be a good idea to change your tone," Frank suggested. "If you haven't figured it out yet, Shane is not in the best of moods. I asked him to not cut on you, but I don't know for how much longer he's going to honor that request."

Ollie looked at Shane through a haze of pain, and he realized Frank was right. *He'll kill me.*

Ollie spit out a bit of bile, straightened up as best he could and asked, "What happened in the prison last night?"

"Ah," Frank said, "that is the right question for you to ask. Well, let me tell you, Oliver. We rescued a member of that amateur group. The Granite State Paranormal Society."

"There were supposed to be four of them," Ollie said, confused. "I mean, that's what the woman, Emma, told me."

"Oh," Frank said. "There were. There were four of them."

"But only one needed to be rescued?" Ollie asked.

"Yes," Frank said, nodding.

"The others were okay?" Ollie asked, trying to understand what the problem had been.

"No," Frank said. "They were about as far from okay as possible. They were dead."

Ollie shook his head. "What?! How?"

"They were murdered by ghosts," Frank said.

Ollie snorted in disbelief. "There's no such thing as ghosts."

Frank looked to Shane and Ollie winced, expecting another blow.

Instead, Shane spoke a single word.

"Courtney."

Chapter 31: Helping Ollie Believe

When Courtney appeared in the kitchen, Oliver Dawson looked as if he was going to faint.

Shane hoped the man would.

He didn't like Oliver, and he wanted to hurt him for what had happened to the women. For what had been done to Emma, and what was most likely being done to others in Gaiman as they stood there. Frank had said it was the best way though, because they were going to need money to do what was necessary, and neither Frank nor Shane had enough cash to do it.

Courtney stood in front of Oliver, her body more defined than usual. Her anger over the fate of the three young women was as great as Shane and Frank's.

"What's this?" Oliver asked, his eyes darting from Shane to Frank. "Some kind of trick? Some little projector one of you has?"

Shane remained silent.

"No," Frank said, his voice patient. "This is Courtney. She is, unfortunately, quite dead. She helped us last night. Courtney was the one who found Emma, and the remains of the others as well."

Oliver shook his head. "I say bull."

Courtney looked at Shane, and he nodded.

She stepped up to Oliver and knelt down in front of him. Without speaking, she reached out with one hand and rested it, palm down, on his thigh. Oliver's eyes widened. He looked at Frank.

"How are you doing that?" he demanded. "How are you making me cold from over there?"

"I'm not," Frank said. "It's all Courtney."

"She's not here!" Oliver yelled. "There's no such thing as ghosts!"

Courtney glanced at Shane, unhappiness plain on her face.

"I'm sorry," Shane whispered. "Please?"

She hesitated, nodded, and then placed her hand on the other the other thigh. Shane watched as she pushed against his thighs.

Oliver's eyes bulged, and his throat seemed to swell as he screamed.

Courtney jerked her hands back, and she disappeared. The now familiar burst of cold from the dog-tags around his neck told Shane she was once more hiding in the steel.

Oliver's head hung down, his chest heaving. After several minutes, he lifted his chin up, his eyes red with pain. In a raw voice, he asked, "Ghosts are real?"

"Yes," Frank said.

"They can't be," Oliver said, his voice frantic. "Come on. I just sent them in there for publicity, you know? Some word of mouth, maybe a viral video. Try to get stuff pumped up for when we finish restoring it. No. No, ghosts can't be real, can they?"

"Yes," Frank repeated. "They can be, and they are."

"And," Oliver said, shaking his head, "they killed those girls?"

"They did," Frank said.

Oliver shuddered. "And the ghosts are loose in Gaiman?"

Frank nodded.

"What do we need to do to stop them?" Oliver whispered.

"A lot," Frank said, his voice low. "And it's going to cost money."

Oliver nodded. "Whatever it takes. Dear God, whatever it takes."

Chapter 32: The Last House on Mulberry Street

Edmund Dumas lived at 31 Mulberry Street, the last house before it joined with an old logging road. He had lived in the house since it had been built, and he had lived there alone. Unlike many professional bachelors, Edmund was not slovenly, nor was he a misogynist.

Edmund didn't want to share his home with anyone. His parents, while they had still been alive, had blamed it on the scarlet fever he had suffered as a child. Friends had blamed it on his dedication to his job. One psychologist had decided he had an issue with his mother, although Edmund had never quite understood that particular rationale.

That psychologist had found Edmund's reliance upon lists curious as well. Edmund kept lists everywhere, in each room of his house. Some rooms, like the kitchen and the bathroom, had more than one. The lists reminded him of what he needed to do, and what order they needed to be done in. Each list helped him to remain calm, to remain focused, and to ignore people.

Because the plain and simple truth was Edmund didn't like people. It was why he had become a prison guard. No one expected him to be sympathetic to the plight of inmates, and any oddities in his behavior could usually be attributed to his work as a third shift guard.

Edmund had enjoyed the work at Kurkow Prison. It had a routine which set him at ease, and he had made it known that he wouldn't tolerate any idiocy. When he said jump, he believed the prisoners should jump. If they didn't, he taught them why they should. The same applied to himself, of course. If his sergeant told him to toss a prisoner's cell, he tossed it. Should the warden tell him to stay on for the day shift, he stayed on for the day shift.

Edmund knew there was an order to the world, and he knew his place in it.

When the accident had occurred at the prison, Edmund had been coming off his shift. The call had come to help the prisoners get out, and so he had helped those he could. He had not panicked, and he had not worried. Instead, he had helped men from 'D' Block get out, and then, when there were no others he could help, he had left.

No real inquiry had ever been made about the accident. And Edmund had been grateful for the State's lack of curiosity. Edmund lacked the ability to lie, and so he would have had to tell the investigators that the accident had been his fault. That he was the one who had gotten angry and lost his temper. Prisoner 11025TK had failed to put the pipe-wrench away, and Edmund had picked it up.

Picked it up and thrown it. The heavy tool had smashed through one pipe fitting and broken the valve on another. The resulting combination had been deadly.

Edmund had seen it for what it was immediately, and he had run, slowing down only when he reached the safety of the stairs.

A stupid mistake, Edmund thought. *Nothing more.*

But it had been enough to cause massive casualties, some of whom had been his coworkers.

And those men who had known about his involvement in it had died. The few prisoners who had been with him were the first to be struck down, their agonized deaths the warning he needed to escape from the gas. He had fled the scene, locking those behind him in, and had the warden not ordered everyone to assist, Edmund would have gone home.

As it was, he had spent hours at the scene, thankful to see that none of the prisoners who had been with him had survived.

There had been suspicions, rumors that perhaps Edmund had been responsible for the accident, especially since he had been the last guard in the basement with a work party. But there had never been any proof. Not so much as a whisper.

And the 'higher authorities' had wanted it to stay that way.

So Edmund had received a significant pension, hush money to not speak to reporters about the incident. The pension, plus the small inheritance from his parents had allowed him to live a comfortable existence in Gaiman.

Each day, for years on end, had been the same. A pleasant rhythm of meals broken only by television and walks.

Until the breaking of the windows at Kurkow Prison.

Somehow, he had known what it meant. The souls of those killed by his mistake had been released, and they would find him soon enough.

His mother had been a superstitious woman, and his father had been a devout Catholic. While his father would have sought the intervention of a priest, Edmund decided to dig into the memories of his mother's folklore to see how to protect himself.

Often his mother would burn sage when he was a young boy, telling him how it was necessary to keep the house clean of any spirits who might wander in from the Merrimack River. She also kept a good supply of salt in the pantry, not only to salt the fish and meat his father procured but to line the window sills and the thresholds with. A barrier, she had told Edmund, to keep the wandering dead away.

And finally, iron. An iron coffin nail, clenched in the hand to strike down the spirits she might meet on dark roads and in cemeteries.

When the windows broke in Kurkow, Edmund changed his routine for the first time in decades. He went to the large Wal-Mart down in Goffstown and bought as much salt as he could. Iron nails had been harder to find, but he had found them at an antique store off of route eighty-nine. Sage, however, was impossible to find in the winter.

Edmund had a decent supply of food and water at home, and a woodstove. Preparing his home against ghostly invaders had been the work of a single afternoon. When it was finished, he had sat down in his chair and looked out the front window onto Mulberry Street. He had the television on in the background, and he watched chaos descend upon the street.

Days passed, and he went about his normal routine, foregoing only his daily walks.

He watched George from down the street run out and assist Merle. The next day, he watched as George and Merle retrieved Evie and her two children. Edmund had watched the murder of the plow driver, and the way the ghosts had kept their distance when the police from Plaistow had arrived to clean up the scene.

The storm had interfered with the police, prohibiting Plaistow PD from doing much more than gather up the body. Edmund had watched them arrive, and he had seen the police remove empty beer bottles from the cab.

Plaistow PD weren't equipped with the necessary gear to protect a scene from the elements, and Edmund doubted they believed it was a murder.

More than likely they believe it to be an accidental death, Edmund thought. *Another drunk plow driver, falling into snow and suffocating.*

The death of a seemingly drunk plow driver, who had managed to smother himself in the snow, wouldn't rank high on the state police's 'to do' list.

Edmund was certain that the state police had their hands full with the roads, and he had watched them seal off Dorothy's house. The news had reported that her murder would be investigated thoroughly after the storm.

On day four, after he had finished his oatmeal and washed and dried the same spoon and bowl he had used for thirty-two years, someone had knocked on his front door.

It was an authoritative sound, hard enough to shake the door in its frame.

Edmund had wiped his hands on the dish towel, hung it up on its chrome bar in front of the sink, and left the kitchen. By the time he reached the front door, the person had knocked a second time. When Edmund grasped the doorknob, he was surprised to discover how cold it was, and how difficult it was to turn it.

And yet he did anyway.

Sergeant Jean Claude Les Hommes, who had died attempting to get the last door open for a group of prisoners, stood on the front step.

"You look terrible," Edmund said, and it was a truthful statement. Jean Claude's skin was green, his tongue black and his lips swollen into obscene shapes. The man's hair, however, was as neat as the day of the accident, although the same could not be said for his uniform. None of the buttons were still attached, and his undershirt had been pulled out. It was as if the man had tried to strip his clothes off as he died.

"You look old," Jean Claude replied. He looked down at the threshold.

Edmund had pulled the threshold up and laced the gap beneath with salt to ensure nothing could disrupt the barrier.

"You don't want me to come in?" Jean Claude asked, a hurt tone in his voice.

"Not at all," Edmund said. "You are dead, Sergeant. You should have the decency to stay in your grave."

"We have no graves," the ghost retorted. "They burned us. All of us. Guards and prisoners alike."

"Ah," Edmund said, nodding. "I had forgotten."

"We have not," Jean Claude said. Anger crept into his voice. "It was not long after our deaths that it became known you were to blame for the accident."

"Yes?" Edmund said, waiting.

"Have you no remorse?" the sergeant asked.

"Not particularly, no," Edmund said. "Do you expect me to have some?"

"No," Jean Claude said, shaking his head. "I suppose not. You were always rather strange, Edmund."

Edmund shrugged and started to close the door.

"We're not going to leave, you know," Jean Claude snapped.

Edmund paused. "I did not imagine that you would."

"And what shall you do?" his former sergeant demanded.

"I shall wait, of course," Edmund said.

"For what?" Jean Claude asked.

"For someone to do away with you all."

Jean Claude laughed. "And how do you know someone will?"

"Someone always does," Edmund answered, and he closed the door. He walked to his chair, sat down and turned the volume up on the television. Jean Claude screamed and pounded on the door, and Edmund was having a difficult time hearing the Price is Right.

Chapter 33: Health and Welfare Checks

Corporal Laura West was sent from the State Police barracks in Concord up to Gaiman to help the undermanned and overwhelmed local police forces and Troopers. The nor'easter which had come down out of Canada had dumped twenty-six inches of snow on the small community, and people couldn't get a hold of their loved ones.

The local police had their hands filled with accidents and downed trees. Volunteers, like Laura, were being sent out to check on particular streets in Gaiman. She was assigned to Mulberry Street. Thirty-one houses, all of which, until the storm had been occupied. There had been a murder earlier on the street, and the scene of the crime had been sealed. Added to that, a plow driver had managed to smother himself after he rammed his truck into a telephone pole.

When Laura turned her Interceptor onto Mulberry Street at 8:15 in the morning, she expected the worst part of her day would involve un-shoveled walkways.

Her vehicle's powerful v8 engine made it through the snow to the first house, a small, white bungalow that looked like every other home on Mulberry. She brought the car to a stop, shut it down and stepped out into the cold.

Laura turned the collar of her coat up, pulled her gloves on and closed the car door.

She glanced at the other houses as she approached the front door of the white bungalow. Lights could be seen in the windows, some still had the exterior lamps on as well.

She frowned and came to a stop. A quick look up and down the street showed all of the lines still ran from pole to pole and house to pole. No wires were down.

Why the hell isn't anyone answering their phones? she asked herself, and an uncomfortable feeling settled at the base of her skull. The hair on the back of her neck stood up, and she dropped her hand to the butt of her pistol.

She moved forward again, but all of her senses were on high alert. The air was crisp with the smell of snow and wood smoke. And the temperature was far colder than it should have been for snowfall. Shapes flickered on the edges of her vision, but when she turned to look, there was nothing to see.

Laura reached the front door, pressed the doorbell and heard the chime sound through the house. She waited to the count of thirty and rang the bell again when no one answered the door.

Laura stepped over to the side and peered through the front window. A light was on in what was once the kitchen, illuminating part of the front room.

A single foot, clad in a blood-stained sock, could be seen.

Laura took her radio off of her belt and pressed down to speak.

Nothing happened.

The battery was dead.

How the hell can the battery be dead? she snapped. Part of her wanted to kick the door in and check on the resident, but she needed to call it in before she did so. Charging in like a rookie could be a death sentence.

Frustrated, Laura turned away from the house and came to a sharp stop.

Several men stood by the Interceptor. Men in prison garb.

Laura drew her sidearm with a single, smooth motion. She brought the weapon to bear, sighting down the length of the semi-automatic and flipping the safety off. The men turned to face her, and Laura's focus vanished.

The men had bloated and distorted faces. A putrescent look about them that caused her stomach to roil. She blinked, shook her head and realized she could see through them. Through each and every one of them.

Laura forced her thoughts into a coherent pattern, demanded her brain to accept what she saw. And when she did, the Glock which had wavered in her hands became steady.

"Stop!" she snapped, keeping her weapon ready.

Chuckles and laughter rose up from the trio of ghosts. The man in the middle, who was gangly and awkward in his movements, led the way.

She heard a voice, and although his lips didn't move, Laura knew it was the middle man who spoke.

"And what will you do about it?" he asked, his voice thick with a Maine accent. "Do you think your little toy can do anything to stop us, pig? We hate cops. We hate you."

Laura glanced at the pistol then back up at the men.

Only one way to find out, she thought.

Laura pulled the trigger, the report of the round echoing off the houses. The sound had rolled through the neighborhood before it was smothered by the snow.

All three of the prisoners laughed, the men on the right and left of the gangly fellow joining him in his approach.

"Do you like what you saw in there?" the middle man inquired. "In the house behind you? She wasn't particularly entertaining. Leon here was a little too rough with her, I am afraid."

The man on the left, who looked only a year or two out of his teens, shrugged.

"Then again," the gangly man said, "he never did have a gentle touch when it came to women."

"You look stronger," the man on the right said. "Much stronger. I wonder, how long do you think she will last, Henri?"

"Hours," the gangly man whispered. "Hours."

Gritting her teeth, Laura emptied the magazine into all three of the men and then turned and sprinted towards the nearest house.

The laughter of the dead men chased her down the street.

Chapter 34: With Ollie

Shane sat on Ollie's back porch, smoking a cigarette in spite of the cold and the snow. His hands hurt from punching Ollie, and Shane had buried them in the snow for a short time to bring the swelling down.

But it was worth it, Shane thought, nodding. *Definitely worth it.*

He tapped the head of his cigarette over the railing and looked back as the door squealed open. Frank stepped out, closing the slider behind him.

"How are you doing?" Frank asked.

Shane shrugged. "Can't complain."

"Sure, you can," Frank said. "Hell, I'll even listen when you do."

Shane grinned and nodded.

In a serious tone, Frank said, "Thank you."

"For what?" Shane asked.

"For asking Courtney to do that."

Shane winced, took a drag off the cigarette and gave a curt nod.

"I know it's not easy," Frank continued, looking out at the snow covered trees lining Ollie's backyard. "I can see it in your face every time she's around. Have you tried to talk to her about how you feel?"

"No," Shane said, his voice hoarse.

"You should," Frank said. He brushed some of the snow off the railing. "You might even want to bring in someone who might be able to convince her to move on if that's what you want."

Shane could only nod in response.

The two men stood in silence for several minutes. Shane finished the cigarette, field stripped the butt and asked, "Any luck with Ollie?"

"Yeah," Frank said. "He's moved some money around. It'll be available in an hour or so. I'm waiting on a call back from my old Abbott. As soon as I hear from him, I can try and get up there, maybe find out if there's a way we can get some help."

"That would be good," Shane said.

"Want to go inside?" Frank asked.

"Yeah," Shane said. They went back into the kitchen, closing the cold out behind them. After they had sat down at the table, Ollie walked into the room stiffly. He winced as he sat down.

"I put out some feelers," Ollie said. "Pete was right. There's a lot of strange stuff going on in Gaiman. Unexplained car accidents. A couple of deaths. No one's gone into the prison yet. The women's bodies haven't been found."

Shane sighed.

"How do we contain this?" Ollie asked. "Seriously. What can my money do?"

Frank nodded to Shane and Ollie turned to face him, his face red as he looked at Shane.

"There are some important questions to answer, first of all," Shane said. He took a cigarette out and tapped it on the table top. "Are the dead bound to the prison, or to something else? If they're bound to the prison, is it possible to get them back in, and once in, is it possible to keep them quiet? You're probably wondering why we need money for this, and the simple answer is mediums don't work for free."

"A medium?" Ollie asked, confused.

"Someone who can talk to the dead," Shane explained. "We're going to need that person to figure out why the dead are doing what they're doing. And while the medium asks those questions, we need to make sure the medium's safe. This means iron and salt. We may even have to call in people who are skilled in binding to grab hold of the hard cases."

Ollie held up his hands and sat back in his chair. "Hold on. Hold on. What in the hell is binding?"

Frank looked at Shane with a confused look as well.

"Binding," Shane said, "is when a ghost is usually forcibly bound to an object, or placed in a specialized lead case. It is extremely difficult to do and as you probably guessed, dangerous. Especially when the ghost you're trying to bind is a formerly incarcerated murderer. Or rapist."

"And these people who can do bindings really exist?" Ollie asked.

Shane nodded.

"Do you know of any?" Frank asked.

"I know a couple. I mean, literally a married couple who can do it," Shane said. "They don't like to do too much of it though because they have their own house full of troubled spirits that they keep under lock and key."

"How is this going to cost a lot of money?" Ollie asked, looking from Shane to Frank.

"Those won't cost you," Frank said. "Getting those people out of Gaiman and putting them someplace safe until we can clean out the whole damned town is what's going to drive the cost up, Oliver."

Ollie's face paled. He licked his lips, tapped his fingers on the table top and said, "Are you saying I need to find a place for people to stay while this whole situation gets taken care of?"

Shane nodded as Frank said, "Not just you, Ollie. We're going to have Pete come by as well. Shane told him not to open the damned doors, and all Pete had to do was listen."

Ollie slumped in his chair and whispered, "Pete's so damned stupid."

"Well," Shane said, putting the cigarette between his lips and lighting it. "You're not the brightest bulb in the pack either, Chief."

Chapter 35: Shots Fired

George had lost another game of Go-Fish to Alison, Evie's youngest daughter when a single shot rang out through Mulberry Street. The television room, which had been filled with the sound of Rachel, Evie's oldest daughter, regaling Merle with stories of first grade, went silent.

The children could sense the tension of the adults, and the two little girls slid over to their mother. Evie wrapped her arms around them, reached down and picked up the cast iron pan she had used to defend them before.

Merle stood up, walked to the window and pulled back the shade.

"I can't see anything out there," she said after a minute, and then a dozen more shots filled the winter air.

George got to his feet, holding onto the fireplace poker with both hands. Merle peered first to the right, then to the left, and then swore under her breath.

"What?" George asked.

"Someone's running this way!" Merle said, letting go of the shade and hurrying to the door. By the time she had unlocked it, George was there. Merle opened the door for him, and he leaped out into the snow, looking to the left.

A female State Police officer was sprinting towards him, three of the dead close on her heels.

"This way!" George shouted, and the trooper shifted her course, aiming for the house.

George stepped out of her way as she barreled past. A young ghost was very close, his hands reaching out for her. George planted his feet and swung, the dead prisoner vanishing as the poker passed through him.

The other two stopped, staring at him.

"That's a neat trick," the taller of the two said.

"Sure it is," George said, turning, so his back faced his own door. A prison guard was advancing from the right. George stepped back, his eyes darting from ghost to ghost.

"You could play out here," the taller man said. "We won't mind."

"George!" Merle yelled. "Come on!"

Without looking around, George twisted and plunged back into the house. Something cold had grabbed at his foot, trying to pull him out, but the state trooper grasped his arms and dragged him in.

Merle slammed the door closed and made certain the salt line was still intact.

"What the hell is going on?" the trooper asked, looking around, her eyes wide.

Alison peered out from behind her mother, wagged a finger at the officer and said, "Hell is a bad word. You shouldn't say it."

Chapter 36: Pete Feels Wanted

Pete was twice divorced, paid too much alimony as far as he was concerned, and liked to drink high-end bourbon.

He was enjoying a fresh bottle and ignoring several angry text messages from his first ex-wife when his phone rang. It rang with the distinctive, antique jingle he had picked out to identify Oliver.

Pete looked at the phone, thought about not answering the call, and then answered it anyway.

"Hello?" he asked, wincing.

"Hey Pete," Ollie said, his voice sounding pleasant.

Pete straightened up and set his drink on the table. "Hi, Ollie. What's going on?"

He was cautious. Pete knew how crafty Oliver could be.

"Not much," Ollie said. "Listen, I've got Frank and his friend over here right now. We're all putting our heads together trying to figure out the best way to resolve this little issue we've got with Kurkow."

"Oh yeah?" Pete asked.

"Yes, indeed," Ollie said. "Since you've got some first-hand experience with what happened when you opened the doors, I was wondering if you could come and help us decide what to do next."

Pete perked up. "Really?"

"Of course," Ollie said. "I know I don't give you a lot of credit, Pete, but there are definitely times when you're needed, and this is one of them."

"Yeah?"

"Yeah," Ollie said, chuckling. "How soon do you think you can be over?"

"Um, I've got Melinda harassing me about her alimony check," Pete said. "Let me call her and get it settled, then I'll be right over."

"Sounds fantastic, little brother," Ollie said, his voice filled with happiness. "See you in half an hour then?"

"Yeah, if not sooner," Pete said. He ended the call, finished his drink and wrote back to Melinda.

Will have your money for you in an hour or two, Pete wrote. And he resisted the urge to swear at her.

Whistling, Pete got up, put his phone in his back pocket and went to pull his boots on. His brother needed him, and the day couldn't get much better than that.

Book 5: Kurkow Prison

Chapter 37: Edmund Has Another Conversation

Soon after he had heard the gunshots, Edmund's front door was knocked upon again. It was a continuous sound as if someone had set up a metronome to pound against the wood. Edmund wanted to wait until "The Little House on the Prairie" ended before he answered the door, but the power went out.

The television flickered and went blank. On the table to the left of the couch, the brass lamp went dark.

For the first time in years, Edmund felt something close to anxiety.

He disliked any interruption to his routine.

The person at the door continued to knock.

Sighing, Edmund got up from his chair and went into the kitchen. He poured himself a glass of water and drank it, ignoring the dead prisoner who stared at him through the kitchen window. Edmund rinsed the glass, put it on the drying rack and returned to the room. He paused, straightened his shirt, and then went on to the front door.

With a flick of his wrist, he undid the deadbolt, and he stepped back as he opened the door.

Jean Claude stood on the step with a semi-circle of prisoners and guards behind him.

"Hello, Edmund," Jean Claude said.

"Hello, Sergeant," Edmund replied.

"Everyone knows you're here now," Jean Claude said.

Edmund shrugged. "Is that all?"

"No," his sergeant snapped. "We cut the power to Mulberry Street."

"I noticed," Edmund said. He scratched his jaw. "Anything else, Sergeant?"

"Did you hear the gunshots?" Jean Claude asked.

"I did."

Jean Claude waited, and when Edmund didn't ask anything else he said in exasperation, "Don't you want to know why you heard the gunshots?"

"It does not matter to me one way or the other, Sergeant," Edmund said.

"It was the cavalry," someone from the semi-circle said. "The State Police had come to save you!"

Edmund looked at the gathered ghosts, then at Jean Claude.

"Well," Edmund said, "it would seem like they did not do the job quite right."

"I'm going to kill you, Edmund," Jean Claude hissed. "I'm going to peel your skin off and hang it in strips from the trees. We're going to tear you to shreds and keep you alive while we do it. Do you understand?"

Edmund scratched his chin, then yawned. "Do you know what I will do?"

"What?" Jean Claude sneered.

"Have some lunch," Edmund said. "And if help does not arrive before my food supply is done, I will blow out my own brains."

"You cannot!" Jean Claude howled.

"No," Edmund said. "I can."

He closed the door on Jean Claude and turned to go back to the kitchen. The entire house began to shake, the dead slamming into it. Pictures fell from the walls and dishes rattled in the cabinets. Edmund felt the tremors rise up from the floor, through the soles of his shoes and into his feet.

Dead faces were pressed against the window over the sink, and Edmund walked over to the drawer to the left of the stove. He opened it, took out a .38 caliber, snub-nosed pistol and a box of ammunition. Without rushing, Edmund opened the cylinder, loaded the weapon, and then placed it within view of the dead men at his window.

From the corner of his eye, Edmund saw them back up. The pounding on his house stopped, and a comfortable silence filled the kitchen. Edmund walked to the stove, took a match and lit the gas burner. He put some water on for tea and wondered how long the dead might linger around his home.

Chapter 38: Shane Reaches Out to a Friend

"Brian can't help us?" Frank asked.

Shane shook his head. "Guy's one bad phone call away from another heart attack. No way I could ask him to come in on this."

Frank nodded. After a moment he said, "Anyone else?"

Shane hesitated, then he said, "Yes. There might be. I haven't talked to him in a long time, but if he's around, he'll help."

"Does he live nearby?" Frank asked.

"Right over the New Hampshire, Massachusetts border," Shane answered. "I'll give him a call."

He stood up, took his phone out and walked into the hallway. In silence, he brought up his contacts, found the name and dialed the number.

It rang three times before it was answered by a woman.

"Hello?" she asked.

"Hi, my name's Shane Ryan, I was trying to reach a friend of mine, this is the last number I had for him."

"Hold on," the woman said.

Shane heard her repeat his name in the background, and then there was a bellowing laugh.

"You're damned right I know a Shane Ryan!" Mason Phillips yelled. A moment later, Mason was on the phone. "Holy hell, Batman! What have you been up to, Gunnery Sergeant Ryan?"

"Slaying bodies," Shane said, chuckling. "You know how it is, Marine."

"I do, I do. Tell me what this phone call out of the blue is for," Mason said. "It's not like you to break radio silence for no reason."

"Yeah," Shane apologized, "there's a reason. I need a hand up in New Hampshire. I'm not sure if you'd be okay doing it, though."

The humor went out of Mason's voice. "Gunny, do you remember that hillbilly punk down in North Carolina who pulled a gun on me?"

"Yeah," Shane said, sighing. "That I do."

"Then I'll do whatever needs to be done," Mason said. "Tell me where you need me to be, Shane."

He nodded and gave Mason the address for Oliver Dawson's place.

Chapter 39: Speaking with the Trapped

Laura holstered her sidearm and fought the urge to reload it. The bullets had not had any sort of effect on the ghosts.

She shook her head at the thought of the prisoners.

Ghosts, she repeated to herself, still in disbelief. *Ghosts*.

George, the man who had rushed out of the house to combat the dead, handed her a cup of hot tea. She could smell a dash of brandy in it, and she nodded her thanks. Laura looked around the small room and saw that the lights which had been on when she had arrived were out.

The room was lit only by the surprisingly cheerful light of the fire burning in the hearth. On the gray suede couch which rested against the right wall, the two little girls played paddy-cake. George sat down on the floor beside Laura and the woman, Merle, occupied an old, cane-backed rocking chair.

Evie had gone into the kitchen to fetch her daughters some goldfish crackers.

"How are you doing?" George asked.

He was a middle-aged man, balding with strawberry blonde hair. Freckles formed a rough swath from his left cheek to his right, bridging his wide nose. Beneath his pale green eyes were dark circles, signs of several sleepless nights and Laura wondered how long he had been trapped in the house.

"Alright," Laura answered. She took a sip of the tea and felt the nip of the brandy. A rush of warmth trickled through her. "Confused, really."

"I'm not surprised," Merle said. The woman was dressed in mismatched clothes, an iron fireplace shovel on her lap. "This is a rather odd situation for any of us to be in."

Evie re-entered the room, handed a bowl to each of her daughters and sat down to the left of the fireplace. She looked at Laura and asked, "How is it out there?"

"Where?" Laura asked. "The rest of Gaiman?"

Evie nodded.

"I don't know," Laura said. "There are accidents, but until just now, there weren't any lines down. People have been concerned about Mulberry Street. I was sent to do health and welfare checks on everyone here. Unfortunately, it didn't go exactly as I thought it would."

"No," George agreed, "I don't imagine it did."

Laura finished her drink and set the cup aside. "When did all of this start?"

"A few days ago," Merle said. "There was a blast of some sort at the prison. I heard the windows break. After that, well, the ghosts showed up."

Laura looked around the room and said, "Whose house is this?"

"Mine," George said. "They're my neighbors."

Laura frowned. "How did you all end up in here?"

They told her.

She learned of the murder of Merle's husband. George's accidental discovery of the power of the iron fireplace poker. Evie's similar salvation with the frying pan. Merle told her of the chase by the fat ghost, and of George rushing to her rescue. Of Merle and George both going to help Evie and her daughters.

"What's the salt for?" Laura asked when they had finished their stories.

"It keeps the ghosts out," George explained.

"How?" she said. "How does salt do that?"

He shrugged. "I don't know."

"I mean, how did you even find out salt could serve as a barrier?" Laura asked.

"The internet," George said. "Before we lost power a little while ago, we had everything. After I got rid of the twin prisoners, I looked up online as to why it happened."

"Excuse me," Evie said.

Laura looked at her.

"Yes?" Laura asked.

"When are the rest of the police going to come and get us out of here?"

Laura could hear the panic in the woman's voice. Evie may have held off the dead with a frying pan, but she wouldn't hold onto her composure much longer.

Laura smiled and lied. "Soon. They'll be here soon."

One of the girls laughed. They were throwing goldfish crackers at each other and trying to catch them in their mouths.

God, Laura prayed, *please let it be soon.*

Outside, the wind howled and railed against the house.

Chapter 40: Getting to Ollie's House

Pete had been forced to switch cars. The front end of the Cadillac had been knocked out of alignment when Frank had smashed Shane's car into it. Pete didn't mind too much, it meant he could take his new toy, his Jeep Wrangler, out in the snow and try it out.

The vehicle had handled the snow like a dream.

With Kenney Chesney blasting out of the radio, Pete had sung along, racing past people stuck in snow drifts or too afraid to put the pedal down.

Pete was not intimidated by the weather.

He chuckled to himself as he took the exit and cut the wheel hard so he could slide down the off-ramp.

Yeah, he thought, nodding, *this is why I bought the damned thing. Serious driving for the serious driver!*

Rock salt and sand popped beneath his tires as he raced along, following the recently scraped and treated pavement towards Ollie's street. Pete wondered what sort of team-up he and his brother would have.

Sure, Kurkow's kind of messed up, he thought, *but we can still save it. I mean, hey, one of those girls is alive, and that's got to count for something. And there's got to be a good way to spin this. Ollie will know what to do. He always does. I shouldn't have freaked out last night, but it's okay.*

Pete rubbed at his face, remembering Frank's punch. Part of him wanted to hit Frank back, but he knew it wouldn't be the best idea.

Frank was a little disturbed at times.

Then Ollie's house appeared on the right, and all thoughts of vengeance slipped away. Pete slowed down, eased the Jeep into the driveway since Beth wouldn't like it if he raced in, and parked beside Shane's car.

Bet old Ollie reeled those two in, Pete thought, smirking. *My brother's always in charge.*

Pete whistled again as he got out of his Jeep, swung the key around on his index finger and hurried out of the cold and into Ollie's garage.

"Hey, Ollie!" Pete called, climbing the stairs to the interior door. He rapped on it twice then opened it, saying, "Hey, Bro, I'm here!"

"Come on into the kitchen," Ollie yelled back.

Humming, Pete made his way down the long hallway, passed the main stairs and entered the kitchen. Ollie was alone in the room, his back to Pete as he looked out the window. Pete wandered over to the breakfast nook and sat down in it.

"How's it going?" Pete asked.

"I've been better, to be completely honest, Pete," Ollie said, turning around.

Pete winced as he saw Ollie's lips. The bottom one was a wreck, split open on the left and a red lump on the lower part of his chin. "Damn, what happened?"

"Shane happened," Ollie answered.

"Why?"

"Because of Kurkow," Ollie said, walking over and sitting down across from him.

Pete noticed how his brother limped. "Did you hurt your legs?"

"No," Ollie said. "Shane did."

"And he's still here?" Pete asked, lowering his voice. "I saw the car, so he and Frank are here? Do you need me to call the police?"

Ollie shook his head. "No. What I need is for us to figure out how we're going to make this right."

"Him hitting you?" Pete said.

"Kurkow," Ollie said, looking hard at Pete. "We need to fix what went wrong with Kurkow. The ghosts got out. We need to put them back in. And then we need to keep them in there."

"How the hell are we supposed to do all of that?" Pete asked, sitting back. "Is there some group we can call?"

"No," a voice said from the doorway.

Startled, Pete twisted in the seat as Shane and Frank entered the room. Their brows were furrowed and the lines around their mouths tight. Frank went to the sink and got himself a drink of water while Shane took out a cigarette and lit it.

Pete glanced at Ollie, but his brother didn't seem to care about Shane smoking.

Tapping his feet on the floor, Pete asked, "Um, then who do we get in touch with?"

"I've already reached out to one friend," Shane said, exhaling the smoke towards the ceiling. "I'll be talking to another soon."

"And I've left a message with the Abbott of my former Order," Frank added. "We'll be gathering our forces. We're hopeful to have everyone in the next few hours."

"Okay," Pete said, shifting himself in the nook. "You don't need me for anything then, right?"

"On the contrary," Ollie said. "We need you to speak with the hotel in Ennis."

"Um, hey," Pete said, clearing his throat. "You know, Melanie works there."

"Exactly," Ollie said.

"Yeah, she's the manager," Pete continued.

Ollie nodded. "I figured it would be best for you to speak with her."

"She doesn't exactly like me, Ollie," Pete said, upset at the whine he heard in his own voice.

"Who is she?" Frank asked.

"Pete's second ex-wife," Ollie explained. "It was a surprisingly peaceful divorce considering the way they used to fight."

"Ah," Frank said. "So you're thinking maybe Pete here could get a deal on some hotel rooms?"

Ollie nodded.

"Why do you even need hotel rooms?" Pete demanded.

"No," Shane said, his voice cold and hard. "The question is why do 'we' need hotel rooms, Peter."

Pete shook his head. "No. You know what, that doesn't sound like the right question at all."

"Why doesn't it?" Ollie asked. "We're both to blame for this situation. We bought the place. You opened the doors. I sent that team in. Something's going on in Gaiman. People are getting hurt. You know this."

"I don't care," Pete said, sliding out of the seat and standing up. "I really don't. I did my part. I called Frank and told him what was going on. They got one of those girls out. So, yeah, way I see it, my part's done."

Pete turned to leave and stopped.

Somehow, Shane had crossed the tiled floor without a sound. He stood between Pete and the hallway. The cigarette was between his lips, clinging to a precarious position in the left corner of his mouth. Smoke drifted out of his nostrils, and the look in Shane's eyes tied an uncomfortable knot in Pete's stomach.

"I need to leave," Pete whispered.

Shane shook his head.

Pete straightened up, forced himself to speak louder and said, "I'm leaving."

Shane remained silent.

"Fine," Pete said, and he tried to push his way past the man.

Shane's right fist was a blur and Pete yelled, staggering back. Pain exploded in his left shoulder, and the arm hung dead at his side.

"You're going to stay and help make this right," Frank said.

Pete shook his head.

Shane's left hand lashed out, and Pete's right ear began to ring and pulse.

"We're not asking you, Pete," Frank said, a mournful expression on his face. "We're telling you."

Pete shook his head.

Shane sighed, gave a shrug, and then punched Pete in the stomach.

Gasping for breath, Pete collapsed to the floor, writhing on the cold tile.

Shane squatted down in front of him, took the cigarette out and said, "Pete, are you listening to me?"

Pete looked at him through tear-filled eyes and nodded.

"Good," Shane said. He took another pull off the cigarette, the smoke slipping out of his mouth as he spoke. "Good. Now I want you to hear me. If you don't make the call to your ex, then I'm going to have to start hurting you."

Pete closed his eyes and let the tears fall.

Chapter 41: Angry at the World

Shane sat on the stairs in the hallway, his hands hurting. A small part of him was disgusted with what he had done, the way he had hurt the Dawson brothers to get their agreement and assistance.

The rest of him wasn't.

The rest of him wanted to bring the two men to Kurkow and show them what had happened.

And that's just what I know happened, Shane thought. He snorted, took his cigarettes out and tapped the pack on his leg. *What the hell's going on in the rest of Gaiman?*

Frank walked out of the kitchen, down the hall and sat beside Shane.

"How are you holding up?" Frank asked.

"I'm alright," Shane said.

Frank raised an eyebrow. "Yeah?"

Shane nodded.

"You're looking a little stressed to me, Marine," Frank said.

"Little bit," Shane confessed. "I don't like waiting. Not when I know something bad is going on."

"Neither do I," Frank agreed. The former monk's phone rang. Frank took it out, looked at the caller ID and said, "It's my Abbott."

Shane nodded and continued to play with his pack of matches while Frank answered the call and stood up. His voice trailed off as he left the hallway. Ollie appeared in the doorway, glanced after Frank and then walked over to Shane. He stopped a few feet away from him.

"What's up?" Shane asked.

"Did you have to go so hard on him?" Ollie asked. There was anger in his voice, his face flushed with the same.

Shane stared at Ollie until the other man looked away.

"That wasn't hard," Shane said, his voice low. "Not hard at all. If I had my way, Oliver, I would have broken his God damned fingers, and yours as well. I still might. Depends on how many bodies end up at your feet when all of this is done."

Ollie took an involuntary step back.

"You wouldn't," Ollie whispered.

"I would. I can, and," Shane said, "I'd like nothing more. Greed and arrogance are two of my least favorite traits. Show me you're different and I'll leave you be."

Ollie shook his head, turned and hurried away.

Frank returned, putting his phone away and asking, "Can I borrow your car?"

"Sure," Shane said. He dug his keys out and tossed them to Frank.

The other man caught them with one hand and said, "The Abbott's got some items we can borrow. I was hoping for some more men, but evidently, there was a situation at a Church in Boston. All of those in the Order who are capable of combating the dead have been sent there."

Shane sighed. "Great. Hey, any word from Asa as to what's up with him and Emma?"

"Not yet," Frank said. "I'll send him a text. Want me to give him your number?"

"Please," Shane said. "Are you going to talk to him about going up to Ennis?"

Frank nodded. "Yeah. Damn, I forgot all about that. I'll call him from the car then I'll have him text you, and the two of you can set up everything once Pete gets those rooms for us."

"Okay," Shane said. "Be safe out there."

"When aren't I?" Frank asked, grinning.

"Given our short friendship," Shane replied, "I'd have to say always."

Frank's laughter followed him as he left the house.

Chapter 42: Becoming Concerned

The snow had stopped, and George was thankful. He was also pleased with the fire, the food, and the pleasant company considering the circumstances. His phone, however, had finally died.

And Evie was becoming worse with each passing hour.

She was no longer content to sit by the fire and watch her girls play. Evie no longer had any desire to engage in conversation or play cards.

Instead, she paced from window to window, always careful of the salt. While she had started doing so in silence, she had begun to mumble after darkness had fallen.

George, Merle and Laura had all exchanged concerned looks. Evie's daughters didn't seem to notice anything was wrong with their mother.

When both Alison and Rachel had fallen asleep, and their breathing was in a steady, deep rhythm, Laura got up. George watched as her face became a mask of concern, a police officer worried about a citizen.

Laura's voice was soft, her words picked with care, her touch gentle on Evie's arm as she stopped her. Evie's eyes darted about, frantic as they moved from one window to the next. Her fingers twitched, and she licked her lips every few seconds.

"Evie," Laura said. "How are you doing?"

Evie jerked her arm away and took a step back as she snapped, "How do you think I'm doing?"

"I don't know," Laura said. "That's why I'm asking."

George started to stand, but Laura shook her hand at him. He sat back down, scooting himself closer to the couch where the girls sat.

"I'm doing fantastic," Evie spat. "I'm trapped in here. My girls are trapped in here. I don't know where my husband is. I don't know where the rest of the police are. Didn't you say they'd be here soon? What's soon to you, huh? Three hours? Six? Tell me!"

"Evie," Laura said. "They'll be here as soon as they can. Why don't you come on back to the couch? Maybe we could play a game with your kids."

"Maybe we could find out where the hell the cops are!" Evie shrieked.

Merle moved from the rocking chair to the couch, wrapping her arms protectively around both girls.

"Yeah, that's what we should do," Evie whispered. "Let's find out where they are."

Laura lunged for Evie as she twisted around for the door. Evie grabbed hold of the door knob as George launched himself off the couch. Laura managed to catch Evie's right arm, but Evie ripped the door open.

Before George reached her, Evie kicked out a section of the rock salt on the threshold.

Cold exploded into the room, a shriek driving a spike of sound into his head. George moaned, clamped his hands up over his ears and dropped to his knees. Evie stumbled backward, her calves hitting him in the head and sending her tumbling over him as Laura let go.

Through cloudy, pain-filled eyes George saw Laura slam the door close, grab the box of salt next to it and refresh the broken line.

The cold lessened, but it wasn't gone.

Evie had gone silent. Laying on her back beside George. Her eyes were closed, and George could hear one of the little girls whimper. Merle was whispering to them, telling Alison and Rachel that everything was going to be alright.

Breathing hard, George rolled onto his side and got to his feet. Laura leaned against the door, the box of salt still in her hands.

"What happened?" one of the girls asked, and George turned and saw it was Rachel who had spoken.

"Your mom's really tired," George said. "And stressed. She just needs to rest for a while."

"We all do," Laura muttered. She put the box down and sat back on the floor. Laura took her hat off, massaged her temples and looked over at the still body of Evie. "Is she alright?"

"I think so," George said.

"Could you check please?" Laura asked.

George nodded, turned and felt for a pulse in the soft flesh of Evie's neck. He found it, the beat of her heart strong and steady. George glanced at Laura, saying, "She's okay."

"Thank God," Laura murmured.

George looked again at Evie, and her eyes snapped open. The whites were bloodshot, the pupils tight.

Evie smiled at him, her lips spreading wide in an unnatural grin.

George pushed himself away from her.

Evie sat up, twisted her head to the left, and then to the right. Some of the vertebrae cracked, and she chuckled.

"That's not my mom," Alison whispered, and the words burned George's ears.

"No," Evie said. "I'm not your mom. But you look sweet."

Evie cracked her knuckles and looked around at everyone. "You all do. And I can touch you."

Evie got to her feet, holding out both hands to keep her balance.

"Who are you?" Merle demanded.

"Who are you?" Evie asked, raising an eyebrow and snickering. "Well, introductions, huh? I'm Pat. Patrick Nett."

"How did you get in here?" Merle asked.

"This one?" the possessed Evie asked. She patted her own behind and chuckled. "Weak. Weak. *Weak!*"

Evie looked around, grinning. "Almost too easy to climb in her head. I wasn't sure I could. But I did. And here I am! Feels a little different, you know?"

"You need to leave her," Merle said.

Evie glared at her. "I don't think so. Besides, I need to get this door open for my friends. We've been trying to get in for a while. There's only a few of you holding out, and you've got the most interesting place. A little taste for everyone."

Evie blew a kiss at her daughters, and there was nothing maternal in the act.

"Well, time to let our friends in, what do you say?" Evie said, and she lunged for the door.

George scrambled after her, but Laura was already there. The State Trooper slammed into Evie, smashing her into the wall, grabbing hold of Evie's arm and spinning her down onto the floor.

"Grab her!" Laura yelled.

George threw himself onto Evie, landing hard on the woman. Beneath him she squirmed, trying to buck him off. A stream of profanity poured out of her mouth, and she threw an elbow into his ribs. His breath rushed out of him, leaving him gasping and trying to hold on.

Then Laura was there.

"Move," she said, and George rolled away.

Laura got on top of Evie, put a knee into the small of the woman's back and with surprising ease had Evie handcuffed.

George managed to catch his breath and looked at Merle. The older woman had turned the girls away from the scene, and she had them pressed close to her.

Laura dragged Evie up and propped her against the wall.

Blood trickled out of the corner of Evie's mouth, her teeth bloody. Evie chuckled, looking from George to Laura.

"What's funny, Pat?" Laura asked.

Evie spat on the floor and grinned and said, "What you're thinking right now."

"What am I thinking?" Laura said.

"Not just you, Pig. All of you," Evie sneered.

"Fine," Laura said, sighing. "Tell me, what are all of us thinking right now?"

"That I'm trapped in here with you," Evie said. "Trapped in her."

"And you're not?" Laura asked.

"Tell me what you think," Evie whispered.

George watched as Evie closed her eyes, twisted her head to the left, and then hammered it against the wall.

The sound of her neck breaking was loud and horrifically clear. As her body slumped over, the temperature in the room plunged. The air between George and Laura shimmered, then Patrick Nett appeared.

He looked like all the others George had seen. Clad in prison garb, face swollen and green, black tongue protruding from his lips. Patrick was short and wiry, and his voice was thin and reedy when he spoke.

"A pity," he said. "I had hoped to get a little taste of her daughters. But I'll have to wait on that, won't I."

George snarled, grabbed hold of the fireplace poker and lunged at the ghost.

Patrick moved out of the way, laughing. As George lurched by, Patrick struck him on the side of the head. The touch was colder than anything George had felt before, and he screamed, dropping the poker to clutch at his injured ear.

Patrick's laugh was cut short, and when George turned around to look, he saw Laura. The trooper's face was pale, her lips pressed into a thin line. In her hands, she held Evie's cast iron frying pan.

She set the utensil down on the floor, turned to George and said in a strained voice, "Let's look at that ear."

Chapter 43: Help Arrives

"Hey, Shane," Frank said.

Shane sat up, rubbed at his eyes and said, "Yeah?"

"Someone's here for you."

Shane blinked, looked around and tried to remember where he was.

Ollie's house, he reminded himself. *You're at Ollie's house trying to figure this mess out.*

Shane stood up and followed Frank out of the guest room he had fallen asleep in.

"Are you feeling alright?" Frank asked.

"Yeah," Shane said, nodding. "You?"

"Feeling a little off," Frank replied. "Kind of strange, but hey, I'll be better."

They entered the main hall, and Shane saw Mason Phillips.

Mason grinned at him, saying, "God, Gunny, you look worse than I remember."

Shane laughed, embraced his friend and pounded him on the back. "You look healthy. And happy. What the hell has gotten into you?"

Mason held up his left hand, and Shane saw a gold wedding band on it.

"What?!" Shane asked. "Someone actually married you? Did you come into money or something?"

"Let's go with the something part," Mason said, chuckling. Seriousness replaced the mirth, and Mason said, "Tell me what's going on."

"First," Shane said, "I need to ask you this. Do you still believe in ghosts?"

Mason nodded. "Believe in them. Afraid of them, when it's necessary. Is it necessary?"

"Yeah," Shane answered.

"Tell me what you've got," Mason said, looking from Shane to Frank.

Shane did so, with Frank adding information Shane left out.

After a short while, they had told Mason everything, and the man stood with his arms crossed. Finally, he asked, "Am I the only help you've got?"

"Yeah," Shane said. "I'm afraid so. I've got a call into some other friends in Nashua. Hoping they can help with binding, but I haven't heard back. They usually don't do big cases like this."

"Don't blame 'em," Mason said. "This is a nightmare. That being said, how do you want to do this?"

"We want to get them all back into Kurkow Prison," Frank said. "Which means we've got to secure the facility, and then hunt down the others that have gotten out."

"Do you know why they're out?" Mason asked.

Shane frowned and looked at Frank.

"No," Shane said. "I mean. I figured it was just to wreak havoc. You know, bottled up in the prison for all that time."

"Might be," Mason said. "Maybe we can find out if that's all it is, or if they're after something more."

"I think there is," Ollie said from the kitchen.

They turned to look at him. Ollie was in the doorway, Pete lurking behind him.

"What is it then?" Mason asked.

"Pete said there were a lot of calls about Mulberry Street in Gaiman," Ollie said. "Almost exclusively so. Sure, a few other accidents and stuff. Those can be explained away by the weather. The only fatalities, other than the murder of the three women in Kurkow itself, well, were on Mulberry Street."

"Can we bind the prison again with iron chains on the doors?" Frank asked.

"I think so," Shane said.

Mason looked at him. "What about the broken windows?"

"The windows have iron bars on them, or in the frames," Shane said. "They couldn't have come out from there. Otherwise the dead would have been causing trouble a long, long time ago. No, it was when the iron was stripped off the doors that did it. The dead came out of them, one right when the inner chains were cut off. There was something about the doors being locked with those chains."

"Alright," Mason said. "We need to get to Mulberry Street."

Frank turned his attention to the Dawson brothers. "Any luck with the hotel?"

Pete shook his head as Ollie said, "Guess his ex isn't in the office yet."

"Keep trying," Frank said.

"What about Asa?" Shane asked. "And the girl, Emma?"

Before Frank could answer, a cold, powerful blow struck Shane in the chest, knocking him backward. He gasped for breath, stumbled, tripped over his own feet and crashed to the marble floor.

His head struck stone, and he grunted, rolling onto his side. A dull roar filled his ears, and beneath it, Shane heard shouts. Pushing himself up, Shane tried to focus. He saw Courtney standing in front of him, her fists clenched at her sides.

"Why are you concerned about Emma?!" she shrieked, and struck him again.

Chapter 44: The Situation Begins to Change

Edmund was becoming anxious.

From every window of his house, he could see the dead. They were not merely gathered around his house but pressed against it. Edmund could no longer see his yard or anything else for that matter.

His heartbeat quickened at the sight of them, so he went around the rooms and closed all of the blinds. With each window sealed off, the dead began to pound on the walls again.

And they didn't let up.

The doors to the kitchen cabinets popped open, and dishes fell onto the floor, shattering on the worn linoleum. Canned goods fell out of the pantry, the windows rattled in their frames. From beyond the walls, he heard the siding crack and splinter. A crash shook the rear of the house and Edmund realized the ghosts had ripped the porch down.

If they keep this up, Edmund thought, *they might rip the house down around my ears.*

He shook his head, picked up his pistol and walked with it into the television room. Edmund sat down in his chair and looked at the blank television set. The clock on the wall above the couch read eleven thirty.

I should be watching a rerun of Antiques Roadshow, he thought. Anger flared up. He hated the disruption of his schedule.

Someone pounded on his front door.

For seventeen minutes, they hit the door until Edmund finally stood up and stalked over to it. He threw back the deadbolt and ripped the door open.

Jean Claude stood there.

The dead ceased their assault upon his house.

"Edmund!" Jean Claude said in mock surprise. "Why I didn't realize you were home!"

"What do you want now, Sergeant?" Edmund asked his voice sharper than he wanted it to be.

"Do you know you only have a few neighbors left alive?" Jean Claude asked.

"I did not know any of them were still alive," Edmund replied.

"There are. Five of them now. Two of them," Jean Claude said, lowering his voice to a conspiratorial tone, "are children."

"Are they?" Edmund asked, wondering what the point of the discussion was.

"They are," Jean Claude said, nodding. "We should be in the house soon."

"Mine or theirs?" Edmund asked.

"Theirs."

"Ah," Edmund said, and he went to close the door.

"Edmund," Jean Claude said. "Do you remember that some of the prisoners enjoyed children?"

"Yes."

"And what do you think they will do when we breach the walls of that house?" Jean Claude asked.

"Why do you think I care?" Edmund asked.

Jean Claude didn't reply.

Edmund shook his head and said, "You confuse me, Sergeant."

"You don't care?" Jean Claude asked in a shocked voice.

"I do not care," Edmund affirmed.

"Then why were you a guard?" Jean Claude snapped.

"I needed a job," Edmund answered, and he closed the door.

The dead assaulted his house again as Edmund sat back down in his chair. He looked at the clock, then at the television and sighed.

I'm missing reruns of Hill Street Blues.

Chapter 45: Madness Reigns

Ollie wasn't quite sure what happened, but he knew it wasn't good.

For a moment he and his brother stood in the kitchen, confused as to what to do next. Mason, Shane's friend, was off to one side, and Frank was close to Shane.

Shane had been laid out on the hall floor with the female ghost standing over him.

All of that, Ollie felt certain he could handle.

When she turned and attacked Frank, he felt immobilized.

"Why is she so important, Shane?!" she shrieked, striking at him.

"Calm down, Courtney," Frank said, ducking.

But she didn't calm down, and it was only when Frank had backed down the hall towards the game room that Ollie felt able to move again.

Ollie rushed out into the hall towards Shane and Mason. Mason, in turn, had gotten down on his knees and was pulling Shane into a sitting position.

"Shane!" Mason snapped. "Gunny!"

At the second word Shane's eyes flickered open, and as Ollie reached them, he could see Shane's eyes. They rolled madly in opposite directions.

"Gunnery Sergeant Ryan!" Mason said, his tone powerful. "Who's the female, Gunny?"

"Courtney," Shane whispered.

"How did she get here?" Mason asked.

"Tags," Shane mumbled, and then his eyelids closed, head lolling to one side.

As Ollie watched, Mason reached into Shane's shirt, pulled out a chain and removed a pair of dog tags. He slid them over Shane's bald head, lowered the man gently to the floor and shot a look to Ollie, asking, "Do you have salt?"

"Yeah," Ollie said, confused. "How much do you need?"

"All of it. And hurry up," Mason ordered. There was no give in the man's tone, a promise of violence in his words.

Ollie turned, saw Pete still skulked in the kitchen and yelled to his brother, "Hey, get the salt out of the pantry!"

Pete hesitated and Ollie shouted, "Now!"

Ollie had no idea why Mason wanted it, but from what he had witnessed in his own house, Ollie wanted to make certain the man had it.

Frank reappeared a moment later, disheveled, breathing hard.

"Where is she?" Mason snapped.

"She should be back in the tags," Frank replied. "I had to hit her."

The former monk held up his hands and showed the dark rings on his fingers.

"What?" Ollie asked, confused.

"Iron," Frank began, but he was cut off as Courtney materialized and launched herself at him.

Frank staggered back, caught himself and thrust his hand through her mid-section. Courtney disappeared, and Mason shouted, "Where is that God damned salt?!"

Pete came jogging down the hall a moment later, a large container of Morton's Salt in his hands. Mason reached out, snatched it from him and tore the container open. He threw the top off to one side and stuffed the dog tags into the salt until nothing could be seen of them.

Only then did Mason seem to relax. He sat down on the floor, set the container on the tile beside him and sighed.

"What the hell just happened?" Ollie asked after several seconds of silence.

Frank plodded towards them and sank to the floor. "Courtney went a little crazy."

"I hope to God it doesn't happen again," Pete whispered.

"It won't," Mason said, nodding at the salt pile. "Not as long as she's in there."

Chapter 46: Unfortunate News

When Shane woke up with a headache worse than any hangover he had inflicted upon himself, it was not to any smiling faces.

Instead, he found himself back in the bedroom he had slept in earlier. Mason was sitting in a chair, reading a newspaper. When he saw Shane was awake, Mason put the paper down and gave him a tight, small smile.

"You could have told me you had a pet ghost," Mason said.

Shane frowned, then he remembered Courtney's attack.

"Damn," Shane grumbled. "Yeah. Well, I would have if I'd had any idea she was going to freak out."

"Who is she?" Mason asked.

Shane gave him an extremely abbreviated version of his time with Courtney. Finally, he said, "I should have seen it, though. She's been a little stranger than usual. I mean, I've heard of ghosts losing their minds. Hell, she even told me I was the only living person in my house."

"You're not?" Mason asked.

"No," Shane said. "My friend, Frank, he lives with me. Ever since he left the brotherhood he had been a monk in."

"Ah," Mason said.

Shane tried to lift his head, winced and closed his eyes. "Has Frank gotten in touch with his friend Asa?"

"Don't know," Mason answered. "He had a hell of a time with your ghost there."

Shane frowned. "What do you mean?"

"After she knocked you out," Mason said, "she turned on Frank. Screaming something about him trying to have her replaced with a living girl."

With a groan, Shane shook his head. "Damn. How did he calm her down?"

"He didn't," Mason sighed. "He tried to talk to her, but when she kept attacking, he hit her with one of those iron rings."

Shane cringed at the thought. He had no idea how it felt for a ghost to come in contact with iron, but he could only imagine that it wasn't pleasant.

"That wasn't the worst part, though," Mason continued.

"No?" Shane asked, surprised.

"No," Mason said. "She kept coming back. Until we stuffed your dog tags into a box of salt."

"Great," Shane said bitterly.

"Hey," Mason said, "let's not lose sight of what's going on here."

"No," Shane said, "you're right. We can't do that. Any luck with anymore help?"

Mason shook his head. "I made some calls, Frank made some calls. We've got nothing. Can your plan work without one?"

"It better," Shane said. "Because there's a whole town that depends on it."

Chapter 47: Choices

George looked at his phone. It was dead. Completely, undeniably dead. There was no power in the house to charge it. Or his laptop. They couldn't charge Laura's cell phone either. And her police issue radio was dead as well.

Food was running out, and there was a corpse in the basement. There were two little girls who had witnessed the possession of their mother and heard her death.

Soon they would begin to starve in the house, and George remembered stories of cannibalism at sea and of the survivors of some Russian city eating the dead during World War Two.

"George?" Laura asked.

He turned and looked at her. It was nearing nightfall again, only the light of the fire illuminating the room. Merle was asleep on the couch, both of the girls wrapped up in a blanket with her. The girls had cried themselves to sleep, Merle battling her own grief through the comforting of the children.

"What's up?" George asked.

"We won't be able to stay here much longer," Laura said.

He nodded. "I was thinking the same thing."

"We can't try to get out of the house with the girls, either," Laura continued.

A cold knot formed in his stomach. *Does she want us to abandon them?*

"I'm going to try to leave soon," Laura said. "Someone should have been here before this. Before Evie died. I don't know why they haven't, it's not right."

Book 5: Kurkow Prison

"How are you going to get away from the dead?" George asked. "They're everywhere. The snow doesn't slow them down."

"I'm not sure," Laura answered. "But I know there hasn't been any sort of activity around the house since Evie died. I'm wondering if maybe they're gone. Or at least focused on someone else. If either one is the case, well, I should be able to get away. Bring some help back."

George rubbed the back of his head. "You know, I'm not a fan of this idea."

"No?" Laura asked, surprised.

"Yeah, I kind of like having you here. You give a lot of strength to us, Laura," he said, the words sounding awkward as they left his mouth.

She smiled. "I appreciate that, George. I do. But this is going to be our best chance. And let's be honest here, without me, the food will last a little longer. Maybe enough until someone realizes what's going on."

George sighed and nodded. "Yeah. You're right."

Laura offered her hand, and George shook it. She glanced at the front door and sighed. "Will you lock the door behind me?"

"What if you need to come back in?" he asked.

She shook her head. "If I know I can come back easily, then I might not be able to do it at all."

"Okay," George said, his throat tight. He felt his heartbeat quicken, and an uncomfortable feeling washed over him. "Feels like I'm condemning you to death."

"You're not," she said. When she stood up, so did George. They walked together to the front door. "I want to think that everything's going to work out. Maybe come back with my husband and meet your wife. Might even have a little barbecue."

"I'd like that," George said.

Laura gave a terse nod, pulled on her gloves, and without another word, she unlocked and opened the door. A blast of cold air hammered into the house, and then she was gone, jumping out of the door and into the snow. George didn't look after her, closing the door as quickly as he could and sliding the deadlock home.

He stood there for a moment, straining his ears to hear something. Anything.

When only silence greeted him, George turned away from the door and walked to the hearth. The flames had burned low, and it was time to put another log on the fire. As he did so, he wondered what would have been worse to hear.

Nothing, or Laura screaming.

Chapter 48: Cat and Mouse

Laura had never been a fan of hide and seek as a child. She had lacked the patience for it on both ends. It bothered her to have to hide, and she despised the search for a hidden player.

Now she didn't have a choice.

Once she was outside of the safety of George's house, she sprinted to a large evergreen bush on the edge of his property. She squatted down behind it and looked out at Mulberry Street. The clouds had passed, and the sky above was clear, the stars and half-moon bright in the cold air.

She looked for any sign of the ghosts, and when she found them she stifled a gasp.

At the far end of the street, the dead had gathered around a house, and it looked as if they were intent upon the destruction of the home. The siding had been stripped off of it, and several ghosts were hammering away at the base of the chimney. Others worked on the foundation while still more slammed against the bare wood like a storm's waves against a seawall.

She found herself caught up in the chaotic scene, finally forcing herself to look away.

Focus, Laura scolded herself. *Pay attention.*

After her admonishment, Laura looked around at the rest of Mulberry Street. To the far left she saw her Interceptor. She suspected that the vehicle's battery had suffered the same fate as the radio's, and as all of the other battery-run items.

Somehow the dead seemed to sap the charges from the various pieces of equipment. There was no need, as far as she could see, for her to run to the Interceptor only to have herself surrounded by ghosts and ripped to shreds.

Or possessed, she thought, shuddering.

The memory of Evie and the mother's painful death was fresh in her mind, and Laura found herself wondering how the children would recuperate from the incident.

How do you tell a grief counselor about watching your mother kill herself by slamming her head into a wall? Laura thought.

She shivered and realized she was cold.

The temperature was lower than she had suspected, and she wasn't dressed for long exposure to it. She needed to move and keep moving. Surviving repeated ghost attacks only to die of exposure would be extremely unfair.

Laura peered around, and when she was satisfied she was alone, began to move. Her steps were careful and well chosen. She set a reasonable goal, the garage of the next house over.

Thirty-three small, cautious steps brought her to the building. Two more and she was in front of the garage door. Another four and she was at a small breezeway.

And then she saw him.

A ghost.

A man who must have been a guard. His back was to her as he stared into the house through the side window.

Laura tried to move past him, but the sound of her footsteps jerked him around.

He looked at her, hands twitching.

"You're a state trooper," he said in the disconcerting way the dead had, his bulbous lips not moving.

Laura nodded.

"And a woman," he stated.

"Yes," she said.

He looked back into the house for a second, and then fixed his attention on her again.

"This was my home once," he said, staying by the building. "Did you know that?"

Laura shook her head. She had no recourse. She could either listen to him speak, or try to outrun him.

"I bought it when it was new," the ghost continued. "I brought my wife up from Hudson. She liked it here. She had family over the border, in Canada. We were happy. We were trying for children."

The man hesitated, and Laura waited for him to continue.

He did after a moment. "She never conceived. And I died. Died because of Edmund and his stupid mistake!"

The anger in his words was accompanied by him smashing his fist against the house, the glass in the window shattering.

"Where is he?" Laura asked.

"Edmund?" the ghost said.

"Yes," Laura said.

"In his house," the man said, letting out a bitter laugh. "In the same damned house he lived in when everything happened."

"He's alive?" Laura asked, surprised.

The ghost nodded. "Of course he is. He made it through. No ill effects or anything. We're going to kill him tonight. Once we get through the walls."

"What about the rest of us?" Laura asked.

"We are trying to get control of them," the ghost explained. "But if I were you, I'd get out now. They'll get bored with Edmund soon, and when they do, they'll start with you."

Laura took the former prison guard at his word and hurried away. The sound of the dead as they tore at Edmund's house followed her down Mulberry Street, as did the sound of the guard breaking the windows of his old home.

Chapter 49: A Mystery

Shane was smoking one of Ollie's cigars. It was a foul, nasty, expensive piece of tobacco, and he hated it.

But Shane was out of cigarettes, and his body was screaming for a fix.

He sat in the spare room, the pounding in his head muffled by five crushed aspirins mixed with water. The door to the room was locked, and somewhere in the house Ollie and his wife were deep in conversation.

Shane tried to imagine the discussion between the husband and wife.

Oh hey, honey, I'm sorry. See, Pete and I screwed up and bought this prison. Then the ghosts in it, yes, ghosts, well, they were let out. And then I messed up and sent some people in and they died. Plus, yeah, yeah, they died. Honestly, how much simpler can I say it?

Shane groaned and pushed the thought away. He'd go crazy if he concentrated on the dynamics of someone's marital relationship.

"Hey."

Shane leaped off the bed and twisted around.

Frank stood by the closet, his hands in his pockets and his shoulders slumped.

Shane took the cigar out of his mouth and said, "You scared the hell out of me."

"Sorry about that," Frank said, grinning. "Bad habit from special forces. I tend to creep up on people."

"Creep is the right word," Shane said. "How are things going?"

"Rough," Frank said. "Sore as hell. Courtney beat the hell out of me."

"So I heard," Shane said. "Sorry about that."

"Not your fault," Frank said. He rubbed at the scar on his face. "Surprising is all, I guess. Didn't expect her to turn violent. At least not against us."

The statement hung in the air for a moment, and then Shane asked, "Any word from Asa?"

Frank shook his head. "I haven't heard yet. I'll give him a call, though."

"Good." Shane forced himself up and off the bed, Frank reaching out a hand and helping to steady him.

"Thanks," Shane said.

They left the room and found Mason sitting in the hallway. He was reading a newspaper, and when he saw them, he folded it up and dropped it to his lap.

"You two look terrible," Mason said.

"Thanks," Shane said, "you're still a real sweetheart, huh?"

Mason chuckled. "Why would I change that much, Gunny?"

"Good question," Shane said. "Tell me, where's Courtney?"

"Right here," Mason said, gesturing towards the floor.

Shane looked down and saw a rectangular box of Morton's Salt. The top had been ripped off, and the thick sea salt chunks could be plainly seen in the hall's light.

"Damn, it really worked," Shane murmured. "Who needs a lead box?"

"So," Mason said, standing up and stretching. "What's the plan now?"

"We wait on Asa," Shane said. "When that happens, we go into Kurkow. Not much more to it."

"Good," Mason said. "Less for us to screw up."

Shane nodded his agreement but kept his eyes fixed on the box of salt. His heart ached to look at it and to know that Courtney was trapped within.

Chapter 50: Cold and Hot

Laura shivered, her collar turned up, and her hands pulled into the palms of her gloves to keep her fingers warm. Her legs ached from her passage through the deep snow, and it had taken her nearly half an hour to get from George's house back to the Interceptor. She had to hide, the occasional ghost appearing to make its way down to the house at the end of Mulberry.

Her thoughts had grown fuzzy from the cold, and she found it difficult to keep herself focused and on track. She stood on the driver's side of the Interceptor, looking in through the window. Laura struggled with the desire to unlock the door and get in, to see if the vehicle would even start.

Don't waste time, she told herself. *It's already too cold. You're too cold. You're going to die. You'll fall asleep.*

Laura let out a low groan. She wanted to be in the Interceptor. She wanted to be warm.

Maybe it'll start, she argued with herself.

"It won't start," Laura murmured, turning away from the vehicle. "It won't start. It won't start. It won't start."

She walked another half a dozen steps, stumbled and fell. Laura landed on her side, the snow cushioning the fall. She lay there, staring. Then she blinked and realized she was hot.

She took her gloves off and felt a little bit better, flexing her fingers. Laura smiled. She slipped her hand into her coat, undid the Velcro and accessed the zipper. For a moment, she fumbled with it, then her fingers locked on the metal tab and pulled. As she did so, the heat trapped within her slipped out into the night air. Tendrils of steam rose up, and through them, she saw a ghost approach her.

He was an old man, smiling at her. His face was bloody and retained a somewhat natural color, unlike the others she had seen. He was clad as a prisoner, and he looked as though he might be in his late seventies.

The man squatted down beside her as she sat up.

"Hello," he said.

Laura nodded and pulled off her coat, dropping it into the snow.

"Too warm?" he asked, his voice pleasant, concerned.

"Too warm," she echoed.

"Yes," he said, "I suspect you are. You may want to remove your shirt, too."

In her cold-numbed mind, his suggestion was completely rational. Perfectly reasonable. Laura was still hot, even with her coat and gloves off. A small part of her screamed, shouted out a reminder about the signs of hypothermia.

No, she thought, shaking her head. *Not hypothermia. Just too hot.*

"Your shirt?" the ghost said, smiling.

Laura returned the smile and began to unbutton her blouse. It was a difficult job, her fingers not responding the way they should. Soon, she had the shirt off, though, her Kevlar vest exposed to the world.

"No wonder you're too warm," the man said. "Look at that vest you're wearing."

"You're right," Laura said, but the words were slurred, and while she knew what she was saying, she had a difficult time recognizing them.

The old man hummed a song, tapping the rhythm out on his thighs.

Laura swayed from left to right, undoing the straps of the Kevlar and letting it fall to the snow. She yawned and stretched.

"Going to lie down?" he asked her, pausing his humming.

"Should I?" she asked.

"Oh," he said, his voice a whisper, "yes, I think you should."

Laura smiled, laid down in the snow and closed her eyes. Beneath her warm flesh, the snow melted, and sleep drew her into unconsciousness.

Chapter 51: Marital Bliss Interrupted

Shane heard doors slam and the questions of children go unanswered.

He and Mason, Pete and Frank, were in the kitchen. Pete had crammed himself into the breakfast nook as far from Shane as humanly possible, without leaving the kitchen. Shane had a bag of frozen peas pressed against the back of his head, Mason was texting his wife, and Frank stood at the sink.

The former monk was lost in thought, and Shane wondered what it was that occupied the man's mind.

Ollie stormed into the kitchen.

"What's up?" Frank asked.

Ollie spun around, jabbed a finger at him and snarled, "She's going to her mother's, with the kids, and she doesn't buy a single line of the story I told her. She thinks I'm trying to get out to a strip club, for God's sake!"

"Calm down," Shane said.

Ollie glared at him. "Who the hell do you think you are? I've had enough, right now, absolutely enough!"

"I will take an eye out in a minute," Shane said. "First one, and then the other. So you better lower your tone and remember what we need to do."

Ollie's face paled, the blood rushing out of his cheeks. Without another word he stalked over to the breakfast nook and sat down.

"So your wife and kids have left," Shane said.

Ollie nodded.

"Good. Pete, did you call your ex again?" Shane asked.

"Yes," Pete said, his voice soft as he pulled apart a paper napkin, piling the bits up on the table.

"What's going on with that?" Shane said.

"We have twenty rooms at our disposal, with the ability to get more, if we need them," Pete said, not looking up at him.

"Good," Shane said. He looked to Frank.

"I sent a text to Asa," Frank said. "He'll be coming along soon. Wants to get Emma settled in."

"When do we go into Gaiman?" Mason asked.

"As soon as we get word that Asa's at the hotel," Shane answered. "That way you can begin shuffling people out if needed and he'll be there to treat them."

"Can't we just pass this on to the State Police?" Pete asked, his voice anxious. "They can deal with all of this, we won't even have to worry about Kurkow."

Shane pinched the bridge of his nose, took a deep breath and closed his eyes. He kept them shut as he spoke.

"Listen to me, Peter," Shane said, keeping his voice flat. "We are all going to go to Kurkow Prison. We are going to secure the inner doors. Then, we are going to secure the outer doors. Afterward, we will go to Mulberry Street and take care of whoever remains."

"I'd really rather not," Pete whispered.

"Let's not get into a whole discussion about rather nots, okay?" Mason said, stepping in. "From what I understand, we're in this situation because of you. So shut your mouth, get a hold of yourself, and get ready to go in and do whatever damage needs to be done."

Pete kept quiet and looked down at the table.

"You still want to do this?" Ollie asked, his voice thrumming with anger. "You still want to go in there with only what, you three and us keeping watch?"

Shane grinned. "I have gone into worse places, with a whole lot less."

He kept his gaze fixed on Ollie until he, like Pete, looked away and at the table.

When neither of the brothers said anything, Shane walked over to the cabinets and began to open them. After a moment Ollie asked, "What are you looking for?"

"Whiskey," Shane answered. "I'm thirsty."

"We're going to go into a prison full of the dead," Ollie said.

"All the more reason to not be sober," Shane replied, and continued his search of Ollie's cabinets.

Chapter 52: Dazed, Confused, and Angry

When Emma woke up, it was to excruciating agony. She had no way to equivocate the pain, no marker. Emma had literally never hurt so much in her life.

A piercing beep, repeated at short intervals, caused her head to ache. As she looked around the room, the memories of Kurkow Prison and the nightmare she had suffered returned to her. Panic welled up inside her, and she fought it down, forcing herself to sit up in spite of the pain.

The door to the room opened, a low light spilling in from the hall beyond. She saw the man named Asa, a concerned look on his face as he stepped in.

"You should lie back down," he said, his voice low and soothing. "You suffered quite a bit of physical trauma. I'd rather not have to treat you for anything else."

Emma groaned and let herself flop back onto the bed. She inhaled sharply as the pain spiked for a heartbeat. Asa came and stood by her side.

"I'm sorry the pain medication wore off," Asa said, "but I am leery of giving too much. I can offer you a little more, however, to make the ride to the hospital bearable."

"That'd be good," she said between clenched teeth.

Asa turned away, went to a small sink and poured a glass of water for her before he took down a bottle of pills from a shelf. He brought a single, small pill and the glass to her.

"Slowly," he said. "Don't rush it."

She nodded and kept herself under control. Her mouth was dry, her throat burning. The water was cool, and the pill was washed down with ease.

"Thank you," she managed to say after a moment.

He smiled at her. "You're quite welcome. I'm sorry, but all I have are hospital scrubs to put you in."

"What hospital are you bringing me to?" she asked.

"Dartmouth-Hitchcock in Lebanon," Asa answered. "It is the closest, and they are quite excellent. I will also be able to continue on to Gaiman from there."

"Gaiman?" Emma asked. "Why are you going into Gaiman?"

"To help whoever Frank and Shane manage to rescue," Asa answered.

"Wait," she said, shaking her head, trying to fight off the effects of the medication as they took hold. "Who else is hurt?"

"I'm not sure," Asa said.

"I want to help," Emma said, struggling to sit up. "I need to help. My friends."

"Shh," Asa said, putting a gentle but firm hand on her shoulder. "You need to rest. You are in no place to help anyone, not physically. Who knows what you will be able to do in a few days, but you need more extensive treatment than I can offer from my humble home."

"I need to help," Emma whispered, closing her eyes. "I have to help."

"And you will, in your own way," Asa said. "Now rest. I will have you in the hospital soon. I have friends at Dartmouth. They will take care of you."

His words drifted away, as did Emma's worries, and through the haze of narcotics, the removal of her IV was nothing more than a pleasant tug.

Chapter 53: No Good News

Fear had blossomed in Edmund's stomach, spread to his spine and crawled up his back to nestle in his skull. He had begun to ignore the steady, insistent destruction of his home. But he found himself focusing on the pistol in his lap.

They will be through the walls soon, Edmund told himself. He opened the cylinder on the pistol, looked at the way the dull brass of the shells glowed in the firelight, and then closed the cylinder.

He repeated the action several times, unable to stop himself.

Edmund knew it for what it was, an attempt to feel safe.

Something he had done as a child and as a teenager. Never as an adult, not even after all of the accidental deaths.

He put the pistol down on his lap and then picked it up. He returned it to his lap and sat on his hands to keep them still.

The front door creaked under an unseen weight, one of the hinges popping loudly as it broke. A cheer went up from the dead and Edmund risked a glance towards the door. It had been pushed partially out of the upper portion of the frame, cold air hissing in.

He wasn't worried about the door, though. The threshold had been salted. Now, the fear he had was focused on the walls.

The dead had ripped down the old siding earlier, and they had begun to work on the old wood clapboard beneath. Soon they would make their way through that, then it would only be a matter of time before they tore into the insulation.

How long do you believe the wallboard will last? Edmund asked himself. *Five minutes? Perhaps as long as ten? You did not salt the walls, Edmund. They are coming for you.*

He looked down at the pistol, the weight of it comforting. Each chamber held a round, but he would need only one. In the end, it would come down to a matter of speed. *Can I pull the trigger faster than they could reach me once they break through?*

Should I even wait? he wondered.

Edmund hesitated before he nodded.

Yes. Who knows, he thought. *Perhaps those children might yet buy me some time until help comes.*

Edmund smiled at the thought, took his hands out from under his legs and picked up the pistol.

He whistled and checked the cylinder again.

Chapter 54: Going into Kurkow

Asa was on his way to the hospital with Emma, with the information about the hotel.

The Dawson brothers were in Pete's Jeep, the engine running and the headlights illuminating the front of Kurkow Prison.

Shane, Mason, and Frank stood off to one side, two of them ignoring the cold while the third didn't feel it at all.

"Are you ready?" Shane asked.

Mason nodded.

"You up to this?" Shane asked, directing the question towards Frank.

The former monk grinned. "Sure I am."

"Pretty straightforward," Shane said, and he repeated the plan. "In order to clear the dead out of Mulberry Street, we need to secure the prison with iron, the way it was before. With that done, any ghosts we get rid of outside of Kurkow's walls will be forced back inside and won't be able to get out again. So, we go into the foyer together. You two keep the dead off of me. I loop the chain back through, we fall back to the outer doors, and I take care of those. With the chains back in place, and the iron still on the window frames, we should be good to go. And we have to do all of this, theoretically, without being killed."

"What about locks?" Frank asked. "Did we ever figure out what to do about them?"

"Someone will have to come back and take care of the locks," Shane said. "No place is open. Not with all of the snow we got."

"Send Pete back here," Mason said. "He needs to grow some backbone. Maybe it'll help."

"Doubt it," Frank said. "Kid never had one."

"Alright," Shane said. "Let's just worry about this and not how much of a coward Pete is or isn't."

Mason checked the shotgun he had taken with him from Shane's car and Frank looked hard at the prison.

"See anything?" Shane asked, a nervous flutter in his stomach.

"No," Frank said after a moment. "Kind of worries me. I know most of them are supposed to be on Mulberry Street from the radio chatter, but I still expected at least one or two to be here, you know?"

"Yeah," he nodded. Reaching up, Shane flicked on his headlamp. "Okay, lights on."

"You sure you're okay without a weapon?" Mason asked, turning on his own light while Frank did the same.

"Yeah," Shane said. "I've got an iron knuckle-duster if push comes to shove."

"Okay," Mason said. "Let's hope it's enough."

"You and me both," Shane said.

Frank led the way, shotgun on the ready, and Shane felt uncomfortable as they walked along the caged in path again. The last time they had come through it, they had been searching for the women. And they had found them, of course.

Remembering the scene brought a bitter taste to his mouth and he shoved the memory away.

You'll die if you don't pay attention, he snapped.

Frank approached the open door well ahead of Shane and Mason, the two men pushing their way through the thick snow. A moment after he had slipped into the prison, Frank reappeared.

"We're good," he said in a low voice.

Shane and Mason entered Kurkow, Mason hissing.

"Christ," he muttered. "This place is terrible."

Shane nodded his agreement. "Just be happy we're not going inside."

"Who says you're not?" a voice asked.

Shane drew his knuckle-dusters out while the shotgun roared, the flash momentarily blinding him.

But a moment was all it took for the unseen speaker to attack.

Chapter 55: Free Advice

A soft knocking at the door woke George.

He sat up and looked around. Merle and the girls were asleep on the floor. The fire had burned low, and there was a distinct chill in the room, one that reminded George of the twin ghosts who had attacked him.

He listened, straining his ears for another knock, and when he didn't hear it, George shook his head. With a sigh, he stood up, went to the stacked wood beneath the window and carried a few logs over to the fireplace. He made sure each step was soft, not wishing to disturb the delicate sleep of either Alison or Rachel. It was a miracle that they were asleep as far as he and Merle were concerned.

George put the wood down on the floor, knelt beside it and arranged the logs on top of the embers. When he finished, he added a small bit of kindling and a twisted piece of newspaper, which quickly caught fire. He sat back and watched as the flames curled the edges of the paper, the newsprint blackening before the kindling began to burn. George adjusted the flue, and a soft knock sounded on the front door again.

With his hand frozen above the flue knob, George looked at the door, his heart racing inside of his chest. His mouth was suddenly dry as he thought, *Please, please let me have imagined that.*

Another knock told him he hadn't.

George got to his feet, glanced at Merle and the girls to make certain they were still asleep, and then walked to the front door. He paused at it, stared at the lock and then reached out and turned it. George lifted the doorknob a little, putting slight pressure on it to keep the hinges from squealing in the stillness. When he did get the door open, he gasped, his breath ripped out of him from the cold and by the sight of the person on the doorstep.

Laura looked at him, a pained expression on her face. She was dressed only in her bra and pants. Her hair was in an untidy mess, strands and locks having freed themselves from the tight bun at the base of her skull. And George realized, she was dead.

Undeniably so.

He could see through her, more so than the others who had been assaulting the house for days.

"Laura," he whispered.

She nodded, a haunted look in her eyes.

"How did you," he said, shook his head and couldn't finish the question.

"Hypothermia," Laura answered. "I couldn't get away fast enough."

"They didn't kill you?" he asked, unable to keep the surprise out of his voice.

"No," she said, but her tone became bitter. "Although one helped convince me that I would feel much better if I undressed."

"What?" George asked, confused.

"Common side effect of hypothermia," Laura said. "Your body becomes so disorientated that you think you're too hot when you're on the verge of freezing to death. But I'm not here for that, George. I'm here to tell you that you're going to need to leave, in the morning, and as quickly as possible."

He looked over at the others, still sleeping through his strange conversation with Laura. "We can't. If you couldn't make it, how can we?"

"Because you're going to get bundled up in everything you have," she said, her voice firm. "You are going to follow my tracks and not let the girls see my body. Then you will continue on to the main road. I drifted that way for a little. There are plows running on it. Once they've cleared the main thoroughfares, then they'll come down Mulberry. You won't have that long, though."

"We won't?" George asked.

Laura shook her head. "No. Not at all. Soon they'll be through the house at the end of the street. When that happens, they'll look for anyone else who can entertain them. And they haven't forgotten about you."

"What if they come after us?" George whispered.

"You'll have your iron," Laura said, a soothing tone coming into her voice. "And you'll have me. I'll do what I can to stop them. Alright?"

He nodded.

"Good," Laura said, and her body seemed to thicken, become less translucent. "Now go start to get ready. It will be dawn soon enough."

Chapter 56: Trouble

Shane was thrown to one side, his light shattering and his head and shoulder smashing into the wall. He groaned and collapsed to the floor, vomiting from the force of the blow. A shotgun roared again, and Shane went deaf. His vision was gone, filled with lights that danced and obscured the foyer. Something cold struck him across the face, and he felt his skin burn.

Spitting bile, Shane lashed out with the knuckle-dusters and grunted with satisfaction as it passed through something cold.

A hand grabbed him by the arm and dragged him to his feet, and Shane realized he was held upright by Mason.

"Secure the God-damned door, Gunny!" Mason yelled, pushing Shane towards the doors. A guard rushed out, faintly illuminated by Mason's red lamp, and Shane took a stab at the ghost.

He missed, by a wide margin, and the blast of Mason's shotgun filled the air. Shane saw more ghosts in the hall, all of them racing towards the doors.

Oh hell, Shane thought, *I've got to get the chains through it, or else they'll keep coming out.* Gritting his teeth, Shane threw himself against the open door. Something broken in his shoulder exploded in pain, but he managed to close the door. Hands reached through, grabbing at his clothes and pulling him against the metal. Shane slashed at them until he was free, if only for a moment, and he looped the iron links back through the handles.

He fell back, gasping for breath. The pain in his shoulder increased exponentially.

Mason fired the shotgun again, and Shane looked to see what he was firing at.

Ghosts were coming in through the front doors, and Frank was fighting them with his iron-fingered hands. Someone had wrenched the shotgun away.

"We need to get the outer doors," Shane yelled, struggling to his feet.

Mason nodded as he reloaded the weapon. Frank threw a punch into a ghost, and the prisoner disappeared.

"I'll take the walkway," Frank said, but the words were faint, difficult for Shane to hear above the ringing in his ears.

Shane could only nod as he picked up the length of chain he had left on the foyer floor from when he had beaten back the first ghost. From when Pete Dawson had let all of them out.

With his left arm hanging limp and throbbing in pain, Shane held onto the cold iron links and dragged them out. Mason followed behind him, firing twice more.

Ahead of him, Shane saw Frank attacked by a trio of prisoners, and as Shane cleared the threshold, Frank went down to his knees.

Chapter 57: The View from the Safe Spot

Ollie heard the gun blasts from inside the prison. Then he saw Frank come outside and watched as he was ambushed.

"Ollie," Pete whispered, pointing at Frank.

"Yeah," Ollie said, "I see him."

Yet even as the words came out of his mouth, Ollie saw it wasn't Frank that Pete had been pointing at. It was the ghosts rushing towards Frank.

There were three of them, huge apparitions. Monstrous in the illumination of the Jeep's headlights. They attacked Frank, and he fought back.

When Shane came through the front doors, though, Frank collapsed.

"Oh Jesus, Ollie," Pete said. "What are we going to do?"

Ollie could only shake his head.

He didn't know, and his attention was focused on Shane and Mason. Ollie watched as the shotgun-toting Mason stepped past Shane, bringing the weapon up and firing off three quick shots. Each ghost disappeared.

Behind Mason, Shane managed to close the doors, and he was threading a length of chain through the handles while Mason was reloading.

And more ghosts arrived.

Not many, perhaps four, if Ollie counted right, but Mason hadn't been able to reload.

One of the ghosts punched Mason in the side of his head, and the man howled with fury. The other two rushed at Shane. The bald man twisted around and defended himself with his knuckle-dusters, all the while his left arm was limp.

"We need to do something," Pete said, and Ollie looked at his brother in surprise.

"What?" Ollie asked, shocked.

"We need to help them," Pete said, his eyes never leaving the scene in front of the prison. "They're going to die."

"Oh well," Ollie said. "You think I'm going to risk my life for them? Hell no, Pete and neither are you. I offered financial assistance, and this was the best plan they could come up with. Oh, that and renting some hotel rooms to help whoever happened to survive the assault on Mulberry Street. Get a grip, little brother. We are not going down there."

"Ollie," Pete started to say, and then he was cut off. A pair of hands reached into the Jeep and grabbed Pete on either side of his head.

Ollie watched, dumbfounded, as his brother shrieked. Pete's head was smashed into the glass, shattering it, and then he was dragged out of the vehicle, legs lashing out awkwardly.

A ghost slid into Pete's recently vacated seat and looked at Ollie. He was a young man, his throat cut and his shirt dark with blood. The ghost gave Ollie a winning smile and said, "So, who are you, my fine-looking man?"

Ollie struggled a moment to find his voice, and when he did it was low and cracked. "Ollie."

"Ollie," the ghost said with a grin. "Short for Oliver, I assume?"

Ollie nodded.

The ghost glanced out the broken window, Pete no longer screaming.

"Friend of yours?" the ghost asked, his tone light and conversational.

"My brother," Ollie whispered.

"Your brother?" the ghost asked, eyes wide in surprise. "Well, I do apologize for the inconvenience. Terrible thing, having to witness a sibling's death. But then, you really didn't see him die. Just the abduction, so that's alright, I suppose. Then again, you don't have to worry about it, do you?"

"I don't know," Ollie said in a low voice. "Do I?"

"No," the ghost said, winking. "You don't."

"Why?" Ollie asked, even though he didn't really want an answer to the question.

"Because," the ghost said, "we're going to kill you next."

Chapter 58: Moving

"Shane," Mason said. "We need to move."

Shane nodded, stumbling away from the door.

They reached Frank and found the man unconscious, black marks on his face and neck from where the dead had struck him. In silence, they grabbed hold of Frank and pulled him to his feet. His head lolled from side to side.

A scream caught his attention, and he and Mason looked simultaneously at Pete's Jeep. They watched as something dragged Pete's body out of the driver's side window, and a moment later, Pete's screams were silenced.

"Damn it!" Shane spat. He went as fast as he could through the snow, Mason beside him. They hadn't gone more than half the distance along the walkway before another scream erupted, this one from inside the Jeep.

The vehicle rocked back and forth for a moment and then stopped.

Shane and Mason continued on towards the Jeep.

A ghost slid out of the driver's door and waved at them. Mason let go of Frank and put a round into the ghost, the prisoner vanishing.

Grunting, Shane managed to hold Frank up until Mason took up the other side again.

When they reached the Jeep, Shane and Mason found the Dawson brothers dead. Pete's neck was twisted around to an unnatural angle, and Ollie, it seemed, had been strangled to death. There were black handprints on his neck, his skin burned from the touch of the dead.

Shane had seen a great many dead men in his time, and it was never easy. His jaw tightened at the sight of the brothers. He hadn't cared for either of the men, but like so many others, neither Peter nor Ollie had deserved to die the way they had.

Shane glanced into the interior of the Jeep, the smell of urine and excrement rank thick in the air. Ollie, Shane saw, had fouled himself before he died.

Shane shook his head and he and Mason stepped away. They opened the back door and put Frank in, Mason bending over to check his pulse. After a moment, Mason said, "We're still good."

"Good."

Mason glanced at Shane, closed the door and shook his head.

"You can't drive with that arm," Mason said, stepping over Pete and getting into the driver's seat.

"No kidding," Shane said. He went around, opened the passenger door, hesitated, and then he dragged Ollie's body out. He stripped the dead man of his jacket and spread it out over the seat. Shane felt the old disconnect in his mind, the little box where he put away his horrific acts, and those that he had seen. He put the images of the Dawson brothers in that place, and got into the Jeep.

"You know where this Mulberry Street is exactly?" Mason asked.

Before Shane could answer, Frank did from the back. His words were slurred, but understandable. "Left. Second right. First right. Left."

"Good enough," Mason said, and he shifted the Jeep hard into drive.

Shane gritted his teeth as the Jeep climbed over curbs, slammed through snow banks and made its own path under the ungentle guidance of Mason. The man drove like they were in a combat zone, and Shane realized that they were.

The whole damned place is, Shane thought. *And we're going to another fight.*

The Jeep's headlights illuminated a street sign, and Shane saw the name on it.

Mulberry.

Mason cut the wheel hard, and the Jeep plowed into the deep loose snow on the street. The first object to catch Shane's eye was a State Police Interceptor, and the body that was near it.

Mason jammed on the brakes, pointed and muttered, "Holy Christ, Gunny. Look."

Shane looked.

At the end of Mulberry Street, a swarm of ghosts was ripping apart a house. Board by board and brick by brick.

Chapter 59: Getting Out

At first, Merle had argued with George. She hadn't seen any logical reason to leave the house. Not until he told her about Laura's ghost, and how the dead officer had come back to warn them.

After the explanation, George and Merle had worked together in silence, Alison and Rachel asleep on the couch. While the two adults gathered all the supplies and clothing they could, George had to fight down a growing fear that Jess would come home.

He had a perfect mental image of her attempting to drive down Mulberry, and of being attacked by the dead. The anxiety caused his stomach to twist into knots, his movements jerky and unsure.

George jumped when Merle put a hand out and touched his arm.

"Are you alright?" she whispered.

George nodded, forced a smile and said in a low voice, "I'm worried. That's all."

She patted his hand, then went back to putting a bag of goldfish crackers into a backpack.

Within a short time, they had packed what food they felt they could bring and still carry the girls. George went to his bedroom and took out the last of the blankets from the closet. As he carried them back, he wondered if they could escape from the house. If the dead would ignore them.

He and Merle would each have to carry one of the children, as well as a weapon. And they would have to put the sisters down in order to defend them.

George shuddered at the thought, set the blankets on the floor and pulled on his jacket, then his backpack as Merle woke the girls up.

He watched as they rubbed the sleep from their eyes, yawned, and listened to what Merle had to say. The girls nodded once they were told what they had to do, and George was amazed at the calm demeanor that each child possessed.

"They're resilient," Merle said, smiling over Alison's head at George. "Children always are."

George could only take her word for it as he held out a blanket and wrapped Rachel up in it. The girl snuggled against him, yawned again and closed her eyes.

Time to go, George realized, and he turned to face the front door with growing trepidation.

Chapter 60: Sights on Mulberry Street

"We've got people coming out," Shane said, leaning forward in his seat.

"Where," Mason started, then he said, "wait, yeah. I see them."

"Can the Jeep make it?" Shane asked.

"So long as the others don't try and stop us," Mason said, and he down-shifted.

"How bad is it?" Frank asked, sitting up, his voice thick.

"Bad," Mason answered.

Wincing, Shane unzipped his coat, pulled his injured arm across his chest and stuffed his hand under his armpit. Stars exploded around the edges of his vision, but he ignored the pain and closed the jacket.

"You hurt?" Frank asked.

Shane nodded.

"Can you handle a weapon?" the former monk asked.

"I've got my right hand," Shane said. "I'll use the knuckle-dusters. What about you?"

"No," Frank said. "I'd shoot someone. I'm useless right now."

"Can you help someone through the snow?" Mason asked.

"What?" Frank said, confused.

"Screw it," Shane said. "We're close enough. Frank, you're with me. Mason, shotgun, protect the Jeep. It's the only way we'll get them out of here."

The Jeep ground to a halt and Shane got out, his arm sending sharp bursts of pain into his skull, which vibrated from the same pain. Frank stepped out a moment later.

"Come on," Shane said, as he started through the thick snow towards the people. He could see two adults carrying large bundles.

"Damn," Frank said, "they have kids with them."

Shane could only nod. The cold was making his injuries throb. Each step and every breath was a challenge. Beyond the people, Shane could see the house, the dead continued to destroy it.

"There's someone in that house!" A woman shouted, pulling the scarf in front of her face down. "There's an old man who lives there."

Shane glanced at Frank and saw the man wouldn't be able to help him. The distance was too far.

"Get them back to Mason and the Jeep," Shane said. "If you see me fall. Don't come for me. Let me go. Get them to Asa."

Frank didn't argue. Instead, he focused his attention on the people in front of them.

"This is Frank," Shane said, walking towards the strangers. "He's going to bring you to the Jeep."

With that said, he passed by them and made his way towards the end of Mulberry Street. In the crisp stillness, he heard the house being torn asunder. He saw prisoners doing the damage, a swarm of them ripping every shred they could off the frame. On the outer edge of the crowd, forming a cordon, there was a thin line of guards. They watched all of it and the idea that the destruction was condoned, and monitored, sent a new tendril of fear into Shane's heart.

A high, sharp scream punctured the air, a gunshot following.

The prisoners surged forward in silence and Shane tried to hurry forward.

One of the guards stopped, turned and faced him.

"This isn't your concern," the dead man said. "We need to be avenged."

"You can't kill him," Shane said. "You've killed enough people."

The guard shrugged. "And how will you stop us?"

Another scream cut off Shane's response.

They had dragged the old man out, his arms and legs stretched. Fear was etched on the man's face, and Shane stepped forward. The guard shook his head, reached out, and Shane slashed the man, the ghost vanishing.

Even as Shane pushed forward, the prisoners began to kill the man.

Chapter 61: Edmund has a Discussion

The cold on Edmund's face was a blast of hot air compared to the hands of the dead.

Anger bubbled at the edges of his thoughts as he remembered his failure. He had sought to save himself the agony of a slow death, and to deny the dead any sort of satisfaction.

Will they expect me to be sorry? Edmund wondered. *Will they demand me to beg for forgiveness?*

He wouldn't of course. And he couldn't. Lying was impossible, and he had never, ever felt badly about the accident.

The only event he regretted, was not being able to pull the trigger fast enough when the dead had broken into the house. They had ripped the pistol out of his hands, a single shot firing as his finger broke in the trigger guard.

Edmund kept his expression impassive as they held him steady.

With slow, maddening movements they stripped his clothes off him, his skin blackening with every touch. Soon he was naked, the dead pressed close around him, and he felt sharp, hideous pinching. He shrieked until his throat was raw and felt as though it was going to burst.

One of the dead held up a piece of bloody meat, pressed between forefinger and thumb, and Edmund knew it was his own flesh.

He closed his eyes against the horror of it, but someone pried them open, finally ripping the lids off in frustration.

When hands reached into his body and broke off a rib, Edmund felt his heart stop. And while the pain continued on for a moment, he relaxed, for he knew he was finally dying.

Chapter 62: A Frenzy of Dead

Shane tightened his grip on his knuckle-dusters and looked at the dead around the shattered house. Some of them turned and focused their attention on him, the remainder were still intent upon shredding the body of the old man.

Adrenalin surged through Shane and he knew he had reached the end.

He wouldn't survive the fight, not with so many of the dead in front of him. Not with only a single piece of iron for defense, and an arm that was next to useless.

Shane grinned and took a step forward.

Book 5: Kurkow Prison

A prisoner came in from the right, and Shane cut him down. As the ghost vanished, the others hesitated, suddenly wary of the knuckle-dusters. Yet even as they hung back, still more turned around.

Shane was now the focus of attention.

Who really wants to live forever? Shane asked himself, and he lunged forward. Dead hands struck him, each blow painful as cold shot through his clothing and into his flesh. Shane found himself laughing, great billows of white issuing from his mouth as he attacked and defended.

The ghosts formed a circle around him as they had the old man, and for a moment, Shane wondered if he, too, would be stripped down and gutted.

The thought was obliterated by the sound of shotguns being fired.

Ghosts vaporized around him and something tore through Shane's left ear. He let out a howl of pain mixed with rage. Blood rushed down his neck from the wound, soaking into his undershirt. A ghost stepped in and Shane snarled as he thrust his hand through it.

The ghosts pressed in closer while Shane continued to fight. Again the shotguns were fired, this time towards the ghosts on either side of him.

"Shane!" Frank yelled. "Drop!"

Shane dropped into the snow, wincing at the pain in his shoulder. The shotguns roared, then another one sounded again.

"You good, Shane?" Frank asked.

"Yeah," he said. "Fantastic. Which one of you meatheads hit me?"

"Not it, Gunny" Mason said.

"Probably me," Frank said. "Still out of it."

Before Shane could answer, the dead rushed at them.

He didn't have time to get out of his sitting position, and he was forced to remain where he was. Fear gripped him as the cold of the snow and the winter air worked into his flesh.

A curious silence fell over him, and Shane heard nothing. Not even his own heartbeat. The world seemed to hesitate, as if someone had pressed pause on a movie. Each ghost moved a fraction at a time, and Shane watched the battle unfold around him.

The shotguns were silent as they fired, the only sign of their existence being the vanishing of ghosts in ones and twos and threes.

Shane forced himself back to his feet, grinding his teeth at the pain in his arm. To remain on the ground would be his death, and Shane found he wasn't comfortable with the idea of dying on Mulberry Street.

A short, thick prisoner, looking more like a sickly toad than a poisoned dead man, delivered a blow to Shane's injured arm, and Shane screamed. Furious, he struck the ghost with the knuckle-dusters, causing it to vanish. Even as he did so another ghost appeared, latching onto Shane's left hand and tearing off his glove.

The sudden cold sent a fresh shiver through Shane, and he punched the iron through the ghost's face. Shane's stolen glove dropped to the churned snow at his feet.

A prisoner and a guard attacked, and before Shane could react, the guard had hold of his left arm, while the prisoner secured his right. The guard held up Shane's left hand, gripping it by his coat, and a second guard arrived. This man was taller and wore captain's bars on his collar. A sense of power emanated from the new ghost, as he whispered, "You shouldn't have tried to interrupt us."

Shane fought against the ghosts holding him. The dead captain reached out and took hold of Shane's exposed left pinky finger.

The pain was immense, and Shane would have collapsed to his knees if the dead hadn't held him up. His vision blurred and when it returned to focus, he saw the captain had let go of the pinky, that particular digit black.

436

"This is our place," the captain said. "And this was our time for retribution. Your interference has robbed us of our pleasure. Do you have any idea of how I've had to work, to keep them all in line? To keep them all focused?"

Shane ignored the question and tried to free himself, but he couldn't. The dead were too strong.

"Reloading!" Mason yelled.

"Damn it, so am I!" came Frank's reply as Shane continued to struggle. In horror, Shane watched as the captain reached out for Shane's ring finger.

When the dead officer grabbed hold of it, Shane screamed. As pain tore the sound out of his voice, Shane saw a shape racing towards them. It was another ghost; a woman.

And she was running straight at the Captain. She was barefoot, and wore only pants and a bra, loose hair hanging about her shoulders. A snarl curled her upper lip, and she slammed into the dead officer. The temperature around Shane plummeted, and he blacked out.

When Shane opened his eyes, the captain and the woman were gone. The ghosts who had held Shane upright dropped him to the snow.

Shane fell to his knees and watched the dead turn to run, but they vanished instead. Frank and Mason passed by him, focused on the last few of the dead who were present. The men pushed through the snow with slow steps. Shotguns were pressed to their shoulders, and Shane could watch the muzzle-flashes. Frank continued to fire as Mason stopped and reloaded with the grace of a dancer, each movement fluid and precise.

Then Mason was firing and Frank was reloading.

And the dead were gone.

Shane could hardly think through pain as the world slammed back into full speed.

"Is that all of them?" Mason asked, his face flushed.

"I hope so," Frank answered.

Mason offered Shane his hand and helped him to his feet.

"How you doing, Gunny?" Mason asked.

Shane held his left hand up in reply.

Mason's eye's widened as he whispered, "Oh hell."

"Shane," Frank said. "Are you in pain?"

Shane shook his head. In a hoarse voice he said, "Not too much. Mostly the ear. I can't feel much in those two fingers."

"Alright," Frank began.

The sound of a car horn interrupted him, and all three of them turned to look toward the noise.

It was the Jeep. Someone was laying on the horn, and a dead guard was rushing towards them. The man slammed into Shane, throwing him backward into Mason, their heads colliding.

And even as Shane collapsed to the ground, Frank fired the shotgun, the ghost instantly vanished. Salt ripping the snow apart only inches from Shane.

"Come on, Frank!" Shane yelled.

With his head pounding, Shane rolled over onto the snow, and felt pain blossom where his left ear should have been and shook his head.

"What is it?" Frank asked. "Are you hurt again?"

"No," Shane said, groaning.

"What then?" Mason asked groggily.

"There's always one more," Shane spat. "Always one God damned more ghost."

Book 5: Kurkow Prison

Chapter 63: A Final Conversation

Shane sat at his kitchen table.

He had finished his cigarette and his whiskey, and he still dreaded the task which stood before him.

On the old, dark wood of the table top, standing between a pack of Lucky cigarettes and a half empty bottle of Jameson's whiskey, was a box of salt. A dark blue, rectangular piece of cardboard with the top torn off.

The current resting place of Courtney DeSantis.

She had been going mad, slowly, but surely. Shane had done some research, digging through internet pages, looking at old books. All of them had said the same thing, that sometimes ghosts lose their minds.

Something broke inside of them. Some became despondent, and could be seen moaning their fate.

Others, like Courtney, became violent.

And from what Shane had read, there was no salvation for them. No way to talk to them and bring them back from the edge of the precipice of insanity.

Courtney would become worse, and there was nothing Shane could do about it. She would lash out, attacking. At some point, she might even kill.

Shane sighed and shook his head.

Part of him wanted to take the coward's way out, to stuff her into a lead box and hide her away. Perhaps take her out years hence when he had worked up enough courage to do so.

But he wasn't one to put things off, as his many scars reminded him.

Shane reached up, touched the bandage over the remnants of his left ear, and felt a small, bitter smile slide across his face. His left hand was heavily bandaged as well, the pinky and ring fingers having been amputated due to terrible frostbite inflicted by the dead captain.

No, you never put things off, do you. He sighed, contemplated another cigarette, and, realizing it was another way to delay the inevitable, pushed the thought down.

Shane pulled the box close to him, shoved his hand into it and searched for the chain of his dog tags amongst the grains of salt. He found it quickly, and as soon as he pulled them free, Courtney appeared in the kitchen.

The temperature plummeted and the lights flickered.

She solidified as the bulbs dimmed and stayed low.

Courtney glanced around the kitchen.

"When did we get home?" she demanded.

"This morning."

"How long was I in there?" she asked, a harsh, dangerous tone in a once pleasant voice.

"Three days," Shane answered.

"You left me in there for three days?" she snapped.

He nodded.

"Why?!"

Shane sighed. "You attacked me."

Courtney glared at him. "Who's Emma?"

"The girl who you helped to rescue," Shane said.

"I should have told you they were all dead," Courtney hissed. "Should have left her there to be butchered. You shouldn't have spoken with her."

"Courtney—" Shane said.

"No," she cut him off, her voice shaking. "I'm dead because of you. Your friends want you with a living woman. Not a dead one. I'll kill them, too. But I'll kill Frank slow. It's his fault. All of it. Every last bit of it. And your fault, too. I'm going to hurt you, Shane Ryan. And when I'm done hurting you, you're going to be with me."

His shoulders sagged.

"Courtney," he whispered.

She took a step forward, the temperature in the room plummeting. Several of the lights flickered out.

"Courtney," Shane begged. "Please."

Courtney moved closer, and tears stung Shane's eyes. He dropped his chin to his chest, and said in German, "Now, my friend."

Screams of rage echoed off of the kitchen's walls as the rest of Shane's dead friends raced into the room. Carl and Eloise, Thaddeus and the dark ones. The sounds were horrific, the cold so terrible that it set Shane's teeth to chattering.

Courtney's screams changed into high-pitched wails, and Shane looked up, blinking away the tears.

Carl and Thaddeus had her, gripping her arms holding her up as she sagged between them, her head bowed. Eloise and the dark ones waited at the open pantry door. Beyond it was darkness, the shadow too deep to be natural. It was then that Shane knew they had opened the trap door into the root cellar.

Courtney lifted her head, locked her eyes onto him, eyes filled with rage, fear, and sadness.

"Shane," she moaned, his name sounding like a curse as it left her lips.

Shane sobbed and squeezed his eyes closed.

Courtney let out a long wail, but it was silenced as the first door to the pantry, and then to the root cellar, were slammed shut.

The light strengthened and Shane opened his eyes.

Carl stood alone in the room. The others, Shane knew, had taken Courtney deep into the house. She would be in the walls, bound and kept from him, kept in some secret place only the dead knew of. A prison for the woman who had gone mad, and who loved him beyond death.

Carl looked at Shane sympathetically.

"Is there anything else I can do for you, my friend?" Carl asked in German.

Shane nodded as he reached out and grabbed hold of the whiskey bottle.

"What is it?" Carl asked.

"Don't ever tell me where you've hidden her," Shane whispered. He removed the bottle's cap, and didn't bother with a glass.

* * *

Lake Nutaq
Book 6

Chapter 1: The Darkness Comes In

Shane woke up panting, his hands shaking. He fumbled as he went to turn on the light, the lamp rocking on its base. Shane grabbed hold of it and held onto the cool metal, forcing himself to calm down.

He had nearly succeeded too, until she screamed.

Goosebumps erupted on his skin as he shivered. Another scream burst from within the walls, rising to a crescendo before being cut off.

A thin, disturbing silence filled his bedroom.

Shane swallowed; his mouth was dry. His heart hammered in his chest, and he hesitated before he turned on the table lamp. He blinked as harsh, bright light exploded in the room. It shined into all of the dark corners.

Courtney was not in his room.

But he knew her screams hadn't been part of his nightmares, which revolved around his past.

God in heaven, Shane thought, letting out a shuddering breath. *I can't do this.*

A knock sounded on his door, and Shane answered, "Come in."

Carl passed through and stood in the room, lowering the temperature by several degrees.

"I'm sorry, my friend," Carl said in German, "but there are times when we lose control of her. Her madness makes her quite strong. You could always bind her."

Shane shot Carl a hard look. "I told you before, I'm not doing that. It's bad enough that I have to keep her locked up in the house. I'm not going to bind her to some little lead box, or stuff her into a bag of salt."

"Then I do not know what to do, my friend," Carl said.

"I do," Shane replied, getting off the bed. "I'm going out for a drive."

"For how long?" Carl asked.

Shane shrugged. "Long as it takes, I guess."

"As long as what takes?" Carl asked, frowning.

"To figure out what to do about Courtney," Shane said. He sighed, shook his head, and walked to the bathroom.

Chapter 2: Lake Nutaq, New Hampshire

Clark Johansen pulled his van up to the chain which stretched across the mouth of Preston Road. He was surprised to see the barrier was still intact. More often than not, he found it cut, with the tracks of snowmobiles having pressed it down into the snow.

Clark put the van into 'park' and let it idle as he forced the door open, climbing out into the bitter cold. He cleared his throat, spat a glob of mucus out, and pulled his custodial keys from his pocket. After several long and miserable seconds, he found the key to the padlock.

It looked like Danny, the plow driver, had already been down Preston Road. Banks close to four feet in height flanked either side of the narrow road, and Clark hoped like hell Danny hadn't forgotten to cover the padlock back up.

Clark sighed in relief as he saw the blue, weatherproof bag around the log. With his breath rushing out in white clouds, Clark bent over, undid the straps, and pulled the bag away. He fit the key into the lock, wrestled with it for a moment, and then grinned at the satisfying sound of the tumblers as they freed the latch.

Clark let the chain fall to the ground, pocketed the lock, and hurried back to the van. He climbed in, slammed the door behind him, and swore under his breath.

Too damn cold, he thought, pulling off his gloves. He turned up the heat and held his hands in front of the vents. As he let his fingers warm up, Clark looked out at the tall pine trees which grew up along both sides of the road. Snow clung to the branches, dull, gray clouds in the sky above them. The winter had been brutal so far, with harsh temperatures and more snowfall than in the past one hundred years.

While there was no prediction of snow in the forecast, that didn't seem to mean anything.

Clark shifted the van into drive and headed down into the community. When it came down to it, he didn't care one way or another about the weather. The Society paid him a decent wage over the off-season months and kept him busy during vacation time. None of the owners could be troubled to fix their own, everyday domestic problems.

Clark snickered and pulled up to the first cottage, the one owned by the Zettels. Clark knew they were well to-do dentists from Cambridge, down in Massachusetts. He remembered when they bought the place, after being approved by the Society of course, and they had brought in some interior decorator. From New York, no less.

He shook his head at the memory and wondered what else the doctors wasted their money on.

Clark nodded in approval at the plowing job. Danny had been a good hire. He took care of everything, same as Clark did.

Different for a kid his age, Clark thought, coming to a stop in front of the door. He put his bag down, opened it, and pulled out a pair of disposable booties.

The interior was warm. A sure sign that the electric heater was running properly. Clark whistled to himself as he moved through the cabin. He checked the main room, the kitchen, the bathroom, and the bedroom. Everything was in order. No broken windows. No sign of leaks or burst pipes. The taps ran, and the toilet flushed.

The wealth of the seasonal residents on Preston Road ensured that their power was always on.

Money makes the world go 'round, Clark thought, nodding to himself.

He finished his walk through; made sure he hadn't left any lights on, and left the house. The cold stung his face as he paused to take off the booties. *Damn, it's so God-awful cold!*

Clutching his belongings, Clark hustled back to the van. He climbed in, shivering, and slammed the door behind him. Clark turned the heat up to high and thought, *Twenty-four more houses, and the damned clubhouse.*

He looked to the far end of Preston Road and saw the clubhouse, a squat, ugly structure sitting like a wart on the face of the lake. It seemed to glare at him, the curtainless windows malevolent in the shadow of the porch.

Clark straightened up.

The front door of the clubhouse was open. Wide open, as if someone had swung it inwards and stuffed a wedge into it.

Frowning, Clark shifted the van into drive and rolled towards the open door.

Chapter 3: Reasoning with the Dead

"Why don't you wait for Frank?" Carl asked, worry clear in his voice, the German words sharp and powerful.

"Because I don't want Frank to come with me," Shane explained again. He yawned, his jaw popping as he did so.

"You need to sleep, my young friend," Carl said.

Shane smiled. "That's why I'm going out. I can't sleep, not with Courtney screaming. Not with the nightmares being worse than they've ever been."

"Perhaps you should see a doctor?" Carl asked. "There must be some medicine he could prescribe?"

"Probably," Shane said as he pulled his rucksack out from his closet and tossed it onto his bed. He opened his dresser, his left hand fumbling with the effort. His mind believed his missing fingers were there, arguing that the pinky and ring fingers hadn't been amputated.

Shane smiled, then winced, the fresh scar tissue on the left side of his head pulling too much. He sighed and tugged out fresh socks and underwear. Shane threw them to the bed, and then a pair of jeans and several tee-shirts as well.

"You look to be packing for an extended stay," Carl said.

"Might be," Shane said. "I'm not sure yet."

A shadow flickered by the bathroom door and Shane twisted towards it, adrenaline surging as he braced himself for an attack.

"My friend," Carl said, his voice low, "what is it?"

"I saw something by the bathroom," Shane replied. "Who else is in here, and why are they hiding from me?"

"No one else is in here," Carl said. Concern was etched on his face as he looked at Shane. "My friend, there is no one here in this room except you and myself."

Shane's eyes told him someone had been in the room. But he could hear the truth in Carl's words, and he could see the honesty in his dead friend's face.

"I need to leave," Shane whispered. He walked to the bed and continued to pack his rucksack.

Chapter 4: At the Clubhouse

Clark approached the front door of the clubhouse cautiously. He didn't see any footprints in the snow, or paw prints either, but that didn't mean something or someone wasn't in the building. The wind could have opened the door. Or a squatter could have found his way down the road and decided the clubhouse was a better option than one of the cabins.

Either way, Clark didn't want to take any chances. In his right hand, he held a two-pound sledgehammer, his left arm extended, palm out and prepared to push anything away from him.

"Hello?" he called, stepping into the clubhouse. Clark glanced around. There was a smattering of wind-blown snow across the polished wood floor. All of the tables were covered with sheets. The backs of the chairs making each table look like a crowned ghost.

"Hello?" Clark called again.

Someone or something whimpered. The sound came from the back, near the kitchen.

He went to the right wall and crept along it, keeping an eye on the closed door to the kitchen.

"If you're in there, it's okay," Clark said, his voice breaking with fear. "I ain't going to press charges. You just need to get out."

He paused, then added, "Hell, if you need it, I'll give you a ride into town."

A pot or a pan rattled in the kitchen, and Clark stopped, a few feet from the door. The sledgehammer shook in his hand, and he switched it from his right to his left.

"Come on out now," Clark said, his voice hoarse, the words painful to speak.

I hope to God it's just a cat, he thought, and he took the last few steps to the front door. *Hell, I'd even be okay if it's a raccoon.*

The closed door was without a handle, a brass push plate instead of a doorknob.

His hand trembled and his fingers touched the cold metal. All the noise behind the door ceased, and Clark hesitated.

Then, with a sharp exhalation, he pushed himself forward, thrusting the door open. It bounced off the wall, rebounded, and cracked against his extended arm, numbing it. In the dim light filtering down through the skylight above, Clark saw a small shape hunkered in the far right corner. A pile of small frying pans was nearby, but Clark focused on the figure.

It looked to be a child, crouched low in the protection of the corner's darkness. The air was harsh and cold, smelling of something wet and foul.

"Hey," Clark said, his courage returning at the sight of the invader's size. "Hey. What are you doing in here?"

The child shook its head, long, dark brown hair hiding its face from him. A long, winding moan escaped from its chest.

"How did you get in here?" Clark asked, lowering the sledgehammer. "Are you alone?"

Still, the child refused to speak.

"Listen," Clark said with as much authority as he could muster, "you're in a lot of trouble. I'm going to have to call the cops, you know."

Clark stepped further into the room, letting the door swing closed behind him. When it had, a shadow to his left caught his eye, and Clark turned to look at it.

It towered above him, reaching from the old boards of the floor to the tin panels of the ceiling. Waves of cold emanated from the shadow and Clark took a horrified, fearful step backward. The sledgehammer fell from his hand, slamming into the floor and denting the wood.

Clark glanced over to the child, who had straightened up. Its face was pale, the features elfin and fine, the eyes wide and light blue. Clark couldn't tell if the child was a boy or a girl, its long, dark brown hair ragged and unkempt. A thick, dark gray, woolen blanket was wrapped around it. From the fabric's depths, a pale, thin hand clutched the blanket closed.

Clark opened his mouth, to ask what the creature was, to see if the child had come with it, but he couldn't.

The air was stolen from his lungs, his mouth robbed of his words as he realized he could see through the child. He caught a faint glimmer of the stovetop through the child's face. A sharp, piercing scream exploded in to the silence of the kitchen, dropping Clark to his knees. He clamped his hands over his ears.

A second later, his own scream joined the first as a cold and brutal hand grabbed his neck from behind, and started to squeeze.

Chapter 5: Driving

Over his lifetime, Shane had gotten used to many things, and he had eventually taken them for granted. One such item was the ability to drink coffee and drive a car at the same time.

When he had first driven as a teenager, it would have been impossible. He would have lived in fear of an accident with another vehicle, or of making a mess in the car itself. By the time he had reached forty-two, he could smoke a cigarette, negotiate the perils of traffic, drink his coffee, and curse roundly at other drivers.

Those days, Shane thought, looking down at the cup of coffee in the console, *are long gone and far away now*.

He hadn't mastered the art of driving the car with the remnants of his left hand, which would have left him with the opportunity to hold his drink with his right.

At least I can still smoke, Shane thought. He tapped the head of the cigarette into the ashtray, put the cigarette back into his mouth, and waited for the light to turn green. In a few minutes, he was following traffic down the ramp onto Route Three, and leaving Nashua behind him.

Nashua, Berkley Street, Courtney. He shook his head. *Leaving it all behind for a while.*

Part of him wanted to leave it all for good. If he didn't get some sleep and figure out how to make his world better, Shane knew he might have to.

He had no desire to die in his own house.

With a sigh, he pushed those thoughts out of his mind and headed north. The comforting sound of traffic, the monotony of it, and the complete lack of pressure allowed him to relax. He blinked, yawned, and felt sleep trying to steal over him.

Better find a place soon, he told himself.

Shane forced his eyes to stay open, and soon, a little distance past Boscawen, New Hampshire, he saw a sign.

Lake Nutaq, he read, nodding to himself. Another road sign after that informed Shane about the presence of a gas station, a McDonalds, and hotels. Shane signaled right and turned off the highway. The exit curved to the right, hooked back on itself towards the left, and in a short distance, Shane was at a blinking red light. An arrow pointed to the right and indicated the presence of the aforementioned hotels.

As he turned towards them, snowflakes began to fall. They struck the windshield and melted almost the instant they landed. Within a few minutes, they increased, and Shane had to turn on the windshield wipers. The sky had darkened, and Shane pulled into the first parking lot he saw.

It was for a Motel 6, and as he neared the front doors, he saw a sign that read, 'CLOSED! Thanks for a Great Season!'

"Damn," he muttered. He shifted into 'park,' turned on the radio and searched the channels until he found a news station.

"—change in the forecast," a man's voice said. "We know there wasn't supposed to be any snow until this evening, but we've had a cold front move down from Canada, right through the green mountains and it's slamming into New Hampshire now. It's looking like we could get those eight to twelve inches over the next four to six hours. Then there's the possibility the storm could spin around and come back at us once it hits the Atlantic. We are definitely looking at a Nor'easter."

Shane turned off the radio and looked at it, shaking his head. He shifted his gaze to the snow as it piled up on his windshield, melting slowly.

No time to get back to Nashua, he thought, turning on the wipers. The world beyond the car was smothered in snow, near whiteout conditions. *I'll die out here.*

He shifted into 'drive' and eased his way through the storm, pausing at the edge of the parking lot before turning onto the main road. Shane continued to creep along, eyes scanning either side for a house, or a business that had lights on.

Nothing, he thought, anger building up. *All the crap I've been through, and I'm going to die on the side of the road in a snowstorm. Nice.*

A sign loomed up out of the snow by a side street.

Preston Road Cabins.

Shane hesitated, then turned down the small road. If he had to break into a cabin, he could report it afterward, suffer the consequences, but at least be alive to do so.

The first of the cabins appeared on the left, and through the snow, Shane could see the shadows of others. He pulled up and then backed into the small driveway on the side of the structure. Grabbing his bag off the passenger seat, Shane turned the engine off and stepped out into the cold. The air was much colder than it had been down in Nashua, and each snowflake felt like ants biting into his face and head.

Book 6: Lake Nutaq

The sound of his boots on the porch was muffled by the snowfall. The door, not surprisingly, was locked. Shane twisted the knob, put his shoulder to the door, and popped the lock. He stumbled in, turned around, and slammed the door closed in an effort to keep out as much of the cold as possible. With the lock broken, he glanced around, saw a nearby side table, and dragged it over, using it to keep the door in place.

Shane stepped back and examined the small cabin, noticing the warmth of the room. From somewhere, an electric heater hummed, fighting the cold. He looked with disdain at the modern décor and the pretentious art, but then he chuckled and dropped his bag to the floor.

Don't judge, he told himself. *Just be glad you found a place to weather out the storm.*

Shane unzipped his coat and shrugged it off. He hung it on a peg by the door and wandered around the cabin. In the kitchen, he found some canned soups and the tap ran.

Well, Shane thought, *at least I won't starve.*

He made his way into the bedroom, found blankets in the closet, and a shelf of *Jack Reacher* novels.

And I won't be bored to death, he thought, nodding. He grabbed a book and went back into the main room. The electric heater, set against the right wall, continued to warm the room. Shane brought his bag, the blankets, and the book over to the heater, and turned an overstuffed chair around to face it.

He sat down, draped one of the blankets over his legs, and picked up the book. A pair of windows flanked the heater, which was designed to look like a stylized antique wood stove. It had smooth lines, too much chrome, and it stood out of place between the curtainless windows.

Beyond the glass, the snow came down in small flakes, thousands of them obscuring the world beyond. The shape of another cabin, perhaps twenty or thirty feet away, was all Shane could see.

He looked at the snow for another minute, then he shook his head and opened up the book.

Before he could get beyond the opening sentence, a scream caught his attention.

The sound sent a blade of fear through his stomach. For nearly a minute, the screaming continued, and in it, Shane could hear fury and rage.

His heart pounded, the pulsing of his blood audible in his ears once the screaming ended. Shane looked down, the book shaking in his trembling hands. He closed it, set the volume on his lap, and looked outside.

Only snow greeted him.

Laughter rang out from the storm, a sound racing through the snow to ricochet off hidden trees and unseen cabins. Voices joined the laughter, speaking in a tongue Shane didn't recognize.

He listened, though, tilting his ear towards the sound. And as he focused on the words, he understood them.

"We've another one," a male voice called out.

"We shall see what he is made of," others said, chanting the words.

"And if he is strong?" the male voice asked.

"We shall eat from his flesh," the others responded.

Shane closed his eyes, dropped his chin to his chest, and wondered what he had wandered into.

Chapter 6: Surrounded by Darkness

Clark couldn't see.

He was in complete darkness.

His arms were numb, pain throbbing in his shoulders.

A voice spoke suddenly, and Clark jerked away.

Laughter from many throats filled the air.

"Who are you?" Clark asked, wheezing, his breathing difficult. "What did I do?"

More laughter answered his questions. Low moans and strange, piercing shrieks served as a backdrop to Clark's new and painful world.

A cold hand reached out and touched his face.

Clark screamed, jerking his head away. Those around him guffawed. His nose detected the sharp, copper smell of blood.

"Please," Clark begged, "please let me go."

Something harsh and cold struck him in the chest, breaking a rib and forcing a scream out of him.

"Oh God," Clark moaned, "what did I do?"

Someone grabbed his jaw and pulled it down as he shrieked. The cold was unbearable, the pain spiking as fingers colder than ice reached into his mouth, took hold of his tongue, and ripped it out.

Blood exploded from the wound, and his head was jerked backward. Clark gagged and choked, trying to breathe. His head was shoved forward, and he vomited, the act accompanied by the laughter of his unseen tormentors.

When he had expelled all of the blood he had swallowed, along with his breakfast, Clark gasped for breath. He couldn't think, and when he tried to talk, the pain was excruciating.

Fingers pinched his nose and began to squeeze. As the cartilage broke, Clark screamed again, and darkness swept over him.

Excruciating pain, blazing into life from his groin, slammed Clark back into consciousness. Light flickered, waxed and waned until he could see. As blood filled his mouth and spilled past his lips, Clark realized he was still in the kitchen of the clubhouse.

The child he had seen was gone. In its place were four men. They were Indians, sitting on their heels. Paint adorned their faces, beaded chest-plates hung down from their necks, and their hair was shaved down to the skin while long, black scalp locks descended in thick tails. Dyed leather and feathers were woven into the hair.

The men smiled at Clark, the effect both gruesome and terrifying. It was worsened when he realized that they weren't quite there. He could see through them, as he had the child, yet as they smiled, their shapes thickened.

A voice spoke from Clark's left, a question from the sound of it.

The men nodded, and the speaker came around to stand in front of Clark. He recognized it as the dark shadow he had seen when he had entered the kitchen. Except now, the shadow had more definition.

It was a man, tall and clad in a bearskin cloak that reached from his shoulders to brush against the kitchen floor. Long, loose black hair hung down to the man's breast. Teeth, both human and animal, were woven into the strands and clacked as the man moved.

Clark could not see his tormentor's face since it was hidden by a large wooden mask, painted red and in a twisted mockery of a man's visage. The long, exaggerated nose was broken, bent at a harsh angle to the left. Through the carved eyes, Clark could see a glint, while a wooden tongue protruded from thick lips and pointed to the right. More hair fell from the mask's top, joining that of the wearer.

Hands slipped free from the cloak. They were large and thick, scarred and brutal in appearance.

And Clark knew he stood before the one who had tortured him.

The man raised his arms up, extending them out to either side, palms facing the ceiling.

Again, the man asked a question, and the laughter of the others filled the room.

The masked man nodded his approval. He stepped forward, and as Clark tried to jerk his head away, the man took hold of his throat.

The pain was immediate and intense, Clark's scream a little more than a gurgle. A single thumb was placed beneath his chin, and the masked man forced Clark's head up.

Clark tried to swallow as much of the blood from the root of his tongue as he could.

But there was too much, and soon he was gasping, coughing, sputtering. The gathered men laughed as Clark slowly drowned in his own blood.

Chapter 7: Stillness

Shane sat in silence, rubbing at the scars on his head as he thought about his current situation. Beyond the windows, the snow still fell. The cabin beyond remained obscured for the most part, and the hum of the electric heater filled the room.

Shane stretched and wondered if he had heard people, or if he had suffered from a hallucination. It was a possibility, considering how little he had been sleeping.

Plus I was seeing things in my own house, Shane reminded himself. He stood up and looked around for a clock, since he had left his phone at home.

He went into the kitchen and found a small digital clock on the countertop.

Four in the afternoon, he read, and shook his head. Shane looked out the window of the back door and could make out pine trees.

As he turned away, he stopped.

Something moved.

He looked back out the door.

A shadow. Nothing more. The barest hint of a shape. Small, and half-hidden by trees and snow.

Then it moved again, darting to the left and vanishing.

Shane shook his head. He reached for the doorknob, his hand hesitating a few inches from it.

That was a kid, he thought. Then he followed up his statement with, *It couldn't be. Not in this storm.*

What if it is? he asked himself. *What if there's a kid out there?*

Shane shook his head. *You know there isn't. There can't be.*

The back door's window had curtains tied up and out of the way. With a shaking hand, Shane undid the knots, let the fabric fall, and made sure he couldn't see out the window anymore.

Either you're losing it, Shane thought, turning to the cabinets, *or there's something out there. Neither one of those sound like a good idea right now.*

He took out a can of minestrone soup, found a can opener in one of the drawers and a pot under the sink. In a few minutes, he had the soup made and he carried the whole pan with a hot pad out into the main room. He went back to the chair, sat down on the floor, and began to eat.

Focusing on the act of feeding himself, Shane thought only about the soup. Mechanically, he moved the spoon from the pan to his mouth and repeated the process until he had finished all of it. The soup was warm in his stomach, and it felt good. He set the pan down on the floor and got back into the chair. Once more, he wrapped himself in the blanket and stared at the stove. The heat it sent into the room comforted him, but there was an itch at the base of his neck. Shane could feel something wasn't right, a strangeness in the air that he could notice on the edge of his senses.

Beyond the walls of the cabin, the wind picked up and Shane was thankful for the small, sound structure.

"Why are you here?" a small voice whispered, destroying Shane's sense of peace and safety.

Chapter 8: Perfect Weather for Sledding

Matt Rushford raced through the snow, bent over the handles of his new snowmobile, its engine screaming. The beam of his headlight refracted in the heavy snowfall as he raced through the snow. Even through all of his gear, the cold bit at him, the chill driven in by the speed of snowmobile's powerful chassis.

Behind him, Matt could hear his brother's snowmobile, the headlight flashing and flickering around him.

Matt grinned beneath the protection of his neoprene mask and revved the engine. He took off, aiming for the side of the road. Soon the plows would be out, and he and Mark would need to find another place to sled.

Through the haze of the storm, Matt saw the sign for Preston Road.

The chain's down, Matt realized, and he pulled over, coming to a sharp stop.

Mark came up beside him, and the two of them turned off the snowmobiles' engines.

"Are you serious?" Mark asked, straightening up and looking at him. Mark, in spite of being younger than Matt by three years, was taller and free of the ravages of acne.

Neither of which Matt appreciated.

"I've never seen the chain down in the offseason," Matt said. "Think Clark screwed up?"

"Naw, not him," Mark answered after a moment. "Probably Danny. He's half spun on meth most days. Anyway, what do you think?"

Matt chuckled. "I think we should go in there. Can you imagine? We'd be able to tear up and down the road, then we could just cut across Lake Nutaq. Ice is thick enough to bear the weight."

"Yeah," Mark said, nodding. "Even if it isn't, hell, we could skip over any wet spots."

"With the new sleds?" Matt said. "Definitely."

"Awesome," Mark said, and the brothers fired up the snowmobiles.

Matt got ready, and then blue lights flashed and danced. A powerful spotlight shined on the brothers and Matt groaned. He leaned back and shut the engine off. A glance over at Mark showed his brother had done the same.

A police pick-up truck pulled up behind them, and Rowan Little got out.

"What in the hell are you boys doing out?" Rowan asked, his hard voice cutting through the storm.

"Trying out the new sleds, Rowan," Matt replied.

The officer pulled his hat down lower, the harsh, angular lines of his face jagged in the glare of the pick-up's headlights. He frowned and shook his head.

"Boys," he said in a voice that brokered no sass, "your mother would kill me if I didn't send you back home now."

"Aww, Rowan," Mark whined. "Preston Road is open. We were going to cut across Nutaq."

Rowan looked over at the entrance to the road, his eyes widening in surprise. He shook his head. "Going to have to talk to Danny about this. Good thing you boys saw it and told me. Old Clark Johansen would have Danny's head if he found it unlocked."

"Can't we just cut across the lake?" Matt asked.

"Hell no!" Rowan snapped. "One of the Dube's lost their ice-house yesterday morning when he went out to check his traps. Ice cracked and took the house right down. Almost took him with it."

"If it was Norbert," Matt said, "he probably had a hundred pounds of meat pie stored in there."

Rowan snorted, grinning. "It was, and he probably did. Point is, there hasn't been enough time for the break to ice back over. I don't want you two boys trying to skip across the water. I don't care how fast those new sleds are, you could lose them, or die."

Matt and Mark remained silent.

Rowan went passed them, dug around in the snow for the chain, and dragged it up. In the lockbox attached to one of the posts, he found the padlock and he secured the chain.

"Now get the sleds started and turned around," Rowan said. "The storm's spun back around from the coast, and it'll be cutting back toward us. They say we've got another foot coming our way. The plows will be through soon, too. I'll follow you back to your mom's house. Unless you're keeping the sleds at your pa's?"

"No," Mark said. "At mom's. Dad doesn't know mom's new boyfriend bought 'em for us."

"Alright then," Rowan said. "Let's get the lead out, boys. Don't want to become news items, now do we?"

The brothers shook their heads.

As they started the snowmobiles, Matt looked at Preston Road.

Later, he thought. *Later on, I'll get onto that road and across the lake. No matter what. This sled can do it.*

With Rowan's pick-up behind them, the Rushford brothers headed home.

Chapter 9: A Voice in the Stillness

Shane held his breath and kept his eyes closed. He waited to see if the voice would speak again, and he hoped it was only a hallucination.

"Why are you here?" the voice asked again.

It was a young voice. That of a child, and it brought back horrible memories of his childhood. Those first nights in his room with Eloise coming through the door.

Shane took a deep breath, opened his eyes, and straightened up. He twisted around, facing towards the voice, but he couldn't see anything.

Maybe I am hallucinating, Shane thought.

A shadow flickered by the front door, behind the table he had propped against it to keep it closed.

"Why are you here?" the unseen child said. "This place isn't safe. Nothing here is safe."

"I'm here by necessity," Shane answered. "Not choice."

"It's still not safe."

"Why?" Shane asked.

"They're here. They don't like us. They hate us," the child replied.

"Who are they?"

"The Micmac," the child whispered. "They'll eat you. They're hungry."

Shane remembered the voices.

"Can I see you?" Shane asked.

The shadow moved, stepped into the room, its form solidifying. A thin child, wrapped in a blanket, stood before him. The hair was ragged, the face androgynous.

"What's your name?" Shane asked.

"Patience," she answered.

"I'm Shane," he said. "You're dead."

Patience nodded. "For long and long."

"May I ask how?" Shane said. He turned the chair around to face her, and he sat down.

"The medicine man, Broken Nose," she said. "He and the members of his lodge. They killed me. And my family. Our servants and all of those who sought refuge in Reverend Ezekiel's house."

"Broken Nose," Shane said. "Well, he sounds absolutely delightful. I suppose he's the one who's here?"

Patience nodded. "You need to leave, Shane. He will find you soon enough. Or one of them will. It doesn't matter. When they do, they will come for you, and they will kill you. They finished with the old man only a little while ago, so you have some time."

Shane began to ask why, and then he remembered the stories he had read as a boy. The tales of Indian captivity, the way some of the prisoners would be tortured to death. All in an effort to see whom among them was the strongest.

"An old man?" Shane asked instead, straightening in his chair. "Someone was screaming, but I thought I was hearing things in the storm."

"Yes," she said, her tone mournful. Patience shifted, adjusting her blanket as a moan penetrated the cabin's walls. "He seemed a kind man to me. But it matters not now. He is dead. Broken Nose is upset, for they can no longer partake of a captive's flesh. Not that he would have been worthy. The old man screamed far too much."

Shane sighed. He glanced down at his bag and remembered that he didn't have any iron with him. Or his phone. Or salt.

Nothing. Shane thought. *Not a Goddamned thing.*

"You need to leave," Patience said.

"I've no way to go," Shane said. "The storm will kill me."

"Better death from the storm than at his hands," the girl said. She opened her mouth to say something else and then stopped.

"He's looking for me," she whispered, and vanished.

Shane sat in the chair, tapped his fingers on the arm several times, and then stood up.

Maybe there's some salt in the pantry, he thought and prayed to God there was.

Chapter 10: Frank Comes Home

Frank opened the door to the house on Berkley Street, shaking his head as he did so. It still amazed him that Shane didn't lock the place up.

But why should he? Frank asked, chuckling as he closed the door behind him. *He's got the best damned security system there is.*

He took off his jacket, brushed the snow off it, hung it up, and sat down on the chair. With quick motions he untied his boots, pulled them off and sat back, sighing. Frank tilted his head to one side, listening.

Silence greeted him.

He frowned. "Shane?"

No answer.

Frank stood up, went down to the study, and peered in.

It was empty.

Frank's pace increased as he made his way to the kitchen. Looking out the back door, he couldn't see Shane's car. The small parking space was empty, filling with rapidly falling snow.

Where the hell would he have gone? Frank asked, letting the curtain drop back into place. He got a Gatorade out of the refrigerator, breaking the seal on the bottle as the door swung closed. *Why would he have gone out?*

An image of Courtney flashed through his mind and Frank winced. Even though the dead had taken her ghost into the depths of the house, her screams could still be heard in the dark hours of the night.

And if I can hear them, Frank thought. *Well, then Shane can hear her.*

Frank took a long drink from the bottle, capped it, and put it down on the counter by the sink. He took a deep breath and called out, "Carl, are you around?"

From a shadow, alongside the refrigerator, Carl appeared. The slim, studious looking ghost gave Frank a short bow, a look of concern on Carl's face.

"Carl," Frank said. "Do you know where Shane has gone?"

"I do not," Carl said, shaking his head. His words were clipped and precise, tinged with a German accent. "He left some time ago."

"I believe," Carl said, his voice taking on a tone of restrained concern, "that Miss DeSantis' nocturnal laments have caused Shane far more distress than he is ready to admit."

"Yeah," Frank said, nodding. "It's bad for me, and I've only ever known her as a ghost."

"Yes," Carl agreed. "We try our best to keep her quiet, but she is far stronger than one would think. Especially given how young she is, for one who is dead."

"Fair enough," Frank said. "I'll take your word on it."

Frank pulled his phone out of his pocket and called Shane's cell. It rang on the other end, and a heartbeat later, the sound of Shane's ringtone filled the hallway.

Surprised, Frank hurried out of the kitchen, his own phone to his ear as he followed the sound of the phone. The noise came from the study and Frank stepped in, ending the call as he did so. Shane's cell was on the coffee table in the room's center.

Frank turned and saw Carl in the doorway.

"Did he say anything to anyone at all?" Frank asked.

Carl shook his head. "All he said was that he wanted to take a drive."

Frank sat down in one of the chairs and rubbed the back of his head. He sighed and looked down at Shane's phone. A small, green light flashed at the top, a reminder of a missed call.

Something in Frank's stomach twisted, and he felt, deep within his guts, that Shane was in trouble. He hesitated, then reached out, picked up Shane's phone and started to scroll through the contacts. When he found the number he was looking for, Frank dialed the number from his own phone and waited for someone to answer.

Chapter 11: Questions Asked

Shane did find salt in the pantry.

Only about a third of a container of it, and not nearly enough to do anything other than make a ghost laugh.

Still, he thought, *what the hell.*

He carried it with him back into the front room, holding the depressingly light cardboard container in his hands as he sat down.

"Hello."

Shane squeezed the box in surprise as he turned to look behind him.

Patience sat on the floor, staring at him.

Shane wrapped the blanket back around him and returned the dead girl's look. Minutes of silence passed, then Shane shook his head and said, "Tell me, does Broken Nose kill people often?"

"No," Patience said. "Hardly ever. We sleep for most years. It is rare for a storm to awaken us, and when it does, we tend not to see anyone."

"How many of you are there?" Shane asked.

Patience thought about the question, shrugged and answered, "I am not quite sure. I have seen close to a hundred in some storms, in others only a handful. We don't matter, though."

"No?" Shane said.

She shook her head. "Only Broken Nose matters. He is the one who has gathered all of our threads together. He is the common link."

"How so?" Shane asked. "Did he kill you all?"

"No," Patience answered. "Not all of us."

"Then how does he link you all together?" Shane asked, frowning.

"He ate all of our hearts," she answered.

The calm, easy way in which Patience spoke the sentence caught Shane off guard, and it took him a moment to get his wits back together.

"Hold on," Shane said, lifting a hand. "You're telling me he ate your heart?"

"Mine and many others," Patience said, nodding.

"Why?" Shane asked, his voice low and thick with horror.

The girl straightened up, a small smile playing on her face. "Because I withstood the torture well. I was judged to be strong enough."

A wave of revulsion swept over Shane. He kept it hidden, though, and he nodded his head. "Of that, I have no doubt, Patience. You seem extraordinarily strong to me."

Her smile broadened.

"Has he eaten any more hearts since his death?" Shane asked.

Patience shook her head. "He must put all of his concentration into consuming their energy. He is like a leech. Broken Nose will latch on to a soul, and sup upon it if he feels it is worthy."

"Why?" Shane asked, confused.

"Power," Patience said. "Life eternal. For himself and his braves. And for me. The hearts he consumed as a living man gave him power after death. Those souls that he feeds upon now, they allow him to thrive. He is like a great bear, yet he hibernates in the mellow seasons and awakes only in the bitterest of winters. It is then that he hunts and seeks out fresh souls. The stronger the soul, the more power he obtains."

"Have there been many others?" Shane asked.

"No," she replied. "We have awoken only a handful of times. And only twice has he kept the newly dead bound to him."

Patience paused, then grinned. "You know, he may keep you close when he has killed you, Shane."

"Wonderful," Shane murmured, and beyond the walls of the small cabin, the wind picked up, howling in the growing darkness. "When will he come for me?"

"He hasn't even noticed you yet," Patience said. "Perhaps, when the storm lessens, he will wander about, but he will not stray when the storm is at its height."

"Why's that?" Shane asked.

"He is afraid of becoming lost in the storm," she confided, her voice low. "I have heard, from others, that he did become lost once, as a child, and it was in a storm. I wish he had never been found."

Shane rubbed his chin with his diminished left hand. "Will he come looking for others?"

Patience nodded. "He has always done so. I hope you can get away, Shane. He will be pleased to find you, and his pleasure is a horror to behold."

"Is there a place where–" Shane began, but the widening of Patience's eyes silenced him.

"He's looking for me," she hissed and vanished.

Shane sighed and looked down at the salt in his hands.

Wish there was more, he thought and stood up. He walked to the window and looked out at the cabin next door. He smiled, nodded and thought, *Maybe there is.*

Chapter 12: On the Phone

"It's Frank, and I need help."

Frank waited, his heart pounding in his chest.

"What's wrong?" Brian Roy asked.

The tension in Frank's shoulders lessened, and he said, "Shane's gone."

"Gone where?" Brian said, and before Frank could answer him, Brian added, "Never mind. Stupid question. You wouldn't be calling me if you knew where he was."

"No, I wouldn't," Frank responded.

"Alright," Brian said. "Obviously, he's not answering his phone. What do you need me to do?"

"Is there a way you can find him?" Frank asked. "I don't know if you have someone you could speak with or not."

"Like a medium?" Brian asked, a dark humor in his voice.

"Whatever works," Frank fought to keep his words free of exasperation.

"I don't have a medium," Brian said, his tone becoming serious. "But I do have a friend who can look into it. He knows Shane."

"How long will it take?" Frank asked.

"Depends on where Shane is," Brian answered. "And how soon I can get in touch with my friend."

"Is he hard to reach?" Frank said.

"Depends," Brian said.

"On what?" Frank snapped.

"On whether or not you think it's hard to get in touch with the dead. I'll call you when I have something," Brian said, and he ended the call.

Frank took the phone down from his ear and looked at it.

He stuffed it into his back pocket and walked over to the fireplace. Carl stood off in a corner, watching him.

"Carl," Frank said, "do you think it would be alright for me to remain in the study while we wait for news on Shane?"

Carl bowed slightly. "I do believe it would be fine. I shall inform the others."

"Thank you," Frank said. Carl left the room through a wall, and Frank went to the fireplace. He took some wood out of the bin, set it in the irons, and soon had a fire going. Frank sat down in the chair nearest to the hearth, pulled his phone out of his pocket, and held it.

He closed his eyes and waited for Brian to call.

Chapter 13: Danny Swings By

The transmission screamed as Danny worked the gears, profanity streaming out of his mouth and filling the interior of the truck. He finally got the pick-up to shift, dropped the plow, angled it to the right, and pushed the snow away from the entrance of Preston Road.

In front of him, Danny saw the remains of snowmobile tracks and a pang of jealousy struck him.

Wish I was out there sledding, Danny thought. He had seen the Rushford brothers at the Kawasaki dealership in Manchester, chatted their mom up and saw the boys were getting new snowmobiles.

Well, Danny thought, getting out of the truck, *after this storm, I should have a good chunk of change to put down on a new ride.*

He hurried to the chain barrier, unlocked it, and brought it to the other pillar, hanging it up so he wouldn't lose it in the snow.

Danny slammed the door shut. He raised the blade and winced at the way the hydraulics sounded, the plow mount shaking on the front of the truck. Danny shifted into reverse, checked the mirrors for lights, and backed up. The plow slammed down onto the pavement, and Danny shifted hard.

Just one pass through, he told himself. *I can do clean-up on it later. Run some salt out as well.*

Danny had a full load in the back of the pick-up, not the cheap salt and sand mix the State wanted him to use. No, Danny had a good, solid load of rock salt prepped, the spreader ready. He could treat Preston Road on his way out, and it would make clean-up easier after the storm ended.

And what the residents and the State don't know, he thought, grinning, *well, then it won't hurt them, will it?*

He angled the blade first to the right, dumping the snow off that way first, and then he stopped. For a second, he thought about the snowmobile tracks.

What if someone follows me in? he wondered. *Oh hell, I better lock it.*

When Danny climbed back out into the storm and started towards the chain, he came to a sharp stop.

A car was parked in the small driveway of the first cabin.

There hadn't been one there before, and Clark hadn't said anything about one of the residents coming up.

Anger flared in him, and Danny shook his head. *Wonder if they're even supposed to be here? Probably not. Probably a teenager looking for a place to get it on.*

Danny stomped back to the chain, ran it across the road, and locked it in place. He glanced at the car, which was covered in snow, and spat in disgust on the ground.

I'll deal with them after, he told himself, getting back into the warmth of the truck. Danny focused on the work at hand, and he went through the routine of getting the road open for his truck.

The visibility was slim, and it wasn't until he was almost on top of the clubhouse that Danny saw Clark's van. Exhaust slipped out of the tailpipe, but there was snow on top of the vehicle's roof, and it had piled up around the wheels.

Where the hell is he? Danny thought, dread infecting him. Then fear for Clark spiked through his chest, wondering if he had had a heart attack or maybe even a stroke.

Danny eased the plow forward, coming to a stop behind the van. He sat in the truck, gripping the steering wheel.

Danny glanced at his cell phone, but he knew Preston Road had miserable reception. He wouldn't be able to get any emergency help unless he was up on the main road.

Maybe he doesn't even need help. What if he's in there fixing a window or something? I'll look like an idiot getting the cops down here. Aw hell, I'd never hear the end of it.

Danny's decision was made for him.

He threw the truck into 'park' and got out, stomping through the snow up to the driver side window of the van.

Clark wasn't in it.

Danny's throat went dry, feeling like sandpaper as he swallowed. His heart thumped in his chest, and he couldn't seem to breathe fast enough.

Suddenly, and for no reason he could understand or identify, Danny was afraid of the clubhouse.

Terrified of it.

Danny backed away from the van, retracing his steps to the pick-up. He stumbled once, caught himself on the cold metal of the plow, then turned and ran for the safety of the truck's interior. Danny scrambled inside, slamming and locking the door behind him. His hands shook as he fumbled for the shifter, and ground the gears. The truck bucked, shimmied, and the engine seemed to gasp as it threatened to stall.

Somehow, it didn't, and Danny forced it into 'drive.'

The pick-up surged forward, the plow smashing into the back of Clark's van. Glass shattered and metal crumpled. The plow's mounting system collapsed and a hydraulic line burst, spewing steaming hot fluid across the white snow.

Danny tried to find 'reverse,' shifted into 'second' instead, and pushed the van forward, the front of it crashing into the clubhouse's porch. He pulled the shifter down, found the right gear, and backed up. Both rear doors of Clark's vehicle came away with the plow. The iron blade of the plow threw up a cascade of sparks, each brilliant, orange flare drowned by the snow.

Gripping the steering wheel with white-knuckled hands, Danny clenched his teeth as he used the mirrors to get back up on to Preston Road. The rear-end of the truck slid from the left to the right, Danny fighting it to keep the pick-up in the center of the road and keeping it from crashing into one of the other cabins.

Adrenaline surged within him, fear heightening all of his senses.

Danny heard the creature before he ever saw it.

He glanced out the windshield and screamed.

A terrible, dark shape moved towards him. It was larger than a man should be and the snowflakes shimmered as they passed through it. The face was hideous, a twisted visage with an equally bent and mangled nose and wild hair which wreathed it.

Danny snapped the wheel hard to the right, tried to shift on the go, and the engine stalled.

Danny's screams were muffled by the snow as the door was ripped off the pick-up, and he was dragged out into the storm.

Chapter 14: An Awakening

The unmistakable shriek of metal being torn shattered the stillness, the noise ripping Shane out of a restless daze.

He straightened up in the chair, his neck throbbing with discomfort. Instinct kicked in, and he sat still, listening.

Over the sound of the heater, Shane heard an engine and something heavy dragging across the asphalt.

Book 6: Lake Nutaq

A single, smooth motion brought him out of the chair and to the door. He side-stepped to a window and hesitated as the thrum of the motor he had heard vanished, swallowed by the storm.

In a heartbeat, a scream pierced the snow, and Shane risked a peek out of the window to the door's right.

A pick-up with a plow mount was cockeyed across the street, the headlights illuminating snowflakes. Shane saw the driver, a young man in his twenties, in the arms of Broken Nose. The dead Indian had a hand wrapped in the driver's hair and dragged him around the front of the plow.

Shane clenched his hands into fists, frustrated as he watched, unable to help. He had no iron, nothing to attack the dead man with, and save the living. Shane ground his teeth as Broken Nose and his newest victim vanished into the storm. There was a chance, albeit a slim one, to draw on the energy of Preston Road. To drain off the power pulsating in the cold air, but he had done so only a few times, and only when the dead were willing.

Too risky, he seethed.

Shane stood at the window only a moment longer, then he backed away, turned towards the chair, and stopped.

Still cautious, Shane returned to the door, peered out the window once more and looked at the truck.

Is there salt in the spreader? he wondered. Shane looked hard at the plow blade, saw the dark metal, and grinned.

The yellow plow was old, a battered, curved piece of metal that had seen better days. And the cutting edge on the plow wasn't made of steel. It was a long, thick piece of iron bolted onto the bottom of the curve.

One piece of the edge was broken, hanging by a single bolt.

Shane wondered if he could manage to get it free. As the question crossed his mind, he felt as though he could, and the lights on the plow flickered and went out. Darkness fell upon the world and obscured the pick-up from him.

Shane left the window and returned to the chair. He picked up the blanket and the salt, and made his way to the small bedroom he had seen. His steps were slow and careful. The cabin was unfamiliar, a place in which to be cautious. After what seemed like several minutes, Shane crossed the threshold and was pleased to see, in the room's near perfect darkness, a single window.

He crept up to the window, took the salt, and poured a thin line out on the sill, sealing it as best he could. He tossed the blanket onto the bed and returned to the threshold. Shane gave the salt container a shake and nodded. He knelt down on the floor and used the last of it.

Shane sighed as he realized there wasn't enough.

Making certain not to disrupt either of his seals, Shane closed first the door, and then drew the curtains over the window. When he finished, Shane retreated to the bed. Lying on his back, Shane stared up at the ceiling.

His mind raced as he tried to force his body to relax. He knew he needed to rest, and he understood that he would be no good to the plow driver, weaponless and exhausted. Stepping out into the storm, where the cold and the falling snow would help hide the signs of a ghost approaching would be tantamount to suicide.

Yet he was tormented by the desire to do something, anything.

With a shudder, Shane repressed the urge to get his cigarettes and forced himself to think about what needed to be done.

Do I have a chance of getting him out? Shane asked. He let the question sit unanswered for some time as he considered his options.

If I can get the iron off the plow, I have a weapon. If, he thought, *the truck has rock salt in the back then I have a way to secure the cabin.*

Shane sighed.

Those are two big ifs, he thought.

And I can't even do anything in the dark, Shane reminded himself. *I have to wait for dawn. A light will bring attention, and I already know Broken Nose isn't a nice guy. Do I even know if Patience is good?* he wondered. *Will any of them be? Will she be the only one?*

The questions caused his stomach to churn and tighten. He took a long, deep breath, exhaled slowly, and repeated the steps several times. When he felt a sense of calm return to him, Shane closed his eyes, put his hands on his stomach, and interlocked those fingers he had left.

Shane knew he needed sleep, but he wouldn't do anything more than allow his body to rest. Sleeping would be too risky, the man might die while Shane dreamed.

Every part of him screamed to go for the driver, tried to convince him it could be done, that he would find the man, and weapons, in the blinding storm.

And Shane almost believed it.

An ululating scream, high and piercing, shattered his thoughts and reminded him of the many unknowns that lurked in nor'easter beyond the cabin walls.

His body tightened, but he kept his eyes closed. The sound rose and fell, grew and shrank. It was in one breath, everything and nothing.

On an instinctual level, Shane knew the scream wasn't one of pain. Rather, it was Broken Nose's announcement of victory.

A sound of celebration.

For the first time in years, Shane prayed, and it was a simple, honest prayer.

Please, God, Shane thought, *let me get to him before he's killed.*

Chapter 15: In Mont Vernon

Frank felt strange as he stood on the porch of Brian's house. Sadness had settled in him on the long, dangerous drive up from Nashua in the snowstorm. Shane's absence felt wrong, as though some darkness was preparing to wrap itself around the man.

With a sigh, Frank shook the thoughts away and knocked on the door. It opened a moment later, Brian Roy waving him in.

"Go on into the den," Brian said, locking the door behind him.

"Thanks," Frank said. He unzipped his jacket as he entered the room, sitting down in one of the chairs. Logs crackled and popped in the fireplace, the room was warm and comforting. Frank wanted to close his eyes and go to sleep.

Brian sat down across from him, rubbed at the stubble on his bald head and asked, "Have you had any word yet from Shane?"

Frank shook his head.

"I didn't think so," Brian said, sinking back into the chair. He picked at a loose thread before he added, "I owe him, you know."

"I didn't," Frank confessed. "All he ever said was that you two were friends."

"Jenny thinks he's great," Brian said with a wry smile. "He did a lot for both of us. I have, well, a friend who can help us find him. If he can be found."

A cold sensation settled into the pit of Frank's stomach. It was the same feeling he had suffered in Afghanistan when he would come upon the bodies of men and women butchered.

"I hope he can be found," Frank managed to say, "and that he's alive. Shane's been good to me."

"Feeling's mutual," Brian said. "So, you've got no issues with ghosts, right?"

"Right. I just need to know he's okay. This storm's tough." Frank said.

"Okay," Brian said. Then, to someone behind Frank, he said, "Come on in."

The temperature in the room plummeted, and Frank shivered. A shape passed by on his right and went to stand beside the Brian. In a heartbeat, the dark shape took on definition, revealing the ghost of a young man. He was a curious looking figure, dressed in a long coat and his hair wild.

"You are the one who is looking for Shane Ryan," the ghost said. His words were clipped, pronounced precisely.

"Yes," Frank replied.

The ghost nodded. "He is a difficult man. Strong, though. Incredibly strong. Has he ever told you about Berkley Street, and what exactly occurred there?"

"Not all of the details, no," Frank answered.

"You should ask Shane Ryan some time," the ghost said. "It would be most enlightening, especially if you are considering a prolonged period of exposure to the dead."

"Okay," Frank said, smiling in spite of the seriousness of the situation.

"Yes," the dead man said, nodding, "yes. You should. But I digress. I must search for Shane Ryan. I wanted to make certain he is all right. You see, I am not inclined to betray his trust. He is a good man."

Before Frank could agree, the ghost vanished.

As the warmth of the fire filled the room again, Frank looked at Brian.

"He's a curious fellow," Frank said.

Brian grinned. "You don't know the half of it. It was a shame, what happened to him, but that's another story, for another time."

"Fair enough," Frank said. He glanced around. "You've got a nice place here."

"Thanks," Brian said. He picked up a cigar from the edge of an ashtray, put it between his lips and lit it. After he let a thick cloud of smoke out, blowing it towards the ceiling, he smiled at Frank. "Jenny's out. Otherwise, I'd have to smoke this in the study. She hates the smell. Do you smoke?"

"No," Frank said. "I did for a while in the service. Especially when I was in Afghanistan. It's a good way to pass the time with the Muj, you know?"

"I'm going to take your word on that," Brian said. "Only interaction I had with the Muj was calling down fire on them, and making sure they didn't figure out where I was."

"Good call," Frank said. He looked around the room, feeling on edge. An irritating feeling of helplessness was settling over him. He wanted to be out, looking for Shane. With a deep breath, he forced a smile and tried to think of something to talk about, something to distract himself from Shane's situation.

"You know," Frank said after a minute, "I saw what the Muj could do when they were really upset with someone."

Brian raised an eyebrow.

"A member of a Pakistani force beat the hell out of one their elders," Frank said. "I don't know why. Sometime in the night, some Muj from the nearby village snuck into the Pakistani compound and grabbed the man they wanted. We found him the next morning."

"What'd they do to him?" Brian asked.

"What the Muj did," Frank continued, "was strip the skin off the Paki. Left him alive, too, nailed to a tree on a little rise. If you were in the house of the old man who was beaten, you would have been able to see the Paki perfectly with a pair of binoculars."

"Christ," Brian murmured. "How long did it take for him to die?"

"Not long," Frank said, looking down at his hands. "I blew his brains out."

Brian cleared his throat and shook his head. "Tough to live with that."

"Yeah," Frank agreed. "Yeah, it is."

"I have found Shane Ryan," the ghost said, causing Frank to jump.

The dead man went and stood by Brian once more.

"What's going on with him?" Brian asked. "Is he alive?"

"He is," the ghost said. He hesitated, then added, "Although I do not know for how much longer. It seems he has stumbled into a bit of trouble."

"Where is he?" Frank asked, his chest tightening.

"Lake Nutaq," the dead man said. "In a cabin on Preston Road."

"What's the trouble?" Brian asked.

"There is a ghost there. Well, more than one in all actuality," the ghost said, then frowned. "They are, for the most part, extremely unpleasant. I was informed, in no uncertain terms, that I was not welcomed on Preston Road. They did not afford me the opportunity to speak with Shane, and I did not believe it would be right to ask them if I could."

"Why?" Frank asked.

The dead man looked at Frank and answered, "Because they were torturing a man to death when I stumbled upon them."

"Torture?" Brian said. "Torturing a man?"

"Yes," the ghost answered, nodding. "They had removed his eyes and had taken his ears as well. The one in charge seemed quite adept at it, actually."

"Damn," Frank said, shaking his head.

"We'll get you ready for whatever's up there," Brian stated. "I've still got plenty of gear kicking around. Couple of shotguns. Plus we can preload shells for them with rock salt."

"Do you have any iron?" Frank asked.

Brian nodded. "Yeah. A set of rings. They're good for close encounter combat, but I'd refrain from that as much as possible."

"Definitely," Frank said. He sighed. "Glad you have the gear. I'd hate to have to go all the way back to Nashua for my gear. Hell, I don't even know where Nutaq is."

"North," Brian said. "Other than that, I don't know. We'll get it all squared away though."

"It would be better to do so sooner rather than later," the dead man said.

"Yeah, usually," Frank said, angry at the situation Shane had put himself in. "But Shane is alright?"

"For now," the dead man said. "When they find him, however, I am quite certain they will torture him as well."

"How," Frank said, his words tight, "can you be certain of that?"

"Because," the ghost said, "there was a corpse hanging beside the man being tortured."

Chapter 16: Shane Gets Ready

"Shane."

He turned his head and looked at the doorway.

Patience stood beyond the threshold, her head tilted to the right. She held her blanket around her as she watched him.

"Hello, Patience," Shane said.

"What is on the floor?" Patience asked. "Is it salt?"

"Yes," Shane answered. He rubbed at the remnants of his left ear.

"Curious, is it not," she said, squatting down to examine the line of the salt.

"What is?" Shane asked.

"This," she said, gesturing towards the salt. "I cannot cross over it. I even tried to come through the window, to see you and to speak with you. But I could not. Do you have salt on the windowsill as well?"

"I do."

"Why?" Patience said.

"I didn't want Broken Nose to come in," Shane said. "At least not this room."

"He won't," Patience said. "Not yet."

"The young man," Shane said. He sat up. "I'm on my way to find him."

Patience raised an eyebrow. "How will you stop him?"

Shane shrugged. "Don't know. I need to get the guy out."

Patience nodded. "Broken Nose is extremely interested in the man."

Shane hesitated, then asked, "Is Broken Nose torturing him?"

"Only a little," Patience said in an offhanded manner. "When they tore off the young man's clothes, they found that he is marked."

"Marked?" Shane asked, sitting up. "What do you mean? Scarred?"

"Pictures," she said. "Some of them are beautiful. Others are frightening. Skulls and the faces of demons."

"Tattoos," Shane murmured. "Broken Nose finds them appealing?"

Patience nodded. "They are finely wrought. I do believe Broken Nose is searching for a way to keep them once he has finished with the young man."

Shane shook his head, checked his pockets, found his cigarettes and lighter, and then lit one. He exhaled smoke and looked at the dead girl.

"You're not bothered by it?" Shane inquired. "The torture? The fact that Broken Nose wants to skin this kid and keep the tattoos?"

"I wish these events would not occur," Patience said. "But I am dead. I lack the strength to go against Broken Nose. Or any of those who side with him."

Shane smoked in silence then asked, "Do you want to be free of him, Patience?"

"No," she answered.

Shane blinked, surprised. "No?"

She shook her head.

"Why not?"

"There is no other world than this one," Patience replied. A hard, surprisingly old look took over her delicate face. Her tone grew harsh. "I was raised to believe in God. A God who demanded devotion, and devotion would be rewarded with a place in His kingdom. This did not happen, Shane. I was good. I went to Church. The commandments were learned. I knew the parables. The psalms were familiar friends."

An angry scowl settled upon her face. "And look at me. My family was killed around me. I witnessed the horrors as Broken Nose tortured us all. Only I was strong, for I had faith in Him. I clung to that faith. I prayed in silence while I smelled human flesh burn. And then, when I was promised by Broken Nose that we would defeat Death, he consumed my heart."

Patience pulled her blanket tighter around her narrow shoulders. "Because he ate my heart, he kept my soul. There is no Heaven. Nor is there a Hell."

She stood up.

"There is only Lake Nutaq, Broken Nose, and the snows which free us," Patience said. "I hope you free yourself. And I will pray for you, because even now it is still a comfort to me, even though I know it should not be. It is nearly dawn, Shane. You will need to leave here when the sun breaches the horizon. This new man will keep Broken Nose occupied for only a short time."

"I can't go," Shane said, pinching out his cigarette and leaving the butt on the floor.

"Why not?" she asked, surprised.

"Because I won't leave the young man to be tortured any more than I have to," Shane said, standing up. "I have to try and help him."

"Then you'll join him." Patience sighed. "I hope your death will be quick, Shane."

She stood up, shuddering. A deep, multi-voiced moan filled the cabin.

"Broken Nose is wandering," Patience said. "Make your peace."

She turned and left, disappearing into the darkness.

Shane waited a moment, then he zipped his coat up all the way, pulled on his gloves and took a deep breath. It was time to try and save the driver.

Squaring his shoulders, Shane stepped over the line of salt and headed for the door.

Chapter 17: Anxious and Concerned

Frank sat at the kitchen table across from Brian, who frowned at his phone.

"Everything alright?" Frank asked.

"Yeah," Brian said, shaking his head as he put the phone on the table. "Worried about Jenny, is all. She's going to stay the night at her sister's place. The roads are terrible in Merrimack. Probably all over the state."

Frank nodded. The weather report hadn't been good. Not only had the storm come back from the Atlantic Ocean, but it had also settled down on the whole of New Hampshire, southern Maine, and all of eastern Vermont. The entire area was getting an average snowfall of an inch to two inches an hour, with some spots getting three an hour. It was worse than the Blizzard of '76.

"We've got a spare bedroom upstairs, if you'd rather stay here than risk the roads," Brian offered.

"Yeah," Frank said. "I appreciate that."

"Wish I could be on the road to Lake Nutaq now," Frank said, "Think we can figure out where it is now? And who the hell might be haunting it?"

"Sure. We haven't lost power yet," Brian said, standing up. "Let's go in the study. We can do a little digging if you want."

"That'd be great," Frank said. He followed Brian out of the kitchen and walked down the short hallway. Brian's study was small, neat, and extremely organized. "Damn."

Brian grinned as he sat down at his desk. "I've discovered that cleaning helps me relax. And that's worth its weight in gold after a couple of heart attacks."

"A couple?" Frank asked, glancing over his shoulder as he went to the hearth. The mantle was a single, long piece of granite. Photographs of Jenny, young men in uniform, and what looked like a World War 2 era wedding occupied places of honor on the mantle. The groom wore an Army uniform with sergeant's stripes and a lot of ribbons.

"Those were the guys in my platoon," Brian said, the keys of his laptop clacking beneath his fingers.

"And the wedding picture?" Frank asked.

"My grandparents," Brian answered. "On my dad's side. Tough man. Fought in Europe during the Second World War, then in Korea."

"That's impressive," Frank said.

"Yeah," Brian said, "he was a hell of a man."

Frank turned away from the pictures, he was anxious, the desire to leave, to do something, was eating at him.

"Hey, take a seat," Brian said, gesturing to a chair by the desk. "I'm connected, and I pulled up a site on the history of Lake Nutaq."

"A whole site?" Frank asked, sitting down. "What is it, a tourist one? Come and swim in our unseasonably cold, dark water?"

Brian snorted with laughter. "No. Looks like it's done by someone who was looking at the supernatural aspect of it."

Brian angled the laptop as Frank shifted the chair as well.

The website was barebones, a generic background of headstones. On the left of the screen was a map. Ads for psychics and tarot readings scrolled by on the right.

But the middle was the meat. Paragraphs of text. A few highlighted words and phrases, embedded links to other sites.

Frank leaned forward, and he started to read.

> *Lake Nutaq, from the Micmac word 'to hear' is said to echo with the voices of the dead. Unlike most theoretical haunted places, Lake Nutaq does not have a long, and storied history of unexplained deaths. What it does have, however, is a brutal history.*
>
> *In 1675, a small community of English colonists was established near the lake. They called their village Williamstown and lived in an uneasy peace with the local Micmac tribe. The Micmacs were heavily influenced by a member of the False Face Society, a medicine man who took the name of Broken Nose. When King Philip's War broke out in the lower sections of the Massachusetts Bay Colony, the Micmacs received word, and Broken Nose convinced his followers to attack the colonists.*
> *The colonists, who numbered only forty-seven, retreated to the house of Reverend Ezekiel Williams. Per tradition, the Reverend's house was the strongest, fortified and prepared in case of an attack.*
>
> *Unfortunately for the colonists, Broken Nose was adamant that the house be taken. After a four-day siege, which was an extremely unusual tactic for the Native Americans of the time, the house was taken. Forty-six of the people within were dragged out. Nathan, the reverend's ten-year-old son, managed to hide himself in the roof, crammed between the thatch and a joist. While he was unable to see what occurred next, young Nathan was quite able to hear.*
>
> *The members of his father's congregation were tortured to death.*
> *The process took three days, and the entire time, Nathan remained hidden. He did not leave the garrison until he heard the King's English being spoken by a group of militiamen.*
>
> *These men were led by Adam Hawkins, a resident of Williamstown, who had managed to slip away from the siege. He made for the nearby town of Reach and gathered a patrol of militiamen.*
>
> *The militiamen approached the rear of the house and made the horrific discovery of the bodies of the colonists. Several accounts remain of what they saw, and all speak of the dead, of how more than a few of their chests had been cracked open, and the hearts removed. It was not unheard of for some of the Native Americans to practice limited acts of cannibalism, especially after dealing with a particularly worthy opponent.*

Jesuit missionaries in New France had reported how the Native Americans believed that by consuming the heart of a man or woman, the cannibal gained both the power of the individual, as well as gaining power over that individual.

Eventually, Broken Nose died, but not at the hands of anyone other than Time. He died of old age, somewhere near Lake Nutaq. The reason for this was simple. Those militiamen who attempted to go after Broken Nose's Micmacs rarely returned. The houses of the slain colonists fell into disrepair, and the forest reclaimed them over the decades.

Nathan was lost to history, being sent back to England to live with relatives in Surrey. It wasn't until the conclusion of the French and Indian War, nearly a hundred years after the massacre of the colonists, that white people returned to Lake Nutaq.

There was no immediate supernatural event when they did so, although six years after they arrived, a pair of hunters vanished in a snowstorm. After the storm had subsided, others in the community sought them out. Three days had passed before the bodies were found. Both men had been stripped naked and tortured to death. One had his chest ripped open, and the heart was gone.

While the deaths were disturbing, they were not the most unsettling aspects for those second settlers. What bothered them was the lack of footprints. It was obvious to the men who found the hunters that the bodies were fresh. No more than a day old, which meant that the storm had finished and no new snow had fallen. Yet the snow was unbroken.

Decades had passed before another incident was recorded in the history of Lake Nutaq. Three men, looking for a new logging site, were swallowed by a storm. These men were found nearly a month later. Their remains had been mauled by the animals, but, like the hunters, the men were bare and tortured.

It was then that the rumors began.

Similarities between the deaths were pointed out. Someone noticed that the men had been killed in a way much the same as those who had died in the raid of Broken Nose's Micmacs.

Over the decades, only a few others have been killed. All have been found like those reported. In addition to that, the bodies are always discovered in the same location, without fail. While there hasn't been a disappearance since the Blizzard of 1976, the authorities knew exactly where to look.

A small, private road, home of the Preston Cabins. They are empty in the off-season, the privileged owners far from the brutal New England cold, and the voracious, vengeful ghosts of Broken Nose's Micmacs.

Frank sank back into the chair.

Brian got up, went to a small cabinet, and took out a pair of tumblers and a bottle of bourbon. He poured a healthy dose into each of them and handed one to Frank.

Frank nodded his thanks as Brian returned to his seat.

"This is not good," Frank said, breaking the silence.

Brian shook his head. "Does Shane have any of his stuff? Anything at all?"

"I don't think so," Frank replied. "I mean, why would he? Carl said he was going for a drive. It's not like Shane expected to run into ghosts."

"No," Brian said, sighing. "No. Why would he?"

Frank took a drink of the bourbon, the liquor strong and smooth as it slid down his throat. "If this snow doesn't stop soon, he'll be dead."

"Well," Brian said. "Here's to it ending soon."

The two men finished their drinks.

"Come on," Brian said, standing up. "Let's get the gear together, so you can get out of here as soon as a plow unburies us."

Frank nodded, stood, and prayed the storm would end soon.

Chapter 18: A Long Night

Shane was familiar with long nights.

And he hated them.

He moved out of the cabin, across the porch and hesitated. In the darkness, he could hear the dead. The voices of the Indians were loud and brazen, drowning out the night sounds of the forest. Shane looked at the wrecked snow plow, and went down the steps. The snow was up to his knees, chilling his flesh.

Shane managed five more paces and froze.

A pair of dead men appeared, their backs to him. They chatted, their words rising and falling. The wind carried bits of their conversation to him, and Shane learned that the driver was still alive.

Shane's eyes darted to the broken piece of iron, his heart racing. He tried to judge the distance, the time it would take him to cover it and tear the metal free.

If it were even possible.

He forced himself to try, and then held his breath.

Two more dead Indians joined the first pair, and Shane knew he had no chance.

His stomach tensed and the adrenaline which had fueled his efforts fled, leaving him with a nauseous feeling. Shane's hands trembled and his heart rumbled. Forcing himself to breathe in a steady, normal rhythm, Shane edged back to the cabin. His eyes never left the dead men, and soon he found the steps to the porch.

Up he went, silently and carefully. He moved across the threshold like a wraith and he managed to close the door without a sound. The effort to move the table quietly into place against the door caused sweat to explode across his brow and down his spine.

But he succeeded.

With his entire body shaking, Shane retreated to the bedroom.

He sat down on the bed, stripped off his jacket, and sighed, both angry and depressed.

"You're still here," Patience said from the doorway.

Shane jumped.

"I didn't mean to scare you," Patience said, sitting down on the floor.

"That's okay," Shane said, forcing a smile. He dragged the blanket up and wrapped it around his shoulders. He got himself a cigarette and lit it.

"So," he said, anger rising up, "Do they talk about anything other than torture?"

Patience shook her head, then looked at him with surprise. "You know their language?"

Shane nodded. "It's a little gift I have."

"Ah," she said. Patience looked at him a moment longer before she said, "No. Torture is all they think of. The four with Broken Nose, they were his most loyal. They know that only through torture, will the strength of the victim be revealed. It is only the strong ones that Broken Nose needs. He has no desire to leave this world, and neither do they."

"Have you ever asked him to let you leave?" Shane asked.

Patience gave him a small smile as she shook her head. "Why would I try and ask for something I know he would not give?"

Shane shrugged. He glanced around and asked, "How's the storm out there?"

"It is worse," she replied. "Broken Nose is angry. The world is not moving the way it should."

"What does that mean?" Shane asked, confused.

Patience nodded. "He feels the storm is too long as if he is being punished. He is fearful too, although he will not show it. But I know."

"How?" Shane inquired. "How do you know he's afraid?"

"We are close," Patience answered. "Far closer than any of the others. I always know when he is afraid."

"Is that why you know when he's looking for you, too?" Shane asked.

"Yes," Patience said. She adjusted the blanket. It was a rough, dark material and looked as if it had been woven on a loom. Her hands clutched it closer, and other than her head, they were the only parts of her which could be seen.

Shane had a sudden, sickening idea of her body's appearance beneath the blanket.

"Were you killed in that blanket?" he asked her.

Patience nodded. "At the end. I was bare before that. It was easier for them to work upon me. To prepare me, I suppose."

"For death?" Shane asked.

"Yes," Patience said. "And Broken Nose felt it would be proper for me to die in something of my own people. My clothes had not survived the ordeal. Nor did my flesh. He was surprisingly considerate when it came to the blanket."

"I'm sorry," Shane said.

"You have no reason to be sorry," Patience said, smiling. "You were not the one who tortured me to death. And you were not the one who ate my heart."

"I'm saddened that you had to suffer," Shane said, and he choked on the words, realizing for the first time how hard it was to look at the girl.

"Thank you," she whispered. "I suffer still."

"Where is your body?" Shane asked her.

Patience tilted her head and looked at him with curiosity. "Why?"

"If you want," Shane said, "I can salt and burn your bones. It would free you."

"Free me?" she repeated, her words so low Shane had a difficult time hearing her.

"Yes," he said, leaning forward. "I can free you. You would be able to go to wherever you're supposed to go next. Even if it's nothingness."

The low, pained moan filled the cabin, and Shane tried to ignore it.

Finally, the sound faded and Patience asked, "And what of them, Shane?"

"Who?" Shane asked. "Broken Nose and his faithful?"

"No," Patience said. "The others. What of them? Those who are bound? What will become of them once I am freed?"

"Patience," Shane said, "I don't know what you're talking about."

The dead girl stood up, her hands tight upon her blanket.

"Will you look upon me?" she asked in a grim voice. "Will you see what was wrought upon my flesh?"

Shane wanted to say no.

He wanted to scream it.

Instead, he nodded and whispered, "Yes."

Patience shifted her grip on the edges of the blanket and extended her arms to either side.

The sight that greeted Shane both revolted and fascinated him.

Her arms had been shredded, flesh hanging in long, curling strips from the bones. Huge chunks were missing from the muscle mass. The bones of her ribs and sternum had been broken, pulled outward to form a brutal, gruesome flower. Each bit of yellowish bone a grotesque petal.

None of these compared in horror to what Shane saw where Patience's organs should have been.

Instead of her stomach and liver, her heart and her lungs, there were faces. Dozens and dozens of faces, all of them stuffed into the small, scraped out cavity. Their eyes were wide. Some in shock. Others with pure terror. A few were outraged. The majority looked numb.

As Shane watched, the faces twisted and moved, swirling in a maddening pattern. At the edge of clarity, he heard whispers. Most were prayers, a few curses. Some babbled, incoherent and insane.

"What of them?" Patience asked, closing the blanket again and returning to the floor. "What will happen to them if I am freed?"

Shane shook his head. He tried to push the image of what he had seen away and found he couldn't.

"How?" he managed to ask.

"I don't know," Patience answered. "Broken Nose stuffed them into me. Each soul. As the years have passed, he has added others. Not many. Only one or two at a time. But there they are, and there they have remained. When he is hungry and feeling weak, I must go to him so he could feed. I let him feast on the strongest, and I make sure none are devoured. So you must tell me, Shane, what will happen to them if I am freed?"

Shane shook his head and whispered, "I don't know."

Chapter 19: Getting Out

Shane had not fallen back to sleep after Patience had left the cabin.

Instead, he had remained upright, chain smoking until he ran out of cigarettes. By the time the light of dawn could be seen around the edges of the curtain, the world had gone silent beyond the cabin. No longer could he hear the screams of the driver. Part of Shane wondered if the man was even alive; if it would be worthwhile to try and rescue a corpse.

I need to know, Shane thought, wincing as he stood up, his legs aching. *I can't leave him.*

Shane walked to the window, trying to forget what had been beneath Patience's blanket.

But he failed.

How? he asked himself. *How could anyone do that to a child? How could it be done to anyone, at all?*

Shane shook the thought away and came to a stop in front of the window. His hand faltered as he reached for the curtain. He chuckled at his fear, took hold of the edge of the fabric, and pulled it back a fraction of an inch.

Beyond the glass, the world was white. Perhaps, in a calmer, safer place the scene would be beautiful. Worthy of a photograph or a painting.

Shane couldn't see the beauty. Instead, he picked out those places where he could be ambushed. Shadows, clumps of trees, hidden corners. The damaged and abandoned truck was a large lump of snow, only a faint glint of silver on one of the mirrors revealing it for what it was. But beneath the white were tools Shane could use.

The iron edge of the plow.

Rock salt, if he had any sort of luck at all.

Sand, he thought grimly, *if my luck holds true.*

Shane looked down at the line of table salt on the windowsill. He let go of the curtain and turned away as it fell back into place. Shane strode out of the room, stepping over the threshold and making sure he didn't disturb the line of salt. He stayed focused on the task at hand. From the back of the chair, he took his coat, pulling it on and buttoning it. Next, came the gloves, the last two fingers on the left empty. His hat came last, pulled down low over the scars and vicious mementos of other battles against the dead.

Finally, Shane turned and faced the door which led out. He moved the table out of the way, the hinges squealing as the door swung in. Shane caught the edge of it, gripped it, and looked out.

The truck was fifteen feet away with almost twenty-four inches of snow.

Shane stepped out onto the porch, and then waded through the snow, pushing his legs forward. The cold slapped him in the face, bit through his jeans and sought to freeze his toes in his boots.

He grimaced and forced himself to the truck. When he reached it, he had driven the cold from his mind, and he was able to concentrate. Quick movements cleared the snow away from the bottom of the plow. He grinned as he found the broken edge of the blade. A cursory examination showed the metal hung only by a single bolt to the plow's frame, the bolt itself sheared more than half way through.

Settling his weight down in his hips, Shane crouched, grabbed the iron with both hands, and twisted. For a heartbeat, the iron refused to move, and then the bolt broke, a sharp cracking sound muffled by the snow.

Breathing hard, Shane held the broken blade up. He looked at it, nodded, and stood up. He took a quick glance around and saw nothing had changed. Rapid steps brought him to the pick-up's side and the snow-covered tarp tied down over the spreader and the treatment in the bed.

Shane grabbed an edge with his free hand and forced the tarp up.

Rock salt, Shane thought. *Rock Salt.*

He moved back to the driver's side door, which hung drunkenly off one broken hinge. Shane glanced inside and saw several empty grocery bags and an equally empty coffee cup. He grabbed them and brought the items to the rear of the truck. Shane set the blade down on the pick-up's rear fender, doubled the bags, and used the cup to scoop salt into them.

He finished in less than a minute, holding the bag in his left hand, and picking the blade up in the other.

Shane turned and faced down Preston Road. Cabins were on either side and at the end was another building. He took a deep breath and listened, hoping the driver was still alive, and that he would make some noise to prove it.

Chapter 20: Mark Makes a Decision

"No school today, guys," Matt's mother said, pulling her coat on.

Matt sat up in bed, rubbing his eyes hard enough to cause stars to explode against the inside of his eyelids.

"No?" Mark asked from across the room.

"Nope," she said. As she buttoned against the cold, she looked at Matt. She had worry lines around her mouth and crow's feet that spread far and wide from the corners of her eyes. Years earlier, her hair had turned gray, and she had clipped it short, a constant reminder of how their dad had left her and the boys, high and dry.

She adjusted her glasses, wrapped a scarf around her head, and said, "Now listen. I need you boys to bring in some wood and clean the house for me today."

Matt groaned and sank back to his bed.

"Why?" he whined.

"One," she said, a harsh note heavy in her voice, "because I told you to. Two, because as soon as you're done, you and your brother can take the new sleds out for a spin."

Matt sprang up, grabbing onto the headboard to keep himself from falling off onto the floor.

"Really?" Mark asked.

"Really," she replied. Their mom smiled at them. "Go eat. Just because school is canceled doesn't mean work is. I'll give you boys a call around two. Make sure you're here for the call."

"Yes, mom," Matt and Mark said in unison.

"Good," she said, nodding. "Love you both. Behave today."

And without waiting for them to lie about behaving, their mother left, closing the bedroom door behind her.

Matt looked over at his brother and saw his own excitement mirrored in Mark's face. Laughing and shouting they got out of bed, changing from pajamas into jeans and sweatshirts. They left their bedroom, and went to the small kitchen, dug out a box of Cheerios and ate cereal for breakfast. Matt got up and went to the sink, washing the dishes while Mark left to see to his own chores. A moment later, the vacuum cleaner started, the whining sound of its engine filling the house.

The two brothers raced through their chores, but they didn't sacrifice quality for speed. Their mother would make them do the work over again, as well as denying them the privilege of riding the sleds if they made a bad job of it.

Soon the inner chores were done, and the only one left was lugging wood in. The two brothers thundered down the stairs, past the wood stove, and into the basement to look at the bin. It was nearly empty, which meant they would have to stock it.

But Matt and Mark had a rhythm.

"Ready?" Matt asked.

Mark nodded.

They pulled their gloves on, and Matt grabbed the canvas carrier they used for the wood. Mark propped the basement door open, a blast of cold air tearing past them. Matt gritted his teeth against the weather and stepped into a knee-high snowdrift. He pushed through it to the cord of wood stacked against the barn.

When he reached it, Matt took hold of the blue nylon tarp that protected their fuel from the worst of the elements and peeled it back. He secured the tarp with a log, and then spread out the canvas carrier. The fabric was a faded brown, torn and frayed from years of use, but the black nylon straps of the handles were still strong.

Matt took down the split wood, a piece in each hand, and tossed it down to the carrier. When he had ten pieces on it, Matt took a handle in each hand and picked all of it up. He struggled through the snow to the open doorway where Mark waited. Matt dumped the wood on the basement floor, turned around and went back to the woodpile to repeat the process.

Halfway through it, Matt switched with Mark, taking the dumped wood and stacking it in the bin.

"One more," Matt said shortly, and Mark nodded. As his brother went back to the barn, Matt closed the flue on the stove. The fire would burn slower, and the house would stay warm enough to keep the pipes from freezing.

When Mark returned, the two of them finished with the bin, put the carrier away, and left the house through the basement. They left the door unlocked and followed the path they had made to the barn. Matt led the way to the front, slid the right door open, and closed it once Mark was in.

Daylight came in through the windows in the old stalls, shining on the new snowmobiles. The brothers opened a slim door, flicked on a light, and pulled their riding gear out. Matt grimaced as he put on the warm outer clothing, his undershirt wet with sweat.

I'll be cold enough, he thought, zipping up his coat and then folding over the protective flap and velcroing it into place. More than one rider had gotten frostbite by not dressing warmly enough.

"Ready?" Mark asked, tossing Matt his helmet.

Matt nodded, tugged his helmet on, and secured it. It had a new visor, a polarized one which meant he didn't have to worry about goggles or neoprene masks.

Once Mark had his helmet on, Matt walked to the barn door and opened it enough for them to get the sleds out. When they started the snowmobiles, the sound of the engines filled the barn and brought a delirious grin to Matt's face. He nodded to Mark, and his brother led the way out.

Matt followed.

He had no idea where Mark wanted to go, and he didn't care. Their mother was working, school was canceled, and the brothers had all day to get into trouble.

They cut through the field connecting them to the Davidson Farm and hit the trails Mr. Davidson had made for his own family. The sleds flew along the snow, approaching a fork. Mark, without hesitation, turned left and Matt let out a laugh.

They were headed towards Lake Nutaq.

Time to see how well this thing skips, Matt thought, leaning over the handles and following as close to his brother without getting buried in the tail spray.

Chapter 21: At Berkley Street

At four in the morning, a plow had shown up on Brian's street, and by six, Frank had made it back to Berkley Street. Frank stood in the study. The weapons and gear he needed were already prepared, but he needed to speak to Carl, to ask a question he had not even posed to Brian.

Frank had kept his idea to himself as Brian had printed out a map to Lake Nutaq, in the event that cell service had been interrupted by the storm and the GPS was unavailable. And while they had looked at the best way to get there, the two of them had made an attack plan.

It was simple and straightforward. Go in, heavily armed, find Shane, and bring him out. There was always the possibility Frank would be too late, and that he would only be able to recover Shane's body, but he would deal with that later. Frank crossed his arms over his chest and thought about what to do next.

The roads had been terrible on the way back from Mont Vernon. It was only seven and Frank wasn't certain how clear the highway would be. The traffic reports online hadn't been encouraging. Multiple car accidents. At least two fatalities. All of Route Three South, from exit six to exit four was shut down as firefighters attempted to extract someone from beneath a tractor-trailer.

I have to wait, he thought. *No matter what. I have to wait. At least a little bit. An hour. No more. No more than that.*

"Frank?" a voice asked.

Frank turned around to see the little dead girl, Eloise, in the doorway.

"Hello," he said, smiling at her as he went and sat down in one of the room's leather club chairs.

"Hello," she said. "May I come in?"

Frank nodded.

When she entered, the room chilled, steam rising from his mug.

"Where is Shane?" she asked.

"Somewhere up north," Frank answered. "I'm going to see him soon."

"To bring him home?" she inquired.

He hesitated, considering, for a moment, a lie. But he decided against it. "I hope to. If it is not too late."

"Is he in trouble?" she asked, her voice and expression serious.

Frank nodded.

"You should bring Courtney," Eloise said.

The girl's suggestion caught him off guard.

"What?" he asked when the surprise wore off.

She nodded. "She'll be able to protect him."

"How do you know," Frank began, but he stopped as Eloise arched an eyebrow.

"There are few people in the world of the living who would be a danger to Shane Ryan. It is the dead we should be concerned about the most, and one who is already dead," she said, "would serve as an excellent defender."

"Hold on," Frank said, shaking his head. "I can think of a lot of better options than Courtney. She's not exactly stable right now and I think you know this."

Eloise gave him a pitying look. "Whether or not her madness controls her is of little importance. She would be more inclined to save him for the sake of being able to punish him herself."

"That," Frank said, sighing, "is some of the most twisted logic I have ever heard. Why couldn't you or Thaddeus or Carl stand by him?"

"We are all bound to the house," Eloise explained. "Our bones are tucked away. She is attached to his necklace, and thus can go where she is needed."

Frank groaned and shook his head. "I can't believe I'm actually saying this, but I think you're right."

"I know I'm right," Eloise said, smiling. The smile faded as she said, "Speak with Carl. He will bring Courtney to you if you demand it. But you will need a way to carry her and to keep her bound. She will kill you if she gets the chance."

"Yeah," Frank said with a sigh. "I figured she would."

"Would you like me to get Carl for you?" she asked.

Frank nodded.

"Frank," Eloise said. "After you're home with Shane, would you play with me?"

The request brought a smile to his face. "Yes. What would you like to play?"

"I want a tea party," she said, straightening up and grinning. "Do you drink tea?"

"I do."

Eloise clapped her hands and vanished, leaving the echo of her dead joy behind her.

Frank shook his head at the curious nature of the request and finished his drink while he waited for Carl.

Chapter 22: Not a Nightmare

When Danny opened his eyes, two thoughts crossed his mind. The first was that he had been stupid enough to drink Jagermeister again. The second was that the nightmares were the worst he had ever suffered through.

After being awake for less than thirty seconds, Danny understood two important facts. One, he hadn't been drinking Jagermeister, or anything else. Two, the nightmares had all been real.

He found himself in a kitchen. Blood was splattered all over the polished floor, the stainless steel appliances, the walls, and the ceiling. Clark was hanging by his wrists beside him.

Or it had at one time been Clark. A large scar ran from the left hip to the right nipple. Clark had told him about how a chainsaw he had been using had struck an unseen nail in a pine tree. The chainsaw had kicked back, cut through Clark's leather apron, sweatshirt, flannel shirt, and a tee-shirt.

Danny could only imagine the chainsaw injury had been the equivalent of a caress in comparison to Clark's final moments in the world.

Panic built up in Danny's chest, trying to force its way out through his mouth, but he clamped down on it. He shuddered as he looked around the kitchen, saw the bits of bone and flesh scattered about like a child's discarded playthings. It was then he realized he couldn't move his arms, and for a split second, he harbored the fear that both limbs had been cut off.

He straightened up and yelped.

His arms weren't gone, merely tied behind his back and, judging from the burst of pain he had experienced, he had been suspended by them.

Gasping, Danny tried to get his feet under him, and it was then he saw the damage that had been done.

All his toes were gone. Only bloody, mutilated stumps remained, and a memory flashed through his mind. The dark creature with the wooden face, the distorted nose, and the cold, freezing touch. Danny recalled the sound of the bones and teeth as they clacked against one another in the beast's hair.

Gagging, Danny dragged his gaze away from his tortured feet and tried again to straighten up. He knew it would be certain death if he waited for the creature to return.

Better to freeze to death if I can't get the truck started, Danny thought.

He twisted his head around to see the cord which held him up, and he vomited. The bile was thin and hot, and it stank as it struck his chest before hitting the floor and his feet.

Danny hadn't been suspended with rope, but rather long strips of skin woven together. And, judging by the state of Clark, the dead man had supplied the raw material. With his eyes watering, Danny turned away, breathing through his nose and ignoring the taste of regurgitated coffee and donuts in his mouth.

Danny tried to pull away from the skin, but it was too strong, tied too well to a hook in the ceiling. The panic built up within him again, and he couldn't fight it. Death would be coming for him in the form of the beast that had grabbed him and ripped him out of his pick-up.

He began to hyperventilate, twisting to the left and the right, desperate to get away. His feet slipped in the vomit, and without the traction of his toes, he jerked forward and down, the skin robe pulling up sharply.

Danny refused to scream; afraid it might bring more attention to him.

Fearful of reminding the creature of his presence.

Danny, close to winning the battle against panic, heard the front door open, and let out a long, fearful shriek.

Chapter 23: Moving Down the Road

It had taken Shane the better part of half an hour to get from the damaged plow to the house at the end of Preston Road. He had focused on a white van as his beacon. Its rear-end smashed in and the front jammed into the shattered remnants of the front porch.

If he's still alive, Shane had rationalized, *then he's got to be in there.*

Why else would he have run from it, to begin with? Shane asked himself.

He had climbed up, around the splintered wood and broken glass, and onto the porch. The front door was closed, and Shane gripped the knob, took a deep breath, and twisted it sharply, thrusting it open before him.

A long groan, the sound of metal grinding on metal, came from the door's hinges.

And in less than thirty seconds, a scream ripped out of the back of the small building.

The driver! Shane thought, and he launched himself forward. The scream had come from behind a door set in the far wall, and when Shane reached it, he lowered his shoulder and barreled through.

He entered a vision of hell and had to close his mind against it.

Instead, he focused on the naked plow-driver suspended from the ceiling.

Shane dropped the bag of salt, snatched a knife out of a butcher's block, and cut the foul looking braid from which the man hung. The man collapsed to the floor, his screaming growing hoarse, but still far too loud.

Shane gave the man several slaps across the mouth, stopping only when he saw the light of reason appear in the younger man's eyes.

Fearful, the naked plow driver whispered, "Who are you?"

"Doesn't matter," Shane hissed. He took the man's hands, cut the ties, and ignored the man's whimper of relief. "Get dressed. Quick as you can."

"My feet," the man sobbed.

Shane glanced at them and repressed a shudder at the sight of the absent toes.

"It looks like your clothes are in the corner," Shane said, ignoring the man's feet. "Get 'em on."

The plow driver nodded, crawled, and started to get dressed.

Shane listened and wondered where the dead had been. Part of him was curious as to how they would react to their missing victim. Shane grinned at the thought and shot a quick look at the driver.

The man had managed to get a sweatshirt on and was struggling with his pants. Shane walked over, grabbed the man's boots and socks, stuffing them into the bag with the rock salt.

"I don't think I can walk," the man said, looking down at his mangled feet.

"I know you can't," Shane said. "I'm going to put you over my shoulder. We're going to the last house on the right. If I have to drop you, that's where you crawl to."

"Drop me?" the man asked, his voice rising.

"If," Shane reiterated. "Now get ready, and let's get the hell out of here."

The driver nodded, and Shane snorted as he got down and put the man in a fireman's carry.

He's not too heavy, Shane thought. *You can do this.*

Ignoring the man's weight, the discomfort, and the growing pain, Shane left the house. He fixed his gaze on his cabin and moved towards it in a straight line. No need for stealth. No need for subtlety.

Shane pushed through the snow, the man on his shoulder weeping.

By the time they reached the porch of the cabin, Shane's entire body screamed in outrage, muscles demanding that he put the man down. Drop him to the floor and stumble into the cabin.

No one gets left behind, Shane thought. It was the Marine Corps' mantra. No one was ever left behind.

No one.

Shane pushed the door open and dumped the man without ceremony onto the couch. The man sobbed as Shane staggered back to the door, pushing it closed, and jamming the end table against it. Without pause, Shane went to the bedroom and put the bag of salt on the mattress. He kept his grip on the iron edge of the plow and stumbled back to the driver.

The young man looked up at him, eyes red and wet with tears.

"My name's Danny," the driver said.

"Shane."

"This is real," Danny said. It wasn't a question, and the desperation in the young man's voice was painful to hear.

Shane nodded. "It is. We need to get you into the bedroom, and it's going to hurt."

"Okay," Danny whispered. He gripped Shane's hands and allowed himself to be pulled to his feet.

Danny bit down on his lower lip hard enough to cause blood to well up and spill out of the corners. Together they crossed the short distance to the threshold.

"Step over the salt," Shane said. "Don't disturb it."

Danny didn't ask why, but did as he was told. Shane got Danny to the bed, eased him down, and set the bag of salt on the floor. It was then that Shane examined Danny's brutalized feet.

The toes had been ripped out of their sockets, shreds of ragged skin visible in the half dried, oozing wounds.

They need to be cleaned, Shane thought. *Cleaned and bandaged. Probably cauterized too.*

Shane straightened up and said, "I'll be right back. Stay on the bed."

"I'm not going anywhere," Danny hissed, his eyes clenched shut.

Shane went to the kitchen, rummaged around, and found a bottle of whiskey tucked in the far back of the pantry, hidden behind a roll of paper towels. He paused at the small, two-burner stove, and wondered if the electric coils could heat up the iron enough to cauterize the wounds.

No, Shane thought, shaking his head. *It's not worth the pain it would cause him. No way to be sure.*

He left the kitchen and went to the bathroom, where he found a first-aid kit in the medicine cabinet. It had the basics, as well as some anti-bacterial cream that had expired but it would have to do.

Shane took the supplies into the bedroom and found Danny breathing hard and fast, clenching the blanket in his fists. Danny's eyes opened and locked onto Shane.

"You've got to clean them, right?" Danny asked, his voice raw.

Shane nodded.

"Okay," Danny said. "Let's get it done."

"Yeah," Shane agreed. "Let's get it done."

Shane unscrewed the whiskey's cap, looked at Danny, and said, "Big breath, Danny."

The younger man nodded, inhaled through his nose, the muscles in his jaw standing out.

Shane splashed the whiskey out of the bottle, onto the ragged, red wounds. Danny let out a muffled howl and fainted. Shane set the bottle down, applied the anti-bacterial cream to the bandages, and wrapped Danny's feet quickly. He had bandaged many wounds, most of them far worse than the younger man's missing toes.

When Shane finished with the first aid, he sat down on the floor, the air in the room thick with the mingled smells of sweat, blood, and whiskey. Shane picked the bottle up and took a long drink from it. The liquor was cheap, burned as it went down, and was perfect.

Well, he thought, looking at the bottle. *If I die here, I hope I die drunk.*

Shane took another shot and wondered how long Danny would remain unconscious.

Chapter 24: A Conversation with a German

"I don't think your idea is particularly wise," Carl said.

The ghost stood by the entrance to the study, his hands by his side, his pose distinctly military.

Frank shrugged. "It probably isn't. I don't see what other options I have, Carl."

"Gott in Himmel, my friend," Carl said, shaking his head. "Do you not know she is a mad woman? Death has made her so. Yes?"

"I'm not going to argue that point with you," Frank said. "I know she's crazy. I think I'm going to need her insanity if the situation is as bad as I was led to believe."

"How will you contain her?" Carl asked.

"Salt," Frank answered. "It seems to have worked so far."

"It did, but it will not always do so," Carl said.

"What?" Frank asked, unable to keep the surprise out of the question.

"She is extremely capable, and she has managed to slip free of our own bonds upon her," Carl grumbled. "And on more than one occasion."

"How?" Frank asked, shaking his head in confusion. "She shouldn't be able to get out. Not at all."

"I know. I agree." Carl sighed. "We are still attempting to discover a permanent way to contain her, without shattering her spirit to the distant corners of the earth."

Frank frowned. "It doesn't matter. I need her with me. I'll have to take the chance."

"There is," Carl said, hesitating as he spoke, "another option. One not as mad, but equally dangerous, I am afraid."

"What?" Frank asked.

"Not 'what,' but 'who,'" Carl said. "And the 'who' is The Englishman."

"Who is The Englishman?" Frank asked, displeased with the chill the word created within him.

Carl walked to the mantle and nodded to a wooden rosette which graced the top of the left column. "Not even Shane knows of him. The Englishman was trapped and sealed long before Shane's family took possession of the house. And he is here, behind this flower, which is appropriate, I suppose, in its own curious way."

"How is he dangerous?" Frank asked, getting to his feet and walking to the fireplace.

"He was a killer, in his youth, as so many of us were," Carl replied. "I am saddened. We learned of him, later on. He was a lover of war. And of death. The urge to kill was strong, and one he chose not to ignore. A lynch mob caught him here and hung him from a tree which is no longer here. When his spirit raged through the halls of the house after it was first built, they found him and bound him. For his freedom, I believe he would help you, Frank. But it is a risky endeavor. He may well decide to harm you both instead."

Frank considered it for a heartbeat, and then asked, "How do I get to him?"

"The fourth petal of the rose," Carl said. "Press it, wait until you hear the click."

Frank did so, and a moment later, the petal clicked. When he removed his hand, the entire rosette sprang out, swinging on a silent hinge to the left.

The back of the decoration was lined with lead. And the interior was the same.

Resting upon the dull gray metal was a bright, gold button. In the light of the room, Frank could see three letters, 'KRR' surrounded by a wreath which met on either side of a crown.

He glanced at Carl, and the ghost nodded.

Frank's skin prickled with anticipation. The small hairs on the back of his hand stood as he reached in for the button. His fingertips touched the cold metal, and a shock raced through his flesh, jolted his bones, and sent him stumbling backward. He hit a chair with his hip, spun on it and fell.

Carl yelled something in German as Frank scrambled to his feet.

In front of the hearth stood a tall man with wild hair, wearing ragged clothes. The man's broad face was a mask of both madness and rage, and Frank felt fear seize him. A primal part of him demanded that he run.

If I run, I'll die, he thought, and he forced himself to stand and wait to see what The Englishman would do.

Chapter 25: Patience is a Virtue

Shane was well on his way to being drunk when Patience called once more to him from the doorway.

He turned to face her, squinting.

"Hello," Shane said, setting the half-empty bottle down beside him.

"You left a blood trail," she said, eyeing the whiskey with disdain. "I covered it as best I could."

Shane pictured the dead girl in the snow, moving it somehow, and wondered if the ones trapped within her had helped as well.

The thought was instantly, and disturbingly, sobering.

He straightened up.

"Thank you," he said.

She nodded. "He is alive."

"Yes," Shane replied.

"Did you see his markings?" she asked, keeping her blanket tight around her as she tried to look into the room.

"I didn't notice," Shane confessed. "I was concerned with his rescue."

"Yes," she said, smiling. A serious, concerned look settled onto her small, elfin face. "Of course. They are quite interesting. But Broken Nose will not be happy when he returns and finds this man gone."

Shane nodded. "I'm sure. This young man is Danny, by the way."

Patience craned her head forward, stopping at the unseen barrier created by the salt.

"Is it short for Daniel?" she asked shortly.

"I assume so," Shane said.

"Daniel is a good, strong name," Patience's tone was one of approval. She sat down, adjusted her blanket, and waited as Shane turned himself around to face her.

Shane reached for his cigarettes, remembered he had smoked them all, and dropped his hand into his lap.

"Are you not well?" Patience asked, tilting her head to one side.

"I'm fine," Shane lied. "When do you think Broken Nose and his friends will be back?"

"I do not know if they are friends," Patience said, frowning.

"The other Indians with him," Shane said, trying not to sound exasperated. "When will they all be back?"

"Sooner, rather than later," she answered. "There was a curious noise coming from the Lake. They went to investigate the sound."

Shane straightened up. "There might be time then."

"To escape?" Patience asked.

"Yeah," Shane said, getting to his feet. "Yes. Definitely. I need to see if the car will start."

Patience shook her head. "Do not leave the room, Shane."

"Why not?" Shane asked, turning away from her and grabbing his car keys out of his bag.

"It isn't safe," she replied.

He glanced over his shoulder at her. "It's never going to be safe. And what's different about today? Yesterday you were telling me I needed to leave as soon as possible. What's changed?"

Patience looked down at the floor and said nothing.

Shane stiffened and turned around. An uncomfortable feeling crept up from the base of his spine, settling in the base of his skull.

"Patience," Shane whispered. "What has changed?"

She looked up at him, tears in her eyes, the brown pupils expanding and retracting. Several minutes seemed to pass, the two of them looking at each other.

Shane opened his mouth to ask her a third time, but instead she spoke.

Her voice was raw. Each word clipped and precise.

"Yesterday," she said, "Broken Nose hadn't told me to keep watch on the driver. Yesterday, he had not wanted me to kill the man."

Dropping his bag to the floor, Shane walked back to the whiskey bottle. He sat down, took it into his hands again, and sighed.

Patience didn't speak or show any dismay as he took three long, noisy gulps from the bottle. When he finished, he wiped his mouth with the back of his hand, put the bottle on the floor, and said, "So, what the hell do I do now?"

"Put him outside," she whispered.

"I can't," Shane growled.

Patience nodded, stood up, and vanished.

For a short time, Shane stared at the place where she had been, then he picked up the bottle. He eyed the whiskey as it sloshed about, and he wondered if there was enough to get drunk.

Chapter 26: Across Lake Nutaq

Matt was disgruntled.

The ride across Lake Nutaq had failed to provide any open spots of water to skip over. Ice had formed over the bare spots some of the other riders had talked about and thickened on the lake. And while he and Mark were able to get up to some decent speed, it wasn't the same as skipping.

Matt took the lead, passing Mark and racing towards the private beach of Preston Road. The wind had whipped the snow off of the lake, forming huge drifts spanning from the frozen shore to the tall, thin pines encircling Nutaq.

When he rode up onto the beach, Matt turned off the snowmobile's engine, lifted his visor, and turned his head to talk to Mark.

His brother pulled in beside him, shut down his own snowmobile, and flipped the polarized visor on his bright orange helmet.

"Where to now?" Mark asked.

"Don't know. Maybe Preston Road. Doubt Danny's been in there to plow more than once," Matt said, looking at the cabins which could be glimpsed through the sparse trees.

"Yeah?" Mark asked. "You don't think we'll get in trouble?"

Matt laughed and shook his head. "Come on. We got almost two feet of snow. You know Danny's regulars are going to be screaming for him to plow them out. Come on. Think about Old Man Willows. Guy drinks a thirty pack of Budweiser a day. He was probably too drunk to get an extra rack in, and now he's going through withdrawals."

Mark grinned, nodding. "Yeah. Right. Sure, let's go in there. Maybe the storm will have knocked in a door or something. Jenny Welsh said when she and her mom cleaned up the cabins at the end of the season, some of the people had left Blu-ray players and flat-screens."

Matt imagined playing Call of Duty on a flat-screen television instead of the old, 1987 tube set they had in the basement.

"That would be awesome," Matt said. "Let's go."

The brothers pulled their visors down and started their snowmobiles.

Matt led the way, creating a small path from the beach to Preston Road. As they breached a small crest, he caught sight of the clubhouse, and a white full-body van smashed into the building's porch. Not only was the front of the vehicle jammed into the broken boards and fore of the structure, but the rear end of the van was a mass of torn and twisted metal.

The brothers came to a stop, engines idling.

Matt looked up Preston Road and saw a vehicle, and in spite of the blanket of snow on it, he could tell that it was a pick-up.

And there was a broken plow hanging from its mounts.

Oh man, Matt thought. *That's Danny's truck. It's got to be.*

He motioned to Mark, who nodded, and together they traveled along the road to Danny's pickup. Matt turned off his snowmobile's engine and climbed off. Mark remained where he was, his head twisting to the left and right, as if expecting someone.

Picking his way through the snow, Matt made his way up to the driver's side where the door hung cock-eyed. He looked at it, filled with a sudden dread of what might be inside. Horrific images of Danny dead flashed through his mind, and Matt's hand had a minor tremble as he reached for the door. The metal of the frame felt cold even through his thick gloves as he took hold.

Open it, he told himself. *Just open it.*

Holding his breath, Matt pulled on the door, a broken hinge letting out a miserable scream. Matt shied away from the truck, expecting the worse, but was surprised to find the interior empty.

Danny wasn't there.

"Matt!" Mark screamed, his voice muffled by the helmet.

Matt jerked his head around to look at his brother.

A huge monster was walking towards them. It had a twisted face and long, black hair. Matt couldn't see arms or legs, both hidden by a long cloak it wore.

Matt slipped as he tried to get away from the truck, and as he fell, he was hit in the face by the fantail of snow thrown up by his brother's snowmobile. Panicking, Matt scrambled to his feet as Mark sped off, leaving him behind.

The wooden face of the monster followed Mark's passage, and Matt tried to get to his own snowmobile. Yet as his hand touched the handle, the creature remembered Matt's existence. It stepped forward as Matt clambered onto the seat, fumbled his attempt to start the engine, and then felt needle-like pain explode in his bicep as the creature took hold of him.

The monster turned him around, twisting Matt's arm around until it felt as though the tendons would tear free. Matt's throat closed up with the pain, and he began to suffocate from his fear.

As Matt's eyes fluttered and consciousness slipped away, he heard a yell. A great, terrible bellow and he wondered who else had come to kill him.

Chapter 27: A Good Drunk Spoiled

Shane hadn't had quite enough whiskey to get drunk, but it had been more than enough for a decent buzz. Danny remained asleep on the bed, and Patience hadn't returned. Shane leaned against the wall, his eyes closed as he thought about his current situation.

The thoughts weren't in any particular order. They tended to drift, from Courtney to the lighthouse, from the Marine Corps to the death of his parents. His mind rambled, opening and closing the doors to memories he didn't want to recall.

During an exceptionally vivid recollection of his first introduction to Eloise, Shane heard the sound of an engine.

He opened one eye, looked at the curtained window and waited.

It took him a moment, but finally, Shane nodded, returned his eye to its previous state of rest, and thought, *Yup. That's an engine.*

A heartbeat later, his eyes snapped open.

An engine, dummy! he screamed at himself. Shane's attempts to get to his feet were clumsy, and in less dire circumstances, would have been extremely funny.

As it was, he only grew angry.

Muttering under his breath, Shane picked up the piece of iron, stepped over the salt, and ran to the front room. A single, vicious kick sent the table flying away from the door. As it swung open, Shane leaped out, springing off the porch and into the snow. He saw the snowmobile, the young rider in the grip of Broken Nose, and Shane let out a furious roar.

Broken Nose jerked around, the rider flailing about like a cornhusk doll.

Shane brought the iron smashing down and through the Indian's arm.

The blow caused Broken Nose to vanish and reverberated through Shane as if he had struck a tree instead of a dead man.

He managed to keep his grip on the iron and catch hold of the rider as he fell. Shane wrapped his arm around the stranger's waist, and movement caught his eye.

Looking down at the house at the end of the street, Shane saw Broken Nose stepping out of the doorway and onto the porch.

"Oh hell," Shane murmured, and he half carried, half dragged the rider back towards the cabin. Patience stood there, frowning. She stepped aside to let them pass.

"What have you done, Shane?" she asked, following him towards the bedroom.

"Saved this kid," Shane grunted, picked the rider up and over the salt.

"You should not have done so," she scolded.

"Why not?" Shane asked, putting the stranger down on the floor.

"Broken Nose wanted him," Patience snapped. "It was not good to take from him. Nor was it wise to strike him. I can hear him. He is displeased with you."

"Tell him to get in line," Shane said, taking the helmet off the rider and revealing the face of a teenage boy.

The young rider was in shock, his brown eyes wide, his acne-marked face pale. His dark brown, curly hair was damp with sweat, and saliva clung to the corners of his mouth.

"Hey," Shane said, snapping his fingers in front of the kid's eyes. "Hey!"

The teen blinked, focused on Shane and muttered, "What?"

"Look at me," Shane commanded. "Pay attention to me. Do you understand?"

The rider nodded.

"Okay. What's your name?" Shane asked.

"My name."

"Yeah," Shane said, taking hold of the teenager's chin and making the rider look at him. "Your name. What is it?"

The teen frowned, then smiled and said, "Matt."

"Matt," Shane started. But he couldn't finish.

Matt's eyes rolled up in his head, exposing the whites. The teen went limp, and Shane had to drop the iron and catch Matt with his other hand, lowering the boy to the floor.

Shane checked Matt's pulse. Checked it again.

He dropped onto the floor and sat beside the teen.

The boy was dead.

Chapter 28: The Englishman

When Frank had been in the Army, he had been on intimate terms with death. After meeting Shane, Frank had been introduced to an entirely new aspect of death. He knew full well how dangerous ghosts could be, and how ghosts were not the powerless images of the past.

The Englishman that was standing before him, Frank saw, would gut him without batting an eye.

In silence, the dead man examined Frank, nostrils flaring as if he could smell Frank.

"Who are you?" The Englishman asked, his voice sounding like metal dragged over broken glass.

"Frank."

"You have a hard look about you, Frank," The Englishman said. "Can you see out of that eye of yours?"

"Most days," Frank said, keeping his voice even, not letting his fear creep into it.

The Englishman chuckled, thin lips parting to reveal yellowed and broken teeth. "What did you wrong?"

"Shrapnel," Frank said.

"Aye?" the ghost asked. "We have a kinship there. You see this?"

The Englishman pointed to a thick scar on his left cheek.

Frank nodded.

"My mate's jawbone did that," the man said. "Round shot tore his head away, sent the jaw through my cheek, took out a few of my gnashers as well. You ever swallow a tooth before?"

"Once," Frank confessed. "But it was someone else's."

For a moment, the Englishman looked surprised, then he let out a loud, braying laugh. "Aye, but I do like you, Frank. The name's Jack. Jack Whyte. I'd shake your hand, but I've seen what my touch does to those still taking air."

"I appreciate that, Jack," Frank said, relaxing a fraction. "How long have you been in there?"

"Who's the King, then, my boy?" Jack asked, crossing his arms over his chest.

"No king right now," Frank said after a moment of hesitation. "Queen Elizabeth the second sits on the throne. Who was the king when you died?"

Jack twisted his face into a scowl. "Fair question that is. Hm, who was on the throne? Ah yes, it was that bonnie tart George. Did my time on the wheel for speaking ill of him."

"The wheel?" Frank asked.

"Punishment," Jack said, winking. "Terrible it was, too. Strapped you down to a tilted wagon wheel and laid into you with a lash. Better than aboard ship, though. Those devils let the cat out of the bag more 'n I care for."

Frank shook his head. "That sounds distinctly unpleasant, my friend."

"Aye, it was at that," Jack said. "So, bonnie King George was on the throne when I came here to the colonies. Yes, 'bout seventy if I recall correctly, though I have a hard enough time doing that without a bit of stout. What year is it now?"

"Two thousand and seventeen," Frank answered.

Jack coughed, shook his head, and repeated the number.

"Yes," Frank said.

"So," Jack answered, rubbing his chin. "I've been tucked away, then."

Frank waited, wondering if he could close the rosette if Jack became violent. Madness danced in Jack's eyes for a moment, a curious, shimmering gleam that set Frank's teeth on edge.

"You're not a foolish man," Jack said, a grim look settling over his face.

"Not usually, no," Frank responded.

Jack glanced at the gold button in the lead-lined compartment.

"You need help, am I correct, my friend?" Jack asked, returning his attention to Frank.

"Yes," Frank answered. "I have a friend who's in trouble. And I need someone who's dead to help me."

A lopsided grin appeared, and Jack said. "Do you now?"

"I do."

"And would you be willing to help old Jack?" the Englishman asked.

"To a point," Frank said.

Jack chuckled. "Oh yes, I do like you, Frank. I do indeed."

The Englishman became serious, his voice hard. "Will you help me leave here?"

"The house or your existence?" Frank asked.

"The latter is preferred," Jack said. "Though I'd take the former in a pinch."

"I'll help you with either one," Frank said. "To the best that I can."

"Well then, Frank," Jack said, straightening up and running a hand through his hair. "I believe that we will be friends, good and true at that. Now tell me, where are we going, and what for?"

"North," Frank said. "And my friend is trapped by the dead."

"Take hold of the button then," Jack said, nodding towards the gold button. "Put it in your pocket to keep me close, and we'll be on our away."

Frank stepped over to the hearth, removed the button, and placed it in his pants pocket. The metal was cold and refused to get warm in spite of its closeness to his flesh.

"Now, Frank," Jack said, "do you know why I'm bound to such a tawdry piece of work?"

Frank shook his head.

Jack beamed at him. "Belonged to the last officer I killed. A nasty, priggish colonel."

"How did you kill him?" Frank asked, looking up into Jack's eyes.

"I twisted his head off his neck, I did," Jack said with satisfaction.

"And did it cure him?" Frank asked.

Jack frowned. "Cure him? Of what?"

"Being an officer," Frank said and walked towards the hallway as Jack let out his strange, braying laugh. The sound raced through the house, and Frank shook his head.

He may be a madman, and a murderer, Frank thought, *but he's still a soldier, and I can work with that.*

Chapter 29: Across the Lake

Fear boiled in Mark.

It pushed him to drive the snowmobile faster, racing across Lake Nutaq.

He didn't look back as he went, for there was a nagging, terrifying doubt eating at him.

Mark wasn't sure if his brother had left Preston Road, and he was too afraid to know the truth. All Mark wanted was to be home, where it was safe, where there wasn't a monster lurking behind him.

A shimmer on the snow ahead caught Mark's eyes, and his mind, smothered by fear, failed to register what it was.

Before he knew it, Mark was skipping.

The open water wasn't large, but it was enough since he hadn't been paying attention. He didn't have time to rev the engine or to swerve to either the left or right. All he could do was hang onto the grips and pray that he had enough speed to get across.

He didn't.

The new sled slammed into the ice shelf, water splashing up and soaking him. With the force of the impact, Mark was launched over the handles. His body spun left to right while his feet began a slow arc up towards the sun.

The world slowed down, and his vision became preternaturally sharp.

He saw, out of the corner of one eye, the snowmobile slip into Lake Nutaq, the headlight shining beneath the water. Each ripple was defined, highlighted by adrenaline. His heart beat like a fist against his chest. He stiffened, felt the world reset itself to its normal speed, and slammed down onto the ice, his right leg bent beneath him.

Mark heard rather than felt his femur snap. The pain was instant and blinding.

Snow spilled down onto him, and when Mark tried to stand, darkness smothered him, and he lay on the shuddering ice.

For a brief moment, he looked as lifeless as his brother did.

His face contorted with pain, and Mark's eyes snapped open. He swallowed back a scream, suspecting but not knowing that the monster was still out there. A small, horrific idea blossomed in Mark's mind. The creature wasn't satisfied with only Matt.

It wanted Mark too.

Mark rolled over onto his stomach and fainted as pain exploded in his leg.

When he came back to consciousness, Mark discovered he had thrown up in his helmet. Vomit splashed across his face and stung his nostrils. Disgusted, Mark ripped the helmet off and scrubbed at his face with a handful of snow. The break in his leg felt like someone was smashing at it with a hammer, and Mark had to fight another faint.

Breathing hard, he pushed himself up and looked around as best he could. It took him several minutes to get his bearings, but when he did, he was able to see where he needed to get off the lake in order to make it home. His hand shook as he reached into his coat, pulled the hood of his sweatshirt out, and managed to put it on.

Home, Mark thought, refusing to acknowledge the silence behind him. *Home.*

Matt will be home soon. He's probably home now, Mark lied to himself.

He started to crawl through the snow, across the ice, and he whispered to himself, "He's probably home now."

Chapter 30: Discussions with the Dead

"Why did he die?" Patience asked.

The sound of her voice jarred him out of his thoughts. He looked at the dead girl. She was in her favorite place, seated on the other side of the salt and staring at him.

"Shock," Shane answered. He twisted around and saw Danny was still asleep, the injured man's chest rising with a slow and steady rhythm.

Patience frowned and shook her head.

"What do you mean?" she asked.

"His body couldn't handle the injury," Shane explained.

"But he was not hurt," she said. "Not grievously."

"It doesn't have to be severe," Shane said. "People react differently to being injured. I've seen men with shrapnel wounds die, their bodies shutting down because of the trauma of being wounded. I've also seen guys with both of their legs torn off and joking with the medics trying to keep them alive. Everyone's different."

"You haven't died of shock," Patience said. "You are missing most of an ear, Shane. And a pair of fingers. You have seen more than a little, I think."

Shane nodded. "You're right. But, like I said, everyone's different."

A groan from Danny interrupted Patience, and Shane stood up and looked down at the young man.

Danny's eyelids opened, his eyes darted around, pupils dilated. It took him a few seconds to focus, but when he did, he looked at Shane.

"Oh hell," Danny croaked.

"What?" Shane asked.

"It wasn't a dream," Danny whispered. "I was really hoping it had all been a dream."

"Sorry," Shane said. "No luck there."

"Figures," Danny muttered, groaning. He turned his head towards the doorway and asked, "Is that a dead girl?"

"Yup," Shane answered.

Danny closed his eyes and said, "I would really like this to be a bad dream."

"You and me both, kid," Shane said. "You want some water, maybe something to eat?"

Danny shook his head.

"You should," Shane said.

"I know," Danny said without opening his eyes. "I'm just not hungry. Not thirsty. I want to go to sleep and wake up at home."

"Not going to happen if you keep moaning and pretending we're not here," Shane snapped.

"I don't believe it is going to happen," Patience said. "Broken Nose is not pleased."

"I don't care if he's happy or sad, or anything else," Shane said. "Danny, open your eyes."

Danny kept them closed.

"Danny," Shane said. "If you don't open your eyes, I'm going to slap you until you do."

The young man's eyes opened.

"Thank you," Shane said. "You're going to need to eat because we're going to need to get the hell out of here."

"We can't." Danny's voice was thick with bitterness. "My truck's destroyed. Clark's van is worthless, and if that's your car on the other side of the cabin, there's no way it's going to make it through two feet of snow."

"I wasn't thinking about them," Shane said. "I was thinking about the snowmobile."

"A snowmobile?" Hope tinged Danny's voice. He turned his face towards Shane. "There's a snowmobile out there?"

"Yeah," Shane said.

"How?" Danny asked, pushing himself up onto his elbows.

Shane pointed at the body of the teen, the dead boy's head hanging to the right.

"Oh God," Danny whispered. "That's Matt Rushford. What happened to him?"

"Broken Nose," Shane informed him. "The ghost who grabbed you."

"What did he do to him?" Danny asked. "I can't see any marks."

"Seems to have died from shock," Shane answered. He looked away from the teen's corpse.

"Broken Nose is looking forward to killing you," Patience said, addressing Danny. "He is extremely upset about you leaving the house."

Danny's complexion went waxen. His voice was hushed when he spoke.

"I've seen you," Danny said. "In there. When he was torturing me."

Patience smiled a broad, happy expression. "I'm pleased you noticed, Daniel. The other man only saw me before Broken Nose took him. And a few times whilst being tested."

Patience frowned. "He failed his tests, I am afraid."

"And what about mine?" Danny asked. "Did I fail mine?"

She shook her head.

"That's good, I guess," Danny said, dropping back to the bed and grimacing with pain.

"I don't think it is," Shane said.

"I didn't finish," Patience said, tilting her head up and looking down her nose at them. "Danny has yet to complete his testing. And yours, Shane, yours has yet to begin."

Chapter 31: Looking for the Boys

Doreen Conroy had reverted to her maiden name after the boys' father had left them. She pulled into the driveway of the small house where she and her sons lived. The building had been a summer cottage, once, long before she ever purchased it, and so it was a rambling collection of additions. It was the type of house which seemed to exist only in New England.

Doreen parked her truck, the old diesel grumbling before she turned the engine off. She got out into the cold, her hips hurting and her right knee aching. From the passenger seat, she took her messenger bag and slammed the door, making sure the lock caught.

"Matt," she called, kicking the door shut behind her. "Mark."

Neither of the boys answered her.

Probably out on their snowmobiles, she thought, smiling.

Doreen dropped her bag on the table and made herself a cup of orange pekoe tea, and brought it into the TV room. The warmth and flavor of the drink soothed her as she sipped at it. Each bad tip, each unpleasant customer, faded from her memory as the cup was emptied. When she finished, Doreen smiled, set the cup down, and relaxed. Her eyelids grew heavy, and at first, she fought it. Then, after several minutes, she gave in. Pulling the bathrobe tight around her, Doreen closed her eyes and rested her head against the back of the chair.

The phone rang and woke Doreen up.

Around her, the house was dark, and she fumbled for the phone, finally picking it up and answering, "Hello?"

"Doreen." It was Lloyd Gibbons.

"Hey Lloyd," she said, straightening up. "What are you calling for?"

"Well," he said, his voice uneasy, "are your boys home?"

"I don't think so," she answered. "They had the day off from school. They're probably out somewhere on their snowmobiles."

Lloyd cleared his throat, the sound uncomfortable and hesitant.

Doreen stiffened. "What's wrong? Why are you asking about the boys?"

"Someone thought they saw them out on Nutaq today," Lloyd said. "Then, a little later, one of the State Police helicopters was doing a flyover of the lake and saw a good sized hole out there."

"Where there any tracks?" she asked, hating the sound of panic in her voice.

"There may have been," Lloyd said. "But the wind picked up. Created drifts all over town, the lake too, of course."

Doreen stood up, carrying the portable with her into the bedroom. She changed her clothes, her movements awkward as she switched the phone from one hand to the next and tried to continue the conversation.

"Why do you think it's my boys?" Doreen asked, tugging on her pants.

"The sleds were bright orange," Lloyd said. "And the guy, Drew Reich, he knew the model. They were the new, Arctic Cat snow-pros. Your boys are the only ones around here who have them."

Doreen felt sick, her stomach threatening to expel the tea she had so recently finished.

"I don't want it to be my boys, Lloyd," she whispered, closing her eyes.

"I know, Doreen," he replied, his voice filled with kindness. "I'll call the sheriff. Notify the State Police barracks. They're probably just out and about, but better safe than sorry."

Doreen nodded. "Yes. Yes, you're right."

"Doreen," Lloyd said, "don't try and go out on the ice. If it's cracking, well, you'd just go in, and then what would your boys do?"

She swallowed, shook her head and said, "Don't worry, Lloyd. I won't go out there."

They said good-bye, and Doreen ended the call. She dropped the portable to the bed, put on her sweatshirt, and wondered if she would need a face mask when she stepped out onto the lake to look for her sons.

Chapter 32: A Bad Call

Rowan Little had spent the better part of an hour with an irate businessman from Bar Harbor, Maine. The businessman, who was named Youssef Kamal, had been an all right fellow. He had been upset with the condition of the roads, and Rowan understood him perfectly well.

Rowan was upset with the condition of the roads as well. They had talked about the state of each particular thoroughfare until the tow-truck had shown up and taken both Mr. Kamal and his damaged Chrysler away.

Then again, he thought, *if I wasn't working, I wouldn't be out and about.*

Rowan knew it was unfair to think that way. Youssef had been on his way to a job down in Nashua, and somehow the man's GPS had shuffled him over near Nutaq. One of the worst errors Rowan had heard of in a while, and it justified his faith in the Rand Road Atlas he carried in the pick-up.

He shook his head, opened the driver's door, and kicked his feet off on the edge of the frame before he climbed into the seat. The engine rumbled and heat poured out of the vents. After so much time outside, Rowan was pleased he had decided to leave the engine on.

He pulled his stiff hands out of the gloves, squeezed his hands into fists several times to move the blood around, and then turned on the stereo. He moved the old dial back and forth until he found a piggyback relay of the weather forecast from Channel Nine news.

As he listened, Rowan looked on the seat for the newspaper. When he saw it and picked it up, Rowan noticed he had forgotten his phone beneath it.

Chuckling, he looked at the cell's screen.

Five missed calls, he thought, rolling his eyes. *Hell, they would have called me on the radio, if it was important enough.*

Rowan looked at the calls and saw all five had been placed to him by Doreen. Frowning, Rowan keyed in his code and listened to the messages.

Each one was the same, with the tension and pitch of Doreen's voice becoming more frantic until the final message was no more than a rush of words.

The boys were missing. Last seen on the lake.

Skipping, Rowan thought, shaking with anger at the idea. *Those stupid kids went skipping.*

He forced himself to remain calm and alert as he shifted the truck into drive. A glance to the mirrors showed he wasn't in any danger of being hit, so Rowan pulled out onto the main road. The truck moved fast, Rowan's foot putting a sufficient amount of pressure on the accelerator. In a few minutes, he turned up Doreen's driveway. By the time he pulled in behind her truck, she was stepping out of the door, closing it behind her.

She looked up in surprise as he got out.

"Doreen," he said, hurrying towards her. "Any word from them?"

She shook her head, and in the glare of the headlights, Rowan saw the redness of her eyes, the swollen tear ducts beneath the orbs themselves.

Doreen had been crying, and that frightened Rowan.

He'd seen her help pull bodies out of the Ridge Road fire, where thirteen people had died in the old Ander's house. Rowan had been there when she had buried each of her parents, when her marriage to her high-school sweetheart had collapsed, and when her brother had drowned in Lake Nutaq.

And she had never shed a tear.

Not once, Rowan thought.

"Where are you going?" Rowan asked, although he knew perfectly well, where she was headed. He would do the same.

"To look for my boys," she answered, her words curt.

"On Lake Nutaq?" Rowan asked.

She nodded.

"Alright," Rowan said. "It's getting colder. Let me grab my gloves and flashlight, then we'll go out together if that works for you."

Doreen nodded.

Rowan gathered his items, tested the batteries to make certain the flashlight worked.

"All set," he said to Doreen.

He followed her around the side of the house, to the back and over to the old barn. From there, Rowan could see the tracks the snowmobiles had left behind. They went straight towards the lake.

Oh hell, he thought.

Doreen straightened her shoulders and followed what little of the trail remained. Rowan could do nothing more than go with her. A sudden, terrible thought flooded through him.

One or both of the boys being dead, dragged down with their snowmobiles into the cold dark of the water. They would have to wait until the spring thaws to even look for the body or bodies. And Rowan pictured it perfectly, the body floating, half-suspended in the darkness, hair and clothing soaked, skin beginning to swell.

Rowan tried to ignore the mental image, and kept pace with Doreen instead, walking out onto the frozen lake in search for her sons.

Chapter 33: On Lake Nutaq

Mark was cold.

Colder than he had ever been.

Each movement was filled with agony. His teeth ached from being clenched, the break in his femur throbbed with a relentless rhythm that threatened to drive him mad.

In spite of it all, Mark continued to drag himself forward. Several times, he had gotten twisted around.

With the coming of night, he knew he was dangerously close to death, and the idea was terrifying. His world had shrunk to consisting of pain, cold, and the frozen lake. For a short time, he had held out the false hope of a rescue, of Matt coming in to save the day as he had always done before. Then Mark had latched on to the idea that his father, who had left them all years before, would pick that day to go ice-fishing.

Mark had pictured it, idealized it. He would get close to an icehouse, a ramshackle affair with a kerosene heater inside. The cheap plywood door would open, and out would come his father. Out to save him, as his father had never done before.

Finally, Mark daydreamed about salvation from any source. A man out for a walk across the lake. Other riders on their sleds. Some smart dog that had spotted him from the bank and led a team of intrepid saviors out to him.

The daydreams had been shattered when the sun began to set.

In the distance, Mark believed he could hear voices. Strange men speaking in tongues he didn't understand, their words racing across the ice towards him, urging him on.

Mark had tried to hurry when he first heard them. Tried to crawl instead of dragging himself forward.

With his broken leg dragging behind him, Mark had managed to slip. He screamed until his voice broke and he couldn't even whisper.

For a long time he had lain in the snow, body wracked with sobs as he tried to ignore the voices. A weak, timid thought filled him.

Maybe they're looking for me, to help me.

As soon as the thought finished, Mark pushed it aside.

He knew that whoever spoke those words didn't want to help him.

Like they hadn't wanted to help Matt.

Mark winced at the thought of his brother. Fresh tears stung his eyes and mucus ran from his nose as he pulled himself forward.

From behind came a whooping cry, a joyous, brutal sound that caused Mark to stop.

The first whoop was joined by others until three or four people were calling out.

"Hello."

Mark looked up, surprise and hope filling him.

A little girl stood in front of him, her face pale and drawn. She held a blanket around her, and she gave him a sweet, tender smile. Beside her stood a tall man, a Native American. In his left hand, he carried a tomahawk and he smiled down with disturbingly white teeth.

"What is your name?" she asked, cocking her head to the left.

"Mark," he croaked.

"Mark," she said. "Are you cold, Mark?"

"God, yes," he hissed.

"Then come," the girl whispered. "Come and be warm."

She spread her arms wide and revealed the nightmare beneath her blanket.

Faces, some screaming and others laughing, peered out of splayed bones and emptiness.

"Be warm," the girl repeated, and hands reached out from her body. Dozens of them, fingers questing.

Mark tried to crawl backwards, but the man beside her sprang forward and grabbed him by the back of his jacket. With a gleeful shout, the man began to run, dragging Mark with him.

Away from the shore and safety.

Terrified, Mark let out a long, hoarse scream.

Chapter 34: Noises in the Night

They had been walking for less than fifteen minutes when a loud whoop went ringing across the ice. At first, it was a single voice, then others. When Doreen looked over at Rowan, her face tight, all he could do was shake his head.

Her guess was as good as his. He was about to say as much when he heard a shout, which was quickly followed by a scream. A horrible cry filled with terror. Before the noise finished, Doreen had left his side. She ran through the snow, and Rowan raced after her, trying not to fall as his boots hit the buried ice.

"Look!" Doreen screamed, pointing ahead of them.

Rowan followed the line of her finger and saw a small shape. It stood in the snow, back to them, and as they got closer, Rowan realized it was a child.

"Hey!" Rowan yelled. But his next words died in his throat as he realized he could see through the figure.

"Doreen," Rowan snapped, grabbing hold of her arm and pulling her to a stop. "Don't!"

"What?" Doreen asked, frantic. "Why not? Maybe she's seen my sons!"

She? Rowan thought.

The figure turned around and proved Doreen's estimation of her gender to be correct. In front of them was a young girl, wearing only a blanket, and she was transparent.

Rowan knew in his gut that it wasn't a trick of the light or the cold. And he knew there was something wrong with her.

Doreen seemed to come to a similar conclusion. She didn't try to pull away from Rowan.

"Your sons?" the girl asked.

"Yes," Doreen gasped, taking a cautious step forward and making Rowan do the same. "My boys. Matt and Mark. Have you seen them out here?"

The girl nodded. "I have. In fact, I was just speaking with your son, Mark. He seemed like a nice young man."

"He is," Doreen sobbed. "He really is. Do you know where he went?"

"Yes," the girl replied. "Broken Nose has him."

"Where does he have him?" Rowan asked as Doreen stuttered and tried to form the same question.

"There," the girl said, gesturing towards the far shore with a small hand.

"And what about Matt?" Rowan asked. "Have you spoken with him?"

"Matt is dead," the girl said, her voice tinged with sadness. "But it is a blessing. It means he won't have to worry about Broken Nose. I cannot say the same for Mark."

Then the girl's expression brightened. "Perhaps he will do well, though. If he does, he can stay with me forever, and he seems like a nice young man. I would like that. I think you would, too."

Before either Rowan or Doreen could disagree with her, the girl vanished.

Doreen's heartbroken wail chased after the strange creature in the cold night.

Chapter 35: Preparing to Leave

Night had settled, and there had been no further sign of Broken Nose, the ghost's accomplices, or of Patience.

Danny sat on the bed, his face puffy and swollen, eyes black. The man looked worn thin, and on the point of breaking.

Shane could understand why.

Only a few minutes earlier, they had put socks and boots on Danny's tortured, toeless feet. Danny had bitten down on the blanket to keep from screaming and drawing attention to them.

Shane trembled, a sign of alcohol withdrawal, and he felt a gnawing anger. He wanted a cigarette, and there wasn't anything to smoke.

Without a word, he left the bedroom, went to the front window, and peered out. In the moonlight, he saw the orange snowmobile. His eyes searched the shadows for any sort of movement. He let his gaze trail along either side of Preston Road, down to what Danny called the clubhouse, and roam over the wreck of the van and the front of the building.

Nothing, Shane thought. *But they'll be looking for Danny. Patience said as much.*

Shane sighed, closed his eyes, and forced the tremors to cease.

He opened his eyes when a sense of calm had come over him, and he turned away from the window. Quick steps brought him back to the bedroom.

Danny's expression was a mixture of anxiety and fear.

"You ready?" Shane asked.

"Yeah," Danny replied, his voice hoarse and raw.

"Good." Shane picked up his bag, slung it over his shoulder, and picked up the iron blade fragment. He had found medical tape in the bathroom cabinet and used it to make a rough grip on the broken metal.

Wish I had my knuckle-dusters, he thought as he stepped over to the bed and offered Danny his hand.

Danny grabbed hold and pulled himself up. The man's eyes widened with pain, muscles dancing along his jaw, and Shane could hear Danny's teeth grind together.

With Danny leaning on him, Shane led the way to the front door. He paused and whispered, "You sure you know how to drive a snowmobile?"

Danny let out a pained laugh. "You don't drive 'em. You ride 'em. And yeah, I know. Had my first one when I was seven."

"Alright," Shane said, moving the table away from the door. "You're in charge when we get there."

Danny nodded, and the two of them went as quickly as the younger man's damaged feet would allow them.

Shane winced at the sound of their footsteps in the snow, each sound an opportunity for the dead to find them. But they reached the snowmobile without incident, and Shane helped Danny onto it.

"Where are you going?"

Shane jerked around, dropping his bag and facing Patience.

A long, agonized scream caused her blanket to flutter.

"We're leaving," Shane answered.

Patience frowned, shook her head, and said, "No. You cannot. Broken Nose is too excited. The three of you may satisfy him, but I doubt it."

"Two of us," Shane said, nodding to Danny.

Danny started the snowmobile, its engine roaring gloriously into life.

"Three," Patience corrected. "I have gathered another for him from Nutaq."

"What?" Shane demanded, taking a step closer to the girl.

She drifted back, a smile dancing across her face. "Yes. The other who had fled. His name is Mark. Matthew was his brother."

A joyous cry, sounding from the clubhouse, caused Shane to tear his attention away from the dead girl.

Five shapes stood by the van, and one of them was undeniably Broken Nose, the moon's light oddly reflected on his mask. The four Indians around him were tall, dressed in deerskins and breastplates made of polished animal bone. They were armed with tomahawks and war clubs.

Shane looked at Danny, the younger man's face rigid with fear.

A warm, thrilling sensation rippled through Shane, and he grinned.

"Get out of here," Shane said, dropping his bag.

Danny nodded, shifted the snowmobile into gear and tore off, a fantail of snow arcing into the air.

"You should run," Patience suggested. "You might make it to the cabin."

"I don't run," Shane said. He walked towards the clubhouse.

"Look at him," one of the Indians said in his own tongue. "He wants to die!"

The others laughed.

"Who are we then to not assist him?" Broken Nose asked. He gestured with a long hand, and two of the men walked towards Shane. Their legs passed through the snow, not a single flake disturbed by their long strides.

One of the men, the top half of his face painted black, let out a yell, raised his war club, and sprinted towards Shane.

Shane, who had fought more than a few men, both living and dead, ducked beneath the blow, and brought the iron in an upward arc. The ghost screamed and vanished, causing his partner to hesitate.

"Will you not come forward?" Shane asked, speaking in their language.

The dead man stopped, glancing back at the others and at Broken Nose.

"Are you afraid of pain?" Shane asked, filling his words with disdain.

The ghost stiffened.

"Ah, you are," Shane said, chuckling. "Go then, little one. Let a better man come forward to speak with me."

Furious, the ghost screamed and dashed forward, feinting to the left and bringing his tomahawk in with an undercut. The blow nearly missed Shane as he stepped into the attack, thrusting his iron forward.

Broken Nose nodded, the bones and teeth jangling as the other two men advanced towards Shane.

Here's hoping their bones are far enough away for me to get back to the cabin, Shane thought. Then before any other ideas could cross his mind, the dead were upon him.

His movements were fluid, muscle memory kicking in from knife training a decade earlier. The heavy, awkward piece of iron in his hand was a far cry from the K-Bar fighting blade he had trained on, but he wielded as if it were.

Shane dropped to a knee and thrust up and through the midsection of one. As the surviving attacker swung at him, Shane rolled beneath the blow and slashed out, the iron passing through the Indian's calf.

And Shane was alone with Broken Nose.

Chapter 36: Questions Without Answers

Doreen had collapsed after Mark had vanished, and Rowan had struggled to keep from doing the same. He forced himself to focus on her, getting Doreen to her feet and bringing her towards the shore. Together they had stumbled along, numb not only from the cold, but also from the sheer horror of what they had witnessed. He had called for help on the radio, for someone from the station to meet him at Doreen's house. Rowan had asked for the State Police, too. Anything and anyone who could help.

When they scrambled up onto the snow-covered beach, Doreen sank down to her knees. Her head hung down, and Rowan hunkered beside her.

"Doreen," he said, hating the cold professionalism in his voice. "Doreen, hon, we need to get you inside. I have people meeting us at your place. We have to figure out what's going on here. What happened?"

She lifted her chin up and stared at him, her eyes barren of any spark.

"He was taken, Rowan," she said, the words flat and without inflection. "He's gone. There's no getting him back. You know the stories."

"It's why they're stories," Rowan responded, forcing her up. "It could have been anything."

She remained silent as they trudged through the snow.

Then she stiffened and refused to move.

"Doreen," Rowan started.

She silenced him with a gesture, her face turning towards the lake.

And Rowan heard it, too.

The sound of an engine. A snowmobile.

Rowan twisted around and caught sight of a headlight. It raced along Nutaq.

With fumbling hands, Rowan pulled his flashlight free from his belt. He managed to twist it on, the beam bursting into life. He waved it back and forth until the snowmobile changed its course towards them.

"It could be Matt," Doreen whispered.

"It's probably another rider," Rowan said, "but they might have seen Matt. Come on."

They followed their tracks back to the shore as the snowmobile roared. In the moonlight, Rowan could see it was an Arctic Cat, a brand new orange Snow Pro.

But the rider was neither Matt nor Mark Rushford.

It was Danny Nordman, crouched low over the controls.

He's not going to stop, Rowan realized, and he yanked Doreen back and to the left before Danny smashed into a small rise in the shore. The young man was thrown over the top of the snowmobile, smashing through the windshield.

Rowan left Doreen, sprinting for Danny. The young man was bleeding from a dozen cuts and slashes, his face a bloody mess. Half of his scalp hung off to the right. His face was bright red, and Rowan saw, for the first time, the thin clothes Danny wore. He didn't have a helmet or gloves. No jacket or hat.

Danny's eyelids fluttered, his lips parted and revealed a mouthful of shattered teeth.

"Rowan," Danny mumbled.

"Yeah," Rowan said, nodding. "It's me, Danny. You're going to be okay."

Danny let out a hoarse croak, and it took Rowan a moment to realize it was a laugh. The young man's mangled lips spread into a grin, blood oozing out of wide splits in the flesh.

"I am," Danny hissed. "I know I am. I'm not there. I'm here. Here!"

The young man's eyes rolled back in his head as he passed out.

Rowan turned to Doreen, but she had curled herself into a fetal position.

"God dammit," Rowan swore. He took his coat off and put it over Danny's still form. Shivering, Rowan took the radio off his belt, keyed it, and called for a pair of ambulances. When he received confirmation of the dispatch, he concentrated on Doreen again.

"Doreen," he said, crouching down beside her.

She stared out at the lake, refusing to respond.

Rowan sighed, sat down beside her, and gently gathered her into his arms. As he held onto her, she began to sob. Deep, wracking sounds, and each one pierced his own heart until he too wept.

Chapter 37: Outside of Preston Road

Frank sat in his car, the engine idling and the hazards flashing. He had his hands resting on the steering wheel while leaning against it, staring down the faint outline of Preston Road. A State plow had built an impressive wall of snow across the entrance of the road.

Not that it matters, Frank thought. The storm had dropped two feet of snow on most of New Hampshire, and Preston Road was included. There were faint signs of a plow's passage, but not enough of the road had been cleared for Frank to risk a drive. Plus there was a chain across the entrance, and Frank didn't carry bolt cutters with him.

Probably should, he told himself. *Should probably keep a whole kit in the trunk if I'm going to make a habit out of this.*

He drummed his fingers on the steering wheel, then sat back. Frank reached into his coat pocket and retrieved the gold button Jack was bound to.

Here goes nothing, Frank thought, and he put it down on the passenger seat.

"Jack," Frank said.

Nothing happened.

"Jack," Frank repeated.

Still, Jack didn't appear.

Frank groaned, let out a long breath and said again, "Jack!"

"What?" came Jack's voice from behind him.

Frank jumped in his seat, the quick jerk of his body causing the seatbelt to snap tight.

Looking into his rearview mirror, Frank saw Jack. The dead man wore an expression of innocence. "You're a pain."

"Me?" Jack asked, and then he grinned. "Aye, Frank, I am indeed. We're here, then, my boy?"

"We are," Frank said, reaching up and adjusting the seatbelt.

Jack looked around, sniffed in disdain, and then gave a predatory smile. "This is a wild place."

"Is it?" Frank asked.

"Oh aye," Jack said, his voice dropping low. "Can you not feel it, Frank?"

Frank shook his head.

"Oh, there are red men here. Savages. Foul beasts that wear the cloaks of men, but have not our hearts," Jack said. He eased forward, through the seat to smile at Frank. "Terrible deeds have been committed here. Tortures and murders. Rapes and pillaging. And not on the savages' part alone. No, my kin have done their share here. This place stinks with it. It would be best to put it all to the match and let the good God purge the land."

"That's all well and good, Jack," Frank said, eyeing the dead man warily. "And you're welcome to put it to the torch, once we get my friend out of there."

"And here is why I like your company so much, my boy," Jack chortled. "Willing to destroy the world for a friend. Aye, I've had a few like that in my day. Bound by the King's shilling we were. Brotherhood of the coin. Course we would have fought for a Hessian lord just as well, but the King, well, he paid better now, didn't he."

"If you say so, Jack," Frank said.

"So I do, so I do," Jack murmured. He turned his attention to Preston Road. "Your friend is down there, in the thick of it?"

"He usually is," Frank answered.

Jack chuckled. "Then old Jack Whyte will find him, so I will. You'll be seeing me shortly."

And with those words, Jack vanished.

"I hope so," Frank said, picking the button up and pocketing it once more. He stared at the entrance to Preston Road, and he waited.

Chapter 38: A Game He Doesn't Want to Play

They stood facing each other, less than twenty feet separating them.

Shane knew in his gut that it was only because Broken Nose wished it to be so.

"You speak our tongue," Broken Nose said into the silence between them.

"I do," Shane responded.

"How?"

"Fate," Shane said.

Broken Nose nodded, and the frozen, twisted smile on the mask disturbed Shane in a way he hadn't felt before. It was a sickening sensation, primal and instinctual. A raw, rank taste burned in the back of his throat and fear choked his thoughts.

"You are here for me?" Broken Nose asked.

"No," Shane answered. "I don't care about you at all."

"Do you not?" Broken Nose's voice carried a hint of surprise.

Shane shook his head. "I would have been gone if Patience hadn't told me about the boy."

"Ah," Broken Nose said, satisfaction filling the word. "You wish to help him."

"Yes," Shane replied.

"What will you do to retrieve him?" Broken Nose asked.

"Whatever I have to," Shane said.

"Even your death?" Broken Nose questioned.

"I'd prefer yours," Shane said.

Broken Nose laughed, his wide shoulders shaking, the bearskin cloak jumping. From behind the man, Patience appeared.

"I wish she had taken you," Broken Nose said, the mirth gone from his voice. "Your heart I would have liked to eat. But I will feast upon your spirit instead. If it be so."

Shane resisted the urge to look around, to make certain the dead he had disrupted hadn't come back.

"I will allow you to try and save the boy," Broken Nose said after a moment.

Shane hid his surprise. "And how do I do that?"

"Here," Broken Nose said, gesturing with his hand at the cabins and the wood, "my bones have been tucked away. He is with them. Find my bones, find the boy. We will hunt you, of course."

"Of course," Shane said. "And I'll hunt you."

Broken Nose chuckled. "I would ask for nothing less. I have not been so entertained since we shaped Patience."

Shane glanced at the dead girl and saw her smile up at Broken Nose. He watched as the dead man put a hand on her small shoulder.

"She helped us, you know," Broken Nose said, looking down at her. "When we came for her people, it was Patience who finally let us in through the back. It was she who helped us take them all and to kill the weakest. And when it was her turn for the trial, she was the strongest one by far."

Shane repressed a shudder of revulsion, and his face burned with anger.

"She helped you?" Shane asked, each word short and clipped.

"Yes," Patience answered. "We had met before when I was tending the sheep with my brothers. They were afraid of him. But not me. He whispered to me, told me what I could become. How strong I would be, if I could be. How none of my family would ever be bigger or stronger. And the minister, he would fear *me*."

Broken Nose looked at Shane. "Are you ready?"

Shane gave a curt nod.

"Then I shall see you in the darkness, stranger," Broken Nose said, and turned to walk back into the clubhouse.

Patience advanced towards him, giving him a smile tinged with madness.

"He likes you, Shane," she said, coming to a stop only a foot away. "Can you not see? Why worry about this boy? Let Broken Nose break him. If he is strong, the boy will be with us. I know he wishes to add you to me as well. We can serve him together. He might even let you out, to range through the snow, to hunt those who are too weak. Would that not be a glorious time, Shane?"

Her eyes gleamed as the moonlight passed through them, her thin face more the visage of death than that of a little girl.

"Come, Shane," she whispered, snaking a small hand out from her blanket and extending it to him. "Take my hand, and we shall go to him together, you will tell him you wish to pass the test, and he will embrace you."

Shane smiled.

"Of course he will," Shane whispered, and he thrust the iron blade through her.

Chapter 39: Humored and Ignored

Few things in life irritated Rowan more than being ignored. One of those was being humored.

In less than half an hour, he had suffered through both, and he knew that it was only the beginning.

Emergency personnel had arrived at Doreen's, and she and Danny had been taken away by ambulance. Which had left Rowan in the company of his colleagues. Men and women he had known for years. People he had worked with and helped through hard times.

And they had looked at him with mixed expressions of surprise and pity as he described what had happened to Mark Rushford on the ice.

It was with little surprise that he saw Captain Allen Higgins enter the State Police mobile command center, where Rowan was seated. Rowan suppressed a groan and stood up.

The captain motioned for Rowan to sit down, and he did so. Higgins took the chair opposite him and smiled, an expression that was meant to show care and consideration.

Rowan took it for what he knew it was; a paternal gesture for a wayward son.

"How are you, Rowan?" Higgins asked, taking his hat off and scratching at the thick, silver hair. Higgins' face was red from the cold, the lines around his mouth and eyes looking as if they had been etched by the harsh New England sun over centuries instead of decades. His eyes were a sharp, bitter blue and could cut through to the quick of a question, like the man's mind.

Too many people had mistaken Higgins for a country bumpkin over the years, and more than a few were up in Concord, still at the prison.

"Upset." Rowan answered.

"Why?" Higgins asked, crossing his arms over his chest and leaning back.

"I should be out on the ice, looking for whatever took Mark Rushford and finding out what happened to Matt and Danny," Rowan snapped.

Higgins raised an eyebrow.

"Sorry, Cap," Rowan muttered.

Higgins nodded. He looked at Rowan and said, "I don't think you should be."

Rowan was too surprised to respond to the statement.

Higgins seemed to have expected Rowan's reaction because he followed the statement up quickly.

"I know you were sweet on Doreen's kids," Higgins continued. "Word gets 'round. You know that. And you always did right by the boys after their father ran out. Not to mention, I've heard from reliable sources, that Rushford senior may have lost a couple of teeth in a Manchester bar because of you."

Rowan felt his face redden.

"Now, putting all of those little facts together," Higgins said, "I don't think you're in much shape to go rushing off looking for the boys. I think the risks you'd take would be unacceptable. You might put yourself in danger, which is bad enough, but you could put your brothers and sisters, here, at risk, too. That would be inexcusable."

Rowan remained silent.

"Now what they've told me so far," Higgins said, "sounds unbelievable. But they're young, the officers out there. Nutaq's just stories to them. Campfire tales to scare each other with. But you and I, we know better, don't we?"

Rowan nodded.

"Yes," Higgins said in a small voice. "You were just a boy, but you remember there's something out there."

"It's where we should go," Rowan said, unable to keep the urgency and fear out of his voice. "If it's the same thing, then we have to."

"I will," Higgins said. "*I* will. I won't be sending anyone out there."

The captain stood up and looked at Rowan. "Remember Rowan, that was my brother Paul who went missing when you and my nephew were just boys. If anyone's going out there to look for those boys, it'll be me. The rest of you will look in the safer places, just in case we are wrong on this one."

Higgins pulled on his hat and left.

Rowan watched him go and clenched his hands into fists as he thought, *We're not wrong. Not with this one. Not at all.*

Chapter 40: A New Ally

Shane stood in the center of Preston Road. His mind still reeled from the revelation about Patience and the fact that there was another boy trapped with Broken Nose.

The strange ghost that appeared before him wasn't the shock that it might have been earlier.

Shane looked at him, tightened his grip on the iron, and asked, "Are you with Broken Nose?"

"With who?" the dead man asked, his English accent was thick and hard on the ears.

"Evidently not," Shane said.

"Are you Shane Ryan?" the ghost asked.

The question caught him off guard and Shane nodded.

"Ah, a good piece of news," the ghost said with a grin that revealed yellowed and broken teeth, and more than a few were missing. "Frank will be pleased to receive it."

Shane's shoulders sagged with relief. "Frank's here?"

"Aye," the ghost nodded. "He is indeed. Well-armed and ready to assist his friend in need, as am I."

Shane narrowed his eyes, examined the rough appearance of the dead man before him and asked, "And what was your price?"

"Hah!" the ghost exclaimed. "You're as quick as your friend, that you are. And Jack appreciates it, so he does."

And Jack's mad, Shane realized as he waited for Jack to answer his question.

The ghost cleared his throat, winked and said, "I would like to leave this bonny land, once and for all. Young Frank has agreed to assist me, so he has."

"Fair enough," Shane said. He shivered, glanced around at the snow-covered area, and said, "Will you bring Frank here, to me? I'll be in that cabin."

Jack frowned. "I thought your friend and I were here to help you leave, not help you stay, Master Shane."

"There's a boy," Shane said, turning and walking towards the cabin. "I won't leave without him."

Jack appeared in front of Shane, anger flashing in his eyes. "What's this? I'm not here to rescue any bloody brat, my boy. Only you. 'Twas all I enrolled for."

"Then go and wait," Shane said, keeping his anger in check. "I won't leave him to be tortured."

"Who has him then?" Jack snarled.

"Broken Nose. The Indians," Shane replied.

Jack's eyes widened, the snarl vanished between pressed lips, and he nodded, saying in a small voice. "Aye, then. We'd heard, so we did, of what the wild savages did to their captives."

"Nothing good," Shane said over his shoulder. "I can tell you that for certain."

He climbed the steps onto the cabin's small porch and closed the door over. Shane walked into the bedroom, picked up the bag of rock salt, and brought it out into the small den. He poured a large semi-circle around the door, wide enough so it could still be opened, but small enough to keep anything dead at bay.

When he had finished, he paced the room. He wanted to go out after the boy, but if Frank was coming to the cabin, and he had weapons, then he would have to wait.

We'll have a better chance of getting him out together, Shane thought. A sudden realization flashed through him, and Shane hurried into the kitchen. He dug around under the sink and found a bottle of starter fluid for a fire. In the cabinets above the sink, he found a box of kitchen matches. He brought both items out to the den and put them down by the rock salt.

He looked at all three for a moment and then nodded.

Broken Nose, Shane thought, *I am going to light up the night sky when I burn your bones.*

Chapter 41: Danny Wakes Up

"Danny."

The voice was soft and insistent.

"Danny."

His name was pronounced a little louder. He felt a hand on his arm.

Danny struggled to open his eyes, but it felt as though there was a cloth on them, too heavy to be moved. When he reached for it, he discovered his arms were held down.

"Danny."

Danny recognized the voice.

"Rowan?" Danny asked, the name came out cracked and broken, the syllables hurting his throat.

"Yes," Rowan Little said, relief in his voice. Danny felt a friendly pat on his arm as Rowan continued to speak.

"Danny," Rowan said, hesitant at first. "Where did you get Matt's snowmobile from?"

A painful memory seared into Danny's mind. The raw image of Clark's mangled body flooded his thoughts, and Danny struggled to get away from it.

Rowan's hand tightened on his bicep. "It's alright, Danny. It's okay. I don't know what happened to you, but I need you to tell me where you got the sled from."

Shuddering, Danny nodded. He swallowed several times to get enough saliva together to moisten his dry mouth, and he managed to whisper, "Preston Road."

Rowan squeezed his arm and then let go. Danny heard metal squeak, and Rowan's voice came from a little further away. "What happened to Matt Rushford?"

"I don't know," Danny hissed. It hurt to talk, but he wanted to tell Rowan what he knew. "A ghost grabbed me. It's crazy, but it's true. It killed Clark. Was going to kill me, too. A guy named Shane pulled me out. He tried to save Rushford, but the kid died of shock. We were going to get away on his sled, but he sent me off. Something about saving a boy."

"This man, Shane," Rowan said, his voice coming closer. "He stayed behind to help someone else?"

Danny could only nod.

"When was this?" Rowan asked.

"Right before I crashed," Danny answered. "I'd only been on the ice for five, maybe ten minutes."

"Alright," Rowan said. "I'm leaving, Danny, but you're in good hands. You're in Elliot Hospital. I'll check on you soon."

"Rowan," Danny said.

"Yes?"

"Why can't I see?" Danny asked.

It took a moment for Rowan to respond.

"They're not sure how much damage you suffered on your ride," Rowan explained. "They're not taking any chances. Your Dad's on his way up from Massachusetts. He'll be here soon to sit with you. Alright?"

"Alright," Danny whispered.

He listened to Rowan leave the room, door opened and closed with a gentle whisper. The lock clicked into place, and Danny was left alone in the darkness. He felt fear creep over him. Weeping, Danny lay in the darkness and waited for his father.

And he wondered, for the first time, if he would ever see again.

Book 6: Lake Nutaq

Chapter 42: The Band's Back Together

Shane heard footsteps on the porch, and he squeezed the handle of his iron.

The door was eased open, and Frank stepped into the room. He smiled at Shane, looked around and stepped over the line of salt. On one shoulder, a duffel bag was slung, and he extended his hand.

Shane shook it, grinning with relief. "I am happy as hell to see you, Frank."

"I would have been here sooner," Frank said, putting the bag on the floor, "if you hadn't been so stupid as to leave without anybody."

Shane shrugged the rebuke off and looked out the door. Jack stood on the porch, back to them. "Your friend came with you."

"Jack?" Frank asked, squatting down to open the duffel bag.

"Yeah."

"Yup," Frank said, pulling out a sawed-off shotgun and handing it to Shane. "He came along. I thought he was going to take off soon as he told me where you were."

"Why didn't he?" Shane asked, opening the weapon and making sure there were rounds in the two chambers. The glint of brass told him it was loaded.

"Here," Frank said, handing Shane a pair of black, iron rings. They were a snug fit on the index finger of each hand.

"Jack told me he wants to see if he can kill a ghost," Frank said, putting a set of rings on his own fingers. He pulled a second shotgun out, and a box of shells, too. "Brian and I loaded up about twenty of them."

"Brian Roy?" Shane asked, surprised.

"Who else was I going to go to?" Frank said, straightening up. "Looks like you have the makings for a good bonfire."

"I hope so," Shane said. He bent down, put a loose knot in the plastic bag of rock salt and then added it, the matches, and the starter fluid to the duffel bag before shouldering it.

"Tell me what's going on," Frank said, and Shane did so.

By the time Shane finished, Frank's face had paled and tightened. A cold, hard look had crept in his eyes, and he said, "Are you ready to get the boy?"

Shane nodded.

Without any other words, they left the cabin. Jack opened his mouth to call out a hello, but he closed it when he caught sight of their expressions. Instead of asking any questions, he fell into step with them.

"Jack," Shane said.

"Aye?"

"Could you scout ahead a bit, tell us what you see?" Shane asked.

Jack gave a lopsided grin and raced ahead, disappearing between two cabins. Shane and Frank continued on in silence. Their feet plunged into the snow, the traveling difficult. Soon, Shane's thighs began to ache, and in the trees around them night birds called out.

They passed between the same pair of cabins Jack had, and then through a small yard and into the trees. The pines and evergreens were old, far older than any Shane had seen before. Passages between the trees were narrow, some piled high with snow that had drifted down, or fallen from the branches above. There was a sense of age to the forest, and Shane understood he had never been in woods as old as the one they walked through.

Jack appeared before them and held up his hands in mock surprise as both Shane and Frank snapped the shotguns up into firing positions.

"Not that lead will hurt old Jack now," Jack said, winking and lowering his arms.

"It's salt," Shane said, "and it'll send 'old Jack' right back to wherever he came from."

Jack looked from Shane to Frank, and Frank nodded. "Salt sends you back to where you're bound, Jack. And while the button's in my pocket, I've heard it's not a terribly pleasant experience."

Jack inclined his head. "I'll take your word on it. I hope, as well, that you'll take mine. You have a way to travel yet, but they're waiting for you. A pair of them, red children of the forest with cruel knives that yearn for your flesh, aye."

"I'm sure they do," Shane said. He wiped at his nose with the back of his hand, the mucus running freely from the cold. "Frank told me you wanted to see if you could kill one of them."

"So I do," Jack said.

"Did you try?" Frank asked.

Jack shook his head.

"Why not?" Shane asked.

"Because," Jack said, wearing an expression of innocence. "There were two and not one of them."

Frank snorted, and Shane shook his head.

"Lead on, my lion-hearted friend," Shane said, gesturing with the shotgun.

"Aye," Jack said, grinning. "That, I shall. We'll fall on these heathens together, and write our names large with their blood. Or whatever it is we have now."

Shane didn't reply. He was focused on the boy, and finding him as soon as possible.

Chapter 43: In Darkness

Mark Rushford woke up in horrific pain. His leg throbbed, and he remembered everything.

He lay in darkness, unable to see anything. With a trembling hand, he felt around his eyes, fearing he had been blindfolded. But he hadn't been. He couldn't see for the simple reason that there was no light.

Mark licked his lips, shifted his weight and bit down hard on the inside of his cheek to keep his scream of pain in check.

The air around him was warm, and he felt sweat trickle down his back. He could smell dirt and rotting leaves. In the darkness, tiny feet skittered across a stone.

"Is anyone there?" he whispered.

"Yes," a voice answered. It was a small child, but whether the speaker was a boy or a girl, Mark couldn't tell.

"Where are we?" Mark asked, his voice trembling. "What's happening here?"

"We are in Hell," the voice responded. "We are being punished for our sins."

"What?" a note of panic crept into Mark's voice. "I'm not dead. I can't be dead."

"No," the voice agreed. "You are not dead, although you may well wish you were before this is done."

The sentence sent a stomach-knotting chill down Mark's back.

For a moment, Mark said nothing, listening instead to the rapid beating of his heart. Trying to keep his mind off the pain of his broken leg, Mark asked, "What's your name?"

"Jonathan. What is yours?"

"Mark," he answered. "How did I get here?"

"Patience brought you," Jonathan replied, and the hatred in his words made Mark shudder.

"I don't know what you mean by that," Mark said after a pause. "How did my patience bring me here? I'm confused."

"No," Jonathan snapped. "Patience is my sister's name. She brought you here. As she brought me. As she brought so many of us."

Mark began to ask how, and then he thought of the little girl on Lake Nutaq.

The hands reaching out from her chest and pulling him in.

"But that wasn't real," Mark whispered. "None of it was real. Not that part."

"Silence!" Jonathan hissed. "Someone is coming!"

Mark whimpered but held his tongue.

The air went from warm to cold in the blink of an eye, and Mark's fear magnified.

A deep, male voice asked a question in a language Mark couldn't understand, but the words were quickly followed by the sound of a young girl translating.

"Broken Nose would like to know how you are doing," she said.

Mark was too afraid to answer.

Broken Nose chuckled and spoke again.

"He says you have nothing to fear, Mark," the girl said. "Someone is coming to help you."

"She lies," Jonathan whispered.

"Leave here, Jonathan!" the girl snapped, and Mark understood that she was Patience, Jonathan's sister. To Mark, she said, "Best to answer him, Mark."

Mark stuttered, and his response tumbled out of his mouth. "I'm afraid, and I think my leg is broken."

Patience translated and Broken Nose's response was both quick and frightening.

"The man, Shane, and his friends will be here, soon," Patience said, "and then you will all suffer together."

Silence followed her statement and warmth crept back into the room. Mark closed his eyes and held back tears. The blood in his head pounded in time to the throbs of pain which emanated from his leg, and suddenly, Mark understood he was going to die.

He thought about Matt and wondered where his brother was. Then a terrible thought crept into his consciousness, and Mark cried.

"Why do you weep?" Jonathan asked in a small voice with a hint of condemnation.

"Because I think my brother's dead," Mark moaned.

"Ah," Jonathan whispered.

As he sobbed, Mark felt a cold, comforting hand come to rest upon his head.

"At least, Mark," the dead boy said, "he is not trapped here, like me. A handful of my teeth scattered in a savage's grave keeps me from God."

And while he cried harder at the thought, Mark understood Jonathan was right.

Chapter 44: Thinking About the Past

Rowan sat in his personal vehicle, parked almost a mile from the entrance to Preston Road. He had the heat turned up to the maximum, and even with the hot air blasting out of the vents, he couldn't get warm.

The idea of going down among the cabins made him feel like a little boy again. Like a frightened eight-year-old who was about to stumble onto something terrible.

For most of his life, Rowan had fought the memories of that blizzard.

Other people liked to chat about the storm, ask one another where they were, what they were doing.

Not Rowan.

Every heavy snowfall reminded him of that blizzard.

He and William Higgins had gone with William's father, Paul, out for some cross-country skiing. Mostly, it had been for Rowan's mother to have a little peace and quiet. He and William were best friends, and they'd been driving her up one wall and down another after being stuck indoors for days. Paul had cut down two pairs of skis for the boys, waxed the wood, and fitted each ski with leather ties to fit around their boots. He had even trimmed some poles for them.

The day had been quiet, the world smothered beneath the snow. And while the air had been cold, stinging what little parts of Rowan's face weren't hidden by his scarf; it was beautiful to be out of the house.

Paul had been trying to tire the boys out, which was why he brought them out as far as Preston Road. If Paul had stopped there, decided to turn around and head back the way they had come, then all would have been well.

But he didn't, Rowan remembered. *And it wasn't.*

Rowan stuffed the memories down, as far as they would go into the back of his mind, and forced himself to think about Preston Road in the present. He needed to go in there, to look for Matt's body, and possibly find out if something truly had grabbed Mark.

The way it had seized Paul.

And the memory was there. Unbidden, unwanted, and relentless.

Rowan was no longer a forty-seven-year-old man, but an eight-year-old boy, standing in the snow beside his best friend. The sun shined down on them, and darkness uncurled from the trees, reached out long, dark tendrils and wrapped around Paul Higgins' limbs. First, a look of surprise settled on the man's face, then terror flashed across it.

Paul was jerked backward, knocked down, and dragged beneath the snow-heavy bows of a pine tree. Someone screamed, a loud, piercing sound, and Rowan discovered later that the scream was the combination of two voices, William's and his own.

Rowan and William had fled from Preston Road. The two boys had been desperate to escape the monster that had grabbed William's father, and they had made it to the safety of the main road. After the nightmare of Paul's death, Rowan lost his best friend, William and his widowed mother moving far from Lake Nutaq.

Rowan shuddered as he remembered Paul. A man who had seemed too tall and vigorous to Rowan to be brought down by anything.

And on a cold, snowy day, Paul had been snatched away as if he hadn't been anything at all.

Enough! Rowan screamed. He slammed the car into gear and drove down to the entrance. When he arrived, Rowan stepped hard on the brakes, shocked to see another vehicle there.

The vehicle was free of snow and ice, the gray paint job dirty with salt and sand from the roads. Rowan knew it couldn't be the man that Danny had told him about. Common sense said Shane's car would be down further along the road, and more than likely covered in snow from the storm.

No, this was someone else.

Rowan put his car into park and turned off the engine.

Do they know what they're getting into? he wondered. Rowan got out of the car and looked at the footprints that lead from the other vehicle down onto Preston Road.

"Hell," Rowan whispered. "Do I?"

He looked down at the thick trees on either side of the road and realized he did not.

Chapter 45: Deeper into the Forest

They walked with a steady rhythm, following Jack through the gloom. The path he led them on was curved, and it didn't take Shane long to understand they moved parallel to Lake Nutaq. Somewhere, along the lake's border, they would find where Broken Nose had hidden away the boy.

And with any luck, they would discover the Indian's bones as well.

Don't forget Patience, Shane thought, the girl's memory bitter to him. *We'll burn her too. Hell, I'll set the whole damned forest ablaze if I have to.*

"Shane," Frank said.

Shane looked over at his friend.

"You okay?" Frank asked.

Shane shook his head. "I'm angry. I'm going to hurt them if I can."

Frank raised an eyebrow. "Let's just get it done with."

"Can we hurt them?" Jack asked, appearing beside them. "Aye, there's a question to be answered, what do you say, Frank?"

Frank didn't answer, looking instead to Shane.

"I don't know if we can hurt them," Shane said. "And I don't care. All I want is to get the boy, and send the dead into the next world."

Jack snorted, a disappointed expression on his face. "And where is the fun in that, aye, my boy? Nowhere, says Jack, and it's a truth to be sure. I'd rather find out if I can stick a blade in and twist it about."

"You're welcome to try," Shane said, "after we get the boy out. Not before. Do it before, and you and I will have a bit of talking to do."

A sneer flickered across Jack's face, and then the ghost was gone.

"He's not exactly right in the head, is he," Shane said.

"No," Frank replied. "Not by any stretch of the imagination. Even Carl said as much."

"Carl knew about him?" Shane asked, surprised.

"Yes," Frank said, and he told Shane what he had learned from Carl.

Shane shook his head and came to a stop. "Where the hell did he go?"

"I don't know," Frank answered. He shifted the shotgun in his hands and dug the bright gold button out of his pocket.

Frank held it up to his mouth and whispered, the words faint.

"Jack," Frank said. "Where are you?"

There was no response from the dead man.

Shane lifted his chin and felt the air. The temperature hadn't changed. Jack wasn't back, but no one else had arrived either.

"This isn't good," Shane said. He slipped the strap of the duffel bag off his shoulder and set it down in the snow at his feet. "I can't say I have a lot of trust in our new friend, Jack."

"That's more than what I have," Frank said.

"What do you mean?" Shane asked.

"I don't trust him at all," Frank said. He sank to one knee, looking out into the depths of the forest.

Shane wracked his memory for any shred of information in regards to Native Americans and their burial habits. He remembered only a little, a vague recollection concerning mounds and pyramids.

"We can't wait for him," Shane said. "If he doesn't come back soon, though, I say we put his shiny button in the salt for him."

"Sounds good to me," Frank said, standing back up. He brushed the snow off his jeans and nodded to the bag. "Want me to carry it now?"

Shane began to say no, but he changed his mind, nodding instead. "Yeah. Best to switch off with it."

"No, that's not why," Frank said, picking the bag up and shouldering it.

"Oh no?" Shane asked.

Frank shook his head.

"Why is it then?"

"It's because you're a cripple now," Frank snickered.

Shane let a small smile creep onto his face as he thought, *It's good to face death with a friend.*

Together the men continued on through the snow, angling their path towards what Shane hoped would be Lake Nutaq.

Chapter 46: Still Awake

Mark had managed to roll over, and he lay on his back, staring into darkness. His throat was dry, and his stomach rumbled, hunger overcoming the unrelenting ache of his broken leg. He felt exhausted, his eyes dry and pained as they moved in their sockets. Mark reached out around him, groping at the cold, hard dirt he found.

His fingers quested for a bit of ice or snow, anything to help slake his thirst and take his mind off the gnawing in his belly.

But there was nothing to find except for old and brittle leaves. Small, unseen creatures scurried away from his hands, and Mark was afraid the animals would nip at him.

"How are you?" Jonathan asked from beside Mark's head.

Mark shuddered. "I'm hungry. And thirsty."

"There is nothing here," the dead boy said. "I am sorry."

"It's okay," Mark said, sighing. Tears welled up in his eyes, but he held them back. He had cried enough. "Have you heard anything?"

"No," Jonathan answered. "Broken Nose sits alone. The others have gone to seek out your savior. They will bring him back alive."

Mark couldn't argue with the statement because he didn't know if it were true or not. He knew he didn't want it to be true. But all Mark had was a name and the affirmation from Jonathan that Shane was indeed looking for him.

"What do you think happened to my brother?" Mark whispered.

"I think he died, and nothing more," Jonathan replied. "For which we must be grateful. He did not suffer at the hands of Broken Nose. Nor was he forced into an eternity of captivity within Patience's foul depths."

"Why do you hate your sister so much?" Mark asked. His throat hurt with the effort to talk, and to keep his voice level, but he was too afraid of the silence and the darkness.

"It was she who betrayed us," Jonathan answered, anger rising in his voice. "The savages had attacked us, and we were safe. Secure within our garrison house. We had only to hold out until the heathens tired of the siege."

"Would they have left?" Mark asked.

"Yes," Jonathan answered, confidence in the response. "They always did. Fields would be set afire, animals butchered. Houses razed. But always they did leave, and always the men went out to exact vengeance. This time, too, it would have kept to its rhythm, had it not been for Patience. It was she who unlocked the back door. She slipped the bar and let them creep in among us. Those that died quick, they were indeed the lucky ones. The rest of us, we suffered. And the strongest of us are trapped here, unable to claim our places in Heaven."

Mark wanted to ask more, but the sound of voices silenced him.

"So I says," a deep, manly voice stated, "I wanted to try my hand at killing one of the savages. Or whatever it is that can be done to our kind. They weren't obliged to let me try. No, not at all. Which is all well and good, now that I thinks on it a bit more."

Mark heard Broken Nose answer, and Patience translated. Her words were too faint to be understood. The stranger's boisterous laugh and the cruel undertone to it made Mark believe that it had not been a funny or pleasant statement in the least.

"Well, 'tis neither here nor there at this point, aye, my girl?" the stranger asked.

Patience's answer was once more too weak to hear.

"Yes," the stranger said, clearing his throat, "send your bucks along with me, and I'll lead them straight, so I will. And I've your word I can stay here?"

Patience's murmur set the man to laughing.

"Oh aye," the man said, "I'll not kill too many, that I promise. I'd scare off the rest of the flock, what?"

Chortling, the stranger left, his voice fading.

Broken Nose and Patience exchanged a few words in the Native American's own language, and left, their voices fading.

"I fear the worse for Shane," Jonathan said. "It seems he is to be betrayed, for the man speaking to Broken Nose was a member of his party."

The thought of being trapped, when rescue had seemed so close, caused Mark to shake. It started as a tremble and transformed itself into something violent. He clenched his jaw to keep his scream of pain and fear trapped in his throat.

"Calm yourself," Jonathan urged. "Keep your body and your mind your own. Do not let fear take them from you, Mark. Find the strength of your name, it is a good name, the name of one chosen by God."

Mark didn't find any strength in his name, but he found a place of comfort in the dead boy's voice. He focused on the gentle rise and fall of Jonathan's words, the lilt in the way he spoke.

In a few moments, Mark was calm. He forced his jaw to relax, rubbing the muscles with one hand, and trying to ignore a throbbing headache that had sprung up behind his eyes.

"Are you calmer now?" Jonathan asked.

"Yes," Mark managed to answer.

"Good." Jonathan paused, then added, "If the worst occurs, then it will be up to you to save yourself. Do you understand?"

"No," Mark responded. "How can I save myself? I'm trapped."

He hated the sound of hysteria as it crept into his voice, but he couldn't seem to stop it.

"Hush," Jonathan said gently. "No one is ever trapped. Not when you have the will. I will help you, and you will be free. My sister and Broken Nose have gathered enough souls to them."

"Alright," Mark whispered, turning his head towards the sound of Jonathan's voice. "I will save myself if I have to."

"Good," Jonathan whispered, and silence fell over them as they waited for news of Shane.

Chapter 47: Going Down Preston Road

Rowan fought his fear with each step he took. He felt watched, the sensation gnawing at what little remained of his confidence. A small part of himself told him to man up, to deal with the fear. It reminded him of when he had gone and pulled people from burning cars, intervened between men fighting, and when he had needed to jump into Lake Nutaq to save a child from drowning.

Yet all of those occurrences had been within the scope of his job as a peace officer. They were, when it came right down to it, mundane.

Looking for monsters, the supernatural kind, was not anything he had considered doing.

Not ever, he told himself.

Rowan reached the cabins of Preston Road and came to a stop.

His eyes took in the entirety of the scene, his training cataloging everything. He saw the snow-covered car at the first cabin on the left, and the churned snow from the steps to the battered remains of Danny's plow. Rowan saw the cabin's door hung askew and open.

Snowmobile tracks ran from the right, arced around the plow, and back down towards the clubhouse. At that building, he saw Clark's van, and the damage done to it and the structure. There was a path from the first cabin to the clubhouse, and Rowan wondered what had happened on Preston Road.

Without knowing why, he lowered his hand to his semi-automatic pistol, slipped the holster's loop off it, and took a deep breath. He let the air out slowly through his nostrils, the steam curling up past him as he considered what to do next.

His thoughts were interrupted by a high-pitched yowl, jerking his head over to the right as he drew the pistol with a single, smooth motion.

A Native American man ran out from between a couple of cabins, a war club raised over his head.

"Stop!" Rowan ordered, steadying his right hand with his left and sighting down the barrel. He kept the weapon pointed at the man's chest, and it was then Rowan realized two facts.

The first was that the man's breath wasn't forming the clouds of white it should have been. Second, Rowan could see through the man, as if the stranger was nothing more than a trick of the light.

Rowan fired the pistol anyway.

The sound of the weapon rang off the cabin walls and raced into the woods.

Rowan knew he had hit the stranger because he never missed.

A hole had even appeared in the wood of the cabin behind the man.

But the Native American kept charging towards him, closing the distance with long, powerful strides.

Rowan fired two more shots, the brass casings spinning through the air before landing in the snow.

After the third shot, Rowan turned to run. A sense of panic was fighting his rational mind for control of his body, and Rowan understood he wouldn't make it to his car before the man caught him.

Instead of turning towards the road, Rowan ran for the open door of the cabin on the left.

With the screaming man behind him, Rowan barreled up the steps, slammed into the open door and slid on a pile of rock salt scattered around the threshold. He tripped, stumbled, and then fell into a chair, knocking something heavy onto the floor which landed with a loud thwack.

Rowan fell on the floor but managed to hold onto his pistol. He twisted around and fired three more useless shots at the figure which appeared in the doorway. The man laughed at him, glanced down at the scattered salt, and frowned.

Rowan tried to steady himself, preparing to push himself up, but his gloved hand smacked a hard piece of metal. Turning his attention to it, Rowan saw it was a rough length of plow-edge, the iron pitted and worn. Someone, he noticed, had wrapped the bottom with medical tape.

Without knowing why, Rowan grabbed the iron, holding onto it as he would a life raft. Gripping the makeshift weapon, Rowan faced the Native American, who was squatting down and looking at the salt. The man rested his war club on his shoulder and scratched at his topknot.

Rowan stood up, holstering his useless pistol.

The movement and the noise caught the other man's attention, and he gave Rowan a smile that caused the hairs on his neck to stand up.

He's a ghost, Rowan thought, the idea strange and foreign to him. *He's already dead. That's why the bullets didn't do anything.*

The dead man used the war club to point at the iron in Rowan's hand. He spoke in a language Rowan couldn't understand, but the meaning was clear.

The iron was not welcome.

Rowan felt a surge of hope, and he switched the weapon from his left hand to his right. He pointed it at the dead man and said, "Come on."

The man snarled at Rowan and gestured to the salt on the floor, making a sweeping gesture.

It keeps him out. Salt.

"You don't like the salt?" Rowan asked, nodding towards it.

Again, the dead man gestured to it, then he beckoned Rowan forward.

"Sure," Rowan said. "Sure."

He took a step forward and squatted down. In the corner of his eye, he saw the dead man raise the war club in a slow arc, and Rowan thrust the iron plow edge forward.

The result was instantaneous and thrilling.

A scream of rage was ripped from the throat of the dead man even as the ghost vanished.

Rowan was left alone with ringing ears and a way to protect himself.

He straightened up, adjusted his grip on the iron, and turned away from the door. Danny had said Matt was dead. Shane, whoever that was, had tried to save him.

It was time to see if Matt's body was in the cabin.

Rowan took only a few steps into the small den, passed the chair he had knocked over and into the doorway of the bedroom.

Matt Rushford lay on the floor, hands folded on his chest, legs, and feet together.

There wasn't a single mark on the boy's body, and his face looked younger than Rowan knew him to be.

Rowan's heart ached for Doreen, but Mark was still alive, and he needed to find her younger son.

Taking a blanket from the bed, Rowan spread it out over Matt. He didn't try to say any prayers. The sadness he felt faded away beneath a growing wave of anger.

With the iron in his hand, Rowan turned away from the body and went to find Mark.

Chapter 48: Jack Returns

Jack appeared from behind an evergreen, and Shane resisted the urge to scatter the ghost with a blast from the shotgun.

Without taking his finger off the trigger, Shane came to a stop, and Frank did the same. Shane noticed that Frank kept his weapon pointed on Jack, too. Jack seemed aware of it as well, looking from one man to the next.

"Why the distrust of old Jack?" the ghost said, a pained note in his voice. "I've not led you astray, now have I? No, not Jack. Did I not bring you to Shane, Frank? And Shane, did I not bring Frank to you?"

Shane didn't answer the question. "Where did you slip away to, Jack?"

"Ahead and to the west, then back to the east, a bit to the north," Jack said, grinning. "All points of the compass did Jack cover, to make sure no trouble would be found."

"What did you find?" Frank asked, easing the duffel bag to the snow covered forest floor.

"Not much, I'm afraid," Jack said. "Little and less. No sign of a boy. No sign of a savage. Nay, nary a one."

"No?" Shane asked, thinking, *You're a terrible liar, Jack. I can see in your dead eyes something happened.*

Frank unzipped the bag with one hand and rummaged around inside. His shotgun rested on one knee and continued to point towards Jack.

"No, no. All Jack saw was the glory of God's creation," he said, offering up an attempt at a winning, confident smile.

The air grew a trifle colder. Shane's breath billowed a little more as it left his mouth.

"Oh, Jack," Shane whispered, "payback is a terrible thing."

The dead man's smile faltered, and then he howled as Frank thrust the gold button into the bag of rock salt. Jack vanished, and from either side of the evergreen, a couple of Indians appeared.

There was no posturing, no screaming, no howls to frighten Shane or Frank. The dead men charged forward, tomahawks ready.

Yet they were men of an earlier time. Creatures from a period when muskets were inaccurate at best. They were confident, and wrongly so. The sound of the shotguns being fired ripped through the air.

As the rock salt passed through the ghosts at a thousand feet per second, the dead men vanished. The shots knocked loose snow from the evergreen, and as it fell to the ground, Shane and Frank reloaded their shotguns in stoic silence.

"Have I mentioned," Shane said, "that I don't trust Jack?"

"You may have," Frank said, picking the duffel bag back up and slinging it over his shoulder. "We'll talk about this later, after we find the boy."

"Definitely," Shane agreed. "And I'll have to have a chat with Carl when we get home. See who else is hidden in Berkley Street."

Frank nodded. "Guess that would be a pretty good idea."

"You think?" Shane asked, sighing. "Like I didn't have enough trouble with the damned dead I knew about."

With Jack imprisoned in the bag of salt, Shane saw a glimpse of an open space ahead and to the right, and took the lead.

Frank followed close beside him, and the men readied themselves to fight off more of the dead.

Chapter 49: Not the Only One Alive

The shots were muffled, but they were undeniably shots.

For a moment, Rowan paused, head tilted as he listened. No further shots came, and for a second he worried that he had heard nothing more than a couple of poachers looking for some venison.

No, Rowan thought, shaking his head and continuing on. *That's Shane. And there's someone else with him.*

Rowan had been following the trail left by Shane, and whomever had driven the car parked near the entrance to Preston Road. The men had a decent pace going. Rowan could tell by the length of their strides in the deep snow.

He wondered if they had fired at ghosts, and if so, how did they manage to keep the dead at bay when firearms didn't work.

Think, Rowan scolded himself. And so he did.

The gunshots had been on top of one another, almost indistinguishable. But they had been separate, and they had also been from shotguns. Shotgun shells could be loaded with either solid lead slugs or pellets of varying sizes.

Rowan also knew a few old timers who kept shotgun shells loaded with rock salt to keep raccoons and skunks out of the trash.

If a line of salt can keep one out, Rowan thought, *what can it do when it's shot through them.*

He looked at the iron in his hand and thought he might know what the rock salt was capable of.

I need a shotgun, Rowan thought and continued on through the snow. He moved as fast as he dared. Not only were the dead out and about, but there were two men armed with shotguns. And while getting hit with rock salt wouldn't kill him, Rowan suspected it would be extremely unpleasant.

His reflecting on the discomfort of rock salt came close to being fatal.

Rowan ducked to avoid a snow-laden branch, and a tomahawk slashed through the air where his head had so recently occupied. The attack surprised him, and Rowan fell, letting go of the iron and losing it in the snow.

A scream was torn from his throat as a sharp pain exploded in his lower back. He tried to scramble away, but he found his legs were unresponsive. Terrified, Rowan dug his hands into the deep snow, sought some sort of purchase, and tried to drag himself forward, away from his invisible attacker.

Keeping his head up, Rowan looked for the iron blade, but it had vanished. From his low vantage, he couldn't see where the weapon had fallen, and then a man stepped into his field of vision.

The stranger was a Native American, not the same ghost as the one he had defeated on Preston Road, but from the same tribe. The man carried a war club, the polished wood caught Rowan's eye and held his attention. Rowan gasped as a bitterly cold hand grabbed him by the back of the neck. Beneath the dead man's grasp, Rowan felt a deep chill penetrate his flesh.

The ghost in front of him said something in a language Rowan didn't understand.

A chuckle was the dark spirit's response, and Rowan felt himself pulled up, his legs hanging loose like a rag doll.

The warclub-wielding ghost took a step forward, the upper half of his face painted black. He grinned as he looked at Rowan. After a moment, he looked past Rowan, spoke again, and the one holding up Rowan replied.

The ghost in front of Rowan laughed, nodding his agreement. He raised his weapon up until the edge of it grazed Rowan's chin. Rowan quivered, the pain of the touch sucked the air out of his lungs.

The ghost took the warclub down, asked a question, and the ghost behind Rowan replied with a single word.

Rowan watched as the dead man raised the warclub up, and then brought it crashing down.

Chapter 50: With Doreen

Doreen lay on a bed, her arms secured by soft, yet strong restraints to the safety rails.

Allen Higgins took a chair, moved it closer to her, and sat down. He set his cap on his knee, pulled his gloves off, and looked at the woman. Her head lolled to one side, and her eyelids were open a fraction of an inch. Allen could see the whites of her eyes and her breathing was slow, ragged.

He couldn't imagine her pain at the loss of her sons.

"Doreen," Allen said, his voice low and gentle. The doctor on duty had told him there was a chance she might not be able to respond. Allen pitched his voice a little deeper, a shade louder. "Doreen."

Her eyelids twitched, flickered, and then the left eyelid opened. Her eye spun around, jerked from left to right, up and down and back again before it fixated on Allen.

"Doreen," Allen said. "I'm Captain Higgins. I'm investigating the disappearance of your boys."

"My boys." Her voice was barely a whisper.

Allen leaned forward. "Can you tell me where you think they may have gone?"

She shook her head, the slightest of movements.

"Do you know anything that could help me? Could you tell me anything, anything at all?" Allen asked.

"There was a girl," Doreen whispered. "On the ice. She said Matt was dead. She was taking Mark. There was a girl."

"A girl?" Allen asked. "Like a teenager?"

"No," Doreen whispered. "A little girl. Grade school. Thin. Terribly thin. She had a blanket on."

Allen straightened up.

"You saw her?" he asked.

"Yes."

"Did anyone else see her?" Allen asked.

"Rowan," she murmured. "Rowan saw her."

"Alright," Allen said. He reached out, patted her on the leg and added, "We're going to find your boys, Doreen. Don't you worry about a thing."

Her only response was to close her eyes. A moment later, the sound of her troubled breathing filled the room. Allen sat by her side for several minutes, thinking. Finally, he stood, sighed and put on his cap. Digging out his phone, Allen walked to the bathroom in her room and entered it. He closed the door over and dialed a number he had memorized decades earlier.

The call rang twice before it was answered.

"Yes?" a woman asked.

"It's Allen," he said. "Patience is out and about."

"Damage?" she inquired.

"At least one boy. Possibly two," Allen answered. "An old man."

"Containable?" she asked.

"Of course," he replied.

"Is this merely a courtesy call?" she asked, a note of annoyance entering her voice.

"For now," Allen said, keeping his own tone calm and patient. "I may have to conduct an investigation."

The woman hesitated, then said, "You'll require a scapegoat."

"Yes."

"Hm." Allen could hear her tapping her fingers on something. "Alright. I will make the necessary arrangements. Inform me immediately when the scapegoat is to be delivered."

"Yes ma'am," Allen replied.

She ended the call, and Allen searched his contacts for Phil Smith's number. When he found it, he called the man.

"Allen," Phil said, answering after the first ring. "What's the situation?"

"Lake Nutaq," Allen stated.

"Damn," Phil said, sighing. "I was hoping it wasn't. What've you got?"

Allen told him.

"Alright, alright," Phil muttered. "I'll meet you there. Half an hour?"

"Make it an hour," Allen said. "I've got to make sure the boys are looking on the other side of the lake, and not Preston Road."

Phil snorted. "Yeah. Might be a little difficult to explain if Broken Nose started killing cops."

"You think?" Allen questioned. "Anyway, one hour. Meet you there."

He ended the call and looked at himself in the mirror. Allen could see the dark circles around his eyes, the stubble coming in.

You've got a long way to go tonight, Allen told himself. *And you'll have to talk to Rowan eventually. Be better if he's the one to tell Doreen her boys are dead.*

With a sigh, Allen left the bathroom and went to prepare for Preston Road.

Chapter 51: On the Edge of Lake Nutaq

When Shane and Frank came out of the tree line, they could look over the frozen expanse of Lake Nutaq. In the distance, they could see houses scattered about on the far shore. Smoke from woodstoves drifted up from fieldstone or brick chimneys. The snow covered landscape and the old homes were a perfect snapshot of the classic New England image of winter.

"There are no houses here," Frank observed.

Shane looked around and realized his friend was right.

There were no buildings at all on their side of Lake Nutaq. Trees grew undisturbed, reaching up to the sky. Yet they didn't grow close to the shore. A wide expanse of land, at least a hundred yards, stretched from the shore to the first of the trees. Between the frozen water and the snow-laden evergreens were small mounds, averaging six or seven feet in height and equal in diameter.

"What are those?" Frank asked, a wary tone in his words.

Shane frowned, a memory picking at the back of his mind.

"I know what they are," Shane muttered, taking a step forward. "I just can't put my finger on it."

He looked around, counting. There were at least fifty, perhaps more tucked behind the larger ones.

"Oh hell," Shane said, straightening up. "I think we found what we were looking for."

"What? Broken Nose's bones?" Frank asked.

Shane nodded. "Yeah. This is how the local Native American's buried their dead. Mounds. Graves beneath frameworks of branches. Almost like pyramids."

"Damn," Frank muttered. "Which one is he in?"

"I don't know," Shane said. "I don't even know how to figure it out. And where's the boy, for God's sake?"

"I don't know," Frank answered, "but we need to figure it out soon. We're running out of daylight, and it's going to get real cold, real fast."

Shane nodded. He walked to the closest mound, brushed some of the snow off, and looked at the dry and brittle grass beneath it. Frowning, he grabbed a handful of the dead vegetation and gave it a tug.

He grunted in surprise as a chunk of dirt the size of his fist came free. Shane threw it down and saw he had made a hole into the mound. He glanced at Frank and saw he had dug a small flashlight out of the duffel bag. Shane took it with a nod of thanks, turned it on and shined the light into the mound.

Ancient branches, interwoven to form a thick framework, could be seen, as could a woven mat partially covered with dirt. But there was no boy in the burial chamber. Nothing at all.

Shane shook his head and stepped away from the mound.

Together they moved on to the next one and were greeted by the ghost of a Native American woman.

She was old, her face wrinkled, and her eyes intense. Her clothing was of fine deerskin, beaded and decorated. She was small, well below five feet, and she looked up at them with a mixture of curiosity and surprise.

"Who are you?" she asked in her own tongue, which was similar to the one Broken Nose had spoken.

"Strangers," Shane answered. She did not seem surprised by his reply or the fact that he was talking her language.

"Why are you here, among the dead?" she inquired.

"We're seeking a boy, a living boy," Shane replied. "He's been taken here against his will. I seek to return him to his family."

She narrowed her eyes. "There is only one here who would take a member of the living, and he is down there."

The old woman gestured towards the end of the mounds.

"You had best beware," she added. "He is not overly fond of the living. Or even the dead. I must not show you the way. He would do terrible things to me."

Shane inclined his head, saying, "Thank you. I would not ask you to endanger yourself."

She smiled and walked away from them.

"What'd she say?" Frank asked.

Shane told him, and Frank nodded. "Alright. Guess we're going to the end."

"Yup," Shane said. He adjusted his grip on his shotgun. "Let's hope it's easy."

"Hope for the best," Frank said, "prepare for the worst."

"Yeah," Shane agreed.

Together they moved through the mounds towards those at the end, and Shane wondered how soon Broken Nose would realize they were there.

Chapter 52: With Phil at Preston Road

Allen had known Phil for thirty years, the two of them introduced by the woman. He knew little about the man other than the fact that he, like Allen, had been paid to protect the sanctity of Broken Nose. And for three decades, they had done just that. Bodies had been disappeared, tracks erased. Cars disposed of.

In the dark hours of the night, when Allen lay awake in his bed, he thought about Lake Nutaq. He remembered when they had found his brother's body, and what it had looked like. It was during those times of reminiscing when the question of 'why' arose.

Why was Allen helping to protect the secret of the thing that had killed his brother?

Why was Allen helping the Watchers, a group that condoned and hid murder in his small town?

And the answer was simple.

Blackmail.

Allen liked expensive food, expensive hotels, and expensive women. He had gotten himself deep into debt with some individuals who liked to run meth and coke through his town on their way to Canada.

Somehow, the Watchers had found out, and they had bought his debt and blackmailed him. They held, and continued to hold, the threat of prison above his head.

It wasn't all threats though. They paid him a significant amount of money for his work, to keep him malleable.

And while he despised the Watchers, Allen consoled himself with the thought that him being in prison wouldn't bring his brother back.

That rationalization allowed him to carry out the duties the Watchers required of him.

The one aspect of his extra-curricular activities Allen didn't enjoy was having to work with Phil.

What Phil did for a living, Allen didn't know, and he didn't want to know. The man was in excellent shape, he was always clean-shaven, and his clothes were perfectly tailored. Even his winter attire was expensive and well fitting. Phil's smile was one of even, white teeth. His brown eyes lacked any sort of warmth, and his nose had the hooked shape of a beak.

Allen knew instinctively that Phil was dangerous. It was a feeling, deep in his gut and from decades of police work that told him Phil was a psychopath.

They parked their vehicles at the entrance to Preston Road, and Allen was angry. There were two other cars on the road. One he didn't recognize, the other belonged to Rowan.

"What's wrong?" Phil asked, pulling his hat down to cover his ears.

Allen pointed to Rowan's car. "Belongs to one of my cops."

"Oh hell," Phil said, frowning. "I'm sorry."

Allen didn't know if the man was sincere, but he appreciated the statement nonetheless. "Thanks."

"What do you want to do?" Phil asked, putting his hands in his pockets.

Allen knew that the wrong answer would mean a bullet in the head.

"We'll put him down if we have to," Allen said. "I like Rowan, but his life isn't worth mine."

Phil nodded and took his hands out of his pockets. "Lead on, Captain."

Allen snorted and took the lead. He followed a well-trodden path through the snow. When they reached the main stretch of Preston Road and saw the situation, Phil let out a low whistle.

"Damn," he said, looking up and down the street. "We've got our work cut out on this one, Allen."

"Yeah," Allen agreed, not trying to hide his bitterness.

"Well," Phil said. "This is why we get paid the big bucks."

Before Allen could answer him, the air shimmered, and one of Broken Nose's Indian friends appeared. He stared at Allen and Phil, raising his tomahawk.

Phil stepped forward, lifting a hand and saying in the ghost's own language, "We're here for Broken Nose."

The dead man lowered his weapon, looking at them warily, asking, "Who has sent you?"

"The Woman," Phil responded.

"And her name?" the ghost asked.

"Abigail," Phil answered, "and she hears everything, from the past to the future."

The dead man grinned and vanished.

Allen realized he had held his breath, so he let it out in a rush.

Phil looked over to him. "Freaks me out every time, too."

Broken Nose appeared, with Patience beside him. Allen was both disturbed and relieved to see her. The dead girl bothered him, although he didn't know why. He suspected it had something to do with the blanket she kept wrapped around herself, and the strange moans and cries which seemed to slip out from beneath it.

He felt relief because she could translate for them, and Allen had a far worse grasp on the language than Phil.

But both he and Phil bowed to Broken Nose, and when they straightened up, Patience asked, "Why are you here?"

"The woman has sent us," Phil answered. "There's a boy you've taken. We need to make sure he dies, and anyone else here, too."

"The boy is alive," Patience said. "Broken Nose will decide if he lives or dies. No one else."

Allen winced at the reprimand in her tone. "Is there anyone else alive here as well?"

Patience asked Broken Nose a question, but she spoke too fast for Allen to understand her.

Broken Nose's response was a simple 'yes.'

To Allen and Phil, she said, "There are two men, Shane and his friend, Frank. They are seeking the boy now. Broken Nose finds it entertaining."

"Anyone else?" Allen asked.

"There was another," Patience said. "Whether he is alive or dead, we do not know. Nor do we care. Broken Nose's warriors went out to find him. You may search for him. He is nothing to us."

Allen winced at the words, at the harsh truth behind them.

"Thank you," Phil said. "We will look for him. May we know when the others are dead as well if that is what Broken Nose chooses?"

Patience asked the question of Broken Nose, and the dead medicine man nodded.

"Thank you," Phil said, and Allen thanked them as well.

Like the Indian before them, Broken Nose and Patience vanished.

Phil shook his head, chuckled and said, "Let's find your cop, Allen."

Allen trailed a few steps behind him as Phil followed the churned snow into the forest.

Chapter 53: Do Not Look to Hope

Mark shivered, tried to curl into a fetal position and bit back a scream instead. The pain in his broken leg was overwhelming.

"Mark," Jonathan said, the dead boy's voice coming from beside Mark's head.

"Yes?" Mark asked in a hushed voice.

"Something is happening," Jonathan said, his voice low. "My sister and Broken Nose have left."

"Do you know where they went?"

"No," Jonathan said, "but it is unlike them to leave when they have a plaything."

Mark realized Jonathan meant him, and he shivered. "Do you know when they'll be back?"

"I do not," Jonathan answered. "The others have left as well."

"What others?" Mark asked, a new wave of fear washing over him.

"There are others who still serve Broken Nose, long past death," Jonathan replied. "My sister is not the only one who is loyal."

"What are they going to do?" Mark asked. "Are they waiting for me?"

"No," Jonathan said, chuckling. "They will be the ones to hunt down Shane, and whoever else is with him."

"Oh," Mark said, unable to keep the dejection from his voice.

"Do not look to hope," Jonathan said. "I would like nothing more than to see you free, to see Patience and Broken Nose disappointed. I do not believe, however, that such an event is likely to occur."

"But–" Mark began, but Jonathan silenced him with a hiss.

Mark's heartbeat was loud in his ears as he waited for Jonathan to speak.

"They're here," Jonathan whispered.

"Who?" Mark asked.

But the dead boy didn't answer. Mark felt the air warm by a fraction, and he understood Jonathan had left.

Frightened, Mark waited. His mouth went dry, and every sound sent a new thrill of fear racing along his spine. Each breath came faster until he was hyperventilating, stars exploding on the edges of his vision.

"Mark!" Jonathan whispered, excitement filling the air.

"What?" Mark asked, his heart thudding against his chest.

"Broken Nose's men," Jonathan said, his words rushing out, "they've returned. They're here. I heard them speaking. The Watchers have come. The Watchers are here!"

"Who are the Watchers?" Mark asked, confused.

"The living who serve Broken Nose," Jonathan said. "I must away. I shall return soon."

"Where are you going?" Mark asked, voice shaking.

"To warn Shane," Jonathan said, and it sounded as if the dead boy was smiling as he said it.

Chapter 54: Unnatural

Shane and Frank stood at the end of the mounds.

Those before them looked no different than any of the others they had passed, and for a moment, Shane was afraid the old woman had lied to them.

Then he felt it.

A crawling, vile sensation filling his mouth with a bitter taste. Shane looked at Frank and saw discomfort on the other man's face.

"This is the right place," Frank said, glancing at Shane.

Shane nodded his agreement. "Thing is, which one is his?"

"Good question," Frank replied. "Wish I knew."

"Bet it's the center one," Shane said, nodding towards the middle mound. It was no larger or smaller than those flanking it, but it made sense to Shane. Broken Nose would have made certain to have his servants on either side of him in the afterlife, as they had been when they were alive.

"Probably," Frank agreed.

"It is," a small voice said, and a little boy appeared from behind it. His face had the same delicate, thin features as Patience, and Frank knew instinctively they were brother and sister.

The boy's eyes were closed, and when he spoke, Shane could see the shattered remnants of teeth.

"This center mound is Broken Nose's," the boy said in a soft voice. "And it is my sister's as well. Which of you is Shane?"

"I am," Shane said, and the dead boy turned to face him. Shane saw how his eyelids were flat. The boy's eyes, Shane understood, were gone.

"The Watchers are coming for you," the boy said. "For both of you."

"Who are they?" Frank asked.

"They are the living," the boy answered. "They serve Broken Nose, as my sister did. As his braves did."

"What?" Frank asked. "Why the hell would they do that?"

"It is a question best left for them," the dead boy responded. "And they are on their way here to deal with you. They will be upon you before you can break through to Broken Nose's bones if those are what you seek."

"They are," Shane said.

"Then it would be best for you to waylay the Watchers before they are here," the dead boy said. And before Shane could ask the child another question, the ghost slipped away.

For a moment, Shane and Frank stood in silence, looking at where the dead boy had been.

"Time to set up an ambush," Frank said.

Shane nodded his agreement, and they turned to look back at their tracks in the snow. He had no doubt that the Watchers would follow the trail.

Because why would we be expecting them? Shane asked himself, a sneer creeping onto his face.

"Ready?" Frank asked.

"Always," Shane answered, and the two of them prepared to receive the Watchers.

Chapter 55: The Watchers

"It's days like this," Phil complained, "that I really, really hate New England."

Allen nodded, but he kept his comments to himself. He was focused more on the trail in front of them, wondering what happened to Rowan.

"Allen," Phil said, his voice uncharacteristically gentle.

Blinking, Allen looked up at the other man. Phil had come to a stop, and Allen brought himself up short. Phil put his hand out and rested it on Allen's shoulder.

"Look," Phil said, pointing.

Allen followed the line of Phil's finger. His eyes locked onto a dark shape in the snow and his shoulder's sagged. He recognized Rowan's dark blue jacket and the battered jeans the man always seemed to wear. Rowan lay on his side, half curled in the snow. A single blue eye stared forward, unseeing.

"Ah hell," Allen muttered. He took a few steps forward, crouched down, and pulled a glove off so he could check Rowan's pulse.

The man's flesh was cold, and there was no heartbeat.

"Oh, Rowan," Allen said, standing up. "I told you to leave it alone."

"Knew him well?" Phil asked.

Allen nodded. "Since he was a boy. Shame, him dying like this."

"We can put it on the fellow, Shane," Phil offered.

"Yes," Phil said, sighing. "I know we can."

He didn't want to put it on Shane. He didn't want to put it on anyone. What Allen wanted was for Rowan to be alive and at the hospital, sitting with Doreen. Not dead in the snow.

"Ready?" Phil asked, taking a stick of gum out of his pocket and popping it into his mouth.

"Yes," Allen said.

A broken path continued through the snow, and they followed it, Phil in the lead. The man hummed as he walked, and not for the first time since having met the man, Allen wondered what Phil thought about. In the back of his mind, Allen knew he was more afraid of Phil than either Broken Nose or the woman. Phil would be the one to kill him if there was ever a time for it.

And Allen wasn't sure if Phil would make it quick or not.

There were rumors down in Massachusetts of a serial killer who made the rounds of the bigger cities, Boston, Springfield, and Worcester, and Allen suspected Phil knew all three of those cities intimately.

"You're pretty quiet back there," Phil said over his shoulder.

"Yes," Allen replied.

Phil chuckled. "Don't worry. We'll be done soon enough, and I'll be out of your hair. I'll be sure to tell her how much extra trouble there was on this little clean-up session. And that it cost you a police officer. She'll make sure you get a bonus in your account."

I'm sure she will, Allen thought. He wondered how he had gotten himself mixed up with the business of Broken Nose. There was no clear-cut path he had taken which led to his status as manual labor for a murderous ghost and his living keeper.

He had never even met the woman. Never even had more than a few conversations with her over the phone.

And yet he was ever at her beck and call.

Phil slowed down, and Allen's attention was focused on the path ahead. The trees had begun to thin out. Ahead of them lay the burial mounds, where he had found his brother's corpse decades earlier.

And why didn't that stop you from ending up here? Allen asked himself bitterly.

Before he could answer, Phil came to a stop. The man's nostrils flared, and he looked around, caution and anxiety flickering across his face.

"What's wrong?" Allen whispered.

Phil shook his head. "Don't know. I can't put my finger on it. Something doesn't seem right here."

"Nothing's ever right here," Allen hissed. "We're in a damned haunted Indian burial ground, getting ready to frame someone for the murder of a cop and two kids."

Phil glared at Allen with such intensity and venom that the rest of Allen's comment was swallowed.

"Keep this up," Phil said, his voice a low monotone, "and I'll be framing him for the murder of two cops."

The utter sincerity with which the words were spoken caused Allen to take a step back. Phil nodded and returned his attention to the burial mounds.

Allen tried to focus on them as well.

The trail left by Shane and his compatriot continued on, weaving between the various plots before vanishing. Allen couldn't see anything out of place, but he felt uncomfortable. The hairs stood up on the back of his neck, a warning that something out there wasn't quite right.

Odd as it was, Allen wished Broken Nose or Patience was with them.

Phil reached into his jacket pocket and pulled out a small, semi-automatic pistol. It looked like a .22 caliber, the metal a flat black. He slid the safety off, eased the slide back to make sure a round was chambered and said, "Better draw your own piece."

Allen hesitated, then drew his personal weapon, a Sig Sauer 9 mm semi-automatic pistol.

"Stay here," Phil ordered. "I don't want anyone slipping around behind me."

"Sure," Allen said. He was all right with staying back.

Phil moved forward with silent steps, the pistol down by his side and hidden. Allen watched the man advance, peering to the left and the right as he passed between the first pair of mounds. Phil continued on, and when he walked through another set of mounds, he stiffened and turned to the left, looking at something behind the burial mound. His pistol, Allen noticed, was still kept from view.

"Hello," Phil said, the word smooth and exuding confidence as he spoke to someone Allen couldn't see. Then Phil's hand was a blur, bringing the pistol up, but the roar of a shotgun ripped a scream out of Phil's throat as he spun away. The gun flew through the air as Phil reached for his face, still screaming.

A figure stepped out from behind the mound and kicked Phil in the chest, knocking the man down into the snow. As the hired killer writhed about, Allen brought his own weapon up, sighting down the barrel.

The click of a hammer being drawn back behind his left ear caused him to stop.

"Now, sir," an easy, polite voice said, "you do not want to be holding onto that Sig. Why don't you let it drop into the snow before you find out what a load of rock salt to the face feels like?"

Allen thought about it for a moment.

The stranger cocked what sounded like a second barrel and Allen understood it was a sawed off shotgun, and at close range, the rock salt might actually kill him.

Allen dropped his pistol.

Chapter 56: Dangerous Men

Shane reloaded his shotgun while the man who had tried to shoot him continued to scream and thrash about in the snow.

"If you don't shut up," Shane said, "I'm going to see how much damage I can really do with two barrels of rock salt."

The man shut up.

Shane watched as he lowered his hands. The stranger's face was a bloody mess, his eyes closed.

"You're dead!" the stranger spat at Shane.

"Could be," Shane agreed.

"Is that one still alive?" Frank called out.

"Yup," Shane answered. He continued to watch the man, eyes focused solely on him. "Put your hands on your chest and interlock your fingers."

The stranger did so.

Frank came into Shane's field of vision less than a minute later, marching a police officer in front of him.

"You're in a lot of trouble," the officer began.

Shane glanced at him, saw the man's rank was a captain, and he addressed him as such. "Captain, you're full of it. You and I both know that we're the only four out here."

The captain didn't respond.

"Good," Shane said. "Now, we're going to go rescue a boy. You two are going to stay here, and you're not going to interfere."

The man on the ground snorted.

"Boots off," Shane said. "Both of you."

"What?" the captain asked.

"Now," Shane replied.

"I can't see," the wounded man stated. "Can't do it."

Shane cocked one barrel back. "You're going to do it, or I'm going to shoot a load of rock salt into your hands, and *then* you're going to do it."

The wounded man snarled, sat up with surprising speed, and unlaced his boots. The captain didn't need any additional persuasion.

"Captain," Shane said. "You've got the honors. Throw your boots, and your little buddy's here, as far as you can towards the woods."

The captain hesitated until Frank prodded the man with the shotgun's barrel.

Shane watched as the captain first threw his own, then the wounded man's a good distance. Both pairs vanished into the deep snow.

"Good," Shane said. "Now, jackets off."

"We'll freeze to death!" the wounded man spat.

"No, you won't," Frank answered. "Not for a good, long while. Temperature's right around freezing. You'll be uncomfortable, but you don't even have to worry about frostbite. At least not yet."

The wounded man ripped his coat off and threw it in Shane's direction while the captain took his off. He held it out to Frank, but Frank only chuckled.

"Drop it," Frank answered.

The captain did so.

"Good. Excellent," Shane said. He had a strong urge to shoot both of the men anyway, just to add a little more misery to their lives, but he stopped himself. "I want you to listen to me. Both of you. You're going to walk, out towards the lake. Make whatever phone calls you want, I don't care. We'll deal with you afterward."

"We can't walk," the captain protested. "Not without boots."

"Pretty sure we've already established what you can and can't do," Frank said, his voice cold. "Help your buddy to his feet, and then get walking."

Shane watched the captain stomp over to the wounded man and pulled him to his feet. The injured man turned his ravaged face towards Shane, saying, "I'm going to kill you."

"No," Shane said. "You won't. I'm pretty sure whoever hired you is going to take care of you and leave me alone."

Shane was pleased to see fear blossom on the man's face while the captain's went pale. He watched as they turned and limped towards the frozen lake.

"Ready?" Frank asked.

"Course not," Shane answered, watching them for a moment longer. "But that doesn't matter, now does it."

"No," Frank agreed. "It doesn't matter at all."

Chapter 57: A Rescue Attempt

Mark lay on his side, not daring to breathe. Jonathan sat beside him, the ghost's cold presence oddly comforting. They listened together, waiting to hear what would happen.

The muffled roar of a shotgun caused Mark to jump and howl with pain. Beneath the agony of the broken leg, there was a spike of joy.

Shane had taken Jonathan's word and waited to confront whoever the Watchers were.

A moment later, the ground shook, though, and Jonathan whimpered.

"What is it?" Mark whispered.

"Broken Nose and Patience," Jonathan cried. "They know what's happened. They know Shane hasn't been stopped, and now they're coming for him."

"How do you know?" Mark asked, feeling panic rise up within him.

"The ground has only shaken once before," the ghost answered. "A long time ago. And they all came out. Broken Nose and his braves, my sister and her arms. Each of them had arrived, and destroyed those who sought to cast Broken Nose out of this world forever."

"No," Mark whimpered.

"Yes," the dead boy answered. "It was terrible. And they are all coming again."

"What do we do?" Mark asked, throat threatening to close. "Can I do anything? Can't I get out?"

"No," Jonathan said. "But if there is silence, if there is a lull in the battle, you must scream."

"Why?" Mark asked, shaking.

"You have to let them know you are still alive," Jonathan said. "You must let them know they do not fight in vain. Otherwise, they might leave you here to suffer at the hands of Broken Nose."

Mark nodded, not knowing if Jonathan could see him or not, and started to prepare himself to scream as loud and for as long as he could.

Chapter 58: Meeting upon the Field

By the time they had returned to the center mound at the far end, Shane knew they were in for a fight.

Broken Nose stood in front of his mound, with Patience on his right and three of his men spread out in front of him. Where the fourth man was, Shane didn't know, and it worried him.

The whole situation bothered him.

Broken Nose's body was in the mound, and for them to defeat the ghost, Shane and Frank would have to get to Broken Nose's remains to salt and burn them. The entire time they would have to fight off the dead, who could be shot with rock salt and sent back to their bones.

Located in the mounds on either side of Broken Nose's, which meant they would return within minutes, if not seconds.

But we need to get the boy, Shane thought, and he knew he would die before leaving the boy to be tortured to death by Broken Nose and his soul imprisoned within Patience's twisted specter.

"You have cast off the yoke of the Watchers," Broken Nose said, his voice deep and melodious.

"We have," Shane replied.

"And you are ready now to face me," Broken Nose said.

"No," Shane said. "But, we will."

Broken Nose's broad shoulders shook with laughter beneath his dark cloak.

"I like your spirit," Broken Nose began, but Shane silenced him with a blast from his shotgun.

The second barrel took care of the closest Indian while Frank knocked the other two out with shots from his own gun. As the sound of the weapon blasts died out, the two men were left with Patience, who let go of the edges of her blanket and screamed at them.

Shane staggered back in surprise as dozens of arms reached out of her, each limb growing and stretching towards them.

"What the hell?!" Frank shouted, reloading while stepping away.

Shane didn't reply, lashing out instead with his diminished left hand. The iron ring came into contact with a hand and Patience howled as the limb disappeared. Frank brought the weapon up to fire at her, but an Indian appeared from the far right mound, racing towards them.

Frank focused his attention on the Indian, and Shane dropped his own shotgun and faced off against Patience. He clenched his hands into fists and felt a dull, black rage settle over him. As each phantom limb sought him out, Shane struck it aside. Fury danced upon Patience's face and madness burned in her eyes. She lunged towards him, and Shane drove his right fist into her head, causing her to vanish.

Broken Nose stepped out of the wall of his mound, arms spread as he began to chant.

Shane threw himself at the dead man and scattered the ghost with the rings on both fingers.

Shane was at the side of the mound. Behind him, he heard Frank fire the shotgun twice more, but then Shane's attention fixated on the snow covered mound.

With his anger barely contained, Shane plunged his hands into the snow.

Book 6: Lake Nutaq

Chapter 59: On Lake Nutaq

Allen's feet were freezing, literally, as he led Phil across the ice. Phil was blind and silent, and Allen was more frightened of the man than he had ever been before.

He held onto Phil as gently as he could, not wishing to seem like he was taking control. Allen suspected Phil was capable of more than he seemed, even when blind.

Neither of the men had used their phones because both of them had kept their cells in their coat pockets. Their only hope lay in making it to one of the houses across the lake, and that alone might cost them both their feet, in spite of the assurances from Shane's friend.

Allen stumbled on his numb feet, and Phil jerked his arm away.

"Idiot!" Phil spat.

Allen straightened up, anger flaring up and his fear vanishing.

"Shut up," Allen ordered. "You want to make it across this ice?"

"What do I care?" Phil demanded. "I'm blind!"

Allen didn't answer.

One of Broken Nose's men had appeared behind Phil.

"Did you hear me?" Phil asked. "I'm blind!"

Allen's breath caught in his throat, his warning dying in his mouth.

The dead man stepped forward, a brutal tomahawk in his hand.

"Allen," Phil said, his voice low and dangerous. "You better answer me."

Allen would never know if Phil intended to elaborate on his threat, for Broken Nose's brave drove the tomahawk deep into Phil's head.

Horrified, Allen watched Phil stiffen, his arms shaking and his hands trembling. Foam appeared at the corners of his mouth, and then it was as if someone ripped the man's spine out as he collapsed boneless onto the frozen lake.

The dead man smiled, his teeth stained bright red. He said something unintelligible, gesturing with his tomahawk.

Allen turned and ran.

But his legs were too stiff. His feet were numb.

He fell, crashing into the ice, snow scattering at the impact. Screaming, Allen turned around onto his back and looked up. His mind raced as he tried to think of a way to defend himself.

But it was no use.

The dead man was upon him, the tomahawk raised above his head and a look of glee on his face.

Allen shrieked as the tomahawk raced towards him.

Chapter 60: Fighting for the Boy

Shane was thrown backward from the burial mound. A sharp, stinging blow had landed on his chest, causing his heart to miss a beat before he struck the ground hard. His breath rushed out of his lungs and his vision blurred for a moment.

When his sight cleared, Shane saw Broken Nose step out of the mound and move towards him.

Shane got to his feet and laughed, calling out, "How weak are you, Broken Nose?"

The question brought the dead man to a halt. Even his braves stopped, looking with surprise at Shane.

Frank reloaded.

"Weak?" Broken Nose asked. "Weak?"

"Look at you," Shane sneered. "Your little boys running around you. A little girl standing by your side. Protected by everyone but yourself."

Broken Nose straightened up. "Weak!"

"Pretty sure I didn't stutter," Shane said, laughing. "You're weak. You can't even defend yourself from me. A cripple."

Shane held up his left hand and wiggled the fingers that remained. He tore his hat from his head, revealed the bald and scarred scalp, and laughed again. "You're weak. And a coward."

Broken Nose's men looked from Shane to their shaman and their arms lowered ever so slightly.

"I am no coward," Broken Nose hissed, stepping forward.

"Prove it," Shane said.

"I need to prove nothing," Broken Nose hissed.

Behind the dead men, Frank crept toward the center mound.

"Sure," Shane said. "Tell yourself that. You don't need to prove yourself at all. You just go on letting others do all the heavy lifting for you. Let them gather your victims. Did you ever collect them yourself, or did you talk them into it? Promise them glory after death?"

Shane looked at the dead braves, a fourth one appearing beside them.

"Did he?" Shane asked. "And is this glory? Coming out only in the cold? And for what?"

"We are power beyond death," the men said in unison, their voices quivering with rage. "All seek to serve us. The fools in their cabins worship us."

"Do they?" Shane asked, looking at the others. "Or do they worship him? Did they ever call your names out? And what weak willed people are doing that? What do they do, Broken Nose? Make sure no one bothers your little burial ground here?"

The sharp expressions that leaped onto the faces of the dead braves told Shane he had hit his mark.

"They did," Shane said, chuckling. "Oh, that's good."

To the other men, he added, "And you've helped to protect him too. You've added to his strength, haven't you? He's fed off those you've brought to him. But have *you* grown stronger?"

Without looking at his men, Broken Nose said, "Take him!"

None of the men moved.

Broken Nose turned halfway and demanded, "Now!"

The men stepped forward and advanced upon Broken Nose. They formed a rough ring around him as he screamed profanities. One of them leaped forward, slamming his war-club down.

Broken Nose spun out of the way, and the five dead men became a swirling mass.

Shane raced past them to the burial mound. Frank raised the butt of the shotgun up and smashed it into the dirt. A hole opened up, and Shane reached his hands in, ripping out clumps of dirt.

Shane glanced behind him and saw the dead men still engaged in a fierce fight, and then turned his attention back to the mound. The opening was wide enough for Shane to put his head and shoulders in.

"Give me a light," Shane said, leaning forward.

Frank pulled out his flashlight and shined the beam into the hole as Shane peered in.

On the small floor, Shane saw a boy; the young teen's face was a pale white mask of fear.

Shane followed the boy's gaze and saw Patience.

Her hands lashed out, latched onto Shane's head, and dragged him into the burial mound.

Chapter 61: Shock and Awe

For a split second, Frank stood still.

Jerking his shotgun up, he aimed the weapon into the mound, the flashlight showing him the scene within.

Shane was fighting with the monstrous little girl, and each time he hit her, she vanished, only to reappear a heartbeat later. A young boy pushed himself against the far wall, letting out a long, hoarse scream.

Shane struck the girl in the head, shot a glance at Frank and yelled, "Get the kid out!"

Then the girl appeared from behind, grabbing onto Shane's face. Shane let out an agonized growl and lashed out, hitting her hand.

Patience disappeared again, and Frank snapped, "Kid! Kid!"

The teen looked at him, his eyes wide, his face a sickly white.

Patience appeared in front of Frank, snarling.

Frank pulled both triggers, blasting the girl with rock salt.

"You need to move!" Frank yelled.

The teen shook his head.

"My leg," the boy whispered.

Shane turned to the teen, grabbed him by the arm, and shouted, "I don't care! Get out!"

As the last word left his mouth, Patience launched herself out of the shadows, striking Shane in the face.

Frank winced at the howl of pain torn from Shane's mouth, but as Shane battled the dead girl, the teen crawled forward.

Dropping the flashlight, Frank reached in, found the back of the boy's jacket, and dragged him up and through the hole. He fell backward, the teen screaming as he landed on top of Frank. From the mound, Frank heard as Shane let out an agonized howl.

A moment later, Shane screamed, "The bag!"

Frank pushed the teen off him into the snow, grabbed the duffel bag, and threw it into the mound. Then, getting to his feet, Frank looked around and saw Broken Nose was held firm by two of the Indians. The other two approached Frank.

He grabbed hold of the teen with his free hand, aimed the shotgun with his right, and pulled the trigger.

Both hammers fell on spent casings.

He hadn't reloaded the shotgun.

Dropping it, Frank dragged the boy backward.

But the dead men didn't follow him.

Instead, they entered the burial mound.

Chapter 62: Help Needed

Shane sank against the inner wall of the mound. Huge portions of his scalp and face were numb, and he knew the flesh was dead, killed by Patience's touch.

A dim light filled the interior, the girl across from him, her eyes narrowed. Her own arms hung limply at her sides, the limbs and hands of her prisoners extended from her shattered ribs. They waited for her to move closer to him.

The temperature in the mound dipped, and a pair of Indians materialized.

Shane's hopes sank as they looked at him. Their expressions were cold and unfathomable.

Shane's heartbeat slowed, and he chuckled, shaking his head.

I'm going to die here, he realized. *Here, in a god damned hole.*

Yet as the thought finished, one of the dead men grabbed Patience. Her eyes widened in surprise, and as she struggled to free herself, the Indian tightened his hold.

The other man turned his attention to Shane.

"Can you free us?" the dead man asked.

Shane could only nod, his shock robbing him of his voice.

"How?" the Indian asked.

Shane cleared his throat, winced at the pain as he swallowed and said, "I have to salt and burn your bones."

"They are here," the dead man said, pointing to the ground. "With Broken Nose's and the girl's. Set us all aflame. We would move on to something else."

"Okay," Shane said, and ignoring the pain, he crawled to the bag. He unzipped it and took out the plastic bag of rock salt, the fluid, and the matches. Quickly, before the dead men could change their minds, he scratched at the floor. Beneath the first half inch of dirt, Shane found a woven mat, and in a few minutes, his fingers pried loose the edge.

He peeled it back and looked down at scattered bones.

Shane's heart thundered in his chest, and he felt a wave of relief crash over him as he tore open the bag of salt. He opened it and poured the contents out onto the human remains. Shane saw the glint of a golden button mixed in with the salt and groaned as he realized what he had done.

"You bloody git!" Jack screamed, freed of the salt. The dead man slammed Shane backward. "I'll have your eyes!"

Before Jack could make good on his threat, the Indian smashed into him.

"The bones!" the brave yelled.

In the dim light of the mound, Shane saw Patience renew her struggle against her own captor. The hands of her prisoners reached out, yet they didn't fight against the dead man. Instead, the limbs stretched into the air, twisted around themselves and back to Patience. Fingers, long and dead, grasped and pulled, stretching the girl's face, and tearing apart her flesh. Her eyes widened in shock as her captives tore her apart. The girl's terrified screams filled the mound for the briefest of moments before her mouth vanished in a child's small hand.

Shaking with exhaustion and pain, Shane ripped his eyes away from her, grabbed hold of the lighter fluid and sprayed the liquid onto the bones. He picked up the matches only to have them knocked out of his hands by Jack, who was screaming profanities, the dead man's voice so loud that it made Shane nauseous.

Shane found the matches, pulled out a trio of them, and struck them on the side of the box. They burst into flames, the smell of sulfur overriding the scent of the lighter fluid. Jack's screams rose to a fevered pitch and then went silent, the fire and salt destroying the ghost's bond to the golden button and returning him to his hidden remains.

Without any ceremony, Shane threw the matches down onto the bones.

A foul, greasy smoke erupted, causing Shane to cough and hack. He struggled through the new darkness, found the hole, and pulled himself free.

Gasping for air as he fell, Shane vomited into the snow. Mucus ran from his nose and tears from his eyes as he climbed to his feet, wavering on unsteady legs.

Frank was off to one side, standing over the teen. He pointed behind Shane, and Shane twisted around.

Broken Nose stood in the snow, alone. A putrid green flame ate at his cloak, racing from the hem towards his knees, then from his knees to his waist.

As the flames devoured him, Broken Nose stared at Shane.

When the edges of the fire nipped at the bottom of the mask, Broken Nose said, "I will wait for you on the other side, Shane Ryan."

Shane turned away and walked towards Frank and the boy, an uncomfortable thought in the back of his mind.

Jack hadn't burned, which made Shane wonder, *Where are Jack's bones?*

Chapter 63: A Visit from an Old Friend

Shane stubbed out his cigarette and took a drink of whiskey. Frank lowered his book and looked at him.

"How are you feeling?" Frank asked.

Shane grunted in response.

"They would have given you medication for the pain," Frank said, closing the book and putting it down on a side table.

"I have enough with being an alcoholic," Shane said. "I don't need to get hooked on pain meds too."

"Seriously, Shane," Frank said, "they must have taken two pounds of dead flesh off of you."

"More than that," Shane said. "Weighed myself this morning. I'm down five pounds."

The doorbell interrupted them, and Frank looked at Shane.

"If you want to answer it," Shane said, "be my guest."

"Sure," Frank said, grinning. "I've never heard the doorbell here before. Didn't even know you got visitors."

"I don't," Shane said. When Frank got up and left the study, Shane closed his eyes and rested his head against the back of the chair.

It had been less than a day since they had brought the boy, Mark, to the hospital, left him in the emergency room, and made their way to Asa's house. The former Special Forces medic had patched Shane up, and Shane had been left with even more scars. In a week or so, Frank would be cutting the stitches out of Shane.

"Shane," Frank said from the doorway.

Shane opened his eyes, frowning. "What's up?"

"The police are here about your car," Frank said.

"Oh," Shane said, closing his eyes again. "Yeah. Bring 'em in, please."

Frank left and returned a moment later.

"So your car was stolen?"

Shane opened his eyes, surprised.

Detective Marie Lafontaine sat across from him.

Shane straightened up in his chair. "Yes, yes it was."

Frank looked from Shane to Marie, and Shane shook his head. Without a word, Frank left the room.

"We found your car, Shane," Marie said.

"Really?" he asked, trying to sound surprised.

"Really," she said, settling back in the chair. "Up at Lake Nutaq."

"Lake Nutaq?" Shane said. "Never heard of it. Where is it?"

"Up North," Marie answered. "Funny, too."

"How is it funny?" Shane asked.

"Two dead cops, a dead teen, a dead maintenance man, and a couple of injured people as well," Marie stated.

"My car did all of that?" Shane asked.

Marie's look hardened. "What happened, Shane?"

Shane topped off his whiskey, looked at it for a short time and then whispered, "I have no idea, Marie."

She hesitated, then asked, "What happened to your face, Shane?"

"I cut myself shaving," he said, gulping down the whiskey.

"And your ear?" she asked, concern in her voice.

"Same," he replied.

Marie shook her head and stood up. "I suppose you have an alibi?"

"Do I need one?" he asked.

"No." Marie sighed. She opened her mouth as if to say something else, then closed it, shook her head and walked out of the study.

Shane heard the front door open and slam shut, and then, from the depths of the house, he heard Courtney wail.

Shane's hands shook as he poured another glass of whiskey. He opened his laptop and stared at the screen. Slowly he typed in 'ghosts going insane.'

There had to be a way to save her.

* * *

Slater Mill
Book 7

Book 7: Slater Mill

Chapter 1: Slater Mill, Nashua, NH

Miguel had crept into the decrepit mill building shortly after midnight. A sharp chill had sprung up in the April air, and he needed a place to sleep. He had managed to hitch-hike from Lawrence to Nashua, but his uncle hadn't been home.

No one had even answered any of the doors in his uncle's building.

And Miguel had been wearing the wrong colors for Vine Street. His blue hoodie, representing his ties to the 'Muerto Brotherhood' had been met with hostile expressions from other young men and women. Most of those he saw were clad in dark green, the color representing the Vaqueros.

Sleeping in the hallway outside of his uncle's apartment hadn't been an option, not if he wanted to avoid a beat down.

The mill had been a decent option. A hole in the wire fence had let him slip away from the ones who had followed him. And he had been pleased that they hadn't pursued him into the building itself.

Miguel knew it meant the place was probably patrolled, but he figured he could outrun any fat security guard who might have the job.

Miguel eased the door behind him shut and waited for a moment while his eyes adjusted to the dim light. The glow of the street lamps was filtered through windows grimy with decades of dust and grit. When he could finally see, Miguel noticed that the worn wooden floorboards were covered with the same.

Tracks of various small animals crisscrossed through the film on the floor.

There weren't any footprints.

Miguel grinned.

He glanced back at the door he had entered, then he moved deeper into the wide passage. Stairs, worn down in the center, led up to a second floor, and he decided to follow them. Staying too close to the door might be risking exposure.

Especially if he had triggered some sort of silent alarm.

Frowning at the idea, Miguel hurried up the stairs. He took them two at a time until he reached the second floor.

Miguel stumbled to a stop, surprised at what he saw.

A cavernous room stretched out before him, one that looked to be the entire second floor. Dark pillars reached from floor to ceiling, and windows ran along the brick walls. Like the glass on the first floor, these windows were filthy.

And while the first floor had seemed warmer than the outside, the second floor felt colder.

Shivering, Miguel took a few cautious steps into the room. He looked from left to right, trying to see if any of the windows were broken.

But the fact that none of them were, brought him to a stop.

All of the windows should have shattered. There shouldn't have been a shard of glass left in the frames.

Miguel had seen plenty of empty buildings in Lawrence, and if they were abandoned, it meant the windows were the targets of any kid who thought he could pitch in the major leagues.

Miguel knew this because he had broken his share of windows as well.

The dust at his feet spiraled up, whipped around the bottom of his jeans, and then dissipated. Another one arose a short distance away, then it died down as well. A third appeared at the left wall, but instead of dropping back to the floor as the others had, it stretched towards the ceiling. Soon it was as tall as Miguel, and a heartbeat later, it towered over him.

He took a nervous step back, trying to see where the air creating the twisting spiral was coming from.

Yet as he did so, the dust exploded in his face, blinding him.

Miguel retched, trying to catch his breath. The filth invaded his nose and tried to plunge into his open mouth. He wanted to shut it out, but he couldn't, the vomit forcing him to keep his lips separated.

Something struck him in the stomach, doubling him over, and a powerful force struck him on the back of the neck, knocking him to his knees.

An angry, male voice asked him a question Miguel couldn't understand. The language wasn't Spanish or English.

The man repeated his question, and when Miguel failed to answer, he was struck on the side of the head. Miguel whimpered as the blow drove him to the floor. His head throbbed, and he couldn't move, he tried to open his eyes, but his eyelids refused to respond.

The man muttered in his unintelligible language, and Miguel felt him grab hold of his sweatshirt's hood. Miguel made an effort to get to his knees, but a boot caught him in the stomach and sent a fresh spike of pain through him.

Miguel found himself being dragged across the floor, the boards rough and harsh against his hands. Splinters drove deep into his flesh, and he whimpered.

The stranger paused, struck Miguel in the head again, and then continued on.

For a moment longer, Miguel was dragged along, and then the man stopped. Hands grasped his left leg and left arm, a brutal cold penetrating his clothes. A sharp, jerking motion brought Miguel up off the floor, and he managed to force his eyes open.

Miguel was in the air, suspended above the stairwell.

Desperate, Miguel twisted in the grip of his attacker and looked down.

But there was nothing to see.

Miguel was held aloft by nothing.

The unseen man asked a single question.

Miguel still couldn't answer because he didn't understand.

The man sneered and threw Miguel.

The stairs, Miguel discovered, were hard and unyielding.

Chapter 2: Myrtle Street Patrol

Kurt Warner and Bill Waters both responded to the call about a break-in at the Slater Mill off Myrtle Street. It was a first for both of them.

No one, in all of Kurt's time with the Nashua Police Department, had ever broken into Slater Mill. Bill, who had five years more on the force than Kurt, hadn't heard of it either. The place was almost a no-go zone for the local kids. Nobody knew why, and no one in the department had ever asked. The Mill was one less place to worry about, and that was fine with Kurt.

Bill parked the cruiser at the front gate, which wasn't even chained or locked.

Kurt took out his flashlight, held it up, and scanned beyond the fence. "Which door was it?"

"Pine Street side," Bill answered.

"Great," Kurt grumbled.

"Yeah," Bill said. "Ready?"

"Sure," Kurt sighed. "Let's do this. Probably a squatter."

Bill nodded and pushed the gate open. They went in together, and Kurt took the lead. The Pine Street Entrance was an easy hundred yards up the right side of the building. As they went,

Book 7: Slater Mill

Kurt noticed the lack of trash on the inside of the fence. In the light of the halogen street lamps, he saw that there were no cigarette butts, no signs of any sort of human passage.

It was as if everyone in the area paid attention to the 'No Trespassing' signs zip-tied to the fence every twenty or thirty feet.

When they approached the Pine Street door, Kurt saw it was ajar, a sliver of darkness apparent. The sight of it made him uncomfortable, and he slipped the catch off of his holster, freeing his pistol.

"That's not good," Bill said, his voice low.

"No," Kurt agreed.

Bill called in their status on the radio, as well as the fact that the door was open. He finished with, "Proceeding inside."

Kurt took a deep breath, settled his suddenly anxious nerves, and stepped forward. He pushed the door open, shined his light into the Mill and called out, "Nashua Police!"

No one answered as Kurt moved the flashlight's beam from left to right, then he stopped. Beyond a set of wide stairs, he saw several fingers.

"I've got somebody," Kurt said. He stepped into the building, Bill following behind him.

"Hello," Kurt said, directing his voice toward the stairs. "Are you hurt?"

A finger twitched.

Bill saw it too, and in a heartbeat, he was calling for an ambulance.

Still proceeding with caution, Kurt advanced towards the person beyond the stairs. When he reached them, Kurt stopped and dropped to a knee.

A young Hispanic male lay on the floor, his body contorted and broken. His neck was twisted awkwardly, his brown eyes rolling in his head, the pupils pulsing without any sense. How the kid was still alive, Kurt couldn't understand, but he knew it wouldn't be for much longer.

"Hey," Kurt said, reaching out and taking the hand he had seen. In Spanish, he asked, "Are you a Catholic?"

Somehow, the boy squeezed his hand.

"Do you want a priest?" Kurt asked.

Again, the boy responded with a weak grasp of Kurt's hand.

Leaning forward Kurt said, "Do you ask God for forgiveness, and repent for your transgressions against Him?"

Again, the boy answered.

"Do you know who did this to you?" Kurt asked.

The boy didn't respond.

"Was it a stranger?"

The boy gripped Kurt's hand, squeezing it with surprising strength.

"Are they still here?" Kurt asked.

The boy didn't answer.

He couldn't. His brown eyes had rolled up to reveal only the whites, and he had breathed his last breath in the filth of the old mill building.

Kurt sat down, took his radio, and called dispatch. In the distance, he heard an ambulance's siren wail, and he asked the dispatcher to send along the priest who was on call.

Chapter 3: Berkley Street

The knock on Shane's door startled him.

"Come in," he called after a moment.

Frank opened the door. Shane saw that Frank was dressed in a suit and asked, "What the hell's going on?"

Frank raised an eyebrow. "You don't remember?"

"Obviously not," Shane said, getting up from his chair and stretching. "Sorry. What's happening today?"

"My brother, Alex, is getting married," Frank said, shaking his head. "I'll be gone for the weekend."

"Oh," Shane said, drawing the word out. "Damn. That's right. Sorry, Frank."

Frank looked at him. "I'm worried about you, Shane. You're forgetting a lot more lately."

"I'm still not sleeping that well," Shane confessed. "Been trying to cut back on the whiskey, too."

"Maybe you ought to go and see a doctor?" Frank asked.

Shane frowned and didn't answer. He and Frank had had that conversation more than once.

Frank sighed. "Alright. Well, think about it. I do know a couple of people up at the Manchester VA who'll be able to help you out."

"Yeah," Shane said. "I know. Let me sleep on it."

"Ha," Frank said without any sort of humor. "Real funny. Take care of yourself this week. The newspaper's on the kitchen table. There's another unsolved murder in Nashua."

"Where?" Shane asked.

"The Slater Mill," Frank answered.

"Again?" Shane said.

Frank nodded. "Yup. The paper has dubbed the killer as the Mill Murderer."

"Because of two bodies?"

"Yeah," Frank said. "Some nice, light reading for you."

Shane snorted. "The way the paper edits, it's more like some light torture."

Frank chuckled, waved goodbye and left the room. Shane turned back to his desk, closed the book he had been reading and pinched the bridge of his nose. He had a slight headache. The lack of sleep made any sort of mental exercise a challenge. He considered getting out a fresh bottle of whiskey.

Part of him wanted to drink himself into unconsciousness, but he knew that it wouldn't be a restful sleep.

I need to figure out what to do about Courtney, he thought. But as soon as it crossed his mind, Shane shoved the idea away. It hurt him to think of her, and so he did his best not to.

Even when she was screaming in the middle of the night.

Sighing, Shane left the room. He walked along the hallway, down the stairs, and into the kitchen. None of the house's dead bothered him, and he was pleased. He needed time alone. Time to think about what he needed to do.

His work as a translator had dropped off, and that was his fault for focusing more upon the dead than the living. He knew he could always find work, but he lacked the desire to seek out new jobs. Courtney occupied a great deal of his thoughts, and he wondered if it would be possible to bring her back from madness, or if he would have to find a way to force her to move on.

Shane took a pack of cigarettes off the counter, fished a smoke out, and lit it. He dropped them onto the dining table beside the paper and sat down. Frank had left the front-page face up, and in bold letters, a headline proclaimed, "Mill Murderer Strikes Again!" A sub-title asked if the police were dragging their feet because of the location of the mill, and Shane shook his head.

It never ceased to amaze him that people thought the police played favorites when it came to death. If someone was murdered, detectives did their best to find the perpetrator.

The article was accompanied by a series of photographs. In the first picture, there was a police officer standing in front of a door marked with yellow caution tape. The second was of a coroner's van. It was the third photograph that caught Shane's attention.

The final picture was a wide shot of the mill itself. It looked like a normal, nineteenth-century mill. Dull red bricks, tall windows, and fading white trim peeling after decades of neglect. Those were expected.

What brought Shane's mind to a sharp, cold focus was what he saw in the window above the door.

A pale shape.

Through the dirty glass, he saw a man, and for a moment Shane thought it might have been nothing more than a trick of the daylight on the window.

He knew it wasn't though. A solid feeling of certainty in his gut, a piercing, cold understanding in his mind. They both told him that he was looking at a dead man, one who was murdering the living.

Shane stared at the picture, smoking his cigarette. He contemplated doing nothing. It would be easy. He could pick up the front page, turn it, and forget he had ever seen the image. Shane could pretend it hadn't been anything at all.

But he knew he couldn't.

The ghost had killed twice in as many weeks, and he felt certain the dead man would kill again.

Shane finished his cigarette, stubbing the butt out in the ashtray. He tapped his foot on the floor and considered what to do.

Mills, he knew, had seen plenty of accidents. The buildings were no strangers to death or violence. Some said the foundations of the structures were soaked in blood. Whether that statement had any truth to it, Shane didn't know.

But he would find out about the Slater Mill. He would learn about deaths which had occurred there before it had ceased to be useful.

And he would find out why it had been abandoned for so many years.

Shane stood up, walked to the phone, and called Brian Roy.

Chapter 4: Santeria

Jose De Los Angeles had been a Santeria priest for seven years. He had even returned to the Dominican Republic for a year to learn at the feet of some of the finest members of his faith. Jose had learned how to summon the dead, read omens, and help care for the living. He was not afraid of ghosts, and he had cast more than a few out of the old and run-down buildings along the Tree Streets of Nashua.

When the teenager from Lawrence had been found dead in the Mill, there had been some mutterings about the place being haunted. Those mutters became grumbles when an old Ecuadorian had been found dead against the fence. The man's eyes had been gouged out, and while the police suspected a crazed man, Jose and the others knew better.

There was an angry ghost at work; one who needed to be checked.

A knock on the door brought Jose back to the present. After a moment, he heard his wife's voice, her words too soft for him to hear. She entered the room shortly, followed by a young woman carrying a large Calvin Klein bag. The girl was pretty, and Jose felt his interest pique, but he forced himself to focus on what she had brought, instead.

"I bring news from Oloricha Dominica," the young woman said. "And greetings. She sends you this gift, and hopes you will be able to accomplish your goal."

"Thank you," Jose said, standing up. He crossed the room and accepted the bag from her. When he opened it, the dark, hollow eyes of a human skull peered back up at him. Jose felt a wave of relief. It was difficult to get any Santeria priest or priestess, an Oloricha of merit, to part with such a prized possession, but Dominica knew his need was great.

Jose suspected that the deaths were not natural. That there was a spirit, perhaps an angry one, or simply misguided, who had committed the crimes. As a priest, Jose could not allow the dead to prey upon the living.

Jose turned away as the young woman gave a short bow and then was led out of the room. He carried the bag to his altar, a long, weathered piece of wood covered with the amulets and icons necessary to execute his tasks as a priest. Jose removed the skull reverently, placing it down in the center. He set the bag on the floor and stared at the remnants of some unknown man.

Jose closed his eyes and whispered a short prayer of thanks, and then he waited for his mind to clear. He would soon have to enter the Mill, but before he could, he needed to be prepared. Turning away from the altar, Jose walked to the closet, opened it, and turned on the light. Several bookcases lined the walls, each of the shelves filled with jars and bottles with various ingredients.

Jose stepped in with nervous hands and selected what he would need to ward off death.

Chapter 5: Visiting with Brian and Jenny

"You look terrible," Jenny said after she had let Shane into the house.

Shane grinned. "What, you don't think the one-eared look is in this year?"

She slapped him on the shoulder, shaking her head. "You better not be here to try and convince my man to go on a little ghost adventure."

"No," Shane said. "I'd like him to stay alive. Nope, I just came for some research help. Nobody's better than you two."

"See," Jenny said, grinning, "flattery will get you everywhere."

From the den, Brian called, "Don't sweet talk her, it just makes it worse for me."

Jenny rolled her eyes and said, "Come on. Let's go see Mr. Congeniality."

Chuckling, Shane followed her into the den where she went and sat down beside Brian on the couch.

"Damn," Brian said, his eyes widening. "You look like you've been worked over."

"A few times," Shane admitted, dropping into the chair across from them. "How have you two been?"

"Evidently better than you," Brian said, his tone serious. "What happened?"

"A lot," Shane said. "Too much. I don't know. It's been pretty rough."

"Looks like it," Brian said. "Anyway, tell us what you need. All you said over the phone was you wanted information."

"That's pretty much it," Shane agreed. "I didn't know if either of you knew anything about the Slater Mill in Nashua?"

Brian shook his head, but Jenny's eyes narrowed. A heartbeat later she said, "Yeah, yeah, I think I do."

She got back up and left the room.

Shane looked to Brian, but his friend shrugged, saying, "Man, I don't even know what she has for information anymore."

Jenny's footsteps rang out on the stairs and then moved across the hallway of the second floor.

"We have a few minutes," Brian said, chuckling. "She went into her library. Place is chock full of books, and articles. I swear she's got way too much on ghosts up there."

"More power to her," Shane said. "I definitely need some help on this before I poke my nose in there."

"Yeah," Brian said. "Tell me what's going on."

"Have you read the Telegraph?" Shane asked.

"No," Brian said. "Thing's a rag. I stopped reading it a year or so ago after I found spelling errors in their headlines."

"Understood," Shane said. He settled back in the chair and told Brian about the two murders, and what he had seen in the photograph.

"Seriously?" Brian asked.

Shane nodded.

"Damn," Brian muttered. "Well, you definitely came to the right place. Jenny's got a ton of stuff on both Nashua and Manchester. Not so much on the little towns around the cities."

"Fine by me," Shane said. "All I need is info on the Mill right now."

Above them, a door closed and a moment later, Jenny was on her way back down the stairs. She appeared carrying in her hand a slim, dark blue book. With a smile, she handed the volume to Shane, and then returned to her seat beside Brian.

There was nothing written on either the book's spine or cover. When Shane opened it, he found he had it upside down and had to turn it around before he could read it. The title page stated the book's name was "Mishaps at the Slater Mill." It had been published in 1911.

"That's a list of all of the deaths that occurred in the Mill," Jenny said. "Both when it was being built, and when it was in operation."

Shane flipped through the pages. The book was arranged by year, starting in 1841, and continuing until the year of publication. In each section, the deaths were arranged alphabetically by surname, with information on the individuals and their manner of death concisely described.

The book was a litany of horrors.

On one page alone, Shane saw three men who had died after having an arm torn off by "Machine Number 5" on the third floor. Blinding was common, as were the loss of fingers and toes. More than one child was listed as a fatality as well.

"This is miserable," Shane murmured. He looked up at Brian and Jenny.

"Yeah," Jenny agreed. "I found the book last year at the Nashua Public Library's annual book sale. I thought it was interesting at first, but then it just got to be too much, even for me."

"That bad, babe?" Brian asked in a soft voice.

"Yeah," she said, sighing.

"May I borrow this?" Shane asked, closing the book.

"Sure," Jenny said. "Do you have to go into the Mill?"

"I think I do," Shane said.

Jenny didn't ask why. Instead, she said, "You're not taking Brian."

"No," Shane agreed. "I am most definitely not taking Brian. He's not exactly the picture of health."

Brian snorted. "Look who's talking. You could star in horror movies now."

"Ha," Shane said. "You're a funny guy."

"I am," Brian said, grinning. The grin dropped away, and Brian became serious. "I hope you're wrong, though, about the photo."

"Me too," Shane said.

"What photo?" Jenny asked, looking from Shane to Brian.

"I'll tell you later," Brian said.

Shane stood up, holding the book in his left hand, still painfully aware of the absence of his two fingers.

"Are you going into the Mill alone?" Jenny asked.

"More than likely," Shane answered.

"What about Frank?" Brian said. "Won't he go in with you?"

"He's at a wedding," Shane said. "And I don't think I can wait on going. I've got a feeling this is going to get worse."

"Okay," Brian said. He and Jenny got up and walked with Shane to the front door.

"I know I can't do anything to help," Brian said, "but I still know some people. If you need anything, don't hesitate to call."

"I won't," Shane said. He shook their hands and left the house. He had a long ride back to Nashua, and he needed to figure out the best way to get into the Slater Mill.

Without being arrested or getting murdered by a ghost.

Chapter 6: Standing on the Corner

Chad Everett had a pocket full of 'H'.

If he sold all of the heroin before the night was through, he could clear a couple of hundred, and that was after what he owed Simone for the buy in.

Grinning, Chad relaxed, adjusted his headphones, and waited to see what the night would bring.

He watched a few cars roll by, but most people were interested in the old Slater Mill. The double homicides had piqued everyone's interest, and Chad had even taken a stroll over there earlier in the night. He hadn't gotten too close, though. The police were still hanging around, asking questions, and Chad had already done a four-year bid in the state prison for dealing.

He took out his cigarettes, shook out a Newport, and lit it. Exhaling the smoke up into the night sky, Chad felt a smile creep across his face. The air felt good, and there was nothing better than a cigarette to help the time slide by.

The hours eased along, and soon he had emptied his pocket. He split the cash from the sales into various places in his jeans and sweatshirt, and then got himself another smoke. Whistling, Chad walked away from the corner. In the clear night air, the wind carried the sound of the old Mill clock down to him as it struck midnight.

The witching hour, he thought, chuckling. *Maybe I'll take a closer peek at the Mill.*

And with that, Chad adjusted his path, crossing Central Street to cut down Ash. The old building loomed up at the end of the street, the old windows sucking in the light of the stars and the moon.

He had never liked the place. It had always made him feel strange, as if someone was behind the glass, waiting for him to come too close.

Chad snorted. He had real problems to worry about. The police finding out he was dealing again. Simone thinking he might be skimming off the top. Somebody learning Chad was shooting up every night.

Nope, he thought. *I've got real issues. Not any boogie man garbage to deal with.*

When Chad reached the end of Ash Street, he looked around, stared past the chain-linked fence, and wondered what had happened.

A can rattled to his right, and Chad turned. Half in the shadows he saw a middle-aged white man staring at him.

Chad reached up, slipped the headphone out of his right ear and said, "Hey man, no more chemicals tonight. I'm sold out. Catch me tomorrow. I'll be all set and stocked up. You can get your nod on then."

The man didn't respond, and Chad felt uncomfortable.

Chad hadn't seen him around before, but that wasn't anything too strange. He knew all of the cops by sight, and this one wasn't anything close to a cop.

Just another junkie looking for a fix, Chad told himself. He waited another few seconds for the man to say something, and when he didn't, Chad shrugged and turned his attention back to the Mill. Out of the corner of his eye, he made sure he could see the stranger. Chad hadn't lived in the projects his entire life to forget that little lesson.

When the man took a step towards him, Chad bristled and turned.

"What's your problem?" Chad snapped, and then all of his thoughts vanished.

The man faded in front of Chad's eyes, disappearing.

Chad backed up until he bumped into a wall. His eyes darted all around, and finally, they found the man.

He was standing on the other side of the chain-linked fence, staring at Chad.

Without a word, the man turned around and walked through the brick wall.

The cigarette fell from Chad's lips, the ashes burning small holes in his sweatshirt as they tumbled down.

"No," Chad whispered. His eyes searched the Mill, and in a window, on the second floor, he saw the half-moon shape of the man's face.

Chad screamed, his voice rising to a high shriek before he went racing from the scene.

Chapter 7: Looking for Something

Jamie Fernandez opened the door to his apartment in time to see the skin-popper Everett running down Ash Street.

"What the hell was that?" his brother Tony called from the kitchen.

"Everett," Jamie answered, going out to sit on the front step.

Tony stepped into the doorway behind him, looking out and watching Everett run.

"Damn," Tony said. "He get a bad dose or something?"

"Who knows," Jamie said. "Get me a beer, will you?"

"Yeah." Tony left and returned with a beer for each of them.

Jamie twisted off the cap, dropped it into the half-filled coffee can of the same by the step, and looked at the Mill building. He had never paid much attention to it before the murders. It had always been there. Like the sun, or the sky. Nothing to think about, let alone worry.

"Think he went into the Mill?" Tony asked.

Jamie shrugged. "Maybe, but no junkies go in there to boot up. Even they're not that stupid."

"Think somebody's in there?" Tony asked.

"Naw," Jamie answered. "Cops would have found him. Building's big, but you can't hide from a cop when they're after you for murder."

"True," Tony said while leaving, his footsteps trailing away.

Their father was doing a life sentence down in Massachusetts for killing a clerk in a robbery. The Nashua police had been relentless. Jamie could still remember when they had raided the apartment and dragged his father out in handcuffs.

No, Jamie thought, finishing his beer. *Cops don't mess around. Not with murder.*

He put the empty bottle down by the coffee can and looked at the Mill.

"Yeah," he muttered to himself, standing up. "I'll do it."

"What's going on?" Tony called to him.

"Going into the Mill," Jamie said.

"What?" Tony asked, disbelief in his voice.

"I want to see what the big deal is," Jamie said, rolling his shoulders. He had enjoyed a good day at the gym. Big Mike had brought in two guys from Billerica to spar with him, and Jamie had beaten both of them. If there was anyone in the Mill, Jamie wasn't worried about him.

Jamie was a hell of a lot better at bare-knuckle brawling than he was in the ring with the gloves on.

No rules outside the ring.

"Don't go now," Tony said. "Ella's asleep. I can't leave her alone."

Jamie almost said something nasty about Tony not being a man, then he remembered how much his niece depended on Tony. Jamie's brother was a better father than theirs had ever been.

"No, man," Jamie said. "Stay home with Ella. It's probably nothing. I just want to stretch my legs. See what's going on."

"Don't start anything," Tony said. "Least not without me. Okay?"

"Yeah," Jamie lied. "Of course. See you soon."

"Yeah," Tony said. "Door'll be unlocked."

Jamie nodded and walked down to the end of the street where the gate to the fence was. For the first time in his life, he reached out and touched the cold metal, flipping the latch up. Jamie realized he had never seen it locked before.

And even after the murders, it still wasn't locked.

Jamie shook his head, pushed the gate open, and entered the enclosure. He walked towards the nearest door, tall and wide. There was no caution tape on it, no sign to stay out.

Jamie reached out, grasped the doorknob, and turned.

It wasn't locked and slid easily, as did the door itself. The old hinges complained, their noises swallowed by the darkness revealed. Jamie stepped into the building, pushing the door out further. He could smell a rank mustiness, but nothing else. A few paces in and his eyes adjusted to what little light there was from the outside.

He was in a wide hallway, and there was a younger man sitting against the left wall. A few feet past him was an older man, and both of them, like Jamie, were Hispanic.

"You two okay?" Jamie asked.

As one, the men turned to look at him, and it was then that Jamie noticed they didn't seem quite right. They were opaque. On their faces, he saw sorrow and desperation.

The younger one opened his mouth and spoke a single word in Spanish.

"Run."

Jamie had never run from anyone. He had built a reputation for standing his ground, no matter what the odds were.

But that word, uttered in a hollow voice, forced him to turn around.

Jamie focused on the door, the rectangle which led to freedom, and gasped as the portal swung closed.

He stood still, too surprised to move.

A pale face loomed in front of him. There was a five o'clock shadow on the man's flesh, highlighting the darkness of his eyes.

The stranger spat a word at Jamie, and before Jamie could reply, the man's hand lashed out and plunged into Jamie's chest.

Gasping for air, Jamie couldn't scream. He couldn't move backward and pull himself away from the terrible, cold fist wrapped around his heart.

The stranger grinned and tightened his hold.

Jamie couldn't think, let alone move.

He was asked a question, but he didn't understand it.

And even if he had known it, he wouldn't have been able to speak it. The pain in his chest was too great.

The stranger waited a moment longer, shrugged, and squeezed.

Jamie felt his eyes roll up in his head, his knees gave out, and a pain he never imagined possible, devoured him.

Chapter 8: Researching the Mill

Shane was in his library, the lights on and the book Jenny had loaned him on the desk. Beside it, Shane had a notebook and a pen, thirty-nine names were written down. Thirty-nine people who might still be haunting the Mill.

Two men were dead, and Shane couldn't understand why.

He had gone to the library and examined reels of microfilm, searching through the old newspapers in an effort to find evidence of more murders. But there hadn't been any. The only reference he had found was an article from the early seventies where the author talked about the haunting of Slater Mill, and of how everyone knew not to go in there.

But how? Shane thought. *How did they know?*

He sighed, leaned back, and rubbed at his eyes. Shane had spent hours at the library, and not waiting for his brain to rest, he had launched himself into an examination of the book.

"Shane?" Carl asked.

Shane dropped his hands and looked at the ghost. Carl stood by the door.

"How are you feeling, my friend?" Carl asked in German.

"I'm as well as can be expected," Shane said, answering in the same language. "Is everything alright in the house?"

Carl hesitated before he nodded.

Shane frowned. "Carl, what's going on?"

"Well," Carl said, looking uncomfortable. "It seems as though a minor situation may have presented itself."

Shane closed the book and straightened up in his chair. In all of the years he had known the ghost, Shane couldn't remember a single occasion where Carl had referred to anything other than a 'bother' at best.

"What," Shane said, choosing his words carefully, "do you consider to be a minor situation?"

"It concerns Courtney," Carl said.

Shane stared at Carl and waited for the dead man to continue.

He did a moment later. "She is no longer a captive."

Anger flared in Shane, and he asked through clenched teeth, "Which one of you sent her on her way?"

Carl looked surprised. With a shake of his head he said, "No, you misunderstood me, my young friend. She has, well, she has escaped her cell."

Shane slumped back into his chair, all of the blood rushing out of his head. The room swam before his eyes, and he took a moment to regain his composure. His hand trembled as he reached out and closed the book.

"Do you have any idea where she is?" Shane asked, his voice as shaky as his hands.

"No," Carl said, his voice wavering. "We are searching the hidden rooms and the places between the walls, but it could be some time. I thought, perhaps, it might be advisable for you to vacate the premises for a short time."

Shane snorted. "No. This is my home, Carl. I'm not going to leave it. Not because of the dead. I didn't do it as a boy and I sure as hell won't do it as a man."

Carl shook his head. "This is not a question of your manhood, my friend, but of the girl murdering you while you sleep."

"She won't," Shane said aloud, thinking, *No, she'll want to look me in the eyes when she kills me. She's insane now.*

Tears welled up in his eyes, and he wiped them away.

"You will not leave?" Carl asked.

"No," Shane answered, shaking his head. "I won't."

"We will watch over you then," Carl declared. "We will ensure your safety."

"Don't," Shane said. Guilt, never far from his thoughts, rose up, a leering monster in his mind. "Look for her. If she comes to me, I will let you know."

Carl hesitated, then nodded. "Alright, Shane. We will listen for you."

"Thanks," Shane said.

Carl bowed and left the room.

The silence in the library weighed upon Shane like a stone. He tapped his fingers on the arm of the chair. Carl's suggestion had been a wise one. Shane had no idea what Courtney might do. He knew she still harbored murderous intentions towards him.

Taking a deep breath, Shane let it out slowly through his nose and then stood up.

To the emptiness of the room, he spoke in a soft voice, "Courtney, can you hear me?"

Silence answered him.

Shane looked around and raised his voice. "Courtney?"

"I can hear you," she hissed, her words coming from the walls.

"Can you hear me?" she asked, her voice moving from right to left.

"Yes," he answered.

"Do you know what I want?" Her voice was harsh, unforgiving.

"No," he lied. "What do you want, Courtney?"

"I want you to love me!" she snarled.

"I've never stopped loving you," Shane said. "I will always love you."

Silence greeted his statement.

Then the room shook, and an unseen hand yanked all of the books off of the left wall. They went hurdling through the air, and Shane ducked down, but not before a thick volume struck him in the ribs.

Grimacing at the pain, Shane moved towards the safety of his desk. When the last of the books fell to the floor, Carl barreled in.

"Where is she?!" Carl demanded.

Shane shook his head. He didn't know.

With a curse, Carl ran and vanished into the bookcases on the left wall, leaving Shane alone in the room.

Shane straightened up and examined the mess around him. Some of the books were open, flat on their backs or face down. Pages were bent, and spines cracked.

Shane shook his head, bent down, and began picking up the books.

Chapter 9: Watching Slater Mill

It was Kurt's one night off from work, and he was sitting in his car on Myrtle Street. Through his windshield, he could see the Slater Mill. A third man had been found dead the night before. Jamie Fernandez, a hard man who had done hard time. He had been a figure of violence in the neighborhood but had been in the process of getting his life together after ten years in a cell.

And now he's dead, Kurt thought. He took a sip of his coffee and winced when the cold brew hit his lips. Kurt hated cold coffee, but he couldn't leave the Mill. He was on a self-imposed 'stake out,' observing the building on his own time.

The initial reports on all three of the homicides were mundane. The Hispanic boy had died from injuries resulting in a fall. Old age was the main contributing factor to the Ecuadorian man's demise. And Jamie Fernandez, according to Doctor Leonard, had a heart issue no one knew about. They wouldn't know anymore unless the family gave the coroner permission to do an autopsy.

They had already rejected it. The thought of him dead had been too much for them, and Kurt understood. He had felt the same way when his first wife had died at the age of thirty because of an ovarian cyst which had turned out to be ovarian cancer.

That no one had caught.

Kurt pushed the thoughts away and focused his attention on the Mill again.

Why now? he wondered. *Why are there deaths now? Not even the owner has gone into the place. He can't tear it down because it's a historical building, and he can't use it because there's something wrong with the structure, although he isn't sure what exactly.*

Kurt shook his head.

None of it made sense. The only thing he did know was that there was a trio of deaths, and none of them made any sense. Maybe spread out over a few years, but not over a week.

A flicker of light caught his eye and Kurt looked at the building.

On the second floor, a pale glow could be seen from one of the windows.

Kurt leaned forward, staring hard at the light. He watched it move from the bottom row of panes to the center, and then to the top. Kurt blinked, confused as the glow disappeared behind a wall to reappear at the next window, at the same height. Then onto the third.

He felt confused. There shouldn't be anyone in the Mill, and he didn't know of anyone who would be able to reach the top of the Mill windows. They were easily ten feet tall, and four feet wide.

An uncomfortable feeling filled him, and Kurt reached for the radio.

But there wasn't one in his personal car.

He contemplated going into the building, but he didn't have any backup, and he couldn't see or hear anything happening inside.

Kurt picked up his phone, hesitated, then put it back down. He wanted to call his brother, but Erick wasn't exactly the soul of discretion. If the two Warner brothers went into the Mill, Erick would be sure to post the experience on every social media platform before they even left the building.

Just observe, he told himself after several minutes of debate. *If someone goes in or comes out, then I can intervene.*

Satisfied with his decision, Kurt got as comfortable as he could in the seat, folded his arms across his chest, and settled in to watch and wait.

Chapter 10: Jose Seeks to Cleanse the Mill

Jose saw the cop in his car, watching the mill.

With a shake of his head, Jose walked past the vehicle and made his way past the side of the Mill. He turned right around the building, approaching it from the back side. As he drew nearer to the fence, he felt the power radiating from the bricks. It was a curious feeling, similar to being on a roller coaster, his stomach felt as if it dropped down to his knees.

Jose hesitated and looked at the building with dread.

Whatever was inside of the Mill was getting stronger.

For years, Jose had passed the structure and never had he experienced the new, charged atmosphere now surrounding it.

A flicker of doubt, an insecurity about his own abilities, occupied his heart. It grew steadily, like a spark bursting into flames and devouring a piece of paper.

Suddenly unsure, Jose stepped back.

It was then that he saw the man standing by the wall.

Jose squinted, recognizing the man. "Jamie?"

Jamie smiled.

"What are you doing in there?" Jose called in Spanish.

"Waiting," Jamie replied.

"Waiting?" Jose asked. "Waiting for what?"

"More." The smile on Jamie's face faltered, then crumbled. "You should run, Jose. You should tell everyone to run."

"Run from what?" Jose asked, feeling confused.

"From him," Jamie answered, a mournful expression accompanied the words as he looked past Jose.

Twisting around, Jose saw a small man standing a few feet away from him. He was dressed in starched jeans and a stiff, khaki shirt. The man glared at Jose. The stranger asked Jose a question, and it took him a moment to realize that the words were French.

Jose's mind scrambled to translate. It had been years since he had traveled through Haiti and the Dominican Republic.

The stranger repeated the question, and Jose was able to understand it.

"Why are you here?"

"There's something wrong with the building," Jose explained, faltering and stumbling on some of the words. "I will cleanse it."

"You are a Catholic Priest?" the man asked, squinting warily.

Jose chuckled, surprised at the question. "No. I am not. I am an Oloricha of Santeria. A priest of Santeria, if you will."

The man frowned, stepped forward, and asked, "Not a Catholic?"

Jose shook his head.

"Not a Catholic," the man repeated in a murmur.

Jose started to speak again but stopped. There was something off about the man. He didn't look quite like a man should, but Jose knew it might be nothing more than an optical illusion. The stars and the city lights could make strange things appear, and people look odd, especially around a place as powerful as the Mill was turning out to be.

"You are a heathen," the stranger said, taking a step closer. "But you look strong. Are you?"

"Strong?" Jose asked, confused. "I don't know."

"Yes," the stranger said, nodding. "You're strong. You'll do well. And you can speak the proper tongue."

Jose stepped to the left and contemplated calling for help. He wondered if the cop he had seen would hear him. There was a disturbing, frightening quality to the stranger. An intensity that caused Jose's knees to quiver in fear.

Then it struck him.

This is the ghost, he realized, and that knowledge was accompanied by the understanding that he would never be able to turn the spirit away.

It was too strong.

Terrifyingly so.

Jose turned and ran, opening his mouth to scream for help when he was struck in the back. The blow was cold and hard, sending him sprawling on the asphalt. He felt his pants tear and his lower lip burst open. Blood gushed down his chin and stars exploded in his eyes. He struggled to get to his hands and feet, to get away from the ghost, but the dead man was waiting.

Jose tried to scream again, but the man grabbed him on either side of the face and squeezed his mouth closed.

"Shh," the man said. "Let us not disturb our neighbors."

Jose tried to twist away, jerking his head from left to right. He struck at the man's hands but only succeeded in hurting himself. Wherever the dead man touched Jose's flesh, an excruciating pain shot through his skin. The stranger's hands were cold, unbearably so.

Frantic, Jose struggled to pull away, but the stranger pinched Jose's nose closed. Jose couldn't breathe. He couldn't do anything. He fought but his efforts were useless. The dead man's hands weren't accessible; Jose couldn't pull the fingers back. When he tried to kick the man, all that happened was a fresh pain. It exploded through his foot and traveled up and into his calf.

Jose would have screamed if he had the air to do so.

The stranger had robbed him of it.

Jose's lungs screamed for air, yet there was none.

As blackness ate away at the edges of his vision, Jose comprehended that he was going to die. And it would not be pleasant.

He struggled to see, and when his vision cleared, he saw three men standing around the stranger. They too were dead, and one of them was Jamie.

"Almost there," the dead man whispered with a smile, "and when you are dead, well, then you can come work with me."

With a last effort, Jose forced himself to focus, reminded himself that it was a dead man he fought, and acted accordingly.

He plunged his hand into his shirt pocket, found the iron dust he had placed there, and grasped it. Jose tore the fabric as he removed his hand and cast the iron into the ghost.

A shriek exploded in the night and the dead man was gone. Jose's body screamed for oxygen and he sucked in great lungfuls of it. Ignoring Jamie and the other two ghosts, he dragged himself to his feet and fled for the safety of his home.

Chapter 11: In the Bedroom

Shane had moved his studying from the library to his bedroom, where he had found Eloise standing at the window and looking outside.

"Hello, Shane," the dead girl greeted him.

"Hello, Eloise," Shane replied, sitting down on his bed.

She turned and faced him, her lips set in a grim line.

"What?" Shane asked, putting the book down. "What's wrong?"

"Carl spoke with you."

"Yes," Shane said. "He often does."

Eloise pointed a finger at him. "Do not get smart with me, Shane Ryan! I died when I was a little girl, but that was a hundred years before you were born!"

Shane held up his hands, palms outward. "I'm sorry. Yes, Carl spoke with me. About Courtney."

It hurt him to say her name.

Some of the anger fell away from Eloise's face. She nodded. "And you will not leave?"

Shane shook his head. "No. I have work to do. Something's happening at one of the mills."

Eloise frowned. "Which one?"

"The Slater Mill."

The dead girl clapped her hands and smiled at him. "I know that mill!"

"Wow," Shane said, blinking. "Really?"

"Yes," she said, skipping around. "Wait. What's happening at the Mill?"

"People are dying," Shane said.

Eloise made a dismissive gesture. "People die all of the time in the mills."

"This one hasn't run for a hundred years," Shane added.

She stopped in mid skip and looked at him. "Ah. Yes. That would be a little different then."

Eloise returned to the window, pulled on one of her braids and then sat down on the end of the bed.

"You should probably speak with my father," she finally said.

"I'm assuming he's dead?" Shane asked.

"Of course he's dead, silly," Eloise said, her laughter filling the room. "He was old before I was killed. But even if he's dead, he'll know what's going on. He always knew what was happening at that Mill. He ran it for Mr. Slater."

"And where might I find your father?" Shane asked, hoping it was some small, family burial ground.

"Edgewood Cemetery," she answered. "That's where everyone in the family is buried. Except for me. Well, most of me is buried there."

Shane didn't ask for clarification.

"Do you have any idea what part your father might be in?" he asked. "Edgewood's a big place."

"By the Andersons," Eloise answered. "They were good friends. When my mother killed herself, they even made certain that the Minister buried her in hallowed ground. Silly, isn't it?"

"What?" Shane asked.

"My mother killing herself," Eloise said, sighing. "She thought she was going to see me again, but instead she went right to the next world."

Leaning forward Eloise gave him a grin as she said in a confidential tone, "I heard her screaming as she went past."

"You're a bit mad, aren't you," Shane said, eyeing her warily.

"Of course, I am," Eloise said. "And I thank you for noticing. Will you visit my father?"

Shane hesitated and then asked, "He isn't buried in a crypt, is he?"

Eloise laughed, shaking her head. "No. Not at all."

"Thank God," Shane murmured.

"He's buried in a mausoleum," she said.

Shane repressed a groan. "Great. And at Edgewood."

Eloise nodded. "By the Anderson Chapel. It's very nice, you know."

"The mausoleum?" Shane asked.

"Yes," she replied. "Will you say hello to him for me?"

"Sure," Shane said. "Wait, how do you know he's still there?"

"There are those among the dead," Eloise said, becoming serious, "who know no bounds. I have heard from them about my father. He and others move freely in Edgewood, close to their bones and bound by the iron fence. But ask him, Shane Ryan, and he will tell you who to look for in Slater Mill."

The girl vanished without another word, leaving Shane alone in the bedroom. Elsewhere, Carl and a few of the others hunted for Courtney. Part of Shane hoped they would find and recapture her. A smaller part hoped he might speak with her again.

Shane got up from his bed, walked to his bureau and picked up the iron rings there. He slid them on before he picked up his knuckle-dusters and slipped them into his pocket. Shane lifted his backpack from the floor, walked with it to the bed, and slipped the Slater Mill book into it.

Well, Shane thought, adjusting the knuckle-dusters in his pocket. *Time to talk to the dead.*

Chapter 12: The Cultivation of a Ghost

She held the dossier on the foreman open and glanced over it. She had read it after the sudden death of a teenager and she was well familiar with the situation. What she found curious about the dead man, and thus the Slater Mill, was how the Watchers had taken an active role in the recruitment of the man.

An early representative of the organization, a man named Elijah Johnson, had sought out Pierre. The mill foreman's propensity toward violence had been legendary in the community. Johnson had learned of the man's enjoyment of industrial accidents. Arms and hands lost. Blindings. Deaths. The foreman had enjoyed the misery caused by every incident, the bloodier the better.

Johnson, according to the field notes, had been on friendly terms with Slater, the owner of the Mill, and he had been granted permission to approach the brute. Johnson had spoken with him and found all of the qualities for a test subject.

The foreman had possessed a level of hatred and rage that had the potential for the man's spirit to remain past physical death.

Unbeknownst to the man, Johnson had arranged for the foreman to be murdered. Considering the man's reputation, it hadn't been difficult to enlist the aid of several disgruntled workers.

She smiled at the idea of it. The organization had never been one to shirk from a distasteful task.

Johnson had written about the beating, and of how he had removed one of the Pierre's fingers once his death had been confirmed. Pierre hadn't materialized immediately, but within five years, he had.

The looms had claimed more limbs and more lives, all under the brutal hand of the dead foreman.

And the Watchers had ensured that as long as the Mill was in operation, the ghost had enough to murder. Even after the Mill had been closed down, they had arranged for the occasional individual to be brought there.

She closed the dossier and put it on her desk.

After Shane Ryan had become a concern for the organization, she considered the troublesome man's removal. She had even played with the idea of kidnapping and killing him.

Too risky though, she decided with a sigh. *He has proven far too adept at staying alive. Best to have him removed and not be a bother any longer.*

She tapped her fingers on the desk, then she picked up the second file.

The one that told her all about Shane Ryan, 125 Berkley Street, and how long the Watchers had kept Shane under surveillance.

Chapter 13: Edgewood at Night

Most people, Shane knew, would refrain from entering a cemetery at night. Especially if they suspected it might be haunted.

Shane was not most people, and he was fully aware of the dangers represented by an angry ghost. Or worse, a crazy one.

He came to a stop at the side entrance to Edgewood on Ashland Street. The gate was ajar and the cemetery lit by the full moon and bright stars. Shane sighed and walked forward, slipping into the burial ground. The place was suspiciously absent of any animal noises. A few cars passed by in front of the cemetery, their lights illuminating the headstones.

Shane stopped and got his bearings. To his right was a large chapel made of stone with stained glass in its narrow windows. On the building's left was a mausoleum, smaller but constructed in the same style. Shane wandered around to the front and saw a name carved into the stone above the chapel's wooden doors.

Anderson.

And there was only the one mausoleum.

Shane took a deep breath and walked to it. The door was built from thick glass with a brass, oriental style grating over it. Shane stepped up to it, and gave it a nudge.

The door clicked and swung back towards him.

In the dim light, Shane saw a trio of stone sarcophagi. Two were adult sized, one on the left and the other on the right. Below the carved image of an angel on the back wall was the third, and much smaller sarcophagus.

Shane stepped into the building, took his backpack off, and set it on the floor. He pulled his knuckle-dusters out and slipped them onto his right hand. Looking around the tight confines of the room, Shane said, "I'm looking for Eloise's father."

A cold wind rippled through the mausoleum, and Shane smiled.

A pale shape, vague and difficult to discern, formed in front of Eloise's sarcophagus.

"Who are you?" a male voice asked. It was faint and difficult to hear, and Shane could only do so by focusing on the words.

"My name is Shane. I live in one twenty-five Berkley Street," he explained.

The shape became defined, took solid form, and revealed a stern man. His jaw was square, his hair cut short all the way around. The man's nose was broad, taking up a good portion of his face, and dominated the same. His eyes were narrow and the irises brown. He looked like a man who was used to being in charge.

"Shane," the dead man said. "Why are you here?"

"Your daughter suggested I come and speak with you," Shane answered.

The man frowned. "You spoke with Eloise?"

"Almost every day," Shane confirmed.

"She is well?" the dead man asked hesitantly.

"As well as can be expected," Shane said, "given the circumstances. She asked me to say hello, by the way."

The man nodded. "Thank you. My name is Trevor. What would you ask of me?"

Shane squatted down, opened up his backpack, and removed the book.

"I'm hoping," Shane said, "that you might be able to help me with the Slater Mill."

"In what capacity?" Trevor inquired.

"There have been some deaths in the main building," Shane explained. "And I believe I saw the face of a man in a window."

"What window?" Trevor asked.

Shane told the dead man what part of the Mill had been photographed and Trevor nodded.

Pointing to the book, the dead man asked, "Is that the Death Book?"

"It is," Shane acknowledged.

"Look up August of 1910," Trevor said.

Shane took his flashlight out, turned it on, and found the date.

"There should be a name there, Pierre Gustav, yes?" the dead man asked.

Shane nodded. "Yeah. Right here, says he died of a heart attack."

Trevor chuckled. "A pleasant lie, I am afraid."

"A lie?" Shane asked. "Why, what happened?"

"Pierre was a brute," Trevor explained. "He was too brutal. There were times to push the workers, and times to let them breathe. Pierre never accepted that fact. One night, when he stayed late, some of the others did as well. They killed him. How, I am not sure, but I have no doubt it was murder."

"Was anyone arrested?"

"No," Trevor said. "Of the three men suspected of the crime, all were related to police officers. Thus the police were well aware of Pierre's excesses."

"And so he died of a heart attack," Shane murmured. He turned off his flashlight, closed the book, and put it away.

"Exactly," Trevor agreed. "I must advise caution if you are going to seek an audience with Pierre. He was a man notorious for his temper, and his violence. He thrilled at the idea of discipline. If he is unquiet in death, then I can only say you should take exceptional care."

"I will," Shane said.

"Know this too," Trevor continued. "I heard Slater speak of Pierre, after the man's death, and of how there was something of Pierre's still in the Mill."

"What?" Shane asked.

"A finger," Trevor replied.

"A finger," Shane repeated.

Trevor nodded his head. "I don't know why it was there, or why it would concern him. Slater's voice had not been pleasant when he spoke of it."

"I think I know why," Shane said, shaking his head. He closed his backpack and slung it over his shoulder.

"And Shane," Trevor said, "I would ask a favor of you."

"Yes?" Shane asked.

"Will you say hello to my daughter for me, please?" the dead father said. "Will you tell her that I miss her so?"

Shane's throat tightened, and he nodded.

"Thank you," Trevor said, smiling. He faded, and in a short time, Shane stood alone among the sarcophagi.

Shane waited a few minutes, collecting himself, and then he turned and exited the building. The door swung closed of its own accord, clicking into place as Shane walked away.

He pushed his hands deep into his pockets and thought of the Mill. Shane looked around at the cemetery and wondered how many of them had died in the Mill, or because of it.

And he wondered if the Mill would kill him too.

Book 7: Slater Mill

Chapter 14: The Super's Office

From his seat, at his desk, Mitch Atherton could see a good deal of the Pine Street and the Mill. He was the superintendent at the Pine Street Estates, which was a nice way of saying 'ghetto housing.' The Estates existed in the old casket company building and specialized in over-fifty housing, which Mitch used to think was funny.

Until he turned fifty.

Now it was a bad joke.

The phone on his desk rang and Mitch wished he had a secretary to answer it for him. He knew it would be one of the old cranks or biddies complaining, as always, about their subsidized housing. Someone always needed the wiring checked, or the plumbing checked, or something of the sort.

Or, he thought bitterly, *it's Mrs. La Flamme needing the toilet plunged again.*

Mitch shivered at the thought and answered the phone.

A dial tone was all he heard, and he thanked God for small favors.

He returned his attention to his window and examined the Slater Mill. Police activity around it had been heavy, and the Telegraph hadn't exactly been forthcoming with any information.

And all of the cops he had known had long since retired.

The screensaver on his computer flickered then went out. A moment later, the desk lamp went dark as well.

He sighed, hating the idea of a blackout, and then he noticed that the traffic light was still running, and the 'Open' sign on the bodega was still lit.

Mitch swore under his breath and stood up.

If it wasn't a power outage, it was wiring. And wiring meant he had to call in an electrician.

Which meant he'd have to justify it to the board at the end of the month.

Rolling his eyes, Mitch left his office and went into the waiting room, where a man sat in one of the two chairs.

"Hey," Mitch said, grabbing his jacket off the coat rack. "I'll be back in about five minutes. Got to check a breaker out."

When the man didn't answer, Mitch looked over.

The man was gone.

Mitch stopped one arm in a sleeve and the other out. His door remained closed, and the stranger hadn't passed by him to go into his office.

Pulling his coat on slowly, Mitch turned around. He couldn't see anything, though. Shaking his head, Mitch shrugged and went to the door. He opened it and stopped.

The man stood in front of him.

A wave of cold air rushed into the room, and Mitch stepped back, surprised.

The man grinned, an act that sent a wave of sickening fear through him. There was something wrong with the man. Something off.

"Who are you?" Mitch asked.

The man shook his head as he held a finger up to his lips.

"What?" Mitch whispered, moving towards his office.

The stranger glided into the room, the door closing by itself behind him.

"Listen," Mitch said, struggling to summon authority into his voice. "You need to leave. If you're visiting a resident, then go. Otherwise, you need to leave the premises."

A laugh, both harsh and grating, escaped the man's mouth and he shook his head. He gestured with his left hand, and Mitch was knocked to the left, slamming into a filing cabinet. Mitch struggled to regain his balance, and the man stepped forward, punching Mitch in the face.

Pain exploded in Mitch's jaw, a tooth exploding from the impact. Mitch screamed as the stranger grabbed him by the hair, jerking his head up. The stranger's face broke into a wide grin, and the man pointed a finger at Mitch. He wagged it to the left, and then to the right.

Mitch watched it move, unable to tear his eyes away.

When the stranger saw he had Mitch's undivided attention, he moved the finger forward. Mitch tried to focus on it, but it struck his forehead, and the pain was excruciating.

Writhing in the man's grip, Mitch let out a shriek as a cold spike drove in through his skull. His vision went black, and the horrific chill pushed deep into Mitch's brain. Within a few minutes, Mitch couldn't move. It hurt to breathe, to even think.

And in a heartbeat, he no longer had to.

Chapter 15: Alone with His Thoughts

Kurt sat in his chair in his studio apartment, the only one he was able to afford after his costly divorce. Lisbeth, his second wife, had taken everything, literally, and the court had decided that he needed to pay alimony.

Which left him just enough to live on if he didn't work any extra shifts.

His apartment reflected his lack of funds, the furnishings sparse and decorative items noticeably absent. Blackout shades hung on the windows, and the digital clock by his bed was set to military time.

It was twelve hundred hours, and Kurt needed to go to sleep. The night had been long, and he and Bill had swung by the Mill a few times. Nothing had cropped up, no lights shined from the building's windows, and no one had been hanging around it.

Then, when Kurt had finished up in the gym after his shift, he had heard some of the guys talking about another death near the Mill. A middle-aged super at the Estates had had a heart attack or a stroke and died in his office.

Hearing about that had started an itch in the back of Kurt's brain. One he couldn't ignore.

Deaths were common in Nashua. It was a city with over a hundred thousand people in it, which meant that people died on a regular basis. What they didn't do was die in a concentrated area.

Kurt had taken a large, tourist map of the city from the foyer of the station, and brought it home. He had tacked it up on the wall across from his chair and used tape flags to identify the known deaths. Each flag had the date and suspected cause of death. He also had a flag for Jamie Fernandez, who was still missing.

Fernandez had lived across the street from the Mill. The teenager, Miguel, had died in the Mill. Paolo, the Ecuadorian, had died on the fence against the mill. The super, a man named Mitch, had died in his office, which faced Slater Mill and was three hundred and twenty-one feet away.

Three known deaths in less than three weeks.

No obvious signs of foul play. No pattern that could be seen.

The only similarity between any of the deaths was with their proximity to the Mill.

But it's spreading out, Kurt thought. *And it's moving faster.*

He didn't know why he felt that the deaths were intentional. It was a gut reaction; an instinctive reflex that he had learned to rely on throughout the years.

When something seemed wrong, he knew that it usually was.

He stifled a yawn, thinking, *I have to go to sleep, or I'm going to be tired as hell for my shift.*

Kurt stood up, stretched out the kinks in his back and legs, and walked to the sink. He filled a cup with water and took his vitamins as his phone buzzed. Frowning, Kurt picked it up off the counter.

It was a text from Bill.

Jamie Fernandez found in the Mill. No signs of violence. Just dead.

Kurt sent a quick reply, thanking his partner for the information, then turned back to the map. He walked to it, picked his pen up off the coffee table, and wrote the new information on Jamie's tape flag.

He stared at the map for a minute longer, then he dropped the pen to the table and walked over to his bed.

I'll worry about it later, he told himself as he laid down.

But he didn't worry about it later.

His mind wrestled with the problem for a long time before he succumbed to sleep.

Chapter 16: Uncertainty about Courtney

Shane had finished with the paper and was pleased to see there were no new fatalities reported in regards to Slater Mill. A man had been found dead nearby, but it hadn't been close to the building, against the fence, or in the Mill.

He still planned to enter the structure, but there was no longer a sense of urgency. People were staying away from it, and so Shane could take his time and determine the best way to deal with Pierre.

Shane's most pressing concern was how to find Courtney, and what to do with her.

The dead in the house had continued to search for the missing ghost, yet she had continued to elude them. Shane had seen Eloise and Thaddeus prowling the third floor, and Carl had begun to loiter in Shane's bedroom.

Courtney remained hidden.

Shane suspected where she might be, and he would face her alone. He twisted the rings on his fingers and stood up from the kitchen table. With his hands shaking from the want of whiskey, Shane left the room. He walked in silence, the house comforting with its lack of noise.

All of the ghosts were hidden, and it made him smile as he climbed the stairs to the second floor. He made his way to the library, entered it, and closed the door behind him. Shane turned on the lights and sat down at the large desk.

The books Courtney had knocked down previously were all returned to their shelves. It had taken Shane the better part of an entire day, but he had finished it.

He made himself comfortable in the chair, put his hands on the desk and said in a low voice, "Courtney."

Several minutes passed without a response, so Shane repeated her name.

The lights flickered, and the temperature dropped.

"Shane," Courtney whispered.

Her voice came from across the room, near the door.

"Hello, Courtney," Shane said, the words difficult and painful to speak.

"Why did you call me?" she asked.

"I wanted to speak with you," he said. Hesitantly, and in a whisper he added, "And I miss you."

"You could be with me," she responded, her voice moving to the right as she spoke. "I tried to bring you to me, but you resisted. You refused."

Her voice grew louder, angrier as she spoke.

"It's not my time to die yet," Shane said, hating the words.

"Was it mine?!" she snarled, the lights going out.

"It shouldn't have been," Shane murmured. "But it was."

"I came for you," Courtney said, drifting to his left. "I tried to save you."

"I know," Shane said.

"And then you locked me up," she continued, her voice rising.

"You're out," Shane said. "And they are hunting you."

"I know," she said, her voice plunging to a whisper. "But you knew where to find me."

"Yes," Shane said. "Close to the oubliette."

"The little place of forgetting," Courtney said. "Because that's what you're doing, Shane. You're forgetting."

"No," Shane disagreed. "I will never forget you."

Courtney didn't answer.

"Will you stay in here?" Shane asked. "In the library?"

"What?" she asked, surprised.

"I would like it if you stayed here, in the library," Shane said. "I will tell the others not to enter. To leave you be."

Courtney flickered into form in front of the desk, a look of surprise on her face. For a moment, her voice sounded as it had when she was still alive. Vibrant and rich.

"You're serious," she whispered.

Shane's voice wouldn't work, so he nodded.

"Then, yes," Courtney said, and she vanished.

The lights snapped back on, and warmth returned to the room. Behind the bookshelf, where the oubliette was hidden, came the sound of weeping.

Shane choked back his own tears, stood up, and stumbled out of the room.

Chapter 17: Frank Returns

"Shane!" Frank called, walking into the house and closing the door behind him.

"What?" Shane yelled back from the kitchen.

"I'm home," Frank said, laughing.

Shane stepped into the kitchen doorway, dressed in his usual sweatshirt, jeans, and boots, and said, "Well, welcome home."

"You're a miserable man, did you know that?" Frank asked, hanging his jacket up in the closet and dropping his bag to the floor.

"Yup," Shane said, leaning against the door jamb. "How was it?"

Frank shrugged. "Eh. Lots of jocks I knew from when I was a kid. Caught up with a couple of friends from high school. Most of them haven't turned out too well though."

"Did you point that out to any of them?" Shane asked, grinning. "Maybe help them realize how small and miserable their lives were?"

"Ah, no," Frank replied, shaking his head. "What about you? Did you look into the two deaths at the old mill?"

"I did," Shane said. "I'll tell you in the study."

"Okay," Frank said, and he went into the room. He dropped down into a chair, and Shane entered a minute later.

Shane looked thinner and paler than when Frank had left for the wedding, and he said as much to Shane.

"Yeah," Shane agreed. "I'm not doing too well right now. But we can talk about it after. I want to tell you what's going on with the Mill first."

When Shane had finished, Frank could only shake his head.

"Definitely deserves some looking into," Frank said. "Any particular time you want to do that?"

"I was thinking tomorrow," Shane said. "I wanted to do a little more research, see if we could find out who owns the building and get their permission to go in. Nashua isn't a small town that's not going to get too hyped up about us being in a place we shouldn't. The cops would be on us in no time."

"That reminds me," Frank said. "I meant to ask you about that female detective."

"Marie?" Shane asked.

Frank nodded.

"What about her?" Shane said.

"How do you know her?"

Shane gave him a small smile. "That's a long story, Frank, and only a little less painful than Courtney's story."

"Ah," Frank said. "Well, moving on, think we should go down to City Hall and see if we can dig up some info on the Mill's current owner?"

"Yeah," Shane said. "I need a quick drink first. My nerves are shot today."

"Tough night?"

Shane nodded. "I'll tell you about it on the way downtown."

"Fair enough," Frank said. "I'll wait here."

"Okay." Shane stood up and exited the room. In a heartbeat, Carl slid through the wall to stand near the hearth.

"Damn," Frank muttered. "You always scare the hell out of me when you do that, Carl."

"My apologies, Frank," Carl said, glancing at the door. "But I am concerned for our friend."

Frank frowned. "Why? What happened?"

"He has granted Courtney sanctuary in the library." Carl's voice was filled with anger.

"What? He let her out?" Frank asked.

"No," Carl answered. "She escaped. For a few days, she wreaked havoc within our home, but we were unable to lay our hands upon her. Then, it seems, she and Shane had a discussion. She now resides in the library, and we are forbidden to remove her."

The thought of Courtney anywhere other than her hidden cell within the walls of the house made Frank uncomfortable. Her past actions had made her a distinctly undesirable houseguest.

And she wasn't particularly fond of Frank.

"What do you need me to do?" Frank asked, glancing at the door.

"We would have you speak with him," Carl implored. "He will not listen to us. We, who have known him longest. I believe he sees our motives as suspect. Perhaps spurned on by jealousy. That is the farthest from the truth."

Frank nodded. "I know. Okay. I'll speak with him. See what I can do."

Carl gave him a short bow. "Thank you, Frank. I am fearful of what she might do to him. We watch his room, but he has taken to spending a great deal of time in the library. And as I said, we are forbidden from entering to deal with her."

"Yeah," Frank said, sighing. "Yeah. We'll see what I can do about her."

Carl nodded and slipped away as Shane's footsteps rang out in the hallway. Frank got to his feet as Shane stepped in.

"Ready?" Frank asked.

Shane gave him a wry grin. "Yup. Let's go deal with some city hall types."

Frank snorted a laugh, shook his head, and the two of them left the house.

Chapter 18: Coming to Terms with the Dead

Jose lay on his bed, still unable to speak. The ghost had damaged Jose's throat, the skin dead and flaking away. His wife had changed the bandage on it a short time before, and he had written instructions on the preparation of a balm for his mouth and tongue.

Nothing thus far had helped. Soon he would request that she send for the Olaricha from Boston, if his voice did not return.

Jose closed his eyes and let his thoughts roam, lifting them above the pain he felt in his throat. His wife had been begging him to go to the hospital, to at least cut away that which was dead.

He had written 'soon', and nothing more.

Jose had to think first.

The dead man had been far more powerful than he had imagined. Jose had been surprised as well at the other ghosts. The one who had attacked him, the small man, that one not only killed the living, but trapped their souls.

With a wince, Jose interlocked his fingers on his stomach and considered the problem. Including the attacker, there were at least three other ghosts. All of them bound to that man. Whether or not they would stand with him in a fight, had yet to be seen. And the killer was strong. He moved beyond the building, which meant he had an ability to project himself, which Jose had not seen before.

The most difficult part of the situation was not the dead man who tried to kill him, or the ghost's bounded companions, but Jose's lack of knowledge in how to deal with such a vicious entity.

He had brought the iron dust, more as an afterthought than any sort of real preparation. Jose had been fortunate. Lucky, and nothing more.

If he was to rid the community of the parasitic ghost, then he would need to learn all he could about ghosts.

On the bedside table, there was a small silver bell, a birthday gift from his wife's Goddaughter. When he needed his wife, Jose rang the bell. He reached out his hand, careful not to strain the muscles in his neck as he took hold of the cold metal. When he had it, Jose rang the bell. A soft tinkling sound filled the room, and his wife appeared a few moments later. She wiped her hands on her apron and looked at him with a worried expression.

He motioned for the writing pad she carried, and she handed it to him. Jose unclipped the pen and jotted down the titles of several books in his office. Ones that dealt only with the dead.

When he handed the pad back to her and she read what he had written, she frowned.

"Jose," she said, "are you certain you can do this?"

Her concern made him smile, and he gave a minute nod.

"Alright," she said, and left the room.

Jose closed his eyes once more. He listened as she searched his shelves. A tiny worm of doubt spread into his heart, one that ate at his confidence and told him he would draw his last breath in the Mill.

Chapter 19: An Introduction to Pierre

Kurt and Bill were parked at the end of the Pine Street Extension. They both had pictures of the boys, Seth and Dylan, who had disappeared after a trip to the bodega on Ash Street. There was no Amber Alert, since the boys were fifteen years old, and they were listed as runaways.

Kurt had his suspicions.

The boys had been in the Estates, where the super had died in the office. And the Estates were close to the Slater Mill. Something wasn't right. Not at all.

It didn't help that the boys didn't have a history of running away. Or of being any sort of trouble. Good students, respectful, and now missing.

Bill tapped his fingers on the steering wheel of the cruiser.

"I don't like this," Bill said after a minute.

"I know," Kurt said.

"There's been way too much weird stuff here, the past couple of weeks," Bill said. "Can't help feeling like it's got something to do with the Mill."

Kurt nodded. "What do you want to do?"

"I want to check the Mill out," Bill said, putting the car into gear. "I know we can't go in, but I want to see if there's any sign of someone messing around."

As Bill drove the car up towards the building, Kurt said, "You know, we could probably go in. If we think the kids are in there."

Bill nodded. "If we see a door open, that's what we're going to do. Agreed?"

"Agreed," Kurt said. A feeling of relief swept over him. He had been anxious for days. There was nothing solid, no rational explanation for why people were suddenly dying or disappearing around the Slater Mill. But it was comforting to know that Bill felt the same way.

Bill guided the cruiser around the back of the Mill, then parked the car. They both got out, looking at the building. It seemed to squat on the earth, a nasty growth in need of removal.

"They should just tear the damned thing down," Kurt said.

Bill nodded his agreement.

Movement caught Kurt's eye, and he turned towards it, pulling his flashlight from his belt. He clicked it on and brought it up in one smooth motion, the beam illuminating a short man.

And passing through him.

"What the hell?" Kurt asked.

Bill turned at the same time, saw the stranger, and cursed.

For a moment, the short man stood there, then he stepped forward.

"Bill," Kurt said. "We should leave."

"No," Bill said, shaking his head. "This is, hell, I don't know what this is. What is that?"

A terrible feeling settled into Kurt's gut.

"Bill," Kurt said again. "We need to get out of here!"

Before Bill could answer, the stranger launched himself forward, latching onto him.

Bill let out a surprised shout that turned into a howl of pain. He tried to pull himself away from the stranger, and Kurt raced to him.

Kurt tried to grab the stranger, but his hands passed through him, a biting cold attacking his flesh as he did so.

The stranger snarled something and shoved Kurt away.

Bill struggled and then stiffened as the stranger plunged his hand into Bill's chest.

Kurt scrambled to his feet as Bill's eyes rolled back in their sockets. Again, Kurt tried to grab the stranger, and once more, his hands passed through him. The pain was terrible, and when the man gave Kurt a backhand, the blow knocked him to his knees.

Kurt's head spun, and his thoughts were confused. He tilted his head up in time to see a pair of men racing towards them. The one in front was bald and missing an ear, and as he ran, he lifted his right hand, metal gleaming in the pale light of the street lamps.

As Kurt watched, the bald man reached the stranger, and struck him, the metal passing through the man. A howl of rage filled the night air, and the stranger vanished.

Bill collapsed to the pavement, his head cracking against it. His eyes stared forward, and Kurt realized his friend and partner was dead.

Chapter 20: In the Car

Shane and Frank sat in Frank's car, parked far away from the Mill so that they wouldn't be noticed, but still close enough to see what was going on.

They had left the dazed officer by the cruiser, the man's partner dead on the ground. Frank had told him to call it in as a heart attack, and Shane had told the man where they would be.

There was the risk the officer would directly involve them, but it was a risk Shane was willing to take.

The lights of the ambulance and other emergency vehicles danced in a maddening pattern across the walls of the old buildings around the Mill. In silence, Shane and Frank watched the paramedics examine the surviving officer. The dead man had been rushed to the hospital. Shane knew the cops should have called the medical examiner to retrieve the body, but the man was one of their own. They would do everything they could to save him.

"Think he'll talk?" Frank asked in a low voice.

"No," Shane said.

Frank glanced over at him. "Really?"

Shane gave a terse nod. "He'll want to know what we did to good old Pierre. I figure he'll think about telling his duty sergeant, but then he might worry about sounding like a lunatic. Especially if we act like he's out of his mind. Sure, I might get picked up for the knuckle-dusters, but he'll get sent off for a psyche evaluation. And that never looks good."

"True," Frank said after a minute. "Plus we won't tell him a thing if he rats on us."

"Yeah," Shane agreed. "There's that too."

Several minutes passed, and Frank swore.

"What?" Shane asked.

"Guess we're not breaking into the Mill tonight," Frank said.

Shane nodded. They had found the name of the current owner of the Slater Mill, but they hadn't had any luck getting in touch with the man. They had agreed to try and do a quick look before waiting for his blessing, especially after hearing about the missing kids on the news.

Shane hoped the kids had been found. Or were at least safe somewhere, but after what he had seen with the police, he doubted it.

Movement caught his attention and Shane watched as the paramedics loaded the officer into the back of the ambulance. Other cops stayed with the cruiser and the fire trucks that had responded had left.

Frank waited a few more minutes before he started the engine. In less than a minute, they had left the Mill behind them. Frank navigated the streets, bringing them back towards the house.

"Think he'll call?" Frank asked as they waited at a traffic light.

"Yeah," Shane said. "He'll call. Might even show up at the door without calling. Either one is fine."

"You really think he knows something?" Frank asked.

Shane nodded. "I do. They were there because they suspected something. I know it. Maybe they saw something before. Anything."

"You don't think this is a one off?" Frank asked, glancing over at him. "That maybe they just happened to be in the wrong place at the wrong time?"

"No," Shane answered, shaking his head. "I don't."

"Guess we'll find out one way or another," Frank said. He turned the car into the driveway and parked it behind Shane's. As he shut the engine off, he said, "Can I ask you something?"

"Sure," Shane said, getting out. "What's up?"

"I heard from some of the dead," Frank said, following him to the front door.

Shane paused and looked at his friend. "About Courtney."

"Yeah," Frank agreed. "About Courtney."

"She's in the library."

"That's what they told me," Frank said.

"I'm good with her there," Shane stated.

Frank raised an eyebrow. "Really? Because last thing I remember was, she seemed to be after my head as well as yours. In fact, you were first on the list."

"Still am, as far as I know," Shane said, turning to the door and opening it.

"You think she's going to let you live?"

"I don't think it matters," Shane murmured.

"What?" Frank asked.

"Don't worry about it," Shane said, sighing. "I'll figure it out."

Frank hesitated, as if he were about to say something else, then he shook his head and closed the door. "Sure. What now?"

"A cigarette and some sleep," Shane said. "Then we'll see whether the cop knows anything else."

Frank nodded and headed towards the kitchen.

Shane stared at the stairs, took a deep breath, and made his way to the library.

Chapter 21: Disbelief

"I'm fine," Kurt snapped.

The nurse looked at him sympathetically as she took a step back. "You need to be examined for shock, Officer. The paramedics wouldn't have brought you here otherwise."

"The paramedics are covering themselves," Kurt argued. "Same thing with the Department. And the damned Union. I'm fine."

Her expression never changed. "Officer, you need to relax a little. The doctor will be in shortly."

He gave her a hard look. "Don't lie to me. I saw victims from a multi-car accident out there. And I heard it called in. No doctor's going to get to me anytime soon."

She shook her head and asked, "Do you want the television on?"

"Please leave," Kurt growled. He had reached the end of his patience.

The nurse recognized it, nodded, and left the room, closing the door behind her.

Kurt stood up and paced around the small room they had placed him in. His eyes kept returning to his phone, which lay on the bed. He was waiting for his shop steward to call, to see if there was a way he could get out of having to wait for an evaluation. It was standard when any officer's partner died, but Kurt felt as though it only made the experience harder to deal with.

He couldn't even tell anyone how Bill had died. Not just because they wouldn't believe him, but also because he didn't believe it himself.

Book 7: Slater Mill

From his back pocket, Kurt took out a business card and turned it over. On the back was a name, a number, and an address.

All belonged to the man who had tried to save Bill, the bald-headed, scarred individual who looked like a gladiator out of some movie about the ancient Romans.

Kurt had seen some hard men in his time, but none of them had looked as brutal, or as ruthless as Shane Ryan.

And Kurt couldn't tell if that was good or bad.

Shane Ryan was a distant second to the disbelief that continued to swirl in Kurt's thoughts. Bill had been a big man. A strong one, too. The thing that had attacked him was nothing more than a ghost.

Ghosts can't kill people, Kurt told himself. He had been repeating the statement since calling for the ambulance. Since he had done as Shane had suggested, telling dispatch it was a heart attack.

Part of Kurt thought that it was.

But then he remembered what he had seen. An image of the map in his apartment had flashed in front of his eyes as well. The people who had died in or near the mill. The boys who were missing.

None of it seemed real.

He had the same surreal feeling as when his ex-wife had filed for divorce. Complete and utter amazement.

A knock sounded on the door and then it swung open, jerking his thoughts back to the present.

"Hello," a younger woman said. "I'm Doctor Himmel."

"Hey," Kurt said.

She was a tall woman, probably a good two or three inches taller than he was. Her shoulders were wide and she had high, prominent cheekbones. She had brown hair clipped close to her head, and her eyes were dark brown. The doctor had the appearance of someone who didn't suffer fools.

Kurt could appreciate that.

"Why don't you have a seat," she said. It was more of a command than a request, and Kurt did so in silence.

Doctor Himmel walked over, pulled a stool close, and sat down on it.

"Your partner died," she said.

Kurt nodded, the three simple words striking him with the force of a slap.

"Preliminary examination says it was a heart attack," the doctor continued. "I'm sorry you had to see it."

"Thanks," Kurt said, his voice raw.

She nodded.

"It's my job," she continued, "to make sure you're okay before I send you home. We both know the symptoms of shock, Kurt. And I have to make sure you're not hiding any of them. Is that understood?"

Kurt nodded, not trusting his voice anymore.

"Good." She leaned back, looked at him and added in a gentler, but still firm voice, "I will do this as quickly and as painlessly as I can. Alright?"

Kurt bobbed his head and ground his teeth to keep the tears locked in his eyes.

Chapter 22: Dangerous Reading

Shane sat in his chair in the library. The lights were off, and he was in darkness. He had closed the curtains, blocking the moon and starlight. In the room's stillness, he heard the rumbling of the oil furnace through the radiators and the pipes in the walls. The room had a hard chill to it. Courtney had come out of the oubliette and was somewhere near the door.

She fluctuated between sadness and rage as she spoke with him.

"You killed me," she hissed.

Shane had his eyes closed and his hands upon the desk's leather blotter.

"I did not," Shane argued. His eyes moved against his eyelids, tracking her by the sound of her voice.

"You might as well have," she snarled.

Shane didn't respond.

A book was knocked off a shelf. Then another, and then a slew of them.

"I'm sorry," she whispered a moment later.

"It's alright," Shane replied.

"There's something wrong with me," she continued. "There's something eating away at my heart."

"I'm sorry, Courtney," Shane said.

"You should be!" she screamed, and he winced.

The sound of books being thrown filled the room. In the darkness, he could hear her panting.

Then suddenly, her voice was in his ear.

"Would you stop me if I tried to kill you, Shane Ryan?" she hissed.

"Yes," he answered.

"Good."

And the chill was gone.

Heat boiled out of the room's radiator, and Shane knew she had returned to the sanctuary the oubliette offered her. He wasn't surprised to find a tremble in his hand as he turned on the desk lamp.

Shane's heart found its natural rhythm and someone knocked on the door.

"Come in," Shane said. He picked up the whiskey bottle and poured himself a drink as Frank entered.

"I thought you were cutting back," Frank asked, glancing at the chaotic pile of books on the floor.

"I am," Shane said. "This is the same bottle I opened this morning."

"You're almost done with it," Frank said, sitting down in a chair across from Shane.

"Ah," Shane said before he knocked the liquor back. "But I'm not done with it. There's the important part. The key ingredient."

Shane poured himself another shot.

"Is it?" Frank asked.

"Yes," Shane said. "I would have finished this bottle around dinner time before."

"That's only about seven hours ago, my friend," Frank said.

"Progression not perfection," Shane chided. He drank the second shot and put the tumbler down beside the bottle. "There. This bottle might even live to see the dawn."

His hand no longer trembled.

"How did it go?" Frank asked.

"I don't know," Shane confessed. "I don't know if she's okay. I don't know if she'll ever be the way she was, right after she died. I've read that some ghosts, well, they deteriorate as time goes by. Some do it quickly. Others take a long time. Some never do. I don't know if

Courtney's had a temporary hold put on her sanity, or if the little sane bits I see are the remnants of who she was. It's confusing as all hell, though."

Frank cleared his throat and then said, "You know, I thought things were in good shape when she was locked up."

"I couldn't stand the screaming. Every night. I could hardly sleep." Shane said, sighing.

"And now?" Frank asked.

"I'm sleeping better," Shane told him.

"Is that because Carl's in the room?" Frank said.

Shane chuckled and shook his head. "No. Carl being in the room means she doesn't murder me in my sleep."

Frank snorted. "That's not much comfort, my friend."

Shane shrugged, what little mirth he felt, leaving him. "I'm having a hard time right now, Frank. Dying isn't something I'm worried about. At least not at her hands."

"You may want to see someone about that," Frank said, his voice filled with concern.

"Probably," Shane said. "But I can't be bothered right now. We've got the Mill to keep me occupied. Maybe after that."

Frank shook his head. "You're not suicidal, right?"

"Right," Shane said. "I just don't know how hard I'd fight if Courtney came at me."

"You've still got the iron on your fingers," Frank pointed out.

Shane nodded. "Like I said. I'm not suicidal. I won't take any unnecessary risks, but, well, I don't even know at this point."

"Okay," Frank said. "Fair enough. You going to try and get some sleep?"

"Yeah," Shane said, standing up. Frank did the same, and they left the room together, Shane shutting the door and locking it behind him.

"What's the point?" Frank asked.

"A little reminder," Shane said, putting the key in his pocket. "I want to make sure the rest of the house understands she's to be left alone. A closed and locked door should do the trick."

"And if it doesn't?" Frank asked.

"Then I'll help them remember," Shane stated.

"Alright," Frank said, turning towards his own bedroom. "See you in the morning."

"You got it."

Shane walked to his room, passed through the open doorway and paused at his bed to strip down. The air was cold on his bare flesh, and as goose bumps rippled along his skin, he slipped between the sheets. He didn't bother with a lamp. The pale light of the moon poured in through the windows. Shane put his hands behind his head and closed his eyes.

In a few moments, he heard Carl.

"I'm here, my young friend," the dead man said in German.

"Thank you," Shane said. He yawned.

"Would you like me to send Eloise to the library for you?" Carl asked. It had been the same each night since Shane had given Courtney sanctuary.

"No," Shane snapped. "Leave her alone. Am I understood?"

"Of course," Carl answered. He didn't sound embarrassed by Shane's sharp words. Shane knew that the dead man would ask the same question the next night, and the one following that as well.

"Good night, Carl," Shane said.

"Good night, Shane," Carl responded.

In the silence of the room, Shane listened to the rhythm of his heart and waited for sleep to claim him.

Chapter 23: The Sounds of Machines

Benjamin Bergen hadn't slept well in decades.

The slightest noise woke him, forcing him to wear ear plugs when he went to bed. His fire alarm was designed for deaf people, a flashing light bright enough to punch through his eyelids and force him out of whatever drug induced haze he had managed to sink into.

While Benjamin never felt rested when he woke up in the morning, his body and mind at least got the sleep he needed. The drugs and the ear plugs were unpleasant, but they worked.

Nothing had woken him up in over seven years.

He was surprised, then, and furious, when a loud, rattling sound interrupted his sleep.

His eyelids, feeling as though they weighed far more than they should, fought him as he sat up in bed. He ripped the ear plugs out and looked around, blinking as he identified the noise was that of machines.

Someone, it seemed, was running construction equipment at three in the morning.

Muttering, Benjamin got out of bed, stumbled to the wall, and jerked the curtain away from the window. Glaring down at the street, Benjamin saw nothing.

Not a single piece of machinery. Not even a car.

There wasn't even someone walking by.

The street below his apartment window was dead.

Benjamin knew he didn't have to worry about the rest of his building because he owned it. All of it. He had taken an old warehouse and built a small apartment in a second-floor office.

Flashing lights caught his attention and Benjamin pressed his face against the cold glass of the window.

Half a block down, he saw the old Slater Mill. Bright white light flickered behind the windows, and it was from there that the sound of machines seemed to originate.

It was a horrible sound. One that made his teeth ache and eyes throb in their sockets. Benjamin stomped away from the window, snatched his phone up out of its cradle, and dialed the police department.

"Nashua Police Department, this is Danielle," a woman said when the phone was answered.

"Hey," Benjamin snapped. "You've got some kids or somebody in the Slater Mill raising all kinds of hell."

"Sir," the woman said, her voice cold. "We have officers there."

"I can see lights coming from the building," Benjamin spat.

"Sir," the woman repeated. "We have officers there."

"What, inside the building with their cars?" he demanded.

"Sir," the woman said, anger creeping into her voice. "I've told you that we have officers on the scene. If you don't get off of the line, I will report your position to a unit, and they will come and speak with you."

Benjamin bit back a curse and slammed the phone into its cradle.

He went back to the window, looked out again, and didn't see a single cruiser near the Mill.

"Bull," he snarled. Benjamin turned around, tugged on his boots, pulled his jacket over his pajamas, and left his apartment. He trudged down the stairs, left the broken peace of his building, and hurried towards the Mill.

When he reached it, there weren't any cruisers. Or police officers. Or anyone. Period.

Told you so, Danielle, he thought. Benjamin came to a stop at the fence that surrounded the Mill and considered what he should do next. The rational part of him said he needed to go back and give the police a polite and intelligent report as to what he had seen.

The irrational part disagreed.

And Benjamin agreed with the irrational part.

He went around the fence until he found a gate, and the gate, he wasn't surprised to see, was open. Shaking his head at the stupidity of others, Benjamin pushed his way in. The door to the Mill was ajar, and he shoved that open as well.

When he stepped into the hall, only a small rectangle of it lit by the moon, he grimaced. The air stank of machine oil and sweat. On top of that, it was cold in the building. As if someone had turned up an air conditioner and set it to sub-arctic temperatures.

Benjamin pulled his hands into his sleeves as he winced at the sound of machinery that ran on the second floor. He tilted his head back and saw lights flicker between the stairs.

Somebody's up there, he thought angrily. Determined to get them to stop their racket, Benjamin stormed up the stairs. The boards of the door were broad and the gaps between them wide. Through those same gaps the racket flowed.

The noise rose and fell, and it sounded like the work floor of Nashua Plastics, where Benjamin had worked when he was still a student in high school.

He knew it couldn't be that because Benjamin had watched when all of the machinery had been pulled out of the Slater Mill. Benjamin had even been there when the chain link fence had gone up.

The work floor, he knew, was empty.

At least it's supposed to be, he thought. Still furious over his interrupted sleep. Benjamin grabbed hold of the bent metal handle of the door and yanked it open.

The noise ceased, and a dull, sick light filled the long room.

Half-formed images of ancient textile looms dominated the cavernous floor. Shapes, roughly similar to people, pulled back into the shadows.

A single man walked down the center of the floor, and as he moved, his old work boots were silent.

Benjamin felt the wrongness of the situation, and he moved back to the door.

The man sprang forward, covering an impossible distance. Before Benjamin could turn to run, he felt a cold, hard weight slam into the small of his back. The blow sent him sprawling to the floor, the rough wood gouging his cheek. Benjamin was too surprised to cry out, even as he felt the rush of warm blood race down his face.

He tried to scramble to his feet, but a boot pressed down into the small of his back, thrusting him again to the floor. The weight remained there, a terrible, debilitating cold settling into his flesh.

Benjamin groaned, tried to crawl away, but the pressure was too much.

With a whimper, he ceased to resist. A cold finger stabbed him in the back of his neck where his skull met his spine. The stranger pushed, and Benjamin gasped in a mixture of horror and pain as the digit pierced his flesh.

Thunderous waves of agony crashed over him, and Benjamin went blind. He heard his limbs hitting the floor rather than seeing them. It was a curious, staccato sound that reminded him of children banging on school desks.

The noise of his own death chased Benjamin into darkness.

Chapter 24: Heightened Concern

Frank had finished his morning prayers and sat in the parlor. He didn't often visit the room, and so each time he went in, there was something new to see.

This morning Frank had discovered a series of small photographs, each one in a small, brass frame. They were of a young boy, starting from a picture of the child as a newborn until what looked like a high school photograph.

The child was undoubtedly Shane.

Shane's eyes had held a mixture of joy and genuine pleasure in the early photographs, those that showed him as an infant and a toddler. Even the few representing the beginning of his school years.

Others, taken when Shane was slightly older, reflected something else. There was sadness and fear in the eyes. Dark shadows revealing a lack of sleep. Fear and grim acceptance in the line of his chin.

For the first time, Frank understood how difficult Shane's childhood must have been, and he wondered exactly how much his friend hadn't told him.

"He was an intense child," a voice said from behind Frank, the words causing him to jump in his chair.

Frank twisted around and saw the little dead girl, Eloise. She stood inside of the door.

"Was he?" Frank asked, watching her as she went and stood by the hearth.

"Oh yes," Eloise said, nodding. "It was ever so difficult to get him to play with me at first. I am afraid I frightened him the first night."

"Did he ever forgive you for it?" Frank inquired.

"Of course, silly," she said, grinning. "Wouldn't you forgive me, Frank?"

Frank smiled and nodded. "Of course, I would."

She sat down on the floor and looked at him.

"Tell me," Frank said. "Did he have many difficult days here?"

"Nearly all of them," she admitted. "It was fear, at first, of me and Thaddeus. The dark ones and the old man. He befriended Carl early, but there was one, the bad one. The one who wanted to hurt him and his parents. And everyone who came into the house."

Frank frowned. "Who was this person?"

Eloise shook her head. "I have said enough and I will say no more."

"Alright," Frank said. He stood up, adjusted the chair so he could face her, and sat back down. "Tell me, what do you think should be done with Courtney?"

Eloise frowned. "I don't want to speak of her either."

Frank looked at the dead girl for a moment and then said, "We have to."

Eloise folded her arms over her chest and glared at him, the temperature in the room plummeting. "We do not."

"Eloise," Frank said in a firm voice. "She's in the library. He won't let anyone go in when she's there."

"So?" she said, raising her head in the air. "I don't care a thing what Courtney does."

Frank raised an eyebrow, and Eloise turned her face away from him.

"I don't," she repeated.

"I do," Frank said. "I need to know what to do about her. I don't want her killing Shane."

"He wouldn't let her," Eloise proclaimed.

"He would," Frank argued. "He's depressed. He holds himself responsible for her death. I think that most days, he would allow her to kill him. Perhaps some shred of him would try to stop her, but I'm not sure. I definitely don't want to gamble on it."

"Then you need to take her from the house," Eloise said. "Find where Shane keeps his necklace and seal it in lead."

"Shane wears his dog tags all the time," Frank reminded her. "I can't exactly sneak in and lift them off of him."

Eloise glowered. "Then we have no way to remove her!"

Frank started to debate the issue with her, but Eloise shook her head and sank down into the floor. Suddenly alone in the room, Frank stared at the section of flooring the dead girl had sat upon.

"No," he murmured. "There has to be a way."

Frank pushed himself up and out of the chair and left the room. He made his way towards his bedroom and grabbed his phone.

It was time to call the Abbott.

Chapter 25: Preparing for the Confrontation

Jose had gone to the emergency room three days after the attack. It had been difficult, the doctors questioning him as to how he managed to obtain frostbite around his neck in warm weather. The police had even been called in, and he had lied to them all.

He had awoken with it, he had told them, and nothing more.

They had not believed him. And he wasn't surprised.

Jose looked at what he had gathered thus far. It was arranged on his desk, with the skull watching over all he did. Salt and iron lay beside charms and pendants. He had read of how some people loaded shotgun shells with rock salt, but it was not something he wanted to attempt.

A Hispanic man carrying a shotgun was sure to attract the eyes of the police. And it would be unwanted attention.

Jose picked up the piece of iron, an old length of chain. He would be able to wrap a portion of it around his wrist and then beat back the dead. With the ghosts away from him, he would cast spells of dispersal. He would cast them into the afterlife where the saints would deal with them.

Yet one point remained unanswered, and he had yet to find a solution in his books.

How was he to keep the dead from returning?

Some spoke of using only the spells. Others advocated the use of spells and prayers. A few mentioned the burning of the dead's bones.

Jose knew there was power in bones, and that great magic could be performed with the same. The ghost who had attacked him had been strong. Frightfully so.

If I could find his bones, Jose thought, *and bind him. Ah, there would be a coup.*

A smile played across his face and Jose opened a book, searching for the best way to bind an unruly ghost.

Chapter 26: An Unexpected Conflict

Kurt was driven from the hospital to the police station so he could change out of his uniform and take his car home. A few of his colleagues offered words of sympathy. More still gave him rough embraces. All Kurt could do was nod his thanks.

He didn't bother to shower before putting on his street clothes. Kurt was going straight home. He stuffed his uniform into his bag, slung it over his shoulder, and left the locker room with his head down.

Without looking where he was going, Kurt walked into Detective Marie Lafontaine. The force of the impact knocked the bag off his shoulder, and the unsecured top allowed his uniform shirt to fall onto the floor.

Marie stooped down to pick up the article of clothing, and when she did so, the business card with Shane's information on it fell out.

"Hold on," Marie said, and she bent down to grab the paper. She hesitated when she straightened up. After a pause, she asked, "Do you know Shane Ryan?"

"I met him yesterday," Kurt said, accepting both the shirt and the card from her. He returned them to his bag.

"Why did he give you his information?" she questioned.

Kurt had never been a good liar.

He felt his face go hot with embarrassment and he cleared his throat. "I have to talk to him about some stuff."

A hard look settled on the detective's face. "Why?"

"Some stuff, that's all," he mumbled.

Marie took a step closer, lowered her voice to a whisper, and asked, "Does this have to do with Bill's death?"

Kurt didn't answer, but he couldn't keep the surprise off his face.

"Bill was my friend," Marie said, her voice barely audible. "I trained him when he was a rookie. And I know Shane Ryan."

"You do?" Kurt asked in a whisper.

Marie nodded. "When are you going to Shane's house?"

"Now," Kurt confessed.

"Head out in about five minutes," Marie said, "and I'll meet you there."

"You know him?" Kurt asked, still surprised.

"Yeah," Marie answered. "I know him. Don't go inside his house until I get there, understand?"

"Sure," Kurt said. He watched Marie walk away and then he continued out to the parking lot. Tossing his bag onto the passenger seat, he drove to the address Shane had given him and parked several houses down from 125 Berkley Street. He watched the house until he caught sight of Marie's car as she pulled in behind him.

Kurt got out and met her on the sidewalk.

"How do you know him?" he asked.

"I'll tell you later," Marie said. "I want you to listen. Shane's house is different. You need to stay with me, or with him. Do *not* wander inside. Do you understand, Kurt?"

Confused, Kurt could only nod.

"Alright," Marie said. "Let's see what Shane wants to talk to you about."

They crossed the street together, and Kurt felt uncomfortable. Shane hadn't told him to come alone, but part of him worried that Shane wouldn't speak freely with the detective around. Few people did.

But clearly, she had also had interactions with Shane before, and Kurt thought her familiarity with the man might be helpful.

Before he could reflect on it much more, Kurt found himself standing at the front door.

Marie reached out and rang the bell.

A minute passed by before the door opened, answered by the man who had been with Shane. For the first time, Kurt got a good look at the stranger. A jagged scar dominated one side of his face, passing through a milky-white eye.

"Officer, Detective," the man said, giving them a genuine smile. "Please, come in."

Kurt and Marie did so. The interior was huge and cold. An unpleasant draft moved past them, and Marie frowned. The man closed the door and said, "Please follow me to the study."

Kurt and Marie did. The room they entered was large, and a fire burned in the hearth.

"My name is Frank," the man said, smiling. "I don't believe we were properly introduced the last time you were here, Detective."

"No," she agreed. "We weren't. It's a pleasure."

"Likewise," Frank said. Turning to Kurt, he said, "Again, my apologies about last night, Officer. We hated to have to leave as quickly as we did, but my friend believed it was best for all involved."

Kurt nodded.

"I don't care," a voice came from the hallway. "You have to put it back."

"Why?" a little girl asked.

"Because it's not yours," was the response.

"But you never play with it."

"Eloise!" the man snapped.

"Fine!"

Kurt focused his attention on the door and saw Shane Ryan walk in. Like Frank, Shane was even more battered in the light of day. Most of his left ear was gone, and parts of his neck and head were a mass of pink scar tissue.

"Kurt," Shane said. "Marie. A pleasure. I didn't know you two were acquainted."

"Shane," Marie said, her voice tight. "What do you know about the officer's death?"

"Ah," Shane murmured. "You didn't tell her. How did you find out, Marie?"

"Kurt dropped a piece of paper with your name on it," Marie answered. "Now answer my question, Shane."

"There is no quid pro quo here, Marie," Shane said.

"Shane," Frank intervened.

"Nope," Shane said, shaking his head. "No. Nothing. She gets nothing on this. She gets nothing on anything. How about that?"

Marie remained silent, but Frank did not.

"Hey," Frank said, his voice becoming sharp. "Get it together. We're not enemies here. And we're sure as hell not fighting with the cops."

"Fine," Shane snapped. "We, Frank and I, that is, were on our way to the Slater Mill. We saw Kurt's partner get attacked. We tried to help, and unfortunately, we were not successful."

"Who killed him?" she asked.

"A ghost named Pierre Gustav," Frank answered. "We were going to do a recon of the building. Were you doing the same thing, Kurt?"

Kurt nodded. "But I didn't think of a ghost. I didn't really consider anything supernatural. I just thought it was odd."

Kurt stopped, cleared his throat, and then continued. "We knew something was up, we just couldn't figure out what. I had seen something or someone in the window on the second floor, so Bill and I were trying to see what was going on. I didn't think it would kill him. I didn't think a ghost could kill someone."

"They can," Shane said, his voice hard. "Some of them even enjoy it. And quite a bit, too. Yours seems a little different, though. As if he's spreading out."

Kurt nodded. "Yes. That's exactly what I was worried about. I told Bill, too. It's why we were checking on the Mill. I needed to know what was going on. Too many people were dead or missing."

"Like the two boys," Frank said.

"They're not missing anymore," Marie interrupted.

Kurt looked at her.

"They were found in the attic of the Estates," she continued. "Behind a locked door. Heart attacks, at least according to the preliminary examination."

"A pair of teenagers with heart attacks?" Frank asked.

Marie nodded.

"That's not suspicious," Shane grumbled. He walked to the fireplace, took a small log from a stand, and added it to the flames. For a moment, the study was filled with the sound of the bark as it popped and snapped in the fire. Then Shane said, "Our plan is to get permission to go in from the current owner of the Mill."

"You can't," Marie said, a curious note of concern in her voice. "Shane, look at you."

Shane gave her a small, sad smile. "Thank you, Marie. I have to, though. There's something going on, and Frank and I can stop it."

Kurt looked to Frank, and the man nodded.

"It'll be difficult," Frank admitted. "But we should be able to. And if we can't, well at least we know how to get the hell out of a situation like that."

"What?" Kurt asked, confused. "You've done this before?"

"He has," Marie said, gesturing to Shane. "I can't speak for Frank."

A grim smile spread across Frank's face, twisting the scar. "I've done it a few times as well."

"Can you show me how?" Kurt asked.

"Kurt," Marie snapped.

"What?" Kurt demanded. "My partner is dead. Killed by a ghost for God's sake. If there's a way to stop them, then I want to know how. I need to know, Marie."

"It could kill you," she said.

"Kurt," Shane said. "You need to understand that some ghosts can gain power from the souls of others. Some ghosts just don't want to leave the earthly plane. And a few, well, more than a few, seem to enjoy killing for the sake of killing. Pierre might be one, two, or all three of the above."

Kurt shook his head, rage building within him. "Bill was my friend. He was my partner. I can't say he took a bullet for me, or anything like that, but I know he would have. And he didn't die of a heart attack. He was killed. And his death, it has to be answered in kind."

"Okay," Shane said.

"So," Frank said, sitting down. "Tell me, Kurt. What do you know about iron and salt?"

Chapter 27: A Sickness Spreads

The two of them had eaten breakfast at a diner just off Main Street. Shane could see the top of Slater Mill from where he sat on a brick wall. Frank was by the car in the parking lot, trying to get a hold of the Mill's owner. Shane lit another cigarette.

Frank put his phone away and walked towards Shane, a satisfied grin on his face.

"You made it through?" Shane asked around his cigarette.

Frank nodded and sat down on the wall beside Shane.

"Yeah," Frank answered. "Mr. Dell's a nice enough guy. He told us to, and I quote here, 'knock yourselves out,' and not to worry about any damage. Seems like he's fighting with the city to have it removed from the historic register."

"Damn," Shane said, "I didn't even think it was on it."

"Guess so," Frank said. "And since it is, Mr. Dell can't develop it, or even unload it on anyone."

"That's tough," Shane said, leaning over and stubbing the cigarette out on the sidewalk.

"Yup."

"So," Shane asked, "is there a place where we can pick up a key?"

"We don't need one," Frank replied. "He's left it unlocked for the past ten years. He's been hoping someone would set the place on fire."

Shane snorted a laugh and shook his head. "Insurance?"

"I asked him," Frank said, grinning. "He said he only had the bare minimum on it. If the place burned down, he'd actually lose money on the structural loss. But he calls the Slater Mill his albatross."

"I like Mr. Dell more and more," Shane said, turning his attention back to the Mill. "Not many people reference 'The Rhyme of the Ancient Mariner' anymore."

A silence fell over them, and they sat for several minutes, each of them lost in their own thoughts. Frank finally ended it when he asked, "So, do we wait for Kurt and your friend, Marie?"

Inwardly, Shane winced at the mention of Marie. His face remained impassive as he nodded. "Yes. I suspect this is going to be a little difficult."

Frank glanced over at him. "Why?"

"Don't know," Shane answered. "Just a gut feeling. I don't like it."

"Great." Frank shook his head. "Want to go back and start packing some salt rounds?"

"Yeah," Shane said. He took out a cigarette, lit it, and exhaled the smoke into the morning sky. "Yes, I do."

They stood up together and walked towards the car, the Mill; a dark stain in the heart of the city.

Chapter 28: A Phone Call is Made

She sat in her office, the room a curious mix of cutting edge technology and antiquity. Her furnishings were, for the most part, antiques. Items worth hundreds of thousands of dollars when grouped together, tens of thousands separately. Along the walls were bookcases, crafted by master carpenters and equipped with sensitive electronics to ensure the protection of the valuable texts. Books on spirits, ghosts, demons and other supernatural phenomenon stood behind shatterproof glass and in a controlled environment.

The room's solitary window, treated to ensure no harmful ultraviolet rays penetrated to damage the antiques, looked out at the row of brownstones which mimicked the one she herself occupied.

Abigail Horn was a powerful woman, although few people knew it. On her tax returns, she was listed as a consultant, and her salary showed she was an excellent one at that.

But what she consulted on, no one outside of the organization knew.

The telephone on the desk rang.

Abigail turned her attention away from her computer screen to look at the phone, waiting for the caller ID to perform its job. It did so in the short span of time between the two rings, revealing that it was Howard Dell on the other end.

She reached out and picked up the receiver before the second ring could finish.

"Yes?" she asked, her voice cold and harsh.

"This is Dell," the man said.

"Situation?" she asked.

"I've had an inquiry on the Slater Mill," Dell answered.

She tapped her nails on her desk as she asked, "Who?"

"A man named Frank Benedict," Dell said.

Abigail's fingers stopped. "Did he say anything else?"

"Only that he and a friend would be entering the building," Dell said. She could hear his desire to ask why it mattered, but he refrained. He hesitated and then added, "I didn't think it would be a problem. Pierre's been active, so he could take care of them if we needed him to."

"No." The word came out flat.

She heard him catch his breath. Abigail waited to see if he would press the issue, and then she spoke.

"Frank Benedict, formerly Dom Francis Benedict of the Benedictine Order, formerly a member of Fifth Special Forces, United States Army," Abigail recited. "Currently resides with retired Gunnery Sergeant Shane Ryan. Together the two men are responsible for the loss of one institution and our holdings in upstate New Hampshire. They are also directly responsible for the loss of a highly effective free agent who had successfully carried out a myriad of tasks for thirty years."

"I didn't know," Howard whispered.

She let a small hint of her anger creep into her voice. "You should have called first, *Howard*. This is a situation that can rapidly get out of hand. How are you going to resolve it?"

"I can call the police," he answered, his voice frantic. "I can report Frank to them."

"We don't have anyone on the Nashua Police Force," she snapped. "And since Pierre is active, we don't want any sort of authority in there, now do we?"

"No," Howard whimpered.

"No, we do not." Abigail pinched the bridge of her nose and closed her eyes. She took a deep breath, let it out slowly and said, "You find someone, anyone, to interrupt them. Do you understand?"

"Um, no," he whispered.

When she spoke a half a second later, her words were clipped and sharp. "The Mill is in a bad part of the city. A dangerous part of the city. You will go to Nashua. You will bring a significant amount of money from your operational funds, and you will hire someone to do bad things. Is that clear enough for you, Howard?"

"Yes, Ma'am," he answered.

"Call me when it is accomplished," she said and slammed the phone down.

Abigail stood up, walked to the rear wall, and looked at the map of New England which hung in a dark wood frame. The map was a few months old. Every quarter it was reprinted and updated. Houses, buildings, plots, and roads which currently harbored the dead were clearly labeled. They were color coded as well, with a legend at the bottom explaining the code.

Blue meant less than five deaths attributable to the resident spirit.

Red corresponded to greater than five but less than ten.

And the numbers and colors continued to one hundred plus. A vibrant green, which only a few places in all of New England boasted.

When Abigail first looked at the map a decade earlier, she had been thrilled and proud. The numbers grew each year, often only by one or two, but they increased. But now, for the first time in recent memory, a place would be removed from the map.

Three, in fact, and that realization drove a spike of rage deep within her heart. One, a lake front community, had boasted a spiritual heritage that reached back to the colonists. A prison, which had shown potential, was the second, and the third drove her near to madness with fury. She had lost a hospital that had been one of the rare, beautiful green spots.

Abigail turned away from the map, went back to her desk, and sat down. She picked up her phone and dialed out to her secretary.

"Yes, Ms. Horn?" Zane asked.

"Coffee. Large," she stated.

"Yes, Ms. Horn."

Abigail hung up the phone and accessed the file on replacements. She would go through the notes on various individuals in the organization.

Abigail would need to replace Howard Dell soon.

Book 7: Slater Mill

Chapter 29: A Difficult Conversation

"You've come back," Courtney said.

"I said I would," Shane replied. He sat in the darkness of the library, a blanket wrapped around his shoulders to ward off the chill which dominated the room. A mixture of fear and excitement raced through him. "I wanted to ask you a question."

"A question?" she asked, surprised. Then her voice lowered as she said, "Tell me, Shane, what do you want to ask?"

"I have to go into the city," he said. "There's a Mill with a spirit in it. He's killing people."

"Do you want me with you?" she demanded.

"I was hoping you could help," Shane stated. "I was hoping it might help you."

"Help *me*?!" she snarled, her voice suddenly in his ear. "I'm dead, Shane! Nothing can help me!"

Courtney slammed into him, launching him out of the chair. He hit the floor hard, rolled and came to a sudden stop as he struck the wall. Several books fell, bouncing off him before landing on the floor. Shane gasped as he sat up, pain flaring through his ribs.

From across the room came Courtney's voice.

"Are you alright?" she whispered.

"Yes," he lied. He stood up, wavered and reached out, grasping one of the shelves.

"No, you're not." Her voice bordered on inaudible, and he had to strain to hear it. "I don't want to hurt you, Shane. Please leave."

Shane hesitated, wanting to argue the point. He wanted to stay in the room with her. But the pain in his ribs caused stars to explode around the edges of his vision.

"Alright," Shane said, sighing. He took small, tender steps, careful not to jar his ribs as he left. "I will see you soon, Courtney."

"I know you will," she whispered and said nothing more as he left the room.

Shane paused in the hallway to close and lock the library door, the hall light harsh in his eyes.

Carl stood a short distance away, and when he realized Shane could see him, the dead man asked in German, "Why do you torture yourself, my friend?"

"I have to make the effort," Shane replied in the same tongue. "I never should have agreed to having her locked up. No matter how badly she was behaving."

"She wants to kill you," Carl reminded him.

"Only sometimes," Shane said. He winced when he started to walk.

"What's wrong?" Carl asked. "Did she hurt you?"

Shane nodded. "I'll get checked out at the hospital soon. Nothing to worry about."

Carl glared at him. "It is something to worry about! You must allow me to accompany you when you speak with her."

"No," Shane snapped. "I will not. She can get better, Carl. I know it. Now if you will excuse me, I am going to go drink a fifth of whiskey and pass out."

"Perhaps you're right," Carl said, his voice filled with bitterness. "Perhaps you shall drink yourself to death first."

"One can always hope," Shane muttered, and he moved on towards his bedroom.

Chapter 30: A Curious Scene

The small mantle clock in his room struck eleven thirty, and Frank stretched. He had spent the majority of the night worrying about how Courtney had injured Shane.

And he still won't have her locked up, Frank thought angrily.

Shane was putting both of them at risk, and Frank knew he'd have to broach the subject of Courtney, as uncomfortable as it was.

Shane's preoccupation with Courtney could lead to more deaths, and the idea of anyone else dying bothered Frank. While Kurt and Marie might provide additional firepower, they would be burdens if they couldn't operate on their own, and if Shane wasn't focused on the problem at hand.

Frank sighed and walked over to his window. From his position, Frank could look down on the back of the house. A wide expanse of yard spread out around a small pond, the water dark and still. It reflected the pale light of the quarter moon, and the stars shining in the sky.

For some reason, Shane avoided the pond, and no one in the house would speak of it. Not even Carl, who had made a point to answer all of Frank's questions regarding Berkley Street and Shane.

The pond was something none of the dead would talk about, and that alone said something.

At the edge of the property, a forest began, stretching out into Greeley Park. As Frank looked at it, he saw a shape move near a pair of tall, thin pine trees. Frank went still, his breathing slowing down as he focused on the stranger. With a patience born from long hours of training, Frank watched and waited.

When the mantle clock struck midnight, the person in the tree line moved forward. Frank's heart leaped with a frenzied beat, but he quickly regained control.

The stranger took several short steps into the open lawn and looked around.

Frank knew who it was, and a mixed pang of fear and rage struck him.

Jack Whyte stood twenty yards away from the pond. He looked thinner than Frank remembered. Too much moonlight passed through the dead man. Jack lacked the vivacity and spryness which Frank had first noticed in the study.

As Frank watched, Jack walked towards the pond, his pace quickening. When he reached the dried reeds along the shore, Jack passed through them and vanished into the dark water.

Frank took a cautious step back from the window, sat down on his bed and looked at his hands. There was a slight tremble in his fingers but nothing more. Frank let a small smile slip out. He took a deep breath and said in a loud voice, "Carl."

In less than a minute, the ghost appeared, sliding through the closed door.

"Yes, Frank?" Carl asked, his voice clipped and polite.

"We seem to have a new problem," Frank said.

Carl raised an eyebrow and waited for Frank to inform him what that problem might be.

Frank did so.

"Jack Whyte's in the pond," Frank said.

Carl's eyes widened, and then he snarled, "Gott in Himmel!"

As the last word rang off the room's walls, Carl vanished. A moment later, the house seemed to vibrate, the walls thrumming. It felt as though every spirit in the house was racing down the stairs at once.

Who knows, Frank thought, standing up. *Maybe they are.*

He walked to the window, and for the first time since he had moved in, Frank drew the curtains closed. He walked to the bed, sat down, and turned on his light before he stretched out on the cool sheets.

As he lay waiting for sleep with his eyes closed, a powerful thought settled into Frank's mind.

Things are only going to get worse.

Chapter 31: The Bearer of Bad News

Shane had been in better moods before.

He had also been sober before.

As he sat on the chair in his study, with one of his whiskey bottles empty beside him, he understood that he was neither sober nor was he in a good mood.

Shane wanted to fight.

Someone knocked at the study door, and he twisted around to look at it.

"What?" Shane demanded.

"Shane, it is Carl."

Shane rolled his eyes and let his head flop back against the chair.

"I'm not interested in your complaints tonight," Shane stated, although he was vaguely aware that his words were probably unintelligible.

"Shane?" Carl asked.

"Go away!" Shane yelled in German.

"My friend," Carl pleaded. "This is important!"

"Everything's important," Shane spat. He pushed himself up in the chair and promptly fell back down into it. His head spun, and his stomach threatened to expel the whiskey with extreme prejudice.

"Jack Whyte has come back," Carl said, still speaking through the door.

"Who?" Shane asked. The name was familiar, but he couldn't place why.

"Jack Whyte. The Englishman," Carl explained. "He is back."

"He can't be back," Shane said, slurring his words. "Not unless his damned bones are buried nearby."

"They are," Carl said, anger creeping into his voice.

That simple, two-word statement forced Shane to sit up. He felt nauseous, but he forced the urge down. "Where?"

"We are not sure," Carl said. "We only know that they are."

Shane gripped the arms of the chair, closed his eyes, and pushed himself to his feet.

A heartbeat later, he realized that he should have kept his eyes open.

Vertigo spun him around, he staggered forward, vomited and crashed into the opposite chair. He landed in his own bile, smelled the stench of the whiskey, and threw up a second time.

Groaning, Shane rolled onto his back and looked up at the paneled ceiling.

It was only then he remembered he hadn't turned any lights on.

The room cooled down, and Carl was beside him.

"Are you hurt?" the dead man asked.

Shane shook his head and answered, "Drunk."

"What do you need me to do, my friend?" Carl asked.

Shane started to answer, but he passed out instead.

Chapter 32: Power Grows

In the early hours of the morning, a strange glow emanated from the Slater Mill.

It wasn't anything people could put their fingers on. Not that many people were looking at it at two AM. But those who did notice, paused. The glow was a flicker on the edge of their vision. A curious light that reminded them of the sickly green of Halloween decorations.

As they turned their heads towards the Mill, they could smell something too. A strange, fetid scent that wrinkled their noses and caused their lips to curl. An instinctual voice told them that Slater Mill was a bad place to be, and they listened to that voice.

Most of them listened.

In any group of people, there are always a few too foolhardy, or too stupid to listen to their own fears.

Marian Davilla and Ruby Cortez were two such people.

They were seventeen and eighteen years old respectively, and they ran their little block of government housing with iron fists. Their prospects for making it out of the inner city were less than zero, and this was something they had cultivated. They knew the city, and they loved it. In their hands, they had power, a power they enjoyed, and their plan was to keep a firm grip on it for as long as possible.

They had watched other girls and women become pregnant, get tied down with kids, and settle for a life Marian and Ruby mocked.

Other girls chased after boys.

Marian and Ruby hunted down the cash. They lived a hard life, and they loved it. Both of them had been picked up on assault and battery charges, and they wore their time in jail with pride.

But being incarcerated meant they couldn't enjoy the fruits of their labor, so both of them made a point to let others do the dirty work for them.

Over the past few weeks, they had become enthralled with the Mill. It had always been there, of course, but it had been boring. Nothing special. Just another empty building.

Now, though, going inside and getting back out would be a mark of respect. People were afraid to go in, and if Marian and Ruby showed they could go in, then it was one more thing people would need to think about.

The two of them stood across the street from the Mill. They had finished a bottle of malt liquor between them and their courage had received the necessary boost.

"Ready?" Ruby asked.

"Ready," Marian answered.

As one, they stepped off the curb and began to cross the street.

They hadn't even reached the halfway point when a pair of headlights, set on high, blasted them.

Ruby let out a string of curses and Marian joined in. Over their angry words, a man called out, "Where are you going?"

Marian let him know what he could do with his question, and the man laughed.

"You two want some money?" he asked.

The inquiry silenced both of the girls.

"Turn your damned headlights off," Ruby yelled.

The lights went out.

Marian and Ruby rubbed at their eyes and Marian said, "What the hell are you talking about?"

"You two were going to go into the Mill," the man said.

Marian opened her eyes and looked at the speaker. He was a short, fat white man dressed in what looked like an expensive suit. The car he stood next to was a black Mercedes. Gold rings decorated his fingers, and Marian wondered if it would be better to just rob the man.

The thought evidently crossed his mind as well, because he pulled open the left side of his suit coat.

From where Marian stood, she could see the grip of the pistol in a shoulder holster.

"How much money are we talking?" Ruby demanded.

"Come a little closer," he said. "I won't bite, and I know you won't."

Not with that nine you're carrying, Marian thought angrily.

With cautious steps, she and Ruby approached the man. When they got within five feet of his car, they stopped.

He smiled at them, a flash of gold teeth. There was a strangeness to the man that set Marian's own teeth on edge, and she knew he was bad. He was someone who liked to hurt people, and for nothing more than to cause pain.

"What do we need to do?" Ruby asked.

"It's easy," the man said, his voice smooth. "Keep an eye on the Mill for me. Soon, probably in the next couple of days, two men are going to come here. One will have a scar down his face, and his eye will look like a damn cotton ball. The other will be bald. No hair at all."

"What about 'em?" Marian asked. "What do you want us to do?"

"Kill them," the man said.

Ruby shook her head as if she hadn't heard the man.

"What?" Marian asked.

"Kill them," he repeated. "Now is this something you can do?"

He asked in the same calm voice Marian's grandmother used when she wanted to know if Marian could go to the bodega for her.

A look in the man's eyes showed he was serious.

"Yeah," Ruby said, putting bravado into her voice. "Sure it is."

The man smiled. A wide, grotesque expression that made Marian's stomach tighten.

"I'm glad to hear that," he said. The man leaned into the car and then took out a briefcase. It was black leather and locked. His thick thumbs spun the correct combination, and he flipped up the latches, the metallic clicks loud in the night.

The stranger opened the case and turned it towards the girls.

Inside, were two stacks of hundred dollar bills, two handguns, and two clips. Everything was wrapped in plastic.

"The pistols are new," the man explained. "They are nine millimeters. Fifteen in the clip, one in the chamber for a total of sixteen rounds. There are ten thousand dollars split into two piles of five. The weapons are cold. They were stolen from a gun store in Maine before you were born. The bullets were prepared by our gunsmith, they cannot be traced via any manufacturer."

Marian had seen weapons and cash before, but it had never been offered to her.

"Will you do it?" the man asked.

"Hell yeah," Ruby said, laughing. Marian nodded her agreement, unable to take her eyes off the money.

"Now," the man said, closing the briefcase and locking it. "The combination is three, two, one. Nice and simple. I will know when the men are killed because someone will be watching the Mill."

The calm way in which he stated the fact brought reality back into focus.

He smiled and handed the briefcase to Ruby.

"Now," he continued, "if you get the bright idea to try and do anything other than that which you have agreed to, I will kill you."

Marian looked at him, heard Ruby inhale to say something and then stop.

There was a mad glint in the man's eyes. Part of him, Marian saw, hoped they would do something wrong. Anything.

"I can assure you," the man said, his voice pleasant, "that you will take an extremely long time to die. And you won't beg for death."

"No?" Marian asked, her own voice sounding faint and strange.

"No," he whispered. "Because the first thing I do is cut out the person's tongue."

He smiled at them again, winked, and got into his car. The engine purred into life, and the man put it into gear. Marian and Ruby watched him back the Mercedes up a few feet, then shift gears again.

The stranger beeped the horn twice in a friendly goodbye and drove off.

Marian looked at the briefcase in Ruby's hands and wondered what it was they had actually agreed to.

Chapter 33: Planning and Preparation

"How's the head?"

Shane winced at the sound of Frank's voice. He squinted and looked across the room to where Frank sat.

"You're pretty damned heavy," Frank said, taking a sip of coffee. "I honestly thought I was going to have to drag you into the downstairs bathroom to get you cleaned up."

Shane closed his eyes and let out a groan. His head ached and something pulsed unpleasantly behind his eyes.

"You're not hungover," Frank said.

"No," Shane agreed, his voice sounding like a tire driving over broken glass. "Hit my head."

Frank nodded. "You've got a bump the size of an egg on your forehead. I'm surprised you didn't split your skull open."

"Too much scar tissue," Shane said.

"Too thick," Frank retorted.

"That, too," Shane said, sighing.

"What do you remember from last night?" Frank asked.

"Nothing," Shane replied. With tremendous effort, he sat up, head hanging down and blood pounding in his temples. "Not a damned thing. What happened?"

"Evidently you drank more than usual," Frank said. "Then you threw up. At least twice, and fell into it. You were a hell of a mess."

"I'm sorry," Shane apologized.

"That's not the worst of it, though," Frank continued.

"What?" Shane asked, lifting his head up. "What else did I do?"

"Nothing you did," Frank answered. "Jack Whyte is back."

Shane blinked, his mind processing information far slower than normal. "Wait. What?"

"Jack Whyte," Frank repeated. "The Englishman."

"You have got to be kidding me," Shane said. "How in the hell is that even possible? His bond with the button was destroyed. Oh no."

Frank raised an eyebrow.

"His bones have to be nearby," Shane said. "Where did you see him?"

"He walked into the pond."

That simple statement sent a chill through Shane. His heart raced, and he forced himself to breathe through his nose, trying to calm down. He cleared his throat and said in a low voice, "The pond."

Frank nodded. "Do you think his bones are in there?"

"Maybe," Shane said. "I sure as hell hope not. He might have a pretty good radius for travel, though."

"Is there a way we can find out?" Frank asked. "Historical society maybe?"

"Yeah," Shane said. He winced as he nodded his head. "Over on Abbott Street. Maybe the library too. They have a pretty good collection of histories about the city."

"Okay," Frank said. He paused and then asked, "Shane, what's up with the pond?"

Shane hesitated, sighed and said, "You know the house is haunted."

"Yeah," Frank said, grinning. "Kind of figured that one out."

"Well," Shane said. "There was another ghost. Someone bad, and she was in the pond."

"How bad?" Frank asked.

Shane glanced at the clock, saw it was only eight, and remembered the historical society didn't open until ten.

"Bad," Shane said. "We've got some time. This will take a little bit."

"Okay," Frank said. "Let's hear it."

Shane took a deep breath and began to tell Frank about Berkley Street.

Chapter 34: Forced to Believe

Kurt and Marie sat in the Main Street Diner next to City Hall. They had finished their breakfast and their coffee. The waitress had taken the dishes away, and the two of them sat in the booth, ignored by the other patrons. Marie knew the owner and had told Kurt they wouldn't be bothered.

He tore his napkin into small strips. A nervous habit he thought he had broken himself of after his divorce.

As he shredded another piece, Kurt realized he hadn't after all.

In a low voice, he said, "Ghosts are real."

Marie nodded.

After the shock of Bill's death, and going to Shane's house, Kurt thought that Marie would reassure him that the whole thing wasn't real. That it was all just madness.

She hadn't though.

"How can they be real?" Kurt asked, picking up another piece of napkin.

"I don't know how," Marie said. "I just know that they are."

"But it doesn't make sense," Kurt said, his disbelief and anger spiking. "None of it does. You die, and you go to heaven, or you go to hell. Damn, maybe even purgatory. But you don't hang around."

Marie watched him, her face impassive.

"It doesn't make sense," he grumbled and tore the piece in his hands apart.

"It doesn't have to make sense," Marie said. "Nothing does. All we can do is accept what our senses tell us in this regard. You saw what happened to Bill. I've seen other things that I don't want to talk about, let alone remember. The point is, Kurt, that we have to accept what we have seen, and what we've experienced."

He grunted but didn't speak.

After a few minutes of silence, he reached up, rubbed the bare skin of his scalp, and asked, "Do iron and salt really work?"

"Yeah," she said. "They work. And so does fire."

He blinked. "What?"

She explained to him how they salted and burned the bones of ghosts. How it was the only way to destroy them.

"What happens if you don't?" Kurt asked.

"Then you don't get rid of them," Marie said. She sat back in her seat and fixed her ponytail. Her face was harsh, her eyes hard. Kurt had worked with her on a handful of cases. Nothing more than grunt work, but he had always been respectful to her. Which she had reciprocated.

"So you think this is something we can do?" Kurt asked. He dropped the last piece of napkin and stuffed his hands under his legs, making certain he didn't pick up another one.

"Of course, it is," she answered. There wasn't a trace of doubt in her voice.

"Is it as dangerous as they said?" Kurt said.

"Yes," Marie replied. "They didn't oversell it, and they didn't understate the dangers. There is a chance we'll be killed. Or worse."

"Worse?" Kurt scoffed, shaking his head. "What the hell could be worse?"

"Your soul might not be allowed to leave," she said.

The idea struck him like a fist, causing him to blink and shake his head. Then a horrible thought arose.

"Marie," he said, pulling his hands out from beneath his legs and putting them on the table. "Is Bill's soul there?"

"It might be," she replied.

"God in Heaven," Kurt whispered, and he dropped his head into his hands.

Chapter 35: Information Gathered

Shane stood with Frank in the kitchen. The afternoon sun poured through the windows over the sink while the two men looked out the glass of the back door. Wind rippled the surface of the pond and bent the stiff reeds back. Branches, still bare of leaves, resisted the wind's efforts, and dark clouds raced by in the sky above.

Shane reached up and scratched the remnants of his left ear. The tattered flesh ached more often than not, and when he was concerned about something, anything, he had a tendency to scratch them. He dropped his hand down to his side and looked at the pond.

It reminded him of his childhood and all the terrible things that had occurred. The water was never restful to his eyes, never peaceful. It held dark secrets and threatened violence.

And now the ghost of Jack Whyte had slipped into its depths.

Shane was certain it meant that Jack could enter the house.

Shane sighed and turned away from the window. He went to the table and sat down in one of the chairs. Frank joined him a moment later. The former monk looked anxious, which was an expression Shane hadn't seen on the man's face before.

"It's supposed to be nearby?" Shane asked.

He had already asked the question twice before, and Frank had answered it the same number of times.

Frank answered it again.

"Yeah," the man said without any hint of aggravation. "No one's sure exactly where the tree was. It came down in some storm, and they harvested the wood. There had always been a rumor that a murderer had been lynched from it, but that was all. Just a rumor."

"Well, we know it's not," Shane said. He rapped his knuckles on the table. "Damn."

"We need to take care of this," Frank said. "Before we even think about going into the Slater Mill. We can't leave him here to wait for us."

Shane wanted to. He wanted to unleash Courtney on Jack, but such a plan could backfire. Given Courtney's tenuous state of mind, she could attempt to destroy Jack, destroy Shane, or sit and watch them tear each other apart.

And for once, unfortunately, Carl was no help. Jack Whyte was stronger than the ghosts in the house. Even combined they wouldn't be able to face him. This, Carl had told him, was confirmed by the fact that he had been able to return to his bones. Not all of the dead, it would appear, could remain after an item they were bound to was destroyed.

"What are you thinking about?" Frank asked.

"How strong he is," Shane answered.

Frank nodded. "The question is, do we try to take him alone, or do we try and do it with Kurt and your friend, Marie?"

Shane's shoulders slumped. "Good question."

Frank was quiet for a moment, and then he said, "We could use it as a dry run."

Shane waited.

"Listen," Frank continued. "You told me Marie can handle herself."

Shane nodded.

"And Kurt's no slouch. I mean he recognized an issue at the Mill. He's got some basic skills as a cop," Frank said, "which means he should have a good baseline for disciplined responses. I think we might be able to work with this."

"I don't know," Shane said, scratching at the stumps of his missing fingers. "Being able to handle a police situation is a far cry from dealing with an enraged spirit."

"I know," Frank said. "And I'm not saying we shouldn't be careful. But seeing how powerful Jack evidently is, we're going to need more than the two of us. And, since we're bringing Kurt and Marie into the Mill with us anyway, we should do a test run."

"This is going from training wheels to a Harley Davidson Panhead," Shane said, unable to keep the doubt out of his voice.

"Well," Frank said. "I was thinking of asking for a little more help as well."

"From who?" Shane asked.

"Carl," Frank replied.

Shane sat back in his chair. "Carl?"

Frank nodded. "If Jack can make it as far as the pond, then it means Carl can make it as far as Jack's bones. What's good for the goose is good for the gander, right?"

"Yeah," Shane said. "Yeah, I think you've got something."

"Now we don't need Carl to do anything other than help run some interference with Jack," Frank continued. "He doesn't have to go toe to toe with him. Carl won't have to do anything other than serve as an early warning system. Just an alarm. He can keep his eyes open, and when, or if Jack shows up, then we can retreat if we haven't gotten close enough to the bones."

Shane thought about it and then grinned. "Damn. I think that might work out."

"We'll just have to ask Carl," Frank said. "And if he says yes, we'll get in touch with Kurt and Marie."

"Okay," Shane said, standing up. "Let's go talk to Carl."

Frank got to his feet, and the men left the kitchen together.

Chapter 36: Impatient for Results

Kurt had met with the psychologist that the Police Department had assigned him. The woman, Dr. Lee, had been compassionate without treating him like a child and Kurt had appreciated that.

She hadn't signed off on a 'Return to work', and Kurt was fine with her decision.

It would give him time to do what needed to be done.

Since his discussion with Marie, Kurt had been wracked with worry. All he could picture was Bill, as a ghost, trapped somewhere in Slater Mill. Imprisoned and kept from Heaven. Shane and Frank hadn't set a time for going into the building, Frank informing him that preparations weren't done yet.

But Bill was Kurt's partner, and there was no way Kurt was going to let the man's spirit continue to be held in the Mill.

Kurt stood in the shadow of the old powerhouse, the smokestack rising up from it to stab at the night sky. From his hiding place, Kurt could watch the Mill. Fewer people than usual walked near the building. Or even within a hundred yards of it. The only sight slightly off was a teenage girl who sat in the playground.

She was by herself, which wasn't unusual for the neighborhood, but she wasn't doing the usual things. On any other day, Kurt would have seen her as a look out. Not a particularly good one, but still, a look out.

She wasn't playing with a phone or talking on one. She wasn't listening to music or even watching any of the cars that drove by. Instead, the girl sat on a bench and watched the Mill.

Nothing else.

A part of Kurt wanted to walk over to her and ask her what she was up to. Even without his uniform on, she would identify him as a cop. Either from having seen him before or from the way he walked and the way he talked.

The kids who grew up in the Tree Streets always knew.

She was watching the Mill for someone, but Kurt couldn't be bothered with it.

He turned his attention away from her and focused again on the building.

A soft glow ebbed and flowed from the dirty windows. Occasionally he could hear the sound of machinery, and he knew that wasn't right.

The building had been empty for years. Until he and Bill had found the dying teen in it a few weeks earlier, Kurt had never even heard of people squatting on the property.

Steeling himself, Kurt walked towards the Mill.

If Shane and Frank had been right, then the old iron spike he had salvaged as a kid would do the trick against a ghost. He pulled it out of his pocket, the metal heavy in his hand. The weight of it was comforting, something real he could focus on. He felt the grind of rust and dirt into his palm, and he squeezed it. Kurt took long, deep breaths as he crossed the street, angling his steps so he would reach the corner of the building without any waste of time.

The fence leaned outward, creaking on unsteady posts with a growing wind.

I need to know he's not in there, Kurt told himself. *He can't be in there. Not Bill.*

Kurt reached the edge of the fence, followed it around to the back of the building and glanced once at the girl in the park.

The phone was at her ear.

Kurt turned his gaze back to the Mill and pushed the thoughts of the child out of his mind.

Chapter 37: Earning their Pay

"Ha!" Ruby said, slamming her phone down.

Marian looked at her. "What's up?"

"Gabriella says some bald dude just went around the back of the Mill," Ruby answered, getting to her feet.

"Is it our guy?" Marian asked, sliding the magazine into the pistol and chambering a round.

"Got to be," Ruby said, tucking her own pistol into the waistband of her pants and pulling her sweatshirt down over it. "Can't think there'd be another bald guy who'd want to go in there."

"Yeah," Marian agreed. She stood up, put her own weapon away, and then frowned. "She say anything about the other guy?"

"The one with the bad eye?" Ruby asked.

Marian nodded.

"No," Ruby answered. "Nothing. Got to figure he's on his way, though."

Marian shrugged. "Guess so. Don't want to have to do it twice."

"Nah, we're good," Ruby said, chuckling. "Come on, girl. Let's do this."

They left Ruby's apartment, worked their way around to the front, and walked down Central Street towards the park where Gabriella waited. In a few minutes, they reached the little girl, Ruby's niece, and came to a stop.

"Anybody else show up yet?" Ruby asked the girl in Spanish.

Gabriella shook her head. "No. Just the one."

"And he's bald?" Ruby asked.

Gabriella looked disgusted. "You think I'd call if he wasn't?"

"Don't get mouthy," Ruby snapped, and then she grinned. "You're good, girl. Get out of here. I'll be around tomorrow to catch up with your mom."

Gabriella nodded and slipped away.

"Alright," Ruby said. "Let's do this."

"Yeah," Marian agreed. "The sooner, the better."

The young women walked along the sidewalk across from the Mill. They kept to the shadows, trying to see if anyone was on the outside of the building, or if they had already gone in.

There was no one by the front door.

"I'm not going in," Marian said. There was no negotiation in her voice.

"Me neither," Ruby declared. "We can shoot him just as easy when he walks out."

"Yup," Marian said.

The girls moved back into the dark shadow of an empty doorway. They leaned against the cold brick walls and watched the front door, waiting for their victim to return.

Chapter 38: Inside the Slater Mill

As soon as the door closed behind him, Kurt knew he shouldn't have entered the building.

It stank of death, and the air was brutally cold. His breath streamed out in long white tendrils, and he shivered as he stood on the old worn floor. From the second floor, he could hear the sound of heavy machines thumping.

With his free hand, Kurt reached into the side pocket of his khakis and removed his flashlight. He thumbed the button, and a red light burst out. His hand shook as he swept the beam back and forth.

The hallway was surprisingly clean, as if someone had swept away the dust of decades, revealing a shining floor. Fine cracks spiderwebbed through the horsehair plaster on the walls and Kurt could feel the vibrations of the equipment rise up through his boots.

He let out a shaky breath and approached the stairs cautiously. When he reached them, he walked along the edge of each riser, cutting back on the amount of creaking each step elicited from the stairs.

Kurt reached the second floor and paused. His heart hammered against his ribs, and he wondered if he would pass out from the fear he felt.

No, he reprimanded himself. *You will not.*

Kurt straightened up, panned the flashlight's beam across the hallway, and found a tall door set in the right wall. It was painted a dull white and set in faded gray tracks. The door would slide to the left and open into whatever workroom was beyond it.

A small, rational part of Kurt refused to believe there was a ghost beyond the old, thick wood. That rational portion of his brain demanded that he accept a logical explanation for the noise.

The Tree Streets were notorious for moving narcotics through the city, funneling the drugs to smaller towns and cities in New Hampshire.

What you're hearing, Kurt told himself, *is someone who got the bright idea to package the product with old equipment in order to get it ready to go out. All you're going to find in there are some punks and a lot of dope.*

But Kurt didn't even believe his own idea.

A large-scale dealer would have been noticed long before the first death. The temperature in the building couldn't be attributed to any sort of machinery.

And finally, Kurt knew there was something far worse in the Slater Mill than a dealer with a couple of hired guns working for him.

Kurt walked to the door, grabbed it by the handle, and jerked it open.

The tracks screamed as the door's wheels scraped down their un-oiled length and Kurt winced at the noise he made.

With the room open before him, Kurt shined the flashlight into its depths and felt his breath catch in his throat.

Dozens of machines filled the long chamber, some of them running, others still. People stood at those machines which ran. A pair of boys at one, an old Hispanic man at another. None of them looked at Kurt or acknowledged him in any sort of way.

At the far end of the flashlight's beam, on the left, at a machine that sputtered and coughed, stood Bill.

He was dressed in his uniform, bent over the machine. The flashlight didn't illuminate Bill as much as it passed through him. As it passed through all of them.

Kurt panned the light toward the opposite wall, the pounding of his blood suddenly loud enough, drowning out the noise of the machinery. From the shadows on the right, a man emerged.

It was the same one who had struck down Bill.

Yet he was unlike the others. He was almost solid, absorbing the flashlight's beam. His smile was crooked, wicked. Hatred danced in the man's eyes and twitched at the corners of his mouth. His black hair was greasy, slicked back away from his forehead and tucked behind his ears.

If he had been a regular man, Kurt would have pulled him over to see what he was up to.

But Kurt knew he wasn't.

And the man knew it too.

At a gesture from Bill's killer, all of the ghosts stopped and turned around to stare at Kurt.

The man asked Kurt a question in what sounded like French, but Kurt didn't know the language. He couldn't answer the undead killer.

Kurt started to hyperventilate. He raised the iron railroad spike up in front of him like a B-movie actor lifting up a gaudy crucifix in a vampire film.

But unlike the movie, Kurt's relic had no effect on the dead man.

On any of the gathered dead.

Terrified, Kurt dropped the spike, turned, and fled from the room. Behind him came the sound of people laughing, and it chased him down the stairs.

Chapter 39: Too Easy

"Did you hear that?" Marian asked.

Ruby straightened up, nodding.

The two of them pulled their weapons out and clicked off the safeties.

They would kill the two men together, so neither one could rat the other out if caught. Ballistics on the weapons would show that the men were shot by both of them.

The girls did everything together, and they'd go to prison together too.

If they had to.

Neither of them planned on prison, though.

That was for chumps who couldn't get the job done.

Marian and Ruby could.

The door to the Mill slammed open, and a man ran out. He raced to the fence, slammed through the gate, and the man's bald head reflected the gleam of the street lamp's light.

The two girls fired simultaneously. The pistols bucked in their hands, and the first shots went wide, striking the side of the Mill. By the time the third and fourth rounds had left the barrels, the bullets found their mark. In silence, the girls advanced on the man as the force of the bullets punched him backward.

He staggered, half spun and fell. Not a noise escaped his mouth, but he struck the pavement with a loud, wet thump.

Marian and Ruby reached him and emptied the pistols into him.

With the thunder of the guns still ringing in their ears, the girls turned away from the body and went home. Around them, the Tree Streets were silent, because no one saw anything, ever.

Chapter 40: A Failure at the Most Basic Level

The phone let out two, abbreviated rings, followed by two long rings.

Without turning on the light, Abigail Horn sat up. In the darkness, she reached out, plucked the handset out of its cradle, and listened.

"A man was killed outside of the Slater Mill," a woman said.

"One?"

"One," the unknown woman confirmed.

Abigail frowned. "Ryan or Benedict?"

"Neither."

"Explain," Abigail demanded.

"A police officer out of uniform. Our observer confirms that it was the two girls hired by Dell."

Abigail contained her rage with difficulty.

"Does Dell know this?" she asked.

"No," the woman answered.

"See that he doesn't find out. And make certain he doesn't leave his home," Abigail said.

"Yes."

The call ended, and Abigail replaced the receiver. For several minutes she sat in the bed, thinking. Finally, with her decision made, she picked up her cellphone and dialed a number she hadn't used in years.

"Hello," a woman said.

"Slater," Abigail stated.

The woman on the other end asked, "Name?"

Abigail gave her all of the information relevant to Shane Ryan and Frank Benedict.

"Collateral damage?" the woman asked.

"Acceptable," Abigail said.

"Preference?"

"Whatever gets the job done," Abigail said through clenched teeth.

"Time frame?" the woman asked.

"ASAP."

"Alright," the woman replied, and she hung up the phone.

Abigail put her cell phone back down on the nightstand and remained upright in bed. She knew she wouldn't be able to return to sleep. Her body throbbed with an anger that bordered on hatred.

Shane Ryan had cost her more than anyone had, and she despised him.

Chapter 41: An Interrupted Sleep

At four in the morning, someone decided it was necessary to pound on the front door. The noise jarred Shane out of an uneasy sleep, one rife with nightmares, and forced him out of his bed. He met Frank in the hallway and in silence, they went down the stairs.

Several of the ghosts were near the front door, interested expressions on their faces.

"Get out of here," Shane said, motioning them away with his hands. When he reached the door, he called out, "Who is it?"

"Marie," the detective said. There was a hard, harsh bite to her voice, a hoarseness that penetrated the heavy wood and rolled through the cool air of the house.

Frowning, Shane opened up the door and saw her. She was dressed in what he knew was her work attire. A no-nonsense suit that didn't hide or accentuate her femininity. Her hair was pulled back into a ponytail, a baseball hat with the brim down low that clashed with her clothing.

"Marie," Shane said, nodding. "What's going on?"

"Why don't you invite me in, Shane?" she asked.

The rough tone of her voice was different than anything he had heard before from her.

The hackles on the back of his neck stood up, and he took a step closer, keeping a firm grip on the doorknob. "Why don't you tell me what's going on first?"

She gave a small shake of her head. "No, Shane. I think we need to have a talk."

"What's going on, Detective?" Frank asked over Shane's shoulder.

"I need to speak with Shane. And you as well, Frank," she said.

"Sure," Frank said. "You going to let her in, Shane?"

"No," Shane replied. There was something strange about her. A wrongness he couldn't place.

"We need to talk," Marie said.

"We can talk right here," Shane responded. "I can hear you just fine from where you're standing."

"This isn't something we can discuss outside," she snapped. "Do you understand me?"

Shane felt a cold grin spread across his face.

"I understand you just fine," he said, his voice low. "Maybe, Marie, you don't understand me. I don't care if you're mad at me. I don't care that you're a cop. I am not letting you into my house until you tell me what's going on."

"Shane," Frank said. "What the hell is up?"

"Look at her," Shane said. "Look at her and tell me something's not wrong with her."

"Frank," Marie snapped. "Will you talk some sense into him, please?"

"Come on, Shane," Frank said.

Shane turned his head slightly toward Frank, and Marie struck.

Her foot lashed out, kicking the door out of his hand and sending the edge of it into his shoulder. He stumbled back, knocking Frank off balance.

Marie was inside in a heartbeat, moving faster than Shane had ever imagined she could. Shane caught himself on the wall and dodged a kick from Marie that would have crushed his kneecap if it had connected.

She slammed the door behind her, the entire frame shaking as wood struck wood. The baseball hat fell from her head, and the ponytail with it.

A woman, slightly older than Marie, was revealed. Her black hair was clipped short, her face sharp and the jaw set.

The stranger's face was a cold, immovable mask as she threw a punch at Shane. He twisted at the last moment, the blow glancing off his left arm. There was a power and strength to it.

She tried to stomp on Frank's ankle, but the man rolled, her booted foot smashing down onto the floor. The woman spun back toward Shane, her right hand sliding into the depths of her suit coat.

Her hand reemerged seconds later, a semi-automatic pistol held in it. The weapon had a suppressor attached to it, the pistol grotesque in appearance as she pointed it at Shane.

The expression on her face never changed as she pulled the trigger.

Chapter 42: Shock and Awe

A sense of cold detachment dropped down onto Frank, and he recognized it instantly. In some of his worst battles, it had appeared. It was a filter; a magnifying glass that afforded him a preternatural ability to focus.

It seemed as though the world slowed down. Frank could see everything.

He saw the brutal determination on the stranger's face, a murderous glint in her eye. Her hand was steady, the pistol rock-like in its stillness. When she pulled the trigger, her finger went backward without the faintest hint of hurry.

Frank watched the slide on the pistol move back and then jerk forward. The spent shell casing spun with all the grace and care of a pinwheel out of the ejection port.

Frank didn't see the round itself, but he watched as Shane twisted his head to the right. A bright red line leaped into life along the left side of his head above his mutilated ear.

The round smashed into the stairs, and the world exploded back into full speed.

So too did Frank.

He launched himself forward, striking the woman in the elbow, forcing the arm up and sending the next round wild. She spun to face him, trying to bring the butt of the pistol down on his face.

But Frank had been in more fights than he wanted to remember, and with killers who had been at their peaks. He had left more bodies than she could imagine in places like Afghanistan and Iraq.

A quick snap of his hand broke her wrist, the weapon dropping to the floor as she grunted. The stranger was skilled, though and focused. Even as she lost her pistol, she brought her left hand around, trying to rake her fingernails down Frank's face. Frank parried, and by the time she brought her right knee up towards his groin, Shane was there.

What Frank and the woman had in finesse, Shane had in pure rage and brute power.

Shane plowed into her, his shoulder catching her in the ribs, breaking them while lifting her up off her feet. She exhaled and grunted all in one motion as Shane drove her into the wall. Pictures fell from their hooks, landing on the floor with a shatter of breaking glass.

Blood ran down the side of Shane's face, some of it slipping along the line of his cheekbone and spilling down over his mouth. The lower half of his chin became a grotesque imitation of a clown's smile and his teeth were stained red as he stepped back.

Frank opened his mouth to speak but didn't have the chance.

Shane stepped forward and smashed his fist into the woman's face. Her head snapped back, putting a dent in the horsehair plaster as her eyes rolled up to show the whites. She slid, seemingly boneless, to the floor.

"Kitchen?" Frank asked, his voice loud and harsh in his ears.

Shane shook his head. "Bathroom. The blood will be easier to clean there."

Together they took the stranger by her arms and dragged her up the stairs.

Chapter 43: A Conversation between Friends

Shane's head pounded, and his hands trembled as he lit a cigarette. He was alone in the bathroom with a stranger. They had searched her and come up with a phone, a small coil of wire, a detective's badge that said she was Lisbeth Walker, and far too much money for a police detective. She lay in the bathtub, bloody and battered, and Shane had no doubt she was still extremely dangerous in spite of her injuries.

Frank leaned in the doorway with a shotgun, a pair of rock salt shells loaded into it.

"She's awake," Frank said.

Shane looked at her. The woman's expression was unchanged, but he didn't doubt Frank's assessment.

"Who are you?" Shane asked.

Her eyes snapped open, and she glared at him. A fine mixture of hatred and anger filled her eyes.

"I'm exactly who it says I am," she said. Her words were cold and flat.

"Detective Lisbeth Walker," Shane said.

She nodded.

"Then why, Detective Walker," Shane said, "did you come here to kill us this morning?"

She looked from Shane to Frank, seemed to assess the situation, and said, "I'm not leaving here alive."

"I haven't decided yet," Shane replied.

Lisbeth scoffed. "I'm going to kill you, Shane. And you, Frank. The first opportunity that presents itself."

"Why?" Shane asked. He was surprised and curious.

"It's what I'm paid to do," she responded.

"By whom?" Frank asked.

"Someone who is extremely upset with you," Lisbeth snapped. "You've stepped on some toes, Shane. And you as well, Frank. You've interrupted a process of cultivation, and they're going to stop you."

"What in the hell are you talking about?" Shane asked.

A cold, calculating look appeared on her face. Her eyes lacked any sort of empathy, any sort of emotion.

His own face must have been easy to read, for Lisbeth gave him a cold and brutal smile.

"Life's not what you thought it was, is it, Shane?" she snickered. "No. Not at all. And here's a little bit of information for you. Something to wrestle with during your sleepless nights.

They've been watching your house since before your parents bought it. They knew about the girl in the pond. They've always known. And when your parents bought the house, they wondered how long you would all last."

"I lasted long enough," Shane hissed. "And I'll last longer than you."

Lisbeth spat a wad of bloody phlegm on the floor.

"You were told to stay away from ghosts," she snarled. "You could have been here, in your house, happy with your little assortment of dead friends until the Watchers decided to move. Instead, you became involved. Sanford, Kurkow, Nutaq. And now, Slater Mill. Pierre Gustav is to be left alone. Someone is going to make you leave him alone."

"No one," Shane hissed, "is going to make me do anything."

"How many more of you are there?" Frank asked.

Lisbeth laughed. "I'm not a true believer, Frank. I'm a hired gun. And there are always more who are willing to pull the trigger. I happened to be closest. Others will come. One will succeed."

"You won't," Shane said, standing up. "What will happen to you if we let you go? How is failure dealt with?"

She grinned. "Failure means I don't get paid."

"Success means money in the bank," Shane said.

Lisbeth let out a laugh, nodding.

"How do you call it in?" Frank asked. "When you succeed?"

She shook her head, a broad, gruesome smile spreading across her face.

"Oh no," she whispered. "That won't do. You won't get away that easily. And I know you won't torture me for it, Frank. I know what you did in Afghanistan. And you, Shane. I know you won't do it either."

Shane nodded, finished his cigarette, and knocked the ashes off into the sink. He exhaled the smoke towards the ceiling and then turned his attention back to Lisbeth.

"You're right," Shane said. "I won't. But there are those who will. Eloise."

The dead girl slid out of the far wall, her face a mask of fury.

For the first time, fear flickered across Lisbeth's face.

"What do you need, Shane?" Eloise asked, glaring at Lisbeth.

"There's a number or a word that we need. It's what she would tell them as confirmation of her having killed the two of us," Shane said, keeping his rage contained. "She'll tell you when you've done enough," Shane said.

"How will I know it's the right thing?" Eloise asked.

"Keep hurting her until she promises that it's the right one," Shane said. He left the room and glanced back at Lisbeth, who had pressed herself into the corner of the tub.

"You can close the door," Eloise called out. "And turn the light out. I can ask my questions in the dark."

Without responding to her statement, Shane turned off the lights and shut the door behind him. Before he and Frank reached the top of the stairs, the first of Lisbeth's many screams punctured the stillness of the house.

Chapter 44: The Dead do not Forget

"Do you think Marie knows about any of this?" Shane asked.

Frank glanced over at him and shook his head. "No. I don't."

"I tried texting her," Shane said. "I mean, I think it was the right number. I don't even know anymore."

"We can figure that out later," Frank said, crossing the room. "Right now, we have a more pressing concern. He's still out there."

Shane looked up at Frank. The man stood by the back door, staring out into the dawn.

The pounding in Shane's head made thinking difficult.

"Who?" Shane asked, the sound of his voice causing him to wince.

Frank glanced over at him and said, "Jack."

Shane groaned and sank back into his chair, closing his eyes. "Hell. I forgot about him."

"Yeah," Frank said. A moment later, the chair across from Shane's desk was pulled back, and the wood creaked as Frank sat in it. "Getting shot at, well that can do it to you."

Shane opened one eye and said, "Correction. Getting shot."

"You were grazed," Frank said gently

Shane let his eyelid sink down again and said, "Still, it qualifies as being shot."

Frank snorted. "What do we do now about Jack?"

"We're going to have to call Kurt and go at him with just the three of us," Shane answered.

"Sounds like a terrible idea," Frank said.

"Agreed," Shane said, sighing. "I don't see much of an alternative."

"No," Frank acknowledged. "I think you're right about that. When do you want to call him?"

"In about an hour or so," Shane answered. "Can't wait much longer. Got a feeling Jack won't."

"You're right," Carl said, stepping into the room through the wall beside the pantry.

The two men looked at the dead man and waited for him to continue.

"Thaddeus and I saw him earlier," Carl said. "Jack Whyte did not so much run as he did turn and stroll away. He was attempting to come in through the study. I do not doubt he will find a place we are not near soon enough."

"Great," Frank muttered.

"If we are to move in on him," Carl continued. "I would suggest we do it soon."

"I'll call Kurt now," Shane said. He straightened in his chair, pulled his phone out, and called the officer. Within two rings, it was answered and a man who wasn't Kurt answered.

"Sorry," Shane began. "Wrong number."

"If you're looking for Kurt," the man said, "it's the right number."

"Oh," Shane said. "Could you pass the phone over to him?"

"I'm afraid not," the man said, sounding decidedly unapologetic. "Who's this?"

"A friend," Shane said. "I'll call back later."

Shane ended the call and put the phone on the table. A moment later, he picked it up, accessed the search engine, and looked for local news. Within seconds, a headline caught his attention.

"Off Duty Police Officer Executed."

"What's wrong?" Frank asked.

Shane slid the phone across the table to him.

"Oh, hell," Frank said, shaking his head.

"I think we can say this entire situation has gone sideways," Shane said, standing up.

"Will you tell me what is going on?" Carl asked a note of exasperation in his voice.

"Sure," Frank said. "We're going to have to go after Jack Whyte on our own."

"Ah," Carl said.

"Yeah," Shane said as he started to leave.

"Where are you going, my friend?" Carl called after him.

"To get some help," Shane replied.

"From whom?" Frank asked.

"Courtney," Shane answered, and walked to the stairs.

Chapter 45: Broken

She lay in the tub, drunk on pain and agony. Lisbeth couldn't move, and every breath was a struggle. The room was an ungodly black. She shivered, but she didn't know if it was from trauma or the residual effects of the ghost's torments.

Lisbeth suspected it was the latter.

She didn't even know if she was alone in the room.

"You're strong," the dead girl said and Lisbeth whimpered. "Not strong enough, though."

Lisbeth didn't speak. She didn't know if she could.

"Tell me again," the girl said.

"Forty-six, ampersand, two," Lisbeth said, her voice as harsh and as broken as she was.

Pain exploded in her right arm as tiny fingers made of ice pushed into her flesh.

Lisbeth screamed, thrashed and screamed again as she struck her broken wrist against the side of the tub.

"Again," the dead girl whispered.

Lisbeth repeated the call-in code for a successful termination. She didn't know how many times she had told the girl the code. Or how many more times the girl would ask her the question.

"Please stop," Lisbeth begged.

"For now," the girl said. "But I'm going to come back soon, and I'm going to hurt you more than I have so far."

"Why?" Lisbeth moaned. "Why? I told you the code."

"Why?" the girl asked with a scoff. "Because you hurt Shane, and you tried to hurt Frank. You tried to do bad things to my friends. And I am going to do bad things to you."

Lisbeth wept, and the dead girl remained silent.

After several minutes, Lisbeth realized the girl was gone, and she contemplated, for the briefest of moments, an attempt to escape.

Then she remembered the dossier on the house. The other ghosts who inhabited it. The idea of suffering more at the girl's hands, as well as that of others, Lisbeth sank into the tub.

She felt a chill creep over her, and she wondered if it was shock.

"Hello my love," a deep voiced man asked. "Mm, you've been a bit broken, haven't you? Yes, old Jack can see that. You're in a bit of a spot, aren't you?"

Lisbeth whimpered.

The man chuckled.

"Oh no, my love, you need not fear old Jack. I'll not do those terrible things the little one did."

Hope sparked within Lisbeth's chest.

"Ah, yes," Jack said, chuckling. "Never fear old Jack. Jack's rough, but he's true. Aye, that, he is. Yes?"

Lisbeth couldn't see Jack, but she nodded nonetheless.

"So I thought, so I thought. 'Tis all well and good," he said, chuckling. "So said I to myself, she's in a spot and in need of a pair of helping hands. Do I speak the truth now?"

"Yes," she whispered.

"And would you like Jack's help?" he asked.

"Yes," she said, her voice growing stronger.

"And Jack would like to give it to you, so he would," Jack said, chuckling.

Suddenly cold hands wrapped around her throat, the touch of them excruciating. Lisbeth kicked out at the walls and clawed at the hands, but she encountered nothing. The hands tightened, squeezing the life out of her.

Lisbeth flailed about, her heels drummed against the old cast iron tub, and above it all, she heard Jack.

He was whistling, a happy, cheerful tune as he slowly, leisurely, tightened his grip.

Chapter 46: Tidying Up

Abigail had showered, dressed, and gone to her office. She sat at her desk, tapping her fingers on the leather blotter and stared at her cell phone, willing it to chime that a message had arrived.

Instead, the phone rang.

Abigail answered it with a cold, "Hello."

"Hello," the woman on the other end replied. "Dell has been confirmed."

"Excellent," Abigail stated, allowing herself a small smile of satisfaction. "Take care of the shooters."

"Yes."

The call ended.

Abigail placed the phone back on the blotter and accessed Channel 9 News in New Hampshire via the internet. She turned up the volume on her speakers and listened to the top stories.

A veteran officer of the Nashua Police Force had been gunned down, execution style, on the same street his partner had suffered a fatal heart attack. In Chelmsford, Massachusetts, a faulty gas line had exploded in the early hours of the morning, killing a husband and wife as well as their three children.

Abigail nodded, pleased with the events, and navigated away from the site. She glanced at the phone.

Aside from the two shooters, which was nothing more than minor housekeeping in the grand scheme of things, Abigail was waiting only on the operative in Nashua. The female detective had been an effective asset for a decade. While the organization had only used her a handful of times, she had always come through.

The tempo of Abigail's fingers increased, beating out a maddening rhythm on the desktop.

Five minutes passed. Then, soon an hour had elapsed, and for the first time, Abigail found herself concerned.

A sound in the front caught her attention and made her reach for the silenced pistol she kept secured under the desk. She was by no means a trained sniper but Abigail knew she could hit anyone who walked through the door of her office.

It took her several moments to recognize the everyday noises her secretary made, and when Abigail did, she let go of the pistol's grip.

The cell phone chimed.

Abigail picked it up with a hand that was steadier than she thought it would be.

The text was from the operative's number.

46&2.

Abigail sank back into her chair, relief flooding her.

She deleted the message and dropped the phone to the blotter. The intercom on her desk buzzed and Abigail answered it. "Yes?"

"I didn't realize you were in this early, Ma'am," her secretary said. "Would you like a cup of coffee?"

"Yes," Abigail replied.

"Right away, Ma'am."

Abigail took a deep breath, cleared her mind, and began to plan how she would bring Slater Mill back under control.

Chapter 47: Focus and Drive On

"Thank you," Frank said to Eloise. He put Lisbeth's phone down on the side table in the study.

"You're welcome," Eloise said, grinning. "What should I do with her now?"

"Keep an eye on her, please," Frank said. "I have to talk to Shane about what to do."

Eloise nodded and skipped out of the room, leaving him alone.

The situation was decidedly sticky, Frank knew. There was no doubt that Lisbeth intended to kill Shane and him. Frank was still taken aback by her initial attempt, by the whole situation. Whomever she worked for had deep pockets, and were well aware of what Shane had done in the past. Why they were concerned about it was worrisome as well.

It meant that there was a group of some sort who concerned themselves with the unruly dead, and they weren't pleased with what had been done in the past, or what he and Shane were attempting to do with Slater Mill.

Frank had little information on the group, and he hoped to get Lisbeth to talk about it. If she even knew.

But Lisbeth was a problem for another time.

The priority was Jack, and only Jack. Lisbeth was, at least for the moment, contained. The dead Englishman was not. Knowing Jack's propensity for violence kept Frank focused. He and Shane could worry about the assassin, and what to do with her, later.

Eloise raced into the room, a look of dismay on her face.

"What is it?" Frank asked, pushing himself out of the chair.

"The woman," Eloise said, her eyes wide, "she's dead."

"Did you kill her?" Frank demanded.

Eloise shook her head.

Without another word, Frank turned on his heel and sprinted out of the room. His footsteps thundered on the stairs, and when he reached the door, Frank wrenched it open.

He reached in, turned the light on, and came to a sharp stop.

Detective Lisbeth Walker was without a doubt dead.

She lay in the far end of the tub, pressed against the back corner. Her head was tilted back and her mouth and eyes open. The glassy orbs stared at the ceiling while black marks, which looked like handprints, wrapped around her throat.

From where Frank stood, he recognized the marks. The curious frostbite so many ghosts left on their victims.

And the prints left on Lisbeth's throat were huge.

He had seen dead hands like those once.

"Jack Whyte," Frank murmured.

"Who is that?" Eloise asked.

"The Englishman," Frank answered.

"Why would he kill her?" Eloise asked, looking up at him.

"He likes to kill," Frank replied. "And it seems like he's getting warmed up."

"What do we do now?" she asked.

"We tell Shane," Frank said, turning off the light and leaving the room. "And then we figure out what to do with her body."

"Oh," Eloise said. Then she smiled, clapped her hands and declared, "That's easy!"

Frank was taken aback, and before he could ask her what she meant, she offered up the information.

"There are so many places to hide her here," Eloise said, skipping around him in the hallway. "In the walls, and the secret rooms. Down in the pantry. Oh, yes! The root cellar! She'll keep for a good, long time there."

Frank shuddered at the idea of the detective's body hidden in the house, but he kept his revulsion to himself as he made his way to the library. The dead girl skipped beside him, humming a happy tune.

Chapter 48: In the Library Again

Shane heard some sort of commotion beyond the locked door of the library, but he ignored it. Instead, he concentrated on Courtney. He had darkened the room and taken his seat behind the desk. The air had chilled, and goosebumps settled onto his flesh.

"Why are you here?" Courtney demanded. Her voice came from behind him, and he kept himself seated, his hands gripping the arms of the chair.

"I need your help," he stated.

She waited a moment before asking, "Why?"

"Because you are the best choice," he lied.

The anger in her voice lessened.

"And," he continued, "I would feel safer with you beside me in this job."

"What is it?" she asked, her voice closer.

He shuddered, remembering when she had been alive. When they had been together. His throat tightened, and he blinked back tears.

"There is a ghost," Shane managed to say. "He is a murderer and was one, long before he was dead. His bones are nearby, and I have to salt and burn them."

"I can't do either one of those," Courtney said. "How do I help you?"

"By keeping him away from us," Shane said.

"Who is 'us'?" she asked, suspicion in her voice.

"Frank," Shane answered, wincing.

"Frank," she murmured. "I remember Frank. I did something to him, didn't I?"

Shane hesitated before he answered. "Yes. You tried to hurt him."

"Oh," she said in a small voice. "Should I have?"

"No," Shane answered. "But you weren't well."

"I'm still not well," Courtney replied, anger creeping into her words. "I am still sick."

"Courtney," Shane started, but Courtney cut him off with a snarl.

"I am sick!" she spat. "How can I be healed? What will make me better?!"

"I don't know," Shane confessed. "But I'm trying to find out."

Silence filled the room, and Shane waited for her to respond. When she didn't, he put his hands on the desk and pushed himself away from it.

"How?" she whispered.

"The internet," Shane answered. "Books. Brian and Jenny. Anyone and everyone."

"Why?" her voice was difficult to hear.

"Because," he said, choking on the word. "I love you."

She answered a moment later, her voice stronger and saner than he had heard in a long time.

"I will."

A loud, hard knock rang out on the door, the sound followed by Frank.

"Shane," Frank called out, "we've got a problem."

"Hold on," Shane said. The room's temperature increased, and Shane realized Courtney had left.

He turned on the desk lamp, blinked at the light and got up, hurrying to the door. Shane unlocked it and pulled the door open. Frank stood in the hall with a harried expression, Eloise beside him.

"What is it?" Shane asked.

"Lisbeth's dead," Frank answered.

Shane frowned. "Damn. How? Was it you, Eloise?"

"No!" she said, tilting her head up and folding her arms over her chest. "Why do you think I would?"

"Nevermind," Shane replied. "What happened?"

Frank told him about the marks on the detective's neck, and his suspicion as to who the culprit was.

"You're probably right," Shane said after a moment. "We need to take care of Jack sooner than later."

"And the body?" Frank asked.

"Eloise," Shane said, turning to the girl. "I'm sorry I thought it was you."

"That's alright," the dead girl answered. "I did want to kill her."

Shane smiled. "Of course you did. Will you tell Carl that I need him to hide the body?"

"What about her car?" Frank asked. "We can't just make a detective and her car disappear."

"No," Shane agreed. "We can't. But I doubt that her car is anywhere nearby. She knew people watched everything in this neighborhood. I wouldn't be surprised if she used a rental and parked it a street or two away. We'll worry about it later. Right now we need to focus on Jack."

"Yeah," Frank said, casting a sidelong glance at the open bathroom door. "I particularly dislike the idea that he was here and we didn't know."

"Right there with you," Shane said.

"Where are you going?" Frank asked when Shane walked away towards his bedroom.

"I need to get the dog tags," Shane answered.

"Wait. Why?" Frank questioned. He looked from the library's closed door and then back to Shane. "Why in the hell are you getting your tags?"

"She's coming with us, Frank," Shane said, and he continued to his bedroom, ignoring the other man's disgruntled mutters.

Chapter 49: The Fruits of Their Labor

Marian half sprawled on the couch, the bass reverberating through the apartment. Ruby was making out with Antoine in the bedroom, and Marian was higher than she had been in a long time. She grinned, took a hit off the bong, and held the smoke in for a long, delicious moment.

When Marian exhaled, she coughed and her eyes watered.

"You good?" Xavier asked, coming from the kitchen with a bottle of Crown Royal.

"Hell yeah, I'm good," Marian said, grinning. Xavier looked good, strong and proud. He was working his way through classes at the University of Massachusetts in Lowell, some engineering program. He talked about it, but Marian never listened. She liked to look at Xavier, and that was about the extent of it.

She passed the bong to him, and he gave her the bottle. Marian had herself a long drink, watching as Xavier took a small hit.

"You need a little more," she said.

He snorted, smoke coming out of his nose as he laughed.

"Nah," he said. "I'm good. I take a big hit, and I'll be asleep before the new Walking Dead episode comes on."

"Don't want you asleep at all," Marian said, blowing him a kiss.

Xavier chuckled and held out his hand. She passed him the bottle, and he took a drink. Cradling the container in a large hand, he settled back into his chair. In the city, the clock on the old church struck nine.

A glass broke in the kitchen and Marian looked lazily towards the room.

"You leave something on the counter for the cat to break?" she asked, glancing at Xavier.

"No," he answered. "I threw the cat out. I'm allergic to the damned things."

Before Marian could sit up, a figure appeared in the doorway. The person was small, dressed in jeans and sneakers and a dark blue hoodie. A black bandana was secured around the lower half of the person's face, and the hood was pulled up. All Marian could see was the stranger's pale skin and bright brown eyes.

Then she saw the weapon.

It was a semi-automatic pistol, equipped with a suppressor.

Xavier stood up, and the weapon moved a fraction of an inch and the person fired. It sounded as though someone coughed and two shell casings spiraled through the air. When they struck the worn carpet, Xavier fell back into the chair, two dark, wet spots blossoming on his chest.

The stranger pointed the pistol at Marian, and it coughed again. Something hard and unforgiving struck her in the left breast. She found she couldn't breathe, her eyes, working on their own, as she watched the person pass by her. Quick steps brought the stranger to Ruby's bedroom and through the open doorway. Through a haze of pain, Marian watched the shooter fire again, then step further into the room and out of her view.

Marian struggled to sit up, managed to roll on her side and felt blood pump out of the wound and onto the couch.

A moment later, the stranger came out of Ruby's bedroom. The shooter paused beside Marian, bending over to pick up a shell casing. For the first time, Marian saw the stranger was wearing black gloves. All of the shooter's clothes were generic. No name brands. Not even on the sneakers.

A pro, she thought, and she understood. They had been played, she and Ruby. When the police came, they'd find the guns from the shooting. No one would investigate the murder of a couple of cop killers.

No one would care.

The stranger took a step forward, picked up the last two rounds, and pocketed them. Then the shooter turned around and squatted beside Marian. The brown eyes looked at her, full of curiosity.

As Marian felt herself dying, she understood it was what the shooter wanted.

Marian wanted to disappoint the killer, she wanted to fight and live, force the shooter to waste another round.

But Marian couldn't.

All she found herself capable of, was exactly what the shooter wanted.

Chapter 50: Looking for Jack

Shane wore the dog tags on the outside of his sweatshirt. The metal was painfully cold against his bare flesh, and he suspected that prolonged contact would cause permanent damage.

He and Frank moved through the woods, a few feet between them. Each of them carried a shotgun in a duffel bag, as well as salt, lighter fluid, and matches. On their fingers, they wore iron rings, and each carried a shovel. Somewhere nearby, Eloise moved among the trees, and Courtney too was near. All of the land, from the house down to the river, had once belonged to the house. The dead were bound only by those barriers that had existed when they were alive. As a child, that idea had worried Shane, but in the hunt for Jack, it added a layer of security.

Shane looked around for Courtney, trying to see her.

And part of him feared Jack sought them out.

All they would have to defend themselves with would be the rings, with only their shotguns as weapons of last resort. The police would frown upon the discharge of a firearm within city limits. And explaining to any responding officers that the rounds were only rock salt and that he and Frank were fighting a ghost, would land them both in a mandatory psychiatric evaluation.

Eloise appeared in front of them, and Shane grumbled a curse under his breath, his heartbeat spiking.

"I've found the tree," the dead girl said. She was disturbingly translucent in the woods, her voice almost tin-like. Her face was a mask of worry, and Shane felt uncomfortable.

He glanced about the woods, fighting the urge to open the duffel bag and remove his shotgun. A look at Frank showed that he too seemed to wrestle with a similar desire.

Shane wanted to ask if Eloise was sure, but her worry answered the unasked question.

"Lead the way," Shane said, "and take it slow. We're not as fast as you."

Eloise nodded and led them deeper into the woods. While she passed through bushes and trees alike, Shane and Frank had to step around them. They drifted apart, then back together, and soon they found themselves in a wide clearing.

Shane didn't know if the tree was an oak or an elm or a chestnut. He only knew that it was big. Bigger than any tree in New England had the right to be.

"Oh no," Frank said in a hushed voice.

"What?" Shane asked. "What's wrong?"

"The tree," Frank answered.

"Yeah?" Shane said. "What about it?"

"Look how big it is."

"So what?" Shane asked.

"Think about it, Shane," Frank said, looking at him, the muscles in his jaw twitching. "Trees grow."

"So?"

"When did Jack die?" Frank asked.

Then it dawned on Shane.

If Jack had died two hundred years earlier, and his bones had fallen at the base of the tree, then they couldn't dig.

They couldn't dig at all.

How tall had the tree grown? How wide over two centuries? The bones would have been encompassed by the roots. Absorbed into the tree itself.

"We have to uproot it," Shane whispered.

"And burn the roots, too," Frank said, "if we're going to get every last bit of bone that might still be around."

Eloise looked at them both and offered up a suggestion.

"I can look," she said.

"How?" Shane asked in surprise.

"I'll go down a bit," Eloise said. "I'll be able to see them. And feel them."

"What if he sees you?" Frank asked.

"I'll be okay," she said, although Shane heard a hint of doubt in her voice. "I'll be quiet. And I'll be quick."

As much as he hated to, Shane nodded his assent.

The dead girl sank into the earth without a sound.

Frank put his bag on the ground and Shane did the same. The shovels were laid alongside them, and then the men removed their shotguns from the duffel bags. Safeties were clicked off, and they stood once more. Minutes passed by, and while Shane knew it was only a short time, it felt much longer.

Around them, the forest was silent. There was no hint of birdsong or the clambering of squirrels.

The creatures had long abandoned the tree and Jack's bones.

Shane wondered how the animals had reacted when they found the ghost among them. Did they scatter immediately, or did it take time for them to flee their nests and their dens?

Eloise rose up from the ground, a look of concern on her face.

"What is it?" Frank asked.

"Most of the bones are here," she said, gesturing towards a spot on the earth to her right.

"Most of them?" Shane asked. "Where are the others, under the tree?"

She shook her head. "The tree grew away from them. Its roots avoided Jack's bones. Animals must not have. There are small bits of him all over this place. I counted twenty-seven of them scattered."

"The lion's share are right here, though?" Frank asked, gesturing towards the spot on the ground with his shotgun.

"Yes," Eloise said.

Frank exchanged his shotgun for a shovel. "Alright. I guess we start digging here."

Shane nodded his agreement, set his weapon down and picked up his shovel. To Eloise, he said, "Keep an eye out for old Jack, alright?"

"Yes, Shane," she whispered.

Within moments, the shovels thudded into the earth, and the stillness of the woods was shattered.

Chapter 51: Unasked for Interruptions

The Watcher network spread far and wide through New England. There was a small town on the coast of Maine, near the Canadian border, that had a single spirit within an old woodshed. Yet that malevolent being was responsible for fourteen confirmed deaths in the past twenty-nine years.

On an island in the Pachaug River, which ran through the state forest of the same name, there was the ghost of a madman. The things he had done when alive had chilled Abigail's cold blood when she had learned of them.

And there were dozens more throughout the six New England states. The Watchers knew where they all were, and were slowly building the spiritual connections between them. It had taken fifty-six years to connect all of the powerful, supernatural places in New Hampshire together. That energy, a subtle, electrifying force, was to be channeled through the last link in the chain and into Maine.

With the power of New Hampshire's unquiet dead funneled into Maine, it would have taken half of the time to harness Maine's spiritual energy.

Instead, Shane Ryan had destroyed that plan. Not once, but twice. The work of decades had been undone in days.

Abigail had managed to maintain her position at the helm of the Watchers through sheer force of will, and threats of violence.

The loss of Slater Mill would have been unacceptable, and she would have had to flee Massachusetts if she wanted to live. As it was, she had been forced to expend a large amount of capital, execute a foolish member of the organization, and bring an asset into play.

All of which would have to be justified at the next meeting of the board. It was that petty, bureaucratic dilemma that occupied her attention as she sat at her desk.

Abigail stared at the spreadsheet on her monitor, tapping her fingers on the desk and wondering where she could move funds from without attracting too much attention.

Her cell phone rang, causing her to raise an eyebrow in surprise. With a deft movement of her hand, she scooped it up and answered it.

"Hello," she said.

"Hello," a female caller said. "The shooters have been taken care of."

"Excellent," Abigail said. She went to put the phone down but stopped when she realized the woman was still on the other end. Abigail brought the phone back to her ear and asked, "Do you have more information?"

"I have a suggestion," the woman said. "Turn on the New Hampshire news."

Then the woman did end the call.

Abigail returned her cell phone to its place on the desk and did as the woman suggested. For the second time in the day, she found the Channel 9 news site and scrolled through the top stories.

The headline screamed at her when she found it.

Police find detective's car abandoned in Tyngsboro, Massachusetts.

Abigail continued to read.

The article was concise and badly written. In spite of the latter, Abigail was able to obtain the information she needed. A longtime Nashua detective, Lisbeth Walker, was missing. She hadn't shown up to work, and she was not at home. The Nashua police were concerned, especially following the murder of another police officer, who in turn was Detective Walker's ex-husband. There was additional information as well. An unnamed source stated that Detective Walker was a person of interest in the murder of the other officer.

Abigail closed the site and sat rigid in her chair.

It could be a coincidence that a female detective had gone missing.

Coincidences were always possible.

Abigail had never known who the asset in Nashua was, but she knew how the organization worked. They tended to recruit from law enforcement. Abigail herself had been the one to recruit Allen in Nutaq. It would have made sense to recruit a detective in a large city like Nashua. And a female asset would have been a coup.

People always underestimated women. It was a psychological defect of American society and one which Abigail had exploited to her benefit on more than one occasion.

So, the disappearance of a female detective could certainly fall under the umbrella of coincidence.

But Abigail didn't think so.

Not at all.

Her hand trembled as she picked up her cell phone and dialed the asset's number.

It rang five times and went to a generic voice mail.

Abigail didn't leave a message.

Instead, she ended the call and put the phone back on the desk.

She sat and counted to thirty, and then she reached out and pressed the intercom button.

"Yes ma'am?" her secretary asked.

"I'd like a coffee from the corner shop," Abigail said, keeping her voice steady. "A bagel as well."

"Toasted with butter?" her secretary inquired.

"Yes."

"Very good, ma'am," her secretary said, and the intercom clicked off.

In less than sixty seconds, Abigail heard her secretary leave the office. When the door closed, Abigail stood up, walked to her closet and opened it. She quickly stripped off her work clothes and pulled on her jeans, sneakers, and sweater. Abigail kicked her good clothes into the closet, removed a plain, battered red backpack, and closed the door. She put on a pair of non-prescription glasses, tugged her hair into a messy pony-tail, and yanked a beaten Red Sox baseball hat out of the back.

She shouldered the pack, which contained power-bars, a change of clothes, a significant amount of cash, and a new identity.

The organization didn't suffer fools, and she found herself with that title.

In less than two months, she had lost three assets and a major link in the supernatural chain.

For a moment, she considered finding Shane Ryan and how she would enjoy killing him.

But only for a moment.

Abigail was nothing if not practical, and seeking revenge on Shane Ryan would only give the organization more time to kill her.

It was time for Abigail to cut her losses.

Without a second glance, Abigail left her office and took the stairs down to the first floor. She exited the building even as her secretary entered it, and neither of them looked back.

Chapter 52: Sweating and Afraid

Shane had faced his share of monsters, both living and dead. He had encountered horrific creatures who pretended to be men, men who killed for pleasure, and who tortured for the same. Shane had seen the dead, and he had lived with the same. He had broken both the living and the dead, and he hoped to do the same again.

Shane had never been stupidly courageous. He knew his limits. Fear was a rational response, and he had suffered through it more often than not. He remembered boot camp, which he foolishly had thought his life in a haunted house had prepared him for. Shane remembered being afraid of the Drill Instructors, believing every horrible threat and nightmarish promise.

He also recalled his graduation from boot camp, the glorious belief, if only for a short while, that he was invincible.

As he dug deeper into the earth beneath the tree, Shane longed for that feeling of invincibility once more.

He paused, straightened his back for a moment, and wiped the sweat off his forehead.

Frank stopped too and looked at him.

"How far down do you think Jack is?" Frank asked.

"Too far," Shane answered.

"No," Eloise whispered. "Only a few more inches."

"Why are you whispering?" Shane asked, a chill racing along his spine.

"Because I don't know where he is," she answered.

"Great," Frank muttered, and he began to dig again.

"Have you found all of the bones?" Shane asked.

She nodded.

"Each and every one?" he said.

"Yes," she said, pouting. "All of them. I didn't miss a single one, Shane Ryan. You're not being nice to me."

"I'm sorry, Eloise," Shane said, and he meant it. "I'm nervous."

"So am I," she said in a small voice. "But we will win through."

"I sure as hell hope so," Shane said.

"Your language is nearly as bad as your drinking," she scolded.

Shane rolled his eyes as Frank laughed.

"What about his smoking?" Frank asked.

"That too," she said, shaking a finger at him.

Shane laughed, the absurdity of a dead girl's ghost lecturing him was too much.

"Go on," Frank said, chuckling. "Would he be better off without tobacco and alcohol?"

Shane shook his head as Eloise warmed up to the subject, and focused once again on the search for Jack's bones.

Chapter 53: The Danger Spreads

Cam Darby wasn't a professional thief.

He wasn't an amateur either. He just couldn't claim the title of 'professional,' although he was working on it.

Cam had heard of the recent deaths near the Slater Mill, and he had also heard from a secretary strung out on meth that people were looking to leave the Clock Tower Condominiums. So many people, in fact, that her boss, the manager at Clock Tower, left the master key with her so she could hand it out to any real estate agents who showed up.

And she had owed Cam a couple of favors.

Cam stood in regular street clothes on the third floor of the condos, the key in his hand. The secretary had even told him which apartments were likely to be empty.

The smile on his face was huge.

Today, he thought, *today is going to be your day, Cameron.*

And he knew it was. He could feel it. In spite of the cold air in the wide hallway, Cam knew it was going to be his day.

He took in a deep breath, felt his lungs expand, and he grinned. A great, big, stupid grin that would have made him the butt of his friends' jokes if they had seen it.

Chuckling to himself, Cam strolled down the hallway as if he belonged there. He aimed for the condominium marked '7,' and he rapped on the door with a firm hand.

When no one answered after thirty seconds, he knocked again.

No one responded to the second, or third knocks, so Cam let himself into the condo. The place was dim, the shades drawn against the sun, and for a moment, he felt a pang of panic. He wondered if someone who worked the third shift was asleep, and a dull droning sound brought him to a standstill.

After a moment, Cam recognized the sound of a refrigerator and felt a wave of relief was over him.

He closed the door behind him and locked it. There would be a second exit down the center hall in the condo, and he followed it towards the bedrooms. A sense of excitement built up within Cam as he approached the open the door to the first room. From the hall, he could see a bureau and an unmade, queen-sized bed. Jewelry was scattered about the top of a small vanity, and the palms of Cam's hands dampened.

He let out a low whistle, reached up under his shirt and took out the pair of thin leather gloves he had hidden there. Cam tugged them on, flexed his fingers and stepped into the room.

He approached the jewelry as if it were alive, a cat that might dash off. His eyes darted around the room, searching for small cameras or anything else that might seal his fate in a courtroom.

Nothing caught his eye, and a smile spread across his face. By the time he reached the vanity, he had grown silent. With deft movements, he picked up each piece of jewelry and examined it. He looked for markings on the gold and silver, chuckled at a small platinum ring he found. Whatever didn't end up in a side pocket of his cargo pants was placed in the exact place and position it had occupied before.

Cam spent less than sixty seconds in the room.

He moved from the first bedroom and into the next. It was a spare bedroom, and he doubted much could be found within it.

But he knew, as an up and coming professional, that he needed to check everything.

A tall, narrow chest of drawers stood off to the right, and Cam made a beeline for it. He started at the top drawer, which held nothing more exciting than folded hand towels with roses embroidered on them. The second drawer held face cloths, and the third, bath towels that were so soft Cam had to fight the urge to steal one for his bathroom.

He slid a hand beneath the towels, as he had done to those in the first and second drawers, and his fingers found something.

It was hard and metallic, and by the time he pulled it out and into the open, Cam knew what it was.

A small caliber pistol. Its barrel was a bright silver, the handgrips a vibrant black. He had seen enough television shows to know better than to look down the barrel of a gun to see whether or not it was loaded. Cam also understood that he didn't have any idea how to open it and check the cylinder.

The pistol's safety was on, he saw, and so he assumed it had bullets in it.

He closed the drawer and straightened up, holding the gun in his hand as if it were a snake. Cam wondered if he should put the weapon back, but at the same time, he knew how much money he could get for it. He wouldn't move it himself. No, he had a few friends from high school who could do that for him, and they wouldn't even take too much of a bite out of the profits.

Cam stiffened, his ears straining.

For a moment, it had sounded as if someone else was in the room with him.

With his heart pounding, Cam turned around.

He was the sole occupant.

His heart rate decreased, and he let out a sigh. The blood pounded in his head, and a wave of dizziness washed over him.

I'm fine, he thought. *Nothing wrong. Just nervous. That's all. Just nervous.*

He turned back to the dresser and shuddered.

A pair of young teenagers stood in front of the piece of furniture.

And Cam could see it through them.

Their faces were emotionless. Dead eyes stared at him and through him.

He couldn't force enough air into his lungs to allow him to think.

Fear and a primal need to flee overtook all of his rational thought, and Cam tried to listen to those baser instincts.

He spun on his heel and dashed for the door.

But another teen was in the doorway. A battered and tortured individual who looked as though he had been thrown out a window, or down a flight of stairs. In the hall beyond, Cam saw a pair of adults and panic swept over him.

He tried to run through the teen in the doorway, but he encountered a wall of air so cold and painful it tore a shriek from his throat. Cam stumbled backward and slammed into the room's small bed.

He struck it with the backs of his knees, forcing him down into a sitting position. The pistol in his hand cracked against the side of his knee, and a bright bolt of pain seared his nerves.

The gun! Cam thought. His fingers fumbled as they searched for the safety. After several clumsy attempts, he found it and switched it off. It took all of his strength to aim at the nearest ghost and pull the trigger.

The pistol seemed to explode in his hands. A tongue of flame leaped out of the barrel of the weapon, and he went deaf from the blast in the small room. The force of the blast caused both of his arms to jerk up, and it sent a reverberating shock into his shoulders.

A large chunk of wood flew off of the dresser's top drawer, the massive splinter tumbling through the air and striking the far wall.

Cam tried to get a second shot off, but he couldn't.

The dead were already on him.

Chapter 54: Frank Gets a Feeling

Frank and Shane had gathered all of the bones from the first hole. They had even dug out six more from places Eloise had pointed out to them.

But it was past noon, and they still had another twenty-one to dig out. All of them before Jack showed up to interrupt them.

He will too, Frank realized. The dead man would show up when it was least convenient, or in the best interest of Frank or Shane's continued well-being, and then the situation would get decidedly unpleasant.

Frank glanced at the shotguns, and once more, he wondered if he should hold onto it while he dug. Or at least keep it closer than it was.

He shook his head.

"You're in the wrong place, Frank," Eloise called from her place by the pile of bones.

Frank wanted to thank her, in an extremely sarcastic fashion, but he knew the dead girl was trying to help.

"Thank you," Frank said. He straightened up. "Left or right?"

"Forward, a few inches," she replied.

Frank nodded and put the shovel down. "Here?"

"Yes," Eloise said. "It's his jaw bone. Not many teeth in it, I'm afraid."

"Excellent," Shane said.

"Be nice," Eloise pouted.

Frank wanted to mimic the girl, but he was too tired. His sense of humor had left the situation when they were halfway through gathering the first batch of bones.

Frank felt exposed.

He appreciated Eloise's assistance, but he didn't think she would be anything more than a canary in a mine. The first to die.

And Frank knew she could die, or as close as ghosts came to a second death. The idea of Eloise suffering again, and for him and Shane, set his teeth on edge. He refused to look at her because he had seen that she knew her situation as well.

Frank often forgot her true age. At times, she acted like a child, but there was an old soul trapped behind her eyes.

He glanced at Shane. The man's dog tags swung with each motion of the shovel. Shane was focused. All of his humor, what little remained, was locked away. The battered man dug until he found a bit of Jack Whyte's earthly remains, and then he went and dug some more.

The fact that Shane had brought the tags with him bothered Frank. As insane as the dead woman was, he didn't want her hurt for his benefit either. Shane's face revealed he felt the same.

What a sorry lot we are, Frank thought. He angled the shovel in the earth, put his boot on the metal lip and pushed down. The cutting edge clipped something hard, and Frank hoped it was the bone he sought and not another rock.

Holding onto the handle of the shovel, Frank sank into a squat and used his free hand to push the dirt near the edge aside. A bit of yellowed bones appeared, and he felt a sense of relief. Frank dug out a little more, gripped Jack's jaw, and gave a tug. It came out of the earth grudgingly, and Frank saw Eloise had been correct in her assessment.

Jack hadn't had many teeth left at all.

Frank remained in his squat, pivoted, tossed the jaw onto the pile of bones by the tree, and let out a sharp curse.

Jack Whyte stood beneath the tree, his arms folded across his chest and a nasty smile on his face.

"What friends has old Jack," the dead man chuckled. "Here to make certain Jack finally has a proper burial, and a send off to go with it, eh?"

"Yes," Shane said, leaning on his shovel and bestowing a cold, brittle smile upon Jack. "We're here to say goodbye to you. You entered my home without permission, Jack. I don't appreciate that."

Jack waved a hand dismissively as he straightened up.

"Come now, Shane," Jack said, grinning. "Is your home not open to a friend such as myself? Do you not enjoy the company of the dead? Speak truth to me now, Shane. Speak it and let me rejoice in it."

"Truth," Shane said in a soft voice. "Honesty is what you want?"

Jack's head bobbed up and down. "Oh aye, Jack wouldn't have it any other way. No, not at all."

"Here's a bit of truth for you then," Shane said. "We've come here to gather your bones, to put them in a pretty little pile, and return them to the ashes from whence we all came."

The smile faltered on Jack's face. A corner of his mouth twitched, and a sneer flashed across his visage before it vanished as quickly as it had arrived.

"You joke with old Jack," the dead man said, his voice strained.

Frank put down his shovel and took a casual step toward the shotguns.

"Not a move, you!" Jack howled. "I know what you can do with yon guns, and I'd not feel the burn of the salt. Wretched mineral that it is. And to think I sought after it when I still took air."

Frank stopped, but he kept a wary eye on Jack as he judged the distance between himself and the first shotgun.

"I can move faster than you," Jack hissed. "Do you understand me?"

"We do," Shane said. "And you'd best understand us. We haven't forgotten what you did."

"Always I am blamed and held accountable for the bad acts of others," Jack said, sighing. "'Tis a pity, it is. Prosecuted, persecuted, punished. All sorts of crimes have been hung about Jack's neck, but my back is like that of Atlas, and I hold the weight of the world upon it. Aye, so I do."

"Not for much longer," Shane said.

At Shane's statement, Jack snarled and lunged for him.

Frank, in turn, made for the shotgun, only to discover Jack's move had been a feint.

The dead man struck Frank a horrific blow on the side of the head, the world darkening around him as he fell towards the ground. As the blackness took over his thoughts, Frank heard Jack's raucous laughter ricochet in his head.

Chapter 55: Alone

"You're alone, eh, Shane?" Jack asked.

The dead man stood beside Frank, who lay crumpled on the earth and less than a foot away from the nearest shotgun.

Shane saw his friend's chest rise and fall, so he forced himself to lean on the shovel.

"No," Shane replied.

Jack eyed him warily. "You seem to be alone to me, so you do."

"You're also an idiot, Jack," Shane retorted, "so I'm not particularly impressed with any observations you have to make."

Jack bristled at the insult.

"You're soon to be dead," the dead man spat. "So I'd not speak so poorly to old Jack, I'd not. He's thought long and hard on your death, aye, old Jack has indeed. Your tongue was sharp and swift away with the savages. We'll see how quick it waggles when I tear it from your ever lovin' head, so we will. Think you'll choke on your own blood, Shane? I think not. Old Jack will keep your head up and straight so you'll last many an hour. Oh, my boy, we'll have a fine time, so we will. You and old Jack, old Jack and you."

"Tell me," Shane said, straightening up and wincing at the tight pain in his lower back, "why did you kill her?"

"Which one?" Jack asked with a leer. "I've killed more than a few girls in my day."

Shane gave him a tight smile. "The woman in my bathroom."

"She seemed rather spent if you don't mind old Jack saying so," the dead man laughed. "If she was your beau you treated her a tad rough. At least I was courteous. I always put mine down when I was done with them."

"No reason then?" Shane asked.

"Pleasure," Jack replied. "Nothing more and nothing less. Murder is a great and wondrous relaxation for me, so it is."

"And your own?" Shane asked, feigning politeness.

All of the good humor drained from Jack's face and vanished from his tone. "'Tis an unpleasantness you speak of."

Shane nodded. "I'm curious as to how you felt about it. Do you think you'll feel the same way when I set fire to your bones?"

Jack's visage became a mask of rage.

"You're alone, you foul man," the ghost hissed, taking a menacing step forward.

"No," Shane disagreed. "I'm not."

Courtney appeared in front of him, her form far more solid and robust than Jack's. The dead man looked at her warily, his hands opening and closing. When Jack realized he was almost a full head taller than Courtney, a wicked grin spread across his face.

"You know," Jack said. "Old Jack wonders if strangling the ghost of a girl will please him as much as the living do. Do you think they'll last longer, Shane? Are you curious as well? Is that why you've invited your wee friend to play with good old Jack Whyte?"

Jack turned his attention to Courtney and blew her a kiss. "Come, my love, my love. Come and play with dear old Jack, will you not?"

Without a word, Courtney sprang at the dead man, striking him in the chest and throwing him backward. His eyes widened in a mixture of shock and anger. He righted himself and let out a string of profanity. With his attention fixed on Courtney, Jack never saw Eloise.

The little girl ran into him and through him, an act which caused him to stagger and come to a stop.

Then Carl appeared out of the woods, as did Thaddeus and the ghost of the Old Man, who Shane hadn't seen for months. Dark shapes flitted out, creatures without definition and that had once been men.

Led by Courtney, all of them converged upon Jack, locking themselves around him and dragging him to the earth.

"Quickly, Shane," Courtney called, her voice strong above Jack's screams of fury. "We will hold him for as long as we can."

The massive, writhing form sank below the surface, and silence filled the world. Only Eloise remained above ground with him, and she went to check on Frank. She leaned over, looked at him, and then smiled at Shane.

"He's breathing," she said. Her smile dropped away, and she nodded at the shovel in Shane's hands.

"Best to start digging, Shane," the dead girl said. "Jack Whyte is stronger than he looks."

Without answering, Shane began to dig.

Chapter 56: A Small Measure of Satisfaction

The shaking of the ground beneath him woke Frank. He felt nauseous, his head pulsing as he rolled onto his side, put his hands on the earth, and pushed up.

Instantly he regretted the decision, and Frank forced himself to get to his knees. The back of his throat went dry, and his stomach threatened to purge itself of what little he had eaten. Instead of vomiting, Frank cursed and spat down between his hands.

He clambered to his feet, took a few tottering steps, and then focused on the sound of a shovel as it struck the earth.

Memory flooded him, and Frank remembered he had gone into the woods with Shane. They were there to dig up Jack's bones and burn them. But Jack had struck him, and done some damage.

The ground shook again, and Frank almost fell.

Dizziness threatened to send him back to the earth, but Frank fought it. He looked around and caught sight of Shane.

The other man dropped the shovel, went down to his knees, and pawed at the earth. Handfuls of rich, dark dirt were thrown aside, and then Shane let out a triumphant yell that caused Frank to wince.

Shane lifted a hand, the flesh dirty, and held aloft a small piece of bone.

A muffled scream ripped through the air, and the earth near the tree rolled as if a great beast was beneath it, struggling to free itself.

"Where's Jack?" Frank asked, his words slow and his throat raw.

Shane, getting to his feet, glanced at Frank.

"Underneath," Shane answered, carrying the bit of Jack's remains to the bone pile.

"Why isn't he up here?" Frank asked.

"Don't worry about that now, Frank," Eloise said, emerging from the center of the tree. "We have to move quickly. He is nearly free."

Shane nodded and picked up a shotgun. Frank went to the same, but Shane stopped him with a sharp, authoritative, "No."

Frank looked at him.

"You're a terrible shot when you've had a head injury," Shane said. "I'll stand guard. You light him up."

Frank gave a small nod, bent over, and steadied himself before he opened the duffel bag. From it, he drew out the kerosene and the matches. He held onto them as he stutter-stepped to the pile. Frank popped the top on the accelerant and sprayed the contents of the entire bottle onto Jack's bones.

He dropped the empty container, lit some of the kitchen matches on the side of their box, and tossed the burning matchsticks onto the bones.

Flames shot straight up.

The earth exploded, dark dirt and leaves raining down upon Shane and Frank. Jack rose up, a demonic expression of pure hatred on his face while he battled the other ghosts. They were a ball of limbs and torsos. Howls and yells filled the air and shook the trees. All the while Jack's bones burned.

"What the hell?" Shane asked.

"You need to get all of the bones!" Eloise called, breaking away from the fight.

"I got them all!" Shane snarled. "Every single one you told me about!"

"I may have missed one," she said in a small voice.

"Where is it?" Frank asked, tearing his gaze away from the fight.

Eloise pointed at Frank's feet. "There."

Frank dropped to his knees and with frenzied motions tore at the dirt with his hands. Another howl tore out and he looked up in time to see Thaddeus thrown aside, the dead boy vanishing.

Jack was stronger than they had thought.

"Leave my bones be!" Jack demanded, striving against the other ghosts.

Frank returned his focus to the dirt.

He continued to dig, further down. Then his hand struck something. He wrapped his fingers around it and pulled out a length of forearm.

"That?!" Shane cried. "That?! How in God's good name did you not see that?"

Eloise turned away and launched herself at Jack. When she struck him, the force of her blow carried all of the dead back into the earth again.

In the sudden stillness, Frank threw the bone onto the pyre, where it landed with a hollow clack and the flames spurted higher.

A high, painful shriek ripped through the air, and a single, pale hand pierced the earth. For a split second, the fingers curled into claws, opening and closing spasmodically.

Then the hand was dragged back down as orange flames turned first pale blue, then dark purple. A foul odor emanated from the bones as they burnt, and Frank turned away. He fell forward and vomited, almost clear bile spewing out in front of him.

Shane remained impassive, the shotgun ready while he watched the fire devour the last vestiges of Jack Whyte.

Chapter 57: Preparing for Slater Mill

Shane handed Frank an icepack before he returned to his seat.

The other man muttered his thanks as he brought the ice up to the side of his head.

In a low voice, Shane asked, "Feeling any better?"

"No," Frank grumbled. "My head's killing me, we stink like death, and we still have to deal with the ghost in the Mill."

"Yeah," Shane agreed. "Sounds about right."

Frank closed his eyes and tilted his head back.

They were both silent for several minutes.

"What's the next step? How soon do we move in?" Frank asked, breaking the silence. "Because honestly, I'm having a difficult time thinking right now."

"Soon, when've recouped," Shane answered. "And then, we burn it to the ground."

Frank opened his eyes and sat up. Although pain flickered across his face, he fixed a hard look on Shane.

"Burn it?"

Shane nodded.

"In the middle of a neighborhood?" Frank demanded.

"I don't have a better idea," Shane snapped. "Jack threw a wrench in our research of Pierre."

Frank straightened up and said, "Then we need to learn what we can. We need to go to the Historical Society and find out where he's buried. Anything. Something. We just can't light a damned building up!"

Shane got to his feet and paced around the room. He knew Frank was right. It wasn't that the idea of burning the place down was offensive. No, he worried about the firefighters, the men and women who would rush into the blaze to try to make certain no one was in there.

Shane couldn't condemn them to death.

Clenching his teeth, Shane went back to his chair and dropped down into it.

"You're right," he admitted.

Frank looked at him. "What do you want to do?"

"I'll go online and look up cemetery databases. In fact, I think there's one called 'Find a Grave.' I'll see if that works," Shane said.

"And if it doesn't?" Frank asked.

"Then we break into the damned Historical Society," Shane grumbled and dug out his cigarettes.

Book 7: Slater Mill

Chapter 58: A Lucky Break

A cool touch woke Shane up from a fitful sleep.

His heart thundered in his chest as he looked around and in the pure darkness, it took him several seconds to realize he was in the library.

He took a deep breath, filling his lungs before letting the air out at a slow, controlled pace. When he felt himself again, Shane said, "Courtney."

"Hello, Shane."

Her voice came from near the door, and there was a curious tone to it. An almost peaceful quality he had last heard when she was still alive.

"Was that you?" he asked.

She laughed. A delicate sound, tinged with madness, but far saner than he remembered. "Yes. What would you have done if it wasn't?"

"Been upset with someone else," he answered. Shane stretched, his eyes adjusting to the darkness. He saw the faint line of light beneath the library door. "I want to thank you."

"For help with Jack?" she asked, and anger filled her voice at the mention of the dead man.

"Yes," Shane said, nodding. He wanted to say more to her. To apologize again for her death, to thank her for her sacrifices. But all of it would sound false, said once too often.

"Jack killed someone in the bathroom," Courtney said.

"He did," Shane said.

"Carl said she tried to kill you," Courtney added.

"And she wanted to kill Frank, too," Shane said.

"Why?" Courtney asked.

"I'm not sure why," Shane said. "But when all of the business with the Mill is done, I'm going to find out."

"You're like a dog, Shane," Courtney said, but there was nothing insulting in her tone. "You sink your teeth into it, and you worry it until it dies."

Shane didn't respond to the statement. Instead, he asked in a small voice, "Will you stay with me?"

She hesitated before she answered.

"Not yet," she said, sighing. "I have trouble. I'm angry, still, and I am afraid it may run its course. I don't want you dead, Shane, in spite of what I've said in the past."

"Okay," Shane said. He cleared his throat, and then repeated the word, louder. "Okay."

A knock sounded on the door, and Courtney said, "Let him in. I'll step away."

Again, Shane nodded, unsure if she could see him in the darkness, and then he turned on the desk lamp and called out, "Come in!"

He was still blinking, his eyes adjusting to the light when Frank stepped in and closed the door behind him. Frank sank into the chair across from the desk and said, "How are you feeling?"

Shane shrugged. "How about you? You're the one who got a solid hit from Jack."

"Better," Frank said. He rubbed at the scar on his face for a moment. "I have good news and bad news about Pierre Gustav."

"Oh good," Shane said. "Love it. Is the good news a slightly less bad version of the bad, or is it actually good."

"Depends," Frank said.

"Of course it does," Shane grumbled. "Hell, let's mix things up and start with the good news."

Frank nodded. "Good news is I found where Pierre's body is buried."

"Damn," Shane said, grinning. "That is good news. Where?"

"That's the bad news," Frank said with a frown. "Lot twelve, row 'F' at Woodlawn Cemetery."

Shane shook his head. "Woodlawn's in the middle of the city. How in the hell are we supposed to dig him up and burn him?"

"Oh," Frank said. "Don't worry about that."

"Why not?" Shane asked, surprised.

"Because Lot twelve refers to the chapel and the ossuary," Frank said, his voice filled with bitterness. "It's where they keep the cremains."

"He's already been burned," Shane said, shaking his head.

"Yeah," Frank agreed.

"Then what in God's name are we supposed to do?" Shane asked.

"I don't know," Frank admitted.

Shane opened his mouth to complain and then snapped it closed, the teeth clicking audibly. "Oh, damn."

"What?" Frank asked, leaning forward. "What is it?"

"When I talked to Trevor," Shane said, shaking his head. "He told me what to look for. He told me!"

"Spit it out," Frank said.

"A finger," Shane said. "He told me he had overheard the owner, Slater, complain about one of Pierre's fingers still being in the Mill. And he wasn't happy about it. Damn it! I just assumed that everything had been buried together."

"Don't worry about that now," Frank said. "Do you think Slater knew about Pierre?"

"Could be," Shane said, disgusted with himself. "But it can't hurt and it gives us a place to look."

"Right, all we need to do is find a finger and then burn it," Frank said.

"All the while dodging Pierre, who's been gathering the dead to him for a couple of weeks now," Shane added. "And I doubt he's going to be easy to take down."

"Yeah," Frank agreed. "You're right about that one. Know anyone we can call on for help?"

"I could try Marie again, but she's about the only one. No one else is really prepared for something like this," Shane said.

Frank looked at him and asked, "Are we?"

"We've faced worse," Shane reminded him.

Frank nodded. "We have indeed. But we also had room to move. And it wasn't in the middle of a city. We've got a lot to take into consideration here. If we didn't think the police would be pleased with us firing off the shotguns in the woods, how happy are they going to be if we start letting off rounds in the Mill?"

"Not happy at all," Shane said. He sighed and shook his head. "You ready?"

"Nope," Frank said, standing up. Then he grinned. "But when has that ever mattered?"

"Never," Shane said, and he felt a grin steal across his own face. "Never."

He got out of his chair, and the two men left the room. Their gear was in the study, and they'd have to make sure they had enough shells for however many dead Pierre had bound to him.

Chapter 59: Getting Dressed

Marie Lafontaine adjusted her uniform, looking at herself in the tall mirror on the back of her bedroom door. The brass buttons on her coat shined against the backdrop of the dark blue fabric. She reached up, fixed one of the bobby pins that held her hair in place and let out a deep breath.

She'd only gotten her uniform back the previous day. A hard rain had fallen on the day of Bill's funeral and she had sent her dress to be cleaned professionally.

And now I'm burying Kurt, she thought, anger and bitterness filled her.

Kurt would be alive if Shane had told him to stay away. To leave the ghosts to someone who at least knew how to handle them properly.

He should have known, she thought bitterly. *Especially after Courtney. Shane should have known.*

It wouldn't have helped Bill she knew, but it definitely would have helped Kurt.

There was word around the station that it had been Lisbeth who had killed Kurt. Marie didn't think so. His ex-wife had been a cold and calculating person. Shooting him down in the middle of the city wouldn't have been profitable.

Lisbeth had already taken him for everything he had.

And Marie knew it couldn't have been the woman, or at least not her alone. Forensics had pulled bullets from two different pistols from the man.

More than likely, Kurt had been in the wrong place at the wrong time.

Marie turned away from the mirror, picked up her dress uniform hat and walked to her bureau. Her phone rang, vibrating beside her wallet.

Frowning, Marie picked the cell up and looked at the caller ID.

It was Shane.

Her thumb rose up, hesitated over the answer button, and then she put the phone back on the bureau. She shook her head.

Later, she thought. *I'll call him later and then we can figure out what to do about the Mill.*

Marie put the phone on mute and slipped it and her wallet into a back pocket.

She fitted the cap down on her head, adjusted it, and left her bedroom. Shane, Frank, and the Slater Mill could wait.

Marie had another funeral to attend.

Chapter 60: The Machine

The looms were constructs of the imagination. And each of them formed part of a whole, massive single entity generating power for the possessor.

For Pierre Gustav.

Souls were bound to the machines, their energy feeding the looms, and those, in turn, feeding him.

He moved up and down the floor on the balls of his feet, as he had when he had still been alive. When he still had feet or anything resembling a body in the true sense of the word.

There had been living people who had visited him. People who spoke French beautifully, potent reminders of his childhood in Canada. They had suggested that he restrain himself, that further expansion of his machine might end badly for him. It had not been a threat, merely a warning. They wanted him to have his power, for whatever excess his workers generated would be sent along the key lines through New England.

But there were others who did not wish Pierre to succeed.

And he knew all about such men.

Three of them had killed him on his work floor. His blood had soaked into the wood, and the building remembered the crime committed against him as well as he did.

The dead crouched at their machines, backs to him, heads bent in submission.

All of it brought a smile to his face and a whistle to his lips.

It was not time to add to the machine. Not yet.

He would prepare for the men who wanted to stop him, and when they failed, when they died beneath his hands or those of his workers, then they too would join the ranks at the looms.

Pierre listened to the thrum of the machines, and he whistled louder.

Chapter 61: Well Planned and Well Executed

Lyndsey, which was the name Abigail now owned, sat in North Station in Boston. She had a Dunkin Donuts coffee in her hand, and a half-finished bagel in the other. Abigail hated them both.

Lyndsey, however, loved them, and if Abigail was going to survive, she needed to be Lyndsey in all things.

All of her credit cards, a checking account, a savings account, and an apartment in Jamaica Plains were all under the name Lyndsey Elwood. Other accounts, established in offshore banks and in countries lacking in extradition treaties, were not part of Lyndsey's history.

They were part of the false trail that Abigail had left. A trail for the Watchers to follow, presumably until her new persona could make it to the mid-West and then up into Canada.

She took a sip of her coffee as an old man sat down next to her. He was far too close for comfort, but it was Boston, and she was in the middle of busy North Station. The old man smelled of aftershave and soap, his clothes pressed. He carried a folded copy of the Boston Globe, and he wore a pair of thick-framed black glasses. From the corner of her eye, she watched him unfold the paper. He selected a section and then folded it again so that only that portion was visible.

After a moment, he turned, looked at her, and smiled.

She forced herself to smile back.

He nodded, returned his attention to the paper, and said in a low voice, "It is quite nice to see you, Abigail."

It took her a split second to realize what he had said, and then it was too late.

Someone sat down beside her, and there was a sharp pain in her left leg. The effects of the toxin were instant, and she found herself pitching forward. Coffee splashed out as the Styrofoam cup was crushed and the bagel went skipping across the stained floor. While she couldn't move or speak, Abigail could hear.

The old man was calling for an ambulance.

From her vantage point on the floor, Abigail saw a pair of EMTs running with a gurney. They were far too quick.

The medics belonged to the Watchers, and she could only wait in paralyzed horror to learn what they would do with her.

A heartbeat later, the old man was kneeling beside her, speaking low and into her ear.

To anyone else, he would have looked like a concerned citizen, a kindly grandfather.

If they had heard him, they would have discovered otherwise.

"You cannot run from us, Abigail," he whispered, a note of pleasure in his voice. "We watch, remember?"

Book 7: Slater Mill

Chapter 62: Preparing to enter the Mill

The plan was simple.

Shane and Frank would enter the Slater Mill and proceed to the second floor, where Pierre had been killed. Somewhere, among the dust of decades, they would find a finger or some other bone fragment. The last vestige of the ghost.

Once it was recovered, they would burn it.

Shane and Frank would have to keep Pierre off balance, a feat which would be difficult considering the ghost's finger was on the same floor. Any effects the salt rounds had on the dead man would be minimal since he would regenerate within a matter of moments.

But Pierre wasn't the only ghost they had to be concerned with.

Shane and Frank had scoured the internet for information on deaths around Slater Mill. What they discovered was that there wasn't much information out there to begin with, and what there was hadn't been good. What was more disturbing was the fact that there hadn't been any reason given as to why it might be haunted. And, from what they could gather, Pierre Gustav had managed to kill at least six people in the past few days. There were rumors that there had been more, random bodies found over the years, but nothing substantial.

Nothing like what had so recently happened.

Shane didn't know if Kurt's death counted. Or if the gangland-style execution of two girls was included. He suspected they might be, and that Pierre had grown strong enough to drag the souls of those who died nearby to him.

The thought was chilling.

With the understanding that they would be facing more than Pierre in the Mill, Shane and Frank had prepared accordingly. They were armed with shotguns and extra shells. Bags of salt and containers of lighter fluid were in backpacks. Matches, too. Iron rings were on their fingers, and Shane's trusted knuckle-dusters were ready as well.

And the last items, for Shane, were his dog tags.

The metal wasn't as cold as it had been. He wore them under his shirt, a reminder of Courtney. Shane also wore them in the hope that she would continue to get better, though he didn't know if such an event could come to pass.

Nothing he had read led him towards that belief.

"You good?" Frank asked, interrupting Shane's contemplation.

"Yeah," Shane nodded. "I'm good. You?"

"Always," Frank answered. "Let's do this."

They climbed out of Frank's car, went around to the trunk, and got their gear out of it. Across from them stood the Mill. Shane saw how the second-floor windows glowed as if the city's ambient light ricocheted off the nighttime clouds and found purchase in the dirty glass.

Shane knew better.

Pierre was behind the glow. Pierre and his captive souls.

Frank pushed the trunk closed, and together they crossed the street towards the Mill.

Chapter 63: An Observation of Tactics

Two men sat in a car parked a block away from the Slater Mill. They each held a small camera, one recording directly to an SD card while the other transmitted the scene to an office in Boston. Neither of the men spoke as they kept the cameras focused on Shane Ryan and Frank Benedict.

Those watching from Abigail's former office had the ability to adjust the camera via a command to the men. None of the observers did so. The men in the car were professionals and to interrupt them could cause a disruption in the feed.

None of the Watchers wanted that.

They were content to observe Shane and Frank, individuals who had significantly disrupted the plans of the organization. Earlier, someone had put forward the idea of another assassination attempt, but it had been cast aside as too risky. Three police officers were dead, one of whom had been an asset. The Nashua PD had already increased its presence in the neighborhood, and an attack on the two troublesome men wasn't worth the risk.

Thus, the Watchers were content with doing exactly what their name implied. They watched as Shane and Frank removed duffel bags from the back of Frank's vehicle. Rings could be seen on the men's hands, and most of those gathered suspected the items were made of iron. The bags themselves more than likely contained the basic tools of any professional ghost killer. Salt, iron, and a means to start a fire.

The observers watched as the men closed the trunk and then crossed the street, the camera keeping them in the center of the frame the entire time. Some of those who watched nodded in approval, appreciating the direct method of Shane and Frank as they walked towards the entrance of the Mill. Others admired the courage of the men.

All of them hated Shane and Frank, for if anyone could disrupt what the Watchers were attempting to build, they saw that it could be the two battle-scarred ghost killers.

In less than a minute, Shane and Frank crossed the road and reached the door. Without hesitation, they entered the building and left the world of the living behind them.

In the office in Boston, an old man with thick glasses and a pressed suit, the one who had been responsible for the apprehension of Abigail, leaned forward. A bony finger reached out, tapped a key on the computer, and said in an old and strong voice, "That is enough, gentlemen. Thank you. Please fall back and return to your assignments."

The view on the monitor winked out, and the old man turned to face the others.

"So," he said, "what shall we do about them?"

In the late hours of the night, earnest and dangerous men discussed the fate of Shane Ryan and Frank Benedict.

Chapter 64: A Brutal Cold

When they reached the second floor, Shane regretted his choice of wardrobe. Before they had left, he had considered a jacket or even a thicker sweatshirt, but in the end, he had sacrificed warmth for maneuverability.

As he shivered outside the door to the work floor, Shane wished he had chosen the jacket.

Pushing the discomfort of the cold out of his thoughts, Shane unslung the duffel bag and put it on the floor. From it, he took his shotgun and stuffed as many spare shells into the front pouch of his hoodie as he could. When he looked like a swollen and pregnant kangaroo, Shane slung the duffel bag back over his shoulder and waited for Frank to do the same.

A soft noise interrupted them both and the two men turned simultaneously and looked at the stairs. From the darkness, a man emerged. His neck was wrapped in a bright white bandage and he looked at them with surprise as he came to a stop a few steps below the second floor.

Shane saw the man had a length of chain in one hand. The old iron links swinging from left to right and back again. He had a fanny-pack on one hip, the zipper half open. Images of various saints hung from cords around his neck.

The man whispered a question to them.

"Have you come for the dead?"

Shane and Frank nodded.

"So have I," he said.

Frank glanced at him, and Shane gave him a thumbs up.

Stepping up to the door, Shane grasped the handle with his diminished left hand and looked back to Frank. The other man held up three fingers, and then silently counted down to zero, and Shane jerked the door backward in its track. By the time it slammed into the stop, Shane and Frank were through the opening and onto the work floor, with the stranger close behind them.

Giant, monstrous looms thrummed and clanked, their noises a curious mixture of real and hollow at the same time. Ghosts worked at the machines, and not a single one of the dead turned their attention to the men.

One of the ghosts, down at the far end, did more than look at them. He started towards them.

"Find the bone," Frank said, and he brought the shotgun up to his shoulder as he advanced on the ghost who moved.

Still holding onto his shotgun, Shane scanned the floor, taking small steps to not miss anything.

Frank's shotgun roared at the same time that Shane saw a pair of tactical boots. He straightened up and found himself in front of Kurt's partner. The man he had tried to save.

"Bill," Shane said, remembering the man's name.

The ghost's eyes widened in surprise. In a voice that was less than a whisper the man said, "Yes."

Before Shane could speak again, Frank yelled out, "Down!"

Shane dropped to the floor, and the shotgun roared again. Scrambling to his feet, Shane twisted around and said, "Bill, I'm looking for a bit of bone. Something that was part of Pierre have you seen anything like it?"

Bill gave a slight nod of assent even as a howl of pain rang out through the second floor.

Shane turned and saw Pierre attack the unknown man from behind. The man let out a grunt of pain, twisted, and swung the chain. When the links passed through Pierre, the ghost vanished.

Frank reloaded the shotgun and fired a single barrel when Pierre appeared on the right. A heartbeat later, the ghost emerged from the shadows and grabbed hold of the unknown man's wrist, above the chain. The man screamed, his eyes widening.

Frank fired the second shot and Pierre vanished. The stranger staggered away, clutching his arm with his free hand. A torrent of Spanish escaped from the man's mouth, and Shane heard them for the prayers they were.

Pierre appeared again, throwing a punch that would have done a professional boxer proud. It connected with the side of the stranger's head, sending him spiraling down. Frank cursed and Shane saw him cast the shotgun down.

The stranger staggered like a drunk, swung his arm in a wide arc and managed to hit Pierre with the chain. A scream of fury exploded from the dead man as he disappeared again.

Pierre appeared behind Frank and kicked him in the back of his knee, causing the man to twist down to the floor, rolling with the blow. As Frank got to his feet, Shane saw the stranger turn on Pierre, the length of chain raised in defense.

Pierre laughed, raced forward, and tried to duck beneath the iron links as they crashed down.

The end of the last piece of metal struck the dead man, and he vanished.

In a heartbeat, Pierre was back, focused again on the stranger. As the ghost grabbed hold of the man's neck, the stranger wrenched one of the icons from around his neck and thrust it into Pierre's chest.

Pierre laughed and then plunged his hands into the back of the man's head. Shane knew the man was dead, and he wondered if the stranger's death had been as painless as it was quick.

As the man collapsed, Frank rushed forward and threw a punch, but the ghost ducked and grabbed Frank's thigh. Frank's eyes bulged, the milky one looking as though it might pop from the pain he was experiencing.

When Pierre yanked his hand back, Frank fell, his shotgun skittering across the floor.

All of the looms had stopped, the ghosts who manned them stared at Frank and Shane with lost, hopeless expressions.

Shane brought the shotgun up to his shoulder and pulled the trigger.

Nothing happened.

The weapon had misfired.

He tried it again, and when it refused to fire once more, he dropped it. Anger flared up in him, and he pulled the knuckle-dusters out of his back pocket, sliding them on. As his rage built up, Shane felt something curious. A sense of power fluctuating around him.

It was a sensation he had last felt at the lighthouse, and before that, it had been when he had faced off against *her*.

An angry, harsh smile spread across his face, and he called out in French, "Come, Pierre, I would have words with you."

The ghost hesitated, surprise flashing across his face.

Whether it was from Shane's knowledge of the man's name, or his ability to speak French, Shane neither knew nor cared.

He straightened up and spread his arms out to either side. The sense of power pulsated around him. It was the strength of the dead, their hatred towards Pierre. Their rage at the prison he had built for them.

Their enslavement.

The dead seemed to feel their energy as it was drawn towards Shane, and they fed it to him. What had been gentle pulses became raw, battering waves. Shane nearly collapsed beneath the weight of it, but he forced himself to remain upright.

To wait for Pierre.

The dead Frenchman seemed to understand what was going on as well, and the look of hate that exploded onto his face told Shane that the ghost would not stand for it.

Up and down the work floor, the dead stepped away from the looms, staring at Shane, funneling all of their energy into him. Shane felt a thousand stings of electricity dance along his flesh, and he laughed.

Pierre Gustav screamed with rage and charged towards him.

Shane stripped off his rings and his knuckle-dusters, dropping the iron to the floor. Then he stepped over them and met Pierre head on.

The ghost slammed into him, rocked Shane on his feet, but didn't knock him down.

Pierre took a surprised step back, his eyes wide.

"Hello, Pierre," Shane whispered, and he punched Pierre in the forehead.

The gathered energy of the dead flowed through Shane and gave force and fury to the blow.

Pierre stutter-stepped backward, his knees wobbling before he fell to the floor. Dazed, the ghost stared up at the ceiling, sinking into the wood.

"No you don't," Shane murmured, leaning over and grabbing the man by the shirt. Shane pulled him back up, dragged him close, and glared at him.

In less than a heartbeat, Pierre realized what could happen to him, and he began to fight.

His blows were ineffective.

They felt like nothing more than the flutter of a butterfly's wings against Shane's skin. There was no bite, no cold.

Shane held him aloft and asked in a cold voice, "Where is your finger, Pierre?"

Pierre shook his head.

Shane reached out with his free hand, put his thumb on Pierre's right eye and said, "Tell me, do you think it will hurt to lose your eye even if you're dead?"

Pierre's lips curled in a sneer, so Shane pressed down on the eye.

The ghost's reaction was instantaneous.

A high-pitched scream shattered the curious stillness of the second floor, and his arms and legs flailed about.

Shane pulled his thumb back and asked again, "Where is your finger, Pierre?"

"Why?" Pierre gasped in French.

"Don't ask why," Shane hissed, and he placed his thumb on the ghost's remaining eye. "Shall I take it? Both of your eyes? Gouge this one right out?"

"No," Pierre moaned. "But you can't have it. You can't."

Shane put pressure on the eye and Pierre screamed.

Easing his thumb back, Shane waited for Pierre to speak.

"To the right," the ghost whispered. "By the policeman."

Shane looked past Pierre to Frank, who sat on the floor, a look of shock on his face.

"Frank," Shane called, "find Pierre's finger!"

Frank hesitated, then nodded. He managed to get to his feet and limp to where Bill stood. In the strange light of the ghostly machine, Frank looked for the bone. A minute later, he dropped down to his hands and knees, dug at a crack, and then held up a small, yellowish object with a triumphant cry.

"Pierre," Shane said, looking back to the ghost, "are there any more bits of you lying about the Mill?"

Pierre shook his head.

"Are you telling the truth?" Shane asked.

Pierre nodded frantically.

"If you're lying," Shane said in a soft voice, "I'm going to tear you to shreds until we find your other parts."

"I'm not lying," Pierre sobbed. "I swear to God above, I am not. But you still haven't told me why. Why do you want it?"

"That's not any of your business, Pierre." To Frank, Shane said in English, "That should be it."

Frank carried the bone back to his duffel bag. As he took out the items needed to burn the last remnant of Pierre, the ghost asked Shane, "What is he doing?"

"Don't worry, Pierre," Shane said.

A moment later, the finger was doused in lighter fluid and set aflame.

Pierre titled his head back and shrieked as bright blue flames erupted from his flesh and clothes. Shane dropped him, although not fast enough. Fire had licked at his arm and set the front of his hoodie ablaze.

"The shells!" Frank yelled.

Without trying to put out the flames, Shane ripped his hoodie off and threw it away from him.

The garment wasn't thrown far enough, and the shells exploded when they struck the floor. Shane found himself falling backward, the blast knocking him down.

He landed on his back, the breath knocked from him. Pierre was beside him, writhing on the floor in agony.

"They'll come for you!" Pierre screamed in French. "They know who you are! They're coming!"

If anything else was said by the ghost, it was lost as Shane passed out.

Chapter 65: Unknown Destination

Abigail awoke in the back of a van. She knew it was a van even though she was blindfolded. Just as she knew her hands and feet were secured with zip-ties. She was on her back, which was painful as well as uncomfortable. Abigail reflected on the fact that she had sent more than a few people to their deaths bound and transported in a similar fashion.

"You're awake," a woman said.

Abigail didn't recognize her, but she still responded. "Yes."

"Good," the woman said. She didn't offer up a rebuke, or condemn Abigail for her attempt to escape the consequences of her actions.

They traveled for a while in silence, the body of the van filled with the steady thrum of the engine and the sound of the wheels on asphalt. Abigail could tell they were on a highway, the noises loud and fast.

"Where are you taking me?" Abigail asked, her voice free of any trembling.

"Do you really want to know?" a man asked.

He too, was a stranger.

"I do," Abigail responded.

Neither the man nor the woman spoke and after several minutes, Abigail resigned herself to the fact that they would not enlighten her.

Then the woman spoke. And she said two words.

"Borgin Keep."

Abigail screamed until her voice broke and she could scream no more.

Chapter 66: Among the Books

Frank had managed to get Shane home and up to the library. Shane had awoken and passed out several times, and Frank was concerned about whether or not his friend had a concussion. He contemplated a phone call to a friend or two with more medical knowledge than himself, but he loathed the idea of involving anyone else in their troubles.

Frank also wanted to know what it was that Pierre had screamed at Shane in the end.

Sitting in the chair across from Shane's desk, Frank had a legal-sized notepad on his lap. He had the numbers one through fifteen written down on the yellow paper. Several names were written in. The two police officers, as well as that of the young man who had been found in the building weeks earlier.

Frank had counted fifteen ghosts other than Pierre in the Mill.

Fifteen bodies that would need to be salted and burned if the souls of the dead were to have any peace.

"Hello," a voice said.

Frank was so startled that he dropped his pen. He looked beyond Shane to see Courtney. She stood behind the unconscious man, her neck slightly crooked. Frank's heart picked up its pace as he remembered how she had wanted to kill him the last time they had been alone together.

"Hello," Frank replied. He still had an iron ring on, and he hoped he wouldn't have to use it.

"What's wrong with Shane?" she asked, looking down at him. She reached out and caressed the side of the man's head, her touch lingering over the mangled left ear.

"We had some trouble," Frank answered.

She nodded.

"You brought him to me," Courtney said after a moment, looking at Frank.

"Yes," Frank replied.

"Why?"

"Because you'll keep him safe," Frank said. "And there are things I need to do tonight. People I need to see. I have to make sure that what was started at the Mill gets finished."

"Yes," she whispered. "I'll keep him safe."

Frank hesitated, then stood up. He clutched the legal pad and asked, "How are you, Courtney?"

She looked surprised at the question, then she smiled and looked down at Shane.

"I am better now that he is here," she answered.

Frank almost spoke again, but instead, he turned away and left the library. He went to his room, to where his laptop was. Frank needed the names of the others who had died.

He wouldn't be able to rest until he knew that they could do the same.

As he entered his bedroom, Frank heard Courtney's voice as she began to sing. Sadness wrapped around his heart and he offered a silent prayer for Shane.

Chapter 67: Awakening

A soft voice, singing an even gentler song, woke Shane up.

He was in pain, and that particular fact didn't surprise him. His attention was focused on the singer, and then on the stunned realization that it was Courtney he heard.

She was beside him, a cold presence pressed close to his own body, and it was comforting. A beautiful, powerful sensation that drove his physical pain into the dark recesses of his mind.

Courtney stopped when she felt he was awake.

"You were hurt again," she said.

"A little," Shane admitted. "Nothing too much though."

She hesitated then said, "You're going to end up dead."

Shane realized it was true.

Is this what I'm trying to do, get myself killed? he asked himself. *And what in the hell would that prove?*

"I don't want you dead," Courtney said softly.

"No?" Shane asked, his voice cracking.

"No," Courtney whispered. "Sometimes, sometimes I do. When I'm here, alone in the library. I remember what it was like to be alive. When you held me. Then I wish you dead. It's like I go crazy, and I try not to. But there's something eating away at me."

She sighed. "In the end, I don't want you dead, Shane. I want you alive. I want you to live. You shouldn't be locked in here with me. With any of us."

"I don't want to leave you," Shane whispered.

"You don't have to," she replied. "But you should rest. I'll be quiet now. No more singing."

"Please," Shane said, his voice hoarse. "Please, don't stop."

"All right," she said, a pleased tone in her voice.

A cool finger caressed the back of his neck, traced the scar that curled up from the collar of his shirt, and Courtney took up the song once more.

Shane closed his eyes, listened to her voice, and dreamed of what life could have been.

* * *

Borgin Keep
Book 8

Book 8: Borgin Keep

Chapter 1: Locked, Barred and Sealed

Borgin Keep was a masterful construction, perched upon a hilltop in Samsett, Vermont. The building dominated the horizon, its stones hewn from the granite hills when the Roaring Twenties were in their infancy and the Great Depression was nothing but a dark nightmare looming in the future.

The various histories written by ambitious members of the Samsett Historical Society described Borgin Keep in less than glowing terms. Emmanuel Borgin was, by all accounts, a wretch of a man. In a time known for brutality and the crushing of workers beneath the combined wheels of progress and industry, Emmanuel exceeded all of his peers. Only the desperate worked for Emmanuel, and in the woods of Vermont and New Hampshire, men were desperate.

Emmanuel's harsh practices filled graveyards even as they raised the walls of the Keep. He was a secretive man who employed over thirty architects for the construction of the Keep, which consisted of ten thousand square feet, and rivaled the gothic structures of Europe. Rumors abounded about secret passages, hidden rooms, and a hallway that felt wrong.

Rich Blonde thought about all of it as he looked at his cameras. He had three of them on the hood of his jeep, each loaded with a high capacity memory card. Rich was clad all in black, not for any fashion statement, but to ensure that his clothes didn't reflect any light.

He stepped back, examined them with a critical eye, and then nodded to himself. From the front seat, he took his GoPro camera, slipped the headset it was attached to into place, and adjusted it. The elastic band fit tight, but it was better than having it loose. A tight fit ensured a great video stream, and live-streaming his adventures paid Rich's bills.

Lots of people, he had discovered, enjoyed the thrill of a life lived vicariously through others. And Rich was happy to provide the thrill.

He had explored abandoned sanitariums, asylums, hospitals, mills, houses, and cemeteries. An entire audience existed for such examinations, especially when it was done illegally. Rich's former life as an accountant was happily forgotten, cast aside for the adrenaline rush of breaking into the building.

He caught himself smiling, and then chuckled. With a swift push he got out of the car, closed the door and locked it. Rich hid the car key in the wheel well of the back tire. With that done, he slipped cameras into the pockets of the black hunting vest he wore. Rich double-checked the laces on his hiking boots, made sure his cell phone was on silent and pulled on his gloves.

Borgin Keep glared down at him from the summit of the hill and Rich gave a nod of respect to it.

The building had claimed its share of urban adventurers. People had gone into it and disappeared. Others had been found half-starved and insane. Plenty had also been caught by the on again off again security service which patrolled the grounds. There was no set schedule kept by the company, and guards were always dropped off so there wasn't a vehicle that could be identified.

Rich had studied Borgin Keep, and he planned on a thorough examination, and documentation of the structure. He even had three hundred dollars to bribe any guards who might interrupt him.

Let's do this, he thought with a nod, and he stepped away from his jeep. He kept to the shadows as the sun set, keeping an eye on the Keep as he moved forward. The closer he drew to the building, the quieter the area became. Soon the only sound Rich could hear was that of his own footsteps, and he was a soft walker.

The lack of birdsong and the silence of the insects sent a thrill of excitement through him. He had read about how animals would abandon a haunted place. Rich had no fear of ghosts. He knew, in spite of the protests of some doomsayers, that ghosts couldn't harm people.

Rich hoped he might catch something on film. Maybe some of the orbs he had seen on various ghost specials on TV, or even a figure.

Shots like those would cause a spike in his audience, which meant more money at the end of the week.

Grinning, Rich was filled with excitement. He forced himself to keep a steady pace and to continue looking out for guards.

None appeared, and in a matter of moments, Rich found himself standing at Borgin Keep.

The walls towered above him, the stones massive and the windows set deep within carved alcoves. Bars were crisscrossed over each window, and wood had been nailed in place from the interior of the building. Broken glass littered the sills and glinted in the last of the day's light. The air was colder near the Keep as if it rejected the sun and the warmth it provided.

The chill stole some of the excitement Rich felt. With a hand that trembled, he reached up and turned on his GoPro camera. He thought about the Keep, remembered the layout of the exterior, and continued on to the right. Some bloggers had said the main entrance was set with an electronic trip alarm, but for some reason, the kitchen door wasn't.

It took him several minutes to make it around to the back of the Keep. He passed dead bushes, and what looked like the rotted remains of a rabbit pressed up against the stone. A hedgerow garden stretched out behind the house, a malignant entity that flowed down several terraces.

Rich paused as he realized the garden was a maze, a dark structure in the center of it. His eye kept returning to the small building, almost a mausoleum, the copper roof green with patina.

Rich's stomach turned and threatened revolt as he looked at it. Finally, he was able to tear his gaze away and hurry with clumsy steps to the kitchen door.

The door looked as though it had been carved from a single piece of dark wood. It was tall and narrow, and Rich wondered if he would have to angle his shoulders to get in. A quick search of the door revealed that it lacked a handle, latch, lock, and hinges.

With his heart thumping in his chest, Rich reached out and put his fingertips on the door.

It swung in without a sound and Rich's breath caught in his throat.

The cold air of the house slammed into him, settled into his bones, and set his teeth to rattling.

For the first time, Rich felt unsure about what he was about to do.

He recalled all of the stories he had read about the Keep and how he had dismissed them.

Maybe, he thought, hesitating at the threshold, *maybe there's some truth to it all.*

Rich shook his head. *Even if there is, ghosts still can't hurt you.*

With a deep breath, Rich walked into the kitchen.

Chapter 2: Making a Decision

"Has she been moved?" the old man asked.

"Yes," Ms. Coleman answered.

"Excellent." He took his thick framed glasses off, picked up a maroon polishing cloth from the leather blotter, and cleaned the lenses. "Do we have an asset willing to take on the assignment?"

"Yes," Ms. Coleman replied. "He'll be down from Bennington tomorrow morning. The assignment should be concluded in the late evening or early morning."

"Very good," he said, smiling. He put his glasses back on and asked, "Tell me, Ms. Coleman, someone has secured a delivery vehicle?"

Ms. Coleman nodded. She knew the 'someone' he spoke of was her. "Yes, sir. We've obtained a DHL van, with the appropriate uniform."

"That, Ms. Coleman," the old man said, "is some of the best news I have heard today. Now, tell me, has there been any news from the team in southern New Hampshire?"

"Yes, sir," she replied. "They report that there is a house on Concord Street which may serve as a replacement stop on the ley line for the loss of Slater Mill. Also, further up in Merrimack along the Daniel Webster Highway. They have not reached out to the dead yet."

The old man nodded, turned in his chair, and glanced out the plate glass window at the world beyond the office.

Ms. Coleman wondered, briefly, what it was the man thought about.

"One last question, Ms. Coleman," he said, facing her once more.

"Sir?"

"When Abigail was here, did she have you make coffee or did she send out for it?" he asked.

The question caught her off guard, and she almost stuttered as she answered him. "It depended on the day. More often than not I made her coffee in the front office."

He nodded. "Would you please make me a cup? Black and strong, if you could."

As pleasant as the request was, Ms. Coleman knew it was a command.

"Yes, sir," she said and hurried out of the room. As she went about readying the Keurig, Ms. Coleman hoped they would find a replacement for Abigail soon.

Ms. Coleman's hands trembled as she poured water into the reservoir, trying not to think of the old man in the other room.

Chapter 3: Thinking of a Threat

Shane sat at his desk in the library. The drapes were tied back, and sunlight streamed into the room. One of the windows was open half an inch, and a cool wind came in, moving through the library while seeming to promise a warm and pleasant spring.

Courtney had been silent for days, and Shane worried about her lack of communication. While she made progress in regards to regaining her sanity, she did have bad days. Shane feared that on such a day, she might decide to kill him and he, in turn, would have to try and do the same to her. The idea of destroying the spirit of the woman he had loved pained him, and so Shane focused on an external problem.

The last ghost he had faced had threatened him. Not with spiritual retribution, but physical. And from someone in the land of the living as well.

The Watchers.

He had done random searches on the web, tightening the questions as he went. Yet regardless of how deep he went, he couldn't find anything other than rumors. Blogs and websites, nothing official, hinted at a widespread organization that focused on the dead. Of how they conducted human sacrifice to obtain the support of spirits. Some bloggers had even speculated that the Watchers practiced ritual cannibalism.

Shane shook his head. Some of what was written could be true. Perhaps none of it. Maybe even all of it. He had come to the conclusion that he was going to have to go deeper. And deeper meant the dark web.

Shane looked at his new laptop. He would need to download software, access the deep web, and then find his way to the dark web. Shane hated the dark web because of the people and things that hid there.

But he had been threatened, and he was going to find out who the Watchers were.

Shane powered up the laptop and lit a cigarette as he waited. He took a pad of paper out from the desk and a pen as well. Whatever information he needed would have to be written down, remembered, and destroyed.

He already knew the Watchers used dirty cops. Leaving an electronic trail wouldn't be the best way to protect himself.

Shane tapped the head of his cigarette into the ashtray by the lamp and typed in his password.

It was time to hunt down the Watchers.

Chapter 4: Inside Borgin Keep

The darkness had swallowed Rich.

His flashlight's thin, powerful beam cut through the dark, but that was the only light he had. He had never been in a place where darkness was so complete. No hint of the sunset crept in through the boarded windows.

Rich was alone in the Keep, the soles of his boots whispering along the polished wood of the main hallway. His heart thumped in his chest, an uncomfortable feeling that made him question his decision to enter the building.

He pushed the doubts and worries aside.

It wasn't only the money driving Rich forward; it was his reputation.

His audience had an expectation, a belief in Rich's ability to go into places no one else would. Confidence in his personal strength.

Rich's ego wouldn't let him endanger his status through cowardice.

You've been in over thirty 'haunted' buildings, Rich reminded himself. *This one's a little darker. A little scarier. Nothing you can't handle.*

He straightened up, squared his shoulders, and forced himself to slow down. In his previous life as an accountant, he had known stress. Real stress. Long hours and irate clients. Angrier full partners who didn't appreciate a talented new hire who could run circles around them when it came to balancing books and making sure the clients came out on top.

Rich smiled at the memory, turned his head, and came to a stop. The beam of his flashlight played along the wall, coming to rest on a door.

In form, the door was exactly that. A tall and wide affair of dark wood with a cut crystal knob set within a silver lock plate.

Attached to the frame was a heavy latch, one which was connected to a ring on the door. And joining the two together was a lock.

A large lock that consisted of both a combination and a key.

It was new. The metal gleamed and kept his eye as he took a step towards it.

Someone had entered the Keep, attached the latch and the lock.

Rich kept the beam on the door and reached out with his free hand, taking hold of the lock. He gave it a gentle tug, but it was secured.

He wiped his hand on his palm, the metal leaving what felt like a trace of oil on his skin.

Rich leaned forward, letting the lens of the GoPro focus on the lock, and then he heard it.

A soft scratching sound at the bottom of the door.

Rich gasped and stumbled back, his boots squeaking across the wooden floor. He hit the far wall and slid down to sit and stare at the door. Terror gripped him, and he was unable to move. He couldn't tear his eyes away from the barred room. An instinct screamed at him to run, howled about a danger beyond the door, but Rich couldn't listen to it.

His eyes were fixed on the door, he could hear nothing but the scratching against the wood.

A moment later, a small shape probed the gap between the wood of the floor and that of the door. It took several seconds for Rich to understand he was looking at a finger. A long, narrow finger. The flesh was pale, almost gray. Its fingernail was a putrid black. Soon the finger was joined by a second, then a third.

Finally, all four fingers were beneath the door, and they curled up, the nails digging into the finish. Rich saw how the nails were ragged, broken, and chipped. When they were settled in, the fingers tensed, and the door shook in its frame.

Gently at first, then violently.

The metal of the doorknob groaned in protest, and soon the latch sounded the same.

Before Rich could react, the latch broke and clattered against the door frame, the lock thumping against the wood.

Rich pushed himself against the wall, his chest rising and falling, his breath racing out of control. He couldn't move, petrified as he watched the door move inward inch by inch. The hinges were silent while the sound of his blood was a thunderstorm in his ears.

When the door reached the end of its arc, cold air streamed out.

Rich's hand shook as he lifted the flashlight up, pointing the beam into the depths.

A room, with sheet-draped furniture, was illuminated. Paintings in ornate frames hung upon the walls and mirrors were shrouded with black cloths.

Not a sign could be seen of the person who had ripped the door open.

Rich tried to move but found his body was mutinous, the muscles refusing to obey his commands. He couldn't get his heart to slow, and he could hardly think with the way his blood pounded in his skull.

With a dry swallow, he closed his eyes, counted to ten, and opened them.

Nothing.

The room beyond was still barren of life, populated only by shrouded furniture.

Rich managed a deep inhalation, then he let it out as slowly as he could. He kept his eyes open and counted to ten once more. A nervous smile twitched on his face. Rich chuckled, shook his head, and got to his feet. His legs were weak, the muscles trembling from fear.

He cleared his throat, shook his head, and took a step towards the open door.

And so did someone else.

A woman.

She wore a ragged gray nightgown, the hem of it dragging on the floor. Her hair, what was left of it, hung in twisted locks. The right corner of her upper lip twitched, and her nostrils flared. She stared at him with empty sockets, black holes where the eyes should have been.

And through those holes, Rich could see the wall behind her.

She opened her mouth, the teeth jagged and broken. The scream which followed filled the Keep. When she closed her mouth and grinned at him, Rich realized it was his own voice he heard.

Rich turned to run, but he was too slow.

Far too slow.

She slammed into his back, and he felt the bones break. He went numb from the waist down, and he tumbled to the floor, his own inertia and gravity driving him into the wood.

His teeth shattered on impact and blood exploded in his mouth. The flashlight smashed and rolled, the light dancing across the walls without rhyme or reason.

While he coughed and sputtered, Rich tried to use his hands to crawl forward.

Instead, he was dragged backward and into the room.

Before he could stop his momentum, the door slammed closed, and Rich was plunged into darkness.

Chapter 5: Ley Lines

The Abbott poured Frank a cup of tea, put the pot down on the stove, and sat down at the small table.

Between them was a large book, nearly two feet long and a foot across. There was no writing to break the smooth leather of the cover, but a silver latch kept it closed. The Abbott reached out, unlocked it, and opened the book. The smell of old paper filled the room, and Frank leaned forward to read the title page.

He found he couldn't. The words were a mixture of both Latin and Greek, and they had been handwritten.

"What is it, Abbott?" Frank asked, sitting back. He picked up the teacup and let the tea-heated porcelain warm his own hands.

"This is a book," the Abbott replied, a grin on his old face.

Frank chuckled. "Fair enough."

"Tell me, Frank," the Abbott said, "where was the first place you worked with Shane?"

"Sanford," Frank replied.

"Alright," the Abbott said. He turned several pages, stopped on an index of place names, and then found the name 'Sanford,' which he pointed out to Frank.

"Yes," Frank said, leaning forward. "That's it."

The Abbott nodded and turned to the page the index indicated.

A well-illustrated map of the hospital's front was on the page. At an angle, a deep blue line was drawn leading up to the structure.

"What is that?" Frank asked.

The Abbott held up a finger and inquired, "The next place?"

"Kurkow," Frank answered.

The Abbott went back to the index and Kurkow was there as well. When he turned to it, there was a drawing of the prison set onto the page. Like Sanford, there was a blue line leading up to the prison, and then through it.

"Next?" the Abbott asked, a concerned tone in his voice.

"Nutaq," Frank replied.

Nutaq was in the book as well.

"And the last?" the Abbott asked.

"Slater Mill."

After the Abbott found it, and the corresponding blue line, he was silent. Frank kept his mouth closed and waited.

Finally, the Abbott closed the book, secured the latch, and looked at Frank.

"You are wondering why they each have a blue line piercing them?" the Abbott asked.

Frank nodded.

"Each place you mentioned," the Abbott said. "Each place you have been with Shane Ryan, where you have fought the angry dead, all of them are on ley lines."

Frank frowned. "What's a ley line?"

"They are paths of power," the Abbott said. "A source of spiritual energy. They are a place where the veil is thin between the worlds. Between Heaven and Earth, Earth and Hell. Many of those who do not move on can be found along these lines."

"Oh," Frank said. "That doesn't exactly sound like a good thing, Abbott."

"It's not," the Abbott said. He shook his head. "It is troubling that you have encountered so many on the same lines. Has anything else occurred, Frank? Anything strange, but could not be described as supernatural?"

"We had a woman try to kill us," Frank said.

The Abbott raised an eyebrow in surprise and waited for Frank to continue.

"She was an assassin, evidently," Frank said, shaking his head. "She showed up one morning, forced her way in, and tried to shoot us both."

"Ah," the Abbott said. "And she wasn't known to him? This wasn't a lovers' quarrel?"

"No," Frank said. "She was there for a job. Someone wanted us dead, and for what we had been doing."

"You need to find out why, Frank," the Abbott said. "You are quite close to something, perhaps closer than most have ever been."

"What?" Frank asked. "Abbott, what are you talking about?"

The Abbott shook his head. "I cannot tell you. To do so might affect the conclusions you come to. You must promise me, Frank, that you will tell me as soon as you know anything. And not by telephone or by email. You must come in person, or, if you absolutely cannot come, mail me a letter."

"Yes, Abbott," Frank said. "I don't understand, though."

"I can only offer you advice," the Abbott said, giving Frank an apologetic smile. "I wish I could tell you more. But as I said, whatever conclusions you come to must be achieved on your own. I will tell you to be safe. And to not take any chances. Do you understand?"

"Yes, Abbott," Frank said.

"I do have one suggestion," the Abbott said after a short silence.

"Yes?" Frank asked.

"If you have any pistols, I would suggest you carry one," the Abbott said. "I feel your most dangerous adversaries are still breathing."

Chapter 6: In the Night, They Came

The sky was free of the moon, and the stars were dulled by the warm temperatures. Beyond them, the house was dark, and in it was a dangerous man and his wife.

The team outside of the house consisted of six men and women. They were all professionals, and therefore nothing was left to chance. One had slipped close to the house, pressed against the stone foundation as he ran a tap on the old phone line box. All outgoing landline calls would be routed on a loop, and the router was crashed with a short pulse. A scrambler on the man's hip ensured that all cell service was disrupted. He was armed with a nine millimeter Glock with a suppressor, as were all of his colleagues.

The house had two entrances, one at the front and one at the back. One pair had positioned themselves at the back, the other at the front. A solo shooter took the left side, the tech with the scrambler covered the right.

There was no signal given. They had the timing of their work finely tuned, and each knew their jobs.

The breaching teams entered through their respective doors. They wore night-vision goggles, and their feet were silent. And while they noticed everything, nothing distracted them.

They were, above all else, professional.

There was no animosity in their acts. All of it was done with a minimal amount of pain to the target. Other teams specialized in torture and terror.

Within less than thirty seconds, they had reached the bedroom, where the target and his wife lay in their bed. The couple slept peacefully, and they died the same way. Two shots each to the head.

The leader of the team stepped forward, handed her pistol to one of her colleagues, and received a surgical saw. With long practiced motions, she removed the man's head. When she finished, both the instrument and the severed head went into a bag brought specifically for that purpose. She exchanged the bag for her weapon, and they left the house in the same silence they had entered it in.

The team had been inside for less than three minutes, and in the same amount of time, they slipped onto the next street. A pair of nondescript sedans were parked in front of an apartment building. The team got into their appointed vehicles, and in a moment, the stillness of the night was broken by the sound of the engines starting.

With the head tucked away from prying eyes, the team drove towards Boston.

They had a delivery to make.

Chapter 7: Making Decisions

"I don't know if it's worth it," Shane said. He lit a cigarette and looked at Frank. "From what I could find out, and I'd only dug around for a little while, is that they're focused on purchasing places where the dead are active. Or have been active. There's no real explanation why."

"It has to be something serious," Frank said. "Come on, they were willing to kill us."

"And I want to hurt them for that," Shane said. "Don't doubt that. But I don't know if we should go after them right away. I need a breather. At least a little bit of time."

"Sure," Frank said. "I get that. But I wonder, if we know about this, Shane, shouldn't we do something about it? And sooner rather than later?"

"No. Because all we know," Shane said, "is that someone's been protecting the dead on ley lines. We don't know why. I don't think we need to look into that right away. Not right now. Like I said, I need a breather, Frank. I'm not going to lie. The Watchers are extremely well organized and they are, without any doubt, extremely dangerous as well. If we're going to take them down, then we need to make sure that we do it right. No mistakes, nothing done halfway."

Then Shane let out a sigh, shook his head, and added in a low voice, "And Lisbeth, she was hard to deal with."

"What made it difficult?" Frank asked. There was nothing malicious in the question, only an honest curiosity.

Shane hesitated, then sighed. "I'm not sure. I did a lot when I was in the Corps. She reminded me of them. What I had to do."

"Yeah," Frank said, nodding. "I get that. I wonder, though, do you think she was watching you for these people, whoever they are?"

Shane shook his head. "Hell, I don't want to think about that."

"Doesn't matter," Frank said. "You need to. I mean, if they've been watching you, do they know about your house?"

Shane nodded in affirmation.

The doorbell rang, and before Shane could stand up, Frank had risen from his seat. "I got it. Need to stretch my legs."

Shane shrugged as Frank left the study. When the door opened, Shane could hear Frank speak with someone, thank them, and then a thump as the world was locked out once more.

"So," Frank said, entering the room carrying a small box. "What'd you get me?"

"A carton of cigarettes so you could start the habit," Shane replied, straightening himself in the chair. "Seriously, though, I have no idea."

"Well, it's got your name on it," Frank said, handing the package over before sitting back down.

"Damn," Shane said in surprise. "It's heavy."

The box was big enough to hold a basketball and had a shipping label from a firm in Boston. Webb and Fenster. Shane read his name on the package, and saw his address. Even the email he used for his translation work was there. DHL had delivered it, same day.

"You're not expecting anything?" Frank asked.

"No," Shane said. "But it's got my work email on it. I might have ordered something. Back before everything went absolutely crazy in my life."

"Come on, no more suspense," Frank said, grinning. "Tell me, what exciting material did you order for your enthralling translating work?"

Shane snorted, stubbed out his cigarette in the ashtray and picked at the edge of the tape. In a moment, he stripped it away, pulled the cardboard flaps open, and looked inside. Greenish white packing peanuts greeted his eye, and Shane shook his head. He picked them out, a handful at a time, and then his fingers hit something hard, almost rubbery.

"The hell?" he murmured. Shane reached both hands in and stopped.

"What is it?" Frank asked. "Shane? Hey, you just lost all of the color in your face."

"Yeah," Shane whispered. He withdrew his hands and looked at them. They were covered in blood. Drying, congealing blood.

"Oh, man," Frank said, standing up. "That's not your blood."

"No," Shane agreed. "It's not."

"Whose is it then?"

"It feels like a head in here," Shane said. He took a deep breath and said, "I'm going to reach my hands back in and get a hold of it. Do me a favor, will you?"

"Sure," Frank said, nodding.

"Grab the box for me, this might be a tight squeeze," Shane said.

"Yeah," Frank said.

Shane pushed his hands in again, grasped the unknown head, and nodded to Frank.

Frank took hold of the box and held it as Shane pulled.

The head came out, packing peanuts dropping lazily to the floor.

Shane turned the head around in his hand and looked into the face of his friend, Mason.

Chapter 8: A Day Disrupted

Frank sat alone in the kitchen.

On the table was an unopened letter. It had come with Mason's head, and Shane had left it in the study. Frank had carried it into the kitchen, following Shane. Shane, who had carried Mason's head into the pantry, then closed the door behind him.

"Is it true?" Carl asked, appearing from the wall beside the refrigerator.

Frank nodded.

"Thaddeus said he descended into the root cellar," Carl said, glancing at the pantry door.

"Maybe," Frank said. "I don't know."

"Do you know of the root cellar?" Carl asked.

Frank shook his head. "No. Didn't even know there was one."

"There is," Carl said. "It is where the dark ones are. The root cellar is where Shane's parents went when he was away for his military training. They never returned."

Frank looked at Carl in surprise. "Why is he down there?"

"I do not know why," Carl answered. "He is safe, though. No one could be safer. Not in this house."

The pantry door opened and Shane stepped into the room, blinking at the light. His hands were empty but still bloody, his face an image of controlled rage. He crossed the room in silence and went to the sink. After he had turned on the water, he tore off a paper towel, used it to open the cabinet and took out a container of sugar. Frank watched in silence as Shane used dish-soap and the sugar granules to scrub the blood from his skin.

When Shane finished, he took several more paper towels and dried his hands as he walked to the table. Frank didn't say anything as Shane sat down.

Carl, too, remained silent, and Frank and the dead man watched Shane pick up the letter. Shane opened it, the muscles in his jaw twitched as he set the envelope down and looked at the document within. When he was done with it, Shane handed the letter to Frank.

> *Dear Mr. Ryan,*
>
> *I trust that this letter finds you well and that you have received our message. In case you are unable to understand it, I shall translate for you.*
>
> *I am going to kill everyone you know, if you continue to disrupt the plans and goals of this organization. I have started with your friend, Mason, and his wife, because they were the nearest targets. I will work my way outward, throughout the country if I have to. And quite frankly, Mr. Ryan, I will kill Mr. Benedict's family and friends as well, should I run out of yours.*
>
> *Now, since I have established my position, I will explain exactly what I want from you. Cease and desist all activities relating to the neutralization or the destruction of any spirits in which you might come in contact with. In simple language, Mr. Ryan, stay home. While I take no pleasure in the death of your friend, I will not hesitate to do what is necessary to ensure the success of this organization's goals.*
>
> *I have included a card with a phone number on it. Should you feel the need to verify the truth of my statement, please, call it. You will find a comprehensive list of men with whom you served, and women with whom you were once on intimate terms.*
>
> *Sincerely,*
> *Harlan Canus*
> *The Watchers*
>
> *P.S. I am sorry that my predecessor activated Lisbeth. She was an exceptionally talented asset and I regret her loss. I hope you have disposed of her body properly. Perhaps Mason's head will join her?*

The letter shook in Frank's hands as he folded it and set it down on the table.

"Why Mason?" Frank asked after a moment of silence. "Why not us?"

"They couldn't get to us after Lisbeth," Shane said, his voice hoarse with rage. "Not with all of the dead around. They want us to dig in here, stay safe, and try to figure out what they're going to do next. Or maybe even believe them and not do anything in order to save our people."

"You don't think they will?" Frank asked.

"They might kill a couple more of mine if I try to do anything," Shane said. His eyes were hard, filled with hatred. "They may even kill a few of yours. If we don't stop, they'll panic. Maybe they'll try to come directly at us again, instead of through someone like Mason."

Frank wanted to disagree, but he couldn't.

Shane was right.

"They will try," Shane said, as he spat out each word. "We'll have to warn them. All of them."

"I don't have much in the way of family," Frank said, "but I do have the Abbot. I'll reach out to those I can. The Abbot should be alright."

Shane nodded. "I'll get in touch with the Roys. They're the closest. I don't think this Harlan will reach out too far. Not yet."

Frank sat and read the letter again while Shane took out his phone and sent a text.

Frank thought about the Watchers, and what the threat meant. If they were willing to kill in order to keep Shane and himself away from their plans, then it meant something terrible was on the horizon.

And it would more than likely kill more than a few people.

Shane's phone chimed and a moment later the man let out a sigh of relief.

"Everything's good?" Frank asked.

"Yeah," Shane replied, putting his phone down. "Brian says he has more than enough protection. His own ghosts won't let anyone near the property. I'll have to dig around to find out the numbers for my older friends."

"Same here," Frank said.

Silence filled the kitchen and then Frank asked, "What now?"

"We find out who they are," Shane said. "We find out what they want to do. And we find out where to hit them next."

Frank nodded, looked at the letter and then to Carl. "Think you could find out about who the Watchers are?"

Carl hesitated and said, "There is a possibility."

"You have someone you can ask?" Shane said, surprised.

"Yes," Carl said, clearing his throat. "Yes. There is."

"Really?" Frank asked.

"Yes," Carl said, and he looked uncomfortable as if the questions bothered him.

"Carl," Shane said. "Is there something you haven't told me?"

Carl answered in German, and Shane shook his head.

"You're kidding me," Shane said, dropping his chin to his chest. "You have got to be kidding me."

"What?" Frank asked, confused. "What the hell did he say, Shane?"

"Tell him," Shane said, without looking up.

"Shane," Carl pleaded.

"*Jetzt!*" Shane snapped in German.

Carl stiffened, turned to face Frank, and said, "We will be able to question Lisbeth."

It took a moment for the statement to register, and when it did, Frank asked, "How?"

Carl looked at Shane, who continued to stare down at the table, and then his shoulders slumped.

"Eloise and Thaddeus," Carl said, his accent thickening with his stress. "They didn't let her spirit leave after Jack killed her. She is trapped here as well. We could question her."

Frank was too shocked to answer.

Shane lifted his head, his eyes red, his muscles standing out along his chin.

"Let's get it over with," Shane hissed, and he got out of his chair.

"Eloise!" Shane yelled as he stormed out of the kitchen. "Thaddeus! Get down here now!"

Carl sighed and shook his head.

"Hasn't he learned yet?" Carl asked, glancing at Frank. "They only hide when he yells."

Chapter 9: In Darkness and Despair

Rich was naked on a cold, stone floor, and he begged God to wake him up.

But God didn't listen.

Curled in a ball, Rich whimpered and tried to remember what had happened. Nothing came to him. All he had was a vague recollection of a voice, a woman's voice, begging someone to spare her.

God hadn't answered her either.

Something cold crawled over his right ankle, and it burned, causing him to jerk his foot away. But whatever gripped him refused to let go. Then a second hand pressed upon his hip, followed by a third and a fourth. Rich screamed at the pain, a sharp cold that drove through his flesh and settled into his bones. As he screamed, the hand on his ankle pulled, extending his leg.

Laughter rang out, and voices spoke in a language he didn't understand, the words painful to his ears. Then something pierced the side of his knee and Rich shrieked. He felt the joint tremble and then give way. Something sawed at his flesh, and a moment later, he heard a horrific pop.

The pressure on his hips vanished, and the grip on his ankle did as well. Within seconds, a rope of some sort was tied around his thigh, cinched down so tight that stars exploded in front of his eyes.

Rich twisted away and into a puddle of warm liquid. The stench of iron filled his nose, and he had a difficult time as he tried to crawl away. His right foot was numb, and he couldn't find any purchase with it. Rich held back a sob as his fingers found gaps in the stone floor and he pulled himself forward. Soon he struck a wall, then he followed it until he found a corner, and he huddled there, curled once more in a fetal position.

A woman babbled nearby, her words unintelligible aside from a few here and there that he understood. She was asking someone for forgiveness. Asking to be let out. Asking to be given a second chance to prove herself.

No one answered her, although laughter occasionally rang out in the room.

Rich was dizzy, his right thigh throbbed, and he wondered what he had done to deserve the pain he was suffering.

Then he remembered the door. And he saw again the figure at the door.

And Rich knew what it was he had done.

He had gone into Borgin Keep, and the dead had been displeased.

Chapter 10: Questions and Answers

Shane was in his bedroom with the dresser moved away from the wall and pushed towards the door. He had torn down the wallpaper his father had put up decades earlier, revealing the secret door. His mouth had gone dry looking at it, remembering the fear he had felt as a child.

Frank sat on his bed, and Carl stood beside it. Eloise and Thaddeus hid in the pantry.

"They said she is in there?" Carl asked.

Shane nodded.

"Behind the door?" Frank asked.

"Beyond it," Shane answered. "Further in. Somewhere in the walls."

"Is it safe for you to go in there?" Frank questioned.

Shane glanced at his friend. "Who knows."

"I shall go with you," Carl said.

"No," Shane said, his tone sharper than he had intended. In a gentler voice, he said, "No. I need you here, with Frank. I will speak with Lisbeth. If she doesn't listen to me, or won't answer any questions, then I will have you go in."

Shane stepped forward and squatted down. He found the hidden trigger at the top of the door, and he pressed it. The house seemed to sigh as the door swung out. Darkness waited for him, absorbing the light of the room.

Carl murmured, "Do you need a flashlight?"

"No," Shane said, getting down on his hands and knees. "I know my way around."

Without another word, he crawled forward and entered the space between the walls. The door remained open behind him as he turned to the right, his hands guiding him. In a few seconds, he was in complete darkness, a solid, impenetrable black. Cobwebs gathered and broke against his face like waves on a sea wall. The passage smelled of stale air with an underlying scent of mustiness.

He continued to move forward, fighting back memories of being chased in the walls. Of screaming for help.

Perspiration broke out on his forehead and along the back of his neck. His underarms became soaked and his breath caught in his throat. He was afraid, and he had no reason to be.

Not true, he told himself. *What if she slipped out, the same way Courtney had? Will Lisbeth kill me here?*

He didn't have to answer the question. Shane knew she would.

Then the passage brightened. A gentle glow at first, then it grew in strength. Soon he found himself in a small, circular room. Windows were covered in heavy drapes, and the room wasn't more than eight feet in diameter. Old toys were scattered around the edges, and a threadbare carpet covered the floor. The walls had built-in shelves, and these too were populated with toys.

A mirror caught Shane's attention. It was small, similar to one that could be found on a vanity, and it rested on an easel. The glass, Shane saw, reflected nothing.

Looking at it made his skin crawl. He hesitated before he moved forward and straightened up. His head bumped into the ceiling, and he grumbled as he sat down on the carpet.

The mirror reflected movement, and he looked at it and stiffened.

The movement hadn't been reflected in the mirror but came from behind it.

Lisbeth glared at him. Her face was puffy and battered, her neck marked with Jack's hand prints.

Shane looked at her and then said, "Hello, Lisbeth."

She didn't answer.

"How are things?"

Lisbeth's answer was a torrent of profanity.

When she finished, he gave her a small, tight smile. "Nice to see you, too. Now I have some questions for you."

"You know what you can do with your questions," she snarled. Her words reached his ears half a second after her lips formed them, like a badly dubbed movie.

"I do," Shane said. "I can ask you, and then you can answer."

She snorted.

"Now," Shane said. "I want to know about the Watchers."

Lisbeth laughed and shook her head. It looked as though she wanted to leave, but she was trapped within the narrow confines of the mirror's frame.

"Tell me about them," Shane said.

She glared at him and answered, "No."

"Yes."

"No," she spat. "I'm already dead. You can't do anything more to me."

"Don't believe that," Shane said, his voice low. "Don't ever believe that."

A look of doubt flickered across her face, but it vanished quickly.

"And why not?" she asked with a sneer.

"Because you are in a house with some angry ghosts," Shane answered. "And you tried to hurt me. They don't take kindly to that sort of thing."

"They can't hurt me," Lisbeth declared.

"They can. They will. And you won't like it," Shane said. He crossed his arms over his chest and said, "Tell me about the Watchers."

"Here's a bit of information about the Watchers for you," she said, her voice hard and angry. "You're out of your league with them. You have no idea what they can do."

"Sure, I do," Shane whispered. "They sent an assassin in to kill me and my friend. When that didn't work, they took the head of another friend and mailed it the next day to me. I can tell you that's not going to work either. In fact, I would consider it to be a significant error on their part. I had just decided to not worry about the Watchers before they delivered Mason's head."

Lisbeth looked surprised.

"Did they move quicker than you expected?" Shane asked.

She didn't answer, which was enough of an answer.

"Alright," Shane said, "since we know where I'm coming from, and you know that I have no qualms about torturing you, tell me about the Watchers."

With a grimace, she said, "They are an organization that watches the dead."

"All of the dead, or just a few chosen ones?" Shane asked.

"Only a few," Lisbeth answered in a halting voice.

"Why?"

She looked away.

"Why?!" Shane yelled.

Lisbeth glared at him. "To restore balance to the world."

"What?" Shane asked, taken aback.

"In this time," she said, "people live long. Far too long. There is no longer a true and healthy fear of death. The Reaper does not walk among the living."

"And they want that?" Shane asked. "To bring the Reaper here?"

"In a sense," she answered. "They want to unleash a few of them. Fifteen, maybe twenty. They've been cultivating the dead for decades, building them up. Some they feed the living to. Others are strong enough already. Your little ghostbusting adventures have set them back by at least ten years. Maybe more."

"And that's why they wanted me dead," Shane said.

Lisbeth nodded.

"They killed Mason because of it," Shane continued.

"Yes," she said.

"Where are they located?" Shane asked. "Boston?"

"I don't know," she said, a note of stubbornness in her voice.

"Yes, you do," Shane retorted. "Where in Boston?"

Lisbeth didn't answer.

"Tell me where," Shane hissed.

She turned her back to him in the mirror.

"Alright," Shane said, nodding to himself. "Alright."

He turned around and crawled back the way he had come. The light from his bedroom soon became visible, and he crawled out a few minutes later. Carl still stood by the bed. Frank sat in the room, silent.

Beyond the windows, the sky was dark.

"How long was I in the walls?" Shane asked, standing up and stretching.

"Six hours," Carl answered in German.

"It amazes me," Shane said, replying in the same language, "to think of how time moves differently within the walls of the house."

"Did you find out anything useful?" Frank asked.

"Yes," Shane said. "But she is hiding more information. I don't know why. She's already dead."

"Stubbornness?" Frank offered.

"Maybe," Shane acknowledged. "Carl, will you do me a favor?"

"Certainly, my friend," Carl replied.

"Find Eloise for me," Shane said. "Tell her I am not angry. But I do need her to torture Lisbeth for a while."

Frank looked away in disgust and Carl shook his head in surprise. "What should she ask her?"

"What do you mean?" Shane asked.

"If she's going to be torturing the woman," Carl said, frowning, "shouldn't she have questions to ask?"

Frank looked at Shane, waiting for his answer.

"No," Shane replied. "I want her tortured, so she'll be ready to answer *my* questions."

Without waiting for Carl's response, and ignoring Frank's disapproving stare, Shane turned and left his bedroom.

He needed a cigarette and a glass of whiskey.

Chapter 11: The Fruits of His Labor

Harlan sat in the office and wondered whether he should pull the surveillance team away from Shane's house. A cocky, confident part of himself said he should.

But there was a small tickle of doubt in his thoughts. A belief that he couldn't count Shane Ryan out yet.

Would he be so foolish? Harlan wondered. *Would he risk the death of another friend?*

Harlan knew if he were in Shane's situation, he would sacrifice any number of friends for vengeance. But Harlan had never truly had any friends. He had people who owed him favors.

Nothing more.

Harlan glanced at the telephone. It was a large affair, with ten separate lines to various individuals. One, however, Harlan had dedicated to Shane. The number he had included with Mason's head. Harlan had spent the better part of the day preoccupied with it, wondering if Shane would be so brash as to call. Part of Harlan wanted the man to telephone in, but suspected he would not. He wanted to get a feel for what the man was like. He believed Shane would be like all of the others, a coward, in the end. A man lacking conviction.

Harlan picked up his pen and jotted down a note. He disliked computers and the ability of others to 'hack' into them and discover the secrets of others. While Harlan was not averse to blackmailing someone, he preferred his agents to gather it in a more physical manner. The idea that a stranger could reach out and touch them put fear into many people.

A smile played on Harlan's lips, and he sat back in his chair. He enjoyed the office, although he had drawn the curtains on the window. The view had been distracting, and he wondered if part of Abigail's abject failure at the helm of the Watchers could be attributed, at least in part, to the scenery.

He pushed the thought out of his mind and picked up the book he had brought with him. It was a leather bound affair and slim, containing only thirty-nine pages. The book had been put together by a long since dead member of the organization, and it focused on Borgin Keep.

Harlan had fond memories of the Keep, for it was his first assignment as a young man, and one he had treasured. The entity there was powerful, a true spiritual force to be reckoned with. He had secured the Keep for the order, a dominant link in the chain of power.

The leather was cool in his hands, the paper thick and strong beneath his fingers. It had the curious, attractive smell of old parchment when he opened it. The marbled paper on the inner boards soothed his eyes, and he let out a soft sigh. Nothing pleased him more than to hold the book, and to look upon what they had achieved.

The known history of the Keep was impressive, the secret history of it even more so. Few people even among the Watchers knew the full potential of the building, or what had occurred there. If a building could drown in blood, then Harlan knew the Keep would have died years earlier.

As it was, the building hadn't died. Instead, it had thrived, demanding lives. The granite walls seemed to exude death to all who came in contact with them. Some in a quick flash. Others were tortured to death. The mad ghosts of Borgin Keep keeping them alive to siphon off their energy.

Many of the organization's enemies had been sent to Borgin. Abigail had been deposited there, and Harlan wondered if she was still alive.

He chuckled at the thought and placed the book on the desk.

If he thought he could capture Shane, Harlan would have sent him to the Keep as well.

Still chuckling, Harlan rested his hands on his lap and looked at the phone, wondering if it would ring.

Chapter 12: Frank Contemplates a Drink

The house had shaken with her screams, and when she finally stopped, Frank found his nerves were frayed.

Shane seemed unfazed. He had a cigarette going and a book in his hand. The man hadn't moved from his seat since it had begun.

Frank cleared his throat.

Shane put the book down, looked at him and asked, "You okay?"

Frank was surprised by the question. "How the hell can you ask that? How are you, okay?"

"I'm fine," Shane said, tapping the cigarette ashes into a tray.

"She was tortured," Frank said.

"She's dead," Shane retorted.

Frank shook his head. "We shouldn't have tortured her."

"*We* didn't," Shane corrected.

Frank frowned. "Shane, we let Eloise torture her."

"No," Shane said, gently, "*I* asked Eloise to do it. You had nothing to do with it. Not only that, Frank, but you wouldn't be able to stop her."

Frank shook his head and looked away, his foot tapping on the floor. After a moment he continued. "I don't like it."

"Then you should put some music on if it starts up again," Shane offered.

Frank could tell the man was serious, and the concern was genuine.

It was also disturbing.

"How can you be okay with it?" Frank asked.

"Two reasons," Shane said. "First, she was going to kill us. Second, she was going to kill us."

When Frank didn't respond, Shane continued.

"Frank, you were okay with this when she was alive, why not now?" Shane asked.

Frank shrugged. "I don't know. This feels worse, somehow. She should be let loose. Sent on her way to judgment. We shouldn't be keeping her spirit imprisoned."

"Once I have the information I need," Shane said, "I'll have Eloise and Thaddeus let her go. Until then, she gets questioned."

A scream tore through the walls, and the mirror over the study's hearth shook.

Carl appeared in the room, his face a twisted mask of anger. In German, he snapped a question at Shane.

"English, please," Shane said putting out his cigarette. "Frank doesn't speak German, remember?"

Carl gave a curt nod as an apology to Frank, and Frank waved it away.

"When is this going to stop?" Carl demanded. "This is absurd, my friend. Can we really trust anything she says after such abuse? Would you not make up any lie you could think of to make your tormentor happy?"

"Of course, I would," Shane said. "Torture hardly ever works. That's why Eloise isn't asking any questions."

Frank looked at him, horrified. "If you don't believe in it, then why are you condoning it?"

"Because I still have questions I want to ask," Shane answered. He got a fresh cigarette, lit it, and picked up his book. Before he opened it, he looked from Carl to Frank and then said, "And because she tried to kill us."

Frank couldn't respond to the statement, so both he and Carl remained where they were, listening to Lisbeth's tortured screams.

Chapter 13: No Time

Rich lived in a world that didn't exist.

There was no light. Only darkness.

He had no sense of time. He slipped between consciousness and sleep in such an uncontrollable fashion that he didn't know what was real, or what was a dream.

When he was rational enough to think about his situation, Rich realized it didn't matter. None of it mattered.

The Keep was killing him, a little at a time. He was thirsty and had nothing to drink. Hungry, with nothing to eat. The cold chewed at him, to the point where he could no longer feel his arms or legs. He was exhausted, unable to move more than a few feet at a time, and that was only through a jerking, rolling motion.

In his dreams and his waking, Rich heard a woman. One who made no sense, and who railed at the dark in a hoarse, broken voice.

He tried to stay away from the madwoman.

Rich only wanted to escape.

He begged to be released.

His supplications weren't to God, but to the Keep. Because it was the Keep which kept him trapped. And it was the Keep alone.

Rich lay on his back, thinking of all of these things when he heard a curious squelching sound. It was as though a piece of raw meat was being rolled across a granite counter.

Then he quivered as something bumped into him.

It was cold, only slightly warmer than himself, and it pressed against him. He wept as it wriggled and wormed its way up his body, long, silken strands dragging across his flesh.

A mouth latched onto his shoulder, teeth and tongue probing. Within a heartbeat, the mouth was removed.

"You're real," a broken voice said.

It took Rich a moment to realize it was the woman he had heard.

"Yes," he replied, his voice nothing more than a croak.

"Have they taken them all?" she hissed.

"All what?" he asked in return.

"Arms, legs. Hands, feet. Little fingers and little toes," she asked, laughing. "Have they left you your eyes?"

She pressed herself against him, licking his flesh again.

"Ah," she sighed. "You taste of salt and sweat. But have they taken them? They've taken mine. They took everyone else's too. Long before me. Long before you."

Rich shuddered, revolted by her touch and the vile images her words produced in his starved mind.

"No," he declared. "I still have everything. I'm just cold. Too cold. And hungry."

"Hungry," she murmured. "Hunger."

Her mouth found his shoulder again, worked its way down and then he lost track of it in the cold.

She chortled.

"Oh no," she said, the words followed by a slurp that made his skin crawl. "No, your arm is not here. It's gone. Like mine. Like everyone's."

"You're insane," Rich snapped, and he tried to move.

He was too weak to do so.

Then he felt a tug on his arm. A rip filled his ears as if someone had torn a wet sheet in half. The woman sighed and pressed against him, the sensation grotesque and revolting.

"Get away!" he howled.

When the woman didn't reply, he tried to move, but a bolt of pain exploded in his arm.

"What are you doing?" he moaned.

"I'm eating," she murmured.

Rich stiffened. "Eating what?"

The woman laughed.

"You," she said. "I'm eating you."

Rich bucked and squirmed, but the woman had clamped down on him again.

In the oppressive darkness, he heard rather than felt her teeth upon him.

Chapter 14: Gathering Information

Shane sat in the small, circular room. Lisbeth's mirrored prison was before him, the dead woman nowhere to be seen.

"Where is she?" Shane asked, looking at Eloise.

The little dead girl put down the doll she had been playing with and stood up. She peered into the mirror and said, "On the floor."

Eloise skipped over to Shane and sat beside him. In a serious voice, the girl said, "She is not very happy."

"Oh, no?" Shane asked.

Eloise shook her head. "Not one bit. When she wasn't screaming she was saying terrible things."

"About you?"

"No," Eloise said. "About you. She said they would lock you up some place bad."

"Really?" Shane asked, looking at the mirror. "Did the place have a name?"

"Yes," Eloise said, nodding. "She called it the Keep."

"Hm," Shane murmured. "Alright. Thank you, Eloise. I'm sorry if it was hard for you."

The dead girl gave him a wide grin.

"It wasn't hard, silly," she said. Then she lowered her voice to a whisper and added, "I kind of liked it."

Shane could only nod. There were times he had enjoyed it as well.

Eloise shrugged and stood up. "Will you be out soon?"

"Yes," Shane said.

Eloise smiled, waved, and left the room.

Shane looked at the mirror and addressed Lisbeth. "Come where I can see you."

She didn't respond.

"I'll call her back," he said.

Lisbeth appeared in the glass. She looked cowed, fear behind her eyes.

"Are the Watchers based in Boston?" he asked.

She hesitated, then nodded.

"Were they really watching this place since before my family bought it?" he asked.

Lisbeth nodded again.

"Is there a way to stop them?"

A sneer crept onto her face and disappeared a moment later. She shook her head.

Shane didn't believe her, but he didn't want to argue about that point.

"What's the Keep?" Shane asked.

Lisbeth looked surprised for a second, but she didn't answer.

"What's the Keep?" Shane asked again.

"I don't know," she replied, and while Shane hadn't doubted Eloise, he could hear the lie in the dead woman's words.

"Okay," Shane said. "I'll have Eloise come back in."

"No!" Lisbeth yelled.

He looked at her.

"No," she whispered.

"What's the Keep?" Shane asked.

"It's called Borgin Keep, and it's a place to get rid of people," Lisbeth said. "A warehouse to store those the organization no longer wants."

"Is it important?" he demanded.

She nodded.

"Good," Shane said.

"What are you going to do, Shane?" she asked, a mocking, sing-song quality in her question.

"Why do you care?" he asked in return. "What do you owe the Watchers?"

"I owe them nothing," Lisbeth said. "They were a paycheck and nothing more."

"So I'll ask again, why do you care?" he said.

"Because it bothers you," she sneered. "And I have taken a sudden liking to things that upset you."

"That can't be all of it," Shane said. "Not with you. You're too smart."

Lisbeth didn't respond, but her eyes flicked away from him for a moment, and then Shane knew.

"They promised you something, didn't they," he said in a soft voice. "Was it power? Life eternal alongside of whatever it is they're really doing with all of those ghosts?"

"You don't know anything!" she hissed. "Nothing! When everything is set on its proper path, the faithful will be rewarded!"

"And what about the ones who are already dead?" Shane asked.

"Our bones will bring us back," she said, lifting her chin up.

"That's going to be a little difficult for you then," Shane said. "How so?" she asked with a sneer.

Shane turned and began to walk away.

"How so?!" she screamed.

He called his answer back to her as he left. "Because no one will find your bones here."

Her curses followed him into the darkness between the walls.

Chapter 15: Another Abandoned Car

Sergeant Jill Murray pulled in behind a Wrangler jeep, the lights of her cruiser illuminating the metallic blue paint of the vehicle. She turned on her work lights, called the jeep in, and waited for the confirmation call-back. After she received it, Jill got out, put on her hat, and took her flashlight out. She flipped it on with a flick of her thumb and advanced on the jeep. The beam reflected off the windows, and as she stepped closer, Jill saw the vehicle was empty.

She shook her head and glanced up at Borgin Keep.

Jill was certain that whomever the owner of the jeep was, had gone up to the Keep.

Another thrill seeker, she thought, frowning.

The Keep squatted on the hilltop. Over the years, she had found her share of cars on the side of the road. Most of the owners were never found. A few people popped up, later on, discovered on side roads and no longer sane.

The abandoned vehicle would mean a search for the missing person's system. It also meant a physical search of the Keep, something Jill despised.

The place never felt *right*. There was always something off. Either a smell or a feeling.

And nothing was ever found.

Not a trace of anyone. No clothes, no belongings. Nothing.

Jill reported the jeep in as abandoned, gave the vehicle identification number, the plate number, and then walked back towards her cruiser. When she reached the door, she looked over the roof at the Keep.

For the first time in her career, Jill saw lights on in the building.

In a pair of windows on the third floor, a dull, yellow light glowed.

A figure passed before them, and then darkness returned.

Jill felt her heart thumping, the familiar sensation of adrenaline coursing through her. Her basic instincts were screaming for her to either fight or run.

Something deeper told her to run, and Jill listened.

She hurried into her cruiser, slammed the vehicle into drive, and tore away from the jeep. A fantail of dirt sprayed up from behind her tires, and Jill didn't care.

She needed to get away from Borgin Keep, and whatever lived in it.

Chapter 16: A Different Tact

"Borgin Keep."

The name caused Frank to sit up and rub the sleep out of his eyes. He had drifted off at some point, and Shane's statement had woken him up.

The scarred, angry man dropped heavily into the chair across from Frank and lit a cigarette. Shane's face was haggard as if he hadn't slept well in weeks. The vivid scar on the side of his neck, as well as the battered remnants of his left ear, didn't make him look any healthier.

Frank watched as Shane poured a glass of whiskey, the man's hand shaking and slopping the liquor onto the table. Shane muttered under his breath, grabbed a napkin, and wiped it up before he lifted the glass to his lips. With one movement, Shane drained the glass as if it had held nothing stronger than water.

Shane lit a cigarette and repeated to himself. "Borgin Keep."

"What's Borgin Keep?" Frank asked. He was still upset with Shane over Lisbeth's continued imprisonment.

"Some place important to the Watchers," Shane answered.

"How'd you find that out?" Frank said, and Shane told him. When he had finished, Frank shook his head. "And what do you want to do about it?"

"Exactly what I told her," Shane said. "I want to burn the place to the ground. I want them to understand exactly what they did when they killed Mason."

The memory of Mason's head caused Frank to wince. "Shane, what about Mason's wife?"

"What about her?" Shane asked.

"Aren't we doing this for both of them?" Frank asked.

"Yes," Shane answered. He looked down and sighed. "For both of them, and for everyone else the Watchers have killed and allowed to be killed. It's easier for me to focus on Mason. He is the face of all the dead."

Frank nodded. "Well, what's your plan?"

"Simple. Get loaded up, bring a hell of a lot of accelerant, and light it up," Shane said.

"And if there are any dead there?" Frank asked.

"All the better," Shane said. "I'm going to reach out to a friend of mine. He specializes in securing haunted items. If there are any dead up there I can take, I want them."

Frank leaned back, surprised. "Why?"

"Because I'm going to turn them loose on Harlan," Shane said through his teeth. "I'm going to hurt him before I rip their little group to the ground."

"And what about Lisbeth?" Frank asked. "When will you let her go?"

"When I have all of the information I need," Shane replied.

Frank shook his head. "You should let her go now. She's waiting on God's judgment."

"God has a lot of time," Shane quipped. "I don't. She's got plenty of time too. When I've had my vengeance, then I'll let her go. Not before that, though."

Frank wanted to argue a little more, but Carl entered the room. The ghost looked flustered and upset.

"What is it?" Shane asked, surprise in his voice.

"There is a man and a woman," Carl said. "They are in the house across the street, but they do not belong there. And, my young friend, they are watching our house."

Frank was out of his chair before Shane, and he hurried to the window. He opened the shade enough to see out of, but nothing more. Frank's eyes scanned the street, then the houses.

A silver Mercedes, with New York license plates, was parked in the driveway of the deep blue Victorian that was home to the Mitchells.

But it wasn't the car the family usually had. Frank watched as a man passed by the front window, and he caught sight of a woman on the second floor. Both were doing an exceptional job at looking like they weren't watching.

Frank had been a professional, though. He knew how to look for someone who wasn't right. What to see when there shouldn't have been anything to see.

And the couple across the street weren't right.

Frank turned to Shane. "Carl's right. We're under surveillance."

Shane nodded. "Good. It means Harlan is still unsure as to which way I'll go."

"Hold on," Frank said, looking to Carl. "How did you find out they were watching us?"

"The building across the street," Carl explained, "was once the guest house. Some of the dead can still move from one home to the other."

"What do you want to do about this?" Shane asked, his voice hard.

"About them?" Frank asked.

Shane nodded.

Frank sighed. When he had been a Benedictine monk, Frank had cultivated peace, and he had sought to find a sense of calm within himself. Since he had left the order, Frank had found himself embracing the violence within his heart with disturbing ease.

And while part of him wanted to let the people watch and report, there was a harder part that knew he couldn't.

"We'll need to take them," Frank said in a small voice. "Both of them."

Shane nodded.

"And no torture," Frank stated.

Shane grinned, the smile frightening.

"No," Shane agreed. "No torture."

Chapter 17: Outside of Borgin Keep

When they entered the strongest places, they always worked in pairs.

David and Blanche had been a team for twenty-seven years; sixteen of them had been concentrated on Borgin Keep. They knew the exterior of the structure as well as their own homes.

The interior contained only two consistent features. The rear entrance through the kitchen, and the main hallway. All other aspects of the multi-storied building, including the stairs, shifted in form and function, depending upon the will of the dead.

This was due to the fact that the home had been built upon the convergence of two ley lines. Somehow, Emmanuel Borgin had created a structure that shifted in the physical plain with the same ease that was said to exist in the ethereal.

David shook the thoughts away.

It was dangerous to enter the Keep with any sort of distractions. The dead had a rapacious appetite, and it would not matter how long either David or Blanche had worked with them. Within the walls of the Keep, all were fair game.

The organization's contact in the Vermont State Police had informed them when the Wrangler jeep had been discovered. It meant that David and Blanche had a limited window of opportunity to get into the building, clean up any remains, and get out.

They got out of the pick-up they had taken from the Bennington safe house and went around to the back to gather up their supplies. As they did so, the work phone sounded, alerting them to a text message. Blanche read the text, swore under her breath, and handed the phone to David.

He adjusted his glasses and read the message.

He looked it over twice more before he looked at her and said, "A light in the windows."

Blanche's tanned skin had a pale look to it as she nodded, tucking a strand of black hair behind her ear.

"There's never been light on here," David said, looking up at the dark building. "Not once."

"I know," she replied. "What do you want to do?"

"Call it in," David said. "If someone in there is getting more active, we're going to need another team up here. This place is dangerous enough as it is."

"You're right," Blanche said, holding her hand out for the phone. David returned it to her, and she dialed the emergency number of the main office in Boston. In the stillness of the night air, David could hear the call ring on the other end. When it was answered, Blanche said, "This is Borgin."

The response was muffled, but in a clear voice Blanche replied, "We have an intruder as well as reports of a light on one of the upper floors."

Blanche stiffened as the person on the other end spoke, and she gave a curt nod before she ended the call.

"What happened?" David asked.

In a strained voice, she said, "I was told we were to continue on with the mission. It was imperative that we do so, and there are no other teams available to assist at this time."

Without a word to her, David went up to the front of the truck, opened the door and reached into glove compartment. He took out a thirty-eight caliber revolver. Silently David swung open the cylinder, made sure all six chambers were loaded and closed it before he tucked it into the pocket of his suit coat.

"Why did you bring that?" Blanche asked.

"Neither one of us is going to end up like any of those we've cleaned up," David stated. "We've given a lot of time to the Watchers. Our souls aren't staying on overtime to work a little longer."

She nodded her agreement, hefted the bag of supplies onto her shoulder, and led the way up the hill to the Keep.

The pistol was a comfortable weight in David's pocket, and he was glad to have it.

Chapter 18: Making His Decision

Courtney was singing in a corner, her voice soothing and gentle in the darkness. The sound made Shane smile, and his burden all the lighter.

He sat in his chair, behind his desk, and with his eyes closed.

Shane found he thought better and clearer when he sat alone with Courtney. She became a little better each day, and it pleased him.

Her song stopped, and Courtney asked, "What are you thinking about?"

"I have to do something bad," he said. "And it isn't going to end well for at least two people."

"Are you one of them?" she demanded.

"No," he said in a soft voice. "Not at all."

She didn't respond, and when she did, it was with another question.

"Will they suffer?" she asked.

"They might," Shane admitted.

"Why do you have to deal with them?" Courtney asked, her voice coming closer in the darkness.

"They're part of the group who killed Mason," Shane explained. "I may kill them to send a message. I may not. I haven't decided."

"Do they deserve to die?" she asked in a whisper.

"Just about everybody does," Shane said. He let out a long sigh. "And I'm not in a particularly forgiving mood."

"You should be," Courtney said. "You're alive, Shane. And you still have friends."

"Friend, singular," Shane corrected. "At least living."

"Am I only a friend?" she asked, and Shane could hear a hint of madness in her question.

He didn't rush his response, though. "You are more than a friend, Courtney. You were, and you always will be."

"Thank you," she whispered.

When she spoke again, she was across the room.

"What will you do to them?" Courtney asked. "Will you torture them as you did Lisbeth?"

"Hm? Oh, no. I already told Frank I wouldn't," Shane said. "I'd like to, but in this case, it wouldn't do any good. In fact, I think it might make Frank withdraw from the whole venture."

"Frank stands by you," she said.

"He does," Shane agreed. "And I respect him too much."

A pleasant silence filled the cold room as Shane contemplated the fate of the two watchers across the street. After a short time, Shane came to a decision, and he stood up.

"What are you going to do?" she asked as he walked towards the door.

"Kill them both," Shane replied.

"How will that help?" The question was a serious one, Courtney's voice lacking any sort of judgment.

He paused at the door, hand on the cold knob.

"It will show a man, named Harlan," Shane said, "that killing my friend was a poor decision."

"Oh," she said, and a moment later lifted her voice up in song.

Shane smiled, opened the door, and left his cold sanctuary.

Chapter 19: Conducting Business

The Keep was colder than David remembered it.

Blanche looked at him.

"This isn't good," she said.

"No," David agreed. "It isn't. I hope it's only one trespasser."

"Me too," Blanche said. "We still need to clean up after the last one we dropped off."

David groaned. "Damn. I'd forgotten about her. Well, here's hoping we have enough bags. I really don't want to go out to the truck again. It'll take us half the night to find the remains."

Blanche nodded her agreement, and they passed out of the kitchen and into the main hall. Ahead and to the right, David saw fresh drag marks. Unfortunately, they led into a wall, which meant the Keep had shifted since the intruder had entered.

David sighed, and Blanche said, "My turn anyway."

He nodded and came to a stop. She did the same a few feet away, standing in the beam of the flashlight. Blanche held her arms out to either side and called out, "Emmanuel!"

The foundation of Borgin Keep shook.

"Emmanuel!" she said, raising her voice.

A cold wind raced through the hallway, knocked an unknown item down in the darkness beyond them, and then rushed back. At the edge of the flashlight's beam, a pair of polished shoes appeared.

Emmanuel Borgin stepped forward, and David clenched his teeth to avoid a startled gasp.

The ghost was thin, face sunken in and eyes nothing more than white dots peering forth from cavernous sockets. When he smiled, gold and silver flashed, most of his teeth covered or filled. He wore a tailored, pinstriped suit that accentuated the thinness of his body. His nails were long, filed to points, and made his fingers look like the jointed legs of a spider. The man's skin was as pale as paper and had no hair of which to speak. His ears were large, almost cartoonish in size.

But when they were added to the overall stature of the man, they only made David more fearful of him.

"Hello, Emmanuel," Blanche said.

"Hello, Blanche," Emmanuel replied.

David relaxed. It was always good when the dead man remembered who they were. The pistol, however, was still a comfort.

"Are you here to clean up?" Emmanuel asked with a chuckle.

Blanche nodded. "How many?"

"One," Emmanuel answered. "Only one. And not much of him. Not nearly as much as when he came in."

"What of the woman?" Blanche asked.

"She's why there's not much left of him," Emmanuel grinned. "You'll see. Three doors down on your right. I'll tell the other guests to leave you be."

Blanche nodded her thanks, and Emmanuel vanished. She glanced at David.

"Are you ready?" she asked.

"Yes," David lied.

Together they walked to the third door, the lock clicking and the doorknob turning for them. Blanche pushed the door open, and they entered an elegant sitting room. All of the furniture looked as if it had recently been dusted, and there was the sweet scent of evergreens.

David shined the light around the room, stopping it on a bloody, naked body.

It had once been a man. Most of the skin was gone, as were all of his limbs. The face was ravaged, in some spots, the meat stripped from the bone. There were teeth marks and chunks of flesh missing from various parts of the torso. A few feet away was a pile of limbs.

From what David could see there were two pairs of legs and two pairs of arms. They had not been neatly removed. Instead, the edges were ragged, as if the limbs had been torn from their joints. The fetid stench of rotten meat filled the room, and David choked back a gag.

"Where is she?" David asked, surprised that he could still be horrified after all of his years with the Watchers.

"I don't know," Blanche said in an awed voice. "How has she even lasted this long?"

"I don't care," David answered, looking around the room. His skin crawled as he imagined her in some dark corner, limbless and mouth covered in red.

After several fearful moments, David asked, "Should we hunt her down?"

Blanche shook her head. "I think we're lucky Emmanuel let us in. There's something going on. If we travel too far from this room, we may end up like him. Food for her."

Suddenly the man on the floor exhaled a long, broken breath and David swore in fear and surprise.

In shocked silence, he and Blanche watched as the body in front of them shuddered, tried to move, and then went still.

"He's still alive," Blanche whispered.

David didn't speak. Instead, he reached into his pocket, pulled the pistol out and walked up to the wreck on the floor. He squeezed the trigger and put the tortured man out of his misery.

"Sometimes," Blanche said, shrugging the bag off her shoulder, "sometimes, I hate this job."

David nodded his agreement and put the pistol away. It was time to work.

Chapter 20: Watching 125 Berkley Street

They had been in the house since the package had been delivered to Shane Ryan. Emilio and Sadie had taken possession of the observation point the night prior to the delivery. The family who had lived there, a husband, wife, and three children, had been removed.

A team had disposed of the bodies.

In spite of the expert removal, or perhaps because of it, the house still stank. It was permeated with the foul odor of the cleaning products used to scour the crime scene. The team would return after the observation of 125 Berkley Street was finished. There was far too much trace evidence for anyone's peace of mind.

Once the house was cleaned for the second time, Harlan would ensure the place was burned to the ground.

Emilio smiled. Harlan was efficient, thorough, and he left nothing to chance.

Looking around, Emilio's eyes found a small, silver Zippo lighter on the mantle. He would pocket it before they left. A little memento of the job to add to his collection. In his apartment, Emilio had a significant number of items he had gathered over the years.

Sadie sat in a chair set several feet back from the picture window, a pair of binoculars at hand should something interesting occur across the street.

Emilio played a hand of solitaire. Neither Shane nor Frank Benedict had left, and the observation bordered on mind-numbing.

Both Emilio and Sadie were professionals if nothing else. They would remain in position until told to do otherwise. It was why they were assets, and why Harlan used them on the most difficult cases.

Sadie lifted the binoculars and examined Shane's house with them.

"What do you want to eat tonight?" she asked, keeping her focus on the building.

"Chinese," Emilio answered.

"You always want Chinese," she complained.

"You always want Mexican," he retorted.

She snorted a laugh. "Yeah. I do. Want to try something else?"

"No," Emilio said, grinning.

The ringing of his cell phone cut off her reply.

Emilio took the phone out of his pocket and answered it. He didn't have to look at the caller. There was only ever one.

"Hello, sir," Emilio said.

Before he could listen to Harlan's question, there was a knock on the front door.

Sadie put the binoculars down and looked at Emilio.

"Hold on, sir," Emilio said. "Someone's at the door."

Without hanging up the phone, Emilio placed it face up on the table. He stood up, and moved to the door, stopping a few feet away and off to the right. "Who is it?"

No one answered.

"Who's there?" Emilio demanded.

When he still didn't receive a response, Emilio turned to Sadie, and their world collapsed.

Chapter 21: A Lack of Patience

In many ways, Harlan was a patient man. He had plotted his movements, his rise through the organization over decades. His accomplishments were many, and they had been meticulously planned each of them.

In other instances, Harlan had no patience whatsoever.

And regardless of his respect and admiration for the ruthless efficiency of Emilio and Sadie, Harlan hated to wait on subordinates.

Harlan had the phone on speaker, and he sat at his desk, hands folded into a steeple as he listened to the observation post in New Hampshire.

After Emilio's second, unanswered query, Harlan was ready to hang up and call Sadie's phone. Instead, he heard something extraordinary.

A fight.

Or rather, Harlan heard one side of a fight. That of Emilio and Sadie. Harlan heard curses, the rapid firing of suppressed weapons. The sickening sound of flesh being struck and of things breaking.

The fight was over in less than a minute, and Harlan found himself leaning over the desk, craning his neck to hear Emilio's report.

Then the line went dead.

Frustrated, Harlan reached out to call them, but even as he did so, their phone line rang.

"What happened?" Harlan demanded when he answered the call.

A heartbeat later, someone spoke, and it wasn't Emilio.

"Hello," a man said. His voice was cold and brutal, and Harlan realized he had heard dead men with livelier tones.

Harlan hesitated, then he demanded, "Who is this?"

"I'm disappointed, Harlan," the hard man said.

The hatred Harlan heard sent a chill down his spine.

"Who is this?" Harlan repeated, and he hated the hint of weakness in his own words.

"You sent me my friend's head."

"Shane," Harlan said, surprised. He sat down hard in his chair. "Shane Ryan."

"Yes," Shane said.

"I told you what I'd do," Harlan said.

"Shut up," Shane snapped, and Harlan was surprised to find that he did.

"I have two of your people here," Shane continued. "And it is not going to end well for them."

Harlan's heart began to hammer a mad beat in his chest.

"I'll kill a dozen of yours for mine," Harlan spat.

"Sure you will," Shane said. "I've got big shoulders, though, Harlan. I'll carry that weight. I'll carry it until I go to my own grave."

Harlan found it hard to breathe.

"I have a number for you now," Shane said. "I'm betting you won't have it changed. Too much effort. Too many people you'd have to reach out to. I'm not sure if I know exactly where you are, but I will. Soon enough. Lisbeth's even told me about a place."

"Liar!" Harlan hissed. "She's dead!"

Shane laughed. A sound reminiscent of steel being dragged through broken glass.

"That, she is," Shane agreed. "It doesn't mean she can't answer questions. Or tell me things she'd rather not."

Harlan snatched up the receiver and screamed into it, "You lie!"

"Think of it," Shane said, his voice dropping to a whisper, forcing Harlan to press the phone to his ear. "Me, with a captive who knows far too much. Think of the damage I did when I didn't know who you were. Consider what I'll be able to do now. All of those places I can destroy. All of your plans shattered."

"You can't," Harlan seethed. "I won't let you. We'll stop you. I will come to your house and gut you like a fish!"

"Good luck with that, Harlan," Shane said.

Harlan heard someone else speak in the background, and he knew it was Frank Benedict.

"What does Frank think of this little plan of yours?" Harlan demanded. "You can tell him I'll be going after his cousin. The little one who lives in Delaware."

Shane chuckled, the sound abrasive. "Funny thing about that. Turns out our Frank is a little more devious than even I thought. He doesn't have any family. Pleasant lies and falsehoods spread to ease the minds of others. His family died years ago. You don't have any leverage there."

"I'm going to kill you," Harlan promised.

"There's always the chance that you could," Shane said, his voice suddenly pleasant. "But here's a question. Do you know this sound?"

There was a soft, metallic click on the other end.

Harlan straightened up in his chair.

He did know the sound.

"Are you going to torture them?" Harlan asked, a grin spreading across his face.

"God, no," Shane said with a chuckle. "These two are professionals. Anyone can see that."

The soft, muffled cough of a suppressor traveled across the phone lines. A thump, the unmistakable sound of a body hitting the floor, followed.

"That would be the female," Shane said. "Whoever she was. And you always kill the females first. Do you know why, Harlan?"

Harlan couldn't answer. He was too surprised. Shane's action was a shock, unexpected. Far more brutal than Harlan had believed the man was capable of.

"Harlan!" Shane snapped.

"What?" Harlan spat back.

"Do you know why you kill the females first?" Shane asked.

"Why?" Harlan asked, genuinely curious.

"Because they're the most dangerous," Shane explained. "They've worked the hardest."

Harlan shook his head. He wanted to say something witty, a cutting statement that would remind Shane of where he stood in the natural order of things.

Nothing came to mind.

"Now," Shane said, "if you'll excuse me, I have to speak with your other employee."

Harlan heard Shane walk away from the phone, and then the distinctive sound of a pistol being cocked.

Chapter 22: Playing the Hand

David and Blanche stood in the kitchen of Borgin Keep. She held the flashlight while he double checked the knots on the plastic bags. They had gathered up the severed limbs and secured the torso of the intruder.

David didn't feel well. For the first time, what he had seen had sickened him. He was nearing retirement age, and according to the records kept by the Watchers, he would be able to enjoy a significant pension. The idea of sitting in a small house down in the Florida Keys and whiling away the hours made him smile. David had waded in blood for the organization, and he deserved retirement.

"What are you grinning about?" Blanche asked.

David chuckled. "I'm going to put in for retirement."

She laughed and shook her head. "You said that every day for a month last year after we had to scrape that family out of the oven in Rhode Island. You'll be fine by the end of the summer."

"No," he disagreed. "Not this time. This was different. This was one person doing it to another. Something wrong about it, Blanche."

Blanche opened her mouth to answer, but not a sound came out. Her eyes widened, and a hand protruded from between her teeth. A second one appeared a heartbeat later.

Horrified, David watched as her mouth was spread apart. A single, dead eye peered out at him, blinked and a voice other than Blanche's let out a callous laugh.

David stumbled back, leaving the bags on the floor. Blanche sagged, held up only by the ghost behind her. He watched her eyes roll up into her head, only the whites showing between the lids. Her arms hung limply from their sockets, her stance bowlegged.

A face peeked around her head, a madman's smile, crazed hair.

David had never seen the ghost before.

And he never wanted to see him again.

"Hello," the ghost said, moving Blanche's mouth to mimic his own. "How are you doing today? This evening? This year? Hm?"

David shook his head, edging towards the door.

"You want to leave, do you?" the dead man asked.

David nodded.

The iron ring on his finger itched, and for the first time, David was afraid that it wouldn't be enough.

"Then you should leave," the dead man said. The grin vanished. "You should leave now before I change my mind. Before anyone here changes their mind."

David didn't hesitate.

He turned on his heel and sprinted out of the kitchen. Blanche was left twitching, hanging like a broken toy on the dead man's hands. The bags of body parts were on the kitchen floor. Thoughts of retirement were discarded.

David wanted nothing more than to die in his own bed, and at his own time.

The laughter of the Keep's dead chased him back to the truck.

Chapter 23: A Bad Time of It

In Harlan's seventy-four years of life he had not suffered worse weeks.

None in recent memory compared to the past seven days.

He was in his office, alone, a fresh cup of coffee on the desk. Steam curled up from the dark green ceramic. Ms. Coleman, who was worth her weight in gold, had quietly brought the beverage in.

She had closed the door behind her, leaving him in a vacuum of silence. From the short time in Abigail's former office, Harlan had come to appreciate the secretary's intuitive nature.

Ms. Coleman would ensure that Harlan remained undisturbed for however long he decided. This, he knew, was a good thing.

New England would suffer if he didn't manage his anger.

Shane Ryan and Frank Benedict were quickly becoming problems that Harlan didn't want to have. He had misjudged the way they would react, and it had cost him. His best observation team had been killed. With the two of them dead, he couldn't risk sending in the cleaning crew to rid the house of trace evidence. Harlan would have to reach out to an arsonist and hope a fire could rid him of that portion of the problem.

Then he had received the phone call from David, a man Harlan had trained and mentored. Someone he trusted with the delicate ambassadorship between the Watchers and Borgin Keep.

The dead were acting up. One of them had killed David's partner, a woman whose name escaped Harlan, and chased David from the premises.

And David had put in his request for retirement at the end of the phone call.

After informing Harlan of Abigail's continued existence.

Harlan snarled at the idea of her alive. She had mismanaged the Shane Ryan affair from the start. With her still breathing, she may have antagonized the ghosts in Borgin, which meant there would be more incidents near the Keep. And more incidents translated to more police activity.

More police activity meant more inquiries, which the Watchers strongly discouraged.

Miserable, Harlan thought, picking up his coffee and taking a sip of the hot liquid. *Wretched.*

He considered the insertion of another team into Borgin, then shook his head. His people were brave. They all believed in the end goal of the Watchers, of finding the One who would crush death for them.

But they were not zealots. They would not throw their lives away cheaply.

No, Borgin would have to wait.

Harlan would focus on Shane, and how he might bring the man to task for his actions. With a smile on his lips, Harlan wondered if he might be able to get an arsonist close enough to 125 Berkley Street, and whether or not the dead might be able to stop him.

Chuckling, Harlan reached out, picked up the phone, and dialed a number in Nashua.

Chapter 24: A Disturbing History

"It isn't good," Frank said.

He had a thick packet of papers in his hands and he looked at Shane with an earnest expression. His milky white eye caught and absorbed the evening light.

Shane sighed. "When is it ever?"

Frank shrugged, leaned forward and held the papers out. Shane took them, the sheaf felt heavy. There were at least fifty pages. Maybe sixty.

And all of it was about Borgin Keep.

"The place has been a nightmare since the beginning," Frank said, settling back into his chair.

"How so?" Shane asked, putting the papers down on his lap. He lit a cigarette.

"It started with deaths during the construction," Frank explained. "Some of the workers left, but more were hired. The owner, Emmanuel Borgin, evidently had the only jobs in town. Or anywhere, for that matter."

"So no matter how many died," Shane said, glancing down at the papers, "others just kept coming in."

Frank nodded.

"Do we have a total number of deaths there?" Shane asked.

"Confirmed, we have twenty-nine," Frank said.

Shane felt a surge of depression wash over him. "And unconfirmed?"

"Rumor has it," Frank said, "that the death toll reaches over two hundred."

"Damn," Shane murmured. He flipped through the pages until he found a picture of the building. "Hell, it's a castle."

Frank nodded. "Evidently Mr. Borgin had a thing for medieval Europe. Some architects were told they were building an exact replica. Dungeons and all."

"Some architects?" Shane asked. "Did he use more than one?"

"Definitely," Frank confirmed. "No one knows how many though. Some people said there were architects in Europe that he conferred with. One page I found said that there are as many levels below ground as there are above."

Shane tapped his foot on the floor, an uncomfortable feeling settled over him.

"Frank," he said after a brief pause, "was there anything in this that talked about changing rooms?"

Frank looked surprised as he nodded. "How did you know?"

"Just a guess," Shane answered.

"Um, yeah. There are diaries from a couple of his household staff who said the house seemed to change from night to night. They knew better," Frank continued, "than to wander out of their rooms after hours. It seemed to be safe in the walls, but that was it."

"Servants' passages," Shane murmured.

"Yeah."

"What did old Emmanuel die of?" Shane asked.

"No one knows," Frank answered. "Seems like he disappeared and that was it. The police and his lawyers went in, looked for him, and couldn't find anything. Not a trace. Everything he owned was still there."

"Did they ever find any evidence of multiple subfloors?" Shane asked.

Frank shook his head. "A regular basement, that was it."

"So," Shane said, letting cigarette smoke out through his nostrils, "things got weird after he vanished?"

"You can say that," Frank said. "Again, there are no firm numbers here. If we take police records, we've got about one abandoned car a year near the building. Occasionally a person will be found with the car, but that's only once in a great while. Most of the cops think that people just like to dump their cars there. Usually the vehicles are stripped of any identification; plates, vehicle ID numbers. All of it. And when they can find the owner, they're usually all well and good."

"Usually?" Shane asked.

"Usually," Frank said. "But not always. Sometimes the owners are found, insane. Wandering around the road, or in the woods, talking about Borgin Keep, and the ghosts, and about barely getting out."

"Are any of them still alive?" Shane asked.

"What?" Frank said, confused.

"Any of the people who were found, are any of them still alive?" Shane said.

"I don't know," Frank said. "I didn't even think about it. Why?"

"Because it may do us some good to talk to someone who's been in there," Shane stated.

Frank nodded. "I'll see what I can dig up. It may be tough getting in to see them."

"We'll get it done," Shane said. He looked down at the papers.

Frank stood up, he turned to leave, hesitated and asked, "How are you doing?"

"I've got a lot of hate in me," Shane replied. "They killed Mason and his wife."

Frank nodded.

"I want to do a whole lot worse."

"Me too," Frank admitted. Without another word, he left the study. Shane picked up the sheaf of papers and began to read.

Chapter 25: Immolation

He enjoyed fire.

To him there was nothing more beautiful, or purer than flame. When he had first discovered matches at the age of six, it had been an awakening. The world had opened for him as he watched the flames consume first one page, then another of his father's Bible. Later, when he turned seven, he had stood and observed how fire had devoured his father's flesh, the man's screams trapped behind a barrier of duct tape.

As always, the memory brought a smile to the arsonist's face, and he felt serene as he finished the preparations for 126 Berkley Street. He set the rudimentary timer, and snuck through the darkness to an elm tree which grew on the sidewalk.

His next task, 125 Berkley Street, waited for him. It was a great and beautiful brick building. The arsonist smiled for he knew everything burned.

When he was certain that no one was peering out at him, he made his way across the street, careful to avoid the street lamps which held back the night. The arsonist enjoyed nighttime, the fires burned brighter. The sound of wood popping and glass shattering would carry so much further.

He would light up the night sky, and if he set the fire properly, it would burn for hours.

The arsonist had plied his trade, his passion, up and down the East Coast for almost a decade. He had eventually come into contact with Harlan, and Harlan had paid him to start fires.

To burn down homes and buildings. Sometimes Harlan even let him set the fires when there were people in them.

The arsonist shuddered with delight. He had never forgotten the heady scent of his father, taped down and roasting in bed.

With a happy sigh the arsonist made it to his next target, sneaking onto the property. The thick grass was damp, rain glistening on the blades. There had been a heavy down pour earlier in the day, which would make the blaze a little more difficult to light.

A little, but nothing he couldn't handle. Buildings always burned, that he had learned.

He traveled along the side of the house, ducking beneath all of the windows, regardless as to whether the blinds were closed or not. To be caught would ruin the fun.

He finally reached the far side of the house and he was pleasantly surprised to find that there were no lights there. Not a single motion sensor, no glaring security light. He was alone in darkness, allowed to play with fire.

The arsonist hummed the tune to 'Camptown Ladies' as he slid his backpack off and sat down on the cool grass. He removed his tools and went about the delicate art of arson. Each action performed was necessary. He didn't waste time or effort on anything unessential. The arsonist was many things, but unprofessional was not one of them. He knew each step needed to be done correctly, and he remembered what one of his many psychologists had told him.

Do it right the first time.

The statement was pure and simple, a verbal twin to fire.

The arsonist repeated the phrase to himself, and leaned over to set the accelerant against the side of the house. An uncomfortable chill wrapped around him and he shivered, a frown creasing his forehead.

He had checked the weather for the evening when he had made his plans. Everything was important when it was time to burn a building down. He couldn't have his hands shaking from the cold while he tried to set the fire.

The arsonist sat back, considered whether or not he should find his gloves and put them on, and rubbed at an itch on the back of his neck.

"What are you doing?" a voice asked.

He let out a squeak of surprise and nearly fell over as he twisted around, looking for the speaker.

When he didn't see anyone, the arsonist tried to get his heart to slow down.

"I asked you a question," the voice stated, coming from a dark clump of trees off to the right.

The arsonist realized the voice belonged to a little girl and his heartbeat calmed down.

"Why don't you come out where I can see you?" he asked, his voice light and pleasant.

"I can see you fine from where I am," she said. "You shouldn't answer a question with a question though. It's rude."

"Well," the arsonist said, straining to see her among the trees. "I'm trying to fix a little part of the wall. Is this your house?"

"There's nothing wrong with the wall," the girl stated. "And no, it isn't my house. But I live here."

"Oh," the arsonist said. He slipped his hand into his backpack, found the grip of the pistol he kept for emergencies and removed it casually. "Do you like living here?"

"I do," she said. "You should leave."

"I can't do that," he said. "I have a job to do."

The arsonist listened and waited for the girl to respond. He didn't like to kill people. At least not in such a straightforward manner. It always felt too *messy* when he had to shoot someone.

Fire was so much cleaner.

After waiting a minute for her to speak again, the arsonist asked, "Are you still there?"

"Of course I am," she snapped. There was a curious maturity to her voice that he found unsettling.

"Then come out where I can see you," he said.

She did.

In the dim light of the stars filtering down, the girl appeared ethereal. She stared at him, anger in her eyes and a hard-set jaw.

"I want you to leave," she said.

The arsonist brought the gun up and fired a single shot into her chest.

While the weapon, a .22 caliber pistol, sounded like the backfire of a car, the girl remained upright.

Her small hands clenched into fists and the arsonist fired off another shot.

He felt panic thunder through him and he emptied the last four chambers.

The arsonist pulled the trigger a seventh time, but the hammer struck a spent casing. He dropped the pistol to the ground and he sat down hard.

The girl walked towards him, the starlight shining through her. Her face was a perfect picture of rage and she came to a stop in front of him.

"I don't like you," she hissed. "Not. One. Bit."

He turned away from her, panic rising in his throat with the realization that she was dead. In his bag was a length of iron and if he could reach it he would be safe.

But the dead girl got to him first. With a snarl, she bent down and thrust her hands into his own. The pain was immediate and excruciating.

He let out a scream as she grabbed hold of bones and tendons, flexing his fingers with her own. The arsonist tried to wrench his hands away from her and found he couldn't. He was helpless as she grabbed hold of his tools. Beneath the pain was the dull sensation of her wearing his hands like gloves, using his fingers unscrewing the cap to the liquid accelerant.

Then he was dousing himself with it. It stung as it struck his face, burned as it landed in his eyes. Unable to control his movements, his hands rose above his head and shook the contents out over his hair and his clothes.

When she was finished, she tossed the bottle aside and searched through his bag for his matches.

"What are you?" he moaned.

"Dead," she answered. She straightened up, used his fingers to open the box of kitchen matches, and took one out. The girl turned and smiled at him.

"I hope you like this," she said, and she struck the match.

For the first time in his life, the arsonist was afraid of fire.

Chapter 26: Awakened by Strife

A car backfired and woke Shane up.

He lay on his back, not wanting to look at the clock when he heard the car again.

Then another four times.

Shane rolled out of bed, half tangled in the sheets as he stumbled for the door. Just as he pulled it open, he heard Frank do the same. The two men entered the hallway simultaneously. Without a word, they rushed down the stairs. Frank reached the front door first, opening it a crack before hurrying outside.

A high-pitched scream rang out from the side yard and the two men broke into a run, bare feet striking the cold, wet grass. More screams filled the night air before they made it to the side yard, and by the time they did, there was a bright light flickering across the grounds.

Turning around the corner of the house Shane came to a sharp stop as Frank threw out an arm. In front of them, standing on the grass and screaming, was a man. The stranger was a giant torch, and Eloise stood a few feet away.

Shane stared at the man, too surprised to move.

The stranger's screams ceased and he looked at Shane and Frank. Shane could see the man's flesh burn, the skin blackening and cracking before splitting open completely. Even as the man's eyes seemed to melt in his sockets, he turned towards the house. He took several tottering steps, and Shane shook the shock away.

The burning man was focused on an object near the wall.

"It will burn!" the stranger screamed, his voice high-pitched with a note of insanity within it.

He staggered forward and before either Shane or Frank could react, Eloise was there.

She sped toward the man, smashing into him and knocking him onto the ground. Stunned, Shane watched as the man tried to get to his feet again, only to have Eloise push him down into the cold, damp grass.

While the burning man didn't speak, he continued to try and rise up, and each time Eloise battered him into the ground. Finally, unable to control himself any longer, the man let out a scream of pure frustration and tried to extinguish himself.

But it was already too late.

In a moment he was still, with Eloise standing near him.

She turned and smiled at Shane and Frank.

"He wasn't a nice man," she explained.

Frank shook his head, unable to speak. He tried to step forward, but it was Shane's turn to hold him back.

Shane cleared his throat, ignored the stench of the man's flesh as it burnt and asked, "How do you know?"

"He was going to light the house on fire," Eloise said, gesturing toward a backpack near the building.

Frank tore his eyes away from the burning man and went to the pack. Shane waited as Frank knelt down, looked at the material and gave a nod of confirmation.

The burning man had ceased his movements and lay still. From the body came the sound of plastic buttons popping and the crack of flesh splitting.

"I saw him across the street," Eloise continued. "He set something over there, too."

An explosion punctuated her statement, the force of the blast throwing Shane forward. He slammed into the earth and found himself near the fresh corpse. Already the dead man's lips had curled back from his teeth, revealing silver and gold caps.

The smell was atrocious and Shane had to hold back vomit as he pushed himself away. A glance to the house revealed that Frank was still upright, sitting, but conscious. Frank rubbed the back of his head, and Shane turned to look at 126 Berkley.

The building was a mass of flames. Windows cracked and shattered. Fire ate at the roof and devoured the front porch. Somewhere, a fire engine's siren called out, and soon it was joined by the wail of a police cruiser. Within minutes several fire trucks had arrived, the fire fighters calling out while racing about their tasks. The cruisers were close on their heels, as were a pair of ambulances.

And it took only a short time for one of the EMTs to notice there was a burning body in Shane's yard.

Shane and Frank were dazed by the explosion, and they were unable to put up any resistance when they were separated by the police and questioned about the situation.

Fortunately, the two of them remembered to leave out Eloise.

Shane slowly regained control over his thoughts while sitting on the back bumper of an ambulance. A female paramedic took his vitals while an older, male detective stood in front of him. The man's face was pale, red 'gin blossoms' on his nose. His hair was graying and clipped short in a crew-cut. The suit he wore was ill-fitting, and Shane wondered if the man had stepped out of a television drama about cops who worked the late shift.

"So you didn't know the man at all?" the detective asked.

"What?" Shane said.

The detective frowned and repeated the question.

"No," Shane said, shaking his head, which he instantly regretted, wincing at the pain. "No, I didn't know the guy. Heard some noises, went outside, and found him rolling around."

"You didn't think to try to put the fire out?" the detective asked.

"No," Shane answered.

"Why not?" Disgust was thick in the detective's voice.

"Because he shouldn't have been in my yard," Shane replied.

The answer took the other man by surprise, and the EMT as well. They both looked at Shane with near identical expressions of shock.

"My house. My property," Shane said. "I came outside because I heard gunfire. Why was he in my yard, firing a gun, and trying to set my home on fire?"

"How do you know that?" the detective demanded.

Shane shook his head as another man approached them. He was a little younger and a little slimmer than the detective, and he had on a uniform with the rank of a lieutenant.

"Dwayne," the lieutenant said, "may I interrupt?"

The detective looked over and nodded, saying, "Sure, Lieutenant."

"Hi," the lieutenant said, offering his hand. "I'm Lieutenant Martin Klein."

Shane shook the man's hand warily. "Shane."

"And a last name?" the lieutenant asked.

"He wrote it down," Shane said, nodding towards the detective.

A brief look of irritation flashed across the lieutenant's face, but it was replaced with an easy smile.

"Shane," the lieutenant said, "I was informed, just a few minutes ago, that you were a friend of Officer Kurt Warner?"

At this, the detective glared at Shane.

Shane nodded.

"Did you happen to speak to him before his death?" the lieutenant asked.

Shane shook his head.

"What's wrong?" the detective snapped. "Cat got your tongue?"

Anger boiled up and Shane said, "Take a good look at me."

He turned his head to the left to show the police the scar along the side of his head and down his neck. Then Shane turned it to the right to show them the remains of his left ear. When he looked at them again he lifted his left hand to allow them to count the three fingers which remained.

"Does it look like I care about a whole lot?" Shane demanded. "I'm a retired Marine Gunnery Sergeant. I have been through the wringer, and more than once. Tonight's really no different than any other time. It just happened to occur on my street. I was asleep. Gunfire woke me up. I found a guy burning to death in the side yard. A house blew up and the concussion knocked me stupid. Now you want to know about Kurt?"

"Shane," the lieutenant began.

"Shut up," Shane snapped, stabbing a finger at the man. "Let me tell you about myself. I've buried a lot of friends. I've killed my share of men and women and children. And I don't care. There are only two things I want to do with the rest of my life, and that's smoke and drink. So that's what I'm going to do. I'm going to smoke my cigarettes. I'm going to drink my whiskey."

Shane looked at the female paramedic who eyed him with a wary mixture of concern and distrust.

"Am I good?" Shane asked.

She nodded.

"Thank you," he said, getting up. His entire body ached. "Am I being arrested?"

"No," the detective said.

"Do you need to bring me in for questioning?" Shane asked.

"Maybe," the lieutenant replied, his voice raw with anger.

"Fine," Shane said. "I'm going back into my house. I may have a cup of coffee. I may have a shot or three of whiskey. Come knock on the door when you've decided what you're doing."

Shane pushed his way between the two surprised policemen and stalked back to the front door. Behind him, he heard the lieutenant swear, and then a crashing sound as part of 126 Berkley collapsed on itself.

Chapter 27: A Curious Conversation

Frank was alone in the house. If the dead could sleep, he felt certain the ghosts were.

Shane had been taken down to the police station for questioning. Frank had not. Unlike Shane, Frank had kept a civil tongue in his head, and he had answered all of the questions put to him in a calm and polite way.

Shane, Frank suspected, was spoiling for a fight.

A tremor rippled through Frank's body as the adrenaline from the explosion burned out of his system. He had a tall glass of water, his third, and he sat in a comfortable chair in the front parlor. The shades were open, the lights in the room off. Frank had plenty of illumination from the fire across the street as well as the emergency beacons of the fire trucks.

The distorted voices and radios of the rescue personnel filtered in through the walls and Frank found the entire situation oddly relaxing.

"How are you doing?" Eloise asked.

Her sudden appearance in the room caught him off guard, and Frank jerked upright, spilling the water on himself. He smiled and shook his head.

"I'm okay," he answered, trying to ignore his wet pajamas.

"The police took Shane away," she said, walking to the window and looking out at the activity across the street.

"They did," Frank agreed.

"He needs to learn how to control his temper," she said. Eloise watched for a moment longer, then she turned away and walked to stand in front of him.

"Do you disagree?" she asked him.

Frank shook his head. "Not at all. I'm a little tired, Eloise."

She smiled. "I'm never tired."

Frank didn't have a reply, so he didn't speak. The dead girl sat down and smiled at him.

"How long will you stay?" she asked.

The question caught Frank off guard and he answered, "I don't know. I hadn't really thought about it. Shane was kind enough to take me in."

Eloise nodded. "Would you stay forever?"

The thought chilled him and Frank hesitated. "Well, I like to think that when I die, I'll go to heaven."

She offered a patronizing smile. "I don't believe in that anymore."

"No?" Frank asked.

Eloise shook her head. "I've been here a long time, Frank. If there was a God, He would have called me to Him by now, don't you think?"

"I don't know," Frank replied. "We can't know the will of God."

The statement brought a flare of anger into her eyes, but she remained calm as she answered, "Believe what you will, and I will do the same."

"Fair enough," Frank said, shifting in his chair. This was a side of Eloise he had never seen before. And one he wasn't quite sure he enjoyed.

She looked down at her dress, smoothed it out as a small grin played across her face.

"I shouldn't tell you this," she whispered, her voice so low that Frank had to lean forward to hear each word. "But I liked killing that man."

The words chilled Frank's blood.

"Why?" he asked, keeping the question light.

"He was going to hurt you and Shane," she answered. "I hurt him first. I wanted him to suffer, though. The way he was going to make you suffer."

Frank examined her face, looked at the intensity in her eyes, the firm set of her jaw which had replaced the grin. He wondered if her enjoyment of the violence was a sign of madness. *Will she go down Courtney's road?* Frank thought, suddenly fearful for the dead girl. *What will she do if she goes mad? Will she have to be bound?*

"Frank," Eloise said, interrupting his thoughts.

"Yes?" he said, forcing a smile.

"Would you like to have a tea party with me?"

Frank let out a relieved laugh and nodded. "Yes. Yes, I would."

The little dead girl vanished. Frank knew she was going to the upper parlor where her tea set was placed. He stood up, his gaze lingering on the fire still raging across the street. Frank thought of the family that had lived there, butchered, and he wondered how many more bodies would pile up before the Watchers were through.

Chapter 28: A Difficult Decision

The phone rang and Harlan answered it.

"Speak," Harlan stated.

"Shane Ryan," a male said. "Forty-three years of age. Permanent address on Berkley Street in Nashua, New Hampshire."

"Continue," Harlan prompted.

"Currently in custody at the Nashua Police Station, Panther Drive, Nashua, New Hampshire," the man said.

"For how long?" Harlan asked.

"As long as you need," the man replied.

"Excellent," Harlan said. "I'll have a man down there to question him, soon."

He ended the call, replacing the receiver back in the holder. Harlan kept his hand on the black plastic, a long, thin finger tapping on the phone. Minutes ticked by on the wall clock and he removed his hand. From the top drawer of the desk he withdrew an old rolodex. His fingers, in spite of their arthritis, nimbly sorted through the worn cards.

When he found the proper card, Harlan withdrew it, placed it face up on the blotter and looked at it.

He had not spoken to the man in several years, and their acquaintance was thin at best. But the man owed the Watchers in general, and Harlan in particular.

A smile crept onto Harlan's face and he picked up the phone. He dialed the New Hampshire number and waited as it rang.

A sleepy male voice answered. "Hello?"

"Good morning, Elmer," Harlan said.

"Who is this?" Elmer asked.

"An old associate," Harlan explained. "We had business together, shortly before you ended up in the hospital with a curious injury."

When Elmer spoke again, all vestiges of sleep were gone from his voice. "Who is this?"

"As I said, an old associate," Harlan stated. "We did attempt to retrieve the weapon that wounded you, but unfortunately it was too well protected. However, we were able to obtain several interesting items. One of which was a broach imbued with the spirit of a rather, shall we say, angry young woman?"

"Harlan," Elmer said, and then Harlan heard a door close. "I remember you now. What can I do for you?"

"I have a favor to ask," Harlan stated. "And in return for the favor, I have several items which you may be interested in."

"Really?" Elmer asked. "What sort of items?"

"A candelabra, with blood in the crevices of some excellent filigree. There is also a tea cup that was used to administer fatal doses of arsenic by a disturbed Irish maid. And, the coup de grace, a battered New Testament carried by a violent soldier in Mogadishu," Harlan said.

Elmer's breath was loud and excited in the earpiece of the phone.

"What do you need me to do?" the collector asked.

"I need you to take something to the Nashua Police Station for me. You will deliver it to a young Lieutenant," Harlan said. "He will meet you in the parking lot."

"What is it?" Elmer asked, his voice cautious, worried.

"Do you remember the piano wire you acquired from us?" Harlan inquired.

"Yes," Elmer answered, his voice sinking.

"Bring it to the Lieutenant," Harlan said, and then, in a reassuring tone he added, "the officer will make sure it gets back to you."

"Alright," Elmer agreed. "When do you want it brought to him, and when do I get the objects?"

"Bring it to him now," Harlan ordered. "He's waiting for you. As for the objects, they'll be delivered via our service by this afternoon."

"Excellent!" Elmer declared. "I'll be leaving in a few minutes."

"Very good," Harlan said, and he hung up the phone.

It was a dangerous game, he knew, to bring in another party, but Shane Ryan was forcing his hand.

Harlan needed Shane dead, and the idea of it brought a smile to his face.

There would be nothing painless in Shane's death, Harlan knew, and that was exactly as it should be.

Chapter 29: At the Station

Shane sat at the table in the interview room and yawned. He had spent plenty of time in a variety of jails and holding cells during his active duty as a Marine. There was nothing for him to fear, and nothing new.

The table was a standard, heavy piece of metal, as was the chair he occupied. Across the table was an identical chair, recently vacated by the Lieutenant who had brought him in for questioning hours earlier. A two-way mirror was set within the left wall, and a small camera was positioned in the upper right corner above the door.

Shane suspected he could get up and walk out of the room, but that might lead to some trouble with the police officers on the other side of it.

And he knew the Lieutenant was attempting to think of some way he could arrest Shane.

Shane grinned at the thought and wondered if it would be worth some jail time to punch the officer. There was something wrong about the man, an itch at the base of Shane's neck that told him the man wasn't what he seemed.

Regardless, Shane told himself, *I should have kept my cool.*

I wouldn't be jonesing for a cigarette or a shot of whiskey if I hadn't run my mouth.

The door opened and the Lieutenant walked in with a cup of coffee and a donut wrapped in a napkin. He flashed a false smile and sat down across from Shane.

Shane watched as the man got comfortable, took a drink, then a bite of the donut, and smiled again.

The Lieutenant swallowed and asked, "How are you doing?"

"Fine," Shane said.

"Good, good," the Lieutenant said. He took another bite, then a second sip. When he finished, he looked at Shane in surprise and said, "Oh, I forgot to ask, are you hungry?"

"No," Shane answered. His stomach was twisting itself into knots with hunger, but he didn't want anything from the Lieutenant.

"No, no," the Lieutenant said, putting the remnants of the donut down on the napkin. "You must be starving. Let me get you something."

The officer put the coffee down beside the donut and stood up, going back to the door and opening it.

"Bob," the Lieutenant called. "Bob!"

When no one answered him, the officer turned back to Shane and said, "Hold on one sec."

The Lieutenant left the room, the door clicking shut behind him.

Shane shook his head and twisted the iron rings on his fingers. The metal was warm to the touch and he smiled.

Book 8: Borgin Keep

After a minute, he stifled a yawn and felt cold. Shane rubbed at his arms, wondering if the officer had gone to turn the heat down. His exhalation came out as a white cloud and Shane stiffened.

Shane looked around the room, searching, and in the mirror, he found what he sought. A tall, thin woman stood behind him. Her clothes placed her in the Edwardian era, her gray hair pulled into a severe bun. She wore a lace-trimmed apron over her dress and glasses were perched on her long, angular nose. Her lips were mere hints and her hands had all of the elegance and frightfulness of a spider's legs.

She was stooped, peering at Shane's neck.

He watched as she reached out a hand, the fingers coming to a stop a hair's breadth from his own flesh.

Then she lowered her arm, dipped her hand into a pocket of the apron and removed a long, shimmering coil. A smile, oddly beautiful on such a harsh face, appeared, and she stepped forward.

Shane kept his eye on her in the mirror and twisted in his seat, lashing out with his left hand. It passed through the ghost, her smile dissolving into a grimace. A shudder raced through the room and Shane got up, stepping away from the chair.

The woman appeared a heartbeat later, standing between him and the door. He could see that in her hands was a length of piano wire.

She had every intention, Shane saw, of garroting him with it.

"You've misbehaved," the woman said in a deep timbre. "You need to be punished."

Shane didn't respond. She raised an eyebrow.

"You don't disagree?" she asked.

"Why would I?" Shane answered.

The woman hesitated, then stepped towards him. She moved through the table.

"It would have been easier to catch you from behind," she said, her hands spreading out and pulling the wire taut.

Shane struck her and the ghost vanished only to reappear by the door. Her lips curled in a snarl.

"It's ever so quick," she said. "A loop around your neck, a quick jerk. The wire cuts through flesh and tendon, slips between the vertebrae. You'll hardly feel a thing. Or so I've been told."

She pounced, trying to snare him. Shane pulled away and lashed out with his left hand.

When she showed up at the door again, her face was a livid mask.

"How are you doing that?" she demanded. "Tell me!"

Shane held up his hands, spreading his fingers wide.

"Iron," he said. "It will beat you back each time."

A smile spread across her face. "Will it? Shall we put your theory to the test?"

"Why not?" Shane spat. "I've got nothing better to do."

Her attack was fast, far faster than he suspected it of being.

Her speed could do nothing against the innate power of the iron, and she shrieked as she vanished again.

When she reappeared, her chest rose and fell, as if even dead she could still breathe and seethe. The woman watched him, waiting.

"Why are you here?" Shane asked, breaking the silence.

The question seemed to surprise her.

"What?" she asked.

"Here," Shane said. "Why are you here, in the police station? Did you die on these grounds?"

"I died in my own house, in Boston," the woman barked.

"Really?" Shane asked. "Because you're pretty far from Boston. You're in New Hampshire."

"Someone took me out of my house," she said. Then, in a voice that rose in anger she demanded, "Why?"

"I don't know. I don't even know how you got in here," Shane said, keeping a wary eye on her.

She threw herself at him again, and this time Shane was too slow. The force of her impact slammed him back into the wall and knocked him to the floor. He scrambled to his feet, throwing a punch that she slipped away from. A blow landed against his kidney and he doubled over, gasping with pain. From the corner of his eye, he saw her slash in towards him and Shane threw himself to one side, crashing into the table. The coffee cup was knocked over, the hot liquid splashing against the floor and Shane's pants.

A shimmer caught his eye and Shane spotted a coil of thin wire in the middle of the spilled coffee.

In a flash, Shane knew what it was and dove for it. The air rushed out of his lungs as he hit the floor, but his hand closed around the painfully cold wire.

Struggling for breath, Shane pushed himself upright and looked at the woman. Her eyes were locked on his.

For several seconds they stared at one another, then the woman said, "Did you bring the coffee into this room?"

Shane shook his head, the pain and lack of oxygen stopping him from responding with words.

"Someone," she said in a low, angry voice, "put my wire into a cup full of coffee. *Coffee*. Who?"

"A police officer," Shane responded after he caught his breath.

"Why?" she demanded. "Why would someone put me in a cup of coffee?!"

"Hold on," Shane said. "What's your name?"

"Mrs. Henderson," she answered. "And yours?"

"Shane," he replied. "I think I know why they put you in the coffee."

She raised an eyebrow and waited for his explanation.

"You're here to kill me."

Mrs. Henderson gave a slight nod. "More than likely. I have killed a fair few since my death."

"That means someone is using you," Shane continued.

She frowned. "The thought had occurred to me."

"Do you want to be used?" he asked.

"No," she growled. "I'd rather kill the one who brought me here."

"Fair enough," Shane said, "because I'd be okay with you doing that as well."

A smile played on her face. "Would you now?"

He nodded. "I'll make a deal with you. I'll make sure you go to a quiet place, where you won't be used, if you won't kill me."

She considered the offer for a moment. "A fair deal. I only require one addition to it."

"And that is?" Shane asked.

"I also kill the one who placed me in *coffee*," she hissed, her voice filled with disgust.

Shane eased himself back into his chair, smiled at the dead woman, and said, "I would sincerely like to see that happen."

Mrs. Henderson bowed her head and stepped towards the mirror.

Shane folded his arms over his chest and stared at the door, trying to will the Lieutenant to walk in.

He couldn't wait for the man to die.

Chapter 30: Losing His Cool

Martin was an up and coming cop. A man who had moved quickly through the ranks, bypassing tried and true officers and making waves among the older detectives before earning his lieutenant's position. He had also been brought along by Lisbeth Walker, who had vanished shortly after the murder of her ex-husband.

Occasionally, Martin thought she might have done the deed. There was something wrong with her, a disconnect in her brain that didn't allow her to make lasting bonds with people. She had told him as much when she had been his training officer. Lisbeth had said more after introducing him to a group called the Watchers, who paid him to do just that.

The delivery of a piece of piano wire to the interrogation room had been something new.

As had the taking in of Shane Ryan.

Martin didn't feel comfortable with what he had been asked to do.

No, he told himself. *Don't kid yourself. I wasn't asked to do anything. I was told.*

And the voice on the other end had told him what to do, and who to call. Martin couldn't risk the exposure of him taking money for information, regardless as to how innocuous it seemed at the time. People generally disliked cops who relayed information to third parties.

No threat had been made. None had even been implied.

But it was there, an unspoken reality between himself and the Watchers.

He didn't even have Lisbeth to talk to about it.

And what the hell was that wire supposed to do? Martin wondered. His instructions had been specific, but without any reasons given.

Take Shane Ryan in for questioning should his house not burn down.

Shane's house hadn't burnt down, and so Martin had brought the man in. That had been easy enough. Shane stunk of whiskey and he had an attitude. Not a single cop at the scene had batted an eye.

A coil of piano wire will be brought to you. Leave it in the room with Shane and walk away. Do not let him see it.

Martin had done that too.

Afterward, he had left the room, turned off the cameras, and waited.

A glance at his watch showed it had been twenty minutes.

He considered making a phone call to his contact in the Watchers, but then decided against it. Martin would check on Shane and see what was going on.

Martin put his false, *Hey, I'm your buddy*, smile on and walked back to the interrogation room. He took hold of the doorknob, which was a great deal colder than he remembered it ever being before, and let himself in.

The coffee cup was on the table, but its contents were spilled across the same and on the floor.

Shane sat on his chair, arms across his chest and a smile on his face.

Martin's own smile almost faltered, but he managed to keep it in place as he closed the door behind him and took his seat again.

"Sorry about that," Martin apologized. "Tried to get you something, but you know how it is."

"Sure," Shane said. "Sorry about your coffee."

Martin glanced at the spilled liquid and shrugged, keeping the false smile on his face. "It's not that big of a deal, right?"

"No," Shane said, shaking his head. "Not really. But Mrs. Henderson is wondering why you put her piano wire in your coffee though."

"What?" Martin asked, confused.

A blurred shape slammed into him, knocking him out of the chair and onto the floor. His head struck the tile and the breath rushed out of him. The room spun out of control and he found himself staring up at the ceiling.

"Don't use the wire," Shane said, and Martin turned to see Shane continued to sit, unmoved. "They'll figure it out."

"Doubtful," a woman replied, her voice vibrating with rage. "But I will do as you suggest."

Martin tried to sit up but he was struck from behind, a hard, painful blow that sent him reeling back to the floor on his stomach. He found he couldn't move, his limbs refusing to respond to his commands. All he could see of Shane was the man's worn black boots.

A cold sensation bit into Martin's neck and the unknown woman whispered in his ear, "This, my fine young man, is going to hurt a great deal."

An excruciating pain erupted in his back and what felt like a vise clamped down on his heart.

As the pressure increased, Martin understood two things.

The first was that he was unable to scream. And the second was that the woman had told him the truth.

Chapter 31: David Brings in the New Team

The women, Gabby and Jenna, were twins. Not particularly young, but not old either. David couldn't place their ages and he found that oddly disconcerting.

"Is this it?" Jenna asked. The red tie she wore with her black suit was the only way he could tell the difference between the women.

David glanced at Borgin, then back to Jenna and wanted to ask if she saw another medieval style home around. But he didn't. He kept his temper because he was almost done. He had to bring them in and make the introduction to Emmanuel, if he could find him.

David wasn't thrilled about the idea, but it was something he had always known he would have to do. It was how it transpired, and had for as long as he had worked for the Watchers. For those ghosts who were cognizant and rational enough to interact on a somewhat normal basis with the living, introductions were absolutely necessary. The pleasantries cut back on unwanted deaths.

"How long are we going to wait here?" Gabby asked.

"Until I say so," David snapped.

The women looked at him in surprise, but they didn't flinch or recoil. They were hard, just as everyone he had ever met in the organization was.

"Okay, Gramps," Jenna said. "No need to get all cranky."

David looked at her and wondered what it would be like to draw his pistol and execute her in front of her twin.

Jenna seemed to sense his desire and she raised her hands up and apologized.

David gave a curt nod, reached into the back of the truck and pulled out his shotgun.

"Do you need that?" Gabby asked, sounding more curious than derogatory.

"You've been briefed on what occurred here on my last trip?" he asked.

Jenna nodded and Gabby said, "Sure, unknown ghost took out your partner."

"Yes," David said, "and I have every intention of making him extremely uncomfortable if he reappears."

The twins shrugged simultaneously and waited for David to take the lead.

Cradling the shotgun, David stepped away from the truck and forced himself forward. He hated the sight of Borgin Keep, the way it protruded from the hill and stabbed at the skyline. David had always known it was a terrible place, and one that might well be the death of him.

For some reason he had never thought it would claim Blanche.

He realized it had been a stupid oversight on his part, as was his attachment to her. But they had been friends, and David had never had many of them.

"Who built this again?" one of the twins asked from behind him.

"A monster," David answered. "He's the worst I've ever met. He doesn't always appear when we arrive. If he shows up tonight, and I hope to God he does, then you'll see it. Even smell it. And let me tell you, I haven't known too many of the dead that I could actually smell. Seems like there's a cloud of death that follows him around. Maybe it's just me."

Gabby came up to his left. "Maybe. Who knows, though. I knew a ghost, little girl, down in Providence. She smelled exactly like peppermint. Couldn't figure it out until I learned she had used a peppermint to choke her nanny to death."

"What a sweetheart," David muttered.

"Hey," Jenna said from behind, "takes all kinds to make a world."

Gabby laughed and David could only shrug at their private joke. His concern for them dropped the closer they got to the Keep. There was a change in the air, a coldness that surprised him. They were still a hundred feet away and the temperature lowered with every step.

The twins became quiet. Finally, Gabby asked, "Is it always this cold?"

David could only shake his head, not trusting his voice to be steady.

"How strong is he?" Jenna asked, coming up on his right.

"It isn't just him," David said, clearing his throat to mask his fear. "No one's sure how many he has killed. Or how many others died after he vanished."

"Hold on," Jenna said. "I thought he was dead and buried on the grounds."

"It's what the organization suspects," David said, wondering why the women hadn't read the dossier on Emmanuel Borgin or his house. "Even now he won't confirm that he died on the grounds. Or even where he's buried. If he is buried. He might be tucked away in one of the rooms no one ever found."

"House of horrors?" Gabby asked.

Jenna snickered as David nodded.

"There were always the rumors about sacrifice and black magic," David said, leading the way towards the back of the building. "They were never confirmed. The journals and diaries of others who were frequent visitors here do mention ritual cannibalism, though. And it seems like it's something the dead here wish they could enjoy again."

"We've heard rumors that this is where our people go when they misbehave," Gabby said.

"It is," David replied. He stopped and looked at the twins. "That's part of your job. To help people disappear."

The women smiled.

"No," David said, shaking his head. "Not in the way you're thinking. That was executing someone. Maybe making it look like an accident. Or a crime. Maybe even digging a grave somewhere, or dumping them in the ocean. That's child's play. This, Borgin, it's the real deal. You do something bad enough, and Blanche and I, we brought you here."

The twins glanced at one another and then Jenna asked, "Like who?"

"Think about it," David said. "This is your job now. Think about someone who the organization would love to have put in here."

"That's easy," Gabby said.

Jenna nodded. "Abigail. But Abigail got away. Scooted right out after that mess she managed to make in New Hampshire."

"She didn't make the mess," David corrected. "She just panicked. She ran."

"Yeah she did," Jenna said. "I heard from one of the accountants that they were able to trace some of her money to the Keys."

David nodded. "That's definitely where some of the money is. But that's not where she is."

"Oh yeah?" Gabby scoffed. "And do you know where she is?"

David gestured towards the Keep.

Jenna raised an eyebrow. "And how do you know that?"

"I put her in there," David said, and he started to walk again.

"What happened to her?" Gabby asked as they hurried to keep up.

"They took her arms and her legs," David answered.

"And then you cleaned up the remains, right?" Jenna asked.

"It never got that far," David clarified.

"Why not?" Gabby asked.

"Because of what happened to Blanche," David said. "Harlan had to call in a few favors. One of the New Hampshire agents showed up at the Vermont State Police impound yard and claimed the Jeep as his own. Plus Harlan had another one of our people working in the yard that day."

"And that worked?" Gabby asked.

David snorted. "Of course it worked. Cops never suspect anything. We've had people in law enforcement for a hundred years. Why do you think no one ever tore the Keep down? Or any of the others?"

"Oh," Jenna said, nodding. "But you've still got to get rid of the body, right. I heard that, from Harlan."

"When he was explaining the job," Gabby added. "Whoever got caught in here, the remains had to be taken care of."

"I didn't clean up her remains," David said as they reached the door to the kitchen.

"Why not?" Jenna asked.

"She's not dead yet," David stated, and he went into the Keep.

Chapter 32: Another Interrogation

Marie Lafontaine sat in the chair across from Shane Ryan and looked at the man she had once been intimate with.

Physically he was no longer the same. He had been beaten and bloodied, shot and burned. His left ear was healed, but a mangled mess. Scar tissue, pink and raw, was pulled tight along the right side of his neck. As he tapped his feet he drummed his fingers on the table, and she saw again how he had only eight remaining.

The skin on his face was stretched thin, as if he hadn't been eating well for months. Beneath his eyes were black circles and a vein thumped rhythmically in his left temple. His eyes watched her and they were guarded.

They were in Interrogation Room 2. Room 1, where Shane had been kept when brought in by Martin was being processed as a crime-scene.

Less than an hour earlier, Shane had opened the door to Room 1, stepped out and informed a passing officer that the Lieutenant was dead.

Shane had been secured in the second interrogation room, and then it was discovered that the cameras focused on Room 1 had been turned off. All of the cameras. It hadn't been a malfunction because the different pieces of equipment ran on various systems, ensuring that at least one was always able to catch the interrogation of a suspect fully.

The Lieutenant was indeed dead. He was without any signs of obvious trauma, and no one quite knew when the man had died. The last anyone had seen of him had been near the coffee pot almost two hours earlier.

"Hello, Shane," Marie said.

"Hello, Marie," Shane said, his voice tight. "Funny meeting you in a place like this, huh?"

There was no humor in his voice and none in his eyes.

She had called him after Kurt's funeral, but Shane hadn't answered, or returned her text messages.

"What are you doing here?" she asked.

"You should ask the Lieutenant," he replied.

Marie kept herself from frowning. "He's dead."

"That, I have discovered, doesn't stop some people," Shane said.

"Well, if I see him around I'll ask him," Marie quipped. "Since he's not here, either physically or spiritually, why don't you fill me in?"

"Evidently, the gentleman in question didn't appreciate my mouth," Shane answered. "So he brought me in to chat about the man who immolated himself in my side yard."

"And did you have anything you could tell him about that?" she asked.

"I told him where he could go," Shane said. "And how to get there. And how most of his friends could go with him."

Marie sighed. "Did you tell him anything pertaining to the man who lit himself on fire?"

"No." Shane yawned. "I did not."

"Alright," Marie said, changing tack. "How did the Lieutenant die?"

Shane shrugged.

"When did he die?" she asked.

He shrugged again, rolling his shoulders and yawning again.

"How long did you wait before you told someone he was dead?" Marie asked.

"Until I was sure he was dead," Shane replied.

"Why did you wait until you were sure?" she asked, surprised.

"Because I didn't like him," Shane snapped. "I wasn't going to perform CPR on him and I sure as hell didn't want anyone else to either."

Marie sat back, stunned.

Shane shook his head. "Don't look shocked, Marie. He was miserable. He's in a better place."

"Did you kill him?" she demanded, leaning forward.

Shane grinned. "No. No, I did not."

"Did he just fall over and die then?" Marie asked.

"Sure," Shane said. He crossed his arms over his chest and closed his eyes.

"What are you doing?" Marie said.

"Going to sleep," he answered. "I'm tired. Your Lieutenant kept me up for a little too long."

"You can't go to sleep," Marie hissed. "That man is dead, Shane."

Shane cracked open his eyes, looking at her through narrow slits.

"He is dead," Shane responded. "And I can go to sleep. I don't care. I didn't care that he fell down. Didn't bother me that he died. Now, do me a favor, Marie. Either send me downstairs to one of the cells so I can at least sleep on a cot, or leave the room and turn off the light. I'm tired."

A knock on the door interrupted her.

In silence, she stood up and left the room.

Detective Dwayne Bright was in the hallway, an unhappy look on his face.

"What's up?" Marie asked, closing the door behind her.

"They got Martin to the hospital," Dwayne said. "No marks on him except for what the coroner swears is frostbite."

"Frostbite?" Marie asked, stiffening.

Dwayne nodded. "Yeah, he says there's a spot of it the size of a fist on Martin's back, like someone put a piece of the Arctic there and held it for a while. Doesn't know what the hell could have caused it, and he won't know the cause of death until he can open Martin up. He's going to get on it today."

"Alright," Marie said, regaining her composure.

"Do you think he had anything to do with it?" Dwayne asked, nodding towards the interrogation room.

"I don't think so," she answered. "But I'll keep asking."

Dwayne gave a sad nod. "Yeah. Okay. I'll let you know if anything else comes up."

Once he turned and left, Marie reentered the interrogation room.

Shane was in the same position, his eyes closed once more.

She slammed the door shut but he didn't react.

"Who did it?" she demanded.

"Who did what, Marie?" Shane asked.

"Who killed him?" she hissed in a voice barely audible. "Carl? Eloise? Was it Courtney?"

At the last name, Shane's eyes snapped open.

"No," Shane answered after a moment of silence. "None of them. Why don't you review the video? See what you get."

Marie almost told him there was no video, but she kept the information to herself.

"I want you to tell me who did it," Marie said, sitting down.

A bitter smile crept onto his face.

"You don't know," he said, straightening up. "There's nothing on the film. Or did he turn it off? He did, didn't he? The Lieutenant was worried someone might see a little something they shouldn't, so he shut it off. Easy enough to explain I'm guessing or he wouldn't have risked it."

Marie clenched her teeth but said nothing.

She didn't need to.

"Yes," Shane whispered. "That was it."

In a louder voice he said, "I really don't know what happened to that fine, upstanding officer. It's a shame really. I was shocked. Surprised. Saddened. Horrified. I don't know, let's put through a few more adjectives out there, shall we? Lock me up or send me home, Marie. I've had about enough for one day."

Marie wanted to put him in a cell. Judge Valade was on the bench for the day and he didn't have an issue with signing a material witness warrant.

But that would only seal Shane's lips permanently and Marie wanted to know what had happened to Martin.

Without looking at Shane, Marie stood up and left the room. She needed to get the okay to let Shane go.

Shane's bitter laughter followed her down the hall.

Chapter 33: In the Keep's Kitchen

The room was an atrocity.

It stank of death, the fetid odor of rotting human flesh polluting the air. The bags containing the remains of the most recent trespasser, as well as the limbs of Abigail, remained where David had left them.

Blanche was face down on the floor. She looked like a child's abandoned toy, and he realized that she had been nothing more than that in the end.

David shined his flashlight around the kitchen.

"What's in the bags?" Jenna asked, pointing her own light at one of them.

"The last person to trespass here," he answered.

"Got it," Jenna said. "We were told there's a landfill with a crematorium nearby?"

David nodded. "West Lebanon. Retired prison guard runs it. Doesn't mind the extra money and doesn't ask any questions."

David stepped further into the room, went around Blanche's corpse, and reached the door into the main hall. He stepped out and held the flashlight up. The hall was empty and he waited in silence until the twins joined him.

"Why aren't there any doors?" Gabby asked.

He didn't look around. "It changes."

"What? That's true?" Jenna asked.

David looked at her. "Listen to me. Listen well. This building changes. Constantly. Whether it's only an effect of the ley lines beneath the foundation, or if it's really some twisted, brilliant architectural masterpiece, the Keep changes. You *will* get lost in here. It has happened to others. And they haven't been found. All of the rumors about Borgin Keep are true, and you need to remember that."

"Alright," Jenna murmured. "We'll remember it."

"How do we meet him?" Gabby asked. "Do we call for him?"

David shook his head. "He doesn't know you. He'd rather take you deeper into the Keep than listen to you. I hope he listens to me."

"And if he doesn't?" Gabby asked.

"I give him a belly full of salt and we run like hell and hope we can get out before he comes at us," David explained.

"Have you had to do that before?" Jenna asked.

"Once," David said.

"Did you get injured?" Jenna asked.

"You could say so," David answered.

"How so?" Gabby inquired.

"Let's just say that before that incident, having children was an option," David said.

Neither of the twins said anything.

David pushed the painful memory away and took a deep breath as he adjusted his grip on the shotgun.

"Emmanuel!" he called out.

There was no echo. The building seemed to devour the sound of his voice.

"Emmanuel!" David yelled again.

From a shadow, the dead man emerged. A wide, manic smile was spread across his face and he laughed as he saw them.

"Hello, David," Emmanuel said. "Blanche is here."

David shivered and said, "I know."

"I'm glad. She misses you," the dead man continued. "She is ever so fond of you. Did you know Abigail is still alive?"

"How?" David asked, surprised.

"A wounded deer," Emmanuel whispered. "It was chased in here by someone, and she's eating it. Right down to the bone! You can hear her gnawing on them, it's so very exciting, David."

Then Emmanuel straightened up and smiled past David at the twins.

"And you are Gabby and Jenna?" the ghost inquired.

David nodded that they were, and then he stopped.

"How did you know that?" David asked.

Emmanuel smiled. "Is he the one then?"

Horrified, David spun around and pulled the trigger on the shotgun, but the hammer merely clicked.

"Sorry," Gabby said without the slightest hint of sympathy. "Harlan doesn't believe you'll be quiet once you retire."

The shotgun was ripped from his hands and thrown aside. A cold hand grabbed him by his hair and jerked him off his feet.

David tried to free himself, twisting to the left and right.

Emmanuel's laughter filled his ears as he dragged him backward.

His flashlight was knocked out of his hand and David was plunged into darkness.

"Relax, David," the dead man said. "There are so many people here that you know!"

Which was exactly what David was afraid of.

Chapter 34: On the Way

Shane had been to many places in his life. He'd traveled the world and drank and fought with some of the best. There had been rough bars in Thailand, taverns in England, and beer gardens in Germany. He had drunk homemade vodka in Serbia and smoked hash with tribal leaders in Iraq.

Never, however, had he set foot in an abbey before.

"You look nervous," Frank said, putting the magazine he had been reading down.

Shane chuckled, adjusted his dog tags under his shirt and nodded. "Little bit."

"Why?" Frank asked. The question was sincere, without a mocking tone.

"I know what I've done," Shane replied. "Kind of feels like it's wrong to be in here."

"Well," Frank said, "first you have to get rid of that idea. You're in an abbey, not a church. Second, if we were in a church, that would be the perfect place to reflect on what you've done. Church is where you can ask forgiveness, and God can forgive, Shane."

"That's the thing," Shane said, clearing his throat. "I don't want forgiveness. I don't feel bad about anything I've done."

Frank's eyes widened and he sat back. "That's a whole different story then."

"Yeah, it is," Shane said. Before the conversation could continue on its uncomfortable course, an older man walked into the small waiting room.

The stranger was tall and what could only be described as well-built. His jaw was square, his eyes bright behind a pair of black framed glasses, and his steel gray hair was cut close to the scalp.

Both Shane and Frank got to their feet, the authority of the man was undeniable. It radiated from him.

"Shane, this is Abbot Gregory. Sir, this is my friend, Shane Ryan," Frank said.

The old man grinned, extended his hand and Shane was surprised to find it callused.

"I like building things," the Abbot explained, holding up his hand to show the breadth of the calluses.

"He's a fantastic carver," Frank added.

"Let us say that I enjoy carving," the older man said with a soft smile. "Now, is this a social visit, Frank, or business?"

"Business, I'm afraid, Abbot," Frank said.

The older man nodded. "I was fearful that it was such. Please, follow me, gentlemen."

They walked into a small study, with a single, narrow window set between a pair of thick bookshelves. No light entered the room, the sun unable to pierce the thick drapery covering the window.

There was a low, wide desk at the far right with a pair of tall, straight-back chairs in front of it. Shane and Frank each sat down while the Abbot went behind the desk, easing out a large, heavily carved chair.

"Tell me," the Abbot said, "what brings you to me?"

Shane leaned forward and said, "Well, sir. We came to find out if you know anything about Borgin Keep."

The reaction was instant.

Shane watched as the Abbot's face drained of color. His hands, which had been steady, trembled on the desk and he moved them down to his lap.

The Abbot gave them a tight smile, his nostrils flaring. He cleared his throat, adjusted his glasses, and said, "I wish you hadn't come for this."

Shane glanced at Frank and saw the tightness in the man's body. Frank looked like a predator ready to pounce.

"Why?" Frank asked.

Abbot Gregory responded with, "It is a terrible place. We have tried, on several occasions, to clear it of the dead. Unfortunately, we were not able to do so."

"How many did you lose?" Shane asked.

Frank looked at him in surprise.

The Abbot shook his head. "Too many. And they were not recruits. They were experienced men. We believed that they had been in the worst places imaginable. We had ourselves disabused of that belief."

"What do you know about the place, Abbot?" Frank asked.

The Abbot took off his glasses, pinched the bridge of his nose, and let out a sigh. He folded the arms of the spectacles, placed them on the desk, and began to talk.

For the better part of three hours, he went into minute details about Borgin Keep and Emmanuel Borgin who had ordered its construction. With every morsel of information, Shane felt worse. Some of what the Abbot told them reminded Shane of his home. The rooms that could shift. Entire floors that vanished. Doors appearing where they shouldn't.

And the numbers of suspected deaths were staggering.

He spoke of an organization that referred to itself as the Watchers. An entity that sought out haunted houses and buildings.

In the nineteen seventies, according to the Abbot, they had even managed to cultivate a contact within the organization. A man from Concord who had told them a great deal about the Keep, and of how the living were fed into the structure. Sacrifices were made, and at times, when the Watchers needed to, problematic people were brought there to disappear.

"And so our contact disappeared," the Abbot said at the end. "Vanished. We suspected he had been discovered, and that he had been brought to the Keep. It was then we decided on the first attempt to rid the structure of its ghosts."

"Had he been brought there?" Frank asked.

The Abbot nodded. "And we found what was left of him."

"What do you mean?" Shane asked. "Was he there for an extended period?"

"No," the Abbot said, shaking his head. "Not at all. Two days. We were hoping to rescue him, if he was indeed in the Keep. He was, but he had died. Horribly."

Shane didn't ask what 'horribly' was. He had seen plenty of deaths and he could picture a horrible one easily enough.

"So," Abbot Gregory said. "I've told you what I know. Now, will you tell me why you're interested in the Keep?"

Shane and Frank did so. They alternated, first one speaking and then the other, until they had told the Abbot everything in regards to their situation.

When they had finished, a silence fell over the room. No one attempted to break it for several minutes. Finally, Abbot Gregory stood up and walked to one of the room's many bookshelves. He adjusted his glasses, peered at the titles, and then nodded to himself. The Abbot withdrew a tall, slim item from the shelf and carried it back to the desk.

He placed it in front of him as he sat down and Shane studied it from where he sat.

From what he could see, the object Abbot Gregory had retrieved was nothing more than a leather folder. It was kept closed by a silver hinge, but there were no other markings or any sort of writing on the cover.

Abbot Gregory put his hands out, rested them on the folder and a sad look settled on his face.

"Once," the Abbot began, "there was a great and terrible man. His crimes were nothing short of diabolic. His vices were the stuff of legend. And one day his penance was the same."

Abbot Gregory looked down at the leather beneath his hands.

"When I first took my vows and learned of the dead," he continued, "I met a man. He was old. Nearly a century, although he couldn't be certain. No one told him when he had been born. He had no marker, no way to know. At the time of our introduction, he was a resident here. The brothers cared for him. In the last years of his life, he had sought the Order out and he had told us what he knew."

Abbot Gregory grew silent and wiped at the edge of one eye. He cleared his throat before he spoke again.

"This man spoke of an organization which sought to harness the natural and supernatural powers of New England," the Abbot said. "And he gave sufficient details to let the Order know that he was not lying. The end goal, he said, was the resurrection of a terrible creature. A beast which had been hunted and hounded until driven into a corner. And once there, it had been slain."

"Who," Shane started to ask, but the Abbot held up a hand and Shane stopped.

"It is said that the place is hidden," the Abbot went on. "Not even our guest knew of the location of its body. All he knew was that it was on a ley line, and nothing more in that regard. There was other information he had and the brothers were slowly mining him for it. The task was difficult, for he was old and his brain was not the sharp weapon it once had been."

The Abbot smiled at both of them. It was an expression full of melancholy.

"As one new to the order, it fell upon me to care for this gentleman," the Abbot said. "Bathing, feeding, and dressing. Those needs we have as infants and as the very aged. We became friends, for he was exceptional and I was impressionable. I believe that this is what my Abbot had hoped for. Our conversations were pleasing, and in the end, he left me this."

Abbot Gregory patted the folder.

"I have never looked into it," the Abbot said. "I was asked not to, by my friend. He told me that as cliché as it sounded, I would know when the right time to open this was. We had a good laugh over that, but after he passed away, I never found the right time. I realize, however, that the moment is now."

He slid the folder across the desk to them and then stood up.

Book 8: Borgin Keep

"I am going to leave for a short time," Abbot Gregory said. "I do not wish to see my friend's handwriting, to do so would be to call up memories of his voice, and that would be too painful for me to bear."

Unable to respond, both Shane and Frank watched the Abbot exit the room.

When the door had clicked shut behind the man, Shane turned to Frank, who shook his head.

"No," Frank said in a low voice. "That's all you, my friend."

Shane shrugged, reached out, and picked up the folder. The leather was warm and smooth beneath his fingers, the silver of the clasp cold and hard. He opened it on the desk, then adjusted his seat so both he and Frank could see the letter.

Quietly the two men leaned forward and started to read.

Chapter 35: The Letter

My Dear Friend,

Who would have thought that I would have become a cliché in the end? A wretched, old malcontented hedonist who has sought refuge within the arms of the Church.

The irony is not lost upon me, and it is not, I am certain, lost upon you.

Before we begin, I must be honest with you. When we first spoke, and you learned of my lack of knowledge of my own age, you asked me what I remembered about my childhood. I had professed a deep and profound ignorance.

It should come as no surprise to you that my statement was an unabashed lie. First, I did not know quite who you were, or whether I should trust you. Second, when I decided I could, we had already become friends and I did not wish to frighten you with my early, troubled beginnings.

My earliest memory, young Dom Gregory, is of war. The Union general Sherman had marched through the South, and war had come to the people. I was but a child, only five years of age, and I can say with honesty that I was a product of brutality and abuse. I shall not bore you with the details, but let it be sufficient for me to say that should I have ever met my natural father, I would have made him suffer exquisitely.

Now, back to my memory.

Yes, war. I remembered moving through the fields of battle. I was neither horrified nor was I attracted to what I saw. Death was merely an aspect of life I was well familiar with, and one, quite frankly, which I found boring.

You might ask why this would be frightening, and herein is where the story turns.

There were wounded upon those fields, Gregory, and at the tender age of five, I found it quite thrilling to sit and watch the light bleed from a man's eyes as he died.

Years passed and I aged, was educated, and traveled the world in such a way as to make Oscar Wilde blush. I sampled a wide assortment of pleasures, indulged in a variety of sins, and learned ten thousand ways to inflict pain.

Book 8: Borgin Keep

I was not a good man, Gregory, and I do not know if my continued discourse on my former employer is an attempt to redeem myself, or merely me seeking to avoid Hell.

It is a terrible feeling to not know what I want.

A frightening sensation, if I am to be honest, and it is one I wish I didn't experience.

Now, since I am being honest, I have come to the main reason for this letter.

For almost a decade, I have spoken with Abbot Patrick about the Watchers. I have told him of their plans, although I do not know their end game. I have also told him of the home of Emmanuel Borgin, which will play a significant role in whatever their coup is to be.

In our many hours of pleasant conversation, I have spoken on a plethora of subjects. Never have I spoken of my business with the Watchers. There is good reason for that, Gregory. At some point, you will learn what true horror is and I would rather that I not be the one to introduce you to it.

That being said, I must speak to you of Borgin Keep.

It is a terrible place.

Your Abbot can fill you in on the details, but when I say to you that the building is a miniature version of Hell, know that I do not exaggerate. Not in the slightest way.

I have seen terrors within those walls, and I have witnessed events which drove others mad.

Recently you learned of the existence of ghosts. Spirits. Specters. Whatever you wish to call them, you know they are real. You know some of them can threaten your physical form. So too you know how to contain them. We have spoken of salt and iron.

And lead.

Let us not forget lead, young Gregory.

Not only can you use a lead box to tuck them away like an unwanted memory, but you can use lead to hide yourself as well.

Emmanuel Borgin considered me a favored guest. When we met it turned out, we had a great many similarities in taste. Quite literally. While it pains me to admit this, I feel I must. I had a longing for human flesh in my younger years, as did Emmanuel. We often dined together on the purloined meat of lesser men. I shared with him methods of harvesting he had yet to consider, and thus I was the fortunate son, if you will, of a despotic and mad king. While the throne was never to be mine, or anyone else's for that matter, I was allowed to come and go as I wished.

Before I came here, I took advantage of my curious station.

While others were molested when they entered the Keep, I was not. Emmanuel's ghost, and those who he had trapped there with him, left me alone. I could wander about and learn the seemingly nonsensical shifting of the building's interior.

I digress. Your Abbot has those details as well.

I must remain focused and tell you all before I am spent.

Within the Keep, there is a room. A single, solitary room, with a small window. The window is made of leaded glass. The frame lead encased wood. Each wall has been covered with beaten lead. As has the ceiling and the floor. The door itself has a leaden shield which drops into place.

It is a safe room. Within it, you are untouchable by the dead.

I have placed items within the room for a man to use to escape from the Keep if necessary. No others know of it. I had intended to go back, at some point when my courage returned, and to destroy the building.

As you can see, my courage has yet to find its way back to me. Or perhaps I have forgotten how to find it.

Regardless of my courage, or lack thereof, the safe room is there.

You may not be the one to enter Borgin Keep, and I would be lying if I said I wished the task did fall on you, but I suspect you will know the one who will have this burden.

Whoever goes in must remember this, Emmanuel despised patterns. The only way to get to the room is to turn in the wrong direction. If your instinct tells you to go down, then find stairs leading up. Should you want to turn right, turn left. Trust no one in that house.

Not the living, should there be any, and certainly not the dead.

I will leave you with what I have become, Gregory, a cliché.

You will know when the time is right to give this, and I will say as much to you when I see you next.

You were a true friend to an old and terrible man. I cannot say how much I enjoyed our games of chess, your abysmal knowledge of Latin, and your ability to make this old cynic laugh.

Ever your friend,
Louis B. Johnson, III

Chapter 36: Another Phone Call

Harlan's days were becoming worse instead of better, and his mood was not improving.

Ms. Coleman stood in his office, her body rigid and tense. She had delivered the bad news and it was obvious she expected his wrath to fall upon her.

Normally it would have, but a dim part of Harlan was impressed with her refusal to run from the room. Courage and intelligence seemed to be in short supply in the organization of late and he didn't want to punish it.

"Ms. Coleman," he said, forcing his voice to remain even and neutral.

"Sir?" she asked, the question a squeak.

"Please take the rest of the day off," he said. "I want nothing, thank you. Only leave the office, do something pleasant, and return to work in the morning at your usual time. I will call if something changes."

"Yes, sir," she replied, and he could hear the relief filling her words.

Her discipline continued to impress him as she walked calmly from the room, easing the door closed behind her.

A few minutes later, he heard the main door thump as she left for the day.

Harlan leaned back in his chair, closing his eyes and trying to ignore his pounding headache.

He was, it seemed, suffering a setback for every bit of ground he gained. Less than an hour before, the phone had rung and Jenna had called in. She had reported the first good news he had heard in days. David had been removed by Emmanuel, which ensured there would be no loose ends in that regard. While Harlan had regretted the necessity which required the death of David, the man had chosen an unfortunate time to leave the organization.

Jenna's good news had been quickly followed by bad news, and from her as well.

Harlan had learned of Abigail's continued existence. Somehow, the woman hadn't died in the Keep. From what he was told she had lost her limbs, and she was more than likely insane, but she was still alive.

And alive meant she was a danger.

Harlan had never had any doubts about her capabilities and her ability to survive in Borgin Keep was justification for his thoughts on her. She would die soon enough, as long as she didn't have any other food, although David might help her in that sense.

And what if Emmanuel manages to trap her soul? Harlan wondered. *What if she decides she wants to stay a little longer? How will that come back on me?*

He sighed and forced himself to examine the second bit of bad news he had received.

Shane Ryan wasn't dead.

Far from it.

The man was alive.

And the Lieutenant was dead, murdered by the ghost who had been brought in to end Shane. Which meant Harlan had lost all of his avenues of influence into Nashua, a city which still had several structures on the ley lines.

Let us not forget the loss of the ghost, he thought bitterly.

And the inability to return the possessed wire to Elmer would mean either a hefty payment in like objects to the collector, or the refusal of the man to help them again.

Harlan snarled and slapped his palms down on the desk, knocking the phone out of its cradle. He snatched it up, slammed it back into the base, and fumed as he sat in his chair.

A moment later, the phone rang and Harlan leaned forward to read the caller ID.

All he could see was a random assortment of numbers.

The phone stopped ringing at ten.

Less than a minute later, it rang again.

Once more, it was the same random numbers.

It stopped ringing at nine.

The pattern repeated itself until Harlan answered the call after it had gotten down to three rings.

"Who is this?" he yelled into the phone.

"My, you're a little testy," Shane Ryan said.

Harlan was shocked and couldn't respond.

"I can hear you breathing," Shane said, chuckling. "Which is good."

"What do you want?" Harlan said, in perfect control of himself.

"I want to chat," Shane said. "See how you are. Find out what the weather's like down in Boston."

"You could always come down," Harlan replied. "You have the address."

"I may," Shane said. "Don't count it out. When I do though, it'll be to finish this whole show up."

"And what if I send someone up there first?" Harlan inquired.

Shane let out a pleased laugh. "Oh, Harlan. You already have. Two observers in the house across the street. Someone to set fire to my house. The Lieutenant. And let's not forget Lisbeth. Did you forget her, Harlan?"

"No," Harlan growled. "I certainly did not."

"Excellent," Shane said. "Fantastic, really. You know, I've been doing a bit of research on your organization. Fascinating stuff. I'm not quite sure what your endgame is, but I'm looking forward to helping you fail."

Harlan's heart beat erratically in his chest. He tried to speak but his anger refused to allow words to form.

"I will find out," Shane said and the joking, playful banter was gone from his voice. It was replied with a cold, hard edge. "I want you to understand that. You need to remember, Harlan, that I have one of your little workers with me. And they like to talk. I like to listen. You should too. Soon, and I mean very soon, you're going to hear something you won't like."

Shane ended the call and Harlan held the phone to his ear until the busy signal beeped.

He returned the phone to the base and sat at the desk, his back rigid.

There were a great many places Shane could strike. Each of them would set the program back. Some more so than others.

The problem then wasn't when Shane would attack, but where.

And if he had someone like Lisbeth trapped and questionable, then there were several structures that would prove to be more enticing targets.

The Watchers had always been a moderate-sized organization, and therefore lacked the numbers to protect all of the properties.

Harlan forced himself to stand, his legs stiff as he walked to the map on the wall which displayed all of the organization's holdings. He stared at it for a long time, trying to decide which places to protect.

Where Shane would strike first.

After a long time, Harlan turned away from the map and returned to his desk.

He had phone calls to make and troops to assemble.

Chapter 37: Preparing for War

"So what now?" Frank asked.

Shane tapped his fingers on his pack of Lucky Strikes.

"Now," Shane said, "I'll have Eloise question Lisbeth again."

Frank shook his head. "I don't like it."

"I know," Shane replied.

"There has to be a better way," Frank said. "We have to let her soul move on."

Shane waited a moment before he responded.

"I agree that her soul needs to be allowed to move on," he said, "but not yet. Not until this thing with the Watchers is done. I'll leave word with Eloise that if something happens to me, she should let Lisbeth go."

Frank frowned. "There's no guarantee that she would do that."

"You're right," Shane agreed. "There isn't. Eloise can be a little difficult at times."

Frank raised an eyebrow and Shane sighed.

"Alright," he admitted, "she can be extremely difficult. But I can make sure she takes care of it."

"I don't believe it," Frank said. "But I don't suppose we have much of a choice at this point."

"Not if we're planning on coming out on top," Shane said.

Frank gave a reluctant nod. "Alright. So we torture Lisbeth for more information about Borgin Keep."

"Yup," Shane said. "Then we arm ourselves as heavily as possible before we go in."

"Why go in?" Frank asked. "We should try to burn the place down."

Shane shook his head. "I don't think it'll be that easy. I think we'll have to find Emmanuel's bones first, then salt and burn them. Otherwise his ghost will linger on the ley lines and the Watchers will still be able to tap into his energy."

Frank snorted, his mouth set in a grim line. "This situation is terrible."

The front door opened and was slammed shut.

In a heartbeat, Shane and Frank were on their feet and moving towards the study door. Neither of them had a weapon. Shane pressed himself against the left wall while Frank did the same on the right. From the hallway came the sound of heels on the floor.

Whoever it was, Shane realized, didn't care if they were heard or not.

And that bothered him.

He clenched his fists and crouched down. Shane lowered his center of gravity and tensed the muscles in his thighs.

The doorknob turned halfway and then stopped. Shane's eyes never left it, even as it returned to its original position.

The door exploded inward, the latch tearing through the jamb and the hinges ripping out of the same.

In an awkward spin, the door arced to the floor and slammed down, bouncing twice.

Shane sprang forward but Frank's arm caught him and pulled him back.

Marie Lafontaine stood in the doorway, glaring at him.

Shane couldn't find any words to speak.

"Shane Ryan!" she snapped.

He shook himself out of his stunned daze and managed a weak, "What?"

"What the hell is going on and what are you planning on doing?" she demanded.

Frank answered before he could.

"Detective," Frank said, smiling and keeping his distance. "We're going to a place called Borgin Keep in Vermont."

"Why?" she asked. "What are you going to do there?"

"We've been led to believe that there is a ghost there who has a considerable amount of strength," Frank explained, "and that a rather disagreeable group of people are seeking to channel his energy."

Marie looked at Shane and asked, "Does this have anything to do with Kurt?"

Shane could only nod.

"When are you two leaving?" she asked.

"We're not sure yet," Frank answered. "We still have some information and equipment to gather."

"Alright," Marie said.

She walked into the room, passing Shane to go and sit in his chair. The detective crossed one leg over the other, picked up a book from the end table, and opened it up.

"Marie," Shane said, finding his voice.

"What?" she asked. She continued to flip through the pages, not bothering to look at him.

"Marie," Shane said again. "What in the hell do you think you're doing?"

Shane heard Frank sigh but he didn't care. Marie was forcing him to retain control as she sat in his chair.

"I think I'm looking at a book, Shane," she said.

"No," Shane said, his voice tight and angry. "What the hell are you doing in my chair?"

"I'm waiting for you," she replied.

"Waiting for what?!" he yelled.

Marie glanced over at him. "I'm waiting for you to get the information and your equipment together."

"Why?" Shane asked, confused.

"Because I'm coming with you," she answered, and she turned another page.

Chapter 38: Surprised and Shocked

Frank stood beside Shane and stared at Marie Lafontaine.

The detective continued to ignore them both, and Frank felt a sudden wave of admiration for the woman wash over him. He grinned and shook his head, a small chuckle escaping. Frank let out a laugh, and then he laughed harder as Shane shot him a disgusted look.

"Come on, man," Frank said as he went and dropped down into his chair. "She got us."

Shane opened his mouth to speak, closed it, and turned around sharply, executing a perfect about-face. He stomped on the broken door as he left the study.

Marie closed the book, returned it to the side-table and eyed Frank.

"Hello, Frank," she said.

"Marie," Frank said, chuckling. "I have to admit it, I'm impressed. Not too many people can get away with talking to him like that."

"No, they can't," she agreed. "It's the Marine in him."

"Partly," Frank acknowledged.

"Yes," she said, glancing at the doorway. "The rest of it is sheer stubbornness."

"Exactly," Frank said. "So, you're in it for the long haul?"

"I am," Marie said. "He got me thinking today when we had him in the station."

"About what?" Frank asked.

"*Why* he was in there," she answered. "See, there was no real reason to bring him in. Not at first. Doesn't matter if a guy immolated himself in the yard. There was enough evidence gathered to support the claim that you and Shane made. Not only that, but why did they only bring Shane in?"

"I don't know," Frank said, watching her. "Why did they only bring Shane in?"

Marie leaned forward and said, "He's the primary threat."

Frank waited for her to continue and she did so.

"I'm not exactly sure what it is you and Shane have done," Marie said. "And at some point, I may, but right now, what I do know is he's gotten rid of a few ghosts. I can only assume that there's some sort of ghost-loving community out there that might not be too happy with him."

Frank nodded. "Bit of an understatement."

"So you've had some trouble," Marie said, and it was a statement, not a question.

"Yeah," Frank said. He hesitated and then asked, "Did Shane ever mention someone named Mason to you?"

She shook her head and asked, "Why? Is this someone I should be concerned about?"

"No," Frank said sadly. "He was a friend of Shane's. Served with him in the Marines and helped us out a little while back. The people who tried to set the house on fire, they killed Mason and his wife."

"What! Why?" Marie asked.

"Scare us off," Frank answered.

"Shane doesn't work that way," she murmured.

"Evidently they didn't know enough about him," Frank said, nodding his agreement with her.

"Tell me everything," Marie said, her eyes boring into Frank. "Tell me everything these people have said and done."

"Alright," Frank said, and he did.

Chapter 39: With Mrs. Henderson

"Who is she?" Eloise whispered from behind Shane's chair.

"Her name is Mrs. Henderson," Shane replied. "She may be living here with us for a while."

The coiled length of piano wire was on the long coffee table, and Mrs. Henderson was on the other side of the room. Her back was to him as she looked out the window. After several silent minutes, she turned around and faced him.

"I can feel death here," she said. Her eyes widened in surprise at the sight of Eloise. "Who is this?"

"Eloise," Shane murmured.

The dead girl crept out from behind the chair and gave a small curtsy. "My name is Eloise, ma'am."

The right-hand corner of Mrs. Henderson's mouth twitched up as she replied, "A pleasure, Eloise. Where are we, Mr. Ryan?"

"My home," Shane replied. "I am hopeful that you will reside here a while until we figure out what best to do."

Mrs. Henderson nodded. "I will be happy to. Are there others, Eloise?"

"Oh, yes!" Eloise beamed. "Many of us, Mrs. Henderson! You need to meet Carl, though, he seems to know absolutely everything about everything."

Mrs. Henderson raised an eyebrow and Shane watched as she struggled to keep a smile from her face.

"Will you introduce me to Carl?" Mrs. Henderson asked.

Eloise nodded and said, "Follow me!"

The two ghosts exited the room, leaving Shane alone. Suddenly the world seemed to weigh down on him, and he yawned, his eyelids far heavier than they should have been. He let his head rest against the back of the chair and closed his eyes. His thoughts raced, and sleep would not come to him, but he refused to look out at the world.

Instead, he listened to the steady beat of his own heart and the way his blood thrummed in his veins. He found his thoughts drifted towards Mason and once more, he wondered if his friend had even known of what had happened. If the man had any knowledge as to the danger lurking in the shadows.

Shane hoped he hadn't.

But thoughts of Mason twisted into a memory of the letter from Harlan. The audacity of the man, his brazenness.

Shane wanted to hurt him. He wanted him to suffer for every breath he had taken after Mason had breathed his last.

Maybe I will, Shane thought. *If I'm lucky enough.*

His thoughts drifted, swung around to Frank and Marie Lafontaine sitting in the study.

Shane didn't want her in the house, but he didn't think the woman would leave of her own accord. He was also curious as to what she knew, if anything, about the current situation. Shane wondered if she had managed to dig up some information on the Lieutenant.

He knew he should ask her, but he didn't want to.

Shane didn't want to talk to her at all.

And Frank's acceptance of her irritated him. On a less visceral level, he knew that Frank's defense of Marie was right. Shane also knew that they would need her in the Keep.

But he didn't want her to know that.

Shane let his mind wander as he stared out the window, not truly seeing anything beyond it. A short time later, there was a noise, and he turned towards it.

Mrs. Henderson had come back. Once more, she walked to the window, but she didn't look out of it. Instead, she fixed her gaze on Shane.

"You have a great many dead here, Mr. Ryan," she stated.

Shane nodded.

"Most were murdered," Mrs. Henderson continued.

"Yes," Shane said.

"There are dead children here," she added.

"That's true as well," he said.

"You didn't kill them," Mrs. Henderson stated, and then she added, "they have no one to care for them."

Shane wondered if he looked as surprised as he felt.

"It would be good," Shane said, choosing his words carefully, "if they had a woman to take them under her wing."

"So it would," Mrs. Henderson said, a small smile playing on her lips.

Shane peered at the murderess for a moment, then he made a decision. "Would you be willing to remain here, for however long you wish, to help me with them?"

The dead woman gave a short bow. "I would be delighted. Where will you keep my wire?"

"Where would you like me to?" he asked.

"Here, if you could," she said, her voice taking on a softer tone. She turned half way and looked out the window. "I like the view. It reminds me of my home."

"Then I'll keep it here," Shane said. "We'll put it on a shelf."

She nodded and then left the room.

After a moment, Shane stood, stretched, and decided it was time for him to leave the room as well. With heavy steps, he made his way towards the library and Courtney.

Chapter 40: The Meeting House

For one hundred and fifty years, the house on Olive Street in Dunstable, Massachusetts had served as the meeting house for the Watchers. The building was small, a single-story structure that was innocuous and unassuming.

A caretaker, employed by the Watchers, lived in the home and kept it ready for their use.

A block away was a warehouse, one that changed in shape and size as need dictated. Every few years a new business moved into the warehouse, but each was a false-front.

Like the house on Olive Street, the warehouse too was owned by the Watchers.

Harlan thought upon the history of the organization as his driver guided their Land Rover into the warehouse. The massive door glided shut behind them and lights flickered into life. Bright, powerful beams illuminated the interior and revealed the other cars parked in neat, orderly rows.

Harlan was the last one to arrive, as was fitting.

He waited until his driver turned off the car engine before he climbed out. The man, whose name Harlan couldn't recall, remained with the vehicle. Using a cane for support, Harlan limped towards the door marked "Caution! Electrical Hazard!" When he reached it, he flipped up a small control pad and placed his thumb upon the reader.

The lock clicked, and the door popped open half an inch.

Harlan took hold of the latch, pulled it, and stepped into a small, wood-paneled elevator. He closed the door behind him, and selected the down arrow. The winch hummed and the elevator descended. When the door opened a minute later, Harlan stepped into a bright hallway.

There was a moving sidewalk set into the long corridor, and Harlan stepped onto it cautiously. Falling on his way to the meeting would in no way impress the others.

It might, Harlan knew, cause them to question his abilities.

And I am sure they are questioning that already, he thought with a grimace.

The corridor, and thus the moving sidewalk, led directly to a second elevator a block away. When Harlan reached it, he rode it to the main floor of the house on Olive Street.

The others were gathered around a long table. Men and women of varying ages. Each had a silver goblet in front of them. An identical goblet waited at Harlan's seat at the head of the table.

He was the first among equals.

No one spoke as he made his way to the dark, carved chair that was his symbol of authority. He was conscious of the way his cane thumped on the floor, and of the weakness in his legs as he walked. When he reached his chair, Harlan managed to pull it away from the table without any semblance of weakness.

He sat down, hung his cane up on the arm of the chair and picked up the goblet. Harlan held it in front of him for a moment before he intoned, "Our watching is nearly done."

The others lifted their goblets and together they each took a sip of the dark red wine.

"Hello, everyone," Harlan said, looking around at the fifteen people. "I trust your travels were uneventful. I apologize for the suddenness of this meeting, but we seem to have a situation which has the potential to get out of control."

"What exactly," Zane Ketch said, "is the situation? We have not had many details, other than the loss of some of our more important facilities."

"I have heard of a gentleman by the name of Shane," Clair Willette said. "Evidently he is causing us a bit of trouble?"

"A bit," Harlan agreed. "He is the reason for this meeting."

"Really?" Zane asked. "A single man?"

Ingrid Brown leaned forward. "He is extremely accomplished, Zane. He is not an amateur. I was with Harlan when we watched Shane, and his compatriot, Frank, enter the Slater Mill. They were prepared, utterly, for the encounter. I've seen few as capable as them."

"So," Clair said, "what have you done to contain him?"

The tone in Clair's voice told Harlan that she already knew. What was more, it told him that she and Zane were working together in regards to the Shane issue.

They were maneuvering to place one of them in Harlan's seat.

Harlan smiled. "We have attempted to contain him several times, but each has failed, I am sorry to say."

Zane seemed taken aback by Harlan's honesty.

Which was what Harlan wanted.

Clair, one of the smartest Harlan had worked with, was not distracted by the naked truth. She fixed a cold glare on him, her thick lips paling.

"I expected better from you, Harlan," she said in a harsh tone. "What is the damage so far?"

"Are you interested in the damage sustained while I have tried to neutralize Shane, or in the damage caused by Abigail's mismanagement?" Harlan asked. "Or perhaps both?"

Clair's eyes widened, and she pushed herself away from the table.

Out of everyone at the table, it had been Clair who had been most vocal in her support of Abigail as the one to lead the organization into the future.

Abigail's abject failure was a direct reflection of Clair's vision.

"Has anyone heard from Abigail?" Zane interjected, seeming to remember where his loyalties lie. "Her vanishing with a significant amount of funds isn't a reflection on anyone."

Clair visibly relaxed, nodding along with several others.

"I doubt," Blaine Worthington said, "we'll ever find her. She was far more adept at hiding her funds than we thought."

"I know where she is," Harlan stated, and he told the gathered leaders about her place at Borgin Keep. Several of the members paled, and Imogene Herdman hurried from the room. Harlan could hear her vomit in the bathroom.

"Harlan," Clair said when he had finished. "Tell me, what damage has the organization suffered after Abigail's removal?"

Harlan nodded. His answer had to be chosen with care.

"It began simply enough," Harlan stated. "I attempted to intimidate Shane and Frank by using the Hitchcock team to send a message. Next, I secured the house across from Shane's with our top observation agents. If you have read the brief I sent along, you'll remember that 125 Berkley played a significant role in the organization prior to the cultivation of Slater Mill as an asset."

Several members nodded, and when no one spoke, Harlan continued.

"They were more than adequate team," Harlan said. "The man and woman had undertaken numerous observation and termination missions."

"Then what happened to them?" Zane asked.

"Shane and Frank happened to them," Harlan said, his tone one of disgust. "They made their way into the structure, took our operatives by surprise, and executed them both."

"Protocol dictates arson," Blaine reminded them all. "Did you follow that, Harlan?"

"Considering I wrote the protocol for such an incident," Harlan snapped, "I should think I did."

"Was the arsonist successful?" Zane asked.

"No," Harlan responded.

Angry murmurs raced around the table.

"What happened?" Zane asked.

"Somehow," Harlan answered, "the arsonist lit himself on fire."

"Now, Harlan," Clair said in a voice heavy with anger, "would be an exceptionally fine time to tell us how you have succeeded in having Shane Ryan assassinated."

Harlan ground his teeth and shook his head.

"I haven't," he grumbled. "Not yet."

"Have we lost anyone else?" Clair demanded.

Harlan nodded.

"Who?" she snapped.

"Another officer in the Nashua Police Department," Harlan replied.

"We only had one more!" Zane yelled, jumping up and knocking his chair back. "My God, you've left the entire southern portion of New Hampshire bereft of assets!"

"What else?" Clair hissed in the sudden silence which dominated the room. "There's something else, I can tell."

For the first time in quite a long while, Harlan felt unsure of his position within the organization.

Such was his fear that Harlan considered, if ever so briefly, a lie.

In the end, he told the truth.

"I had to use Mrs. Henderson," he said.

Murmurs filled the air, and more than a few of his compatriots wiped their brows. First one, then another chuckled.

"Harlan," Blaine said with relief, "you could have led off with that, old man. We all would have felt considerably better about the situation."

Harlan shook his head, and the murmurs were silenced.

"She was unsuccessful," Harlan said. "At least in regards to Shane Ryan. While I have no way to confirm it, I believe he managed to speak with her, and she was the one who killed Lieutenant Owen."

"Then Shane is still alive?" Clair asked.

Harlan nodded.

"Shane is alive," Clair said again, "and you have effectively neutered the organization in Southern New Hampshire."

Anger spiked in Harlan, and he straightened up.

"You listen to me, Clair," he began.

Clair held up her goblet, and Harlan went silent.

Every person around the table, except Harlan, lifted theirs as well.

"No," Harlan growled. "No. You will not oust me. I have obtained this position by right, and I will keep it by the same."

Clair took a sip, and the others followed her example.

Before Harlan could protest, a length of rope was looped around his neck. The fibers were sharp and painful as the cord dug into his loose flesh. He tried to fight but his old body couldn't. His killer pulled him out of his chair, sending the heavy bit of furniture crashing to the floor. Harlan was dragged backward, away from the table.

As he gasped and desperately tried to breathe, he saw Clair stand up. She walked to the head of the table, picked up the chair, and straighten it before she took her place in it. Someone took Harlan's goblet away, and another handed Clair hers. She lifted it up and said, "Our watching is nearly done."

They were the last words Harlan heard, as his life was choked out of him.

Chapter 41: Listening to Death

David could hear her crawling somewhere in the darkness.

He sat on the floor, backed into a corner. The dead had stripped him of his clothes, but they had yet to touch his limbs.

He took it as a blessing.

David ignored the way the cold of the stone seeped into his flesh or the way his joints throbbed with pain. Instead, he focused on the chair he had found.

It was old, held together mostly by dowels.

But he had cut his finger on a nail. Not only a steel nail, but an iron one.

David had touched the metal with his tongue and tasted it.

So as he sat in the darkness, he used his fingers to pry the nail free, a centimeter at a time. He would remove it. The effort might last hours, perhaps days.

David wouldn't be able to tell. Time was too fluid. Trying to count the minutes would plummet him into madness.

Something scraped along one wall nearby and then a woman let out a wordless moan.

The sound caused David to shudder and his fingers to slip on the iron, tearing a bit of his fingernail away. He winced but kept his mouth clamped shut.

With great care, he sought out and found the head of the nail again. He tried to ignore the sounds Abigail made as he moved the iron back and forth, attempting to loosen the grip of the old wood upon it.

The nail wouldn't be much, but it would be something to use against the dead, and something was all David needed.

Just a little bit of an edge, and if he had an edge, David believed he could get out.

"Where are you?" Abigail hissed, her words difficult to understand.

David tilted his head to the left, angling it so he could hear her better. His fingers continued to wiggle the nail free.

"I can smell you," she said, her words tinged with mania. "And I'm *hungry*."

The nail came free, and David sighed with relief. He squeezed it in his palm for a moment, then he swung the chair and shattered it against the wall. David was left with a single leg in his hand, and he listened.

The sound of skin being scraped against stone filled the air. David closed his eyes in the darkness and tried to visualize the distance. Abigail drove herself forward, shimmying and dragging herself along.

David held his breath, listened past the sound of his heartbeat, and then brought the leg of the chair down with a crash.

Abigail's shriek told him he had judged the distance correctly.

Again and again, he smashed the chair leg into her. He kept it up until her shrieks became grunts, and until there was nothing at all.

David sank to the floor, dropped the leg and sought Abigail's throat. He found it, and a faint pulse as well.

David sat down beside her, wrapped his hand around her neck and choked the last bit of life from her.

Chapter 42: A Steadier Hand

Harlan's body would be found in the South End of Boston. The man would be seen as a victim of a robbery, another senseless death. One amongst many.

Clair nodded to Jenna and Gabby as the women picked the corpse up off the floor.

"Send me a status report as soon as you're complete," Clair said.

"Okay," Jenna answered, and the two of them dragged Harlan to the elevator.

Clair turned her attention to the group still seated at the table.

"Shane Ryan and Frank Benedict have proven to be too much of a drain on this organization's resources," Clair said, looking around the table. "Now, we have two acceptable options before us. The first is to ignore them both, to allow them to continue on with what they're doing. As far as we know, they don't have much more than a basic grasp of what the organization's purpose is."

"And our second option?" Blaine asked.

"We send in a team and have them killed," Clair said. Those around the table nodded their heads in agreement.

"Harlan used the Hitchcock team," Blaine said. "We've had excellent results from them in the past. Occasionally a job may run over, but they haven't failed."

"I don't think they will," Clair said. "It doesn't matter how much training Shane or Frank received during their military careers."

She looked around the table, meeting each member in the eye. "Do we all agree that this is an acceptable course of action?"

Each person gave their assent.

"Excellent," Clair said. "I'll call their broker shortly and establish all of the logistics necessary."

Imogene, who had been with the organization for almost forty years, looked at Clair and asked, "And what if Shane and Frank defeat the Hitchcock team?"

Clair and several of the others burst out laughing. Wiping a tear of mirth from her eye, Clair said, "I don't think that Shane, regardless of his skills, will be able to resist the talents of the Hitchcock team."

Imogene opened her mouth to protest, but Clair held up a hand. "Let us not dwell any longer on the issue of Mr. Ryan. I believe we have some news regarding the One."

A hushed silence swept through the room.

Zane nodded.

"We have received word," he said, "of the discovery of a burial ground in Amherst, New Hampshire. It is tucked away on private property, and the landmarks correspond roughly with the documentation that we have."

"When will we know for certain?" Clair asked, trying to control her excitement.

"The research firm is establishing ownership," Zane replied. "Once that is done, we can see about obtaining the property."

"At any cost," Clair stated.

Zane gave a short bow. "Of course."

"Until such time that we have confirmation of the burial ground," Clair said, "we will continue to prepare the House. What free time we have will go in the securing of Shane and Frank."

Clair took a deep breath and smiled at her compatriots. The unpleasant removal of Harlan was pushed out of her mind as she said, "Remember, we are almost done. We are close to realizing the goal which has driven this organization for one hundred and fifty years."

Clair lifted her goblet high and said, "To the One!"

They emptied their goblets as one and brought them down with a simultaneous crash to table. Clair grinned, the warmth of the wine rushing through her.

The future, she knew, would be as dark as they hoped.

Chapter 43: Not Quite Asleep

Shane spent more time in the library than in any other room of his house. He had brought in blankets and a pillow, choosing to sleep there on most nights. Carl disliked it, but the dead man was overprotective most days.

Shane stripped down and slid between the blankets, pulling them close. No sooner had his head reached the pillow than he heard Courtney.

The noises of her passage came from the corner with the oubliette. As Shane got as comfortable as the floor would allow him, the room's temperature decreased significantly.

Courtney moved about the room, rattling the shades and moving books.

Shane waited for her to remember he was there, or to return to the oubliette.

She walked closer to him, the cold causing him to shake.

"Are you sick?" she asked.

"No," Shane replied. "I'm concerned."

"What's bothering you?" she inquired.

Shane gave her a brief synopsis of everything that had happened since the discovery of the two observers in the house across the street.

"They'll be coming back," Courtney said after he had finished.

Shane nodded. "I hope so. I may not be here when they come."

She snorted dismissively. "They will receive a cold welcome."

"I believe it," Shane said, adjusting the dog-tags around his neck.

"Wherever you go, Shane," Courtney said, then hesitated a moment before she continued on, "you go, will you take me with you?"

"Yes," Shane answered.

"Thank you," she said, a pleasant sigh escaping from her.

"We're going to a bad place," Shane said after several minutes of silence.

"Don't you always?" she asked, and even though there was no humor in her question, Shane chuckled.

"That's a fair point," he replied.

"What do you think you'll find in this new place?" Courtney asked.

"I don't know," Shane answered truthfully. "It's supposed to be bad. Really bad. I'm kind of worried about you going in there."

"I'm already dead, Shane," Courtney reminded him. "Not a whole lot more can be done to me."

"Don't believe that," Shane murmured. "There's always something that can hurt us, whether we believe it or not."

"And what's going to hurt you?" she asked.

"Losing you," Shane answered.

"I'm dead," she whispered.

"But you're not gone," he replied.

"Shane," she started.

"No," Shane said, getting into a sitting position and interrupting her. "It was bad enough losing you the first time. Then I almost lost you to madness."

"I haven't beaten the insanity yet," she said, her voice quivering. "It is a struggle each day. Sometimes I don't think I can hold out. Other times never seem to end. It is a terrible situation."

Shane shook his head, the sadness sweeping over him. He dropped his head into his hands, his shoulders shaking as he wept.

Behind him, Courtney began to sing, and the pain was nearly too much to bear.

Chapter 44: 125 Berkley Street

At 3:20 in the morning, the Hitchcock team approached Shane Ryan's house through the woods. They moved cautiously, wary of any alarms.

The building, they discovered, was unprotected.

In a matter of minutes, they had secured the front and rear exits. The lines of communication were cut. A cell phone disrupter was set into position and turned on.

Each member of the team had memorized the layout of the house, although some of it had seemed strange. Rooms identified with question marks, the legend at the bottom of the original map explaining that the map maker didn't know if the rooms existed or not.

The team leader approached the front door, reached out and tested the doorknob.

It was unlocked.

She hesitated, not trusting what she found.

But the map had mentioned the lack of security as well. No windows or doors would be locked. The long dead mapmaker hadn't explained why.

The team leader pushed the thought out of her mind, twisted the doorknob and let the door glide open on silent hinges. Nothing out of the ordinary appeared in front of her. The night-vision goggles she wore flickered, surprisingly temperamental.

She brought her pistol up and stepped across the threshold. Her partner moved with her, holding a pump action shotgun loaded with salt rounds. Intelligence on the house had stated that there were several ghosts who resided within the structure. How friendly the ghosts were with the owner was unknown, but it always paid to be prepared.

She had learned that more than once.

The bedrooms, she knew, were upstairs, and twenty-three long strides carried her to the main stairwell. She walked at a steady pace, weapon at the ready. When they reached the second floor, the rear team appeared from the back stairs.

In perfect coordination, the four of them maneuvered in silence. The rear team established themselves outside of one of the bedrooms while the team leader and her partner took up position by the second. She held up her left hand, the fingers spread wide. One after the other she folded her fingers down until only the index finger remained. Then she extended all of them again and motioned her team forward.

In perfect unison, they opened the doors.

The bedroom was empty.

In the green tinted glow of the goggles, she looked around the room.

There was no one to be seen. A quick check confirmed the initial assessment.

She stepped out of the room, still wary.

The other team did the same.

Howls of fury filled the air as at least ten ghosts raced towards them. Shotguns roared and several of the dead disappeared, but others came through the walls. The dead were everywhere and she had a cold realization that there were too many to stop.

She opened her mouth to call to her team to fall back, when her attention was drawn to a large ghost who ran towards her.

The other ghosts fell upon her team and ripped into them.

Her team's shocked and pained screams ricocheted off the hallway's walls even as the man reached her. He yelled at her in what sounded like German, his hands striking her in the chest and pushing her backward. Reflex forced her to bring her weapon up and she emptied the magazine into the man.

Only to watch the rounds strike the ceiling, great clumps of horsehair plaster exploding from the impact of the bullets.

Then she was going through a window, the sound of glass shattering dim in the background of her mind. As gravity pulled her relentlessly to the earth, she understood she would soon be dead.

The team leader struck the earth stretched out, the gun knocked from her hand as bones were shattered. She felt them all for a moment, and then her spine was severed, and she felt nothing at all.

Her lungs struggled to supply her body with oxygen, and her eyes continued to take in the hazy green world of the night vision goggles. She watched with growing horror as the rest of her team was hurled out of the window. Screams started and were cut off in a heartbeat.

The green glow of her goggles flickered and went out, leaving her in darkness. Her lungs strived to take in air, her heart-rate increased as it tried to keep her alive. While she struggled to live, the team leader heard a voice.

"Carl doesn't like strangers," a little girl said.

Small, icy fingers crept around the team leader's throat and squeezed.

"And neither do I," the little girl whispered, and the child's grip tightened.

Chapter 45: Looking Upon the Keep

As dawn lit the horizon, Shane, Frank and Marie stood beside Frank's car.

The night before, Carl had woken Shane up. The dead man had been uneasy, concerned about people on Berkley who had an odd interest in the house. After Shane and Frank had talked it over, Frank had called Marie and the decision had been made to leave for Vermont as soon as possible. Harlan, Shane suspected, might decide on a preemptive strike.

The decision was made to leave sooner rather than later, and he and Frank had gone to Marie's apartment where they had finished the preparations for the journey.

In the end, it had taken the better part of three and a half hours to get to Borgin Keep. Once they had established where it was, they had doubled back, found a road stop diner, and had a quiet somber breakfast.

With their stomachs full and the entire day ahead of them, they were prepared. They carried iron and salt, shotguns, and the means to set Borgin Keep ablaze.

Without any words, they walked to the Keep. The air around it stank of death and decay, of putrefying flesh and a deep rot that left a foul taste on the tongue. Waves of cold lapped out from the stone structure, and nothing could be heard.

Not the hum of insects or the chatter of animals in the forest nearby.

The world around Borgin Keep was silent and dead.

Shane was surprised to see the evergreens and firs were still alive, or that grass would even grow.

As they passed along, first the front of the building, and then along the right side, Shane kept his eyes away from the windows. He could feel people watching him.

Not one or two, but twenty or thirty.

Maybe even more.

They did not look at him with hope, or out of idle curiosity.

He could *feel* their malice. The entire structure pulsed with it.

When Shane turned the corner to the rear of the house, he saw the kitchen door. It looked exactly as it had in the photos he had found online. A battered and rotten piece of wood that hung cockeyed from its hinges.

From what he had read, Shane knew it was the only safe entrance into the Keep.

Safe was a relative word, and Shane doubted that he, Frank, or Marie would have anything close to resembling safety within the stone walls.

Shane pushed the door aside and felt a shock roll through him. It was unpleasant and dirty as if some wretched man had touched him. For the briefest of moments, Shane hesitated, then he quelled his fear and stepped in.

His stomach roiled at the stench of death in the room. In the dim light, splotches of what looked like rust were splashed about the kitchen. Old, defunct appliances lurked in the shadows, and an open doorway led into the rest of the Keep.

Shane took a deep breath to steady his sudden onset of nerves and walked deeper into the house.

He crossed the threshold of the kitchen and entered a long hallway. Shane took out his flashlight and thumbed it on. The bright LED beam illuminated the corridor. The wall on the left seemed too short while the wall on the right stretched to an almost obscene height. He felt as though he had walked into a funhouse mirror, and the sensation was unsettling.

Doors lined both sides of the hall. The corridor was longer than the building was.

"What in God's name is this?" Frank asked in a low voice.

"That," a voice said in the distance, "is not a name you should speak here, young man. It will bring you nothing but sorrow."

The words were followed by a chuckle that raced along the edges of the walls and vanished into the far end. Shane's flashlight flickered and went out, leaving them in darkness.

"Now," the voice said, coming closer. "I can sense you've come prepared. Iron and salt. The trusted friends of the living who know about the dangers of the dead."

Cold air curled up around Shane's feet and stung his legs beneath his jeans.

"I will introduce myself," the voice said, "and then I hope you will do the same. I am Emmanuel Borgin, and I welcome you to my, oh so humble home."

"My name's Shane," Shane replied.

Marie and Frank added their names as well.

The sound of clapping filled the air, and when Emmanuel spoke again, it was with distinct pleasure.

"Well, I must assume you are here to send me on my way?" the dead man asked, laughing.

"That's the basic plan," Shane agreed.

"Anything else to it?" Emmanuel asked. "Shall you seek to save my soul as well?"

Shane snorted out a laugh. "Hell no. I don't care if you're saved or not. From what I read, you deserve to rot in Hell. No. I'd like to set fire to this place of yours and watch it get wiped from the face of the earth."

When Emmanuel spoke again, it was without mirth.

"You would destroy my home?" the dead man asked, his voice harsh.

"We would," Frank answered.

Emmanuel let out a sharp laugh. "I always admired honesty. It was far more potent than any lie I could ever tell. The truth was eminently more powerful. A brutal tool, if you knew how to wield it. I can say, in all honesty, then, that I appreciate yours. I hope you shall, in turn, appreciate mine when I tell you that I plan on driving each of you mad. Are you ready?"

Before Shane could respond, Marie spoke for them all.

"Do your worst," she said, and brought her shotgun up to her shoulder.

And the building shuddered in response, knocking the three of them to the hallway's floor.

Chapter 46: And Each is Alone

Frank pushed himself up onto his hands and knees as he said, "Shane."

When Shane didn't respond, Frank spoke Marie's name, and when she too didn't answer, Frank got to his feet. He reached out in the darkness, and his hand struck a wall where there shouldn't have been one. Frank turned to the right, arm still outstretched, and it remained in contact. He continued to pivot, stopping only when his hand came into contact with a door.

With his right-hand stationary, Frank reached out with his left and found another wall, closer than the first. Cautiously he extended his left hand above his head and found a wooden bar.

I'm in a closet, he thought.

Part of him wanted to take his backpack off and get out a match to confirm his suspicion. All that would do, he knew, was waste a match. And he didn't know if he would need them all.

Frank trailed his right hand down the door, found the cold metal of a doorknob and turned it. First to the left, then to the right. The catch resisted and didn't open until he twisted the knob hard and put his shoulder against the door.

With an audible groan, the door popped open, swinging out and smacking against a wall. Light filtered in around the edges of boards haphazardly nailed to a window.

Frank remained where he was, taking in the entire room before moving into it.

There was an old bed extending from the right wall. Battered and dust covered furniture occupied the free space.

After he stepped out of the closet, his attention was drawn to an antique vanity. Beneath a fine coating of gray dust, were the various accouterments of a lady. Art Deco jewelry, makeup, silver combs and brushes.

Frank was both fascinated and repelled by them. A strong, demanding part of him was screaming for him to reach out and pick them up. At least one of them.

He shook his head and took a step back.

A sigh caught his attention, and he turned around. His eyes darted about the room, seeking the source of the sound.

Yet he saw nothing.

He took a step away, and it was then that his gaze fell on the bed. Beneath the old blankets, he saw a form. The barest hint of a person.

A body, hidden and tucked away from the light of the day.

Frank was about to turn away when the sigh sounded again.

It came from the body.

Without knowing why, Frank took a step towards the bed.

What if there's someone under there? he asked himself. *What if they're trapped here and need help?*

Frank reached the bed, grasped the edge of the top blanket, and pulled it back. Dust rose up in a huge cloud, momentarily obscuring his view.

He covered his mouth and nose with his free hand, waiting for the dust to settle enough for him to see.

When it did, he found there was still another blanket to be turned up. This one was a deep red, unaffected by the passing of time. Once again Frank stretched out his hand, took hold of the blanket, and pulled it back.

A sheet, silver and shining like the moon might in a summer sky, greeted his eyes.

The form of a woman was revealed, the chest rising and falling in a slow, easy rhythm.

"Hello?" Frank whispered.

The sleeper didn't respond.

"Hello?" he repeated, a little louder.

Beneath the sheet, the woman moved slightly, but then returned to the same position.

Frank didn't bother asking a third time. Instead, he eased the sheet back, away from the face, and took a surprised step backward.

The woman was dead.

And not recently dead.

She had been dead for decades.

Her cheeks were sunken in, as were her eyelids. The lips were smeared with a dark red lipstick that matched the second blanket. Blonde hair, the color of straw, lay sprawled across a silk pillowcase.

The thin straps of a nightgown rested against the stark lines of her bony shoulders. Her chest, still covered by the sheet, continued to rise and fall. The scent of cinnamon greeted his nose, and Frank wondered what he had revealed.

As if in answer to his question, the woman's head turned, her dead and closed eyes fixed upon him.

The lips parted, and a foul air was expelled as she said, "Hello."

Fear, raw and unforgiving, crashed over Frank and he fought against a primal urge to run.

Instead, he planted his feet, ignored the terror, and managed a weak, "Hello."

The dead woman's mouth formed a smile, nothing more than a slash in skin that cracked and crumbled with the movement.

"How did you get into my room?" she asked.

"I don't know," Frank answered.

"Did you not come through the door?" she questioned.

"The closet," Frank replied. "I came in through the closet."

The woman let out a small giggle.

"Oh," she said, "then it was Emmanuel who sent you. My, what a pleasant host he is. Always so thoughtful. So considerate. He always sends me someone, well, tasty. Mr. Borgin sent me a woman before. A delightful girl. She went quite mad, I am afraid. I was disappointed that she didn't last longer. Will you?"

"Will I what?" Frank asked.

"Last longer," the dead woman said. She rose into a sitting position, the sheet falling down to her wasted lap. Stick thin arms and near skeletal hands appeared, the fingers toying with the fabric.

"Tell me," she whispered, "that you'll last longer. So much longer than the last one."

Frank clenched his hands into fists, felt the cold, hard comfort of the iron rings he wore and nodded.

"Yes," he said, nodding. "I'll last longer."

Frank stepped towards the dead woman and swung. His right fist crashed into her skull, which collapsed beneath his hand and plunged the room into darkness.

Chapter 47: Drinks in the Parlor

"How was your ride up this evening?"

Marie blinked and looked around, confused. Bright light dazzled her, making it difficult to see.

"Hello, Marie," the unknown man repeated. "I say, are you quite all right?"

"Um, yes," she lied. "I'm fine. Everything's okay."

"I don't think it is," the man said. A hand, firm and confident, took her by the arm and helped her to sit down.

"Here," he said, "take a sip of this."

A cold glass was pressed into her hands, and Marie accepted it. The stranger guided it to her lips, and she obediently took a drink. She recoiled, the liquor bringing tears to her eyes and a cough to her lips.

"Let me turn a light out," the man said.

A moment later, a click sounded, and the light that had made it impossible for her to see was gone.

Marie blinked, pink and red dots flickering through her vision.

The sound of something being dragged across the floor caused her to wince, and the stranger chuckled.

"You know," the stranger said, "I think your ride up was a bit more distracting than you're letting on."

Marie shook her head and was finally able to see the man who was speaking.

He was handsome and familiar. The man, who looked to be in his early thirties, had a square jaw and fine cheekbones. Blue eyes were marked by laugh lines and his dark black hair, short on the sides and a bit longer on the top, was combed to one side.

"Drink up, Marie, drink up," he said, holding up his own glass.

Marie nodded and took a drink, the second sip of the strong liquor going down easier than the first. She relaxed and looked around.

Beautiful paintings hung on wood paneled walls while stone busts stood among leather bound books. Heavy, dark draperies concealed a pair of windows, and a large, well-stocked liquor cabinet dominated the entire left wall.

"Our friend Francis has gone to see Genevieve," the man said, finishing his own drink and setting the glass down on a marble table to his left. "I suspect she may keep him a bit. She's always been sort of fond of dashing young men."

Marie nodded, took another, longer drink and settled down into the comfort of the chair.

"Now," the man said. "Tell me, did you have a long ride up?"

"No," she said.

"I'm surprised," he said. "Getting out of Boston can be so difficult."

"We didn't come out of Boston," Marie corrected, her words slurred. "Nashua. In New Hampshire."

"Ah," the man said, nodding knowingly. "No wonder you had a rough ride. Half of the roads aren't fit for a horse let alone a Ford. And the recent thaw hasn't helped the conditions at all. You know, the three of you could have left a message for me at the post office. They would have sent a runner to inform me if you had to cancel."

Marie was horrified at the thought. "No. I wouldn't do that."

"Well," he said, smiling. "I appreciate you keeping your engagement. I do so enjoy the company."

Marie watched as he stood up, went to the bar, and took down a bottle of what looked like cognac. He carried it over, winked at her as he uncorked it, and topped off her glass. The aroma was potent and appealing.

She waited until he had returned to his chair before she took another drink.

"Tell me, Marie," he said. "Do you like my home so far?"

She looked at the elegance of the parlor, vaguely recalled a stone building that resembled a castle, and nodded.

"So do I," he said with a sigh. "It cost me a terrible amount of money to build. But it was worth it. It was terrible that I had to marry for the money, she was a wretched woman, mind you. However, in the end, it was worth it. Decidedly so."

Marie nodded her agreement.

"You're a very amicable woman, Marie," he said. "I hope your friends are as pleasant as you are."

"They are," Marie assured him. "Well, Frank is. Shane can be testy. A little difficult."

"You know," the man said, leaning forward, "I suspected as much. He looks like, how do they say, like a hard case? I must say that while he would probably be a good man in a fight, that's not really what we look for here."

"He can fight," Marie agreed. "He likes to fight."

"Of course he does," her host said, sitting back once more. "You only have to catch the glint in his eye to realize that."

"Frank's a nice man," Marie continued. "Used to be a monk."

"Really?" the man asked, a conspiratorial grin on his face. "You don't say."

Marie nodded. "And a soldier."

"My," the man said in a soft voice, "he's duality in the flesh. Peace and violence combined in one body. I do hope Genevieve is careful with him."

"He's good," Marie said. She took another sip of the cognac.

"Do you like that?" the man asked, grinning.

Marie nodded.

"It's a Croizet," the man said. "Exceptional. Monsieur Croizet began producing it shortly after Napoleon seized power."

"It's good," she said.

"Yes," the man said, chuckling. "It certainly is."

A tremendous bang sounded, and the door in the wall behind her host shuddered in its frame.

Marie, drunk as she was, felt certain the look of surprise on the man's face mimicked her own.

The door was slammed into again, and then it burst open.

A tall, naked man ran in. He was old and lean, his body muscular and the skin scarred and pockmarked. In his right hand, he carried a small, black object that looked like a coffin-head nail.

"Hello, Emmanuel," the naked man said, and he sprinted at her host.

Emmanuel sprang to his feet, yet even as he did, the old man reached her host and lashed out with the nail. It struck Emmanuel's temple, and the man vanished.

And so too did the façade of the parlor.

Marie was in a poorly lit room, the only semblance it had to the well-appointed parlor was the liquor cabinet and the naked man.

Horrified, Marie looked down into the glass she held and saw an ancient, fetid liquid. Small insects squirmed at the surface of the liquor.

Marie hurled the glass across the room, leaned over the frayed arm of the decrepit chair she was in, and vomited onto the threadbare carpet.

Chapter 48: In the Basement

Shane stood in darkness so complete it was as if the sun had never existed.

Around him, he heard scratching, a steady, repetitive noise. A dank, mildew smell filled his nostrils, and he could almost taste rot on the back of his tongue.

His heart thumped, and his blood picked up its pace within his veins.

He adjusted the rings on his fingers, shrugged his shoulders beneath the straps of his pack and closed his eyes.

An unknown creature moved towards him, the sound of scratching joined by that of dragging.

Shane slipped his right hand into his back pocket and withdrew his knuckle-dusters. They clicked against his iron rings, and he resisted the urge to take off the pack and retrieve his shotgun. Firing it would be counterproductive, he knew. The noise would deafen him, and the blast itself would do little if any good.

A soft voice spoke to him from the darkness.

"Hello?"

It was a woman. There was fear and panic in her voice.

"Hello," Shane replied.

"Oh my God!" she sobbed. "I've been down here for days!"

A chill washed over him, and Shane knew she had been down there for longer than a few days.

"Why don't you do me a favor and stay where you are?" Shane asked. He put no comfort in his words and the woman sensed it.

"Why?" she asked in a low, pitiful tone.

"It'll work out for the best," Shane said.

"I need help," she pouted, and he heard her move towards him.

Shane grinned, and the woman stopped.

"Why are you smiling?" she demanded.

"How can you see me?" he asked in return.

She hesitated, then laughed.

"Oh, I see you very well," she said. "What's your name?"

"Not anything you need to worry about," he responded.

"I want your name," she spat, all humor gone from her voice. "Give it to me."

"No," he answered.

When she spoke again, it was from only a short distance away, her voice near the floor.

"Tell me your name!" she hissed.

Within Shane, he felt a tug, a desire to step forward and to crush the dead woman.

But he remembered Mr. Johnson's letter.

Shane remembered the man's warning of doing the opposite of what his instinct told him.

With a chuckle, Shane turned around and walked away.

The dead woman let out a stream of profanity, most of which he couldn't understand. She screamed for him to turn around, to return and to name himself.

Shane ignored all of it, just as he ignored his own primal urge to destroy her.

Her voice fell away as he continued on. The echo of his footsteps came closer and closer, and he realized that the walls had begun to close in. He found himself in a narrow passage, his shoulders brushing against the stone on either side of him. Occasionally his feet tripped over an unseen object, and he would stumble.

But he never fell.

The temperature continued to drop until his teeth chattered as he walked. In spite of the chill in the air, Shane could still smell the foul, rank odor of mildew. Then the pungent scent of vinegar was detected a moment before the walls fell away and Shane came to a stop.

He listened and heard murmurs.

"Why are you here?" a man asked. "Have you come to fetch a bottle?"

"No," Shane answered. "I'm passing through."

"You've come the wrong way then," a woman said. "You're in the wine cellar."

"Still," Shane said, "I'm passing through."

There was silence for a short time, and then the woman said, "Won't you ask us for directions?"

"No," Shane said.

"Do you know where you're going?" the man asked.

"No," Shane said.

"You can't see anything," the man added.

"Nothing at all," Shane confirmed.

Suddenly the woman's voice was near his right ear.

"And you're not afraid," she murmured. "Robert, he's not afraid."

"I can see that, Marta," Robert said, sighing.

"You're not blind, are you?" Marta asked.

"No," Shane answered. "Leastways, not yet."

"Tell me," Robert said. "Why are you here?"

"I'm going to burn this place to the ground," Shane stated.

The man and woman laughed, but the laughter trailed off quickly. When the woman spoke again, it was from a little further away.

"You're serious," she said.

"Yes," Shane agreed.

"Why?" Robert asked. "Why are you going to do that?"

"Because it needs to be done," Shane answered.

"That, it does," Robert said in a low voice.

"Someone's taught you the trick," Marta said. "About not listening."

"Yes," Shane said.

"Good," Marta said. "Very good. We never learned. Robert and I came here to visit Emmanuel. We had become good friends when he would summer in Newport. He invited us up to see the Vermont foliage."

"We never left," Robert said, his voice thick with bitterness. "His servants brought us down to the wine cellar, and they left us here. Emmanuel said he enjoyed our company so much that he wanted to see if we would age as well as his fine wines."

"We did not," Marta added.

In the distance, Shane heard a scraping sound. The first ghost he had encountered was on the move.

"That's Abigail," Marta said with disgust. "A new arrival. Far too gauche. She has an interest in you?"

"So it would seem," Shane said. He resisted the desire to go into the passage after her.

"Follow your path," Robert said, "and burn the rotten heart out of the Keep."

"Not everyone will want you to," Marta said.

"I know," Shane said. He started forward again, focused on the opposite of what his heart told him.

"We will, however, pass the word along to those who want Emmanuel to suffer," Robert added. "There are more than a few of us here."

Shane nodded his thanks.

"Will it hurt him?" Marta called after him.

Shane hesitated and said over his shoulder, "I don't know."

"I hope it does," Marta said, her voice filling with hatred and rage. "I hope he feels every last moment of it."

Shane nodded and continued on his way.

I hope he will too, Shane thought.

Ahead of him, he saw a faint light, and in a moment he came to a fork in the passage. To the left, he could see a hint of a door. The passage to the right was black.

Shane plunged on into darkness.

Chapter 49: An Ally

"Hey," the naked man snapped. "Pull yourself together."

His voice was hard and commanding, in spite of the fact that he stood in front of Marie without a shred of clothing on.

Marie nodded, tried to spit the lingering aftertaste of vomit out of her mouth and got to her feet. She wavered for a heartbeat, but she got herself under control and looked about the room.

It was a far cry from the beautiful parlor she had imagined herself in a few minutes earlier.

"We need to get out of here," the man said. "Before Emmanuel comes back. He's not going to be happy with me."

"Do you want my sweatshirt?" Marie asked, starting to remove her backpack.

"Why?" the man inquired. "Is it bothering you that much?"

"No," she said, shaking her head. "I wasn't sure if you were cold or not."

"Can't worry about the cold right now," he replied. "Name's David, by the way."

"Marie," she responded. "Thank you."

He gave a curt nod. "Thank me after we get out. What do you have in that bag of yours?"

She gave him a quick run-down of the pack's inventory, and he gave a small, tight smile of appreciation.

"Mind if I have something a little bigger than my nail?" he asked, holding the small piece of iron up.

It was then Marie saw the cuts and scrapes on the old man's flesh. Some of it was fresh, others were scabbed over. He was dirty and looked exhausted.

"How long have you been here?" she asked.

"I'm not sure," he said. "Probably between four and five days."

Marie examined him and saw none of the tell-tale signs of dehydration or starvation.

"Are you hungry?" she asked.

He shook his head.

"Have you eaten?" she said.

David nodded. He held up a hand though and said, "Don't ask that. Now, about that extra bit of protection?"

Marie took off her pack, dug through it and removed a length of iron chain. When Shane had given it to her, he had muttered something about the Slater Mill and had left it at that.

When she passed it over, David dropped the nail to the floor, wrapped part of the chain around his hand and nodded in approval.

"Good," the man said. "Let's get out of here. Do you know where we are?"

She shook her head. "No, but I didn't come alone. There were two others with me. Emmanuel said something about Frank being with a woman named Genevieve?"

David shuddered, and in the thin light, Marie saw goose-bumps erupt across his flesh.

"If he's lucky, she killed him quickly," David said, glancing at the ceiling. Then he looked back at Marie and asked, "Were your friends armed like you?"

"Yes," she answered.

"Maybe he made it out then," David muttered to himself. He nodded. "Yes. He could have. And what about your other friend? Did Emmanuel say anything about that one?"

"I don't know about Shane," Marie replied. "He didn't say where he was."

The house shuddered, and Marie reached out and steadied herself with the help of the chair.

A high, keening wail went ripping through the air, and Marie felt a cold wind as it went racing by her face.

David let out a grim chuckle. "Evidently your friend Shane was in the basement."

"How do you know?" Marie asked.

"That was Abigail who went by," he answered.

"How can you tell?" Marie asked, shaking her head.

"I just can. Come on. Genevieve's on the fourth floor," David said, adding, "if Emmanuel hasn't shifted the house again."

Without waiting to see if she would follow, David turned and left the room. Marie shook her head and questioned her sanity as she followed a naked man out of the parlor.

David led her into a murky hall, a narrow affair with gray wallpaper hanging in curls to reveal horsehair plaster. A few picture frames, each askew, hung on thin wire from the walls.

"Straight to the end," David said over his shoulder. "If everything is right we should find a stairwell."

"And if it's not?" Marie asked.

"Then it's not, and we don't," David said.

Marie rolled her eyes. The man sounded exactly like Shane, and another Shane was not what she wanted.

She passed a large, gilt frame, most the gold stripped from it by time. Within the frame itself was an old mirror, the silver backing spotted and faded. When she looked into it, she saw a careworn version of herself, and then a black hand snapped out of the mirror and grabbed her by her hair.

Before she could pull herself free, the hand yanked her forward, smashing her forehead into the wall.

Marie felt her legs give out, her hair was released, and she slid to the floor, unconsciousness rolling over her.

Book 8: Borgin Keep

Chapter 50: Another Good Deed

David didn't know why he did it, but when he heard Marie's head smash into the wall, he turned and went back for her.

While she slid down to the floor, the thing in the mirror climbed out.

He had seen it once before, and only from a distance. A teenage boy had gotten into the house, and David and Harlan had heard the boy's screams. They had been there for a routine check on the property, to clean up whatever debris the dead had turned the living into. David and Harlan had the unfortunate experience of seeing what some of Emmanuel's darker friends had been capable of.

David's dreams had been plagued by the experience for years.

The black form which stood above Marie was sexless, its face without features.

David remembered the way it had stripped the flesh off of the boy's face, and he lashed out with the chain.

The iron hummed through the air, ripped through the dark creature and smashed into the wall. Horsehair plaster exploded, dust and particles raining down on the unconscious woman as the creature vanished with a shriek that left David's head pounding.

He staggered back, the sound striking him like a blow. The chain bounced off his leg, cold and painful as a bit of skin was pinched between a pair of links. David forced himself forward, and he dropped down into a squat beside Marie.

Blood dripped from numerous small cuts on her forehead, and when he lifted up her eyelids, only the whites were revealed. David stayed beside her for a moment and considered what he should do. Every ounce of him screamed for him to strip her of her equipment, take at least a few items of her clothing, and get out.

David didn't though. It felt *wrong* on a deep, primal level and in a way he had never heeded before. He took a deep breath and picked Marie up, slinging her into a fireman's carry. David staggered a little, more from bearing her weight with his bare feet than anything else. With his free hand he steadied her, and with the chain dragging on the floor in the other hand, David made his way towards the door he hoped would be there.

Chapter 51: Through Borgin's Keep

Frank hated to fight the dead.

In his mouth, he could taste the fetid dust of Genevieve and for a moment, he wondered how much of her he had inhaled.

He remembered the lighter in his back pocket, reached for it, took it out, and flicked it into life. The small flame produced enough light to show him that Genevieve's remains were scattered on the bed, beneath the sheet. He shrugged his pack off, knelt down and rummaged through it, pulling out the salt and lighter fluid.

"That wasn't nice," Genevieve said with a pout.

Frank stiffened as he snapped the lighter shut, extinguishing the flame. Her voice came from across the room.

"Did you think striking me with iron would cast me from the house?" she asked.

Frank stood up, holding onto the lighter fluid and the salt.

"No," he answered, opening the salt container and spreading some of it out over her remains.

"What's that for?" Genevieve asked with a laugh. "Are you planning on eating me? While you may have come to the right home for that, I'm not exactly an appealing meal anymore."

"Sure you are," he replied. "You just have to be basted."

With a flick of his hand he opened the lighter fluid and sprayed the liquid onto her remains.

"And will you cook me?" she asked, her voice filled with humor. "Even then I won't make much of a meal."

"No," he agreed, "you won't."

He flicked the lighter, watched the flame burst into life, and then tossed it onto the bed.

The result was instantaneous.

A deep blue fire engulfed the bed and illuminated the room. Across from him, on the other side of the burning bed stood Genevieve. In life, she had been a stunning woman, her features pale and powerful, her cheekbones standing out.

Yet even as he admired her, Frank watched as the flames devoured her form.

He took a step back, the fire on the bed growing hotter. A quick glance around the room showed an old blanket crumpled on the floor and he snatched it up. The old fabric was harsh and sharp in his hands, but he clenched it in his fists as he waited.

With a final scream Genevieve vanished and Frank leaped forward. He threw the blanket onto the burning bed. While smoke caused his eyes to water and his throat to burn, he extinguished the flames, smothering them with the blanket.

When he was finished, Frank staggered back from the bed, picking up his gear before turning his attention to the door.

It was locked.

His booted foot served as an effective lock pick as he kicked the door out of its frame. Rotten wood sprayed out into a bright, circular room where decrepit chairs were positioned against the walls. Two other closed doors offered a passage out, or perhaps into another room.

Or nowhere, he thought.

Frank took off his backpack, opened it and removed his shotgun. He double-checked that it was loaded, flicked off the safety, and then stuffed his pockets with shells before he put the backpack on again. A glance up showed the room's illumination came from a glass ceiling. Steel lines formed a spider's web with panes of dirty glass in each.

Frank brought the shotgun up and fired both rounds of rock salt into the ceiling.

Whether it was due to the age of the glass, or the force of the blasts, Frank didn't know, but several of the panes shattered. Fresh air raced into the room and helped him to focus.

As he took deep breaths, Frank reloaded the weapon and looked at the two doors. He discovered an urge to try them both, and he knew that neither was what he wanted. Yet they were the only way out of the circular room, except for the door he had entered from. Frank half turned and looked at the room he had exited and saw that it wasn't the same.

Instead of the boudoir he had left, Frank found a set of stairs.

That's not right, he thought, a prickling sensation racing along his spine. He knew the room shouldn't have changed. And as his instinct had urged him to try the doors, so too did it scream that he should ignore the newly revealed stairs.

"Oh, Hell," he murmured, and he turned and entered the small stairwell.

The air smelled of cedar wood as if he had stepped into a closet, and he shivered, remembering the closet he had recently left. In front of him, the stairs descended into darkness, the lack of light further down raising the hackles on his neck.

Clutching his shotgun, Frank fought his fear and walked down the stairs. Old boards creaked beneath his feet, and a faint noise reached his ears. The farther he traveled, the darker the stairwell grew, and the louder the strange sound became.

Soon, Frank realized the noise was a voice, and that person was speaking. He hesitated, tried to decipher the words and found he couldn't. Frank moved down a few more steps and discovered the unseen speaker was engaged in a discussion in a foreign language, although Frank didn't understand it.

He stepped down and the stair gave way beneath his feet. With a curse, he stumbled and crashed into a wall. His face slammed into something hard, and he felt a hot rush down his left cheek. He threw out an arm to catch himself but it twisted, and he felt his forearm break. Frank ground his teeth together to keep back a shout of pain and curled in to brace himself for the rest of the fall.

He bounced from stair to stair, cradling his broken arm against his chest and trying to protect it. After a few seconds, he slammed into another wall and came to a stop. His broken bone throbbed relentlessly, and his head roared with pain. Frank's right hand still held onto the shotgun, and while he may have lost a few shells, he could feel the remainder in his pockets.

Get up, he commanded. *Get up and get moving.*

Frank pushed himself up, and a cold, driving force struck him in the stomach. He spun, crashed into the wall with his broken arm first, and fought to maintain his balance.

Using the wall as a support, Frank managed to stop himself from another fall, but whatever had hit him, did so again.

This time the blow was aimed at his right arm and landed on his forearm. The muscle went numb, his fingers relaxed, and the shotgun clattered onto the floor. Before he could bend down and try to find it, he heard it kicked away.

An unseen fist drove into the side of Frank's head and sent him to the floor with a thud.

Stretched out prone in the darkness, Frank struggled and failed to get to his feet.

"Now," a man said, "let's see how strong you are without your weapon, shall we?"

Before Frank could answer, a cold hand wrapped around his broken forearm and squeezed.

The pain was enough to thrust him into madness.

Chapter 52: Not Stopping

Shane walked into a dining room. It was almost fifty feet in length, and at the far end was a tall white door. A long table, smeared with dust, occupied the center of the room. The walls on the left and right were lined with built-in china cabinets and behind the glass were hundreds of pieces of dinnerware.

By the time Shane had taken a dozen steps into the room, he noticed there were no chairs around the table. Part of him wanted to know why, and he hesitated a split second to think about it.

When he did, the door behind him slammed closed.

Centered in the tin ceiling above him was a huge chandelier. Cut crystals hung from the arms and they rattled as the dishes in the cabinets did the same.

On the far wall, a mirror shimmied on its hook and then fell to the floor. It bounced, spun, and landed on its back, the glass facing up.

The white door opened, and Emmanuel Borgin entered.

Shane watched as the dead man went to the head of the table and sat down as if in a chair. Emmanuel gestured, and the dark light fixtures on the walls burst into life, causing Shane to blink and resist taking a step back.

Emmanuel grinned at Shane, a great, toothy gesture which revealed the man's teeth. Each was a disturbing yellow, and each had been filed down to a fine point.

"Would you care to join me?" Emmanuel asked.

Shane shook his head.

Emmanuel shrugged and mimed the act of removing a napkin from the table and placing it on his lap.

"I have been assured by my cook," Emmanuel continued, "that this evening's meal will be exceptional. We have a leg of lamb that has been allowed to season, and she informs me that it couldn't be a finer piece. Aged just right, you know."

Shane stepped up to the table, took his backpack off and set it down on dusty wood. He opened the pack, made certain the shotgun's handle was accessible and looked at Emmanuel.

"Where are your bones?" he asked.

Emmanuel was caught off guard by the question and let out a delighted laugh.

"Oh, you're a forward one," the dead man said, nodding with pleasure. "Oh, you are, you are. I must admit, I was surprised when you made it up and out of the wine cellar. When you slipped away from Abigail, it wasn't unsuspected. She's rather new you see, to this whole death business. David did her in, which I suppose was a kindness in the end. To the both of them. She didn't need to squirm around anymore and, well, David did need to eat after all."

When Shane didn't react to the hint at cannibalism, Emmanuel clapped his hands and laughed.

"I know who you are!" the dead man crooned.

"You do?" Shane asked, managing to keep the surprise out of his voice.

Emmanuel nodded. "You're trouble. My mother always told me to watch out for trouble, but you are entirely too appealing to ignore. And my goodness, your scars! You look, if you will forgive me, as if someone has staked you down in the road and ridden over you a few times."

"Feels that way," Shane admitted.

"Now," Emmanuel said, "what was your question again?"

"Your bones," Shane said. "I want to know where they are."

"And what would you do with my bones?" Emmanuel asked, and then he pouted. "Nothing pleasant, I suppose."

"You'd be right," Shane agreed. "I'm going to salt them down and burn them."

"Ah," Emmanuel said. "That would explain why the Shaws let you out of the wine cellar. They wouldn't have, you know if they thought you didn't mean it."

"It's good that I do mean it then," Shane said.

Emmanuel snickered. "It is. Now, how about a riddle?"

"Sure," Shane said. "Why not."

Again Emmanuel looked surprised, and again the dead man laughed. "You know, I don't really have a riddle? So often when I've offered a guest that they've hemmed and hawed and chosen the alternative."

Shane didn't ask what the alternative was, so Emmanuel sighed and offered it.

"Well, the alternative," the dead man said, "is to go and speak with the cook."

Shane looked at Emmanuel's sharpened teeth, remembered the casual reference to cannibalism, and smiled. "And they ended up as your meal."

"Oh," the dead man whispered. "You're so very pleasant to speak with. I'm almost tempted to let you have my bones. But then that would rather spoil the evening."

"It would," Shane said. "I can guarantee that."

"Well," Emmanuel said. "I won't give you the bones, but I will tell you this. You can find them where an old friend hid them, although he didn't know they would be there when he made the wall."

"That," Shane said, "was exactly less than helpful."

"Then I'm afraid you won't appreciate this either," Emmanuel said.

The doors to the china cabinets exploded open, and hundreds of dishes sped towards Shane.

He snatched his pack off the table and raced for the door as cups and saucers, bowls and plates smashed into him. Some broke against him, and others shattered against his knuckle-dusters. More still bounced off him to spin away and roll on the floor.

Out of the corner of his eye, Shane saw Emmanuel, and the dead man grinned his sharpened grin as Shane tried to flee the room.

A few steps away from the white door a large shape caught Shane's attention, and he turned in time to see a soup tureen race towards him. He turned his head away at the last moment, the china cracking against his skull and sending him crashing into the mirror on the floor.

Chapter 53: In the Dressing Room

Marie came to and gasped for breath. She was bouncing on the shoulder of David, and when she struggled, he stopped to put her down.

"Can you walk?" he asked.

"I can run if I have to," she answered. She struggled to remember what had happened, but she couldn't. Part of her thought that was probably for the best, especially considering her drinks with Emmanuel.

David nodded, rewrapped the chain around his hand, and gestured towards a door a few feet away.

"Where does that lead to?" Marie asked, ignoring the pulsating pain in her head.

"Don't know," David answered. "Could lead to anywhere."

"Great," Marie muttered. "I do not want to go in there."

"Me neither," David said. "We don't have a whole lot of choice, though. If we can meet up with your friends, then that'll give us a better chance of getting out of here."

"Can we?" Marie asked, looking hard at the man. "Has anyone?"

"More than a few," David said. "More than that have died in here, though, I won't lie about that. You may want to get your shotgun out, too."

Marie did so, flipped off the safety, and looked at David.

"You ready to go?" he asked.

Marie nodded. "I'll take the lead."

"No argument from me," David said, stepping aside.

She went to the door, reached out and tested the knob.

It was unlocked.

Marie wrapped her hand around the cold metal, squeezed and turned as she pushed against it. The door opened a sliver at a time, and in a moment the room was revealed.

Light, filtered through green glass in the ceiling, filled the room. The walls were all lined with dark blue curtains and benches with cracked leather seats were set in a haphazard fashion in the room's center.

David came in behind her, and the door clicked shut, the lock tumbling into place.

"How do we get out?" Marie asked, keeping her voice low.

"I'm hoping the exit is behind one of the curtains," David said.

"Great," Marie said, sighing. She watched as he walked to the nearest piece of fabric and pulled it down.

It fell and landed with a soft thump, a cloud of dust spiraling up from it.

"Oh no," David whispered, staring at what he had uncovered.

All Marie saw was a mirror, and she said as much.

"No," David said in the same hushed tone. "It's worse than that. So much worse than that. Hurry, pull the rest down. We need to find the door. We need to get out of here."

Marie didn't ask why. Instead, she went to the nearest curtain and pulled it down, revealing another mirror. By the time the fabric was on the floor, she had already moved on to the next. In a matter of moments, every curtain had been torn down, and not a single door had been revealed.

Marie's murky reflection stared back at her, dizzying in its multiplicity as each mirror showed the other.

"Break them," David whispered.

She looked at him, confused. "What?"

"Break them!" he screamed as he lifted his arm up, the chain rising up with it.

But it was too late.

Black shapes hurtled out of the mirrors, broken glass launching out like shrapnel. The creatures were humanoid but lacked features. Long arms reached out while thin legs launched them across the room.

Marie fired blindly, first one barrel, then the second, and she was fighting for her life with iron rings and nothing more.

Chapter 54: A Reunion of Sorts

When Shane hit the mirror, he felt the glass break, and then he continued to fall.

It was as if there was no floor.

He fell for what seemed like several minutes, and then he was thrust into light and in the middle of a brawl. Shane struck the floor with enough force to leave him breathless and dazed as he tried to make sense of what had happened.

Around him were black shapes, tall and frightening. They attacked a naked man and Marie, both of whom had a hard time keeping the creatures at bay.

Shane regained his breath, scrambled to his feet and became dimly aware that he was bleeding from multiple cuts. He had landed on broken glass and a glance at his legs and chest showed his clothes glittered with what looked like hundreds of slivers.

One of the black beasts sensed him, turned and reached for Shane.

Without thinking, Shane punched it in the head with his knuckle-dusters, and the creature vanished.

They're ghosts, Shane thought, and he stepped into the fight. He lashed out with both hands, rings, and knuckle-dusters dispatching the dead as he moved forward. In a moment, all of them were gone, and only he, Marie, and the naked man remained.

Marie's pupils fluctuated in size while the man looked around as though he suffered from PTSD.

"Who are you?" the man asked.

"He's Shane," Marie answered. Her words were slurred. "This is David."

It was then Shane noticed the blood on her forehead.

"I think you have a concussion, Marie," Shane said.

"She probably does," David interjected. "She was knocked out."

"I'm fine," she argued.

Shane ignored her and asked the man, "Do you know anything about this place?"

"Too much," David answered. "We need to get out. Before Emmanuel sends anyone after us."

"What were the black things?" Shane asked.

"They used to be part of something," David said. "Then they weren't. I can tell you about that later. We need to go, and we need to go now."

Shane shook his head. "I need to find Frank, and I need to burn Emmanuel's bones."

"Nobody knows where his bones are," David snapped. "They're probably not even here."

"They're here," Shane said.

"How do you know?" David demanded.

"He told me," Shane replied.

David looked surprised. "Oh."

After a moment David asked, "Did he say where?"

"This is what he told me," Shane said, and he repeated what Emmanuel had said.

"Mr. Johnson," David murmured.

"What?" Shane asked.

"Johnson," David said louder. "Mr. Johnson was the only person Emmanuel ever considered a friend. As far as I know, though, Johnson never built anything here."

"He did," Shane said.

When he didn't elaborate, David said, "Well, what?"

"I need to find Frank," Shane said, twisting around. "Is there a door out of here?"

"No," Marie answered. "Nothing we could see."

Shane closed his eyes tried to clear his mind and felt a tug in his gut. When he cracked an eye open, he saw that he stood on a carpet, albeit one littered with broken mirrors.

"There's a door of some sort under here," Shane said, tapping the floor with a foot.

"Let's pull it up then," David said. "Before he sends anything else after us."

"No," Shane replied.

"No?" Marie snapped. "What the hell do you mean, Shane?"

"I mean no," he said again. "We go up."

And as he spoke, he turned his attention to the ceiling, in the middle of which was a small, circular trap door.

"How are we going to get up there?" Marie asked.

Shane grinned at her. "You get to go first."

"And what if there's someone up there?" she asked.

"Jump," Shane said.

David nodded. "We'll catch you."

"Maybe you will," she said to David. "He won't."

Shane's response to her statement was to interlock his fingers as he said, "Step on in."

Marie looked at him with an expression of mixed disgust and anger before she put her foot into the stirrup he had made. David did the same, and in a moment, she had a hand on each of their heads, balancing herself.

"Okay," Marie said.

Together Shane and David lifted, the muscles straining in the older man's neck as they lifted her towards the ceiling. She kept her hands outstretched, and when they reached the small trap door, she pushed up. The wood creaked, resisted for a second, and then popped. She slid it aside as a cloud of dust drifted down towards them.

Shane and David both watched her, waiting until she got her hands up and into the darkness before they lifted her the rest of the way up. As her feet left their hands, the two men straightened and she climbed into the unlit room above.

A heartbeat later, her scream pierced the air and shook the house to its foundations.

Chapter 55: Mutual Terror

A terrified scream pierced the pain which smothered him and Frank jerked up. His broken forearm was still grasped by an unseen, cold hand. Frank struck out, and the iron rings on his fingers broke the hold.

It was only then that Frank realized he could see.

Enough light came up from a hole in the floor to show him Marie Lafontaine as she struggled against a dark shape. While Frank couldn't make out the details of the creature, he saw that it held her wrists up and away with one hand. It slowly pushed its free hand into her mouth, stifling her scream and choking her at the same time.

Without looking for his shotgun, Frank scrambled to her, the creature twisting to howl at him. A blast of cold air slammed him in the face, the sensation one of excruciating pain as he inhaled. The beast let go of Marie, jerked its hand out of her mouth and launched itself at him.

Frank swung at it, and the creature ducked beneath the blow. It struck him in the chest, sending him sprawling backward and letting out a joyous cry.

Then the room was plunged into darkness as a figure plugged the hole in the floor.

A cold hand latched onto Frank's ankle, and he twisted around and slammed his fist into it, the iron on his finger causing the creature to vanish.

"Marie," Shane called from where the hole had been.

"I'm here too," Frank said.

"Oh, hell," Shane said. There was a rustling sound, and then a match was lit.

"You look like hell," Frank said, sitting up.

"Like looking in a mirror then," Shane said. He tossed a box of matches and Frank caught them one-handed. "I've got to help David up. Hold on."

"Who's David?" Frank asked.

"My naked friend," Shane replied.

Frank lit another match off the first before it could sputter out and he watched as Shane passed Marie, went back to the hole, and stretched himself out on the floor. He lowered his arms and grunted.

A moment later an older, naked man climbed into the room. Frank nodded, as Shane introduced them.

Frank lit another match, and David found a candelabrum with the nubs of old candles in it. The wicks soon flickered with flame. The light offered by the tarnished piece of silver was one of comfort as shadows flickered on the wall.

Shane bent over Marie, checked her pulse and shook his head.

"She's in bad shape," Shane said, sitting back. "And your arm looks like garbage."

Frank nodded. "Pretty much junk."

David, Frank noticed, was covered in a multitude of scratches. Bruises seemed to blossom on the older man's pale skin. He shivered as well, and Frank knew it was from shock more than the cold of the room, although that wasn't helping matters.

Shane was the only one of them who looked as though he was fine. He had a few cuts on his face and head, other than those, he seemed unperturbed by the world around him.

Frank took a deep breath and said, "I think we need to find that room, Shane. We need to get out of here."

"We did find it," Shane said. "Look behind you."

Frank did so, and he saw an open door. It was tall and narrow, and the light of the candelabra illuminated a room lined with a dull metal.

They had found the way out, but not Emmanuel's bones.

Chapter 56: Forcing Them to Leave

Shane lit a cigarette and said, "I don't care. The three of you are going."

Marie remained unconscious, and David had helped to splint Frank's broken arm. The older man had also finally agreed to wrap Shane's sweatshirt around his waist and to wear Frank's.

"You can't stay here," Frank argued.

Shane looked at his friend and smiled. "You have a bad break. It needs to be set, and soon before you go into shock. We also don't know what's wrong with Marie. The two of you need a hospital. I'll be fine."

Frank opened his mouth to disagree, but it was David who spoke.

"You'll die here," the older man said.

Shane nodded. "Always a possibility. But I could die anywhere and at any time. Death here, at least, would be worthwhile."

Frank looked at him, and Shane shook his head.

"I'm not doing a suicide by ghost," Shane assured his friend. "I don't think we'll have another opportunity, and, to be perfectly blunt, you three are dead weight at this point."

Neither of the men responded.

"David," Shane said, "can you get the window open in there while I bring Marie into the room?"

The older man nodded and went into the lead-lined room.

With Frank watching, Shane picked up Marie and carried her limp body into Mr. Johnson's safe room.

David managed to pop the window open and murmured, "Damn."

Frank stepped past Shane, looked outside and then back to Shane.

"This is on the first floor," Frank said. "I never saw a window like this."

"The house moves," David said. "Each room, every day, multiple times a day. Only the kitchen and the hall remain in the same place."

The older man grasped the edges of the window frame, pulled himself up and out of the Keep. Shane passed Marie through the window to David.

"Shane," Frank said, "you shouldn't do this."

"I have a shotgun, salt, and enough lighter fluid to turn this place into a bonfire," Shane replied.

Frank frowned and hesitated before he said, "We'll wait for you then. At the car."

"No," Shane replied. "You can come back after you get yourselves squared away. But you can't wait. The three of you need to get seen by a doctor."

David peered in. "Come on."

Frank nodded and said, "Good luck."

"Thanks," Shane responded. He helped Frank out through the window, and then pulled it closed. Lead clamps were around the frame, and he tightened them down before he looked out the warped glass. The two men supported Marie between them, and the trio made for a pitiful sight.

Shane turned away from the image, walked to the exit, closed the door, and pulled the lead shield into place. Then he turned around and looked at the room he was in.

Mr. Johnson had described it well in the letter. Various sized sheets of lead were tacked into place around the room. The only light available was that which the window let in. At the far end of the room was a low, narrow cot with an olive drab woolen blanket on it. Beneath the cot were several boxes, and to the left of the bed was an equally tall and narrow door.

Shane walked to the bed, squatted down and pulled out the boxes. Each was made of lead and kept closed by a latch. In the first box, Shane found a length of rope and a pair of leather gloves with iron studs. When he opened the second container, Shane discovered a large and well-thumbed Bible. The gold leaf had been rubbed off the pages in most places, and the leather cover was soft and supple beneath his fingers.

Beneath the Bible was a small, moleskin journal. Shane picked it up and slipped it into his pack.

The last box was wider and longer than the other two, and the latch gave him some difficulty as he opened it. When he did, he let out a sigh and shook his head.

The interior of the box was divided into small squares. Seventy in all.

Each space was occupied by a single piece of bone, yellowed and cut into a neat, almost perfect circle. A letter and a date were carved into every bone. The earliest, in the far left, read, *E. 1892*. In the last box, the information inscribed was *H. 1917*.

Shane rubbed at his jaw as he looked at the bones, wondering to whom they had once belonged.

Don't go down that hole, he told himself as he got to his feet. *Start thinking about them, and you may never get out of here.*

As safe as the room was, Shane knew he had to leave soon. He doubted Mr. Johnson's safe-room would last long against a concerted effort by Emmanuel. And if the Watchers should arrive and Emmanuel assisted them, then Shane knew he would be trapped there forever.

Shane stepped to the door, found it unlocked and opened it.

"Hello," Emmanuel Borgin said, and he grinned as he punched Shane in the face.

Chapter 57: Less than a Gentlemen's Duel

The blow was powerful and caught Shane off-guard, sending him staggering back into the room. His shotgun fell from his hands and bounced, then slid under the bed. Beyond Emmanuel, Shane saw a cot, similar to the first, but spread out on the woolen blanket were mummified remains of a man in a black suit.

"I look good, do I not?" Emmanuel asked, doing a little dance as he came out of the room. "Mr. Johnson, my dear, sweet Mr. Johnson, suffered under the delusion that I didn't know about this room."

The dead man chuckled and shook his head. "There's nothing I don't know about in my own home. When he was done with his little modification, a delightful man by the name of Harlan carried my corpse upstairs and placed it here for me. Eventually, someone might have stumbled on my remains, but not here. Not in this special room, oh no."

Emmanuel stepped over to place himself between Shane and the window, and Shane smiled.

"Why are you smiling?" Emmanuel asked with a frown.

"You think I want to leave," Shane said.

"I know you do now," the dead man snorted. "You've seen what is in my house. You know what we are capable of. Of course, you want to leave."

Shane glanced into the room where Emmanuel's bones lay. Lead lined the walls, floor, and ceiling of that room as well.

"No," Shane said. "I don't want to leave."

"Of course, you do," Emmanuel snapped.

"Tell me," Shane said, gesturing towards the box of bones. "Who did those belong to?"

"Ah," Emmanuel said, a leer spreading across his face. "Those are from the breasts of children. They always had the softest flesh, you know. So many ways to prepare them, unlike adults. Too few options with older, stringy meat. My chef always struggled with men, try as he might."

"Children," Shane murmured. His shoulders sank, sadness pressing down on him. "You ate children."

"Of course I ate them," Emmanuel said. "All of my guests did. Good God, man, we weren't pedophiles."

Shane glared at him, hate building up.

"Now I see it," the dead man said, laughing. "The fear is coming out. Oh, you will be fun."

Shane shook his head. "I'm not afraid."

"Yes, yes you are," Emmanuel said, wagging a finger at Shane. "Admit your fear, you're terrified to be trapped in this room with me."

"Is that what you think?" Shane asked.

"It's what I know," Emmanuel crowed. "Oh yes."

"You have it backward," Shane whispered.

"What do I have backward?" the dead man asked, leaning in, his smile broadening.

"I'm not trapped in here with you," Shane said. "*You're* trapped in here with *me*."

Shane lashed out with his left hand and caught Emmanuel off-guard. The ghost vanished, and Shane shook off his backpack. By the time it hit the floor, Emmanuel had reappeared in the doorway, his smile not as broad as it had been a few seconds before.

Before the dead man could speak, Shane struck again.

With Emmanuel gone a second time Shane opened the pack, found his lighter fluid, and was knocked to one side.

The dead man had rematerialized behind Shane and hit him on his left ear.

Shane twisted and rolled as he hit the floor, his left knee going numb as it struck the steel frame of the cot. For a moment, he lay there, a wave of exhaustion smashing into him. He felt as though he couldn't stand up. That even the effort to lift his head would be too much.

With his head pressed to the floor Shane considered, for the first time, doing nothing more than dying.

"What?" Emmanuel asked, a look of surprise on his face as he stared at his own hands. "How did I strike you? Why didn't it pass through you?"

Then, as the dead man questioned himself, it was as if a door opened deep within Shane. He felt strength flow back into him. Determination filled his chest.

The sense of exhaustion and desire to quit fled from him.

As the energy pulsed through him, Shane knew it for what it was.

The power he felt was that which ghosts like Borgin fed off, the strength they stole from their victims.

And it was an energy, it seemed, that some of the dead gave freely to Shane.

Robert and Marta had done it, he realized. They had passed the word along to the rest of the dead, and they were there to help.

"They're here," Shane said. "Aren't they? The children. Some of them are ghosts."

Emmanuel nodded. "Of course they are. They feed my spirit as their flesh fed my own."

"They don't feed you anymore," Shane said, his body vibrating with the power of the friendly dead. He stood up, slipped his knuckle-dusters off, and tucked them into a back pocket. His iron rings followed.

"What are you doing?" Emmanuel demanded. "Why are you stripping your iron off?"

"Because I don't need it," Shane answered. "Not with you."

Shane's bones thrummed within his flesh, the power of the children surging through him. Indecipherable whispers filled his ears, and he knew he was hearing their voices. They poured their strength into him and Shane felt his body pulse with it.

The dead man sneered at him. "You think you can fight me without iron? You're mad, or you're playing at it. I will not take any pity on the insane."

"Don't," Shane replied. "Now come here, will you, I want to show you something."

With a derisive hiss, Emmanuel leaped at him, and Shane sidestepped, driving a fist into the dead man's suddenly firm stomach.

Emmanuel squealed as he folded over, falling onto the floor. The dead man tried to push himself up, but Shane delivered a kick into the base of Emmanuel's spine, driving him down again.

"You can't do this," Emmanuel moaned. "No one can."

"I can," Shane assured him. "And I will."

He squatted down beside the ghost, reached out, and wrapped a hand around the dead man's cold neck. Shane increased the pressure until he saw fear burst into the man's eyes.

"You know it now," Shane whispered. "I have a question, Emmanuel Borgin."

"What?" The dead man shook in Shane's grasp.

"Did you eat them all here? All seventy?" Shane asked.

Emmanuel nodded.

With sudden force, Shane squeezed the dead man's throat, forcing his mouth open. When it did so, he took hold of Emmanuel's tongue and smiled.

"Now," Shane whispered, "let's see how long it takes me to tear this out at the root."

The dead man's screams filled Mr. Johnson's room.

Chapter 58: From the Tree Line

Shane sat beneath the boughs of a fir tree with his back against its trunk. His stomach grumbled, and his hands shook, not only for want of food but also for want of a cigarette. He had smoked his last cigarette before the fire trucks of several nearby towns had arrived.

From where he sat, Shane watched as the firefighters wet down the grass around Borgin Keep as the massive structure burned. The flames were a strange green at their base, and fire licked at the stone walls from the windows. Some of the old granite blocks even seemed to burn.

The firefighters, Shane realized, were focused on containment. They didn't seem too concerned with saving the structure. He couldn't blame them. The foul aura of the building could be felt all the way down the hill, across the road and into the forest on the other side.

Shane shifted his pack in his lap, an odd clacking sound emanating from it. With a gentle reverence he reached in and removed one of the carved bones. He put it on the ground beside him, and repeated the process until all of the remains were in the open. In silence, he dug a small hole with his hands, and then placed the bones within it. As dirt fell from his fingers he reached into his pack, removed the salt and the matches and the lighter fluid.

In a moment, the remains of the children were burning, the small, greenish blue flames hidden by the sagging limbs of the tree.

When the flames had gone out and nothing remained of the bones saved charred ash, Shane pushed the dirt back into the hole. He tapped it down and then he wrapped his arms around the pack and pulled it to him, resting his chin on the rough fabric. He wondered if the others had made it to a hospital as the wind shifted and carried to him the smell of Borgin Keep.

It stank of wood and burning flesh, and Shane smiled as he watched it burn.

Chapter 59: West Lebanon Hospital

Marie lay in a hospital bed, unconscious and connected to a slew of monitors. Frank, his arm in a cast, sat in a chair beside her. His thoughts were fuzzy, made so by the Vicodin the emergency room doctor had prescribed. But the break had been severe, and Frank had found he needed the pain killer.

David was in the room as well. He had on a new pair of dark blue pants, a gray sweatshirt and cheap running shoes. Frank had bought them all on the way to the hospital, despite Marie's condition or Frank's arm. Public nudity was generally frowned upon, and David still had to return to Borgin Keep to see if Shane had made it out.

Frank looked at Marie, her face pale and her eyelids twitching.

He and David had lied to the triage nurse, and to the doctor. In Frank's version of events the three of them had gone for a walk, Marie had fallen, and like the old television commercial, she hadn't gotten up. He too, Frank had admitted with feigned humility, had gotten hurt. His injury, however, had been when they were trying to get her into the car.

The hospital had her stabilized and soon they would run additional tests to see what they could do for her.

"Frank," David said.

"Hm?" Frank asked, looking at the older man.

"I'm going to go see if he made it," David said, standing up.

"See who made it?" Marie asked, her eyes closed and her words slurred.

Frank let out a relieved laugh and David smiled before he answered, "Your friend, Shane."

"Not really my friend," she mumbled. "He's a pain."

"Most friends are," David replied. "But I'll go and see if he's there. I'll be back as soon as I can. I suspect they'll want to keep you for observation anyway."

"I told them we went for a walk and you fell down," Frank said with a glance at the room's open door.

"Doesn't matter," Marie muttered. "Can't remember what happened after we pulled up."

"Good," David said. He looked at Frank. "Best to keep it that way."

Frank nodded his agreement.

"Can I get either one of you anything on the way back?" David asked. The question, spoken louder than his normal voice, seemed forced.

It took a moment for Frank to realize it was meant for ears other than his. So he tailored his response the same way.

"No," Frank answered. "I'm good. Pretty sure we'll have to wait for the docs to clear Marie before we pick something up."

David gave Frank a slight nod, and as he turned to leave a nurse hurried into the room. Frank watched the older man slip out of the room as the nurse began to fuss over Marie, who didn't respond to any of the woman's questions.

The Vicodin caused Frank's eyelids to grow heavy, and he realized he was exhausted.

Another nurse, as well as an older doctor, entered the room. But Frank's eyes were closed by the time they reached Marie's bed.

The memory of Borgin Keep reared up in his mind, yet Frank ignored it as he plummeted into sleep.

Chapter 60: A Harsh Truth

She had torn all of Harlan's effects out of the office and had them donated to the local Goodwill. Not because Clair was moved by any sense of compassion for those less fortunate, but merely for the fact that it would have irritated Harlan had the man still been alive.

Watching the man's garroting had been exceptionally satisfying. It had also been one of the few times Clair had regretted the lack of recording equipment in the meeting house.

A soft rap on the office door interrupted her thoughts.

"Come in," Clair called. She despised intercoms and she had forbidden Ms. Coleman from the use of the one in the office.

The door swung open and the secretary stepped in. "Jenna is here to see you, Ms. Willette."

"Send her in, please," Clair replied.

A moment later, Jenna stepped into the office, Ms. Coleman closing the door behind her.

Jenna wore a mixed expression of anger and sadness.

"What's going on?" Clair asked.

Jenna cleared her throat. "We've received information from our contact in the Vermont State Police."

"And?" Clair said, frustration leaking into the word. Harlan had left the organization in shambles with his bumbling, and she had a tremendous amount of work to do.

"Borgin Keep is gone," Jenna said in a hushed voice.

It took a heartbeat for the words to process, then another three for the information to sink in.

Finally, Clair cleared her throat. "How?"

"Arson is what they believe," Jenna answered. "The fire marshal on scene has called for a forensic unit. Our informant is on the police detail keeping traffic away from the building."

"There are people there?" Clair asked, confused. "First responders?"

Jenna nodded.

"They shouldn't be able to get close to it," Clair said, shaking her head. "Emmanuel would never let them."

"There's more," Jenna added. "Our informant saw a bald man walk away from the scene. He was missing half of his left ear as well."

"Shane Ryan," Clair whispered.

"Do you want me to get my sister?" Jenna asked.

Clair shook her head. "Not yet. I need to speak with the research team. I have to find out how many buildings are going to be needed to replace Borgin Keep on the line. Then we're going to have to seed them. If that's going to happen, I want Shane Ryan to be one of the first."

Jenna nodded and left the room.

Clair stared at the open door, her body shaking with rage.

When it came time to sacrifice a victim to the dead, she would strangle Shane herself.

* * *

Amherst Burial Ground
Book 9

Book 9: Amherst Burial Ground

Chapter 1: Out for a Hike

Madison strolled along the game trail. The air was warm, a pleasant change to the cold winds which had ushered in May. She had found little time to get out and into nature, the demands of her law office and life in general cutting into her alone time. Madison chuckled at the thought.

Alone time had vanished with the birth of her son Felix, and her husband Mitchell still didn't understand why she was cranky some nights.

Madison had been a self-sufficient individual ever since she had left for college when she was seventeen. Her marriage at thirty, and the subsequent offspring produced, had done nothing to curb her individuality.

Which was why on some days she ended up in Amherst for a quick hike. Her law office, located in Milford, was only a few minutes from her favorite hiking trails. She could take half a day, hike for a few hours, shower at her fitness club and be home without Mitchell being any the wiser.

Madison rolled her eyes at the complaints he would issue. While he had relished the idea of being a stay-at-home father when she was pregnant with Felix, the reality of it was far less entertaining.

Mitchell complained on an almost daily basis about how his work suffered. More than once, she had been tempted to inform him that a writer who didn't get steady work to begin with, couldn't complain.

She shook her head and turned her thoughts to the path before her. It was a narrow game trail, wide enough for her to move along without disrupting any plants growing between the thick trunks of the oaks and elms around her. The trees had a curious aura to them, and part of the reason she enjoyed hiking in Amherst. They were among the few, old forest trees she had seen.

This particular path, off General Amherst Road, was new to her. She had read about it online from a few blogs. Most of the articles had been about going to visit the trail, and none of those had been about the hike itself.

The whole trail had an air of mystery to it, and it thrilled Madison. There was no mystery in her marriage, no excitement. Nothing thrilling at her workplace. She had even considered a membership with the Ashley Madison website, in spite of the security risks attached to a site dedicated to extramarital affairs. In the end, with the pros outweighing the cons, she had decided against it.

So Madison was left with the trails.

She adjusted the straps on her backpack as she came to a fork in the path and stopped. The trail to the right showed more use, the dirt packed down and the branches of a few bushes broken and pushed back.

On the left, Madison saw the complete opposite.

The trail was faint, almost as if it hadn't been used in years. Not even the prints of animals marred the loose earth.

Left it is, she thought, and followed it.

For nearly an hour, she moved along the trail as it skirted granite boulders and ran along streambeds. When the path dipped down she slowed her pace, careful not to twist an ankle. She had injured herself in the past on a lone hike, and the return trip had been horrifically painful.

Madison looked around as the trail leveled out and widened. The trees were farther and farther away from the sides of the path, and the underbrush faded away. Soon it disappeared altogether, but within twenty feet, it was replaced with thick, twisted brambles. Ahead of her, a dark shape caught her eye and Madison paused to look at it and get a drink of water.

Book 9: Amherst Burial Ground

A huge, flowering chestnut tree towered at the end of a small clearing. It was massive, perhaps a hundred feet tall and without a doubt, the largest she had ever seen. Unable to take her eyes off it, Madison walked towards the tree.

Soon she found her way blocked by the brambles. Madison ignored them, pushing her way through even as the long, sharp thorns pierced her skin and snagged her clothes. Around her the forest darkened, the long boughs of the chestnut blocking out the sun. A gray twilight wrapped around her and it seemed as though the brambles pushed in closer with each drop of blood she spilled.

Then she was through them, stumbling into a small burial ground.

The grave markers were old. Tall, thin pieces of slate with arched tops and images of death carved into them. There were only twenty or thirty of them, standing upright in perfect order. Dead grass clung to the earth around each stone, and beyond the markers was a house.

The building consisted of a single floor, the roof sagging in the middle and a large, brick chimney protruding from the center. Heavy shutters hung on the windows flanking either side of the doorway, which lacked any sort of door.

And all of it was beneath the tree's tremendous limbs. An entire world separate from the rest of New Hampshire.

Madison smiled, a warm, joyous feeling wrapping around her. It was then that she noticed the little boy. He sat on a rock by the doorway. His face was cherubic and his hair was pulled back in a small ponytail. The boy's clothes looked handmade, and they were cut in a fashion Madison had only seen in history books about the early New England colonists. He seemed to be somewhere between eight and ten years of age, and he smiled at her when their eyes met.

Several of his teeth were missing, which gave him an even more endearing appearance.

"Hello," he said, waving at her.

"Hello," Madison replied, offering a little wave.

"Are you on your way to meeting?" the boy inquired.

"Meeting?" she asked, confused.

"To town," the boy said, grinning. "Are you going into town?"

"No," Madison answered. "I'm just out walking."

"Ah," the boy said, nodding.

In a dull, absent way Madison understood she couldn't look away from the child. He commanded all of her attention.

And she was fine with that, smiling at him.

He smiled back.

"What's your name?" he asked, the gentlest of lisps in his pronunciation.

"Madison," she answered.

"Would you like to know my name?" he said.

Madison nodded.

"I am Samson," the boy said, his lips hardly moving as he spoke. His eyes narrowed and for the briefest of moments, there was a cruel glint to them.

Then it was gone and Madison knew it had been some sort of twist of the light.

"Would you sit with me?" Samson asked. "My mother has been gone a long, long time."

Madison nodded, choking back a sob at the idea of the beautiful boy being alone and without his mother. A faint memory of her own child tugged at her, but it wasn't enough to stop her from entering the burial ground.

The air vibrated as she stepped past the first headstones, the slate shimmering on the edges of her vision.

Samson's smile broadened and he clapped his hands with enthusiasm.

The joyous look on his face quickened her step, and in a few heartbeats, she stood before him. Madison stared down at him, her heart pounding in her chest.

"Will you sit with me?" he asked.

Madison sat on the ground, folding her legs under her. A hard object pushed into her thigh and she reached down, pulling it out from beneath her. It was a bone, nearly a foot in length and yellow with age.

"You could throw that inside, along with the others," Samson said, nodding towards the doorway.

Madison did so, the bone vanishing into the darkness and landing with a clatter. It sounded as though it had struck a pile of the same.

At the noise Samson laughed, clapping his hands again as he fixed an intense stare upon her. Smiling, the little boy leaned forward and said, "Are you excited to sit with me?"

"Yes," Madison replied, her own voice sounding distant in her ears. Then she asked, "Are you excited?"

"Oh, yes," he said with sudden, mock seriousness. "And do you want to know why?"

Madison gave a nod.

"Because," Samson whispered, "I've been alone for an awfully long time."

Chapter 2: Remembering the Past

Shane stood on his back porch in the warm sunlight, staring down into the pond. He looked at the cats' tails as they bent in the wind, watched the water ripple from the same. The water remained dark, impenetrable. Even after Vivienne had been chased away, there was no escaping the memories she had left with him.

A shudder rippled through him and Shane took his cigarettes out. His hand trembled as he lit one and returned the pack to his pocket.

The back door opened and Frank stepped out of the kitchen, a bottle of water in his hand as he walked over to a deck chair and sat down.

"You alright?" Frank asked.

"That's a tough question to answer," Shane said, tearing his attention away from the pond and sitting down in the other deck chair.

"Not really," Frank replied. "You either are, or you're not. Pretty basic."

Shane shrugged. "Guess I'm not then."

"What's bothering you?" Frank asked.

"Everything about the Watchers," Shane answered. "I want more information on them. I want to know why exactly they're gathering up haunted buildings. How long have they been doing it? What's the real end game? And I don't feel like I achieved what I wanted, not for Mason and his wife. Not for anyone who's died because of the Watchers."

"How much more can you do?" Frank asked, his brows furrowed with concern. "Hell, Shane, you've taken some serious beatings. Honestly, you look like someone stuck you in a fire, changed their mind, and then dragged you back out over broken glass."

"Thanks," Shane grumbled.

"Hey, it's the truth," Frank said. "Why don't we find someone a little younger, maybe some of Abbot Gregory's brothers. They can start to dig around more. See what's out there and what can be done."

Shane shook his head. "I can't do that. I know what's out there, Frank. I won't send them into it. The Watchers are my responsibility."

Frank's cellphone rang and cut Shane off.

"Hold on," Frank said, putting his water down and digging his phone out of a pocket. "Hello?"

Shane waited as Frank nodded and said, "Yeah. No, we're both here. Come on by."

"Who was that?" Shane asked after Frank had ended the call.

"Hm? Oh, that was David," Frank said. "You know, the naked guy in Borgin?"

Shane snorted, repeating, "The naked guy."

After a moment he asked, "Just David?"

Frank looked away as he replied, "Far as I know."

Shane sighed and shook his head. "He almost never goes anywhere without Marie."

Frank sagged in the chair and turned his head back to Shane. "Strength in numbers."

"It's aggravating," Shane snapped, pushing himself to his feet.

"We need all the help we can get," Frank stated. "And she can definitely handle herself."

"That's never been in doubt," Shane said over his shoulder. "I don't like having her around. Seems like she still blames me for Kurt Warner's death, the cop killed at Slater Mill. Not to mention all the emotional baggage."

"On her end or yours?" Frank asked.

"I don't have emotional baggage," Shane grumbled.

Frank didn't respond to the statement, remaining silent as Shane pulled out another cigarette and lit it off the first. As he exhaled into the warm air, Shane twisted around to face Frank. "Do you think today would be a good day?"

Frank hesitated, then nodded. "Might as well. My arm's healed up. Marie's in good shape. David doesn't seem any worse for the experience up in Borgin. And you, man, I think you're made of steel sometimes."

"No," Shane responded. "I'm just stubborn is all. Think David will want to talk about the Watchers?"

"I'm hoping that's why he's on his way over," Frank admitted.

"Good," Shane said, facing the pond once more. He glared at it for a few moments, waiting until he finished the fresh cigarette before turning away.

Shane knew she wasn't around anymore, but the child in him still hid in the dark and whispered about her.

"What are you looking for?" Frank asked in a low voice.

Shane forced himself away from the railing and gave his friend a small smile before he said, "Something that isn't there anymore."

And with his back to the nightmares of his past, Shane went into the kitchen.

Chapter 3: Stocking Up

Clair never doubted herself in regards to the Watchers. She had seen that the organization was faltering under the doddering leadership of Harlan, and the necessary steps had been taken. Had there been someone more suitable than herself to run the organization, she would have backed them.

There hadn't been, and Clair was fine with that as well.

The pressures of the Watchers were acceptable to her, and she thrived under them.

Over the past few months, the organization had suffered setbacks from Shane Ryan, but she recognized them for what they were; setbacks, and nothing more.

Everything could be overcome with the proper application of available resources.

The resources of the Watchers were limited, which was why she found herself back in a role she hadn't played in nearly twenty years.

She wore her work clothes, standing in nylons with her work heels and purse on the hood of a dark blue Lexus. The car was jacked up, the left front tire off the rim and on the pavement. There was no spare. Clair held a cellphone and waited.

She was in a small car park in Chelmsford, Massachusetts, and there were only four cars in the lot, including the Lexus. As Clair stood and waited, reflecting on the task at hand.

A taxi pulled into the lot, dropped a man off by silver BMW. Clair waited until the man had gotten his door open before she said, "Damn it!"

The mild curse rolled across the pavement and caused the man to pause. In her peripheral vision she saw him turn to face her and then open his door. She continued to watch, wondering if he would get in and leave, or if he would stay and help.

He put his messenger bag in on the front seat, closed the door, and walked to Clair.

"Hello," he called out when he was a short distance away. "Everything okay?"

"No," Clair said, shaking her head. "The tire's flat and my damned son didn't put the spare back when he took the car into Boston and slashed the tire on a curb. And now, now he won't answer his phone!"

"It's alright," the man said, "Do you have Triple A or anything like that?"

She nodded. "They told me it will be at least two hours, they have only one truck on the road."

"I have a garage that I trust," the stranger said, trying to speak soothingly. "I can call them if you like. They'll send their truck out and tow it anywhere you want."

"Oh, could you?" Clair asked, pouring relief and excitement into her voice. "Thank you so much!"

The man grinned, took his phone out of his pocket, and Clair lashed out with her right hand. Her fingers were curled in partially, knuckles extended as she struck. The first blow hit him at the junction of his right shoulder and his chest, causing him to drop the phone. Before he could utter a syllable, her second blow caught him in the right temple.

His eyes rolled up into his head and he sagged to the pavement.

Off to the right, the engine of a battered, maroon Mercury sedan rumbled and the car's lights switched on. Clair stood over the unconscious Good Samaritan, rubbing the knuckles on her hand.

The sedan rolled to a stop beside her and the trunk popped open as a pair of men stepped out. They nodded to Clair before they bent over and zip-tied the man's hands behind his back, then did the same to his ankles. She watched as they picked the Samaritan up, dumped him into the car, then slamming the trunk down over him. The two men got into the car and drove away, the entire process lasting less than thirty seconds.

Her earpiece clicked and Clair said, "Yes?"

"Will we wait here or move on to another site?" a man asked.

"We'll wait for another half hour," Clair answered.

"Is it safe?" the man questioned, hesitation in his words.

"Of course not!" Her tone was harsh. "We have properties that need seeding. If you lack the ability to perform the task, leave."

The man cleared his throat and mumbled, "No, ma'am. I'll stay."

Clair shook her head and wondered about the future of the Watchers as another taxi pulled into the lot.

Chapter 4: In the Enemy's Camp

The office was dark, the sun not yet risen above the horizon. Pink light painted the skyline, and soon the city of Boston would come to life with the morning commute.

She left the door of the new director's office open, as she had done to the set of office suites. In the palm of her hand, she carried a small camera, one she could tuck into the sleeve of her blouse. Her phone was in her bag, and any glance through the device would reveal it free of compromising photographs. Even if they stripped the phone down and accessed her online data storage, there would be nothing to incriminate her.

While she had a few weaknesses, stupidity was not one of them.

Her steps carried her to Clair Willette's desk, but instead of attempting to access the files and downloading material onto a thumb drive, she turned to the wall.

The newest map, she had learned, had been brought into the office the previous morning. It revealed two essential changes in the landscape of the Watchers' organization.

The first was that they had indeed lost Borgin Keep. Burnt to the ground by a man they had described as an 'amateur ghost hunter.' The second, more important piece of information was that they may have found the One.

The idea of the location of that vile creature's home turned her stomach. Knowing that they planned on feeding it almost caused her to vomit.

She was surprised at the steadiness of her hands as she lifted the camera up, focused on the map, and took a picture. Without any hesitation, she moved from left to right, sectioning off the map mentally so she could gather close up information to pass along.

In less than a minute, she had taken sixteen photos. Calmly she tucked the camera away and left the director's office, easing the door shut behind her. Then she proceeded to do the same for the outer office.

She left the building at a casual pace, descended to the 'T' and climbed aboard the Red Line. After eight stops, she got off, pushed her way through the growing press of commuters, and climbed the stairs to the street above. An all-day internet café was crammed between a high-end shoe boutique and a guitar store. Both of which were dark.

She removed a twenty-dollar bill from her wallet and handed it to the twenty-year-old at the door of the internet café. Instead of asking for her license or proper identification, he gave a nod and muttered, "Eight's open."

Without responding to his statement, she hurried to the numbered terminal.

Her fingers typed in the necessary web addresses and passwords, and in less than a minute, she had the camera connected to a USB port, the photos uploading to an information drop. When it was finished she ended the connection, and logged out, then ejected the memory card from the camera. From her pocket, she removed a pair of gloves and a tack cloth.

She pulled on the gloves and with careful movements, she rubbed her fingerprints off the camera. Finished with it, she placed the camera down, on its back. She removed the memory card and broke it before she stood up.

By the exit was a trash can and she dropped the card's pieces into it before she left.

The cool air of the morning stung her cheeks and a sense of exhaustion crept over her. She pushed it aside, straightened up and walked to a nearby coffee shop. Caffeine and food would help her focus, for she had a few more tasks to complete before the day ended.

She put her hands in her coat pocket and started down the street, listening to the soothing sounds of Boston and wondering if any of the Watchers knew what she was doing.

Chapter 5: Visiting Rights

David rapped on the main entrance of the house at 125 Berkley Street and Frank answered it a minute later, an amused expression on his face.

"No Marie?" Frank asked, stepping aside.

"Physical therapy appointment," David explained as he entered the house.

"How's she doing?" Frank asked. "Any better?"

"A little bit," David said, nodding. "She can walk without a cane now, which is good. Still has a bit of trouble with stairs and getting into and out of the bed and bath."

Frank closed the door and gestured to the study.

"How's Shane doing?" David inquired.

"Shane's Shane," Frank replied with a shrug. "Who knows what goes on in his head? Man's a little different."

David snorted. "He's a tough one, that's for sure."

The door to the study was closed and when Frank opened it, David hesitated for a moment. Shane sat in his chair, drink in hand and Carl stood beside him. The dead man looked at David with an expression that showed he was not impressed.

And David, who had once stood in front of Emmanuel Borgin, found himself afraid of the old, dead German who lived in Shane's home.

"Come on in," Shane said. "What brings you over?"

"I have some news I think you'll appreciate," David said as he sat down. "I've told you before that I'm not happy with the way I was treated."

Shane and Frank, in addition to Carl, nodded.

"I have a few friends in the organization," David continued. "I've been wanting to hit back at the Watchers. Every property they've gathered over the years is essential to their plan."

"Their little strategy to unleash some of the stronger ghosts?" Shane asked, leaning forward, his eyes filled with hatred. "Yeah. I know that much. What I want to know though, is what else do they plan on doing? There has to be some bigger play here. What more do they want to do?"

David sat back, surprised. "You don't know the end game?"

"I thought I did. But obviously not," Shane started, but Frank put a hand on the man's shoulder.

"No," Frank said. "We're not sure what's going on. We can't tell what's true and what isn't. I'm not a big believer in information gathered by torture."

Shane frowned at him, but remained silent.

"I'm surprised," David murmured, shaking his head. "I thought you knew and that it had pushed you into making a move against them."

Shane's face paled and his lips formed a tight line.

"No," Frank said, "That's not why. Something else happened."

"Alright," David said, and he let the subject drop. He well-remembered the types of messages the Watchers had sent to people. David cleared his throat. "I received a phone call this morning. Just a quick call to tell me that my mother was fine."

The two men waited and David shook his head and gave them a rueful grin.

"Sorry," he said. "I forget I'm not with others like me anymore."

"Don't worry about it," Shane said. "What's your mom got to do with it?"

"Nothing," David said. "She's dead. Has been since I was four. It was a call-in code to check an email account."

"Did you check it?" Shane asked.

"Yes," David said, grinning at the men. "Do you have a laptop? It'll be easier if you see it."

"Sure," Frank said. "I do. It'll take a few minutes. I think it's still packed up."

The man exited the room and left David alone with Shane.

"Why are you doing this?" Shane asked in a low voice.

Carl, who hadn't moved from Shane's side, had a harsh expression on his face. David felt certain that Carl would kill him if Shane told him to.

"I want revenge," David said. The statement was both blunt and truthful. He wanted nothing more than to rip apart decades of the Watchers' work.

"How much?" Shane asked. He drummed the remaining fingers of his left hand on the arm of the club chair.

"How much what?" David asked, uncertain as to what Shane meant.

"Revenge," Shane explained. "Is there a limit, and if so, what is it? I want to leave them in ruins. Both literal and figurative. And I want scalps, David. I want to stretch their scalps and leave them to dry in the sun. And if I get angry enough, I'm going to kill everyone they know as well."

David looked at Shane and understood the man's words were the truth. There was hatred in his eyes, a dry, brutal honesty in his words that told him Shane would gut each and every one of them.

David smiled. "I like the idea of scalping them."

Shane nodded. "Let's drink to it then."

While David watched, Shane stood up, took a bottle of whiskey from a shelf, and filled a pair of glasses. He brought one to David and kept the other for himself.

Shane raised his glass and said, "To the death of the Watchers."

"To their death," David agreed, and he downed the strong, brutal liquor. He nodded to Shane and asked, "What happened to your fingers?"

The grin that appeared on Shane's face stretched his skin and highlighted the sharp angles of his face.

"Have you ever heard of Kurkow Prison?" Shane asked in a whisper.

"Yes," David answered.

"Then listen," Shane said, the grin fading away. "I'll tell you a story while Frank finds his laptop."

And the story chilled David.

Chapter 6: With Samson

Madison hadn't been hungry.

And she knew she should be hungry, but she wasn't. She didn't want to eat. Or to drink.

She only wanted to sit with Samson, to look at the boy and to speak with him. Time was lost when she did so, leaving her alone with him. Beneath the sweet smell of the forest, there was a foul, wretched scent. Its acrid bite pained her at times, as did the vague realization that she was the cause of the smell.

Madison knew she had soiled herself. She couldn't remember when, but she knew she couldn't leave him.

"How are you, Madison?" Samson inquired. His sweet young voice was full of concern and curiosity.

Her own words came out as a croak, difficult to hear and hardly intelligible.

"I'm wonderful," she answered, and she was. To look upon him was everything.

He smiled at her. "I'm so glad to hear that. You know, I'm extremely impressed."

"Why?" she managed to ask.

"No one has ever stayed with me as long as you have." His wholesome expression made her feel as though she would weep with joy.

Yet Madison couldn't move.

Her body was too heavy. Each article of clothing felt as though it were made of lead. Breathing had become a chore, a laborious process that she wanted to stop, and sometimes she did, if only for a few seconds.

Her heart beat in an irregular pattern, sometimes fast, at other times slow. When she tried to shift herself, to be comfortable, her joints exploded with pain.

A cold drop fell on her, then another. Water came down from the branches of the tree. While the rain struck her, it passed through Samson.

Of course it does, she thought, chiding herself. *He's a little angel. The water doesn't want to bother him.*

Samson leaned forward, putting his elbows on his knees and his chin in his hands.

"Madison," he said, "I want to hear a story. Would you tell me one?"

"What type of a story?" she managed to ask.

"A ghost story," was his reply, and a mischievous smile appeared. "A scary one. How about one with the ghost of a little boy in it?"

Madison nodded. She ignored the rain, or the way her body shook as her clothes became wet. For a long time she sat in silence, Samson patient across from her. Finally, Madison smiled, and she started the story.

"Once upon a time," she began. "There was a beautiful little boy named Samson, and he was a ghost."

Samson let out a tremendous laugh and clapped his hands with pleasure.

"Tell me more," he said, winking at her. "Tell me all there is."

Madison's voice continued to break, but Samson wanted a story, and she would tell him one.

Chapter 7: Choosing a Target

Frank had found his laptop, and he had brought a television downstairs as well. In a short time, he connected the two devices together. When he finished, Frank sat down next to Shane.

Shane glanced over at him while David accessed the email account.

"I didn't know you had a television," Shane said.

"I try not to have the volume up," Frank replied. "I know you have a hard enough time sleeping."

Shane nodded. "Thanks."

"My friend," Carl said in German, his voice low. "I do not know if I trust this David."

"That's why you're in here," Shane said, speaking in the same language. "If something goes wrong, I expect you to hurt him."

"I will," Carl stated.

"Here we go," David said, clicking on an email. He selected an attachment and opened it. A picture of a large map appeared on the screen. While David used the laptop's mouse, Shane stared at the image.

It was detailed, with small, marked places.

"What are we looking at?" Frank asked.

"That's part of the map," David said. He dragged his chair over. He used the cursor to illustrate what he spoke of. "This is Rhode Island, part of Massachusetts, part of New Hampshire, and most of Maine. It's the coast line."

"What map, though?" Shane asked. "I can see that it's New England."

"Sorry," David grumbled. "This is the map that hangs in the headquarters of the Watchers. The information on it is updated every quarter. It tells them what buildings are still haunted, which ones are active, and how active they are."

Shane chuckled. "So we can find out where their locations are?"

"Not with just the map," David said. "I'm hoping my contact can get me the alpha file."

"Which is what?" Frank asked.

"It's an index to every location, and it has all of the applicable information." David turned and faced both of the men. "With the map and the index, we'd be able to destroy the organization."

Shane scratched at the scar on the back of his neck. "Frank?"

"Yeah?" Frank asked.

"Do you think we could get a copy of the ley lines from Abbot Gregory?" Shane inquired.

"Sure," Frank answered. "I don't think it would be a problem at all."

"What are those?" David asked, sitting back and looking at them.

Frank explained the basics quickly, and David was nodding by the end.

"Makes sense," David murmured. "All of the seeding."

Shane straightened up as he asked, "What are you talking about?"

"You would hear it sometimes," David explained, "from the higher ups. Places would be 'seeded.' Certain buildings picked out, people sacrificed there. Sometimes, like with Borgin, they were feeding the living to the dead."

Frank muttered a curse under his breath and Shane clenched his teeth.

Shane took a deep breath, cleared his throat, and asked, "How many houses are out there?"

"I don't know," David answered. "If we can get the alpha file, then we'll have everything we need."

"What are the other attachments?" Frank asked.

"Hold on," David replied. He turned back to the laptop and clicked through the other four attachments. Each one contained another section of the map. Frank got up and he manipulated the images to form a single composite.

A large, comprehensive map, showing all six of the New England States, was revealed. In some spots, there were one or two dots. In others, cities like Boston and Concord, the marks were on top of one another.

There were hundreds of them.

Possibly even a thousand, Shane realized. To Carl he spoke in German, "Make sure someone is watching the house at all times."

"We have been," Carl replied.

"Thank you," Shane said, sighing. "Will you check on everyone for me, please?"

Carl responded with a short bow and vanished from the room.

"Is there a way we can strike at one, maybe two of them while we wait for the file?" Frank asked David.

The older man shook his head. "No, not that I know of. Only a few people knew of those outside of their own area of operations. Borgin had been mine for years. And I didn't handle any others before it."

"We may have someone who does know," Shane said, standing up.

"Who?" Frank and David asked in unison.

"Lisbeth," Shane answered.

David looked confused and Frank's face revealed his disappointment.

"When will you let her go, Shane?" Frank asked.

"Soon," Shane replied.

He just didn't know when soon would be.

Chapter 8: Ben and Jesse

At thirteen years old, Ben was tall for his age, almost six feet. He was heavier than he should be, according to his doctor, and the high school football coach had already come to the house to talk to him about playing his freshman year.

Jesse, his fraternal twin, was everything Ben was not. Short, thin, and completely lacking in any athletic ability, she preferred to be left alone to read in her room. While people thought her brother was older and already in high school, no one believed Jesse when she said she was in middle school.

She didn't know if she loved, liked, or hated her brother anymore. When they had been younger, they had been the best of friends.

Most of the time she didn't bother thinking about him, and when she did, it was with no enjoyment.

Jesse put her bookmark in the newest Richard Matheson book she had checked out from the library and shivered. It had gotten cold in her room. She sat up, searched around for her blanket, and stopped as something strange caught her eye.

A shadow stood in the corner of her room where there shouldn't have been one.

It seemed to solidify and a young boy stepped forward.

Her heart skipped a beat at the boy's beauty and her initial surprise and concern at a stranger being in her room vanished.

He smiled at her and she smiled back.

"Good evening to you," he said, bowing.

"Hi," Jesse whispered.

"You know," the boy said, looking around. "it has been quite some time since I traveled out of my own yard. I do believe that I am getting stronger."

"How does it feel?" Jesse asked in a low voice.

"Good," the boy replied, nodding. "Quite good."

She smiled.

"You were reading," the boy said with a grin.

She nodded.

"Of what is the subject of the book?" His voice was as beautiful as he was.

"Vampires," she said.

He frowned and asked, "What are vampires?"

Jesse told him everything she knew, and when she finished the boy smiled at her.

In a low voice he said, "There's a boy in the room next to yours. Is he your brother?"

Jesse nodded.

"You know," the strange boy whispered. "I believe he is one of these vampires you describe."

And as the words left the boy's mouth, Jesse knew it to be true. She felt her eyes widen and she asked, "What should I do?"

"You are a strong girl," the strange boy confided in her. "I have no doubt you know what to do about this vampire."

The boy was right.

Jesse knew exactly what to do.

She got out of her bed and walked to her desk. In silence, she flipped her chair over and with a strength she had never before possessed, she broke off one of the legs. The end of the leg was sharp, a jagged piece of wood sufficient to put down a vampire.

"Yes," the strange boy whispered. "Do it quickly, before he suspects anything."

Jesse nodded, more to herself than to him, and left the room. She felt the boy behind her as she walked to her brother's room. Ben's door was open and he lay sprawled on his back. He had on his Beats, deaf to the world as his music played.

Jesse approached him with firm steps. Grasping the broken chair leg in both hands, she raised it above her head.

Ben's eyes opened, and then widened in surprise as she drove the makeshift stake down and into his undead heart.

As her brother screamed, Jesse felt the strange boy's hands wrap around hers and she smiled as they pushed the stake in deeper together.

Chapter 9: Damage Control

Clair Willette stood in her office, staring at the new map on the wall where a bright, silver pin marked the small town called Amherst in New Hampshire.

And the One might be there. The chance was high, and the possibility made her drunk with anticipation.

For nearly two centuries, the Watchers had tracked the house down. Once, when Borgin had still been alive, they had managed to steal it out from under him. But his retribution had been quick, and the property had vanished. The few people who had even known of its existence had ended up in shallow graves along the eastern seaboard, if the stories were true.

Clair had no reason to doubt their veracity.

She needed to find a team that could go into the marked off territory, find the One and supplicate themselves before him.

Clair would have to be among them, and it had been twenty years since she had last gone out to meet with one of the dead.

Will we have enough power? she wondered. With the loss of Borgin and the Mill, their ability to provide the energy the One would need, had been severely diminished. Part of her wanted to rush through the process, but to do so could have disastrous results for all of them.

Still, she needed to know.

Clair went to her desk, sat down, and called Ms. Coleman on the intercom. When the secretary answered, Clair said, "Connect me to Rousseau, please."

"Yes, ma'am," Ms. Coleman replied. In less than a minute, the phone rang and Clair answered it.

"Clair," Rousseau said. His voice was thin and pinched, as if he forced each word through his nasal passage before he spoke it. It conjured up a memory of him, dressed in his perennial running suit with his strawberry-blonde hair swept back and held in place with too much gel. "What can I do for you?"

"I need you to check out a location for me," she explained.

"Hm, where?" he asked, and Clair gave him the particulars.

"That's a haul for me," he said after a moment of silence. "A good two hours, minimum. Connecticut State Police are cracking down on speeding this month. Not to mention the business I'd lose down here."

"I understand," Clair said, allowing her annoyance to seep into her voice. "However, you are held on retainer for the Watchers, and you are required for this particular investigation."

He grunted on the other end but said nothing else.

"Excellent," Clair said, dismissing the conversation. "I expect to see you in a week, no later. I'd rather not have any more unexpected issues occur among the rank and file."

"Sure," he said with a snort. "Whatever you say, Clair. I'll go up there. Dig around a bit. See what I can come up with. Anything I should know about before I go into Amherst?"

"Nothing that comes to mind," Clair answered. "It is merely a new acquisition. I expect you would need to take the proper precautions and nothing more."

"I'm an extremely careful man, Clair," Rousseau stated with pride. "It's why I'm on retainer, and why I'm still in the business."

"My thoughts exactly," she said. "Call me when you have information."

Without waiting for his response, Clair ended the call. She logged into her computer, brought up her email and frowned at the number of inquiries from various section heads.

All were about Borgin Keep. Each sought information, from the bare bones of 'how' to the more thoughtful 'who' may have done it.

Clair had spent a good portion of the previous evening with a bottle of wine and a pad of paper. By midnight, she had crafted what she believed to be a firm response that covered all of the questions.

It also avoided giving them anything remotely close to the truth.

> *My Dear Colleagues,*
>
> *You have all heard about the Keep, and I regret to inform you at this time that we have no information to pass on. I have placed a mole within the State of Vermont's forensic sciences division and our operative has successfully accessed the State's server. As soon as the State has determined what happened to the Keep, I will let you know.*
>
> *Until that time, however, we must continue on. As you may have heard, there is the real and thrilling possibility that the One has been found. We are in the process of reaching out to the entity and we are hopeful to have information regarding it sometime in the next two weeks.*
>
> *Our patience, and the patience of those who went before us, has nearly paid off. Soon we will no longer need to fear our mortality. Soon, my friends, we will dine at the table of the One and outlive humanity.*

When she finished, Clair read the email over several times, adjusted sentences and grammar, and then pressed send.

In a split second, the message was sent, and she exited out of the account. Chuckling to herself, Clair stood, walked back to the map, and stared at Amherst.

Will he find the One? she wondered. *Are we finally at the end?*

If he did, Clair knew he wouldn't survive the experience, in which case no news would be good news.

Smiling, Clair hoped she would never hear from Rousseau again.

Chapter 10: Securing the Alpha File

She knew it existed.

Not from word of mouth or any such nonsense, but she had actually seen the file. A glimpse only, to be sure, yet it had been there. Plainly listed as such on the screen of Director Cesare before he too had been removed in the tradition of the Watchers.

Cesare had never been adept when it came to the use of a computer, and his inability to close files had leaked information out to the wrong people. In the end, it had cost him his life, when an assassin had slipped an awl between a pair of vertebrae in his neck.

She pushed the thoughts from her mind as she slipped into the office. For the second time that week, she had made her way past security through the outer office and into the director's inner sanctum. She was frustrated with her lack of foresight. Had she been thinking beyond the map, she would have considered the significance of the alpha file, and how useful it could be.

With a deep breath, she reminded herself of the importance of the task at hand. A small, tickle of fear settled into the base of her neck. The hour was late, far later than was acceptable for her to be in the office.

And there was no reason why she should be standing in front of Clair's computer. In the darkness, she stood still, staring at the hard drive, waiting.

Her patience was rewarded a few moments later when a dull green light flashed on the drive's front.

The system was on.

She stepped closer to the desk and with a gloved hand, she turned on the monitor. When the image of the desktop appeared, she smiled. She typed in Clair's username and password quickly, having acquired both of them weeks before through a backdoor program in the system.

She bent down, pulled a thumb drive from her pocket, and plugged it into an available port. She proceeded to search for the information she needed, a growing fear of discovery gnawing at the back of her thoughts.

In less than a minute she found the alpha file, clearly marked and named in a folder labeled 'Important.' She made a copy of the file and then transferred it to the thumb drive and pocketed it.

She reached the outer office and heard footsteps in the hallway.

With her heart pounding in her chest, she stepped to the left of the door. Her palms began to sweat and her mouth went dry.

Someone swiped an entrance key through the reader, a confirmation beep sounded and the door swung open.

She pressed herself close against the wall, the door stopping only a few inches from her feet. Her eyes were closed as she listened, trying to hear who it was.

Then the door was swinging away from her, clicking shut. In the semi-darkness, she saw a person walk to the director's office. Another key was swiped through and Director Clair Willette stepped into her office. She passed through the evening glow that came through the window and walked to her desk to turn on the light, not looking back as it settled into place.

The thief wasted no time and let herself out, easing the main door shut as she stood in the hallway. Her vision pulsed as she stepped away and hurried down the hall towards the stairs. The thumb drive in her pocket felt like a lead weight as she realized that she could have died because of it.

The Watchers, as she had seen in the past, were not fond of thieves.

She knew what was done to them, and it was an experience she preferred not to have.

Composing herself, the thief left the building, turned down a nearby alley, and made her way towards the nearest T stop.

David needed the alpha file, and she was going to get it to him.

Book 9: Amherst Burial Ground

Chapter 11: Rousseau Goes to Amherst

The town of Amherst was small enough that people noticed when Rousseau pulled up and parked his Volvo by the village green in front of the Congregationalist Church. He nodded and waved to a few, a smile on his face as he walked around to the back of the car. From the trunk, he removed a few cameras, a camera bag, and a floppy sunhat that made him look ridiculous.

When the curious town folk saw his equipment, they lost interest in him.

He was another person from out of state looking to get some pictures of their beautiful town. Someone, therefore, of absolutely no concern.

Rousseau whistled some piece of pop music he had heard on the radio, shut the trunk and adjusted the hat. While he did so, he brought up the memory of the maps he had studied. He positioned himself with the church on the left and looked at the town hall. Beyond it, he knew, was a path that would lead into a small neighborhood. From there a street would lead to an entrance into conservation land.

And it was in the virgin woods that he would find the parcel the Watchers were concerned with.

Putting his hands in his pockets Rousseau strolled along, smiling at people he saw, pausing to snap a picture here and there. In a short time, he passed the town hall, and after half an hour, he made it through the neighborhood. He stopped at the edge of the conservation land. A pair of crooked granite posts flanked either side of a narrow entrance that led into the land. Between the two posts was a length of thick, one-inch chain. The steel was painted orange and served as a barrier to anyone who tried to drive into the woods.

Beyond the barrier was a path, wide enough for a single vehicle, but grass grew in the tire ruts and he doubted anyone had driven on it in recent memory.

Rousseau climbed over the chain as awkwardly as he could for the benefit of anyone who happened to watch him enter the forest. Tall trees pressed close to the road and he felt a shift in temperature after he had traveled twenty yards along the path.

It wasn't from the shade of the trees, he knew. The cold was deep, far more penetrating than the weather dictated.

Rousseau recognized the chill as the mark of the dead. Either a great many of them, or a particularly strong one.

He didn't like either option. For a moment, he hesitated, considered a retreat from the wooded lane, and then he shook his head.

As Clair had pointed out, he had a job to do and he would do it.

Rousseau continued along the path. It wound on, the forest tight on either side. Eventually the trail he followed grew wider. The ruts vanished. He shivered as the temperature plummeted, his breath coming out in great white clouds as he exhaled.

Rousseau paused, stripped the cameras off, and left them on the ground before he continued. From his pocket, he took several iron rings, fitting them on his fingers while walking deeper into the forest.

Part of him screamed to stop, demanded that he go back into town, and find a place to buy a shotgun.

But he couldn't stop.

Something tugged at him. A deep seeded curiosity demanded him to follow the path.

Ahead of him a giant tree loomed, the likes of which he had never seen before. The branches were tremendous, each one filled with leaves and he knew, deep within his gut, that he needed to be there.

He knew he had to walk beneath the boughs of the tree.

Rousseau quickened his pace, stumbling over the occasional root or fallen branch, but he never stopped.

The forest darkened and he broke into a jog.

Then he was there.

Before him stretched a small burial ground and at the back was an old house. Almost ancient.

In front of it was what he had come for. Rousseau knew that.

The boy had called him, somehow, and that, Rousseau felt, was wonderful.

The boy sat on a rock and smiled. When he saw Rousseau, he waved and Rousseau, with excitement surging through him, returned the gesture.

Across from the boy was a woman. Or what had been a woman. She was emaciated, her clothes filthy and ragged on her thin frame. When she turned to face Rousseau, it looked as though someone had stretched plastic wrap over a skull. Her lips were cracked and her eyes sunken in their sockets. It seemed as though her head was the only part of her which moved.

"Hello," the little boy said.

"Hello," Rousseau said, smiling at the child.

"What's your name?" the boy asked.

"Rousseau."

"How nice," the boy said with a grin. "This is my friend, Madison. Have you come to talk with me, too?"

"Yes," Rousseau whispered. "Oh yes, I have."

The boy smiled. "Come then, Rousseau, sit with us."

And Rousseau stumbled forward, a sense of joy burning within him as he sought the company of the boy.

Chapter 12: A Vengeance of His Own

Shane had never pretended to be a nice man. Or a kind man. He had flat out refused to consider himself as a hero.

Heroes didn't do the sort of acts Shane did.

Or those he planned to do.

Every day that he could, Shane kept to the habits and rituals that had helped him survive years of nightmares and memories. The destruction of Vivienne, his childhood tormentor, had eased those pains, but had not erased them. Walking helped him to think, and so he walked.

When he could.

For the past week he had been able to get out before the sun set. He smoked a few cigarettes, walked out to Concord Street and then up to Greeley Park. The Park, a hundred acres set aside in the center of the city for public use, had several paths he found perfect for contemplation.

Two days prior, he had discovered he wasn't alone on his walk.

A man and a woman followed him.

They were young and trendy, wearing the latest fashion trends and pushing a stroller.

Shane might not have paid them any sort of attention if he hadn't had to tie his boot. They passed by, he nodded, and noticed how they hurried past him.

It was odd, and at first, he assumed it was only because of his fearful appearance.

But as they moved away and he straightened up, he noticed their clothes were brand new. The fabric still creased from where it had been folded on store shelves.

He also noticed the stroller was empty.

There was no child in it.

The next morning they had followed him again. And as he turned into Greely Park, lighting a cigarette, he caught sight of them once more.

Shane kept his pace steady though his heartbeat quickened. With the empty stroller and the new clothes, he suspected they were Watchers. Though apparently new to the task of trailing someone.

Which didn't make them less dangerous.

In fact, Shane felt it made them more so. They would be more inclined to take risks, to try to complete their objective, whatever it might be.

When he reached the trail he wanted, Shane quickened his pace.

"Stop!" the man behind him barked.

Shane broke into a sprint.

A loud cough sounded and something slammed into the tree to his right.

Suppressed weapon, Shane thought, and he leaped off the path and into the woods.

Neither the trees nor the underbrush were sufficient to hide him, so he looked for a place to defend himself. Several shots hit the trees around him, and one cut close by his ear. Shane didn't stop running.

It seemed that they meant to take him alive, which would mean torture and eventual execution.

Shane had no intentions on letting that occur.

Ahead he caught sight of a large boulder, and he knew it was there that he could make his stand. He sprinted for it, feet flying over gnarled roots and down trees. When he reached the tall boulder, he scrambled up it to stand and look down as the man and the woman raced to him.

They had semi-automatic pistols with suppressors and their faces were flushed with the exertion of the run. Yet their hands were steady as they pointed the weapons at him. Their faces wore expressions of determination.

"Shane Ryan," the woman said. "Come down."

Shane's hand trembled as he removed his cigarettes and lit one. Exhaling he replied, "No. I don't think so."

"You need to come down," the man stated. "I have no issue with blowing your knee caps out."

Shane nodded. "I appreciate your honesty."

The woman frowned. "Where's Frank Benedict?"

"Busy," Shane replied, catching his breath.

She glanced at her colleague. "We can't wait any longer. We need to take him now."

"Agreed," the man said, bringing his pistol up.

"Hold on," Shane said, holding up a hand. "I have a statement to make, for the next time you use the stroller on someone. Make sure you have a kid in it."

"What are you talking about?" the man asked.

"Kids," Shane said with a sigh. "You should have brought one. I brought my own."

Shane gave them a grim look, reached into his pocket, and clasped the small finger bone he had placed there before his walk. He took a deep breath and hoped his plan would work as he whispered, "Eloise."

The dead girl appeared in front them and smiled as she said, "Hello."

Shane watched as both the woman and her companion fumbling in their pockets.

Before Shane could warn Eloise about iron, the dead girl was in motion, a blur that struck both man and woman down.

Sitting on the boulder, Shane shook his head, lit a fresh cigarette, and watched the little dead girl murder his attackers.

Chapter 13: At Marie's

"How are you feeling?" David asked, helping Marie into her chair.

The detective shrugged. "Same. Be better when I can get back to work. *If* I can get back to work."

"You will," David reassured her. He lifted the cozy from the teakettle and filled Marie's cup. When he returned to his own seat, he found her eyes on him.

"What?" he asked, grinning.

"You," she replied. "I'm still surprised at how graceful you are."

David shrugged, saying, "I keep telling you, I used to be a dancer. Before the Watchers."

Marie chuckled, winced and let out a sigh. "They keep telling me the pain will go away eventually."

"I don't know," David said. "I've never had to come back from an injury like yours."

She grunted. "Neither did they. The doctors have it randomly categorized as a traumatic brain injury."

"I think they're spot on," David admitted. "It was traumatic, and it occurred to your brain."

His phone chimed and interrupted his next comment. Frowning, David picked the cellphone up from the table and saw it was a text about the alpha file. Surprise must have shown on his face as Marie asked, "What is it?"

David had kept her up to date as to the informant within the Watchers' organization, so when he told her what the text concerned excitement filled her eyes.

"Will she bring it here?" Marie asked.

"It would be for the best," David said. "Boston is too dangerous. As is Shane's for her. She is too prominent in the organization. I'm afraid she would be recognized instantly."

"Then have her come here," Marie said. "Where is she right now?"

David sent a text asking the same. The reply came in less than thirty seconds later.

"A town called Hudson," he said.

"It's the next town over," Marie said. "Give her my address. Tell her to come on up."

David smiled as he typed the message in.

After he had sent it Marie asked, "Why are you grinning?"

"You continue to impress me, Marie," he said.

"All my years as a cop," she said, grinning.

A pleasant silence fell over the two of them and they drank their tea. It was good, David realized, to be in the company of someone he had fought beside. And he recognized that Marie reminded him of Blanche, murdered in Borgin.

By the time David finished his tea, there was a knock on the door of Marie's apartment. He glanced at her and she gave a nod. David stood up, unlocked the door and opened it.

His informant stood in the hallway, her face pale and her hair in disarray. David stepped aside and let her in, securing the deadbolt behind her.

"Marie," David said, "this is my God-daughter, Shirley Coleman."

Chapter 14: The Truth

Shane sat in the small, circular room within the house's walls. The mirror was in front of him and Lisbeth was in the mirror. She watched him as she moved with nervous energy within the glass boundary of her prison.

"What do you want?" she demanded, and there was a shrill, fearful note in her words.

Shane said nothing.

Lisbeth sneered at him. Then the sneer faded, replaced briefly by a nervous grin. "Are you here to visit?"

"Not quite," Shane said. "I need information."

"I need to not be a prisoner," she retorted. A genuine look of desperation appeared on her face.

"Let me go," she begged.

Shane felt no mercy towards her.

"I need information," he repeated. "When I have everything I need from you, then I will let you go."

A whimper escaped her lips and she gave a small nod.

"I have a map," Shane said, "which shows the location of all the Watchers' properties. What I want to know is, if they were to lose a property, which one would hurt the Watchers the most?"

Lisbeth hesitated and her face contorted before she made a decision to speak. "There's a house, one that belonged to a school teacher. They've made sure to keep him well supplied."

"Are there others?" Shane asked.

"Yes," she answered.

"Tell me," Shane demanded.

Lisbeth winced at his tone and nodded. She spoke to him about various properties, some nearby, others in the far corners of New England.

"You have to understand," she finished, the words coming out slowly, "that these ghosts, some of them have been fed and cared for by the Watchers for over a hundred years. The organization helped them to perfect killing, and taught them how to properly siphon the energy of the dead."

"Did that help them?" Shane asked. "Did the dead benefit from it?"

"You faced Emmanuel?" Lisbeth asked.

Shane nodded.

"Then tell me, Shane," she said, saying his name as if it were a curse, "did it work for him?"

Shane nodded.

"He was the strongest," Lisbeth finished. "But by no means the only one."

After a moment of silence, Shane asked, "And that's it?"

She looked up, surprised. "What do you mean, 'that's it?' Isn't that enough? The more bodies mean the stronger the ghost."

Shane shrugged as he stood up. "How strong they are doesn't really matter to me."

"Why not?" she demanded. "You actually think you could face them?"

Shane looked at her and said, "I grew up with worse."

Lisbeth blinked. "Impossible."

"Next time Eloise feels like talking," Shane said, "ask her about the pond."

Lisbeth threw herself at the mirror, the glass humming in the frame as she bounced off it.

"What will happen to me if you die going after the Watchers?!" she screamed at him.

"Then you'll stay here," Shane said, "until someone lets you out."

Silence followed him out of the room.

Book 9: Amherst Burial Ground

Chapter 15: A Corner Lot

The house was small and set at the back of a corner lot in Pepperell, Massachusetts. Starlight supplemented the weak glow of the streetlights and the other houses in the neighborhood were dark, the residents fast asleep.

The house Shane and Frank were interested in was as dark as the others, but for a different reason. Its wood siding was painted a bright blue, the shutters a horrific shade of green. There was a 'For Sale' sign on the front yard and the windows were absent of any light.

Shane sat in the driver's seat, smoking a cigarette while Frank double-checked the loads on the shotguns.

They had received word from David earlier about the arrival of the alpha file. The man also said he would be by as soon as possible to share the information.

Frank had told the older man it was fine, and it was.

While the stolen file would help them find the location of the One, neither Shane nor Frank needed it to wreak havoc on the Watchers.

The map David had brought over would help with that.

They had zoomed in on the image, found a nearby house, and discovered that there was a ghost in the structure. Exactly as Lisbeth said there would be.

The spirit had accounted for seven deaths in the past twenty-three years. Not much when compared to the other ghosts Shane and Frank had faced. Or even when held up to those Shane had squared off against as a child. Yet Lisbeth said that this one was strong, and well fed by the Watchers.

And that the organization would be hurt by its removal. Which was perhaps the most important reason for Shane.

"So, what information do we have on this house?" Frank asked, handing a shotgun to Shane.

"From what I could find," Shane said, putting the weapon on his lap, "there was a school teacher, Cody Gray, who used to live here. By all accounts, he was a great guy. Teacher of the year, donated time and money to underprivileged kids. Then, when he died, they found a hidden room with home movies and photos that showed him committing horrific acts. Hell, they even found the tools he used to torture people still hanging on the walls."

"When was this?" Frank asked. "When did he die?"

"Nineteen sixty-two," Shane answered. "House went unoccupied for a few years. Then someone from out of town bought it, and two years into their ownership, the husband strangled the wife and then killed himself. He left a note, apologizing for what he had done, but Mr. Gray had been telling him to do worse. Much worse, so he ended it before Mr. Gray could make him."

"Damn," Frank murmured.

Shane nodded. "It went on. Seven deaths in all, plus eight people in psychiatric facilities."

"Why don't they just raze the building?" Frank asked.

"When it goes up for sale," Shane explained, "I think the Watchers buy it. They sit on it for a couple of years, and then they put it on the market. There's no state law saying that the seller has to disclose if a crime was ever committed in the house, so a lot of people pick it up at a cheap price and move right in."

Frank let out a long breath and said, "Any idea where his body's buried, if there are no bones here?"

"He was cremated, but there's got to be a bone here somewhere. It's the only thing that makes sense," Shane replied. "There was an article from the local paper about his body being mutilated prior to cremation. A toe was missing. Some of the people interviewed thought it was his wife that did it. She was crazy about him. I think if we find that hidden room, we'll find a piece of him tucked away in there."

Frank nodded. "Alright, let's go see who's in there."

Shane got out of the car, took his bag out of the back seat, and slung it over his shoulder. He looked at the cape and wondered how such a small building could have housed someone so terrible.

"Ready?" Frank asked.

Shane took one last drag off his cigarette, stubbed it out, and nodded as he let the smoke curl out of his nose.

"Yeah," Shane said. "I'm ready."

In silence the two men left the car and headed up the driveway, shotguns in hand and hatred in their hearts.

Chapter 16: Necessary Information

David was surprised to notice a tremble in his hand after Shirley turned off the laptop.

He was still in shock over the tremendous number of properties the Watchers owned. Through a fog, he realized that the organization was larger than he had thought, that its pockets were deeper than imagined. He understood his insignificance in comparison to them, and how Harlan's attempt at removing him was nothing more than the mistake of an old and foolish man.

"Does this 'One' truly exist?" Marie asked, looking from Shirley to David.

"The Watchers think it does," Shirley said.

"And that's all that matters, unfortunately," David said. "They will move heaven and earth to see if the One's powers to extend life are true or not. There is a mythos around it. Everyone, from the lowest soldier to the highest district member has been spoken to about the reward of serving the One. Some never lose faith. I didn't, not until Borgin Keep."

"What would you gain?" Marie asked. "A few years of extra life? And how?"

"The Watchers were founded a hundred and fifty years ago," Shirley explained. "Some of the original members noticed how some ghosts fed off the energy of other spirits. A few of the members started to sacrifice people they considered undesirable, trying to see how strong the dead could become. As the years progressed more, well, research was put into the study of the dead."

Shirley cleared her throat, and then continued. "Then they discovered the ley lines, and that the strongest of the dead were on there. Someone then theorized that a ghost at the junction of the northeastern lines would be the strongest, and that it would be possible for a spirit to become powerful enough to extend the life of those still living."

"So there's no proof," Marie said.

"None," Shirley agreed. "It's literally a matter of faith. A cult has been built up around this theory, and we've all been part of it."

"But the file," David said, gesturing toward the laptop, "it holds a good deal of information. It should also tell us where the One is. The only question now is, do we dig through the file ourselves, or wait until we're with Frank and Shane?"

"I'd wait," Shirley said, "I'm not certain about the extra security the Watchers have. They may have embedded a deletion program in the file that would erase it after a single use."

"Alright then," David said, "we'll wait until we're with them."

"What's the Watcher's next step then?" Marie asked. "How do we stop them?"

David looked at her and grinned.

"What?" she asked.

"I'm impressed," David said. "That's all. I'm just impressed."

"Their next step," Shirley said, grinning at them both, "is to find out if the ghost at the intersection of the ley lines is really as powerful as they think. If it is, then they'll try to reach out to it. If it isn't, the Watchers will attempt to make it strong enough to test out their theory."

"More deaths?" Marie asked. Her voice was hard, unforgiving. David could sense the anger in her.

It was difficult for him to feel the same. He had brought the Watchers' own disavowed members to Borgin Keep and fed them to the dead. While he had never considered that others like himself might have been engaged in similar actions at different locations, it wouldn't have bothered him.

So long as those beings offered up had been adults. David had refused to sacrifice children.

He doubted those in charge of the organization suffered from similar qualms.

"When will they start the investigation?" Marie asked. Her questions, David realized, were those of a detective. She needed all of the information to process the situation and to move forward.

"They've already started it," Shirley said. "The director has sent an investigator out there. He should report back by the end of the week. I'll pass along whatever information I can glean. I don't think I should risk accessing the computer again directly. The director almost caught me this morning."

David heard the slight shudder in her voice and he understood. There would have been no excuse for Shirley to have been in the office so early, even if she was Clair's secretary. She would have been questioned, and not gently. David had been witness to more than a few interrogations.

Shirley would, in the end, have ended up dead. Either after a short 'interview' as they called the interrogations, or after a lengthy torture, if they didn't believe her answers.

One more body amongst a thousand others. Another spirit to feed the dead.

"How will you get the information to us then?" Marie asked.

"I'll send an email," Shirley said, and before either David or Marie could protest, she held up a hand. "Not from my own account. Not even from the one I used to send the map. I'll make a new one. You'll know it's mine. I'll put something about a baptism in the subject line."

David nodded. "I don't like you doing this."

His god-daughter looked at him with a maturity he didn't realize she possessed.

"Someone has to," she said. "Or a lot more people are going to die."

David remained silent, for what Shirley said was a hard and bitter truth.

Chapter 17: In Cody's House

The interior of Cody Gray's house had a fresh coat of paint on the walls. A bright white that magnified what little light came through the bare windows. The carpets were new, as were the wooden risers on the stairs.

Shane and Frank had entered the house through the front door. They stood in the main room. The stairs led up to the second floor and an entryway opened onto the kitchen, where new appliances gleamed in the starlight coming in through the bay window behind the sink.

And like so many other homes and buildings Shane had been in, Cody's house was cold.

"Hello," a voice whispered in Shane's ear.

It was a man's voice. Confident and friendly, the voice of a man in whom a young man could confide. A father figure for the lost and the lonely.

Shane turned his head towards the speaker.

"What is it?" Frank asked in a low voice.

Shane held up a finger.

"Ah," the man said. "You can hear me. That's wonderful. It's been a long time since someone came to visit me. It's difficult, and lonely if I'm being perfectly honest. I find that I just feel better when I can talk to someone. Don't you?"

Shane nodded.

"I knew you would," the man said cheerfully. "What's your name?"

Shane told him and Frank stepped to one side, giving a short nod towards the kitchen. A slight movement of Shane's hand sent his friend away, leaving Shane alone with the ghost.

"I'm Cody, Shane," the man said. "That's a great name, you know. One of my favorite characters had your name. He was in a book by Jack Schaeffer. Do you know it?"

"No," Shane answered.

"Ah well," Cody said. "You'll get to read it someday, I'm sure. Is that your friend who came in with you?"

"Yes," Shane answered.

"He doesn't look very trustworthy," Cody confided. "Have you noticed that?"

Cody's words pushed their way into Shane's mind. Each syllable seemed to latch onto him and it was a struggle to keep his mind focused on why they were there.

"Terribly untrustworthy," Cody continued, not noticing that Shane hadn't agreed with him. "I'd be cautious. That's all I'm saying, mind you. Be careful. You seem like a nice young man and I would hate for you to be *hurt*."

With the last word, Shane shivered. A deep, powerful urge to harm Frank surged through him and he gasped at the strength it took to fight the desire off.

Cody let out an exclamation of surprise.

"Who are you?" Cody demanded. "Who?!"

Shane turned towards the sound of Cody's voice, and for the first time he saw the ghost.

Cody was tall with stooped shoulders. Light blonde hair fell to the shoulders of his blue cardigan and his head seemed unnaturally large. The man's eyes were wide-set and his face was broad and flat. There was a look of shock on his face.

"Tell me who you are," Cody ordered.

Shane resisted, managing a grin. "No."

"Got it!" Frank yelled from the kitchen.

Cody twisted toward the sound of Frank's voice and when he did so, Shane leaped at the ghost. He slammed his hand through the dead man's body, the iron ring on Shane's finger dispersing the ghost.

An enraged howl filled the house and a heartbeat later Cody was back. He shimmered with energy as he glared at Shane but kept his distance.

"How did you do that?" Cody asked.

"It's a secret," Shane whispered. "I can't tell you."

"I'll make you tell me," Cody hissed. "You don't know what I can do."

"Wrong," Shane snapped. "I don't care what you can do."

"When I'm through with you, you will care," Cody corrected.

With a scream that penetrated Shane's skull, Cody charged forward again. Shane twisted away, throwing a punch at the dead man. Cody twisted away from the blow, snarled and kicked out, the strike catching Shane in the thigh and sending him spinning back.

Shane caught himself against the wall, spun around to face the ghost.

Cody crouched down and grinned.

Then the ghost straightened up, a look of surprise on his face. He shook his head, unsure what to do.

Light flickered in the doorway to the kitchen and the curious odor of burning bone filled the house.

A small spot of blue, tinged with orange, appeared on Cody's left cheek. It spread like wildfire, and then Cody seemed to understand what was about to happen.

The ghost let out a shriek, clawed at his own face and then his voice reached a pitch Shane didn't think was possible. Cody's fingers were devoured by flames that burst forth from the dead man's cheeks.

Shane watched, the shotgun held in his hands. He kept the barrel pointed towards Cody and part of him wondered if the ghost would make an effort to attack Frank.

But the dead man didn't seem to realize that it was Frank who had lit his remains on fire.

Shane winced as Cody's voice rose to a crescendo, and then ended as the dead man vanished.

A moment later, the sound of water running came from the kitchen.

Frowning, Shane walked into the room to see Frank at the sink. A cloud of noxious smoke hung about the ceiling above him.

"Where'd you find the bone?" Shane asked.

"Looks like Cody's secret room was in the pantry, behind a false wall," Frank answered as he turned on the water and splashed it about the stainless steel of the sink.

"What are you doing?" Shane asked.

"Washing the ash out," Frank replied.

"Why?" Shane asked, feeling confused.

"Why wouldn't I?" Frank asked in return. "Who wants to see bone ash in a sink?"

Shane shook his head and laughed at the absurdity of the statement.

A whisper filled the kitchen and he looked over to Frank, all mirth gone.

"Oh, hell," Shane muttered.

A shape barreled past him, the blurred image of a woman. She screamed as she slammed into Frank, throwing him into the countertop. When she attacked Frank again, the former monk smashed a fist through her, the iron disrupting her and casting her away.

Frank sank to the floor and gasped, "Pantry."

Shane nodded, ran towards the open pantry door, and narrowly missed the ghost as she raced out into the kitchen. He pushed himself into the small closet, felt a loose panel in front of him, and shoved it open. From a small skylight came the dim glow of the moon, casting enough of light for Shane to see by. The sounds of the fight in the kitchen increased and it seemed as though Frank wasn't doing well.

Shane's eyes stopped on a small plate on top of a shelf that stood at eye-level. Pinned to the wall above the dish was an old and worn wedding invitation.

He reached out, tore the invitation away, and found a small, dark hole behind it. Shane plunged his hand into it, grasped something cold and metallic, and pulled it out.

In his hands, he found the remains of a severed finger with a wedding band on it.

Mrs. Gray, Shane thought. He ran with the grotesque item back into the kitchen and had to duck as Frank was thrown against the far wall.

Mrs. Gray ignored Shane until he dropped her remains into the sink and set them on fire.

Unlike her husband, Mrs. Gray didn't stand still.

She abandoned Frank and charged at Shane. Her punch caught him squarely on the chin and dropped him to his knees, his head screaming in agony.

No other attack followed, for the flames devoured her.

Frank stumbled over to the sink, waited until the fire had extinguished itself and then washed her remains away the same as he had her husband's.

Shane pulled himself to his feet and looked at his friend. The left side of the man's face was swollen, blood trickling from the left corner of his mouth.

"You good?" Shane asked.

Frank nodded, turned the water off, and dried his hands on his pants as he asked, "Now what?"

"We go on to the next house," Shane replied. "We should be able to do another two tonight, since we know where they are."

"What about after that?" Frank inquired.

"Then we go home," Shane answered.

"And will you free Lisbeth's soul?" Frank asked in a soft voice.

The question caught Shane off-guard.

"No," Shane said. "I'm not done with her yet. And we've got more ghosts to burn."

With that, he shouldered his shotgun and left the house, Frank silent behind him.

Chapter 18: More Bad News

Jenna and Gabby sat in Clair's office. Their eyes were sunken, their faces drawn. They looked as if they hadn't slept well in days and Clair didn't care.

Clair took pills each night to sleep. And it had gotten bad enough that she washed them down with a glass of wine. Only she and the twins knew what was going on, what it was that Shane and Frank were doing to the organization.

It has to be them, she thought, stifling a curse.

"How many?" Clair asked, hating the stiffness in her voice.

"Three on Monday night. Two more on Tuesday," Jenna answered.

"They took a breather on Wednesday and Thursday," Gabby continued, "and then hit us again yesterday."

Clair glared at Gabby until the woman added, "Another three."

"Damn it!" Clair snarled, slapping the top of her desk.

"At least they're small," Jenna said.

"The size doesn't matter here," Clair spat. "Every single one of them is necessary now. Rousseau didn't return. We have the One. We're not losing one ghost in each house. Oh no, we're losing all of the dead it siphons energy from. It is a horrific ripple in our little pond."

"Do you want us to go to Shane's house?" Jenna asked.

"Are you serious?" Clair asked after a stunned moment of silence.

"Sure," Gabby said, nodding and glancing at her twin. "It's just him and his buddy, right?"

Clair took a deep breath, let it out slowly, and said, "Were either of you ever informed as to why these two gentlemen are an issue for us?"

"No," Jenna said. "We only know that they were causing some trouble."

The phone on the desk rang before Clair could enlighten the sisters. A look at the base showed a button labeled "Emilio and Sadie" flashed. Something about the pair tugged at her memory but it wouldn't reveal itself. Frowning, Clair reached out and answered the call.

"Hello?" she asked, her voice sharp.

"Why hello," a man said. His tone was harsh and unforgiving. "Who's this?"

"Evidently the wrong number," Clair retorted and slammed the phone back into its cradle.

Before her hand had left the receiver, the phone rang again.

The same line flashed.

Feeling anger flare within her, Clair snatched up the phone.

"You have the wrong number," she began, but the man on the other end cut her off before she could finish.

"Where's Harlan?"

"He's not here," she replied, warily. "Who's this?"

"This is Shane Ryan."

Clair straightened up. "Shane."

"Yes," he said. "Who are you?"

"I'm Clair." The twins leaned in, all hints of exhaustion gone as they listened intently to the part of the conversation they could hear.

"You're in charge now," Shane said. It was a statement, not a question.

"I am," Clair replied.

"What happened to Harlan?" Shane asked.

"I had him strangled," she responded.

A snort of laughter came through the line. "Good. Well, I have to ask, how do you like my work so far?"

Hatred boiled within her. Gritting her teeth together, she replied, "I'm not. When are you going to stop?"

"Just as soon as I've crushed your organization," Shane replied in a voice so low as to be almost inaudible.

"You can't," Clair stated.

"Maybe not," Shane conceded. "But I'm going to try. And now, I know how."

He left an unasked question in the dead space between them and when Clair didn't speak, he did.

"I know about the One," Shane said. "I know where it is. And while I figure out what to do about it, how to go about destroying it, I'm going to continue to disassemble the Watchers. A single ghost at a time."

"And what makes you think you'll succeed?" Clair hissed. "What makes you think we can't stop you?"

"I don't know if I'll succeed," Shane said. "But I know you haven't been able to stop me yet. Let's not forget, Clair, that you've got an awful lot of real estate to cover. I don't think you've got the personnel to protect everything, and I know for damn sure you don't have the ability to come at me again."

He chuckled, a grim, painful sound.

"I almost forgot," Shane added. "Lisbeth sends her regards."

The phone went dead and Clair's hand shook with rage as she put the receiver back.

"What did he say?" Jenna asked.

Clair gave the twins a synopsis of the conversation.

"We need to kill him," Gabby said, standing up and pacing about the office.

Clair shook her head. "No. Not yet. Our first priority is protecting access to the One. As soon as we've established that we can send out teams to try and intercept him."

"What do you want us to do?" Jenna asked.

"Do you know Linda Grace?" Clair asked, taking a notepad out and jotting a message down upon it.

"No," the twins answered in unison.

"I didn't think so," Clair said. She tore the page free, folded it, and handed it to Gabby. "Take this to her. Ms. Coleman will give you Linda's contact information on the way out."

The twins nodded and left the room, closing the door behind them.

Clair stared at the phone, a mixture of fear and hate churning in her stomach. Shane was far more dangerous than she had believed.

And once more, she realized how essential it was to kill the man.

Chapter 19: In Amherst with Linda

Linda Grace stood at the edge of the woods in Amherst, New Hampshire.

She was a young woman. Unlike those she knew, Linda existed in a world of silence. She had been born deaf and thus was immune to the verbal assaults of the dead. Linda had discovered that talent the hard way, when as a child she had watched her mother succumb to the ghost of a young man who had convinced her to drink drain cleaner.

Later in life, Linda had discovered the Watchers by accident, and when they learned of her previous experience, she had found herself employed.

She was no longer considered half a person. No one she worked with thought she did less, or was treated special.

Where she went, others truly feared to tread.

A tap on her right shoulder got her attention and Linda turned to face one of the twins. She didn't know if it was Jenna or Gabby, but it didn't matter. The twin held up a whiteboard with the question, *Are you ready?*

Linda checked the straps on her harness and nodded.

The twins had secured her in a five-point harness, with the catch/release at the back instead of on her chest. She was connected to a tether of high-tensile rope, which would play out from a massive reel in the back of a box truck. Linda motioned to her head and the twin nodded, her mouth moving.

The other twin appeared and checked the camera on Linda's helmet. Whatever she saw would be fed back to a monitor in the back of the truck, and a second one in the main office in Boston.

If the image went dead, or she started to act in a way they didn't like, the twins would rescue her. Three men had also accompanied them, and they would help the twins reel Linda back in should it be necessary.

They didn't treat her differently.

They treated Linda with respect.

She confronted dangers none of them could. And while the danger to her was lessened, it was by no means absent.

As the harness attested.

The twin picked up the whiteboard and replaced the first question with a second.

Now?

Linda nodded.

The twin gave her a thumbs up, and stepped out of the way.

Linda moved forward.

She had on thick hiking boots that helped her keep a steady pace on the narrow trail. In addition to that she wore a padded, one piece suit. On more than one occasion, the Watchers had been forced to drag her out of a house or a building, and her injuries had been extensive. Now, in spite of the warmth of the day, Linda was fully protected.

Well, she thought as she continued forward. *As much as I can be.*

Linda followed the path. She knew that there was a ghost somewhere ahead of her. Another investigator for the Watchers had vanished a week before, and there was a rumor in the organization that this ghost might be the One.

A shiver of excitement raced through her as she considered it.

Immortality, or close to it. The ability to outlive all of those who had made her suffer.

She smiled at the idea and quickened her steps.

Linda paid careful attention to her surroundings as she went. The farther she traveled, the more focused she became. Soon she passed from the forest and into a glade, and then she found herself beneath the boughs of a tremendous tree.

The smell of rotting flesh struck her, causing her head to jerk back and to stagger to a stop.

It was then that she noticed the old, colonial cemetery, the house beneath the tree, and the death around the house.

A quick scan of those in front of the house churned Linda's stomach.

She counted five people. Two men, one woman, and two others who were so close to death she couldn't tell what gender they were. All sat on the ground, staring at a young boy who sat on a stone beside the open doorway. Two more lay on the earth and Linda knew they were dead, and that it was the odor of their putrefying flesh filling the air.

The boy turned and looked at her, and Linda knew he was dead. His clothes and his sickening grin spoke to her, telling her that he had died a long time in the past, and that he reveled in the death around him.

His mouth moved and he gestured warmly to her.

When she didn't respond, the grin on his face faltered.

His lips moved again, and his hand beckoned to her.

Even without being able to hear him, she felt a tug in her stomach. An instinctual urge to go and sit beside the others. To look upon the boy and to converse with him, regardless of her inability to do so.

The boy spoke a third time and any hint of amiable intentions vanished when she didn't respond.

He stood up, his face twisting and contorting. She watched as he stomped forward, up to the edge of the graveyard. He came to a stop and opened his mouth wide. From within him, something dark and hideous exploded out.

Even as Linda twisted away she felt the harness tighten for a split second, and then she was yanked backward.

The dark mass chased after her, twisting along the path at a speed she didn't think was possible. As it neared her, Linda felt a wave of uncontrollable fear rip through her.

She squeezed her eyes against the darkness and howled when it caught hold of her foot.

Chapter 20: Getting His Hands Dirty

David recognized the man at once.

Elliot, David thought, an angry, cold feeling filling his gut.

While the man had only been with the organization for a short time, and was nothing more than a low-level scout, David wasn't pleased to see him. It didn't matter that Elliot only knew the basics of the organization. Elliot's job was to find new houses that might be haunted. Chat up the neighbors. Nothing too serious, just the basic legwork.

The man's arrival on Berkley Street would be due to one of two reasons. First and simplest would be the man was doing nothing more than his job. Replying to a request from someone higher up to investigate Berkley.

The other possibility was that the Watchers had decided to keep tabs on Shane and Frank, and that meant that Elliot was a danger to David.

If the Watchers knew David was alive, they would make it a point to take him alive.

At a little past two in the afternoon, David had been parked in a beaten up Chevy sedan, two blocks down from Shane and Frank's place. He had arrived, prepared to deliver the alpha file and the email footage to the men when Elliot had pulled in front of him.

David had watched as the man bumped the curb with the car's tire. Then, with a loud grinding of gears, the man had slammed it into park and proceeded to watch Shane's house.

Elliot never bothered to look behind him, or to check his mirrors. Instead, he seemed focused on a cigar and rolling all of the windows of his large SUV down.

When David was certain that Elliot was focused on Shane and Frank and not there for some other reason, he got out of the Chevy. He closed the door but didn't latch it. For a moment, he stood still, waiting to see if Elliot would notice the movement behind him.

He didn't.

Large clouds of cigar smoke rolled out of the driver's side window as David approached the vehicle. He could hear Elliot humming, and it was then David noticed the man had headphones on.

For a moment, David paused, unable to comprehend the level of stupidity he was seeing. Then, with a shake of his head, David walked up, reached through the open window of the driver's side rear door, and let himself into the car.

"What the hell?!" Elliot demanded, half-turning in his seat.

What he saw wasn't David so much as it was David's pistol.

Granted, it was only a thirty-eight revolver, but it was enough to keep Elliot's attention focused on. The man couldn't look away from the opening of the barrel.

"I have money," Elliot said, not taking his eyes off the weapon.

"I don't want your money," David replied. "Turn around and drive."

"You can have the car," Elliot stammered, frozen in place.

"Turn around and drive," David repeated. "Or I'm going to neuter you."

Elliot turned around and tried to start the car.

The engine sputtered and refused to run.

Swearing, Elliot tried it again, and the vehicle roared to life.

"You're going to drive now," David said, "and I'm going to ask questions. You need to answer each question truthfully. Do you understand?"

Elliot nodded.

"Good," David said. "Start driving."

"To where?" Elliot asked, his voice trembling.

"I don't care," David said, lowering the pistol and pressing the barrel into the back of the driver's seat.

Elliot shifted into gear and eased off down the road, passing by Shane and Frank's place.

In the rearview mirror, David saw Elliot's eyes flicker toward Shane's house.

David's shoulders sagged.

"Why are you here?" David asked.

"I'm looking for properties in the area," Elliot replied, regaining some of his composure. "I was trying to find a place for me and the wife."

"You don't have a wedding ring," David retorted.

"Oh," Elliot said, flustered. He turned left, then left again.

David saw the sign for a dead end and said nothing about it.

"Say," Elliot said, "why don't I let you out here and we call it quits, okay? No hard feelings. Figure you're with some neighborhood watch group, right?"

"You could say that," David said. "But you'd be wrong."

When Elliot's eyes met his in the rearview mirror, David pressed the barrel of the pistol deep into the back of the seat and pulled the trigger.

Elliot tried to twist himself out of the way but it was too late.

There was no place for him to go.

The blast of the weapon was muffled by the foam and cloth of the seat. Elliot grunted as the bullet passed through the material, and then cut its way through his organs. It shredded his innards as it ricocheted off of ribs. The man slumped over the wheel, his foot slipping off the gas pedal and causing the standard to stall out.

The vehicle rolled forward for a few more feet before it bumped into a thick pine tree and came to a sharp stop. David put his pistol away, glanced around the back seat, and saw a clump of napkins from a Dunkin Donuts. He picked them up and used the rough paper to scrub at the door latch, the only part of the car he had touched.

From the front seat came the familiar rattle of death from Elliot's lungs. David knew from experience that Elliot would bleed out soon enough. There was no need for a second bullet, as merciful as one might be.

Another shot wouldn't be silenced as the first.

David held onto the cleaned latch with a napkin and let himself out.

There would be trace evidence on the back seat and elsewhere, but it would be minimal, and not nearly as damning as fingerprints and the pistol itself.

David sighed and shook his head.

He would have to get rid of the weapon, scrub his hands with a caustic solution to get the residue off and destroy his clothes.

He walked away from the vehicle, his hands in his pockets as he thought, *Homicides are never easy.*

Behind him, Elliot breathed his last, a harsh, guttural noise that caused David to give a nod of satisfaction.

Yet with the satisfaction came a sense of worry.

If the organization is sending people like Elliot out to keep tabs on Shane and Frank, David wondered, *where are the others? Where are those damned twins, Gabby and Jenna?*

The idea that something was commanding the attention of the Watchers' killers caused an uncomfortable sensation to settle in the pit of David's stomach.

He glanced at Elliot and shook his head. Clair was planning something, and David suspected it would be worse than anything Harlan had dreamed up.

Chapter 21: A Problem Arises

Clair had watched the interaction between Linda and the One when it was streamed live to her office. She had watched it perhaps forty more times since then, and she had sent it out to several others for their take on the situation.

No one had replied, and she found herself frustrated but not surprised by their failure to respond.

Clair had been surprised at the number of people around the One. Granted, they were close to death, but the fact that they were there was disconcerting.

She had spent several days researching current events in Amherst, New Hampshire.

There had been little to go on at first.

A missing persons report concerning a new mother. Rousseau was there. Clair had seen his body. Then there had been the possibility of a runaway. From the next town over, an elderly man had vanished on his walk. The same for a younger man who had broken down on the side of the road in a town called Milford.

Lacking any sort of intelligence assets in the southern New Hampshire police forces after Harlan's debacle, Clair had been forced to outsource the job. She had dipped into the Deep Net, found a hacker who was reasonably bored and in need of funds, and had the anonymous individual retrieve the information she needed.

With a map of the area around the One laid out before her, Clair had been able to pick out a pattern. Combined with what she had witnessed on the video, she knew the One was strong and getting stronger. Despite the havoc Shane and Frank had recently wreaked.

What disturbed her the most was the black shape which had exploded out of the One's mouth. It was as though there was some tremendous darkness within the One, as if even the semblance of his former body was too small to contain it.

Clair leaned back in her chair and looked at the map of Amherst and the surrounding towns.

The first pin in the map represented the new mother, a woman known to be an avid hiker. Clair could only assume that the woman had come upon the One by accident and paid the price. The dead boy's strength had only been increased by a small margin by the new mother.

Then Clair had sent in Rousseau, and that seemed to have bolstered the One even further. The possible runaway was a male teenager who lived a quarter of a mile from the One and was reported to have been a disciplinary issue at both home and school. Clair's hacker had said the police were looking in Nashua and Manchester, but not Amherst.

Three tenths of a mile from the teenager's home was the spot from where the next victim vanished. The old man was known to walk along Dell Road as part of his morning routine. He had left, a neighbor said, at his usual time of seven thirty, and never returned.

The last person to disappear had done so only two days ago, and he was a further half-mile away from the One. Someone had witnessed the young man on the side of the road, trying to change a flat tire.

Clair looked away from the map and back to her computer screen. The video of the interaction with the One was paused. His mouth was open and the dark creature had just emerged.

Clair had to find a way to speak with the One. To facilitate a conversation where they could feed him, and thus gain access to what was theirs by right of patient devotion.

She would need a sacrifice. Someone from within the organization and who was faithful. Clair could send Linda along with them so that they could see the One's reaction.

The woman was in poor condition, but Clair knew Linda would do it. She was dedicated. A true believer.

And Clair only needed one more to go with her.

She sat in silence for several moments, and then it came to her. A smile spread across her face and she leaned forward, pressing the intercom button.

"Shirley," Clair said.

"Yes, Ma'am?" Shirley replied.

"Could you come in here, please? I need to speak with you about something," Clair stated.

"Yes, Ma'am," Shirley said.

Taking her finger away, Clair relaxed into her chair.

Shirley Coleman was perfect. She had served several heads of the Watchers, and with a focus and determination that Clair found impressive. But should Shirley die at the hands of the One, well it was for the greater good.

And besides, Clair thought as the door to her office opened. *I can always get another secretary.*

Book 9: Amherst Burial Ground

Chapter 22: Questions without Answers

"What will you do?" she asked.

He shrugged.

"That's not an answer," she said into the darkness.

Shane sighed. "I know."

"Are you going to continue to destroy their houses, one at a time?" Courtney asked.

"I don't know," Shane said. And he didn't.

The alpha file, despite its impressive name, had yielded little evidence and even less information concerning the Watchers' endgame in regards to the One. What it did contain was an extremely comprehensive list of properties seeded, ghosts cultivated, and a list of newly discovered hauntings. For disruption purposes, the alpha file was a gold mine. There had been no extra security in the file, no self-destruct program that would have destroyed or corrupted the information.

Massive amounts of information had been there for the taking.

There was also a recent batch of files indicating heavy activity in Amherst. David had a vague recollection of investigating the disappearance of a girl there, back in the mid seventies but nothing more.

It was the lack of information on the One that concerned Shane. He shook his head, ground his teeth in frustration and tried to keep his anger to himself. Amherst, Shane had discovered, was big and filled with a lot of woods. That meant roughly thirty-five square miles, and almost twenty three thousand acres to search.

In the downtime between raids on the Watchers' holdings, he had tried to find some information, *any* information about Samson and the family in Amherst. To try and see what they might be up against.

But there was nothing.

It was as though someone had stricken all information about it from the various histories.

"Shane," Courtney said, interrupting his musing.

"Yeah?" he asked.

"Do you have to do this?" she asked in a low voice.

Shane twisted in his chair, looking towards the oubliette in the library's corner. "Stop them?"

"Stop them by going there," Courtney said. "I have listened to your description of it. I have even spoken with Frank. It, well, it doesn't sound good. Can't there be someone else who does it?"

Shane hesitated before he answered her. He couldn't tell her how depressed he had become. How worthless he felt. There was so little left for him.

Courtney was dead.

Mason was dead.

Frank and Marie had been injured, Marie severely.

It seemed as if everyone who was close to him suffered for him, or because of him. His decisions had killed Courtney. His friendship with Mason had caused the man's death. The guilt weighed upon him, pressed down upon his heart, and threatened to overwhelm him.

The only motivation he had in life was revenge, and that, some nights, was only barely strong enough to keep him from pulling the trigger.

"There can't be anyone else," Shane answered. "I'm the only one. But this will be the last. I promise you that, Courtney. As soon as I put them into the ground, I'm going to stay here. I'm not going out anymore. I don't want to hunt anymore."

Her voice came closer as she spoke.

"Do you promise?" she whispered.

Shane nodded. "I promise."

A knock sounded and Shane straightened up.

"David's here," Frank said through the door. "He said he has something we're going to want to see."

"I'll be back," Shane said.

Courtney responded with silence.

Shane sighed, stood up, and exited the library. He hurried down the stairs, meeting up with Frank, David and Marie in the study.

"What've you got?" Shane asked, dropping down into his chair.

David nodded to Frank, saying, "I got this at lunch time. This is footage of the Watchers gathering information about the One. They're as blind as we are when it comes to the history of this place, this person. All of it."

Frank brought up the email footage David had brought, cued the video and hit play.

The image on the screen flickered, and then came into sharp focus. They watched in silence as someone with a camera mounted to their headgear progressed through a forested area. Soon the individual arrived at a burial ground and a house.

It took Shane a moment to understand that the people sitting on the ground weren't propped up corpses, but still living and breathing. Their attention was focused upon a little boy.

The sight of the people as they rotted away churned his stomach.

But his repulsion at what he saw was quickly replaced by shock as the boy raced towards the camera.

Then the image flickered out as the camera went dead.

Shane stared at the screen, focused on it as David began to speak.

"I've been told that something came out of the dead boy's mouth," David said. "I'm not sure what. It was strong though. And black, similar I'm guessing to those creatures we saw in Borgin. It latched onto the investigator's leg and managed to dislocate her ankle before she was pulled far enough away."

Frank started to ask a question but Shane interrupted him.

"I know him," Shane whispered.

He could feel the eyes of everyone on him.

"What?" Frank asked.

Shane couldn't take his own eyes away from the screen.

"The boy," Shane said. "I know him."

"You can't possibly know him," Marie said. "Shane, he looks like he's been dead for three hundred years."

"That's about right," Shane murmured.

"How do you know him?" David asked.

"Because," Shane whispered, "we're family."

Chapter 23: A Cold Silence

Everyone stared at Shane.

"How?" Frank asked, breaking the silence. "How is that even possible?"

Still stunned at the image of the boy, Shane couldn't answer. Instead, he got to his feet, crossed the room, and went to a barrister bookcase set against the right wall. He took an old brass key from atop the case and unlocked the cabinet. His hands trembled as he replaced the key and then squatted down, then lifted the glass door up.

Old brass hinges squealed in protest and Shane could appreciate the complaint.

The last time it had been opened was in 1985, when he had been eleven years old.

As he remained in front of the cabinet, staring at the contents, the smell of aged papers and old books drifted out. The scent brought back memories of his mother, of the hours she would spend pouring over their family's history.

With difficulty, he pushed the memory away, reached in, and removed a small, dark gray cardboard box. He held it against his chest, the smell of his mother's perfume, faint and delicate, caused his breath to hitch in his throat.

Shane returned to his seat and held onto the box for a moment longer. The others watched him, surprise etched on Frank and Marie's faces.

Lowering the box to his lap, Shane tried to speak. His voice failed him, and he cleared his throat twice before he found the words.

"My mother," Shane explained, "was an amateur genealogist. She had told me our family had been in the area since the beginning, but I didn't understand that. Plus my dad would tell me not to get her started on the subject. He hated to hear about it. Said it was like someone reading the numbers of the stock market out loud."

Shane took a deep breath, let it out, and forced a smile.

"Anyway," he continued, "I would sit with her, watch her go through old books and letters. Back before the internet. Every once in a while, she would get a picture or something in the mail, and I'd look at it with her. Then, one day, she got this old portrait."

Shane opened the cardboard case. He withdrew an object wrapped in tissue paper. The crinkling sound the paper made was loud and abrasive as he removed it from the item. Soon he held a black, oval frame. The glass was bright, and beneath it, the portrait was stark and crisp and as frightening as it had been thirty years before.

The boy from the video stood beside a chair, his hand resting on the back of it. There was no joy in the child's smile. His eyes lacked any mirth, filled as they were with hatred. If the portrait had been a photograph instead of a painting, Shane would have sworn the shadow in the chair was a trick of the eye.

But the long dead artist had gone to the trouble of placing the image there.

It was nothing more than a hint of darkness.

Yet it was enough to know it was real, especially with the evidence on the film.

"This is Samson Coffin," Shane said, handing the portrait to Frank.

"What did he do?" David asked as the image was passed along to him for inspection.

"I don't know," Shane replied. "But a journal came with the portrait, and after she read it, she stopped her research."

The image of Samson made its way back to Shane, and he returned it to the box.

"I found her in here one night, the portrait in one hand, and a glass of wine in the other," Shane said as he closed the box and stood up. He walked over to the barrister bookcase, put the box away, and closed the cabinet door. "There was an empty bottle on the desk beside her. It was one of the few times I saw her drunk. I didn't think about that then, or why she might be. I just thought she'd had a few more drinks than usual. I asked her if she had found out any more about Samson."

Then he sighed and shook his head. "My mom said she knew enough."

"And what was that?" David asked.

Shane turned around and faced the others before he answered.

"She said she knew where the bodies were buried, and she didn't want to know anything more."

Chapter 24: With His Dogs

Larry Wilton stumbled a little as he walked along the dirt path to the kennel. He had run out of whiskey and had to switch to the back-up bottle of red wine he kept in the cupboard for emergencies.

Like when he ran out of whiskey.

His stomach gurgled and Larry grimaced.

The wine never sat well on top of hard liquor, and it was always a challenge to keep it down. He didn't appreciate vomiting.

It was a waste of good alcohol.

Well, he thought, reaching the kennel door, *maybe not good, but at least it's alcohol.*

Larry's hands shook as he undid the latch and let himself in. The dogs howled as he flicked on the light, the fluorescents sputtering like old gas lanterns. His dogs, all fourteen of them, were Kentucky hounds.

And they were loud.

"Oh, hell, shut up!" Larry hollered as he closed and locked the door behind him. "Ain't none of you gonna eat if you don't shut it."

It was an empty threat. Larry loved his dogs, and his dogs loved him. In spite of his issues with alcohol, Larry always took care of the canines. He raised them and bred them, taught them to be trackers and sold them only to hunters he knew, or who were recommended to him.

And anyone new had to be vetted first.

His dogs didn't go to people he couldn't trust.

"Hold on, hold on," Larry grumbled as the dogs whined in their individual stalls. He turned to the control box on the wall and punched in the code that opened each kennel door. The locks released with loud clicks and the doors swung wide.

Yips and yaps, and howls of joy filled the air as the dogs rushed toward him. When they had almost reached Larry, they came to a stop.

The happy sounds vanished and deep, guttural growls of fear emanated from their throats. Their ears flattened against their skulls and tails dropped down and were tucked between their legs.

Frowning, Larry looked at them and said, "What in the absolute hell is your problem?"

"I think they're afraid of me," a small voice said behind him.

Larry spun around and nearly fell doing so.

He looked in surprise at a small boy who stood in front of the door. The child was dressed in clothes that made Larry think of the American Revolution.

And the little boy was beautiful. A perfect child. Like something out of a painting or a drawing.

The small boy was perfection personified.

"Why don't they like you?" Larry asked.

The boy shrugged. "They never have, I'm afraid. You look tired. You should sit down."

Larry smiled. He was tired.

He sat down on the floor, his back to the dogs.

The boy grinned.

"Aren't you hot, with that shirt on?" the boy asked.

And suddenly Larry was hot. He could feel sweat on his back and chest, under his arms and soaking the fabric of his shirt.

"I don't mind if you remove your shirt," the small child said.

"Thank you," Larry murmured with relief. He stripped off his shirt and dropped it to the floor.

The boy looked around for a moment before he asked, "Do you have a knife, or something sharp?"

"I have a knife," Larry answered. He reached into his pocket and withdrew his old Swiss Army knife. It was a battered tool. While the blade was no longer as keen as it used to be, it was still sharp.

"Now," the boy said, sitting down, "why did you come in here?"

"To feed the dogs," Larry answered.

The boy nodded. "They seem quite hungry. Do you love your dogs?"

"I do," Larry whispered.

"Will you show me how much you care for them?" the boy asked, leaning forward. "Will you show them?"

Tears sprang into Larry's eyes as he said, "Yes."

"Share with them what you ate," the boy said, winking. "show us the depths of your affection."

Larry grinned, opened the knife blade, and plunged it into his stomach. He didn't make a sound as he cut himself from left to right, his intestines spilling out onto his lap.

And he stroked the heads of his dogs as they buried their snouts in his stomach and ate their fill.

Chapter 25: A Discussion on Mental Health

"He seems like he's getting worse," Marie said.

Frank sat with her and David at the dining table, the remains of a take-out meal spread out before them. A guilty feeling crept over Frank as he looked at the other two. It felt wrong to talk about Shane behind his back, yet at the same time, he knew she was right.

Shane was far more emotional than when Frank had first met him, and the man was spending too much time in the library with Courtney. There were even moments when Frank was certain he would find Shane dead or hear a gunshot in the middle of the night.

"I can't say," David said. "I've only known him a short time."

"He's taking more risks," Marie added, taking a sip of her water. "And it can result in more danger for us."

Frank rubbed at the scar on his face. After a moment he spoke.

"I'm worried about him," Frank confessed. "I won't deny that. But he's our best bet in finishing the Watchers off. He always survives. No matter what."

"And what if he doesn't?" Marie demanded. "What if he makes the situation worse?"

"He can't," David said.

Frank and Marie looked to the older man.

David shrugged. "It literally cannot get any worse. Either we defeat the One, who the Watchers seem to have found. Or we don't, in which case they continue on with their plan."

"I don't like it," Marie snapped.

"No one does," Frank said. "But we need him, and he needs us. If we can get this done, I think he'll be alright."

She snorted and shook her head. "He'll never be alright. There's something wrong with him."

There was a bitterness and pain in her voice that spoke volumes about Kurt Warner's death, how she had felt about Shane Ryan, and their brief relationship that had ended poorly.

"Regardless of how we feel about him," David said, raising an eyebrow at Marie's tone, "he seems to be our best chance right now. Frank, do you think he'll be stable enough to make it through to the end?"

Frank's gut impulse was to say no, but he squashed it and forced himself to think about it.

"Yes," Frank finally said. "I do. It may be rough. But we'll get through with him."

Marie snorted in disgust and looked away.

"Well," David said. "now that we've got that settled, we need to figure out what we're going to do while Shane finds out more about Samson."

"Keep it simple," Marie replied.

"How so?" Frank asked.

"Keep hitting the Watchers," she said. "Hurt them until it's time to go to Amherst."

"Do we have enough information on the various places?" Frank asked.

"The map gives us most of what we need," David said. "But when it comes down to which locations are most important, no, we're on our own there. Most of the work we did was focused on bigger places. Kurkow Prison, Lake Nutaq, Slater Mill and Borgin Keep. Doesn't really apply anymore."

Frank nodded, the names of the places bringing up difficult memories. "What happened to your source?"

David frowned and a concerned look flashed across his face. "I don't know. I'll call later. Try and connect. As of right now, we're on our own."

Frank hesitated, then said, "Maybe not."

David and Marie looked at him and waited.

"There may be someone else," Frank said, getting to his feet. "I'll see if I can reach them."

"Who?" David asked.

Frank shook his head and left the room. He walked along the hallway to the stairs and climbed them at a quick pace.

He needed to find Eloise, to see if she would take him into the walls to speak with Lisbeth.

Chapter 26: Family History

Shane sat in the study, the room cold and dim. Carl stood by the hearth, his form waxing and waning. The dead German eyed Shane for several minutes in silence.

"What is it?" Shane asked in German.

"I am concerned," Carl replied in the same language. "You do not seem well to me, my young friend."

"I'm not," Shane stated. "I'm miserable. Courtney is dead, because of me. Mason and his wife are dead, because of me. Hell, I had to bring my friend's head down into the root cellar and have it tucked away. I'm just thankful he moved on. I don't think I'd be able to handle it if he was trapped here."

"What will make you feel better?" Carl asked, stepping forward. "Those many years ago, when you found my bones in the oubliette, you saved me. I would do the same for you."

Shane smiled. "Thank you. For now, all I can do is try to learn about Samson Coffin."

Carl nodded. "I am afraid I cannot help you there. I know nothing about your family."

"I know," Shane replied. "Keep an eye on the others, will you? Marie didn't look too pleased with me today. She may speak to the other two about me."

Carl gave a short bow. "I will."

The dead man slipped through the walls of the room and Shane was alone. For several minutes, he stayed in his chair, staring at the barrister bookcase. He knew what he needed to do, but it hurt him to think of it.

Taking out the portrait had been difficult. He had last seen it with his mother. Going into the case meant touching the items she had, at one time, loved and cherished.

Shane closed his eyes and pinched the bridge of his nose in an effort to keep the tears at bay. Each day he thought of his parents and tried not to imagine the different ways in which they could have died. Searching for Samson's history would be a painful reminder of Shane's own status as an orphan.

Finally, with a sigh, Shane stood and crossed the room. He found the small, leather-bound journal which had come with Samson's portrait and returned to his chair. From the small side table, Shane retrieved his glass and filled it with whiskey. He emptied the cup with two long gulps and placed it back on the table.

The liquor burned in his stomach, and he allowed himself a bitter smile as he lit a cigarette. When he was finished, he reclined in his chair and opened the journal.

The handwriting was delicate and graceful, the old ink looking like frozen waves upon the old paper. On the first page was a name.

Sarah Coffin, June 10th, 1733.

Shane scanned the lines of text and saw that it would take some time for him to decipher it all. The words were written in the style of the time, with 'f's' similar to 's's' and abbreviations he didn't recognize.

He knew he would learn about them soon enough.

Shane lifted the book, knocked the end of his cigarette off into the ashtray, and began to read.

The first few pages were slow and boring. He learned of the family's move from Dunstable to what was known as 'Narragansett Number 3.' Isiah Coffin had been rewarded with a land grant there for his service in Dummer's War. Sarah, his third wife, was twenty-six years his junior, but the marriage was a good one. She cared for the children of his second wife, who had died during childbirth, as his second wife had done for the children of the first.

Sarah and Isiah had a child as well, Samson, who was five years old when they made the move.

Samson, Shane discovered, had been born with a caul. Not only did Sarah keep this information from the new settlement, but from her husband as well. She feared the superstitions of some of the more religious-minded in her community.

On February 2nd, 1734, Shane read a line that caused him to close his eyes. He was sure it had caused his mother to do the same.

> *On this day, I found Joseph dead. He had cut out his stomach and removed that which God had placed inside. Samson alone saw his half-brother do this thing. I asked if Joseph had said why, but Samson had told me that they had wanted to see the unseen.*
>
> *We buried Joseph in the evening.*

Shane stubbed his cigarette out in the ashtray and poured himself another drink.

He read the journal quicker, his eyes darting over words that became more crowded together. It was as though Sarah was scrawling her thoughts out onto the page.

At the end of March, Shane read how a local indentured servant, a German girl by the name of Henrietta, had gorged herself to death on the warm flesh of a sow she had butchered.

The horrors marched on across the pages.

Isiah, her husband, was found sitting beneath the chestnut tree in front of their house. Sarah had written, with her words hardly legible,

> *He was naked. Long strips of his skin lay in coils about his legs. His body gleamed with blood, and when I found him, he was cutting out*

> *an eye. Samson sat with him, watching each move his father made with an intensity that frightened me.*
>
> *I started to ask Isiah why he had done it. What devil had made him do it? His answer had been to grin at me in a most hideous and savage way, and to hold up his left hand, in which he held his own tongue.*
>
> *Samson turned to me then, nodding and saying, 'You see, mother, your husband has learned that if he cannot keep a civil tongue in his head, he will not keep it there at all.'*

Shane closed the journal and put it down on his lap. He tapped his fingers on the cover, the leather smooth beneath his skin.

After a moment of hesitation, he stood up and carried the journal back to the bookcase. He searched among the books and letters until he found a notebook. Its cover was blue and faded. In his mother's bold handwriting the words, *Atherton Family Tree*, were written.

Shane put the journal down and opened the notebook. In it was a long, folded piece of paper taped to the inside of the cover. He stretched the paper out, revealing the well-diagramed family tree his mother had come close to completing. Shane searched the individual branches. By following the matrilineal lines, he was able to trace his family back to Samson.

The names and dates were all written in neat, block letters.

All except for Samson's.

His were scrawled. As if Shane's mother had felt compelled to write the information in, but wanted nothing more to do with it afterward.

Shane looked at the date of death for the young sadist.

June 12, 1739.

Shane sat down on the floor and opened the journal again. He leafed through the pages until he came to the right date, and he read his relative, Sarah's entry.

> *No one would blame me for what I have done. Had they known what he was, what foul acts he had committed, they would have done far worse. By his mother's hand, he is dead, and it is right. He lies with them all. His body shall return to the dust from whence we have all come, and I will play the grieving mother.*
>
> *Samson is dead, and I shall sleep well because of it.*

Chapter 27: Setting Up a Cordon

Clair was unsure of how the One could exert his will over such distances. So, lacking any firm information, she started by doing the obvious.

Members of the organization from around New England were tasked with salting the area around the One's house. They worked in teams of three. Each person was equipped with a pair of industrial headphones to reduce noise intake. One person was responsible for spreading the salt while in a harness similar to the one Linda had worn. Should the one establishing the barrier pull away, the other two would reel them back.

Or that was the theory.

By the third day, they had lost four teams.

On the fifth day, they had lost another two, and Clair realized it was time to send in Linda and Shirley.

Linda had been compliant, eager to please as always. A doctor in the organization had written a prescription for Oxycodone for her, not only for the pain she suffered from, but also for the additional injuries she was sure to sustain.

Shirley had been less than enthusiastic. While she had not been violent in her protests, she had sought to have the 'privilege' passed on to someone else.

Clair had not allowed her to defer.

The organization had few individuals left who could be spared, and Shirley was one of them.

Clair had also learned of the death of another member. Elliot Bretford, who had been tasked with observation of Shane and Frank, had been found dead a few streets away from Berkley. Shot from behind in his rented vehicle.

Which meant she would have to dispatch someone else to cover the house.

Shane and Frank had also struck at two more buildings owned by the organization. Each structure had been a total loss. The dead expelled from it and the buildings, being abandoned and in desolate locations along the ley lines, had been burnt to the ground.

Clair wanted to swoop down on the two men. To drag them outside, stand them against the wall of their house and execute them.

But she didn't have the time or the manpower to do so.

Events were happening far faster than she had ever believed they could.

With a sigh, Clair picked up her phone, dialed Jenna's number, and waited for the woman to pick up. When she did so, Clair asked, "Are you ready?"

"Yes," Jenna replied. "We'll have the link up to you in a minute. Send a confirmation text, and we'll get them on their way."

"Good," Clair stated, and she hung up the phone.

Clair relaxed into her chair and looked at her monitor. As she waited for the signal to upload, she wondered where she would find a replacement for Ms. Coleman.

Chapter 28: Success at Last

For the better part of the week, Frank had argued with Eloise. In the end, he decided to go to the newest member of the house's dead residents, Mrs. Henderson.

She had taken up a permanent place in an empty bedroom on the second floor, and both Eloise and Thaddeus were known to be with her more often than not.

The bedroom's windows were hidden by thick draperies, and the air had a brutal chill to it. In the dim light, Frank could make out a bed and other items of furniture, but nothing distinctive.

"Mrs. Henderson?" Frank asked the silence.

"Yes?" the dead woman responded. Her voice had a regal air to it, a sense of power and authority.

"My name is Frank, ma'am," he said. "I was wondering if I might ask you for your help."

"Certainly," she answered.

He quickly explained the situation to her, and when she spoke again, there was a hard and brittle tone to her words.

"And Eloise knows of this you say?" Mrs. Henderson asked.

"Yes," Frank confirmed.

"Please wait here a moment," she said, and the room warmed up slightly.

Several minutes passed, and then the temperature plummeted, causing Frank's skin to erupt into goose bumps. Shivering, he waited for her to speak.

But it wasn't Mrs. Henderson who spoke.

It was Eloise.

"Frank," Eloise said in a small voice. "Will you follow me?"

Before he could ask where, a door opened on the right side of the room. It was tall and thin, the doorway a sliver of darkness. Not certain where Mrs. Henderson was in the room, Frank said, "Thank you."

"You're welcome," the older woman replied, close to his left side. "Be careful when you speak with her."

"I will be," Frank assured her. He stepped over to the wall and slipped into the narrow passage behind it. A hard, unpleasant smell washed over him as cobwebs struck his face and hands. He felt a spider scurry across the back of his neck, and then vanish. Frank ignored the uncomfortable sensation it left him with and asked Eloise, "Left or right?"

"Right," she answered. "You'll know when we arrive."

Frank took small steps, his hands outstretched to guide him along the wall. They brushed against studs and old wires and items for which he had no name. A curious sense of claustrophobia tried to take control, but he fought it back. He focused on his steps, counting each one he took.

By the time he had reached two hundred, he understood that he shouldn't have been able to go as far as he had, considering how small his steps were.

At three hundred, he spoke up.

"Eloise," he said.

"Yes?" she asked.

"Where are we?" he asked.

"On our way to Lisbeth," Eloise replied.

"How can we even be in the house anymore?" Frank said. "It's not this big."

"The house doesn't want you to get to her," Eloise said.

"Why not?" he asked, trying to understand how a house could *want* anything at all.

"It doesn't want Shane to be mad," she answered.

The appearance of a faint light cut off his reply. It took another one hundred steps to reach the source of it, an open, oval doorway. Frank had to get down and crawl through it, entering a circular room. The toys and possessions of a little girl were scattered about, and a single, tall mirror stood among them.

"This was my secret place," Eloise whispered. "I would hide here and play."

Frank sat down and looked around.

"She's in the mirror?" he asked after a minute.

"Yes," Eloise answered.

"How do I talk to her?" he said.

"Just say her name," Eloise said.

Frank nodded. He took a deep breath and thought about what he was about to do.

"Hello, Lisbeth," he said.

The reflection within the mirror's depths roiled and churned. A heartbeat later, Lisbeth was peering out at him, a look of surprise plain on her face.

Then the expression was replaced by one of wary expectation.

"Frank," she said. "Where's Shane?"

"Busy," Frank replied. "He'll be along shortly."

Her eyes flicked past him to the door and then back to his face.

"What do you want?" she asked. "Why are *you* here? Don't you trust, Shane?"

"I trust Shane implicitly. Unfortunately he hasn't been exactly in his right state of mind lately," Frank said. "However, I do question what he might and might not share with me. Especially when it comes to what information he might get from you."

"So what do you want?" Lisbeth asked.

"Information," Frank answered. "The same you gave to Shane."

"And what will you give me in return?" Lisbeth demanded.

"What do you want?" Frank retorted.

"Freedom," she hissed. "I want to be let go."

He nodded. "I can do that for you."

Her eyes widened in shock even as Eloise spoke up from behind Frank, saying, "You can't! Shane wouldn't like it!"

At the mention of Shane's name, Lisbeth winced within the glass, and Frank wondered what his friend had done to her.

"Shut up, girl!" Lisbeth snarled, pressing herself close against the mirror.

"Yes," Lisbeth said to Frank. "Yes, I'll tell you, if you let me out."

"Then it's a deal," Frank said. "Tell me."

Lisbeth did so.

She explained to him the significance of the houses on the ley lines, and how there was a juncture, somewhere in southern New Hampshire. The buildings with the most deaths attributed to them were the strongest, and those further along the lines were more powerful still.

Frank listened to it all intently, forcing himself to remember everything she said.

The telling didn't take long. Perhaps ten minutes. Maybe twenty. And when she was done, Lisbeth looked at him with painful hope.

When he straightened up and moved toward the mirror, Eloise whispered, "Don't!"

Frank ignored the dead girl and smashed his fist into the mirror.

A rush of cold air slammed into him, catching him off balance, and knocking him onto the floor. Shards of glass raced towards him as he curled away, shielding his face with his forearms. From the depths of the shattered mirror came a deep, tremendous roar followed by pure silence.

Blood spilled from his arms, face, and scalp. A glance at his forearms revealed that multiple pieces of glass protruded from his flesh. Wincing, Frank got to his feet and resisted the urge to pull the shards from his arms. Instead, he staggered towards the exit, bent down, and made his way out.

The trip back to Mrs. Henderson's room took only a few minutes, the house evidently eager to expel him from between the walls.

When he stumbled into the open space, he sat down hard on the floor. The overhead light came on, and he blinked, tried to focus, and finally saw Shane. He stood in the doorway, his face a mask of anger. Eloise stood beside him.

Shane's lips moved, but Frank couldn't hear them.

He couldn't hear anything at all.

Chapter 29: Without Options

Terror gripped Shirley, squeezing her heart and threatening to cause her to faint.

She stood between the twin killers, the sisters who had brought her godfather to what they had thought was his death. If they knew what she had done, the information she had passed on to him, they would torture her to death.

That realization did nothing to help her calm down.

She had seen what the One had tried to do to Linda. Shirley had seen the dead and the dying around the boy as well.

She had no illusions as to what her chances were of surviving the encounter.

There was a slim possibility she might live. The One might decide he approved of the message Clair had crafted, but Shirley doubted it.

"Are you ready?" Jenna asked.

Shirley looked at the woman. "No."

Gabby snorted with laughter. "At least you're honest. What'd you do to deserve this?"

"Clair called it an honor," Shirley said, unable to keep the bitterness out of her voice.

Neither of the twins scoffed at that.

"We thought you had volunteered," Jenna said after a moment. "Thought you were one of the sheep."

Shirley didn't beg them not to send her in. They took their orders from Clair, as she did.

"No," Shirley explained. "I've been loyal and true. There was no choice here. She made that abundantly clear. I was going. She put it politely and made it sound like a reward for my faithful service, but it's not."

"You're right," Gabby agreed. "It's not."

"Well," Jenna said in a gentle tone that surprised Shirley, "ready or not, it's time for you to go in."

"Yeah," Shirley whispered. She leaned forward and vomited onto the ground, the remnants of her meager breakfast splashed onto her running shoes.

But she had nowhere to run. Even if they did let her go, which she knew they wouldn't.

She straightened up, and one of them handed her a napkin. Shirley wiped the tears out of the corners of her eyes, scrubbed the vomit off her lips and spat on the ground.

She stuffed the napkin into her pocket, cleared her throat and said, "Alright, let's get on with it."

Chapter 30: Following the Leader

Linda didn't know who the woman was in front of her, and she didn't care. In a short time, Linda knew the woman would be dead, and the best that could be hoped for was that the One would listen to the message *before* he tried to kill the messenger.

One of the twins stepped away from the unknown woman and withdrew a small, flat black, semi-automatic pistol. She showed it to Linda and carefully mouthed the question, *Do you know how to use this?*

Linda did. She nodded.

The twin turned, put her finger to the back of her own head, placing the tip of it at the junction of her neck and skull. Then she dropped her hand and turned back to Linda. *When it is time,* the twin mouthed, *you put her down.*

Linda felt her eyes widen.

The twin nodded and pressed the pistol into Linda's hand. Linda checked to make sure the safety was on and pocketed the weapon.

When the messenger started forward, Linda followed. The pain of the injuries she had sustained in the previous encounter with the One was dulled by medication. She was able to keep up with the messenger's stumbling, frightened gait.

Linda was equipped the same way she had been on the first attempt to see the One. A full, five point harness and a helmet. And, like the time before, she had a camera live-streaming the event to Clair.

Soon the two of them came to the giant tree and passed beneath into the shadow of its boughs. In a moment, they were at the edge of the burial ground. There were fresh mounds of dirt around the house, and the dead bodies that had laid there before were gone.

More people sat around the dead boy, staring at him. Linda didn't bother to count them. Instead, she put her hand on the pistol and slipped the safety off. She could see the One's lips moving, but she forced herself to keep her attention on the messenger. Linda could see the woman's jaw work, muscles tightening and relaxing in her neck and along her temple.

The One tilted his head back, mouth open in what Linda assumed was a laugh. He nodded, then and beckoned the messenger to him. The unknown woman took a hesitant step towards him. Linda looked from her to the emaciated dead around the boy, and then back to the messenger.

Then Linda lifted the pistol, put the barrel where the twin had shown her, and pulled the trigger.

Chapter 31: A Chat with David

David accepted a cigarette from Shane and glanced up the stairs, asking, "How is he?"

"I don't know," Shane answered, motioning towards the open door of the study.

They entered the room in silence, sitting down in chairs across from one another and smoking their cigarettes.

Shane exhaled and let the smoke out through his nose. After several moments he said, "I've stitched up the worst of the cuts."

David raised an eyebrow. "You didn't take him to a doctor?"

Shane snorted and shook his head. "I've done enough emergency field medicine to do some stitches. No, the only injury I'm concerned about is his hearing."

David lowered his cigarette and said, "Come again?"

"From what Eloise told me," Shane said, "when Frank broke the mirror and released Lisbeth, there was a huge blast of air. Some sort of pressure. Lisbeth is gone. Straight on to Hell, I hope. Right now, I'm waiting for her body to be returned to me by the dark ones. Once I have it, I'll burn the remains. Make sure she's gone. Anyway, I felt the blast of her release in the library, and when I found the door to Mrs. Henderson's room open, I went in. Frank was coming out of a servant's entrance at the same time. He couldn't hear a word I said. Still can't. I've given him enough whiskey to help him pass out."

"Do you think he needs a doctor?" David asked. "For his hearing?"

"More than likely," Shane answered. "The better question is, do we have time for it?"

The older man hesitated before he responded, "Probably not."

"Have you heard from your source at all?" Shane asked.

David shook his head.

"We have an idea as to where the One is supposed to be," Shane said. "So our only questions are, how bad is he, and where is he exactly?"

"I thought you were looking into that?" David asked.

"I did," Shane replied. He gave the man a quick recap of what he had read in regards to Samson.

"And he did that as a boy?" David asked in a low voice.

Shane nodded. "Kind of why I want to see what he's up to now. If he's strong enough to talk to someone and get them to stay though, well, that's going to make it a little harder to accomplish."

Neither of the men spoke for several minutes, Shane finally breaking the silence. "Don't suppose you have another person you could speak with about this?"

David shook his head. "No, not specifically about the One. Plenty I could call up, but they'd put a bullet in my head as soon as they see me. And that would be them doing me a favor. Best I can do is try and get in touch with my source. I'll head out in a little while and see what I can do about that. What about you?"

"I'll check on Frank," Shane said. "Then wait on you. See what you find out. If anything."

"Fair enough," David said, getting to his feet. "I'll give you a call in a few hours. Let you know what's going on."

Shane nodded and waved good-bye as David left the room. A few moments later Shane heard the man drive away. With a sigh, Shane got out of the chair, left the study and went upstairs.

A quick peek into Frank's room showed the man was asleep. Nodding to himself, Shane went to the library, gathered up his dog tags and slipped the cold necklace over his head.

"What are you doing?" Courtney asked from the darkness, startling him.

"I need to go check out an area," Shane replied. "I want you with me."

She stepped forward, a waxing and waning figure of the woman he loved.

"You're going after this 'One,' aren't you," it was a statement, delivered in a flat, angry voice.

Shane shook his head. "I'm going to see if I can find where he is. But I'm not going to confront him. I can't. Not yet. We need to know the layout though."

"What about Frank?" Courtney asked. "Why aren't you taking him with you?"

"He's hurt," Shane answered.

"Oh." His answer had caught her off guard. "Will he be alright?"

"I hope so," Shane said, the words coming out roughly. He cleared his throat. "I really do. We can't wait on the One. I think he's getting stronger with each day."

"Alright," she said after a moment. "I'll go."

And she vanished, the dog tags growing colder against his chest. The feeling was both comforting and heartbreaking.

Swallowing back his emotions, Shane left the library. By the time he reached the bottom of the stairs, Carl was there.

The dead German had a stern expression on his face as he said in his native tongue, "Where are you going?"

"Out," Shane answered, disliking the tone of his friend.

"You are leaving Frank alone?" Carl demanded.

"I'm leaving him with you," Shane snapped. "That's not alone. Far from it. I expect you and Eloise to watch over him. Especially Eloise. She knew better."

"And what of Mrs. Henderson?" Carl asked.

"What of her?" Shane responded.

"She bears a burden of responsibility in regards to Frank's current state, does she not?" Carl said.

"She does in that she commanded Eloise to show Frank the room, but nothing more," Shane said. "Eloise should have come to me as soon as Frank asked. And I bear some responsibility for it as well. I shouldn't have kept Lisbeth locked up for so long. But my part is to find out what's going on in Amherst. You and Eloise are to make sure Frank is okay, and to help him if necessary."

"You're taking *her*," Carl growled.

"Of course, I am," Shane answered. "She can travel with me. She's strong, as you well know. The two of us will be able to get a basic idea of what's going on, with both the Watchers and Samson."

For a heartbeat, Carl looked as if he might speak again, but instead, he turned and walked into the hallway's left wall.

Shane felt his shoulder's sag, and his head dropped a fraction of an inch. Then he took a deep breath, straightened up and went into the hall closet. Within was a coded gun safe. He punched in his pass code, pulled the door open, and retrieved his pistol.

It was a Springfield, 1911, .45 caliber semi-automatic. The weapon had been a gift from his unit when he had retired from the Corps.

In silence, Shane removed the trigger lock and retrieved a magazine from the safe. He checked the spring on it, and then removed a box of rounds. Shane loaded the magazine, then slid it into the weapon and chambered a round.

The .45 was heavy in his hand. A weight of responsibility and harsh understanding.

He held death in the form of polished steel, and laser cut grips. A machine designed for the sole purpose of killing.

And he loved it.

Shane took out his holster, put it on his right side, and then made sure the grip safety was in place before he holstered the weapon. He loaded two more magazines and then secured the safe.

Shane slid the magazines into his back pocket, pulled his sweatshirt down over his weapon, and left his house.

It was time to see how many people needed killing.

Chapter 32: David Goes Looking

"Still no word from her?" Marie asked as he helped her into the small TV room.

"No. Nothing," David said. He was worried, and he knew it came through regardless of how hard he tried to keep control of it.

He eased her down onto the couch and then sat in a recliner. As he reached for the remote control for the television, Marie stopped him with a gesture.

"You don't have to stay here with me," Marie said. "I'm a big girl. I'll be alright for a while. You need to find out what's going on with Shirley. Just be careful."

"I will be," David replied.

"Good," Marie said. "Make sure she's okay and laying low or something."

David nodded. "I'll see you soon."

Within a few minutes, he was out of her apartment and making his way out of the building. When he got to the lobby, he had to stop as a pair of mothers and six screaming children came in the front door.

The harried women saved David's life.

Beyond the glass doors, David caught sight of a dark blue sedan. An early two thousand model that wasn't of any particular interest.

Which was why he noticed it.

He saw the driver and stiffened.

It was one of the twins.

Either Jenna or Gabby.

David stayed back, smiling at the mothers and children as they went streaming past him. In a minute he was alone in the lobby, the exterior door closed.

He knew the Watchers didn't suspect his existence. If they had, they would have made every effort to seize him, or at the least, they would have killed him.

But with the twin parked outside it meant that the Watchers had Marie under observation.

Something David should have considered the entire time.

He cursed himself for his own stupidity and thought about what needed to be done. Killing the twin wouldn't be easy, not in the way Elliot's death had been. The twins were professionals, and it would be difficult to catch her unaware.

Yet even as the thought crossed his mind, he saw the twin put her phone down and step out of the car. David reached for his pistol, and then remembered he had gotten rid of it after Elliot. He looked around the room, his eyes falling on an abandoned dog leash pinned to a bulletin board.

Without hesitating, he tore it down. He stepped close to the elevator, pressed the down button, and then slipped over to the front door. Standing to the right of it, David waited.

The door to the elevator opened and revealed there were no travelers the same time as the twin walked into the building.

With the leash held stretched between both hands, David looped the leash over the woman's head.

Her reaction was instant, twisting to the right and dropping down.

David, while he was slower and older, had decades of experience on the young woman. He snapped the leash tight, instantly cutting off her oxygen before she could get a hand up between the woven fabric and her neck. With a grunt, he hauled her into the elevator, slamming her into the wall as the door was closing behind them.

The twin fought, twisting and clawing at him with one hand, the other reaching for a weapon. David ignored the pain as it blossomed in various parts of his body, and smashed her head into the wall, stunning her.

He leaned over and hit the emergency stop with his elbow.

Without knowing whether or not the stop was tied in with an emergency alarm system, David tightened the leash.

The twin whipped up, arms striking at him. She hit him twice in the side of the head, causing him to stagger into the back of the wall. The leash loosened and she twisted around, driving a knee up towards his groin. He shifted his right thigh and took the blow on the muscle.

"You!" she snarled. She slipped a hand up between the leash and her neck while she drove a fist into his ribs.

David grunted, bent to the right and he snapped a quick punch into her larynx.

She dropped her weight down as she gasped, and her hand slipped away from the leash.

David tightened the leash again, trying to twist her around and away from him. She fought, punching him in the knee. Pain exploded in the joint and he dropped to the floor. Her hand came up towards his face, fingers searching for his eyes.

David, with a last surge of strength, got behind her once more and twisted the leash. Her blows missed as he kept the pressure up. He recovered his breath, ignored his pain and watched without pleasure or satisfaction as her efforts to fight back slowed, then stopped. Slowly her tongue protruded from her mouth, and her eyes bulged.

For several minutes, he continued the pressure until he was certain there was no way for her to have survived the attack.

When he loosened the tension on the leash her head lolled to the left, and she collapsed to the floor.

David stared down at the body, then, with a great deal of stiffness in his hands and his damaged body. He slipped the leash off her neck and freed his hands from it as well.

With the improvised garrote hanging from one hand, David wondered how he would dispose of the newly minted corpse.

Chapter 33: Nothing Works the Way It Should

Clair had watched Shirley deliver the message to the One.

The One had accepted the offer from the Watchers, with Shirley serving as the coin of the realm. She was to be another soul upon which the One could feed.

And then Linda had ruined it.

Perhaps, Clair thought with bitter hindsight, *I should have told Linda the purpose of Shirley Coleman as the messenger.*

Clair shook the thought away.

The One's reaction to the destruction of his gift had been unpleasant, it had been expensive. Instead of one member of the organization, Clair had also lost another three-person team.

Yet he had agreed to accept the delivery of sacrifices.

Clair's intercom buzzed and interrupted her train of thought.

Frowning, she reached out, pressed the button, and asked, "Yes?"

"I'm sorry, Ma'am," Kevin, her new secretary, said. "There's a woman named Gabby here to see you. She said it's important."

Clair held back her anger as she said, "Fine. Tell her she can come in."

A few seconds later, Gabby stormed into the room, slamming the door behind her. The woman's face was a mask of rage, spittle gathering at the corners of her mouth.

"What in God's name is going on?" Clair demanded.

"She's gone!" Gabby yelled, kicking a chair across the room. "My sister's gone!"

"What?" Clair asked. "Where did she go?"

"She's dead," Gabby hissed. "Someone murdered her. I just got a call from the Nashua Police. They just fished her body out of a dumpster in the back of the high school!"

Clair was too stunned to respond.

Gabby threw herself into a chair and shuddered.

"Did they tell you anything?" Clair managed to say after a minute.

Gabby shook her head. "No. I went and identified her body. Whoever killed her knew what the hell they were doing."

"How did she die?" Clair asked, still trying to get a grasp on the situation.

"Strangled," Gabby spat. "They tried to hide the marks, but I spotted them. This was no half-done job. No hesitation. A damned *professional!*"

"Could it have been the detective she was watching?" Clair asked.

Gabby shook her head. "No. No way it was her. That detective still has to use a walker to get around. Impossible for her to choke out my sister."

"Boyfriend?" Clair asked.

"Had to have been," Gabby said. "I went up to the apartment."

"What?!" Clair asked. "You did what?"

Gabby pointed a thin finger at her and said, "Shut up. I don't care if you are the boss. This was my sister. Yeah, I went up to the apartment. I knocked on the door. Nobody answered. I broke in. The detective left in a hurry. Most of her clothes and stuff are there. Looks like there was a man staying there too. Deodorant. Shaving gear. All men's scents. They were in the spare bedroom."

"Do you think they went to Shane's?" Clair asked.

"Maybe," Gabby said, nodding. "We can't risk putting anyone else there. Not since Elliot was ventilated."

"No," Clair agreed. "But I don't want them watched. I want them erased. Scrubbed from the face of the damned planet."

Eagerness mingled with Gabby's rage-filled expression.

"How do you want to do it?" Gabby asked in a low voice. "We lost a team."

"We do it the same way," Clair replied. "With ghosts of our own."

Chapter 34: A Painful Awakening

Agony launched Frank out of sleep, or unconsciousness, he wasn't sure which.

He was no longer in whatever state he had been in, and he was miserable.

His entire body throbbed, pulsed, and screamed. Sitting up brought tears to his eyes, causing his breath to catch in his throat. Stars exploded around the edges of his vision, and he shuddered while he tried to remember what had happened.

The memories were dim.

A circular room and a mirror. Lisbeth bound within.

And breaking the glass.

Frank dropped his chin to his chest and sighed, instantly regretting it as the pain went lancing through his lungs.

Every part of him screamed to lie back down, to surrender to the pain, and pass out.

But the same drive, discipline, and determination that had helped him pass the selection course for Special Forces required him to stay upright. So he did.

Frank took deep breaths until the pain was manageable. He reached out and turned on the light. He cringed as light filled the room, a headache bursting into life.

His skin felt stretched as if someone had pinned it back. When he looked at his arms, he saw they were wrapped in bandages, his face, when he touched it, was tender and sore.

"Damn," he muttered.

But he heard nothing.

It took him a moment to realize he hadn't heard his own voice, and when he understood what the lack of sound meant, his heart began to race.

Frank cleared his throat and spoke again.

And again.

And once more.

Nothing.

Not a single sound.

Panic rose up, and he crushed it, without mercy.

It's probably not permanent, he told himself. *It can't be. Look at Marie. She's recovering. This is temporary. Nothing more and nothing less.*

Carl appeared in the bedroom, startling Frank. The dead man's mouth moved, a look of concern on his face.

Frank shook his head, pointing to an ear and saying, "I can't hear anything."

Carl nodded and gestured for Frank to follow him. Wincing, Frank got off the bed and limped after the ghost. They entered the hall and Carl brought him to a window that overlooked the driveway.

A yellow, DHL delivery van had pulled in and backed up to the front door. Two people, a man and a woman in company uniforms, stood by the rear doors.

Frank frowned and then stiffened.

He recognized the woman from the video David had shared with them.

She worked for the Watchers.

The Watchers, who had sent Mason's head to them by DHL.

Frank turned away from the window and said, "Get the others together, and I need a gun. With real bullets, not salt."

Carl nodded and headed toward the library. For a moment, the dead man hesitated outside the door, and then he shook his head and passed through it. Frank opened it and followed him.

Carl stood by a bookcase, and he pointed to a leather bound collection of Shakespeare's works.

Frank reached out, gave a gentle pull on the first volume, and found the entire set moved as a single piece. Surprised, he took the set down. He found a small, silver latch on the back of the books.

Placing the set on the desk, Frank examined the books. There was a thin line running through the center of the collection from left to right. He freed the latch and pulled up on either side. The books opened again as one, revealing a felt lined interior. Within it were two large, six shot revolvers, dark metal affairs with wooden grips. Bullets of heavy lead with bright brass casings were held in place by leather straps, same as the pistols.

The rounds were small, possibly .38s.

But they would do the job.

Frank removed the pistols, loaded each chamber, and placed extra rounds in the pockets of his pajamas. He was barefoot and bare-chested.

"Get the others now," Frank said.

Carl gave a short bow and vanished.

Frank cocked each pistol, left the library, and headed for the stairs. For a moment, he wondered where Shane was, and then Frank saw the front door open.

Crouching down he took aim and waited for someone to enter.

Chapter 35: Cutting Down the Enemy

Gabriella 'Gabby' Belanger shifted between rage and numbness. While she understood that her twin was dead, and rationally accepted that fact, a dull pain still swept over her when she thought about Jenna.

It was a strange sensation, and she didn't quite comprehend it. Of all the many experiences she and her sister had enjoyed, emotions tended to be absent from that list.

She wondered if rage was an emotion, and then she didn't.

They were there to work.

She and an agent named Aaron stood on the doorstep, wearing DHL uniforms in an effort to blend in with normal society. Of which they were not.

Nor were the others with them. They were clad as movers. Plain, dark blue coveralls that concealed weapons and more dangerous items.

Clair had pulled out all of the stops. She had called in the last of the killers. The ones who took care of some of the bigger stations along the ley lines. Five of them, whose names Gabby hadn't bothered to get.

Like Gabby, they carried small, semi-automatic weapons with suppressors. Small caliber rounds to bring down whoever was inside, and then a few more to finish the job.

And as for the dead, Gabby had what she needed for them as well.

Each of the five who accompanied her and Aaron had an item. Some small token to which a ghost was attached.

They were to be used against the dead who lived with Shane and Frank.

Gabby only hoped that the one who had killed her sister was in the house as well.

Then her attention shifted to the door as Aaron opened it. She watched as he nudged it further into the house until a long hallway lay before them.

No one greeted them.

The house was still and silent.

Aaron entered first, followed a moment later by two of the killers, who were then followed by a second pair. Gabby came in last with the fifth killer, a young man who looked as though he had never smiled.

The door slammed behind them, and the back of the young man's head exploded as the sound of a pistol being fired ripped through the air.

Something struck Gabby in the shoulder, spinning her around and causing her to lose balance.

"Let them out!" Aaron screamed as he scrambled past her, trying to get a door open.

Gabby twisted around, reached up and jerked open a closet door, pulling herself behind it. A wet sensation was spreading down from her shoulder, and she knew she had been shot. Pressing her hand against the wound, she risked a small glance around the door's edge and saw the shooter.

It was Frank, and he was at the top of the stairs, half hidden behind a large, dark wooden banister. The young man and one other were dead on the floor. A third man, wounded, tried to move to the side, and Frank fired again.

The third man no longer moved. His brains were spilled onto the floor.

Of the four of them who had survived and managed to find some sort of cover, only two had bound objects with them.

Gabby watched one of them, an older woman, remove a comb from her coveralls and throw it like someone might a grenade. As the small, dark brown object left the woman's hand, a shot rang out again.

The bullet caught the woman squarely in the wrist, blood spraying out as the bullet smashed into the wall.

Aaron reached out, took hold of the woman with one hand, and tried to drag her into the safety of the doorway he had taken shelter in. With his free hand, he brought his pistol to bear, firing several times in Frank's general direction. A single shot roared from the top of the stairs, and another bullet slammed into Aaron's chest. The impact of the round knocked him backward, and his hand lost its grasp upon the woman.

Frank had the high ground, Gabby knew, but he could still be killed.

And it was time to do that.

Chapter 36: A Dark Thrill

Frank reloaded a revolver one handed while he kept an eye on the hallway.

Of the seven who had entered the house, three were dead and three were wounded. One of the wounded, a woman, had thrown a comb before he put a bullet in her wrist. A nagging feeling at the back of his head drew his eyes back to the comb. In the new silence of his world, Frank saw the fourth, uninjured man move out of a doorway on the left. A small object, the size of a wallet landed beside the comb, and then there was a pistol in the man's hand.

The weapon was a small caliber, and it was equipped with a suppressor. The pistol was steady, the man carefully drawing aim.

Blind men can't shoot straight, Frank thought.

Frank let off two quick shots, each striking the woodwork around the doorway and sending splinters into the man's face.

The unknown assailant retreated, his weapon unused.

Frank finished reloading the first pistol, switched it out for the other and reloaded that one. His eyes remained focused on the hallway. The woman whom he had shot in the wrist had moved into a doorway on the right, part of her boot visible.

Frank took stock of his situation.

One on the left. Two on the right. The twin, who was the fourth, was behind the open closet door. Frank had twelve rounds left. Six in each pistol. He had to assume all of them were armed, and soon they would start to work in unison.

Frank needed to get down the stairs and finish them off.

He wanted to call out to Carl and the others, find out what they were up to, but he thought better of it, and then the temperature in the hallway plummeted.

A smile spread across Frank's face, and he relaxed, and then stiffened.

On the floor beside the comb and wallet, a pair of shapes appeared. They were hazy at first, then they became more defined. Sharper.

Two dead men stood in the hall.

They wore three-piece suits and fedoras. Patent leather shoes, and cufflinks in their shirts. Their chests were bloody messes, for the men had been gunned down.

They were killers as surely as those who had brought them into Shane's house were.

The dead men saw him and headed for the stairs, smiles playing on their faces.

Thaddeus barreled out of a shadow, throwing himself at the man on the left. The larger ghost's lip curled in a snarl, and for a moment he and Thaddeus were engaged in a struggle. Then the other man joined in and together they threw Thaddeus back the way he had come.

Eloise appeared a moment later, a dark, gleeful look on her face as she attacked the same man Thaddeus had. Frank watched as the dead man's eyes widened in surprise before he vanished. Before Eloise could turn her attention to the other ghostly intruder, the first returned, springing into existence beside the comb.

In a moment, Eloise was gone. The two men turned their attention to Frank and started toward him.

Frank, nodded to himself, stood up and retreated towards his bedroom.

He hoped he could get his shotgun and the salt rounds before the dead got to him.

Chapter 37: Chasing Frank Down

Gabby heard movement and risked another glance around the corner of the door. Two of the dead men made their way towards the stairs. Frank was backing away.

Aaron screamed.

It was a high, piercing sound that penetrated Gabby's head, and when she turned to glare at him, she froze.

A pair of small arms protruded from the door he was pressed against. Tiny, child-like thumbs were buried in his eyes, the fingers drumming playfully on his face.

Gabby watched as Aaron reached up with a ringed hand to strike at the ghost who attacked him, but another set of hands grabbed hold of his wrist. An adult male ghost, dressed in a black suit appeared and looked down at the injured female killer that Gabby and Aaron had brought with them.

"Und wer bist du?" the ghost asked as he knelt down on the woman's arms, pinning them down. He looked at her for a moment, then he pinched her nose, closed and covered her mouth.

Gabby dropped her hand from her injured shoulder and tried to move it.

Pain exploded, and she gasped. Panting, Gabby put her hand back up to staunch the fresh blood flow. She looked to the last killer, the one who had thrown the wallet.

She shouldn't have.

A matronly looking ghost stood over him and through her, Gabby watched as the dead woman strangled the man.

No, Gabby thought, stunned. *Garroting. She's garroting. Just like Jenna was.*

And with that, Gabby's will broke.

She scrambled to her feet, made it to the main entrance door, and ripped it open. Bright sunlight caused her to stumble, but she didn't fall. Instead, she slammed into the rear of the van, groped her way around to the driver's door and climbed in. The keys were in the ignition, and she started the engine.

Jamming the van into drive and stomping on the gas, Gabby tore out of the driveway, narrowly missing a car that was about to turn in. A familiar man was behind the wheel. But it wasn't Shane, and she just didn't care.

It was only when she reached the highway and was headed towards Boston that Gabby realized where she knew the man from.

David had been behind the wheel.

David, who she and Jenna had left for dead in Borgin Keep.

Chapter 38: In His Room

Frank didn't bother closing his bedroom door behind him.

It wouldn't stop the two ghosts making their way towards him.

He didn't know if the living would follow the dead up the stairs, or if Carl and the others had finally gotten involved in the fight. Neither of those were pressing enough to occupy his attention.

What Frank had to worry about was the dead.

He put both of the pistols on the bed, reached beneath the same and pulled out his gun bag. From that, he removed his shotgun, double checked to make certain the weapon was loaded, then dragged the case of shells out. He carried both the shotgun and the extra rounds to his chair and sat down.

His adrenaline rush had begun to fade, dumping the chemical into his stomach and giving him a nauseous feeling. Frank shivered from the combination of coming down from the high of combat and being less than half dressed.

A minute passed, and the two men appeared in the doorway.

Frank fired both barrels of the shotgun, the ghosts vanishing.

He reloaded quickly and winced as his fingertips were singed. Dropping the spent shells to the floor, Frank snapped the shotgun to the floor and waited.

The ghosts rushed through the wall to the left of the door and made it three feet into the room before Frank shot them both.

He could smell his own flesh burn as he withdrew the casings and reloaded again.

Forcing his heartbeat to remain steady, and his breathing to stay calm, Frank sat patiently in his chair.

One minute passed.

Then another.

He kept his eyes on the open door and hoped they hadn't found another way into the room.

Chapter 39: Entering the House

"You have to stay here," David said to Marie.

She nodded. He placed her Glock in her hands.

"I'll be back in a minute," David said. "If you so much as think you see her you call 911, and then you shoot her if she steps out of that van."

"I can't shoot straight anymore," Marie said in a strained voice.

"You don't have to," David said. "Keep putting rounds down range and keep her guessing. The way she tore out of here says she didn't like what happened."

When Marie motioned for him to go, David did so.

He jogged up to the open door and hesitated in the entrance.

The scene in front of him stunned him.

There were six dead on the floor. Multiple gunshot wounds.

They weren't the strangest part of what he saw.

That was reserved for the battle being fought between the dead in the center of the hallway. He only recognized two of them, Eloise and Carl. They were leading an attack on two ghosts in the midst of the others.

Those two were men, dressed as gangsters from the thirties or forties. Complete with fedoras and multiple gunshot wounds.

And the two men were losing.

The fight was vicious and guttural. His ears ached, and his head pounded with the cacophony voiced by the combatants. Some ghosts were knocked back by the dead gangsters while others stood firm. David watched as Eloise darted in and tore a hole through the stomach of one of the men.

The gangster stumbled and shrieked as Eloise literally pulled herself into him. Other ghosts continued to press the attack.

David stood there, watching the battle, until he heard sirens in the distance.

The police, whether he wanted them there or not, were on their way.

Within seconds, the gangster Eloise had climbed into let out a howl and then he and the other dead man the Watchers had brought were torn to shreds beneath the onslaught of Shane Ryan's undead housemates. Moments later, all of the ghosts disappeared, leaving David in the hallway with multiple corpses and a crime scene he wouldn't be able to explain away.

At that moment, Frank appeared at the top of the stairs, armed with a shotgun and a revolver that looked like a prop for a Civil War movie. Judging from the dead, David knew it wasn't.

"What happened?" David asked Frank as the man descended the stairs.

Frank shook his head.

"Oh hell, you're still deaf," David grumbled. Frowning, he gestured towards the bodies.

"They broke in," Frank stated, his voice too loud. "They brought their own dead."

David nodded and said in an exaggerated manner, "The police."

"No," Frank said. "I didn't call them."

David rolled his eyes as the sirens drew nearer.

"No," David said. "They are almost here."

Frank narrowed his eyes and said, "What?"

David pointed at the floor and said, "Here."

"Oh," Frank said, his eyes widening with understanding. "They're on their way here."

Before David could correct him, the police pulled into the driveway. They blocked in Marie's car, parked in front of the driveway, and multiple units stopped along the street. Men and women emptied out of the vehicles. They wore tactical vests over their uniforms and several carried M4s at the ready. At least two others carried shotguns.

When David looked back to Frank, he saw the man had taken a seat on the floor, directly in a spreading puddle of blood. Frank had placed the pistol and the shotgun on the floor and had his hands raised above his head.

David heard booted feet on the driveway and sat down as well. He shrugged and put his hands into the air, even while an officer told him to do the same.

David didn't resist as someone pulled his arms down and handcuffed him.

He watched as the same was done to Frank, and David sighed.

It was going to be a long and tedious day.

Chapter 40: Fear is an Infection

When Clair walked into the small operating room, she felt the line of her jaw tighten at what she saw.

Gabby lay on the surgical table while a doctor, in the employ of the organization, and his assistant worked on Gabby. The now singular twin stared at the ceiling, her face a complete blank while the two men inspected the wound one last time before they stitched it up. In silence, they tilted her onto her side so the doctor could then stitch the exit wound.

Gabby had been fortunate in that the bullet looked to have passed through without doing any serious damage, leaving her in pain, but nothing more.

When the two men finished they nodded to Clair and left the room, closing the door behind them. Clair saw a small, rolling stool and brought it over so she could sit down beside Gabby's bed.

It was not done out of compassion, but a need to know what had gone wrong.

For several minutes, she sat there, looking at the evidence before her. Gabby's sleeve and most of the upper portion of the DHL uniform had been cut away by the doctor. The remainder of the yellow clothes were stained and spotted with blood. Gabby's own as far as Clair could surmise.

"Gabby," Clair said.

The woman didn't respond.

Clair repeated her name, and Gabby continued to ignore her.

Frowning, Clair switched her small, clutch purse from her left hand to her right, and then reached out. With a large amount of force, she pushed her thumb down onto the freshly stitched wound.

Gabby inhaled sharply and with obvious pain, sitting up and letting out a string of curses. Her head snapped towards Clair, and pure hatred blazed in her eyes, the corners of her mouth twitching.

"Pay attention," Clair said in a grim voice, "or I will gut you here and leave you to bleed out. Do you understand?"

Quivering with rage, Gabby nodded.

"Excellent," Clair said as Gabby returned to her position on the bed. "Now, I want you to tell me what happened."

Gabby did so. Her sentences were short, brutal, and exactly to the point. The story ran along a familiar theme, that of Shane and Frank destroying whomever the Watchers sent out for them.

"That's not all," Gabby said, and for the first time, Clair heard the emotion in the younger woman's voice.

"What else?" Clair asked.

"David," Gabby answered.

Clair frowned. "Who the hell is David?"

Gabby shook her head. "Never knew his last name. Jenna and I went with him to Borgin's. He was the old caretaker, the one who dealt with Borgin all the time. We were there as David's replacements, or that's what Harlan told him. We were supposed to hand David over to Borgin alive, and we did. Evidently, the guy was tougher than anyone thought. He made it out."

"Well, what about him?" Clair asked.

"I saw him pulling into the driveway of Shane's house," Gabby hissed. "He was driving that detective, Marie Lafontaine's car. Which means he's probably been hiding at her place."

Clair nodded, understanding what Gabby was implying. "You think he killed your sister?"

Gabby nodded. "I'm going back for him. Soon as I can get my hands on a weapon."

Clair stood up. "I wish you the best of luck on that. I doubt the police will let you get anywhere near him."

Gabby's head snapped over, and she glared at Clair.

"The shooting is all over the New England news channels," Clair explained. "And national as well. Frank's the new face of the NRA as far as gun proponents are concerned. It's not often a half-naked man defends himself against seven assailants. Even if he is former Special Forces."

"They're taking his word on it?" Gabby snarled. "We can't spin this?"

"Of course they're taking his word on it!" Clair snapped. "After Harlan's arsonist blew up one house and then died at Shane's, people became paranoid. Home security systems were installed. Did you notice the neighborhood as you went through it? That's old New England money in those houses. You and the others were supposed to keep it clean. Contained to the confines of the house. Instead, your images were captured on a dozen different security cameras."

Clair shook her head angrily. "One of them even shows all of you entering the house. Someone leaked the footage to New England Cable News. You'll be recognized anywhere you go. They've got still shots of you going into and coming out of 125 Berkley Street, Gabby. The fallout on this will be tremendous, and, if we're both very, very lucky, we won't lose our heads because of it. Or end up meeting the One before everything is in place."

Clair crossed her arms over her chest and continued. "Because of this, we've lost the DHL van. It's a total loss. We've got a shop chopping it, as we speak. The corpses left behind will be identified, their jobs and lives investigated. With all of our financial resources focused on the One, we won't be able to pay off the necessary forensic technicians at the New Hampshire lab. Or fund any hackers to go in and change certain files. In addition to that, we lost four possessed items. Four of them. They are all now under the lock and key of the Nashua Police Force."

"There has to be a way I can still get at David," Gabby said.

Clair sighed. "There is, of course. Before I tell you how, I need to know if you've left out any other information regarding the event."

"Nothing," Gabby said bitterly. "There's nothing else to tell. We went in, and Frank butchered us."

"You're certain of that?" Clair asked.

"Yes," Gabby said.

"Excellent. Well, let's see," Clair said, opening her clutch. "I have some cash and a weapon in here for you."

Gabby's eyes widened with grim pleasure as she sat up.

"Now," Clair said, holding up the small, black .22 caliber revolver. "it's not a large weapon, but it will get the job done. Don't you agree?"

Gabby nodded, extending her hand for the pistol.

Clair smiled and shot the woman twice through the left eye.

The orb exploded, spraying blood out as Gabby went tumbling over the side. She struck the floor with a hard, wet smack. Clair walked around and put the other four bullets into the back of Gabby's skull, just to be certain.

"For your failure," Clair said in a low voice to the corpse. "And your lack of foresight."

The door to the operating room opened, and the doctor came in. He looked neither surprised nor concerned. Which was why the Watchers paid him so well.

"You'll dispose of it?" Clair asked, putting the pistol away.

"Yes," the doctor replied. "I'll dig out the bullets as well."

"Excellent," Clair said. "You'll find a little more in your retainer at the end of the month."

He gave her a short bow and turned to his work as she left the room.

By the time Clair reached the end of the hallway, she heard the dull whine of a bone saw start up. She was smiling by the time she left the private operating room.

Chapter 41: In the Hospital

Frank had spent a lot of time in hospitals through his life.

He had found that he didn't enjoy hospitals, and this particular time was no exception.

Frank had awoken in the hospital, hours after the incident on Berkley Street. He had no memory of anything after the arrival of the police, so he could only assume he had passed out. Frank was certain it was from a lack of sleep, food, water, and from the injuries sustained with the release of Lisbeth.

Earlier, when a nurse had come into the room, Frank had seen that he wasn't alone. A uniformed police officer was stationed outside of his door. He was surprised that the police hadn't handcuffed him to the bed, but he didn't think it was unreasonable that they might do so in the near future.

He had shot seven people in the house. One of whom had been the twin, and he didn't know if she was among the dead or not.

An anxious fear settled into his stomach as he thought about her on the loose. Frank doubted she would return for him, but there was always the possibility. And it wouldn't be hard for her to figure out which of Nashua's two hospitals he was in. With that in mind, he wondered how he could get himself a weapon. Granted, there was an armed officer at the door, but Frank had a suspicion that the twin would be the resourceful type. A police presence wouldn't prove difficult for her to overcome.

Frank was not in a situation that he felt was best for his personal well-being.

With a grimace, he adjusted himself on the bed and read the subtitles on the news program he had on the television. The flat-screen unit was mounted on a ceiling bracket which allowed him to look but not touch.

He didn't know what was worse, having only a few channels to choose from, or the fact that all of the subtitles were a good thirty to forty seconds behind what the people were saying. Frank found himself trying to read the lips of the newscasters and failing.

Finally, he gave up on the television, took up the remote attached to his bed and turned the unit off.

A moment later the door to the room opened, and an older, male doctor walked in with a young woman dressed in nurse's scrubs. The woman wore the green work uniform well, and her dark brown hair was pulled into a neat bun on the back of her head. Her face was soft, with gentle lines, and her eyes a chestnut color. She smiled at him, and Frank felt himself return it.

The doctor was shorter than the nurse and in need of a shave as Frank's drill sergeants would have said. Frank watched the man run a thick-fingered hand through his gray hair and then put a pair of bifocals on.

The doctor spoke, and the young woman's hands moved.

Frank slumped back into his bed. Looked at them both and said, "You need a writing pad."

Both the doctor and the nurse looked at him in confusion.

"I wasn't deaf yesterday morning," Frank said. "But I am today. You need to get a writing pad, so I know what the hell you're saying. I don't know sign language."

The doctor turned to the nurse, spoke to her, and the young woman nodded, hurrying away. She returned less than a minute later with a notepad attached to a clipboard. The doctor took it from her with a nod of thanks, pulled a pen from a pocket, and wrote something down on the paper. He held it up so Frank could read it.

"What happened yesterday?" was the question.

"I got hurt," Frank replied.

The doctor frowned and wrote the next question.

"How?"

"That's not important," Frank said.

"It is. I need you to tell me how you lost your hearing, and how you came to be covered in lacerations," the doctor wrote.

"And I told you," Franks snapped, "that it's not important. I want to go home. Sooner rather than later. So, if you could, I can really use your help calling for a ride."

The doctor and the nurse looked at each other before the doctor wrote a longer response.

"You can't go home. You can't leave here. The police are going to question you about the incident at your house. Then they're going to decide whether you get released or remanded into custody for a clinical evaluation."

Frank forced himself to keep his temper in check as he asked, "What type of clinical evaluation?"

The nurse's cheeks reddened, but the doctor's expression was bland as he wrote the answer down and then showed it to Frank. "You were saying some rather strange things, Mr. Benedict. The hospital wants to make certain that you are both physically and mentally at your best when you leave us. The clinical examination will be conducted by our on-staff psychologist."

Frank shook his head. "No. I'd rather not."

The nurse looked down at the floor while the doctor frowned and jotted down a quick reply.

"Mr. Benedict," the note said. "you don't have a choice."

Too stunned to respond, Frank shook his head while the doctor wrote an additional note.

"Of course, I have a choice," Frank managed to say.

The doctor shook his head and wrote, "We will be holding you for a seventy-two-hour evaluation."

"No," Frank said. "Just no."

"This is for your own safety as well as for others, Mr. Benedict. I'm sorry."

And with that, the doctor and the nurse left the room, closing the door behind them. Frank remained upright on the bed, struggling to comprehend what was happening.

Then, with disturbing clarity, he understood one important fact.

He wouldn't be able to help Shane. The man was on his own.

Chapter 42: At the Holiday Inn

Marie lay asleep on the bed of their hotel room. David sat in a chair, his cellphone on the table behind him, a new laptop beside that. He was exhausted. It had taken witness statements from most of the residents on Berkley Street, as well as some private home security footage, to convince the police he hadn't been part of the shooting. In addition to that, he still hadn't been able to get in touch with Shirley. His concern for her grew as more time passed.

Once the Watchers understood he was alive, they would begin to search for any sort of handle they could get on him. It was how they operated. Only a little work would be required to discover the connection between himself and Shirley, and then she would be used as leverage on him. A way to get him to come in.

And he would have to.

Shirley couldn't be allowed to suffer because of him.

He had wanted to stay at Shane's house to speak with the man, but the police hadn't allowed that. They were processing the entire home as a crime scene, and they were actively searching for Shane. No one in the Nashua Police Department seemed to believe that Frank, by himself, could have done the damage he had.

David had been fortunate in the fact that he had been with Marie. If she hadn't been in her own car, in the driveway, with her weapon, David was confident he would have been arrested as well. Or at least brought down to the police station for questioning.
That would have been unfortunate, especially since his fingerprints were undoubtedly linked to several unsolved murders and disappearances.

He and Marie had followed the ambulance with Frank to St. Joseph's Hospital. A police guard on the man's hospital room had refused them entry.

David's level of frustration had been on the rise ever since.

He had sent Shane several texts. A pair from his own phone and two more from Marie's.

The man hadn't responded to any of them.

In the end, fearful of a return of the Watchers to Marie's apartment, David had rented a hotel room. They had spent the better part of the morning in it, wondering what was going on, until Marie had taken her medication and fallen asleep.

David glanced at his phone and his email, and when he saw that neither Shirley nor Shane had responded, he sank back into the chair with a grunt of disgust.

He hated the fact that neither of them had replied to him. David hated it even more that they were losing time. The longer they waited to hit the Watchers, the better chance the organization had of regaining its footing. They would establish themselves with the One, and once a bargain was struck, it would be difficult as hell to break.

David, Shane, and Frank had done some damage to the Watchers, but if they don't keep the pressure up then it would be pointless. The organization hadn't survived and thrived for decades because of a refusal to act when necessary.

David sighed, pushed the thoughts out of his mind, and tried to think of a way to distract himself.

Finally, he shook his head and picked up the remote control of the television. He turned it on and lowered the volume, not wishing to disturb Marie. While her medication had a tendency to make her sleep, it was by no means guaranteed that she would remain in that state. And he had made the mistake of waking her up once, and his jaw had hurt for the rest of that weekend.

For a few minutes, he flipped through the channels until he found a news network. David closed his eyes and listened to the weather report and then the sports recap. After that, a man, with far too much enjoyment, spoke about several other crimes.

"And there's still no information on who may have killed Shirley Coleman, the young woman discovered in Jamaica Plains yesterday morning," the newscaster stated.

David's eyes snapped open, and he sat up, staring at the screen.

A picture of Shirley smiling, taken at her parents' house the Christmas before last, was shown on the screen.

"As we reported yesterday," the newscaster continued. "Ms. Coleman was found yesterday with a single gunshot wound to the back of the head, killed execution style. Police are asking for any help with her murder. Her employer, an internet security company, has offered a reward of ten thousand dollars for information leading to the arrest and conviction of her killer."

David shut the television off, the sight of his goddaughter unbearable.

His shoulders shook, and tears stung his eyes.

For the first time in decades, David cried.

Chapter 43: On the Village Green

Shane sat on a park bench in Amherst's Village Green. He had a cup of coffee in one hand, a cigarette in the other. The clock on the Congregationalist Church struck four in the afternoon, and a warm breeze curled around him, whisking the cigarette smoke away.

His back ached, and his eyes felt like a pair of pitted steel orbs as they moved in their sockets.

He had spent hours researching Samson. First in the thinly lit archives of Amherst Town Hall, and then far longer in the Amherst library. He had turned up nothing in regards to the family. Or even that particular parcel of land.

It was as though all history concerning the family had been stripped out of Amherst's history.

And Shane could understand that too.

He only wanted a way to find the cemetery. Shane didn't care about the delicate sensibilities of an old New England town. They could keep their skeletons hidden from the rest of the world so long as they gave him a peek at them.

But they weren't going to.

Shane doubted a dozen people in the town even knew anything about what happened with Samson.

He had one more avenue of research, and that was through the land deeds given out to men like Samson's father. Whether the man's name would be found in the papers wasn't a concern. The absence of a name, as much as the presence of one, would help Shane locate the plot buried in the thousands of woodland acres.

And with a location, Shane could begin to hunt the dead boy down and finish him.

That research meant another two hours in the Amherst library, which in turn would require Shane to finish his cigarette and walk quickly back. The library closed at 8:30 and he still needed to convince a stubborn reference librarian to allow him to even see the copies of the original deeds.

A flash of motion caught his eye and Shane looked up.

The Amherst Police had driven by him four times in the past forty-five minutes. Part of him wanted to get up and go find where the One was. Another childish aspect thoroughly enjoyed the concern he had caused the small town police force.

Give them a few more minutes, he thought. *If they haven't approached by then, I'll head out and see what I can find.*

Shane didn't have to wait a few more minutes.

Before he could take another drag off his cigarette, a cruiser pulled up and parked across the green from him.

He heard another car park behind him, and he knew it had to be a second officer.

The police officer in the car he could see stepped out, adjusted his hat and belt and started toward him.

"Shane Ryan?" a voice asked from behind him.

Shane glanced over his shoulder and saw a tall, solid, older man in a State Police uniform. The man had sergeant's stripes on his sleeves and a hand on a holstered pistol.

The safety loop, Shane noticed, was off the weapon and would allow a free, unencumbered draw.

Shane looked back at the Amherst police officer who had almost reached him.

"No," Shane said.

"No?" the State Police officer asked. "That's not your car parked here?"

"Nope," Shane answered. He finished his cigarette and field stripped it, stuffing the remnants into his pants pocket.

"So you won't care if this vehicle gets towed?" the sergeant asked.

"Not a bit," Shane said. "Knock yourself out."

"Could we see some ID?" the Amherst officer asked as he came to a stop a few feet in front of Shane.

"No," Shane said.

"That's not really a request," the Amherst officer said.

"Sure it is," Shane replied. "See, you're wearing a body camera, which means that this is all being recorded. Also, did you look outside of the gas station over there?"

The Amherst officer glanced over, and a frown flickered across his face. A group of teenagers sat on a stone wall, drinking soda, eating snacks, and filming the police and Shane.

"Great," the Amherst officer muttered.

"Yeah," Shane said. "Exactly. Those kids are watching everything you're doing. And you know they're recording too. Hell, I bet a couple of them are even live streaming it. You may even become a viral hit, officer. So, since I haven't done anything wrong, and since all of this is being recorded for posterity, no, I don't want to show you my ID. Or any ID."

Silence settled on them for a minute, and then the sergeant broke it.

"What's in your coffee cup, sir?" the man asked.

"Nothing," Shane answered.

"Then why are you still holding onto it?" the Amherst officer asked.

"Didn't see the trash," Shane said truthfully. "Figured I'd hold onto it until I found a place to throw it out."

"Not because you had alcohol in it?" the sergeant asked, baiting him.

Shane almost rose to it, but he shook his head. "No. Just a black coffee."

"You need to show me some ID," the Amherst officer said, a frustrated tone in his voice.

"I need to take a walk," Shane responded. He stood up. "You officers have a nice day."

He started to leave when the sergeant said, "Sir, is that a weapon?"

"Yes," Shane said. "Yes, it is."

"Then I definitely need you to show me some identification," the sergeant said.

Shane turned around. Anger filled his voice as he answered.

"No," Shane said. "You don't. Now if you'll excuse me, I'm going now."

The Amherst officer stepped over to the right, and Shane knew what they were about to do. One of them would draw a Taser, hit him with it, then bring him in. He didn't know why they were so intent on speaking with him at the police station, and he didn't care.

Shane knew he hadn't done anything wrong, and he was going to make them work for everything they had to get.

"Gentlemen," Shane said, pouring all of the steel and hate he had learned in the Marines into his voice, "you are both going to stand down and take a long, deep breath before you do something you're going to regret."

"Sir," the sergeant said. "You need to put your hands behind your head and interlock your fingers so we can disarm you, do you understand?"

"That," Shane said between clenched teeth, "is not going to happen."

A small group of people had gathered on the other side of the park, a mix of men and women. Some of them had cellphones up as well.

"Sir," the sergeant barked. "This is not a request. Put your hands behind your head and interlock your fingers. Do you understand me?!"

Shane opened his mouth to reply even while the Amherst officer's hand dropped down to the yellow Taser he carried.

And then the world went cold as Courtney burst out of the dog-tags.

Chapter 44: An Unpleasant Surprise

The force of Courtney's exit from the dog-tags sent Shane tumbling. He rolled, got to his feet, and saw he hadn't been the only one impacted by her movement.

Both of the officers were down, but they were getting up again. Branches were knocked off of several of the town trees, and there were exclamations of dismay from the bystanders.

Shane found out why a moment later when the Amherst officer drew his Taser and fired it.

As the darts pierced his sweatshirt, Shane braced himself for the shock to follow, but it never did. The Amherst officer squeezed the trigger several times even as Shane ripped the darts out.

Without hesitating, Shane turned and ran, leaping over the sergeant as he got to his knees.

Both officers called for him to stop, but Shane didn't. It would be better to deal with the ramifications later than wind up in jail for the night.

And there was the real worry about whether or not the officers were working for the Watchers. Shane didn't want to have to try and survive another assassination attempt. He might not be as lucky as he was before.

Twenty steps into his run and Shane was coughing, decades of cigarettes wreaking havoc on his lungs. He ran through the pain, the officers' footsteps loud behind him.

He reached a small, dark green house and ducked behind the back of it.

Courtney appeared in front of him, a grim expression on her elfin features.

"Stay here," she said and raced past him.

Shane came to a stop, sucking in huge breaths while trying not to throw up. The coffee swirled and turned in his stomach, his throat tightened, and a moment later, he lost his battle with it. Beneath the sound of his vomiting, he heard a crash and two dull thuds.

Courtney returned, waited for him to straighten up and said, "They won't bother us now."

"What did you do?" Shane asked, more out of curiosity than concern for the officers.

"I knocked them out," she replied. "Do you know where to go?"

Shane shook his head. "I was hoping to look at some maps, but that's not going to work now."

"No," she said, agreeing with him. Courtney looked down at the ground. "But I can help. I can find him for us."

"Are you sure?" he asked her. "There's a lot of territory to cover."

Courtney nodded. "I'll find him, Shane. Follow me."

The faint sound of sirens in the distance reminded Shane that he needed to move quickly.

"Alright," he said softly, "lead the way."

Courtney glided into the forest behind the house and Shane followed her. He watched her as they made their way; something was different about her. An attitude that he couldn't identify. Part of him was fearful that she might slip away from him, lose all that she had gained in the past few months. While he didn't want her to leave him, Shane also didn't want her to stay.

She needed to be healed, and to leave for whatever was next.

Shane pushed the thoughts away and forced himself to focus on the path they followed.

He noticed, suddenly, that the deeper he moved into the woods, the stronger he felt. Energy pulsed up through the ground, penetrated his shoes, and worked its way up through his legs and into his chest. His heart thumped, and a curious, cheerful smile made its way onto his face.

Shane couldn't understand why since he knew that eventually, he would have to meet Samson.

And meeting Samson, Shane knew, wasn't something to smile about.

Chapter 45: Hope Springs Forth

Clair sat at her desk with her eyes closed and in darkness. It was her preferred way to contemplate a situation. Especially one as difficult as her current predicament.

Shane Ryan had not been killed.

Frank Benedict had not been killed.

Clair had lost an entire section of seasoned professionals, haunted items, and been forced to execute one of her most effective assassins. Gabby had been unstable following the death of Jenna, but the knowledge of who had killed her sister had made her useless. Clair would have gotten nothing from the woman until vengeance had been enacted. Gabby would have been a risk, in regards to not only the security of the organization but to the limited resources that remained. With the execution of Gabby, Clair had been left with only thirty-four effective members.

Which brought Clair back to the situation concerning the One.

She had to review his terms and to review them with care. The devil, as people said, was in the details. A mistake on her part would undo too much work. Too much sacrifice. She had spent almost her entire adult life in the service of the Watchers. Clair had waited for her opportunity to shine, and she had seized it when the moment had come. One of her greatest memories was the murder of Harlan.

A smile graced her lips as she remembered the man's death.

She shooed the pleasant recollection away and focused on the One.

While she had not revealed to other members of the organization any doubts or questions in regards to the boy in Amherst, she had suffered from them. The Watchers had been seeking the One for decades and there had been several false starts. The schoolteacher who Shane and Frank had recently dispatched had been one of them.

According to the calculations made by the early Watchers, the One would be found at the intersection of multiple ley lines. The spirit would be powerful, feed easily from both the living and the dead, and when strong enough, the One would be able to share its strength. Each of the faithful would gain nourishment from the One, energy and sustenance that would hold the ravages of age and time at bay.

Clair had never delved into the reasons behind these statements. She, like all of the Watchers, took the words of the organization's founders on faith. And she had never experienced anything to shake her convictions.

The child in Amherst fit everything the early Watchers had said to seek. He was on the ley lines and powerful. With words only, he could convince the living to do his bidding. And his power expanded exponentially with each individual fed to him.

Anger spiked in Clair for a moment as she thought about the current situation. She was upset with her predecessors as well as herself. Someone should have sought out the intersections of the ley lines decades ago. Such examinations would have revealed buildings, if there were any, and one definitely would have shown them the presence of the Amherst burial ground.

Where the boy, the One, resided.

The boy wanted a new person each day. It would build up his strength, which was weak after so many years without any real sustenance. She estimated thirty to forty days before he would be powerful enough to even begin to try and extend one person's life. And neither the Watchers nor the One knew how much energy it might require of him.

It could drain him to the extent that they would never be able to work with him again, in which case the quest would continue.

Clair didn't believe it would come to that.

The boy was on the intersection of the ley lines. His property was the one Emmanuel Borgin had tried to purchase nearly a century earlier. And Borgin had been far from stupid.

No, Clair thought. *I have to find out how much the One really needs. When I do that, then we can start to extend ourselves.*

The memory of Shane Ryan's voice filled her mind suddenly, and forced her to straighten up, her eyes opening.

Before the extensions could begin, Shane Ryan would have to be killed.

The only question for Clair was *how*.

A knock sounded on the door, and Clair snapped, "Hold on."

She straightened her blouse, switched on the desk lamp, and said, "Come in."

The door opened, and her secretary stepped in on silent feet. His face was pale as he said, "I think you need to turn the news on."

She kept her comments to herself, silently promising him a miserable day if he had disturbed her for some foolish reason.

He hadn't.

Clair watched the news for several minutes, then when the story changed, she moved on to a new channel. There she received the same information as the other.

An unidentified man had been confronted by police in Amherst, New Hampshire, and then somehow managed to knock two officers unconscious, escaping afterwards. Clair did an internet search and discovered some uploaded video footage that showed the start of the altercation.

A bald man sat on a park bench on the town green, and while there was no sound, the body language of all three men involved was plain enough to read. The air seemed alive with hostility. Clair watched as the bald man stood, walked away, and then stopped to turn and face the officers.

Then there was a flash, and the footage ended. Clair scrolled down and saw there were nearly a thousand comments on the video. Some claimed it was footage of a ghost. The majority ridiculed the rest, saying what they saw was nothing more than a hoax. There were, according to the comments, no ghosts, and the footage's abrupt ending confirmed that the video was a hoax. The original poster defended the footage, replying that the reason the video was cut short was the sudden draining of the phone's battery.

Clair, however, watched it again. And then a third time.

Frowning, she pulled up a magnification program, applied it to the film clip, and managed to zoom in on the bald man.

Clair managed to repress a gasp as the man's face leaped into clarity.

It was Shane Ryan.

He was in Amherst.

He knew about the One.

Forcing herself to remain calm, Clair turned to her secretary. "Pull everyone. From everywhere. Shane Ryan is in Amherst, and he needs to die."

Chapter 46: In the Hotel Room

Marie and David sat at the small table in the hotel room. The curtains were closed against the dusk, and the television was off. David felt drained, as if there had been a plug in his soul and someone had yanked it out. He hadn't realized how much he had depended upon Shirley for his own future happiness.

David had hoped his goddaughter would get away from the world of the Watchers. That somehow the organization wouldn't taint her.

In that sense, his desire had come through. She had died unsullied by the Watchers, having never fully subscribed to their curious brand of faith. Yet only through death had she been able to escape it.

And that realization broke his heart.

"What do you want to do?" Marie asked him, squeezing his hand.

"I want to hurt them," David muttered. "I need the weapons in Shane's house."

"You won't be able to get them," she told him. "At least not yet. With a crime scene this large, it may take a week for them to process it. You'd be better off buying what you need in the morning."

David grimaced and didn't answer.

After a moment of silence, she asked, "Have you heard back from Shane at all?"

David shook his head. "Nothing. Not a damned, single thing. Every call I make goes to voice mail. None of the texts get responded to."

Marie frowned. "That's not like him. I mean the voicemail. Not with you being out of the house. He may be obstinate, David, but he's not stupid. He wouldn't isolate himself that way. He'd be concerned about you. And Frank. Have you found out what's going on with Frank, yet?"

"No," David said with a sigh. "I forgot about it."

"Give him a call," Marie prodded.

David nodded, picked up his cellphone, and called St. Joseph's Hospital first. When he asked if a Frank Benedict was a patient there, he received an affirmative answer. His next question, asking to be put through to Frank's room, was answered with a polite request for him to hold.

Horrible elevator music, intermixed with advertisements for services provided by the hospital, assaulted David's ear as he waited. After several minutes, someone picked up.

"Hello," a man said into the receiver.

"Hello," David replied. "Can I speak with Frank, please?"

"May I ask who's calling?" the man inquired.

"David," he answered.

"David who?" the man on the other end asked.

"Don't worry about who, just put me through to Frank, please," David said, keeping his temper under control.

"No," the man responded, his voice becoming hard. "You need to tell me your last name and your relationship to Frank Benedict."

David ended the call and swore under his breath.

"What is it?" Marie asked.

"They won't let me speak to Frank," David said. "At least not without giving them a name."

"Why didn't you, then?" she asked, looking as though she wasn't quite sure what the issue was.

"Because," David replied, "they'd want a phone number. And then they'd want an address. When they realize I was the same witness from the house, they might decide to have a little bit longer of a chat with me. I don't need that. I've got enough prints at enough murder scenes to put me away for life."

Marie's face paled a shade.

David nodded regretfully.

"So," he continued, "if they decide at some point they need to talk to me a little longer, and I don't want to, I'd be hard pressed to get away in your car. No, it's better not to do anything. I don't like the idea of leaving Frank alone in the hospital, but I don't see anything else I can do."

"We need to find Shane," Marie said.

As the last syllable passed her lips, Marie's cellphone rang. Surprised, she picked it up and answered.

David leaned back in the chair, looking at the curtains and trying to formulate a plan of action while half listening to Marie's conversation. He heard several 'yes's, a few 'no's, and a pair of 'I don't knows.' By the time she had ended the call, David still didn't have any idea of what they should do.

A look at Marie brought his attention back to focus and the front legs of the chair back onto the carpet.

"What's wrong?" David asked.

"That was the Amherst Police Department," Marie said in a tight voice. "Nashua PD had given them my number. They wanted to know if I might have any information as to where Shane might have gone off to, or where he might hide out."

"Hideout?" David asked, shocked. "What the hell from?"

"They didn't say," Marie said with a sour expression, "but it could be anything as serious as a gunfight to something as simple as giving a cop a hard time at a traffic stop. You really never know with him."

David straightened up and asked, "Did you say it was the Amherst Police?"

Marie nodded. "Why?"

"Amherst, that's the town where the One is supposed to be," David muttered, half to himself. "God have mercy, is he going after him by himself?"

A knock on the hotel room door was a loud and unwelcome intrusion.

Neither of them moved as they waited.

The unknown individual knocked again, louder and insistent. A voice followed at the end.

"Marie," a man said. "Marie Lafontaine. This is Richard Blanchard. Got a minute?"

David looked at Marie, and she shook her head. In a whisper, she said, "Nashua detective."

David sighed and sank back into the chair.

"Hold on, Richard," Marie said, getting to her feet.

David stood as well and helped her towards the door.

There was nothing else he could do.

Chapter 47: In the Woods of Amherst

Shane knew he was in Amherst, New Hampshire, but precious little beyond that.

He had stumbled into someone's back yard as the sun had begun to set. Only a few steps out of the tree line he had come to a complete stop, listening for any sound that would tell him if he could rest or if he should continue moving.

After a few minutes of silence and a lack of lights on in the house, Shane risked a few more steps into the yard. When no dog howled inside of the house, and the lights bracketing the back door entrance remained dark, Shane crept up to the faucet. He was thirsty and hungry. And while the first could be helped by the spigot that protruded from the house, the second would be a little more difficult to appease.

When he had drunk his fill, Shane stood up and wiped his mouth on the back of his hand. His stomach rumbled loud enough for him to hear, and Shane looked hard at the back yard in the dim light of dusk.

The grass was unkempt, the bushes wild. An old and rusted swing set stood haphazardly off to the left, and a shed that tilted to the right was beside it.

Shane faced the back door again. The cement steps looked to be older than him, and he moved up them with the appropriate amount of care. When he opened the screen door, un-oiled hinges squealed, and Shane came to a complete stop. His heart thudded in his chest as he waited for a light, or a sound to emerge from the shadows of the house, and when none did, he reached out and took hold of the doorknob.

It was locked, of course, but with enough pressure on it from his arm and his shoulder, with his legs adding to their strength, Shane popped the door open.

He waited a moment, listening for any sound. Shane strained his ears, yet there was nothing to hear. Not even the ambient sounds of a house.

He stepped into the house and eased the door closed. The jamb was broken where the latch plate had torn through the old wood. After a moment of effort, he managed to force the door to remain closed and looked around the room.

It was a kitchen, with old, yellow wallpaper and appliances that had been new in the seventies. There was no table, and a thick layer of dust was on the floor. The tracks of mice could be seen on the edges, while those of cats stretched across the center and the Formica counter. His nose wrinkled at the smell of ammonia, another sure sign of cats.

Shane had smelled worse, and he dismissed it as he moved deeper into the house.

Beyond the windows clouded with grime, the sun continued its descent. The next room he passed through was a den or family room, then he was up a flight of stairs and onto the second floor. Nothing but dust and dirt and animal scat could be found.

Shane returned to the first floor, considered a quick inspection of the basement, and then decided against it. Night had arrived and going through the darkness would be both foolish and dangerous.

He groped his way into the first-floor bathroom and sat down. Shane reached into his shirt, found his dog-tags and removed them. The metal was no colder than it should have been, which meant Courtney had yet to return. He sighed, put the tags away, and took out his phone. Two attempts to turn it on reminded him of Courtney's exit from the dog-tags and he gave up, stuffing the phone back into his pocket.

Shane closed his eyes, rested his head against the plaster wall and tried to relax. If he could get a few hours of sleep he would be able to move deeper into the woods. Why the police hadn't found him yet nagged at him, making him nervous that the Watchers were around.

He twisted the iron rings on his fingers and thought about his current situation.

Shane hadn't gotten more than a minute or two into his self-reflection when there was the sound of someone walking up the basement stairs.

All desire to sleep fled as he got to his feet, watching the dark rectangle of the doorway. The basement door opened, closed, and the unknown individual advanced down the short hall to the bathroom. A moment later, the footsteps stopped in front of the door.

"Who are you?" The voice sounded like it belonged to an old woman. Each word was pronounced with difficulty as if it pained her.

Shane felt fear creep through him, and he shoved it down as he answered, "My name's Shane."

"Are you a friend of Herman's?" she asked.

"I'm not," Shane apologized. "Who is he?"

"He's my little boy," she whispered. "I'm waiting for him to come home."

"When did he go away?" Shane asked.

"Seventy years ago," she said, and her voice was so low Shane had a hard time understanding her. "Perhaps eighty. I, I have no way to know anymore."

"How old was he, and where did he go?" Shane asked.

When the woman spoke again, her voice broke with sorrow, anguish making the words thick.

"He was seven," she sobbed. "And he was called away. Herman heard the boy, and we told him not to go, but he went. He was a willful child, and the boy kept him."

"What boy?" Shane asked although he knew the answer. "Who kept him?"

"The boy in the woods," the woman whispered. "It was the boy in the woods."

Chapter 48: Clair Goes on the War Path

"You're going to do it," she said.

The older man looked at Clair with undisguised hate in his deep-set brown eyes. The lines around those eyes were etched into pale skin, his silver hair cropped short. Clair watched as the right corner of his mouth twitched, and a nervous hand stole up to loosen the collar of his dark blue, uniform shirt.

"I can't," he said after a minute of awkward silence. His eyes dropped from her face and focused on the floor.

She snorted.

"You can, Dana," she retorted. "And you will. You've given your support to the Watchers for decades."

"Passive!" he snapped. "I allowed nothing overt to be done."

"You didn't have to," Clair said. "Your silence has made you an accomplice. And, to be quite honest with you, we've arranged for the creation of certain evidence that shows you've been far more active than you were."

"Are you threatening me?" he asked in a hoarse voice.

"No," Clair said, sighing. "I'm making you a promise, Dana. If you do not give us the access I need, then some rather disturbing images are going to surface regarding you and some impressionable young men. Then some of these same men will step forward to testify against you. You will be tried, convicted, and executed in the court of public opinion. Someone may even attempt to introduce you to vigilante justice."

She shrugged. "Who knows. However, I can assure you that if you do help us in this matter, then you will never hear another word about it."

"You can't expect me to believe that," he sneered, but she heard the surrender in his voice.

"I don't care what you believe," she told him. "It's the truth. Accept it or don't. But understand this, we are going in there after Shane Ryan, and you are going to have your men stand down. Form a perimeter along the lines I told you. Feed them a lie about this being a domestic terrorism concern and that they're to keep him from getting out. Tell them that he's Santa Claus and that he's trying to hide the toys he kept from good little girls and boys. The fact of the matter is this, Dana, I don't care what you say so long as I get what I need."

"Fine," he snapped, pushing himself out of the chair in the command center. "You'll get your line. And I hope you go to Hell."

He stormed out, leaving her alone among the equipment.

Clair smiled to herself, straightened up and thought, *Not likely*.

She left the command center, and men and women filed past her, not looking as they returned to their posts. Clair paid no attention to them as she walked to the several SUVs that contained the rest of the Watchers she had been able to muster.

While the organization enjoyed a large, silent group of supporters, it had always had a small cadre of active participants. Operatives who ensured the safety and growth of properties, and who took care of any unnecessary unpleasantness. They were a hard and tested group.

And Shane Ryan and his friends had whittled that number down to a paltry thirty-four people.

When Clair reached the vehicles, the operatives got out. They were dressed in dark blue utility uniforms that were the standard of police departments and government organizations across the United States. Semi-automatic pistols were worn on belts and serious expressions on their faces.

The men and women gathered close to Clair to listen.

She didn't raise her voice to talk to them because she knew they were paying attention. Every eye was on her.

"The New Hampshire State Police, courtesy of their Colonel, will ensure that a perimeter is established and maintained," Clair stated. "They will not interfere. All other municipal law enforcement agencies have been seconded to the State Police, and in such a capacity they are bound to follow the decisions of the Colonel. Thus they too will be in the perimeter."

Clair looked around to see if anyone had questions.

None of them did.

She nodded and continued on.

"They will ensure that Shane Ryan does not escape," Clair said. "They will not, of course, kill him for us, but we can worry about that after he's been detained. If he is caught by them. I doubt that will happen. Shane is direct in his approach to certain problems, and I do not believe he will change in that regard."

Clair took a breath and said, "We will shoot to kill. I do not want him taken alive. I am not interested in learning anything more about him, or how he has managed to do what he has done. He is a threat to everything we have strived for. We have lived into the time of the One, and I refuse to let him destroy what is ours."

Several of the operatives nodded their agreement, but the majority waited for the word.

So Clair gave it to them.

"Bring me his head," she told them. "I want to mount it on the wall in my office."

Chapter 49: After Nightfall

The hospital's clinical psychologist didn't get to Frank's room until after the sun had set.

Frank was not in a good mood, and he didn't mince any words with the woman when she came in. The officer at the door looked as though he might enter, but the doctor smiled and waved the cop away.

She was a young woman, possibly in her late twenties. While she was pretty and had a small amount of make-up on that highlighted her eyes and lips, Frank wasn't distracted by her.

He wanted to leave, and he told her as much.

The doctor had brought in a whiteboard and a marker. She jotted down several lines.

"I know you do. But that's something we have to figure out, Frank. My name's Lynn Waltner. And the sooner you and I talk, the sooner you'll be going home."

Frank bit back his response and gestured for her to continue.

"Great. So, how about you tell me how you got those cuts and lost your hearing."

"I had an accident," Frank said.

"What kind of an accident?"

"I don't know," he lied. "I hit my head pretty hard. When I came to, I was bleeding."

"What hospital did you go to for your stitches?"

"No hospital," Frank said. "Had a friend who knows some basic first aid. He came over and helped me out."

"And what about the concussion?"

"I didn't get a concussion," Frank said, his voice tight. "I just knocked myself out."

She smiled at him, the expression patronizing and infuriating.

"That is a concussion, Frank. Now, you share the home you were found in with a friend?"

Frank nodded.

"Was that friend with you when you hit your head and got cut?"

"No," Frank replied. "I was alone."

"Okay. Could I call him now? Maybe have him come and talk to me about the accident?"

"He doesn't know anything about it," Frank snapped.

"How about you tell me what you told the triage nurse when you were brought in?"

"I don't know what I said," Frank stated. "So I can't tell you."

"Why don't you try."

Frank shook his head.

"Will this help?" Frank watched as she wrote down the word, "Ghosts."

Again he shook his head.

"It won't help, or you didn't say it?"

"Both," he replied.

She nodded.

"You see, a lot of people say strange things after a particularly stressful situation. You're a man who's seen combat, Frank. Your accident shouldn't have rattled you at all."

Frank remained quiet.

"No?"

"I want to go home," Frank stated.

"I know."

She wrote something else down on the dry whiteboard and stood up. Still holding it, she started for the door.

When she had gotten half way there, Frank yelled, "Hey!"

Dr. Waltner hesitated and looked over her shoulder, raising a questioning eyebrow.

"What's going on with me?" Frank demanded.

She threw the whiteboard to him, and he caught it as she reached the door.

Frank looked down at what she had written.

"We'll hold you for 72 hours before we kill you. Will Shane last that long against the One?"

Shocked, Frank switched his gaze from the whiteboard to the door.

Dr. Waltner was about to leave when she saw him looking at her. She smiled, winked and mouthed the words, "He won't."

And the officer closed the door behind her, trapping Frank in the hospital.

Chapter 50: A Decision is Made

David stood in the bathroom and washed his face at the sink. It was ten at night, and Marie was at the hotel room's table. Detective Richard was still with them.

Richard and another, younger detective named Phil had questioned them for nearly two hours. Most of the questions had been directed towards Marie. She had known Shane for longer, and there was the chance that she might know something and not know that she knew it.

Which was how they had phrased it.

David knew it wasn't true. The pair of detectives in the other room were real cops, and not on the payroll of the Watchers. They were investigating not only Shane, but he felt certain they were waiting for information on him as well.

During the questioning, David had watched the three officers. The men had asked questions and Marie had answered to the best of her ability. It was a game the detectives had to play, and the three officers thought they were the only ones who knew what the game was.

They were wrong.

David himself had played along a few times. He had been questioned in regards to murders in the past. Thefts and assaults. He had learned how to answer a question without giving information when cops still beat up guys behind the station or in a cell.

Richard and Phil had been friendly towards him, introducing themselves when they had come in.

But David had seen how they kept an eye on him. How their hands never strayed far from their weapons. Phil sat closer to the door, blocking any quick exit from the hotel room. Richard sat in a corner, beside Marie, but from his place, he could cover the bathroom and the beds.

David sighed, took a white, overly large face-cloth down from the stainless steel rack above the toilet and wiped the water from his face. He held it for a moment, then set the damp cloth on the countertop. Unexpectedly sorrow welled up within him. He saw Shirley's face, her smile. He remembered her baptism, her tenth birthday when he had been allowed to bring her a puppy as a gift.

David shook his head, took a deep, shuddering breath and forced himself to focus.

David knew that the detectives suspected something in spite of the perfect, fake license David had provided them. His last name on the identification was not the one he had been born with. The birth date wasn't his own either.

It wasn't the license, of *that* David had no doubt.

No, the problem lay with Shane's house.

The police would have processed the scene. All of the fingerprints would have been lifted and sent for analysis. With Shane's house being the site of a multiple homicide, they would have rushed the prints out. Some of them would have come back with hits.

All of the ones brought in and left dead on the hall floor would have kicked back names and criminal histories. Shane and Frank's prints would have returned information that concerned their military background. Marie's prints would have confirmed that she had, in the recent past, been in the house as well.

And then there would be David's prints.

The first name would come back properly, but not the family name. Or the birth date, or his current residence. A photograph and a physical description would have been sent along.

The investigators working the crime scene at Shane's house would have realized that David matched the description, even if his information didn't.

The police didn't look at information when it came to murder, and David had a couple of murders they could tie him to.

He knew the two detectives were waiting for an arrest warrant to be written out against him. One of them would get a call or a text, get up, excuse himself, and leave the room. Within a few minutes, the man would return, and there would be several officers with him.

And nothing could be done about it.

David ran his fingers through his hair, wiped his hands off on the towel and left the bathroom. Marie smiled at him, and he returned it. He walked over to the dresser, took a bottle of water from the top of it and had a drink.

As he set it down, Phil's phone chimed, and David glanced over at him.

Phil took the phone out, chuckled and said, "It's my mom. I've got to give her a call."

"Sure," Richard said, "tell her I said hello."

The banter was good, but David heard the tension beneath it.

Phil stood up to leave, and David attacked.

He launched himself at the younger man and took him by surprise. As Phil reached for his pistol, David punched him in the shoulder, numbing the entire arm. David yanked the semi-automatic out of the holster and grabbed Phil, throwing him out of the way.

The weapon in David's hand was a police issued Glock 9 mm. He chambered a round as he twisted towards Richard. The older detective was slow to get to his feet, trying to pull his pistol at the same time.

But David was fast, and he was a professional killer.

David squeezed off two rounds that hammered into Richard's chest. Deep red splotches blossomed on his white shirt over the left breast as the shell casings rattled on the floor. David spun on his heel, saw Phil on his feet and fired twice more, dropping the young detective with the same ease as he had the older.

David lowered the pistol, wondered how long he and Marie had until the first uniformed police showed up, and gasped.

A terrible blow had struck him in the back.

Then two more, and then a fourth, which dropped him to his knees. The pistol fell from his fingers. Its thunk onto the carpeted floor was dull and lifeless.

A fifth round was fired, and David tumbled forward. He landed on several still hot casings, his face against Phil's calf.

It was then that David heard Marie. She was chanting in a whisper.

"I'm sorry. I'm sorry. I'm sorry."

As darkness devoured his vision, David wondered if she was sorry for having shot him, or for him having shot them.

David died with the question unanswered.

Chapter 51: A History of Death

The ghost of the old woman drifted in and out of the bathroom. At times, Shane heard her in the floor above. Occasionally he heard her in the kitchen, the faint scent of coffee reaching his nose.

His stomach rumbled, a bleak reminder of him having not eaten since the morning. He rummaged through the kitchen and found a single, solitary can of baked beans among a collection of small, empty liquor bottles. There was an empty pack of cigarettes and a tattered blanket.

Someone had squatted at the house, and recently, Shane realized as he turned the can over and read the expiration date. The beans were good for another month.

Well, he thought, *I've eaten worse.*

When the dead woman returned again, Shane had finished the beans and he spoke to her.

"What's your name?" he asked.

For a heartbeat, she solidified enough for him to see her, but then it was gone as she answered, "Amelia Pine."

"Amelia, do you mind if I ask you some questions about the neighborhood here?" he asked.

"No," Amelia said, "I don't mind."

Shane cleared his throat, tried to think of the most delicate way he could put the question, and failed. With a sigh, he asked, "Were there any other people who disappeared before your son."

"Yes," she whispered, the temperature in the room racing to the bottom of the thermostat and set Shane's teeth to chattering.

"Can you tell me what happened?" He tried to keep the eagerness out of his voice.

"They were just rumors," she said in the same low voice. "We didn't pay any mind to them. Who would? The woods are large. People get lost. It is sadness, but it is also a truth. When we moved in, one of the older folk, Jonathan Engberg, came to our house to warn us of the boy in the woods. We laughed it off until he told us that his wife and daughter had both succumbed to the boy in the woods."

Amelia sighed. "After that visit, we assumed he had been devastated by grief. We gave him our pity, silently, and wished him the best aloud."

"Did Engberg live nearby?" Shane asked.

"Yes. Several houses up. When he passed, it was a terrible day. We all went to his funeral, and they placed him in the ground between his wife and daughter. They had been declared dead, and the bodies had never been found. So instead of waiting for resurrection with his loved ones, Jonathan was alone." She went silent, and Shane waited several minutes before he attempted to talk.

Her choked sob cut him off as she continued. "Herman left us a week later. And never returned."

Shane, unable to comfort the woman, refrained from speaking until she was done. When he was positive she wouldn't break into tears again, he asked, "Are there more ghosts on this street?"

"Yes," she whispered. "Lots of them. Whoever lost a loved one or a friend to the boy remained here."

"Shane," a voice whispered in his ear, causing him to jump. Twisting around, he caught sight of Courtney and slumped back down. "Scared the hell out of me, Courtney."

"I'm sorry," she replied with sincerity. "You're on an old street. Only the dead are here now. There are Jersey barriers at either end of the end of the street."

"Why the hell would a street be closed off?" Shane wondered out loud.

"I don't know," Courtney said. "But there's more."

Shane groaned as he asked, "What now?"

"Local and state police units have shown up," Courtney said. "They've got the entire area cordoned off. Only one group is allowed to enter and exit. No one knows who they are, but they're armed and I know several of them were talking about you. I heard them."

"Alright," Shane said, rubbing at the back of his head.

"Shane," Courtney said hesitantly.

He looked at her. "Yeah?"

"I've been feeling different," she said in a soft voice.

His heart skipped a beat and he moistened his lips before he asked, "What do you mean?"

"I don't feel as bad as I did before," Courtney said, giving him a small smile. "It doesn't feel like I'm going crazy."

Shane relaxed and grinned at her. "Good. I thought you were going to tell me that you were feeling worse."

Courtney shook her head.

"Good," Shane said, nodding. "That's really good."

They were silent for several minutes before Shane said, "I need to do something."

He reached into his pocket, took out his cellphone and remembered with a frown that there was no power to it.

"Damn it," he grumbled, stuffing the phone back in his pocket. "Okay. No phone calls."

He looked at Courtney. "Will you follow me into the houses?"

"Yes," she answered without hesitation. "Why would you need to?"

"According to Amelia, they're here still because they lost people to Samson," Shane replied. "I'm hoping some of them might be willing to seek a little revenge on my distant relative."

Courtney nodded. "Okay. Do you want to do it now?"

He shook his head. Shane was exhausted and he hadn't slept well in days. A quick rest, even one that was only twenty or thirty minutes in length, would help him remain focused. It was a trick he had learned in the Marines, one that had helped him survive long deployments and short, brutal firefights.

"In a little bit. I need at least a few minutes of rest, or I'll never make it," Shane explained to her.

"As much as you need," she said. "I'll watch over you."

With a tired nod, Shane slumped down, closed his eyes and tried for at least twenty minutes of sleep.

Chapter 52: A Harsh and Terrible World

Marie had been moved into an empty room next to the one she and David had shared in the hotel. Someone had wrapped a blanket around her, and someone else had brought her water.

Lieutenant Wayne Hammett came into the room and sat down beside her at the table.

"How are you doing?" he asked, care and concern evident on his broad face.

"Terrible," she replied.

Wayne nodded.

Marie glanced at the closed door, the one that concealed the hallway from her, but didn't block the sounds of the forensics teams as they moved back and forth.

"I didn't know what he was going to do," she whispered.

"No one is saying you did, Marie," Wayne replied.

"I know that," Marie sighed. "I don't know what he was thinking."

"Who knows? He was a bad man, Marie. We've got his prints on murders that are decades old," Wayne said. "We're going to have to question you about what you know."

She nodded. "I think I surprised him, at the end."

Wayne looked at her and stayed silent, letting her speak without interruption.

"The shooting was over in seconds," Marie continued, "and he lowered the pistol. It was as if he was thinking about how we were going to get out of there, and not just himself. I wish I was quicker, that I could have seen what he was going to do. They might be alive if I had thought about who David really was, about what he had done in the past."

"Marie, don't tell anyone he had lowered his weapon," Wayne advised. "It'll go from a righteous kill to murder in the blink of an eye. And popular opinion has definitely swung against us recently."

"I won't say anything," Marie said.

"Now, Marie," Wayne said, clearing his throat. "we're going to have to talk about why this man was here, staying with you and helping you. You know that, right?"

Marie grimaced as she nodded. After a moment of thought, she added, "I think he forgot, at the end."

"Forgot what?" Wayne asked.

"That I'm a cop," she said, closing her eyes. "First, last and forever. And no one gets to shoot a cop."

Wayne put a hand on her shoulder, and when she started to sob, he pulled her close.

No matter what anyone said, Marie knew killing never got any easier.

Chapter 53: Manhunt

Clair had equipped every member of her team with headsets and sent them out in ten groups of three and two of two. She had turned the back of one of the SUVs into a small command center from which she could monitor the progress of each team. They had hundreds of acres to cover and little time to do it. Clair didn't know how long the Colonel would allow her to run the operation, regardless of the dangers to his career.

If he had a sudden attack of morality, she and the rest of the Watchers would be driven out of Amherst. In that scenario, Shane would have the opportunity to close in on the One.

Clair doubted he could succeed against the dead boy.

But she had also doubted he would come out victorious in Borgin. Or in any of the other encounters he had engaged in.

Her cellphone rang and Clair glanced at it. When she recognized Dr. Waltner's number, she picked it up, asking harshly, "Situation?"

"Taken care of," the doctor responded. "I've written my report, stated that he needs at least three days of observation in a safe and controlled environment and that he shouldn't be released. The hospital and the Nashua police have agreed with me."

"Excellent," Clair said, some of her tension slipping away. "Well, done, Doctor."

"Thank you," Dr. Waltner replied. "Do you need me out there?"

Clair considered the question for a moment and then answered, "Yes. Head out here."

She gave the doctor the directions and ended the call.

Clair allowed herself a small smile. With Frank detained at the hospital for three days, Shane would be robbed of his biggest supporter. How much Shane had relied on the other man would be known soon enough, and even if it was only a small amount, it was still something.

And any edge over Shane Ryan was worth its weight in gold.

Chatter on the police band caught Clair's attention, and she reached out to turn the volume up.

Two detectives have been killed in a hotel room in Nashua. Their assailant has been brought down by Marie Lafontaine, a detective from the Nashua Police Force on medical leave. Tentative reports over the radio stated the shooter had been a man named David. His documentation had been falsified, so they had no real information on who he was.

Clair sat back, her eyebrows raised in surprise.

She hadn't thought anyone would be able to catch David. Clair had also thought he would have been smart enough to leave the area after his encounter with Gabby.

Clair chuckled, shook her head, and straightened up in her chair.

Shane, she realized, had no more allies left.

His ghosts were in his home and not with him in Amherst. There was a cordon of police officers stretched around the entire perimeter of the One. And teams of Watchers were actively hunting Shane in the woods.

For the first time in weeks, Clair relaxed.

Smiling, she adjusted her headset and wondered where in her office she should mount Shane's head.

Chapter 54: The Second House

Shane had been in difficult places. Areas of the world that had made him uncomfortable. Bosnia in Europe, and Fallujah in Iraq. The Korengal Valley in Afghanistan and his own bedroom as a child.

When he stepped out of Amelia's door that same sensation of dread and fear settled on his shoulders. Fifteen houses stood on the dark street. Their windows stared at him with all of the empathy and liveliness of a dead man's eyes. In the moonlight, Shane could see overgrown yards and litter. It looked as though someone had reached down and plucked all of the residents out of their homes at the same time one evening, and the people had never returned.

Courtney materialized beside him, and once his heart had settled back to its normal rate he asked, "Which one do we go to first?"

She frowned and then pointed at the second house on the left. "There is a woman there. She has been there for a time. Not as long as Amelia. Not as short as some of the others."

"Is she a madwoman?" Shane asked.

Courtney shook her head. "I don't think so. But she could be."

Shane rolled his eyes and offered up a less than sincere, "Thanks."

"I didn't speak with her," Courtney said. "There was no need. I don't think she even realized I was there."

"Even better," Shane muttered. In a louder voice, he said, "Okay. Second house on the left it is."

The night sky was full of stars, and the moon was full. There was plenty of light by which to see, and more than enough of it to populate the abandoned street with shadows.

Shane wondered if there was a way he could get word to either Frank or David. Even Marie if he had to.

But he knew the battery of his phone wouldn't recover, and he knew there would be no electricity in the houses. Not with the street dead and blocked off. Which made him wonder again why the police hadn't found him.

He hadn't made good distance from the Amherst town green to Amelia's house. And it would be common sense for the police to check the street itself. There was no helicopter searching for him, and no dog handlers and their canines out seeking his scent.

Everything was wrong.

And he knew why.

Somehow, the Watchers had gotten into the mix. They had taken control of the situation, and it seemed as if they were determined to ensure his disappearance.

If they left Shane alive, he could talk. Even if the majority of people thought he was completely out of his mind and a paranoid schizophrenic, there would be some who did believe. There always were. Someone, the Watchers knew, would believe him. Someone would start to dig.

Digging would be an unnecessary interruption. Curious individuals or, heaven forbid, a few curious reporters, would put a halt to their activities in regards to Samson.

Shane dead, on the other hand, meant there would be no one alive to speak embarrassing truths.

Those thoughts receded as he reached the cracked cement sidewalk that lead to the closed-in front porch of the second house on the left. Shane stood there for a moment, looking at it. His eyes strained to see movement, or a face, or anything.

Nothing.

Shane squared his shoulders and marched up the walkway, hurried up the front steps and opened the porch door. The wood rotted and tore free from its hinges, knocking him off balance and leaving him grasping for a hold on the door jamb. His fingernails managed to dig into soft wood, and as his heart thundered in his chest, he pulled himself up.

He shook his head at the bad start and stepped onto the porch. A board sagged beneath his feet, and he hurried across the floor to the front door. The door was unlocked, and he let himself in. Moonlight filled the room, and Shane looked around.

He waited for several minutes to see if the ghost would reach out to him. When nothing occurred, he said in a low voice, "Courtney."

Courtney appeared a moment later.

"She's upstairs," Courtney whispered, nodding to a narrow set of stairs. "The room on the right."

"Thanks," Shane whispered, and he took small, light steps across the floor. He listened for the telltale sound that would threaten the collapse of the subfloor, but it never came. The stairs were solid beneath his feet, and he walked along the edge of them. He avoided the center, knowing that it was the loosest part of each tread. Shane wanted to make as little noise as possible.

Shane reached the second floor and found himself in a short hallway. There was a bathroom ahead of him, a room to the left, and a second to the right. He turned towards the second and stepped through a doorway.

Like the main floor, the room in front of him was well lit by the moon. There was no furniture and what glass had been in the windows had been broken and scattered onto the worn carpet. Cracks and holes broke up the uniformity of the walls, and long strips of paint hung from the ceiling.

A faint sound reached his ear, and Shane bent his head, listening.

Footsteps.

Not from outside or downstairs, but from within the room. Someone paced from the back to the front, front to the left side, left side to the right, right side to the back. And then to the front.

An endless loop.

If the ghost wasn't mad, she was close to it.

"Hello," Shane said in a soft voice.

The pace of the unseen woman quickened.

"Is there anyone here?" Shane asked, raising his voice slightly.

The footsteps became louder.

"My name is Shane," he said. "I want to talk to you about why you're still here."

A force slammed into him and launched him backward. His back cracked against the wall and he fell to his hands and knees, gasping for breath.

The sound of footsteps was gone.

"Who are you?" a woman hissed in his ear. "What have you done with my mother?"

Shane pushed himself up and sat with his back against the wall. His blood pounded in his ears. A bitter cold pressed against the side of his head and sharp fear settled into his gut as he remembered the terrible sensation of frostbite.

When he answered the dead woman's questions, his voice was smooth and controlled.

"I haven't done anything with your mother, and I told you my name is Shane," he said. "I want to find her for you. I want to find everyone."

There was silence for a moment before she said in an angry voice, "There are others?"

"Yes," Shane said. "Many, from what I was told. I spoke with a woman who said her son was taken by the boy in the woods."

A high-pitched shriek caused Shane to wince and slap his hands over his ears as he clenched his eyes shut. The noise went on for several minutes, and as he prepared to get up and escape the room, the woman stopped.

"I didn't believe her," the woman sobbed. "I thought she was seeing things. I didn't believe her."

The dead woman's lamentations filled the room and all Shane could do was sit and listen.

Chapter 55: Seeking to Establish Contact

Clair was out of the SUV, pacing up and down along the side of the vehicle.

Midnight had arrived without any sign of Shane. Her teams were dangerously close to reaching the One, which meant Shane could be near it as well if he had continued to move forward. She didn't know if there were other places where he could have hidden himself. Clair couldn't risk bringing anyone from Amherst into the situation. There was already a tremendous potential for exposure as it stood.

Finally, with an angry snort, she picked up her phone and sent a two-word text.

Bring her.

A short while later a car appeared, the headlights bright as it parked behind the SUV. The lights cut out and a moment later, the doors opened. Linda was escorted forward by an older man named Gordon, and the two of them stopped in front of Clair.

Clair typed a message into her phone and held it up for Linda to read.

I need you to bring a camera and microphone to the One. I have to speak with him.

Linda's eyes widened and she shook her head.

You don't have a choice, Clair wrote.

"Gordon," Clair said. "You'll be escorting her to the One."

The man looked at her in surprise as he stuttered, "What?"

Clair took out the small .22 caliber pistol she had used to kill Gabby. "It's not a request, Gordon. Not for either of you. In your case, the decision is simple. If you bring her, I don't shoot you. If you don't, I execute you right here, and you serve as an example of what I am willing to do. If she refuses, I shoot her in the shin. Painful, but it will leave her capable of fulfilling the task I need done. Am I understood?"

Gordon nodded.

Clair turned her attention to Linda and saw that the woman had understood the essence of what had been said. The deaf woman's face was pale and drawn in the moonlight, but she nodded her assent.

"Excellent," Clair said, without putting away the pistol. "In the back, there's a small camera and an earpiece. You'll wear the earpiece, Gordon, to act as the middle-man. As for the camera, it will broadcast a live feed. Bring it with you and start down the main path. Turn them on when you're about to approach the One. I don't need twenty minutes of trail time. I'll have another team meet you shortly. They'll meet up with you on the trail and then escort you to the chestnut tree. After that, Linda can go about her business."

Clair took a half step back and gestured towards the SUV with the pistol. Linda remained where she was while Gordon did as he was told, the moon shining on the top of his bald head. Clair wondered if he would survive the One, and Gordon, it seemed, was curious as well.

The older man turned around, holding the earpiece and the camera. Both shook in his hands. When he spoke, his voice was weak and tremulous.

"What if he keeps me?" Gordon asked. "I've heard he does that. He keeps them at his house and feeds off them."

Clair gave him a cold look and then lied. "He only feeds off the dead. So don't die."

Gordon opened his mouth to speak again, and Clair pointed the pistol at his head.

She cocked the hammer back and watched with satisfaction as both Gordon and Linda stumbled towards the main path.

Once they had slipped into the darkness of the woods, she shook her head. Even if the two made it back from the One, they might need to be put down.

It made Clair hate Shane all the more. She should never have to get her hands dirty.

Ever.

Easing the hammer back into place Clair returned to her seat in the SUV and waited for Linda and Gordon to make contact.

Chapter 56: In Engberg's House

A terrible weight of sadness settled onto Shane's shoulders as he stepped into the house that had belonged to Jonathan Engberg.

Like the other houses on the street, it was a small, New England-style cape. And, like the others, no one had lived in it since Jonathan had passed away. The temperature was colder than the others, and Shane's breath raced out of his mouth in great plumes of white.

He had visited six houses before Jonathan's, and he had spoken with the dead who inhabited the homes. All except for Jonathan, the one man who had tried to warn each and every person. Some he visited when he was alive. Others, those who had taken up residence after his passing, when he was dead.

All of the dead on the street had two items in common. The first was that they had ignored Jonathan's pre and post-death warnings. The second was that they had each lost at least one family member to Samson.

Unlike the other homes on the street, Jonathan's front door hadn't been locked or difficult to open. There had been no danger. No rotten boards or holes. Nothing to trip a visitor up, or knock them down.

Shane closed the door behind him and waited.

He knew Jonathan's house would be different.

He could feel it.

Less than a minute had passed when a male voice asked, "Who are you?"

Shane introduced himself and explained why he had come.

Book 9: Amherst Burial Ground

A creak sounded from a corner of the room as if the house remembered the way it should react to a person sitting down.

"You know of him," Jonathan said.

"Yes," Shane answered.

"Why?" the dead man asked.

"I've dealt with others similar to him," Shane replied.

"Not as strong," Jonathan warned.

"I hope that's not true," Shane stated. "But I need to end him. And I need to end those that would help him."

"What?" Jonathan's question was sharp and hard.

Shane kept the explanation simple and told Jonathan all that he knew about the boy, the Watchers, and what they wanted.

After a moment of silence, Jonathan stated, "You cannot handle all of them alone."

"I'm not completely alone," Shane said. "But I would like help if I could get it."

"What are you thinking of?" Jonathan asked a note of eagerness in his voice.

"Well," Shane answered, "let me tell you."

And he did.

Chapter 57: Finally Afraid

Up until she and Gordon had spoken with Clair, Linda hadn't been afraid. Her faith in the Watchers hadn't been shaken or even tested. Not even when she had put Shirley Coleman out of her misery.

What Clair wanted Linda to do, and the violence she had promised, had shocked Linda. To go into the presence of the One, without any reason or justification given, was too much.

But Linda knew there was nothing she could do.

She was trapped as Shirley had been trapped, and all of those who had been ensnared by the One. And it seemed as though she would soon count herself amongst them.

Gordon, who she had worked with several years earlier prior to him being relocated to a small home on a ley line in Connecticut, staggered beside her. His fear was palpable. He stank of it, and Linda wondered if he could smell hers as well.

She felt certain he could.

After crossing through the tree line, Linda began the process of counting her steps. She had reached three hundred and nineteen when Gordon tripped and fell. His fingers had been intertwined with hers, and he dragged her down.

It took them a few moments to untangle themselves and after they remained seated on the path. Gordon took his phone out, hit the flashlight app and placed it on the path. He looked at her and mouthed the question, "Are you okay?"

She gave him a thumbs up.

He graced her with a weak smile and glanced up and down the path. She could see him working the problem out, trying to find a way they could get out of going to see the One. In a moment his shoulders slumped, and she knew he had come to the same conclusion she had earlier.

There was no way out.

Not at midnight in the woods.

She and Gordon had passed through a police cordon, and he had explained to her that all of the active members of the organization were in Amherst. They were hunting for the man known as Shane, attempting to keep him from the One and the rest of the world.

Clair had told her about Shane. How he had brought down Borgin's Keep. The loss of the Mill and smaller homes. Rumor had it that Shane had wiped out several teams single-handedly and that he was unstoppable.

Linda hadn't believed the stories Clair had told. They had seemed to be too much for any one person to be capable of. It was physically and mentally painful to understand that there was more than a little truth to what Clair had told her.

If anything, Linda knew, the stories hadn't done the man justice.

He was destroying an organization, and all of its work, which had lasted for over one hundred and fifty years.

Linda shivered at the thought.

Gordon reached out, touched her hand and mouthed the question, "Ready?"

She nodded.

Before he could pick up his phone, the light flickered and died, plunging them into darkness.

Cold air raced around her and Linda stiffened with fear.

Something dead was coming.

Chapter 58: In the Darkness of the Woods

Keith and Moe were a two-man team, called back by Clair to pick up the deaf girl and an old guy and escort them to see the One. Or as close to the One as they dared. Keith, like Moe, was a shooter. It was what he specialized in.

Got a nosy neighbor? Keith thought, *I'll make him disappear.*

Got a mom looking into her runaway? he snickered. *Oops, mom vanishes too.*

But the snicker faded. Keith did his work in cities and towns. The woods freaked him out.

"Weren't we supposed to meet up with them by now?" Moe asked. He was younger than Keith, and he talked in that pinched, nasally Boston way that drove Keith crazy.

"Sure," Keith responded. "Who knows, maybe she's slow as well as deaf?"

"Dummy, that ain't got nothing to do with it," Moe snorted.

Keith stopped himself before he punched Moe in the back of the head. If the whole situation went south on them, then he was going to shoot Moe. Just on principle if nothing more. Keith could always go out west and find a job with some gang. There was always someone who needed to be killed.

"What the hell was that?" Moe asked, coming to a short stop.

Keith bumped into him and cursed. "What the hell was what?"

"I saw something on the trail," Moe said.

"Probably them, stupid," Keith spat. "What the hell is wrong with you?"

He pushed past Moe and went up the path. There was a pair of dark shapes sitting upright against a pair of trees.

"Hey," Keith called out, drawing his pistol. "Hey!"

When neither shape answered, he approached to within a few steps.

In the faint amount of moonlight that filtered down through the leaf canopy overhead, Keith saw them. An older man and the deaf girl.

They were both dead.

Their eyes were too large as if pressure in their skulls had popped them part way out of their sockets. Each one's tongue protruded from between their lips. Neither had a weapon, but there was a phone on the path between them.

"What the hell?" Moe asked.

"Don't know," Keith said, not lowering his weapon. The hairs on the back of his neck stood up as he looked at the bodies.

The One hadn't killed the two people in front of him. They would have been still alive and listless, slowly drained of their life. Keith had seen the footage and knew what to expect. Throughout his time with the Watchers, he had also seen the bodies of people murdered by ghosts, and more than a few had looked like the older man and the deaf woman.

Without much hope Keith said, "Check the phone."

Moe, with his own pistol at the ready, eased past Keith and dropped down into a crouch to retrieve the phone.

"Dead," Moe said after a moment. "Like the two of them."

"Definitely not good," Keith said. "Got your iron?"

"'Course I do," Moe snapped.

Keith stuffed his free hand into his pants pocket, withdrew his iron ring and slipped it over a finger. The metal was warm and reassuring. He reached up and touched the earpiece and spoke into the microphone that hung by his larynx.

"Keith to base."

"Go," Clair said on the other end.

"We've got a problem," Keith stated, and he summed up the scene on the trail.

Her silence was worse than any curses she could have spoken.

"What do you want me to do?" Keith asked.

"Take the camera," she ordered.

Keith shined his light on the bodies.

"There is no camera," he replied.

She did curse then, and Keith realized he was wrong. Her silence hadn't been worse.

"Backtrack towards me," Clair said when she had finished. "See if it was dropped before they were killed."

"Copy that," Keith said, and he dropped his hand from the radio. "Did you hear her?"

Moe nodded. He looked up the trail and said, "This is bad."

"Of course it is," Keith snapped. "If it wasn't, hell, we wouldn't be here."

Moe shrugged in agreement.

Keith took his flashlight out, flicked it on, and aimed it at the path ahead. He had no idea what the camera might look like, and he had no desire to waste time in an effort to find it.

When Moe turned to follow the trail back to Clair, the flashlight went out.

Neither of the men said anything.

Keith dropped the flashlight, holstered his weapon, and tried to anticipate the attack.

Whoever it was, came up through the trail and ended his anticipation.

Chapter 59: Traveling in Darkness

Shane moved along a trail through the darkness with only Courtney beside him.

The other ghosts had fanned out from their street, searching for the Watchers and anyone foolish enough to enter the woods.

Shane held his .45 and listened as he traveled.

The forest was silent.

Neither bird nor beast, as the saying went, could be heard.

And he knew why.

The animals had abandoned the forest, given it over to the dead. If Shane had his way, he would have done the same.

But there was a relative to speak to, and family relationships could be difficult affairs to handle.

He doubted there would be anything easy about Samson.

Courtney moved ahead of him on the slim game trail. She returned several minutes later, whispering, "Two women up ahead. Watchers."

Shane nodded his thanks and slowed down. His footsteps became silent. He blended in with the darkness. The women were loud, obscenely so. Their feet cracked twigs, legs and arms pushed aside branches, and they spoke in low but clearly audible voices.

"This is ridiculous," one said.

"I know," the other agreed.

"Come on, we couldn't just push him towards the One?" the first asked.

Before the second could reply, they stepped into a shaft of moonlight.

Shane let off two quick shots, and the women dropped. He waited a moment for his night vision to return. When it had, he moved forward. Both women were down, the slugs from his .45 having punched through their breastbones. He stepped in, drew one of their 9 mm pistols, and stood up. He put two more rounds in each woman's head, just to make sure.

Shane wiped his prints off the 9 mm, and dropped it onto the stomach of the closest body.

"Ready?" Courtney asked.

"Yes," Shane replied, and she took off again as he continued down the trail.

It took her longer to return, and when she did, it was with grim news.

"Two more teams, three each," Courtney said. "They're in a glade ahead of us."

"Are they stationary or moving?" Shane asked.

"Stationary," she answered.

"Good," Shane muttered. Within a few minutes, he could see the tree line and the glade beyond. They were speaking, but their voices were muffled, making it impossible to decipher what was being said.

But it didn't matter.

Shane left one round in the chamber, ejected the magazine, and slipped a fresh one in, giving him a full eight. He edged up to the tree line, got into a good firing position and took control of his breathing. The shots would be long for a .45, but not impossible. Not if he followed the old Marine mantra of 'slow is smooth and smooth is fast.'

And Shane followed it.

The pistol barked six times, shell casings ejecting into the darkness.

When Shane had finished no one remained.

He walked out to the bodies, mindful of the two rounds he had left. Several of the Watchers were still alive. One, a younger man, was even attempting to draw his weapon.

Shane did it for him, and like the first two he had put down, he finished off the rest.

He cleaned the weapon as he had the first, dropped it down, and looked at the bodies. There was no sense of guilt. No feeling of remorse.

"I've killed better men than you," he whispered to the dead and headed out once more for the home of Samson.

Chapter 60: Alone

Clair threw the handset out of the SUV with a snarl. She ignored the way it smashed into Gordon's car, and she stepped out to stand in the night air.

She had lost contact with all of her teams.

Whether they were alive or dead, she didn't know, although she was certain most of them had been killed. She had heard gunfire and lots of it. A heavy caliber weapon, possibly a .45, followed by the higher pitched report of a 9 mm.

Clair felt certain that the .45 belonged to Shane, and she doubted any of her people had managed to shoot him. Especially since the heavier pistol had been fired first. Eight times. And then single shots from the lighter pistols. Those sounded more like people being finished off than the mad rush of fire from a prolonged gunfight.

Muttering to herself, Clair went to the lead SUV, opened the trunk. She removed a sidearm for herself and a Daewoo shotgun. She slapped a 20-round drum magazine into place, each round loaded with 00 buckshot which consisted of nine small iron balls.

Clair took out a second magazine, placed it into an ammunition bag, and then slipped the strap over her shoulder.

She was going to have to go in after Shane.

He couldn't be allowed to get to the One.

The situation, she felt in her heart, was still salvageable. She, if no one else, could still come out on top. The One would see to that.

He would see her fealty. The One would know.

All Clair had to do was stop Shane.

She could do it.

She had to do it.

And she knew she should have done it before.

Armed and braced with fervent devotion, Clair went into the woods.

Chapter 61: The Chestnut Tree

Shane felt an electrical current run out of the woods on the other side of the glade in pulsating waves. He knew the sensation. He had felt it before.

Standing amongst the dead in Jonathan Engberg's house.

Their energy had infused him with a renewed determination to see the job done. It had expelled all doubts.

And as he drew nearer to his relative's house, the energy increased.

He knew it for what it was, the power of the innocents trapped by Samson. The dead boy had fed off it for centuries, and the Watchers wanted him to have more of it. Shane didn't.

It was as if the innocents knew Shane was approaching. For every step closer to the opposite tree line gave him increased strength. By the time he left the glade, Shane felt as though he could have leaped the distance to Samson's house if he had only known where it was.

As he passed along the trail people appeared in the woods on either side.

Young and old. Male and female. They were from every period of New England's history, and they watched him. In their eyes, he saw a desperate hope, and Shane knew he would either kill Samson or remain with the innocent, although he could not count himself among that number.

Courtney was beside him, a comforting presence of bitterly cold air. On her delicate features was an expression of grim determination, and Shane knew she would stay with him until the end.

He wished he could take her hand and hold it.

Shane holstered his .45 as he drew nearer, the darkness becoming deeper as he crossed under the boughs of a magnificent chestnut tree. Soon he could see only a few feet in front of him.

He didn't slow down.

He knew the path would be clear.

Samson wouldn't want there to be any obstacles for his victims to trip over.

Shane was glad for that.

When he reached the trunk of the chestnut, a strange, green tinted glow appeared. It illuminated the front of a battered house, and the stones of a small, colonial burial ground.

The light also revealed bodies. Some sitting upright, others prone upon the ground.

And Samson sat among them, smiling like a beneficent king.

"Hello," Samson said, his voice sweet and pleasant to the ear. "Who are you?"

"I'm Shane."

"Shane," Samson said, nodding. "What a nice name. I do not believe I have heard it before."

Shane didn't respond to the statement.

Samson evidently didn't expect one. "Will you come and sit with me, Shane, and keep me company?"

Shane nodded and moved forward. Courtney went with him.

He sat down in front of Samson, and the little boy smiled at him.

"Isn't this nice?" the boy asked.

"Sure," Shane replied. He twisted the iron rings on his fingers.

A perplexed expression flitted across Samson's face.

"Are you not happy to be with me?" Samson asked, a playful, hurt tone in his voice.

"I don't care if you're happy or not," Shane replied.

The pleasant smile vanished from Samson's face as he demanded, "What did you say to me?"

"Pretty sure you heard me," Shane said. "Unless you've gone deaf after all these years, Uncle."

Samson opened his mouth to reply, and then closed it, a confused look on his face. "What did you say?"

"You're my uncle," Shane said. "Many times removed, but an uncle still."

"We are not related," Samson spat. "All of my relatives are dead. You lie."

Rage blossomed on the dead boy's face and he whispered, "I shall smother your falsehoods and you will choke to death upon them."

Samson's body began to dissipate, the edges of it shifting into a dark mist, a fog that grew around the dead child.

"I don't lie, Uncle," Shane whispered, and he drove an iron-ringed fist into Samson's face.

The mist that had built up around the boy snapped back into him, and the child himself didn't disappear. He tumbled backward, jumped up and snarled, "How dare you? How can you?!"

"Because, and because," Shane said, getting to his feet.

Samson sprang forward, striking Shane in the midsection and sending him tumbling over an emaciated man.

Shane let out a curse as he got up. Samson stared at him, surprised.

"Why didn't I go through you?" Samson asked, looking at his small hands. "I should have plunged them deep into your innards."

Shane didn't respond with words. Instead, he moved forward and tried to grab Samson. The boy slipped away, passing through a seated person. Shane watched as the stranger shuddered and collapsed.

"That's what should have happened," Samson hissed. "You should have died. Everyone I pass through, dies. Why are you different?"

Shane answered with a kick, driving his foot into Samson's thigh and sending him spinning backward. The dead boy passed through a trio of headstones and shrieked, "Answer me!"

Shane grinned.

Samson howled and jumped at Shane, who caught him easily and threw him through the wall of the house.

The boy reappeared in the doorway a moment later, with several ghosts behind him.

"Now," Samson spat. "Kill him!"

The ghosts rushed at him, and Shane's hate brought a grin to his face.

Samson's dead were why he had worn the iron rings.

His fists smashed into them, casting them back to their bones.

In silence, Shane advanced on Samson and wondered what the boy might do next.

"Save me!" the dead boy screamed, and those who still lived clambered to their feet.

And that was something Shane had not expected.

Chapter 62: On the Move

Clair had come across multiple bodies, the last remnants of the Watchers, stretched out in death. Some had been slain by ghosts, the marks obvious to one who had spent so much time with the dead over the years.

The rest had been killed by Shane Ryan.

She found the last of the bodies in the glade, six of them.

He had murdered them with a cold and brutal efficiency that Clair both admired and despised. Each one he had killed had been dropped by a single shot to the chest, with another to the head to make sure they wouldn't get back up.

Clair considered, for a moment, what an asset he would have been for the organization.

And then she was out of the glade and into the woods. She could hear yelling in the distance, the voice of a child, outraged and furious.

Shane had reached the One.

A sense of panic welled up in her, and she sprinted down the narrow, dark path.

Someone lunged out at her and Clair staggered to a stop as she brought the shotgun up. The weapon roared in her hand, the iron buckshot dissipating the ghost that had sought to stop her.

Others appeared as well, but the shotgun was up, and she pulled the trigger again. She fired as quickly as she could, shooting anything that was potentially threatening.

In less than a minute, she had taken down nine ghosts, and there was silence around her.

Clair waited to see if any more would appear.

None did.

With her heart thundering in her chest, she moved on.

Chapter 63: Out of Options

Shane backed away from the living who were under Samson's spell.

Some walked towards him, others crawled, and a few dragged themselves across the earth. All who could, obeyed, and those who couldn't and were still alive filled the air with moans of anger and sadness.

Shane knew some of the people who approached him had to be Watchers, those caught within the snare of Samson's voice. Others would be innocents, and Shane could not bring himself to draw his weapon and fire at them.

A woman stumbled into him, her eyes feverish in the dim light, her skin hot to the touch as she grabbed hold of him.

Shane tried to shake her off, but in spite of her frail appearance, she was strong. Her fingernails dug into his flesh, and she opened her mouth. Fetid breath engulfed him as he peeled back her fingers. Several fingers broke in his hands before he was able to free himself and push her to the side.

By then the others had reached him.

They clawed, and bit, and punched at him, and Shane replied in kind, with greater strength and violence. Ghosts came at him as well, their blows more powerful and far colder than that of the living.

In the doorway Samson stood, watching with a smirk on his face.

Someone or something struck Shane in the back of his knee, and he dropped down, the joint crashing into the ground. The living defenders of the One tried to swarm over him, and he drew his pistol.

He reversed the weapon in his grip and used the butt of it. Again and again, he smashed it down on noses and cheeks. He shattered teeth and broke jaws. Some fell to be clambered over by their brethren, others continued to fight on. Shane felt himself losing control, lashing out with greater fury, giving way to his inner rage.

Skulls cracked, and the living died, shuddering heaps of skin wrapped bones.

Chapter 64: A Brief and Exuberant Joy

When Clair reached the house of the One, she felt a wave of joy wash over her. Not from the scene in front of her, which she enjoyed, but from being in the presence of the One. Of knowing that she had done right in coming to Him.

But the battle she found herself witnessing sent a thrill of excitement through her.

Shane Ryan was on his knees, being beaten by both the living and the dead.

His dying would be long, painful, and well deserved.

Yet as she watched, her belief in his eventual demise faded.

He was beating them. All of them. Body after body hit the ground, and the dead vanished beneath his blows. They returned within moments, but never long enough to press the attack.

Clair looked past Shane to the house and saw the One in the doorway.

He was the most beautiful child she had ever seen.

The grunts and curses of the battle disappeared. Even the sight of it vanished.

Clair saw nothing except the One, and He saw her.

He spoke, and His voice, clearly that of an angel, rolled out to her.

"Will you help me?" the One asked.

"Yes," Clair whispered.

"Then kill him," the One said, His eyes large and breathtaking. "Before he kills me, dear one."

Clair dropped the shotgun to the ground and reached for her pistol.

A cold hand took hold of her own and wrenched it away. The pain was enough to force her attention away from the One, but not to drive his command out of her head.

She twisted around to face her attacker, trying to wrench her hand free and failing.

Clair found herself facing a ghost. A small woman with elegant features, her head at a curious angle, the neck with a disconcerting crick in it.

In a vague way, Clair felt her hand going numb and she understood that the ghost's touch was destroying her flesh, one cell at a time.

Clair tried once more to pull her hand free and couldn't.

She brought her left hand up and struck at the ghost, the iron ring on her index finger missing her as the dead woman dodged the strike.

Clair tumbled to the left, off balance from the blow and the sudden disappearance of the dead woman's grip.

With a hand disturbingly numb, Clair reached again for the pistol, and again she was stopped.

Surprised, Clair looked and saw the same dead woman.

"No," the ghost said. "You're not going to hurt him."

And Clair screamed as her arm was twisted and pulled from its socket.

Chapter 65: His Distant Relation

Shane fought in silence, clubbing the living down and battering away the dead. His mind registered a scream, but he didn't give the sound any attention.

He regained his feet, kicked a woman away and felt waves of pain undulate through him. Parts of his body burned, and others were moist with blood. Yet like the scream he had heard, Shane ignored his body.

Instead, he focused on Samson.

The boy in the doorway of the house.

Samson pointed a small finger at him, a foul, wretched sneer on his face as he said, "You're going to die here."

A man struggled to stand, and Shane shoved the man aside.

"Speak to me!" Samson hissed.

Shane remained silent as he stalked forward, his eyes locked onto the boy.

The dead child took a step back into the doorway.

Again the ghosts of the Watchers appeared, advancing on Shane.

Yet from the headstones and around the chestnut tree more ghosts appeared.

Shane recognized Jonathan Engberg and Amelia, as well as the others who he had met on the abandoned street. Other ghosts joined them, and together they attacked the dead Watchers.

The path to the One was cleared for Shane, and he walked along it as quickly as his damaged body would allow him.

When he crossed the threshold of the doorway, he felt energy ripple along his skin. His heart stuttered, missed a beat, and then kicked into overdrive. Samson was waiting for him, a light blue luminescence pulsating around him.

The boy stood in a corner in the center of a pile of bones and rotted clothes.

"You cannot touch me," Samson declared.

Shane stepped closer.

The dead boy bared his teeth and shouted, "I have killed hundreds!"

When Shane was less than a stride away from Samson, the dead boy charged at him, and Shane caught him by the arms. Samson kicked out, each blow strong and powerful, deadening Shane's thighs.

Shane stiffened his legs, refusing to allow himself to fall. Samson snarled and grabbed hold of Shane's chest, twisting the fabric of Shane's sweatshirt in his small hands.

"Feel it?" the boy asked.

A painful sensation exploded throughout Shane's body. His joints shuddered with agony. He looked at his hands and saw the knuckles swell. Shane's fingers locked in place and then the pain burrowed into his wrists.

Unwillingly, Shane dropped Samson, who landed on his feet.

He peered up at Shane.

"Yes," the boy said with a mocking laugh. "Oh yes, you do feel it! Do you think I've lasted this long by my wits alone, Nephew?"

Shane, grinding his teeth against the pain, didn't respond.

The dead boy walked around Shane, and Shane forced himself to follow him. The pain was excruciating. It felt as though someone had clamped down on each and every joint. His blood pounded in his ears and it was difficult to hear the boy speak.

"Do you know what I'm going to do to you?" Samson asked in a singsong voice.

When Shane didn't answer, Samson continued.

"I'll have them drag you into my house," the dead boy whispered, dancing around him. "And do you have any idea how hungry the starving are? They will sup on your flesh, if I ask it of them. Can you imagine that, the feel of their teeth sinking into your tender parts? I will have them feast on your tongue first, so you'll be able to scream but not speak so insubordinately to me."

Samson came in closer, leering as he said, "How do you think that will feel, my false Nephew? When they silence your lying tongue?"

Shane stared at the dead boy, forced his mouth into a smile, and lashed out. Both of his hands slammed onto the child and Shane screamed with pain as he forced his fingers to lock upon him.

Samson let out a scream of mixed surprise and rage and he fought against Shane. Every blow landed, and every one brought a burst of excruciating pain. Shane felt bruises blossom and blood explode out of cuts. Dragging the boy in closer, Shane saw his own fingers going white.

The nails on his thumbs turned blue, then purple, and finally they became black. A gut churning pain drove black spots into his eyes and Shane heard a terrible shriek.

A heartbeat later, he realized the shriek was his. Samson continued to struggle, to fight and strike out. But Shane, gasping for breath, tightened his grip, and Samson ceased all movement.

"In a moment you'll be frozen in place, and I will be freed," Samson whispered. "Tell me, how well will you move when your joints are locked and your throat open to my teeth?"

Shane didn't answer, because he knew he didn't need to move.

He lifted the child above his head and smashed him down into the earthen floor.

The effort brought blackness to the edges of his vision and stars burst before his eyes. Yet the result was worth it.

Samson screamed a sound that was taken up and repeated by his followers beyond the house. He struck out with his feet again, but his kicks lacked the strength of only a moment before.

Shane picked Samson back up and drove the boy's head into the nearest wall.

The dead boy sagged in his hands, his efforts to escape weakening.

On stiff legs Shane staggered out, Samson's form curiously hot in his hands. He looked around at the dead, and the living held back by those ghosts who had suffered at the hands of Samson.

And then he saw Courtney. She had a woman on the ground, one arm twisted up behind her back.

"Save me," Samson whispered.

Shane watched the woman lift her head up, staring at him with eyes full of hatred. She struggled against Courtney, but Shane's dead love kept the woman down.

Without loosening his grasp on Samson, Shane limped to the woman. He looked at her dark blue uniform, the disjointed appearance of her shoulder, and the weapons on the ground near her.

"Who are you?" Shane demanded, his voice ragged and raw.

"I hate you," she said, her voice flat and dead.

But he recognized it.

"Clair," Shane said. "You're Clair."

Her lip curled in a sneer. "And you're dead, Shane Ryan."

"Not yet," he replied. Shane looked to Courtney and said, "Let her go please."

Courtney shook her head.

"Please, Courtney," Shane said, his voice soft with affection. "I need you to let her go."

"Why?" she asked.

"Because of what I'm going to do," Shane answered as Samson squirmed in his hands.

Courtney hesitated a moment, and then released Clair's hand.

The woman gasped with pain and fell forward. When she hit the ground, she did what Shane expected.

Clair picked a pistol up with her left hand and tried to get to her feet.

As she did so, Shane slammed Samson down into her.

The pistol spun free out of her hand and Shane held the dead boy up. Samson's form faded in and out of solidity, pulsing with Shane's heartbeat.

I can control his form, Shane realized with surprise.

And, unlike Shane, Clair was not protected by the power of the gathered innocents.

Shane held the dead boy up high for a moment longer, and then slammed him down again. The dead boy passed through her skin as easily as her clothes, and Shane held him there. Clair's agonized shrieks were the stuff of nightmares, and as she died with Samson writhing around inside of her, Shane knew he would hear her forever.

When the screams stopped and she no longer moved, Shane dragged Samson out of her and looked at him.

Samson chuckled as Shane dropped the pistol beside Clair's lifeless form. There was a mixture of fear and admiration in the boy's eyes.

"I see it now," Samson whispered.

"See what?" Shane asked, the statement catching him off guard.

"The familial resemblance," Samson grinned. "Only one of my blood could be so heartless."

The truth of the statement bit deep, and with a howl, Shane tore the dead boy to shreds.

Chapter 66: On the Gurney

The click of a door brought Shane awake.

He blinked his eyes at the bright light above him, and when he could finally see, he found himself in the back of an ambulance. His mind felt muffled as if swaddled in cotton. The last memory he had was of destroying Samson.

Shane tried to sit up and found he was strapped down to a gurney. He turned his head to look at the EMT but instead saw an older man dressed in the uniform of the New Hampshire State Police.

The man had silver eagles pinned to the collar of his dress shirt, the mark of a colonel.

In his hands, he held Shane's .45.

The man's bronze nameplate read 'D. Currier.' He looked at Shane for a long time. Shane's throat hurt, and he remained silent, which, he decided, would probably be for the best until he could get a lawyer.

The colonel took his hat off and placed it on the bench beside him. Then he did the same with the pistol.

"You have, according to the EMTs," the man said in a deep voice, "multiple bite wounds, abrasions, bruises, and at least several cracked if not outright broken ribs. Compared to your half an ear and eight fingers, I'd say you were still coming out ahead of the game in this particular fight."

Shane remained silent, waiting to hear the rest.

The colonel cleared his throat and continued.

"We found you at a rather troubling scene. And I'm curious as to what happened, but," the man said, holding up a hand, "I don't really want to know. From what I can tell, this woman, Clair, imprisoned, tortured, and starved those people at the house. Some of them to death."

Shane felt his eyes widen in surprise.

"And," the colonel added, "she seems to have stolen your weapon and used it on some of her own people. No doubt to frame you after the failed attempt to kill you and your friend at your home."

Shane was too stunned to either agree or disagree with the officer's statement.

"I will, unfortunately, have to keep your pistol with me," the man continued. "Chain of evidence and all of that. You understand."

Shane nodded.

The colonel put his hat back on, picked up the .45 and looked at Shane.

"I understand why you ran from the police earlier, Mr. Ryan," he said, his voice taking on a hard edge. "But let Clair's fate remind you that it is not a wise decision to upset a cop."

With those words, the colonel left the ambulance.

Shane closed his eyes. His thoughts racing.

"Shane," Courtney whispered.

Shane's eyes snapped open, and he saw her.

She sat where the colonel had.

"Hey," Shane said, his voice raw. "Thank you."

Courtney nodded and gave him a small smile. The smile faded, and she looked as if she wanted to speak, but couldn't.

"Are you okay?" he asked her.

"Yes," she said, not meeting his gaze. "It's just that I have to tell you something, and part of me doesn't want to."

Shane's heart quickened its pace.

"What is it?" he managed to ask.

She sighed and whispered, "I'm ready to leave."

"Well, yeah," he said, chuckling. "Me too."

"No," she said, looking at him. "I'm ready to *leave*."

"Oh," he said, but the word was barely audible.

"I don't want to, but I know it's time," she said. "It's the best path, for both of us."

Shane's heart roared, and his head ached.

"I don't want to hurt you, Shane," Courtney said in a low voice, "but that's all I'll be doing if I stay. I understand that now. And I've thought about it, for a while. I've had a lot of time to think, seeing as how I don't need to sleep anymore."

Shane tried to speak but he couldn't. The words wouldn't come out.

"I want this to be clean, well, cleaner than it has been," she whispered. "Please don't make it any harder."

Shane nodded, found his voice, and forced himself to say, "Alright."

"Do you understand that this is the best for both of us?" Courtney asked him.

"Yes," Shane answered, choking on the word. "But I don't have to be happy about it. I know you need to go. I know that I *need* you to go. It doesn't mean I want it."

"I know that," Courtney said, smiling at him. "But, Shane, I want you to be happy. You're alive and you need to be with someone who is alive too. I want you to find happiness, Shane Ryan. I love you."

Before he could say the same, the ghost of Courtney DeSantis began to fade. Her smile remained in place as she slowly became nothing more than a faint hint of herself.

Then her smile widened, and the last faint remnant of Courtney DeSantis slipped from the world.

Chapter 67: Two Weeks Later

Frank Benedict walked into the house on Berkley Street, past a pair of carpenters replacing the woodwork around the doors, and headed towards the kitchen.

Shane wasn't in the room, but the back door was open.

Down by the pond, Shane sat in one of two, dark blue Adirondack chairs.

Frank joined him.

Shane was smoking a cigarette and holding a half-filled water glass of whiskey.

"You look like hell," Frank said. "And you smell like death."

"Thanks," Shane said wryly. "The dark ones brought up Lisbeth's remains today. I had to burn them. Hence the delicate aroma. I'll shower soon. I just really needed a drink."

"Other than burning corpses, how are you feeling?" Frank asked, the sound of his voice still thin in his damaged ears.

"Better," Shane replied. "And you?"

Frank shrugged.

"How was therapy?" Shane asked.

"Okay," Frank said. "I hear a little better each day. How are you holding up, with Courtney being gone?"

"It's tough," Shane answered. "I miss her. I miss her a lot. It's selfish, I know, but with her being around, I didn't have to really deal with the fact that she was dead. I couldn't grieve."

Frank looked at him and said, "What?"

Shane chuckled. "You're not the only one in therapy, Frank."

"Guess not," Frank said, surprised.

Shane finished his cigarette and Frank watched him field strip the remnants. Then the bald man finished the whiskey and set the glass down in the grass beside the chair.

"Shane," Frank said after a moment of silence.

"Hm?"

"Why are you in therapy?" Frank asked.

Shane didn't answer immediately, but when he did, it was with a thoughtful and deliberate tone.

"There's a lot wrong with me," Shane said, looking at the pond. "It started here, in this house, with a terrible ghost. I didn't help myself get better over the years. Made it worse most of the time. But I want to be better. I need to be."

"I don't disagree," Frank said, scratching the back of his head, "but why now? Is it because of Courtney?"

"Partly because of Courtney," Shane admitted. "And partly because of Marie."

"Marie Lafontaine?" Frank asked, unable to hide his surprise.

"Yes," Shane said. He looked at Frank with sincerity. "She tried to help me before, and I didn't let her."

"What about ghost hunting?" Frank asked, feeling confused. "We have the alpha file and there are still all of those houses out there. The ghosts who the Watchers had been grooming. What are we going to do about them?"

"I can't do anything about them," Shane said, looking down at his hands.

Frank saw how they trembled, how the fingers curled in and the knuckles were swollen. The missing nails. "My hands haven't healed from the fight with Samson. I don't think I can do it anymore. I can't find any more bodies. I can't see any more tortured people and tortured souls. I was thinking maybe we could reach out to your Abbot, pass the houses on to him. I think they could handle it."

"And what about you?" Frank asked. "What are you going to do?"

"Remember what I said," Shane whispered. "Marie Lafontaine tried to help me, and I rejected it. Now she needs help. Both physically and mentally. She needs my help, Frank. Hell, I need to help her, too."

Frank didn't know how to respond.

Shane smiled at the silence. "Yeah, I know. It'll be rough, for both of us. She doesn't like it when I drink or smoke. I like to drink and smoke. I don't think either of us are looking for a love connection here. Not this time. But I think we'll be happy helping each other out."

"How is she going to help you?" Frank asked.

"The same way you do," Shane said, standing up. He bent over and picked up the glass.

"How's that?" Frank said as Shane walked back towards the house.

"You help me remember that there are good people in the world," Shane answered over his shoulder, "and that I might be able to become one of them."

* * *

FREE Bonus Novel!

Wow, I hope you enjoyed this book as much as I did writing it! If you enjoyed the book, please leave a review. Your reviews inspire me to continue writing about the world of spooky and untold horrors!

To really show you my appreciation for purchasing this book, please enjoy a **FREE extra spooky bonus novel.** This will surely leave you running scared!

Visit below to download your bonus novel and to learn about my upcoming releases, future discounts and giveaways: **www.ScareStreet.com**

See you in the shadows,
Team Scare Street

Printed in Poland
by Amazon Fulfillment
Poland Sp. z o.o., Wrocław